A
HISTORY
OF GREEK
LITERATURE

A
HISTORY
OF GREEK
LITERATURE

ALBIN LESKY

Translated by James Willis
and Cornelis de Heer

Published in the U.K. by
Gerald Duckworth & Co. Ltd.
London

Published in North America by
Hackett Publishing Company, Inc.
Indianapolis/Cambridge

First published as Geschichte der Griechischen Literatur
by Francke Verlag, Bern
Copyright © A. Francke 1957/58
Second edition 1963
English translation first published by Methuen & Co. Ltd 1966

This edition published, with permission, in 1996 by

Gerald Duckworth & Co. Ltd
The Old Piano Factory
48 Hoxton Square, London N1 6PB

and by

Hackett Publishing Company, Inc.
P.O. Box 44937
Indianapolis, Indiana 46244–0937

U.K. edition:
ISBN 0-7156-2761-9
A catalogue record for this book
is available from the British Library

U.S. edition:
ISBN 0-87220-350-6 (pbk)
ISBN 0-87220-351-4 (cloth)
LC number 96-078783

The paper used in this publication meets the minimum
requirements of American National Standard for Information
Sciences - Permanence of Paper for Printed Library
Materials, ANSI Z39.48-1984

Printed in the United States of America

CONTENTS

PREFACE TO THE SECOND EDITION

I was encouraged to produce a second edition of this book by the kindness of some friends and colleagues, who said that they had found it useful in their studies and that they would welcome even fuller references than in the first edition to problems still unsolved and to accepted solutions. To meet these requirements meant a great deal of labour, but the labour has brought pleasure in its train, for the quantity and quality of recent work has attested the vigorous life of a scholarship which means to keep alive the classical inheritance of our own time. Two things need only be stated in passing: the selection could only be a narrow one, and the wish to bring out the essential must needs contain a subjective element. But the end before my eyes has always been to select from the literature what would enable the serious researcher to follow up the earlier history of the problems.

Rather reluctantly I have fallen in with the wish of friends and critics (often, I was glad to see, the same) and printed the notes at the bottoms of the pages, thus spoiling the simplicity of the printed page. Where the formula 'see below' occurs in them, it normally refers to the bibliography at the end of the chapter.

Not many pages have remained unchanged. The sections on Homer and Plato were among those which demanded large-scale rewriting, and one on pseudo-Pythagorean writings has been added. In so far as the new treatment is an improvement, I am indebted for it largely to the help of others. Errors have been corrected and valuable references given by careful and nearly always constructive critics. It is not through ingratitude to those not named if I single out J. C. Kamerbeek and F. Zucker as having been particularly helpful. I benefited not only from printed critiques, but also from private correspondents to a degree which caused me both delight and shame. In this connection I should mention above all Wolfgang Buchwald and Franz Dollnig, who also lent me their services in correcting the proofs and devoted more pains to the book than I can well express.

There are two important principles in which I have remained true to the positions which I took up in the first edition.

I have remained sceptical of the value of summings-up which try to finish a section by characterizing a great author in a couple of sentences. The ideal of synthesis is very well, but I think it better served by an exposition which tries to group the multiplicity of phenomena around a firm core, or, if necessary, to show them as the end of a long development.

The different scale of treatment given to different periods had to be retained if only for practical reasons. Otherwise it would have been impossible to compress the work into one volume of (I hope) still manageable size. In any case,

I still believe that this inequality of emphasis can be justified on the grounds which I gave in the first edition. An acute but kindly critic brought up against me the passage of E. R. Curtius (*Kritische Essays zur europäischen Literatur.* 2nd ed. Berne 1954, p. 318) which describes late antiquity as the age of harvest and sweet fruitfulness, of wide horizons and of unfettered choice. Certainly no one would deny the amount of beautiful and significant literature produced from Theocritus to Plotinus. But there can be no doubt where Europe's spiritual foundations lie. If it is wrong to deplore the dominance of rhetoric in late antiquity, the author must enter a plea of guilty. It is not perhaps absurd to suggest that Curtius' words mark a milestone on that road which led him to those utterances on the sinking light of Hellas which many must wish that he had kept to himself.

In our day also we look with hope on the light of Hellas, and possibly this book in its new form may help to prevent the realization of that distressing possibility which is hinted at in the *Historische Fragmente* of Jacob Burkhardt: 'We can never be free of the ancient world, unless we become barbarians again.'

VIENNA   ALBIN LESKY

xii

INTRODUCTION TO THE FIRST EDITION

> Art is the true interpreter. If we talk about art we are trying to interpret the interpreter: yet even so we profit greatly thereby.—GOETHE, *Maxims and Reflexions on Art.*

> The organs of recognition, without which no true reading is possible, are reverence and love. Knowledge cannot dispense with them, for it can grasp and analyse only what love takes possession of, and without love it is empty.—EMIL STAIGER, *Meisterwerke deutscher Sprache.*

To write literary history is reckoned nowadays by some to be a menial, by others almost an impossible, task. The latter view has something to be said for it, but the situation resulting from such pessimism is far from pleasing. We have short outlines of Greek literature, among which the little masterpiece of Walter Kranz stands high above the rest, while at the other extreme we have the five volumes produced by the gigantic industry of Wilhelm Schmid, of which the last brings the story to the end of the fifth century B.C. Between these two extremes lies a vacant space. There is no convenient work in English or German which presents our knowledge of the subject so as to give a broad outline for the student, initial guidance to the researcher, and to the interested public a speedy but not a superficial approach to the literature of Greece.

I hope that my work may fill this gap. But the compression of such extensive material within the intended compass has only been possible because of certain deliberate restrictions, which need to be explained.

The first of these touches Christian Greek literature, which would have strained the limits of this volume, and which is important enough to demand separate treatment. To leave out parts of Jewish Greek literature was a harder decision; but they could only be treated marginally in relation to the main subject. Furthermore, no history of a literature can be expected at the same time to be a history of philosophical thought and of science in the language concerned. Where the Greeks – especially the earlier Greeks – are concerned, this distinction is harder than elsewhere. Consequently these subjects have been included, although this history of Greek literature is neither desirous nor capable of being a history also of Greek philosophy and science.

All this is largely self-explanatory. One point, however, must be given special prominence. This book deliberately emphasizes literary achievements which were great and decisive in the rise of western civilization. One can only avoid a brief and cataloguing manner by not putting equal stress on all the phenomena – or, to put it differently, by not drawing the map on the same scale in all parts. I have no intention of chronicling the names of all the 2000 or so Greek writers known to us, or of listing mechanically works of which we know nothing beyond the title. Nor are different periods treated in equal detail. The archaic and classical periods are given the fullest treatment possible within this compass, and the major achievements of the Hellenistic age are also handled in detail; but the enormous literary production of the Empire has to receive shorter shrift. I think that this can be reconciled with the purpose originally stated for this volume. Our knowledge of antiquity can never deny its debt to the historical method, which demolished the narrow classicistic image of the Greeks and brought learned research to bear on every phenomenon as and where it occurred. But since the end of the war one has again felt aware of the duty and the right to evaluate the significance of what the historical method has established. A work which aimed at the utmost completeness would have to treat Cassius Dio in as much detail as Thucydides, to give as much space to Musaeus as to Homer. In a history which aims at bringing out essentials this would be absurd.

I decided on restrictions of this sort in order to be able to treat on a basically uniform method the great works of Greek literature whose influence has been felt over the ages. In discussing these I had no intention of sparing detail. Our age has become too lazy in its attitude to history: behind all the ingenious subjectivism and the often wrong-headed popularization one detects a shrinking from honest discussion and a contraction of real knowledge that reminds one uncomfortably of certain features of late antiquity. This book is meant to play its modest part in opposing such tendencies. It takes as a maxim what Werner Jaeger once wrote (*Gnomon* 1951, 247): 'It is the problems that are really important: we have done our best if we leave them open and hand them on still living to future generations.' An author's right to his own opinion can always be reconciled with the appreciation of other points of view, and often enough it becomes the scholar's duty to confess either that we simply do not know or that there is still doubt.

Today more than ever literary history is torn between conflicting points of view, and for this reason many writers of it go astray. Some of the opposing attitudes, each claiming validity, may be briefly indicated: the tracing of genetic developments and the recording of phenomena in their own right; allowance for environmental factors and recognition of individuality; subordination to the genre and rejection of its limitations; a feeling of closeness to the works described, arising from our common human viewpoints – although Nietzsche warned us against 'impertinent familiarity' – and one of remoteness from the Greeks as people who in many ways thought very differently from ourselves. I do not intend a long theoretical discussion: I merely record my conviction that there are real oppositions here and that each of the attitudes mentioned has something to be said for it. We can only usefully come to grips with them in the course of the history itself.

The most difficult, and in a sense the most distasteful task, has been to divide the subject into epochs and to subdivide these, since as soon as we start doing so, living threads begin to be severed. Where Greek literature is concerned, the large divisions are at once obvious, but to divide them further is both difficult and dangerous. It seemed best, therefore, not to adopt a rigid system, but to vary the principle of division according to the nature of the material. In the archaic period, the great epoch of birth and growth, it seemed desirable to make the division mainly one of literary genres; the age of the city-state demanded a chronological treatment; in the Hellenistic period, at least in the beginning, we find the different fields of study strongly associated with particular places. In general it seemed important not to adopt any scheme of articulation which would build weirs in a river that flows sometimes faster, sometimes slower, but is never at a standstill.

My wish to leave problems open has led to the relatively high proportion of bibliography. Naturally only a selection was possible, and this at once brings in a subjective element. The basic principle has been to quote as far as possible the latest contributions to learned controversy; and while I have tried to judge the intrinsic worth of the items, I have also considered how far they enabled the student to pursue the subject further afield. Without making any claim to completeness, even for the more recent years, the bibliographical references may serve the more serious researcher as stepping stones on the first stages of his journey. Works frequently cited will be found in the index of abbreviations. The ominous *op. cit.* is only used when the work has been cited very shortly before: usually both that and *vid. sup.* refer back from the footnotes to the preceding bibliographical section.

This is not the place to list the copious bibliographical resources available to the modern scholar, but I should like to mention, in addition to the indispensable *L'année philologique*, both J. A. Nairn's *Classical Hand-List* (Oxf. 1953) and the very useful *Fifty Years of Classical Scholarship* (Oxf. 1954).

Among works which I quote in the course of the book I may perhaps refer to two which have given us a better understanding of wide areas of Greek literature: Werner Jaeger's *Paideia* and Hermann Fränkel's *Dichtung und Philosophie des frühen Griechentums*. There is another work, outside the strict philological tradition, which I will mention for the original and stimulating way in which it discusses a variety of topics: Alexander Rustow's *Ortsbestimmung der Gegenwart*, Zürich 1950.

VIENNA   ALBIN LESKY

LIST OF ABBREVIATIONS

AfdA	*Anzeiger für die Altertumswissenschaft*
Am. Journ. Arch.	*American Journal of Archaeology*
Am. Journ. Phil.	*American Journal of Philology*
Ann. Br. School Ath.	*Annual of the British School at Athens*
Ant. Class.	*L'Antiquité classique*
Arch. f. Rw.	*Archiv für Religionswissenschaft*
Arch. Jahrb.	*Jahrbuch des Deutschen Archäolog. Instituts*
Ath. Mitt.	*Mitteilungen des Deutschen Archäolog. Instituts zu Athen*
B.	*Poetae Lyrici Graeci. Quartis curis rec.* Th. Bergk. vols. 2 & 3 (vol. 1 contains Pindar) Leipzig 1882. Reprinted with indices by H. Rubenbauer 1914–15.
BKT	*Berliner Klassikertexte* herausg. von der Generalverwaltung der K. Museen zu Berlin
Bull. Corr. Hell.	*Bulletin de correspondance hellénique*
Class. Journ.	*Classical Journal*
Class. Phil.	*Classical Philology*
Class. Quart.	*Classical Quarterly*
Class. Rev.	*Classical Review*
Coll. des Un. de Fr.	*Collection des Universités de France*, publiée sous le patronage de l'Association Guillaume Budé. Paris, Société d'édition 'Les Belles-Lettres' (with French translation)
D.	Ernst Diehl, *Anthologia Lyrica Graeca.* 3rd edition: fasc. 1, Leipz. 1949, 2, 1950. 3, 1952. Otherwise in the second ed.: fasc. 4, 1936. fasc. 5 and 6, 1942 with supplement.
F Gr Hist	Felix Jacoby, *Die Fragmente der griech. Historiker* 1 ff. Berl. 1923 ff. (normally referred to by Jacoby's numbers)
Fränkel	Hermann Fränkel, *Dichtung und Philosophie des frühen Griechentums*, New York 1951; 2nd edition enlarged Munich 1961
GGN	*Göttinger Gelehrte Nachrichten*
Gnom.	*Gnomon*
Gymn.	*Gymnasium*
Harsh	Philip Whaley Harsh, *A Handbook of Classical Drama.* Stanford and London 1948
Harv. Stud.	*Harvard Studies in Classical Philology*
Herm. (E.)	*Hermes* (Einzelschriften)
Jaeger	Werner Jaeger, *Paideia*, 1, 4th ed.; 2 and 3, 3rd ed. Berl. 1959
Journ. Hell. Stud.	*Journal of Hellenic Studies*
Kitto	H. D. F. Kitto, *Greek Tragedy.* 3rd ed. London 1961
Lesky	Albin Lesky, *Die tragische Dichtung der Hellenen.* Göttingen 1956

LP	Edgar Lobel and Denys Page, *Poetarum Lesbiorum Fragmenta*, Oxford 1955
Mnem.	*Mnemosyne*
Mus. Helv.	*Museum Helveticum*
N.	*Tragicorum Graecorum Fragmenta* ed. A. Nauck. 2nd edition Leipzig 1889.
N. Jahrb.	*Neue Jahrbücher für das klassische Altertum*
Öst. Jahrh.	*Jahreshefte des Österr. Archäolog. Institutes in Wien*
Ox. Pap.	B. P. Grenfell, A. S. Hunt, H. I. Bell, E. Lobel and others, *The Oxyrhynchus Papyri*, 1 ff. London 1898.
P.	Roger A. Pack, *The Greek and Latin Literary Texts from Greco-Roman Egypt*. Ann Arbor Univ. of Michigan Press 1952
Pap. Soc. It.	G. Vitelli, M. Norsa ed altri, *Pubblicazioni della Società Italiana per la Ricerca dei Papiri Greci e Latini in Egitto*. 1 ff. Florence 1912 ff.
Pf.	Rudolf Pfeiffer, *Callimachus*. 2 vols. Oxf. 1949–53
Phil.	*Philologus*
Pohlenz	Max Pohlenz, *Die griechische Tragödie*. 2 vols. 2nd ed. Göttingen 1954
RE	Pauly-Wissowa, *Realenzyklopädie der classischen Altertumswissenschaft*
Rev. Ét. Gr.	*Revue des études grecques*
Rev. Phil.	*Revue de philologie*
Rhein. Mus.	*Rheinisches Museum*
Riv. Fil.	*Rivista di Filologia e d' Istruzione Classica*
Schmid	Wilhelm Schmid, *Geschichte der griechischen Literatur*. I. Müllers Handbuch der Altertumswiss. VII: 1, Munich 1929. 2, 1934. 3, 1940. 4, 1946. 5, 1948
Schw. Beitr.	*Schweizerische Beiträge zur Altertumswissenschaft*
Severyns	A. Severyns, *Homère*. 1, 2nd ed. Brussels 1944. 2, 1946. 3, 1948
Stud. It.	*Studi Italiani di filologia classica*
Suidas	*Suidae Lexicon* ed. A. Adler, 5 vols. Leipzig 1928–38
Symb. Osl.	*Symbolae Osloenses*
Tebt. Pap.	B. P. Grenfell, A. S. Hunt, J. G. Smyly, E. J. Goodspeed, *The Tebtunis Papyri*. 1 ff. London 1902 ff.
Trans. Am. Phil. Ass.	*Transactions and Proceedings of the American Philological Association*
VS	H. Diels – W. Kranz, *Die Fragmente der Vorsokratiker*. 3rd ed. Berlin 1954. I refer to the authors by the numbers assigned to them in this edition
Wien. Stud.	*Wiener Studien*
Zet.	*Zetemata*. Monographien zur klass. Altertumswiss. Herausgegeben von Erich Burck und Hans Diller

A HISTORY OF GREEK
LITERATURE

CHAPTER I

The Transmission of Greek Literature

The extent of Greek literature as we have it, together with the accidents of its transmission, has been determined by historical events stretching over several thousand years, in which the most diverse political and cultural factors have been at work.[1] Since we shall often need to mention particular instances of these, the more important deserve to be outlined at the very beginning.

Until well towards the end of antiquity the Greeks wrote on papyrus. This material had been known to the Egyptians since the third millennium B.C., and they enjoyed a monopoly of its production, since the papyrus reed grew only in the Nile valley. This reed had many uses: the most valuable was in making a material for writing. The stalk was first cut into thin strips, then two layers were superimposed on one another with the grain running at right angles, the recto having it horizontal and the verso vertical. When pressed together and allowed to dry, the layers stuck firmly together. Several sheets of this substance, glued edge to edge, produced the roll, the standard form of book in antiquity. This was the medium both for preliminary drafts and for finished work, unless indeed the first sketches might be made on writing-tablets – hinged leaves of wood with the inner surface covered with a dark wax. All such material was of course extremely perishable, and in consequence the author's original autograph, common enough in modern literature, is almost never to be found among the writings of the ancients. Here and there we might hazard a guess that some scrap of papyrus could have been in the author's own writing, but such a survival as that in the Bibliotheca Marciana of Eustathius' commentary on Homer, in the author's own hand (Eustathius was archbishop of Thessalonica in the twelfth century), finds no parallel in the classical period. Nevertheless, we can know a good deal about the way in which the great classical authors wrote their works.[2] They wrote throughout in capital letters without word-division, and since they used neither accents nor breathings, they would have given incomparably greater difficulty to the reader than the modern printer does. Punctuation was equally neglected: in Attic prose texts of Isocrates' time (cf. *Antidosis* 59) we know that ends of sentences were indicated by a sign in the

---

[1] A. DAIN, *Les Manuscrits*. Paris 1949. G. PASQUALI, *Storia della tradizione e critica del testo*. 2nd ed. Florence 1952. Id. *Gnom*. 23, 1951, 233. H. HUNGER, O. STEGMÜLLER, H. ERBSE, M. IMHOF, K. BÜCHNER, H. I. BECK, H. RÜDIGER, *Geschichte der Textüberlieferung der antiken und mittelalterlichen Literatur*. Bd. I: *Antikes und mittelalterliches Buch- und Schriftwesen*. Zürich 1961.

[2] A. BÖMER-W. MENN, 'Die Schrift und ihre Entwicklung'. *Handb. d. Bibliothekswiss*. ed. 2, 1/1, Stuttg. 1950. The other sections of this work (2nd ed. 1950 onwards) also contain relevant and useful material.

margin. In Attic drama a mere horizontal dash (*paragraphos*) served to mark a change of speaker – a practice which has not helped the preservation of the text. The practice also of writing lyric parts continuously, like prose, gave later grammarians many problems. There is no need to stress the many kinds of mistake possible in copying such texts.

We can only guess when literary works were first put about in the form of books.[1] Aristotle was able to study Heraclitus in writing; Hecataeus began his *Genealogiae* with a pompous introduction clearly intended for publication. These facts suggest that the origin of the Greek book is to be looked for in the early Ionian scientific school. Both these authors take us back to the close of the sixth century: how much further back we must put the book as a vehicle of literature we cannot say. It must have reached Athens by the fifth century, when she became the cultural centre of the Greek world, and we may well think that some part was played in its introduction by Anaxagoras, who came from the Ionian city of Clazomenae and was specially influential in Athens. Technical literature in several fields can be shown to have existed in Athens from the mid-fifth century onwards, and most probably it was in the form of books. The frequent use of tragic parody in Aristophanes seems also to assume in his audience a knowledge of the great tragedians such as they could scarcely acquire without reading; and the references in Old Comedy to booksellers (βιβλιο-πώλης)[2] put the matter beyond any doubt.

The oldest Greek book known to us is the *Persae* of Timotheus (no. 1206 P.), found in a tomb at Abusir in Lower Egypt. The poet belonged to the 'new dithyramb' school and lived *c.* 450–360 B.C., while the papyrus is of the fourth century, possibly before Alexander's invasion. There is no other manuscript of a classical work so near the writer's lifetime as this. The papyrus is written in a clumsy hand in extraordinarily broad columns, and Turner has recently shown good grounds for not taking it as typical of the Greek book of that date.

The fourth century saw a great increase in the popularity of the book. Plato (*Phaedr.* 274 C ff.) speaks of the shortcomings of written works as a means of teaching. There was no literary copyright, and widely read texts were inevitably tampered with or corrupted. It is significant that the speaker and statesman Lycurgus tried to protect the works of the great tragedians by providing an official state text – although actors' interpolations were probably the greatest evil here. We shall see later how the Homeric texts fell into disorder at this time.

It is against this background that we should try to weigh up the achievement of Alexandrian scholarship, with its vital importance to Greek literature. It was

---

[1] TH. BIRT, *Das antike Buchwesen in seinem Verhältnis zur Literatur.* Berl. 1882. Repr. Aalen/Württb. 1959. W. SCHUBART, *Das Buch bei den Griechen und Römern.* 2nd ed. Berl. 1921. G. KENYON, *Books and Readers in Ancient Greece and Rome.* 2nd ed. Oxf. 1951. E. G. TURNER, *Athenian Books in the fifth and fourth centuries B.C.* Lond. 1952. T. E. SKEAT, 'The use of dictation in ancient book-production'. *Proc. Brit. Acad.* 42, 1956 (Oxf. 1957), 179. H. L. PINNER, *The World of Books in Classical Antiquity.* Leyden 1958. There is a splendid introduction to the subject with bibliography by H. Hunger in the first volume of the *Geschichte der Textüberlieferung* (*v. sup.*).

[2] Theopompus fr. 77K. 77E. Nicophon 19K. 9E. Aristomenes 9K. 9E.

Ptolemy I in the last years of his reign who founded the 'Museum' in Alexandria: this was intended, with the addition of a great library,[1] to become the general centre of literature and scholarship. The foundation may well have been influenced by the precedent of the Peripatos and Demetrius of Phalerum, who arrived in Alexandria as a refugee in 297. The library was designed by Ptolemy II Philadelphus with the intention of assembling Greek literature in its entirety: enthusiasm, foresight and a complete lack of scruple went into the amassing of 500,000 volumes, which must have risen to some 700,000 by the time of the disaster in 47 B.C. The gigantic catalogue (*Pinaces*) compiled by Callimachus thus amounted to a stocktaking of Greek literature as it then existed. The reign of Ptolemy II saw also the setting up of a smaller library in the Serapeum, intended for a wider public. The Museum, however, became the accepted place for the definitive establishment of classical texts and the issuing of critical editions. The activity of the Alexandrians as commentators will concern us elsewhere.

It is not hard to understand what the burning of the library in 47 B.C. must have meant. If we are to believe the propaganda of his enemies, Mark Antony had the library of Pergamum brought to Alexandria, supposedly as a replacement (cf. Plut. *Ant.* 58). We can only suppose that it went to the Serapeum, which in turn suffered destruction through the activities of the patriarch Theophilus in A.D. 391. After the destruction of the Museum an important role was played in the transmission of Greek literature by the library of the Gymnasium Ptolemaeum in Athens. This collection was presumably incorporated in the library of Hadrian, which was built in Athens in 131–132.

But there was no replacing what had been lost for all time. With the decline of Hellenistic scholarship went a wider decline of interest in books and texts, and from the first century of our era onwards we find ever-increasing losses in the literature transmitted. Two other factors soon came to be important – Atticism with its love of revived classical forms, and the 'Second Sophistic', reaching its height under the Antonines, which also kindled new interest in the great authors of the past. Largely, however, intellectual life had withdrawn into the schools, and in consequence excerpts, abstracts and anthologies were the order of the day. In this period the selection was made that determined which works of the Attic tragedians were to come down to us.

Another cause of heavy losses was the change in the physical form of the book, which began in the late first century A.D. and was completed by the end of the fourth. The roll was ousted by the codex, the form of book to which we are now accustomed, made up of many pages stitched into gatherings or fascicules. Naturally in this shape a book was easier to read and refer to: it was the difficulty of finding one's place in a roll that made the ancients quote mostly

---

[1] C. WENDEL, 'Geschichte der Bibliotheken im griech.-röm. Altertum'. *Handb. d. Bibliothekswiss.* 3, 1940, 1 (in the same volume K. Christ on medieval libraries). Id. in *Reallex. f. Ant. u. Christentum*, s.v. 'Bibliothek'. E. A. PARSONS, *The Alexandrian Library*, Amsterd. 1952. C. A. VAN ROOY, 'Die probleem van die oorsprong van die groot Alexandrynse biblioteek'. *Roman life and letters. Studies presented to T. J. Haarhoff.* Pretoria 1959, 147.

from memory. C. H. Roberts[1] has recently given some striking figures which illustrate the gradual changeover from roll to codex, with its numerous determining factors. In pagan literature the codex accounts in the first century for 2·31 per cent, in the second 16·8 per cent, and only in the third for 73·95 per cent of texts found in Egypt; but biblical fragments are almost exclusively in codex-form from the beginning. The explanation that Roberts offers is surprising: he suggests that St Mark, when he was writing his gospel in Rome in the first century, became familiar with the parchment notebook among Christians of the lower orders and adopted it as a convenient form. At all events it was the law and the church which caused the codex form to become dominant in the fourth century. The material itself also underwent a change. Papyrus stayed in use a long time for books in codex form, but more and more it came to be replaced by parchment, which suited the new make-up better. *Pergamene* had long been known as a writing-material: its etymological connection with Pergamon only arose from its manufacture there at a time when the Egyptians were jealously restricting the export of papyrus (Plin. *Nat. Hist.* 13, 70).

Once the new form of book had replaced the old, any text not rewritten in codex form was lost. The late fourth and early fifth centuries brought a certain revival of scholarly tastes, which soon faded, however, as a watered-down encyclopaedism became the general ideal of culture. The nadir in the copying of texts was reached in the 'dark centuries', the seventh and eighth. The stage was set for the total disappearance of classical literature, had it not been for the movement led by the patriarch Photius in the ninth century – a movement which is often spoken of as a minor Renaissance, and which the Byzantines themselves called the δεύτερος ἑλληνισμός. This learned friend and protector of ancient literature was recently brought closer to us by a happy manuscript discovery. In the autumn of 1959 Zinos Politis discovered in the monastery of Osios Nikanor in Zanorda (southern Kozani in Macedonia) a paper manuscript of the thirteenth century which contained *inter alia* the complete text of Photius' *Lexicon*. The text is to be published by the scholars of the university of Thessalonica.[2] The significance of this revival was enhanced by its coinciding with a radical change in handwriting. The uncial hand, with its large separately written letters, gave place to the cursive minuscule, which could be written much faster. The 'Uspensky Gospels' (Petropolitanus 219), written in 835, are the earliest dated example of the new hand, which rapidly replaced the old. Those ancient authors and works which were thought worthy of preservation were written out anew: among them were some which were saved from the very verge of oblivion. An example is offered by a distinguished pupil of Photius, archbishop Arethas of Caesarea, who has recorded how, some time shortly after 900, he had the *Meditations* of Marcus Aurelius transcribed from a manuscript that even then was old and damaged. From that transcript come all our extant manu-

---

[1] 'The Codex'. *Proc. Brit. Acad.* 40, 1954 (Oxf. 1955), 169 (figures p. 184).

[2] The 'Bibliotheca' of the patriarch Photius, a monument of indefatigable excerpting, is currently available in the edition (with tr.) of René Henry in the *Coll. Byz.* 1: 'Codices' 1-84. Paris 1959. 2: 'Codices' 84-185. Paris 1960.

scripts. The making of such a copy involved separating the words and adding accents and breathings – a task demanding both knowledge and patience – and would normally be done only once for any given text. Dain has conjectured with great plausibility that a transcript of this sort would then be kept in a large library as a reference copy, like the corrected texts of the Museum, and that it would serve as a master for other copies. This theory would explain why our textual tradition so often goes back to a single archetype. Where variants exist in quantity, they may arise from the incorporation in the master copy of some of the results of ancient textual research, and Byzantine manuscripts show a text constantly in a state of flux through comparison with other manuscripts, alterations and additions made from time to time. The 'metacharacterismus' was of course attended with further losses, and the process went on in the succeeding centuries. The sack of Constantinople by the crusaders in 1204 was particularly destructive. This period saw the loss of many authors who had been extant in Photius' day, such as Hipponax, much of Callimachus, Gorgias and Hyperides, together with many historians.

While the capital was occupied, scholarly work was to some degree carried on in Thessalonica and other cities, and from 1280 Constantinople also saw renewed activity. The movement was led by men like Maximus Planudes and Manuel Moschopulus, while from Thessalonica came Thomas Magister, whose pupil Demetrius Triclinius made metre his main interest.

As early as the thirteenth century cultural connections became closer between Byzantium and Italy: Palermo, Messina and Naples were the chief points of contact. Scholars like Manuel Chrysoloras brought Greek manuscripts to the west, and by the mid-fifteenth century the Vatican library already possessed 350. Thus a movement began which acquired vital cultural importance from the fall of Constantinople in 1453. The west now became for all time the repository of the Greek tradition. Between 1450 and 1600 in every city boasting an intellectual life Greek manuscripts were busily copied; they multiplied in the great libraries[1] – the Vatican, the Laurentian in Florence, the Ambrosian in Milan – and soon printing came to take the ancient texts under its wing. In the late fifteenth century Aldus in Venice and Froben in Basle introduced a printing technique which at first simply imitated manuscript by means of print.

There is no need here to speak of the great achievements of modern editing which have come since that time; but a word may be spared for the way in which papyrus discoveries have enlarged our view of Greek literature.[2] Apart

[1] W. WEINBERGER, Wegweiser durch die Sammlungen altphilologischer Handschriften. Akad. Wien 1930. E. C. RICHARDSON, A Union World Catalogue of Manuscript Books. Preliminary Studies in Method. New York 1933–37 (III: A List of Printed Catalogues of Manuscript Books). M. RICHARD, Répertoire des Bibliothèques et de Catalogues de Manuscrits Grecs. Paris 1948. L. Bieler, Les Catalogues de Manuscrits, premier supplément aux listes de Weinberger et de Richardson'. Scriptorium 3, 1948, 303.

[2] K. PREISENDANZ, 'Papyruskunde'. Handb. d. Bibliothekswiss. 2nd ed., 1/3, Stuttg. 1950. R. A. PACK, The Greek and Latin Literary Texts from Greco-Roman Egypt. Univ. of Michigan Press 1952, with full bibliographies on the individual pieces. R. STARK, 'Textgeschichtliche und literarkritische Folgerungen aus neueren Papyri'. Annales Univ. Saraviensis. Philos.-Lettres 8, 1/2, 1959, 31. On palaeographical aspects: C. H. ROBERTS, Greek Literary Hands 350

from the charred remains of a library in Herculaneum, it is the dry sands of Egypt covering classical sites which have furnished such material. After several chance discoveries in the latter half of the nineteenth century, the nineties witnessed systematic excavations which greatly advanced classical learning in all fields. The particular richness of Oxyrhynchus in literary texts has received an illuminating explanation from Turner.[1] It was a town favoured by writers and scholars from the Alexandrian circle such as Satyrus and Theon, and we may suppose that they were in regular touch with the libraries of the capital. The interest taken by the writer of *Pap. Ox.* 2792 in the handling of learned books is very instructive in this connection. Many of the papyri that have been found seem to have been personal copies from the working libraries of such men. We shall find some authors of whom we had no knowledge before these discoveries, while significant additions have been made to the works of those already known. A particular interest attaches to those papyri which allow a comparison with the current manuscript tradition: the text of Homer will have to be discussed in this connection. In general the papyri have shown the relative fidelity of medieval copies. An extreme case, but an impressive one, is a third-century papyrus (no. 1083 P.) of Plato's *Phaedo*: a comparison shows a considerable balance of better readings in the medieval tradition.

B.C.–A.D. 400. Oxf. 1955. The Byzantine Commission of the Austrian Academy of Sciences, under H. Gerstinger and H. Hunger, is working on a collection of firmly dated papyri and manuscripts.

[1] *Journ. Eg. Arch.* 38, 1952, 78 and *Mitt. aus d. Papyrussamml. d. Öst. Nat. Bibl. N.S. 5 Folge.* Vienna, 1946, 141.

CHAPTER II

The Beginnings

Greek literature for us begins with two works of mature achievement, the *Iliad* and *Odyssey*. Fifty years of research, begun by the pioneering work of Schliemann, has revealed the dim outline of a thousand years of Greek history behind the brilliant light of this first poetry.[1]

We cannot say with certainty when the first waves of Greek-speaking stock began to push in from the north towards the southern Balkans; but we can be fairly sure that the movement was under way by the beginning of the second millennium B.C.[2] Those immigrants who drove to the south found themselves in a country which had been strongly articulated by recent geological events.[3] Heavy folding and faulting had given rise to a landscape of isolated and self-contained units, favourable to the development of highly individual cultures, usually dominated by one large settlement.[4] Arms of the sea penetrate deeply into the land, while the interior is a mass of mountain ranges. This kind of articulation reaches a maximum on the east coast, which is connected by a chain of islands to the no less indented west coast of Asia Minor. Here were obvious routes mapped out for trade and intercourse which were to have the profoundest influence on the development of Hellenic culture.

The Greeks were not the first to inhabit this land. The results of excavations have shown that the immigrants found an old civilization which had attained a very considerable height. A great deal of work has been done to separate out the various cultural levels and to trace influences from different quarters: for our purpose the important fact is that the original inhabitants were peoples of quite different ethnic origins. The Greeks themselves preserved traditions of people whom they called Pelasgi, Cares and Leleges: modern scholars have

[1] A copious bibliography is given in H. BENGTSON's very sober account, *Griechische Geschichte*, 2nd ed. Munich 1960. See also the reports on recent work compiled by F. SCHACHER-MEYR, *AfdA* 6, 1953, 193; 7, 1954, 151; 10, 1957, 65; 11, 1962; id. 'Prähistorische Kulturen Griechenlands'. *RE* 22, 1954, 1350; *Die ältesten Kulturen Griechenlands*. Stuttg. 1955; *Griechische Geschichte*. Stuttg. 1960.

[2] An attempt to date the decisive folk-movements several centuries later was made by F. HAMPL, 'Die Chronologie der Einwanderung der griech. Stämme und das Problem der Träger der mykenischen Kultur'. *Mus. Helv.* 17, 1960, 57.

[3] A. PHILIPPSON, *Beiträge zur Morphologie Griechenlands*. Stuttg. 1930; *Die griechische Landschaften*. Bd. I Der Nordosten der griech. Halbinsel. Teil 1-3. Frankf.a.M. 1950–52. Bd. II Der Nordwesten der griech. Halbinsel. Teil 1 and 2, 1956/58. Bd. III Der Peloponnes. Teil 1 & 2. 1959. Bd. IV Das Ägäische Meer und seine Inseln. 1959.

[4] The connection between soil fertility and settlements is well brought out by A. R. BURN, *The Lyric Age of Greece*. London 1960, 15.

7

spoken of an 'Aegean' stratum of population.[1] This fusion of Indo-European immigrants with the existing inhabitants was vital in the development of the Greek people. Modern assessments have sought to lay the major stress on one racial element or the other; but it would be more reasonable to consider the confronting and interpenetration of the two stocks as the decisive event which was to set the stage for the rise of European civilization. From this point of view we can understand the antinomies and inner tensions with which Greek cultural life was full. The long period of juxtaposition must have passed through many phases, peaceful and warlike, just as the migrations themselves were spread over a very long time.

It is only recently that scholarship has thrown light upon a civilization which first emerges about the sixteenth century B.C., and which has been given the name 'Mycenaean'. Its great centres are the strong fortress-cities of the Argolid, the western Peloponnese and the Boeotian basin. The archaeological material shows that this early Greek civilization was very strongly influenced by the rich and alien culture of Crete, whose naval power in the second millennium B.C. had carried her influence far and wide. The Cretan empire was overthrown about 1400: in all probability there were Greeks strongly established on the island much earlier. Two hundred years later the hour struck for Mycenae also. For a long time the Dorians were held mainly responsible for the catastrophe. Even now the great folk-migration in which they came southward is often called the Dorian invasion. But more and more scholars now think that the Dorians came to their later habitations following in the train of the barbarian tribes who about 1200 B.C. burst in from the north into the Mediterranean area, spreading terror and destruction to the borders of Mesopotamia and Egypt. Their ethnic affinities cannot easily be determined:[2] Illyrian and Phrygian elements may have played an important part. These 'northern peoples' or 'sea-peoples' who destroyed the Hittite empire in the east, probably extinguished also the centres of Greek life in the late second millennium. The overthrow of the Mycenaean world was complete, and it was followed by several centuries that are more dark to us than any others in Greek history. But at the same time this violent immigration was the starting-point of the powerful new movement which led in the eighth century to the perfection of the geometric style and to the full bloom of epic poetry.

Greek literature is divided very much on dialectal or ethnic lines, which makes it necessary to consider briefly the way in which the Greek nation was split into groups. We shall have to set aside the numerous local subdivisions and deal in broad outlines only. In the historical period we find a broad band of Ionian settlements stretching from Euboea over the Cyclades to the central and southern west coast of Asia Minor. Attica, with all its individuality and its

[1] For a short account of the remains of pre-Greek language see F. SCHACHERMEYR, *RE* 22, 1954, 1494.

[2] A vigorous offensive on this front was launched by P. KRETSCHMER, 'Die phrygische Episode in der Geschichte von Hellas'. *Miscellanea Acad. Berolinensia* 1950, 173; now cf. F. SCHACHERMEYR, *Griech. Gesch.* (see p. 17, n. 1) 69. On the questions involved see also D. GRAY, in J. L. MYRES, *Homer and his Critics.* Lond. 1958, 278.

destined central position in Greek cultural life, was simply one of these settle-ments. To the north of this broad belt was an area settled mainly by Aeolic tribes, comprising essentially Boeotia and Thessaly, Lesbos and the northern part of the west coast of Asia Minor. About 1200, in the train of the great folk-migrations, Dorian and Northwest Greek stocks broke into new areas of settle-ment, the Dorians taking firm possession of the south and east Peloponnese, together with the islands, particularly Crete and Rhodes, and the southwest coast of Asia Minor. The location of the Northwest Greeks is obvious from the name: they also mingled with and influenced the Thessalian and Boeotian population to a great extent. In the north and west of the Peloponnese they took possession of the districts of Achaea and Elis. Thus the Arcadians, cut off from the sea by Dorians and Northwest Greeks, were left as an island of pre-Dorian population: their archaic dialect, known to us from limited and sometimes problematical remains, shows a kinship with that of Cyprus and with that of Pamphylia in the south of Asia Minor.

In the historical period there is no difficulty in distinguishing the dialects, and they can be readily shown on a map (cf. Schwyzer's *Grammatik*, I 83). We can also easily see from the later distribution how dialectal areas were overlaid or isolated in the 'Dorian' invasions. But the earlier history of the Greek dialects poses a series of problems which have recently once again been earnestly debated.[1] The basic questions are: after what date can we think in terms of clearly distinguished tribes and dialects in the later sense? What is the relation of the Mycenaean Greek in the Linear B tablets to the known dialects? How are we to interpret the relation of Arcado–Cyprian to these latter? To Mycenaean Greek we shall have shortly to return.

Most scholars take it as proven that there were two great invasions of migrant peoples in the latter half of the second millennium, in the course of which various different stocks came into the south of the Balkans. But how far are we justified in this connection in speaking, as Paul Kretschmer first did, of an earlier Ionic and a later Aeolic invasion?[2]

We must first make it clear that the long-popular theory which viewed languages as spreading out like branches on a tree is now out of favour. One cannot trace the individual languages in a straight line back to a primitive

---

[1] F. ADRADOS, 'La dialectología griega como fuente para el estudio de las migraciones indoeuropeas en Grecia'. *Acta Salmanticensia* V/3, Salamanca 1952. M. S. RUIPÉREZ, 'Sobre la prehistoria de los dialectos griegos'. *Emérita* 21, 1953 (1954), 253. W. PORZIG, 'Sprachgeo-graphische Untersuchungen zu den altgriechischen Dialekten'. *Indog. Forschungen* 61, 1954, 147. E. RISCH, 'Die Gliederung der griech. Dialekte in neuer Sicht'. *Mus. Helv.* 12, 1955, 61. J. CHADWICK, 'The Greek Dialects and Greek Prehistory'. *Greece and Rome* 3, 1956, 38. V. PISANI, *Storia della lingua greca* in *Encicl. Class.* 2/5/1. Turin 1960, 3. VL. GEORGIEV, 'Das Problem der homerischen Sprache im Lichte der kretisch-mykenischen Texte'. *Minoica und Homer*. Berl. 1961, 10.

[2] Apart from Georgiev op. cit. this view of KRETSCHMER'S (cf. e.g. GERCKE-NORDEN, *Einleitung in die Altertumswissenschaft*, section 'Sprache'. 3rd ed., Leipzig 1927, 75), has been recently supported by A. TOVAR in Μνήμης χάριν. *Gedenkschrift P. Kretschmer* II. Vienna 1957, 188. KRETSCHMER spoke not of an Aeolic, but of an Achaean invasion, but we shall see that this is virtually a distinction without a difference.

Indo-European unity: no more can one trace the Greek dialects in this way back to a unitary Old Greek. The postulate of original unity has been replaced by that of a multiplicity of isoglosses, with remarkable variation in their geographic distribution. The truth of this view as regards Greek emerges most strikingly from the work of Ernst Risch, who has shown that characteristic features often cross the boundaries of dialects.[1] In the beginning was not unity, but a richly varied multiplicity. Pursuing this approach, Risch detects relatively late linguistic forms in two important dialects: Ionic and Doric, he thinks, developed their distinctive features in the migrations and the dialectal stratification which came after the Mycenaean period. We must of course remember that Kretschmer, when he reckoned the Ionians as the oldest stratum, was thinking not of the Ionians of Asia Minor, but of their remote antecedents. It was he, after all, who taught us to regard the tendencies towards unity and towards diversity as forces whose constant interplay is the perpetual cause of change. Risch further postulates in the second millennium an old Southern Greek dialect group of which the purest representative is Arcado-Cyprian, and distinguishes this from another group best attested in East Thessalian. Here again we find the two early invasions, and we find it possible to reconcile the new results with the picture drawn by Kretschmer. We must, of course, never overlook the influence of neighbouring groups and linguistic substrata in the development of dialects.

It has proved difficult to classify the type of Greek that we have found in the Linear B tablets. Partly this is due to the nature of the tablets and their writing (this again must be discussed later), partly the trouble is that besides obvious similarities to Arcado-Cyprian there are connections with other dialects also. There are two rival theories. Risch,[2] in accordance with his views on the genesis of the dialects, sees in Mycenaean Greek a little of the early history of the Greek language: here it has not yet developed its characteristic features, especially in phonology and the declensional system. Georgiev, on the other hand, reckons the language to be the result of an overlaying of Ionian by later Aeolic elements, thus giving rise to a mixed dialect ('Achaean'), which is the basis of the Cretan-Mycenaean koine of the tablets. Georgiev's theory is brought a little closer to the other by the fact that he means always proto-Ionian and proto-Aeolic. The question is still under discussion, but the approach used by Risch seems to hold out the possibility of a solution.

As for Arcado-Cyprian, that has virtually lost the unique and peculiar position among the dialects that could still be claimed for it by Eduard Schwyzer (*Grammatik*, p. 88); but it has maintained a place of its own in view of the valuable relics of early Greek that are found in it.[3]

---

[1] For an impressive table see op. cit. 75.

[2] 'Frühgeschichte der griech. Sprache.' *Mus. Helv.* 16, 1959, 215; Georgiev loc. cit.; cf. also E. VILBORG, *A Tentative Grammar of Mycenean Greek*. Stud. Gr. et Lat. 9, 1960. A special place for Mycenaean is claimed by A. HEUBECK, 'Zur dialektologischen Einordnung des Mykenischen'. *Glotta* 39, 1960/61, 159.

[3] A threefold division of the pre-Dorian dialect is still maintained by C. J. RUIJGH, 'Le Traitement des sonants voyelles dans les dialectes grecs et la position du mycénien'. *Mnem.* s. 4, 14, 1961, 193.

We must spare a word now for the settlement of the west coast of Asia Minor, which played such an important part in the cultural life and in the literature of Greece. A radical attempt to date it as late as the eighth century[1] has evoked a reaction which tries to put the effective settlement of the area back into the Mycenaean period.[2] Early Greek remains have now come to light on the west coast of Asia Minor, particularly in Miletus and Rhodes which prove Greek occupation in the Mycenean age; but on the other hand the main stream of Ionic and Aeolic settlers must be considered as a consequence of the 'Dorian' invasion and dated accordingly.[3] Roland Hampe[4] has tried to maintain that Attica was a point of assembly and departure for the colonists coming from the Pylos area: although his arguments from mythology are not wholly convincing, it remains perfectly possible that Attica played an important role in that way.

The pre-Homeric period saw two developments which were of supreme importance for Greek literature – the first appearance of Greek writing[5] and the origin of Greek mythology.[6]

It is not long since our ideas about writing in the second millennium B.C. were rudely shaken. In Cnossus and in the mainland fortress cities of Pylos and Mycenae many hundreds of clay tablets have been discovered, written in a uniform script commonly known as Linear B, and dating partly from around 1400, partly from around 1200.[7] Thanks to the genius of Michael Ventris, we now know that

---

[1] G. M. A. HANFMANN, 'Archaeology in Homeric Asia Minor'. *Am. Journ. Arch.* 52, 1948, 135. id., 'Ionia, leader or follower?' *Harv. Stud. in Class. Phil.* 61, 1953, 1.

[2] F. CASSOLA, *La Jonia nel mondo miceneo*. Naples 1957.

[3] F. SCHACHERMEYR, *Griechische Geschichte*. Stuttg. 1960, 78 and *Gnom*. 32, 1960, 207.

[4] 'Die hom. Welt im Lichte der neuen Ausgrabungen: Nestor'. In: *Vermächtnis der antiken Kunst*. Heidelb. 1950, 11. Apart from CASSOLA loc. cit. the thesis is opposed by M. B. SAKEL-LARIOU, *La Migration grecque en Ionie*. Athens 1958. But see T. B. L. WEBSTER, *Die Nach-fahren Nestors. Mykene und die Anfänge der griech. Kultur.* Janus-Bücher 19. Munich 1961, 32.

[5] A. REHM, *Handb. d. Archäologie* I, 1939, 182. R. HARDER, 'Die Meisterung der Schrift durch die Griechen'. *Das neue Bild der Antike*. Leipz. 1942, 91. The literature on Linear B is already immense. The greatest milestone is still the first complete publication by M. VENTRIS and J. CHADWICK, 'Evidence for Greek Dialect in the Mycenaean Archives'. *Journ. Hell. Stud.* 73, 1953, 84. A comprehensive presentation is given by the two authors in *Documents in Mycenaean Greek*. Cambr. 1956. For the history of the decipherment: J. CHAD-WICK, *The Decipherment of Linear B*. Cambr. 1958. For a convenient collection of the published material from the different sites: E. RISCH, *Mus. Helv.* 16, 1959, 216, 3. We should mention the detailed account of work from 1952 to 1958 given by F. SCHACHERMEYR in *AfdA* 11, 1958, 193. References to current literature in the periodical *Minos. Revista de filología egea*. Salamanca 1951 ff. and the *Studies in Mycenaean Inscriptions and Dialect* published by the Institute of Classical Studies of the University of London. Prompt and detailed reports of new discoveries and new literature in *Nestor* (distributed by Bennett in the form of single sheets). For an able summary with abundant references see now J. A. DAVISON, 'The Decipherment of Linear B: The Present Position'. *Phoenix* 14, 1960, 14. The most recent comprehensive treatment is by L. R. PALMER, *Mycenaeans and Minoans. Aegean Prehistory in the Light of the Linear B Tablets*. Lond. 1961.

[6] M. P. NILSSON, *The Mycenaean Origin of Greek Mythology*. Berkeley 1932. L. RADER-MACHER, *Mythos und Sage bei den Griechen*. 2nd ed., Vienna 1943. H. J. ROSE, *Griech. Mytho-logie*. Munich 1955.

[7] The dating of the Cnossus tablets around 1400 hinges on the correct dating of excavated material: recently it has been challenged by L. R. PALMER as being too early, and the question

this writing is a development of the earlier Cretan Linear A, rudely adapted to the writing of Greek. The value of this discovery for our knowledge of the political and economic condition of the Mycenaean world can scarcely be over-rated, but the light it casts on Greek literature is disappointingly small. The mass of inventories, accounts and receipts shows the existence of a class of scribes in the service of the administration: we should be less ready to assume the literacy of the rulers themselves. If we adopt the view that these scribes were probably unfree and came from different parts of the Mycenaean world or its environs, and if we also bear in mind the purely utilitarian character of these documents, we are brought face to face with a distressing paradox. These tablets in Greek of the second millennium are of inestimable value for the history of the language, but the circumstances mentioned make their evaluation difficult and often uncertain. The knowledge of this script, unsatisfactory as it is when applied to Greek, perished with the catastrophe of the 'Dorian' invasions[1] and Greek writing had to start all over again. Some unknown had the inspiration to modify the north Semitic consonantal script so as to permit the indication of vowels. This was the genesis of the Greek alphabet: its oldest monument is an Attic jug from the first half of the eighth century, to which we may now add a drinking-vessel from Ischia (Acc. Lincei 1955) – both inscriptions are metrical. The writing on the Dipylon jug is already fluent and stylized, so that the develop-ment of the alphabetic script needs to be put at least 100 years earlier.[2]

It was Nilsson who first suggested that the main lines of Greek mythology were laid down in the Mycenaean age. We can hardly imagine that the aristo-cratic society of Mycenae had no songs and sagas of ancient derring-do, but it remains very questionable whether much of the known mythology originated in that period. It is far more likely that Greek heroic legend attained its known form in the 'dark centuries', between the twelfth and the eighth. It became connected, of course – here Nilsson is unquestionably right – in a special way with the great centres of Mycenaean civilization. They spoke to posterity in a hundred voices of tradition, and their great ruins impressed the ages which followed their overthrow. With a certain over-simplification one might say that saga postulates ruins. The nature of the problem is well illustrated in this fact: when in the Mycenaean tablets such well-known names in mythology as Ajax, Achilles, Hector and Theseus repeatedly came to light, this was at first

is under discussion. A quick outline of the essentials is found in F. SCHACHERMEYR, 'Aufregung um Arthur Evans'. *Wiener human. Blätter* 4, 1961, 27.

[1] A. J. B. WACE suggests that it survived: cf. the introduction to Ventris-Chadwick, *Documents* (*v. sup.*). A different view in STERLING DOW, 'Minoan Writing'. *Am. Journ. Arch.* 58, 1958, 77.

[2] There can be few supporters of the late date advocated by RHYS CARPENTER, *Am. Journ. Arch.* 37, 1933, 8. G. KLAFFENBACH, 'Schriftprobleme der Agäis'. *Forsch. u. Fortschr.* 1948, 195, suggests that the Semitic characters were taken over about the tenth century. See also the works cited in p. 11, n. 5. For the oldest inscriptions: T. B. L. WEBSTER, 'Notes on the writing of early Greek poetry'. *Glotta* 38, 1960, 253, 1, where the reading of the beaker from Ischia is discussed. On this see also W. SCHADEWALDT, *Von Homers Welt und Werk*. 3rd ed. Stuttg. 1959, 413.

taken as a confirmation of Nilsson's theory; only later was it realized that these were everyday names,[1] and that only a later age, when they were no longer in common use, could appropriate them for the great heroes of the past. Greek mythology focuses the rays of that dazzlingly brilliant light with which the world is mirrored in Greek literature, both in its content and in its form. Attempts to derive all Greek mythology from one basic source are doomed to failure: we have learned now to distinguish the strands of the fabric one from another, and we can see that Greek mythology brings the most heterogeneous materials together into an enduring form. Memories of historical events, often wildly distorted, rub shoulders with primitive myths of the gods; aetiological myths stand cheek by jowl with ancient fairy-tale elements, or with stories seemingly invented for the sheer love of a good tale. Nature-symbolism in Greek myth is the exception.

Greek mythology, like the Greek people, comes from a fusion of Indo-European and Mediterranean elements. The fact that a large number of gods and heroes have non-Greek names indicates in itself the size and difficulty of the problems involved – problems further complicated by the addition of a third element in the influence of oriental culture and cults. This influence must have been particularly important in the period following the successive overthrow of Cretan and of Mycenean power, when the Phoenicians, dominant in commerce, were the obvious intermediaries.[2]

To say that literature, as something written down, is not found before Homer is not to say that there was no poetry before that time. Myths may certainly have been circulated in bald prose; but it is reasonable to suppose that their true medium was epic poetry. Presumably epic poetry goes back to Mycenaean times: the Homeric evidence points that way,[3] since we learn that marriage and funerals, dances and celebrations of victory, the worship of the gods and indeed everyday work were all accompanied by songs, of types with which we are familiar from a later age. All this is lost. Certain sects in Greece did indeed try to glorify their supposed founder – an Orpheus or a Musaeus - by giving them an antiquity more remote than Homer's; but we can detect the motive and reject the invention.

[1] Cf. A. HEUBECK, Gnom. 29, 1957, 43; 33, 1961, 118.

[2] A. SEVERYNS, Grèce et Proche-Orient avant Homère. Brussels 1960. For the eighth and seventh centuries: T. J. DUNBABIN, 'The Greeks and their eastern neighbours'. Society for the Promotion of Hellenic Studies. Suppl. Pap. 8, 1957.

[3] W. SCHADEWALDT, Von Homers Welt und Werk, 3rd ed. Stuttg. 1957, 62.

CHAPTER III

The Homeric Epic

A The *Iliad* and *Odyssey*

1 EPIC POETRY BEFORE HOMER

The progress of scholarship [1] has made it impossible nowadays to speak of Homer without implying the 'Homeric question'. For discussing the latter there are two possible starting points only – a consideration of pre-Homeric epic as far as we can know it, and the study of the *Iliad* as we now possess it. The basic problems have raised their heads mainly in connection with the older epic, and we shall discuss them after giving some account of the *Iliad*. Most of the results are applicable to the *Odyssey*, although it has also many problems of its own.

When Homer was rediscovered in the eighteenth century in England, he was regarded as a child of nature, naïve and unreflecting. Robert Wood's view of him (*An Essay on the Original Genius of Homer*, 1769) as a poet who was a law to himself was accepted by the classical German writers also. Nowadays we hold different views: we see the form and manner of the poems in a context. Homer is a beginning – and not merely from our viewpoint. We may with fair confidence place him in the eighth century – the century which released the pent-up forces of the dark age to develop freely and to breathe life everywhere. The archaic period already witnessed a development away from the spiritual world of epic poetry, but nevertheless Homer was in truth, as the Greeks always considered him, the fountainhead of many of the most important streams of intellectual life. Yet if we change our viewpoint, we see these poems, with all their later influence, not as a beginning, but as the culmination of a long development. The absence of any surviving pre-Homeric poetry is readily understood once we realize its nature; and in this enquiry the Homeric poems themselves provide the starting point.

In both the epics we find mention of songs celebrating the deeds of heroes, but under very different circumstances. The embassy to Achilles finds him singing of 'the deeds of men' and accompanying himself on the lyre (9. 186). Patroclus sits beside him, ready to take up the song if Achilles leaves off. In the *Odyssey*, however, the singers are professionals – Demodocus at the Phaeacian court, Phemius entertaining the suitors at their banquets. The conclusion has of course been drawn that the *Iliad* reflects an earlier stage, when the heroes

---

[1] The modern literature on individual aspects of the Homeric problem is immense: I refer the reader to my summaries in *AfdA*. Three of these from vol. 4, 1951 and 5, 1952 are printed together in *Die Homerforschung in der Gegenwart*, Vienna 1952. Continuation in *AfdA* 6, 1953, 129; 8, 1955, 129; 12, 1959, 129; 13, 1960, 1. H. J. METTE, 'Homer 1930–1956'. *Lustrum* 1956/1, Göttingen 1957; addenda in *Lustrum* 1959/4, Gött. 1960. A. HEUBECK, 'Fachbericht zur neueren Homerforschung'. *Gymn.* 66, 1959, 380.

sang for themselves; but one might more plausibly explain the difference by the different milieux in which the poems are set. The professional bard is quite in place at home in peacetime, but would hardly accompany an army on active service. At all events the power of poetry to move the hearts of men, and hence the probability of a class of singers to wield this power is attested even in the *Iliad*, where Helen laments to Hector that she and Paris will be sung of among later generations (6. 357). In this connection we should also notice *Il*. 20. 204: Aeneas says to Achilles that they know each other's pedigree by report – by πρόκλυτα ἔπεα. Heroic poetry, dealing as it did with noble deeds, by its very nature gave scope for a good deal of genealogy: the *Iliad* is full of it.

The *Odyssey* tells us a good deal about the bard's status and the nature of his performance.[1] Eumaeus (17. 381) defends himself against the charge of having brought a useless beggar into the house. 'No, of course one does not invite people of that kidney: one invites into the house a man with a trade (δημιοεργός) – a physician, a seer, an architect or a singer who brings joy by his divine gift.' Here we see singers as an organized guild. Mostly the singer would wander from place to place, as we find Homer himself doing in later legend; but he might attach himself to the court of a prince and gain there a respected position. When Agamemnon sailed for Troy, he left his wife in the care of a singer (3. 267) – Aegisthus made him rue the honour. Demodocus is summoned to the Phaeacian court when there is occasion for song to adorn some great festival (8. 44). A herald is sent to escort the blind singer, whose name implies that he is 'esteemed by the people'. One cannot but recall the 'blind man of Chios' in the hymn to the Delian Apollo, commending himself to the maidens as preservers of his memory. A blind singer must have been not uncommon in real life: Homer was so represented, and his name was falsely etymologized as ὁ μὴ ὁρῶν, 'he who sees not'.

Demodocus has a place of honour at court: he sits on a seat of wrought silver near one of the roof-pillars; his lyre hangs by his head; he is brought food and drink on a handsome tray. When everyone has finished eating, he begins his song. He sings and plays several times in the Phaeacian scenes (8. 261, 471; 13. 28). There is, however, a striking feature in the first such passage. Demodocus sings to the lyre the story of the illicit love of Aphrodite and Ares, and of the trap set for them by Hephaestus. As he sings, youths dance around him. Was this a representation in mime of the story? We have no way of telling: the only parallel to this scene is that depicted on the shield of Achilles (*Il*. 18. 590), where there is a singer with his lyre and a chorus of youths and maidens.

An important passage for understanding the nature of primitive epic is the first appearance of Demodocus in the eighth book of the *Odyssey* (72). He takes his theme from the great events around Troy, and sings of the quarrel between Odysseus and Achilles at the feast. In a later passage (487) Odysseus supplies a theme by asking to hear about the Wooden Horse. There follows the song which brings tears into his eyes and leads to his recognition.

[1] W. SCHADEWALDT, 'Die Gestalt des hom. Sängers' in *Von Homers Welt und Werk*. 2nd ed., Stuttg. 1951, 54. R. SEALEY, 'From Phemios to Ion'. *Rev. Et. Gr.* 70, 1957, 312.

We should also notice the terms in which Odysseus praises Demodocus. The Muses or Apollo himself must have taught him: to sing well is impossible without divine inspiration. And, we may note, Demodocus knows how to sing 'according to the rules' (κατὰ κόσμον). This praise implies not only truth in narrative – always claimed by this kind of heroic lay – but also skill on the singer's part in putting the elements together.

What we must decide is whether we think that Demodocus and his like improvised or sang from a fixed text. This question is more profitably considered by first going outside the purely Homeric field. Even when the written book was fully developed, we know that the Homeric poems were current in oral recitation by rhapsodes at religious festivals.[1] In Plato's time rhapsodes were often self-confident virtuosi: he draws a lively sketch of one in the *Ion*. They had long ceased to carry a lyre: a staff in the hand was now the badge of office. They no longer sang, but recited in a loud speaking voice: they had prodigious memories and followed a fixed text – a text which perhaps in early times used to be the prized possession of a particular family or guild. Their strictness in following the text was probably not absolute, and this kind of transmission was the main cause of many difficulties in the Homeric text. What is important for us, however, is that the rhapsodes got by heart a ready-made text.

If we now return to pre-Homeric bards like Demodocus, we find one obvious difference: singer and lyre take the place of reciter and staff. But whence comes the material for the singer's performance? On his first entrance (8. 74) Demodocus sings of the quarrel of Achilles and Odysseus, taking it from a 'song sequence' (οἴμη) 'of which the fame reaches from earth to heaven'. We may compare this with the passage at the beginning of the *Odyssey*, where the Muse is enjoined to begin somewhere in the eventful career of Odysseus – in fact, of course, the starting-point is selected with great artistry. Demodocus is also able on request to sing of a favourite incident in the siege of Troy – the Wooden Horse. This shows clearly enough that there was a detailed corpus of sagas behind the bards. Now did the bards have the words ready-made as well as the theme, or did they improvise anew at each performance? Was this the respect in which they most differed from the later rhapsodes? We could not be sure, were it not that the comparative study of literature has provided us a reliable and detailed picture of this kind of oral epic.

The first steps in this direction were taken forty years ago, when the Slavic scholar Mathias Murko pointed out some features of current South Slavic epic which have a vital bearing on the understanding of early Greek heroic poetry. Murko made little impression on a world that was hotly chasing the hare of Homeric analysis. A better reception was given in the English-speaking world to the work of Milman Parry and his followers.[2] Three years of field-work

[1] The derivation of ῥαψῳδός from ῥάβδος is untenable. H. PATZER, *Herm.* 80, 1952, 314, starts from ῥάπτειν and the notion of tacking together.

[2] Parry's researches (with bibliog.): ALBERT B. LORD, 'Homer, Parry and Huso'. *Am. Journ. Arch.* 52, 1948, 34. 'Composition by Theme in Homer and Southslavic Epos'. *Trans. a. Proc. Am. Phil. Ass.* 82, 1951, 71. *The Singer of Tales.* Harvard Stud. in Comp. Lit. 24. Harv. Univ. Press., Cambr. Mass. 1960. JAMES A. NOTOPULOS, 'The Generic and Oral Composi-

(1933-35) in the Serbo-Croat area yielded about 12,500 texts, some recorded with modern equipment, others taken down by dictation. These now repose in the Harvard University Library under the title 'Milman Parry Collection of Southslavic Texts'. The collection includes a great many epic lays as well as popular lyrics: the examination and assessment of these is still going on. Parry himself died young, but his work was carried on by his companion and assistant, Albert B. Lord, who travelled in Yugoslavia in 1937, 1950 and 1951, making new recordings and checking the material gathered earlier. His book *The Singer of Tales* gives a detailed picture of the various forms of popular oral epic in the southern Slav area, and tries to use the knowledge thus gained towards the better understanding of Homeric poetry. The scope of such research has been considerably widened as a result of Bowra's *Heroic Poetry* (1952), which examines epic poetry from all parts of the world as a basis on which to establish the essential characteristics of oral epic.

Poetry of this sort is found among most of the peoples of the world – in some parts down to the present day. Naturally the differences between Russian *bylin*, Norse saga and Sumatran song are very great in detail; but in the mass they present striking similarities. The central feature of such poems is the hero, distinguished above all men by courage and bodily strength: his conduct knows no restraint but that of honour – a notion which in primitive times offered few difficulties. The ties of friendship may also be very strong in his mind. The origin and continuance of this kind of poetry comes from the existence of a knightly upper class delighting in warfare, hunting and the pleasures of the table (the latter including the performance of the singer himself). The songs originally sung in this aristocratic milieu would later become common property. The background of the hero's activities is usually a heroic age – a past which is larger and brighter than the present. There is a naïve delight in the physical world, expressed in elaborate descriptions of chariots, ships, arms and clothing: the element of magic is largely wanting. It is possible to posit a development from a magical or shamanistic level of thought and narrative to a heroic level: or we may prefer to think that the two elements exist together and touch or overlap at various points.[1] Heroic poetry of this type always claims to be telling

tion'. Ibid. 81, 1950, 28; 'Continuity and Interconnexion in Homeric Oral Composition'. Ibid. 82, 1951, 81; 'Homer and Cretan Heroic Poetry'. *Am. Journ. Phil.* 73, 1952, 225, with interesting details of the composing and writing down of a poem on the Cretan revolt of 1770; *Modern Greek Heroic Oral Poetry*. New York 1959. 'Homer, Hesiod and the Achaean Heritage of Oral Poetry'. *Hesperia* 29, 1960, 177. C. M. BOWRA, *Heroic Poetry*. London 1952. Id., *Homer and his Forerunners*. Edinburgh 1955. S. J. SUYS-REITSMA, *Het Homerisch epos als orale schepping van een dichterhetairie*. Amsterd. 1955. G. S. KIRK, 'Homer and Modern Oral Poetry: Some Confusions'. *Class. Quart.* 54, 1960, 271; 'Dark Age and Oral Poet'. *Proc. of the Cambr. Phil. Soc.* no. 187, 1961, 34. MILMAN PARRY and ALBERT LORD, *Serbocroatian Heroic Songs. Novi Pazar*. 2 vols., Cambridge (Mass.) and Belgrade 1954. These two volumes are the first of a series which is to publish the material collected by PARRY and LORD in more than 20 volumes. The next volume is to contain the 12,000 or so verses of the poem of Avdo Mededović on the wedding of Smailagić Meho.

[1] The shamanistic aspect is stressed by K. MEULI, 'Scythica'. *Herm.* 70, 1935, 121. BOWRA (op. cit., p. 8) favours a development of heroic poetry from a magical to a more anthropocentric outlook on the world. K. MARÓT tries determinedly to derive epic poetry from the

the truth: this claim is supported by saying either that the story has been reliably transmitted or that it has been divinely inspired.

The form of the narrative is usually verse, the unit being the single line, not the stanza. Speeches play an important part in the tale. Perhaps the most striking feature is the predominance of 'typical' elements of language – stock adjectives and recurrent formulae – and 'typical' scenes – arming for the fray, parting, marriage feasts and funeral rites.

These features are bound up with the essence of this kind of epic. It is a work of art and craftsmanship, transmitted from master to pupil, often from father to son. The studies cited above have taught us much about the composition of such poetry. The singer has two basic weapons in his armoury – knowledge of his national folk-stories and a ready mastery of all the formulaic elements. He needs no more. He is innocent of any set text and makes up his song freshly for each occasion. Naturally he goes mainly on what he and others have sung before, but he is in no way bound to a fixed text which he must simply reproduce. He makes constant changes, usually in the direction of amplifying what has been sung before. It is a poetry essentially based on the spoken word – the Americans call it 'oral composition' – and it is no less so in a largely literate society. To take it down in writing or on tape is basically unnatural: one is compelling a flowing stream to freeze at one point.

There are so many bonds of kinship between oral composition of this kind and the Homeric poems that we can reasonably think of their early stages in some such terms. Thus we reach an answer to our former question. What Phemius and Demodocus sang was not a text fixed and settled for all time, but an improvisation made up for each occasion with the help of stylized elements of diction. The subject would be taken from an existing body of myth, the form dictated by a craft tradition.

Thus by comparing the data afforded by various national epics, we gain a very good notion of the earliest stages of Homeric epic as we may suppose them to have existed in Greece and the Greek colonies of Asia Minor several centuries before the present *Iliad* and *Odyssey* took shape. We can hardly suppose that there were no minstrels in the aristocratic society of Mycenae. But even without the recent discoveries we could infer a good deal from such things as the remains of a lyre in the beehive tomb of Menidi in Attica and the fresco from Pylos – whether the lyre-player be a mortal or (more probably) a tutelary god.[1] We can form no clear notion of the content and form of this Mycenaean poetry[2]:

sphere of magic, in particular from narratives with magical purpose and from long enumerations in the manner of a litany – the latter being the origin of the epic catalogue. Of his work *A Görög Irodalom Kezdetei* (1956) the first part is available (revised) in a German translation: *Die Anfänge der griechischen Literatur. Vorfragen.* Budapest 1960. It gives references to other works by the writer on the same theme. His evidences are not, however, sufficient to support his bold conclusions, cf. *Gnom.* 33, 1961, 529.

[1] References in T. B. L. WEBSTER, *From Mycenae to Homer.* London 1958, 47 n. 1 and 130 n. 2; cf. id., *Die Nachfahren Nestors.* Janus-Bücher 19. Munich 1961, 57.

[2] For a lively discussion of the possibilities see Webster, op. cit. W. KULLMANN's book, *Das Wirken der Götter in der Ilias.* Berl. 1956, contains much that is excellent, but his statements on pre-Homeric poetry are mere surmise.

in all probability it dealt in orally transmitted tales of the heroes. For this very reason we cannot hope to be further enlightened about it by the tablets.

One question still demands our attention: What is the relation between the poems as they now exist and the practice of oral composition? This is the form taken by the 'Homeric question' now that we can no longer shut our eyes to the results of the comparative method in literary studies. This question will arise in our chapter on the origin of the *Iliad*: for the moment we must turn to the materials and structure of the poem.

2 THE *ILIAD*: MATERIALS AND COMPOSITION

When we ask what the materials of an epic poem are, we are necessarily asking what the historical background of the narrative is. In this field also we have learnt much from the comparative method. German national poetry well exemplifies what we often meet elsewhere:[1] the events behind the saga are historical, but treated with the utmost freedom as regards person, time and action. The treatment of Theodoric and Attila shows this very clearly. An equally apposite parallel, though on a smaller scale, has been pointed out by J. Th. Kakridis.[2] It comes from the last century, and is a perfect test case to illustrate the forces at work in the growth of legend. A girl from a good family in Zacynthus presented Queen Olga with a piece of beautifully worked embroidery representing traditional themes. Ten years later a water-carrier on the island was singing of the happening and of the little work of art. The bare fact had been preserved, but the details as sung had no connection with reality, or at best a very tenuous one.

Homeric scholars have not yet learned to draw the right conclusions from instances of this kind: they still go to extremes. Rhys Carpenter in his book *Folk Tale, Fiction and Saga in the Homeric Epics*[3] virtually denies any historical kernel to the poem beyond a vague *mise en scène*, and makes the war itself a fiction. Denys Page in his recent book *History and the Homeric Iliad*[4] (an equally purposeful title!) exploits Hittite texts to the limit to prove the historicity of the narrative: for him the *Iliad* reflects the conflict between the Achaeans, with their base in Rhodes, and the league of Assuwa, to which Troy belonged, at the time when Hittite power was waning.

Scholarly opinion is still in flux, and our knowledge of history in the second millennium is steadily growing. At all events, the ruins of Troy, discovered by

[1] D. V. KRALIK, 'Die geschichtlichen Zügen der deutschen Heldendichtung'. *Almanach Ak. Wien* 89, 1939, 299.

[2] In a lecture given in Vienna, shortly to be published.

[3] *Sather Class. Lect.* 20. 2nd ed. Univ. of Calif. Press 1956.

[4] *Sather Class. Lect.* 31. Univ. of Calif. Press 1959. More recently FRANZ HAMPL has published a vigorously polemical article, 'Die Ilias ist kein Geschichtsbuch' (*Serta Philologica Aenipontana.* Innsbr. 1961, 37), in which he is critical (for the most part justly) of our attempts to get at history through the epic. Nevertheless, one may surely suppose as much historical background to Greek as to German epic; and Usener's hypothesis that the heroes are degraded gods has to be applied with extreme caution. HAMPL's historical survey of the various attempts to extract history from Homer is useful and welcome. The question is also discussed by L. PARETI, *Omero e la realità storica*. Milan 1959.

Schliemann, interpreted by Dörpfeld and recently re-examined by Blegen, are evidence far too massive for us to evade the question: What connection is there between the epic narrative and the reality? Mycenaean sherds attest relations between Troy and mainland Greece – relations which can scarcely have been always friendly. The rich treasures of Mycenae and the overthrow of the Cretan maritime empire suggest large-scale plundering expeditions by sea. The sixth city to be founded on the hill of Hissarlik met its end by violent destruction. It was an easy inference that a joint enterprise of mainland princes against Troy, under the more or less unified command of the ruler of Mycenae, formed the historical core of the legend. Blegen's researches, however, have raised some problems afresh. Troy VI, it now appears, was destroyed not by hostile attack, but by an earthquake about 1300 B.C. The new candidate for the position of Homer's Troy is Troy VIIa, destroyed apparently about 1200.[1] The ancients commonly reckoned the fall of Troy at 1184 – a striking coincidence. On the other hand, the conquerors were more likely to have been barbarians crossing the straits in the train of the great migrations than Greeks of the mainland, whose overthrow was then at hand. The difficulty is a serious one. Schachermeyr has tried to meet it by supposing that Troy VI was after all the Homeric Troy, and that the story of the wooden horse is a distorted tradition of the destruction wrought by Poseidon – Poseidon the 'Earthshaker', whose animal symbol was the horse.

In our general approach to these questions we must not forget how loose the connections between myth and history usually are. A Mycenaean expedition against Troy is credible enough in itself, but this would not necessarily have caused the great fortress city in north-west Asia Minor, whose ruins long attested its former greatness, to become the nucleus of a great cycle of legend. In the *Iliad* we can often see the way in which legends could grow. One of the centres of power in the Mycenaean world was Pylos in the western Peloponnese, which we may recognize in the palace of Ano Englianos on the north shore of Navarino Bay. This palace, partly excavated in 1939, was the scene of the great discovery of clay tablets inscribed in Linear B.[2] This part of the Mycenaean world has found its way into the *Iliad* in the person of Nestor; and the old man's garrulous ways enable the poet to bring large draughts of Pylian legend into his epic (11. 670 battle with the Epeans; 7. 132 battle with the Arcadians). Another example is the important role of Lycian heroes like Glaucus, Pandarus and Sarpedon.[3] Mycenaean Greeks had already colonized Rhodes, and they thus inevitably made contact with Lycians – witness the legend of Bellerophon, whose grandson Glaucus from Lycia meets the Argive Diomedes on the battlefield

---

[1] F. SCHACHERMEYR, *Poseidon*, Berne 1950, 194. For a survey with bibliog. see D. L. PAGE, *History and the Homeric Iliad. Sather Class. Lect.* 31. Univ. of Calif. Press. 1959.

[2] R. HAMPE, 'Die hom. Welt im Lichte der neuen Ausgrabungen: Nestor'. *Vermächtnis der alten Kunst.* Heidelb. 1950, 11; cf. *Gym.* 63, 1956, 21. The identification of Ano Englianos with Pylos is not wholly certain; cf. E. MEYER, 'Pylos und Navarino'. *Mus. Helv.* 8, 1951, 119, who adheres to Dörpfeld's identification of the Homeric Pylos with that in Triphylia (bee-hive tombs; citadel of Kakovatos).

[3] M. P. NILSSON, *Homer and Mycenae.* London 1933, 261.

before Troy. They recognize the ties of friendship between them through their grandparents (6. 119), and exchange armour – gold against bronze. Memories of war with the Lycians find their way into the Trojan saga, where they appear as allies of the Trojans, despite their living so far away. Tlepolemus of Rhodes, who falls in combat with the Lycian Sarpedon, may belong to the Mycenaean period: on the other hand, the incident may reflect the struggles of the later Dorian colonists. The last instance shows how extensive a mass of legend we have to reckon with as possible material for inclusion in the Trojan saga. Scholars have constantly been exercised by indications linking Paris with Thessaly and Hector with central Greece: Pausanias (9, 18, 5) says that the latter's grave was shown in Thebes.[1] It is hard to say what these notices are worth. What we must always bear in mind is that the epic of the siege of Troy involves heroes of many different places and times.

The rape of Helen as the motive of the siege represents a very different element. Undoubtedly Helen was once a goddess: she was worshipped in the Menelaeion at Therapnae, while in Rhodes she had a cult as a tree-goddess (δενδρῖτις). Strangely enough, there is a myth of another rape of Helen, by Theseus, in her girlhood. Nilsson[2] compares the stories of the rape of Persephone and the adventures of Ariadne, and comes to the interesting conclusion that behind the alleged motive of the siege of Troy there lies an old Minoan myth of the rape of a vegetation-goddess.

A good deal of the Homeric poems is concerned with the gods, and the action hinges on their intervention. It was through the epic that Greek poetry acquired as part of its stock this pantheon of gods loosely united under the rule of Zeus. We have to ask ourselves on what this pantheon is modelled. Nilsson[3] again invokes the Mycenaean age: the Mycenaean overlord is for him the original of Zeus; and certainly we cannot deny a resemblance between Homer's scenes in Olympus and the scenes involving Agamemnon and the other princes. In both the attitude towards the overlord varies from respect to noisy opposition. We must admit that the Mycenaean kingdom, as regards its origin and extent, is rather an unknown quantity. We ought not to underestimate its importance in this connection, but at the same time we must reckon with near eastern influence in the Greek representation of the divine hierarchy. Such a view is well supported by the Hittite texts of which we shall have something to say in connection with Hesiod: the Hittites in their turn were influenced from Babylon.

The Homeric epics do not confine themselves to presenting the story of Troy, but allude often to other legends. We may reasonably suppose that these also can be traced back to the tradition of oral heroic lays which we have postulated as an earlier stage of the existing epics. We have already mentioned Pylos and Nestor. A particular interest, however, attaches to those passages which refer to the other great heroic cycle, centring on Thebes. Here also, behind the highly wrought romance, lies the historical reality of rivalry between the two great power centres of the Mycenaean age, in central Greece and the

---

[1] References in HAMPL, op. cit. 44.
[2] Op. cit. 252.   [3] Op. cit. 266.

Argolid respectively. In the *Iliad* Diomede is reminded once by Agamemnon (4. 370) and once by Athene (5. 800) of his father Tydeus, one of the wildest blades of the ill-fated Seven against Thebes. His companion Sthenelus, whose father Capaneus also bore his part in the siege, has a retort ready (4. 404): what the fathers could not do was carried through by the sons, the Epigoni. This strikingly shows how myth may be intertwined with historical data. The genealogical connection, which is tied up with a host of mutual relationships, gives us a chronology of the different myth-cycles. The expedition of the Seven was one generation before the siege of Troy, while the successful exploit of the Epigoni came only a short while before it. In the same connection we may recall the passage in the *Odyssey* which mentions the Argo as being the only ship to endure the peril of the Symplegades. The Argo is πᾶσι μέλουσα, which can only mean that she figured in some widely known poem – now of course long since vanished.

There are references to other myths in those passages also where a speaker needs an example to make his point. An instance is the story of Niobe, finely told by Achilles in the twenty-fourth book of the *Iliad*: after all her sufferings the bereaved mother at last consented to take food, and Priam should do likewise. The most highly wrought example is the story of Meleager in the ninth book of the *Iliad*,[1] a passage which drags a whole train of problems behind it. Three speeches – a triptych of the greatest artistry – are delivered to win over Achilles. Phoenix speaks second, and one of his two main points is the history of Meleager, the hero of the Calydonian boar-hunt. Because he had killed her brother, Meleager's own mother cursed him and prayed for his death. In the war against the Curetes he withdrew from the battlefield in anger at his mother's curse, so that Calydon was in grave danger. Priests sent by the elders, his father, his sisters, his mother herself and his dearest friends besought him in vain. Only at the entreaties of his wife Cleopatra did he return to the field, but too late to enjoy the gifts of a grateful people. Was Homer freely inventing, or did he have some model to follow? The question has been much debated. The episode is so independent of the plot of the *Iliad* that it seems most likely to have been taken directly from earlier poetry. We may well suppose that the 'wrath theme' occurred in the earlier saga; but in any case Homer would naturally have retold the tale so as to stress the parallel that Phoenix's argument demands.

Once we have supposed a pre-Homeric 'Wrath of Meleager', we have to ask ourselves whether Homer was influenced by it in choosing the wrath of Achilles as the *leit-motiv* of the *Iliad*. Learned fancy has not shrunk from making such a poem the whole inspiration of the *Iliad*, nor from trying to account for the latter's form and design on this basis. We need not be so courageous. We must grant the possibility that the 'Wrath of Meleager' was in Homer's mind, but without assuming that he took anything from it beyond the most general outline.

Another question bearing on the structure and themes of the *Iliad* has lately

[1] J. TH. KAKRIDIS, *Homeric Researches*. Lund 1949. W. KRAUS, 'Meleagros in der Ilias'. *Wien. Stud.* 63, 1948, 8. For a sceptical view: A. HEUBECK, *Gymn.* 66, 1959, 399.

been vigorously debated.[1] The Trojan cycle included an epic called *Aethiopis*. Its plot is known to us: it dealt with the later deeds and death of Achilles, in which his battle with the Ethiopian prince Memnon played an important part. Many elements in the plot recur in a similar form in the *Iliad*. In both epics there is a scene in which Nestor is in great danger: his chariot has been slowed because Paris has wounded one of the horses. In the *Iliad* (8. 90) Diomede rescues him, taking the old man into his own chariot: in the *Aethiopis* Nestor's son Antilochus rescues him at the cost of his own life. Achilles kills Memnon to avenge a friend, as he kills Hector to avenge Patroclus. In both poems a god weighs the fates of the two heroes before the decisive meeting. In both Thetis warns her son that, although victorious in the coming encounter, he must shortly die. The removal of Memnon's body by Sleep and Death corresponds to that of Sarpedon's body in the *Iliad* (16. 454, 671). In the *Aethiopis*, after the death of Memnon, Achilles assaults Troy and is wounded by a spear from Paris before the Scaean gate. It may be a reflection of this episode that Achilles in the *Iliad*, after Hector's death, leads an attack on the city but then changes his mind and returns to camp. There is thus good ground for thinking that Homer may have been influenced by the story of Memnon in choosing the wrath of Achilles as the central theme of the *Iliad*.

Before accepting this view, however, we must weigh up the arguments against it. The *Aethiopis* is one of the 'cyclic epics', which we have reason to date later than the *Odyssey* (*v. inf.* p. 79). This of course does not mean that it did not preserve ancient material: the cyclic poem no doubt had its models as the *Iliad* did. In general, when we find the same narrative element fully worked out in one instance and only in rudimentary form elsewhere, it is natural to suppose that the line of evolution has been from the imperfect to the more satisfactory form.

We shall now give a short outline of the contents of the *Iliad*, mainly intended to show the coherence of the overall structure, which few nowadays would be inclined to dispute. There will, however, be no attempt to gloss over the difficulties and inconsistencies which first encouraged the rise of the analytical school: these we shall discuss more fully in the next section. Both epics have come down to us divided into twenty-four books. The book-length in the *Iliad* varies between 424 lines (19) and 909 (5). This division must be fairly old: possibly it was made by Zenodotus. The ends of the books usually come at a

---

[1] H. PESTALOZZI, *Die Achilleis als Quelle der Ilias*. Zürich 1945. W. SCHADEWALDT, 'Einblick in der Erfindung der Ilias. Ilias und Memnonis.' *Von Homers Welt und Werk*. 3rd ed. Stuttg. 1959, 155. For criticism of this theory see KAKRIDIS, op. cit. 65, 1; F. FOCKE, *La Nouvelle Clio* 1951, 335; especially the detailed examination by U. HÖLSCHER, *Gnom.* 27, 1955, 392. After a series of individual studies (*Mus. Helv.* 12, 1955, 253. *Phil.* 99, 1955, 167; 100, 1956, 132), W. KULLMANN has dealt with the relation of the *Iliad* to other epics in a broader context in *Die Quelle der Ilias (Troischer Sagenkreis)*. *Herm. E.* 14, 1960. He overestimates the extent to which definite conclusions are possible; but his observations and inferences possess considerable value as long as we bear in mind that, when we think of Homer as using pre-existing themes, there is no need to suppose that one of the cyclic epics was his source. These poems presuppose an extensive epic tradition; and it is this that may have influenced Homer.

fairly clear break in the action, and names were given by the ancients to indi-vidual books (cf. Thuc. 1, 10, 4 νεῶν κατάλογος). Presumably this more or less natural division goes back to the practice of the rhapsodes in reciting Homer.

The first book leads quickly up to the quarrel between Achilles and Aga-memnon. The word μῆνις in the first verse strongly accentuates the central theme: the poem then flashes back to the first cause of the quarrel, the injury done by Agamemnon to the priest of Apollo. From this point it goes forward again in continuous narrative.[1] The commander has incurred Apollo's wrath by failing to restore the captive Chryseis to her father, and the arrows of the god are smiting the host. In the general council Agamemnon cannot but obey the seer's pronouncement: but he compensates himself by taking Briseis, who is Achilles' prize. Thereafter one striking incident follows another: the leaders quarrel, Athene dissuades Achilles from rash action, Achilles swears never to take the field again, Briseis is led away. Achilles calls his mother from the depths of the sea and asks her to obtain from Zeus some gratification of his resentment. Thetis agrees to do so when the gods shall have returned from their twelve-day banquet among the Ethiopians. Meanwhile Odysseus has returned Chryseis to her father, who placates the god towards the Greeks. Thetis lays her request before Zeus, who nods assent. His intentions are kept secret from all, including Hera, despite her bitter complaints. It is left for the cupbearer Hephaestus – lame and the butt of everyone's joke – to bring back the laughter which should accompany the feasts of the immortals.

We were told in the fifth line of book I that the will of Zeus was fulfilled in all that came to pass.[2] The working of the divine will begins the next night, when Zeus sends a dream commanding Agamemnon to attack Troy. The king tells the elders and assembles the army. It is now near the end of the ninth year (2. 134, 295), and it seems advisable to sound the feelings of the warriors. Agamemnon pretends a desire to return home, and the idea is more popular than he had thought. The attitude of the army delays the joining of battle, but Odysseus and Nestor rally the ranks for war: Thersites rails against the leaders, but is put to silence. A succession of highly wrought similes now describes the marshalling of the army: then follows a fresh invocation of the Muses to give an accurate account of Greek strength in the 'Catalogue of Ships', which is followed by a shorter catalogue of the Trojan and allied forces. (2)

Despite these elaborate preliminaries, general battle is not yet to be joined. A new delaying device holds up the increasing pressure of events. Paris declares himself ready to settle the issue by single combat with Menelaus, and at the last minute an armistice is declared. Iris takes human form, speaks to Helen, and the latter goes up to the wall over the Scaean gate, where Priam and the elders are gazing onto the plain. At the king's request she names and points out the greatest

[1] Cf. A. LESKY, Göttliche und menschliche Motivation im homerischen Epos. Sitzb. Heidelb. Phil.-hist. Kl. 1961/4. 16.

[2] W. KULLMANN, Phil. 99, 1955, 167; 100, 1956, 132; Herm. E 14, 1960, 47, n. 2. 210, takes Διὸς βουλή as the plan mentioned at the start of the Cypria to free the earth from an excessive human population. I cannot agree: the βουλή is simply Zeus' intention to hurt the Achaeans in response to Thetis' prayer: cf. Lesky op. cit. 15.

warriors of the Achaeans. Priam is then called into the field to swear that he will abide by the issue of the single combat. Menelaus' sword breaks on Paris' helmet: he seizes him by the chinstrap and drags him towards the Achaean lines. Paris' fate seems sealed, but Aphrodite makes the strap break, and rescues Paris in a cloud, taking him back to his own house. Then, taking the shape of an old woman, she bullies Helen and drives her into Paris' arms. This striking deliverance of Aphrodite's favourite has created an ambiguous situation: Paris is dallying with Helen, while Menelaus rages over the field seeking him. Agamemnon claims victory for his brother and the return of Helen and the booty: the war, he declares, is at an end. (3)

The Achaean king may be in earnest in this view, but in the ensuing scene in Olympus Zeus propounds it only to anger Hera and Athene. Both demand the destruction of Troy; but we are not yet told the cause of their hatred. At Hera's request Zeus agrees – there is no other way of keeping his promise to Thetis – to send Athene to the Trojan field, where she provokes Pandarus to break the armistice by shooting at Menelaus. The latter is wounded, but speedily healed by Machaon, son of Asclepius and physician to the army. Fighting is to be renewed: Agamemnon urges on the heroes with words of praise or censure. Last to be addressed is Diomede, whom Agamemnon singles out for reproach. Unlike Achilles, Diomede takes rebuke patiently; but Sthenelus retorts sharply. (4)

Diomede is now to the fore: Pandarus' arrow cannot hurt him; Athene strengthens him; his prowess is not content with mortal adversaries. He wounds Aphrodite in the hand as she intervenes to protect her son Aeneas: she flies to Olympus to be comforted by her mother Dione. Next Apollo protects Aeneas: Diomede prepares to attack him too, but the god's warning voice keeps him back. With the encouragement and support of Ares the Trojans attack boldly. Hera and Athene plunge into the fray – the latter even serves as Diomede's charioteer. With their help he wounds Ares, who flees to Olympus, and the goddesses also withdraw. (5)

The Trojans' danger grows greater. The seer Helenus calls on Hector and Aeneas to rally the ranks; then he sends Hector into the city, where the women are to propitiate Athene with offerings and vows. Meanwhile Glaucus and Diomede meet on the field of battle, recognize each other as guest-friends, and exchange armour – the Lycian's gold against the Argive's bronze. This encounter in the midst of the fighting serves as an example of knightly courtesy: it has another function also – to hold up the swift development of the action in the fifth book and to let us see what is happening in Troy. Hector hastens to his mother, and the Trojan women fall to their ineffective prayers. He next looks for Paris, to recall him to the field: he wishes to bid farewell to his wife and child, but they are not at home. He finds them by the Scaean gate, to which Andromache's fears have driven her. There is a conversation between husband and wife, full of love and grief, as if Hector were never more to return home. Andromache goes back to the house and mourns him as if he were already dead. Paris now joins Hector, and they return to the battle. (6)

Fighting now flares up again; but Athene and Apollo agree that it has gone far enough for the day, and that Hector should challenge one of the Achaeans to single combat. The seer Helenus transmits their decision, and Hector sends out his challenge. Ajax is chosen by lot to be his opponent. At the approach of night the combatants are separated by heralds, and the day ends as indecisively as it began. The Greeks decide to bury their dead next morning and to build a wall round their ships. The Trojans for their part ask for the return of the bodies of the fallen, and are willing, since Paris will not give up Helen, to return at all events the treasure. The Greeks reject the overture, but next morning the dead are collected and burned. The wall round the ships is built in the course of the next day. (7)

Zeus forbids the gods to take part in the battle, which he surveys from the summit of Ida. The fighting begins with the dawn, and at midday Zeus weighs the lots of the opposing armies: the scales decide for the Trojans. In the varying fortunes of the battle Diomede remains the mainstay of the Achaeans, while Hector, confident of ultimate victory, is the champion of the Trojans. Hera is obstinate in her determination to break the commands of Zeus: she tries unsuccessfully to persuade Poseidon to intervene in the fighting, and gives fresh courage to Agamemnon, who prevails upon Zeus to spare the hard-pressed Achaean host. Hera tries to help them, but Iris brings her a peremptory command from Zeus. Now the Thunderer himself comes and explains his plan for the future: the next day is to bring even more misfortune to the Greeks, and Hector will remain unchecked until Achilles takes the field in defence of the ships and fighting rages round the corpse of Patroclus. Night ends the still indecisive battle, and Hector camps with his followers on the plain. (8)

In his despondency Agamemnon now inclines to the counsel which in Book II he had proposed only to test reactions – to break off the war and go home. He is vigorously opposed by Diomede: in a council of the princes Nestor suggests an appeal to Achilles. Agamemnon is willing to provide the necessary gifts for an embassy to Achilles, and Odysseus, Ajax and Phoenix set out to his tent. They are well received, and make speeches to win him over. Odysseus speaks with skill and address; Phoenix is more human and emotional, with well-chosen examples; the speech of Ajax is brief and soldierly. They move Achilles' feelings, but his resentment still cannot be assuaged: he will fight when Hector attacks his ships, not before. The ambassadors return with their bad news, but Diomede urges all to be calm and confident. (9)

Everyone is asleep except Agamemnon and Menelaus, who wander anxiously about the camp. Meeting each other outside, near the sentinels, they decide to send Odysseus and Diomede to reconnoitre. Hector also has sent out a spy, Dolon, promising him the horses of Achilles. He falls in with the two Greeks, who find out all that he knows and then despatch him, having thus learned of the arrival of the Thracian king Rhesus with his splendid horses. They kill Rhesus and twelve of his followers, and ride back to camp with the horses. (10)

The next day's fighting (the description of which lasts until book 18) begins with the *aristeia* of Agamemnon. His arms are described in great detail. Once again the expected development of the action is held up: Agamemnon's prowess seems likely to unsettle Zeus' plan for the discomfiture of the Achaeans, but the god knows what he is about. He sends Iris to Hector, telling him to hold back while Agamemnon is fighting: his time will come when Agamemnon is wounded and leaves the field. So it comes to pass, but Odysseus and Diomede maintain the battle on equal terms. The wounding of Diomede leaves Odysseus in sore straits, and even Ajax now gives ground before the numbers of the enemy. Nestor takes the wounded Machaon onto his chariot: Achilles, viewing the battle from the prow of his ship, wants to know whom Nestor is rescuing, and sends Patroclus to find out. The old man holds Patroclus long in conversation and urges him to persuade Achilles to fight, or alternatively to give his arms to Patroclus and send him into the fray. Patroclus, moved by this appeal, hurries back: on his way he meets the wounded Eurypylus, who needs medical help and gives but a poor account of Greek prospects. (11)

The first verses of book 12 begin a new section – lasting until the end of 15 – of the great battle. At the start we find the Achaeans fighting to defend the wall round their ships, although their retreat from the battlefield has not been described. In fact, by a technique unusual in epic, it has taken place while Patroclus has his scenes with Nestor and Eurypylus. By the end of 15 Hector is about to set fire to the Greek ships. The intervening four books contain a sequence – only substantially interrupted by the machinations of Hera in 14 – of fluctuating fortune in general and individual encounter, deeds of heroes and deaths of lesser mortals, clearly composed as an artistic whole.[1]

After the retreat of the Achaeans to their ships, the Trojans try to storm the wall. Hector's first proposal, to drive at it headlong in their chariots, is opposed by Polydamas, who more wisely wishes to leave the chariots at the edge of the ditch. This is his first appearance as adviser and amender of Hector's counsels – a role which he sustains up till book 18. The fate of Asius, who assaults the wall singlehanded in his chariot, shows that Polydamas cannot be disregarded with impunity. The Trojans, attacking in five companies, are appalled by an evil omen, and Polydamas counsels withdrawal. Hector rejects the warning and renews the attack. Sarpedon breaks down part of the palisade, and Hector shatters one of the gates with a great stone. (12)

Despite the commands of Zeus, the gods who favour the Achaeans can remain onlookers of their peril no longer. Poseidon, in the guise of Calchas, encourages them to fight bravely: later, in the shape now of Thoas, he is further grieved to see his grandson Amphimachus slain by Hector. In the long drawn-out battle that follows, in which Idomeneus, king of Crete, plays a dominating part, Achaean resistance grows stiffer. Polydamas calls for a concentration of the Trojan force and in a council of war warns Hector that Achilles will not remain idle much longer. Hector accepts the advice to call his men together, but disregards the reference to Achilles. The battle goes on. (13)

[1] This is shown in detail by F. J. WINTER, *Die Kampfszenen in den Gesängen MNO der Ilias.* Diss. Frankf.a.M. 1956 (phototype). On the technique of the less important episodes: Gisela Strasburger, *Die kleinen Kämpfer der Ilias.* Diss. Frankf.a.M. 1954.

Nestor now leaves Machaon, whom he has been tending in his pavilion, to find how the battle is going. He meets Diomede, Odysseus and Agamemnon, all returning wounded from the fray. For the third time Agamemnon speaks of withdrawal, now in terms of flight under cover of darkness. Odysseus and Diomede disagree: Poseidon encourages the king, and his voice puts heart into the army. Female cunning now enters the lists: Hera borrows Aphrodite's enchanted saltire[1] and rouses Zeus' passion on Mount Ida, where he soon enough falls asleep. Her helper Hypnus hastens to the plain to tell Poseidon that he can now help the Greeks without thought of Zeus. The god vigorously encourages them, and soon a stone from Ajax lays Hector low. He is long senseless, and meanwhile the Trojans suffer other setbacks. (14)

The Trojans have been driven back over the ditch when Zeus wakes up and sees how he has been deceived. Hera has to obey his command and send Iris and Apollo to him. Now for the first time she fully learns his plan: Iris is to summon Poseidon from the field; Hector, strengthened by Apollo, will drive the Greeks back to the ships of Achilles, whereupon the latter will send Patroclus into battle. Patroclus will have many successes – he will even slay Sarpedon – but in the end he will fall by Hector's hand. In revenge Achilles will kill Hector, and from then on the fate of the Trojans will be sealed. In the end their city will be overthrown by a device of Athene's (the wooden horse). Hera conveys the commands of Zeus to Olympus, where Athene restrains Ares from a rash intervention in the battle. Poseidon unwillingly obeys the command brought by Iris, and Hector with renewed strength drives the Greeks back into their camp. Apollo himself levels the ditch and breaches the wall: the Greeks are panic-stricken as he shakes the aegis. As the Trojans enter, Patroclus leaves the wounded Eurypylus and runs to Achilles. Already the Trojans bearing firebrands are approaching the nearest ships, and only Ajax still offers effective resistance. (15)

Patroclus' tearful entreaties are wasted on Achilles, who still cannot forget the injustice done him and has no time for Achaean self-pity. Nevertheless he sends Patroclus with the Myrmidons and lends him his own armour, telling him to repel the Trojans from the ships, but to go no further, lest he diminish Achilles' reputation or meet some god who favours the Trojans. Ajax is now exhausted, and Achilles urges Patroclus to make haste, praying to Zeus of Dodona to grant him a safe return. Patroclus drives back the Trojans from the ships and performs prodigies of valour. Sarpedon falls by his hand, the son of Zeus himself. The battle rages around his body; Zeus allows Apollo to shield it, and Sleep and Death convey it to Lycia. Patroclus forgets his friend's warning and attacks the very walls of Troy. He is repulsed by Apollo, who takes the form of Asius and summons Hector to fight him. As the sun sinks, the god himself comes behind Patroclus and strikes him between the shoulders, so that his arms

---

[1] Not a girdle: see C. BONNER, ' Κεστὸς ἱμάς and the Saltire of Aphrodite'. *Am. Journ. Phil.* 70, 1949, 1. He has traced the lucky saltire over the breast from the naked fertility goddesses of Ksich and Susa (3rd millennium B.C.) down to Venus and Mars in a Pompeian wall-painting.

fall from him. Euphorbus wounds him from behind with a spear, and Hector transfixes him with his lance. (16)

A furious battle rages round the corpse. Menelaus slays Euphorbus, but retreats before Hector, who strips Achilles' armour from Patroclus' body and puts it on. The Achaeans defend the body, stoutly led by Ajax. Thick darkness overtakes the combatants. Achilles' divine steeds, mourning for Patroclus, are given fresh heart by Zeus. Athene and Apollo add further fury to the fight around the corpse. At the prayer of Ajax, Zeus takes away the darkness: now Menelaus can look for Antilochus, the son of Nestor, and send him to Achilles with the fatal tidings. Victory inclines towards the Trojans, but Menelaus and Meriones drag away the body, while the two Ajaxes defend them from the angry onslaughts of the enemy. (17)

Achilles is seized with such violent grief that Thetis and the Nereids come from the sea to comfort him. His mother offers him new arms, but says that Hector's death must shortly be followed by his own. The body of Patroclus is still in the gravest danger, and Achilles, directed by Iris and endowed with fearful stature by Athene, runs to the ditch, where his war-cry appals the Trojans. Hera hastily makes the sun set, and the battle ends. Polydamas repeats his warning, but Hector makes the Trojans camp in the field so as to renew the battle next day. Achilles bewails his dead friend, while Hephaestus at Thetis' entreaty makes new arms for him, in particular a wondrous shield with metal inlays displaying all the scenes of human life.[1] (18)

At dawn Thetis brings these arms to her son, and preserves Patroclus' body with ambrosia. Achilles calls for a meeting of the host, briefly renouncing his resentment, while Agamemnon in a long speech laments the folly that Zeus had sent upon him and promises reparation. He also swears that he has never touched Briseis. Achilles' impatience will hardly brook delay while the army eats. The forces are marshalled and Achilles arms himself. His horse speaks, prophesying his death. (19)

For the last battle, the most ferocious of all in the *Iliad*, Zeus leaves the gods free to do what they will. As they enter the lists, Zeus thunders, Poseidon sends an earthquake; but as yet they are spectators. Achilles first meets Aeneas, whom Poseidon rescues. Hector also is once more saved from death by Apollo. Achilles rages like a forest fire in dry woods. (20)

The battle beside the river is on a level of elemental savagery. Achilles fills the Scamander with corpses, and takes twelve youths prisoner to be sacrificed

---

[1] P. J. KAKRIDIS ('Achilleus' Rüstung.' *Herm.* 89, 1961, 288) has recently shown that the exchanging and losing of the armour is a late thematic element, probably invented by Homer, and that it gives considerable possibilities, but some difficulties as well. He rightly reminds us that Achilles' first armour was a divine gift and of divine workmanship (*Il.* 17, 195. 18, 84). – On the shield: W. SCHADEWALDT, *Von Homers Welt und Werk.* 3rd ed. Stuttg. 1959, 352. K. REINHARDT, 'Der Schild des Achilleus'. *Freundesgabe für E. R. Curtius.* Berne 1956, 67, makes much of the contrast between the festive scenes on the shield and the events which follow in the narrative. He also notes the absence from the shield of scenes of contest – an element which was to be provided by the Funeral Games. W. MARG, *Homer über die Dichtung.* Orbis antiquus 11. Münster 1957.

for Patroclus. Lycaon, Priam's son, pleads in vain for his life: he too is slain and thrown into the river. The river god protests, Achilles rages on unheeding, and Scamander now threatens him with his waters. The gods now take a hand; Hephaestus with his fire dries up the plain and defeats the river. By now the gods are fighting after their various fashions: Athene wounds Ares with a stone, but Apollo declines to fight with Poseidon over mortal men. Artemis is more bellicose, until Hera breaks her bow and arrows over her head. All the gods now return to Olympus. Agenor posts himself before the gate to withstand Achilles' assault, but Apollo rescues him, takes his shape, and lures Achilles away, so that the fleeing Trojans can withdraw within the walls. (21)

Hector remains in the field, despite the prayers of Priam and Hecuba that he should take refuge in the city. He recalls now how he was thrice warned by Polydamas and how he led his countrymen to destruction. Achilles approaches, and he flees from him three times round the walls of the city. Zeus weighs the fatal lots: that of Hector sinks. Apollo now deserts his favourite, and Athene checks his flight by appearing in the form of Deiphobus and promising help. Hector falls at the hand of Achilles. As in his anger, so in his revenge Achilles knows no bounds. The dying Hector had begged that his body be given back for burial: Achilles drags the corpse to the ships behind his chariot. Priam, Hecuba and Andromache break into wild lamentation. (22)

Two corpses now await the purifying flames. Three times the Myrmidons march round the corpse of Patroclus; finally they hold the funeral feast. His shade appears to Achilles and prays for speedy cremation. Next morning the pyre is made ready: the flames are fed with sumptuous offerings – among them the twelve Trojan captives. The next day the bones of Patroclus are gathered together, and elaborate funeral games with costly prizes are celebrated. In the various contests Odysseus and Ajax are pitted against each other – craft against strength. The indecisive wrestling-match is a foretaste of the later 'judgment of arms' – a theme probably known to Homer. It is significant that Achilles, not hitherto noted for temperance of emotion or expression, plays the part of the peacemaker in a dispute over the chariot-race. Here we have an anticipation of the Achilles of the ransom scenes. (23)

The anger and grief of Achilles are far from assuaged. Every day he drags Hector's body three times round Patroclus' grave. On the twelfth day the gods intervene. Against the wishes of the gods who hate the Trojans – it is here that we are first told of the judgment of Paris[1] as the cause of Hera's and Athene's hatred – Thetis is sent to Achilles to ask him to return the body of Hector. Iris persuades Priam to face a visit to the Greek camp. By night he sets out with rich gifts for the man who slew the noblest of his sons. Achilles thinks of his own father: both men weep and dismiss their anger and resentment. The angry and implacable Achilles has learned to open his heart to another's grief.[2] Priam

[1] K. REINHARDT, Das Parisurteil. Frankf.a.M. 1938 (= Von Werken und Formen. Godesberg 1948, 11).

[2] This is well brought out by Walter Nestle, 'Odyssee-Interpretationen'. Herm. 77, 1942, 70. He points out the contrast between the Achilles who refuses to eat in his grief and anger and the Achilles who tells the story of Niobe to encourage Priam to take food.

returns with Hector's body and the promise of an armistice of twelve days. Andromache, Hecuba and Helen bewail Hector. For nine days the Trojans gather wood; then Hector's pyre is kindled and his burial mound is built.

The architectonic grandeur of this plan has never been more truly appreciated than it was by Aristotle. In the *Poetics* (23. 1459a30, cf. 26. 1462b10) he contrasts the genius of its plan with the cyclic epics: Homer does not recount the whole history of the war – he selects one part and enlivens it with numerous episodes. We may add that these episodes meet Aristotle's requirement of being pertinent (οἰκεῖα 17. 1455b13): the single exception, the *Doloneia*, will be discussed later. We can make Aristotle more explicit: the central conception, that of assembling and articulating a series of events around the theme of Achilles' anger, is realized in such a way as to turn the narration into a 'tale of Troy' at the same time. The duration of the action has been reckoned as fifty days; but if we deduct intervals of inactivity such as the nine days' plague, the twelve days in which the gods are with the Ethiopians, the twelve days of insulting Hector's body, there remain only a few days which receive detailed narrative treatment. In this short compass Homer contrives to mirror the entire war against Troy. He does so by two methods. The brief narrative of the quarrel is followed by more spaciously managed scenes of the Trojan war. Among these is the sounding of opinion in the army – a scene which would be strange out of its context, but makes good sense where it is: nine years have passed, the Greeks are war-weary, and new efforts are needed to set the siege in train once more. This start of a new phase enables the poet to bring in elements which would normally belong to the opening of the war – the *teichoscopia* and the proposal to settle the issue by single combat.

On the other hand Homer uses forward-looking references, scattered throughout the poem, which make the tragic issue of the action a characteristic element in the narrative. He does this both for Achilles and for the Trojan people – the principal actors in the drama – without any narration in the poet's own words. Under the impact of Pandarus' treachery, Agamemnon speaks confidently of the city's downfall (4. 164): on Hector's lips (6. 448) the same words seem the expression of a gloomy certainty. Diomede also, on hearing the proposal to meet half the Greek demands, cries out that any simpleton can see that the Trojans are in the toils of destruction (7. 401). This kind of anticipation comes more often in the latter half of the poem,[1] and we so completely identify the Trojan resistance with Hector that his end seems the end of the city. Achilles stands in the shadow of early death from the very first conversation with his mother (1. 416); and from passage to passage the threat of his death is ever more sharp and definite.[2]

Thus through all the various episodes of this great poem interest is concentrated on a few leading themes and on a few leading actors. On these Homer bestows that strongly marked personality which the Greeks called 'ethos'. The shape that he gave to the characters earned the praise of Aristotle (*Poet.* 24.

---

[1] W. SCHADEWALDT, *Iliasstudien*. Leipz. 1938, 156, 4.
[2] *Iliad* 1, 416. 18, 95. 19, 408; 416. 21, 110. 22, 358.

1460a10) and became the norm in Greek poetry and the whole western literary tradition.

Three of them receive from the poet a destiny with strong tragic colouring. Achilles[1] in particular treads the path of his own uncontrollable passions. The decisive hour comes for him when the three ambassadors beg him to alter his decision. He himself declares (9. 645) that his judgment is not master of his resentment: and in consequence he has to lose his best friend and hasten his own death by taking revenge on Hector. He is depicted as not without insight. It would be wrong to speak of repentance; but the speaker does show awareness of the fatal interconnection when he tells Thetis (18. 98 ff.) that all his prowess has done is to spread misery around him, and he curses strife and anger which darken men's counsel. The same theme is alluded to in his words to Agamemnon where they are first reconciled (19. 56). Hector[2] is driven by his success to overstep the bounds marked out for him. He hears Polydamas' threefold warning, yet goes his way to his own death and the ruin of those whom he loves. A passage of book 17 justifies us in using the word 'tragic': Zeus looks down at Hector, putting on Achilles' armour which he has won; he pities the poor mortal as he delights in his splendid equipment while the gates of death open before him. In his soliloquy before the Scaean gate, when he expects to die by his enemy's hand (22. 99), he also has his moment of insight: he sees that he has been wrong, and significantly enough Polydamas and his warnings come back to his mind. Equally so Patroclus knows no restraint in victory; his friends too warned him in vain, and he paid for it with his life.

The kind of destiny allotted to these three personages invites comparison with tragedy, and the comparison is important if we are properly to appreciate the *Iliad*. The poem does not merely fulfil the demands of epic poetry: it goes far beyond them towards the realm of tragedy. Instead of uniform flow and unhurried narration of events, we find an artistic scheme of interconnection and cross-reference, happenings sometimes briefly sketched, sometimes elaborately worked out. This applies to the main themes. Many sections, however – blow-by-blow narratives of battles, standard scenes and descriptions, etc. – belong to the ordinary stock of epic. Aristotle (*Rhet.* 3, 9. 1409a24) divides style into two main classes – the flowing and the periodic. We may apply this conception to the construction of the *Iliad*: a structure of elaborate artistry contains considerable stretches of simple, flowing epic narrative. The reasons for this mixture of naïve and artificial elements will be discussed in the next section.

3   THE HOMERIC QUESTION

While it is necessary for the student of Homer to appreciate the structure of the *Iliad* as it deserves, it would be wrong to overlook the many difficulties which strike us when we look closely at the text. In the search for inconsistencies

---

[1] LUCIANA QUAGLIA, 'La figura di Achille e l' etica dell' Iliade'. *Atti della Accad. delle Scienze di Torino* 95, 1960/61.

[2] E. WÜST, 'Hektor und Polydamas'. *Rhein. Mus.* 98, 1955, 335. LUCIANA QUAGLIA, 'La figura di Ettore e l' etica dell' Iliade'. *Atti della Accad. delle Scienze di Torino* 94, 1959/60.

criticism has sometimes set standards far too high for works of art; but there remains enough to deserve serious consideration. A few examples will show the general nature of these problems.

There is one Palaemenes, king of the Paphlagonians, who in 5. 576 is slain by Patroclus, but is later (13. 658) found mourning the death of his son Harpalion. In 15. 63 we hear Zeus' pronouncement that Hector will pursue the fleeing Achaeans to the ships of Achilles; but at the end of the book (704) his attack is on the ship of Protesilaus. In the twenty-fourth book (182, cf. 153) we read that Iris promises Priam in the name of Zeus safe guidance at the hands of Hermes; but in the following scenes – the conversation of Priam with the anxious Hecuba and his later meeting with the god – the promise is entirely forgotten. Again, one finds themes so completely isolated and disconnected as Aeneas' animosity against Priam (13. 460), for which other passages (20. 180. 306) provide no more than the shadow of a context. But the greatest stumbling-block in the *Iliad* is the notorious dual number,[1] used in 9. 182-198 referring to the three ambassadors – Odysseus, Ajax and Phoenix. None of the attempted explanations is satisfactory.

We may add some passages intended to show what totally different interpretations are sometimes possible according to the standpoint of the critic. A theme of the first importance to the analytical critic is the building of the wall[2] around the ships, advised by Nestor (7. 337) and carried out in one day (465). The analysts have roundly declared that there is no good ground for this wall-building, or at any rate none that we are clearly told. The unitarians, taking the general plot of the poem as their starting-point, have maintained that the very purpose of the wall theme is to underline the desperate plight of the Greeks in consequence of Achilles' anger. They take the wall as being a personal invention of Homer's, and point to the care the poet takes to explain why no remains of the wall were to be found in the neighbourhood of Troy (7. 459; 12. 10). Further objection has been taken to the Greeks' deciding to protect their camp with a wall just when Diomede is forecasting the speedy overthrow of Troy (7. 401). On the other hand one could maintain that the two contrasting ideas are significantly representative of the two main themes – wrath of Achilles and fall of Troy. It might be argued that at this nadir of the Greek fortunes the poet intended to preserve a balance by affording us a reminder of the actual outcome. The scene between Hector and Andromache[3] in book 6 also sets critics at variance. Some find their taste offended because after this scene of anxious farewell Hector in fact returns home again. (His return can be inferred, though it is nowhere specifically stated.) Consequently this is an example of an old 'lay'

---

[1] M. NOE, *Phoinix, Ilias und Homer. Preisschrift Jablonowski-Gesellschaft.* 1940, 12. D. L. PAGE, *History and the Homeric Iliad.* Sather Classical Lectures 31. Univ. of Calif. Press 1959, 324.

[2] W. SCHADEWALDT, *Iliasstudien.* Abh. Sächs. Ak. Phil.-hist. Kl. 43, 6, 1938, 124, 2. An analytical standpoint is adopted by PAGE (op. cit. 315), who compares Thuc. I, 11 and infers that the wall-building sequence was not incorporated until after Thucydides' time.

[3] G. JACHMANN, 'Homerische Einzellieder'. *Symbola Coloniensia.* Cologne 1949, 1. But cf. W. SCHADEWALDT, 'Hektor in der Ilias'. *Wiener Studien* 69, 1956, 5.

rather clumsily fudged into the *Iliad* by a compiler who got it into the wrong place. Others will maintain that we should attach no importance to matters which are not stressed or indeed mentioned at all by the poet. What is important, they say, is that the scene should give as forcible an impression as can be of Hector's character; that the hero, who now has but a few days to live, should for the rest of the poem seem to us a symbol of his own fate, assured of the reader's interest and already pointing a moral. The question that Achilles puts to the weeping Patroclus at the beginning of book 16 – 'Has some bad news come from home?' – must to the eye of logic seem senseless and incomprehensible where it stands. But anyone who compares it with other passages in which intractable obstinacy is stressed as an element in Achilles' character will see that his very manner of putting the question is a masterpiece of characterization.[1] Opinion is divided whether or not Achilles could say what he does in 11. 609 and 16. 72 after receiving the embassy.[2]

These few examples show the problems that are raised if individual passages are subjected to logical scrutiny. This kind of criticism began with the Alexandrians, but did not go so far as to take the poems to pieces. The analytical movement had only one precursor in modern times[3] – the abbé François Hédelin d'Aubignac, whose motive was to defend Homer against the depreciation which was fashionable in the France of his day. The poetical value of the *Iliad*, he suggested, lay in individual passages, which some unknown hand put together into a whole. This view was expressed in 1664, but not printed until 1715, as *Conjectures académiques ou dissertation sur l'Iliade*. It has been validly urged against Friedrich August Wolf that he made no due acknowledgment to this study. It is beyond dispute, however, that the whole subsequent development of the Homeric question stems from Wolf's *Prolegomena ad Homerum* (1795). His main theses, that writing was unknown in the Homeric age, that the poems had a long oral tradition, and that the Pisistratean recension was of great importance for the text, long remained central pillars of Homeric studies. The profound effect of this theory on the world of scholarship was not matched by its effect on contemporary literature. Goethe's attitude was typical of most: he acknowledged the force of the criticism, but sometimes deplored the subjective element in the constantly varying theories.

For a long time the history of Homeric scholarship was one of analysts striving with various success to breach the walls of the unitarians. No purpose would be served by attempting a detailed account of the analytical theories, which are of bewildering complexity:[4] it must suffice to outline a few typical

---

[1] Analytically treated by G. JACHMANN, *Der Hom. Schiffskatalog und die Ilias*. Wiss. Abh. Arbeitsgem. Nordrhein-Westfalen 5. Cologne 1958, 59 (agrees with GODFREY HERMANN). But cf. A. LESKY, 'Zur Eingangsszene der Patroklie'. *Serta Philologica Aenipontana*. Innsbr. 1961, 19.

[2] For the opposing views see W. SCHADEWALDT, *Iliasstudien* (*v. sup.*) 81 and 129: Jachmann op. cit. 56 and 80.

[3] G. FINSLER, *Homer in der Neuzeit von Dante bis Goethe*. Leipz. 1912.

[4] We need only mention one or two of the older works which have valuable observations as well as representing different analytical schools: U. VON WILAMOWITZ, *Die Ilias*

positions of leading exponents. It has been supposed that the poem was planned as a unity, and that around an original *Iliad* of moderate compass gradual accretion took place which eventually brought the poem to its present form. This 'expansion theory', long the arena of fierce conflict, claimed Gottfried Hermann (1772–1848) as one of its first exponents. Contemporary with this great critic and linguist was Karl Lachmann, who had previously worked on the Nibelungenlied: he propounded the 'lays' theory, the *Iliad*, on this view, being made up of some sixteen separate poems. Learned criticism here went hand in hand with romantic notions of the 'national spirit' at work in poetry, causing the gradual organic growth of the epic. Victor Hehn's lecture on Homer[1] gave exaggerated expression to this view. The 'lay' theory was made less tenable as Germanist scholars[2] stressed the difference between lays and epic episodes. In consequence an attempt was made to separate out as constituents of the *Iliad* not lays, but small-scale epics of varying extent and merit – the 'compilation' theory. This conception grew out of the analysis of the *Odyssey* in the hands of such men as A. Kirchhoff; but in course of time it became the fashionable theory for the *Iliad* as well. It became fused with the expansion theory, according as one took this, that or the other epyllion as the kernel round which the others accrued.

As regards the critical tools employed by the analysts, it must be admitted that some turned in the operators' hands. Logical inconsistencies became less and less cogent as the unitarians were able to point to many such discrepancies in modern literary works whose unitary authorship no one denies. Attempts to achieve a satisfactory dismemberment on the basis of linguistic and cultural levels entirely failed, for reasons which we shall see in the relevant sections. All that remained was stylistic differences; and the danger of subjectivity in using such criteria cannot be overemphasized. This is not to say that such differences do not exist, only that their interpretation is a problem in itself.

The situation had become one to which Goethe's rather over-confident words in his *Annals* in 1821 now fully applied: 'It would need a revolution in all our notions of the world to set the old views on their feet again.' It was not until after the first world war that growing dissatisfaction with experiments in analysis made it possible again to regard the Homeric epics as a unity.[3] The time was ripe for the *Iliasstudien* of Wolfgang Schadewaldt (Leipzig 1938), in which the old types of analysis were given some very hard knocks.[4] From the very beginning the unitarians had defended the general unity of the *Iliad*'s plot: now the structure of the poem was defended in detail. A study rivalling in minuteness those of the analysts sought to establish numerous correlations, references

und Homer. Berlin 1916. E. BETHE, *Homer.* I. Leipzig 1914; 2. 2nd ed. 1929; 3, 1927. E. SCHWARTZ, *Zur Entstehung der Ilias. Schr. d. Strassb. wiss. Ges.* 34, 1918. See also under *Odyssey.*

[1] K. DEICHGRÄBER, *Aus Victor Hehns Nachlass. Akad. Mainz. Geistes- u. sozialwiss. Kl.* 1951/9, 814.

[2] A. HEUSLER, *Lied und Epos in der germ. Sagendichtung.* Dortmund 1905.

[3] C. M. BOWRA, *Tradition and Design in the Iliad.* Oxf. 1930.

[4] *Von Homers Welt und Werk,* by the same author.

back and forth, economy of narrative or deliberate slowing up of the action, as indications of the conscious design of a single creative artist. This artist may be our old Homer again, although Schadewaldt supposes as the author of our *Iliad* not an individual creating the whole scheme according to his fancy, but a man using a rich stock of precedents and a tradition going far back into antiquity.

As Willy Theiler expressed it in the *Festschrift für Tièche* (1947), for a long time it seemed as if 'the enormous influence of Schadewaldt's book in Germany had brought a century and a half of analytical scholarship down in ruins'. But appearances were deceptive: in late years Homeric analysis has vigorously claimed attention in almost all the old forms.[1]

If we want to see at all clearly in this perplexing battlefield, we have first to dismiss some obsolete and mistaken notions. In one isolated passage (*c. Apion.* 1. 12) Josephus remarks that Homer left nothing in writing. For Wolf it became a central thesis that the poet could not write. The view is no longer tenable since our discovery of the early use of writing in Greece (p. 20). Of course the questions whether Homer could write and whether he did must be kept distinct.

For Josephus and Wolf the Homeric poems were not put together until a late date; and ancient references to the Pisistratean recension seem to state this expressly.[2] But the statements are late and probably reflect guesswork in antiquity. Authors such as Dieuchidas of Megara[3] (ap. Diog. Laert. 1. 57) may speak of interpolations made in the Homeric text by Pisistratus, but this is quite another thing. The same Dieuchidas speaks of a decree of Solon's (some ascribe it to Hipparchus) which presupposes the existence of a definite text of Homer:

[1] An expansion theory, for example, is defended by P. MAZON in his useful *Introduction à l'Iliade*. Paris 1942. W. THEILER, 'Die Dichter der Ilias'. *Festschrift f. E. Tièche*. Berne 1947, 125; 'Noch einmal die Dichter der Ilias'. *Thesaurismata. Festschr. I. Kapp.* Munich 1954, 118, supposes an original *Iliad* overlaid with various additional strata. JACHMANN (op. cit. p. 33, n. 3) applies the lay theory particularly to the battle scenes. P. VON DER MÜHLL, *Kritisches Hypomnema zur Ilias.* Schweiz. Beitr. z. Altertumswiss. 4, Basel 1952, distinguishes an original *menis*-cycle composed by Homer from later additions; cf. J. TH. KAKRIDIS, *Gnom.* 28, 1956, 401. More recently W. H. FRIEDRICH, *Verwundung und Tod in der Ilias.* Abh. Ak. Gött. Phil.-hist. Kl. 3. Folge, 38, 1956, has drawn analytical conclusions from his study of the material. D. L. PAGE's book *History and the Homeric Iliad* (v. p. 38, n. 1) has an appendix *Multiple Authorship in the Iliad*, in which the analysts' case is supported from the embassy and the building of the wall. An extreme view is taken by G. JACHMANN (v. p. 33, n. 3), who reckons the compiler of our *Iliad* to be a clumsy botcher: on this see J. TH. KAKRIDIS, *Gnom.* 32, 1960, 393. The almost simultaneous appearance of two important discussions of the problem brings out clearly the unbridgeable gulf between the opposing positions. W. THEILER's article 'Ilias und Odyssee in der Verflechtung ihres Entstehens'. *Mus. Helv.* 19, 1962, 1, lives up to its title, and is full of confidence in what analysis can do. The unselfish labour of UVO HÖLSCHER has put into our hands K. REINHARDT's book 'Die Ilias und ihr Dichter'. Göttingen 1961, carefully put together from the unfinished manuscript. The title is no less challenging than THEILER's. We can do no more than refer in general terms to this study as the most determined unitarian defence of the *Iliad* since SCHADEWALDT's *Ilias-studien* of 1938 and an attempt to reconcile all the different aspects of the epic within the conception of an individual Homer.

[2] R. MERKELBACH, 'Die pisistratische Redaktion'. *Rhein. Mus.* 95, 1952, 23, tries to establish its historicity. J. A. DAVISON, 'Peisistratus and Homer'. *TAPhA* 86, 1955, 1.

[3] J. A. DAVISON, 'Dieuchidas of Megara'. *Class. Quart.* 53, 1959, 216.

viz. that at the four-yearly Panathenaea the rhapsodes should recite the epics of Homer in order, one taking up where another left off.

The notions of an illiterate Homer and a Pisistratean recension have long been given up. Their place has been taken, behind all the modern theories of contamination, interpolation and patchwork, by other notions scarcely less questionable. Anyone who takes up Wilamowitz's *Die Ilias und Homer* (Berlin 1916) and reads the last pages, expounding such a complex theory of the origin of the *Iliad*, will be unable to conceive of such a bewildering chain of events without presupposing the wide use of writing. One has not merely to assume that the author of the *Iliad* was literate, but that he operated with books as his basis, excerpting, adapting and pasting together. We have now come to the point where we must bring to bear on this whole mass of problems the light shed by comparative literary studies from Murko to Parry. How the great epic itself was composed is still hard to say, but at least we have a clear idea of what must have gone before.

Certainly we have to postulate many centuries of epic poetry before Homer, and we must think of this poetry as 'oral composition' of the type whose techniques we have outlined above.[1] We now have a clearer idea of the broad mass of material on which Homeric poetry is based; and our new knowledge does nothing to support the conception of written earlier forms rehandled by compilers. The form in which we have to put the Homeric question today is, 'What is the connection between the epics as we have them and oral composition?' A few moments' consideration of the techniques of oral composition will show that they are all present in the *Iliad* and *Odyssey*. The most striking technical feature – the use of repetitive formulae – is particularly strongly marked in Homer. Difficulties of metre may be partly responsible.

How shall we answer this question? Shall we say that the Homeric poems belong solidly in this context of poetry orally conceived and orally transmitted? Some of Parry's school seem inclined to draw this conclusion. Pure oral poetry, however, is never repeated twice in the same form[2]: thus they have to explain the fixity of the text by supposing that an oral performance gained such striking success that an immediate transcript was made. This is a new approach and a dangerous one, leading to the misinterpretation of great poetry.

Admittedly the length of the *Iliad* is no argument against this view. Among oral heroic poems we find such examples as the epic of Avdo Mededović with more than 12,000 verses. We can do better by looking at the plot of the *Iliad*. There is indeed a parallel here also from south Slavic poetry, but the differences are so great that we are justified in thinking that the poet of the *Iliad* could write. The decisive arguments for this view are drawn from the many cross-references, often widely separated, which modern scholars have pointed out.

[1] See p. 16 f.

[2] The dictum of STERLING DOW (*Class. Weekly* 49, 1956, 197) 'Verbatim oral transmission of a poem composed orally and not written down is unknown' has been challenged recently by G. S. KIRK, 'Homer and Modern Oral Poetry: Some Confusions'. *Class. Quart.* 54, 1960, 271. From observations of contemporary oral epic on its own ground he concludes that faithful transmission is possible. But even if this were applicable to the *Iliad* and *Odyssey*, the burning question would still be whether they could possibly have been orally conceived.

In our summary of the *Iliad* we spoke of the pronouncements of Zeus in books 8, 11 and 15, each more explicit than the last; the threefold warning of Polydamas (books 12, 13 and 18); finally of the dexterous management throughout the poem of those passages which foretell the fall of Troy and the death of Achilles. A few further examples may not be out of place, since some scholars have roundly denied the existence of any such deliberate planning and cross-referring in the design of the *Iliad*. In 17. 24 Menelaus refers to the death of Hyperenor, which happened three books earlier (14. 516). Contrariwise 2. 860 gives us an anticipation of Achilles' fury beside the Scamander in book 21. In the Catalogue of Ships, while speaking of Pandarus, the poet dwells on his wonderful bow, which is to figure so fatally in the breaking of the truce in book 4. Even the repetition of verses is made artistically effective, as in the two prayers of Chryses (1. 37, 451), or in the verses 11. 357 *sq.* and 18. 35 *sq.*, which underline a correspondence between the scenes in the two books – a parallel referred to by Thetis herself (17. 74). When Hector issues the challenge to single combat (7. 77), he stipulates that his body be returned in the event of his death – a pregnant allusion to what followed his defeat in the end. Likewise Achilles' pious care for the body of Eetion (related, oddly enough, by Andromache in 6. 417) serves as the foil to his rage against the dead Hector. We must admire the skill in composition which in 2. 780, after the long and static description of the forces, takes up again the beautiful simile which had been used before the Catalogue (2. 455) to describe the army's advance. There is a good example of a deliberate variation of emphasis in the *teichoscopia* of book 3. Helen names the principal heroes, Agamemnon, Odysseus, Ajax and Idomeneus, but not Diomede who plays so prominent a role in the following books. He is not described until the fourth book, where the characterization forms the culmination of the *epipolesis*, Agamemnon's review of his forces. Conversely, in her laments over the dead Hector (22. 447; 24. 725) Andromache never dwells on the lot that awaits her: the theme has already been unforgettably touched on by Hector in 6. 450. K. Reinhardt (see p. 29, n. 1) has pointed out that the absence of an element of contest in the scenes on the shield of Achilles shows unwillingness to anticipate the funeral games in book 23.

Much more might be said, but the foregoing is enough to support the view that the poem was constructed with the help of writing. Such delicate touches as the variation in sequence from Achilles, Ajax, Odysseus (1. 138) to Ajax, (Idomeneus,) Odysseus, Achilles (1. 145) in Agamemnon's speech – the first time alluding to the taking away of the gift, the second to the important task of restoring Chryseis; or the different ways in which Priam and Antenor address Helen – Priam calls her 'little daughter' (3. 162), while Antenor, who later urges that she be given up, addresses her as 'woman' (3. 204) – such attention to detail is only conceivable in a poet familiar with writing. A. B. Lord[1] suggests

---

[1] 'Homer's Originality: Oral Dictated Texts'. *Trans. Am. Phil. Ass.* 84, 1953, 124, and *The Singer of Tales* (*v.* p. 16, n. 2). The view here espoused is supported in detail in my 'Mündlichkeit und Schriftlichkeit im hom. Epos.' *Festchr. Kralik.* Horn 1954, 1, and is adopted essentially by PER KRARUP, 'Homer and the Art of Writing'. *Eranos* 54, 1956, 28

a halfway house – a Homer who dictated his poems. We do find today singers in Greece and Yugoslavia who sometimes allow their poems to be thus recorded. But while there is nothing against such a supposition in Homer's case, equally there is nothing for it. In any case, Madvig's words[1] remain valid: 'utrumque poetam . . . scribendi arte atque auxilio usum esse persuasum habeo'. We must admit one thing: we have no notion what an eighth-century manuscript of Homer would have looked like. This is not an argument against our theory: we are simply recognizing the limits of our knowledge.

To sum up: Homer is at once a beginning and a fulfilment, and many inconsistencies in the poems are thus to be explained. The roots of his creative work lie deep in the old soil of oral epic, and he uses many of the older techniques. Such was his source, and we must suppose that a very great bulk of this oral epic was available for his use. If we suppose such a process as this, we shall not be surprised any longer at numerous contradictions, and we shall see why it is that large parts of the poem are in the old simple narrative form. Examples of the old heroic style are particularly common in the endless descriptions of combat, with their long lists of names. But what Homer owed to this early poetry cannot be reckoned exactly. No one can doubt that he used much material that lay to hand: here could be common ground between unitarians and the more moderate analysts. To justify this hope at all, we must part company with simple-minded unitarians who imagine Homer creating in a vacuum and with those analysts who show no understanding of the nature and laws of the genre, and who ply their scalpels in an endless vivisection of the living body of the *Iliad*.

While we look at what Homer inherited, we must not forget what he created. We cannot say for certain that the *Iliad* was the first great written epic. Parry and Lord have shown us that epics of considerable compass occur in oral poetry. What is certain is that the *Iliad* and *Odyssey* owed their preservation and their immeasurable influence to their possessing those qualities in which Greek epic reaches its consummation – or rather transcends the limits of its form; that is to say, the dramatic handling of the incidents (of which we spoke when discussing the plot) and above all the humanizing of the old heroic saga: it is this which wins Homer a place in our hearts. The scene in which Priam and Achilles, after all the pangs of battle, all the grief and cruelty of unmeasured vengeance, learn to understand and respect each other as men, is at once the culmination of the *Iliad* and the starting-point of the western conception of humanity.

and C. M. BOWRA, *Homer and his Forerunners*. Edinburgh 1955. Both these scholars consider dictation as a possibility, as does C. H. WHITMAN, *Homer and the Heroic Tradition*. Harv. Univ. Press, Cambr. Mass. 1958, 82, despite the stress which he lays on the poems' being essentially oral composition. The use of writing in their composition is vigorously asserted by H. T. WADE-GERY, *The Poet of the Iliad*. Cambr. 1952: he thinks (p. 11) that the adaptation of the Semitic alphabet was occasioned by the needs of poetry. See also T. B. L. WEBSTER, *From Mycenae to Homer*. London 1958, 272. D. L. PAGE, *The Homeric Odyssey*. Oxf. 1955, 140 is more reserved. Further references in K. Marót, *Die Anfänge der griech. Literatur*. Budapest 1960, 314, n. 121.

[1] *Adversaria Critica* 3, 1884, 4.

Two factors contributed to the success of what was new in the *Iliad*: the transition from the lyre-playing *aoidos* to the rhapsode with his staff, and that from orally composed heroic lays to poetry conceived as writing. We cannot say **how** long before Homer these two things happened: the latter most likely came in with Homer himself.

It should be added that the view here outlined does not exclude the possibility of later insertions. We no longer reckon among these the Catalogue of Ships,[1] but follow Dieuchidas and many modern writers in supposing Attic interpolations (e.g. 2. 558). The tenth book, containing the *Doloneia*,[2] is so unconnected with the main narrative that it serves by contrast to emphasize the unity of the rest, and suggests a late interpolation.

Now that we can once again think of the poet of the *Iliad* as an historical person, and take 'Homer' as a proper name, not as a description (='hostage'), we cannot help wishing to know something of his life.[3] He must have been a rhapsode, and as such would have seen something of the world – not as the poor schoolmaster and wandering singer of legend, but in close association with the princely courts of his day. The treatment which he gives to Aeneas (esp. 20 307) and Glaucus suggests that he was attached to the Aeneadae of the Troad and the Glaucidae of Lycia.[4] We are in no position to settle the conflict

---

[1] V. BURR, Νεῶν κατάλογος. Klio Beih. 39, 1944; see A. HEUBECK in *Gnom.* 21, 1949, 197; 29, 1957, 40; 33, 1961, 116. He denies any historical Mycenaean background, and in the last-named review especially assails D. L. PAGE, *History and the Homeric Iliad* (*v.* p. 20, n. 1) 118, who shares with WEBSTER, *From Mycenae to Homer* (*v.* p. 18, n. 1) 132 and 175 the view that the Catalogue of Ships might go back to Mycenaean times. At the other extreme G. JACHMANN (*v.* p. 34, n. 1) reckons it as a late interpolation. Further bibliography in HEUBECK, *Gymn.* 66, 1959, 397.

[2] HEUSINGER, *Stilistische Untersuchungen zur Dolonie.* Leipz. 1939. F. KLINGNER, 'Über die Dolonie'. *Herm.* 75, 1940, 337. This view is critically examined by F. DORNSEIFF, 'Doloneia'. *Mél. Grégoire. Ann. de l'Institut de phil. et d'hist. Or. et Slav.* 10, 1950, 239. W. JENS, 'Die Dolonie und ihre Dichter'. *Studium Generale* 8, 1955, 616. S. LASER, 'Über das Verhältnis der Dolonie zur Odyssee'. *Herm.* 86, 1958, 385. K. REINHARDT, *Tradition und Geist.* Gött. 1960, 9.

[3] There are seven ancient biographies, all of imperial times, but possibly going back to an older tradition. Text: WILAMOWITZ, *Vitae Homeri et Hesiodi.* Bonn 1916; T. W. ALLEN in the fifth vol. of his Oxford text: both also give the 'Contest of Homer and Hesiod' (Ἀγὼν· Ὁμήρου καὶ Ἡσιόδου), which is equally an imperial redaction of an earlier narrative. On the literary genre see L. RADERMACHER, *Aristophanes' Frösche.* 2nd ed, Sitzb. Oest. Ak. Phil.-hist. Kl. 198/4, 1954, 29. E. VOGT, 'Die Schrift vom Wettkampf Homers und Hesiods'. *Rhein. Mus.* 102, 1959, 193. K. HESS, *Der Agon zwischen Homer und Herod.* Winterthur 1960 (cf. E. VOGT, *Gnom.* 33, 1961, 697). On Proclus' *Life*: A. SEVERYNS, *Recherches sur la Chrestomathie de Proclos, III.* Paris 1953. Germ. transl. of the pseudo-Herod. *Vita* and the *Certamen* in W. SCHADEWALDT, *Legende von Homer dem fahrenden Sänger.* Leipz. 1942. On the life of Homer and the activities of the Homeridae see H. T. WADE-GERY, *The Poet of the Iliad.* Cambr. 1952. Some questions concerning the person and personality of Homer are discussed in an important article in *Herm.* 68, 1933, 1 by F. JACOBY, who returns to the subject in *F Gr Hist* IIIb (comm.) 2 (notes), 407. On the name see M. DURANTE. 'Il nome di Omero'. *Acc. dei Lincei. Rendiconti d. Cl. di Sc. mor. stor. fil.* 8, 12, 1957, 94. On portraits of Homer: BOEHRINGER, *Homer. Bildnisse und Nachweise.* Breslau 1939. On such portraits we may mention once for all K. SCHEFOLD, *Die Bildnisse der antiken Dichter, Redner und Denker.* Basel 1943.

[4] L. MALTEN, *Herm.* 79, 1944, 1.

of the seven cities (*Anth. Pal.* 16. 295 *sqq.*) about his birthplace. Smyrna seems to have had a strong claim, which suggests origins in Ionia or Asia Minor. That he was originally called Melesigenes seems doubtful; but his long residence in Chios and death on the island of Ios may well be historical. If he used writing in composition, we have to reject his blindness as a stereotyped myth-motiv. The period of his creative activity must be reckoned as the eighth century, which has been well styled 'the century of Homer'.[1] The relation between Homeric epic and Hesiod gives us a lower limit, while an upper limit is fixed by the use of writing and by archaeological arguments drawn from the poet's knowledge of temples and cult images.

4 THE *ODYSSEY*: MATERIALS AND COMPOSITION

Many things that distinguish the *Odyssey* from the *Iliad* arise from the nature and origins of its subject matter.[2] This falls at once into two classes. We find quite widely spread a folktale, not necessarily having any supernatural element, on these lines: a man who has been on a far journey for a long time and is given up for dead, finds on his return his wife beset by suitors: often the wedding date is already fixed. He is recognized, fights and comes into his own again.[3] The name Penelope was variously and unsatisfactorily explained in antiquity. Paul Kretschmer derives it from πήνη, πηνίον 'bobbin-thread, woof', and ἐλοπ- as found in ὀλόπτω 'unravel'. If this is right, then Penelope took her name from the trick by which she deceived the suitors, unravelling in the night what she had woven in the day. In this case the word πηνέλοψ for the common wild duck must be taken from the heroine's name, and conferred on the bird for its supposed monogamous habits. Ancient etymologists went astray by supposing the contrary.

The second element in the *Odyssey* is travellers' tales, which must have been many and varied in the second millennium B.C. while Crete was a great sea power. An Egyptian tale from about 2000 B.C.[4] contains such striking anticipations of the *Odyssey* as a shipwreck in which the hero, as sole survivor, floats ashore on a piece of timber onto an island full of marvels. Such stories have a way of building up into a whole cycle centering round some particular personage – a Sinbad or an Odysseus. The name Odysseus defies Indo-European derivation: outside Homer it occurs as Olysseus. The peculiar epic form may come from an attempt to make it more Greek: cf. *Od.* 19. 406. The facts suggest that Odysseus figured even in the pre-Greek world as the hero of fabulous adventures by sea. The view constantly advanced which makes him into an ancient divinity, usually a sun-god, cannot be made good.

---

[1] W. SCHADEWALDT, 'Homer und sein Jahrhundert'. *Von Homers Welt und Werk.* 2nd ed. Stuttg. 1951, 87.

[2] L. RADERMACHER, 'Die Erzählungen der Odyssee'. *Sitzb. Akad. Wien. Phil.-hist. Kl.* 178/1, 1915. K. MEULI, *Odyssee und Argonautika.* Berl. 1921. P. KRETSCHMER, 'Penelope'. *Anz. Akad. Wien. Phil.-hist. Kl.* 1945, 80. GABRIEL GERMAIN, *Genèse de l'Odyssée.* Paris 1954. L. A. STELLA, *Il poema di Ulisse.* Florence 1955. F. WEHRLI, 'Penelope und Telemachos'. *Mus. Helv.* 16. 1959. 228.

[3] W. SPLETSTÖSSER, *Der heimkehrende Gatte und sein Weib in der Weltliteratur.* Berl. 1899.

[4] RADERMACHER, op. cit. 38.

The story of the homecoming must have been tied up from the beginning with tales of adventures which kept the hero so long from hearth and home. In the Mediterranean world these tales would have been predominantly of adventure by sea, so that the hero was ideally cast for the role of the long-lost wanderer returning.

Both these classes of material are a long way from the aristocratic world of the *Iliad*. If we consider the *Odyssey* as the later work – later in composition, of course, not in material – we must admit a certain shifting of the audience to whom it is addressed. Goethe made this point well in the first Epistle:

> '. . . und klinget nicht immer im hohen Palaste,
> In des Königes Zelt, die Ilias herrlich dem Helden?
> Hört nicht aber dagegen Ulysseus wandernde Klugheit
> Auf dem Markte sich besser, da wo sich der Bürger versammelt?'

But all these differences cannot obscure the fact that the *Iliad* and *Odyssey* belong to the same genre. There is an important addition which we must make to our sketch of the basic subject matter of the later epic: the hero of the 'homecoming' story is not only made identical with him of the sea adventures, but he is also brought into the sphere of the Trojan saga. Odysseus becomes one of those who fought before Troy – and indeed one of the foremost, as the *Iliad* tells us. Yet amidst the world that there surrounds him he still keeps many of his old characteristics. The epithet of 'long-suffering' is applied to him in the *Iliad* also, where he is sharply contrasted with Achilles: patient subtlety against noble rage, supple compromise against angry intransigence, the calm appraisal of the best route against the headlong following of the most direct. It is significant that in the ninth book of the *Iliad* it is Odysseus, of all the three ambassadors, who least succeeds in establishing contact with Achilles. The two men personify the contrasting elements that went into the history of the Greek nation.

To these three ingredients – novel of homecoming, novel of sea adventure, saga of Troy – we must add a fourth: the spirit and standpoint of a new age, which, without destroying the old one, yet looked at it in many ways through very different eyes. We shall have something to say on this score when we discuss men and gods in Homer: here it must be enough to point out the large part which the rising tide of Ionian ways of thought played in the innovations of the *Odyssey*.

The geographical element in the *Odyssey* demands a word.[1] Eratosthenes (ap. Strab. 1. 23c) hit the nail on the head. Hesiod, he says, placed Odysseus' wanderings in the general area of Italy and Sicily, but Homer had no thought of either of these or of any other real place. This view has been received very unwillingly both in antiquity and in modern times. Obstinate attempts to trace Odysseus'

---

[1] A. LESKY, 'Aia'. *Wien. Stud.* 63, 1948, 52. V. BÉRARD, *Les Navigations d'Ulysse*, 4 vols. Paris 1927–29 (and other works), tries to place Odysseus' wanderings in the western Mediterranean: R. HENNIG, *Die Geographie des homerischen Epos*, Leipz. 1934, favours the 'ex-oceanist' school. For wider aspects of the question see A. KLOTZ, 'Die Irrfahrten des Odysseus und ihre Deutung im Altertum'. *Gymn.* 59, 1952, 289. For some similar discussions cf. *AfdA* 13, 1960, 20.

wanderings on a map were dismissed by Eratosthenes with the ironical suggestion that such researchers should first find who the cobbler was who made Aeolus his leather bag for keeping winds in. The Hellenistic period saw schools of thought which placed these wanderings in the Mediterranean, and others which placed them in the Atlantic. This idle enquiry has been taken up in modern studies, which will no doubt reach results as satisfactory as those of the Atlantis-seekers. The truth is that the adventures of Odysseus take place in a fairytale land, far outside the boundaries of the world as it was known when the story was first told.

The poet tells us clearly enough when we cross from the real world into fairyland: we shall note the passages in the summary which follows. Some indications, as we shall see, point to the far west, while on the isle of Circe we are suddenly in the east. The island is said to belong to Aea: Aea is that far-eastern land on the borders of the stream of Ocean which was the fabled goal of the Argonauts before the Black Sea was opened up and Colchis became known. Here we meet the fact which has been made clear by the researches of Karl Meuli – that large parts of the *Odyssey* are modelled on an old poem, now lost, of the journey of the Argonauts to Aeetes, the ruler of Aea. Circe's allusion to this poem (11. 70) can then be taken as a valuable datum for literary history.

The following sketch will deal in greater detail with the articulation of the poem and will go into individual points more deeply than our sketch of the *Iliad* did.

The poem begins with Odysseus on the island of Calypso, the furthest point of his wanderings. Until he shall arrive home, Poseidon remains implacable towards him; but at the moment the god has gone to the land of the Ethiopians, while the other Olympians are assembled in the palace of Zeus. The latter inveighs against the criminal folly of mankind, his text being Orestes' recent revenge upon Aegisthus. This act of violence serves to contrast the character of Telemachus – a contrast which is kept in view in the early books (3. 306; 4. 546). Athene wins the permission of Zeus, notwithstanding Poseidon's resentment, to help Odysseus in his return, and asks to have Hermes sent to Calypso on Ogygia. She herself visits Telemachus in Ithaca, taking on the form of Mentes, king of the Taphians. In a long conversation with him she discusses his present position – his father missing and the suitors revelling in the house. She gives him two pieces of advice: to demand before the assembled people of Ithaca an end to this persecution, and to seek out old comrades of his father's and enquire after his fate. On Athene's departure Telemachus realizes that he has been speaking with a goddess, and his words to his mother and to the suitors show that from this moment on he is facing his problems in a new frame of mind. (1)

The next day he forcibly presents his views in the assembly. He quarrels, of course, with Antinous and Eurymachus, who derides the idea of a divine warning (Aegisthus, we remember, had been warned by the gods). It becomes clear that the suitors hold the upper hand. Telemachus' request for a ship is not even considered, and Leocritus dismisses the assembly with arrogant contempt.

Athene takes the form of Mentor, and leads Telemachus to a ship, on which he embarks by night. (2)

On the shores of Pylos the voyagers find Nestor sacrificing to Poseidon. He receives Telemachus hospitably, and is able to tell him what befell many of the heroes returning from Troy. Of Odysseus, however, he can tell nothing. In the evening Athene departs in the form of an eagle. Next morning Telemachus sets out for Sparta with Nestor's son Pisistratus. They arrive on the evening of the next day. (3)

They find Menelaus celebrating the weddings of his son and his daughter. He and Helen relate Odysseus' deeds before Troy and in the city itself.[1] Next morning Telemachus asks after his father's fate, and hears of the adventures of Menelaus on his way home. Among these is a meeting with Proteus, the old man of the sea, who tells him of the deaths of the Locrian Ajax and of Agamemnon, and finally informs him of Odysseus' sojourn on the island of Calypso. In Sparta a banquet is prepared: in Ithaca the suitors are planning the murder of Telemachus on his return. Penelope hears of the plot, but Athene comforts her by a dream-vision. (4)

The gods take counsel again, and again Athene complains of Odysseus' hardships. Zeus now sends Hermes as messenger (as suggested before by Athene) to tell Calypso what the gods intend. The nymph unwillingly tells Odysseus to build a raft, and lets him go his homeward way. On the eighteenth day, when he is near Scheria, he is seen by Poseidon (now returning from the Ethiopians), who sends a storm and shatters the raft. Leucothea's veil protects Odysseus, and on the third day after the shipwreck he reaches the shore of Scheria, where he sinks into a deep sleep. (5)

A dream sent by Athene causes the king's daughter Nausicaa to go with her maidens to the shore, where they play and wash clothes. Odysseus wakes up, and the girls flee in terror. Nausicaa, however, helps him to wash and clothe himself, and takes him to the grove of Athene before the city. (6)

Under cover of a cloud which Athene wraps round him, Odysseus passes through the streets of the Phaeacians and enters the palace. As he clasps the knees of the queen, Arete, the cloud disperses, and Alcinous bids him welcome. When the nobles have left, Arete, who recognizes the clothes, asks Odysseus how he came by them and where he has come from. He relates his misfortunes since leaving Calypso, and obtains from Alcinous the promise to send him home the next day. (7)

But the next day does not bring the desired consummation. Alcinous orders preparations to be made, but in the meantime there is a banquet, at which Demodocus sings of Achilles and Odysseus. Odysseus hides his face, and the king gives the word for games, in which Odysseus humbles the braggart Euryalus. Next follows Demodocus' lay of the loves of Ares and Aphrodite, and the revenge of the injured Hephaestus. In the evening Demodocus sings of the wooden horse: Odysseus weeps, and Alcinous asks him his name and history. (8)

[1] On the contradictory role of Helen in these stories see J. T. KAKRIDIS, 'Helena und Odysseus'. *Serta Philologica Aenipontana*. Innsbr. 1961, 27.

Odysseus now declares himself and tells his tale. After the fall of Troy he destroyed Ismarus, but had to flee after suffering heavy losses through attacks from the Cicones (we are still in the quasi-historical world of the *Iliad*, where the Cicones feature in the Catalogue of Ships). A storm compels him and his companions to land and rest for two days; then they try to round Malea. A frightful storm from the north scatters the fleet and drives them for nine days over the waves (the figure of nine days indicates a long interval, sufficient to pass over into fairyland). On the tenth day they land among the Lotus-eaters, and the magical powers of the plant almost make them forget their homeland. Next they come to an island off the shore of the Cyclopes' land. (This island is important in the plot: Odysseus still commands a fleet, although only a small force is dramatically necessary for the adventure with Polyphemus.) Odysseus approaches the mainland with one ship only, loses many of his comrades in the monster's den, but wins in the end through his cunning in making Polyphemus drunk and giving his own name as Noman. The blinded Cyclops calls down the wrath of his father Poseidon upon Odysseus. (9)

Aeolus sends a favourable west wind, which wafts Odysseus towards his home. (The scene of action is therefore the far west.) After a nine-days' journey (the same period of transition to bring him back to the real world) the comrades of Odysseus untie the bag of winds which Aeolus gave him. The unchained tempests drive them back to Aeolus, who sees that Odysseus has incurred some god's displeasure, and withdraws his favour. Six days bring them to the land of the Laestrygones, a land of short nights. (We are in fairyland again, despite the spring Artacia which reappears at Cyzicus.) In a little bay they are attacked by the gigantic Laestrygones: all the other ships are lost, and that of Odysseus alone sails on to the island belonging to the land called Aea. Here Eos has his home and his dancing-floor; here also Helius has his rising (12. 3: we are therefore in the farthest east). The island is the home of Circe, who turns an advanced reconnoitring party into swine. By the help of Hermes and the magical herb *moly* Odysseus rescues his comrades and lives for a year with Circe. When he asks to return home, she sends him first to the land of the dead. (10)

One day's sailing takes them to the far shore of Ocean, the land of the Cimmerians,[1] who live in perpetual darkness. Blood is poured into a hole in the ground, and the shades gather round it: Elpenor, who met his fate on Circe's island, Odysseus' mother, the seer Tiresias, who prophesies the difficulties of the hero's homecoming, his trials on account of the Sungod's oxen, his victory over the suitors and his death in a distant land. Next comes a catalogue of heroines, conversation with Agamemnon and Achilles, a show of dead heroes and great sinners. The return journey over the Ocean is uneventful. There is a kind of intermezzo between the catalogue of women and the interview with Agamemnon. Odysseus tries to break off his narrative, and tactfully reminds his hearers of the promise (7. 317) to convey him to Ithaca. They prevail on him

---

[1] P. VON DER MÜHLL, 'Die Kimmerier der Odyssee und Theopomp'. *Mus. Helv.* 16, 1959, 145, takes 11. 14–19 as referring to the historical Cimmerii, and therefore dates the passage late. But it is possible that Homer's Cimmerii are a people of pure fable.

to continue his story, and Alcinous gives a firm undertaking to send him home next day. (11)

After Circe's island, the sequence of adventures takes us past the Sirens, through Scylla and Charybdis to Thrinacia and the oxen of Helius. Odysseus' comrades, pinned down by adverse winds and tormented with hunger, lay hands on the cattle, and in the next stage of their voyage run into a storm sent by Zeus at Helius' request. Odysseus clings to the mast, barely escapes Charybdis, whither he is driven by a south wind, and is carried by the waves for nine days until he lands on Ogygia, Calypso's island. (Once again Odysseus is nine days in the immensity of the seas (cf. 5. 100), while the return from Ogygia takes eighteen days. On this voyage he has the north star on his left (5. 272), so that Ogygia must lie in the extreme west. How Odysseus came here from the Aeaean island in the east is never related. Clearly adventures in the east, drawn from the saga of the Argonauts, have been thrust in among those depicted in the west.) (12)

Odysseus is sent off with gifts by the Phaeacians, and brought during the next night, by a miraculous voyage, to Ithaca. Poseidon turns the returning vessel to stone. Odysseus wakes in a cloud, and does not know his native land until he is informed by Athene in the guise of a young shepherd. She reveals her identity, and man and goddess join in hiding the gifts of the Phaeacians. They plan their tactics against the suitors, and Athene gives the hero the appearance of an old beggar. (13)

Odysseus next seeks out the swineherd Eumaeus, to whom he introduces himself with a long and imaginary story of his sufferings. He is given food and a blanket for the night. (14)

Athene urges Telemachus, who is still in Sparta, to return home. On his return journey he picks up at Pylos the seer Theoclymenus, who has had to flee Argos. By Athene's guidance Telemachus avoids the plot of the suitors. Meanwhile in Eumaeus' cottage Odysseus hears of his father Laertes, and the swineherd tells of his own life. Next dawn Telemachus lands and comes to Eumaeus. (15)

The swineherd goes to acquaint Penelope with her son's return. Odysseus reveals himself in his true shape (restored by Athene) to Telemachus, and they plan the punishment of the suitors. The latter plot a new attack on Telemachus. Eumaeus returns to the cottage. (16)

In the morning Telemachus goes to the city first, then Eumaeus with Odysseus, who is again the old beggar. Telemachus greets his mother, and Theoclymenus prophesies that Odysseus is already in the country. As Odysseus approaches the city, he is met by the goatherd Melanthius, who insults and ill-treats him: but before the palace Odysseus is recognized by his old dog Argus, now on the point of death. He begs from the suitors, Antinous throws a stool at him, hitting his right shoulder.[1] Eumaeus obtains an interview for the beggar with Penelope that evening, and returns to his cottage. (17)

In a fist-fight Odysseus vanquishes the impudent beggar Irus, and warns

[1] H. REYNEN, 'Schmährede und Schemelwurf im ρ und σ der Odyssee'. *Herm.* 85, 1957, 129, takes a rather different view from that expressed in the next section.

Amphinomus, the least arrogant of the suitors. Penelope shows herself to the men in the hall, makes clear her readiness to wed again, and thus receives rich gifts. Odysseus is treated with scorn by the serving girl Melantho; Eurymachus hurls a stool at him, but hits the cupbearer. (18)

Odysseus and Telemachus remove all weapons from the hall while Athene holds a lamp for them.[1] Penelope enters, and Odysseus prepares her for his return by some invented narratives. As his feet are being washed, the old nurse Euryclea recognizes him from a scar: her silence and co-operation are obtained. Penelope relates a dream portending the punishment of the suitors, and talks of her decision to hold a contest in archery next day, the winner receiving her hand. (19)

Full of resentment against the servant girls who have been lying with the suitors, and anxious about coming events, Odysseus is consoled by Athene, and sleeps awhile in an anteroom. On waking he is heartened by good omens. Euryclea and the serving girls prepare for the banquet on the day sacred to Apollo. Eumaeus and Melanthius arrive, together with the faithful oxherd Philoetius. A bird of omen sent by Zeus deters the suitors from their plan to kill Telemachus. At the feast Ctesippus throws a cow-heel at Odysseus, but it only strikes the wall. The foolish laughter of the suitors and the prophecies of Theoclymenus prepare us for the scene of revenge. (20)

Penelope brings the bow, and Telemachus sets up the axes as target. He first, then some of the suitors, try in vain to string the bow. Odysseus reveals himself to Eumaeus and Philoetius. The suitors put off the contest until next day, but Odysseus, against their opposition, tries the bow himself. Euryclea locks up the servant girls, and Philoetius shuts the door leading out of the hall. Odysseus strings the bow with ease and shoots through the loops of the twelve axeheads.[2] (21)

The second shot lays Antinous low, and the hero shows them who he is. Eurymachus tries in vain to arrange a settlement: he also is slain. Telemachus brings arms: so does Melanthius for the suitors, but he is seized and bound by the two loyal herds. Athene helps in the fight, and all the suitors are slain. Only the bard Phemius and the herald Medon are spared. Odysseus forbids the nurse Euryclea to rejoice at the punishment of the wicked, and has the hall cleansed. The faithless servant girls are hanged; Melanthius is mutilated and killed, and the loyal servants welcome their master. (22)

Euryclea cannot bring Penelope to believe in her husband's return. Even in his presence she has her doubts. He orders lyre-music and dancing for the Ithacans to celebrate a marriage in the palace. Bathed and made more handsome by Athene, he returns to the hall; but Penelope's doubts and delays are still not at an end. She only believes when Odysseus shows knowledge of a secret in the

---

[1] Athene's lamp has been a stumbling-block to critics since the Alexandrians. R. PFEIFFER. 'Die goldene Lampe der Athene'. *Stud. It.* 27/28, 1956, 426 (= *Ausgewählte Schriften*, Munich 1960, 1), has shown that in this golden lamp we have a cult-object associated with the goddess probably from Mycenaean times.

[2] B. STANFORD, 'A Reconsideration of the Problem of the Axes in Odyssey XXI'. *Class. Rev.* 63, 1949, 3.

construction of the royal bed. The night brings man and wife together, and they tell each other of their sufferings and experiences. In the morning Odysseus goes off to find his father in the country. (23)

Hermes leads the shades of the suitors to the underworld, where Agamemnon speaks to Achilles and Amphimedon, a conversation contrasting Penelope's fidelity and the crime of Clytemnestra. Odysseus finds his father Laertes on his farm and declares himself. Meanwhile Antinous' father has aroused the people of Ithaca to revolt: fighting flares up, but Athene makes a lasting peace. (24)

In the *Poetics* (24. 1459b15) Aristotle makes simplicity the keynote of the *Iliad*'s plot, complexity that of the *Odyssey*, thinking probably in particular of the part played by disguise and recognition. This verdict has been often repeated, and it deserves careful consideration.

The *Odyssey*, like the *Iliad*, has a very compressed time-scale: all the events occur within forty days. But this concentration is effected by very different means. In the *Iliad* the wrath theme forms a solid core round which all the other elements are ultimately wrapped. This is concentration in the truest sense: the way in which the fates of Achilles, Patroclus and Hector are bound up one with another and with the central wrath motif allows us to speak of a weaving together of several thematic strands in a manner that is not parallelled in the *Odyssey*. There the devices of composition are basically simpler, easier to grasp, and consequently more effective. A continuous narrative of events is broken up into sections and put together anew, without losing the continuity. Odysseus relates to the Phaeacians his adventures from the beginning until his landing on the island of Calypso. The poet is thus enabled to put much of the narrative into the first person. The first four books – the so-called *Telemachia* – can also be said to serve a useful end in the structure as a whole. Apart from the picture they give of the suitors and of Odysseus' character, the events in Ithaca make a kind of picture-frame around the wanderings related in the middle books. Equally, *en revanche*, Odysseus' story of his adventures at the end of 23 closes the brackets after the scenes in Ithaca.

The two epics do not differ only in the manner of their construction: we shall later discuss differences in outlook on the world of men and gods. It is by no means impossible to consider the *Odyssey* and *Iliad* as being products of one individual's old age and maturity respectively – many ancient critics did so. But it would be easier to side with their opponents, the chorizontes, and ascribe the *Odyssey* to a poet who lived later than Homer, and composed this work under his influence about 700 B.C.[1]

---

[1] A. HEUBECK, *Der Odyssee-Dichter und die Ilias*. Erlangen 1954. The widely differing importance of moral elements in the two epics is strongly stated by K. REINHARDT, 'Tradition und Geist im hom. Epos'. *Studium Generale* 4, 1951, 334 (now *Tradition und Geist*. Gött. 1950, 5). The differences in vocabulary and phraseology are presented very fully in D. L. PAGE, *The Homeric Odyssey*, Oxf. 1955, 149; but his conclusion that the *Odyssey* comes from a quite different cultural background from the *Iliad* goes much too far: cf. T. B. L. WEBSTER (p. 18, n. 1) 275 and 354 respectively. The belief in two poets is shared by W. BURKERT, *Rhein. Mus.* 103, 1960, 131, 1 (with bibliog.). The view of the chorizontes has much to be said for it, but in assessing stylistic differences we must take into account the

5 THE *ODYSSEY*: ANALYTICAL THEORIES

The analytical approach has been applied to the *Odyssey* no less than to the *Iliad*, and here again valuable insight has been gained into the composition: indeed it is only thus that its problems have been clearly seen. As we have noticed, Kirchhoff espoused a 'compilation' theory,[1] and his footsteps have been followed by many others. The *Odyssey* has been variously resolved into three or more original poems, but there is little agreement on drawing the boundaries. A different line is followed by P. von der Mühll and W. Schadewaldt, who work on the supposition that an original *Odyssey* (written by Homer) was substantially rehandled. Schadewaldt has published some preliminary studies[2] to a book on the *Odyssey*. In these he strikes out several passages as later additions, and shows the soundness of the remaining structure. In his view the man who made the additions was no mean poet, although not on a level with the original writer where loftiness of conception and strength of construction are concerned. In these studies Schadewaldt often rehabilitates ideas of Kirchhoff's. K. Reinhardt[3] is among the whole-hearted unitarians.

Just as with the *Iliad*, the analysts have sometimes overreached themselves. A theory which holds that the genuine plot of the *Odyssey* has been tampered with, and which proposes as part of the original a scene in which Nausicaa strolls towards the city by the naked stranger's side, is quite beyond acceptance, even if it has such a scholar as E. Schwartz to support it. One must ask the analysts to tolerate in the *Odyssey* such inconsistencies as are inevitable in so long a poem. It is true that in 15. 295 Odysseus tells Telemachus to leave armour for

differences in the nature and sources of the subject matter. R. HAMPE, *Die Gleichnisse Homers und die Bildkunst seiner Zeit*. Tübingen 1952, Taf. 7-11, publishes an Attic geometric pot of the middle eighth century, probably representing the shipwreck of Odysseus. This does not of course date our *Odyssey*, but it would be valuable to have secure evidence that the story was known on the Greek mainland at this time. The interpretation is disputed by H. FRÄNKEL in *Gnom*. 28, 1956, 570.

[1] Leading exponents are: E. SCHWARTZ, *Die Odyssee*. Munich 1924. U. VON WILAMOWITZ, *Die Heimkehr des Odysseus*. Berl. 1927. More recent analysis: P. VON DER MÜHLL, *Odyssee*. *RE Suppl*. 7, 1940, 696. F. FOCKE, *Die Odyssee*. Tüb. Beitr. 37, Stuttg. 1943. W. SCHADEWALDT, 'Die Heimkehr des Odysseus'. *Taschenbuch für junge Menschen*. Berl. 1946, 177, now with some stylistic alterations in the book *Von Homers Welt und Werk*. 3rd ed., Stuttg. 1959, 375. W. THEILER, 'Vermutungen zur Odyssee'. *Mus. Helv*. 7, 1950, 102. R. MERKELBACH, 'Untersuchungen zur Odyssee'. *Zet*. 2, Munich 1951. B. MARZULLO, *Il problema omerico*. Florence 1952. D. L. PAGE, *The Homeric Odyssey*. Oxf. 1955. B. STOCKEM, *Die Gestalt der Penelope in der Odyssee*. Diss. Cologne 1955. Further references in the report quoted above (p. 14, n. 1). R. PFEIFFER's review of Schwartz' and Wilamowitz' books on the *Odyssey* (*D.L.Z*. 49, 1928, 2355) is of basic importance (now repr. in *Ausgewählte Schriften*. Munich 1960, 8).

[2] (i) 'Der Prolog der Odyssee'. *Festschr. W. Jaeger. Harv. Stud. in Class. Phil*. 63, 1958, 15, (ii) 'Kleiderdinge'. *Herm*. 87, 1959, 13. (iii) 'Neue Kriterien zur Odyssee-Analyse. Die Wiedererkennung des Odysseus und der Penelope'. *Sitzb. Ak. Heidelb. Phil.-hist. Kl*. 1959/2. (iv) 'Der Helioszorn der Odyssee'. *Studi in onore di L. Castiglioni*. Florence 1960. vol. 2, 859. Schadewaldt has put at the end of his translation of the *Odyssey* (Rowohlt's Classics 1958) a list of the verses which he ascribes to the diasceuast.

[3] 'Homer und die Telemachie'. *Von Werken und Formen*. Godesberg 1948, 37, and 'Die Abenteuer der Odyssee'. ibid. 52 (the best introduction to the inner structure of the *Odyssey*). For a literary judgment: L. A. STELLA, *Il poema di Ulisse*. Florence 1955.

the two of them when he clears the arms from the hall, and when the time comes, at the beginning of 19, the armour is not there: it is true that in 5. 108 Hermes alleges the anger of Athene as the cause of Odysseus' shipwreck, which contradicts the facts:[1] but this is the kind of thing that a poet might well happen to overlook. The writer of the *Odyssey* is very likely to have worked in sections. There are, nevertheless, real difficulties and problems affecting important aspects of the composition.

Fierce dispute has raged around the *Telemachia*. As early as 1832 it was held by Gottfried Hermann to be an addition. There are indeed serious objections to the way the narrative proceeds, particularly as regards the failure to distinguish and to develop the two themes of Telemachus' appeal to the people against the suitors and his wish to have a ship to go seeking news. Recently the four books (especially the much-maligned first with Telemachus' self-discovery) have been the subject of a careful and unprejudiced study by F. Klingner,[2] and their virtues have emerged clearly enough to outweigh the weaknesses. It is indeed surprising that the dispatch of Hermes to Calypso is requested by Athene in the assembly of the gods in book 1, but is not carried through until she repeats her complaints at the beginning of book 5. Analysts will claim that an original single assembly of the gods has been split into two by the insertion of the *Telemachia*: unitarians will contend that the council of gods in 5 aptly introduces the scenes in which Odysseus figures, and that the *Telemachia* is as neatly framed by the two councils as the wanderings are by the *Telemachia* and the later scenes in Ithaca. It is worth notice also that in the first council Athene makes a request, and in the second Zeus gives his command, so that the two complement each other fairly well. We must bear in mind that the poet is here managing several strands of simultaneous narrative, and this problem greatly affects the composition of the *Odyssey* as a whole, as Édouard Delebecque[3] has shown. An epic poet cannot describe several sequences of action at once, and going back to pick up the thread is a thing that he cannot do more than once or twice. Most likely the rules of oral recitation played their part here. Thus in the *Odyssey* there is a 'dead period' for Telemachus in Sparta, for Odysseus at the hut of Eumaeus, and for the suitors in Ithaca after Telemachus has left: only one place can be the scene of action at any one time. Nevertheless we do find the poet trying to establish cross-connections in such passages as 4. 625-687 or 16. 322-451. In this light the scenes in Olympus in 1 and 5 can readily be understood: each sets going a different, even if simultaneous, train of happenings.

In his work on the prologue of the *Odyssey* Schadewaldt makes the important observation that Odysseus' homecoming is determined by the gods' decision and by his own – the typical Homeric 'double motivation', in the divine and

[1] More examples of this kind in M. VAN DER VALK, *Textual Criticism of the Odyssey*. Leyden 1949, 226. A good summary of the principal analytical arguments is given by Page (op. cit. p. 449 n. 1).

[2] 'Ueber die vier ersten Bücher der Odyssee.' *Ber. Sächs. Akad. Leipz.* 1944.

[3] *Télémaque et la structure de l'Odyssée*. Annales de la Fac. de Lettres Aix-en-Provence. N.S. 21. Gap 1958. Older discussions of the treatment of simultaneous happenings in epic are cited in my report in *AfdA* 13, 1960, 17.

the human sphere. I cannot agree with Schadewaldt, however, in thinking that this balance is destroyed by the repetition of the Olympian council, and that the *Telemachia* is therefore spurious. If it is a later addition, then its author proved himself to be a supreme master of epic composition.

A more general problem touches the wrath of Poseidon as the driving force of the action. It is not dwelt on consistently throughout the wanderings: this would only have led to tedious repetition. After leaving Aeolus' island it is the crew's distrust that brings disaster; and Zeus is incensed with them after their sinful killing of the oxen of the sun. This is no grist for the analyst's mill. Divine displeasure is a secondary element in epic: the old adventure-stories made no use of it. We should also note the skill with which a twofold divine anger is indicated at the end of book 10, when Polyphemus' prayer is heard by Poseidon, and Zeus rejects the offering of Odysseus.[1]

Many of the analytical arguments can be turned to contrary effect. On three occasions (17, 18 and 20) different suitors, swollen with arrogance, throw things at Odysseus in his beggar's guise. If we consider the subtle variation on this theme, and the mounting effect of each anticlimax, we shall recognize the artistry that is at work in the narration.

The *Phaeacis* too has been very vigorously assailed as impairing the unity of the poem. Schadewaldt,[2] like Kirchhoff, would delete 7. 148-232, and thus make Arete's question in 237 relevant to Odysseus' request in 146. Yet we must reflect that Arete's enquiry after the clothes that she instantly recognizes fits very well into the more intimate scene when the Phaeacian lords have gone away. Schadewaldt goes on to athetize the second day in Phaeacia as an invention of the redactor's. Demodocus' singing and Odysseus' narrative belonged origin-ally, he thinks, to the day of his arrival. It has always been a stumbling-block for analysts that in 7. 318 Alcinous promises to send Odysseus home next day, but in fact the promise is not discharged until the day after that. An opposite interpretation has been spiritedly urged by Wilhelm Matte.[3] In our outline of the plot we suggested that the 'intermezzo' in book 11 might explain this delay. But there is still a surprising contrast between the close-packed narrative of the second day and the vacuity of the third. Can we explain it by supposing that the second day restores the tempest-tossed wanderer to the company of his fellows and to all that life has in store, while the third is wholly absorbed by thoughts of going home? Or have we here a detached sequel to the coherent narrative of the day before? Such questions lead inevitably to subjective answers: but they must be seriously posed.

The *Nekyia* of the eleventh book is particularly troublesome.[4] There is much

---

[1] See REINHARDT, op. cit. 85. SCHADEWALT also in the fourth of his studies mentioned above accepts the wrath of Helius as original, but ascribes the oath-taking in 12. 296-304 to the arranger.

[2] In the second of the studies cited. Opposed by U. HÖLSCHER, 'Das Schweigen der Arete'. *Herm.* 88, 1960, 257.   [3] *Odysseus bei den Phäaken.* Würzburg 1958.

[4] For a unitary view see M. VAN DER VALK, *Beiträge zur Nekyia.* Kampen 1935; more recent works are cited in his book mentioned above (p. 50, n. 1), p. 221. An analytical view: MERKELBACH, op. cit. 185.

that is remarkable in the prophecies of Tiresias and the conversation with Odysseus' mother, and the catalogue of heroines and penitent sinners fits its context rather loosely. Yet we should not assume that this visit to the under-world was entirely lacking in the original version of the *Odyssey*. This is a passage where suspicion of interpolation is particularly strong. Traces of older versions can be seen here and there, as in 20. 156, 276; 21. 258, where a festival of Apollo is mentioned, which once no doubt played an important part in the saga of the hero's return.

There remains one passage in which we may reasonably say that traces of an older version are visible. There is no clear motivation of Penelope's appearance before the suitors in book 18, in order to receive their gifts. In addition, the scene of washing the feet in the next book seems as if it ought to lead up to a recognition of Odysseus by Penelope. The avoidance of this by Athene's inter-vention is as violent as the sudden breaking off of the dream vision, which cannot be allowed to reveal too much. The story would be much more intelli-gible if recognition followed the foot-washing, and if Penelope then in concert with Odysseus went in to the suitors, so as to take their gifts as some compensa-tion for the damage they have done. If we are right in supposing an old version like this, and if the poet of our *Odyssey* altered it, we should not overlook the advantages gained – in particular the wonderful sequence of scenes which leads to the recognition in book 23.[1] In his analysis Schadewaldt assigns 23. 117-172 (measures to clean up after killing the suitors; Odysseus' bath) to the diasceuast. Again the poem as Schadewaldt leaves it flows smoothly and faultlessly: but must we really give up our bath scene? Is it not alluded to plainly enough in 115, where dirt and rags are spoken of? Is it not likely that the poet would have wanted Odysseus to look his best for the final reunion with his wife?

We cannot, however, deny, that some passages raise difficulties which cannot be dismissed as subjective. The speech in which Athene advises Telemachus (1. 269-296) is so confused that we can hardly tell what she wants him to do; and Odysseus' request to the Phaeacians (7. 215) to be allowed to have his dinner is very odd, since he had already had it (5. 177). The elaborate introduction of Theoclymenus in 15 strangely contrasts with his unimportant role in the plot. This may be partly accounted for by the poet's delight in story-telling as such. But the way in which the second attack of the suitors on Telemachus is dis-missed in a few verses (20. 241-247), and the thread starting at 20. 371 is rudely broken off, simply does not cohere with the remaining narrative. These diffi-culties concern individual passages and could be removed by slight emendation. Their appearance in the text is perhaps owing to rhapsodic tradition. The analytical zeal that is displayed in devising hypothetical origins trips over the fact that the epic poems, as long as they were virtually the exclusive property of the rhapsodes, were exposed to alteration or interpolation far more than tragedy ever was to actors' interpolations. Yet we know that the actors did interpolate. The brevity, or rather headlong haste, with which the last book is

---

[1] On the management of the scenes in the books preceding the recognition see O. SEEL, 'Variante und Konvergenz in der Odyssee'. *Studi in onore di U.E. Paoli*. Florence 1955, 643.

brought to an end could easily be explained if we inferred from the scholium to 23.296 that the genuine *Odyssey* ended there. The statement that Aristophanes and Aristarchus reckoned this point as the τέλος (πέρας) of the epic has often been taken as meaning that the Alexandrians knew of manuscripts that ended at 296. But there is no hint that they athetized either the end of the *Odyssey* or the passages anticipating it, as they must necessarily have done if the scholium were talking about the end of the genuine transmission. Accordingly we fall back on an interpretation found as early as Eustathius: namely that the Alexandrians considered that the real subject of the *Odyssey* (the wanderings and the slaying of the suitors) had here reached its conclusion.

This does not, of course, guarantee the genuineness of the 24th book as a whole. The end section and the second *Nekyia* are open to grave doubt. But one would be very happy to leave as genuine (with Schadewaldt) the résumé with which Odysseus talks himself to sleep.

The questions we have alluded to give a general picture of the problems. In sum, we can be more confident with the *Odyssey* than with the *Iliad* in assuming earlier treatments of the same material. The poet of the *Iliad*, by introducing the wrath motif as an organizing principle, created something new out of the mass of epic material before him. In the adventures of Odysseus the present state of the poem allows us to infer the existence of older treatments. How specific we can be is quite another matter. Certainly this is not the cobbling together of older poems by a mere compiler. The *Odyssey* as we have it betrays a strength in composition and a mastery of narrative that mark the great work of art. In this sense it is a unity.

6 CULTURAL LEVELS IN THE HOMERIC POEMS

The Alexandrian critics[1] were the first to remark that such things as riding, signalling by trumpet and boiling of meats occur in the *Iliad* only in similes. If these come from the poet's own world, it becomes necessary to posit at least two distinct cultural levels[2] – one to which the actions narrated in the poem are

---

[1] Schol. *Il.* 15. 679; 18. 219; 21. 632.

[2] On the different cultural elements: M. P. NILSSON, *Homer and Mycenae*. Lond. 1933. A. SEVERYNS, I. 7; 2. 13. W. DEN BOER, 'Le Rôle de l'art et l'histoire dans les études homériques contemporaines'. *Ant. Class.* 17, 1948, 25. J. L. MYRES, 'Homeric Art'. *Ann. Br. School Ath.* 45, 1920, 229. H. L. LORIMER, *Homer and the Monuments*. Lond. 1950. W. SCHADEWALDT, 'Homer und sein Jahrhundert'. *Von Homers Welt und Werk*. 3rd ed. Stuttg. 1959, 87. D. H. F. GRAY, 'Metal Working in Homer'. *Journ. Hell. Stud.* 74, 1954, I. L. A. STELLA, *Il poema di Ulisse*. Florence 1955. C. M. BOWRA, *Homer and his Forerunners*. Edinburgh 1955. R. HAMPE, 'Die homerische Welt im Lichte der neuesten Ausgrabungen'. *Gymn.* 63, 1956, I. A. HEUBECK, *Gnom.* 29, 1957, 38. There are important sections on Mycenaean elements in Homer in T. B. L. WEBSTER'S books *From Mycenae to Homer*. London 1958, and *Die Nachfahren Nestors. Mykene und die Anfänge griechischer Kultur*. Janus-Bücher 19. Munich 1961. C. H. WHITMAN, *Homer and the Heroic Tradition*. Harv. Un. Press 1958. D. L. PAGE, *History and the Homeric Iliad*. Sather Classical Lectures 31. Univ. of Calif. Press 1959 (repr. paperbound 1963), on which see the important review by A. HEUBECK in *Gnom.* 33, 1961, 113. SP. MARINATOS, 'Problemi omerici e preomerici in Pilo'. *Parola del Passato*. 16, 1961, 219. There is a good summary (although it cannot but be problematical here and there) in G. S. KIRK'S article 'Objective Dating Criteria in Homer'. *Mus. Helv.* 17, 1960, 189. On the phratries (*Il.* 2. 362) see A. ANDREWES, *Herm.* 89, 1961, 129.

referred, and a second in which the poet lived. Nothing useful has been achieved by attempts to refer these cultural differences to a transitional period in which old and new occurred side by side.

Homer himself makes it plain that he is telling of a far distant time and of greater men (e.g. *Il.* 12. 447). How far we may attribute archaism to Homer, has yet to be discussed. It is certainly true that the epics preserve an almost unbroken silence on the great revolution wrought by the Dorian invasion. Once only in the *Odyssey* (19. 177) are the three tribes of the Dorians mentioned: Hera in the *Iliad* (4. 51) bids Zeus destroy her three favourite cities, Argos, Sparta and Mycenae, and possibly the poet is alluding to historical events. We now have historical data about the Mycenaean kingdom of Agamemnon and that of Nestor in Pylos, and about the wealth of Orchomenus (*Il.* 9. 381); and we know that several centuries separate them from the poet's time. This lapse of time can be seen in the part played by bronze and iron respectively. Iron objects are among the valuable prizes given by Achilles at the funeral games (23. 261, 834, 850). The rarity and costliness of iron is underlined by the fact that weapons in the *Iliad* are almost wholly of bronze. The only exceptions are the iron club of Areithous in 7. 141 and the iron head of Pandarus' arrow (4. 123). From the second passage we can infer that Homer was acquainted with circumstances in which iron was easily enough obtainable to be used for arrowheads. These were of course the circumstances of his own time. Further evidence is the free use of 'iron' in metaphorical and proverbial expressions: 'a heart of iron' (*Il.* 24. 205, 521); 'iron (i.e. an iron weapon) tempts a man to use it' (*Od.* 19. 13).

How are we to explain this relation of the poet to a past in which his heroes live and move? We saw earlier (p. 17) that it is part of the stock-in-trade of heroic poetry to set its stories in a more or less remote past. This is easy to explain. In most cases such poetry has a historical background which remains a living memory despite great liberties in reshaping. Very probably Homer had seen the ruins of Troy. But we must not speak in his case of deliberate archaizing, such as a modern historical novelist might practise. There was an epic tradition going back hundreds of years, and in consequence Homer was tied to precedent in what he said and how he said it. His language makes this plain. But on the other hand, the poet alludes to things of his own time far more than a deliberate archaizer would do.

The two epics are set in a remote past; but it is inconceivable that they do not reflect the social structure of his own time.[1] The world of the great leaders is sharply separated from a lower stratum which is only represented in similes or in the persons of servants. The independent proprietor is the central feature: only a few craftsmen – smiths, potters, carpenters – and itinerant physicians, seers

---

[1] H. STRASBURGER, 'Der soziologische Aspekt der homerischen Epen'. *Gymn.* 60, 1953, 97. ÉMILE MIREAUX, *La Vie quotidienne au temps d'Homère*. Paris 1955 (Engl. trans. London 1959). M. I. FINLEY, *The World of Odysseus*. London 1956. A. FANFANI, *Poemi omerici ed economia antica*. Milan 1960. On the general background: H. M. CHADWICK. *The Heroic Age*. Cambr. 1912.

and minstrels have established their independence. We can see where the centre of gravity of this social order lay from the scene in *Il.* 23 where Achilles offers a large disc of iron as a prize: the winner will ensure his supplies of iron for five years, and will not need to send herd or ploughman into the town in search of it.

Scholars have rightly been unwilling to draw too close a parallel between this society and medieval chivalry. Homeric society is much more closely tied to farming and the work it involves. It is possible for Odysseus (18. 365) to challenge Eurymachus to a contest in mowing and ploughing: even in the *Iliad* the scenes depicted on the shield of Achilles include a noble proprietor (*basileus*) standing contentedly among his harvesters.

But the fact remains that it is a world of chivalry, in which fighting is the ultimate self-fulfilment of the nobles. Only they count in warfare, whether they drive their chariots over the battlefield or seek each other out in single combat. The mass of the people, as listed in the Catalogue of Ships, through all these duels appears only in the poet's similes.

The warrior ideology is strongly brought out in the *Iliad* from the very nature of the material. In the *Odyssey*, however, when Odysseus disregards Circe's warning and proposes to meet Scylla in armour with two spears, we can reckon this as heroic colouring laid on to a primitive story of adventure by sea. We must of course not overlook the fact that the *Odyssey* brings wider ranges of human life within its purview.

The ways of life and thought of aristocratic society are more in Homer than part of his inherited material; he saw them alive in his own age. The proud lords of Chalcis called themselves Hippobotae, rearers of horses, and when in about 700 war broke out with Eretria over the Lelantine lands, bringing noble warriors from all over Greece, there was an agreement to ban all missile weapons, so as to leave the decision to gentlemanly man-to-man duels (Strab. 448).

One of the particular instances that mark the two epics as products of their own time is the fact that Diomede and Odysseus, in one special case, ride horses (*Il.* 10. 513, 541): this, however, in the suspect *Doloneia*. The difference between the two ages comes out amusingly in another connection: Homeric heroes live on roast meat, and are only reduced to fishing by the direst necessity; but in similes fishing in various forms appears with the frequency of an everyday pursuit.[1] Many perplexities and false datings are associated with the question whether a Homer of the eighth century could have had knowledge of temples and cult-images like those in the sixth book of the *Iliad*. He could have had[2] – but it was primarily to his own age that he was indebted for knowledge of this kind of divine worship. In both epics we meet the Phoenicians as traders and pirates. It was between 1000 and 800 that they received the maritime inheritance of Mycenae in the Mediterranean: they are far removed from the age of Agamemnon. Cremation also in the epics is a feature from Homer's own day: the Mycenaeans buried their dead in shaft graves or beehive tombs.[3] There are

[1] Passages cited in A. LESKY, *Thalatta*. Vienna 1947, 18.
[2] Schadewaldt op. cit. 93, n. 5. W. KRAIKER, *Gnom.* 24, 1952, 453. G. S. KIRK op. cit. 194.
[3] E. MYLONAS, 'Homeric and Mycenaean Burial Customs'. *Am. Journ. Arch.* 52, 1948, 56.

sometimes difficulties in referring particular items to the poet's own age. We are probably right in doing so with the armour taken by Agamemnon from the Cyprian king Cinyras, with its snakes twining up to the neck (*Il.* 11. 20).

Against features coming from the poet's time we may set others derived from Mycenaean, or even Cretan, civilization. There are not very many, and not all are certain. It was reasonable to hope for much in this connection from the decipherment of Linear B. This hope has been disappointed, and not merely because the new texts are concerned with the economic records of the seat of government. Rather, it is because the knowledge thus gained of social and economic structure tends to widen the gap between the Homeric and Mycenaean worlds. Rodenwaldt's conclusion,[1] that Homer has many historical, but no archaeological links with Mycenaean culture, has been confirmed in its second part, but weakened in its first. The connections between the Mycenaean world and the civilizations of the Near East seem to be multiplying, but this does not imply that Homer's links with it cannot be traced any more. The classical instance is Nestor's cup, described in *Iliad* 11. 632 seqq., which has been considered Mycenaean on the strength of a golden vessel found in the fourth shaft grave at Mycenae. Recent writers have stressed the differences more than the resemblances;[2] but they are close enough to justify the older view. In the description of the palace of Alcinous (*Od.* 7. 87) there occurs a frieze of *kyanos*, i.e. lapis lazuli or imitation of it in blue glass: this material is found in ornamental work at Tiryns. Since this type of ornament was of Cretan origin, we are in touch here with the culture of Crete – a rare thing in Homeric epic. Such reminiscences may partly account for the special position enjoyed by the queen Arete among the Phaeacians, and the dancing floor that Daedalus made for Ariadne in Cnossus. The knowledge which both epics display (*Il.* 9. 381; *Od.* 4. 126) of the wealth of Thebes in Upper Egypt must go back to a time before the barbarian invasions. Such passages as *Od.* 3. 318; 4. 354, 482 show us how shadowy a notion of Egypt was current later. A clear instance is the leather helmet, oversown with rows of boar's teeth, which Meriones gives to Odysseus (*Il.* 10. 261), which certainly connects with an ivory head and pierced boar's teeth from Mycenae. We have already seen how significant the use of bronze in Homeric weapons is, taken together with the rarity of iron. Metal inlay will deserve a word or two later. Swords with silver-studded hilts are known from the fifteenth and seventh centuries: very likely they were also used in between. The common formula φάσγανον ἀργυρόηλον includes a word for 'sword' which occurs in Linear B as *pa-ka-na* (plural) but goes out of use later, and it is a likely guess that the formula and the thing itself go back to the Mycenaean age. This instance shows how much may be surmised and how little proved in dealing with these materials.

Twice in the *Iliad* (6. 320; 8. 495) we are told that Hector's spear had a golden ring round its head. Socket-type spearheads, secured to the shaft with a ring,

---

[1] *Tiryns* 2, 1912, 204.

[2] Thus HAMPE, 'Die hom. Welt' (*sup.* p. 2, n. 20) p. 20, against MYRES and DEN BOER opp. citt.

are known to us from Mycenaean and Cretan graves. Since W. Reichel published his book on Homeric weapons[1] it has been widely believed that, of the two kinds of shield appearing in Homer, the long one protecting the whole body is Mycenaean, while the small round one belongs to Homer's own time. This view has recently been called in question, and geometric vases have been brought to light in which the small round shield and the large 'figure-of-eight' shield appear side by side. In fact the long shield appears in two shapes in the carved dagger-handle from the fourth shaft-grave at Mycenae: as well as the figure of eight there is the 'fire-screen' type without any narrowing at the waist.

In the *Iliad* the long shield is particularly associated with Ajax: the fact that he is spoken of in a repeated formula (7. 219; 11. 485; 17. 128) as 'moving his shield like a tower' makes us think rather of the second of the major Mycenaean forms.

We have seen that not all the alleged Mycenaean features in Homer can be claimed as certain; but beyond doubt there are some. How does this happen in poetry of the eighth century? C. Robert, in his *Studien zur Ilias* (1901), written under the influence of Reichel's study, tried to establish cultural levels on this difference of armaments. The approach has shown itself delusive. How unfortunate that the splendid Mycenaean boar-tooth helmet should occur precisely in that *Doloneia* which is generally agreed to be a later addition! A more credible theory regards these 'Mycenaean' objects as ancient heirlooms: the helmet in question had belonged to many men, and was left to Meriones by his father. But even so, the survival of such things over several centuries seems unlikely, and the explanation will hardly fit all the cases.

Modern scholars are still divided into two camps on this question. Some maintain that Greek epic poetry with Troy as its theme can be traced back to beginnings in the Mycenaean age. The various thematic and linguistic elements that can be referred to this period are derived from it (they think) by direct tradition. This view is espoused in varying ways, but with considerable confidence, by Webster, Page and Whitman. The opposite attitude is taken by Heubeck, and Kirk also is more circumspect. For them it is the differences between the Mycenaean and Homeric worlds which are of prime importance, and they stress the possibility that the 'Mycenaean' elements are derived not from a poetical tradition going back to that time, but to memories that survived the overthrow of Mycenae and later found their way into epic poetry. The 'dark age', in their opinion, is the formative period for both the legend and the epic.

If the author is to put forward a view of his own, it must of course be no more than hypothesis. There must have been songs and legends of heroes in the feudal world of Mycenae, as we have said before. Possibly they were in a dactylic metre; in the very nature of things their themes must have been battle and adventure; it is conceivable that many of the characters known to us from Homer played a part in them. But there is nothing to suggest that the expedition against Troy was the main subject matter and that we have thus to postulate contemporary poetical accounts of an historical undertaking. It is much more credible

---

[1] Vienna 1894, 2nd ed. 1901. Further literature in H. TRÜMPY, *Kriegerische Fachausdrücke im griechischen Epos*. Diss. Basel 1950, 6 and 20; cf. Schadewaldt op. cit. 94.

that the development of the Trojan cycle of legends in the form of oral epic took place essentially in the 'dark age'. The economic depression of the period is not a valid argument against this view, as has been rightly pointed out.[1] It is impossible to delimit accurately the contributions made by the Ionian and the mainland Greeks, but that of the latter should not be underestimated. The part played by Athens must be borne in mind, even if we cannot go with Whitman in making Athens the cradle of the epic. Hampe and Webster have skilfully traced the strands that lead from Pylos by way of Athens to the colonies. Certainly it would be a great mistake, as Schadewaldt has rightly pointed out, to suppose that the Aegean kept those two areas poles apart.[2]

As for Mycenaean elements in Homeric poetry, we must keep open both the possibilities mentioned earlier, without trying to reach a definite solution in any one specific instance. That words and formulae should have come down from the Mycenaean age is quite conceivable; but at the same time we may be dealing with floating memories from the age immediately following, in which all the devastation was not able wholly to snap the thread of tradition. At the same time we must take account of regional differences. Thus the author also envisages the stream of oral poetry as flowing for many centuries before it pours at last into the wide sea of the Homeric epic: it bears with it many fragments from a remote antiquity, but on its way it has picked up many of a recent date.

There is a striking and, as it were, symbolic mixture of elements in the shield of Achilles. The description of its manufacture takes us back to the Mycenaean dagger-handle with its ornament of metal inlay, but the nature of the scenes portrayed is most closely parallelled by bronze shields of oriental type from the eighth century.[3]

To sum up: the world of Homeric poetry contains many references to the vigorous life of the poet's own time, while also having features that come from a remote past, survivals that are enclosed in their context like flies in amber. There is truth in Myres' paradox, that the world of Homeric poetry is immortal for this very reason, that it never existed outside the poet's imagination.

7 LANGUAGE AND STYLE

Nowhere is language more conditioned by metre than it is in Greek epic. We have no knowledge of any earlier stage in which some other metre than the hexameter was used: rather the extreme antiquity suggested by some of the formulae leads us to believe that the metre goes back to the earliest days of Greek epic. The peculiar position which it holds among Greek metres, and such phenomena as lengthening *metri gratia*, implying difficulty in employing it, incline one to accept Meillet's theory of its pre-Greek origin.[4]

The danger of monotony involved in the use of strict metre in unbroken

---

[1] G. S. KIRK, *Mus. Helv.* 17, 1960, 189 and *Proc. Cambr. Phil. Soc.* 187, 1961, 46.

[2] *Von Homers Welt und Werke.* 3rd ed. Stuttg. 1958, 98.

[3] SCHADEWALDT op. cit. 94, n. 7.

[4] *Les Origines indo-européennes des mètres grecs.* Paris 1923. K. MAROT, 'Der Hexameter'. *Acta Ant. Acad. Scient. Hungar.* VI. fasc. 1/2, 1958; *Die Anfänge der griech. Literatur.* Budapest 1960, 212.

sequences of verse was countered in various ways. The first of these was the substitution of spondees for dactyls: this is exceptional in the fifth foot, and in the fourth it is uncommon when a break follows. The monotony could also be relieved by varying the point where the sentence ended: Homer often runs over the end of the line (enjambement). An important word can be given special emphasis by thus placing it at the beginning of a line. But the hexameter is really made usable as a metre by the many possible caesurae: a feature which earned the praise of Friedrich Schlegel. It is not a question of necessary pauses to take breath, but rather of devising a means to make the sense-divisions coincide in certain recognized ways with the metrical divisions. The following diagram indicates the admissible caesurae.

$$\overset{1}{-}\mid\cup\mid\cup\mid\overset{2}{-}\mid\cup\cup\overset{3}{-}\mid\cup\mid\overset{4}{\cup}-\mid\cup\cup\overset{5}{\mid}\overset{6}{-}\cup\cup-\circ$$

There are three clearly divided groups, of which the middle group includes the two most important caesurae. In 27803 hexameters there are 11361 examples of the break after the long syllable of the third dactyl (penthemimeral caesura) and 15640 of the break after the first trochee of the third foot (trochaic caesura). In other words, almost every verse in the poems has a sensible break in the middle, dividing it into two halves, one beginning with a falling, the other with a rising tone. There are various subsidiary breaks on either side of the principal caesurae, dividing up the halves of the line and thus resulting often in a fourfold division.[1] Since, however, the break in the first half of the line is often either weak or completely obscured, it is not unusual to find a hexameter divided by sense and metre into three parts. In fine, the metre presents a free play of possibilities within sharply drawn boundaries; and as such typifies at an early stage the Greek principle of freedom under law which was to fulfil itself in the classical period.

An historical study of Homeric language[2] discovers at the outset a mixture of different dialects. The latest elements are Attic: but they arise from circumstances not of the composition, but of the transmission of the poems. Since an important stage of the transmission took place on Attic soil, it is easy to see how Atticisms have crept in.[3] Another explanation must be sought for the numerous

---

[1] On the structure of the Homeric hexameter see FRÄNKEL 39. Id., *Wege und Formen frühgriechischen Denkens*. 2nd ed. Munich 1960, 100. H. N. PORTER, 'The Early Greek Hexameter'. *Yale Class. Stud.* 12, 1951 with tables for the individual structural types. Abundant material on the same theme in H. J. METTE, 'Die Struktur des ältesten daktylischen Hexameters'. *Glotta* 35, 1956, 1.

[2] K. MEISTER, *Die homerische Kunstsprache*. Leipz. 1921. M. P. NILSSON, *Homer and Mycenae*. Lond. 1933, 160. P. CHANTRAINE, *Grammaire homérique*. I, 3rd ed. Paris 1958; 2, 1953. Id., *Introduction à l'Iliade*. Paris 1948, 89-136. C. GALLAVOTTI – A. RONCONI, *La lingua omerica*. 3rd ed. Bari 1955. J. S. LASSO DE LA VEGA, *La oración nominal en Homero*. Madrid 1955. V. PISANI, *Storia della lingua greca* in *Encicl. Class.* 2/5/1. Turin 1960, 25. P. J. KAKRIDIS, Ἡ παράταξη τῶν οὐσιαστικῶν στὸν Ὅμηρο καὶ στοὺς Ὁμηρικοὺς ὕμνους. Thessalonica 1960. See also the works cited on the dialect problem (*sup.* p. 9, n. 1).

[3] The opposing positions: J. WACKERNAGEL, *Sprachliche Untersuchungen zu Homer*. Gött. 1916 (1-159, also *Glotta* 7, 1916, 161) and U. VON WILAMOWITZ, *Die Ilias und Homer*. Berl. 1916, 506.

Aeolisms[1] in the basically Ionic language of epic. This co-existence of Aeolic and Ionic forms is remarkable. The Aeolic modal particle κε(ν) occurs three times as frequently as the Ionic ἄν; ἄμμες and ὔμμες occur beside ἡμεῖς and ὑμεῖς; the Aeolic infinitive endings -μεν and -μεναι compete with the Ionic -ναι and -ειν; in the perfect participle the Aeolic inflection like that of the present participle is found beside the Ionic forms, and Aeolic datives like πόδεσσι beside the Ionic ποσσί and ποσί, to give but a few examples.

On the west coast of Asia Minor the Ionians pushed northwards and overlaid old Aeolic settlements, which, like Smyrna, came to be associated with Homer. Hence it was tempting to imagine that the two epics were originally composed in Aeolic and later underwent an Ionic redaction. This view was taken to its logical conclusion by August Fick, who attempted in 1883 and 1886 to turn them back into Aeolic. This is a good example of a mistaken view bringing real benefits in its train. It was only thus that scholars recognized two kinds of Ionism – those which might easily be a substitute for an Aeolic form, and those for which no Aeolic replacement was possible. The result in brief was to show that we have not successive layers of dialect, but Aeolic and Ionic forms in close and often inseparable connection. Attempts to carry out Homeric analysis on a dialectal basis have consequently achieved little of note. The complexity of the problems can be seen from the *Doloneia*. Late forms in it have been eagerly seized upon, but here, and only here, occurs the old Aeolic ἀβροτάξομεν – a linguistic counterpart of the boar-tooth helmet!

A difficulty in the investigation of Homeric language lies in our ignorance of Aeolic or Ionic at the time of composition, so that we have to rely on knowledge of later forms in these dialects. What can be said with confidence is that the language of these poems, with its mixture of dialectal forms, does not represent the language currently spoken at the time.[2] In this sense it can be called an artificial language. This does not mean that it is a deliberate mixture of different dialects, but rather that it arose as a by-product of the formation of the Homeric poems. We cannot follow this development in detail nowadays. The more carefully one studies the mixture of forms in this epic literary dialect, the more complicated does it appear. The different elements can be classified into a horizontal and a vertical dimension: horizontal in that dialectal forms current at the same time in different places are found together: vertical in that old and young forms occur side by side. A particularly clear example of the latter is the use of contracted and uncontracted forms of verbs. In the present state of our knowledge it would be too much of a simplification to separate out an older Aeolic from a later Ionic stratum, or to talk unqualifiedly of one's overlying the other. The mixture is both older and more intimate than used to be

[1] K. STRUNK, *Die sogennannten Aeolismen der homerischen Sprache.* Diss. Cologne 1957, tries to get rid of the Aeolisms by referring them as archaisms to a Peloponnesian and central Greek dialect; but this is not workable, cf. P. CHANTRAINE, *Athenaeum* N.S. 36, 1958, 317, and F. R. ADRADOS, *Kratylos* 4, 1959, 177.

[2] Georgiev's theory (cf. *sup.* p. 9, n. 1 and *Klio* 38, 1960, 69) explaining Homer's language with its multiplicity of forms as the last phase of a Mycenaean *koine* incorporating Ionic and Aeolic elements is not likely to make many converts.

assumed. Nevertheless, some observations point to the great antiquity of certain forms considered as Aeolic. It is also untrue to suppose that parallel forms are always interchangeable. Thus the intensive prefixes ἀρι- and ἐρι- are not interchangeable in the same word, and the latter is especially frequent in formulae at the ends of verses, which are probably very old.

We are greatly helped towards understanding how this epic language originated by the observations of Vittore Pisani[1] on the poetic diction of the Ottocento, which has picked up from the preceding centuries elements of the most diverse origin – Sicilian and Tuscan especially, but also Provençal in many cases.

Attempts have recently been made to separate out different levels of Homeric language chronologically – Mycenaean, Pre-migration and Post-migration diction.[2] But these elaborate studies have served to show how hard it is in a thorough mixture like this to sort out linguistic levels, let alone to date individual passages and sections by them. In the perpetual flux of epic language new formulae were being invented even at a late date, and old formulae were still being pressed into the poet's service. In this way epic language developed its peculiar richness: much that was old remained amid the inrush of the new, and forms of widely diverse age and origin were used side by side. It is obvious that such a rich variety of forms was very welcome to the bards who extemporized heroic lays, while for later poets it made the mastery of the hexameter much easier to attain. The coexistence of different linguistic periods is well illustrated by the varying use of the later definite article. The same may be said of the optional use of the digamma, a discovery which we owe to the genius of Bentley. In both epics we find this sound regarded or disregarded at will in prosody. The degree to which it was sounded in Greek at the time no doubt varied, and thus the poet was allowed to be inconsistent.[3]

As we saw above (p. 9) the decipherment of the Linear B tablets has set everyone asking what relation there is between this Mycenaean Greek and the known dialects. At the same time one would be glad to know how it stands to the epic literary language. Our ideas are very far from settled, and what was said about cultural levels in Homer can be said again in this context. Some scholars, like Denys Page, are confident that we can sort out the Mycenaean elements in Homer's language: on the other hand Kirk prudently points out that it must still have been possible for formulae of the type we have in mind to find their way into oral poetic tradition after the Mycenaean age. Two factors contribute further to the uncertainty. On the one hand

---

[1] Op. cit. (p. 9, n. 1), 38.

[2] T. B. L. WEBSTER, 'Early and Late in Homeric Diction'. *Eranos* 54, 1956, 34. G. S. KIRK, 'Objective Dating Criteria in Homer'. *Mus. Helv.* 17, 1960, 197. Great vigour and confidence is displayed by D. L. PAGE, *History and the Homeric Iliad. Sather Class. Lect.* 31, Univ. of Calif. Press 1959, especially c. 6, in identifying Mycenaean elements in Homeric language.

[3] Apart from the standard grammars, see also A. PAGLIARO, 'Il digamma e la tradizione dei poemi omerici' in *Saggi di critica semantica*. Rome 1952, 65.

Manu Leumann[1] has declared that a great many glosses attributed to Arcado-Cyprian (the group closest akin to Mycenaean) which we find in inscriptions or in the grammarians are not genuine dialect forms, but reminiscences of epic language. On the other, the interpretation of the Linear B tablets is often uncertain and debateable because of the defects of the system of writing (*v. sup.* p. 10). But even bearing all this in mind, we find a good many indisputable connections between Homeric and Mycenaean Greek. This fact emerges from such a careful and valuable study as that of Vittore Pisani.[2] We are no more able to date the entry of individual elements of language into the epic tradition than we were able to date the entry of material objects. But just as we were able confidently to assume the existence of Mycenaean heroic poetry, without supposing it to have been a lineal ancestor of the *Iliad*, so we are free to suppose that a number of formulae (such as our φάσγανον ἀργυρόηλον and words like αἶσα, λεύσσω, ἤπύω) go back to this period.[3]

The assumption of an extremely long period of development for epic language is supported by the fact that we meet forms and meanings which can only be accounted for as misunderstandings of some old linguistic inheritance. Examples are ὁ ἀγγελίης 'the messenger', and the adjective ὀκρυόεις. Leumann has shown wonderful acuteness in tracking many of these down but they will not serve as tools for the analyst. The coexistence of old and new ways of using the same linguistic inheritance need surprise no one who bears in mind the type of development that we postulate.

The most obvious feature of the language of both epics is the large part played by formulaic elements, which we must take to be part of their inheritance from oral composition. Recent studies have brought out ever more clearly the connection of these formulae with the metre.

First we have the 'perpetual epithet' with persons and things.[4] Very often these adjectives have their own particular place in the verse, and some of them occur in only one case, through the exigencies of the metre. We also find in Homer a good many formulae for the beginning and end of a speech, for standing up and sitting down, for incidents in battle, etc. Many of them are as long as half a verse, and by slight alterations can be made to fit different places in the line and to suit other circumstances. A third class is made up of the stock scenes which recur frequently, often running to several verses, such as banquet,

---

[1] *Homerische Wörter. Schweiz. Beitr.* 3. Basel 1950, 262.   [2] *Op. cit.* (*sup.* p. 9, n. 1).

[3] From what we have said about the dialects it is plain that we cannot any longer talk about an 'Achaean' level in this connection. This is a drawback in C. J. RUIJGH's book *L'Élément achéen dans la langue épique*. Assen 1957. E. RISCH in *Gnom.* 30, 1958, 87 deplores the confidence often shown in establishing 'primitive' elements of language, and doubts in particular whether Mycenaean elements can be proved in Homer.

[4] K. WITTE was first in the field: *Glotta* 1, 1909, 132 and his article on Homer in *RE* 8, 1913, 2213.   More recent observations by M. PARRY, *L'Épithète traditionelle dans Homère*. Paris 1928. His later work in J. LABARBE, *L'Homère de Platon. Bibl. de la Fac. de Phil. et Lettr. Liege*. 117, 1949: Labarbe's own contributions are considerable. Severyns 2, 49. D. L. PAGE, *History and the Homeric Iliad* (cited p. 35, 2) 222. E. DIAS PALMEIRA, 'O formalismo da poesia homerica'. *Humanitas* N.S. 8/9, 1959–60, 171. W. WHALLON, 'The Homeric Epithets'. *Yale Class. Stud.* 17, 1961, 95. See also the works earlier cited (p. 37 ff.) on oral poetry.

sacrifice, warriors arming, ships setting sail and the like.[1]

That these elements are important does not mean that they are all-important. It is wrong to look on Homeric poetry as a cento of formulae, or to think that these are component elements in the same way as individual words are in modern poetry.

Any assessment of the formulaic elements which considered simply their technical aspect would go only halfway to understanding them. The perpetual epithet and the stock scene make what is important and valuable stand out from the repetition of what is the same: and thus help effectively to build up the picture of a world in which men and things have their appointed place. Moreover, these elements are used in very different ways. Often they are formulae and nothing more: a ship is 'swift-sailing' even when it is hauled up on the beach (*Il.* 1. 421), Achilles is 'fleet-footed' when he is sitting in his chair (16. 5). This adds nothing to the sense, but it is not of course nonsense to mention a man together with a quality inseparably attached to him. In other places these traditional elements receive the breath of life: as Achilles draws near to Hector and puts him to flight by his appearance, he is given the epithet 'monstrous'; when Polydamas takes the field, he is the 'lance-shaking Polydamas' (14. 449), but when he gives the right advice (18. 249), he is the 'sage Polydamas'; when Odysseus' crew bend to their oars, an often repeated verse gives the epithet 'grey-white foaming sea'. As for the stock scene, we may note the elaborate description of the smooth return voyage in *Il.* 1. 477 after Apollo has been placated: it is in striking contrast at once with the outward voyage, in which the landing at Chryse is the only point emphasized, and with the immediately following scene of Achilles' anger.

In so saying, we have already committed ourselves in regard to a question which has become more important lately. Those who reckon the Homeric poems as pure 'oral composition' have drawn the conclusion that the use of formulaic elements is to be explained on purely technical grounds, and that interpretations which appeal to literary judgment are an illegitimate application of modern standards.[2] As the author does not accept the view that the Homeric poems had a purely oral composition, he rejects this interpretation. We must never forget how much free and original poetry there is in both the *Iliad* and the *Odyssey*, apart from traditional formulae. It is where his creation is relatively free of the traditional that we most catch the tones of his voice; as in the first and last books of the *Iliad*, and where his similes give us pictures of his own world.[3] To evaluate the findings of Parry and his school it is high time

---

[1] W. AREND, *Die typischen Szenen bei Homer*. Problemata 7. Berl. 1933. On the battle-scenes: G. STRASBURGER, *Die kleinen Kämpfer der Ilias*. Diss. Frankf.a.M. 1954. W. H. FRIEDRICH, *Verwundung und Tod in der Ilias*. Abh. Ak. Gött. Phil.-hist. Kl. 3. F. 38, 1956.

[2] A vigorous exponent of this view is F. M. COMBELLACK, 'Milman Parry and Homeric artistry'. *Comparative Literature* 11, 1959, 193. For a different view: R. SPIEKER, *Die Nachrufe in der Ilias*. Diss. Münster 1958. Both he and C. H. WHITMAN (*sup.* p. 53, n. 2), go too far in detecting artistry and symbolism. Both extremes should be avoided.

[3] In this connection the researches of G. P. SHIPP (*Studies in the Language of Homer*. Cambridge 1953) deserve attention.

that we considered not only what we have learned about the formulaic element in Homer, but also those parts which are outside the sphere of the formula.

The double aspect of Homeric poetry is visible also in the language. Beside the old and the traditional we find a fresh immediacy, a springlike abundance, a magic that is always new. The day of abstraction has not yet dawned: the Homeric way of seeing and describing the world is the gift of an age in which, to use Victor Hehn's expression, none of the qualities which determine general concepts had become isolated and hardened. Two examples are enough to illustrate this lively response to the impressions of the senses: in Homeric language there are nine verbs meaning 'to see'; their nuances range from merely catching sight to deliberate scrutiny.[1] Secondly the richness of vocabulary to describe the sea: the limitless plain, the watery path, the salt flood foaming on the beach.[2]

All that we have said of the language applies with special force to the similes.[3] In them the poet opens the frontiers of the 'heroic' world to admit the whole fullness of the world in which he himself lived. The similes do not exist simply to point out one basis of comparison: they create many correspondences, include a brilliant wealth of detail, and give depth and colouring to the action they describe. They have a life of their own. They reflect the Greek attitude to the world in laying bare the essential qualities of things. This double aspect becomes apparent in their linguistic form, passing over readily from comparative to independent clauses.

There is an obvious difference between the *Iliad* and *Odyssey* in respect of similes. The later poem is more sparing of them, and the poet more often takes his comparison from the familiar world of everyday life, while in the *Iliad* the similes reflect a broader reaction to the world of nature and its elemental powers.

The epic style is consistent in avoiding banality, although the *Odyssey* is in closer contact with the earthiness of life, as in the fight between the two beggars, or the simile of the blood-pudding (20. 25). Sentimentality also is absent. Even so moving a scene as that with the dog Argus proceeds by simple factual narrative.

There are considerable variations in the tempo of narration. The uniform flow characteristic of epic style is not always present. Rapid development of

---

[1] BRUNO SNELL, 'Die Auffassung des Menschen bei Homer' in *Die Entdeckung des Geistes*. 3rd ed. Hamburg 1955, 17 (Eng. ed. p. 14).

[2] A. LESKY, *Thalatta*. Vienna 1947, 8.

[3] H. FRÄNKEL, *Die homerischen Gleichnisse*. Göttingen 1921. W. SCHADEWALDT, 'Die homerische Gleichniswelt und die kretisch-mykenische Kunst' in *Von Homers Welt und Werk*. 3rd ed. Stuttg. 1959, 130. R. HAMPE, *Die Gleichnisse Homers und die Bildkunst seiner Zeit*. Tübingen 1952. J. A. NOTOPULOS, 'Homeric Similes in the Light of Oral Poetry'. *Class. Journ.* 52, 1957, 312. M. COFFEY, 'The Function of the Homeric Simile'. *Am. Journ. Phil.* 78, 1957, 113. Against Fränkel, who stressed the functional character of the simile, JACHMANN (*sup.* p. 34, n. 1) p. 222 brings the tertium comparationis into the foreground again. On p. 220 he objects (not unreasonably, to my mind) to the ready postulation of a close affinity between Homeric similes and Geometric art. On this subject see T. B. L. WEBSTER, 'Homer and Attic Geometric Vases'. *Ann. Brit. School Ath.* 50, 1955, 38.

situation, as in the opening of the *Iliad*, alternates with endless series of single combats (in which we catch the tone of the old *aoidoi*) and long descriptive catalogues.

Another feature in which we detect the interplay of the individual and the traditional is the frequency of speeches, which take up so much of the poem that Plato, in the third book of the *Republic*, reckons epic as a mixed literary form halfway between narrative and drama. The large part played by speeches is an inheritance from the old oral epic. Another archaic feature is 'ring composition',[1] which brings the speech ultimately back to the theme with which it began. An elaborate specimen of this (noticed by ancient critics, cf. schol. *Il.* 11. 671) is Nestor's account of the battle with the Epeans. But at the same time the speeches illustrate a new technique – that of making the speech appear to come naturally and necessarily from the character of the speaker. This 'ethopoeia', as it was later called in the rhetorical schools where it was taught, is already completely mastered in our earliest surviving poem. The technique reaches its height in the triptych of speeches from the ambassadors in the ninth book of the *Iliad*. The differentiation of the speeches, the speakers and the listener, the range of tones – all shows the poet's art at its height.[2] In its compass and its subject matter it is the middle one which bears the main emphasis – a principle of composition which can be seen at work elsewhere in the *Iliad*.

8 GODS AND MEN

The gods of the Homeric pantheon have a long history behind them before they form that society which has its difficult moments in the *Iliad* (although it goes smoothly enough in the *Odyssey*). Nilsson's view that the position of the Mycenaean overlord may have provided the model for their relations one to another has much to recommend it: the influence of the east, however, cannot be disregarded, where rather similar societies of gods occur long before Homer.

So much has been said of anthropomorphism in Homer's gods that there is sometimes a danger of forgetting the great gulf which divides them from men. This does not only consist in their immortality, but in that notion of supernatural power associated with them, which puts their activities under a law of their own.[3] Homeric belief extended to an impersonal fate, sometimes on a level with the gods, sometimes above them: a fate by which the lot (αἶσα,

[1] W. A. A. VAN OTTERLO, 'De ringcompositie als opbouwprincipe in de epische gedichten van Homerus'. *Nederl. Akad. Afd. Letterkunde* 51, 1, 1948.

[2] J. L. MYRES, 'Homeric Art'. *Ann. Brit. School Ath.* 45, 1950, 229.

[3] E. EHNMARK, *The Idea of God in Homer*. Uppsala 1935. H. SCHRADE, *Götter und Menschen Homers*. Stuttg. 1952 – a justified but rather one-sided reaction against classicism: see the review by W. MARG, *Gnom.* 28, 1956, 1. P. CHANTRAINE, 'Le Divin et les dieux chez Homère' in *Fondation Hardt, Entretiens I*. Vandœuvres (Geneva) 1954, 47. W. KULLMANN, *Das Wirken der Götter in der Ilias*. Berl. 1956. G. FRANCOIS, *Le Polythéisme et l'emploi au singulier des mots* Θεός, δαίμων. *Bibl. fac. de philos. et lettres de l'Univ. Liège* 147. Paris 1957. H. STOCKINGER, *Die Vorzeichen im homerischen Epos*. Diss. Munich. St Ottilien Obb. 1959. W. K. C. GUTHRIE, 'The Religion and Mythology of the Greeks'. *Cambr. Anc. Hist.* revised ed. vol. 2, c. 40. Cambr. 1961 (with bibliography).

μοῖρα) of the individual is determined.[1] Here we have a juxtaposition of two ways of thought, between which no logical reconciliation is possible. In the opening of the *Iliad* we are told that the will of Zeus was fulfilled in the events to be related: the same Zeus in 16. 458 cannot save his son Sarpedon from the decree of fate, even if he momentarily thinks of doing so. In those two scenes also where Zeus takes up the balance (8. 69; 22. 209) it is impossible to explain away the conflict of the two beliefs by trying to turn the weighing of the lots into an expression of the will of Zeus. But in Homer this notion of fate does not lead to a rigid determinism. Not only does Zeus think of saving Sarpedon, but even human beings are spoken of either actually or potentially as doing or suffering something beyond their fate (ὑπὲρ αἶσαν, ὑπὲρ μόρον). The fluidity of the boundaries of these two conceptions is clearly shown in 20. 30, where Zeus expresses fear lest Achilles should break down the walls of Troy contrary to fate.

It has been a mistake of modern critics to relegate the action of the Homeric gods to the level of an aesthetic and literary device. They form in fact a loose system of powerful fields of force, in which the life of man is wholly subsumed. The question of the relation between gods and men is central in the world of Homer. The poet, instructed by the Muses, is well able to speak on the subject, although his actors seldom speak of the gods with anything like clarity.

The relations of these gods to men cannot be conveyed in one or two ethical or religious formulae. The greatest diversity reigns here also, and the strong will of these Olympian masters is often their ultimate law. So as not to impose a forcible simplification, we shall deal with gods and men in their mutual relations by means of three antinomies.

The first pair of opposites is distance and nearness. The gods often and in various ways enter into relations with men. Zeus sends messengers or signs; other gods put on human form, which they sometimes wear only as a loose garment. Whenever they wish, they approach their favourites without any such disguise. When Diomede in the middle of his exploits is in need of encouragement, standing as he does by his team with his wound growing cold, Athene comes to him and 'grasps the yoke', which can only mean that she leans on it supporting herself with her arm. The attitude of easy familiarity is consonant with her speech, which begins with stinging rebuke but ends by heartening him with the promise of help. But this familiarity is nowhere more strikingly displayed than in the scene in the thirteenth book of the *Odyssey* where the goddess comes up to the recently awakened Odysseus. She appears first as a slender young shepherd lad from the royal house – one immediately thinks of the Athene of Myron – and listens in amusement to the tissue of lies that the crafty wanderer tells her. Then she reveals herself, silences the hero's modest reproach that she should have left him so long to fend for himself, helps him to bury the

---

[1] W. C. GREENE, *Moira*. Cambr. Mass. 1944. W. KRAUSE, 'Zeus und Moira bei Homer'. *Wien. Stud.* 64, 1949, 10. U. BIANCHI, ΔΙΟΣ ΑΙΣΑ. Rome 1953. A. HEUBECK, *Der Odyssee-Dichter und die Ilias.* Erlangen 1954, 72. W. PÖTSCHER, 'Moira, Themis und τιμή im homerischen Denken'. *Wien. Stud.* 73, 1960, 5.

treasure he has brought with him, and finally sits down with him, man and goddess together, under an olive tree to make plans for the future. When a man is thought worthy of such honour, it is expected that he will know his place and keep it. At the beginning of the nineteenth book Odysseus and his son are concealing the weapons from the hall. Without showing herself, Athene sheds light upon them, and a boundless radiance is diffused over beams and pillars. Odysseus checks his son's curious enquiries by telling him that the Olympians have their own ways of working.

The counterpart to this familiar nearness is the unbridgeable distance to which the gods are ready at any moment to relegate mortals. The god who for the later Greeks remained the great teacher of reverence, whose maxim, 'Know Thyself', reminded them of the inescapable limits of human existence, appears in this role in a scene from the aristeia of Diomede.[1] Three times has the hero attacked Aeneas, over whom Apollo holds a protecting hand; three times does Apollo thrust him back: the fourth time[2] he calls to him and says, 'Come to your senses and give up! The human race cannot equal the immortal gods' (5. 440). The hero yields and retreats a little – a significant concession in that heroic world. This other side of the divine nature is nowhere in Greek literature so fully brought out as it is in Hölderlin's *Hyperions Schicksalslied*. In the *Iliad* it constantly recurs and throws a tragic colouring over the whole of human existence, which for all its richness and variety stands at the last under sentence of death. Hephaestus speaks (1. 573) of the folly of gods' conflicting over mortals: but he himself earns a like rebuke from Athene for his heated interchange with Scamander. When in the battle of the gods Apollo meets Poseidon (21. 461), he refuses to fight with another god for the sake of wretched mortals. The other gods are ready enough to take part, but it is simply as a wild frolic, underlining again the great gulf between them and men. In the same book we find the episode of Lycaon, which brings out strongly the notion of inevitable doom. The young warrior pleads for his life, but Achilles is obdurate. His beloved Patroclus is no more – and in any case, why such anxiety for life? 'You see how I stand before you, tall and strong, a goddess' son. And yet there waits for me an hour, be it morning, noon or evening, which shall take away my life (106).' On hearing these words, Lycaon sinks to the ground and opens his arms to death. Where the gods take part, they do so almost jokingly. Hera laughs as she breaks Artemis' bow about her ears (489), while the father of the gods sits on Olympus and smiles at the comedy of the battle. Yet this very same Zeus in 17. 443 pities the immortal horses for their being involved in the fate of

---

[1] The Apollo of the *Iliad* is already the lord of Delphi, but his central importance was to come later. His oracle is mentioned in *Od.* 8. 79, its treasures in *Il.* 9. 904. In both we hear of the 'stone sill', but we cannot tell whether it is that of the temenos or of the temple. JEAN DEFRADAS, *Les Thèmes de la propagande delphique. Études et comment.* 21. Paris 1954, gives too late a date to the installation of Apollo in Delphi; he is rightly opposed by H. BERVE in *Gnomon* 28, 1956, 176, who supposes that it was completed before the seventh century.

[2] On 3 and 3 + 1 see F. GÖBEL, 'Formen und Formeln der epischen Dreiheit in der griechischen Dichtung, *Tüb. Beitr.* 26, 1935.

men, of the most wretched creatures that crawl upon the earth. This tone occurs only in the *Iliad*: in the *Odyssey* men know how far below the gods they are and how subject to their power (16. 211; 18. 130; 19. 80). They are, on the other hand, more long-suffering, more able and determined to keep their heads above a sea of troubles. The gods of the *Odyssey* are more closely bound to moral values.

Closely connected with the first is the second of our antinomies: kindness and cruelty. The gods show kindness to their favourites, particularly in the *Iliad*, with some capriciousness. The nature of Homer's gods comes out clearly in Athene's action when she gives a harmless direction to the arrow of Pandarus (4. 130) as easily as a mother brushes away a fly from a sleeping child. When Diomede is driving his chariot, she picks up for him the whip which Apollo had struck from his hand. But this kindness and help shown by Athene towards her favourites has a reverse side of pitiless cruelty to those she hates. Nowhere do we feel this more strongly than in the death of Hector, who is delivered up to the sword of Achilles by her deceit and treachery. The behaviour when angered of a goddess like Aphrodite, who is still felt as an elemental force, the fire that can flash from her when a mortal opposes her will, is shown in a scene of true tragedy at the end of the third book of the *Iliad*.[1] Aphrodite has snatched Paris from the wrath of Menelaus and taken him back to his chamber, where she now, true to her function, wants Helen to join him. Helen, however, is unwilling to give herself again to the lesser man. The goddess flames into fury, and threatens the mortal woman so angrily that she follows without a word where she is led by the goddess (δαίμων is Homer's word).

If we take as the third of our antinomies justice and self-will, we come straight to the central question of the morality of Homer's gods.[2] Here the *Iliad* and *Odyssey* diverge sharply. The decisive importance of the unqualified will of the gods comes out clearly in the dispute among the gods at the beginning of book 4. Zeus rebukes Hera for her hatred of the Trojans: she would like to eat Priam and the Trojans raw. In reply she attempts no denial: she merely tells Zeus that he may destroy Argos, Sparta and Mycenae if he likes, the cities which she loves above all, if only he will let her have her way with the hated Trojans. Scholars have repeatedly sought some explanation of such an amoral attitude, referring it sometimes to the supposed origin of the Homeric gods as forces of nature.[3] This view is not convincing. Neither is the derivation in itself wholly satisfactory, nor are we in Homer's world near enough to the presumed origin. In any case, it is better not to leap to an evolutionary explanation, postulating incomplete development in Homer's day. In these gods who pursue what they

---

[1] Well brought out by W. BURKERT, 'Das Lied von Ares und Aphrodite'. *Rhein. Mus.* 103, 1960, 141.

[2] ERIK WOLF, *Griech. Rechtsdenken* I. Frankf.a.M. 1950, 70. M. P. NILSSON, 'Die Griechengötter und die Gerechtigkeit'. *Harv. Theol. Rev.* 50, 1957, 193. M. S. RUIPÉREZ, 'Historia de θέμις en Homero'. *Emérita* 28, 1960, 99. We may add ERIC VOEGLIN's analysis (from the viewpoint of the history of philosophy): *The World of the Polis. Order and History* II. Louisiana 1957.

[3] W. K. C. GUTHRIE, *The Greeks and their Gods*. Boston 1951, 117.

want by violence and fraud, whose love-relations are wholly promiscuous, and whose feuds and factions find a temporary truce at the banqueting table, we may with some probability discern features of the feudal nobility who ruled Homer's world.

It would be wrong to suppose that this amorality of the gods was a reflection of the eighth century in general. The *Iliad* itself counters such a view in one of those similes which bring Homer's own world into his poetry. 'A cry from the deep' is what Nilsson calls it.[1] The simile (16. 386) is of a storm of rain which Zeus in his anger sends upon men who give perverse judgments in the market-place, who drive out justice, and do not fear the eyes of the gods upon them. The passage is entirely in the manner of Hesiod, and it would pass without notice in the *Odyssey*, where we find the opposite picture of the virtuous king, in whose land prosperity and plenty reign (19. 109). But is the simile referring to a god of righteousness wholly isolated in the *Iliad*? Does not the poet, within that short space of time in which he has framed the whole Trojan war, show the guilt of Troy as being renewed? The truce so solemnly sworn is violated by Pandarus, and scattered references (7. 351; 401) show that this deed has sealed the doom of Troy. Already by his sin Paris had brought down the wrath of the greatest of Gods upon the city (13. 623). Admittedly these sins were against hospitality and the sanctity of oaths, two spheres in which Zeus had always held sway.

It is undeniable that in the *Odyssey* the notion of morally directed action on the part of the gods is much more developed.[2] The most striking passage comes at the beginning, where Zeus condemns those men who ascribe their sufferings to the gods, and yet, like Aegisthus, pull them down on their own heads. Aegisthus was warned by Hermes, just as the suitors are repeatedly warned in the course of the action. The result is that the poem as a whole becomes a moral paradigm, and as such is sharply distinguished from the dark and tragic tone of the *Iliad*, where all ends in annihilation. At the end of the *Odyssey* (24. 351) Laertes declares: The gods yet live; for the suitors have indeed paid for their intolerable sins. Similarly the shipmates of Odysseus received their warnings, but earned death for their hybris. There are many detached incidents in the *Odyssey* pointing in the same direction. Ilus is hesitant to give poison for the tipping of arrows, since he fears the gods (1. 262); Zeus gives the Argives an evil homecoming, for they were not all wise or righteous (3. 132); we are told in a beautiful line (6. 207; 14. 57) that the guest and the beggar are from Zeus, and in 17. 485 we learn that the gods love to visit the cities of mortals, taking on human form, to learn who is righteous and who sinful. These are very different gods from those Olympians who quarrel and fight one with another; and their mutual relations are different. Poseidon certainly stands out against the other gods; but how civilized their disagreement is! How courteously Athene holds

---

[1] *Gesch. d. griech. Religion* I, 2nd ed. 1955, 421. As a model for Hesiod *Erga* 221: W. SCHADEWALDT, *Iliasstudien*. Leipz. 1938, 118, 1; a different view: Walter Nestle, *Herm.* 77, 1942, 65, 2.

[2] Well brought out by REINHARDT op. cit. (*sup.*, p. 48, n. 1).

back from her favourite as long as Poseidon has a claim on him! The human actors also are more subject to that moral restraint which the Greeks called *aidos*. In the hall yet reeking with the blood of the suitors Euryclea raises a cry of triumph; but Odysseus checks her, saying that it is sinful to exult over the slain (24. 412). Here we have a sharp contrast to the paean that Achilles raises over the corpse of Hector. But we should not forget that there also (24. 53), when Achilles' revenge passes all bounds, Apollo warns him that by such behaviour, for all his bravery, he will earn the hatred of the gods.

These differences can only in very small part be explained by the difference in date of the two poems. The decisive factor seems to us the following: while in the *Iliad* we have the reflection of a compact and exclusive noble class, the social range of the *Odyssey* is much wider. In the later work epic poetry had opened its doors to the wishes and beliefs of classes whom the *Iliad* excluded.[1] It should also not be forgotten that many of these differences arise from differences in subject matter. We expressed agreement earlier (p. 48) with the view that the *Odyssey* is from a different hand.

Throughout the Homeric poems we never find it forgotten that man stands in strict subordination. This conception is conveyed by the word θέμις which has a wide range of meanings. It can denote the power given by Zeus to kings, by which they declare right and justice; it can also mean everything that becomes obligatory on men through the bonds of nature or usage. It can also refer to the commerce of the sexes (*Il.* 9. 276; 19. 177). The powers that be come always from God. Themis herself dwells as a goddess in Olympus, summons the assembly at Zeus' command (*Il.* 20. 4) or offers the cup of welcome to Hera (*Il.* 15. 87).

As W. F. Otto has pointed out in his book *Die Götter Griechenlands*,[2] this world of the gods is bathed in a clear sunshine like that of the Greek landscape. One might be justified in tempering this picture by reference to the daemonic and elemental force that sometimes flashes forth from these supernatural beings;[3] but we should then be adding detail, not altering the main lines. We may add that crass superstition and the practice of magic, if not wholly banished from this world, are removed very far into the background. In the story of the death of Meleager through his mother's anger the magical brand of the old tale is replaced by a curse, more appropriate to the dignity of epic;[4] the custom of increasing the fertility of a sown field by sexual intercourse on it is reflected only in a story about Demeter (*Od.* 5. 125); violations of the laws of nature occur only in unimportant parts of the narrative: all these features show the spirit of a type of poetry that belonged essentially to the courts of the great and was powerfully influenced by the spirit of Ionian culture.

The qualities of Homeric man – his simplicity and compactness, his unqualified

---

[1] F. JACOBY, 'Die geistige Physiognomie der Odyssee'. *Die Antike* 9, 1953, 159. WALTER NESTLE, 'Odyssee-Interpretationen'. *Herm.* 77, 1942, 46 and 113 and esp. 136. M. J. FINLEY, *The World of Odysseus*. Lond. 1956.   [2] 3rd ed. Frankf.a.M. 1947.

[3] Pointed out by H. SCHRADE op. cit., but with too much emphasis here and there.

[4] First demonstrated by P. J. KAKRIDIS in his book Ἀραί, Athens 1929.

acceptance of all the powers around him – have been eloquently expounded by Hermann Fränkel.[1] The new and different elements in the *Odyssey* should not be so overstated that we differentiate its actors from those of the *Iliad* as being less transparent, less open to the outside world. But we cannot fail to recognize new colourings: above all, the potentialities of psychology are more deeply explored. The most impressive example is the delicacy with which Nausicaa's budding attraction towards the stranger is hinted at rather than stated. The scenes of their encounter and parting are the more effective as love between the sexes is not elsewhere in the poem an independent theme. Everyone knows how Goethe was inspired by this episode to write his drama of Nausicaa. With the utmost economy of means the poet of the *Odyssey* heightens the emotional content of the episode of Calypso. Visited by Hermes, the nymph has received the command of the gods which will mean the loss of her lover and a renewed solitude. She must obey, but she wants Odysseus to receive as a favour from her what is in fact a concession from the Olympians. Accordingly she does not tell him of the command and of Hermes' visit. Homer says nothing of all this, but how relevant is the detail (5. 195) that in the nymph's cave Odysseus sits down on the same seat from which Hermes had just arisen!

A problem of central importance is raised when we try to reach some conclusion about Homer's notions of the soul. Homeric Greek knows no word fully corresponding to our word 'soul'. That which is meant by ψυχή makes its appearance above all at the death of a man, when the breath-soul or shadow-soul quits the dying body to lead a wretched life amid the mould of Hades. In the living man the psyche is the basis of all thoughts and desires, but of its nature and operation we know virtually nothing. We tend to see instead particular aspects, which have been called with some exaggeration 'organs of the soul': θυμός, concerned especially with the emotions (e.g. it overcomes Achilles' judgment); φρήν, the midriff as the seat of intellectual activity, hence intellectual activity itself; νοῦς, imagination, conception.[2]

The use of these terms cannot be systematized, since none of them has a clearly defined sphere of application. Mental life may be referred to paratactically by the phrase κατὰ φρένα καὶ κατὰ θυμόν; yet in *Od.* 5. 458, when the hero awakes from a swoon, we are told, ἐς φρένα θυμὸς ἀγέρθη; and a change of mind is oddly expressed in *Od.* 9. 302 by the words ἕτερος δέ με θυμὸς ἔρυκεν. A parallel has been drawn between these expressions for 'soul' and those which Homer's characters apply to the body. The later word for body (σῶμα) means in Homer 'corpse':[3] in the living man we find only partial aspects denoted – trunk, limbs,

[1] 107 ff.

[2] B. SNELL, *Die Entdeckung des Geistes*. 3rd ed. Hamburg 1955, 17. O. REGENBOGEN, 'Δαιμόνιον ψυχῆς φῶς (Erwin Rohdes Psyche und die neuere Kritik). Ein Beitrag zum hom. Seelenglauben.' Synopsis. *Festgabe für A. Weber*. Heidelberg 1948, 361. R. B. ONIANS, *The Origins of European Thought*. Cambr. 1951, gives plenty of material, but his conclusions are often rather doubtful. E. L. HARRISON, 'Notes on Homeric Psychology'. *Phoenix* 14, 1960, 63, with illustrations which show the fluidity of the conception.

[3] H. HERTER, 'Σῶμα bei Homer'. *Charites* (Festschr. *Langlotz*). Bonn 1957, 206, draws attention to a probable exception (*Il.* 3. 23); cf. H. KOLLER, *Glotta* 37, 1958, 276.

head. Snell has the chief credit for this observation, which is an important one; but we should not leap to the conclusion that Homer's world did not see any person as a complete entity. In fact the characters in his poetry possess individual personality in a high degree: otherwise they would not have made an impression lasting three thousand years. Man was felt as a whole, immediately and intuitively understood at the mention of any part. When Odysseus at the beginning of book 20 commands his 'barking heart' to be still, the heart is treated like a bodily member giving pain. But that which compels it to be silent, Odysseus, is an undivided whole. It is the same Odysseus who in the *Iliad* (11. 402) rallies his failing courage by the consciousness of his duty. Partial aspects do appear, but they are subordinated to the personality of the man as a whole, which always underlies the parts and guarantees them their existence and meaning.

This question of awareness of personality is tied up with another: to what extent do these characters arrive at decisions that are their own and their own responsibility?[1] Human behaviour is so interpenetrated by constant divine intervention that Homer's characters have sometimes been thought to have no power of decision at all, and his poetry has been charged with forgetting that decisions, indeed all mental activity, are rooted in man himself. What Homer's men do is activated by the gods.

In answering this difficulty we must first point out that genuine decisions, without divine prompting, do occur, like that of Odysseus (6. 145) on the way in which to secure Nausicaa's help. But what of those numerous cases in which a god suggests or restrains or inspires? Is the man in such cases simply a marionette actuated by the god? Such an interpretation would show a total failure to understand the Homeric world. If we formulate the question so as to leave no middle ground between human beings acting in their own right and gods pulling the strings of puppets, we miss the real point. Human will and divine purpose are in fact closely interwoven: they have an inner bond such that any attempt on grounds of pure logic to separate them tears asunder the unity of the Homeric world-picture. When Achilles returns to its scabbard the sword which he had half drawn against Agamemnon, he does it on the advice of Athene; but at the same time he does it in his own right as Achilles, that Achilles who flames into anger, but holds back from the extreme step. In the same way his last and greatest victory, victory over his own passionate heart, belongs at once to the gods who intervene on behalf of the slain Hector and to Achilles himself, who raises the old man from the ground, mingling his tears with those of his enemy. Divine command and human action, which are seen unmistakeably in the essence of these characters, appear as two spheres which complement each

[1] H. GUNDERT, 'Charakter und Schicksal hom. Helden'. *N. Jahrb.* 1940, 225. H. RAHN, 'Tier und Mensch in der hom. Auffassung der Wirklichkeit'. *Paideuma* 1953, 277 and 431. K. LANIG, *Der handelnde Mensch in der Ilias.* Diss. Erlangen 1953. A. HEUBECK (cf. p. 48, n. 1), 80. H. SCHWABL, 'Zur Selbständigkeit des Menschen bei Homer'. *Wien. Stud.* 67, 1954, 46. E. WÜST, 'Von den Anfängen des Problems der Willensfreiheit'. *Rhein. Mus.* 101, 1958, 75. A. LESKY, 'Göttliche und menschliche Motivation im hom. Epos'. *Sitzb. Ak. Heidelb. Phil.- hist. Kl.* 1961, 4. Homeric comprehension of reality in verbal expression is examined by M. TREU, *Von Homer zur Lyrik. Zet.* 12, Munich 1955.

other, but can yet come into conflict. Normally they are concurrent and share any transaction in a way that forbids any attempt to isolate either. The inter-relation of these two spheres in Homer's world is quite unreflecting and poses no problems. But it does not remain so. Later, especially in Attic tragedy, we shall see the intensity of the problems that had their roots in this Homeric soil.

Here again there is a difference between the *Iliad* and the *Odyssey*, though not a total change. In the later poem much more emphasis is on man acting on his own decisions and taking responsibility for them. The suitors are not made blind by divine agency; they wilfully blind themselves. The same may be said of Odysseus' shipmates when they kill the cattle of Helius, or of Aegisthus, of whom Zeus speaks at the opening of the poem. Not only are the human actors more independent, but also the gods; whose function now is often to warn and watch over the virtuous. It is characteristic that there are five passages in the *Odyssey*[1] in which it is discussed whether an impulse comes from the realm of the gods or that of men, and only one to any extent comparable in the *Iliad*. We catch the first glimpses of a road that leads through Hesiod to those problems of dike which were to be central in Greek thought.

9 THE TRANSMISSION

We share with most scholars the view that the composition of the two epics presupposes writing. In Homer's time this must have been a recent invention. Even if he was not the first epic poet to use writing, the peculiarities of his manner and the number of oral elements support such a view. But it would be wrong to regard this use of writing as initiating a written transmission, tied wholly to books. Rather, it was for a long time in the hands of rhapsodes, who were organized into guilds (often, no doubt, on a family basis). What we hear of the Homeridae of Chios[2] is to be interpreted in this sense. Light is thrown on the activity of these men by the tradition that Solon or Hipparchus[3] the son of Pisistratus arranged to have all the Homeric poems recited at the Panathenaea by relays of rhapsodes.

The basis of all these recitations must have been a written copy, which we may suppose to have been the valued possession of such a guild. Aelian (*Var. Hist.* 9. 15) tells us that Homer gave the *Cypria* to his daughter as a dowry: a statement absurd enough in itself, but indicating that the rhapsodes were involved in the transmission of the text.

For the archaic period, then, we have to assume a mainly oral transmission on the basis of a fixed written text. The accuracy of the recited text would thus only be guaranteed within certain limits. The frequent recurrence of formulae led to interchange of metrically equivalent words and phrases, and to additions and omissions; and this factor must have had its influence. To some extent an opposite influence would have been exerted by the schools as soon as Homer became a principal object of study.

---

[1] *Od.* 4. 712; 7. 263; 9. 339; 14. 178; 16. 356. *Il.* 6. 438.
[2] H. T. WADE-GERY, *The Poet of the Iliad*. Cambr. 1952, 19.
[3] On these see J. D. BEAZLEY, *Journ. Hell. Stud.* 54, 1934, 84 after Friis Johansen.

We have already seen (p. 36) that the later reports of a Pisistratean recension do not prove that the poems first took shape in his day. But on the other hand, the complete recitations at the Panathenaea point to the importance of Athens in the transmission, and it is possible that at the same time something was done towards the fixing of the text. We must not forget that there are traces of a stage where Attic influence was strongly felt. There is no reason to suppose a complete transcription into the Attic alphabet, since the Ionic alphabet was in use side by side with the Attic long before its official introduction by Euclides in 403. But Attic has left its mark in details, particularly in aspiration: thus beside the un-Attic ἦμαρ we find in our Homer ἡμέρη with the rough breathing. We must also bear in mind the possibility of Attic interpolation, although there is no decisive evidence.

The exegesis of the epics soon became a battleground. Attacks on their morality called forth an apologetic literature which understood them allegorically. This movement began as early as the sixth century with Theagenes of Rhegium, who seems to have been the first to write on Homer. It was continued by such men as Stesimbrotus of Thasos (fifth century), by Crates of Mallos, head of the Pergamene school, in the second century, and persisted through late antiquity until the time of Tzetzes.[1] The sophistic movement also saw studies on the language and interpretation. Democritus wrote *On Homer, or on Correctness of Language and Difficult Words* (VS 68 B20a); and from the manner in which difficult passages are discussed by Aristotle we may infer a long tradition of such studies.

Here again it was Alexandrian work that was decisive.[2] Three of the greatest Alexandrian scholars devoted themselves to Homer: Zenodotus of Ephesus, the first head of the great library (first half of the third century), Aristophanes of Byzantium (c. 257–180) and Aristarchus of Samothrace (217–145). The last named, in addition to special monographs, prepared two editions of the text (such, at least, is Lehrs' view, which has been widely accepted). Recently H. Erbse has put forward a revolutionary theory which has great internal probability. He thinks that Aristarchus did not bring out an edition of the text in the modern sense; he probably compared different manuscripts to check the

---

[1] F. WEHRLI, *Allegorische Deutung Homers*. Diss. Basel 1928. For a more general treatment: F. BUFFIÈRE, *Les Mythes d'Homère et la pensée grecque*. Paris 1956. P. LEVÊQUE, *Aurea catena Homeri. Une étude sur l'allégorie grecque*. Ann. Litt. de l'Un. de Besançon 27, 1960.

[2] P. MAZON, *Introduction à l'Iliade*. Paris 1948, 17. V. STEGEMANN in the Tusculum-Bücherei edition of the *Iliad*. Munich 1948, 2, 420. The vulgate is valued more highly by M. VAN DER VALK, *Textual Criticism of the Odyssey*. Leyden 1949. A study of fundamental importance is G. JACHMANN's 'Vom frühalexandrinischen Homertext'. *Nachr. Ak. Gött. Phil.-hist. Kl.* 1949, 167. H. ERBSE, 'Ueber Aristarchs Iliasausgaben'. *Herm.* 87, 1959, 275. His conclusions are broadly shared by J. A. DAVISON, 'The Study of Homer in Graeco-Roman Egypt'. *Mitt. Pap. Rainer* N.S. 5, 1956, 51. For a convenient summary see G. M. BOLLING, *The Athetized Lines of the Iliad*. Baltimore 1944. On the indirect tradition: J. LABARBE, *L'Homère de Platon*. Bibl. de la Fac. de Phil. et Lettres Liège. Fasc. 117, 1949; criticized by G. LOHSE, *Untersuchungen über Homerzitate bei Platon*. Diss. Hamburg 1961 (typewritten). The collected fragments of Aristophanes of Byzantium were edited by NAUCK (Halle 1948): a reprint by Olms is shortly forthcoming.

vulgate, and later published commentaries in which he presented his critical proposals to the learned public with constant reference to the work of his predecessors. Much of their work can be identified in the present scholia. Two vexed problems illustrate their methods of work and the quality of their editing.

The readings of the Alexandrians differ a good deal from the vulgate, which the scholia call the 'common tradition' (ἡ κοινή etc.). Did such men as Aristarchus get their variants from conjecture or from comparison of what they thought the best manuscripts? Inevitably the great collections of the Alexandrian library must have been the basis of their researches. They found a large number of different texts, some (πολιτικαί) named after cities where they had been edited for use in schools or for recitation at festivals, others (κατ' ἄνδρα) called after a man in whose possession they were, who sometimes (like Antimachus of Colophon) had contributed his own work to their preparation. We can suppose that most of Aristarchus' readings were obtained in this way, without ruling out conjecture in individual cases.

The question how far this work in fact influenced the tradition could for a long time only be decided on the basis of the medieval manuscripts and the scholia.[1] Concerning Aristarchus, of whom we know the most, it can be established that of 874 readings bearing his name only 80 appear in all our MSS., 160 in the majority of them, 76 in about half, 181 in a minority, 245 are very much scattered and 132 occur nowhere. Such data do not suggest that Alexandrian scholarship was widely influential. Yet this picture was misleading, as the progress of papyrology has shown us.[2] Among the hundreds of fragments with pieces from Homer the most interesting are of course those which come from pre-Alexandrian texts, or at any rate from a time when Alexandrian influence was very slight. They give a picture of a fluctuating transmission in which differences from the post-Alexandrian texts consist not so much in alternative readings as in the varying number of the verses. This uncertainty in transmission is easily understandable in the hands of the rhapsodes; and it was here that the critical work of the Alexandrians was of decisive importance for posterity. In other words, apart from some miserable fragments, the Alexandrian text is as

---

[1] Outline with summary of the older literature: P. CAUER, Grundfragen der Homerkritik. 3rd ed. Leipz. 1921/23.

[2] Given most fully in PACK; cf. P. COLLART, Les Papyrus de l'Iliade in MAZON's Introduction (v. sup. p. 94, n. 2), with lists and index of variants. V. MARTIN, Papyrus Bodmer I. Iliade, chants 5 et 6. Bibl. Bodmer 1954. Griech. Pap. der Hamb. Staats- und Univ.-Bibl. Hamb. 1954, nr. 153 f. H. J. METTE, 'Neue Homer-Papyri'. Rev. de Phil. 29, 1955, 193. Every new papyrus publication brings new Homer-fragments, but most are of no interest; e.g. Pap. Soc. It. 14, 1957 has nine such. The oldest have been carefully examined by DARIO DEL CORNO, 'I papiri dell' Iliade anteriori al 150 a. Chr.' Ist. Lombardo. Rendiconti, Classe di Lettere 94, 1960, 73; id., 'I papiri dell' Odissea anteriori al 150 a. Chr.' ibid. 95, 1961, 3. The papyrus material is systematically treated from several different points of view by J. A. DAVISON in the book cited above (p. 74, n. 2). There are small fragments of a commentary on the 17th book of the Iliad in Ox. Pap. 24, 1957, nr. 2397; bits of a glossary on Iliad 1 ibid. nr. 2405. Good summary and bibliography: AUG. TRAVERSA, 'I papiri epici nell' ultimo trentennio'. Proc. of the IXth Intern. Congr. of Papyrology. Norweg. Univ. Pr. 1961, 49.

far back as we can go. We can trust the judgment of the men on whom we are so dependent. Concerning the way Aristarchus went to work we have some useful information. He struck out superfluous verses and thus removed them for all time from the text, presumably doing so after carefully examining all the evidence. This we can gather from his quite different practice in passages where language or subject matter led him to doubt whether a verse was genuine. There he was content to put a horizontal stroke as a critical sign (obelos). He has earned our gratitude by not deleting such lines.

The Alexandrians defended and expounded their text in elaborate commentaries, often with a polemical tone, such as Aristarchus adopted against Zenodotus. The mountain of scholarship thus built up gave scope for the mining work of later generations. Exegetical works and lexica, of which the extant one of Apollonius Sophistes[1] gives some idea, battened on the Alexandrian inheritance. The last manifestations of such labours are the masses of scholia, either marginal or interlinear, which go with the text in various manuscripts. The great work of the Alexandrians is here covered by whole layers of accretions. The task of sorting out this confused transmission is very hard, but recent years have seen some successful attacks upon it.[2] The most important scholia on the *Iliad*, whose publication by C. d'Ansse de Villoison in 1788 opened a new chapter in Homeric studies, are found in the Venetus 454 (A) of the tenth century. In a subscription occurring at the end of most of the books the sources of the principal scholia – those accompanying the text in the margin – are said to be four scholars who were influential in transmitting Alexandrian learning to posterity: Aristonicus, who lived under Augustus and wrote a book on the critical signs used by Aristarchus; his contemporary Didymus, whose immense industry won him the nickname of 'Brass-guts' (Chalcenterus), and who devoted one of his many Homeric studies to the work of Aristarchus; Herodian, who lived under Marcus Aurelius and wrote a general treatise on prosody in which he also discussed Homeric accentuation, and his contemporary Nicanor, who wrote on the punctuation of Homer. The commentaries of these four men, written from such differing standpoints, were put together into a single volume by an unknown hand (possibly one Nemesion). The use of scissors and paste on this work produced the marginal glosses of the so-called 'four-man commentary', from which most of the A-scholia are derived; but when the selection was made is a problem in itself. Evidence has recently been brought to suggest that it was made in the Byzantine period on the basis of an uncial codex which preserved the work of the four men through the Dark Age. The scholia which

---

[1] H. GATTIKER, *Das Verhältnis des Homerlexikons des Apoll. Soph. zu den Homerscholien.* Zürich 1945. F. MARTINAZZOLI, *Hapax Legomenon I/2. Il Lexicon Homericum di Ap. Sof.* Bari 1957.

[2] H. ERBSE, 'Zur handschriftlichen Ueberlieferung der Iliasscholien'. *Mnem.* s. IV, 6, 1953, 1. Id., *Beiträge zur Ueberlieferung der Iliasscholien.* Zet. 24, 1960, a most devoted monument of learned labour on the tradition of the scholia and their connection with ancient works of grammar and lexicography. Cf. w. BÜHLER, *Byz. Zeitschr.* 54, 1961, 117. A very useful work is J. BAAR'S *Index zu den Ilias-Scholien. Deutsche Beitr. z. Altertumsw.* 15. Baden-Baden 1961.

we find in the Venetus A between the main scholia and the text and between the lines of the text seem to come from the same source. While in the scholia of this manuscript the emphasis is mostly textual rather than exegetical, the reverse is true of the scholia to Venetus 453 (B) of the eleventh century and B.M. Townley 86 (T, dated 1059). At least three ancient Homer-commentaries were the basis of this compilation. How far they may be derived from the Pergamene school can only be conjectured. The existence of other remains of ancient exegesis in the middle ages is attested by the scholia to Genaviensis 44 (G) of the thirteenth century on the 21st book of the *Iliad*, which show resemblances to *Pap. Oxyr.* 2. 221 (nr. 942 P.). We need not concern ourselves much with the smaller scholia formerly known as the Didymus-scholia: they are also of ancient origin, as the papyri have shown, and are mostly explanations of single words.[1]

The remains of ancient work on the *Odyssey* (principally in the two manuscripts Harley 5674 (H) and Venetus 613 (M), both of the 13th century) are fewer than on the *Iliad*. Presumably scholars in antiquity concerned themselves more with the greater of the two epics. An indication of its higher esteem is found in the Platonic *Hippias* (363b), where the *Iliad* is said to excel the *Odyssey* as much as Achilles excels Odysseus.

In the commentary on the two poems compiled by Eustathius, archbishop of Thessalonica from 1175, a good deal of ancient criticism and exegesis survives, embedded in a prolix exposition.[2] The work of the four men was known to him through the commentary of Apion and Herodorus.

In speaking of the scholia we have already mentioned the principal manuscripts. It may be added that the Venetus A of the *Iliad* was acquired by Cardinal Bessarion from Joannes Aurispa, and that Severyns[3] thinks it was written for Arethas of Caesarea.

There are very many manuscripts of the *Iliad*: Allen reckons 188, but his list is not likely to be complete. We have rather less than half as many for the *Odyssey*: among them we may mention the two Laurentiani of the tenth century, 32, 24 (G) and Abbat. 52 (F), and the Palatinus Heidelb. 45 (P), dated 1201.

We have already noticed that our manuscript tradition is not purely the text of the Alexandrians. Yet at the same time it is not that which the ancients called the vulgate. Rather, we find a number of floating variants in a very scattered distribution. To a large extent they are the same variants which we now find in the Homeric papyri, although differently distributed. In these circumstances it is impossible to arrive at a clear family-tree of the manuscripts. The reason lies in the copiousness of the transmission. Unlike the other poets, who mostly survived the critical centuries from the seventh to the ninth in a single uncial codex, Homer seems to have come through that period in several manuscripts.

---

[1] H. GATTIKER (*v.* p. 76, n. 1).

[2] Stallbaum's edition in seven volumes with index by M. Devarius (Leipzig 1826–30) is about to be reprinted by Olms of Hildesheim.

[3] 'De nouveau sur le Venetus d'Homère'. *La Nouvelle Clio* 3, 1951, 164; but cf. H. ERBSE, *Zet.* 24, 1960, 123 and D. MERVYN JONES, *Gnom.* 33, 1961, 18. A splendid photographic facsimile of the MS. by Sijthoff, Leyden 1901.

Consequently, when letters revived in Byzantium there were different threads of tradition which later became variously entangled.

The oldest edition of Homer is that of Demetrius Chalcondyles (Florence 1488). The Aldine followed in 1504. We cannot here trace the history of the editing of Homer: we can only mention work that is recent or of practical importance. The most convenient complete edition with critical apparatus is that of D. B. Monro and T. W. Allen for the *Iliad* (3rd ed. Oxf. 1920), and of T. W. Allen for the *Odyssey* (2nd ed. Oxf. 1917–19), each in two volumes. A fifth volume (Oxf. 1912, with corrections 1946) contains the hymns, the fragments of the *Margites*, the *Batrachomyomachia* and the lives. Both the epics, with texts by E. Schwartz, tr. by J. H. Voss (*Iliad* rev. by H. Rupe, *Odyssey* by E. R. Weiss), ed. Br. Snell, Berlin-Darmstadt 1956. The *Iliad*, in three volumes with a copious critical apparatus, by T. W. Allen, Oxf. 1931; text and trans. by P. Mazon (*Coll. Univ. Fr.* Paris 1947–49); with German translation and useful supplements in the Tusculum series, Munich 1948, the text by V. Stegemann, the version by H. Rupe. Among commentaries the old one of W. Leaf (2nd ed. London 1900–02 reprinted 1960) is still useful: so is that of K. Fr. Ameis and C. Hentze (Teubner), with somewhat old-fashioned, but still indispensable critical appendices (often reprinted: last edition revised by P. Cauer 1910). Commentaries on individual books: I: E. Mioni, Turin n.d.; IX: E. Valgiglio, Rome 1955; XXIV: F. Martinazzoli, Rome 1948. On the *Odyssey* now see A. Heubeck, 'Neuere Odyssee-Ausgaben' *Gymn.* 63, 1956, 87. The *Odyssey* has been edited with French translation by V. Bérard (*Coll. des Univ. de Fr.* 2nd ed. Paris 1933), with a separate *Introduction* (Paris 1924). A valuable critical edition is that of P. Von der Mühll, Basel 1946: the apparatus is most carefully set out. With German translation: A. Weiher, Munich 1955–61. For the exegesis, in addition to Ameis-Hentze-Cauer (*v. sup.*) we may mention that of W. B. Stanford, Lond. 1947. (2nd ed. 1958). Editions of the scholia: on the *Iliad* W. Dindorf, 4 vols. Oxf. 1875–77; vols. 5 and 6, E. Maass, ibid. 1888; on the *Odyssey* W. Dindorf, Oxf. 1855 repr. 1961 (all these need re-editing; a new edition of the scholia is being prepared by H. Erbse). J. Baar, *Index zu den Ilias-Scholien. Die wichtigeren Ausdrücke der gramm., rhetor. u. ästhet. Textkritik.* Deutsche Beiträge zur Altertumswiss. 15. Baden-Baden 1961. Lexica: H. Ebeling, Leipz. 1880–85 repr. by Olms, Hildesheim forthcoming; A. Gehring, *Index Homericus*, Leipz. 1891. The first three fascicules (1953/9) of a *Lexikon des frühgriechischen Epos* have now appeared, compiled by Snell, Fleischer and Mette on the widest possible basis. G. L. Prendergast, *A Complete Concordance to the Iliad.* Lond. 1875; repr. with additions by B. Marzullo, Hildesheim 1960. H. Dunbar, *A Complete Concordance to the Odyssey and Hymns of Homer.* Oxf. 1880; reprint by Olms forthcoming. Translations in addition to the editions with translation mentioned above: the German translation by J. H. Voss has deservedly gone through many reprints: it is handsomely printed by P. Von der Mühll in the Birkhäuser classics 23 and 24 (Basel 1946). There are many more recent translations: we may mention Th. v. Scheffer (vols. 13 and 14 of the Sammlung Dietrich) and R. A. Schroeder, who has translated both poems in the 4th volume of his collected works, Frankf. a.M. 1952. A prose translation of the *Odyssey* by W. Schadewaldt in Rowohlt's Classics 1958. A delightful curiosity is A. Meyer's translation of the *Odyssey* into the Bernese dialect, Berne 1960. The French translation of the *Iliad* by R. Flacelière and of the *Odyssey* by V. Bérard was published in the Bibl. de la Pléiade 115, Paris 1955. A translation of the *Iliad* into modern Greek by N. Kazantzakis and I. T. Kakridis appeared in Athens 1955. In English: G. Chapman, Lond. 1616. 1624 (often repr.); A. Pope, *Iliad*. Lond. 1715-20. *Odyssey*. ibid. 1725. E. V. Rieu, *Iliad*. Lond. 1950; *Odyssey*. Lond. 1946. On the influence of Homer G. Finsler's *Homer in der Neuzeit von Dante bis Goethe*. Leipzig 1912, remains indispensable. Other interesting studies are: W. B. Stanford, *The Ulysses Theme. A study in the Adaptability of a Traditional Hero*. Oxf. 1954. R. Sühnel, *Homer und die engl. Humanität*. Tübingen 1958. Bibliographies: H. J. Mette, 'Homer 1930-56'. *Lustrum* 1, 1956 (1957), 7, with supplements ibid. 319; 2, 1957, 294; 4, 1959 (1960), 309; 5, 1961, 649; A. Lesky, *Die Homerforschung in der Gegenwart*. Vienna 1952, and subsequent progress-reports in *AfdA*, of which the last appeared in no. 13, 1960, 1, where references are given to earlier reports.

B The Epic Cycle

Passages in both *Iliad* and *Odyssey* attest the existence of heroic poetry on other themes: the siege of Thebes, the voyage of the Argonauts, the hunting of the Calydonian boar. Much of this poetry has been lost to us, and was already lost in Alexandrian times. Other such poems, however, lived to reach the great library and were not lost till later. These are to some extent known to us by report and by surviving fragments. In the *Peace* (1270) Aristophanes quotes the beginning of the *Epigoni* as something well known, indicating that the poem was still in circulation. We need not mourn the loss in these of poems equal to the *Iliad* and *Odyssey*. All that we know of their loosely-knit structure, the style of surviving fragments, such judgments as that of Aristotle (*Poet.* 23. 1459b1), all point clearly to the great gulf that separated them. We also know that these epics presupposed Homer and were complementary to him in subject matter. The term 'epic cycle' occurs in ancient writers: in two rather late passages we find it defined in different ways. A passage from the *Chrestomathy* of Proclus, quoted by Photius (*Bibliotheca* p. 319A17), tells us that the cycle comprised everything from the marriage of Heaven and Earth to the death of Odysseus. The scholion to Clement of Alexandria *Protrept*. 2. 30 makes it rather less comprehensive, saying that the material of the epic cycle was the antecedents and sequel of the *Iliad*. We know nothing of how the notion developed, and it seems never to have been so sharply defined that it might not be applied to collections of different compass.

The few scattered references to a *Titanomachia*[1] leave it as shadowy as other

---

[1] For fragments of the cyclic epics the old and inadequate edition by G. KINKEL, *Epicorum Graecorum fragmenta* (1877), is now partly replaced by the 5th volume of Allen's OCT edition (1912, repr. with corrections 1946) covering the cycle in the wider sense, while

epics on the earliest history of the gods. Allusions in Homer to past battles of the gods (e.g. *Il.* I. 396) give us some inkling how much may have been consigned to oblivion by the success of Hesiod's *Theogony*.

We are little better informed about the epics of the Theban cycle, for which we have not Proclus' summaries. The use of their themes by the tragedians, statements in mythographers, and a handful of works of art afford us very unsafe ground for reconstruction.[1]

One general remark must be made on the fact that particular epics are sometimes ascribed to Homer, sometimes to other poets. Besides the individual ascriptions, we find the whole epic cycle sometimes atrributed to Homer, although notices to this effect[2] are late and unreliable. Doubt of Homeric authorship was early expressed, as we shall see in discussing the *Epigoni* and the *Cypria*. Aristotle (*Poetics* loc. cit.) speaks, without giving any name, of ' the man who wrote the *Cypria* and the *Little Iliad*', and the scholia suggest that Alexandrian views were the same. In later notices various different names are given.[3] How far these were the deliberate inventions of pretenders to learning, or how far they come from older tradition, we cannot tell. We can, however, take as trustworthy the statements about the number of books and verses, which go back to the Alexandrian indices.

Of the three Theban epics the first in respect of subject matter is the *Oedipodea* with 6600 lines. Cinaethon is sometimes named as the author. It dealt with the defeat of the Sphinx and Oedipus' marriage with Jocasta. It probably made him remain king in Thebes and contract another marriage after the discovery of his blood-guilt. But the curse of his mother, who had taken her own life, pursued him until after many domestic calamities he fell in battle against the Minyae.

Next came the *Thebaid*, with 7000 lines according to the round figure in the *Contest of Homer and Hesiod*. Pausanias (9. 9, 5) tells us that as early as the seventh century it had been ascribed to Homer by Callinus, and that many agreed with him. We may thus infer the great age of this epic, which Pausanias valued next only to the *Iliad* and *Odyssey*. Its opening, ' Sing, goddess, of parched Argos, where the princes . . .', shows a close similarity to the opening of both the Homeric epics. This may well be taken as imitation,[4] and the passage of Callinus has not come down to us. Thus we must look on the attribution to Homer as sceptically as in other cases. We know that the subject matter included the

---

E. BETHE, *Homer* 2, 2nd ed. Leipz. 1929, gives those of the Trojan cycle with an attempted reconstruction. An edition of the epic fragments is being prepared by W. KULLMANN. What can be reconstructed of the epic *Titanomachia* is collected by O. GIGON in J. DÖRIG and O. GIGON, *Der Kampf der Götter und Titanen*. Olten/Lausanne 1961.

[1] E. BETHE, *Thebanische Heldenlieder*. Leipz. 1891, corrected in many points by C. ROBERT, *Oidipus*. Berl. 1915. Cf. L. DEUBNER, 'Oedipus-probleme'. *Preuss. Ak. Phil.-hist. Kl.* 1942/4, 27.

[2] E. BETHE, *Homer* 2, 150.

[3] On the various names associated with authorship of the Cycles see W. KULLMANN, *Die Quellen der Ilias. Herm.* E 14, 1960, 215. 2.

[4] A different view is held by E. KALINKA, 'Die Dichtungen Homers'. *Almanach d. Ak. Wien* 1934, p. 22 of the separate printing.

repeated curse called down by Oedipus on his sons and fulfilled in their mutual slaughter, which put an end to the expedition of the Seven against Thebes. Echoes of this epic in later poetry suggest that the siege was described with much episode and elaboration.

For the third Theban epic, the *Epigoni*, the same source as for the *Thebaid* gives the same round figure of 7000 lines. The ascription to Homer is mentioned by Herodotus (4. 32) with obvious misgivings. The successful siege of Thebes by the sons of the first attackers is known to Homer (*Il.* 4. 406); although this could not of course be referring to the treatment of it later incorporated in the epic cycle.

We are best informed about the poems of the Trojan cycle, thanks to the extracts from the *Chrestomathia* of Proclus which are preserved partly in the *Bibliotheca* of the patriarch Photius, partly in some of the manuscripts of the *Iliad* (particularly the Venetus A).[1] Some scholars have been so sceptical as to deny any value to these summaries. While this academic Pyrrhonism has deservedly fallen out of fashion, we should not underestimate how much uncertainty is still left. Whether the Proclus concerned wrote in the second century or the fifth, it is quite certain that he did not have the poems themselves to hand: what he tells us is what he has picked up from the mythographers. Two questions pose themselves. First: do these excerpts give an accurate account of the starting and finishing points of the various epics? Secondly: is the very smooth joining of each to each the work of the original poets or of later compilers and arrangers? We shall return to these questions later.

The *Cypria* (Κύπρια sc. ἔπη: the title has never been satisfactorily explained) in eleven books told what happened before the *Iliad*. The author is variously given as Stasinus, Hegesias or Hegesinus. There is an interesting passage raising a problem of over-population: Zeus sees the world groaning under the weight of human beings, and decides to relieve the burden by a great war. The poet casts his net wide. He tells us all the background: the marriage of Peleus and Thetis, the judgment of Paris, the rape of Helen and the events in Aulis up to the first mistaken landing in Teuthrania. Then follow episodes from the war before the *Iliad*. The style must have been rather inconsequential, to judge from one particular scene. Menelaus, recruiting for his expedition, comes to Nestor, prince of Pylos. The old man tells him the story of Epopeus, who ran off with another man's wife, of Oedipus, of the madness of Heracles, of Theseus and Ariadne. There is a certain bond between these tales—each tells of things going

---

[1] Whether this was the Neoplatonist of the fifth century or a grammarian of the 2nd is uncertain. M. SICHERL, *Gnom.* 28, 1956, 210, 1, rightly points out the weakness of the case for equating this Proclus with the Neoplatonist: it rests solely on the statement of a Byzantine writer (Tzetzes?) in Ottob. gr. 58. Summary of the manuscript evidence and a new version for the *Cypria* in A. SEVERYNS, 'Un Sommaire inédit des chants cypriens'. *Mel. Grégoire. Ann. de l'inst. d'hist. Orient. et Slav.* 10, 1950, 571. Id., *Recherches sur la Chrestomathie de Proclos* I. *Études paléographique et critique.* Paris 1938. II. *Texte, traduction, commentaire.* Paris 1938. III. *La vita Homeri et les sommaires du Cycle.* Paris 1953. Severyns' earlier work on the *Chrestomathy* is referred to in *Gnom.* 28, 1956, 210, 5. For a history of the problem of the cyclic epics see KULLMANN, op. cit. (p. 23, n. 1) 18.

wrong between man and woman—but the prolixity of this string of narratives goes beyond anything which the Homeric Nestor would have allowed himself. The poet has presumably, however, taken the Homeric character as his model. This poem also was ascribed to Homer, as we see from the criticism voiced by Herodotus, who is by no means so uncritical as he is sometimes represented in contrast to Thucydides. He contests the Homeric authorship, since in the *Cypria* Paris and Helen arrive at Troy after three days' easy sail, while in the *Iliad* (6. 290) they take a devious route by way of Sidon. Proclus' excerpts give the Homeric version—which shows how far he is to be trusted.

The *Iliad* was followed by the *Aethiopis* in five books, ascribed to Arctinus of Miletus. It dealt with the last exploits of Achilles: his victory over the Amazon Penthesilea and the Ethiopian prince Memnon, his death at the hands of Paris and Apollo – the human and divine archers – and his funeral. The erotic element that later attached itself to the episode of Penthesilea seems to have been kept out. We mentioned earlier (p. 23) how the *Aethiopis* figured in a recent theory which extracted from it a *Memnonis* as a model for the *Iliad*.

It is very hard to date any of these epics. For the *Aethiopis* we know that the battle of Achilles and Memnon was depicted on the 'Cypselus chest', the chest of cedarwood richly adorned with scenes from mythology which the ruling house of Corinth dedicated at Delphi (Paus. 5. 17, 5). Probably this gives us a lower limit for the dating, although it is possible that the carving reflected an older version of the saga of Memnon. On the other hand, in the epic Achilles kills Thersites for insulting the body of Penthesilea, and is absolved of blood-guilt by Odysseus on the island of Lesbos after sacrifice to Apollo. This episode points to an increasing influence of the notion of blood-guilt and its connection with Delphi – a notion so influential later – and we can probably refer the *Aethiopis* to the late seventh century. With greater reservations we might suppose the epic cycle in general to have taken shape about this time. It should again be emphasized that the material in them was much older, and that the cycle arose from a later re-handling, under Homeric influence, of traditional themes.[1]

An epic in two books entitled *The Sack of Troy* ('Ιλίου πέρσις) is also associated with Arctinus. What we know of its contents, together with representations on pots, suggests that the fate of the city was depicted in a series of detached episodes.

The *Aethiopis* and *Iliu Persis* collaborate in telling the events after the end of the *Iliad*. This fact in itself raises difficulties, since we know of another epic relating the Posthomerica: the *Little Iliad*, in four books, ascribed to Lesches or some-times to others, including Cinaethon. Some scholars have supposed that the *Little Iliad* was a kind of epic fragment, telling what befell between the *Aethiopis* and the *Iliu Persis*, while Bethe makes these two the component parts of a

[1] W. KULLMANN op. cit. (*sup.* p. 23, n. 1) devotes a chapter to the structure of the epic cycle and examines the relation of the cyclic epics to the *Iliad*. He dates the former too early; not only the *Aethiopis*, but also the *Cypria* is older, he thinks, than the *Iliad* – a view I cannot share.

Little Iliad in eleven books all told. In this way both Antehomerica and Posthomerica would be comprised in eleven books; but this may be mere coincidence. The most probable supposition is that the *Little Iliad* stood side by side with the other two, and related the events following Hector's death in a more concise form.

The plot of the *Odyssey* is simply one hero's return, albeit the most celebrated, out of many. This much we can see from the poem itself, where in the *Telemachia* and *Nekyia* much is told of the fate of the other heroes. This material was related at length in a poem of five books, ascribed to Homer or to Hagias of Troezen and entitled *Homecomings* (Νόστοι). The element of catalogue must have been very prominent in the construction of such a poem.

The most surprising shoot from this stem is the *Telegonia*,[1] commonly ascribed to Eugammon of Cyrene. It was designed as a continuation of the *Odyssey*, and it combined old tradition with new invention. Its account of Odysseus' wanderings in the district of Thesprotia in Epirus, of a second marriage and a victorious campaign against the Bryges may well come from an older *Thesprotis* mentioned by Pausanias (8. 12, 5). The wanderings that Odysseus undertakes in order to placate Poseidon are obviously associated with the prophecy of Tiresias in the *Odyssey* (11. 121). A second part of the epic contains that tragic father-and-son theme which finds its greatest expression in the *Hildebrandslied*. Telegonus, son of Odysseus by Circe, lands in Ithaca in search of his father. On a plundering foray he meets and kills Odysseus, not knowing him, with a spear tipped with a sharp flint. The many absurdities in detail, not least the elaborate wedding scene at the end in which Penelope is united with Telegonus and Circe with Telemachus, suggest that the poem was written very late, and we are disposed to accept the statement of Eusebius, who says that Eugammon flourished in the 53rd Olympiad (568–565). This date may well be the lower limit for epic poetry of this kind.

Here we must return to the question whether the epics of the Trojan cycle were conceived by their original authors as supplementing the *Iliad* and making the story complete. Despite all the uncertainties associated with the excerpts of Proclus, we can answer that they were. The closeness of the joins is shown by an alternative form of the last line of the *Iliad*, preserved in the T scholium to 24. 804. Hector's epithet 'tamer of horses' was left out at the end of the verse, and the words 'but there came an Amazon . . .' replaced them, so that one passed immediately in recitation from the *Iliad* to the *Aethiopis*.[2] This is the same trend towards unification which we meet on one of the 'Homeric bowls',[3] which shows first Priam before Achilles, next Priam receiving Penthesilea beside the grave of Hector, and finally the battle of Achilles and the Amazon. The same desire is evident: to make a link between *Iliad* and *Aethiopis*. The new

---

[1] A. HARTMANN, *Untersuchungen über die Sagen vom Tod des Odysseus*. Munich 1917. R. MERKELBACH, *Untersuchungen zur Odyssee*. Zet. 2. Munich 1951, 142.

[2] Ὥς οἵ γ' ἀμφίεπον τάφον Ἕκτορος· ἦλθε δ' Ἀμάζων Ἄρηος θυγάτηρ μεγαλήτορος ἀνδροφόνοιο.

[3] C. ROBERT, 50. *Berliner Winkelmannsprogramm* 1890, 26.

ally gives the Trojans hope that they may yet make good the loss of their best defender.

Scattered references to other epics show how fertile the field was in which those already mentioned sprang up. The *Capture of Oechalia* (Οἰχαλίας ἅλωσις) told of the sack of the city by Heracles and the abduction of Iole – a theme which influenced the *Trachiniae* of Sophocles. Legend has it that Homer gave this epic to Creophylus of Samos in gratitude for his hospitality; from which Callimachus (epigr. 6 Pf.) drew the correct conclusion that Creophylus wrote it. An *Alcmeonis* dealt with the fate of the Theban counterpart to Orestes – that Alcmeon who slew his mother Eriphyla to avenge his father Amphiaraus. Other epics, such as *Phocais*, *Minyas*, *Danais*, are little more than names.

C The Homeric Hymns

A group of hexameter hymns addressed to various gods and ascribed to Homer has been preserved, as it seems, through its having been formed into a corpus together with those assigned to Orpheus and later with the hymns of Callimachus and Proclus. So at least it appears from the manuscript transmission. There are thirty-three of these 'Homeric hymns',[1] and the remains of one more in Diodorus 3. 66, 3. They were written at very different times and places: some of them cannot be firmly dated at all, nor can we say when the present collection was formed. It may be of fairly late origin: certainly the eighth hymn (to Ares) with its astrological trappings is scarcely conceivable before the Hellenistic period. Of course it may possibly have crept into the collection after the others. What we have here in effect is a small and random sample from the great number of hymns written in Greek antiquity. Right down to the end of the ancient world we find allusions to early poetry under such names as Olen (Herod. 4. 35), Pamphos, Orpheus and Musaeus. In most instances the reference would be to cult-hymns in lyric metre; but presumably there were other hymns, like that which brought victory to Hesiod (*Erga* 657), composed on the same lines as those which we find under the name of Homer. These hymns are wholly in the rhapsodic tradition, borrowing their language from Homer even to complete phrases. Of their conception we may say the same as of their execution, except that individuality is a little more apparent here. Many of these poems have a charm of their own, arising from their application of the epic manner to themes and audiences not normally associated with great heroic poetry.[2] The circles to whom this 'sub-epic' poetry was addressed come out clearly in those verses (146 ff.) of the *Hymn to the Delian Apollo* which depict the crowds of Ionians coming with bag and baggage to the festival on the sacred island, and the unrestrained merriment and delight which accompanied the dancing of the maidens. Here we can see what the great religious festivals meant in the life and art of Greece. It is a long step from this communal Ionian

---

[1] Counting separately the hymns to the Delian and the Pythian Apollo.

[2] Pointed out by K. DEICHGRÄBER, 'Eleusinische Frömmigkeit und homerische Vorstellungswelt im hom. Demeterhymnus'. *Akad. Mainz. Geistes- u. sozialwiss. Kl.* 1950/6.

celebration to the feast of Adonis in the great Hellenistic cities (Theocr. 15), with the chattering wives of the bourgeoisie pushing through the throng on their way to the palace to gape at the decorations of the court. In the archaic and classical periods the festivals kindled a true community spirit.

The great Delian festival is mentioned by Thucydides (3. 104), where we find the first reference to this hymn. He calls it προοίμιον᾽ Ἀπόλλωνος. This designation of the hymns as prooemia (preludes) occurs elsewhere, and it is noticeable that they often end with a reference to other poems. Thus for example does the hymn to Demeter, with a formula that recurs several times. Wolf in his Prolegomena ad Homerum drew the inference that these hymns served the rhapsodes as preludes to their recitation of the epics.

Thucydides is also our witness for the ascription of such hymns to Homer. Numerous references,[1] going down to the close of antiquity, make such claims either for individual hymns or for a collection of them (which should not of course be equated with ours). On the other hand, a scholium to Nicander's Alexipharmaca 130 speaks of 'the hymns ascribed to Homer', and the fifth of our Vitae Homeri expressly denies the attribution. From the total neglect of the hymns[2] in scholia to Homer we may infer that the Alexandrians shared this view.

The hymns vary in length as much as they do in subject. Four of them are about as long as books of the Odyssey. A Hymn to Dionysus is known to us from a fragment in Diodorus (3. 66, 3), and from its last twelve verses on the first page of the Mosquensis. Since the hymns coming after it are all long ones, we may suppose that the lost hymn was long also.

The manuscript just mentioned is the only one to give the Hymn to Demeter, which in it is the first of the long hymns. The story of the rape of Persephone, of Demeter's grief, and of the reunion of mother and daughter is here so closely tied up with the immemorial mystery cult of Eleusis that the poem can be taken as a sacred history of the great religious centre. The passages where Demeter fasts in her grief, where the maid Iambe spreads a fleece for her to sit on and makes jokes to cheer her up, all serve to illustrate usages of the mysteries. The conclusion describes the founding of that secret cult which the Greeks received as an inheritance from the pre-Hellenic past, and which still held its followers under the Roman empire.[3] The author is no great poet, but he can certainly adapt the epic style to express intimate and delicate feeling, as when the king's daughters run to the fountain to call Demeter, bounding like does or heifers over the spring meadows, or when the mother embraces her recovered child and Hecate sympathetically shares her joy. And when the king's daughters anxiously take care of the kicking and whining child that Demeter has left behind, a smile flits over the lips which tell the rest of the story in all seriousness.

---

[1] Conveniently assembled in the introduction to the Oxford edition.

[2] With one possible exception: cf. Allen's ed. LXXIV.

[3] Historical account of the mysteries: O. KERN, RE 16, 1209. K. KERENYI, 'Ueber das Geheimnis der eleusinischen Mysterien'. Paideuma 7, 1959, 69. On one particular feature: A. LESKY, Rhein. Mus. 103, 1960, 377.

The hymn shows an immediate acquaintance with the Eleusinian cult and presumably was composed not far from Eleusis. It also postulates a time when Eleusis was not yet under Athenian control. If we assign it to the late seventh century, we shall not go far wrong. A Berlin papyrus (Kern, *Orph. frag.* p. 119) relates the rape of Persephone in prose, but quotes whole verses from this hymn.

The *Hymn to Apollo*[1] begins with an imposing picture of the long-striding archer-god before whom even the Olympians tremble: one might be looking at a painting in a temple. It continues with the wanderings of Leto, who at length found the tiny island of Delos as the place to bring forth the radiant brother and sister. The god grows wondrously, he roves over many lands, but his heart is always with the island of his birth, where the Ionians celebrate their splendid national feast. The poet then turns to the chorus of Delian maidens: if anyone should ask them who the singer is who most delights them, they should say it is the blind man of Chios. After a brief and not very smooth transition comes a scene in Olympus, depicting Apollo not as the threatening archer, but as the god of the lyre. We then follow him as he seeks a seat for his oracle; we are told how the stream Telphusa cunningly, but much to her own hurt, dissuaded the god from establishing himself by her side. Apollo now storms into the mountains, and chooses the foot of Parnassus for his great sanctuary. A huge serpent living by the stream hard by is slain by his arrows. Transforming himself into a dolphin, he summons a ship on the old trade route from Crete to Pylos. In Crisa, the harbour of Delphi, he declares himself by miracles and takes the Cretans into his holy oracle to be its priests.

In the second edition of his *Epistola critica I* (1781) David Ruhnken first expressed the view that in our transmission two originally independent hymns have been combined. This theory has been variously modified or rejected by more modern scholars. But the unmistakable end of the Delian section, the new start with the Delphian legend, together with the peculiarities of the transition, are all on Ruhnken's side. L. Deubner[2] considered vv. 179-206 as a variant intended to replace 140 ff. (dealing with the Delian festival) when the hymn was being recited elsewhere than in Delos. There is much to recommend this view, and the author of 179-206 may well be the same as the writer of the Pythian section.

For the hymn to Apollo we have an ancient attribution: in the scholium to Pindar *Nem.* 2. 1 it is ascribed to Cynaethus, the head of a successful school of rhapsodes which forged extensively under the name of Homer. In the 69th Olympiad (504–501) he is said to have been the first to recite Homer in Syracuse. This may well have been in consequence of some official provision for such performances. At all events, both parts of the hymn are much older than 504, since there is no mention in them of the Pythia or of the games and other

[1] Stylistic analysis in B. A. VAN GRONINGEN, *La Composition littéraire archaïque grecque.* Nederl. Akad. 65/2. Amsterdam 1958, 304.

[2] 'Der hom. Apollonhymnos'. *Sitzb. Preuss. Akad. Phil.-hist. Kl.* 1938/24. A unitary view: F. Dornseiff, *Rhein. Mus.* 87, 1938, 80. Cf. O. REGENBOGEN, *Eranos* 54, 1956, 49.

important elements of the Delphic cult. The only solution is to regard Cynaethus as the composer of the hymn in the sense that he put the two parts together:[1] the parts we must still refer to the seventh century. It was inevitable
that the 'blind man of Chios' should be taken as Homer. The *Contest of Homer
and Hesiod* tells how Homer declaimed this hymn standing on the horned altar
at Delos, after which it was written down by the Delians on a white tablet and
preserved in the sanctuary of Artemis. In this last detail there may be preserved
a fragment of historical truth.

With the *Hymn to Hermes*[2] we are in quite different country. It tells of the
adventures and pranks of this divine infant prodigy: how he made the first lyre
out of a tortoise-shell, stole the oxen of his big brother Apollo, and met Apollo's
anger and the judgment of Zeus with such a disarming impertinence that his
brother's affection was now entirely regained, purchased by the gift of the lyre.
Its fresh and sparkling humour is the particular charm of this poem – humour of
a different kind from that twinkle in the eye and that pleasure in intimate detail
which seems a peculiarly Ionic feature in the other hymns. The poet of the
Hymn to Hermes delights in boisterous action and makes one think of the uninhibited laughter of Old Comedy. After the theft of the cattle, the infant
Hermes, all innocence, wraps himself again in his swaddling clothes, and when
Apollo snatches him up in a fury he makes such an ominous noise that his
brother, in hasty alarm, puts him down again. The ill-matched brothers stand
before Zeus, and the child defends himself most ingeniously while he is held by
the napkins. Zeus can only burst out laughing, and the reader with him. The
poet knows central Greece well, and probably came from there, where he
would have had an unsophisticated, largely peasant audience for his tale. He tells
it in epic language, but the frequency of asyndeton and parataxis, the many
parentheses, the occasional vulgarisms, together with a frequent looseness of
expression, show that the old garment was beginning to fit rather badly. The
hymn to Hermes is the most recent of the longer poems, and may well be as
late as the sixth century.

The *Hymn to Aphrodite*,[3] with its undisguised Ionic colouring, offers a lively
contrast. In it Zeus humbles the goddess who makes trouble even for the
Olympians by giving her a taste of her own medicine, making her fall in love
with the handsome shepherd prince Anchises. She approaches his camp in the
guise of a young maiden. The poem, the most graceful of the collection, ends
with the promise of the birth of Aeneas and a stern injunction to keep the
secret. This Aphrodite may sometimes lack majesty and divinity, but the poet
may well have been connected with the family of the Aeneadae in the Troad.

---

[1] Thus H. T. WADE-GERY, *The Poet of the Iliad*. Cambr. 1952, 21.

[2] Edition with commentary by L. RADERMACHER, *Sitzb. Akad. Wien. Phil.-hist. Kl.* 213/1,
1931.

[3] Good analysis of the hymn, which he thinks to be by the poet of the *Iliad*, in K. REIN-
HARDT, 'Zum hom. Aphroditehymnos'. *Festschr.f.Br.Snell.* Munich 1956, 1; ibid. on the
Aeneas episode in the 20th of the *Iliad*. F. SOLMSEN, 'Zur Theologie im grossen Aphrodite-
Hymnos'. *Herm.* 88, 1960, 1.

Certainly he cannot have lived far away. A beautiful scene depicts the goddess wandering through the wooded slopes of Ida to meet her beloved, while he tarries in the mountain pasture among the shepherds. The wild beasts follow and fawn upon her – wolf and bear, lion and panther – and the goddess lights her flame in all their hearts. It is clear that Aphrodite here has some of the attributes of the Great Mother worshipped on Ida, who was mistress of all the beasts.

Of the other hymns two emerge more sharply than the rest: those to Dionysus and to Pan. The first strikingly describes how the handsome young god punished the pirates who tried to carry him off. Here we can see perhaps most clearly a connection between these poems and archaic Ionian art: the friezes and pediments of the Delphic treasury come readily to mind. The hymn to Pan brings us back to central Greece, where the cult of the goat-god was well established. The rest of the hymns consist mainly of ritual invocations, or they celebrate the power and describe the functions of individual deities.

Joannes Aurispa in a letter to Ambrogio Traversari mentions among the Greek manuscripts which he brought to Italy 'laudes deorum Homeri, haud parvum opus'. It has often been thought that this was the ancestor of our various MSS. Allen disagrees (IV. 1) on the ground of sharp divergencies between the MSS., and posits two classes. Another line of transmission became known when C. F. Matthaei discovered in Moscow the MS. which is now in Leyden and is the only one to give the hymn to Demeter and the end of that to Dionysus.[1] No papyrus text of the hymns was known until *Ox. Pap.* 23, 1956, n. 2379 (*Hymn. ad Cer.* 402-407). The standard edition with introduction and commentary is that of T. W. Allen, E. E. Sikes and W. R. Halliday, 2nd ed. Oxf. 1936. The text is given also in the fifth volume of Allen's OCT Homer. With Germ. trans.: A. Weiher, *Tusculum-Bücherei.* Munich 1951. With French trans.: J. Humbert, *Coll. des Un. de Fr.* 4th ed. 1959. O. Zumbach, *Neuerungen in der Sprache der hom. Hymnen.* 1955, has collected the instances of late linguistic usage in the hymns; V. Pisani, *Storia della lingua greca in Encicl. class.* 2/5/1. Turin 1940, 48, points out some anomalies in epic usage in the hymn to Demeter.

D Other Works Attributed to Homer

The relief of Archelaus of Priene having 'Homage to Homer' as its subject shows a frog and a mouse by the poet's throne. Hence it appears that in Archelaus' time (second century B.C.) the *Batrachomyomachia*, a poem in 303 hexameters describing the war of the frogs and mice, was taken in all seriousness to be a work of Homer's. Another tradition,[2] assigning it to a Carian called Pigres, is scarcely more trustworthy. The cause of the war is amusingly related. The king of the frogs, Cheekpuffer (Physignathos), full of friendship and good feeling towards mice, is carrying Crumbsnatcher (Psicharpax) on his back across a lake, when a watersnake appears. The frog dives in alarm, and the mouse is

---

[1] On the interpretation of the latter see DEICHGRÄBER, cf. p. 84, n. 2.
[2] Notices about *Batrach.* and the *Margites* in Allen's fifth volume OCT.

drowned. A hard-fought war now takes place, in which a comic effect is obtained by the parodying of epic scenes and formulae. Our ignorance of other examples of parody in Greek literature[1] makes it hard to date this one. But since the Hellenistic age reckoned it as Homeric, it must have been composed some considerable time before, despite many marks of degeneracy in language and metre.

There are other examples of animal parodies of Homeric battle-scenes, since we hear of such titles as *Geranomachia*, *Psaromachia* and *Arachnomachia*, which Proclus and the *Vitae* give as Homeric *paegnia*. The *Epicichlides* seems by its name to be concerned with quails, but it was not epic travesty: according to Athenaeus 14. 639A it had a mostly erotic content.

Homer and Pigres again appear as authors of the poem about the simpleton *Margites*[2] – a work whose loss we much regret. In this poem, a precursor of the Ionic prose romance, the leading figure was the blockhead who does everything topsy-turvy: a character with many cousins in folk-tales all over the world. In Greek literature we hear of other similar figures, such as Coroebus and Melitides. The theme, that Margites can only with great difficulty be prevailed upon by his young wife to discharge his marital duties, recurs in medieval fabliaux. The hero, whose qualities of mind are betokened by his name ($\mu\acute{\alpha}\rho\gamma o\varsigma$= demented), was the son, according to a notice in Eustathius (1669. 48), of very rich parents. Perhaps, then, there was some element of social satire in the poem, and its author may have been someone like Hipponax. Its unusual form – hexameters with iambics scattered at random – has now had some light cast on it by the Ischia bowl (*Acc. Lincei* 1955). Some of the statements about the metrical form of the *Margites* speak simply of alternation between hexameters and iambi; others give the impression that a sequence of hexameters would be broken by a single iambic line. If we accept these statements at their face value and do not suppose them to reflect misunderstandings of a remark by some ancient metrician, then we shall be in serious doubt whether to ascribe the new papyrus fragments (showing a very free change of metres) to the *Margites* or not.[3]

Eustratius on Aristotle *Eth. Nic.* 6, 7. 1141a12 declares that Archilochus, Cratinus and Callimachus reckoned the *Margites* as genuine work of Homer's. But since Cratinus, Aristophanes' great predecessor, wrote a comedy entitled *Archilochoi*, it is quite possible that the mention of Archilochus comes from his

---

[1] The scanty remnants in P. BRANDT, *Corpusculum poesis epicae Graecae ludibundae*. I. Leipz. 1888.

[2] L. RADERMACHER, *RE* 14, 1930, 1705. New fragments: *Ox. Pap.* 22, 1954, nr. 2309; cf. K. LATTE, *Gnom.* 27, 1955, 492. W. PEEK, 'Neue Bruchstücke frühgriech. Dichtung'. *Wiss. Zeitschr. Univ. Halle* 5, 1955–56, 189. A. HEUBECK, *Gymn.* 66, 1959, 382. H. LANGERBECK, 'Margites. Versuch einer Beschreibung und Rekonstruktion'. *Harv. Stud.* 63, 1958 (*Festschr. Jaeger*), 33. M. FORDERER, *Zum homerischen Margites*. Amsterdam 1960, has many acute observations, and attempts to greater dimension of depth to the figure of Margites as 'the pure fool', relating it to the heroes of the great epics. This attempt, as the author admits, must remain hypothetical.

[3] This conclusion is reached by FORDERER, op. cit. 5, after examining the ancient notices.

having appeared as a character in Cratinus' play. This supposition would leave us free to date the *Margites* later – say about the sixth century.[1]

We may mention here the short hexameter poems attributed to Homer in the life of him which bears the name of Herodotus. Many of them are quoted to establish biographical points; they are not bad verses, and they go back no doubt to the rhapsodic tradition. This biography, to which the not very meaningful name of 'Volksbuch' has been given, also contains the *Eiresione*, a charming traditional begging song for children. We can see here what a wide range of foundlings was fathered onto Homer. In Alexandria the Homeric critics took no account of any of this material.

[1] Cf. J. A. DAVISON, *Eranos* 53, 1956, 135.

CHAPTER IV

The Archaic Period

A Hesiod

It was common in antiquity to mention Homer and Hesiod in the same breath, and the saying of Herodotus (2. 53) has often been repeated, that these two gave the Greeks their gods. But in fact the resemblances in metre, in use of the epic vocabulary, in rhapsodic tradition, are out-weighed by the one fact that Hesiod lived socially and spiritually in a totally different world. At the very outset they are in contrast, since the personality of Homer remains, even for those who accept his historicity, a gigantic shadow; while of Hesiod's life and circumstances we are remarkably well informed from his own works. He is the first poet of the western world to have a social context. If we date his poems about 700, as is very likely, we find ourselves not far from the time at which the Homeric epics took shape. Since various passages in Hesiod show some affinity to parts of Homer, some writers have tried to assign to him some parts of the *Odyssey*. No such attempt has been able to carry conviction or to invalidate the generally held view that in all such cases Hesiod was the borrower.[1]

The striking difference between the spiritual world of Hesiod and that of the great epics cannot be explained as resulting from historical developments. Rather, what is new and different in Hesiod comes from the difference in his social and geographical background. In this connection we must remember that the *Odyssey* already shows a breaking down of the aristocratic scheme of values and a stronger tendency to think in ethical terms, such as characterizes the work of Hesiod.[2]

We think of the Homeric epics as having taken shape in Ionian Asia Minor, and the stamp of the Ionic spirit is visible upon them. Hesiod, on the contrary, is as un-Ionic as he could be. His father came from Cyme, and thus from the part of Asia Minor which was colonized by Aeolians. Like many of his contemporaries, he sought wealth in overseas trade, but his plans miscarried and he left his home to settle in Ascra, a village of Boeotia near Thespiae. Here Hesiod grew up, and even if not a native Boeotian, he nevertheless was greatly influenced in his ways and in his poetry by this highly individual area of central Greece, with all its peasant self-sufficiency, its richness in ancient tradition and that uncouth strength which we see in the early plastic art of Boeotia.[3]

---

[1] F. SOLMSEN, op. cit. 6, 3. W. SCHADEWALDT, *Von Homers Welt und Werk*. 3rd ed., 1959, 93 n. 1.

[2] The difference between Hesiod and the *Odyssey* where ethics are concerned is rather overstressed by D. KAUFMANN-BÜHLER, 'Hesiod und die Tisis in der Odyssee'. *Herm.* 84, 1956, 267.

[3] R. LULLIES, 'Zur frühen boiotischen Plastik'. *Arch. Jahrb.* 51, 1936, 138.

There were aristocratic landowners there as elsewhere. Hesiod came into contact with them, but their world was not his. In his youth he lived as a shepherd on the mountains; later he worked the land that he inherited from his father. His world is that of the small peasants who were indeed free, but had a hard struggle for their living. The soil was so unproductive that Hesiod (*Erga* 376) recommends the farmer to have only one child. There is no romantic light cast on the toil and suffering of peasant life. Ascra is bad in winter, unbearable in summer, never good (*Erga* 640). It was not until the days of the great Hellenistic cities that men first felt that romantic affection for the world of nature which finds expression in Theocritus.

The most important event of Hesiod's life is described in the prooemium to the *Theogony*. As he was watching his flock on Helicon, the Muses came to him, veiled in thick mist, from the top of the mountain where they wove their dances. Their voices awoke poetry in him; they crowned him with laurel, and he felt called to sing of things past and things yet to come. This is a poet describing the moment when he recognized his vocation; and we should be rather foolish if we examined too closely the historical and factual content of the verses. But that it reflects a genuine experience cannot be doubted.[1] Later he tells us (*Erga* 654) how at the funeral games of Amphidamas in Chalcis he won a victory with a hymn: the tripod which was his prize he consecrated to the Heliconian Muses on the place where they first set his feet on the path of verse and song.

It was the Muses who made Hesiod a poet. But he had to learn his craft, and in this respect, as his verses plainly show, Homeric influence was paramount. Only in the epics could he find the form in which to express what the Muses bade him. But he did more than learn: what he studied often aroused him to doubt and disagreement. In the prooemium to the *Theogony* the Muses are not very friendly to the shepherds: they call them idle wretches, bellies and nothing more. This is the first time that the arts appear in opposition to the lower sphere of everyday necessities: a note is sounded which will be heard again and again in Greek literature. Of their own activities the Muses say that their language is often falsehood bearing the appearance of truth; but they speak truth too if they are inclined. It seems then that there are different kinds of poetry: while Hesiod feels called to enshrine truth in his verses, he gives a sideways glance at those who make such a promise without fulfilling it. Thus this important prooemium provides the first example of literary polemic. The way in which the early philosophers took each other or the poets to task for untruthfulness (VS 22 B40. 57), or in which Hecataeus of Miletus ridicules the beliefs of the Greeks (fr. 1 Jac.), are prefigured in these words. In the mouth of Hesiod they betoken the great gulf by which he was separated from the Homeric world.

Hesiod learned of the Homeric poems from wandering rhapsodes. From them he learned his trade, and he himself became one of their number. We

---

[1] K. LATTE, 'Hesiods Dichterweihe', *Ant. u. Abendl.* 2, 1946, 152. Parallels from poets of other lands: C. M. BOWRA, *Heroic Poetry*. Lond. 1953, 427. K. V. FRITZ, 'Das Prooemium der hesiodischen Theogonie'. *Festschr. Pr. Snell*. Munich 1956, 29.

cannot infer that he gave up his farm: certainly he was never far from it. His visit to the funeral games in Chalcis was something quite unusual, and his voyage over the narrow straits of Euripus was his only journey by sea – a thing for which he had no more love than most Greeks of the archaic period.[1] Nothing shows this so clearly as the single detail that the inhabitants of the just and happy city do not have to go to sea.

But even if Hesiod was not a rhapsode in the same sense as the wandering Homeridae, he was still closely connected with them. In consequence his poems soon came to be recited by rhapsodes – an important but ominous factor in the transmission.

The strongest indication that he was reckoned as a rhapsode is the *Contest of Homer and Hesiod* (cf. 45. 14). The story in its present form has additions dating from the late empire, but a papyrus of the 3rd century B.C.[2] shows that the main lines were already there; and Wilamowitz[3] wants to put the *Certamen* back into classical times. It arose basically from the Greek passion for comparative judgments (*syncrisis*) of literary figures, and begins with a game of question and answer in hexameters between Homer and Hesiod. Next each recites the most beautiful passages from his work; and the audience decides in favour of Homer after hearing battle scenes from the *Iliad*. But Panades, who as brother of the dead Amphidamas presides over the contest, awards the prize to Hesiod's verses describing peaceful country life.

There are all kinds of fables about the poet's death, as in ancient biography the deaths of famous men were favourite subjects for anecdotal embellishment. The story that his tomb was shown in Orchomenus may well be true.[4]

The *Theogony* is hard to understand mainly because its contents are so varied. Added to this is a thought-sequence in which main lines do exist, but are so interlaced and surrounded by side-issues that they often escape our gaze. These features, as well as the associative rather than logical development of some parts and the frequency of digressions, contribute to the strikingly archaic impression that the poem gives. There are also difficulties arising from the transmission. Since the text was in the hands of rhapsodes, it was bound to become riddled with variants and interpolations. In consequence the text in modern times has been vigorously assailed and many passages have been far too readily denounced as spurious.[5] Parts such as the so-called 'hymn to Hecate' and the battle with

---

[1] Passages given in *Thalatta*. Vienna 1947, are enough to show this.

[2] *Flinders Petrie Papyri*, Dublin 1891 nr. 25; in ALLEN's edition 5, 225. To these add *Papyrus Michigan* 2754 (late second or early third century) found in the excavations at Karanis: J. G. WINTER, 'A New Fragment on the Life of Homer'. *Trans. Am. Phil. Ass.* 56, 1925, 120. The papyrus has the ending of the *Certamen* and the subscription Ἀλκι]δάμαντος περὶ Ὁμήρου Bibliog.: *Gnom.* 33, 1961, 697, 2.

[3] *Ilias und Homer*, 400. Recent lit. p. 40, n. 3. Cf. G. WALBERER, *Isokrates und Alkidamas.* Diss. Hamburg 1938.

[4] Sources on Hesiod's life and works in Jacoby's edition (*v. sup.*). O. FRIEDEL, 'Die Sage vom Tode Hesiods nach ihren Quellen untersucht'. *Jahrb. f. class. Phil. Suppl. Bd.* 10. Leipz. 1878/79, is still valuable.

[5] Opposing views are expressed in JACOBY's edition and in P. FRIEDLÄNDER, *Gött. Gel. Anz.* 1931, 241.

Typhoeus[1] are still under suspicion, and so are a number of shorter passages. Inevitably in poetry of this kind definite criteria can only rarely be established; and consequently the reserve shown by modern scholars is well justified.

In the next paragraphs we shall attempt to bring out a few constituent elements of the *Theogony*; but in simplifying it as we needs must, we should not forget how prolix the archaic narrative is, with its perpetual conflict between order and freedom.

In the *Theogony* we find every kind of mixture of traditional stories with Hesiod's own invention. Recent researches have made it much easier for us to pick out leading threads. The *Theogony* depicts partly a development, partly a situation that has arisen in the course of time in the world in which we all have to live. In the *Erga* also being and coming-to-be stand side by side. In the *Theogony* the main line of development follows the succession of three divinities as world rulers: Uranus, Cronus and Zeus. The transfer of power is always violent. Cronus castrates his father Uranus and thus wins the kingdom. He devours his own children, but his wife Rhea saves the new-born Zeus from him and conceals him in Crete, where he grows up to be the future ruler of the world. In battle with the Titans he wins the throne for all time.

In recent years Gustav Güterbock and Heinrich Otten[2] have brought to light two religious poems of the near east, which help to illustrate the origin of certain Greek myths. The texts, written in Hittite, are from the great find of cuneiform tablets at Boghazköi, and are from the period 1400–1200 B.C. Various peculiarities of the texts strongly suggest that behind the Hittite version is an older Hurrian form of the legend, to be dated in the flowering period of that culture in the middle of the second millennium. The main lines of the two myths can be established fairly clearly. The first, whose title is unknown, may be called the *Myth of the Kingdom in the Sky*. It tells of a sequence of four divinities – Alalu, Anu, Kumarbi, Skygod – the last of whom has been convincingly identified as the Hurrian-Hittite Teschub. This is a succession-myth, in which changes of rule are brought by violence. It is the fate of Anu which particularly attracts our attention. His name is connected with Sumerian 'an'='sky'; and the manner in which he is driven from throne and power reminds us of the castration of Uranus by Cronus. The tablets relate how Anu fled from Kumarbi, who seized him by the feet, bit off his genitals and swallowed them. This brought on him Kumarbi's curse, that he should be pregnant with three dreadful deities. One of these is the skygod, who wrests power from Kumarbi in the next phase of world history. How he did so we do not know: the text is missing here. The second myth is called the *Song of Ullikummi*. In it Kumarbi finds an

---

[1] F. WORMS, 'Der Typheous-Kampf in Hesiods Theogonie'. *Herm.* 81, 1953, 29. The hymn to Hecate is defended by B. A. VAN GRONINGEN (*v. inf.*) 267, the fight with Typhoeus by H. SCHWABL, *Serta Phil. Aenipontana*. Innsbr. 1961, 71, who promises a larger-scale investigation.

[2] H. OTTEN, 'Mythen vom Gotte Kumarbi'. *D. Ak. d. Wiss. Berl. Inst. f. Orientf.* 3, 1950, G. GÜTERBOCK, 'The Song of Ullikummi'. *The Amer. Schools of Oriental Research*. New Haven 1952. A. LESKY, *Eranos* 52, 1954, 8; *Saeculum* 6, 1955, 35. On the whole complex of problems see F. DORNSEIFF, *Antike und alter Orient*. Leipz. 1956.

avenger in the dreadful monster Ullikummi, and the gods of the new régime are hard put to it to overcome this threat. This diorite monster is rather different from the serpent-footed, fire-breathing Typhoeus of Greek legend, but here as there the new ruler of the world, the conqueror armed with the thunderbolt, has to face a desperate struggle to defend his throne. A particular interest in this connection attaches to the texts from Ras Shamra,[1] the ancient Ugarit in northern Syria, which restored the credit of an author long suspected of forgery. Philo of Byblus, a Greek-speaking littérateur of the Hadrianic period, wrote among many other works a *Phoenician History* (Φοινικικά), in which he referred to the work of one Sanchuniathon who is alleged to have lived before the Trojan war. In his *Praeparatio Evangelica* Eusebius gives some long fragments of cosmogony from the first book of Philo's history. For a long time Philo was reckoned a swindler who had stolen his material from Hesiod's *Theogony*. But a different complexion was put on the case by the appearance in the Ras Shamra tablets – coming from 1400–1200, the times of the alleged Sanchuniathon – of myths and cult texts agreeing with various of Philo's statements. In these tablets also we have a near eastern myth of successive divine rulers, which, despite individual variants, belongs essentially to the class we have described. More recently the 'creation-myth' of the Babylonians (called *Enuma eliš* from its opening words) has been recognized as a particularly old representative of this type of myth.[2]

All these striking discoveries have proved beyond doubt that Hesiod's narrative of Uranus, Cronus and Zeus is in the main stream of an ancient tradition. The Hittite and Ras Shamra texts belong to the same tradition, but its origin is now lost to us. How was it brought to Greece? There are two possibilities: that the Phoenicians were intermediaries, or that Greeks in Asia Minor (say around Miletus or Rhodes, where they had been established since Mycenaean times) learned the succession-myth and others from their neighbours. We must be careful not to simplify the problem unrealistically: we must remember that Hesiod may have been in touch with old traditions going back to pre-Hellenic times, and that Boeotia would have been the most likely place for such survivals. For the *Theogony* we must suppose a multiple tradition, which is expressed in the heterogeneous nature of its contents. And we should not forget that Hesiod's father came from Asia Minor.

One feature may be mentioned which clearly shows how closely Hesiod adheres to ancient tradition. In relating the history of Uranus and Cronus the *Theogony* exhibits several individual features. The children of Uranus and Gaea are hated by their father from the first. As soon as they are born he conceals them in a hollow in the earth. The earth, resenting this treatment, causes iron to grow, and with it she makes a sickle-shaped knife (the *harpe* of the Near East), which Cronus uses to emasculate his father as he is about to have intercourse

[1] C. H. GORDON, *Ugaritic Literature*. Rome 1949. K. MRAS, 'Sanchuniathon'. *Anz. Oest. Ak. Phil.-hist. Kl.* 1952, 175. Text of Herennius Philo in *F Gr Hist* III C2, 802–804.

[2] G. STEINER, *Der Sukzessionsmythos in Hesiods 'Theogonie' und ihren orientalischen Parallelen*. Diss. Hamb. 1958 (typewritten); id., *Ant. u. Abendl.* 6, 1957, 171.

with Gaea. Here we have a myth of the separation of heaven and earth that recurs all over the world,[1] and which is represented in the Hittite texts that we have mentioned. At the same time this episode brings out clearly an important element in the *Theogony* as a whole. Uranus and Gaea are deities who think and act and are accordingly thought of in anthropomorphic terms. But at the same time they stand for sky and earth as parts of the physical world: Uranus conceals the children in a hollow in Gaea, and Gaea brings iron into existence. This complete fluidity of the boundaries between the concrete natural phenomenon and the anthropomorphic picture of the gods is characteristic of archaic Greek thought in general and of Hesiod in particular. In the realm of the so-called 'lower mythology', with its rivers and river-gods, mountains and mountain-gods, woods and wood-nymphs, the old ways of thought lasted a long time; and Hellenistic sophistication – with Ovid treading in its footsteps – found here many opportunities for light-hearted invention.

Such new discoveries as these have given impetus to the search for ancient tradition as a component part of the *Theogony*. But the importance of such elements should not be overstated. On the contrary, the new material has at last enabled us to fix upon Hesiod's own achievement as the decisive factor in the poem. His original contribution is not always easy to define, but the individual tone of many passages and the forceful way in which they are presented make us think that we must recognize here the original genius of the author.

Above all, Hesiod takes a great step forward from the succession-myth as known to us from the Near East. In the *Theogony* the theme is not the bare succession of different divine rulers, but an evolution leading up to Zeus. The Olympian sky-god is no vulgar tyrant, as the others were: in him a great and everlasting ordinance is fulfilled. Early in the poem (73) the author shows awareness of such an ordinance and of the distribution of spheres of power among the immortals. The victory of Zeus over Cronus and the Titans confirms this ordinance, and thus the *Titanomachia* is the culminating point of the poem. In putting this valuation upon the governance of Zeus Hesiod goes a great deal farther than Homer. The scenes of married strife in Olympus would presumably have been taken by Hesiod as exemplifying the falsehood spread by the Muses. With him a line of development begins which is to culminate in the sublime Aeschylean conception of Zeus. But he did not in consequence regard this world as the best of all possible. The profound pessimism which he consistently displays in the *Erga* is lurking in the background of the *Theogony* also, as we shall soon see. We can recognize here two opposite tendencies whose conflict imparts a constant movement to both poems.

The story of the succession, Uranus-Cronus-Zeus, in the deeper meaning which Hesiod gave it, forms a basic element to the *Theogony*. But how vast the material is in which it is embedded! After the prooemium, when the poet begins his narration, he tells of the origin of the world. At the beginning of his cosmogony stands Chaos. It was not until much later that this word acquired the meaning of lawlessness and confusion. We should avoid any speculation that tries to turn

---

[1] W. STAUDACHER, *Die Trennung von Himmel und Erde*. Diss. Tübingen 1942.

Hesiod's chaos into some startling abstraction. This tendency began as early as Aristotle (*Phys.* 4. 1. 208b28), who took *chaos* to mean 'space'. But in Hesiod nothing more is meant than the yawning deep (χάος from χαίνω) as the origin of all things: a conception which recurs in oriental cosmogonies and is certainly not an invention of Hesiod's.[1]

Another indication that Hesiod is working here with borrowed elements is the often fragmentary nature of his story. 'First came Chaos into existence...': whence it came we are not told. And when the earth, the scene of the later events, and Eros make their appearance, all that seems clear is that they arose of their own, not by an act of creation. Eros also – as we can infer from Philo's *Pothos* – is derived from ancient speculative cosmogonies: certainly Hesiod has not made a great cosmic deity out of the god whom men worshipped in the form of a stone at neighbouring Thespiae.

Now the sequence of begetting and pairing begins. Chaos gives birth to Erebus (darkness) and Night. The union of the two gives rise to their opposites Aether (the pure upper air) and Day. Earth in her turn gives rise to the starry heaven, the mountains and the raging sea. Hesiod goes out of his way to tell us that the last was produced without sexual union; but it was so also with the heavens and the mountains.

The births now follow each other more and more swiftly. Eros is not credited with any progeny, but we may assume his activity in all the couplings, despite Hesiod's silence. The increasing posterity is divided into three branches: the descendants of Night, of Uranus and Gaea, and of the Sea. The second and third groups interbreed extensively; the first remains sharply set apart from them.

As the number of the entities increases, so the main lines of cosmogony recede into the background. Hesiod does not in fact devote any more space to coming-to-be; rather to the explanation of the existing, to the representing of the beings and powers of this world. For this purpose the genealogical scheme[2] remains the dominating form. His explanations range from the purely superficial to such significant strokes as making Eris (strife) the mother of Sorrow, Oblivion, Hunger and Pain.

The central place is still occupied by the progeny of Uranus and Gaea, leading through Cronus and the Titans to Zeus. For the rest, the poem is like a timber-framed house, with a bewildering multiplicity of uprights, crossbeams, braces and struts. In this attempted picture of the world myth and reality are inextricably interwoven; or more accurately, the age was one which saw the reality of the universe only in the shape of myth. The statement frequently made that Hesiod represents the beginning of Greek philosophy can only be accepted with great reservations.

This is not to say that such a poem could not be a vehicle for philosophy. The opposite is in fact shown by the progeny of Night. Among them (211 ff.) Hesiod numbers all those formless powers that work so much suffering in human life: the powers of death, Reproach, Poverty, Wrath, Deceit, Age and

---

[1] On the representation of chaos: U. HÖLSCHER, *Herm.* 81, 1953, 398.
[2] P. PHILIPPSON, 'Genealogie als mythische Form'. *Symb. Osl. Suppl.* 7, 1936.

Strife with her frightful brood. A hint of such a conception may be found in the *Iliad*, as in the words of Agememnon in 19. 91 about Ate (fatal blindness), or in Phoenix's allegory of the *Litae* (prayers) in 9. 502; but Hesiod goes much farther and opens to us a social milieu in which the darker side of life was more immediately and deeply experienced than among the nobility.

We mistake the sense of this archaic poetry if in this and similar passages we talk of personification.[1] In the phenomena of the world, in the forces that actuated them and in the relations between them, the Greek of this period had an immediate perception of divine power. A striking example is provided by the recognition scene in Euripides' *Helen*, where the husband and wife cry (560): 'O gods! For a god is it to find again one's love.'

The section which we have considered well illustrates how freely Hesiod applies his chosen system of division. Among the children of night we also find Sleep – assuredly no evil in itself, but mentioned by Homer as the brother of Death, and associated with night-time. Even less expected in this company are the Hesperides. The reason for their inclusion is quite superficial: they guard the golden apples on the far side of Ocean; hence they belong to the west, the realm of Night (275). We may easily see why Love (Philotes) rubs shoulders with Deceit. Hesiod was sternly critical of women: in the *Erga* (375) he observes that anyone who trusts a woman, trusts a betrayer – an anticipation of the misogyny of Semonides. A similar attitude makes the point of the story about the punishment of Prometheus, son of the Titan Iapetus (521). In the division of a sacrifice he cheated Zeus, giving him only bones and fat. But according to old legends (although the Muses are capable of lying) in fact Zeus was well aware of the deceit, and avenged himself on the human race by withholding the gift of fire. When Prometheus stole it for them, he had the Titan chained and riveted to a crag where an eagle devoured his liver. In due course Heracles killed the eagle and freed Prometheus – not of course without the will of Zeus, as the pious poet insists. But thereupon Zeus sent woman into the world, formed by the gods to be a beautiful evil, first of a useless and idle race of women, a plague to men.

Among the progeny of Earth and Sea we find such personal deities as the Titans or the old man of the sea, Nereus with his lovely daughters, such fabulous monsters as the Cyclopes and the hundred-handed Briareus, or again such natural phenomena as the sun, moon, dawn and the winds. In reading of the great family of the rivers, which are listed by name (337), we are again dealing with entities halfway between concrete phenomena and anthropomorphic divinities.

Presumably so systematic a genealogy must be mostly the poet's own work. We see him most clearly when he remodels old conceptions so as to display the world as the scene of action by divine powers. To speak of Hesiod as a pure pessimist would be to misunderstand him. He sees the world as full of the children of Night, plaguing humanity; but his language here as in the *Erga* bids them a

---

[1] L. PETERSEN, *Zur Geschichte der Personifikation*. Würzburg 1939. K. REINHARDT, 'Personifikation und Allegorie'. *Vermächtnis der Antike*. Göttingen 1960, 7.

sturdy defiance. Lies and falsehood, sickness and hunger lie in wait for mankind, but there are also good powers which sustain and bless. These powers are grouped around Zeus.

The Seasons are ancient forces of nature, by which things are ripened and made beautiful. The names given to them – Thallo, Auxo and Carpo – identified them with flowering, growth and fruition. But Hesiod brings them wholly into the realm of moral powers. Zeus begat them together with Themis (righteousness): their names are Eunomia, Dike and Eirene – Lawfulness, Right and Peace. The Graces also, Aglaia, Euphrosyne and Thalia, are children of Zeus, and they shed around him brightness, happiness and enjoyment. Mnemosyne (memory) bore him the nine Muses, the bringers of wisdom and learning, as they declare themselves in the opening of the *Theogony*. The poet's thought develops further in what follows. Before the decisive battle, Zeus promises everlasting honour to the deities who will fight on his side. After the victory Styx gives him her children to be his inseparable companions. Their names (384) are Ardour and Victory, Strength and Force. Neither good nor bad in themselves, these powers are now ranged with Zeus and associated with his enduring empire. Before the great battle he also freed three Cyclopes from the chains into which Uranus had thrown them. Their names are Thunder, Lightning and Brightness. It is they who give him the weapons with which he wields his powerful sway in the universe. Thus both the powers of beauty and light and those of darkness and fear are for ever linked to Zeus.

The union of Zeus and Themis produces not only the Seasons, but other and still more important progeny. Themis bears him the Fates (Moirai, v. 904), which bring good or bad luck to men. Thus the goddesses of fate are affiliated to Zeus, and an answer is given (at least where precedence is concerned) to the old question of the relation between the personal deities and an impersonal fate.

Formal analysis of the *Theogony* recently took an important step forward with the work of Hans Schwabl,[1] who has found in one section of the *Titanomachia* a number of recurring patterns (which can hardly be accidental) in words and themes. He has not followed the lead of O. F. Gruppe or G. Hermann in trying to force the whole poem into a framework of stanzas, but he has succeeded in showing a tendency towards ten-verse units in the part that he has studied. Structural analysis of this kind shows the great difference between Homeric and Hesiodic hexameter poetry. At the same time it gives fresh grounds for defending the text against too facile assumptions of interpolation. It is nevertheless very hard to explain the phenomena for which Schwabl has made out this prima facie case. Rhythmic principles must be involved which we find difficult to grasp; and no doubt the musical element (as something perceived by the mind's ear) played a larger part than we would readily suppose. The fact that Hesiod was working with a stock of formal elements provided by the epic tradition may have contributed in some way to this peculiar type of

---

[1] 'Beobachtungen zur Poesie des Hesiod.' (*Theog.* 29-42; 829-835; 617-724) *Serta Philol. Aenipontana.* Innsbr. 1961, 69.

composition. Recent misconceptions[1] make it necessary to say once more that the part played by formulae in Hesiod does not instantly make him an 'oral poet'.

In the *Erga* we are dealing with a work of the most singular nature. The poem is commonly called the 'Works and Days', although the section on the choice of appropriate days cannot be assigned to Hesiod. The genuine part can only be called a didactic poem if we make allowance for all the archaic qualities of profusion and variety. The sequence of thought is rather like that in the *Theogony*, but to a more marked degree. One can see the connection between one step and the next, but any firm main lines of composition are lacking. The poem darts hither and thither; yet certain ideas do recur with some frequency and emphasis.

In the first part of the *Erga* the inner structure is determined by two antitheses. The occasion of the poem is nominally a particular circumstance: the dispute between Hesiod and his brother Perses over the division of their father's land. The poet has had unhappy experience of the justice of aristocratic owners. But the particular here is only an excuse for the general, and Hesiod plunges into a discussion of all the powers to which human life is subject. The second antithesis is one which we met in the *Theogony*, and it holds a central position in Hesiod's thought: the conflict in the poet's mind between a pessimistic view of the world and a pious belief in absolute moral values.

The *Theogony* is essentially a glorification of the might of Zeus; and it is with a hymn to Zeus that the *Erga* opens. It is nothing new to be told that the god has the power to raise and to cast down; but when we read that he 'straightens the crooked without difficulty', we are brought into touch with two fundamental notions of archaic ethical terminology. One of the characteristic notes is struck when the poet calls upon Zeus to establish the rule of justice. The last line of the prooemium declares Hesiod's intention to teach his brother the truth; and in consequence he repeatedly thereafter turns aside from his general treatment to address him in person.

In the *Theogony* (225) Hesiod numbered among the children of Night the goddess of strife, Eris. Now he gives striking indication how steady and persevering his thought-processes were: he corrects himself—characteristically in the form of a myth. It was wrong, he says, to speak of one Eris: in fact there are two, of very different qualities. The one is evil and is sent by the gods to plague mankind; it is she who stirs up quarrels and warfare. The good Eris, however, has been sunk by Zeus deep in the earth, so that she should become a living force active among men. This Eris is honourable competition, which makes the achievement of one man act as a stimulus to another to equal or (more truly Greek) to surpass him.

This is the point of departure for the two basic ideas of the poem. Perses ought to abandon the evil strife between the two brothers. This introduces

---

[1] A. HOEKSTRA, 'Hésiode et la tradition orale. Contribution à l'étude du style formulaire'. *Mnem.* s. 4, 10, 1957, 193. J. A. NOTOPULOS, 'Homer, Hesiod and the Achaean Heritage of Oral Poetry'. *Hesperia* 29, 1960, 177.

what Hesiod has to say about the power and value of justice. Perses ought to be directed by the power of the good Eris into gaining his livelihood by honest toil. This leads to the section on the life and work of the peasant.

Toil and hardship have been decreed once for all as the lot of man: the gods have denied him an easy inheritance. This state of affairs is explained by two myths, partly complementing each other. Just as in the myth of the two Erides, we see here Hesiod's mind grappling with the problems of human life. Certainly the myths could hardly have been intended to claim unqualified credence as factual narrative.

The poet takes up again the story which he had told in the *Theogony* about Prometheus' theft of fire and its punishment by Zeus who sent woman onto the earth. Here he takes the story further. Woman was made by Hephaestus out of earth and fire; all the gods endowed her with captivating and dangerous gifts. In consequence she received the name Pandora (in all probability this was the name of an ancient earth-goddess). Despite the warnings of Prometheus, Epimetheus received the bewitching stranger. When she opened the lid of the box (*pithos*) that she presumably brought with her (we are not told where it came from), out flew every evil and plague to infest the world. Hope alone was left in the box when Pandora shut it again. A great many subtle interpretations of this passage have been put forward, but the explanation is quite plain. Hope is naturally meant as a blessing for suffering humanity. As such it has its place in a parable like that told by Achilles in *Iliad* 24. 527 of the two jars in the palace of Zeus, which contain good and evil respectively. The closing of the jar containing good things means the withholding of them; the opening of the other means the release of evils upon the world. In Hesiod's story of Pandora the two have become fused, and some obscurity has been caused thereby.[1]

The miseries of the world form the subject of another of Hesiod's myths. He depicts five successive ages in which the human lot becomes steadily worse. Such a view of history is in the sharpest contrast to the evolutionary optimism that we shall find in the age of the Greek enlightenment. Four of the ages are associated with metals. The first or golden age is that of Cronus, from which, by way of silver and brazen ages, one descends to the age of iron, in which we are condemned to live. The myth stands by itself and apart: Cronus as the beginning of a steady decline from paradisal conditions is irreconcilable with the picture in the *Theogony*, in which there is an upward trend to the reign of Zeus. The myth can hardly have been Hesiod's own invention, as is shown by the difficulties that it gives him. His age was still strongly influenced by the epics with their tales of the heroic deeds of ancient days. On all sides were cults of heroes; even their graves were pointed out. Hesiod could hardly assign such

[1] A. LESKY, *Wien. Stud.* 55, 1937, 21. Different interpretation: H. FRÄNKEL, *Wege und Formen frühgriechischen Denkens.* 2nd ed. Munich 1960, 329 (slightly modified in the *Festschr. f. Reitzenstein* 1931). O. LENDLE, *Die Pandorasage bei Hesiod.* Würzburg 1957; cf. J. H. KÜHN, *Gnom.* 31, 1957, 114, and G. BROCCIA, *La parola del passato* 62, 1958, 296. Pandora's 'box' is a Renaissance myth going back to Erasmus: D. and E. PANOFSKY, *Pandora's Box.* New York 1956, 15.

figures to the brazen age, which destroyed itself by its own lawless violence. Thus he had to interpolate between the brazen and iron ages an age of heroes who fought before Thebes and Troy, of whom many after their death still enjoyed a blessed existence on the margins of the world. This adjustment involves a breaking of the sequence of ages and metals at one point. If we add the consideration that the connection of the metals with the several ages is rather superficial, we shall be the more ready to postulate a foreign origin of the myth. In all probability near eastern influences are at work here also.[1]

Hesiod throws his main energies into depicting the miseries of the iron age, in which we live. It is here that the evils of Pandora's box, sickness and all the other hardships, find their culmination in the moral depravity of this generation, which aims at the breaking of all restraints and at universal licence. Its fate will be sealed when Aidos (sense of shame) and Nemesis (righteous anger) leave the world.

Neither in Hesiod nor elsewhere does Greek pessimism imply a resigned scepticism. The poet sees a light shining beyond all the darkness; and in the succeeding sections he makes it cast a radiance that spreads far into the spiritual history of the Greek people. He expresses this confidence in v. 276 ff.: for fish, beast and fowl Zeus has appointed an existence based on mutual slaughter; but for man he has provided a means of avoiding this battle of each against all. Its name is Justice.[2] There is the force of religious conviction in Hesiod's persuasion of the holiness, the indestructibility, the saving power of Dike; and this conception becomes one of the basic themes of Greek thought and literature. Here again we must be on guard against taking Dike as a personification. Rather, Dike is the anthropomorphic expression of that divine power which is felt to be at work in every righteous judgment and in justice as an absolute value.

To this picture of the miseries of the iron age Hesiod significantly subjoins the earliest animal-fable in European literature – the nightingale whose moans are useless in the talons of the hawk. Here the opposite of justice is brought before us: the unreflecting violence ($ὕβρις$) against which he warns Perses. It is good for a man to honour Dike, for her power is great. The poet speaks of her in impressive images, which dissolve one into another in the archaic manner. She laments loudly when gift-devouring men, corrupt rulers, try to turn her aside from her way. Wrapped in mist, she brings mischief to the men who have banished her, and she accuses them before Zeus of the wickedness they have done. In this poem also Hesiod's philosophy is fulfilled in the supreme deity. Zeus sees all (267), yet he has also appointed 30,000 watchers over the human race: the spirits of those who lived in the Golden Age. In the juxtaposition of these various conceptions we see again the freedom which the mythological treatment allowed. The contrast of the righteous city, prosperous in all

---

[1] R. REITZENSTEIN, 'Altgr. Theologie und ihre Quellen'. *Vortr. Bibl. Warburg* 4, Leipz. 1929.

[2] E. WOLF, *Griechisches Rechtsdenken* I. Frankf. a. M. 1950, 120 – a large-scale work dealing with a central concern in Greek thought, but rather unequal in its interpretations. K. LATTE 'Der Rechtsgedanke im archaischen Griechentum'. *Ant. u. Abendl.* 2, 1946, 63.

things, with the unrighteous, in which hunger, disease and war are the rulers, also belongs to this great group of images built around the figure of Dike.

It would be wrong to class Hesiod as a social revolutionary. Certainly in him the sufferings of the small peasants find expression, having been previously unheard; certainly he sets up the ideal of justice and honourable toil against the pride of status shown by an aristocracy of birth: but he does so not in order to change the social structure of his day, but to heal and purify it by the standards of an absolute morality.

At the beginning of the passage about Dike Hesiod addressed himself emphatically to Perses. With the archaic device of framing, he now addresses him again at the end. This time he continues his exhortations by representing labour as a god-given necessity for men: he speaks of the sweat which the gods demand of the industrious before granting them success. Then follows a string of injunctions in concrete terms directed towards relations with gods and men, leading finally to the description of the peasant's year and its demands which occupy vv. 381-617. We can hardly say that Hesiod has now reached his real subject, since all this section can be taken as an elaboration and amplification of the injunction to Perses that he should work hard. We ought rather to bear in mind the peculiarities and the freedom of archaic composition. The consequence is that we have here, not a systematic instruction in husbandry, but a mixture of practical advice and hints from general experience. The whole is certainly still poetry, as we are reminded by such pictures as those of summer joys and winter hardships. He has a sympathy with the animal kingdom too.[1] The harsher side of peasant life and labour is never glossed over or disguised, but for this very reason it is here in the first poem of rustic life in European literature, that a true value is assigned to the work that wins us our bread.

An interesting light is thrown on the economic structure of that day by Hesiod's including some advice on seafaring (618-694), although he has neither experience nor inclination (cf. 650). The poem then dissolves into a series of detached pieces of advice: the right age to marry, how to behave towards one's friends, and the like. Among these we find a number of maxims which in their form and in their narrow superstitious spirit are so strikingly at variance with their context that they cannot be assigned to Hesiod. The same may be said of the final section, on the choosing of the right days, interesting as it is for the history of religion.

The *Theogony* ends with the announcement of a new theme. The poet promises to sing of women whom the gods made into mothers of great peoples. This ending was a device of the rhapsodes to effect a transition to a poem which was very influential in antiquity and was almost universally reckoned[2] as a genuine work of Hesiod's. It is referred to as the *Catalogue*, or *Catalogue of Women* or *Ehoiai* (*Eoae*): the last title because each new heroine's story begins

---

[1] On the sepia, the 'boneless one' who gnaws his own foot in the idle winter time, see J. WIESNER's excellent article in *Arch. Jahrb.* 74, 1959, 48.

[2] An exception is Paus. 9, 31, 4, who says that the Boeotians on Helicon will allow only the *Erga* to be genuine.

with the formula ἢ οἵη 'or like as . . .'. This fact suggests a simple sequential arrangement – the catalogue form inherited from ancient epic poetry. The *Odyssey* has a catalogue in the *Nekyia* (11. 235-330) of women who had noteworthy careers. We have a fair knowledge of what was in the five books of the *Ehoiae*, and particular passages can be reconstructed, notably the story of Coronis, the ill-fated mother of Asclepius,[1] and of Cyrene, whom Apollo carried off from Thessaly to Libya and made the mother of Aristaeus.[2] Some fragments of a *Suitors of Helen* (a catalogue within the catalogue) are preserved in a Berlin papyrus (nr. 380sq. P.), and they give us a good idea of the very unpretentious style. *Ox. Pap.* 23, 1956, nr. 2354 has given us the beginning of the *Ehoiai*.[3]

It is hard to say who wrote the *Ehoiai*, and it would be wrong to pretend that we knew. It is certain that much of it cannot be by Hesiod. The story of Cyrene, for example, must be put after the founding of the colony Cyrene from Thera in 630. It is obvious that a poem dealing with the origins of princely houses offered a standing invitation to the forger. The question is whether there was ever a genuine core to the poem. Since Hesiod practised the trade of a rhapsode, and since the genealogical principle was congenial to his ways of thinking, there seems no good ground for doubting that there was such a core. But we cannot be certain, and the question is not made any simpler by the circulation of a *Great Ehoiai* under Hesiod's name. A poem about Tyro, found in a papyrus (nr. 398 P.) by R. Pfeiffer,[4] has been assigned by him to this latter collection.

An *ehoie* dealing with Alcmena, certainly not by Hesiod, appears as an introductory piece (1-56) to the *Aspis*. This poem of 480 hexameters relates the battle of Heracles (here fighting on behalf of Apollo) with the monster Cycnus, assisted by its father Ares. The poet tried hard for a purple patch in the scene describing the arming of the hero: the account of his shield has given the poem its name. The imitation of Homer is obvious; but whereas the shield of Achilles depicts life in all its variety, in that of Heracles all the horrors of war and the demons of destruction are displayed. A poet of limited gifts has tried to elevate and ennoble a standard feature of epic, but has merely defaced and distorted it. The first *hypothesis* tells us that ancient critics were fiercely divided over its genuineness. It could hardly have imposed upon such a man as Aristophanes of Byzantium. We are surprised, however, to find it accepted by Stesichorus: can this Stesichorus really be the choral lyrist? If so, the *Shield* must have been put about under Hesiod's name by 600 B.C. It is just possible; for Heracles appears here without the club and lion's skin which afterwards became his standard equipment.

---

[1] WILAMOWITZ, *Isyllos von Epidauros*. Berl. 1886. Towards defining the limits of the poem: A. LESKY. *Sitzb. Ak. Wien. Phil.-hist. Kl.* 203/2, 1925, 44.

[2] L. MALTEN, *Kyrene*. Berlin 1911.

[3] Cf. M. TREU, 'Das Proömium der hesiodischen Frauenkataloge'. *Rhein. Mus.* 100, 1957, 169. J. T. KAKRIDIS, Ἑλληνικά 16, 1958, 219. On pap. Berol. 7497 + *Ox. Pap.* 421: K. STIEWE, 'Zum Hesiodpapyrus B Merkelbach'. *Herm.* 88, 1960, 253. MERKELBACH's edition of the papyri and J. SCHWARTZ' book are listed below.

[4] *Phil.* 92, 1937, 1.

Fate treated Homer and Hesiod much the same. Under the latter's name we hear of a great many works, known now mostly by title alone. The attribution is understandable where the *Maxims of Chiron* (Χίρωνος ὑποθῆκαι) are concerned. The wise old Centaur, the specialist in the training of heroes, was ideally suited to give moral precepts which presumably resembled much that we find in the *Erga*. Geographical and astronomical works also were ascribed to Hesiod (Γῆς περίοδος,[1] 'Αστρονομία): when they were written no one knows. He was also credited with narrative poems, such as an *Aegimius*, dealing with the exploits of Heracles when fighting on the side of that Dorian king. It seems to have included other matters also. A narrative poem of the deeds of Melampus (*Melampodia*) also went under his name; it featured a competition in riddles between Calchas and Mopsus – reminiscent of the *Contest of Homer & Hesiod*. A *Marriage of Ceyx* is also mentioned; but it was probably part of the *Catalogue of Women*. What the *Idaean Dactyls* were we can only guess.

The manuscript tradition is discussed in the large edition of A. RZACH, Leipz. 1902. On the papyrus finds (nr. 360-399 P.) see R. MERKELBACH, *Die Hesiod-fragmente auf Papyrus*. Leipz. 1957 (from *Arch. f. Papyrusf.* 16, 1956): they have been helpful on the *Catalogues*. Small edition by RZACH with app. crit. and fragments, 3rd ed. Leipz. 1913; repr. together with the *Certamen* 1958. With translation: P. MAZON, *Coll. des Un. de Fr.* 1928 (last repr. 1951). H. G. EVELYN-WHITE, *Hesiod, the Homeric Hymns and Homerica* (Loeb Lib.) Lond. 1936. F. JACOBY, *Hesiodi Carmina I. Theogonia.* Berl. 1930 (analytical). Commentary on the *Erga*: P. MAZON, Paris 1914; WILAMOWITZ, Berlin 1928. T. A. SINCLAIR, Lond. 1932. A. Colonna, Milan 1959. A. TRAVERSA, *Catalogi sive Eoarum fragmenta. Collana di stud. gr.* 21. Naples 1951. C. F. RUSSO, *Hesiodi Scutum. Bibl. di Studi sup.* 9. Florence 1950. Scholia: GAISFORD, *Poetae Minores Graeci.* 3rd ed. Oxf. 1820. H. FLACH, *Glossen u. Scholien zur hes. Theog.* Leipzig 1876. A. PERTUSI, *Scholia vetera in Hesiodi opera et dies.* Milan 1955 (these scholia are largely influenced by the Neoplatonist interpretations of Hesiod). J. PAULSON, *Index Hesiodeus.* Lund 1890 (reprint by Olms of Hildesheim 1963). German trans.: TH. V. SCHEFFER, Leipz. 1938. Special studies: INEZ SELLSCHOPP, *Stilistiche Unters. zu Hesiod.* Diss. Hamburg. 1934. F. SCHWENN, *Die Theogonie des Hesiodos.* Heidelberg 1934. H. DILLER, 'Hesiod und die Anfänge der griech. Philosophie'. *Ant. u. Abendl.* 2, 1946, 140. F. SOLMSEN, *Hesiod and Aeschylus.* Ithaca N.Y. 1949. BR. SNELL, *Die Entdeckung des Geistes.* 3rd ed. Hamb. 1955, 65. H. SCHWABL, *Gymn.* 62, 1955, 526: see also p. 99 f. There is an elaborate stylistic analysis of the *Theogony, Erga* and *Shield of Heracles* in B. A. VAN GRONINGEN, *La Composition littéraire archaïque grecque. Verh. Nederl. Akad. N.R.* 65/2. Amsterdam 1958. J. SCHWARZ. *Pseudo-Hesiodea. Recherches sur la composition, la diffusion et la disparition ancienne d'œuvres attribuées à Hésiode.* Leyden 1960. The forthcoming vol. 7 of *Entretiens sur l'antiquité classique.* Fondation Hardt,

---

[1] Did this belong to the *Great Ehoiai*? R. MERKELBACH, *Aegyptus* 31, 1951, 256.

Vandœuvres-Geneva will contain: I. K. V. FRITZ: 'Hesiodisches im Hesiod'. II.
G. S. KIRK: 'Hesiod, the Theogony'. III. W. J. VERDENIUS: 'Die Erga des Hesiod'.
IV. F. SOLMSEN: 'Hesiod and Plato'. V. A. LA PENNA: 'Esiodo e Vergilio'. VI.
P. GRIMAL: 'Hésiode et Properce'. H. MUNDING's book, *Hesiods Erga in ihrem
Verhältnis zur Ilias*. Frankf. a. M. 1959, is full of baseless speculation. On Hesiod's
innovations in form and vocabulary see V. PISANI, *Storia della lingua greca* in
Encicl. class. 2/5/1. Turin 1960, 51.

B Archaic Epic after Hesiod

The surviving works of Greek literature have to be thought of, singly and all
together, as the remains of a vast empire: islands still rising from a sea which
has swallowed up whole countries. There is the more truth in this picture since
it is normally the peaks that still survive.

Corinth, not otherwise productive in the arts, found her epic poet in Eumelus,
a member of the great family of the Bacchiadae, who told the mythical ancient
history of his city in the *Corinthiaca*. The poem had its importance as a source-
book, and it was paraphrased in prose (Paus. 4. 2, 1), just as Hesiod's genealogical
poems were by the logographer Acusilaus. In Eumelus' *Titanomachia* the sea-
god Aegaeon figured as an ally of the Titans.[1] His *Europia* and *Bugonia* are little
more than names; but we have two hexameters of his in the Aeolic dialect, from
a processional hymn written for king Phintas of Messenia on the occasion of a
festival of Apollo. The ancient history of the Argolid was told in the anonymous
Phoronis; the *Naupactica*, attributed to a Carcinus of Naupactus, dealt at some
length with the expedition of the Argonauts, as we learn from the scholia to
Apollonius Rhodius, but this cannot have been its main theme. We may suppose
that poetry of this kind was strongly influenced by Hesiod: of the Laconian
Cinaethon we learn from Pausanias (4. 2, 1) that his epic was genealogical in
structure. The saga of Theseus, backed by Athenian national feeling, competed
with the Heracles-cycle as a subject for epic. Among several indications[2] of this
the most important is in Aristotle (*Poet.* 8. 1451a19): he finds fault with the
writers of epics such as the *Heracleid* or *Theseid* for not limiting their subject
matter as they ought to have done. One has the feeling that he is speaking of
fairly old poems.

The influence of Greek mainland epic made itself felt in the poetry of Greek-
speaking Asia Minor. In the work of Asius genealogies play an important part,
and the popularity of the Heracles-cycle is evinced again and again. A Rhodian
epic on this theme is ascribed to one Pisander. An earlier Pisinus of Lindus, who
also wrote an epic on Heracles, is a very shadowy figure. Poetry of this kind
seems to have come more or less to an end with the fourteen books of the
Heraclea of Panyassis. This poet, born at Halicarnassus, who fell in battle against
the tyrant Lygdamis in 460, was the uncle of the historian Herodotus. His

---

[1] W. KULLMANN, *Das Wirken der Götter in der Ilias*. Berl. 1956, 16, 2; cf. also WILAMOWITZ,
Hellenistische Dichtung 2. Berl. 1924, 241, 2.
[2] L. RADERMACHER, *Mythos und Sage bei den Griechen*. 2nd ed. Vienna 1943, 252.

Heraclea must have been above the average level of such works, since ancient critics (Dion. Hal. *de imit.* 2; Quintil. 10. 1, 54) praised its construction and placed its author together with Homer, Hesiod, Antimachus and Pisander in the canon of the five epic poets. The poems of Pisander and Panyassis must have contributed to the formation of a definite Heracles-cycle; but the notion of twelve labours (the dodecathlos) does not crystallize much before the Hellenistic age.[1] We know almost nothing about Panyassis' *Ionica*, a poem in distichs relating the founding of the Ionian colonies.

The kind of didactic and proverbial style that we meet in Hesiod was continued and developed by Phocylides of Miletus.[2] It is hard to say when he lived: the early sixth century seems most likely. His sayings were in hexameters, with his trade mark καὶ τόδε Φωκυλίδου ('Here's another by Phocylides') at the beginning of each. At some time in the first century of our era a gnomic poem in 230 hexameters was put about under his name. Its author shows knowledge of the Old Testament.

C Early Lyric Poetry

I ORIGINS AND TYPES

Greek lyric poetry has fared much the same as Greek epic. Here again we find creations of a supreme artistry, never afterwards rivalled: here again there are many earlier stages which are lost to us: we can only prove that they existed. In dealing with the beginnings of Greek poetry (p. 13) we had to consider the many types of song attested in the Homeric poems. This approach enables us to recognize many of the origins of lyric poetry, which among the Greeks were basically the same as among other peoples. An important role is played by cult: the Achaeans placate the wrath of Apollo by the paean (*Il.* 1. 372); his sister is honoured by maidens in song and dance (*Il.* 16. 182). Cult also has its part in the songs which accompany marriage or death: the bride hears the *hymenaios* (*Il.* 18. 493); the long lamentations of the *threnos* echo round the death-bed of Hector or Patroclus.

There is another important fountain-head of lyric poetry (not quite, however, to be reckoned all-important) which we meet in Homer: the work-song. When goddesses like Calypso or Circe sing at their weaving, they are behaving just like mortal women. In the shield of Achilles a boy sings the Linus-song to accompany the work of the vintagers. Songs for all occasions were known to the ancients, from water-carrying to bread-baking. A tiny fragment (*Carm. pop.* nr. 30 D.) – a little Lesbian song at meal-time – which can be dated roughly by its mention of Pittacus, gives us some conception of the mass that has perished.

In the third place we must rank folksongs. Such songs certainly existed among the Greeks, as among other peoples, but they were pushed into the background

---

[1] F. BROMMER, *Herakles*. Münster 1953.
[2] Genuine fragments in DIEHL, *Anth. Lyr.* fasc. 1, 3rd ed., 57. Pseudo-Phocylides (vv. 5–79 recur as *Orac. Sibyl.* 2, 56–148) ibid. fasc. 2, 3rd ed., 91 and D. YOUNG, *Theognis*. Leipz. 1961, 95.

by high poetry. Many of these folksongs were tied to particular usages:[1] we might almost speak of cult at a lower level. We have already mentioned the *Eiresione* (p. 90): to it we may now add the Rhodian begging song (*Carm. pop.* nr. 32 D.), in which the children pretend to be swallows, and if they are refused a gift, comically threaten to fly away with the door or the housewife herself. The Hellenistic age took a great interest in such things, and Phoenix of Colophon wrote his *Song of the Crows* (fr. 2 D.)[2] wholly in the folksong tradition. There were also popular songs giving simple expression to personal feeling. If Sappho is indeed the authoress of the little poem (94 D.)[2] in which a girl laments being alone at night, then she looked to folksong for her inspiration; but more likely it is a folksong itself. Much in Sappho's *Marriage Poems* is influenced from this source; but in the Locrian aubade (*Carm. pop.* nr. 43 D.) it is doubtful whether we can assume a folk origin. In discussing the individual types we shall have something to say about the origin of each; but first we must consider the classification.

The lyric as an idea striving for realization within a defined form of composition[3] is not found in ancient theories of art.[4] The term 'lyric' (λυρικός) is a Hellenistic coinage, and expressed a definite and concrete notion: poetry accompanied by the lyre. When the Alexandrians made up a canon of nine lyric poets, comprising the masters of personal lyric Alcaeus, Sappho and Anacreon and the choral lyrists Alcman, Stesichorus, Ibycus, Simonides, Bacchylides and Pindar, they had in mind any poetry that was meant to be accompanied by stringed instruments (λύρα, φόρμιγξ, κίθαρις)[5] or by the flute, either separately or in combination. The term is used in the same sense in the treatise περὶ λυρικῶν of Didymus, who in this respect as in others served as a bridge between the Alexandrians and imperial Rome.

It emerges from what has been said that the ancient conception of lyric poetry embraced two important types – the choral lyric and the individual lyric sung to the lyre; although the distinction between the two, which seems to us so important, did not seem so to the ancients. At the same time we see that two types which we think of today as lyrical were not included – namely elegiac and iambic poetry. We may suppose that in both of these forms singing was given up fairly early, while lyric (in the old sense of melic) poetry presupposed singing. Where elegy is concerned, there is another important difference: the accompanying instrument was the flute (αὐλός), and thus it was

---

[1] L. RADERMACHER, *Aristophanes' Frösche. Sitzb. Oest. Ak. Phil.-hist. Kl.* 198/4, 2nd ed., 1954, 7 f.

[2] It is attributed to Sappho by B. MARZULLO, *Studi di poesia eolica.* Florence 1958; cf. A. W. GOMME, *Journ. Hell. Stud.* 77, 1957, 265; 78, 1958, 85.

[3] E. STAIGER, *Grundbegriffe der Poetik.* 4th ed. Zürich 1959.

[4] H. FÄRBER, *Die Lyrik in der Kunsttheorie der Antike.* Munich 1936.

[5] On instruments, modes etc.: C. SACHS, *Die Musik der Antike. Handb. d. Musikwiss.* Potsdam 1928. Id., *Handbuch der Musikinstrumentenkunde.* 2nd ed. Leipz. 1932. H. HUCHZERMEYER, *Aulos und Kithara.* Diss. Münster 1931. J. W. SCHOTTLÄNDER, *Die Kithara.* Diss. Berl. 1933. O. GOMBOSI, *Tonarten und Stimmungen der antiken Musik.* Copenhagen 1939. M. WEGNER, *Das Musikleben der Griechen.* Berl. 1949. A. E. HARVEY, 'The Classification of Greek Lyric Poetry'. *Class. Quart. N.S.* 5, 1955, 157. R. P. WINNINGTON-INGRAM, 'Ancient Greek Music 1932-1957'. *Lustrum* 1958/3 (1959), 5.

formally excluded from the class of lyric poetry. The iambos, as we learn from Athenaeus (14. 636 B), might be accompanied by such stringed instruments as the *iambyke* and the *klepsiambos*; but this seems not to have been usual. It is interesting, however, that Theocritus (*epigr.* 21) praises Archilochus as an iambic poet and as a singer to the lyre. Xenophon (*Symp.* 6. 3) speaks of the recitation of trochaic tetrameters to the flute.

This classification of accompanying instruments must not be made too hard and fast. The flute and lyre make their appearance (albeit separately) in the Cretan cultural sphere, on the sarcophagus of Hagia Triada. The wedding scene on the shield of Achilles (*Il.* 18. 495) shows them used together to accompany the dancing of boys and girls. Greek choral poetry, despite its 'lyric' character, could not dispense with the flute as an accompanying instrument. We can learn a good deal from the history of the Delphic festival. There the citharodic *nomos*, a ritual song for a single voice, had long been established. In 582 the competitions were widened to include *aulodike* (singing to the flute) and *auletike* (solo flute-playing). One celebrated piece was the *Pythian nome* of the Argive Sacadas, a song with flute accompaniment depicting Apollo's conflict with the Python. Not long afterwards (558) the lyre played by itself, without any singing, was allowed to compete in the citharistic contests.[1]

It was a foregone conclusion that the two instruments should come into technical competition. A choral lyrist (Stesichorus fr. 25 D.) speaks significantly of the flute 'rich in strings', and Plato (*Leg.* 3. 700 D) condemns the folly of those who try on the lyre to imitate the flute. The stringed instrument, weaker in volume and restricted in the number of notes (it had no fingerboard) was at a great disadvantage compared with the aulos or double flute. But the competition was not purely on a technical level. The lyre was reckoned the aristocratic instrument, and the flute as a thrusting parvenu. Alcibiades refused to learn it (*Alc.* I. 106 E). The ritual associations of each instrument also differed: the lyre belonged to Apollo, the shrill tones of the flute to the orgiastic cults. Consequently flute music was much encouraged by the great wave of Dionysiac enthusiasm in the archaic period. It is against this background that we must see the story of Apollo's contest with Marsyas. This same 'battle of the instruments', with its social and religious implications, explains also the attempt to assign as early a date as possible to the Phrygian flute-teacher Olympus: he was even reckoned older than Homer (Suidas s.v. Olympus).

Ancient subdivisions of lyric poetry, such as we find in Photius (319b. B), are purely mechanical, but they provide a number of individual notices, to many of which we shall refer in the following sections.

2 IAMBOS

According to the statement of Pausanias (10. 28, 3), when Polygnotus was painting his celebrated picture of the underworld for the council-hall of the

---

[1] For the historical background of the subdivisions of lyric poetry and for their development we have now A. R. BURN's book *The Lyric Age of Greece.* Lond. 1960. There is useful material on the language of individual genres and writers in V. PISANI, *Storia della lingua greca. Encicl. Class.* 2/5/1. Turin 1960.

Cnidians at Delphi, he depicted Tellis and Cleoboea crossing the river of the dead. In both these figures he was alluding to the history of his native Thasos. Telesicles (Tellis is a hypocoristic form) founded the colony of Thasos from Paros: he was an ancestor – Pausanias says the great-grandfather – of Archilochus. The Cleoboea depicted with him brought over the mysteries of Demeter in the track of the first colonists. In Paros, which was once called Demetrias, there was an ancient mystery cult of the goddess. At the end of the Homeric hymn to Demeter the island is spoken of as belonging to the goddess.[1] It is significant that the culmination of iambic poetry should have come from such a cultural background as this; for it is there that we must look for the origins of this particular form. In fertility-cults a very widespread feature is coarse, often violently obscene, invective. Such expression of ugliness, just as much as visual display of it, was in the last analysis intended to ward off evil. This kind of apotropaic obscenity was used in the iambos, so that to speak in iambs came to mean the same as to abuse or revile.[2] Indications of the part played by such invective in the cult of Demeter are the figure of the girl Iambe, whose jokes amuse the mourning goddess, and the γεφυρισμοί of the procession to Eleusis.

The poet who turned this traditional cult-element into a great artistic form without blunting its cutting edge, was Archilochus of Paros. Various topical allusions in his poems, notably one to Gyges in fr. 22 D., make it plain that the eclipse of the sun which he mentions (fr. 74 D.) was that of April 6th 648 B.C. Attempts at an earlier or a later dating have not been able to shake this identification,[3] which gives us our first precise date in Greek literature. Thus Archilochus lived in the great age of colonization, an age of vigorous intellectual movement, which did not leave unchallenged the status and ideas of the aristocracy. But if to us he appears as being in revolt against traditional values to a degree far transcending the particular issues of his time, the explanation lies in his origins. Archilochus was a bastard. His father was called Telesicles, like his celebrated ancestor the colonist of Thasos; his mother, he tells us, was a slave named Enipo. Critias, the complete Junker, was outraged by the freedom with which Archilochus spoke of things which were shameful and disgraceful by aristocratic standards (VS 88B 44); and it is from him that we hear that the poet left Paros in dire poverty to go to Thasos, where again he made enemies. He earned a living abroad as a mercenary: in a pithy couplet (1 D.) he describes himself as gifted by the Muses and a servant of Ares. He experienced military life in all its aspects, and he may have risen further than we can now establish. He met his death in battle against the Naxians, and a pleasing legend tells us that the Pythia expelled his slayer Calondas from the temple of Apollo.

The external unrest of this career reflects the opposition between the man and his world. Battle was his element, whether he waged it with the spear or the

---

[1] But cf. o. KERN, RE 16, 1271.

[2] E.g. Arist. Poet. 1448 b 32.

[3] E. LÖWY, Anz. Ak. Wien. Phil.-hist. Kl. 70, 1933, 31. 557 B.C.: A. BLAKEWAY in Greek Poetry and Life. Oxf. 1936, 34. 711 B.C.: F. JACOBY in Class. Quart. 35, 1941, 97 (= Kl. Schr. I 249).

pen. Anything that was treated as an unchallengeable assumption by aristocratic circles at once spurred him to contradiction, and tradition meant nothing
to him if he thought it was an illusion which he could see through. In many of
his poems we detect a delight in demolishing cherished fallacies. It is an extraordinary spectacle to see how his whole being drives the seventh-century
mercenary to attack ideas which still flourished generations later.

Fame was of enormous importance to the Greeks. Some saw in it the only
triumph over death. But Archilochus cynically declares that no one enjoys
honour after his death: favour attaches itself only to the living (64 D.). He must
often have experienced the truth expressed in fr. 13 D.: a mercenary is valued
only while the fighting lasts. He candidly tells us (61 D.) the truth behind stories
of great feats on the field: seven of the enemy are slain; a thousand claim to have
killed them.

To the world of Homer the outer and the inner man were inseparably linked.
How accurately externals were observed appears from *Il.* 3. 210, where Antenor
describes the effect produced by Odysseus and Menelaus sitting and standing.
Archilochus deliberately derides such a view (fr. 60 D.). He ridicules the officer
who prides himself on the elegance of his coiffure, and prefers the man who may
be short and bowlegged but has some courage. These words would hardly come
from a man who showed any of the elegance which he derides.

The fiercest of Archilochus' attacks was against the ideals of chivalry as he
had seen them in the lords of Euboea (3 D.), and he embodied it in the poem
(6 D.) which frankly avows the loss of his shield. He abandoned it in battle with
the Saians, in a battle which was to contest the possession of his unloved Thasos
(18; 54 D.) with the Thracians of the mainland. 'Shield-dropper' (ῥίψασπις)
was a word of deadly reproach: Spartan mothers used to send their sons off to
battle with the affectionate injunction, 'Come back either with it or on it!'
Archilochus met with severe censure (e.g. Plut. *Inst. Lac.* 34. 239B) for his
willingness to buy his life at such a price. Yet the same theme is taken up by an
Aeolic aristocrat like Alcaeus (49 D. 428 LP), and possibly by Anacreon also
(51 D.). The theme of *relicta non bene parmula* was admirably suited also to the
spirit in which Horace looked back on the adventure of Philippi.[1]

Themes common to lyric poetry at all times, such as wine and love-making,
occur in Archilochus, but, in keeping with the individual flavour of his writing,
he always gives the concrete experience in all its immediacy, without any touch
of literary convention. He is on watch, and whiles away the tedious hours with
a jar of red wine (5 D.); or he plumes himself on his ability to lead a dithyramb,
the song of the lord Dionysus, when wine is raging like a thunderstorm in his
head (77 D.). We are well informed about his love for Neobule, the daughter
of Lycambes. He speaks of her with a tenderness that scarcely recurs elsewhere
in ancient Greek literature. Only once could he touch Neobule's hand (71 D.).
The beautiful picture of the girl playing with roses and myrtle branches, with
her hair covering her shoulders and back (25 D.) is unfortunately drawn from

---

[1] On the distance between Archilochus and the heroic world: B. MARZULLO, 'La chioma
di Neobule'. *Rhein. Mus.* 100, 1957, 68.

a hetaera, if we are to believe the late classical Synesius (*Laud. calv. 75*). With Neobule, however, he did not find his happiness. Lycambes broke off the engagement and so earned the hatred of the poet, who told him that he was a breaker of oaths and had made himself the laughing-stock of his fellow-citizens. In fr. 74 D. someone says that he is no longer surprised at anything since Zeus darkened the sun on a clear day. The context suggests that Lycambes was brought in declaring that he would no longer be surprised at anything his daughter did. Probably in the course of this attack Archilochus introduced the story of the fox and the eagle (Aesop. 1 Hausr.), which deals with the punishment of unfaithfulness.[1] A story also told of Hipponax attached itself to Archilochus: his verses drove Lycambes or his daughters to suicide.

Archilochus is capable of other tones than those of tender affection, as we see in the coarse eroticism of frr. 34 and 72 D. We may perhaps believe Critias' charge that the poet was his own model in this portrayal of vulgar lust. A matter more worth notice is that a theme becomes prominent in Archilochus which remains dominant in erotic poetry until the end of antiquity: that love is not a blessing to man, but a passion that seizes upon him with the violence of a dangerous disease. It crawls into the heart, blinds the eyes, takes away the understanding (112 D.); its piercing anguish strikes to the very marrow (104 D.); it looses the limbs (118 D.) – a description previously applied to Eros by Hesiod (*Theog.* 121), and to be applied again by Sappho (137 D.).

It was mainly his capacity for intense feeling that drove Archilochus into lyric poetry. The clearest indication of it is found in those passages in which he describes himself as capable of unmeasured and devastating hatred. When he boasts of his power to punish those who injure him, he is of course only professing what the Greeks down to Socrates' time all reckoned as a virtue. His blood is never hotter than when he thirsts for battle with his foes like a thirsty man panting for water (69 D.). Critias remarks that he abused friend and foe alike: no doubt a malicious simplification; but we can see the point when we find that one Pericles, whom he addresses elsewhere in friendly terms, is vilified as an uninvited sponger (78 D.). His wildest outburst is in a poem preserved in a papyrus at Strasburg (79a D.), which poses a difficult problem.[2] It seems very likely that another fragment belonging to the same papyrus is from Hipponax. If then we range ourselves with those who nevertheless assign the first to Archilochus, we may indeed feel confident that we detect the authentic tones of the poet, but we must remember how subjective the grounds for this belief are. We must also suppose that the papyrus contained an anthology – a supposition which the author does not find so unlikely as others do. The poets of antiquity were fond of addressing poems (*propemptica*) to their friends when the latter were facing the hazards of a sea voyage. Here we have the direct opposite. The

---

[1] J. TRENCSENYI-WALDAPFEL, 'Eine äsopische Fabel und ihre orientalischen Parallelen'. *Acta Antiqua Acad. Scient. Hungaricae* 7, 1959, 317.

[2] New comparison of the text and discussion of the authorship: J. SCHWARTZ and O. MASSON, *Rev. Ét. Gr.* 64, 1941, 427. The question is fully discussed by M. TREU in his edition (*v. sup.*) 225, who gives both the Strasburg fragments to Archilochus.

poet describes with furious delight how his enemy is shipwrecked: pinched with cold, covered with weed, he is captured on the beach by top-knotted Thracians, who make him earn the bitter bread of servitude. At the end the writer cries: 'He injured me without cause, broke his plighted word – he who was once my friend!' This is the expression of a heart looking for love and confidence, and flashing into fury at deception or disappointment. If it is not Archilochus, it is someone well able to imitate his manner. French excavations in the agora of Thasos have recently brought to light a valuable witness to the poet's life and times in a funerary inscription to Glaucus, who is often addressed in the poems.[1]

Archilochus took part in the sung worship of Dionysus and Demeter (77 and 119 D.), and we know also that he wrote a hymn to Heracles. So far as we can judge from the surviving fragments, myth remained in the background, and the problems of divine governance did not greatly exercise a poet who lived so intensely in the present. But a theme seems to have come up in it whose importance in ancient lyric has been pointed out by Rudolf Pfeiffer:[2] the helplessness of man before the power of the gods and of fate – his ἀμηχανίη. At the beginning of the *Erga* Hesiod tells us that Zeus has power when he wills to raise up and to throw down. Here the same idea recurs, but with the emphasis on the destiny of man, who may, as the gods will it, either prosper or fall into hopeless adversity. Yet Archilochus is not led thereby into either resignation or scepticism. In the elegy on Pericles (7. D), written under the impact of a disaster at sea, he speaks of the resource that the gods have given to men against all adversity – courageous endurance (τλημοσύνη). And so the elegy ends in urging a return to those pleasures which are conceded to mankind. The finest expression of his convictions is given by the poet in those verses in which he addresses his own heart (67 D.): it must show courage towards enemies, be not boastful in success nor despairing in adversity, but be always mindful of the uncertainty of human life. Thus the fiery passions of the poet sink down at the end into the wisest maxim of all Greek thought – that due measure must be observed in every sphere of life.

All the condemnation voiced by writers in the aristocratic tradition, such as Heraclitus (VS 22 B42), Pindar (*Pyth.* 2. 54: Archilochus' ἀμαχανία is the cause of his bitterness) and Critias was not able to lessen Archilochus' reputation with posterity.[3] A good indication is the elaborately inscribed monument erected to him in Paros by Sosthenes in the first century B.C. (51 D.); to which may be added the considerable remains of an old inscription (3rd century B.C.) from the same place. This also gives large extracts from his poems together with a pious biography. The most striking part of this recent discovery is the charming story of the poet's being called and endowed with talent by the Muses.

The rich variety of his poetry in content and tone is matched by that of its

[1] J. POUILLOUX, *Bull. Corr. Hell.* 1955, 74.

[2] 'Gottheit und Individuum in der frühgr. Lyrik'. *Phil.* 84, 1929, 137 = *Ausgewählte Schriften.* Munich 1960, 42. Cf. BR. SNELL, 'Das Erwachen der Persönlichkeit in der frühgr. Lyrik'. in *Die Entdeckung des Geistes.* 3rd ed. Hamb. 1955, 83.

[3] A. V. BLUMENTHAL, *Die Schätzung des Archilochos im Altertum.* Stuttg. 1922.

form. Archilochus' favourite metres are iambic trimeter and trochaic tetrameter but he also wrote elegies, made up long verses from combinations of various rhythmical elements, and constructed short strophes in which a long verse alternated with a shorter one of the same or sometimes a different type – the form now called epodes. There are occasional Homeric elements in his vocabulary, particularly in the elegies; but his language always flows surely and naturally, without our ever noticing how strict the laws of his metres are – metres which he took over, as he did the iambos, from popular tradition.

The iambic poet Semonides was born in Samos, but his founding a Samian colony in the island of Amorgos has associated his name with the latter. We have no good ground for doubting that at least some part of his life was lived in the seventh century, and that therefore he was roughly contemporary with Archilochus. But as a poet he falls far short of him. We may learn this much from a long fragment (1 D.) preserved, like the *Iambos on Women*, in Stobaeus. Here again the conviction is uppermost that man is an outcast: like the dumb animals he is the creature of a day (ἐφήμερος), not knowing what the end is that god has appointed. Here, however, we do not hear the tones of the Parian poet, undismayed amid the storm, but the distressed and distressing cries of one who sees only misery in the world. We do indeed find at the end a tendency to advise us to make the best of life; but this can hardly have altered the basic tone of the poem. The notion of the nullity of human hopes also plays a part in an elegy (29 D.), which cites *Il.* 6. 146 (men are as transitory as leaves) as the finest utterance of 'the man of Chios', adds some reflections on the fleetingness of human life, and ends with a rather lame appeal to men to enjoy themselves. Stobaeus assigns the poem to Simonides. Such a confusion of the two names was inevitable after etacism had made them sound alike. With Wilamowitz and others I take the poem as an example of the elegiac poetry which Suidas expressly attests for Semonides. If it is smoother than his iambics, that may be attributed to the different metre and the wider use of Homeric forms.[1]

Pessimism is also the underlying tone of his long *Iambos on Women*, which has been preserved in all essentials. The denigration of women was a theme that we met in Hesiod (p. 101), and the myth of Pandora in both forms represents her as an evil. Behind such attacks lies the mutual vituperation of the sexes which is a universal folklore element, and which certainly played an important part in those festivals in which the iambos was immemorially in use. In Semonides' poem we are not far from these ancient roots. On such an occasion the comparison of female types with animals was ready to hand: it occurs with more brevity in Phocylides (2 D). Verbal resemblances compel us to infer direct borrowing, probably by Phocylides. The beast-fable may have contributed to the devising of such comparisons as these.

The poem begins with the assertion that God has endowed women with their faculties in a variety of ways. The word χωρίς at the very beginning has the ring

---

[1] The attribution is far from certain. Arguments for Semonides are put forward by O. VON WEBER, *Die Beziehungen zwischen Homer und den älteren griechischen Lyrikern*. Diss. Bonn 1955 (typewritten).

of polemic against the supposition that women had a unitary origin. Next come nine evil types: the women sprung from earth and sea are flanked on one side by those arising from swine, fox and dog, on the other by those from ass, weasel, horse and ape. The earth-woman is a creation of the gods – like so much in Semonides, this comes from Hesiod (*Erga* 60. 70) – but the sea-woman, who has all the sea's inconstancy, is a symbolic and mythic anticipation of later philosophies deriving all things from one basic substance. In these nine classes actual observation of female failings is combined with the attribution of typical qualities based on the animal in question. Finally comes the one good type of woman, sprung from the bee. She brings joy and happiness, but she is quickly forgotten in the following section, an example of archaic ring-composition: 'woman is the worst of all evils' begins and ends the passage (96. 115).[1]

Another name in the tradition of iambic poetry, yet one with a place of its own, is that of Hipponax of Ephesus. According to Suidas' account of his life he was compelled by a tyrant to leave his homeland, and went to Clazomenae. His name and political status have led scholars to suppose that he came of an aristocratic family. If this is so, his destiny was wholly to estrange him from his class. Reduced to poverty, he lived miserably as one of those exiles who were plentiful in all ages as the victims of Greek political strife. Thus Hipponax complains of the blindness of Plutus (29 D.) – a theme which Aristophanes was to make into a comedy – and prays to Hermes for a coat and warm boots, for he is bitterly cold and frostbitten (24sq. D.). He had become a hungry cur, snapping at people's ankles. His attack on the sculptor Bupalus was famous: according to a story also attached to Archilochus it drove its object to suicide. Later it was said that the poet attacked him in revenge for a statue caricaturing him, but fragments 15-17 D. suggest that the trouble was over a woman called Arete. This disagreement with Bupalus, in which the latter's brother Athenis is supposed to have been involved, gives us ground for putting Hipponax's main activities in the middle of the sixth century (cf. Marm. Par. 42).

The papyri have given us much material for Hipponax, but not in a form from which we can learn a great deal. One large papyrus fragment, however (14A D.),[2] shows us how uninhibited Hipponax could be. This startlingly erotic passage reminds one of the experiences of Encolpius in Petronius (c. 138); and since Hipponax was widely read throughout antiquity, there may well be a connection here. Extensive but badly damaged fragments[3] came to light in the 18th volume of *Oxyrhynchus Papyri* (1941), including scholia of doubtful value which bring a great deal of dictionary-thumbing to bear on the text. It has been possible to identify an abusive poem against one Sannus,[4] which gives us some help on a question of form. While all the other known poems of Hipponax are

---

[1] J. T. KAKRIDIS, in a study to be published in *Wiener humanist. Blätter* 5, points out some modern Greek folktales, certainly independent of Semonides, which suggest that the poem on women incorporated themes from folklore.

[2] K. LATTE, *Herm.* 64. 1929, 385. Id., *Gött. Gel. Anz.* 207, 1953, 38, dating the poet in the second half of the sixth century.   [3] Fr. I-XII D.

[4] Fr. X, D., cf. E. FRAENKEL, *Class. Quart.* 36, 1942, 54. K. LATTE, *Phil.* 97, 1948, 37.

in choliambics (i.e. in trimeters which have a limping effect from the spondee in the sixth foot), we find here an epodic form used also by Archilochus: a regular iambic trimeter is followed by an iambic dimeter. We also find hexameters (77 D.) in which high pathos is brutally parodied.

What sharply divides Hipponax from Archilochus is his wholly different way of seeing himself in relation to his world. In both poets the immediate impulse is to seize the concrete situation in all its force and fullness. But Archilochus does not stop here: he views the whole of human existence, or at least the whole of his own life. How must man behave in this outcast condition, in this constant misfortune, this endless vicissitude? These are Archilochus' ultimate questions. But Hipponax asks no questions: his verses express the momentary perception and nothing more. He is essentially a poet of realism, and he introduces a movement which finally led to the mime. What supported him in his life as a beggar was that wit which saw through all suffering. He drinks with his Arete taking turns from one bowl, since the slave has broken the cup (16 D.); he laughingly describes a painter who has painted a snake on the side of the ship so that it appears to be biting the helmsman (45 D.); when he pleads in tragic tones for a bushel of barley (42. D), he is probably not taking himself too seriously.

One feature of realism in Hipponax is the number of foreign loan-words used in the everyday speech of the Lydian hinterland. *Palmys* for 'king' is a favourite word of his: even Zeus is called *palmys*. We also find the Phrygian *bekos*= 'bread', which, according to Herodotus (2, 2) was shown by Psammetichus through his experiment with the children to be the oldest word of human speech.

Hellenistic taste found the earthy verses of Hipponax a welcome change. Callimachus invoked his ghost in the opening of his own iambi (fr. 197 Pf.), and later (fr. 203. 65 Pf.) says that writers of choliambics all took their inspiration from Ephesus. But his main contribution was to secure by his own writings a long and influential career for the choliambic.

The credit for writing in choliambics – even for inventing them – is also claimed for Ananius, who lived, like Hipponax, in the sixth century and in the Ionian world of culture. He wrote a list of foods according to the seasons of the year, in iambics – most of them choliambics. This is our first example of a poem on gastronomy.

Text of the fragments: *Anthologia Lyrica Graeca* by E. DIEHL, 3rd ed., fasc. 3, Leipzig 1952, with parallel passages and bibliographies – a work indispensable for Greek lyric poetry. J. M. EDMONDS, *Greek Elegy and Iambus*. 2. (Loeb Lib.) Lond. 1937 (repr. 1954). F. R. ADRADOS, *Líricos griegos. Elegíacos y yambógrafos arcáicos*. 1. Barcelona 1956 (with Spanish trans.). – Archilochus: Editions: F. LASSERRE, A. BONNARD, *Coll. des Un. de Fr.* Paris 1958. M. TREU, *Tusculum Bücherei*. Munich 1959 (with trans., comm. and bibliog.) The new inscription: W. PEEK, 'Neues von Arch.' *Phil.* 99, 1955, 4. To Treu's bibliography we may add R. MERKELBACH in *Rhein. Mus.* 99, 1956. New fragments: *Ox. Pap.* 22, ʾ954, nr. 2310-2319; 23, 1956, nr. 2356; on which see K. LATTE, *Gnomon* 27, 1955, 492. W. PEEK, 'Die Archilochosgedichte von Oxyrhynchos'. I. *Phil.* 99, 1955, 193. II, 100, 1956, 1. Id., 'Neue Bruchstücke frühgr. Dichtung'. *Wiss. Zeitschr. Univ. Halle* 5, 1955-6, 191. Full bibliography in Treu's edition. See further: A. GIANNINI, 'Archiloco alla luce dei nuovi ritrovamenti'. *Acme* 11, 1958 (1960), 41. H. J. METTE, 'Zu Arch. Pap. Ox. 2310 fr. 1 col. 1'. *Herm.* 88, 1960, 493 (with bibliog.). – H. GUNDERT, 'Archilochos und Solon'. *Das neue Bild der Antike.* I. Leipz. 1942, 130. F. LASSERRE, *Les Épodes d'Archiloque.* Paris 1950, is overbold in his reconstructions. Verbal index: A. MONTI, Turin 1905. S. N. KUMANUDES, Ἀρχιλόχου γλωσσάριον. *Platon* 11, 1959, 295. E. MERONE, *Aggettivazione, sintassi e figure di stilo in Archiloco.* Naples 1960. – Semonides: Iambos on women: W. MARG, *Der Charakter in der Sprache der frühgr. Dichtung.* Würzburg 1938, 6 (comm.). L. RADERMACHER, *Weinen und Lachen.* Vienna 1947, 156 (trans. and explanations). A. WILHELM. 'Zu Semonides von Amorgos'. *Symb. Osl.* 27, 1949, 40. Imitations in German poetry: J. BOLTE, *Ztschr. d. Ver. f. Volkskunde* 11, 1901, 256. – Hipponax: A. D. KNOX, *The Greek Choliambic Poets.* Lond. 1929. O. MASSON, 'Nouveaux Fragments d'Hipponax'. *La parola del passato* 5, 1950, 71; *Rev. Et. Gr.* 66, 1953, 407. The most recent ed. is by W. DE SOUSA MEDEIROS Diss. Coimbra 1961; see P. VON DER MÜHLL, *Mus. Helv.* 19, 1962, 233.

3 ELEGY

In the *Ars poetica* (77) Horace alludes to the inconclusive battles of the grammarians over the inventor of elegy. He gives the original matter briefly as lamentation – a view also held by Didymus (schol. ad Ar. *Aves* 217), and presumably the current one. We have to admit that we are no wiser today. The word *elegion* occurs first in Critias in the fifth century (VS 88 B4, 3), where it is applied to the so-called pentameter (in fact two dactylic penthemimers) which combined with the hexameter to make the short elegiac strophe. At the same time we meet *elegos* in the sense of 'lament', 'song of lamentation' in (e.g.) Euripides *Tro.* 119. Thus we cannot brush aside the statements of the ancients who, like Didymus, represent lamentation over the dead as the original function of elegy. This view may well be right as regards the districts of Asia Minor such as Lydia and Phrygia, from which the Greeks received the original impulse towards the development of the form, as in all likelihood they took over the accompanying flute music from there also. But we have to make the reservation that elegy, as it first becomes known to us, has subjects of a very different kind.[1] It is certainly so with Archilochus, who provides the oldest known elegiacs. The metre served him for expressing all sides of his life and activity – even for the story of his throwing away his shield. At other times, as in the elegy to Pericles, it takes on a tone of advice and admonition which often recurs in early elegiacs. But we can easily see why Archilochus made his name with posterity

[1] D. L. PAGE, *Greek Poetry and Life.* Oxf. 1936, 206. P. FRIEDLÄNDER – H. B. HOFLEIT, *Epigrammata.* Univ. of Calif. Press 1948, 65.

as a writer of iambi rather than as an elegist. Some of his spirit infuses his elegies; but its most characteristic expression was in the iambic poems.

Chronologically we must begin the history of the elegy with Callinus of Ephesus, who is also more typical of the genre than Archilochus. He belongs to a period in which the Greek settlements in Asia Minor were gravely threatened by attacks from the barbarous Cimmerians. Since these attacks must be dated around 675 B.C., Callinus is an older contemporary of Archilochus'. In that time of troubles he saw the Phrygian kingdom overthrown and the temple of Artemis in his own city destroyed by fire. Himself presumably a member of the military aristocracy, he urged in his elegies the utmost exertion and readiness for the supreme sacrifice. The only lengthy piece of his that we possess is an address on a particular occasion, as this form of lyric often is in antiquity. He comes among the young men, who seem to him to be hanging back, and urges them into the fray. These verses very well show what it was that determined the character of early elegiac poetry, whatever its ultimate origins may have been: its content and verbal form are so strongly influenced by epic, that in some sense (as Wilamowitz[1] put it) elegy is an offshoot of epic. In the nature of things it was inevitable that dactylic poetry should inherit all the formal elements which lay to hand and which were familiar to everyone from the Homeric poems. The similar structure of the epic and elegiac hexameter worked in the same direction. But Callinus' thought also is rooted in that Homeric world which Archilochus rejected. Death will come when Fate, in the shape of the spinning Fury, has appointed it. This reminds us of Hector's words to Andromache (6. 487). And when we read of the gallant warrior who is like a tower to his countrymen, who does the work of many men, we find ourselves again thinking of the hero in whom Homer embodied the ideal of patriotic self-sacrifice.

Just like those of Callinus, the elegies of Tyrtaeus have as their occasion and subject the defence of the city in the arbitrament of war. The historical circumstances are clearly told by the poet himself. The grandfathers of his generation had won the rich lands of Messenia after a bitter struggle of twenty years, and had recklessly treated the enslaved inhabitants like beasts of burden. But about the middle of the seventh century the oppressed had risen, and the second Messenian war compelled Sparta to exert herself to the utmost in order to survive. The man whose poems contributed to ultimate victory has been the prey of ancient anecdote-mongers: he figures now as a Spartan general, now as one sent by the Athenians to help Sparta in her distress, now as a lame schoolmaster and composer of inspiriting songs (Paus. 4. 15, 6). If we dismiss all this, the question still remains: was Tyrtaeus a Spartan by birth or a foreigner? Suidas gives him as either a Laconian or a Milesian. Now in the seventh century Sparta was open to foreign influence to a degree that was inconceivable later: at the same time many scholars would hesitate to ascribe elegies in this form to a Spartan. But these rather vague considerations are put out of court by the Dorisms of his language. Their very sparseness[2] shows that they were the slips

---

[1] *Griech. Verskunst.* Berl. 1921, 38.

[2] Some first decl. accusatives in -ᾰς and a fut. in -εῦμεν.

of a man who had learned to write in another dialect, but occasionally relapsed into his own. Therefore we do not need to suppose that a foreigner would have become so completely assimilated to the spirit and conditions of Spartan life. We may instead take the elegies of Tyrtaeus as expressing the convictions of a man who was immediately involved, probably as a soldier, in the events which decided the fate of his country.

Tyrtaeus' debt to Ionian elegy is obvious. The one poem of Callinus is enough to prove similarity in language and themes. We can trace an interesting line of development if we compare the exhortation to advance with spear held high (1, 52 D.) with a similar formula in Callinus (1, 10 D.) and with a passage from the *Iliad* (21. 161). In addition the language of Tyrtaeus is influenced by epic style in such a way that we have to consider in some places the possibility of direct imitation.

The poems are devoted to one single exhortation: to go forward in the battle line and wager life for victory. If he sings of Sparta's past, it is only to draw a moral for the present. Quite consistently in his *Eunomia* he considers Sparta's internal constitution as inviolable, a body of laws laid down by the oracle of Apollo (3 D.). His words are of great importance for determining the historicity of the *Great Rhetra*. We are inclined nowadays to believe that there was such a constitutional enactment, and to date it about the end of the eighth century.[1]

Above all it is as the advocate of steadfastness in battle that Tyrtaeus appears in the extant poems. His kind of poetry, never fearing to repeat itself, has been well characterized as propaganda-poetry. The hearer is constantly exhorted to march forward boldly, to grit his teeth, to fight bravely hand to hand, to endure until death, which is the warrior's greatest glory. But we are not concerned here, as in the *Iliad*, with the individual hero, whose great deeds render all else secondary: rather we see the beginnings of the phalanx, and it is only consideration of the whole, sacrifice of self for the common interest, that can win the reward of immortal glory. Yet, as we see with Callinus, there is a thread connecting the figure of Homer's Hector with the poetic philosophy of Tyrtaeus.

Apart from small fragments we possess four elegies devoted to this martial exhortation. Each can be taken as an independent whole. They show an archaic manner of composition: the connection of thought is largely associative; ring – composition is common, beginnings and endings being accentuated by the weight and emphasis of what is expressed there. Two of these elegies (6 and 7 D.) are quoted in one of the speeches of Lycurgus against Leocrates; the contents show that they must be two separate poems. The third elegy (8 D.) is a cry de profundis, and shows how closely this type of poetry is tied to the immediate situation. The longest of the elegies (9 D.) is rather different. It begins with what seems like a preamble enumerating various personal advantages – ability at games, handsome appearance, royal blood, eloquent tongue – none of

---

[1] H. BENGTSON, *Griech. Gesch.* 2nd ed. Munich 1960, 100. A. G. TSOPANAKIS, *La Rhètre de Lycurgue*. Thessalonica 1954. On the part played by Delphi in the Rhetra see J. DEFRADAS, *Les Thèmes de la propagande delphique*. Paris 1954, and on the other side H. BERVE, *Gnom.* 28, 1956, 18).

which, in the poet's opinion, is a guarantee of manly virtue (ἀρετή). This quality can only be proved by courage and tenacity in face of the enemy. Such a quality will receive the highest honour in death as in life.

Attempts to prove other parts of Tyrtaeus' poetry spurious have now mostly been forgotten, but in the controversy over the genuineness of this elegy swords have not yet been sheathed.[1] Wilamowitz thought it spurious, and his view has had many followers, most recently Fränkel. I cannot share this opinion. Certainly this poem has not the immediate reference to the decisive hour of battle which the others have: it is in more general terms. But we have no reason to suppose that Tyrtaeus never wrote except in the trenches. It is quite conceivable that this elegy was composed in a time of relative quiet, which permitted a more general topic, instead of the urgent call to arms. If its composition seems more carefully thought out than the others, we must remember that we have very little of Tyrtaeus and cannot rule out different stages of development. What connects the disputed elegy with the others is not only their similarity in themes and treatment: the decisive feature is the role played in them all by the notion of manly fortitude, whose fulfilment for the true hero is death on the battlefield. This conception of the ἀνὴρ ἀγαθός is at the very core of all Tyrtaeus' poetry, and through him it had a wide influence on Greek literature and thought: we need only mention Simonides' *Encomium on those Fallen at Thermopylae* (5 D.). Scholars have in fact been denying to Tyrtaeus a poem in which he found the most mature form for enshrining this ideal above all other values and beliefs of his time.

Callinus and Tyrtaeus mark the creation of that political elegy which was to be heard as long as the Greek polis had a life of its own and while the orator had not yet replaced the poet. But it is a quite different tone that we catch in much of the surviving poetry of Mimnermus of Colophon. We are by now used to being unable to fix precise dates in early Greek poetry, and we must be content to put Mimnermus' life and writings about 600 B.C. Like Semonides (29 D.) he quotes (2 D.) the verse of the *Iliad* which compares human beings with falling leaves; and as in the first iambic fragment of Semonides, so here man is depicted in all the troubles coming from his pitifully limited knowledge. But the emphasis is differently placed. While in both the poems of Semonides the futility of all human hope is the dominating theme, in Mimnermus the stress is on the contrast between the carefree joys of youth and the miseries of old age, which the poet here and elsewhere paints with a sombre palette. This lamenting of the imminence of old age and its trials is sometimes combined with the exhortation to enjoy youth to the full while one can. But in this particular poem there is no reason to suppose that Mimnermus did so. A poem in which the writer pities the human race who vanish like last summer's leaves, who enjoy for a brief moment the delights of youth, without knowledge of good or evil, can hardly have ended with the sentiment that one should enjoy life to the full. Mimnermus had not the defiant spirit of Archilochus. We must consider it

[1] Clear account of the problems in E. MAIER, 'Tyrtaios', *Jahresber. fürstbisch. Gymn. Graz* 1946/47.

possible that some of his poems were elegiac in the modern sense, and that the poet who wished to die a painless death at sixty may have felt and expressed sorrow at the fleetingness of life more strongly than pleasure in its present joys. The element of myth comes into its own more decidedly with Mimnermus. A piece of charming poetry (10 D.) describes the nightly journey of the sun-god in a golden bowl, which bears him round on the stream of Ocean to the east again.[1] The bowl appears in pot-painting as a large round dish or cup. Another passage tells of Jason, who according to the old legend carried off the golden fleece from the wonderland of Aea on the shore of Ocean, where Helios has his palace and guards his radiant beams. Of the first of these fragments we are told that it came from the *Nanno* of Mimnermus, to which not only 4,5 and 8 D., but also 12 belongs, with its references to the early history of Colo-phon. At the time when it was general to bestow titles on books of poetry[2] someone named a book of Mimnermus' elegies after the flute-girl Nanno. What part she played in it, or how far the poems of that book had a unifying theme, we do not know. At all events, it must have contained illustrative episodes, and if we understand Callimachus (fr. 1, 12 Pf.) rightly, the *Nanno* is spoken of in opposition to the shorter poems of Mimnermus. Apparently what we have here is the beginning of narrative elegy. The surviving remains of Mimnermus may perhaps give us too narrow a notion of his work: witness the fragment (13 D.) in which he describes a doughty warrior who distinguished himself in battle against the Lydians. The passage might come from a *Smyrneis*, to which we have some scattered allusions.[3] What survives of Mimnermus is enough to show him as a master of language and metre, who well deserved his place in the ancient canon of elegists along with Philitas and Callimachus.

Anth. Lyr. 3rd ed. fasc. 1, 1949, 1. 4. 48. J. M. EDMONDS, *Greek Elegy and Iambus*. Loeb Class. Lib.) Lond. 1931 (repr. 1954). F. R. ADRADOS, *Líricos griegos. Elegíacos y yambógrafos arcáicos.* I. Barcelona 1956 (with Spanish trans.). Analysis: B. A. VAN GRONINGEN, *La Composition littéraire archaïque grecque. Verh. Nederl. Akad.* N.R. 65/2. Amsterdam 1958, 124. C. M. BOWRA, *Early Greek Elegists.* Cambr. 1938; repr. 1959. S. SZADĔCZKY-KARDOSS, *Testimonia de Mimnermi vita et carminibus.* Szegedin 1959; 'Ein ausser acht gelassenes Mimnermos-testi-monium und -Fragment'. *Acta Antiqua* 7, 1959, 287 (on Mimnermus in Apol-lonius of Tyana, *epist.* 71). JOSÉ S. LASSO DE LA VEGA, 'El guerrero tirtéico'. *Emerita* 30, 1962, 9 (discusses, among other things, the authenticity of fr. 9 D.).

4 SOLON

We put Solon here to make plain a development which was of decisive impor-tance in the history of the Greek people. The Athens which Pindar was to call

[1] A. LESKY, 'Aia'. *Wien. Stud.* 63, 1948, 24.
[2] E. NACHMANSON, 'Der griech. Buchtitel' *Göteborgs Högsk. Årsskr.* 47, 1941.
[3] Paus. 9. 29, 4. Antimachos ed. Wyss p. 83.

the stay and support of Greece, which Thucydides was to describe as its spiritual centre, which is spoken of in a funeral inscription as the very essence of Hellas ('Ελλάδος 'Ελλάς),[1] was late in reaching maturity. On all sides we have seen new intellectual life finding great art-forms for its expression, while Attica remained mute. But when her hour came, she showed herself able to receive and to remodel all that was growing and blooming around her. From every part of the Greek world lines of force converged in Attica to produce that great epoch in history, the classical age of Greece. Of that age the Parthenon, with its harmony of diverse elements, is the witness: the Athenian Solon is its precursor, and the first of Attic poets.

Solon said what he had to say in iambic and trochaic metres, which Archilochus had raised to an artistic form, and in elegiacs like those of Callinus and Tyrtaeus, whose influence can be seen in his poems. It is also important that we should not underrate the spiritual legacy of Hesiod in Solon's works. But Solon was wholly typical of Attic art – indeed of Greek art in general – in that despite all dependence, imitation and borrowing, he emerged as a poet with his own individual personality and ways of thought. We should have to examine subsequent literature very carefully to find another personality in whom life and work were equally integrated into one whole.

Solon was born about 640; that is to say, his life fell in a time of bitter social struggles. The development of trade and a money economy heightened to an unbearable degree tensions which we saw beginning in Hesiod. The ownership of land lay mostly in the hands of the aristocracy, and new and tempting opportunities for amassing capital were coming into existence. Free wage-earners and small peasants could no longer make head against these economic forces. The small man was liable in his own person for debts which he could not help incurring, and his ultimate loss was that of freedom. It was one of those periods in which unrestrained acquisitiveness sows the seed of long-lasting social conflict. Wretched as our information is, we can still see how violent the outbreaks were that occurred in different places. At about the time when Solon was born, the mass of the small peasantry in Megara rose against the great landowners and killed all their flocks. In the class-struggles which later raged in Miletus we hear of atrocities on both sides, such as the massacre of innocent children, which can scarcely be parallelled in Greek history. At Megara we learn that the instigator of this attack on the flocks of the wealthy was Theagenes, one of the first Greek tyrants. The situation is typical: the people, ripe for revolt, are guided by a gifted individual, who overthrows the aristocracy and establishes a tyrannis. The word τύραννος in Greek is a loanword from some language of Asia Minor. Being used to denote the sole ruler, as the East knew him, it necessarily carried the germ of that bad sense which it later developed. But we must not forget the blessings which the tyrants often brought to their cities: we need only think of Corinth and Athens. Not a few of these were true patrons of the arts, and poetry flourished at their courts. Not the least important thing they did was to encourage the religion of the common people, especially

[1] Pind. fr. 76. Thuc. 2, 41. *Anth. Pal.* 7, 45.

the worship of Dionysus, in whose service the fairest flower of the Greek genius, Attic tragedy, was to bloom.

There was, however, another possibility apart from a tyrannis: a reconciliation of the conflicting elements. Arbitrators, such as the individual might invoke in a lawsuit, were sometimes appointed by the parties to civil strife and entrusted with the settlement of the conflict. Thus Pittacus was chosen as *aesymnetes* in Mytilene; thus Solon in 594/3 was given full powers to arrange a settlement in Athens, and was given the title of διαλλακτής – the arranger or reconciler.

It was inherent in the economic structure of the ancient world, that any programme for the socialization of production remained purely utopian.[1] Ancient revolutionary movements aimed at redistribution of wealth, and consequently abolition of debts and reallotment of land were planks in every revolutionary platform. With such demands Solon found himself confronted when he began his work as arbitrator. The confidence placed in him was essentially the fruit of his behaviour during the struggle over Salamis. In her development as a naval power Athens had fallen behind her neighbours: if she wanted to catch up, she must bring Salamis and Aegina within her sphere of influence. Aegina was not captured until much later (456); Salamis was finally won for Athens under Pisistratus, but only after a long struggle with Megara for the possession of the island. Then it was that Solon produced his elegy which was later called *Salamis*. Four extant distichs show that Solon spoke as a herald from Salamis, declaring that, if Athens yielded, he would sooner be a citizen of a tiny island than one of the 'betrayers of Salamis'; finally in Tyrtaean tones he urged the Athenians to war.

Of the two demands – abolition of debt and redistribution of land – Solon complied only with the first. What precise measures were comprised in his 'shaking off of burdens' (σεισάχθεια) is debatable;[2] but he certainly abolished retrospectively the lien on the person of the debtor, so that many enslaved for debt recovered their freedom. From his own words (24 D.) we learn that he took the credit for the disappearance of the mortgage notices from the fields of Attica. He continued his work by reforming measures and coinage, and completed it by his code of laws which reformed the constitution of Athens in many important points.

It is one of the most impressive experiences in the study of Greek literature to hear Solon himself describing his political actions. But something even more important is that in a long elegy (1 D.)[3] he unfolds that philosophy of life which gave rise to all his thoughts and actions. This poem has every feature of archaic

---

[1] F. OERTEL, *Klassenkampf, Sozialismus und organischer Staat im alten Griechenland*. Bonn. 1942.

[2] M. MÜHL, 'Solons sogenannte χρεῶν ἀποκοπή im Lichte der antiken Ueberlieferung'. *Rhein. Mus.* 96, 1953, 214.

[3] R. LATTIMORE, 'The First Elegy of Solon'. *Am. Journ. Phil.* 68, 1947, 161. A. MASARACCHIA, 'L' elegia alle Muse di Solone'. *Maia* N.S. 8, 1956, 92. G. MÜLLER, 'Der homerische Ate-Begriff and Solons Musenelegie'. *Navicula Chiloniensis*. Leyden 1956, 1. B. A. VAN GRONINGEN, *La Composition littéraire archaïque grecque*. *Verh. Nederl. Ak. N.R.* 65/2. Amsterdam 1958, 94. K. BÜCHNER, 'Solons Musengedicht'. *Herm.* 87, 1959, 163, who makes the sequence of thought more logical and necessary than it appears to me.

composition. In one place a multitude of ideas crowds into a single passage, sometimes bringing the reader to a halt by the repetition or multiplication of examples; in another place the poem passes swiftly from one idea to another without making the connection explicit. Thus, if we take particular passages out and consider them, we shall not be doing violence to an elaborately planned structure.

Solon begins by invoking the Muses; but what he asks of them is not a song, but the blessings of life. His poetry is part of his work in the world, which is to advance what is good and just. Accordingly he may hope to receive his reward at the hands of the Muses, as intermediaries of the gods.

The lines on the blessings of life do not rise above conventional morality. He wishes for prosperity and reputation. To his friends he wishes to do good, to his enemies harm – the old moral code of the aristocracy, to which Solon belonged as one of the Medontidae. In the second half of the elegy a section (33-70) stands out as having themes already familiar to us from Ionic poetry. Once more the subject becomes the narrow limits of human thoughts and hopes, and a long string of examples illustrates what a hard struggle men have in all departments of life. Whether a man will succeed is known only to the gods: no-one can escape his destiny. Destiny in Solon's thought is inseparable from the will of the gods.

We can see that it is possible to take out parts of this elegy and put them together into a form wholly within the Ionic tradition. But this would not be Solon: in the other parts of the poem ideas of a very different nature appear. In the opening words Solon asks for prosperity, but expressly that prosperity which the gods concede; and immediately he speaks of the other kind of prosperity, which only gives itself unwillingly to the man who has been seduced by evil courses. Such expressions remind us of Hesiod, and indeed we are in his spiritual world. In the *Erga* (320) he contrasts god-given wealth with that acquired by violence and treachery. Solon likewise speaks of the ill-luck attendant upon riches of this sort. Here we find those ideas prominent which until far into the classical period are part and parcel of Greek ethical and religious thought. In *hybris*, the impious and violent disregard of justice, man goes over the boundaries laid down for him; but he is found out by Dike, the personified power of right. In the epic world of the aristocracy it is Themis who rules, Themis the law divinely appointed to regulate the behaviour of men, finding fulfilment in the decisions of the just king. The Dike whom Hesiod proclaims comes from a different social milieu. In her the oppressed victims of *hybris* cried out for justice with a voice that was never again to be stilled in the Greek world. The instrument used by avenging Dike was Ate, that blindness that is sent upon men by the gods and yet arises from their own guilty hearts. At the same time Ate signifies the destruction which inevitably follows such blindness.[1]

As for Hesiod, so for Solon Zeus is the supreme guarantor of the moral law. Where the elegy sings of his power, its earnest didactic tone rises to a pure and elevated poetry: the judgment of Zeus comes upon the works of *hybris* like

[1] K. LATTE, *Arch. f. Rw.* 20, 1920–21, 255.

the spring gale which lashes the sea and lays waste the meadow, but at the same time cleanses the sky of clouds, so that the sun shines again from an unstained heaven. The simile has a special function: it is a specific medium for the interpretation of reality and at the same time contains the first beginnings of scientific analysis.[1] In this instance what is meant is that the vengeance of Zeus falls with the weight and inevitability of a natural phenomenon. This trick of Solon's of illustrating ethical and political statements by comparison with the world of nature comes out most strikingly in fr. 10 D.: as storm-clouds discharge themselves in snow or hail, so does the concentration of power in one man's hands lead to a tyrannis.

It is easy to see that in the archaic sequence of ideas embodied in this great elegy two basically diverse ways of thought are united: insight into the limitations of human endeavour and the absurdity of human hopes, together with a profound persuasion of the moral government of the universe. If we can see in the poem no perfect reconciliation of these two themes, it is because Solon does not offer us a ready-made system, but reveals the living thought-processes of a man coming to grips with the prevailing beliefs of his time and struggling to lay the spiritual foundations of his political work. When we see Hybris, Dike and Ate as agents, when we see a confidence in the moral government of the world side by side with grief at the outcast condition of man, we feel ourselves already in the intellectual climate of early tragedy; and in Solon, who is in many ways Hesiod's heir, we see the spiritual ancestor of Aeschylus.

Solon's strong tendency to justify the ways of God is shown in fr. 29 D., where he tries to explain the good fortune of the wicked. Zeus is often slow to punish, and his vengeance may fall on children or grandchildren. In a striking simile (*Choe.* 506) Aeschylus compares a man's surviving children with the corks which prevent a fishing-net from sinking in the waves. Such a feeling for the unity of a family may have helped the Greeks towards accepting the notion that God visits the father's sins upon the children.

At the end of this section comes the one we have already mentioned, with hope as its theme; then finally the poem turns determinedly back to Zeus once more. The connection is to be supplied thus: the life of man is full of sorrows, but often of his own making. Men do not recognize any limits to acquisitiveness: the rich have only one wish – to be richer yet. Human greed brings Ate into play, sent by Zeus to punish the impiety of those who cannot be satisfied. Thus at the end of the elegy stress is put onto a basic element of Solon's ethics, one which constantly recurs in Greek poets and thinkers – wise moderation and the golden mean. Such a view leaves no room for asceticism. Solon clearly did not condemn honest gain, and individual passages speak explicitly of the things that make life comfortable. But there are limits in all things, and to overstep them is *hybris*, delivering man up to Ate. This doctrine of due measure was Solon's guide in politics also.

[1] O. REGENBOGEN, 'Eine Forschungsmethode der antiken Naturwissenschaft'. *Quellen und Studien z. Gesch. d. Math.* 1, 193), 131 (= *Kl. Schr.* 141). B. SNELL, *Die Entdeckung des Geistes.* 3rd ed. Hamb. 1955, 258.

What best shows the consistency of Solon's mind is that he rigorously applied to the life of the community those principles which he thought valid for the individual. He faces the problems of society in an elegy (3 D.) depicting the evils which he hoped to mitigate by his reforms.[1] The poem last discussed ended by stressing the source of covetousness: it is the same thought which occurs at the beginning of this elegy, here applied to the polis. Solon's Attic piety recognizes that the city is under the protection of the gods, especially of Athene. The dangers come from the community itself. Her citizens are too foolish to be content with a happy sufficiency. Satiety breeds *hybris*, which bursts all bounds and drags them into unrighteousness. To their lust for gain nothing now is sacred. We seem to hear the voice of Hesiod: the impious disregard the basic laws of Dike, but she is silently aware and awaits the moment for their punishment. These poisoned wounds infect the whole community; slavery comes in and inner conflicts lay waste the city. No one can protect himself: even if he creeps into the innermost corner of his house, the universal evil breaks down the gate or overleaps the walls. Solon is as little addicted to simile as to ornamental epithets: such passages are hardly to be called similes; rather they have the force and value of immediate expression.

The section ends with the poet's avowal that a command from within himself has called upon him to teach the Athenians the evils of *dysnomia*. Next follows the praise of the opposite quality, *eunomia* – a basic notion in Solon's political thought. The word occurs first in the *Odyssey* (17. 487), where the gods in disguise make trial of man's moral sense; in Hesiod (*Theog.* 902, cf. 230) it features with Dike and Eirene as a daughter of Zeus; Alcman (44 D.) makes Eunomia the daughter of Promatheia (forethought). The meaning is 'government by good laws',[2] and Solon sings its praises in elevated strains at the end of the poem.

Werner Jaeger has well shown that this poem significantly develops certain elements of Hesiodic thought. Hesiod also (*Erga* 225) paints in striking colours the condition of the righteous and of the unrighteous community. There, however, happiness or misery are wholly external. The success or failure of crops, of cattle or of children, the blessings of peace or the horrors of war are Hesiod's theme. But with Solon the causes and effects are intimately associated with the inner life of the polis. Greed and injustice destroy first of all certain areas of political life, then they lead to a universal infection, in which peace and freedom are lost. In this recognition of certain regularities and laws in the life of a community we find the germ of an idea which found its fulfilment in Plato's *Republic*.

The surviving parts of those poems (5. 23-25 D.) in which Solon takes stock of his political achievements reflect the basic features of his work as a statesman. A fragment (5) of an elegy has survived in which he professes to follow the

---

[1] Literature on the very uncertain chronology of the poems: SOLMSEN (*v. inf.*) 120, 66.

[2] W. JAEGER, 'Solons Eunomie'. *Sitzb. Ak. Berl.* 1926, 69. K. HEINIMANN, *Nomos und Physis.* Basel 1945, 64. SOLMSEN (*v. inf.*) 116. Later usage of the term: G. GROSSMANN, *Politische Schlagwörter aus der Zeit des Pelop. Krieges.* Zürich 1950, 30.

middle way; and he tells us that the best leadership is that which neither puts fetters on the people nor gives them an excessive freedom. Once again we see the link between Solon and another great Athenian, Aeschylus. The doctrine is the same as that which Athene in the *Eumenides* gives to the Athenians as she founds the Areopagus (696).

In Solon's poems also we find no sharp distinction between the themes of elegy and iambus. In both he speaks in his own person, but we can detect that the elegies are more concerned with general themes, the iambics and trochaics with particular events. He uses trochaic tetrameters (23 D.) to answer those who deride him for not having drawn the net tight and secured the tyrannis for himself. The most attractive of the extant pieces is the sequence of iambic trimeters in which he gives a retrospect over his political achievements (24 D.). Justifiable pride, deep piety and a vigilant determination to repulse the enemy give these verses a stormy tempo unparallelled in archaic poetry. Hermann Fränkel has well compared them with the great speeches in Attic tragedy. Solon has accomplished what he set himself, and before the bar of posterity he calls to witness the dark earth, the mother of the Olympian gods. It is she whom he has freed from the stones of guilt which everywhere had been fixed in her. She was formerly a slave, but is now free. Here again it would be wrong to talk of simile or personification in the later sense. The pious beliefs of the old Athenian had an immediate perception of divine force behind objects and happenings. He also speaks of the men whom he has rescued from slavery for debt. It is interesting to see what strikes him as the greatest disgrace of all: many who had been sold into slavery abroad had by now forgotten their Attic tongue.

The final description that Solon gives of his achievement is at bottom little more than a variation of the doctrine of measure: with strong hand he has united power and justice,[1] and has thus established that union which is so rare and so transient in the history of nations, but is yet the ultimate goal of all political wisdom.

There is one short poem preserved in its entirety which does not immediately seem to fit into our picture of Solon. It makes a rather prosaic appraisal of human life, dividing it into ten sections of seven years each, giving the characteristics, mental and physical, of each one. We take the poem to be a deliberate rejoinder to Mimnermus' gloomy picture of old age. In the ninth heptad of his life Solon still has power of intellect at his service; when he is seventy, he can close his eyes with the consciousness of achievement. His vital powers are not spent in the pleasures of the senses: what he values is that human excellence found in the just man (ἀρετή), not the purely military qualities that Tyrtaeus admires. This *arete* alone is enduring: unlike Archilochus, Solon believes in an afterlife in the memory of one's friends. This view he professes in an elegy (22 D.) which politely but firmly corrects Mimnermus: he does not wish to die at sixty; a man would wish to live until eighty, if only he might continue to learn as he grows old.

---

[1] In v. 16 we should read ὁμοῦ with Plutarch, *Solon* 15; cf. HEINIMANN, op. cit. 72, 41. On the thought cf. Aesch. fr. 381 N.

The extensive travels which ancient tradition makes him undertake when his political work was completed also left their mark in his writings. One hexameter (6 D.) mentions the estuary of the Canobic branch of the Nile; three pleasant distichs (7 D.) are a farewell to Philocyprus, the ruler of Soloe in Cyprus.

Solon is the first representative of the Attic spirit. We are still some way from the classical achievement, but in his poetry lives some of that light in which all things achieve beauty and simplicity.

Anth. Lyr., 3rd ed., fasc. 1, 1949, 20. W. J. WOODHOUSE, *Solon the Liberator.* Oxf. 1938. H. GUNDERT, 'Archilochos und Solon'. *Das neue Bild der Antike I.* Leipzig 1942, 130. F. SOLMSEN, *Hesiod and Aeschylus.* New York 1949, 105. A. MASARACCHIA, *Solone.* Florence 1958. E. MEYER, *Mus. Helv.* 17, 1960, 240, has reservations on historical points.

5 THE LESBIAN LYRIC

In the *Erotes*[1] of the Hellenistic poet Phanocles we are told that, when Orpheus was torn to pieces by the Thracian women, his head and his lyre were carried on the waves to Lesbos and there buried. The island's reputation for poetry and music, which is thus traced back to the great legendary singer, was won for it by Alcaeus and Sappho. A little time before them the name of the island had been made widely known by Terpander of Antissa on Lesbos, but his achievement, important and influential as it must have been, is very imperfectly known to us. At all events the victory which he gained at the Carneia in the 26th Olympiad (676/673) may be considered historical.

Ancient tradition makes Terpander the inventor of the seven-stringed lyre. The Greek desire to trace the origin of everything led to the compiling of whole catalogues of inventors[2] – catalogues whose statements we treat with justified caution. Here, however, the historical nucleus of the story can still be detected.[3] Certainly Terpander was not the first 'inventor' of the seven-stringed lyre, since we know of it in Crete in the second millennium, where it appears in a scene on the sarcophagus of Hagia Triada depicting funeral rites. There is Mycenaean evidence also for the lyre of seven or eight strings. But it is quite unlikely that the use of the instrument should have survived the fall of Mycenaean culture, and ancient authorities (e.g. Strabo 13, 2. p. 618) state that Terpander increased the number of the strings from four to seven. The four-stringed instrument belonged to the realm of speculation until Deubner collected the evidence for its existence in the Geometric period. On the other hand we have an excellent

[1] J. U. POWELL, *Coll. Alex.* p. 106.

[2] A. KLEINGÜNTHER, πρῶτος εὑρετής. *Phil. Suppl.* 26, 1933.

[3] L. DEUBNER, 'Die einsaitige Leier'. *Ath. Mitt.* 54, 1929, 194. *Phil. Woch.* 1930, 1566. M. WEGNER, *Das Musikleben der Griechen.* Berl. 1949, 48. 141. 227. H. L. LORIMER, *Homer and the Monuments.* Lond. 1950). R. P. WINNINGTON-INGRAM, *Lustrum* 1958/3 (1959), 14.

representation of a seven-stringed lyre on a pot from Old Smyrna[1] which may be dated in the second half of the seventh century, thus bringing us to precisely the time at which Terpander won his national reputation. Thus there is good evidence to connect him with the innovation. Pindar (fr. 125), in connection with Terpander's invention, says that the Lesbians became acquainted with the many-stringed Lydian lyre in drinking parties with Lydians. Certainly Lydian influence on the Greeks of Asia Minor is not at all unlikely, and the view chimes well with Athenaeus' statement (14, 37. 635 e) that Sappho used the Lydian *pectis*.[2]

Terpander's activity is particularly associated with Sparta, where he is said to have founded the first of the schools (καταστάσεις) of music which we shall have to discuss in the next section on the beginnings of choral lyric. Of his own contribution to choral lyric we know nothing; what we hear of his methods is in connection with solo singing to the lyre. There are all kinds of statements about the rhythms and melodies of his songs, particularly in the pseudo-Plutarchian *De Musica*, which derives its material mostly from Aristoxenus of Tarentum and Heraclides Ponticus. The few surviving fragments[3] under Terpander's name, even if genuine, teach us very little. Pseudo-Plutarch (c. 4) attributes to him citharodic prooemia in epic metre. These must have resembled in some degree the Homeric hymns. According to the same source (c. 3) Terpander also set Homeric texts for musical presentation; and his name is closely associated with the development of the nome, an old form of song sacred to Apollo. Normally the nome had seven parts, of which the first four, called the 'beginning' and the 'turn' (ἀρχά, μεταρχά, κατατροπά, μετακατατροπά) showed choric responsion. The middle section, the most important, was called the 'navel' (ὀμφαλός): it contained the narrative, and in the earlier period was strongly influenced in its form by epic. The 'seal' (σφραγίς) was a section in which the poet was permitted to sing of his own person and concerns. This kind of self-expression is by no means confined to the nome: we need only remember the hymn to the Delian Apollo and the blind man of Chios. The seventh and concluding section was the ἐπίλογος.[4] We saw earlier how extensively the nome was influenced in its form by the competition between vocal and instrumental music and between lyre and flute.

The fragments of tradition concerning Arion of Methymnus in Lesbos are even harder to put together than those concerning Terpander. He has a place in the citharodic tradition established by the older poet, but the achievements which concern us most nearly lie in another field. About 600 we find him at the court of Periander in Corinth, where his innovations raised the Dionysiac dithyramb to an artistic and elaborate form of choral song. This was one of the

---

[1] G. M. A. HANFMANN, *Harv. Stud. in Class. Philol.* 61, 1953, fig. 5. J. M. COOK, *Journ. Hell. Stud.* 71, 1951, 248 f. fig. 8. H. GALLET DE LA SAUTERRE, *Bull. Corr. Hell.* 75, 1951, 128 f. fig. 21.

[2] Cf. Sappho 156 LP, Alcaeus 36 LP. [3] *Anth. Lyr.* 2nd ed., fasc. 5, 1.

[4] On ἀρχά, ὀμφαλός, σφραγίς as parts of the nome see B. A. VAN GRONINGEN, 'A propos de Terpandre'. *Mnem.* S. IV 8, 1955, 177.

decisive events in the pre-history of tragedy, and we shall discuss it in that connection. His travels took him also to Sicily and southern Italy, and we shall later have to consider the possibility that his innovations exercised some influence upon the art of Stesichorus.

Arion is well known for the story of his being rescued by a dolphin. This charming tale reflects the fusion of two themes. The dolphin is sacred to Apollo, and we are meant to understand that the god did not desert his singer in his hour of need. In addition the story is one of the many told by the Greeks about the helpfulness and friendliness towards the human race shown by dolphins.[1] Herodotus (1. 24) knew of a brazen statue of Arion and his dolphin on Cape Taenarum, and Aelian (*Hist. anim.* 12. 45) cites an epigram on the subject together with a hymn expressing the poet's gratitude to Poseidon: both are later inventions.

Thanks to new discoveries, which have fortunately been more numerous in the last few years, we have so much material concerning Alcaeus and Sappho, that in the two poets, 'a yokepair of opposites', we can see the whole of Lesbian poetry. They were contemporaries, and it does not matter which of them one considers first. We begin with Alcaeus, since the biographical information and the remains of his poems bring before our eyes that world in which we see the figure of Sappho as a creature of her time and yet of all time.

Alcaeus belonged to that Aeolic nobility whose character has been sketched in bold lines by Heraclides Ponticus in his work on the history of music.[2] A proud race, delighting in wealth and happy to display it in horseracing and lavish hospitality; not stupid, but the very reverse of modest; high-spirited men, devoted to drink and women and to all the unrestrained pleasures of life. A little before, Heraclides had described the gloomy earnestness of the Dorians, and we can see that he is striving for antithesis; but undoubtedly he does hit upon the leading features of the social class in which Alcaeus lived.

His lifetime was a period of bitter civil struggles, particularly in his native city of Mytilene, the political centre of the island. After the overthrow of the kingdom, power was at first in the hands of the Penthilid house, who derived their descent from Penthilus, son of Orestes and fabled colonizer of Lesbos. Their violent rule provoked their adversaries twice to revolution: the second uprising was successful. What now followed (7th century) was a struggle for power among the proud aristocratic families, in which repeated attempts were made by individuals to become tyrant. This is the background to Alcaeus' life and to much of his poetry. Ancient and modern interpretations have often grossly simplified this period of history and have romanticized the part played by Alcaeus.

The fortunes of the poet in the struggles for power of the various noble families gave rise in antiquity to a tradition founded mainly on the writings of Alcaeus himself, eked out by local legends, and certainly incorporating a strong element of guesswork to fill up the holes. It is advisable to bear in mind the

---

[1] Some examples in LESKY, *Thalatta*. Vienna 1947.
[2] Fr. 163 WEHRLI (Ath. 14, 19. 624 e).

uncertainty that prevails on several points, and to emphasize the few ascertainable facts rather than make up a continuous narrative.

Alcaeus' chronology is given by his association with Pittacus, which brings us to the time around 600. According to Diogenes Laertius (1, 75. 79) Pittacus flourished (which in the usual practice of ancient authors means he was forty years old) in Ol. 42 (612–609). Later he ruled Mytilene for ten years, spent ten years in retirement, and died in 570. In the article in Suidas his floruit is given as the time of his first important political action – his expulsion of the tyrant Melanchros. Again Diogenes tells us that he did this in concert with the brothers of Alcaeus. Pittacus then can hardly have been the plebeian of many modern accounts. Certainly after their quarrel Alcaeus assails him as a man of low birth (κακοπατρίδας 348 LP[1]), but this may be easily explained. Pittacus' father Hyrras was a Thracian and of ill repute for drunkenness. The remains of a poem (72 LP) suggest that Alcaeus may have attacked him from that quarter also.

The question why Alcaeus did not take part in the overthrow of Melanchros is most simply answered by assuming that he was too young to join in with the men. The words 'while yet a child I witnessed . .' are found in a fragment (75 LP) which certainly refers to political events. From these considerations we should hardly go far wrong if we put his birth about 630–620.

We find Alcaeus himself at Pittacus' side in the battles waged between Mytilene and Athens over Sigeum at the entrance to the Hellespont. His performance was not uniformly creditable. Once he had to make a hasty retreat, leaving his arms behind him: they were subsequently consecrated as spoils in the temple of Athene at Sigeum. Alcaeus took his misfortune in the spirit of Archilochus, and described it in a poetical epistle to his friend Melanippus. The miserable remains (428 LP) indicate that, like his literary prototype, he attached a proper value to having come off with a whole skin.

The same story is told by Herodotus (5. 94 sq.) where he describes the battles over Sigeum. He there names Hegesistratus, son of Pisistratus, as the leader of the hard-pressed garrison. This fact has led a number of scholars radically to revise the chronology of Pittacus and Alcaeus, and to put them both in the mid-sixth century.[2] It is worth noting, however, that in the same book Herodotus speaks of a truce (apparently temporary) arranged by the intermediacy of Periander. Periander was at his most powerful about 600. Now Page has put forward what is probably the correct solution of the difficulty. Herodotus is describing various different phases of this long struggle, and his methods allow him to bring in also the early phase around 600 where Pittacus and Alcaeus belong.

Pittacus distinguished himself more than Alcaeus. He slew in single combat the Athenian general, the Olympic victor Phrynon, whose name appears in a newly discovered fragment (167 LP). The chronicle of Eusebius puts this event in 607/6. The war continued none the less, until the two parties, according to

---

[1] Alcaeus and Sappho are cited according to the edition of LOBEL and PAGE.
[2] Bibliography in TREU (see below); PAGE (see below), 155.

the custom of antiquity, asked Periander to arbitrate. He did so, and Sigeum remained in Athenian hands.

The establishment of peace abroad was presumably the signal to the aristocratic factions at home to renew their conflicts. Events took a course reminiscent of medieval Italian city states. The new man who returned from defeat and exile to bring Mytilene under his rule was Myrsilus of the Cleanactid family. The hetaeria which conspired against him may well have been the same which overthrew Melanchros, except that this time Alcaeus took an active part. The narrative which we shall shortly consider speaks of 'the followers of Alcaeus', giving the impression that he was the leader of the conspiracy. This is possible: but it is equally likely that later writers, acquainted with his literary reputation, magnified his part in the affair.

A papyrus (114 LP) gives us some sorely mutilated verses with the remains of a scholium speaking of a first banishment, when Alcaeus' group had prepared an attack on Myrsilus and escaped punishment by fleeing to Pyrrha, a settlement at the landward end of the gulf of Lesbos. At first Pittacus was in the conspiracy again, but he changed sides and for some time shared the supremacy with Myrsilus (cf. 70 LP).

In the time of the flight to Pyrrha Alcaeus composed the longest of the surviving pieces (129 LP): it is an impressive warsong, known only since the publication of Ox. Pap. 18 (1941). In a temple the poet prays to the Lesbian trinity – Zeus, Hera and Dionysus – to be delivered from the fate of banishment. The son of Hyrras is loaded with execrations: at a solemn sacrifice they had sworn to stick together come good or bad; but now 'the fat-guts' cares nothing for his pledged word, and has now himself become the murderer of his city. The last word still legible is the name Myrsilus.

A like theme recurs in another of the same group of new texts (130 LP), which is full of complaints about the hardships of exile. Far from the business of the state, he has to live like a peasant, like an animal. He has found refuge in a shrine: of what deities he does not say. But we are told that every year the temple rings to the happy cries of Lesbian women when they present themselves for the contest in beauty. Such a practice is known to us in connection with the rites of Hera on the island,[1] and it is very likely that this poem, like the one before, is connected with the sanctuary of the three gods.

There is one particular feature common to these two poems which deserves consideration in forming our picture of Alcaeus. In the first he refers to the sworn purpose of the hetaeria to liberate the people ($\delta\hat{a}\mu o s$), and in the second we hear how he misses the voice of the herald summoning him to the assembly ($\dot{a}\gamma\acute{o}\rho a$) or the council ($\beta\acute{o}\lambda\lambda a$). He speaks of the citizens as people who do evil to each other, but he would still like to be living among them like his father and father's father. The passages are of interest as showing that even such a Junker as Alcaeus was Greek enough to exemplify Aristotle's saying that a man is a $\zeta\hat{\omega}o\nu$ $\pi o\lambda\iota\tau\iota\kappa\acute{o}\nu$. But it would be a mistake to take them as betokening a democratic streak in Alcaeus, and to make him a forerunner of classical political

[1] Cf. E. DIEHL, Rhein. Mus. 92, 1943, 17.

theory. It is common in all ages that a man who aims at violence should claim to be a liberator of the people. And we must think of the assembly and council not in terms of Athens in Cleon's time, but in terms of the assembly in the second book of the *Iliad*. There also the herald summons the assembly and the old men take their places, but what happens is dictated by the 'kings'.

We have two verses (332 LP) from the beginning of a song in which Alcaeus hails the death of Myrsilus with wild exultation. Horace made this passage the model for the opening of his ode (1. 37) on the death of Cleopatra. How Alcaeus' poem went on we do not know; but we shall hardly be unfair to him if we think it inconceivable that it contained anything like the magnanimous restraint of the Roman towards the dead foe.

Alcaeus' jubilation was premature; the people now chose Pittacus as *aesymnetes*. The role of regent with full power and the task of ending the intolerable tensions by an arranged reconciliation provides a parallel to Solon's position in almost contemporary Athens. Although Pittacus in his earlier career had been deeply involved in the factions of the nobility, nevertheless he was the man to bring himself and the state back from error into order. After ten years he laid aside that office in which his conduct had earned him a place among the seven sages.

There is little to be said with certainty about Alcaeus' fortunes in this period. We recall that a scholium (114 LP) spoke of his first exile, which he spent in Pyrrha. Other periods of exile must have followed.

In the fragments there are occasional flashes that throw light on particular details. Alcaeus warns his reader against the man who in his thirst for power will bring the already crumbling city to destruction (141 LP) again, he warns the Mytileneans to pour water on the wood while it is still smoking, so that it does not burst into flames (74 LP schol.). When what he feared has come about, he inveighs against the choice, whose unanimity he does not deny (348 LP). We could not expect him to call the *aesymnetes* anything but tyrant; but it is characteristic of his fiery temper that he reproaches the citizens for lacking gall. There is a similar expression in Archilochus (96 D.), and we see a certain similarity between their characters.

An opportunity for attacking the arch-enemy Pittacus was afforded by the latter's marrying a girl from the great Penthelid family (70 LP). Later anecdotes make the marriage an unhappy one, and attribute to Pittacus a warning against marrying above one's station. The tale is the coinage of an age which saw Pittacus as the simple man of the people.

A considerable piece of contemporary history lies behind the few verses (69 LP) which begin by invoking Zeus, then relate in sober narrative tone that the Lydians had given 2000 staters to the conspirators to subsidize a *coup d'état*. Like the poems of Sappho, but in a different way, those of Alcaeus conjure up the seductive yet ominous presence of the Lydian kingdom behind the eastern Greeks.

We can scarcely doubt that Alcaeus travelled abroad, but we cannot go much beyond conjecture. His celebration of Athena Itonia in a hymn (325 P) may point to a stay in Boeotia; his praise of the soft waters of the Hebrus (45 LP) suggests a visit to Thrace; all the inferences, however, are rather vague. According to Strabo (1, 37) Alcaeus himself spoke of a sojourn in Egypt.

The story of the friendship and enmity between Alcaeus and Pittacus is for us an unfinished one. The story is certainly told[1] that Pittacus, when Alcaeus was in his power, pardoned him with the noble words that to forgive was better than to retaliate. But so many edifying anecdotes were made up about the magnanimity of Pittacus that this story seems to us doubtful. We may nevertheless suppose that Alcaeus returned home in the end. In some delightful verse (written, if we are not mistaken, with a deliberate comic exaggeration) he greets his brother Antimenidas, who has served in the Babylonian army and has performed prodigies of valour (350 LP). It seems natural to suppose that Antimenidas was returning home to Mytilene and that the poem was written there.

In a drinking-song (50 LP) he proposes to pour myrrh over his head and his grey-haired chest. This is the only reference to his reaching old age.

So far we have seen Alcaeus from only one side: as a member of a political club of Lesbian nobles, a man to whom the fluctuating struggle for power, anger and hatred, exultation and despair supplied the themes for unpremeditated poetry. The portrait needs a few more strokes.

The poems of Alcaeus are not crowded with simile and metaphor. This quality is part of their nature, to which we shall later return. But there is one image of his, worked out in elaborate and detailed allegory, which has gained currency in all later ages, although he was in part anticipated by another. Some verses of Archilochus (56 D.) speak of high rolling waves and threatening clouds, and Heraclitus, a writer of the early empire, tells us that the poet was speaking figuratively of danger in battle. If the verses of a London papyrus (56a D.) belong here, the poem contained an exhortation to bring the ship to safety by right management. Alcaeus (326 LP) gives a gripping scene of peril at sea: the winds blow all ways, water is slopping round the foot of the mast, the sail is in rags. Heraclitus declares this passage also to be allegorical, and it would show great misunderstanding of this type of poetry if we offered to disbelieve him. The remains of a commentary enable us to augment the already known fragment by two or three verses.[2] Considerable difficulties are raised by a fragment (73 LP) which has often been made immediately to follow 326 LP (as Diehl has done). There is still no satisfactory explanation. We can, however, discover the same imagery in another poem (6 LP). High waves threaten the greatest peril to the ship, it is time to strengthen the bulwarks and to run for safe harbour. Let no one weakly hesitate, but let all show themselves to be good men, worthy of their fathers asleep in the earth.

This allegory which Alcaeus found so useful a means of expression has a long and varied history: we need only mention classical tragedy and Horace 1. 14. In modern times it has been finely revitalized by Jean Anouilh in his *Antigone*. The two poems of Alcaeus have sometimes been interpreted with

---

[1] Diog. Laert. 1, 76. Diod. 9, 12. [2] 305 + 208 LP; cf. PAGE (*v. inf.*), 186.

unconscious reference to their many imitations, as if he had meant the ship of state as it is spoken of by Eteocles in the *Seven* and Creon in the *Antigone*, or as Horace speaks of his new participation in the state as a whole. But we must not overlook the difference in time and circumstances. Alcaeus is not speaking of the state in the sense of the later *politeia*: he is talking of the situation of his group among the perils involved in the struggle for power.

In a very singular poem – singular in that it consists of an enumeration of facts and is yet very effective – Alcaeus takes us into a place which must have been a very important part of his world: the armoury of his house (357 LP). There is the gleam of bronze, horse-hair plumes nod from shining helmets, greaves, coats of mail and Chalcidian swords lie ready to hand. The end of the extant piece is made very neatly to bend back and echo the beginning. There is no mention of the bow. We are in the company of nobles very like those of Eretria and Chalcis who in the Lelantine war outlawed the use of missile weapons.

If we enquire into Alcaeus' personal surroundings, we find that, next to the armoury, he loved the men's hall as the scene of happy revelry. In all ages fighting and drinking have gone hand in hand. We have also the testimony of Athenaeus (10. 430) that at all seasons and in all circumstances the poet might be found at the bowl. In the usual manner of such dusty erudition, he follows the statement with examples, for which we are very grateful. Here we find the pretty winter song on which Horace modelled his *Vides ut alta stet nive*, and the poem in which Alcaeus starts by speaking of the approach of spring. And promptly comes the injunction: 'Fill the flowing bowl!' The summer drinking song is in many ways remarkable. 'Wet your lungs with wine',[1] is the theme, 'The dog star wheels his course, the season wearies us, all things thirst with the heat; the cicadas shrill their song and the artichokes are in bloom. The passions of women are kindled, but men are apathetic: Sirius' heat weakens their heads and limbs.' With immense force and immediacy these lines bring before us a scorching mediterranean summer day with its shimmering light; yet not a single touch in the description is original. Its model is in Hesiod (*Erga* 582 seqq.). Once again we see the force of tradition in an art which did not concern itself wholly or even predominantly with unqualified new creation.

This Aeolian aristocracy was in many aspects of its life the true inheritor of Homer's world. Here again there is no comfortable belief in a life beyond the grave. Indeed they are a little worse off in this respect, for we find no reflection of the confidence which epic heroes had of surviving in reputation. Yet another song (38 LP) begins with praise of the winecup, and Alcaeus reminds his boon companions that the journey across Acheron is a journey out of the sunlight for ever. Horace echoes the theme in the fourth ode of the first book. In Alcaeus' poem we find also a rare ingredient – mythology. The story of Sisyphus is told to show that even the most cunning cannot escape death.

What we now have of Alcaeus is miserable fragments compared with the edition prepared by the Alexandrians Aristophanes and Aristarchus, which

[1] On the curious anatomy see Gellius 17. 11. 1; Macr. *Sat.* 7. 15. 2; Plut. *Quaest. conv.* 7. 1.

comprised at least ten books arranged according to subject. We shall therefore consider carefully anything that enables us to enlarge our picture of his poetry. The first book of the Alexandrian edition contained the hymns, beginning with that to Apollo (307 LP). A prose abstract of it in a speech of Himerius makes it clear that the poem was filled not so much with religious feeling as with highly wrought mythical narrative. Its climax was the epiphany of the god at midsummer at Delphi, where all nature greeted his appearance. The quality of this poetry is best illustrated by three strophes which can still be reconstructed belonging to the *Hymn to the Dioscuri*. The twin brothers are praised as giving succour at sea, bringing deliverance on stormy nights to the imperilled ship. We may compare this hymn with the Homeric and Theocritean hymns to the Dioscuri. There are a number of similar features, but the especial beauty of the Lesbian hymn lies in the description of the epiphany: the divine youths manifest themselves in the St Elmo's fire which glows reassuringly from the rigging on nights of peril. We have the opening of Alcaeus' *Hymn to Hermes*, and from a note of Porphyrio's on the relevant ode of Horace we learn that the latter was indebted to Alcaeus *inter alia* for one charming touch: the impudence of the child Hermes, who casually stole Apollo's quiver, and was able to dissolve into laughter his brother's anger over the theft of the cattle. Fragments can be recognized of other hymns (as to Hephaestus and to Athena Itonia): one to Eros (327 LP) contains the pleasing and apparently original touch that the god is a son of Zephyrus and Iris, the west wind and the messenger of the gods who comes down the rainbow to earth. The anonymous fragments of a narrative that may come from a *Hymn to Artemis* have been attributed to Alcaeus by the Oxford editors. It would be good to know with more certainty, since the delightful scene in Callimachus where Artemis obtains from her father Zeus the promise of perpetual virginity is modelled upon this piece.

The most recent texts, known to us since the publication of *Pap. Ox.* 21 in 1951, add appreciably to our knowledge of Alcaeus' use of epic material.[1] One fragment (283 LP) tells of the sorrows which Helen's lust brought upon Troy; another (298 LP) of the impiety of the Locrian Ajax in carrying off Cassandra from the temple of Athene. We spoke earlier of a drinking song in which Alcaeus used the story of Sisyphus as an example. We might suppose that the last-named fragments belonged in a similar context, if such a view were not negatived by another poem (42 LP), in which Helen and Thetis are compared and judgment given for the latter. The end of the poem is clearly marked in the papyrus, and the piece itself, with its strongly marked ring-composition, is obviously complete. We must then consider the possibility that Alcaeus took little ornamental elements from the general stock of epic themes and arranged them for informal performance in his circle. The verses from a very short poem (44 LP) which describe the intervention of Thetis for the injured Achilles may also be so interpreted.

Tiny fragments sometimes suggest how much we lack towards forming a

---

[1] *Ox. Pap.* nr. 2378 has been ascribed to Alcaeus, but this is doubtful: M. TREU, *Phil.* 102, 1958, 13; *Gnom.* 32, 1960, 744, 2.

general assessment of the poetry of Alcaeus. The most noteworthy of these (10 LP) may be called the *Maiden's Complaint* to underline the connection between it and a known Hellenistic poem (*Anth. Lyr.* fasc. 6. 197). The opening verse is concerned with the complaints of a female person about some great sorrow; next the subject is the belling of a stag. No one has satisfactorily explained the connection. So far as we can tell, this is Alcaeus' only lyric piece not written in his own person.

Horace (*carm.* 1. 32, 9) says of Alcaeus that he sang of Bacchus, the Muses, Venus with her inseparable son, and Lycus with his dark eyes and dark hair. Other Roman authors also speak of Alcaeus' erotic poetry.[1] But in what survives there is no mention of the lovely Lycus, nor are there any themes of this kind Probably his affections were directed towards some of those named as his boon companions.

Once he seems to strike a philosophical note. But the proposition that nothing comes of nothing (320 LP) might well occur to a mind not profoundly philosophic, despite the fundamental role it played in some later systems.

That the art of Alcaeus had a great influence is undeniable; but it is hard to say why. The life of this Lesbian junker was mostly spent between the struggles of power-hungry factions and the carousals of the men's hall: scarcely subjects attractive for their own sake. If we had Alcaeus' works entire, we might greatly widen our knowledge of his themes and methods of expression, but our impression of his personality could hardly be affected. One could not without reservation call his poems 'class literature'. Certainly they are in so far as their whole body of assumptions is determined by the actions and passions of a restricted social stratum. On the other hand the poet does not make it his business to advertise in his poems the beliefs and ideals that animate his class: at all events that is not his main business, and in this respect he is in sharp contrast with such a poet as Pindar, whose work is purely an embodiment of aristocratic values. An obvious indication of this difference is that the *gnome*, or sententious saying, is very prominent in Pindar, but is almost wholly lacking in Alcaeus.

This comparison with Pindar, the greatest representative of choral lyric, is also instructive when we consider the formal elements. Pindar's pompous burden of adjectives, his long drawn and sometimes inextricable sentence structure, the strained and strutting sublimity of his language could hardly find a sharper contrast than the unpretentious poetry of Lesbos. True, Alcaeus varies to some degree. Dionysius of Halicarnassus (*de imit.* 2. 2, 8) very truly observes that sometimes if one only removed the metre from Alcaeus' poems, one would be reading a political speech. Certainly the report that the Lydians subsidized the conspirators reads like a passage from an historian. But in the hymns the language is much more elevated, and in the poems which bring in mythology the indebtedness to epic is as obvious in language as in matter. But on the whole Alcaeus' verses are well girt up, and their easy flow forms a delightful contrast to the rigidity of the extremely elaborate, syllable-counting metre.

If we now enquire into the real reason for the influence of these poems, which

---

[1] Cic. *Tusc.* 4. 71. *De nat. deor.* 1. 79. Quintil. 10. 1, 63.

we approached at first with every reservation and caution, we find it in the singular immediacy with which a robust temperament put into words, with strong light and sharp outlines, all the impressions of the world about him. To understand this quality of immediacy we should compare Alcaeus' winter drinking song with Horace's imitation of it. Let us put the short sentences, 'Zeus is sending rain; there is a great storm from heaven; the streams are frozen', alongside the polished smoothness of Horace's poem, which artistically imposes the careful structure of its sentences upon the Alcaic strophe. Alcaeus is above all concerned with the lively individual impression; his verses reflect them with a seeming artlessness which we find only in great art. The big painted bowls wink from the table at the thirsty poet; he admires the gold-bound ivory haft of the sword that his brother has brought home with him; he sees St Elmo's fire glow from the rigging. And even where he speaks to us in allegory, in the images of a ship in peril, everything is endowed with that immediacy which has led some to deny the allegorical sense altogether. We have already mentioned the passage in Hesiod from which the individual elements of the summer poem were borrowed. But here again it is impressive to see how the epic description is reflected in the short and crowding sentences of Alcaeus. Dionysius was right when he gave brevity, sweetness and force as the characteristic of Alcaeus' poetry.

Sappho came from the same aristocratic circles as Alcaeus, little as their worlds had in common. Her life also was affected by the struggles for power in Mytilene, and for a time she was in exile. This passage of her life affords us the most reliable indication that we have for the determining of her date. The statements of the Marmor Parium (36) enable us to put her flight to Sicily between 604–3 and 596–5. Various indications derived from the chronicle of Eusebius put her floruit in 600–599 or 595–4. She seems then to have been a slightly older contemporary of Alcaeus'.

Sappho was widely read throughout antiquity, and in consequence we find many biographical details about her, mostly derived from her own writings. What has survived still gives us a certain amount of biography. Where we no longer have a reflection in her poems, the reports are of limited interest and worth relating only in outline: her father Scamandronymus, her mother Cleïs, and her place of birth Lesbos (the latter disputed). We may perhaps suppose that Sappho was born in Eresos but spent most of her life in Mytilene. Her name appears in the remains of the ancient texts and on coins in the undissimilated form Psappho.[1] We are told that in her poems she referred with pride to her brother Larichus who on festal occasions poured the wine in the council chamber. Sappho's brothers were not always a source of pride to her: there is a story told by Herodotus,[2] and supported by some valuable verses of Sappho herself, that her brother Charaxus engaged in trade and sailed with a cargo of Lesbian wine for Naucratis, the Greek trading city in the Nile delta. Such a venture was common at the time: it need not be connected with the wave of

---

[1] In the poems: 1, 20. 65, 5. 94, 5. 133, 2 LP. G. ZUNTZ, 'On the Etymology of the Name Sappho'. *Mus. Helv.* 8, 1951, 12.

[2] 2. 135, where the hetaera, however, is called Rhodopis.

banishments in Lesbos. Beginning in the late seventh century, Naucratis had rapidly reached great prosperity, and was consequently noted for its accomplished hetaerae. One of these, Doricha, soon had Charaxus in her toils. He bought her freedom and was bled white by her. We possess a poem restorable in its main outlines (5 LP) in which Sappho hails the return of her brother. She invokes Cypris (who as Aphrodite Galenaea makes the sea calm) and the Nereids to bring her brother safely home. He must abandon his former errors and return to a position of honour: i.e., in the aristocratic ethic, he must be a delight to his friends and a bane to his enemies. His sister he must hold in honour and free her from the anxieties which he formerly caused. The warmth of sisterly love in these verses is as affecting as if the poem had been written today. We can enjoy it by itself, but we must not forget that it was one of a series of events, now imperfectly known, leading to a striking peripeteia. A second poem (15 LP) probably accompanies the brother's departure on a new voyage: of this we cannot be sure, but certainly she reviles Doricha and prays that she may not have a second victory over Charaxus. One of the most remarkable sources for Sappho's biography is the letter to Phaon which Ovid composes for her in the fifteenth of the *Epistulae heroidum*. It is a strange mixture, with credible elements amid an accumulation of anecdote. To the first class we may assign Sappho's complaint that her brother has added disgrace to misfortune and that he sails the sea in poverty. He has returned her well-meant advice with hatred. Herodotus also mentions that Sappho took her brother seriously to task after his return from Naucratis. Thus the charming propempticon may represent a ray of hope doomed to disappointment.

Such singular interpretations of Sappho's character have been put forward by modern scholars that there has seemed to be no place for a husband in her life. Thus the rich Andrian Cercolas has been deleted from the story, and with him the daughter Cleïs. Now that the new discoveries have delightfully brought to life the relations between Sappho and her daughter, we may consider that chapter closed. First we have some verses which will be important later (132 LP): 'Mine is a beautiful child, her face like a golden flower, Cleïs my beloved. I would not exchange her for all Lydia nor for lovely . . .' A papyrus at Copenhagen and one at Milan give us welcome knowledge of a poem[1] as charming as it is in many ways noteworthy. Sappho first speaks of advice which she once gave her daughter concerning a young girl's toilet: a purple band suits dark hair very well, but for fair hair a garland is a better adornment. But recently the fashion has come in from Sardes of wearing gaily coloured bonnets: one of these (we may suppose) is now the object of Cleïs' wishes. But Sappho cannot think where she is going to find one. Next comes a passage damaged beyond restoration, but clearly containing references to the Mytileneans, to the Cleanactids and to exile. Clearly Sappho here must be referring to the troubles in Lesbos which we know of from the poems of Alcaeus. It is striking that nowhere else in the extant writings do we find so specific a reference to politics. Sappho's

---

[1] 98 LP; cf. SCHADEWALDT, *Studies presented to D. M. Robinson*. Saint Louis 1951, 499, and PAGE (*v. inf.*), 97.

reference to the political struggles of her menfolk in connection with a question of fashionable headwear delightfully illustrates her exclusive and immediate concern with the feminine. And even this grave bonnet-controversy illustrates the background of Lydian culture behind the life of the eastern Greeks.

In Ovid Sappho lets her fame console her for nature's having denied her bodily beauty, in particular tall stature and a fair complexion. This lack of beauty is a consistent feature in the biographical sources,[1] and it may well be true.

In several fragments[2] we seem to be hearing a complaint of the poetess over the passing of her youth: but do not know how long she lived and we can do without the knowledge. Gundolf remarks in his book on Goethe that we tend to picture the world's great literary figures at a particular time of life. For Sappho it is a woman's ripe maturity, with youth and beauty, its brightness yet undimmed by the thought of its transience.

The ancients were not content with picking out one biographical detail or another from the poems of Sappho: her personality seemed to invite wholesale invention. Her death was romantically embellished. Our oldest indication is found in Menander's *Leucadia* (Strab. 10. 452), where he alludes to the story in a way that suggests it was already a traditional tale. We ought not be surprised to find Middle Comedy already making free with her character. Menander relates (unusually for him in anapaests) that Sappho set her cap at the haughty Phaon, and then set the example of jumping from 'the precipitous cliffs' into the sea. He is referring to the promontory of Leucas, on which there was a temple of Apollo Leucatas. This fable, which Ovid translated into bourgeois terms, and which supplied the theme for Grillparzer's drama, is extremely interesting if we trace the history of its elements. It is apparent that this Phaon was originally a creature of mythology. Ancient tradition (211 LP) knows of him as a sturdy ferryman plying his trade between Lesbos and the mainland, who won the especial favour of Aphrodite. The mask of historicity is laid aside when we read that Aphrodite loved him and hid him among some lettuces (Aelian *V.H.* 12. 18). What we have here is a vegetation-spirit, one of those associated with Aphrodite, very much akin to Adonis. We are expressly told that Sappho often sang of this Phaon; and it is easy to see how this would have given rise to the fable of her love for the handsome youth. Comedy would very likely have taken the lead in putting such an interpretation on the poems. The leap from Cape Leucas is harder to understand. Such a notion occurs elsewhere: the most helpful passage is a distich of Anacreon's (17 D.), where the poet in a frenzy of love wishes to leap from the Leucadian rocks into the white-foaming sea. The cape was originally a legendary locality associated with notions of death (*Od.* 24. 11), and a leap from it was synonymous with a sinking into nothingness and oblivion. Was this element in the story suggested by Sappho's having used some such expression in her own poems? It is quite possible.[3]

---

[1] PAGE (*v. inf.*), 133. 0.   [2] Thus 58 LP, cf. SCHADEWALDT (*v. inf.*), 157.

[3] J. CARCOPINO, *De Pythagore aux apôtres*. Paris 1956, supposes without good grounds that Sappho's leap from the Leucadian cliff was a Pythagorean invention from fourth-century Tarentum.

Thanks to the numerous discoveries in papyri, we are well enough acquainted with Sappho's work to know that one group of poems had a special place in it: the *Epithalamia*, a genre much favoured in antiquity, as Catullus' elegant imitation shows. If in no other way, these songs have a place of their own as having been composed by Sappho, a supreme artist of the individual song to the lyre, for performance by a chorus.

The Alexandrians classified the poems of Sappho, unlike those of Alcaeus, not by subject matter, but by metre. Understandably the first book contained those written in Sapphic strophes. It is, however, only a conjecture that the last book contained the marriage songs. Some support for this view is given by a new papyrus (103 LP) with the remains of a sort of *catalogue raisonné* of Sappho's works.

Rewarding as the finds of papyri have been, we still possess only small fragments of Sappho's lyrical achievement. It is very regrettable that the *Epithalamia* should have been perhaps the worst sufferers, considering the impression we are able to form of them. They strikingly illustrate how a popular and traditional song for particular occasions, in all its natural freshness and bloom, can be transformed through the medium of great art into the perfection of literary form without losing the charm of spontaneity. Songs of this kind accompanied the bride on the way to her new home or were sung outside the chamber of the newly married couple.[1] They celebrated the good luck of the bridegroom and the beauty of the bride; and Sappho, never as sparing of imagery as Alcaeus, here embodies some of her most striking beauties: 'Like a rosy apple on a high branch is the maiden; the pickers have forgotten her – no, not forgotten: they have simply not been able to reach her' (105 a LP). This may be taken as praise of unsullied virginity; but in view of the comic element in this kind of poetry, we might suppose it to refer to a bride no longer in the first bloom of youth. There is another image in 105c LP: the hyacinth on the mountain side sinks to the ground, trodden under the careless foot of the shepherd. This may refer to the roughness of a lover who does not properly value what he takes: but Fränkel's view deserves consideration, that the purity of the bride is accentuated by the contrasting image of one who has given herself unreflectingly. Two verses of a dialogue (114 LP) are as tender in their feeling as anything in Greek poetry, the girl complains: 'Maidenhood, maidenhood, whither goest thou from me?' Maidenhood replies: 'Nevermore come I to thee, nevermore'. One can compare this only with the young man's farewell as depicted by Raimund: the comparison needs no apology, for in both instances true poetry has drawn from the same stream, very near its source. There are examples too of light-hearted raillery, such as was common on these occasions. One of the young men kept guard before the door, otherwise the maidens might easily rescue their companion who is being taken from their number. They are ill-disposed towards the janitor, and they sneer at him (110 LP): 'he has feet seven fathom long: it takes five ox-hides to make his sandals, and ten shoemakers have to sew them.'

---

[1] On the character of the songs: R. MUTH, 'Hymenaios und Epithalamion'. *Wien. Stud.* 67, 1954, 5.

There is no parallel in Sappho to a poem (44 LP) which has been declared spurious, although with little ground. The Trojan herald Idaeus appears, announcing the arrival of the ship which is bringing Andromache to Troy to marry Hector. The female heart again betrays itself in the delight taken in enumerating costly furnishings and ornaments. Now everyone goes to meet Andromache, and after a lacuna we hear of the entry of the young couple with music and acclamation. What is the purpose of this poem? Its end has been preserved, and there is no question of its turning from the narrative to something else. Nevertheless it has repeatedly been explained as a marriage-song, in which the narrative element has been allowed to overshadow the principal purpose. But it would hardly have been a good omen at a marriage feast to sing of the wedding of the man whose corpse was mutilated by Achilles and the woman who became Pyrrhus' slave. It is very hard to decide; but since among the fragments of Alcaeus we have found passages showing little more than a pleasure in epic scenes for their own sake, we may leave such a possibility open for Sappho also.

Several of the marriage songs are dactylic, and we notice that in such poems Sappho makes wider use than elsewhere of epic elements of language.[1] The phenomenon is easily explicable: we noticed it in Archilochus also. The account of Andromache's wedding is in Aeolic dactyls, and its metrical affinity to epic explains why it is so rich in Homeric features, particularly in the use of compound adjectives as *epitheta ornantia*. On the other hand, the syntax, with its simple sequence of short sentences, is Sappho's own.

The choral epithalamia were only a small part of Sappho's output. Her favourite form was the individual song to the lyre, and her personal experience was the stuff of her poetry. Before we enter upon this inner region of her art, we should mention a rather difficult passage. Aristotle in the *Rhetoric* (1367 a. 137 LP) quotes parts of a dialogue in Alcaic metre, the speakers being Alcaeus and Sappho. The man says: 'I would fain say something to you, but modesty prevents me.' The woman replies: 'If you had any love for what is good or beautiful, if your tongue were not brewing hateful words, shame would not lie upon your eyes, but you would speak of what is virtuous.' Now among the fragments of Alcaeus there is one (384 LP), a twelve-syllable line, addressing the 'violet-tressed, stately, purely-smiling Sappho'. If one adopts Bergk's emendation of the line in Aristotle, making it a dodecasyllable, 384 LP goes neatly before it. There is one formal point that deserves note:[2] the name is spelt Σάπφοι instead of the Ψάπφοι which one would expect. Now it is after all Aristotle who assigns the dialogue to Alcaeus and Sappho, and Page has rightly observed that there is no real reason to reject such an idea. There is a red-figure pot of the fifth century[3] depicting Sappho and Alcaeus in animated interchange: the painter seems to have known our lines and to have taken them as Aristotle did. But doubt on this point is not confined to modern scholarly scepticism. The scholia

---

[1] Details of this sort are pointed out with great industry by DIEHL in all the authors in his *Anth. Lyr.* On Sappho 44 see PAGE (*v. inf.*), 66.

[2] PAGE (*v. inf.*), 108. 1.   [3] Furtw.-Reichh. T. 64.

to Aristotle seem to reflect a debate whether this was not a purely poetical representation of the 'rejected suitor' theme: but we do not know who held the rival views.

It would be rash to manufacture a piece of biography out of the fragment 121 LP, in which an over-young suitor is rejected. The passage is noteworthy for the sharp distinction it draws between the friendship of a man and woman and their physical relation as lovers. But it may refer to anyone: lyric poetry put into the mouth of another person is found elsewhere in Sappho. For example, the maiden's lament to her mother (102 LP), a piece with a strong atmosphere of folksong, can hardly be written in Sappho's own person, complaining as it does that she cannot mind her spinning for thinking of her absent lover. These are poems akin to that one (94 D.) in which a maiden laments in the night the loneliness of her couch. They reflect a literary genre, not Sappho's personal experience.

In the surviving pieces Sappho mostly sings of her own world, and the voice that we hear is that of a loving heart. Maidens of her circle – we know the names of many of them – awake in her the longing of a heart that is always seeking: they delight and disappoint her, bring her sorrow and happiness. This is the realm of feeling from which those two poems come (1. 31 LP) on which alone Sappho's reputation was based before the papyrus discoveries. The *Prayer to Aphrodite* calls on the goddess as a helper in the pain of unfulfilled longing: the prayer for her appearance and help is emphasized at the beginning and end of the poem, which is preserved in full. Now in ancient poems of invocation it is normal to remind the god of some earlier occasion on which he granted favour or help. In the true manner of Greek art Sappho has taken over a traditional element and made it all her own. Within the framework of the initial and final invocation she has enclosed a picture of the goddess' earlier epiphanies. On a golden car Aphrodite sailed down to the dark earth, drawn by sparrows with energetic flapping of wings, and granted Sappho's desire. Laughingly, as one would speak to a rather troublesome child, the goddess asked what had gone wrong this time that she was calling on Aphrodite; what was it that she so earnestly desired? As the goddess then made a promise, so let her now fulfil it! The magic of Sappho's poetry is hard to capture in words, but an especial charm of this prayer to Aphrodite arises from a remarkable contrast. The poem is full of warm and insistent passion, and yet is cast by Sappho in a form which makes her take part and look on at the same time. The construction of the poem, with a frame set in the present enclosing a central core recalling the past, is the outward expression of an antinomy which is a distinctive characteristic of Sappho's poetry.

In essence it is found again in that poem which the writer of the treatise *On Elevated Language* quotes as a perfect example of the depiction of feeling, and which Catullus chose for imitation. Sappho thinks that man as happy as the gods, who sits quietly opposite the maiden and hears her talking and laughing. But Sappho's heart is quite undone by a glance at the beloved's face: her tongue will not move, a subtle fire burns under her skin, her eyes see no longer, her ears ring, she breaks into a sweat, she trembles, she is as pale as the death which seems so near. The text breaks off with the mysterious words: 'Yet all must be endured, since . . .'

This description of the symptoms of love has had the most persistent influence over more than a thousand years. Aristaenetus even, the late writer of erotic pastiche, shows many traces of dependence on Sappho when he describes the passions of a girl in love. The ancient conception of love as an irrational power, falling like a sickness upon men, found a complete expression in the verses of Sappho.

Do these lines come from a marriage song, as many believe? Certainly not in the sense that she made her plight the theme of a song performed at a feast, in order to glorify the bride's beauty. In these verses a human being is alleviating an intolerable situation by giving it objective existence in art. The situation envisaged may indeed be a wedding-feast, since these are the circumstances most readily imaginable for such an intimate relation of man and woman.

Hardly anywhere else do we find Sappho in such a white heat. She speaks of the fire of longing (48 LP), and of Eros who shakes her inwardly like the mountain-wind shaking the oak-trees (47 LP). In another passage (130 LP) she describes the god, with unforgettable verbal imagery, as the bitter-sweet monster against whom there is no help. Her wish (95 LP) to go down to the dewy lotus-covered banks of Acheron probably comes from a context like that of the poem we have just considered. But Sappho's lyre has many tones. She makes fun of her own longings in a poem (16 LP) that begins by considering the diversity of human judgments. To serve in the cavalry, the infantry, or in the fleet, seems to one or another the finest thing on earth: but to Sappho the finest thing is that which she loves. So she would sooner behold the graceful walk of Anactoria and the light of her countenance than all the chariots and arms of the Lydians: that is a land to which many of her maidens have been taken as wives. The same theme recurs in another poem, again one of her most charming (96 LP). She converses with Atthis about a friend,[1] a girl now living far away in Sardes. Now she outshines the women of Lydia as the moon out-shines the stars. The simile is followed by a passage that has exercised an incom-parable influence on later poetry: a moonlit night is described, with the light falling on sea and plain, on the shimmering dew and the luxuriant flowers. The whole proportioning of the stanzas makes it clear that this is not an elaborate descriptive simile, such as we find in Homer. The moonlit night depicted here is the night on which Sappho and Atthis send their tender thoughts far across the sea.

If we are not content with a purely aesthetic enjoyment of these poems, then at every step the question becomes more burning: What kind of love is it that they express? For centuries the answer has fluctuated between extremes, repre-sented by the total depravity so roundly attributed to her by Pierre Bayle in his article 'Sappho' (1695) and the view of Wilamowitz that she was the principal

[1] Her name may have been Arignota, but this is disputed, cf. PAGE (v. inf.), 89.

of a *pensionnat de jeunes filles*.[1] In antiquity also interpretations differed widely. Maximus of Tyre compares her with Socrates, while in Seneca we find the question put *an Sappho publica fuerit*.[2] It is quite understandable that some ancient grammarians fancied there were two Sappho's, and made one of them the scapegoat: the view is exemplified in Suidas.

A complete picture of the Lesbian society is not now possible. It seems reasonable, however, that the absorption of the male nobility in fighting and drinking led the women to wish for some form of association which would prevent the extinction of intellectual life. Sappho's poems attest such an association, and despite the fragmentary transmission they give us valuable details of it. Scholars are careful nowadays not to imagine Sappho's group as a kind of educational institution. But at all events the facts show her as the centre of a closely-knit group of young girls. Suidas speaks of them as pupils of Sappho's, and gives some names. We must not attach too much importance to late reports, but there was a circle of young people around Sappho; and we may add the important fact that it was by no means unique in contemporary Mytilene. We know of Andromeda and Gorgo, whom Sappho felt to be her rivals: she often shows bitter animosity towards them. Andromeda lured Atthis away from her (131 LP) – Atthis, whose unpretentious maiden grace had won Sappho's heart, and who recurs elsewhere in the poems. Andromeda is also the object of the attack (57 LP) on the peasant woman who does not know how to arrange her robe about her ankle. Propriety of appearance was valued highly in that circle, and the point is well illustrated by the archaic figures of girls on the Acropolis.

We can form a picture of the life of Sappho's circle which is clear enough to put out of court several modern interpretations. There is a poem with many touches of tenderness (94 LP), whose surviving portion begins with Sappho's wish to die, so deeply is she hurt by the loss of the friend who must leave her. Her consolation is in remembering the hour of parting, when she herself was strong and self-controlled, while the sobbing girl remembered all the joys they had shared. The poem speaks of fragrant garlands and perfumes, of precious peace, and in the mutilated latter part we hear of a sacred place or festival which she never failed to attend. Almost the last readable word is 'grove'. We may connect this with another poem (2 LP, *Pap. Soc. It.* nr. 1300) preserved on an ostrakon.[3] Aphrodite is invoked in her sacred grove: again the repeated invocation frames an inner portion, here a description of the grove, and a description only comparable with that of the night in the poem to the distant friend. The

---

[1] On the history of attitudes to Sappho: H. RUDIGER, *Sappho. Ihr Ruf und Ruhm bei der Nachwelt. Erbe der Alten.* 21. 1933. Id., 'Das sappische Versmass in der deutschen Literatur'. *Ztschr. f. Deutsche Philol.* 58, 1933, 140. R. MERKELBACH, 'Sappho und ihr Kreis'. *Phil.* 101, 1957, 1. See also the work by several hands, *El descubrimiento del amor in Grecia.* Madrid 1959.

[2] Max. Tyr. *Diss.* 18. 9. Seneca, *ep.* 88. 37.

[3] Bibliography on this poem in K. MATTHIESSEN, *Gymn.* 64, 1957, 554; cf. G. LANATA, 'L' ostracon fiorentino con versi di Saffo'. *Stud. It.* 32, 1960, 64. E. RISCH, 'Der göttliche Schlaf bei Sappho'. *Mus. Helv.* 19, 1962, 197, on the corrupt and difficult κατάγριον in v. 8.

altars smoke with incense, cool streams murmur among the apple branches, the ground is carpeted with roses and sleep drops from the trembling leaves.

We must not jump to conclusions and make Sappho a kind of priestess or her circle a cult-association. The fragments do indeed show that it was concerned with worship and that the festivals on holy days were the high points of its life. All we know of Greek life suggests that the girls themselves sang and danced on such occasions. Singing was common at other times also in the Sapphic circle: we may suppose that the girls learned from her, without making her into a schoolmistress. Sappho herself indicates what view she took of their function in life: when her daughter is mortally ill she forbids loud wailing: no such sound must be heard in a house dedicated to the service of the Muses (150 LP). The purpose and the pride of her life is to be an attendant on the Muses (μουσοπόλος), since the powers of song which the Muses gave her will endure. Her name will be on the lips of men and even death will not extinguish it (65. 193 LP). When she wants to speak evil of an enemy, she promises her a miserable shadowy existence in Hades – the lot of men and women who have no share in the roses of Pieria (55 LP). It is probably more than an accident of transmission that the comforting belief of the aristocracy in survival by reputation comes out more strongly in Sappho than in Alcaeus, who lived for the here and now. The value also that she attributes to being remembered is far greater.

Towards one or another in this fluctuating group of female companions Sappho always cherished a particular affection. She sings of the passions of her heart in a way which precludes the interpretation of her feelings as purely maternal. Her love is a desire for spiritual domination and possession, capable of the tenderest longing and again of the most complete, almost annihilating torment. There is nothing to suggest that it had any base origin. There is no distinction here between the beauty of outward appearance and the inner beauty of the soul. Of this there could be no clearer proof than the manner in which Sappho speaks of her daughter Cleïs in the passage which we discussed earlier.

A whole world separates Sappho from Plato, and yet the first stage on the philosopher's road to the last and highest recognition of virtue which he embodies in the Symposium is provided by the appearance of beauty in the sensible world and by the longing that it excites. Sappho had formerly written some striking verses embodying a line of thought which leads beyond her world and her age (50 LP): 'one who is beautiful has the beauty which is accessible to sight; but he who is good must also be beautiful'. In καλός and ἀγαθός she is using the two words which later were combined in the ideal of καλοκαγαθία.

For anyone to whom the foregoing interpretation of Sappho's love for her friends seems inconceivable there is a more convincing argument available. In a papyrus (nr. 1612 P.) we have the remains of an ancient biography in which we read that 'some writers' accused Sappho of immorality. In that case neither her poems nor reliable tradition could have offered any support for the gossip which later ages repeated from the bawdy inventions of comedy.

Sappho's art displays the same immediacy as that of Alcaeus: but while in the one we are shown the armoury and the banqueting-hall, in Sappho we are taken into a very different world. Here feeling is everything, and we perceive its fluctuations, its power and intensity as immediately as if the artistic and technical means, through which of course they have to be conveyed, were not there. We have seen that Sappho had a great faculty of self-observation. Often her attitude in some past situation is the theme of her poetry. But even then the living warmth of the expression makes no concession to the coolness of reflection. Her language is simple: every verse is direct and unaffected. Homeric elements are seldom used except in the dactylic verses, almost never as pure ornaments of style. The domination of her poetry by feeling has its formal counterpart in the musical qualities of the language, shown especially in the use of vowel-sounds. The same quality has determined the structure of her sentences, which are always simple. Everything has the spontaneity of nature itself.

The world around her is depicted by Sappho with the same immediacy as her own feelings: the grove of Aphrodite, the moonlit night, the flowers, the sea. In Alcaeus the outlines are sharp and defined: here over all there is a gentle shimmering light like that of the moon. We go out of the armoury into the twilight gardens of Aphrodite. Ancient literary criticism again showed its grasp of essentials when Demetrius (de eloc. 132), speaking of the charm of description, gives Sappho's work in general as an example of it.

Much of Sappho's work survived the end of antiquity, as the remains of her fifth book in the Berlin papyri show. According to Themistius she was read in school in the fourth century. Himerius was well acquainted with Alcaeus: cf. R. Stark, *Annal. Saravienses* 8, 1959, 43.

Text: for Sappho and Alcaeus: E. LOBEL and D. PAGE, *Poetarum Lesbiorum fragmenta*. Oxf. 1955, with the new papyri and a verbal index; to these add *Ox. Pap.* 23, 1956, nr. 2358 (Alcaeus) and 2357 (Sappho): on 2378 see p. 159 n. 1. Diehl's *Anthologia Lyrica* is still valuable for its references. J. M. EDMONDS, *Lyra Graeca* 1. Loeb Lib. Lond. 1922. TH. REINACH and A. PUECH, *Alcée. Sappho. Coll. des Un. de Fr.* Paris 1937, repr. 1960. C. GALLAVOTTI, *Saffo e Alceo* 2 vols. Naples 1947–48. M. TREU, *Alkaios*. Munich 1952. Id., *Sappho*. 2nd ed. Munich 1958 (both with trans., comm. and bibliog.). E. STAIGER, *Sappho. Griech. u. deutsch*. Zürich 1957. Interpretation: A. TURYN, *Studia Sapphica. Eos Suppl.* 6, 1929. C. M. BOWRA, *Greek Lyric Poetry*. Oxf. 1936, 141. 186 (2nd ed. 1961). W. SCHADEWALDT, *Sappho*. Berl. 1950. D. L. PAGE, *Sappho and Alcaeus*. Oxf. 1955. On early lyric in general: M. TREU, *Von Homer zur Lyrik. Zet.* 12, Munich 1955. Literary history: C. GALLAVOTTI, *Storia e poesia di Lesbo nel VII–VI secolo a.C., Alceo di Mitilene*. Bari 1949. A. COLONNA, *L' antica lirica greca*. Turin 1955. B. MARZULLO, *Studi di poesia eolica*. Florence 1958. M. F. GALIANO, *Safo*. Madrid 1958: see also his 'La lírica griega a la luz de los descubrimientos papirológicos'. *Actas del Prim. Congr. Esp. de Est. Clas*. Madrid 1958, 59. Language: C. GALLAVOTTI, *La lingua dei poeti eolici*. Bari 1948. A. BRAUN, 'Il contributo della glottologia al testo critico de Alceo e Saffo'. *Annali Triestini* 20, 1950,

263. H. FRÄNKEL, 'Eine Stileigenheit der frühgriech. Literatur', in *Wege und Formen frühgriechischen Denkens*, 2nd ed. Munich 1960, 40 (=*Gött. Nachr.* 1924, 63). C. A. MASTRELLI, *La lingua di Alceo.* Florence 1954. A. E. HARVEY, 'Homeric epithets in the Greek lyric'. *Class. Quart.* 7, 1957, 206. EVA-MARIA HAMM, *Grammatik zu Sappho und Alkaios. Abh. Ak. Berl.* 2nd ed. 1958. IRENA KAZIK-ZAWADZKA, *De Sapphicae Alcaicaeque elocutionis colore epico.* Wrocław (Breslau) 1958 (*Polska Ak. Nauk. Archivum Filol.* 4.) Translations: H. RÜDIGER, 'Geschichte der deutschen Sappho-Uebersetzungen'. *Germ. Stud.* 151. Berl. 1934. E. MORWITZ, *Sappho.* Berl. 1936 (Greek and German). Individual passages translated in SCHADEWALDT (*vid. sup.*), FRÄNKEL and in SNELL's *Entdeckung des Geistes.* 3rd ed., Hamb. 1955 (ZOLTAN V. FRANYO).

6 CHORAL LYRIC

Numerous archaeological discoveries in the Eurotas valley, particularly those from the sanctuary of Artemis Orthia,[1] have greatly increased our knowledge of Sparta in the seventh century. We receive the impression of a community readier to live life to the full and to accept foreign influences than the later militaristic state, which hardened into the form of a beleaguered garrison. The findings are in accordance with what we know of the music and poetry of that time.

One of the most valuable sources for the history of music is the treatise *On Music* going under the name of Plutarch. It speaks of two 'schools' (καταστάσεις) in the Sparta of the seventh century. The first was founded by Terpander of Lesbos, who was said to have won the prize in music at the first celebration of the Carnean festival in the 26th Olympiad (676–3). The rise of the second school was associated with the development of another festival of Apollo, the Gymnopaediae, instituted in 665. The names and origins of the various artists show how open to foreign influence Sparta was at the time. We find Thaletas of Gortyn named beside Xenocritus from the south Italian state of Locri, Xenodamus of Cythera beside Sacadas of Argos and Polymnestus of Colophon, the latter mentioned by Alcman and Pindar (*de mus.* 5). What these men achieved has been lost to us; in particular we cannot tell what of their work was individual lyric and what was choral. But it cannot be doubted that choral lyric was extensively composed at the time, and that Alcman, the first writer of it known to us, had already a considerable tradition behind him. It is also obvious that from the beginning the choral lyric was closely connected with worship. The same is true of tragedy, which developed out of the choral lyric. In all periods the latter is referred to as μολπή, i.e. it was associated with dancing. If the loss of the music is a sad blow to our understanding of ancient lyric, we must especially remember in discussing choral lyric that we possess now only a part of what was once an artistic unity of sound and movement. The rapid development of the choral lyric in the Doric areas, which stamped the genre for all time with Doric features of language, was intimately connected with the development of the music that accompanied it. In addition to the stringed instruments, the flute determinedly claimed a place.

[1] R. M. DAWKINS, *The Sanctuary of Artemis Orthia in Sparta.* Lond. 1929.

Alcman also came to Sparta from abroad. Later indeed Sparta claimed his birth: the story probably goes back to the Laconian Sosibius, who wrote a considerable treatise on the poet under the second Ptolemy. But to us some verses from his *Songs of Maidens* (13 D.) are decisive. In the elaborate cataloguing manner that he loves, Alcman enumerates various places that a certain man does not come from, leading up to a proud assertion that he comes in fact from Sardis. It is an easy assumption that the poet himself is here spoken of. Was he then a Lydian? If we remember what the African Terence became in Rome, we shall not exclude the possibility. But more probably he was a Greek – most likely an Ionian, in view of the regular intercourse between the Lydian hinterland and the Greek coastal settlements.[1] Ancient datings of Alcman vary, but they all put him in the seventh century. His mention of Polymnestus seems to put him into its second half.

The Alexandrians took a lively interest in the poet of early Spartan choral lyric, and they published his poems in five books. But he was not congenial to the taste of the Atticists, and so his work perished. Fortunately however, apart from the fairly numerous quotations in other writers, one of the earliest papyrus discoveries gave us about 100 verses from the *Songs of Maidens* – sufficient to show their picturesque charm; sufficient also to raise a whole series of difficult problems. Mariette found the papyrus in 1885 in an Egyptian grave: the date of writing is not precisely known, but is decidedly pre-Christian.

What remains of this *Partheneion* shows the presence of three elements which remain important in the subsequent history of choral lyric: firstly myth, which we find in the damaged beginning of the poem. It was concerned with the sons of Hippocoon who were slain by Heracles. The long and highly wrought catalogue of names shows us that this early choral narrative followed different lines from the epic: a fact which we shall see better in Pindar and Bacchylides.

The narrative is followed by the general truth – the gnome. The poet speaks of Aisa, our personal destiny, and of Poros, the satisfactory way out, as ancient deities deserving of worship. Then comes the warning against *hybris*: man must not wish to fly up to heaven, nor to have Aphrodite to wife. The sons of Hippocoon found out whither their ambition had led them. Alcman now goes on to speak of the vengeance of the gods. 'Happy the man who ends his days without tears: but for me, I sing of the light of Agido –'. Here in the middle of the verse, with an abruptness that cannot be disguised he passes over to an entirely different section, which continues until the end of the poem. In it the personal element predominates: it is made up of remarks addressed directly to the girl singers and to the onlookers. Special praise is given to an Hagesichora and to the Agido previously mentioned. They are virtually rivals, and have a special function in the chorus. In these loosely constructed verses, in which we seem almost to hear the happy chatter of the young girls, we could easily forget that the occasion is

---

[1] *Ox. Pap.* 24, 1957 (appeared 1958), nr. 2389, fr. 9 contains the remains of a commentary on Alcman: it appears that Aristotle thought he was a Lydian, and that the commentator disputes this view.

one of worship. The papyrus contains scholia – a token of Alexandrian literary labour – and one of these refers to the festival of Artemis Orthia: it is to her that the maidens bring a robe on the feast-day, in her honour that they compete with other choruses. There are many reasons for believing that in the Pleiads, coming as Sirius rises through the ambrosial night (v. 60), we are to identify one of these rival choruses. The verses of this hymn have repeatedly been assigned to two alternating hemichoruses. The content suggests as much, and a scholium on v. 48 seems to require it; but so far all the attempts have cut the poem up in an intolerable manner. Despite the resemblance of some parts to dialogue, we have to assign them to only one chorus. The external form is very simple, with recurring strophes of 14 lines in a mainly trochaic and dactylic rhythm.[1]

The numerous unsolved questions do not stop us from enjoying this piece of beautiful poetry. It has all the freshness of youth, and its language has a bloom and an unselfconsciousness in its reflection of Homeric elements that is wholly unconventional. Like a noble steed among grazing herds stands the beautiful chorus-leader among the other maidens, and she is likened to a race-horse with thundering hooves, accustomed to victory, one of those from the realm of dreams, living among the rocks.

A new volume of *Oxyrhynchus Papyri*[2] has a most valuable item – two leaves giving the remains of another song for a chorus of girls. Here again the words used by the singers, the light-hearted chaffing of one group by another, the happy colouring of the language and the freshness of expression are quite delightful, and we can better appreciate the stylistic treatment. Like the *Partheneion* found by Mariette, it has a monostrophic structure based on a nine-verse system.

Among the surviving fragments of the Alexandrian five books there are many indications that Alcman often made the chorus sing about himself. We have already heard that he was born in Sardes: in other places (49. 50 f. 55 f. D.) he talks of the gluttony of the Dorians, which Heracles raised to an heroic level. The ageing poet speaks rather touchingly to the maidens of the chorus: his legs will not carry him, and he would fain be a kingfisher, which is borne over the waves by its mate when it grows old. Here as elsewhere there is something of a fairy-tale flavour in his poetry: he knows all the ways of birds, and knows how to imitate the partridge in song (92 f. D.).

Much discussion has been caused by the verses (58 D.) quoted in the Homeric lexicon of Apollonius Sophistes. The fragment in fact, which describes the stillness of night, is one of the most evocative in Greek poetry. The whole slumbering world is conveyed in this broad and tranquil picture: mountain and valley are lapped in sleep, along with all the creatures of land or sea or air.[3] The attribution

[1] Some have thought to detect signs of a triadic structure within the strophe, but see D. L. PAGE, *Alcman, The Partheneion.* Oxf. 1951, 23.
[2] *Ox. Pap.* 24, 1957 (1958), nr. 2387. A. GIANNINI, 'Alcmane Pap. Ox. 2387'. *Rendiconti dell' Istituto Lombardo. Class. di lett.* 93, 1959, 183. M. TREU, *Gnom.* 31, 1959, 558. W. PEEK, 'Das neue Alkman-Partheneion'. *Phil.* 104, 1960, 163. *Ox. Pap.* 24, nr. 2388 gives only some inconsiderable fragments; the ascription of nr. 2394 is uncertain.
[3] R. PFEIFFER, 'Vom Schlaf der Erde und der Tiere'. *Herm.* 87, 1959, 1.

of these beautiful lines to Alcman has been disputed. We should not take too seriously the objection that such a feeling for nature is unthinkable before the Hellenistic age: that doubt may be removed by remembering the way in which Sappho makes her description of the night correspond to her own feeling (96 LP). But the language certainly is peculiar. Elsewhere Alcman uses the Laconian dialect of his day, slightly modified by epic influence. Ancient grammarians such as Apollonius Dyscolus certainly exaggerated the role of Aeolisms in his language: these are partly of epic origin, partly they may have been taken over into current Laconian.[1] But this fragment shows more of epic and less of Laconian colouring than any other piece. This may be attributable to the transmission: also of course we do not know how wide Alcman's range may have been. However, the lines are certainly not 'nature poetry' in the style of modern descriptive lyrics: such passages as Theocritus 2. 38, Apollonius Rhodius 3. 744, Virgil *Aen.* 4. 522 suggest that Alcman also was making a contrast between the peace of nature and the unrest of a human heart.

The name of Stesichorus is associated with one of the sorest gaps in our knowledge of archaic poetry. He is the first literary representative of western Greece, which rapidly achieved economic prosperity in consequence of the colonizing movement in the eighth century.[2] The name of Xenocritus from Epizephyrian Locri has been mentioned already: Xanthus also, who wrote an *Oresteia* before Stesichorus,[3] may have been a west Greek. Stesichorus (who was originally called Tisias, according to Suidas, and got his later name from his work as chorus-master) was born in Matauros, a Locrian colony in southern Italy, but Himera on the north coast of Sicily became his real home. Thucydides (6. 5) tells us that this city showed a mixture of Doric and Chalcidian elements in population and language. If there is not much Doric in Stesichorus, this is to be explained by the nature of conventional lyrical language at his time. The most varied dates are assigned to him, probably through confusion with later bearers of the same name. We can feel fairly confident that he belongs to the late seventh and early sixth centuries. In Cicero's *De Senectute* (23) he is mentioned as one of those who kept their intellectual powers unimpaired into extreme old age. Suidas speaks of his tomb in Catana, where he is said to have gone as an exile from Pallantium in Arcadia. After what we hear about the composition of the *Palinodia*, we have every right to mistrust biographical data on Stesichorus. But he did take part in politics, and according to Aristotle (*Rhet.* 2. 20 1393 b), he tried to prevent Phalaris from becoming tyrant of Agrigentum; so the story of his exile may contain some truth.

Stesichorus writes choral lyric: but what gives a special quality and effect to his work is the dominance of mythical narrative, which we saw was one of the components of Alcman's art. His poetry is thus closely related to the epic: a fact

---

[1] E. SCHWYZER, *Griech. Gramm.* I. 110. PAGE (*v. inf.*), 155 and p. 159 on fr. 58 D.

[2] On the rise of the Greek colonies in the west: G. VALLET, *Rhégion et Zancle. Histoire, commerce et civilisation des cités chalcidiennes du détroit de Messina.* Paris 1958.

[3] Ath. 12. 513a. Stesich. fr. 57 B. PAGE, *Poetae Melici Graeci* nr. 229.

which Quintilian expresses with a Roman brevity: 'Stesichorum . . . epici carminis onera lyra sustinentem' (10. 1, 62). A contributory factor may have been that literary tradition in west Greece was less dominated by the epic, and thus the lyric poetry which came later had the narrative field more open to it. A parallel may be found in the reform of the dithyramb by Arion, who carried through his innovations at the court of Periander in Corinth about 600, securing a place for narrative in the dithyramb and thus making possible the wider development of the form in later times. Arion, according to Herodotus (1. 24), went also to Italy and Sicily; so that some connection with the work of Stesichorus cannot be ruled out.

The ancients collected the poems of Stesichorus into twenty-six books. Enough of the titles later bestowed on the various poems have survived to give us at least an idea of the subjects. Most come from the realm of the cyclic epics: thus Stesichorus brought out an *Iliu Persis* and a *Nostoi* on the homecomings of the heroes. A papyrus fragment[1] has now afforded us two scenes from the latter poem. Both show a close connection with the *Odyssey*: Helen's interpretation of a sign in conversation with Telemachus reminds us of the farewell scene in the fifteenth book (171), and the description of an *objet d'art* recalls the splendid mixing-bowl which Menelaus presents to Telemachus. In the passage of the *Odyssey* (115 f.) gold and silver are mentioned together, as they are in the papyrus. Poems that dealt with these subjects must have been fairly long: we note that his *Oresteia* was in two books. Despite the paucity of the remains, we can still see what a significant intermediary stage such choral lyrics occupied between epic and tragedy. The dream of Clytemnestra, the role of Orestes' nurse – both of them important elements in Aeschylus' tragedy – appear to have been in Stesichorus' *Oresteia* also. The problem of matricide was simply solved: the Erinyes pursued Orestes, but he was able to keep them off with a bow given to him by Apollo.[2] Two poems concerned with a central figure of the Trojan cycle, a *Helena* and a *Palinodia*, became the basis of a legend about Stesichorus. The first comprised everything unfavourable to Helen in the myth-cycle. After writing it, Stesichorus went blind. Prompted by Helen herself, he composed a poem in retractation, and thus regained his sight. It is a very plausible conjecture of Bowra's, that these two poems, together with certain features in the *Oresteia*, are to be connected with the Spartan cult of Helen. The Theban cycle gave him the theme for the *Eriphyla*, the story of the faithless wife who betrayed her husband and suffered the revenge of her son Alcmeon, and for the *Europeia*, dealing with the foundation of the city. Another subject beloved of the old epics, with their delight in descriptions of contests, was the *Funeral Games of Pelias* (Ἆθλα ἐπὶ Πελίᾳ); the *Boar-hunters* (Συοθῆραι) told of the Calydonian

---

[1] *Ox. Pap.* 23, 1956, nr. 2360). W. PEEK, 'Die Nostoi des Stesichoros'. *Phil.* 102, 1958, 169. H. LLOYD-JONES, *Class. Rev.* N.S. 8, 1958, 17. C. M. BOWRA, *Greek Lyric Poetry.* 2nd ed. Oxf. 1961, 77.

[2] P. ZANCANI-MONTUORO, 'Riflessi di una Orestia anteriore ad Eschilo'. *Rend. della acc. di arch. lett. e belle arti.* Naples 1952, 270, discusses a metope from the Heraeum at the mouth of the Sele (latter sixth cent.) with Orestes pursued by an Erinys in the form of a serpent. Its connection with Stesichorus is still uncertain.

hunt. For this poem also we now have a papyrus fragment[1] – two columns of writing, of which the first gives a list of the hunters; so that the catalogue seems to have been a part of Stesichorus' choral lyric no less than of epic. The epithets are wholly Homeric. In view of the great part played by the cult of Heracles in West Greek life, it is not surprising that many poems celebrate the hero's deeds. Thus the *Geryoneis* tells how he carried off Geryon's cattle, the *Cerberus* how he dragged away the guardian of Hades, while the *Cycnus* was named after the brigand and son of Ares whom Heracles killed. Little is known of the *Scylla*, whose attribution to Stesichorus has been disputed.

Sometimes Stesichorus took his inspiration from the popular legends of his country, and developed erotic themes out of them. The *Calyce* (there had previously been a song for women under the same name: cf. Ath. 14, 619 d) and *Daphnis*, named after the handsome lover of a nymph, were both concerned with unhappy love. There is a poem about Rhadina, a woman betrothed to the tyrant of Corinth, but killed by him together with her cousin, which has been attributed to Stesichorus; but this may well have been a younger Stesichorus from Himera, a dithyrambist of the fourth century (Marm. Par. ep. 73).

The influence of Stesichorus, particularly in subject matter, was extraordinarily strong. We seem to detect it in a number of instances in the visual arts of the archaic period:[2] thus the statement of Megacleides in Athenaeus 12. 512f., that Stesichorus was the first to equip Heracles with club and lion's skin, squares well with the evidence of pots from that time. Of course, in so rich a mythographical tradition we must not try to simplify things too much. In some particulars his influence on later poetry, especially tragedy, can be fully demonstrated: but in the main we can only guess. Stesichorus is the great representative of that stage of choral lyric which has a place between epic and tragedy in the transmission of Greek myth and which was of enormous importance in its development.

We know virtually nothing of the form of his poetry. Quintilian (10. 62) praises him for the moral worth (*dignitas*) with which he invests his characters in word and action. In this he seems to have followed the epic manner; the prolixity ascribed to him was no doubt part of the general elaborate character of choral lyric. If Suidas is to be trusted, he replaced the single strophes of Alcman by the triple division of the epodic structure.[3] His indebtedness to Homer, now proved by recently published papyri, was noted by 'Longinus' (13. 3).

Anth. Lyr., 2nd ed., fasc. 5, 6. 44. J. M. EDMONDS, *Lyra Graeca*. I. (Alcman) 2. (Stesichorus). Loeb Class. Lib. Lond. 1922–27. C. M. BOWRA, *Greek Lyric*

---

[1] *Ox. Pap.* 23, 1956, nr. 2359, fr. 1. B. SNELL, *Herm.* 85, 1957, 249. C. M. BOWRA, op. cit. 96. C. GALLAVOTTI, *Gnom.* 29, 1957, 420, assigns nr. 2359 f. to Stesichorus, the first to the *Nostoi*, the second to the *Suotherae*.

[2] BOWRA (*v. sup.*), 123.

[3] Cf. W. THEILER, *Mus. Helv.* 12, 1955, 181. On Ibycus see below, p. 208.

Poetry. 2nd ed. Oxf. 1961, 16. 74. W. SCHADEWALDT, *Sappho*, Potsdam 1950, 59. D. L. PAGE, *Alcman. The Partheneion.* Oxf. 1951. A. GARZYA, *Alcmane.* Naples 1954 (with comm. and trans.) E. RISCH, 'Die Sprache Alkmans'. *Mus. Helv.* 11, 1954, 20. *Ox. Pap.* 24, 1957, nr. 2389f. has remains of a commentary on Alcman, No. 2393 also (fragments of an Alcman-lexicon) shows that Hellenistic Greeks took a considerable linguistic and antiquarian interest in this poet. On 2387 (bits of a new Partheneion) see above. A fragment previously unnoticed is dealt with by K. LATTE, *Phil.* 97, 1948, 54. J. A. DAVISON, 'Notes on Alcman'. *Proc. of the IXth Congr. of Papyrology.* Norw. Univ. Pr. 1961, 30. The standard edition now is D. L. PAGE, *Poetae Melici Graeci.* Oxf. 1962, with some previously unpublished fragments of a commentary from *Ox. Pap.* J. VÜRTHEIM, *Stesichoros. Fragmente und Biographie.* Leyden 1919. F. RAFFAELE, *Indagini sul problema stesicoreo.* Catinae 1937.

D Folk-tales

Of all departments of Greek life our information is worst about the extensive repertoire of folk-song and folk-tale of which parts were made immortal as the themes of great art. We said something about folk-song in connection with lyric. We can hardly doubt that there must have been very many stories circulating in a prose medium, and we would gladly know how much mythology was passed on in this form. But it is only where the beast-fable is concerned that we can reach definite conclusions.

It is interesting to see in what authors we first find it. Homer has no example; the first is in Hesiod's tale of the hawk and the nightingale (*Erga* 202); Archilochus tells of the fox and the ape (81 D.) and of the revenge taken by the fox on the eagle who broke his word (89 ff. D.); a fragment of a poem of Semonides (11 D.) comes from the story of the dungbeetle who punished the arrogance of the eagle.

It is unlikely that these stories were invented by the poets themselves: far more likely they were taken from an extensive repertoire of folk-tale. So even at this early period we have to suppose that the beast-fable was popular and widespread. Almost certainly it must have come to a large extent from the East.[1] The importance of the beast-fable in India has long been known: more recently we have come to recognize its antiquity in the Mesopotamian civilizations. If an Ionian spirit seems to inform many of the stories, this is because the Ionians, in their Asiatic settlements were the great intermediaries. The part played by native Greek invention should not be underrated, although it can hardly be defined with accuracy.

Another fact emerges from the early poets. Hesiod and Archilochus make it plain that the whole feeling of these tales (αἶνοι) is one of social criticism. In a disguise very easily penetrated it speaks for the weak and declares for justice

[1] A fragment from Assur in W. G. LAMBERT, *Babylonian Wisdom Literature.* Oxf. 1960, 213, is from the fable of the midge and the elephant, which recurs in Babrius with an ox instead of the elephant.

against the arbitrary rule of the great. Later every conceivable purpose was served by the fable: inculcation of moral lessons, provision of themes for rhetorical exercises; but in its origins it is a way of pointing out what is true and right in a given situation without giving offence by expressing it openly.[1]

In the old eastern story, the *Romance of Achiqar*,[2] we can see how tales and fables of various kinds can attach themselves to the person of some well-known sage. The same thing appears to have happened in the Greek romance of Aesop, which we may date in the sixth century. It was already known to Herodotus (2. 134). It is on this type of traditional tale that the rather unclear name of 'Volksbuch' has been bestowed: we meet it, for example, in the *Contest of Homer and Hesiod* and the various lives of Homer. The historical core of Aesop's life, if any, has been overlaid entirely by the free flights of fancy which lead the Phrygian slave through the most various countries and circumstances until he meets his death through envy and treachery at Delphi. But Apollo himself avenges his death and establishes his reputation.

We may suppose that this life of Aesop was associated from the first with a large collection of fables – indeed that it was itself the earliest of such collections. Later separate collections were made. The oldest of which we now know was the λόγων Αἰσωπείων συναγωγαί of Demetrius Phalereus.[3] The extant collections are all considerably later, and so are the forms in which the biographical romance has come down to us. The situation is the same as with the *Contest of Homer and Hesiod*: a tradition beginning in the infancy of Greek literature is now accessible only in forms dating from very much later.

The oldest known collection of fables has survived only in a fragment – a John Rylands papyrus (nr. 28 P.) of the first century of our era – *Collectio Augustana*, named after a manuscript preserved formerly in Augsburg, now in Munich (gr. 564). Perry dates it in the first or second century A.D., Adrados rather later, but it is very hard to date any of these collections accurately. The *Collectio Vindobonensis* is more colourful, but the language is more debased: it comes from a later period, probably the sixth century. Some of its fables are told in verse. The *Collectio Accursiana* enjoyed the widest circulation until the *Augustana* took its place. Bonus Accursius brought out the first edition in 1479 or 1480. It is sometimes called the *Planudea*, but it is not certain that Maximus Planudes had anything to do with compiling it (*Phil. Woch.* 1937, 774). It arose from a revision of the Vindobonensis and to some extent from the Augustana. Hausrath's theory that the different versions represent rhetorical exercises done in the schools has not been convincingly demonstrated. In addition to these collections there are side-transmissions of various sorts. The transmission of the romance of Aesop was first examined with decisive results by Perry. The manuscript 397 in the Pierpont Morgan Library in New York, which has been identified with the Cryptoferratensis A33 that disappeared in Napoleon's time, is the oldest of our manuscripts (10th century) and contains the *Collectio*

---

[1] K. MEULI, 'Herkunft und Wesen der Fabel'. *Schweiz. Arch. f. Volkskunde* 50, 1954, 65.
[2] Bibliography in Meuli op. cit., 22.
[3] F. WEHRLI, *Die Schule des Aristoteles* 4, fr. 112.

Augustana preceded by the Life in its most elaborate form (G). There is also a version found in manuscripts of the *Collectio Vindobonensis*, which shows some shortening of G's narrative and some new material. Perry was the first to edit it on a broad manuscript base: its earlier editors called it the Westermanniana (W). The papyrus fragments (nr. 1614–1617 P. and Rylands 493) point to the circulation of both versions in the first century of our era. A striking part is played in G by Isis Musagogos; in addition, elements derived from the *Romance of Achiqar* clearly point to an Egyptian redaction. Thus the prototype of our versions, which itself testifies to a long period of development, may well come from Egypt in the early empire.

Editions of the fables: E. CHAMBRY, *Aesopi fabulae*, Paris 1925 (repr. 1959) Id., *Ésope. Fables* (with trans.), Coll. des Un. de Fr. 1927. Repr. with additions by H. HAAS 1957 (fables 1-181); I/2 2nd ed. by H. HUNGER, Leipz. 1959 (fables 182-345 and those found in the rhetoricians). Indices to both parts by H. HAAS, H. HAUSRATH, *Aesopische Fabeln*. Munich 1940 (with trans.). A. HAUSRATH. *Corpus fabularum Aesopicarum* I/1, Leipz. 1940. Fables and romance: B. E. PERRY, *Aesopica*. Un. of Illinois Press. 1952. Monographs etc.: B. E. PERRY, *Studies in the Text History of the Life and Fables of Aesop*. Haverford 1936. F. R. ADRADOS, *Estudios sobre el léxico de las fábulas esópicas*. Salamanca 1948; id. *Gnom*. 29, 1957, 431. A. WIECHERS, *Aesop in Delphi*. Beitr. z. klass. Phil. herausg. von R. Merkelbach 2 (Diss. Cologne) 1959.

We have already seen how important myth was in Greek narrative literature. The beast-fable shows us that there were other elements also. In the *Odyssey* itself one of the leading themes – the home-coming and revenge of a man whose wife is sought by other suitors – belongs to a class of stories telling of striking turns of fate and owing their origin simply to the pleasure taken in a good story. Fictional narratives of this kind – 'novels' as we may call them – were current among the Greeks from the earliest times, and we should not underestimate their numbers simply because so few have found literary expression. The spontaneity and abundance of such elements in the work of Herodotus should be proof enough of their importance, which must have been greatest in Ionia. Like the fairy-story, the novel must largely have had an existence below the level of great literary creation. Both were originally floating unattached, but later were tacked on to well-known characters in myth or history.

The period around 600 was an age of strong men. As moralists, legislators, even as despots they had many achievements to their credit; and they were remembered also for actions of more dubious moral value. When they became the target of the Greek passion for compiling lists and cycles, a tradition arose of the deeds and the sayings of the Seven Sages: a tradition which was most interestingly developed and rehandled and reinterpreted right down to the end of antiquity. The number seven is probably due to oriental influence: we find seven wise men as early as the epic of Gilgamesh (tab. 11), there concerned with the building of the walls of Uruk. The Greeks gave an historical and intellectual content to the age-old myth-motif; and it is very interesting to see how in the middle ages the legend of the Seven Masters, a creation of oriental fairy-tale, displaced in turn the classical tradition.

The names of the seven vary alarmingly, but four men firmly maintain their place in this distinguished circle: the philosopher Thales of Miletus, Bias of Priene who was renowned for the justice of his verdicts, Pittacus, known to us through Alcaeus, and the Athenian Solon. In the oldest tradition we find also Periander of Corinth, but he lost his place when tyrants went out of favour. Diogenes Laertius (1. 30) says it was Plato who expelled him: certainly he is not in the list given by Plato in the *Protagoras* (343a). It is notable that in the fourth century the Scythian Anacharsis[1] makes his appearance in the list: he exemplifies the ideal of the noble savage.

In the older notion of the Seven Sages the contemplative and the active life, which the Sophists so sharply contrasted, were not thought of separately, and thus their maxims are directed mainly towards practical, every-day wisdom. The emphasis laid on the mean is a universal Greek feature, perhaps to some degree under Delphic influence.

From reflections in later literature it seems safe to infer the early existence of a *Supper of the Seven Sages* in a popular form. Their scolia or drinking songs, as given in the first book of Diogenes Laertius, seem by their form to belong to the fifth century. A collection of their sayings was made by Demetrius Phalereus, who did the same for the fables of Aesop. A good deal of it is preserved in Stobaeus (3, 1, 172).[2] Theophrastus[3] is the first writer in whom we find the pretty story of the tripod which was to be given to the wisest of the wise. Each in turn awarded it to another whom he held wiser than himself: after going round them all, it was consecrated to Apollo. The same theme is found in the story of the golden bowl, which Callimachus (fr. 191 Pf.) makes the ghost of Hipponax relate to the quarrelling scholars. To give an idea of the wide and varied influence of these traditional stories and sayings, we can point to the *Letters of the Sages* – a kind of novel of which pieces are preserved in Diogenes Laertius – and to Plutarch's *Supper of the Seven Sages*, in which Aesop also takes part, sitting on a little foot-stool, and finally to the rather wooden *Ludus Septem Sapientium* of Ausonius.[4]

VS 10. B. SNELL, *Leben und Meinungen der Sieben Weisen*. 3rd ed. Munich 1952, with notes and translation; cf. *Thesaurismata. Festschr. f. Ida Kapp*. Munich 1954, 105.

[1] On the fables that collected around Anacharsis: F. H. REUTERS, *De Anacharsidis epistulis*. Diss. Bonn 1957.
[2] On their genuineness or otherwise see WEHRLI op. cit., 69.　　[3] Plutarch, *Solon* 4.
[4] The story of the tripod going round all the sages recurs in the *Historia Monachorum*; see A. J. FESTUGIÈRE'S valuable article 'Lieux communs littéraires et thèmes de folk-lore dans l'hagiographie primitive'. *Wien. Stud.* 73, 1960, 123 (144).

E Religious Literature

We have seen great individuals like Archilochus and Solon against a background of important social changes. Such changes did not come to pass purely on the plane of economics and politics: the rise of new social strata had its counterpart in religious questions and demands which the world of Homer was unable to meet. After the passing of that age, two strongly diverging tendencies appear in the expression of the Greek national spirit. A trend towards realism, such as we found in the Ionian poets of the seventh and sixth centuries, has its antithesis in a leaning towards the marvellous and towards deeper religious speculation. We must also bear in mind that the changes in social structure may well have brought into sight a great many attitudes and ways of thought which were covered up and concealed by the aristocratic strata of Homer's world.

The sixth century, which brought the rise of Ionian philosophy and with it the beginnings of European science, yet took a delight in such fabulous personages as Aristeas of Proconnesus. Some good illustrations of the mass of legend that accumulated round him are given in Herodotus (4. 14f.). He once fell seemingly dead in his own country, but his body disappeared, and at the same time he was seen by different people in widely separated places, apparently hale and hearty. At Metapontum, however, he was seen as a raven, following in the train of Apollo.

Aristeas is dated by Suidas under Croesus and Cyrus:[1] his name was attached to a hexameter poem called the *Arimaspea* (sc. ἔπη). The plot of this travel fantasy took Aristeas, possessed by Apollo, northwards as far as the Issedones. The few surviving fragments show that the poem contained a remarkable mixture of Ionian exploration and pure fable. Among the Issedones he writes, like any real traveller, a notebook on the northern peoples, and gives a long account of the one-eyed Arimaspians, the treasure-guarding griffins and the Hyperboreans, the dwellers on the northern sea who were the darlings of Apollo.

It is impossible to say how far Aristeas is historical and whether he wrote the *Arimaspea*. But K. Meuli[2] has pointed out the context in which all these tales fit. We hear of a man whose soul can leave his body when it chooses (according to Suidas); in a possessed state he goes on marvellous journeys; he sometimes assumes an animal form: all this belongs to the realm of shamanism. Meuli has convincingly demonstrated to its importance in the Scythian world, where shamanistic ideas and practices were very widespread, and has pointed out the lines of connection between the Scythians and the early Greeks.

A comparable figure was the supposed Hyperborean Abaris. According to Herodotus (4. 36) he was said to have carried an arrow with him all round the world. This is a rationalized form of a myth told by Heraclides Ponticus in his dialogue *Abaris*,[3] in which the wonder-working priest flew to Greece on one of

---

[1] On the date: E. ROHDE, *Kl. Schr.* I, 136, 2.
[2] 'Scythica'. *Herm.* 70, 1935, 121.　　　　　　[3] MEULI op. cit. 159, 4.

Apollo's arrows. The list of alleged works of Abaris in Suidas gives a striking impression of the extent of this species of literature: we find such titles as *Scythian Oracles*, *Wedding of the Rivergod Hebrus*, *Songs of Atonement* and *Arrival of Apollo among the Hyperboreans*.

A *Theogony* in prose is attributed both to Abaris and to Aristeas, which suggests that works of the kind were circulating in great numbers. Where we have any knowledge of them, they seem to be basically in the Hesiodic tradition, although much of the material is new. They try to be cosmogonies, not just divine histories. Naturally they have some points of agreement with Ionian philosophy, which in return could not be uninfluenced by the religious ideas of the time.[1] A *Theogony* in 5000 hexameters is ascribed to the Cretan Epimenides (VS 3), the priest who is said to have purified Athens after the killing of Cylon. This report may be historical, but beside it we find stories of his sleeping many years in a cave and of other exploits reminiscent of Aristeas. We find καθαρμοί and oracles circulating under his name also. The last form part of a tradition which was particularly productive in the sixth century. There were collections of Delphic oracles and of many others besides, among which a particular repute was enjoyed by those ascribed to Musaeus (VS 2) – also the alleged author of a *Theogony*.

In ancient tradition Musaeus stands next to Orpheus, and thus brings us to all the questions connected with the latter. The name of the mythical Thracian singer, dated by his followers before Homer, became attached to a religious movement whose importance has sometimes been immensely over-estimated, sometimes, at the hands of radical sceptics, almost wholly denied.[2] We know of more than half a hundred poems to which the name of Orpheus was attached, and those that survive – the *Hymns*, *Argonautica*, *Lithica* (on stones and their working) – show how much was being added even in late imperial times. The only guide through all this rubbish-dump is a few early references, particularly in Pindar, Euripides and Plato. In antiquity there were several *Theogonies* in circulation which claimed to be Orphic. The Platonist Damascius in his treatise Περὶ τῶν πρώτων ἀρχῶν gives a brief survey (fr. 28. 54. 60 Kern). The most highly esteemed was the poem we now call the *Rhapsodic Theogony* in twenty-four

---

[1] See the next chapter. On the post-Hesiodic Theogonies, esp. that of Epimenides, see U. HÖLSCHER, *Herm.* 81, 1953, 404 and 408.

[2] The pioneer work in evaluating the mystery religions was C. A. LOBECK'S *Aglaophamus*. Königsberg 1829. WILAMOWITZ roughly expelled Orphism from his picture of Greek civilization. Material in O. KERN, *Orphicorum Fragmenta*. Berl. 1922. For a sceptical view: J. LINDFORTH, *The Art of Orpheus*. Calif. Univ. Press 1941. E. R. DODDS, *The Greeks and the Irrational*. Lond. 1951, 147. An early origin is reasonably advocated by M. P. NILSSON, 'Early Orphism and Kindred Religious Movements'. *Harvard Theol. Rev.* 28, 1935, 181 (= Opusc.: Sel. 2, 628); see also his contribution to *Gnom.* 28, 1956, 18, against the exaggerated scepticism of L. MOULINIER, *Orphée et l'orphisme à l'époque classique*. Paris 1955. W. K. C. GUTHRIE, *Orpheus and Greek Religion*. 2nd ed. Lond. 1952. Id., *The Greeks and their Gods*. Boston 1951, 307. For a thorough and judicious account: K. ZIEGLER, 'Orpheus' and 'Orphische Dichtung'. *RE* 18, 1200 and 1321. Some interesting points are raised by W. JAEGER, *Die Theologie der frühen griech. Denker*. Stuttg. 1953, 69. R. BOHME, *Orpheus*. Berl. 1953, stands almost alone in adopting a very early dating.

books.[1] The extant fragments show that its formal side was much influenced by Hesiod. At the beginning is Chronos, who creates Aether and a silver egg, out of which the wonderful hermaphrodite being Phanes is hatched. This deity, among whose many names is Eros, begins the series of reproductive acts which give rise to Uranus, Cronus and Zeus. It is widely agreed nowadays that this whole portentous construction is of late origin. It is another question, however, whether the pedigree of this *Rhapsodic Theogony* may not go back a very long way. Sextus Empiricus informs us (test. 191 Kern) that the *Orphica* of Onomacritus, who played an important, if ambiguous, role in the careers of the Pisistratids,[2] had cosmogony as one of its themes. It is highly probable then that there should have been Orphic cosmogonies among the large number that we may postulate for the sixth century. The parodied cosmogony in Aristophanes (*Birds* 685) is very interesting; but it is very hard to identify the Orphic elements in it.[3]

Here the burning question is: did the central myth explaining the nature of man belong to such an early level of Orphic literature? The myth makes the Titans tear to pieces and devour the infant Dionysus; the thunderbolt of Zeus burns them to ashes; from these ashes man arises, combining in his nature a divine element from Dionysus and an evil earthly element from the Titans. This myth is not attested before Clement of Alexandria (fr. 34 Kern); but Plato (*Laws* 3. 701c) speaks of the old Titanic element in those who defy divine and human laws, as if the reference were immediately intelligible. Nor can we lightly reject the testimony of Pausanias (8. 37, 5) that Onomacritus took over the word 'Titan' from Homer, founded the orgiastic worship of Dionysus, and represented the Titans as the authors of the latter's sufferings. We may reasonably suppose that the essential elements were already in existence in the sixth century. At all events that period witnessed the rise of a number of views on the nature and destiny of the human soul differing greatly from those of Homer.[4] In these views the soul carried the essential nature of man, the divine spark, and after death it did not go like a fugitive shadow to the gloom of Hades, but had to give an account of itself. It was tied to a succession of rebirths, leading either back to its divine habitation or to everlasting damnation. Invaluable information is given on this doctrine by Pindar (*Olymp.* 2. 63; cf. fr. 129-133). He does not directly label it as Orphic, but there can be doubt that he is moving in that particular framework, especially as his verses refer to king Theron of Agrigentum, and as such belong to the area of Magna Graecia, which was particularly given to mystical doctrines. A token of this is the little leaves of gold ('death-tickets', as Diehls has called them) which were buried in the graves of sectaries to help them find their way in the hereafter.

Thus, despite all the defects of our information, we can see that the fifth century witnessed an Orphic movement which urged men to purify the soul,

---

[1] Suidas *s.v.*: Ὀρφεύς· ἱεροὶ λόγοι ἐν ῥαψῳδίαις κδ'.
[2] Herodotus 7. 6, on his forging of oracles of Musaeus.
[3] Cf. H. SCHWABL, 'Weltschöpfung'. *RE* S 9, 1433.
[4] Jaeger op. cit. 88.

to free it from the trammels of the body,[1] and to unite it eternally with the Godhead. We can also show that there was an extensive literature associated with these themes. Apart from the theogonies the Orphists wrote *Songs of Atonement* (καθαρμοί) and probably a *Catabasis*, a poem dealing with the descent of Orpheus into Hades. All that we know of the underlying forces and tensions of the sixth century suggests that we have to refer the beginnings of the Orphic movement and Orphic literature to this period.

The very paucity of the evidence is a warning against over-estimating the extent of the movement. Like most sects, it would have drawn its followers from the most varied levels of society: deep religious feeling would have co-existed from the beginning with formalism and external rituals of purity. The question how far it arose from pure y Greek roots, or how far it derived from eastern doctrines of metempsychosis, does not permit a simple solution. One must deprecate the view which sees Orphism and possibly even Platonism as being foreign flowers grafted on to a Greek stem. Orphism is part and parcel of our picture of the Greek world: what its relation was to Pythagorean teachings we shall discuss later.

This branch of literature which we have been discussing includes also the *Theologia* of Pherecydes of Syros (VS 7), which is reckoned the first book in prose and can be placed about the middle of the sixth century. What we know of its cosmogony and theogony illustrates the tendency for ancient myths, speculation and elements of the most various origin to form ever new combinations. The beginning tells us of Zas, Cronus[2] and Chthonia, the primal forces which have existed for ever. This marks a step forward from Hesiod, who gives even to Chaos a beginning in time. The immemorial marriage of heaven and earth is turned by Pherecydes into a marriage of Zeus and Chthonia, the depths of the earth. Zeus gives her a garment on which he has embroidered the earth and the ocean. Here we have a mythical prototype for the gifts to the bride in the Anacalypteria, the feast of unveiling. The earth thus is a possession of Chthonia: the depths are clothed with the many-coloured surface. Cronus creates from his own semen fire, air and water, out of which, in five caves or holes (μυχοί) in the universe, all the multiplicity of the gods takes form. Conflicts between these beings for the rulership of the world were also narrated: many features, such as the transformation of Zeus into Eros in the act of creation, remind us of Orphic teachings.

F The Beginnings of Philosophy

In strong contrast to western Greece, with its leaning towards mysticism, the great Ionian centre of Miletus in this eventful sixth century became the

---

[1] The formula σῆμα-σῶμα is Orphic, at least in its meaning, as ZIEGLER op. cit. 1378 and GUTHRIE, *The Greeks and their Gods* 311, 3, demonstrate against WILAMOWITZ. For a different view: NILSSON, *Gnom.* 28, 1956, 18.

[2] So instead of Chronos with H. FRÄNKEL, *Ztschr. f. Aesth.* 25, 1931, Beilage p. 115 (= *Wege und Formen frühgriech. Denkens.* Munich 2nd ed. 1960, 19); for Pherecydes the names were probably equivalent.

birthplace of philosophy, numbering Thales, Anaximander and Anaximenes among its citizens. Miletus had sent out colonies in large numbers, and was open to all the influences that streamed in upon it from far and wide.[1] The rich endowments of the Ionian people, fated to reach full development only on Asiatic soil, enable us to see why it was here particularly that a new kind of question began to be asked about the world. The importance of this intellectual development makes us sadly conscious of the limits of our knowledge. Of the views of these men only one single sentence can be reckoned to have come down to us, and that imperfectly. Numerous notices are derived from the lost work of Theophrastus on the *Teachings of the Natural Philosophers* (Φυσικῶν δόξαι).[2] In other words, to a large extent we know of their doctrines only through the interpretation and refutation of their views by Aristotle and his school.[3]

The circumstances outlined explain why we find conflicting interpretations of these first steps of philosophy. Their importance as the beginnings of western science explain the emotions with which many writers look on this abandonment of all mythical elements as a radical break with the past, a deliberate and conscious step forward onto new ground. On the other hand, we find a strong tendency to take this passage in the intellectual life of the Greeks out of the context where it belongs. Thus the picture drawn by Aristotle of this archaic natural philosophy as a rather restricted quest for the primal substance has been significantly broadened in two directions. Werner Jaeger[4] has shown us that this early philosophy still contains an element of theology, that the enquiry into the basic stuff of the world implies a search for what is divine in it. On the other hand, the greater readiness with which classical scholars now accept the notion of eastern influence has had important effects. Such works as Uvo Hölscher's[5] show that these thinkers did indeed free themselves from the myths of epic tradition, but that the decisive stimulus to their thought came from the great cosmogonic myths of the East, with their strong element of speculation.

If Thales ever wrote a book expounding his views, it was lost very soon. In the *Metaphysics* (1. 3; 983b20) Aristotle makes him the originator of a doctrine that all things were derived from one primal substance: this substance he took to be water. The earth he considered as floating on water, and he explained earthquakes as arising from fluctuations in this supporting medium (A 15).[6] It is not at all likely that at such an early date Thales posited a basic substance transmuting itself into all others; but we may believe the tradition that he considered water as the origin of all things and as supporting the earth. The passages in the *Iliad* (14. 201, 246) which make Ocean the origin of the gods or of everything could hardly in themselves have been an adequate stimulus to this view: we

[1] On the economic prosperity of Ionia see C. ROEBUCK, *Ionian Trade and Colonization*. New York 1959.

[2] O. REGENBOGEN, *RE* 7, 1535. How far later writers were indebted is discussed by U. HÖLSCHER, *Herm.* 81, 1953, 259.

[3] H. CHERNISS, *Aristotle's Criticism of Pre-Socratic Philosophy*. Baltimore 1935.

[4] *The Theology of Early Greek Philosophers*. Oxf. 1947.

[5] 'Anaximander und die Anfänge der Philosophie'. *Herm.* 81, 1953, 257 and 385.

[6] The numbers refer to VS unless otherwise stated.

have rather to reckon with the influence of Egyptian and Babylonian doctrines on the origin and disposition of the universe. This is made easier by the quite credible accounts of his having visited Egypt, where he is said to have learned to measure the height ᴏᶜ pyramids by their shadows and to have evolved a theory of the Nile's annual flood.[1] This later became a traditional problem of ancient science. Either there or from the Near East he learned an approximate rule for solar eclipses, whereby he was able to predict that of 585. It indicates the nature of his studies that a *Nautical Astronomy* was attributed to him. There is no decisive evidence that Thales broke fresh ground by using geometrical theorems; but modern scholars would not underestimate his contribution in this connection.[2] Others ascribed it to Phocus of Samos. If we take seriously the report, derived from the 5th-century epic writer Choerilus of Samos, that he taught the immortality of the soul (A 1), Egyptian influence was probably at work here also. We have of course no knowledge of Thales' conception of the soul. Consequently his statement (A 22) that the magnet has a soul may refer to nothing more than a force capable of producing effects. He is also supposed to have said that everything is full of gods: a statement (whether truly his or not) which could serve as a trade-mark of this early philosophy.

The conception of the Milesians as influenced by eastern cosmogonies only brings out the more clearly their own achievement: they freed scientific speculation from its immemorial swaddling-clothes of myth, and they retain beyond cavil the credit of having founded western science.

Anaximander of Miletus, according to ancient reports (A 1, 11), was born about 610 and died shortly after 546. Thus he was roughly Thales' contemporary: later tradition made him his pupil. Reports of his taking part in founding the colony of Apollonia on the Black Sea and of his visiting Sparta show him as a true Ionian, taking a busy part in the life of his world. He published a book, later known as Περὶ φύσεως (a title given to many such works), which was still extant and accessible to the early Peripatetics.

Anaximander, like Thales, enquired into the first origin of things: it is uncertain whether he used the word ἀρχή to designate it (cf. A 9, 11). This origin he found in the *apeiron*, which can mean infinite as well as formless. This *apeiron* is not an element with physical qualities, nor yet is it a mixture[3] which contained all things from the beginning. According to Aristotle (*Phys.* 1. 4; 187a20) he held that all things came from the *apeiron* by a separating out (ἐκκρίνεσθαι); but the interpretation of this as the unmixing of a mixture is probably secondary. Anaximander meant by it a true coming into existence from the undefined and inexhaustible basic stuff that is prior to any individual existence. Thus the unfathomable deep, the abyss, from which Being proceeds in eastern cosmogonies, has been converted by Anaximander, using the abstracting power of Greek thought and language, into an ideal conception – the undefined. A purely material interpretation of the *apeiron* is impossible: it has

---

[1] A 16 with Gigon (*v. sup.*), 48.

[2] Thus O. BECKER, *Das mathematische Denken der Antike*. Studienh. z. Altertumswiss. 3. Göttingen 1957. K. V. FRITZ, *Gnom.* 30, 1958, 81. [3] HÖLSCHER op. cit. 263.

too many attributes of divinity. It is immortal and eternal; it has no beginning (a respect in which it differs from the Chaos of Hesiod, who is really not a cosmologist at all); it embraces and determines all that is divine (A 15).

Out of this infinite and undivided substance the seeds of generation separate themselves; and from them come the individual existences (A 10). A sentence of Anaximander's preserved by Simplicius (B 1) shows that he viewed this coming into existence from an ethical standpoint closely related with *dike* and its problems: 'And the source of coming-to-be for existing things is that into which destruction too happens necessarily, for they commit injustice and perform atonement each to other according to the determining of Time.'[1] Many attempts have been made to settle which words are meant to be Anaximander's.[2] At all events it is he who speaks of the atonement which all things that come into existence have to make by their passing away. He does not mean that individuation is a sin: it is the fact that things 'thrust themselves into space' which causes each to take away or lessen the others' viability.

In the endless coming-to-be and passing-away in the *apeiron* numerous universes take their rise. At the middle of our universe is this earth, motionless because it is equidistant from all the boundaries. It is shaped like the drum of a column, the height being one third of the diameter. Hence Anaximander's map of the world – the first drawn by a Greek – showed it as a circle. We must imagine it as one of those simplified diagrammatic maps such as Herodotus ridicules (4. 36). A Babylonian example[3] represents the eastern forerunners of such maps. From the east also came the idea of the sun-dial that Anaximander built (A 4).

Anaximander was following Thales' precedent when he made earth come into being out of the water which originally covered it by a process of drying-out. Life also began in the water; man was at first a kind of fish, who later on land shed the scales necessary for aquatic life and altered his way of living (A 30).

A bold and fanciful theory is advanced to account for the stars (A 10f. 21f.) Around the earth with its envelope of air there was formed originally, like the bark round a tree, a shell of fire. This 'tore off' and broke up into wheel-shaped formations having a core of fire and an outer layer of air. Where the latter has a hole in it, the inner fire is visible as a star: closing of the aperture cuts off its light. Anaximander is said even to have estimated their magnitudes. The sun, he thought, had about the same circumference as the earth – a remarkable view, since as late as Pericles' day a thinker of Anaxagoras' stamp could reckon the sun as 'a little larger than the Peloponnese' (VS 59 A 42).

The third Milesian, Anaximenes, comes a little later, and was of course represented as the pupil of Anaximander. He died in the Olympiad 528/25. Until recently he was overshadowed by his predecessor, and it was reckoned a

---

[1] On this expression see HÖLSCHER op. cit. 270.

[2] R. MONDOLFO, *Problemi del pensiero antico*. Bologna 1936, 23. F. DIRLMEIER, *Rhein. Mus.* 87, 1938, 376; *Herm.* 75, 1940, 329. K. DEICHGRÄBER, *Herm.* 75, 1940, 10. G. VLASTOS, *Class. Phil.* 42, 1947, 168. W. KRAUS, *Rhein. Mus.* 93, 1950, 372.

[3] BENGTSON-MILOJCIC, *Grosser hist. Weltatlas* I. Munich 1953, 8.

retrograde step that he took air to be the primal substance instead of the feature-less *apeiron*. In reality, however, he makes an important step forward in the struggle towards a scientific world-picture. His views also had oriental proto-types. In the cosmogony of Sanchuniathon[1] the 'interweaving' of air in motion gives rise to Mot, the wet primeval earth; and when he differs from Anaxi-mander in making the sky once more press on the rim of the earth, and in making the sun and moon run round the rim of the earth's disc at night, con-cealed behind high mountains, he is carrying on a Babylonian tradition. More important than these borrowed doctrines is his attempt to derive the origins of the cosmos from a substance whose capacity for changing its properties can be experimentally known. Through changes in its temperature and humidity, air can become visible (A 7). The process of condensation leading from air through cloud, water and earth to stone is very rationally thought out. In the other direction, rarefaction of air gives rise to fire. To Anaximenes air has no end, and we meet again the word *apeiron* which Anaximander applied to the primal substance. It is air that supports the earth's disc (which is now rather thinner than before), and the human soul also is part of the air (B 2). It is easy to see how this could come from the old notion of the breath-soul, even though it is doubtful whether we possess the words of Anaximenes himself. Of his language we are told (A 1) that it was an unpretentious Ionic. If ever he uses similes – comparing the rotation of the stars around the earth's disc to the turning round of a cap on one's head (A 7), or comparing lightning with the phosphorescence of water round oar-blades at night (A 17) – it is not stylistic adornment, but a way of grasping reality which plays an important part in archaic thought.[2]

Chronology alone connects the three Milesians with a man who powerfully influenced the spiritual life of antiquity. We hear of Pythagorean brotherhoods enjoying high repute in cities of southern Italy in the late sixth century and pursuing an aristocratic line in politics.[3] Two rather difficult expressions which recur in our extant references to the Pythagoreans can be best interpreted as follows: the *mathematici* were full members of the fraternity, while the *acusmatici* were followers of the doctrine without being full members. No doubt the latter were responsible for the wide influence and political overtones of the movement in southern Italy. The democratic factions sometimes hit back, and in the middle of the fifth century a conflict of this kind led to the burning of the Pythagorean meeting-house in Croton. But shortly after 400 we find Archytas, a distinguished member of the school, in power in Tarentum. Plato visited him on his travels, and was greatly stimulated by his Pythagorean teaching. We hear little of the Pythagoreans in the Hellenistic period, but under the surface their teaching continued. They had a revival of strength in the first century B.C., and the late Empire saw a revival of what we should now call Pythagoreanism.

[1] Philo ap. Euseb. *P.E.* 1. 10.

[2] B. SNELL, 'Gleichnis, Vergleich, Metapher, Analogie', in *Die Entdeckung des Geistes*. 3rd ed. Hamburg 1955, 258; with further references 284. 2.

[3] Bibliography in H. BENGTSON, *Griech. Geschichte*. 2nd ed. Munich 1960, 139. 3. K. v. FRITZ op. cit. *inf.* and 'Mathematiker und Akusmatiker bei den alten Pythagoreern'. *Sitzb. Bayer. Ak. Phil.-hist. Kl.* 1960/11.

The man who began this movement is very imperfectly known to us. The biography given in Diogenes Laertius (8. 1), like those by Porphyry and Iamblichus, all compilations of late date, shows us just as the more detached references do what a mass of anecdote and miracle had submerged the historical personality.[1] Pythagoras was born in Samos, but the scene of his activities was southern Italy, where he founded his brotherhood in Croton and died in Metapontum. We can accept the story that he fled from the tyranny of Polycrates, which was established about 530.

The absurdities of the later tradition make the few early notices all the more important. In the first place come the verses in which Xenophanes ridicules him, which must have been written either in his lifetime or shortly after his death (VS 21 B 7): Pythagoras, he says, on hearing the cries of a beaten dog, recognized the voice of a friend whose soul now inhabited the animal's body. This passage confirms metempsychosis as one of Pythagoras' own doctrines, and casts light on the various accounts of what he had been in previous incarnations. We can also say with certainty that the chain of re-births had an ethical and religious objective in the complete purification of the soul. Ion of Chios, who lived in the fifth century, not so very long after Pythagoras, attributes to him the doctrine that a courageous and moral life earns a better lot for the soul in the hereafter (VS 36 B 4). It follows that the strict rules of living of the Πυθαγόρειος τρόπος come from the earliest stages of the movement. It is easy to see why believers in metempsychosis should forbid the eating of flesh and the wearing of woollen garments, but the celebrated abstention from beans is more difficult, and other of their prohibitions seem quite senseless. It is not of course possible to date all the elements of this amorphous mass of rules.

The question of the relation of early Pythagoreanism to Orphism raises its head, but with our present knowledge we cannot give a simple answer.[2] There may be connections here and there, but seen as a whole, the momentous achievement of Pythagoras seems to have consisted in his raising those doctrines of the nature and destiny of the human soul, which came out of obscurity into the light during the sixth century, into the realm of scientific thought, and handing them on as a philosophic heritage to posterity. It is an obvious possibility that foreign influences played a part in his mental development. Ancient tradition – admittedly untrustworthy – speaks of extensive travels; a stay in Egypt is first mentioned by Isocrates (*Bus.* 28).

Strangely enough, the Pythagorean circle, with its strong leaning towards mysticism, did more than all the Ionian philosophers for the development of the exact sciences. It was a momentous step forward when number was declared (probably by Pythagoras himself) to be the informing principle of the universe. From this point the most various lines of thought branched out, leading to the development of mathematics, the elaboration of a matter-form dualism, and to

---

[1] J. LEVY, *Recherches sur les sources de la légende de Pythagore.* Paris 1926.

[2] W. RATHMANN, *Quaestiones Pythegoreae Orphicae Empedocleae.* Diss. Halle 1933. K. KERENYI, *Pythagoras und Orpheus: Präludien zu einer künftigen Geschichte der Orphik und des Pythagoreismus.* 3rd ed. Zürich 1950.

numerical speculations of the most diverse kinds. Compared with the great impetus thus given, the fact that the theorem named after Pythagoras was known earlier is quite unimportant. The supreme importance of number as the element of unity in the diversity of phenomena could be recognised most immediately in the relation between the lengths and notes of stretched strings. The discovery that musical pitch was determined by numerical relations must have made a great impression and thus opened the door to the general theory that only those things expressible as numbers have a real existence. Music always had a high place in their circles, and the very perfection of harmony was thought to accompany the well-proportioned revolutions of the heavenly spheres. We are not well able now to answer the questions how far the important discoveries and theorems belong to the early days of the movement, or to distinguish the contributions of Pythagoras himself from those of his followers. But little is gained by an excess of scepticism which minimises Pythagoras' own achievement.[1] The thesis advanced by E. Frank, that the so-called Pythagorean mathematics did not arise until the end of the fifth century, can now be safely disregarded.

According to individual prepossessions, Pythagoras was either praised for the extent of his learning or condemned (as for example by Heraclitus) for barren polymathy. His followers explained the range of his accomplishments by a special dispensation which preserved him from the normal oblivion between one incarnation and the next (A 8 with Empedocles VS 31 B 129). The great reputation of his learning makes us suspect the report (A 17) that he left nothing in writing. But possibly we are now so accustomed to books that we underestimate the potentialities of oral tradition.

O. GIGON, *Bibliographische Einführungen in das Studium der Philos.* 5, *Antike Philos.* Bern 1948. D. J. ALLEN, 'A Survey of Work Dealing with Greek Philosophy from Thales to the Age of Cicero 1945–49'. *Philos. Quart.* 1, 1950, 61. E. L. MINAR, 'A Survey of Recent Work in Pre-Socratic Philos.' *Class. Weekly* 47, 1953–54, 161. 177. A book still indispensable for ancient philosophy in general is E. ZELLER's *Die Philosophie der Griechen in ihrer geschichtlichen Entwicklung.* A reprint of the last edition (Leipz. 1920. 3 parts in six volumes) is shortly due from Olms of Hildesheim. A valuable new edition of the first two volumes in an Italian translation by R. MONDOLFO 1932–38. The first volume of UEBERWEG's *Grundriss*, revised by K. PRAECHTER (last edition 1923) is still valuable for its very full bibliographies. O. GIGON, *Grundprobleme der antiken Philosophie.* Samml. Dalp 66. Berne 1959. W. K. C. GUTHRIE, *The Greek Philosophers from Thales to Aristotle.* Lond. 1950. Texts with bibliog.: Diels-Kranz VS. G. S. KIRK and J. E.

---

[1] Pythagoras is thought to have been very important in the history of mathematics by G. MARTIN, *Klassische Ontologie der Zahl.* Cologne 1956, and O. Becker, *Gnom.* 29, 1957, 441, agrees with him. On the other side: E. FRANK, *Platon und die sogenannten Pythagoreer.* Halle 1923, and K. V. FRITZ op. cit. (p. 163, n. 3) 19.

RAVEN, *The Presocratic Philosophers. A Critical History with a Selection of Texts.*
Cambridge 1957. Students' ed. 1961. – Studies: W. NESTLE, *Vom Mythos zum
Logos.* 2nd ed. Stuttg. 1942. O. GIGON, *Der Ursprung der griech. Philos.* Basel 1945.
F. M. CORNFORD, *Principium Sapientiae.* Cambr. 1952. K. DEICHGRÄBER, 'Persön-
lichkeitsethos und philosophisches Forschertum der vorsokr. Denker', in *Der
listensinnende Trug des Gottes.* Gött. 1952, 57. J. B. MCDIARMID, 'Theophrastus
on the Presocratic Causes'. *Harv. Stud.* 61, 1953, 85. WILHELM NESTLE, *Vor-
sokratiker. Ausgewählt mit Einleitungen.* Cologne 1956. Q. CATAUDELLA, *I frammenti dei Presocratici. Traduz.* 1, Padua 1958. – Anaximander: N. RESCHER,
'Cosmic Evolution in A.'. *Studium Generale* 11, 1958, 718. CH. H. KAHN, *A. and
the Origins of Greek Cosmology.* New York 1960. C. I. CLASSEN, 'Anaximander'.
Herm. 90, 1962, 159. G. S. KIRK – J. E. RAVEN, *The Presocratic Philosophers.* Camb.
1960 (select texts with valuable criticism). – On the Pythagoreans: A. DELATTE,
La Vie de Pythagore de Diogène Laërce. Brussels 1922. K. V. FRITZ, *Pythagorean
Politics in Southern Italy.* New York 1940. J. E. RAVEN, *Pythagoreans and Eleatics.*
Cambridge 1948. L. FERRERO, *Storia del pitagorismo nel mondo romano.* Turin 1955.
J. S. MORRISON, 'Pythagoras of Samos'. *Class. Quart.* 6, 1956, 135. M. TIMPANARO
CARDINI, *I Pitagorici. Testimonianze e frammenti.* Fasc. 1. Florence 1958 (Bibl. d.
studi sup. 28). J. A. PHILIP, 'The Biographical Tradition: Pythagoras'. *Trans.
Am. Phil. Ass.* 90, 1959, 185. To these we may now add: W. K. C. GUTHRIE, *A
History of Greek Philosophy. I: The Earlier Presocratics and Pythagoreans.* London
1962. W. BURKERT, *Weisheit und Wissenschaft. Studien zu Pythagoras, Philolaos
und Platon.* Erlanger Beitr. z. Sprach- und Kunstwiss. 10. Nuremberg 1962 – a
monumental treatment of the whole set of problems with correspondingly full
bibliography. K. V. FRITZ' article 'Pythagoras' for Pauly is now in the press.

G Mature Archaic Lyric

I THEOGNIS

The name of Theognis of Megara is attached to a collection of about 1400
elegiac verses which raise difficult problems concerning their content and
structure. The poems are generally of short compass: some are mere distichs;
few are of more than twelve lines. They are mostly concerned with the symposium – the male drinking party. Some parts of the collection give a striking
picture of the development of a drinkers' code of practice, combining enjoyment of the gifts of Bacchus with decency of form and respect for one's table
companions. This picture comes out best in the elegy 467-496, which deprecates
heavy drinking and earnestly urges a companion to observe moderation. It
persuasively advocates that state poised between sobriety and complete drunkenness which the poet finds most congenial. The maxim 'in vino veritas' makes its
appearance here (499).[1]

At the symposium it was usual to honour the gods with some little songs.
Four of these begin the collection: two to Apollo, one to Artemis, the fourth
to the Muses and Graces.

[1] V. 501 in a better form in Stobaeus, cf. Alcaeus 333. 336 LP.

The codex Mutinensis gives us as Book II of the elegies a collection of poems dealing with the love of boys. It is possible that these rather uninspired productions were at one time scattered throughout the poems, and were brought together later. Women are less often mentioned, but a pretty distich (1225) contains the poet's avowal that there is no better fortune than to have a good wife.

An unusually intimate note is struck in the short poem 783-8. The poet represents himself as a widely-travelled man, who has never found such happiness as in his own beloved country. The whole collection has concern for the situation of the state as one of its main themes. But they do not speak of external foes and of open war in self-defence, as Tyrtaeus and Callinus do. A small group of elegies is concerned with the growing threat of Persian power, but here as elsewhere one poem may contradict another close to it: thus in 763 the growing danger need not hinder the enjoyment of one's wine, while in 773 Apollo is urgently enjoined to protect the city whose walls he himself raised up.

The circles from which these poems originate took a very different attitude to the tensions and movements inside the state. We find ourselves in the midst of that great reshuffling of society that can often be detected as the background of archaic lyric. It had proved impossible to check the economic and political rise of new social elements. Nouveaux-riches were met on all sides, and at any moment the discontent of the masses might help a tyrant to supreme powers in the state. Thus these elegies echo the resentment and complaints of the nobility. Once everything was in its proper place: the 'good' (ἀγαθοί, ἐσθλοί) were the great landowners, of noble descent, brought up as befits a gentleman. Wealth and worth went hand in hand. A deep gulf divided them from the 'bad' (κακοί, δειλοί), who had nothing and were nothing. But now everything is reversed. Those who once dwelt out of doors like beasts of the forest now come forward as the 'good', while the former owners of that name are in poverty. These are hard times for the aristocrat whose heart was with boys, horses and dogs (1255). This wretched money now compels them to form marriage alliances with the 'bad' people for the sake of indecent profit. One takes pains to get suitable mates for horses, asses and sheep, but now marriages are contracted in which the old inheritance of blood is lost (183). This complaint arises from the conviction (forcefully expressed in 535) of the absolute permanence of inherited abilities: a cornerstone of aristocratic philosophy which we shall find again in various contexts.

It is very hard in this age of revolution for a man of standing to hold his own. His best weapon is the friendship which unites people like him. Consequently we are told much about making and keeping friends.

We have given a survey of the collection as a whole, without touching on the problems that it raises. The very diversity of it – although we have left out a good deal, such as a dialogue between a woman in love and a man who does not want her (579) and a versified riddle (1229) – forbids us to suppose that we have here a literary work following a definite sequence of thought. In addition, differences in tone and content point to the participation of different poets.

Thus in one place (1181) the hatred of tyrants goes so far as to recommend their murder, while another poem (824) condemns tyrannicide. Virtue (ἀρετή), whose soul is righteousness, is more highly lauded than wealth (145), but a little earlier (129) we read that the only thing that matters is to have good luck. There are some especially interesting passages in which the aristocratic doctrine of the permanence of inborn qualities is treated as uncertain or even as exploded: the bad are not bad from their mother's womb; they have been made so by circumstance (305); this is a thing against which one cannot be too much on guard (31). Cleverness is better than virtue (1071); once even (1117) wealth is called the greatest of the gods, capable of making bad men good.

Such gross contradictions in sentiment are the most striking proof that the poems come from several hands. It has long been recognized that in the Theognidea we have a collection which has a rich gnomological literature behind it. The little that we know of Phocylides, or Demodocus of Leros, who seems to have been both witty and quarrelsome, from the miserable fragments that survive gives us some conception of this sort of literature in the sixth century (fasc. I p. 61 D.). If we find in the Theognidea some progress from one theme to another over various individual poems, it is not the sequence of thought of one author but the principle adopted by a compiler, who occasionally puts a statement and its contradiction side by side.

This interpretation of the collection may be reckoned as proven, but we should go too far if we denied it any unity at all. The themes of the individual poems may often be unrelated, even at variance with each other, but despite everything there is a basic unifying element. Virtually all these poems are the expression of a world in which aristocratic ideals of life are fighting for their very existence, sometimes with confidence sometimes with misgivings, sometimes with singleminded conviction, sometimes with a willingness to compromise. This is essentially the situation in the sixth century: much may be more recent, but with the end of the classical period questions of this kind had lost all real relevance and significance.

There were numbers of collections like ours, and we wonder why this one should have gained such reputation. It became proverbial in antiquity to say of anything that 'it was known before Theognis was born'.[1] The simplest answer is still that our collection began with some genuine poems of Theognis of Megara, who appears in Suidas as the writer of various works in elegiacs with a gnomic content. However that may be, there certainly was a poet Theognis, and the determining of his contribution is a task of perennial fascination, in which for a long time no decisive success was achieved.

The starting-point of all enquiries must always be the 'seal' which Theognis himself set upon the book of poems to his beloved boy Cyrnus. This seal (σφρηγίς) is mentioned in verses 19-26 of our collection. In the Delphic nome the seal was the part in which the poet spoke of himself. Consequently we must take the poet's mention of his own name as being the seal of authenticity; not (as has been repeatedly supposed) the address to the boy Cyrnus. It is of course

---

[1] Lucilius 952 M. Plut. Mor. 777 C.

obvious that neither method was capable of safeguarding the integrity of the poems. We may confidently reckon as authentic those verses (237-254) in which the poet tells the boy that he has given him wings through these poems, and has rescued him from the oblivion of posterity. The final complaint that the boy has been ungrateful is wholly personal in tone. We can also attribute to Theognis the verses referring to his career, to external dangers and to the unfaithfulness of his friends.

The ancients placed the height of Theognis' career in the middle of the sixth century, but more probably he lived in the late sixth and early fifth. We can easily believe that exile and poverty may have fallen to his lot. It is very hard to find evidence to date our present collection. Plato (*Meno* 95d)[1] quotes under the name of Theognis lines found in our collection. This does not of course mean that he had precisely that one before him. We can hardly think of their origin as coming from a single deliberate act. More probably the genuine poems of Theognis were the starting-point of a process which may have lasted for centuries: they may have been variously cut down or enlarged; verses from such poets as Solon or Mimnermus may have been added in, until finally the collection took its present shape. The process took place outside the realm of great literature: the Alexandrians did not take Theognis under their patronage. An extreme position is taken up by Aurelio Peretti,[2] who has the credit for setting our collection in its gnomological context and for collecting and evaluating the indirect evidence. In his theory the genuine Theognis had been lost shortly after Isocrates' time; Hellenistic and early Byzantine authors quote him purely from florilegia; the extant collection was a result of Byzantine compilation. Hence our first papyrus Theognis (*Ox. Pap.* 23, 1956, nr. 2380) is very important: it was written in the second or third century of our era and gives verses 254-278 in the same order as our texts. A more plausible theory is that of Adrados: a loose collection of Cyrnus-poems was made by Theognis in his old age, and was enlarged with other men's work in the fifth century; from these materials the existing selection was made in Hellenistic times. A rather similar view is that of Carrière, who supposes that our collection came from the fusion of an Athenian collection of about 400 and an Alexandrian of the first century A.D. It is impossible to be sure, and one respects the reserve which Burn[3] shows in his recent treatment of the subject.

The most important MSS. are: Mutinensis (now Parisinus Suppl. gr. 388) of the tenth century; Vaticanus gr. 915 of the thirteenth (according to D. C. C. YOUNG, *Parola di passato* 10, 1955, 206 this MS. comes from the school of

---

[1] On the meaning of ὀλίγον μεταβάς PERETTI (*v. inf.*). 74. 2.

[2] In the work cited in the bibliography to this section.

[3] The reader should particularly consult Burn's useful list (p. 258) of fourteen quotations from Theognis in which verses from our corpus are referred to other authors, likewise his collection of quotations from Theognis in authors before 300 B.C. (p. 260) and the list of verses quoted in Athenaeus and Stobaeus which are missing in our present text.

Planudes. The collation, according to C. GALLAVOTTI, *Riv. Fil.* 27, 1949, 265, leaves much to be desired); Marcianus 522 of the fifteenth. On a MS. in Brussels see A. GARZYA, *Riv. Fil.* 1953, 143. – Text: *Anth. Lyr.* 3rd ed. fasc. 2. J. CARRIÈRE, *Coll. des Un. de Fr.* 1948 (with comm. crit. and trans.); on which see J. KROLL, *Gnom.* 27, 1955, 76. A. GARZYA, Florence 1958 (with trans. notes, testimonia and index). F. R. ADRADOS, *Líricos griegos. Elegíacos y yambógrafos arcáicos* 2. Barcelona 1959 (with trans.). D. YOUNG, Leipz. 1961 (with verbal index). – Analysis: J. KROLL, *Theognis – Interpretationen. Phil. Suppl.* 29/1, 1936. J. CARRIÈRE, *Théognis de Mégare.* Paris 1948. L. WOODBURY, 'The seal of Theognis'. *The Phoenix. Suppl.* 1, 1952, 20. AUR. PERETTI, *Teognide nella tradizione gnomologica.* Pisa 1953, with good bibliography. M. VAN DER VALK, 'Theognis'. *Humanitas* 7/8, 1956, 68. B. A. VAN GRONINGEN, *La Composition littéraire archaïque grecque. Verh. Nederl. Ak. N. R.* 65/2. Amsterdam 1958, 140. C. M. BOWRA, *Early Greek Elegists.* Lond. 1938, repr. 1959. F. S. HASLER, *Untersuchungen zu Th. Zur Gruppenbildung im 1. Buch.* Winterthur 1959. A. R. BURN, *The Lyric Age of Greece.* Lond. 1960, 247.

2 THE EPIGRAM AND THE SCOLION

We have pursued the history of elegy as far as the problems of the Theognidea, and now we must consider two phenomena which are closely related to elegy – the one in its form, the other in its content.

The early Greek epigrams stood in much the same relation to great poetry as a sketch does to the paintings of a Polygnotus. But it is one of the distinguishing features of Greek civilization that handicraft in it has more of art, and art more of handicraft, than anywhere else in history. Thus we can justify a word here on archaic inscriptions in verse.

The oldest of these (53),[1] which we previously (p. 12) mentioned as the earliest monument of the Attic dialect, is on a Dipylon vase, which it promises as a prize to the best dancer. An interesting and exceptional case is the bowl from Ischia, of only slightly more recent date, with an inscription made up of an iambic trimeter with irregular opening and two hexameters. Epigrams of one or more hexameters are fairly common in the sixth century. They are far more frequent on the mainland than among the eastern Greeks: Corinth and its colony Corcyra are best represented. The inscriptions are mostly funerary or dedicatory: the hexameters accompanying the mythological scenes of the chest of Cypselus, described by Pausanias (5, 18 f.), are so far as we know exceptional.

Our material is very sparse, but the evidence points to an introduction of the distich type of epigram from Greek-speaking Asia Minor. On the mainland it was Athens that particularly took up and developed this form. If we call Solon to mind, we shall see that the elegy followed precisely the same path.

The technique of the rhapsodes can be seen behind the inscriptions in hexameters, but the distich type is essentially a short elegy, very seldom exceeding the favourite length of two lines. The precise connection is obscure, but it is a reasonable conjecture that as a lament for the dead the elegy had its effect on

---

[1] Numbers according to FRIEDLÄNDER-HOFFLEIT (*v. inf.*).

funerary inscriptions, and that its religious associations fitted it for dedications. The oldest fragment of a votive inscription (94; 7th century) has elegiac features of language.

Iambic and trochaic epigrams are much less common. One of these deserves special mention: an inscription in the Boeotian temple of Apollo Ptoeus, in which Alcmeonides, the son of Alcmeon, a member of the clan which played such a significant part in Athenian history, dedicates a statue of the god in return for victory at the Panathenaea. Obviously the name necessitated iambic metre.

The early epigrams are all anonymous; consequently it was inevitable that the more effective specimens should be attributed to well-known poets. The process began with Homer, and in many cases it is so palpable that a thorough-going scepticism is justified.[1]

We previously mentioned that the Theognidea contain a great deal of table-poetry, and that the elegy to a large extent belonged to the dining-hall. But the all-male gathering, an important feature in Greek social life, developed in the scolion a special form of song to accompany drinking. The scholium to Plato's *Gorgias* 451e has preserved the statements of Dicaearchus and Aristoxenus (both pupils of Aristotle) which give us the picture of a song which did not go round the table in regular sequence, but was taken up in turn by the best singers, wherever they happened to be sitting. From its pursuing this irregular course around the company it was called σκολιόν (=crooked). The interpretation is rather laboured; but modern scholarship has devised nothing better.

In the beginning such songs were presumably improvised – a practice which can be paralleled today in folk-song. But in addition considerable poets wrote scolia. A passage in the *Protagoras* has made famous the scolion of Simonides in which he gives his views on Pittacus' saying about the difficulty of virtue. Scolia as good as this one were very soon written down: at the same time a great many anonymous songs which found favour were snatched from their context and buried in anthologies. Besides many scattered examples, we have in Athenaeus (15. 694c) a short collection of 25 of these Attic drinking songs, a very valuable survival. They are mostly of four lines, some of two, and there is one distich (23), all in simple lyric metre.

It is not only the first four little hymns at the beginning of the collection that remind us of the Theognidea. In the other songs also we hear the aristocracy singing between bumpers of their joys and cares and the principles that govern their life. One song (14) urges us to keep company only with the virtuous: this it represents as a wise saying of Admetus, king of the aristocratic Thessalians; Theognis gave the same advice to his boy Cyrnus. Another anticipates Euripides' ideas for improving the world and would like to be able to see into a man's heart before making a friend of him. The best poetry comes in two poems of two stanzas each expressing the wish that their writer might be a lyre in the hands of boys at the Dionysia or a golden ornament worn by a beautiful and virtuous woman. The political element is strong in these songs. Four of them

---

[1] Some good examples in FRIEDLÄNDER, op. cit. 67.

(10-13) praise Harmodius and Aristogiton, according to the common view (refuted by Thucydides 1, 20; 6, 54 ff.), as the founders of Athenian freedom.[1] The 24th song laments those fallen at Leipsydrion in the battle of the Alcmeonids against Hippias.

There are many indications that this little collection should be dated in the late sixth and early fifth century. It shows again those qualities which in Solon's poems impart beauty to wholly different material: they display with compelling clarity a sincere and immediate response to the things and forces of this world. Something of the magical quality of Attic literature that reached fulfilment in the classical period shines out in these little poems.

A very different note is struck in a scolion of Hybrias from Crete. The poem is more recent; we mention it here because it gives a good impression of what these songs would have sounded like among serious-minded Dorians at an earlier time.

P. FRIEDLÄNDER – H. B. HOFFLEIT, *Epigrammata, Greek Inscriptions in Verse from the Beginnings to the Persian Wars.* Univ. of Calif. Press. 1948. W. PEEK, *Griech. Vers-Inschriften I. Grab-Epigramme.* Berl. 1955; see the exhaustive discussion by L. ROBERT, *Gnom.* 31, 1959, 1; ib. *Griechische Grabgedichte. Griech. u. deutsch.* Berl. 1960. The Ischia bowl: G. BUCHNER – C. F. RUSSO, *Acc. Lincei. Rend.* 10, 1955, 215. Scolia: *Anth. Lyr.* 2nd ed., fasc. 6, 16; fasc. 5, 159. C. M. BOWRA, *Greek Lyric Poetry.* 2nd ed. Oxf. 1961, 373; on Hybrias 398. On the scope of the genre 'scolion' (much narrowed in Hellenistic times) see A. E. HARVEY, 'The Classification of Greek Lyric Poetry' *Class. Quart.* N.S.5, 1955, 157.

3 ANACREON

More than half a century divides the flowering of Lesbian Lyric from the time of Anacreon, who was placed by the Alexandrian canon of lyric poets beside Alcaeus and Sappho. His poems belong to a wholly different world. The Lesbian poets shared the ideals and way of life of an aristocracy whose mortal enemy was the tyrant. But in the middle of the sixth century all this was enormously overshadowed by a new development. The Lydian kingdom, which the men of Lesbos looked towards with admiration, was shattered by Persian attack. Sardes fell in 546, and its fall settled the fate of the Ionian colonies in Asia Minor. Only Miletus was able to secure a renewal of the terms which she had made with the Lydians, and in Samos Polycrates, the most adroit politician of all the tyrants, maintained his position supported by a powerful fleet and extensive commerce. Persian imperialism found an Ionia that had reached a full-blown maturity. Economic prosperity, the fertile influence of external cultures, and not least a tendency towards the love of pleasure and calculated aloofness had quickly ripened her. It is to this world that Anacreon belongs. He

[1] V. EHRENBERG, 'Das Harmodioslied'. *Wien. Stud.* 69, 1956, 57.

was an Ionian from Teos, a city which was the birthplace of another lyric writer, Pythermus, of whom we know scarcely more than the name.

As the Persian danger came nearer, the inhabitants of Teos, like those of Phocaea, left their homes by ship. Abdera in Thrace provided a new home, but amid perpetual dangers. When Anacreon went with them he was a young man, and his earliest verses were written at Abdera. He mourns in trochaic metre a young friend who had died in the fighting for Abdera (90 D.). The same fate befell a man mentioned in a funeral inscription (100). A single verse (51) mentions one who threw his shield into 'the waters of the sweetly-flowing river', and it would be typical of Anacreon to trick out in pompous epic language a personal narrative which Archilochus despatched more concisely. It was not only danger, however, that came from the Thracians. In this period Anacreon wrote the charming poem (88) describing the shy Thracian filly that gambols over the meadows with awkward leaps, and calls for a skilful rider – a job which the poet would like to have. His knack of expressing erotic concepts under a thin veil of imagery is in this poem already fully developed.

The more distinguished tyrants had the ambition to be patrons of the arts, and so Anacreon, like Ibycus, found his way to Polycrates of Samos. It may be a pure invention that the messenger of the satrap Oroetes found the tyrant at table with Anacreon (Herod. 3. 121); but at all events the story reflects the position which the poet was commonly thought to hold. These palmy days came to an end when Polycrates fell a victim to the treachery of his Persian opponents (c. 522). Anacreon now betook himself to the court of Hipparchus at Athens: an ancient report (Ps.-Plat. *Hipparch.* 228c) says that the tyrant had him conveyed to Athens in a penteconter. A good many of the extant poems were written in Athens, but attempts to show Atticisms in vocabulary or idiom[1] have not achieved consistent success owing to the shortage of material for comparison. We know that one of the herms with inscriptions set up in Attica by Hipparchus bore an epigram of Anacreon's (103).

His activities in Athens left other important traces behind them. Among the many boys whose beauty melted Anacreon's heart was one Critias, an ancestor of the politician and poet who was Plato's uncle. Thus we interpret the ten hexameters (8 D.=VS 88 B4) in which the younger Critias eloquently proclaims the fame of Anacreon. He is the spice of the banquet; he makes women run mad; he puts the flute to shame by his masterly singing to the lyre. Here once again the social distinction between the two instruments is underlined. It is remarkable that Critias prophecies Anacreon's lasting fame as long as choruses of women attend the sacred nocturnal festival. We must take Critias' word for it[2] that Anacreon wrote choral odes for such occasions. His reputation is well attested in the visual arts also. Red-figure pots[3] show him playing the lyre to a young and enthusiastic audience, and Pausanias (1, 25, 1) saw a statue of him on the Acropolis. We know almost nothing of his later years. He may well

[1] BOWRA (*v. inf.*), 304.
[2] Cf. Pap. nr. 942 P.
[3] References in J. G. GRIFFITH, *Fifty Years of Classical Scholarship.* Oxf. 1954, 68. Pl. 3. 5.

have stayed in Thrace for a time: epitaphs forged later[1] put his grave in Teos.

The setting of Anacreon's poetry is the aristocratic symposium – as popular a feature of life at the courts of tyrants as it had been among the Aeolian or Megarian nobles. More importance is now attached to elegance of manners. The poet wants no drunken uproar after the Scythian manner, and the instructions (43) which he gives to the wine-waiter – to add ten parts of water to five of wine – show that he desired a very restrained jollity as the background to his singing. The tone of the conversation, whether at the Samian or the Athenian court, must have been very different from that in Lesbos. Aristocratic pride of place could not of course have found free expression where one man held all the power. Political questions in general are less prominent. There is a striking contrast between Alcaeus singing to his carousing club-mates of his well-stocked armoury, and Anacreon at the wine-bowl expressing distaste for the mention of conflict or hateful warfare (96). The Attic scolion in honour of Harmodius and Aristogiton is equally in contrast to Anacreon's tones. His favourite subjects are outlined in the same poem: the glittering gifts of Aphrodite and the happy delights of festival – that $\epsilon\vartheta\phi\rhoo\sigma\upsilon\nu\eta$ which Solon (3, 10 D.) wished for his citizens. For Anacreon and his circle this kind of pleasure necessarily had an erotic colouring. Beautiful boys served at table: many of the poems are addressed to them; some are even known to us by name, as Cleobulus and Smerdies. Women also occur, and play no small part in Anacreon's life and writings (the poem of Critias spoke only of women). Mostly these women were unfree, flute-girls or the like, such as commonly attended banquets. Romantic love with its tragic overtones has no place here. Anacreon's amours should not be taken too seriously; nor can they be dismissed as pure pretence. There is no toying or trifling with love in these poems: its sweetness is expressed with an intensity which sometimes goes close to pain. The peculiar charm of this mature Ionic art consists in a singular union of opposites. The poet who hates all excess and maintains such a careful balance between love and indifference, between drunkenness and sobriety (79), is always master of his medium; yet the magic of his art lies in that gentle resignation which invests everything with an unconscious inevitability. In his poetry lights and outlines move behind a shimmering veil. Sappho demands affection with a heart of fire, and her poems echo many a shrill cry of pain: but Anacreon throws himself from the Leucadian rocks 'drunken with love' (17). The unexpected image of the fatal leap is here used to describe a yielding to delight. Yet at the very moment of his fall the poet is perfectly conscious of the pleasure of such intoxication.

We have occasionally remarked that Greek art normally contains a large and healthy element of craftsmanship. We find this again with Anacreon, and here again his art reaches to the limits of Greek achievement. The epithets that crowd his poems are sometimes quite individual, as in the poem (2) invoking Dionysus, who frolics over the mountains with the young heifer[2] Eros, the dark-eyed Nymphs and purple-robed Aphrodite; or where Eros looks at the poet's greying chin and flits over his head in a drift of pinions flashing gold (53).

---

[1] *Anth. Pal.* 7. 23-33.   [2] Reading Δαμάλης.

The colour-epithets are all chosen with propriety, and a feeling for colour is displayed which we do not otherwise meet till much later. A similar individuality appears in many of his images. Eros sets to work on his victim like a smith: he forges him with a heavy hammer and quenches him in the mountain torrent (45). He plays with dice, but their names are Folly and Confusion (34). The poet's feeling for anything tender and fragile comes out in the verses in which he compares the shyness of youth to that of a fawn abandoned by its mother, trembling amid the forest (39). Even where the poet laments his old age[1] (5. 44, 53), the expression is mild and restrained.

The Alexandrians knew of songs, iambs and elegies of Anacreon, and they edited his works in five books. The later image of the poet does less than justice to his range, as we see from a venomous invective in verse against the newly rich Artemon, hurling Archilochian thunders against the 'whoreson knave' who now rides in a luxurious coach and swaggers with his ivory parasol (54). The new fragments give examples of ironical pathos, particularly in the lament for the hair of Smerdies.

An art like Anacreon's defied continuation. Where any such attempt was made, divorced from the historical circumstances of Ionia, charm gave way to insipidity, the bitter-sweet enjoyment of love to a superficial pleasure in wine and women. It is characteristic of the later imitations that they choose, out of all the rich metrical variety of the genuine poems, by preference metres like the catalectic iambic or the anaclastic ionic dimeter,[2] which with conventional handling give a monotonous humdrum effect. Anacreontic verse was being written right down to the Byzantine age. Sixty of these poems are preserved in a collection which comes in manuscripts after the Palatine anthology. The poems vary in date and quality, but in general they are feeble effusions, partly responsible for the false view of Anacreon which was long current. But as it happened, the mediocre had a powerful influence and gave rise to whole movements such as the Anacreontic movement in Germany. Goethe demonstrates that the breath of genius can call roses into bloom on the thornbush.

Text in *Anth. Lyr.*, 2nd ed., fasc. 4, 160. (references are to this edition). BR. GENTILI, *Anacreonte. Introd. testo critico, trad. studio sui framm. pap.* Rome 1958. New fragments: *Ox. Pap.* 22, 1954, nr. 2321f., cf. K. LATTE, *Gnom.* 27, 1955, 495. W. PEEK, 'Neue Bruchstücke frühgr. Dichtung'. *Wiss. Zeitschr. Univ. Halle* 5, 1955/56, 196. BR. GENTILI, *Maia* N.S.8, 1956, 181. Analysis: C. M. BOWRA, *Greek Lyric Poetry*, 2nd ed. Oxf. 1961, 268.

4 SONGWRITERS ON THE MAINLAND

If we treat a group of poetesses together here, it is only to get out of a difficulty. We are concerned with personalities for whom our information is as

---

[1] Cf. J. A. DAVISON, 'Anacreon, Fr. 5. D'. *Trans. Am. Phil. Ass.* 90, 1959, 40.

[2] ◡−◡−◡−−; ◡◡−◡−◡−⚊.

scanty as it is unreliable, so that it would be difficult to place them in the historical development.

Corinna is the authoress of some verses (15 D. 5 Page) reproving Myrtis for denying her feminine nature and entering into competition with Pindar. The simplest interpretation of her expressions is that they refer to a contest between contemporaries. Thus we obtain a date for the poetess Myrtis, who came from Anthedon on the north coast of Boeotia; whether her competition with Pindar was historical or merely one of many literary inventions is another question. In Plutarch (*Quaest. Graec.* 40, 300f.) she is called ποιήτρια μελῶν; one would readily take these as being individual lyrics, and her reputed pupil Corinna certainly wrote such songs. But the possibility of their being choral lyrics cannot be excluded, and the story of competition with Pindar points that way. Plutarch (loc. cit.) tells us the content of one of her poems: it was concerned with the unhappy love of Ochna for the chaste young Eunostus, who died as a result of her calumnies. This is one of the many Greek versions of the Potiphar theme: to us it is a valuable indication how rich local legend was in love-motifs which later supplied material for great poetry.

We have been able to form a much better picture of the poetry of Corinna of Tanagra since a papyrus from Hermopolis (nr. 162 P. 1 Page) brought some appreciable groups of verses to our knowledge. We find here a 'contest' theme that occurs elsewhere:[1] the contest of Helicon and Cithaeron. The hills engage in a musical contest: we can still make out that Cithaeron ended her song with the tale of the infant Zeus and the Curetes. The Muses, who are at once audience and mistresses of ceremonies, invite the gods to decide the contest. Cithaeron wins amid an angry shower of rocks from Helicon – a bad loser.

A second part of the papyrus tells how the seer Acraephen assuages the anxiety which Asopus is feeling about his daughter by bringing joyful tidings: great gods have found her worthy of their love, and she will become the ancestress of great princely houses. Then Acraephen, whom we may suppose to be in the service of Apollo Ptoeus, tells how he came to have his job.

What else we know of Corinna's poetry is all concerned with Boeotian myths, some purely local, others more widely known. She wrote of the Seven against Thebes and of the slaying of the Teumessian fox by Oedipus, who was the hero of many Boeotian legends. Heracles of course could not be omitted, and one poem was devoted to his faithful helper Iolaus. In individual features we find a very close adherence to local tradition. A poem *Orestas* is a seeming exception: its title and opening are preserved in a papyrus (nr. 161 P. 2 Page). It describes the rising of the moon, but the last word refers to seven-gated Thebes, and we can be confident that the theme was linked up to her native soil, probably via the cult of Apollo.

In a fragment (2 D. 4 Page) the reading seemed to be that Corinna prided

---

[1] The length of the tradition behind such literary contests is shown by Sumero-Akkadian examples in J. VAN DIJK, *La Sagesse sumère-accadienne*. Leyden 1953. Babylonian wrangles between tamarisk and datepalm, cornel and poplar, barley and wheat, and between various animals are referred to by G. LAMBERT, *Babylonian Wisdom Literature*. Oxf. 1960.

herself on the beautiful γεροῖα that she told to the women of Tanagra. The word recurs as the title of one of Corinna's works in Antoninus Liberalis 25; it was interpreted as 'old wives' tales', and Corinna was thought to be referring thus, with a charming irony, to her own poems. But now comes a new papyrus (Ox. Pap. 23, 1956, nr. 2370)[1] with the form Ϝεροῖα, which must consequently be restored in Antoninus. We do not know what the title means, but we are better off than thinking that we did. In the new fragment Corinna speaks proudly of her poems and of their success: she is inspired by Terpsichore, and Tanagra is delighted with her.

A careful study of what remains has shown that Corinna's language cannot be taken as reflecting her native Boeotian. It contains elements obviously drawn from the common stock of Greek poetical language. The Boeotian colouring is nevertheless perceptible, particularly in spelling, which consistently uses a phonetic system. Comparison with inscriptions shows that our text of Corinna in its present form was written down between 225 and 175 B.C.

While we can form a fair idea of Corinna's poetry, her dating poses a difficult problem. She enjoyed some celebrity in the ancient world, she was added to the Alexandrian canon of nine lyric poets,[2] Ovid named after her the central figure of his love-elegies: yet we have no reference to her before the first century B.C. The great Alexandrian grammarians did not concern themselves with her, and apparently it was one of their successors who first collected her poems into five books.

This disquieting circumstance can be explained in two ways. It is conceivable that Corinna wrote in or about Pindar's time, but that her poems were for a long time preserved only locally, until in late Hellenistic times her primitive manner of narrative and the individuality of her language found admirers. The alternative – seriously urged in recent years – is a radical one: to put her date about 200 B.C. There are no absolute criteria available, and seeming parallels in other poets give no certain results.[3] Corinna's metres are as simple as her language: she uses stanzas of five or six verses made up of ionic or choriambic dimeters. The latter are used in a comparable manner in the middle plays of Euripides more than anywhere else, but no argument can be based on this fact: both might have been building upon a popular metrical form.[4] If we decide to date Corinna in the time of Pindar, it must be on rather inconclusive grounds. Suidas names Corinna as a pupil of Myrtis, and says that she was victorious over Pindar five times. The story turns up in various forms: Plutarch in particular tells a charming tale of their rivalry (Glor. Ath. 4, 347). Corinna found fault with Pindar for neglecting myths, which she said were the soul of poetry: when he carried out her advice in good earnest, she told him he was sowing by the sackful.

---

[1] Cf. C. GALLAVOTTI, Gnom. 29, 1957, 422; Boeotian poetry also appears in Pap. nr. 2371-2374, but it is doubtful whether it is by Corinna.

[2] Reference in PAGE (v. inf.) 68. 1.

[3] Euripides before Corinna? Material in PAGE 20. 5. Corinna before Antimachus of Colophon? See B. WYSS, Antimachi Coloph. reliquiae. Berl. 1955, praef. p. III.

[4] Thus WILAMOWITZ, Griech. Verskunst 227.

Pausanias, who saw Corinna's monument and portrait in Tanagra (9, 22, 3) knew of an alleged victory over Pindar, which he attributes to the ease and intelligibility of her dialect and the beauty of her person. Now we know that the ancient world was much addicted to anecdotes of this kind, and we must not take Corinna's contest with Pindar as an historical fact. But it is very hard to suppose that this kind of story, at least partly developed in the time of Plutarch and Pausanias, could easily have attached itself to a poetess who in fact lived at the time of the Roman wars against the Macedonians, and could have made her a contemporary of Pindar's. Propertius' phrase *antiqua Corinna* (2, 3, 21) is not very precise, but it fits the early dating better than the late.

In the shrine of Aphrodite near the theatre at Argos Pausanias (2, 20, 8) saw a stele with a representation of the poetess Telesilla. She was depicted having just thrown her books aside, and putting a helmet on her head. The reputation of Telesilla was indeed based on the widely recurring story that in a crucial hour for Argos she had led the women of the city victoriously against the Spartans. She lived in the first half of the fifth century. Of her poems all we can say is that they were closely connected with divine worship. In the shrine of Asclepius at Epidaurus stones have been found inscribed with various hymns to the gods (IG 4/1, 129-134), one of which tells how the mother of the gods roams angrily over mountain and valley, demanding her share in the kingdoms of the world. The rather damaged verses exhibit a metre[1] which the Alexandrians later named Telesillean after the poetess, and since we know that she wrote hymns to the gods, it is quite likely that this is some of her work. Her style is very simple, more unassuming even than Corinna's: the only animation comes from the immediate juxtaposition of statement and counter-statement. Her language, with a few exceptions, is the common language of contemporary lyric. A papyrus (nr. 1163 P.) has a scholium on Theocritus 15, 64 ('Women know everything: they even know how Zeus took Hera to wife') which says that the verse alludes to Telesilla. At all events we may credit her with a poem on the marriage of Zeus and Hera.

It is in Boeotia and the Peloponnese, not in Athens, that women achieve a lasting reputation for poetry. This reflects a freer social position of women than that which we know from Athens. Corinth's neighbour Sicyon had its Praxilla, whom we may suppose to have been roughly contemporary with Telesilla. Her personality eludes us: to make her into a hetaera would be rash. Her memory was held in honour, and in the fourth century her countryman Lysippus cast a statue of her in bronze. A verse (1 D.) from a dithyramb *Achilles* is attributed to her. It is possible that Praxilla wrote dithyrambs of a narrative content; but it is remarkable that the verse in question, in which someone blames Achilles for hardness of heart, is a hexameter. Three hexameters are preserved from a poem called *Adonis* (2 D.). Adonis, dead and in the underworld, is asked what he reckons fairest of the things he has left behind: he says the sun and moon and various different fruits. In antiquity this was taken as the expression of a remarkable naïveté, and 'simpler than Praxilla's Adonis' became a proverbial saying.

It is more likely that the proverb ridiculed Praxilla herself than that she was representing Adonis as an idiot.[1] Of those Attic scolia which we mentioned earlier Praxilla was given credit for Admetus' advice to keep good company and for the warning against scorpions that lurk under every stone (14 D.; 20 D.). In this connection 'drinking songs' (παροίνια) are mentioned: this probably means no more than that some of her poems were found suitable for singing at table.

Corinna: *Anth. Lyr.* 2nd ed., fasc. 4, 193. K. LATTE, 'Die Lebenszeit der Korinna'. *Eranos* 54, 1956, 57, goes into the question of the dating and of the μεταχαρακτη-ρισμός, and comes to the conclusion expressed here. D. L. PAGE, *Corinna*, Lond. 1953. Telesilla: *Anth. Lyr.* 2nd ed., fasc. 5, 72. P. MAAS, 'Epidaurische Hymnen'. *Schr. d. Königsb. Gel. Ges., Geisteswiss. Kl.* 9/5, 1933, 134. Praxilla: *Anth. Lyr.* 2nd ed., fasc. 5, 160. A Boeotian bowl, to be dated c. 450, has the beginning of two verses (3 D.) in the metre called Praxillean after the poetess (P. JACOBS-THAL, *Götting. Vasen* 1912, T.22 nr. 81); but since the verses are not ascribed to Praxilla by name, this is not a firm base for dating. Fragments of these poetesses now in D. L. PAGE, *Poetae Melici Graeci.* Oxf. 1962.

5 CHORAL LYRIC

Ibycus represents a highly individual development within Greek choral lyric: like Anacreon he follows a line that goes no further. His date is fixed by his visit to the court of Polycrates, who was overthrown by the Persian invasion of 522.

He hailed, like Stesichorus, from the Greek west, from Rhegium with its mixed Chalcidian and Messenian settlers. His father's name is variously related: Phytius seems the most likely. Whether this was the same man whose legislative activity was still remembered (Iambl. *Vit. Pyth.* 130. 172) we cannot tell. He was probably of a distinguished family: so at least the story suggests which tells us that he might have been tyrant in his native city. At all events he spent his earlier years in his homeland, and he must naturally have been deeply impressed by the art of Stesichorus. Ibycus, of whom we know desperately little, is very different from the great Sicilian choral lyrist, but the few surviving fragments allow us to posit an early period in which he imitated Stesichorus. Many of them show references to myth, with a predilection for out-of-the-way variants. He tells us of Menelaus that the sight of Helen's beauty made him drop the sword with which he was about to punish her infidelity; he refers to a liaison between Achilles and Medea in Elysium; sometimes local elements creep in, such as Heracles' bathing in hot springs (which must be those of Himera), but a great deal of course comes from the well-known myth-cycles. It is in Ibycus that we find the first poetical allusion to Orpheus (17 D.): not perhaps surprising if we remember the importance of Orphism in southern Italy. In all these particular instances we have no means of knowing whether

[1] Cf. W. ALY, *RE* 22, 1764.

they are passing references or full-length narration of myths, after the manner of Stesichorus. The large number of names and themes speaks for the latter possibility, and the report (2 D.) of the slaying of the sons of Moliona, Siamese twins who had grown to maturity in a silver egg (the speaker is apparently Heracles), can only have belonged in the context of a long mythical narrative. In addition we find among later writers a great number of expressions and themes ascribed to Stesichorus and Ibycus.[1] For the most part these are very unusual features, unlikely to have occurred in both poets: the situation was probably like that of the *Games at the Funeral of Pelias*, of which Athenaeus (4, 172) could not say whether Ibycus or Stesichorus wrote it. This presupposes poems of Ibycus' which so closely resembled the choral narrative odes of Stesichorus that there was room for this kind of doubt.

We may suspect that the great change in Ibycus' life brought with it the great change in his work. His road led to the court of Polycrates of Samos – the very tyrant from whose grip Pythagoras had fled to southern Italy. In Samos Ibycus must have met Anacreon at the height of his favour, but there is no report of their mutual relations. Under Polycrates' roof the poetry of Ibycus took that strange turning towards erotically coloured choral lyric which seems to have been determined by many factors. In this world of Ionian maturity men already felt themselves more remote from the old mythology than the mainlanders did, among whom choral lyric was the successor to epic. Also choral lyric must have felt the impact of Lesbian monody as the great vehicle of love-poetry: in Alcman the chorus was already speaking the poet's innermost thoughts. But the decisive influence was the direction of Ibycus' own interests: the remains, wretched as they are, of his mythical narratives yet suffice to show his predilection for the erotic.

What Ibycus wrote in Samos fixed his image for posterity. When Cicero (*Tusc.* 4. 71) and Suidas speak of him as the poet of passionate love, both are echoing the common verdict. His art is exemplified particularly in two fragments. One (6 D.) speaks of the regular rhythm of the seasons, which in the spring makes the young vine and the quince-tree bloom in the garden of the nymphs. A violent change brings in the antithesis: there is no season in the poet's life in which Love falls asleep; Love lashes him mercilessly like a storm from the Thracian north laden with thunderbolts. In the second fragment (7 D.), with melting glances from beneath his dark brows Eros lures the poet towards Aphrodite's net. But he shies away from the approaching god like a racehorse who has won many races, but now, old and weary, shrinks from new contests. In both poems a conception is embodied which was widespread among the Greeks: Love comes to man as a dangerous and maddening power, stealing away his very self; grief is of its essence. In both we hear the poet in old age – for so we are to interpret the complaint against the god who spares no season of human life.

The sorrows of love had been Sappho's theme also: the difference between her verses and those of Ibycus is that between the Lesbian monody with its

[1] PAGE (*v. sup.*), 167.

force and immediacy and the heavy opulence of choral lyric. This elaboration, showing itself most in the number of the adjectives, is not there to trick out the inner emptiness of the poetry. Rather it appears in these verses as the appropriate expression of a great passion holding sway over all mankind.

It is difficult to reconcile what we know so far of Ibycus' poetry with the evidence of a longer passage preserved on papyrus (nr. 967 P.). Four triads are discernible, and if this is really the work of Ibycus, then this is the first example known of the species of composition in which strophe and antistrophe are followed by an epode. Suidas ascribes the 'invention' to Stesichorus.

The end of the poem is preserved, and enough of its beginning to make it impossible for any new discovery to alter the general picture. Down to the last triad the poet enumerates persons and events of the Trojan war merely to assure us that he will not sing of them. This sounds like a rejection of narrative heroic poetry, either as formerly attempted by Ibycus, or as he saw it attempted by others. The narration of such stories is the task of the learned (σεσοφισμέναι) Muses of Helicon; no mortal can aspire to it. Then, after the greatest of the heroes, he mentions the most beautiful – an otherwise unknown son of Hyllis and, outshining all others as gold does brass, Priam's son Troilus. In three lines comes the ultimate point: 'You, Polycrates, will share with these the imperishable fame of beauty, just as my fame is immortal in song.'

This long enumeration that makes up most of the surviving verses is in its composition and linguistic expression alike unsatisfactory, and it is in striking contrast to the ending so hastily clapped on to it. There is not a spark of that emotional colouring that imparted such a sombre splendour to the other two fragments. Either this poem (which does not bear any author's name) is not by Ibycus, but by a later poet trying to plough with his team, or Ibycus dashed it off hastily and without any real feeling as an occasional piece. In any case it is apparent that we have here a piece of courtly flattery addressed to a handsome and well-born youth, not (as in the previous fragments) the expression of an all-consuming passion for an attractive boy. If in the face of all these arguments we still decide for Ibycus, the mention of Polycrates is the reason. It is not, of course, the tyrant who is referred to: an excerpt from Himerius,[1] who lived in the fourth century of our era and both read more and knew more of the lyric poets than we can, puts our poem into its proper setting. The tyrant had a son of the same name, who lived in Rhodes as his lieutenant, just as Periander of Corinth sent his son to Corcyra. This younger Polycrates was a lover of the arts, and his father gave him Anacreon as a tutor. It is to him then that we must suppose Ibycus' flattery to be addressed.

An argument not very strong in itself, but fitting well with the others, is the agreement on dialect between this poem and the rest of the fragments. As with Stesichorus, so with Ibycus it has been thought that the mixture of different elements in his language reflects the dialectal situation of a colony made up of different peoples. But such features as the omission of the syllabic augment or the use of the digamma according to metrical exigencies point rather to a

[1] *Herm.* 46, 1911, 422.

literary dialect strongly influenced by epic, with a thin veneer of Doric and an occasional Aeolic form.

If it is Polycrates' son who receives this tribute with its mythological adornments – just as Ibycus is said (schol. ad Apoll. Rhod. 3, 158) to have complimented one Gordias with references to the rape of Ganymede – this goes very well with Eusebius' dating of Ibycus' floruit in the 61st Olympiad (536/33): the tyrant would have been his contemporary.[1] We do not know whether the poet survived the overthrow of his patron (c. 522). His death was embellished with legend. The well-known story of the cranes which led to the detection of his murderers is dismissed by Iamblichus (*Vit. Pyth.* 126) as a story told of many different people.

In the mature archaic period choral lyric was an important force in education. It might certainly be largely dependent on the favour of ambitious rulers; sometimes, as with Ibycus, it might renounce a wider effectiveness for the sake of intimacy: but where it was an adornment of divine festivals and of the supreme hours of human life, it could not fail to have such repercussions. We may consider choral lyric as holding an important place in Greek cultural life between epic and tragedy. It spoke indeed with many voices, and it is fascinating to compare the figure of Simonides – individual, many-sided and often anticipating later developments – with that of Euripides. In the Ionian world Anacreon and Ibycus achieve a peculiar sweetness that allowed of no further development. But Simonides shows a wholly different side of the Ionian spirit of his time: he sows a vigorous seed which is to bring forth an abundant harvest both in the mainland and in the Greek-speaking west.

Simonides was born about 556 on the island of Ceos, the nearest of the Cyclades to Attica: according to Herodotus (8. 46) it had an Ionian population, coming largely from Athens. The island set its face against the luxury of Ionian Asia Minor, and had the reputation of being without any prostitutes or flute-girls. Simonides, whose art has a strong simplicity that gives it a special place in choral lyric, grew up in a society that banished all luxury from its confines.[2]

Athenaeus (456c ff.) has preserved two riddles in hexameters, couched in language of oracular obscurity. The rather complex circumstances to which they seem to allude may or may not be rightly interpreted in the explanations offered by the Peripatetic Chamaeleon, whose biographical reports are as numerous as they are untrustworthy. But, as related by Athenaeus, the first referred to Simonides as a young man, the second to his activity as chorus-master at the temple of Apollo at Carthaea, one of the main centres of the island. If so, this would agree with the supposition that he began with performances of this kind, and came to write choral lyrics himself through his experience in rehearsing the songs for the sacred festivals of his country.

Once established as a poet, he led a wandering life, which took him through many parts of Greece, and in particular to the tables of the great. Pisistratus' son Hipparchus is said to have induced him with expensive presents to come to Athens. It was commonly said of Simonides that he was a good business man,

---

[1] Suidas says the 54th Olympiad (564/1).   [2] *Syll. Inscr. Graec.* 1218.

and knew how to coin his talent into gold. After the fall of the Pisistratids he went to their friends in Thessaly, where Anacreon also may have lived for a time. He had particularly close relations with the house of Scopas, and we will hear of poems attesting this friendship. During the Persian wars he lived in Athens again, and took part through his poetry in the events of those years. We may suppose that he was close to the leading men and there may be some truth in the story which associates him with Themistocles. The latter had incurred the bitter animosity of the poet Timocreon from Ialysus in Rhodes through refusing to forward his return from exile. We have some remains of poems (probably scolia) in which Timocreon fiercely attacks Themistocles. Under the name of Simonides we find an epigram (99 D.) purporting to be the epitaph of the toper, glutton and scandal-monger Timocreon. But he outlived Simonides: consequently the epigram, if it is genuine, can only be interpreted as a malicious joke. It would, however, be a valuable indication of the poet's readiness to attack Themistocles' enemies on his behalf. But since this account of Timocreon's slanderous character does not occur before the imperial period, the ascription to Simonides must remain as doubtful here as in numerous other cases.

At the age of eighty, in 476, Simonides trained a chorus of men which won the prize: so much he says in one of his own epigrams (77 D.). Shortly afterwards we find him at the court of Hiero in Syracuse. On his first arrival he reconciled Hiero with Theron of Acragas, when they had already decided on war. This would not have been his least recommendation at court. The relations of the despot and the poet were adorned by the inventions of later ages: an illustration is the *Hiero* of Xenophon. Simonides brought his nephew Bacchylides to Sicily, and doubtless he himself met Pindar there. There could not but be rivalry between them: we shall see its reflection in Pindar's work. In 468 Simonides died, certainly in Sicily, probably at Acragas.

Among the poems of Simonides there were some intended for religious use – Suidas speaks of *Paeans*. But the information on them is so scanty and uncertain, that we can consider such hymns as forming an insignificant part of his output. His reputation was won on other fields. The victors in great athletic contests had certainly from time immemorial been wildly acclaimed and variously honoured on their homecoming, and inevitably songs must have been improvised at such times. But there is no example before Simonides of a chorus singing a prepared song written especially for the occasion by a considerable poet, and we may assume that it was he who first laid hold of this new field for choral lyric as an art-form. This step led the way to an unparallelled connection between sport and art in Greek life. The great games were in themselves human events of a kind which we can scarcely appreciate nowadays, despite the revived Olympic Games. We must consider that in this instance the primitiveness of their technique was a singular blessing to the Greeks. They had no mechanical means of timing the best performances and thus readily comparing them. Consequently in their sports meetings it was not a question of beating records previously established; the attention of a whole nation was not riveted upon a few outstanding performances. Rather the object at every meeting was there and then to strive for the goal which young men found defined in Homer: always to be the first and to be distinguished beyond others. This kind of competitive spirit bound the athletes and the spectators together, making them share one common excitement. The great importance of these games in fostering a Greek national consciousness, which was denied a regular political embodiment, has been often and rightly stressed.[1] When the choral lyric, in the form of the Epinicion, brought athletic events into the sphere of high poetry, it did this in a very remarkable way. We never find the technical details of the contest occupying the foreground: it is sketched often with the very lightest touches as part of a world that is basically of the spirit, that feeds upon the traditional myth, and puts everything into a living connection with the basic problems of human existence. This attitude explains the frequency of gnomae, or maxims of general validity, in the epinicia. But since we are still in the world of archaic art, we shall find the various elements connected not by some readily perceived principle of articulation, but strung together very often by mental associations of one kind or another.

Pindar gives us abundant opportunity to study the particular charm of this kind of composition: the fragments of Simonides' victory odes are not sufficient to give us a clear picture. The small remains do, however, show that he differed greatly from Pindar. In the early period of his poetry he wrote an *Epinicion for Glaucus of Carystus*, who won the boys' boxing contest at Olympia in 520. A fragment of it (23 D.) declares that not even Pollux, the great boxer of mythology, nor the iron-fisted Heracles himself could have stood against Glaucus. If this is to be taken seriously, it betokens a considerable change of religious feeling, since in the old days such praise of a mortal over the sons of gods would have been reckoned blasphemy. But it is after all only a boy who has won, and there is no difficulty in taking the words in a joking sense, particularly since Simonides begins another epinicion in a like spirit. He tells us (22 D.) that the wrestler Crios was 'regularly shorn' when he came to the Nemea. Since the name means 'ram', there is obviously a pun, although it is hard to explain it. The attempt to make it allude to the wrestler's crew cut is best forgotten; many have thought that it referred to the severity of the contest which the victor had to endure; but it is simplest to think of the defeated contestant as the one who was violently shorn.[2] This Crios was an Aeginetan, probably the same mentioned by Herodotus (6, 50. 73): after the first Persian attack had been repulsed, the Spartans deported him to Athens in the course of reprisals against Aegina. Herodotus also has a pun on the man's name. If we are right in supposing him to have been the loser at the Nemea, then the joke about his shearing is appropriate to Simonides' political position on the side of the Athenians. Scanty as the fragments of these epinicia are, they show elements quite irreconcilable with the heavy seriousness of Pindar's victory odes.

---

[1] Cf. now BR. BILINSKI, *L' agonistica sportiva nella Grecia antica. Aspetti sociali e ispirazioni letterarie*. Accademia Polacca. Biblioteca di Roma. Conferenze Fasc. 12. Rome 1960. JULIUS JÜTTNER's posthumous work on Greek sport and gymnastics is to be published by the Austrian Academy of Sciences.　　　　[2] PAGE (*v. sup.*), 140. H. FRÄNKEL 495. 20.

The Alexandrians classified Simonides' epinicia, unlike Pindar's, not according to the place, but to the nature of the contest. We have on a papyrus (1139 P.) some miserably mutilated remains of those on victories in the foot-race. Among the new papyri, *Oxyrh.*[1] 2431 fr. 1 a has the opening of an epinicion, probably by Simonides. It refers to the sons of one Aeatius, members of a noble Thessalian family, who had won a foot-race.

If our surmise is right, Simonides established choral lyric in many other departments of human life. Laments for the dead and consolations in bereavement, such as Archilochus expressed in his elegy to Pericles after a disaster at sea, found a new form in the choral *threnos* of Simonides. The development parallels the one by which themes of Lesbian monody were taken over into the choral lyric of Ibycus.

The *Threnoi* also have survived only in a few small fragments. We know the strange and horrifying circumstance which gave rise to one of them. At a banquet of the Scopads the house collapsed and buried the assembled members of the clan. The poet begins his lament by touching on the uncanny speed with which human fortunes change. The idea is often enough expressed elsewhere, but the image that Simonides uses is unique, and is effective through its very lowness, which at first is repellent: as quickly as a fly buzzes from one spot to another, so quickly are human fortunes reversed.

This catastrophe can be seen as the starting-point of a widely diffused legend. In an epinicion celebrating a boxer's victory Simonides is said to have devoted a great deal of space to the Dioscuri. (We might indeed expect that myth would play a considerable part in the epinicia.) The recipient of the ode thereupon told him to apply for his payment to the gods who had been his main theme. At the banquet two young men called the poet outside, and then disappeared. The house fell and buried all the others. Thus the gods showed their gratitude. The variations in the name of the victor and the place of the event, as they are conscientiously reported by Quintilian (11, 2, 14), show clearly enough the character of the story.

Some verses (7 D.) specifically assigned to the *Threnoi* convey the unhappy truth that not even the sons of gods are granted a life free from care and mutability. The words contain the seed of that tragic conception of Heracles which reaches maturity in Euripides.

The theme of the transitoriness of all that is earthly is often found in Greek lyric, but it is nowhere expressed so uncompromisingly as in the fragment (8 D.) which speaks of the deadly Charybdis as being the one and final end of all in this world: courage and virtue no less than riches come to her at last. Survival in reputation, to which the poet elsewhere attaches great value, is here forgotten. With a gloomy pessimism he speaks in another fragment (59 D.) of posthumous fame as being the last to sink into the grave: that also is transitory, he well knows. And what indeed could be exempt from mortality? Was there not an inscription on a grave, boasting that its statue of bronze would not pass away while nature's forces were still at work (*Anth. Pal.* 7. 153)? The words

---

[1] On these see the appendix to this section.

were even ascribed to Cleobulus of Lindus, one of the Seven Sages. Simonides does not mince words: it is pure folly, he says, to compare the duration of a bronze statue with that of the forces of nature (48 D.).

If we assign to the *Threnoi* of Simonides the remains of thirty lines of choral lyric on a papyrus (1138 P.), to which Bacchylides also lays claim, it must be because the *Threnoi* and *Epinicia* seem to have been the only parts of his work that were later read. If the attribution is right, then the *Threnoi* will appear to have had separate titles, like the dithyrambs of Bacchylides; for we find *Leucippides* written over the opening words of a new poem. But it is all very uncertain.

In celebrating the memory of those fallen at Thermopylae, Simonides strikingly united the threnos with the encomion, or rather the lament into a song of praise (5 D.). Their lot is glorious, their destiny noble, their grave is the altar, instead of wailing they have remembrance, for pity, praise. This sequence of contrasted pairs, in which one component first differentiates and then replaces the other, has been taken by some as showing the beginnings of sophistic thought and style.[1] The point is valid, but it must be remembered that these words – which for all their art are extremely simple – attest a very real respect for the magnitude of the sacrifice. The complaint of the fleetingness of life is here suppressed, with some inconsistency: decay and all-conquering time can have no power over this monument.

The poem beautifully illustrates Simonides' participation, through his poetry, in the great struggle for freedom. In the ancient biography of Aeschylus we read that the great tragedian wrote an elegiac epitaph on the dead of Marathon, but was judged inferior to Simonides since he lacked 'tenderness of sympathy'. The words go to the heart of Simonides' poetry. The attribution to him of two epigrams in an inscription in the Athenian agora (88 AB D.) is very questionable. He devoted a poem to the sea-fight at Artemisium: the few surviving words (1. 2 D.) suggest that it was a choral lyric. At the promontory the north wind had done great damage to the Persian fleet, and it is an attractive suggestion that[2] Simonides' ode on Artemisium was sung at the dedication of a temple which the Athenians erected to Boreas shortly after 479. The day of Salamis also furnished him with a subject for an ode (83 Bergk: 536 Page).

It was his epigrams that won Simonides a particular reputation, and in consequence many were falsely attributed to him. He marks an important stage in the development of the epigram to a perfect work of art in miniature. During the Persian wars there were certainly many great events to be celebrated or lamented. It is a pity that the only epigram which we can confidently attribute to him is the epitaph (83 D.) on his friend Megistias, who fell at Thermopylae. Even that most famous of all Greek epigrams, 'Tell them at Sparta . . .' cannot any longer be considered his.

At the tables of tyrants Simonides had to sing for his supper: he composed drinking-songs. One of them (4 D.) is quoted by Plato and interpreted in a

---

[1] WILAMOWITZ, *Pindaros*. Berl. 1922, 458.

[2] WILAMOWITZ, *Sappho und Simonides*. Berl. 1913, 206.

very Platonic manner.[1] Setting this aside, we must consider what the poet in fact meant in this scolion addressed to Scopas. He starts with the saying of Pittacus of Mytilene, that it is difficult to become a truly perfect man. This is very true, but it does not go far enough: God alone enjoys such well-being; a man may be stripped of his worth by a mischance against which there is no help or resource (ἀμήχανος). So we ought to set a more modest target, and praise a man who does not evil of his own free will. Everything which has no admixture of ugliness is beautiful. In his interpretation of the poem Hermann Fränkel has shown that the old connection between outward success (v. 10 πράξας εὖ) and inward qualities is here given up, and with a humane toleration a goal is proposed that is accessible to honest endeavour. This scolion is partly parallelled by the poem of which 21 mostly legible verses are now known from Ox. Pap. nr. 2432.[2] Here also we find the same moderation and mild scepticism towards the moral capacities of mankind. Another noteworthy feature of the poem is that we find here for the first time a notion that was later very important in Greek ethical doctrines: the βίος φιλοχρήματος, the φιλήδονος, and the φιλότιμος appear as forces inimical to practical morality.

We have seen Simonides as the master of various forms of poetry. We must, however, confess that a considerable part of his work is quite beyond our knowledge. Towards the end of his activity in Athens, he boasts in an epigram (79 D.) intended for a votive tablet, that he had gained sixty-five victories with male choruses. In other words, he had composed dithyrambs to compete in the Dionysia. The discoveries of Bacchylides' poems have given us some notion what these narrative choral lyrics were like. A passage of Aristophanes (Vesp. 1410) lets us infer that in this field he would have come into conflict with Lasus, the reformer of the dithyramb. But only some unexpected discovery could take our knowledge further. We are rather perplexed by the statement in Suidas that Simonides also wrote tragedies. He was an older contemporary of Aeschylus, so how can the possibility be excluded? But since the dithyramb often contained elements of dialogue, as those of Bacchylides show, the statement is more likely to refer to his dithyrambic poetry. We shall find a similar tradition concerning Pindar.

Simonides gives clear expression to certain sides of the Ionian character, and looks forward in many ways to the sophistic movement, which in the next generation revolutionized the spiritual life of Athens. The prominence of the human element in his choral poetry is one of these features. In the scolion for Scopas and the protest against Cleobulus we detect a penchant towards a critical approach which sets up the results of individual reasoning against traditional ideas. Cicero's anecdote of him (De nat. deor. I. 60) is characteristic: questioned by Hiero about the nature of the gods, he asked for longer and longer periods to consider his answer; at last he said that the question became the more obscure the more he thought about it. The closest parallel is in the

---

[1] H. GUNDERT, 'Die Simonides-Interpretation in Platons Protagoras'. Festschr. O. Regenbogen. Heidelb. 1952, 71.

[2] See M. TREU, 'Neues zu Simonides (P. Ox. 2432)'. Rhein. Mus. 103, 1960, 319.

words of Protagoras (VS 80 B4), that the difficulty of the subject and the shortness of human life prevents us from knowing anything about the gods. In his scheme of values, so far as we know it, he expressed a realistic sense of the immediate actuality of life. There are a few details to fill in. His powers of memory were renowned, and he is said to have devised a system of training the memory[1] – a faculty on which Hippias of Elis so prided himself. What truth there may be in the report that he interested himself in various matters of orthography, we do not know: even this, however, is consonant with a reforming spirit. His abilities in practical life also rank him with several of the great sophists

These traits in Simonides cannot be overlooked, but it would be wrong to assess him mainly on the rational element in his creative work. He was an artist who knew how to create out of the power of genuine feeling, and to move his hearers by so doing. The most impressive example of his art is the 'Danae fragment' (13 D.). We do not know its context, but it can stand by itself as a great piece of poetry. Locked up in the wooden chest, mother and child are tossed on the stormy sea. Danae pours out the sorrows of her heart. Her wild grief finds its echo in the roaring of the waves, and the sweet slumbers of the innocent child[2] are in striking contrast to the uproar all around. She prays that Zeus, the first cause of all her sorrows, will change her fortunes, and ends by asking forgiveness if there is any impropriety in her request. The myth here is merely an occasion for depicting human emotion with the utmost force and pathos.

The simple language of this passage, its clear word-order and the consistently meaningful choice of epithets helps us to understand the judgment of Dionysius of Halicarnassus (de imit. 2, 2, 6) – that Simonides excelled even Pindar in the expression of sorrow through his use not of grandiose words, but of words going right to the heart.

Another indication of Simonides' lively critical faculties is that he reflected on the whole basis of his creative work, and came to a conclusion that expresses one of the main characteristics of his own poetry: painting is silent poetry; poetry is spoken painting (Plut. de glor. Ath. 3). The dictum has had its effects in modern times, and the element of misconception in it has found its critics. But to Simonides this statement of the relation between poetry and painting expressed something essential. It is well illustrated by the Danae fragment, and we greatly regret that another celebrated example of his graphic presentation has perished: namely the scene in which Achilles appears before the Greeks when they have already decided to return home – a passage which is singled out for praise on this score by the author of the treatise Περὶ ὕψους.

Pindar is the second of Boeotia's great poets. As a literary artist he represents a different tradition from Hesiod's, and he comes from a very different social level. Nevertheless, in those passages where his native qualities come out most strongly, we can see his affinity with the author of the Theogony. Both have the

---

[1] On memory-training in antiquity see W. SCHMID, Lit. Gesch. I, 521, 12.

[2] The text of v. 11 is uncertain and cannot support the notion that the child shines in the dark by his own light: see now D. L. PAGE, Poetae Melici Graeci. Oxf. 1962, nr. 543.

same religious attitude towards all phenomena, the same uncompromising severity in their assertions.

He was born at Cynoscephalae, a settlement belonging to Thebes, during the Pythian festival, as the great venerator of the Delphic god tells us himself (fr. 193). The festival must have been that of 522 or of 518, since his floruit, i.e. his fortieth year, was reckoned in antiquity as coinciding with Xerxes' attack on Greece.

We possess four manuscript *Lives*, in addition to the article in Suidas. These are all either late antique or Byzantine, but they continue a teaching tradition that goes back to the earliest attested biographies of Pindar, compiled by the Peripatetic Chamaeleon and by Callimachus's pupil Ister. As so often, we find here a little that is useful wrapped up in a mass of fable, including such a pretty anecdote as that of the bees which prophetically deposited their honey on the lips of the slumbering child.

The difficulties of interpreting Pindar are exemplified in the question of his birthplace. In *Pyth.* 5, 76 he speaks of the Aegeids, a clan associated in mythology with Thebes and with Sparta and Therae: 'my fathers', he calls them. This raises the problem of the use of the first person in choral lyric: sometimes in Pindar it means the poet, sometimes the chorus, sometimes the generalized 'one'. In this passage the most distinguished exponents of Pindar have embraced directly opposed views.[1] To take it as meaning the chorus seems the most likely, but it is quite conceivable that Pindar as a Theban might have named the Aegeids as his ancestors. The passage certainly cannot be taken as proving his aristocratic connections, and the various names given for Pindar's father in the ancient biographies make the whole question very obscure.[2]

We can certainly believe that he came of a good family, and if he was sent to Athens as a boy, in addition to education in the arts he would have made contact with the old Attic nobility. Their position had been threatened for some time by the rise of new classes, but power was still largely in their hands, and aristocratic values were still in possession of the field. Even in the classical period these values remained largely current: indeed they never wholly faded from Greek consciousness. A stay in Athens in his youth would explain Pindar's close connection with the Alcmeonids, a family whose political activities were important rather than uniformly beneficial in Athenian history. The only epinicion which Pindar wrote for an Athenian (*Pyth.* 7 in 486) was for the Alcmeonid Megacles, who had been ostracized a little before. According to a scholium on v. 18 he composed a threnos for Megacles' father Hippocrates, a brother of Cleisthenes. Four years after Marathon the poet praised Athens, not for the defeat of the Persians, but for the magnificence with which the temple of Apollo at Delphi, burnt down in 548, had been rebuilt by the Alcmeonids.

---

[1] Bibliography in SCHWENN, *RE* 20, 1950, 1614, 24.

[2] The new papyrus *Ox. Pap.* 26, 1961, nr. 2438 with the remains of a life of Pindar tells us that a lively controversy raged about the name of his father: Corinna (an important witness) says it was Scopelinus, while κατὰ τοὺς πλείστους ποιητάς it was Daiphantus. In another tradition it occurs as Pagondas or Pagonidas.

The biographies speak of Apollodorus and Agathocles as instructors of the young Pindar. Only the second of these names has much meaning for us, since Agathocles also trained the musical theorist Damon. A more important fact is that the men's choruses in Athens had a new and vigorous development after 508 as an officially recognized part of the Great Dionysia. It was thanks to the reformation of the dithyramb by Lasus of Hermione that it was able to maintain its place beside the rapidly maturing tragedy. Now since we can hardly suppose that Lasus was in Athens after the fall of the Pisistratids, the tradition that he was Pindar's teacher cannot be true in an immediate sense. The same holds good of Simonides, who despite the deep differences between the two men cannot have been without influence on the young Pindar.

Pindar's poetry brought him into contact with many of the political and cultural centres of his day, and in the course of his work he travelled widely. But unlike so many wandering poets of the archaic period, he remained always true to his native land. In his *Paean for Ceos* (32) he speaks of the value to a man of his homeland and kinsfolk, and the words apply to his own life also.

The earliest of the surviving epinicia, *Pyth.* 10, shows Pindar associated with Thessaly, whose noble families had enjoyed the services of many of the older poets. In the Pythia of 498 the double foot-race for boys was won by Hippocleas of Pelinna, and Thorax, the oldest of the great family of the Aleuads, commissioned Pindar to write an ode in celebration. The young poet, who was a guest-friend of Thorax and probably came in person to the performance, might have built great hopes for the future on this commission. We know nothing, however, of any continuance of their relations. In general Pindar does not seem to have had any sudden success. It was not until he went to Sicily that he made his name.

In his early period Pindar seems to have written mostly songs for religious usage, and since these have perished except for a frew fagments, we know very little about his work at that time. Some papyri, however, (nr. 1069-1071 P.) have acquainted us with bits of his *Paeans*, in particular of the one which he had performed at the Theoxenia in Delphi (probably in 490), no other chorus being at his disposal. It is only a surmise that the singers were Aeginetans, but certainly Pindar here sings the praises of that island, which meant so much to him all through his life. Aegina, which like Boeotia had a mixed Dorian and Aeolic population, was at this time a dangerous rival to Athens and politically connected with Thebes. Power lay in the hands of an aristocratic upper-crust made up of wealthy and sport-loving families. This was the true world of the Pindaric epinicia. In this paean, despite all his flattery of the Aeginetans, Pindar wounded their feelings. Of Neoptolemus, a descendant of their national hero Aeacus, he related how for his cruel killing of the aged Priam he was punished by Apollo, who made him die a miserable death at Delphi. A few years later, in the *Seventh Nemean*, celebrating the victory of Sogenes of Aegina in the boys' pentathlon, Pindar included a retraction, and dwelt at length on the honour enjoyed by Neoptolemus in the Delphic sanctuary. But his relations with Aegina, which became so close later, seem not to be much in evidence before the Persian wars. There is, however, another connection, later to be very important, which is attested in 490: Xenocrates, brother of the tyrant Theron of Acragas, had won a chariot-race at Delphi, and the *Sixth Pythian* celebrates his son Thrasybulus, who had come from Sicily to compete. At this time Pindar had won some recognition as a poet, but he could not afford to be too particular, and so in the *Twelfth Pythian*, the only ode on a victory in music, he celebrated the flute-player Midas of Acragas, who had probably come with Thrasybulus to Delphi.

Pindar and his city played a rather special part in the time of mortal danger when Xerxes attacked Greece.[1] The Thebans had 'Medized', and were threatened with annihilation by the victorious Greeks. The danger was averted by delivering up the most prominent pro-Persians: a god graciously moved aside the stone of Tantalus which had been poised above the city. This image is used by Pindar in the *Eighth Isthmian*: it is relevant that the ode celebrated the victory of an Aeginetan in the pancration. We can hardly doubt Pindar's connections with the pro-Persian nobility in Thebes. Even at the very height of his fame he repeatedly wrote in praise of members of the families who had been associated with the Persians (*Isthm*. I. 3. 4).[2] But in the years following the Greek victory his political mistakes were a heavy burden on him, and from Aegina's special position we can understand why it was there that Pindar looked for support and encouragement. He found it particularly in Lampon, whose son he had celebrated in the *Sixth Isthmian*, shortly before the great war.

It was his success in Sicily that determined Pindar's pan-Hellenic reputation. There in the west, after the successful repulse of the Carthaginian threat, the Greek world had developed under the leadership of capable tyrants into a political structure far beyond the small dimensions of the old city-states. The first place was taken by Hiero, who in 478, as regent of the twin state of Gela-Syracuse, had stepped into the inheritance of Gelo. In Acragas was his kinsman Theron, with whom his political relations were not always friendly. We have heard of the reception of Simonides: Pindar formed a close association with both courts. Despite the absence of immediate testimony, we can fairly certainly infer that he arrived in Sicily between 476 and 474, and lived a long time at the courts of Hiero and Theron. The multitude of new impressions that he received from the power and brilliance of this west Greek world is reflected in verses like those of the *First Olympian* celebrating Hiero's victory in 476. This was a victory in the horse-race: the more coveted victory in the chariot-race had fallen to Theron. For him also Pindar wrote an epinicion which was sung in Acragas at a great religious feast (*Ol*. 3). The same victory is alluded to in the *Second Olympian* in a very different, intimate and personal tone. The ode is not so much concerned with the event itself as it is to console Theron in sickness and cares. Apparently Theron was a follower of Orphic and Pythagorean doctrines, which provide Pindar with themes of consolation. We can easily understand that the mystical teachings concerning the destiny of the soul made

---

[1] JOHN H. FINLEY JR., 'Pindar and the Persian Invasion'. *Harv. Stud*. 63, 1958, 121.

[2] WILAMOWITZ (*v. inf.*), 331. 337.

a great impression on the poet: his strong Delphic background makes it unlikely that he was himself an initiate.

The two Ceans, Simonides and Bacchylides, must have crossed Pindar's path in Sicily. Many passages have been taken as polemic against them: thus the ancients interpreted the attack in *Ol.* 2. 86 upon the 'journeymen' who are like ravens croaking at an eagle. Other examples are the warning against flatterers and calumniators (*Pyth.* 2. 74) and the attack on those who serve the muses with an eye to profit (*Isth.* 2. 6). The view may be true of individual passages, but it is impossible to be sure of them all. Simonides and Bacchylides were certainly not the only ones who courted the Sicilian despots.

At the time of his return from Sicily Pindar could claim the first place among the choral lyrists of his day, and he had no doubt profited as much in pocket as in reputation from his stay in the west. Thence came the resource which enabled him to build near his house that temple of Rhea and Pan which was still there in Pausanias' time (9, 25, 3). We still possess remains of a song for a chorus of girls in honour of Pan, who was associated with the Great Mother as a companion and doorkeeper (fr. 95 ff.).

There followed a particularly creative period, in which the poet's services were sought from all quarters of Greece. His connection with the Sicilian courts was kept up for some time. The two odes already mentioned (*Pyth.* 2 and *Isthm.* 2) show the poet's fear that enemies were at work against him in Sicily and in fact he was not able to celebrate either Hiero's second victory in the horse-race in 472 or the coveted victory in the Olympic chariot-race in 468. The latter commission was given to Bacchylides. The ode on the victory in the Pythian chariot-race of 470 was Pindar's last poem for Hiero (*Pyth.* 1.) The tyrant had had himself proclaimed at Delphi as the founder of Aetna, and thus had shown how much importance he attached to the new settlement under the rule of his son Dinomenes. Aeschylus wrote a play to celebrate the founding, and Pindar's ode is full of prayers for its success.

Now at the height of his career, Pindar could not close his eyes to the greatness of Athens in her confident development following the victory over the Persians. In the late 460's he published the dithyramb whose opening is so well known (fr. 76): 'Shining, violet-garlanded, song-renowned, glorious Athens, bulwark of Hellas, city of the gods!' Another passage (fr. 77) declares that the Athenians have laid the foundations of freedom. Ancient tradition relates that the Thebans fined the poet a thousand drachmae for thus praising the enemy city, while the Athenians made him a *proxenos* and gave him a large honorarium. There may be an element of truth in this, but the statue of Pindar in the Athenian agora (Pseudo-Aeschines *ep.* 4; Paus. 1, 8, 4) was not brought into the story until later.

Pindar was now constantly making new friends. Among the victorious athletes who wanted to secure a monument of their achievement in his poetry were Rhodians (*Ol.* 7) and Corinthians. The Xenophon who won the foot-race and pentathlon in 464, a member of a rich and distinguished Corinthian family was not content with an epinicion (*Ol.* 13), and wanted a poem to glorify his ostentatious gift to Aphrodite. The temple of the goddess in Corinth was associated with ritual prostitution – itself a very unusual feature in Greek life – and for this purpose Xenophon gave fifty female slaves. Pindar can never have had a more singular assignment. He discharged it in a poem which is entitled Σκόλιον in the manuscripts, writing with an elegant superiority and delicate humour.

Hiero died in 466, and with his death the hour had struck for the Sicilian tyrants. Pindar, however, soon found the way open to another prince's court. In 474 he had celebrated the victory in the chariot-race of Telesicrates of Cyrene, the most flourishing Greek city in Libya; twelve years later king Arcesilaus IV won with his chariot at Delphi, and the event called forth two poems from Pindar. One (*Pyth.* 5) was intended for performance in Cyrene at the feast of the Dorian Apollo Carneius in celebration of the victory; the other (*Pyth.* 4), the longest of all extant choral lyrics, was sung at a feast in the palace. The victory is hardly mentioned, but the story how Battus came to found the city from Therae leads Pindar to relate at great length the tale of the Argonauts in the manner of choral lyric. At the end of this long ode Pindar sides with the exiled conspirator Damophilus and makes a plea for wise moderation. Such interference is seldom welcome: when Arcesilaus won the chariot-race at Olympia two years later, Pindar received no commission.

In all these vicissitudes friendship with Aegina remained a sure and permanent possession. Again and again Pindar had Aeginetan victors to celebrate, and the last word that we have from him (*Pyth.* 8 in 446) refers to the beloved island. In the concluding section of the ode we find one of those gloomy reflections which often darken the sunlight of Greek thought: 'What is man? The dream of a shadow; no more. But God can send his light upon all the weaknesses of our life, and the heavenly ones can keep the city on the path of freedom.' Freedom Aegina had partly lost already, when in 456 she was forced into the Athenian maritime alliance. The final catastrophe, the expulsion of the Aeginetans in 431, was one which death saved Pindar from experiencing.

Pindar's crown of glory was not without its thorns. The envious grudged him his Sicilian successes: he was traduced as a friend of tyrants, a neglector of his homeland. The rather violent manner in which in the *Ninth Pythian* – dedicated to a Cyrenean, but sung in Thebes – he drags in an account of his poetical activities on his country's behalf shows how seriously he took reproaches of this sort. But in the last years of his life he must have suffered much more deeply from the political developments. As the days of common danger receded into the past, so the rivalry of Sparta and Athens ate deeper into the vitals of Greece. The battle at Oenophyta (457) confirmed for a decade the oppressive Athenian dominion over Boeotia. Only two epinicia are known from this period. The recovery of Boeotian freedom at Coronea (447) came within Pindar's lifetime. Ancient tradition says that he died in Argos, and it is a happy invention which makes this priest-like poet of beauty breathe his last on the knees of a boy whom he loved.

In the classical period such a poet as Pindar was fated very soon to be considered old-fashioned. He shared this fate with Alcman, Stesichorus and Simonides, as we see from a passage of Eupolis (*Ath.* 1, 2d and 14, 638d). We can just as easily understand, however, that the Alexandrians took a great interest in the difficult and allusive poet who yet had a deep sense of his creative mission. Here again it was Aristophanes of Byzantium who made the definitive contribution; he divided the lyrical text into cola and edited all that then survived in seventeen books. The *Vita Ambrosiana* gives us the best synopsis of what the Alexandrians had before them. Eleven books were composed of songs connected with worship: first and foremost the *Hymns to the Gods*, next the *Paeans*, both of these in one book each; then *Dithyrambs*, *Processional Hymns* (*Prosodia*), *Songs for a Chorus of Maidens* (*Partheneia*) and *Songs for Dancing* (*Hyporchemata*), each of these groups composing two books, except the *Partheneia*, which had another book of separate songs for girls added to it: there are obvious difficulties in the subdivision here. The provinces newly won for choral lyric by Simonides are represented by four books of *Epinicia* and one each of *Threnoi* and *Encomia*.

A glance at this list shows us how miserably little has survived. We have reason to believe that the same factors which caused tragedy to be represented now only by a small selection were at work in Pindar's case also. The age of the Antonines, with its strong concentration on the requirements of the schools, was content with an edition of Pindar which comprised only the *Epinicia*. When Eustathius of Thessalonica was preparing a commentary on Pindar in the twelfth century – the introduction still survives – he justified this limited selection on the ground that the victory-odes were the most intelligible part of Pindar's output.

To some extent our knowledge of Pindar has been helped by the papyrus discoveries,[1] and the larger fragments have given us some impression of his other work. Often, of course, we have to content ourselves with titles and citations in later writers. For one of the hymns these are enough to give us some inkling how much we have lost. In the *Hymn to Zeus* written for Thebes[2] a song sung by Apollo (or by the Muses to his lyre) is related, which is said to have been performed at Cadmus' wedding and to have related the creation of the world and the ordering of it by Zeus. When the work was finished (so the song related) Zeus asked the gods if anything was lacking to this beautiful world. They replied: a divine nature to sing its praises. Thus Pindar elaborately displays

---

[1] Nr. 1063-1081 P.: cf. IRIGOIN's chapter (*v. inf.*) and the index in SNELL. The new volume *Ox. Pap.* 26, 1961 consists wholly of fragments of Pindar, partly from unknown works, partly assigned conjecturally, and some fragments of commentaries (esp. on the *Isthmians* nr. 2451) and bits of a new life of Pindar. We mentioned its polemical nature in connection with the name of the poet's father: in another part the statement that he died at the age of fifty when Habron was archon (458/7) is rejected on chronological grounds. Fragments from the poems are almost all very small in this volume, but LOBEL has done wonders with them. Nr. 2441 deserves a mention – a larger fragment, possibly from a prosodion; so do nr. 2450 fr. 1 (from a dithyramb?) describing the feats of Heracles, and nr. 2442 fr. 7, the best of all, with some verses about the birth of Heracles.

[2] B. SNELL, *Die Entdeckung des Geistes*. 3rd ed. Hamb. 1955, 118 (Eng. ed. p. 79).

in mythical form the poet's place in the world, as he saw it and maintained it.

It is of the *Paeans* mostly that our knowledge has been advanced by the papyri. We have already mentioned the one with which Pindar stepped into the breach at Delphi in 490. The *Paean for the Abderites*, a very difficult poem, implores divine assistance for the Ionian colonists, who were in constant conflict with the Thracian population. Another paean reflects the terror felt in Thebes at the solar eclipse of the 30th April 463. With a disregard of Ionian science Pindar, the lover of light, prays to the rays of the sun, which he calls 'mother of the eyes'. Even Ceos, the home of his rivals Simonides and Bacchylides, had a paean written for it by Pindar, in which he praised the island for its fame in the arts. Two of the dithyrambs were composed for the Athenians. One contained the passage already mentioned in praise of the city. These poems had their own titles: thus one composed for Thebes was entitled *Descent of Heracles into the Underworld* or *Cerberus*. In the surviving verses Pindar turns against the long-windedness of the old dithyramb, almost certainly under the influence of Lasus. Suidas mentions δράματα τραγικά in his list of Pindar's works: he means of course the dithyrambs.

The remains of the *Prosodia* are very scanty, but those of the *Partheneia* are much better. Among these were included the *Daphnephorica*, sung at Thebes when a staff wreathed in laurel, flowers and ribbons (the κωπώ) was carried in procession to Apollo Ismenius. We have appreciable remains of one of these poems (fr. 94 b.), and we know of another, which Pindar composed when his son Daiphantus had the honour to be chosen as a daphnephorus. We can find out very little with certainty about the *Hyporchemata*: we do not even know what they were. Ancient interpretations are confused, and they show how much we depend on the classifications and definitions of the old grammarians. There is much uncertainty, so that many things are cited as from scolia, which Aristophanes apparently put under the *Encomia*. At all events, poems of the last-named variety were performed at banquets in praise of individuals.[1] Some historical interest attaches to an encomium on the phil-Hellene Alexander, king of Macedon, and a special personal interest to a poem on the beautiful boy Theoxenos of Tenedos. Pederasty is here spiritualized: the beams that dart from the eyes of Theoxenos kindle a flame in the poet's heart. Some remains of the *threnoi* remind us of the second Olympian (addressed to Theron) with its Pythagorean elements of thought: here consolation is sought in the assurance of a happy life hereafter. The Orphic and Pythagorean themes of metempsychosis and judgment after death (fr. 129 f. 133) rub shoulders with the beatification of those dedicated at Eleusis (fr. 137). One fragment (131 b) shows a remarkable juxtaposition of the Homeric notion of the likeness concealed within the body and the belief in an immortal soul proceeding from the gods. We do not know its context, but the verses show that in these realms of religious thought Pindar was no more than an occasional visitor.

Among the surviving fragments scarcely any has so singular an atmosphere

---

[1] B. A. VAN GRONINGEN, *Pindare au banquet. Les fragments des scolies*. Leyden 1960 (fr. 122-128 SNELL with commentary).

as the *Cerberus-dithyramb* (fr. 70 b) with its depiction of the wild ecstasy which at the feasts of Dionysus seized even upon the gods. But passages of such individual colouring are the exception. In general the style (taking the word in its widest sense) of the fragments is very similar to that of the *Epinicia*, so that we can feel confident that the latter enable us to grasp all the essentials of Pindar's personality as a poet.

The Alexandrians arranged the four books of the *Epinicia* according to the festivals: one book each for the great Olympic and Delphic games which recurred every four years and for the smaller Nemean and Isthmian games which were held biennially.[1] The supposition that the Nemeans once brought up the rear of the collection, explains the appearance of alien elements in the third book. The *Ninth Nemean* celebrates a victory of Chromius of Aetna at Sicyon, the *Tenth* a victory of one Theaeus at the games of Hera in Argos, while the *Eleventh* is not even an epinicion, but was written for Aristagoras of Tenedos to celebrate his appointment as prytanis. Apparently in the change from roll to codex the last two books changed places: the *Isthmians* came at the end and in this exposed position suffered damage at the closing sections. The *Olympians* include one spurious piece—the *Fifth*, in which a contemporary of Pindar's, probably a Sicilian poet, sings the praises of Psaumis of Camarina, whose victory in the chariot-race is celebrated in *Ol.* 4.

A passage such as *Nem.* 4. 13 shows that after the celebration the *Epinicia* might sometimes be performed by a single singer to the lyre. It is not impossible that some of them were intended from the beginning for solo performance,[2] but it seems unlikely. These songs of victory were sung by a chorus to the accompaniment of flute and lyre, only occasionally on the scene of the success, generally at the celebration held in the victor's city.

There are certain elements which appear in almost every epinicion. The purpose of the song demanded some statements about the victor, his family, his sporting achievements at other festivals. We are seldom told anything about the course of the contest itself. The Pindar of the 'Wanderers Sturmlied', revelling in the rumble of chariot-wheels and the crack of whips, had no existence outside the mind of the young Goethe.

Another element, varying greatly in extent, but usually taking up a good deal of space, is mythical narrative. The poet and his employer might very well take different views of the relative importance of these two parts, as we see in the story that Simonides' fees were reduced because he had given too much space to the Dioscuri. Several different considerations may govern the introduction of myth. It may have a relevance to the place of the victory – this was particularly common in the odes written for west Greeks, who had not many family myths of their own. It may be prompted by the victor's own circumstances. It

---

[1] Dating of the individual epinicia: SCHWENN, *RE* 20, 1950, 1613. On the difficult question how far Pindar's development can be seen in the form and content of his poems: F. SCHWENN, *Der junge Pindar*. Berl. 1940. W. THEILER, *Die zwei Zeitstufen in Pindars Stil und Vers*. Halle 1941. SCHADEWALDT (*v. inf.*), 337.

[2] Thus WILAMOWITZ (*v. inf.*), 233. 240. 254.

may contain an inner meaning which serves as a great example to the victor himself. Choral lyric narrative is essentially different from epic narrative. Such an elaborate passage as the story of the Argonauts in the *Fourth Pythian* gives us an especially good opportunity to see its characteristic features. The point of departure is not the beginning of the story, but some later stage in it, from which the poet ranges, or rather jumps, backwards and forwards. The object is not to tell a straightforward story, but to elaborate within the framework of the poem something in the tale which seems important and presents itself to the mind as a separate picture. One cannot forget Pelops standing at night on the seashore and calling the god from the sea (*Ol.* 1), the bold huntress Cyrene, who wins Apollo's heart, so that he goes and takes counsel with the wise Centaur before his cave (*Pyth.* 9) or the young Jason coming down from the mountains and standing in the market-place of Iolcus like a radiant god among the astonished townsfolk (*Pyth.* 4). The poet is fond of framing his scenes and sections by the archaic device of ring-composition.[1] There are a good many speeches, giving some element of drama. The narratives end as suddenly as they begin, with some brief formal phrase. But with all its changes in tempo and texture, Pindar's narrative is by no means formless;[2] rather it has to be understood in reference to some definite value which the poet is particularly concerned to illustrate.

A third constituent element is that of proverbial wisdom. All the separate poems are shot through with it, and gnomae recur constantly. Usually the poet gives the impression that he is conveying the fruit of his own reflections. Consequently the gnomic elements are closely connected with another constituent, which can therefore only be separated out if we bear this in mind: namely expressions of Pindar's own views, usually on the value and purpose of the poet's calling, but sometimes rising in hymn-like strains to the expression of his religious convictions.

The *Partheneion* of Alcman allows us to see that the individual elements which we have here enumerated were already found in the earliest choral lyric; and when we see how Alcman follows the myth of the sons of Hippocoon with the gnome about the avenging power of the gods, passing immediately to, 'But I sing of the light of Agido . . .', we can conclude that these sudden transitions were all part of the style. Pindar himself occasionally speaks of his rapid changes of subject as if they were a stylistic feature demanded by the rules of his art. It is striking that his testimony (*Pyth.* 10. 54; 11. 41) is supported by that of Bacchylides (10. 51) and probably of Stesichorus (fr. 25). In the very nature of the epinicia it was inevitable that the question of their unity should in recent times have become once more a central problem in the interpretation of Pindar. August Boeckh, whose great edition of 1821 laid the foundations of Pindaric research, was the first to look for dominating themes in this poetry whose manner of composition is so hard to grasp. The method was brought into disrepute by the speculations of L. Dissen and others, and the house had to be put

---

[1] W. A. A. VAN OTTERLO, 'Untersuchungen über Begriff, Anwendung und Entstehung der griech. Ringkomposition'. *Meded. Nederl. Akad. afdeeling letterkunde* 7/3. Amsterdam 1944.   [2] L. ILLIG, *Zur Form der pindarischen Erzählung*. Berl. 1932.

in order by A. B. Drachmann.[1] Then for a long time the most fashionable type of interpretation was that which aimed at discovering the associative connections which seemed predominant between the different parts. Wilamowitz' *Pindaros* paved the way for change, and Schadewaldt has recently brought the question of unity back into the foreground.

The problem is as follows: Pindar's *Epinicia* give the impression of a sometimes kaleidoscopic mixture of diverse elements, tied together by loose and even wilful transitions. Yet anyone who has any feeling for poetry cannot escape the feeling that in the last resort all this multiplicity is subsumed under a great unity. Now where does this unity reside? The decisive answer has been given by Hermann Fränkel:[2] the epinicion elevates the significant event of victory into the realm of values, the world from which the poet's creation flows. This world of values is displayed and exemplified in its various spheres: in the divine itself, in the tales of the heroes, in the rules of conduct and not least in the poet's own creative activity as an artistic realm in its own right. Once this is understood, we shall not find it difficult to find a unity in Pindar's poetry which is comparable (although distantly so) with the unity of classical works of art. Observations like those of Dornseiff in particular on the peculiarities of his composition – sometimes gliding smoothly, sometimes desultory and abrupt – are entirely justified. On the other hand, the lines of thought emanating from the individual elements are all within a realm provided by the personality of the poet and his way of seeing the world. Thus the unity of these poems lies not in their internal structure, but in the consistent relevance of their constituent parts to that firm world of aristocratic values which Pindar felt to be immovable.

We can only mention the most important of his convictions. A central feature of the aristocratic view of humanity was the firm belief that innate and inherited qualities ($φυά$)[3] were decisive. 'It is a vain struggle, if one seeks to hide one's inborn character' (*Ol.* 13. 13). Pindar speaks throughout in the spirit of the aristocracy when he looks down on those who have acquired skill compared with those who have inherited it. The Olympic victor needs a trainer, certainly, but the trainer's job is only to 'sharpen' the inborn abilities (*Ol.* 10. 20). One who only possesses acquired ability is always a man in darkness, who never walks with a sure foot (*Nem.* 3. 41).

The direct light of this world of ideas falls first on the myths of the heroes. The characters they depict, with their deeds of supreme bravery, are all illustrations of that noble quality that shows itself also in the hard-won successes achieved in the great games. Very frequently these two realms touch one another, since the heroes were the putative ancestors of the noble houses from which the athletic victors sprang.

---

[1] *Moderne Pindarfortolkning.* Copenhagen 1891.

[2] *Gnom.* 6, 1930, 10, now in *Wege und Formen frühgriechischen Denkens.* 2nd ed. Munich 1960, 366. See also the splendid chapter 'Die "Mächte" bei Pindar' in *Dichtung und Philos. des frühen Griechentums.* 2nd ed. 549.

[3] W. HAEDICKE, *Die Gedanken der Griechen über Familienherkunft u. Vererbung.* Diss. Halle 1936.

Next to the athlete's achievement, and of equal merit, was the poet's. Through it the victory achieved permanence, since the words of the poet elevated his victory into the realm of the noble and valuable. Just as in Homer, the worth of a man is first authenticated by the recognition that it finds in the bestowal of honours and in words of praise. Pindar is conscious of his important office, and speaks of it often and emphatically. 'Noble deeds must perish if none speak of them' (fr. 121). Goethe expressed the same view when in *The Natural Daughter* he puts into Eugenie's mouth the words, 'Das Wesen, wär' es, wenn es nicht erschiene?'

Both these things, however, the victories that come from innate ability and the gift of poetry that defies time, depend on the basic condition of all successful achievement – the blessing bestowed by the gods. In other words, Pindar's outlook on the world is essentially religious. 'From the gods come all possibilities of mortal achievement; by them men become wise and strong of arm and mighty in speech' (*Pyth.* 1. 41). Zeus is lord and giver of all. Next place to him in the poet's heart is held by the Delphian god, the protector of aristocratic qualities. Pindar's pantheon is not so colourful as Homer's. His gods are less individual: he sees them rather as powers that penetrate the whole universe. Hence we find a great part played by such figures as Tyche, Hesychia, Hora, which represent a crystallization of the divine into particular powers or around particular aspects of human life. It would be wrong to speak of personification. The most impressive expression of this *Weltanschauung* is the proemium of the *Fifth Isthmian*. In Hesiod's *Theogony* Theia is the mother of Helios, Selene and Eos: in Pindar she has become the primal source of the world of beauty and splendour, the ultimate, divine basis whence all that shines and gives light derives its magical power, whether it be gold or victory in holy places.

There is another respect in which Pindar's view of the gods differs yet more profoundly from Homer's. The poet himself declares (*Ol.* 1. 35) that it becomes a singer to speak good of the gods. This involves abandonment of several features of Homer's mythology, and we see how in practice Pindar purified the traditional tales. His suppressing the story of the dismemberment of Pelops and his replacing it by the theme – blameless by contemporary standards – of Poseidon's carrying the boy off provides the best-known example.[1] This procedure is very different from the passionate protest of a Xenophanes or the struggles of Aeschylus to justify the ways of Zeus, but ultimately it is rooted in the same dissatisfaction with the religion of the epics. The poet's attitude to this world of the divine contains an antinomy which is surprising and yet typically Greek. It finds striking expression in the opening of the *Sixth Nemean*: the poet is well aware of the impotence of men, which must ever set them apart from the power and certainty of the gods. But he knows the other side of the medal: in spite of everything, power of mind and greatness of soul can make man comparable to the gods. They are two eternally distinct races, yet both are children of the same mother. The *Eighth Pythian* also speaks of the two sides of human life. We find there the gloomy dictum that man is only the dream of a shadow;

---

[1] Other examples in DORNSEIFF, *Pindars Stil*, 126.

but at once comes the comforting reflection that if light from the gods shines on this troubled existence, it can rise to success and glory. To embody this light in poetry and to impart it thus to men – this for Pindar is the duty and purpose of the poet.

Pindar's language falls essentially within the framework of the literary dialect of choral lyric: that is, it adopts the epic inheritance, displays a Doric colouring (stronger in Pindar than in the two Cean poets of Ionian extraction), and includes Aeolic elements. Our evaluation of the latter depends on the degree of faith that we have in the transmission. The style enjoined by the genre was less binding on Pindar than on an epic poet. He did not let tradition prevent him from the effective deployment of his individual manner of expression. His massive sentence-structure, in which the heavy load of ornament scarcely lets the framework be seen, his renunciation of the antitheses and particles beloved of Greek authors in favour of a wilful violence in stringing together and interlacing his clauses, the weight which he places on the noun, so that the verb in contrast is little more than a colourless prop to the sentence, his wealth of images, aimed at the nature of the thing, not at its sensible properties, and mingling one with another with a head-strong recklessness – all these qualities went into Pindar's creation of that ornate style which has characterized the ode right down into modern times.[1]

Despite all his generic propriety, Pindar is essentially the great individualist. We must therefore kill a cock to Tyche for the great papyrus discovery which acquainted us with a choral lyrist who was Pindar's rival, although he never arrived at Pindar's greatness. In 1896 the British Museum acquired the remains of two papyrus rolls containing poems of Bacchylides (nr. 109 P.), which had been found in a grave. A few small fragments were later added (nr. 110-112), and now Ox. Pap. 23, 1956, nr. 2361-68 have given a little more.

Bacchylides, who had before been only a name, came like his uncle Simonides from Ceos. Eusebius puts his floruit in 467, which fits quite well. He died probably around the middle of the century.

The Alexandrians adopted him into the canon of the nine lyric poets and classified his work. They seem to have done so in nine books, of which six contained hymns for religious uses, namely dithyrambs, paeans, hymns, prosodia, partheneia and hyporchemata, while three others, entitled *Epinicia*, *Erotica* and *Encomia* were addressed to human beings. Thus with Bacchylides as with Pindar, we have access only to a relatively small part of a very large production.

One of the two rolls of which portions survive contains the epinicia in groups which are not arranged according to place, like Pindar's, or according to the type of athletic event, like those of Simonides. We have fourteen of them, which, despite considerable gaps and mutilation, are essentially readable, and so we receive a fair idea of Bacchylides' qualities in this genre. Comparison with

---

[1] This tendency stems to some extent from a misconception going back to Horace, as F. ZUCKER has shown: 'Die Bedeutung Pindars für Goethes Leben und Dichtung'. *Das Altertum* 1, 1955, 180 f.

Pindar is particularly interesting when both poets are celebrating the same victory. This is the situation in the oldest of the known epinicia of Bacchylides, to be dated probably about 485. It is concerned with a victory in the pancration at the Nemean games, won by the Aeginetan Pytheas, one of the sons of Lampon. The island and the family had close connections with Pindar, as we have seen, and he celebrated this victory in the *Fifth Nemean*. It was at Hiero's court especially that the paths of the two poets crossed, at least as concerned their poetry: it is not certain that Bacchylides was personally present in Sicily, although his close ties with Simonides make it very likely. When Hiero entered a winning horse at Olympia in 476, Pindar wrote the *First Olympian* to celebrate it, and Bacchylides also sent an ode from Ceos (5). The next commission from Hiero – following on his first victory with a chariot at Delphi – fell to Pindar, and Bacchylides had to be content with a short expression of good wishes in choral lyric form (4). But the Cean finally was victorious, since he and not Pindar wrote the ode to celebrate Hiero's victory with the chariot in the Olympics of 468.

Bacchylides wrote also for his own island: five of his epinicia refer to victories of his countrymen. It is surprising that about 458[1] Pindar received the commission to write for the Ceans a paean to the Delphic Apollo. Thus we may have to take seriously the statement of Plutarch (*de ex.* 14. 605 c) that Bacchylides lived for a long time in the Peloponnese as an exile.

In the epinicia of Bacchylides we find the same elements as in those of Pindar. The construction also is comparable in so far as the myth, in an elaborate form, occupies the central position and is framed round by the other parts. He sometimes goes into the details of the victory more than Pindar does, and in the closing sections he is very free with gnomic expressions. In these we can see his inferiority to Pindar: it is very everyday philosophy that he imparts, usually in everyday language. Nowhere do we find the profundity of Pindar's perception of values. There are passages also in which the poet speaks of his art. In one place (5, 16) he does this in a pompous and Pindaric vein, flapping eagle's wings in Hiero's face: but we find him more convincing as the Cean nightingale which he claims to be in another passage (3, 98). An epigram (9, 184) in the Palatine anthology, with rather delicate appreciation, addresses Pindar as Μουσάων ἱερὸν στόμα but Bacchylides as λάλε Σειρήν.

The epinicia are sufficient to show that Bacchylides' strength lay in his gift for narrative. The earliest of them (13) bears witness that he draws upon Homer much more than Pindar does. His dexterity is visible in little touches: the superiority of the Trojans and their collapse when Achilles re-enters the battle are depicted from the Trojan side. The besieged rushing forward to the attack evoke a simile drawn from seafaring which is wholly Homeric in subject and treatment. Bacchylides appears less derivative in his two long odes to Hiero (3 and 5), even if we suppose that he had originals now lost. In the second of these, on the victory in the Olympic horse-race, he makes the meeting of Heracles and Meleager in the underworld an impressive illustration of the frailty

---

[1] Cf. *Isthm.* 1, 7 f.

of all heroic greatness. The sudden ending of the scene is only superficially reminiscent of Pindar. It is not one of Pindar's bold transitions, but rather a simple abandonment of the subject, more in the style of Alcman. In the third poem on the victory in the Olympic chariot-race of 468, Bacchylides addresses a Hiero who was gravely ill and died shortly afterwards. It is rather a fine touch that he consoles him with an elegant version of the story of Croesus: the Lydian king, who like Hiero had won the favour of Apollo through his sumptuous gifts to the temple at Delphi, was not deserted by his god in the hour of mortal danger. When Sardes fell, he rescued his protégé from the pyre, which had been quenched by rain from Zeus, and took him to live a blessed life among the Hyperboreans.[1] Here and in many other passages it is not hard to discover the relation between the narrative and the circumstances of composition.

The other pieces of the London papyrus belong to a second roll, which contained the dithyrambs. The word Διθύραμβοι as the collective title is confirmed by occasional citations and by the label (σίλλυβος) of a papyrus (nr. 110) containing this text. Under this heading the Alexandrians had collected choral odes of a narrative content: it did not matter to them that two of them (16, 17) were manifestly addressed to Apollo. But in learned theory and in practical religious use the distinction between paean and dithyramb had ceased to be clear.[2] The individual poems had titles and were arranged according to the initial letter. Six of them survive in one condition or another: the *Sons of Antenor* or the *Demand for the Restoration of Helen*, with the embassy of Menelaus and Odysseus to Troy as described in *Il.* 3. 205 ff.; the *Heracles* (the title is only an inference), which does not so much relate as allude to the death of the hero at Deianira's hands – the subject-matter of the *Trachiniae* of Sophocles;[3] the *Youths* (᾽Ηΐθεοι) and the *Theseus*, two poems which we shall have to discuss a little later; the *Io*, a dithyramb composed for Athens containing the story of Zeus' love for that heroine and giving that prominence to Dionysus which one expects in the genre; finally the *Idas* (only a few verses of this survive) which Bacchylides wrote for the Spartans probably during his banishment. The subject was the rape of Marpessa by Idas.

Among these poems it is the two based on the legend of Theseus that best exemplify the narrative skill of Bacchylides. Like Pindar, he does not follow the chronological order, but seizes upon situations. It has been truly remarked that there is a ballad-like quality about much of his poetry. That earnest and powerful impressiveness, the statuesque beauty of the figures that we find in Pindar is wholly lacking in Bacchylides. This is typical of his Ionian nature: he did not write his poems as Pindar did, surrounded by all the divine powers which permit themselves to be perceived in their images by the wise in this world. In Bacchylides all this was superficial, and in consequence his sententiae

---

[1] On this poem and on the Delphic and Lydian variants of Croesus' death see B. GENTILI in the second chapter of his book *Bacchilide. Studi.* 2nd ed. Urbino 1958.

[2] Ps.-Plut. *de mus.* 10. 1134e. A. V. BLUMENTHAL, *RE* s.v. Paian 2351.

[3] On the relation to Sophocles, whose handling of the story is probably the later, see POHLENZ, *Griech. Trag.* 2nd ed. 2. 88.

have no depth. But he knew how to work with a well-filled stage, on which there was always something to captivate or to move, one that was the scene of many-coloured life and of a movement that held the attention captive.

In the 'Ηίθεοι we are on the ship which carried the unhappy children of Athens to Crete as an offering to the Minotaur. Minos, the great son of Zeus, is boldly defied by Theseus as protector of one of the maidens. Theseus also is the son of a god: he proves that Poseidon is his father by producing from the deep a ring which Minos had thrown into the sea. Dolphins convey him to the god's abode; he is alarmed at the bright light that streams from the daughters of the sea as they dance, but Amphitrite bestows on him a purple mantle and diadem of roses. The scene is depicted on two vase-paintings, which it is instructive to contrast. A masterly bowl of Euphronius[1] shows on its inner surface the young Theseus led by Athene, stretching out his hand to receive the gifts of the enthroned Amphitrite: a solemn and dignified treatment, such as Pindar would have given. A more recent bowl in Bologna[2] depicts the same scene in an operatic manner, with a stage crowded with life and movement, the gods striking effective poses rather than showing true nobility. This scene probably illustrates Bacchylides' narrative.

While the 'Ηίθεοι shows an extensive use of direct speech in the narrative, the dithyramb *Theseus* is wholly in dialogue form. One of the speakers is Aegeus, king of Athens. He has just heard news of the approach of a young hero who has done great deeds on the Isthmus: he does not yet know that it is his son Theseus. It is hard to know who the other speaker is, whose questions invite the king to relate the facts and to give an elaborate word-picture of the approaching hero. The simplest supposition is that the questions come from a chorus of Athenian citizens. The triadic strophe-division of the other dithyrambs and the larger epinicia is here given up in favour of the question and answer, which is maintained through four similarly constructed strophes. One is very greatly tempted to see in this structure, otherwise unparalleled, the kind of dithyramb which Aristotle saw as the precursor of tragedy. But if we consider the time at which Bacchylides wrote, we will more readily suppose that the form of the poem is influenced by dramatic forms already well developed.

Among the dithyrambs we have evidence that there was a *Philoctetes* and a *Laocoon*. One of the surviving fragments (fr. 20 A.) is interesting: it comes from a drinking-song written for King Alexander of Macedon. The Alexandrians classified these songs under the *Encomia*, as we saw them doing with Pindar, who also wrote one for the Macedonians. The description of the banquet at which fancy spreads its wings without restraint is quite masterly. A comparison with the treatment of this theme in Pindar (fr. 124 a. b.), which Fränkel has made in detail, is very instructive, and shows us certain standard features of the genre.

The style of Bacchylides is easier and lighter than that of Pindar. Instead of Pindar's measured tread we find a rapid flow, instead of his heavy articulation, pregnant with meaning, there is a rainbow haze of verbal ornament never

---

[1] E. BUSCHOR, *Griech. Vasen*. Munich 1940, fig. 169.
[2] E. PFUHL, *Malerei und Zeichnung der Griechen*. Munich 1923, fig. 590.

concealing any great profundity. A characteristic feature is the excessive use of epithets, in which he contrasts sharply with Simonides – as far as the latter is known to us. He borrows more from Homer than Pindar does, but his borrowings appear in altered contexts which give a different tone from that of the epic: Bacchylides' technique is to form unusual compounds out of current elements and thus to impart a new colouring. The dialect which he uses is the artificial one of choral lyric as we find it elsewhere. In general there are few Ionisms, although the Marpessa poem (fr. 20 A.) provides a striking exception.[1]

Of the other choral lyrists we met Timocreon, with his enmity towards Themistocles and his polemical scolia, in connection with Simonides. Lasus of Hermione had to be considered when we were discussing Pindar. More knowledge of him would be very welcome, since his activity in Athens under the Pisistratids was of great importance for the artistic development of the dithyramb and for the beginnings of musical theory. The Athenian Lamprocles is known to us through the beginning of a powerful hymn to Athene. Of Antigenes all we know is an epigram in which he celebrates his success as chorus-master in the Athenian Dionysia. Tynnichus of Chalcis long enjoyed a reputation based on one of his paeans.

Ibycus: *Anth. Lyr.* 2nd ed. fasc. 5, 58. C. M. BOWRA, *Greek Lyric Poetry* 2nd ed. Oxf. 1961, 247. D. L. PAGE, 'Ibycus' Poem in Honour of Polycrates'. *Aegyptus* 31, 1951, 158. Simonides: *Anth. Lyr.* 2nd ed. fasc. 5, 76; ibid. Suppl. 49, 59. After a few fragments in *Ox. Pap.* 23, 1956, volume 25, 1959, has brought important new evidence. LOBEL confidently attributes 2431 to Simonides, of 2430 and 2432 he is less sure. BR. GENTILI in *Gnom.* 33, 1961, 338 claims all three for Simonides, and he is probably right. MAX. TREU (see p. 189 n. 2) has convincingly shown this for 2432. On the epinicion nr. 2431 see p. 187, Nr. 2434 has remains of a commentary on some verses of lyric: the connection with Simonides is uncertain. On the new texts see also BR. GENTILI, 'Studi in Simonide' (Pap. Ox. 2431). *Riv. di cultura class. e medioev.* 2, 1960, 113 (a second part is to follow). C. M. BOWRA, op. cit. 308. Id., *Early Greek Elegists*. Lond. 1938 (repr. 1959), 173. G. CHRIST, *Simonides-Studien*. Diss. Zürich 1941. D. L. PAGE, 'Simonidea'. *Journ. Hell. Stud.* 71, 1951, 133. G. PEROTTA, 'Simonidea'. *Maia* 5, 1952, 242. BR. GENTILI, *Simonide*. Rome, 1959. Texts of Ibycus and Simonides: D. L. PAGE, *Poetae Melici Graeci*. Oxf. 1962.

Pindar: report on published work 1945-1957 by E. THUMMER, *AfdA* 11, 1958, 65. Detailed study of the transmission: J. IRIGOIN, *Histoire du texte de Pindare*. Paris 1952, who thinks that the archetype of our recension, represented by Ambrosianus C222 (thirteenth century) goes back to the fourth century. Id., *Les Scholies métriques de Pindare*. Bibl. de l'École des hautes études 310. Paris 1958. H. ERBSE, 'Beiträge zum Pindartext.' *Herm.* 88, 1960, 23. On the papyri see

---

[1] B. SNELL, 'Bakchylides' Marpessa-Gedicht'. *Herm.* 80, 1952, 156. Can it really have been an invective?

p. 196 n. 1. The best edition is that of BRUNO SNELL, 2nd ed. Leipz. 1955; the third edition (Leipz. 1959) only contains the *Epinicia*: SNELL has been waiting for the publication of the new Pindar papyri by LOBEL. See also C. M. BOWRA, 2nd ed. Oxf. 1947. AIMÉ PUECH, *Coll. des Un. de France.* 4 vols. 3rd and 2nd ed. Paris 1949–58. A. TURYN. Oxf. 1952. M. F. GALIANO, *Olímpicas. Texto, introd. y notas.* 2nd ed. Madrid 1956. J. SANDYS, *Loeb Lib.* Lond. 1918 (repr. 1957). ST. L. RADT, *Pindars 2 u. 6. Paian.* Amsterdam 1958 (text, scholia, comm.). L. R. FARNELL, *The Works of Pindar 2* (comm.) 1932, repr. 1961. R. W. B. BURTON, *Pindar's Pythian Odes. Essays in Interpretation.* 1962. - A. B. DRACHMANN, *Scholia vetera in Pindari carmina,* I. Leipz. 1903; 2, 1910; 3, 1927. J. RUMPEL, Lexicon Pindaricum. Leipz. 1883 (reprint by Olms, Hildesheim 1961). Add to this the supplementary index in SNELL's edition. - On the language and style: F. DORNSEIFF, *Pindars Stil.* Berl. 1921. U. VON WILAMOWITZ, *Pindaros.* Berl. 1922. H. FRÄNKEL, 'Pindars Religion'. *Die Antike* 3, 1927, 39. W. SCHADEWALDT, *Der Aufbau des pindarischen Epinikion.* Halle 1928. H. GUNDERT, *Pindar und sein Dichterberuf.* Frankf. a. M. 1935. G. NORWOOD, *Pindar.* Berkeley 1945 (repr. 1956); his theory that individual poems were separately given their premiere is very uncertain. E. DES PLACES. *Le Pronom chez Pindare.* Paris 1947. Id. *Pindare et Platon,* Paris 1949. M. UNTERSTEINER, *La formazione poètica di Pindaro,* Messina 1951. F. SCHWENN, *RE* 20, 1950, 1606. J. DUCHEMIN, *Pindare poète et prophète.* Paris 1955. J. H. FINLEY JR., *Pindar and Aeschylus.* Cambr. Mass. 1955. E. THUMMER, *Die Religiosität Pindars. Comm. Aenipont.* 13, Innsbruck 1957. B. A. VAN GRONINGEN, *La Composition littéraire archaique grecque. Verh. Nederl. Akad. N. R.* 65/2. Amsterdam 1958, 324. G. PERROTTA, *Pindaro.* Rome 1959. S. LAUER, *Zur Wortstellung bei Pindar.* Winterthur 1959. Bibliog. on the metrical structure of periods in Pindar: ST. L. RADT, *Gnom.* 32, 1960, 223, 1. ASTA-IRENE SULZER, *Zur Wortstellung und Satzbildung bei Pindar.* Zürich 1961. G. NEBEL, *Pindar und die Delphik.* 1961. - Translations: Eng.: R. LATTIMORE, Chicago 1958; R. FAGLES, New Haven. Lond. 1961 (foreword by C. M. BOWRA, Introd. and Notes by A. M. PARRY); Germ., R. DORNSEIFF, Leipzig 1922; Ital., L. TRAVERSO, Florence 1956. ATHANASIUS KIRCHER (*Musurgia universalis* 1, 1650, 541) published a melody for *Pyth.* 1, which he claimed to have found in the cloister of San Salvatore at Messina. The genuineness has been keenly debated; for an outline of the controversy see R. P. WINNINGTON-INGRAM, *Lustrum* 1958/3 (1959), 11: he is inclined to think it spurious, but P. FRIEDLÄNDER in *Herm.* 87, 1959, 385 has recently spoken up for Kircher.

Bacchylides. Text. BRUNO SNELL, 7th edition (after F. Blass and W. Suess), Leipz. 1958. On particular papyri: id., *Herm.* 75, 1940, 177; 76, 1948, 208. Of the new texts *Ox. Pap.* 23, 1956, nr. 2361-68, the last two contain fragments of an exegetical commentary. C. GALLAVOTTI, *Gnom.* 29, 1957, 421, basing himself on nr. 2364, assigns Pindar fr. 336 SNELL (=342 BOWRA) to Bacchylides. *Pap. Soc. It.* 14, 1957, nr. 1391 contains fragments of a commentary on choral lyric, but we cannot tell whether it refers to Pindar or to Bacchylides: cf. H. LLOYD-JONES, *Gnom.* 31, 1959, 112. A. SEVERYNS, *Bacchylide: essai biographique.* Paris 1933. BR. GENTILI, *Studi bacchilidei.* Messina 1953; 2nd ed. Urbino 1958.

A new Eng. transl.: R. FAGLES, New Haven/Lond. 1961. (Preface by C. M. BOWRA, introd. and notes by A. M. PARRY.)

H Philosophy at the End of the Archaic Period

Amid the plaudits which the epinicia bestowed on wrestlers, boxers and charioteers, one man of independent thought and the courage to express it dared to reckon intellect as being greater and more useful to the state (VS 21 B2). This man, who thus anticipated the words of Euripides (fr. 282 N.) and Isocrates (4. 1) and brought out into the open the basic opposition of two ways of life, was Xenophanes of Colophon. According to his own story (B8) he left home at the age of twenty-five when Harpagus was attacking the coastal towns, and wandered about the Greek world for sixty-seven years. He must have died about 470. His path led him, like Pythagoras, to the Greek west, where he had especially close connections with Elea. For his fellow-citizens in Asia Minor he wrote a history of the founding of Colophon (Κολοφῶνος κτίσις), and for the new Ionian settlement in Lucania he composed the *Colonization of Elea* (ὁ εἰς Ἐλέαν τῆς Ἰταλίας ἀποικισμός). This is the oldest known epic of contemporary history. For the rest he conveyed his thoughts mostly in the elegiac metre, which was well adapted to subjective expression; but he also devised a new and individual form in the *Silloi*. These poems in hexameters with occasional iambic lines were directed against false or obsolete values. They were imitated by Timon of Phlius in the third century, and to a large extent they were forerunners of Hellenistic popular philosophy and of Roman satire.

Diogenes Laertius (9. 18) tells us that Xenophanes recited (ἐρραψῴδει) his own poems. It would be rash, however, to picture him as a wandering rhapsode who recited Homer and Hesiod to a wide public, only to fall upon them and rend them in more select circles. It is not now possible to gain any notion of his status in society. We detect something of his personality in the fine elegy (B 1) which deals with the value of a properly celebrated symposium.

The clear and sober language of the surviving verses does not attest a great poetical genius, nor yet does Xenophanes' greatness lie in his philosophy. His far-reaching influence is based on the depth and strength of his theological thought. We can still see how his own elevated conception of the deity arose out of his merciless exposure of the immoral and criminal gods of the epics (B 11) and his ridicule of anthropomorphism. These Homeric gods are of human handiwork, just as oxen and lions, if they had hands, would make themselves gods after their own likeness (B 15): the Aethiopians imagine their gods as black and snub-nosed, the Thracians theirs as blue-eyed and red-haired (B 16). But in reality there is one god only – the greatest, all eye, all ear, all mind: without effort he moves all things by the force of the spirit; remaining in himself, without movement, which would be unbecoming to his greatness (B 23-26). This adumbrates already the unmoved mover of Aristotle. It is an intellectual conception unheard of in the early Greek world; the anthropomorphic picture of the gods is abandoned and a supreme being is posited, ruling the universe from outside it. If we take B 23, 1 literally (one god is the greatest among gods and men[1]) then Xenophanes would have assumed the existence of other gods alongside this supreme deity, and thus made his peace with the popular religion. We can only guess. The much disputed Peripatetic treatise *On Melissus, Xenophanes and Gorgias* cannot be relied on to give a more detailed picture of Xenophanes' theology.[2]

Some of the fragments deal with natural phenomena, and show a marked scepticism towards unsupported hypotheses, together with a striking gift for observation. From the finding of shells and fossil sea-creatures in rocks Xenophanes inferred a period in which the land was covered by the sea (A 33), and the alternation of flooding and drying-out was an important feature in his physical cosmology. It is often said that he wrote a special treatise on this subject, which was later given the title *On the World of Nature* ($\pi\epsilon\rho\grave{\iota}$ $\phi\acute{\upsilon}\sigma\epsilon\omega s$); but the evidence for it is weak (B 30. 39).[3]

The fear that the Olympian gods might be called in question in the light of new ways of thought evoked a defence which was repeatedly essayed down to the end of antiquity. Theagenes of Rhegium, whom Tatian (VS 8. 1) makes a contemporary of Cambyses, is reckoned as its originator. The gods and the stories about them, he wrote, were to be understood allegorically. Mostly it was natural phenomena that were to be understood in them: no one could take exception to their behaviour if it were realized that Apollo signified fire and Hera air. This doctrine found its way (through men like Stesimbrotus of Thasos) into the Stoa and has had a wide influence even on modern theories of mythology.[4]

Ancient historians of philosophy made Xenophanes the teacher of Parmenides and thus the founder of the Eleatic school; although Theophrastus (VS 21 A 31)[5] makes the qualification that Xenophanes did not teach the unity of all that exists, only the unity of his deity. In his book on Parmenides[6] Karl Reinhardt has disproved the immediate dependency which had been supposed, and has thus re-established the uniqueness of Parmenides, without of course lessening the stature of a theologian like Xenophanes.

In Plato's *Theaetetus* (183 E) Socrates tells how as a young man he met the veteran Parmenides, and he describes him as Homer does Priam: powerful and awe-inspiring. Parmenides' lifetime falls in the late sixth and early fifth centuries. Elea, his birthplace in southern Italy, came our way in connection with Xenophanes, and its nearness to the centres of Pythagorean teaching puts it beyond

---

[1] In the elegant banquet-elegy also (cf. C. M. BOWRA, *Problems in Greek Poetry*. Oxf. 1953, 1) we find $\theta\epsilon\acute{o}s$ and $\theta\epsilon o\acute{\iota}$ side by side. G. FRANÇOIS, *Le Polythéisme et l'emploi au singulier des mots $\theta\epsilon\acute{o}s$, $\delta a\acute{\iota}\mu\omega\nu$ dans la littérature grecque d'Homère à Platon*. Paris 1957, 160, which is relevant to the other thinkers discussed here as well.
[2] Problems: W. JAEGER, *Theologie der frühen Gr. Denker*. Stuttg. 1953, 65. Text: VS 21 A 28.
[3] JAEGER op. cit. 52.
[4] JACOB BURKHARDT rejects it: *Griechische Kulturgeschichte* (Kröner) I. 326. I. F. WEHRLI, *Zur Geschichte der allegorischen Deutung Homers*. Basel 1928. F. BUFFIÈRE, *Les Mythes d'Homère, et la pensée grecque*. Paris 1956.   [5] Cf. FRÄNKEL 297. 17.   [6] Bonn 1916.

question that he was influenced by those doctrines. A close relation to Heraclitus has been repeatedly asserted, but it is still problematical. At all events he knew the older Ionians, and much of his teaching presupposes Anaximander and Anaximenes.

The philosophy of Parmenides does not exist in a vacuum. If he was more than just a disciple of Xenophanes, that does not mean that the latter's theological doctrines had no influence on him. But a fact more important than any postulated relations of this sort is that no other Greek thinker ever laid claim so radically and resolutely to a new intellectual territory. He broke new ground also in not being content with assertion, but advancing proofs of his doctrines. The early Ionians started from what their senses told them about the world, and looked for a basic principle underlying this multiplicity and for the mechanism by which it arose. Now came a man who with a single bound passed beyond this sensible world and used the power of his intellect to seek the truth beyond its confines. He found it in the one unique existent, which knows neither coming-to-be nor passing away. Its eternity in time meant that it had no past and no future, but endured always in a pure present. The perfection of this being suffers no division and no alteration. It is an unmoved, homogeneous continuum, comparable to a sphere (B 8, 43), nowhere interrupted by not-being. That not-being, as the opposite to true being, is unthinkable and therefore non-existent is a point to which Parmenides constantly returns. Although he arrives at this absolute being beyond the sensible world by the path of the intellect, although he even equates being and thought (B 3), yet his supreme existent does not fade into a mere idea. Rather what he means is something possessing actuality, although we cannot have detailed knowledge of its nature. It is important in this connection that Parmenides treats the true existent as finite (B 8, 30), a notion which caused difficulties to his followers and was soon given up. On the other hand those who came after him laid considerably greater stress on the principle of unity.[1]

The world of being is contrasted with that of appearance: the former is accessible to the intellect of the wise man while the latter is the creation of human opinion. On one side is the one true ὄν, on the other the many δόξαι. Yet in this universe of opinion there are different levels. In a second part of his didactic poem Parmenides includes a detailed cosmology,[2] which, while belonging to the realm of δόξα, nevertheless claims the highest rank in it for systematic perfection (B 8, 60). It is the basic mistake of mankind that instead of the One which is without parts they have posited a duality made up of fire and night. But from this mistake, perpetuating itself through all things, the world of appearance can be systematized with inner consistency. Fire and night have this in common with the true being, that they cannot alter their nature. This of course rules out such cosmogonies as that of Anaximander, and in all subsequent philosophies the fundamental notion of mixture was well in the foreground.

---

[1] M. UNTERSTEINER, 'L' essere di Parmenide è οὖλον, non ἕν'. Riv. critica di storia della filos. 1955, 51. But he goes too far in rejecting ἕν in B 8, 6.

[2] Cf. GIGON, Ursprung (sup. p. 168), 271.

The manner and proportion in which the two principles are mixed determine the cosmology of the world of appearance.

The relation between the world of *doxa* and true being is the most difficult and yet unsolved problem that Parmenides poses. This section of the poem can certainly be explained as an exposition of the views of others or a polemic against them, but still the problem remains: to what extent did Parmenides claim that his cosmology based on the elements fire and night represented an approach to the truth or a participation in true being?[1]

Parmenides conveyed his doctrines in a didactic poem in hexameters, of which considerable parts are extant. We may say that he takes his place in a tradition going back to Hesiod; from echoes of Pindar[2] we may infer the influence of early choral lyric, but even so the decisive quality of the man is his uniqueness. The harshness and lack of connection of his verses has sometimes been remarked by critics and can hardly be denied: we prefer, however, to salute the poet who in his proemium conjures up the image of the journey into the bright realm of truth. Divine maidens, the Heliades, escort the car in which Parmenides is speedily borne along. From the realm of night he comes to the gate which separates darkness from light. Dike, who holds the key, lets herself be persuaded by the daughters of the sun to open the great door. A goddess whose name is not given receives the bold traveller and reveals to him the world of truth and the world of appearance.

In these verses Parmenides bodies forth his spiritual experience. Southern Italy early became a land of mystery religions, and the opening up of truth in the kingdom of light must be partly derived from them. What Parmenides experienced was an enlightenment, but the chariot with its shrill-squealing axles bears him along as 'the man who knows' (B 1, 3). Here in the realm of knowledge we find again that juxtaposition of human faculties and divine intervention which we met in the actions of Homer's characters.

This is not the place to deal with the way in which the Eleatic school, in the persons of such men as Zeno,[3] maintained and modified the ontology of Parmenides in a way that led to pure dialectic. Melissus of Samos, who held command for his country against Pericles in 441, faithfully defended the basic doctrine, but explicitly abandoned the finiteness of the supreme being (VS 30 B 3).

Heraclitus of Ephesus was in the prime of life about 500; i.e. he was roughly contemporary with Parmenides. We cannot be more precise than this. Reinhardt's view that Parmenides was the elder need no longer concern us. If we consider that the reverse is possible, then Parmenides may have been in reaction against Heraclitus. He has often been contrasted with Parmenides as the philosopher of coming-to-be as against the philosopher of being, and in fact he did not depreciate the sensible world, like Parmenides, and consider it a world of

[1] H. SCHWABL, 'Sein und Doxa bei Parmenides'. *Wien. Stud.* 66, 1953, 50.

[2] *Ol.* 6. 22 ff. On the proemium see BOWRA op. cit. 38.

[3] J. ZAFIROPULO, *L' École éléate.* Paris 1950. Id., *Vox Zenonis.* Paris 1958. W. KULLMANN, 'Zenon und die Lehre des Parmenides'. *Herm.* 86, 1958, 157. H. FRÄNKEL (*v. inf.*) 198. O. GIGON, *Sokrates.* Berne 1947, 214. M. BLACK, *Zeno's Paradoxes.* Ithaca 1954.

appearance only; rather he made it with all its incessant change the basis of his philosophy. Such sayings as that one can never step twice into the same stream (B 91, cf. 12. 49 a) show us how the flux of all things came to be reckoned as a cardinal point of his philosophy; although in fact the celebrated πάντα ῥεῖ is not one of the direct quotations, but was apparently formulated by later writers on the basis of such passages as that quoted.

But the difference between Heraclitus and Parmenides should not be more highly stressed than their affinities. The philosophy of Heraclitus also transcended the world of sense-perception, although in a different way. He saw the change and decay of things principally as the continuous mutual resolution of opposites – day and night, winter and summer, peace and war, hunger and satiety (B 67): but his most characteristic doctrine, which he inculcated repeatedly and often paradoxically, is the recognition behind all things of an ultimate, all-embracing unity. Our experience shows us the world as a mass of conflicting tensions, in which war reigns as the king and father of all (B 53); but at the same time all contraries are bound together in a firm unity: 'the unseeen bond is stronger than the seen' (B 54). The 'back-stretched connection' of bow and lyre is the most strongly expressed symbol of this philosophy, which pierced the surface of the sensible world not less boldly than Parmenides' did.

This unity of opposites is the central element of that logos whose eternal validity Heraclitus felt himself called upon to proclaim. This logos[1] is the word of his writings, it is the thought working in that word, it is above all the great governing principle of the world. It is the divine law which nourishes all human laws (B 114); it resides with God, who alone has the insight denied to humanity (B 78), it is the One only Wise, which is named and not named by the word Zeus (B 32). We are here reminded of Aeschylus' hymn to Zeus, and we can see the similar way in which very different types of religious thought approached the greatest name of traditional belief.

The passages just quoted bring before us the picture of a thinker proclaiming his doctrines under a strong ethical impulsion. Recognition of the great cosmic law, which embraces the path of the sun (B 94) as well as the life of man, must be our purpose unless we are barbarous of soul. Can we go one step further, and assume that Heraclitus posited as the ultimate end of human wisdom harmony with this law that works through all things? By doing so we touch on a central element of Stoic ethics and at the same time on a difficult basic problem in the interpretation of Heraclitus. His thought became to a considerable degree the basis of Stoic philosophy, and inevitably there is a dangerous temptation to paint his portrait in Stoic colours.

We can see what a special place fire occupied in Heraclitus' cosmological thought. 'Fire's turnings: first sea, and of sea the half is earth, the other half scorching breath' (B 31). In another passage (B 90) he speaks of the exchange of all things with fire and of fire with all things. But it would be premature to

[1] W. KRANZ, 'Der Logos Heraklits und der Logos des Johannes'. *Rhein. Mus.* 93, 1949, 81. U. HÖLSCHER, 'Der Logos bei Heraklit'. *Festgabe f. Reinhardt.* Cologne 1952, 69. W. BRÖCKER, *Gnom.* 30, 1958, 435.

rank Heraclitus as a hylozoist with the older Milesian thinkers. His fire is not simply the basic stuff from which all else arises. His fire is endued with reason,[1] and when he talks of the lightning which rules the cosmos we can see its divine nature: we can establish a close relation between the three notions, logos, god and cosmic fire. The human soul also partakes of this fire, and from such a notion it is easy to see why the driest soul is said to be the wisest (B 118). It has rightly been inferred that this fiery nature enables the soul to recognize the logos; and we need only remark in passing how close this train of thought already is to Stoicism.

Heraclitus appears to us as a great solitary. He came from an old family of royal degree, but he renounced the privileges of his rank in favour of a brother. He kept himself aloof from the generality of mankind, for whom he had only contempt: he often refers to them as sleepers. But he felt himself also widely severed from other Greek poets and thinkers, from Homer as much as from Archilochus and Hesiod, from Pythagoras, Xenophanes and Hecataeus. If we enquire into the sources of his teaching we can only take his own words for answer: 'I have sought my own self' (B 101). It was this path that taught him how immeasurable are the realms of the spirit, whose boundaries no one can reach.[2]

If the thought is individual, its expression is no less so. We know of a treatise which Heraclitus is said to have deposited in the great temple of Artemis in Ephesus. It was later given various titles, including the common 'On the Nature of the World'. The remains are extensive enough to tell us that it took the form of a continuous exposition of his doctrine. Brick was laid on brick in a style of the utmost brevity: short noun-clauses are very common. These sentences bursting violently through the hindrances of language, come from the heart of a man who was a miser with words and despised the incurious multitude. The way in which the sentences are strung together may be distantly influenced by old collections of proverbs (hypothecae). Their interpretation has been difficult in all ages: Heraclitus has always been called 'the obscure' (σκοτεινός). We hear of a devoted soul called Scythinus of Teos who turned these enigmatic sentences all into trochaic tetrameters, probably in the fourth century B.C.

The life of Empedocles of Acragas extends over the first half of the fifth century and well into the second. The reason for mentioning this contemporary of Democritus and Anaxagoras here is that he displays very much more archaic features than either of them.

In the ancient cultural soil of western Hellas his life developed to a richness and variety which greatly encouraged the rise of legend in later times. He was active in the politics of his city, appearing as a democratic party-man after the overthrow of the oligarchical régime which had followed upon the tyrannis. As a physician and wandering priest he collected disciples and admirers who followed him from city to city. In the opening of the Catharmoi he speaks of himself as the leader of a religious thiasos (B 112). In another passage (B 111)

---

[1] B 64. K. REINHARDT, 'Heraklits Lehre vom Feuer'. Herm. 77, 1942, 1; now in Vermächtnis der Antike. Göttingen 1960, 41, where see also 'Heraclitea' on p. 72.

[2] B 45. B. SNELL, Die Entdeckung des Geistes. 3rd ed. Hamb. 1955, 36.

he promises his adepts not only knowledge of healing arts but the secret lore of commanding the winds and the weather. His work, of which we possess a good many fragments, mirrors the many-sidedness of his life. In a didactic poem of some two thousand verses in two books (A 2), later known as 'On the Nature of Things', he expounded his cosmogony in the archaic manner, professing to teach his pupil Pausanias. He also sought true Being, but he did not need to go beyond the sensible world: he found it in the four 'roots' – the four elements of which all is built: earth, water, air and fire, all having an eternal existence and continuing unperturbed in a circular motion (B 17, 13. 26, 12). Thus his world-picture combines the eternal rest of Parmenides and the eternal movement of Heraclitus. But in these four elements the basic substance of the old Ionians was changed in more than simply number. It is not now a question of a basic substance causing all things to arise out of itself: rather the forces that determine all coming-to-be and passing away are found in the principles of mixing and separating. At the same time this rationally constructed system can be understood as the play and interplay of divine powers. To see pure allegory here would be wholly to mistake the man with whom we have to deal. The four elements appear under the names of Zeus, Hera, Aedoneus and Nestis, and are called divine.[1] Divine also are the two great movers which produce union and separation: their names are Philotes and Neikos, love and strife. As one or the other has the upper hand, the world varies from happy unity and completeness in its rounded sphere (B 27, cf. Parmenides B 8, 43) to warring disunity and vice versa.

If we form a just estimate of the mythical element in this cosmology, we shall not be surprised that its author wrote also a poem entitled *Catharmoi* (*Purifications*). It seems to have been an extended work: Diogenes Laertius gives the combined length of it and the other as five thousand verses. The extant fragments enable us to see common traits in the two poems, but, so far as we can see, the subject matter of the *Catharmoi* was quite different. It deals with the destiny of a human soul: he speaks of it as his own. He avers the divine origin of this soul, and his supposed career of thaumaturgy was probably connected with this belief.[2] But in another passage (B 115) we hear that he had incurred guilt and therefore had been driven from the presence of God into long wanderings. Thirty thousand 'hours' (probably=years) must be spent by such fallen daemons in wandering about the cosmos in ever new forms of mortal creatures, tossed from one element to another. In earlier lives Empedocles claims to have been a boy, a girl, a bush, fowl and fish (B 117). His opposition to the sacrifice of animals and the eating of their flesh comes from the same source. If we understand B 120 aright, this earth, as the seat of darkness and misery, came to be for Empedocles the 'roofed-over cave', and the body the 'alien fleshly covering' of the soul (B 126).

---

[1] On the distribution of these names see VS 31 A 33 with the note.

[2] For B 112, 4 f. W. KRANZ's interpretation (*Empedokles* 27) is to be preferred. On the shaman-element in such a figure as Empedocles cf. E. R. DODDS, *The Greeks and the Irrational*. Berkeley 1951, 145.

It is obvious that all these views fit immediately into the context of the Orphic and Pythagorean tenets of immortality and metempsychosis which were so widely current in the Magna Graecia of that time.[1] To explain the relation of the *Catharmoi* to the cosmological poem scholars have devised a variety of hypotheses which make Empedocles develop from scientist to mystic or vice versa. None of these has any secure basis. We should do wrong to underestimate the range of his genius, which was capable of embracing at once the inquiring spirit of Ionia and the mystic beliefs of the Orphists. His strength cannot be said to have lain in the construction of a wholly consistent system; but as a poet he displayed considerable skill in the modification of old epic elements and in the devising of new forms. In everything that he wrote we feel heat rather than light from the fire that burnt within him.

For bibliography see p. 167 f. Texts in VS. Apart from the works of DEICH-GRÄBER, GIGON, HOWALD-GRÜNEWALD, JAEGER (loc. cit. n. 3), NESTLE and SNELL (p. 186 n. 4), see on Xenophanes: M. UNTERSTEINER, *Senofane. Testi monianze e frammenti*. Bibl. di studi super. 33, Florence 1956. A. LUMPE, *Die Philosophie des Xenophanes von Kolophon*. Diss. Munich 1952. H. THESLEFF, *On dating X*. Helsingfors 1957. H. FRÄNKEL, 'Xenophanesstudien' in *Wege und Formen frühgriechischen Denkens*. 2nd ed. Munich 1960, 335. A section on X. in the treatise of Aš-Šakrastānī, trans. by F. ALTHEIM and R. STIEHL, *Geschichte der Hunnen* 3, 1961, 138. A. FARINA, *Senofane di Colofone. Ione di Chio*. Naples 1961 (with trans. and comm.). – Parmenides: survey of modern work: H. SCHWABL, *AfdA* 9, 1956, 129. Editions: J. BEAUFRET, *Le Poème de P*. Paris 1955 (with Fr. trans., text from VS). M. UNTERSTEINER, *Parmenide. Testimonianze e frammenti*. Bibl. di studi super. 38. Florence 1958. Monographs etc.: W. J. VERDENIUS, *Parmenides, some comments on his poem*. Groningen 1942; *Mnem*. 4, 1949, 116. M. BUHL, 'Zum Stil des P.' *Festschrift Regenbogen*. Heidelb. 1956, 35. U. HÖL-SCHER, 'Grammatisches zu P.'. *Herm*. 84, 1956, 385. H. SCHWABL, 'Zur "Theogonie" bei P. und Empedokles.' *Wien. Stud*. 70, 1957, 278. K. DEICHGRÄBER, 'Parmenides' Auffahrt zur Göttin des Rechts.' *Abh. Ak. Mainz. Geistes- u. sozialwiss. Kl.* 1958/11. V. GNAZZONI FOÀ, 'Le recenti interpretazioni italiane e straniere dell' essere eleatico.' *Riv. di filos. neo-scolastica* 50, 1958, 326. K. REIN-HARDT, *P. und die Geschichte der griech. Philosophie*. 1916, repr. Frankf. a. M. 1959. W. R. CHALMERS, 'P. and the beliefs of mortals.' *Phronesis* 5, 1960, 5. R. FALUS, 'P.-Interpretationes' *Acta antiqua Acad. Scient. Hungar*. 8, 1960, 267. J. H. M. M. LOENEN, *P., Melissus, Gorgias. A reinterpretation of Eleatic Philosophy*. 1960. H. FRÄNKEL, *Wege und Formen* (v. sup.) 157. – Heraclitus: Bibliog.: R. MUTH, *AfdA* 7, 1954, 65. A. N. ZOUMPOS, βιβλιογραφικὰ περὶ ʽΗ. Πλάτων 9, 1957, 69. Editions: H. WALZER, Florence 1939 (with trans.) C. MAZZANTINI, Turin, 1945.

[1] On particular problems see W. RATHMANN, *Quaestiones Pythagorae Orphicae Empedocleae*. Diss. Halle 1933. On the relation between the two works see H. SCHWABL, *Wien. Stud*. 69, 1956, 50, 6.

Trans.: BR. SNELL, 4th ed. Munich 1944. Studies: O. GIGON, *Untersuchungen zu H.* Leipzig 1935. MISCH, *Der Weg in die Philosophie I.* Berne 1950, 335. G. S. KIRK, *Heraclitus. The Cosmic Fragments.* Cambr. 1954, with a detailed commentary, including interpretation of H's forerunners. A. JEANNIÈRE, *La Pensée d'Héraclite d'Éphèse.* Paris 1958, with trans. of the fragments. E. KURTZ, *Interpretationen zu den Logos-Fragmenten Heraklits.* Diss. Tübingen 1959 (typewritten). CL. RAMNOUX, *Héraclite ou l'homme entre les choses et les mots.* Paris 1959. P. WHEELWRIGHT, *Heraclitus.* Princeton 1959. K. REINHARDT's studies 'Heraklits Lehre vom Feuer' and 'Heraclitea' are now to be found in *Vermächtnis der Antike.* Göttingen 1960, 41. 72. H. FRÄNKEL op. cit. 237. 251. 253. M. MARCOVICH, *Heraclito I.* Mérida-Venezuela 1962 (full bibliog.); 'H. und seine Lehre. Materialien des Koll. über den altgr. Philos. H. 30. 10. 1961 in Leipzig'. *Wiss. Zeitschr. d. Karl-Marx-Univ. Gesellsch. u. sprachw. Reihe.* Heft 3/1962. Empedocles: W. KRANZ, *E. Antike Gestalt und romantische Neuschöpfung.* Zürich 1949 (with trans.). K. REINHARDT, 'E. Orphiker und Physiker'. *Class. Phil.* 45, 1950, 170; now in *Vermächtnis der Antike.* Gött. 1960, 101. MARIA SOPHIA BUHL, *Untersuchungen zu Sprache und Stil des E.* Diss. Heidelb. 1956 (typewritten). J. BOLLACK, 'Die Metaphysik des E. als Entfaltung des Seins'. *Phil.* 101, 1957, 30. B. A. VAN GRONINGEN, *La Composition littéraire archaïque grecque.* Verh. Nederl. Ak. N.R. 65/2. Amsterdam 1958, 201. M. DETIENNE, 'La "Démonologie" d'Empédocle'. *Rev. Et. Gr.* 72, 1959, 1. G. NELOD, *Empedocle d' Agrigente.* Brussels 1959. G. CALOGERO, 'L' eleatismo di E.' *Studi L. Castiglioni* 1, 1960, 129. C. H. KAHN, 'Religion and Natural Philosophy in Empedocles' Doctrine of the Soul'. *Arch. f. Gesch. d. Philos.* 42, 1960, 3. An outline of the contents of the *Catharmoi* is given in the treatise of Aš-Šakrastānī (*v. sup.* Xenophanes).

I The Beginnings of Science and Historiography

Some of the most credible traditions about Thales refer to his mathematical interests. The achievements of the Pythagoreans in this field can be assessed in their general outlines only. Anaximander drew a diagrammatic map of the world, and either the Pythagoreans or Parmenides discovered that it was a sphere. Empedocles' activities as a physician have just been discussed.

These few examples serve to show that the beginnings of Greek philosophy embrace also the beginnings of the individual sciences, and that to separate them is to apply quite unhistorically a modern distinction. It is only with this reservation – and with the further one that such questions remain necessarily on the fringe of our treatment – that we add the following observations.

Some of the instances mentioned remind us of important historical connections. Unquestionably Thales' mathematics were under Egyptian influence, and we were able to find a Babylonian forbear for Anaximander's map of the world (p. 164). The Ionians of Asia Minor, who were mainly responsible for cultural advances in the archaic period, were influenced by old and highly developed civilizations: in the sciences as elsewhere they learned much from them. With increasing knowledge of such indebtedness the conviction that the Greeks were the originators of European science has seemed to become more questionable. We certainly do not propose here to treat the Greeks as inventors out of nothing. But despite all that we have learned of Egyptian medicine or Babylonian mathematics, we must never overlook the basic difference which divides Greek science from all that had gone before, and which guarantees its fundamental importance in the history of western civilization.[1] It was among the Greeks of Asia Minor that there first arose that form of intellectual work, directed purely towards the acquisition of knowledge without consideration of practical utility, which we call science. Those characteristics which we see most clearly in the history of Greek mathematics, with its apparatus of axiom, postulate and definition and with that leaning towards systematization which so soon showed itself, belong to Greek science in general, including the writing of history, which sprang from similar intellectual attitudes. The will towards critical examination and comprehension of truth and actuality embodies itself in a way of approach to certainty through the testing and rejection of hypotheses – an entirely new form of intellectual procedure which has been the basis of all subsequent advance in the sciences.

The late sixth and early fifth centuries witness the work of a man who exemplifies impressively the efforts made to master one science within the stream of contemporary culture. The man is Alcmeon of Croton. He may well have known Pythagoras: at all events the latter's teaching had a profound influence on him.[2] His book, written in the Ionic dialect under the title Περὶ φύσιος, is the first known medical treatise in Greek. It calls itself a manual of instruction for three of his pupils, and begins (B 1) with a sentence which sets its whole tone: a man can only approach that wisdom possessed by the gods through drawing conclusions from what he can see. This sentence looks backwards to Xenophanes' modest disclaimer (VS 21 B 34) and forward to the famous dictum of Anaxagoras (VS 59 B 21 a): Phenomena give us a glimpse of what is not seen.[3]

Alcmeon's work shows a mixture of theory and empiricism which is characteristic of his time and of a wide range of Greek science. Health he considers as a state of balance between opposing qualities such as wet and dry, cold and warm, sour and sweet. The loss of this equipoise produces illness. This way of interpretating the condition of microcosm and macrocosm as coming from the interplay of opposites either in equal or unequal proportions is wholly in harmony with the intellectual climate of the age. Yet its author took a giant stride in the realm of physiology when he recognized the brain as the central organ of sense-perception. He did, however, overstep the limits of observation when he propounded, in discussing a much-debated question of ancient medicine, the view that human semen originates in the brain.

[1] Cf. the works of NEUGEBAUER and VON FRITZ cited below.

[2] Discussions of this influence are cited by ERNA LESKY, Herm. 80, 1952, 250, 5. On the date of Alcmeon: L. EDELSTEIN, Am. Journ. Phil. 63, 1942, 371, and W. JAEGER, Aristoteles Metaphysik. Oxf. 1957 in the apparatus to 986 a 29 f.

[3] H. DILLER, Herm. 67, 1932, 14.

Despite his great importance, Alcmeon is by no means unique. Scanty as our knowledge is, we cannot doubt that there were technical treatises in prose in the late archaic period. We are still able to form some conception of such a man as Menestor of Sybaris, who lived about the same time as Empedocles. He wrote on botany, and like Alcmeon he made a dualism of opposites the basis of his system.

Just like the sciences, historiography in the later sense of the word first arose among the Greeks and from very diverse beginnings. For a long time their mythology served the Greeks for history, and it took a long, hard struggle, not fully successful before Thucydides, to replace the mythological interpretation of the past by one that was critical and rational. It was not simply a matter of something true and right replacing something wrong and false. In fact those very elements of Greek thought which were already to be found on the mythological level became of vital importance for later developments.[1] It is quite conceivable in itself that the Greek epics contained a good deal of historical material, although often altered almost beyond recognition. But nevertheless all the events of epic are treated as occurring in a definite spatial and temporal setting widely separated from that of the narrator. Furthermore a start had been made, within this setting, to tie the events and personalities together into a temporal sequence by means of genealogical cross-links. By this means two great myth-cycles were brought into a firm chronological sequence: Diomedes and his charioteer Sthenelus, fighting before Troy, are made the sons of heroes who took part in the expedition of the Seven against Thebes. But more important than all else, epic poetry was already looking beyond the unique and individual happening and asking what relevance it had in the world as a whole, asking also after the causes and the connections of things, and looking for some ultimate meaning in the course of events. Homer is in this sense the 'father of history'; and here again he is a beginning.

We come up against another of the springs of Greek historiography when we trace the history of the word itself. We start with the root *vid*, meaning 'to see'. We first find the word ἴστωρ, which signifies one who has seen a thing and can relate it as an eye-witness. Thus history ((ἱστορίη) first means relating something and vouching for it by ocular testimony. But in a wider application it ceases to be confined to immediate personal experience: the knowledge may be won by the questioning of witnesses. The latter are of course not of equal value, and their reports may conflict. Thus here, just as in the domain of the natural sciences, the object becomes the establishment of truth by rational criticism. Once again Ionian Asia Minor takes the first steps along the road which Thucydides was to follow to its end.

---

[1] Cf. w. SCHADEWALDT, 'Die Anfänge der Geschichtsschreibung bei den Griechen'. *Die Antike* 10, 1934, 144; now in *Hellas und Hesperien*. Zürich 1960, 395. K. DEICHGRÄBER, 'Das griech. Geschichtsbild in seiner Entwicklung zur wissenschaftlichen Historiographie'. In: *Der listensinnende Trug des Gottes*. Göttingen 1952, 7. K. V. FRITZ (*v. inf.*). B. SNELL, 'Die Entstehung des geschichtlichen Bewusstseins'. In: *Die Entdeckung des Geistes*. 3rd ed. Hamburg 1955, 203 (cf. Eng. ed. p. 191).

The normal vehicle for such collection and evaluation of testimony is prose: first of all a prose which makes no pretence to ornament, which lets the facts speak for themselves.[1] The simple and straightforward manner that is most common is the appropriate expression of the intellectual process by which the facts that present themselves are taken and strung upon a thread of narrative. Since this manner of seeing and reporting things first developed in Ionia, the earliest prose is written in the Ionic dialect even outside the normal Ionic-speaking areas, e.g. by Alcmeon of Croton.

Nowhere could this kind of reporting be more fruitfully prosecuted than on travels in foreign lands. The Ionians of Asia Minor carried their colonizing and trading activities very far afield, but travels like those of Hecataeus and Herodotus were probably taken deliberately for the sake of knowledge. The great importance which knowledge of foreign countries had for nascent Ionian historiography led to two of its most important ancillaries: geography and ethnography.

Since most sailing in antiquity was coastwise, practical considerations soon led to the description of voyages undertaken. The situation and distance apart of harbours and rivermouths, navigational hazards, watering-places and the like had their obvious utility. But the men who made these journeys were Greeks, who had their eyes open, and their interest often went beyond the merely practical. It was above all the *nomos*, the manners and customs of foreign peoples, that held their interest, and we shall later have to consider how far the development of Greek thought was influenced by such observations and comparisons.

The most common form of such descriptive accounts was the *periplus*, a description of the coast seen from the ship in the sequence enjoined by the course of the voyage. This form was used by Scylax of Caryanda to describe the voyage which he took in the service of Darius I towards the end of the sixth century from the Indus to the Arabian Gulf. The scanty remains still let us see how wide his geographical and ethnographical interests were. He is said to have written other descriptions of coastlines, but he has nothing whatever to do with the Pseudo-Scylax – a name given to a description of the Mediterranean coast drawn up about the time of Philip II of Macedon. Roughly contemporary with Scylax was the old *periplus* which can still be partly reconstructed from the *Ora Maritima* of the late Latin versifier Avienus. The author, who probably hailed from Massilia (Marseilles), wrote an accurate account of the coast from Tartessus to Massilia. The same colony appears in connection with one Euthymenes who in the late sixth century wrote a periplus describing his journey from Massilia to the west coast of Africa. The competition of the naval powers in opening up new coasts becomes obvious when we hear of the navigation of the Carthaginian Hanno about the same time. His periplus was written in Punic, but we have a Greek translation of Hellenistic date.

In considering the various factors contributing to the rise of historical writing,

[1] H. FRÄNKEL, 'Eine Stileigenheit der frühgr. Lit.' GGN 1924, 63; now in *Wege und Formen frühgr. Denkens*. 2nd ed. Munich 1960, 40.

we found no reliable indication that annalistic records, such as we find among other peoples, played any special part. There are indications of the compilation of annals in certain places (e.g. Samos), but we have no means of dating such works reliably. But it does deserve consideration that Charon of Lampsacus, who wrote after the Persian wars, in addition to two books of Persian history (Περσικά) wrote four books entitled Ὧραι Λαμψακηνῶν. This may have been a literary writing-up of old yearly chronicles (ὧροι). But Greek historiography certainly does not originate in the compilation of annals.[1]

A striking indication of the unity of cultural life in archaic Ionia is that the natural philosopher Anaximenes as well as the geographer Hecataeus could be reckoned pupils of Anaximander. All three came from Miletus, the centre of Ionian spiritual life: Hecataeus belonged to the old nobility of the city. At the time when he appears as the counsellor of the Ionian revolt, he must have been an old man. His proposal that the costly votive offerings of Croesus to Apollo Didymaeus should be used for the construction of a fleet expressed the rationalism that we shall find embodied in his work.

He widened his view of the world by travel. His Egyptian journeys are the best known to us, mainly through Herodotus' second book. We read there (143) the invaluable account of the meeting between two civilizations of different antiquity: Hecataeus with his sixteen generations of ancestors, going back to a god, was outdone by the Egyptian priest who could reckon his ancestors back through 345 generations!

Hecataeus drew a map of the world (γῆς περίοδος), in which he took over from Anaximander the ultimately oriental notion of a disc with Ocean flowing round its edge. As early as Herodotus (4. 36) the notion was ridiculed. The Mediterranean and Black Sea formed an east-west axis, the Nile and the Ister a north-south axis, thus dividing the world into four neat quadrants. We must suppose that the map was filled in with details taken from the various *periploi* or from Hecataeus' own experience. Thus here again we find speculation and empiricism side by side. The map was accompanied by a description of the earth in two books – a work later usually cited as his *Periegesis*. The method was a periplus of the Mediterranean and the Black Sea starting from Gibraltar, following the northern coast as far as Phasis and then returning by the southern coast. He sometimes included the hinterland in his purview also. Mostly one geographical fact followed another in dry sequence, but here and there detailed ethnographic information attested the keen interest of the Ionians in such matters. In Herodotus 2. 70–73, where various peculiar Egyptian customs are described, including crocodile-hunting, we seem to catch very clearly the tone of Hecataeus' simple, flowing narrative.[2]

---

[1] The question is handled with proper reserve by F. JACOBY, *Atthis*. Oxf. 1949, 176. H. STRASBURGER, *Saeculum* 5, 1954, 398.

[2] As an illustration of the style: K. LATTE, *Entretiens sur l'antiquité class.* 4. Vandœuvres-Genève 1956, 5, 1, seems to be right in rejecting a conjecture in JACOBY fr. 217 which would result in a relative clause. In the surviving fragments Hecataeus has only relative adverbs of place.

A wish to collect and digest all kinds of knowledge also led him to compile four books of genealogies (Γενεαλογίαι). He did not lead the way towards a rejection of the myths: rather he modified them here and there on rationalistic grounds. Cerberus he held to be a formidable serpent in Taenarum, which had been nicknamed the hound of hell; the cattle of Geryon, which Heracles drove back from the ends of the earth, are located on the Ambracian Gulf; the fifty daughters of Danaus are reduced to a more credible number – about twenty. Such rationalism as this destroyed the charm of the old myths without deriving any history from them. But we cannot deny that the same critical spirit, which is here wasting itself on unsuitable material, was capable later of inspiring effective historical research. Hecataeus' chronology was probably constructed on the same basis of generations which had already been established in the epics. He seems to have adopted a period of forty years as an average generation.[1]

Hecataeus and other forerunners of Herodotus appear generally as 'logographers' in histories of literature. Herodotus calls Hecataeus 'logopoios' (2. 143; 5. 36, 125), which means no more than that he wrote in prose instead of writing epic. Thucydides (1. 21) speaks of 'logographoi', contrasting their methods with his own: he means essentially Herodotus.

Hecataeus does not stand alone. Dionysius of Halicarnassus (de Thuc. 5) gives an imposing list of old writers of the history of particular lands and peoples. Charon of Lampsacus we have met before. Dionysius of Miletus, who wrote yet another Persica, is a very shadowy figure. About a generation later than Hecataeus came the hellenized Lydian Xanthus of Sardes, the son of one Candaules; he wrote a history of the Lydians (Λυδιακά) which went on being read for a long time and was excerpted in the Hellenistic period. The Μαγικά, on Persian religion, may have been part of this work or a separate book: we cannot tell.

We mentioned above (p. 106) Acusilaus of Argos, who made prose versions of epic poetry. He wrote shortly after Hecataeus, and like Pherecydes used the Ionic dialect which was the language of archaic prose. He seems to have taken his subjects from the Greek-speaking east, but his fragments contain nothing comparable with the powerful critical grasp of Hecataeus. A large fragment containing the story of Caeneus is preserved in a papyrus.[2]

Among those who came after Acusilaus was Pherecydes of Athens. The best that we can do towards dating him is to say that his work (written in Ionic) must be placed before the Peloponnesian War. At all events it is pre-classical in form. He made even greater use of the old epics; did not concern himself with cosmogony, but put in its place various tribal and national myths – particularly of course those of Athens. In the transmission his work was divided into ten books. Titles such as Theogony and the like cannot be trusted, since in this early period there was probably no such thing as a title to a book.[3] The main

---

[1] D. PRAKKEN, Studies in Greek genealogical Chronology. Lancaster 1943.

[2] Ox. Pap. 13, nr. 1611. F Gr Hist 2, 22; cf. L. DEUBNER, Sitzb. Ak. Heidelb. Phil.-hist. Kl. 1919/17.

[3] E. NACHMANSON, 'Der griech. Buchtitel'. Göteborgs, Högsk. Årsskr. 47, 1941.

lines of history for Pherecydes were provided by pedigrees of heroes, which gave him an opportunity for more of the syncretism which we saw already at work in the epics. Basically Pherecydes starts the line of development which leads through later handbooks of mythography up to the Pseudo-Apollodorus: indeed, until such handbooks came into existence, his work remained a basic source for all who concerned themselves with the old mythology.

Matter relevant to the beginnings of science will be found in the literature cited on early philosophy. See further: K. v. FRITZ, 'Der gemeinsame Ursprung der Geschichtsschreibung und der exakten Wissenschaft bei den Griechen' *Philosophia Naturalis* 2, 1952, 200. 376. B. SNELL, 'Gleichnis, Vergleich, Metapher, Analogie und die naturwissenschaftliche Begriffsbildung im Griechischen'. In *Die Entdeckung des Geistes*, 3rd ed. Hamburg 1955, 258 and 299 (cf. Eng. ed. p. 227). G. SARTON, *A History of Science. Ancient Science through the golden Age of Greece*. Lond. 1953. There is a useful collection of sources (in trans.) with good bibliog. on all the fields: M. R. COHEN – I. E. DRABKIN, *A Source Book in Greek Science*. New York 1948. A. REYMOND, *Histoire des sciences exactes et naturelles dans l'antiquité gréco-romaine*. 2nd ed. Paris 1955. M. CLAGETT, *Greek Science in Antiquity*. New York 1956. In the collective work *Histoire générale des sciences*. Paris 1957 the sciences other than medicine are treated by P. H. MICHEL, while L. BOURGEY deals with medicine. G. DE SANTILLANA, *The Origins of Scientific Thought. From Anaximander to Proclus*. Chicago Univ. Press. 1961. - Mathematics: B. L. VAN DER WAERDEN, *Erwachende Wissenschaft*. Basel 1956. O. NEUGEBAUER, *The Exact Sciences in Antiquity*. Princeton 1952. 2nd ed. Providence. Brown Un. Pr. 1957. J. E. HOFMANN, *Gesch. der Mathematik*. Sammlung Göschen 226. Berl. 1953. G. MARTIN, *Klassische Ontologie der Zahl*. Cologne 1956. O. BECKER, *Das mathematische Denken der Antike*. Göttingen 1957. CH. MUGLER, *Dictionnaire historique de la terminologie géométrique des Grecs*. Études et commentaires 28/29. Paris 1958/59. - Astronomy: H. BALSS, *Antike Astronomie* (with texts and trans.) Munich 1949. B. L. VAN DER WAERDEN, *Die Astronomie der Pythagoreer*. Amsterdam 1951. - Alcmeon: text in VS (24). L. A. STELLA, 'Importanza di Alcmeone nella storia del pensiero greco'. *Acc. d. Linc.* 6/8/4. 1939. On the connection between philosophy and early medicine: J. SCHUMACHER, *Die naturphilosophischen Grundlagen der Medizin*. Berl. 1940. ERNA LESKY, *Die Zeugungs- und Vererbungslehren der Antike*. Akad. Mainz. 1950. On the periplus: R. GÜNGERICH, *Die Küstenbeschreibung in der griech. Literatur*. Münster 1950. - Ethnography and geography: K. TRÜDINGER, *Studien zur Geschichte der griech.-röm. Ethnographie*. Diss. Basel 1918. J. O. THOMSON, *A History of Ancient Geography*. Cambr. 1948. E. H. BUNBURY, *A History of ancient Geography among the Greeks and Romans*. 2nd ed. 2 vols. 1960. Fragments of the early historians with commentary in F. JACOBY, *Die Fragmente der griech. Historiker*. I. Berl. 1923 (repr. with additions Leyden 1957). See also L. PEARSON, *Early Ionian Historians*. Oxf. 1939. G. NENCI, *Hecataei Milesii fragmenta*. Florence

1954. K. LATTE, 'Die Anfänge der griech. Geschichtsschreibung.' In: *Histoire et historiens dans l'antiquité. Entretiens sur l'antiquité class.* 4. Vandœuvres-Genève 1956, 3. J. B. BURY, *Ancient Greek Historians.* London 1958. GIAMPOLO BERNAGOZZI, *La storiografia greca dai logografi ad Erodoto.* Bologna 1961. On their style: H. FRÄNKEL, *Wege und Formen frühgriech. Denkens* 2nd ed. Munich 1960, 62. Full bibliography in *Fifty Years of Classical Scholarship.* Oxf. 1954, 177. A. HEPPERLE, 'Charon von Lampsakos.' *Festschr. Regenbogen.* Heidelb. 1956, 67. On Xanthus: H. DILLER, 'Zwei Erzählungen des Lyders X.' *Navicula Chilonensis* (Festschrift F. Jacoby). Leyden 1956, 66.

K Beginnings of Drama

I TRAGEDY

While the archaic period witnessed a vigorous intellectual life in many different spheres in the east and west of the Greek world, the mainland remained very quiet. But in fact developments were there taking place which led to the perfection of dramatic forms on Attic soil and to the creation of the basic conceptions of European drama. This was a process of vigorous growth which is unfortunately known to us neither through the survival of the works themselves nor yet by clear and comprehensible accounts. Consequently, ever since the age of the Alexandrian savants, the origins of tragedy have posed one of the most difficult and most violently disputed problems.[1]

Modern opinion has been divided on the *Poetics* of Aristotle. To scholars of an ethnological bent who come to the problem from the dances and mimicry of primitive vegetation-rites, his statements seem either false or trivial. But in recent years a reconciliation has been achieved. All the ethnological material has its value for what we may call the sub-structure of the drama.[2] This level includes particularly the mask as the device to effect that transformation which is the first requirement of any genuinely dramatic performance. Here also we find the phenomenon of possession, whereby the man who is trying to imitate daemonic powers imagines that he finds them within his own breast. All this is important, but we find it in many places and among many peoples. As a piece of pre-history it is to be kept distinct from that development which occurred on Greek soil, which there and only there led to the fulfilment of tragedy as a work of art, and which, despite all variations in subject matter, has determined its structure down to the present day.

When we look for the basic features of this development, we face the decisive question whether we are to follow Aristotle or to reject his testimony. There is no adequate rejoinder to the simple consideration that Aristotle was in infinitely closer contact with the things he discusses than we are, and that he certainly did

[1] Clear summary in GRANDE (*v. inf.*) 255.
[2] See the article under that title by K. T. PREUSS, *Vortr. d. Bibl. Warburg* 1927/28. Berl. 1930, 1. Material from the east in T. H. GASTER, *Thespis. Ritual, Myth and Drama in the Ancient Near East.* New York 1950. We should be very careful about assuming ritual as a previous stage of literary drama. DIETERICH and others are wrong in dragging in the Eleusinian mysteries in this connection.

not take any less pains to study these problems beforehand than he is known to have done with the *Politics*. The decisive question is whether the other indications can be combined with those of the *Poetics* to make a consistent and convincing picture. And, as we shall see, this is in fact the case. The element of theorizing is still quite big enough; but certainly in facing the problem we ought not to disregard or distort the ancient tradition.

In the fourth chapter (1449 a 9) Aristotle derives the drama as a whole from improvisation: the starting-point was with the 'precentors' of the dithyramb (οἱ ἐξάρχοντες τὸν διθύραμβον). The Greek word may signify the singers who began or introduced the singing and were thus distinguished from the chorus. We must think of Archilochus in this role when he prides himself on his ability to lead (ἐξάρξαι) the dithyramb even when his senses were reeling with wine (77 D.). Clearly Aristotle thought that the opposition of chorus and precentor provided the starting-point for the development of dramatic dialogue.[1]

The dithyramb – a word which has long defied accurate interpretation and is probably not Greek – was the song sung in the service of Dionysus. What we have of Bacchylides under this title (p. 204) shows an already developed artistic form, which was probably influenced in its turn by tragedy which had been by then established and partly developed. The history of the dithyramb is full of changes. We shall shortly have to speak of the process by which it became an art-form of great potentialities; and later, in connection with Euripides, we shall have to consider its most mature form, the late Attic dithyramb.

What makes the situation more complex is that Aristotle speaks also of another precursor of tragedy. It was once concerned, he says, with trivial subjects and composed in a jocular style; it only attained its full dignity when it transformed itself out of the 'satyricon'. Shortly afterwards we read that its metre was trochaic tetrameter before it was iambic; trochees fitted better with the 'satyrical' and dance-like character of the poetry. A serious difficulty seems to have been caused as early as Alexandrian times by the report that the inventor of the satyr-play was Pratinas, whose work comes after that of Thespis. This led to a peculiar Alexandrian theory of the origin of tragedy, differing from Aristotle's view: with this we shall shortly have to concern ourselves. But in reality there is no problem, if we rightly interpret Aristotle's 'satyricon'. He is not speaking of the developed satyr-play, but of an early forerunner of it. It was driven into the background by the rise of tragedy, and more and more absorbed by it; finally it would have fallen into oblivion, if Pratinas had not restored and reformed it. He restored the comical antics of the satyrs to their rightful place, and did it so effectively that, when the tetralogy was devised, the satyr-play had a regular position as the closing piece after the three tragedies.

Historical considerations then do not conflict with the Aristotelian view that satyr-drama was an original element of tragedy, and his view receives considerable support from another side. Within Greek poetry the various genres are clearly defined and rigidly separated. Where tragedy and comedy are concerned,

---

[1] The way in which the individuals are opposed to the group in the threnos in *Iliad* 24 is also of interest in establishing the meaning of this expression.

the closing speech in Plato's *Symposium* is a well-known testimony to this effect (223 d). The possibility that the same writer might compose comedy and tragedy, which is roundly denied in the *Republic* (395 a), is here entertained purely as a theoretical postulate. But the position of the satyr-play from the earliest times is quite different: it is always written by a tragedian. The two in fact spring from the same root.

Now how can the statements of the *Poetics* be reconciled, which give in one place the dithyramb, in another the satyr drama as the starting-point of tragedy? We must be grateful that the tradition, so miserly elsewhere, here gives us the point at which these two lines of development were united. Herodotus (1. 23) tells us that Arion, so far as anyone knew, was the first man to write a dithyramb, to name it, and to prese·it it in Corinth. Suidas goes into more detail, calling Arion the inventor of the tragic manner, and telling us that he was the first to train a chorus, to sing a dithyramb, to give a title to what the chorus sang, and to bring on satyrs speaking in metre.[1] This very late notice has been strikingly confirmed by a passage in Johannes Diaconus' commentary on Hermogenes,[2] where a statement that Arion presented the first tragic drama (τῆς τραγῳδίας πρῶτον δρᾶμα) is ascribed to the elegies of Solon.

Now it is quite obvious that Arion did not invent the ancient ritual hymn to Dionysus. His contribution must then be that he raised the dithyramb to an artistic form of choral lyric. The reports that this happened in the Corinth of Periander agrees well with what we otherwise know of the tyrant as having fostered the cult of Dionysus – a cult deeply rooted in popular life. The statement that Arion gave a name to what was sung by the chorus can hardly be taken otherwise than as meaning that he gave titles to his choral odes. Presumably then they had a narrative content: this squares well with the later history of this form (Bacchylides). But the most important point for our reconstruction of the prehistory of tragedy is that Arion had his dithyrambs performed by satyrs. The point at which dithyramb and satyr-drama converged is thus quite clearly marked, and the double origin assigned by the *Poetics* thus receives historical backing.

Arion may be reckoned one of the creative personalities on the path to tragedy as an artistic form, and it was not perhaps unjustified if the Peloponnesians contested with the Athenians the honour of claiming tragedy as a native growth.[3]

We have seen how integral a part is played in the early history of tragedy by the satyrs, those blood-brothers of all the various fertility-daemons of different countries. In consequence the interpretation of the word tragedy as 'goat-song' (τράγων ᾠδή) is still the most probable. It is of course rather troublesome that the satyrs or silens (as they are also called) on pots of the fifth century have horses'

---

[1] The unclear λέγοντας in Suidas cannot be taken literally. The chorus sang.

[2] Ed. H. RABE, *Rhein. Mus.* 63, 1908, 150.

[3] Aristot. *Poet.* 3. 1488 a 29. Pseudo-Plato, *Minos* 321 a (indirect). JOHANNES DIACONUS (see the previous note), who says that the controversy could be traced back to Charon of Lampsacus.

ears and tails, and that all attempts to find goat-satyrs from the Peloponnese have been unconvincing. The satyrs of plastic art, with goats' tails and ears, are Hellenistic, and show the influence of the Pan type. We cannot go into the details of this very complex question: it must be enough to say that on various grounds it is quite credible that satyrs even of the archaic period should have been described as goats. The father of the satyrs, Papposilenus, always wears a kind of knitted garment garnished with tufts of hair ($\mu\alpha\lambda\lambda\omega\tau\grave{o}s$ $\chi\iota\tau\acute{\omega}\nu$), which in his high-spirited sons appears in rudimentary form as a kind of furry loincloth surrounding the phallus. This feature, like the long beard on which every true-born satyr prided himself, is not proper to the horse, but to the goat. These satyrs are wild beasts, and are often so designated ($\theta\hat{\eta}\rho\epsilon s$).[1] Their sexual urges know no restraint, and it is not the most stupid of explanations when the Etymologicum Magnum (s.v. $\tau\rho\alpha\gamma\psi\delta\acute{\iota}\alpha$) derives the appellation of 'goats' from their devotion to the service of Aphrodite.

We should have to give up the preceding interpretation if E. Buschor[2] were right in his theory (partly anticipated by G. Löschcke) that the dancing daemons with fat bellies and buttocks whose antics form the subject of many archaic pot-paintings are the true and genuine satyrs. But they are nowhere directly so named, nor is there any other support for the theory, which involves some very complicated inferences. We cling to the old view which connects such dancers with the early history of comedy.[3]

The Hellenistic savants, who reckoned Pratinas as the inventor (in every sense) of the satyr-play, naturally could not accept tragedy simply as 'the song of the goats'. With their general interest in everything primitive and rustic, they derived tragedy from Attic village customs. Thus they at once took sides in the dispute between Attica and the Peloponnese about the origin of drama. 'Tragedy' they interpreted as 'the song at the sacrifice of a goat', or 'song competing for a goat as prize'. We find an echo of this Hellenistic theory in Horace's *Ars Poetica* (220). In consequence they made satyr-plays a later invention than tragedy.

Dithyramb and satyr-play are closely connected with the worship of Dionysus. The basic element of transformation came from the realm of a god who took a different and a deeper hold on men than the gods of the Homeric Olympus. But the outward features of tragedy also declared its Dionysiac origins. The principal occasion of tragic drama in Athens was the feast of the Great (or City) Dionysia, instituted by Pisistratus, in which tragedy occupied the days 11-13 of the month Elaphebolion (March–April). The feast was in honour of Dionysus Eleuthereus, whose ancient statue had been brought to Athens from Eleutherae on the Athenian-Boeotian border. His shrine in the city was at the southern slope of the Acropolis, where there stood for a thousand years the theatre of Dionysus[4] with its many changes in architectural design, including even a Roman adaptation for shows of wild beasts. The pan-Ionic Dionysus was

---

[1] *Ichn.* 141. 215 (113. 168 PAGE, *Greek Lit. Pap.* I).
[2] 'Satyrtänze und frühes Drama' (*v. inf.*).
[3] So also HERTER (*v.* p. 240), 13.   [4] PICKARD-CAMBRIDGE (*v. inf.*).

celebrated at the Lenaea in the month Gamelion (January–February). This was the festival of comedy, but from c. 432 onwards tragedy was also admitted to a limited degree:[1] two tragedies without a satyr-play instead of the complete tetralogy of the City Dionysia. There are Dionysiac features also in the dress of the players: the sleeved chiton and the cothurnus, which did not become a heavy, thick-soled boot until Hellenistic times – originally it was a soft, high-fastened shoe such as the god himself wore.

But however much in tragedy may be Dionysiac, one thing is generally not: that is the subject matter. 'Nothing to do with Dionysus', was a proverbial phrase among the ancients, and the various explanations offered of it show that the question exercised them also. Occasionally the birth of the god or attempts to oppose him (e.g. Lycurgus, Pentheus) provide the plot, but there is no evidence for a stage of development in which the content of tragedy was essentially Dionysiac. Thus the statements of Aristotle, while we do not reject them, leave us puzzled, and we have to supplement them with other information that can help us to understand the non-Dionysiac character of developed tragedy. Here again a single notice throws some light on rather complicated processes. Herodotus (5. 67) tells us of the religious innovations of Clisthenes of Sicyon, who was the maternal grandfather of the Athenian Clisthenes. Being at war with Argos, he resolved to put an end, if possible, to the cult of the Argive hero Adrastus in Sicyon. Adrastus had a heroon in the market-place and was honoured with tragic choruses (τραγικοῖσι χοροῖσι) referring to his unhappy destiny. Clisthenes now brought over from Thebes the cult of Melanippus, Adrastus' mortal enemy, and appointed feasts and sacrifices to him, but made over the choruses to Dionysus. There is much obscurity in detail. We have no means of deciding whether Herodotus meant tragic-choruses in our sense or whether the word meant to him simply 'goat-choruses'. But the essential fact is clear. We are dealing with another example of that religious policy pursued by the tyrants which in the sixth century so strongly forwarded the cult of Dionysus, the god of the peasants, the looser of care and grief, the great transformer.[2] Even though Herodotus tells us nothing about the content of the choruses which were thus transferred to the cult of Dionysus, it is clear that his report provides an example of that union of songs attached to hero-cults with the worship of Dionysus in a manner that decisively influenced the content of tragedy as it was then developing. Songs in the worship of heroes were sung in many places: usually they were laments for their death. This fact explains the considerable part played in tragedy by the *threnos*.

We have very uncertain information about an Epigenes of Sicyon, said to have been the first tragedian and to have had Thespis as the sixteenth (sometimes the second) in succession after him. We may reasonably suppose that he had something to do with the innovations of Clisthenes.

Both myth and tragedy were profoundly influenced by the effect which hero-cults had in making tales of the heroes the normal subject of tragedy. In

---

[1] On the date: C. F. RUSSO, *Mus. Helv.* 17, 1960, 165, 1.
[2] Dionysus was worshipped in Mycenaean times, as the Linear-B tablets show.

this way the myth, after its epic and choral-lyric phase, entered on its tragic phase in which poets made it the vehicle of ethical and religious problems.[1] Tragedy gained in return by having a type of subject which already lived in the consciousness of the people as a part of their own history, while at the same time it gave a distance and perspective to the matters treated which is an invariable postulate for the greatness of any work of art.

All that we have been able to reconstruct of the development of tragedy so far is concerned with choral singing. Now we have to consider that decisive step which led to the introduction of dialogue. We have had hitherto to find most of our early stages in the Peloponnese, but we now find ourselves once more on Attic soil. Attempts to trace dialogue back to an early Peloponnesian stage have been unconvincing: appearance of the so-called *alpha impurum* in dialogue metres is unable to support such a theory.[2]

Some scholars[3] have supposed that the spoken part originated from the choral ode by way of a sung dialogue. This theory, however, conflicts with the general differences in language and style between choral and spoken parts. A much better interpretation is that which supposes that the dialogue was an addition from outside, and in fact we have explicit testimony to support such a view. Themistius (*orat.* 26. 316 d) gives it as an opinion of Aristotle's that at an early stage only the chorus sang, and that the prologue and the speech (ῥῆσις) were added by Thespis. It is no longer fashionable to doubt the trustworthiness of Themistius. He paraphrased Aristotle, who obviously knew far more than he put into the *Poetics*.[4] Thus we come to a view which can lay every claim to internal probability: in the course of its development the choral ode came to include themes presupposing more and more knowledge on the part of the audience. It was an obvious step to prepare the hearers for what was coming by means of a prologue. Similarly a sequence of choral odes dealing with the various phases of a mythical narrative could be made possible by the simple device of bringing on a speaker between two odes. The next step was to have the narrator and the chorus-leader speaking to each other.

The conclusions regarding the development of the spoken part which have been drawn from the designation of the actor as *hypocrites* are wholly lacking in cogency. The interpretation of the word as 'answerer' is by no means as sure as one would infer from the confidence with which it is commonly advanced.[5]

---

[1] B. SNELL, 'Mythos und Wirklichkeit in der griech. Tragödie'. In: *Die Entdeckung des Geistes.* 3rd ed. Hamb. 1955 (Eng. ed. p. 90).

[2] E. BICKEL, 'Geistererscheinungen bei Aischylos'. *Rhein. Mus.* 91, 1942, 134. G. BJÖRCK, *Das Alpha Impurum und die tragische Kunstsprache.* Acta Soc. Upsaliensis 39 : 1, 1950.

[3] See especially W. KRANZ, *Stasimon.* Berl. 1933. My own reservations: *Phil. Woch.* 1937, 1404.

[4] 1449 a 29. 37; b 4.

[5] Cf. A. LESKY, 'Hypokrites'. *Studi in onore di U. E. Paoli.* Florence 1955, 469. The same position with some variations is taken up by H. KOLLER, 'Hypokrisis und Hypokrites'. *Mus. Helv.* 14, 1957, 100. H. SCHRECKENBERG, ΔΡΑΜΑ. Würzburg 1960, 11. The meaning 'answerer' is defended most recently by M. POHLENZ, *Herm.* 84, 1956, 69, 1 and G. F. ELSE, 'ΥΠΟΚΡΙΤΗΣ'. *Wien. Stud.* 72, 1959, 75. The latter defends the view which he proposed earlier (*Trans. Am. Phil. Ass.* 76, 1945, 1), that the term ὑποκριτής came into use first when

It cannot be squared with a fragment of Pindar (140 b), and such passages as Plato *Tim.* 72 b lend themselves more to the translation 'interpreter, explainer'.

Our researches have now brought us up against the name of the first writer of tragedy of whom we can form any notion – albeit a limited one. In the tradition there are two distinct views of Thespis discernible.[1] One makes him the great innovator, repeatedly styled the inventor of tragedy: he belongs in the Peripatetic picture of the development, with which the one we have outlined largely coincides. The other image is of the rustic Thespis, associated with simple village customs,[2] whose place in the Hellenistic theory of the rise of tragedy is owed wholly to his singing for a goat around the Attic villages. His coming from the Icarian deme (the modern Dionyso) could only assist the rise of such notions. The story of Icarius, who received the vine-stem from Dionysus and was murdered by drunken peasants, was dragged in constantly by Hellenistic writers on the origins of all kinds of festal customs. This was particularly emphasized in the *Erigone* of Eratosthenes, which dealt with the suicide of Icarius' daughter and the atonement for his murder. Even Thespis' famous cart – a household word ever since Horace (*Ars poet.* 276) – was explained as a folk-element in his drama. We have to think rather of the boat-cars of Dionysus or better of the carts full of merry-makers which drove around during the great Athenian spring festival.

We have at least one solid and important date in connection with Thespis. The Marmor Parium (ep. 43), in agreement with Suidas (s.v. Θέσπις) gives the 61st Olympiad (536/5 – 533/2) as the date when Thespis became the first to present a tragedy at the Greater Dionysia. That then was the time at which, under the influence of Pisistratus' wide-ranging innovations, tragedy became an integral part of official religious life. This important date can be made a little more precise, since the fourth year of this Olympiad can be excluded on the basis of the partially preserved name of the archon on the Marmor Parium. It is possible that there was a dramatic competition at the time of this first official presentation, but we have no knowledge of it.

We have one or two titles[3] and a few verses attributed to Thespis. Our pleasure in possessing them is diminished by our knowledge that the Peripatetic Aristoxenus (fr. 114 W) reproaches Heraclides Ponticus with having put tragedies of his own about under the name of Thespis.

According to Suidas Thespis at first painted his face with white lead, then later introduced the buckram mask. This cannot be literally true, since the mask belongs to the prehistory of drama, but it is quite conceivable that Thespis made innovations in this field and that these were associated with the introduction of masks for the actors.

---

the second actor was introduced. The way in which the Syracusan introduces and explains the following pantomime in Xenophon's *Symposium* (9. 2) illustrates the function which I think was the original one of the ὑποκριτής.

[1] E. TIÈCHE, *Thespis*. Leipz. 1933.

[2] On the 'Eratosthenic' theory see K. MEULI, *Mus. Helv.* 12, 1955, 226.

[3] Ἄθλα ἐπὶ Πελίᾳ ἢ Φόρβας, Ἱερεῖς, Ἠίθεοι, Πενθεύς.

Among the various inscriptional records[1] of festivals, which serve the function of official archives, we find a list of winners in the dramatic contests in Athens, covering both festivals and giving the poet and the comic actor in the sequence of their first victory. It is hard to say when the list started, but it was somewhere in the last decade of the sixth century, the first years of Athenian freedom. The extant remains of the list of victors shows us that Aeschylus had some ten predecessors. Only a few of these are in any way known to us.

Choerilus is still a very shadowy figure. Ancient lexicographers date his first presentation in the 64th Olympiad (i.e. the Dionysia of 523–520), and they make him compete with Aeschylus and Pratinas in the 70th Olympiad (499–496). This occasion remained in men's minds, since the wooden seats for the spectators collapsed. We have no reason to doubt these dates, of which the second attests the earliest known competition in tragedy. Choerilus' thirteen victories may also be taken from the records of performances (didascaliae). We confess ourselves sceptical of his 160 plays: the number could very easily have been corrupted. We know of a tragedy *Alope* dramatizing an Athenian local legend: Poseidon makes the heroine the mother of Hippothoon, after whom one of the phylae was named. The subject recurs in Euripides.

We are somewhat better acquainted with Phrynichus, son of Polyphrasmon. Suidas credits him with a dramatic victory in the 67th Olympiad, i.e. the Dionysia of 511–508, and it is likely that this victory was carefully recorded, since it was his first. The same includes the beginning of an alphabetical list of his pieces, showing many of the themes used in later tragedy. The *Egyptians* and *Daughters of Danaus* have the same titles as two of the plays of the Aeschylean trilogy from which the *Suppliants* only survives. Of his *Alcestis* we are told[2] that Euripides borrowed from it here and there. The *Women of Pleuron* was concerned with the Calydonian hunt and the fate of Meleager.

More importance attaches to those reports which tell us that Phrynichus also made contemporary history the material of his dramas. Herodotus (6. 21) relates that the *Capture of Miletus* (Μιλήτου ἅλωσις),[3] which aroused in the Athenians the most painful memories of the destruction of their kinsmen's city, brought the poet a fine of a thousand drachmae and a ban on the play itself. Miletus fell in 494, and it is likely that Phrynichus submitted the play to the archon of 493/92. This was Themistocles, and it can hardly be an accident that we have a second opportunity to connect him with the presentation of an historical drama by Phrynichus. In his life of Themistocles (5) Plutarch gives the text of a votive inscription dedicated by Themistocles to celebrate a tragic victory in 476. At this time he was choregus, and had to bear the costs of production and staging, while Phrynichus was the writer of the play. The title is

---

[1] PICKARD-CAMBRIDGE, *Festivals* (*v. inf.*), 103. We must not forget that here everything rests on the foundations laid by A. WILHELM in his *Urkunden dramatischer Aufführungen in Athen.* Vienna 1906.

[2] Schol. Dan. *Aen.* 4. 694. The resemblances seem to have been mostly in marginal scenes; cf. *Sitzb. Wien. Phil.-hist. Kl.* 203/2, 1925, 63. There is little to be gained from L. WEBER, Φρυνίχου ᾿Αλκῆστις. *Rhein. Mus.* 79, 1930, 35.

[3] G. FREYMUTH, 'Zur Μιλήτου ἅλωσις des Phrynichos'. *Phil.* 99, 1955, 51.

not given, but we may suspect that it was the *Phoenissae*, with Themistocles' great achievement, the victory of Salamis, as its subject. In the hypothesis to the *Persae* of Aeschylus we find a valuable piece of information about this play. In a book on Phrynichus Glaucus of Rhegium had said that the *Phoenissae* had a prologue spoken by a eunuch, who prepared the places for a meeting of the council of state and at the same time related the defeat of Xerxes. This defeat could only be Salamis, and despite all contrary suppositions[1] we can take it that the piece included a report on the battle and lamentation over the Persian defeat. It is hard to say in what character the Phoenician women of the chorus appeared. It has been suggested that they were widows of those slain in the sea-battle, or perhaps *hierodulae*. The councillors whose arrival the eunuch is expecting in the prologue were either mutes or a subsidiary chorus. In Suidas' list we find also a *Persae* with two alternative titles (Δίκαιοι ἢ Πέρσαι ἢ Σύνθωκοι). Obviously there is much confusion here, and we must leave it an open question whether we have here an alternative title for the *Phoenissae* or something quite different.

If we consider these two historical dramas of Phrynichus' together with Aeschylus' *Persae* of 472, we can see that the period provided abundant material for composing dramas of contemporary history. Pericles was the choregus for the *Persae*, which reminds us of the double connection of Themistocles with the works of Phrynichus. It seems quite possible that the occasional application of tragedy to contemporary history did not occur without influence from some leading statesman, who wanted either to warn the Athenians by recalling their past mistakes or to encourage them by recalling their great achievements. But we must never forget that for the Greeks of that time myth was a part of history: the distinction has for us a sharpness which it did not have for them.

Pratinas of Phlius has already been mentioned for his greatest achievement, that reform of the satyr-play in which he embodied the Doric spirit of his birthplace. From a formless harlequinade he turned it into an artistic form of enduring qualities. Suidas speaks of 32 satyr-plays and eighteen tragedies. The figures may be unreliable in detail, but with this poet the higher proportion of satyr-plays may well be accepted. If we date this reform about 515, our view is supported by the observations of Buschor,[2] who has found frequent reflections of satyr-plays in vase-paintings after 520.

Athenaeus (14. 617 b) quotes as from a *hyporchema* some verses of Pratinas in which a chorus of satyrs makes a delightfully animated attack on the flute music of a rival chorus. The god belongs to them alone; he is their master, whom they follow through woods and mountains with the Naiads: let the flute content itself with the role of a handmaiden to the art of song. A probable assumption, although recently disputed, is that these verses come from a satyr-play of Pratinas and reflect the battle that he fought for this form of drama.[3] It is

---

[1] F. MARX, 'Der Tragiker Phrynichos'. *Rhein. Mus.* 77, 1928, 337. F. STOESSL, 'Die Phoinissen des Phrynichos und die Perser des Aischylos'. *Mus. Helv.* 2, 1945, 148.

[2] 'Satyrtänze' (*v. inf.*), 83.

[3] Thus also E. ROOS, *Die tragische Orchestik im Zerrbild der altattischen Komödie*. Lund 1951, 209, with excellent bibliography but uncertain conclusions.

usually (and plausibly) assumed that there were two competing choirs. But A. M. Dale[1] now thinks in terms of one choir attacking its own flute-player. We may also feel sure that in the comparison of the flute with a toad (φρυνέος) there is a pun on the name of Phrynichus.

In the hypothesis of the *Seven against Thebes* we read that in that year (467) Aristias the son of Pratinas won second place with the *Perseus, Tantalus* and the satyr-play *The Wrestlers* (Παλαισταί) of his father. The passage has commonly been taken to mean that Aristias, who was himself a playwright and according to Pausanias (2. 13, 6) had a statue in the market-place at Phlius, took only the satyr-play from his father. But we now have to take the notice as referring to all three plays, since a recently discovered papyrus (*Ox. Pap.* 2256 fr. 2), speaking of the same victory, says: 'Second Aristias with tragedies of his father Pratinas.'

The surviving verses of Phrynichus show Ionisms. The poet, who was known for the soft sweetness of his odes, and who appears in Aristophanes as a handsome but rather dandified man,[2] is obviously Ionian in his outlook. He stands in contrast to Pratinas, the man from Phlius, the friend of satyrs, who in the verses already quoted makes his speakers call on Dionysus to hear their Dorian song. We have here an incomparable picture of those two elements and traditions juxtaposed whose synthesis was to give rise to Attic classical art. The Parthenon with its Ionic frieze and Doric columns is the impressive symbol of this synthesis.

A. W. PICKARD-CAMBRIDGE, *Dithyramb, Tragedy and Comedy.* Oxf. 1927. Id., *The Theatre of Dionysos.* Oxf. 1946 (good introduction to the Greek stage). Id., *The Dramatic Festivals of Athens.* Oxf. 1953. T. B. L. WEBSTER, *Greek Theatre Production*, Lond. 1956. AURELIO PERETTI, *Epirrema e tragedia.* Florence 1939. M. UNTERSTEINER, *Le origini della tragedia e del tragico.* Turin 1955. E. BUSCHOR, 'Satyrtänze und frühes Drama. *Sitzb. Ak. München Phil.-hist. Abt.* 1943, 5. F. BROMMER, *Satyrspiele* (2nd ed., corrected and enlarged) Berlin 1959. P. GUGGIS-BERG, *Das Satyrspiel.* Zürich 1947. C. DEL GRANDE, Τραγωιδία. Naples 1952. See also the sections in POHLENZ, LESKY and D. W. LUCAS, *Greek Tragic Poets.* 2nd ed. Lond. 1959. G. F. ELSE ('The Origin of Tragodia'. *Herm.* 85, 1957, 17) presents a radically different view from ours, rejecting the testimony of Aristotle and discounting any Dionysiac element in the origins. The beginnings are also discussed by T. B. L. WEBSTER, 'Some Thoughts on the Pre-History of Greek Drama'. *Inst. of Class. Stud. Univ. Lond. Bull.* Nr. 5, 1958: he seeks to provide new evidence for the theory that tragedy arose from rites in honour of the year-god (propounded first by J. HARRISON and G. MURRAY); cf. id., 'Die mykenische Vorgeschichte des griech. Dramas'. *Ant. u. Abendl.* 8, 1959, 7. G. THOMSON'S *Aeschylus and Athens.* 2nd ed. Lond. 1946, repr. 1950, has been translated into several languages (Germ., Berl. 1957). The first part tries to derive the beginnings

[1] *Words, Music and Dance.* Inaugural Lecture at Birkbeck College. London 1960, 11.

[2] Aristoph. *Vesp.* 220, *Av.* 750, *Thesm.* 164, *Ran.* 1298, where his style is contrasted with that of Aeschylus.

of tragedy from initiation ceremonies. κ. κεréνyi, 'Naissance et renaissance de la tragédie'. *Diogène* 28, 1959, 22 (now also in the volume *Streifzüge eines Hellenisten*. Zürich 1960), clings to the testimony of Aristotle and the Dionysiac connection, but works out the details otherwise than we have done. H. SCHRECKENBERG, ΔPAMA. *Vom Werden der griech. Tragödie aus dem Tanz*. Würzburg 1960, follows out through thick and thin the notion contained in his title. H. PATZER, *Die Anfänge der griech. Tragödie*. Wiesbaden 1962. RINSYO TAKEBE, *Wien. hum. Blätt.* 4, 1961, 25, draws some interesting parallels with the development of the Japanese Nō-drama.

2 COMEDY

In the fourth chapter of the *Poetics*, in the same sentence in which he traces tragedy back to the leaders of the dithyramb, Aristotle makes phallic songs the origin of comedy, and says that such processions with the phallus were a living custom in many cities in his own time. In the following chapter he declared that, unlike those of tragedy, the rudimentary stages of comedy remain obscure, since it was not until much later that the archons granted a chorus for comedy. This can be confirmed from epigraphical dramatic lists and other evidence. The true home of comedy was the Lenaea (Διονύσια τὰ ἐπὶ Ληναίῳ), the festival which the Archon Basileus celebrated in the month Gamelion to that Dionysus who has a longer-established cult in Athens than the Dionysus Eleuthereus of tragedy. If we want to explain the name of the feast, its connection with Bacchantes (λῆναι) is more convincing than that with winepresses (ληνοί).[1] It was long assumed that the festival was celebrated in the shrine of Dionysus 'in the swamps' (ἐν Λίμναις), a view supported by Hesychius (s.v. Λίμναι), but Pickard-Cambridge[2] has shown that there are arguments for assigning it to the Lenaion in the Agora.

Comedy did not become an officially sponsored feature of the Lenaea before the mid-fifth century – probably about 442. Provision was made for a contest not only of dramatists, but also of actors. Since the City Dionysia was by far the more elaborate festival, the presentation of comedies there became an official part of the cult much earlier, starting in 486. Contests for the comic actors were introduced later, between 329 and 312, whereas the tragic actors had had a competition and prizes at the City Dionysia since 449. The competition for comic actors, the basis of selection for the coming Dionysia, took place on the third day of the Anthesteria (February/March) which was called *Chytroi*. The practice was re-established by Lycurgus in the third quarter of the fourth century.[3]

This brief summary of the various relevant dates suggests that comedy was for a long time the realm of free improvisation. The name itself is a valuable indication of what it was at first. Aristotle (*Poet.* 3. 1448 a 37) rightly explains it as the song of a train of revellers (κῶμος), such as were formed above all when the

---

[1] On the so-called Lenaean vases see PICKARD-CAMBRIDGE, *Festivals* (v. p. 232), 27.
[2] Op. cit. 36.   [3] [Plut]. *Vit. dec. or.* 841 f.

service of Dionysus brought his followers together in wild festivity. But the false derivation from κώμη (=village), which Aristotle here rejects, and which was connected with the claims of the Peloponnesians to be the originators of comedy, has also a grain of truth in it.

We know nowadays of very widespread usages (particularly well described and attested by students of folklore) which are all connected with the pre-history of comedy as a literary form. In this field a great deal has been learned by the study of paintings and plastic art, without which philological research is very ineffective. We also owe much to ancient treatises on comedy,[1] of which several survive and give us valuable information side by side with much that is rather silly.

Starting with Aristotle, the first thing we hear of is processions with the phallus, accompanied by appropriate songs. The antics of Dicaeopolis in the *Acharnians* (263) are a kind of miniature of what went on at the country Dionysia (τὰ κατ᾽ ἀγροὺς Διονύσια). A fuller picture is given by Semos of Delos, a Hellenistic writer quoted by Athenaeus (14. 622). Unfortunately he does not tell us anything about the places in which he had met these customs, but there can be no doubt that they were widespread. The *phallophoroi* whom he describes may well be those of Sicyon. Garlanded with leaves and flowers, they were led by a youth with soot-blackened face wearing the phallus, and marched into the orchestra, into which observances of that kind had by then been transferred. Closely akin to these performers were the *ithyphalloi*, whose dress included masks representing drunkenness. Semos has very little to tell us about a third class of these maskers, the *autokabdaloi*. All these processions were accompanied by singing, and it is particularly noteworthy that the *phallophoroi* used to direct raillery and abuse towards individual members of the audience.

Our researches have now led us to the Greek carnival – a word which can justly be used if we trace all these customs back to their original source. There it was that expression was given to an abounding vitality and every conceivable rite was performed to stimulate young growth. Obscene raillery directed against the participants in the festival is a constant feature. We find it in a specialized form in the Attic spring-festival of the Anthesteria, from which these practices were taken over into the procession at the Lenaea. Clowns and jesters drove around in wagons and kept up a lively fire of abuse against the bystanders. The gross obscenity that characterized this humour has a ritual origin. Behind all the hearty laughter lay a belief (forgotten by later ages) in the apotropaic power of obscenity. The Fescennine verses sung at Roman weddings, the filthy jokes which assailed the triumphant general on the proudest journey of his life, are good illustrations of this belief. Thus we are able to see that the astounding obscenity of Aristophanes and with it the strong leaning of Old Comedy towards personal invective was rooted in ancient and still living usages.

A different view is presented by a seemingly Hellenistic theory[2] of the origin of comedy, based on κώμη=village. Peasants used to come by night into the city and sing insulting songs outside the houses of citizens who had used them

---

[1] Texts in KAIBEL (*v. inf.*); lists in KÖRTE (*v. inf.*) 1212.
[2] KAIBEL (*v. inf.*), 12. HERTER (*v. inf.*), 53. 135.

ill. The social benefits of this procedure were appreciated, and the peasants were told to repeat their performance in the theatre. They did so, but concealed their identity by smearing their faces with wine-lees. This is quite absurd: we have a theatre before there was any comedy, and the wine-lees as a substitute for a mask shows that the inventor of this theory took seriously the notion that *trygodia* was a name for comedy. In fact it is a facetious formation, punning on *tragoedia* and τρύξ=must or lees.[1] All this is very perverse, but when taken together with what Aristotle in his *Constitution of Naxos* (fr. 558) tells us about the rebuking of the wealthy Telestagoras, it does give us some insight into the problem. The Greeks had the same kind of popular justice which is known nowadays from the Italian *charivari*, as Usener[2] has taught us to understand it, to the *Haberfeldtreiben* of the Bavarian peasants. It is perfectly credible that the personal invective of comedy, the ἰαμβικὴ ἰδέα, derived its impetus from this quarter. The activities of begging parties also, like those who 'go a-gathering with the swallow',[3] were associated with abuse of people whom they met, and we can see from this how in common belief such abuse had a benfiecial effect.

Animals would often be led along with processions of this kind. This brings us to choruses of men in animal costume, which were once performed in Athens, according to the testimony of the vases.

What we have found out so far is all concerned with processions, dancing and singing of choruses, and in fact comedy begins with the chorus just as much as tragedy does. Its particular function, as we see it in developed form in the plays of Aristophanes, is the parabasis,[4] its march on to the stage singing verses of cheerful invective.

This basic element acquired additional features which soon postulate the use of actors. Of the two best-known of these elements one is the altercation (ἀγών). This is a type of scene which is traceable through the literature of many peoples and countries:[5] it occurs in many forms in Greek. Here, as with the parabasis, we find the first developed example in Aristophanes. Since in both cases these are found in epirrhematic syzygy (cf. p. 251) it is an easy inference that the agon developed in very close connection with the chorus. Possibly the evolution began as altercation between choruses or semichoruses.[6]

There is a clear distinction between the agon and the episodic scenes. These are much less closely connected with the chorus, and have repeatedly invited comparison with the adventures of Punch and Judy. Here again we are luckily able to form some conception of the contexts from which such scenes originally come. Athenaeus (14. 621 d) has preserved a description from the Laconian Sosibius of the Spartan *deikeliktai*, who acted in everyday language such scenes

---

[1] K. KERÉNYI, *Symb. Osl.* 36, 1960, 5 has shown good grounds for taking τρύξ as lees.

[2] 'Italische Volksjustiz'. *Kl. Schr.* 4. 356.

[3] Hesych. s.v. χελιδονισταί, and see the 35th sermon of St John Chrysostom, cf. RADER-MACHER (*v. inf.*), 7.

[4] On the meaning of the word see HERTER (*v. inf.*), 31. POHLENZ (*v. inf.*), 42, 18.

[5] RADERMACHER (*v. inf.*), 23.

[6] T. GELZER, 'Der epirrhematische Agon bei Aristophanes'. *Zet.* 23. Munich 1960, devotes an appendix (p. 187) to the origins of the epirrh. agon.

as the stealer of fruit or the travelling quack. In the *Anabasis* (6. 1) Xenophon describes various miming dances, including the so-called *karpaia* of Aeniae and Magnesia: one man represents a peasant sowing and driving his team, another a robber attacking him; they fight in rhythmic movement to the sound of the flute. Finally the victor drives off the loser together with the team. A third example is afforded by the Corinthian *crater* in the Louvre[1] which on one side depicts two men caught stealing wine and on the other their imprisonment in the stocks. The figures have fat bellies and buttocks and the phallus is larger than life-size. The actors are certainly human, as is shown by the group of a flute-player and dancer with obvious masks. These paunchy figures represent daemons of fertility. Like the satyrs, they embody to ancient Greek eyes the growing and fertilizing forces of nature.

Our evidence has led us largely onto Dorian soil, partly supporting the claims of the Dorians in Aristotle (*Poet.* 3. 1448 a). We may add further the Megarian farce, whose obscenity, compared with their own work, was often remarked on by Attic comedians – hardly with perfect justice. The influence which this Megarian improvised drama supposedly exerted on Attic comedy seems to have been embodied by ancient theory in the person of Susarion, a poet of whom we otherwise know nothing. The Dorian farce was probably a drama of stock figures much more than the political comedy of Athens. We know the names of two of them – Maeson and Tettix, the cook[2] and his assistant. Another offshoot from this Dorian stem was the 'phlyax farce'[3] of lower Italy, which later (c. 300 B.C.) was given a sort of literary existence by Rhinthon of Syracuse as *Hilarotragodia*. There are few fragments, but a great number of phlyax pots, which mostly depict travestied myths. The well-stuffed paunches and posteriors of these figures, together with the use of the phallus, make them obviously akin to the paunchy figures which we saw on the Corinthian *crater*. It must be admitted that the great confidence with which it used to be assumed that a strong Doric element had gone into the making of Attic comedy has recently been shaken somewhat. The difficulty is mainly that we have no material to date Doric farce earlier than Attic comedy.[4] The possibility of influence is not thereby ruled out, but in general one must approve of the modern tendency to interpret Athenian comedy as a native growth.

Alfred Körte has put forward a theory of the origin of Attic comedy which has received much attention.[5] He thinks that the indigenous Attic chorus which

[1] M. BIEBER, *History of the Greek and Roman Theater*. Princeton 1939, fig. 84 f. Bibliography in HERTER (*v. inf.*), note 33 f.

[2] On this personage see A. GIANNINI, 'La figura del cuoco nella commedia greca'. *Acme* 13, 1962, 137.

[3] L. RADERMACHER, 'Zur Geschichte der griech. Komödie'. *Sitzb. Ak. Wien. Phil.-hist. Kl.* 202/1, 1924. Bieber op. cit. 258.

[4] L. BREITHOLZ, *Die dorische Farce im griech. Mutterland vor dem 5. Jahrhundert. Hypothese oder Realität?* Stockholm 1960. His scepticism is shared by T. B. L. WEBSTER, *Gnom.* 33, 1961, 452.

[5] E.g. *RE* 11, 1921, 1221. The opposite views: BUSCHOR (*v. inf.*) and HERTER (*v. inf.*). KÖRTE's theory is supported by POHLENZ (*v. inf.*) and by T. B. L. WEBSTER, *Wien. Stud.* 69, 1956, 110.

performed various mumming dances, usually in animal costume, received the addition of actors who came from the Peloponnese, bringing with them the dress of the pot-bellied Dionysiac figures. Recent researches have thrown doubts on this theory. Buschor has been able to produce from Attica representations of such dancers from the first half of the sixth century, and we must face the question whether such representations do not have a genuine Attic substratum. Herter has objected to the over-sharp division between chorus and actors in comedy. We have in fact to consider the possibility that the paunchy figures belonged to the chorus as dancers. On the other hand, simple scenes are found represented in the dance even nowadays: in the ring dances of Alpine countries we still find Sosibius' itinerant quack, now working as a dentist. Xenophon's account also attests the linking of such primitive dramatization with the dancing of a chorus. The difficulty of deciding whether the costume of the actor had already been in use in the chorus is heightened by our ignorance of the chorus' costume in Attic comedy. From *Plutus* 295 we learn only that the chorus sometimes wore the phallus, which could hardly be combined with the usual animal masquerade. In general we should imagine the costume of the chorus as brightly coloured and capable of easy change. The chorus may sometimes have been attired as phallic pot-bellied dancers: with our defective knowledge we can neither affirm nor deny it. As for the comic actor, the pots and terra-cottas make it plain that he normally wore the grotesque padding called the *somation* and had the phallus. It is impossible to say whether this costume had its origin in the ithyphallic choruses of the Athenian comic stage, as Herter thinks: but certainly in the last resort it goes back to the Peloponnese and thus to a Dorian origin. This supports Körte's thesis, but the limitations of our knowledge call for great caution.

The elements out of which Attic comedy grew are rather loosely linked together even in their classic exponent Aristophanes. In the archaic period there was no unifying treatment at all: only the joyous spirit of the Dionysia tied together the heterogeneous parts. The development which led to unitary treatment is connected by Aristotle (*Poet.* 5. 1449 b) with the names of the Sicilian poets Epicharmus and Phormis, who are supposed to have influenced Attic comedy. We can lay stronger emphasis on the native Athenian contribution than he does, while not excluding Sicilian influence.[1]

In another passage (1448 a 33) Aristotle says that Epicharmus lived a good while before Chionides and Magnes. Chionides won the victory at the first official contest in comedy at the City Dionysia in 486. One of the eleven victories of Magnes is dated to the Dionysia of 472. Thus the beginning of Epicharmus' activity is to be put in the sixth century.[2] However, he was famed

---

[1] Influence from this quarter is posited by B. GENTILI, *Gnom.* 33, 1961, 338, against E. WÜST, *Rhein. Mus.* 93, 1950, 337.

[2] T. B. L. WEBSTER, *Gnom.* 33, 1961, 453, gives up the dating of Epicharmus before Chionides and Magnes. But if we suppose that he lived from about 550–460, we need not sacrifice any of the various data. B. GENTILI, *Gnom.* 33, 1961, 338, also supposes a Sicilian comedy which had attained some development by the end of the sixth century.

in antiquity for his long life, and survived until the time of Hiero, with whom he is connected in many anecdotes. Epicharmus (fr. 88 K.) speaks very respectfully of a predecessor, Aristoxenes of Selinus, of whom we know practically nothing. But his coming from a Megarian colony squares well with our notices of Doric farce in Megara, and may not be accidental.

It is hard to see what his main features were and to assign them a place in the development. The first difficulty is that he is named by Aristotle and others as contributing to the development of comedy, yet his plays are not referred to as comedies, but as dramas (δράματα). Thirty-seven titles are known to us, and together with the few fragments they point to great variety in his dramatic production. Travesties of myths seem to play an important part: we saw that this material recurred in the phlyax farces. In both Heracles is a favourite figure: a true Dorian Heracles, a clumsy bull of a man, who displays superhuman powers also in eating, drinking and wenching. This is brought out very clearly in the *Marriage of Hebe* (˝Ηβας γάμος)[1] with its lists of delicacies and in the *Busiris*, where an astonished onlooker describes the hero's noisy enjoyment of his victuals. *Heracles' Journey to fetch the Girdle of Hippolyte* (Ἡρακλῆς ὁ ἐπὶ τὴν ζωστῆρα) and *Heracles' Visit to Pholus* (Ἡρακλῆς ὁ παρὰ Φόλῳ) occur among the titles. Epicharmus was fond of bringing Odysseus onto the stage. Among his various adventures his spying expedition into Troy was made the subject of a happy comedy (Ὀδυσσεὺς αὐτόμολος), in which the crafty hero tries to wriggle out of the difficult task. This guess at the subject matter has been rather shaken by the new papyri. The view hitherto current, propounded by Kaibel, was built mainly on the verses of a papyrus in Vienna (fr. 99 K. 50 Oliv.) which were construed as a soliloquy of Odysseus in anxious reflection. But now *Pap. Ox.* 25, 1959, 2429, with seven fragments of a commentary on the play, shows that the verses were in fact part of a dialogue. B. Gentili[2] thinks that it may be a conversation of Odysseus with a companion, possibly Diomede, in which a plausible story is being devised for the Achaeans to explain the failure of the undertaking.

The new Epicharmus papyri include (in *Pap. Ox.* 25, 1959, 2426) the remains of a catalogue of his plays. The list seems from the fragments to have been in trimeters, which reminds us of Apollodorus of Athens, who drew up his *Chronica* in verse. We may suspect that the same man was the author or the source of the commentary mentioned above.

The fragments of this catalogue give us a variant form of a title already known (Προμαθεὺς ἢ Πύρρα) and also an Ὀδυσσεὺς ναυαγός (the restoration seems fairly certain). Another new item is a Μήδεια; the only comedies of this title previously known were by Dinolochus of Syracuse or Agrigentum (a poet in the tradition of Epicharmus) and Rhinthon of the *Hilarotragodia*.

Pap. Ox. 25, 1959, 2427 has part of the *Prometheus or Pyrrha* with the remains of a dialogue between Pyrrha and a partner, presumably Deucalion, concerned with the ark which was to save them in the flood. This rekindled an old prob-

---

[1] Among the new papyri those fragments collected under *Ox. Pap.* 25, 1959, 2427 contain one (fr. 27) that may be from the ˝Ηβας γάμος, although the Μοῦσαι can also stake a claim to it.   [2] *Gnom.* 33, 1961, 336.

lem: Kaibel¹ was the first to conclude from the *Amycus* that Epicharmus used three actors. Lobel, who has edited the papyrus, and Gentili want to draw the same conclusion from the fragment of the *Pyrrha*. But Webster has made a tentative reconstruction of the very fragmentary passage which avoids any such inference. We are in the dark here, since there is no clear indication anywhere that Epicharmus could not have used more actors. Epicharmus was also a keen observer of everyday life. It is extremely interesting to know that he used stock characters which are familiar to us from the later development of Attic comedy, as the parasite in *Hope, or Riches* (’Ελπὶs ἤ Πλοῦτοs) and the rustic ninny (’Αγρω-στῖνοs). We find also the altercation, which we met as one of the primitive constituents of Attic comedy. One piece is entitled *Earth and Sea* (Γᾶ καὶ Θάλασσα), and another *Mr Argument and his Wife* (Λόγοs καὶ Λογίνα), names which remind us of the contest between the just and the unjust argument in Aristophanes' *Clouds*. There is no indication of personal invective, but the fragments are exceedingly varied. Side by side with ribald portrayals of Heracles (which, however, fall a great deal short of the obscenity of Attic comedy) we find echoes of the epics; then again Heraclitus' doctrine of universal flux is used for an amusing story of a debtor and creditor each trying to cheat the other by maintaining that they are not the same men they were yesterday. Sometimes (e.g. fr. 170) one almost has the feeling of being at a Platonic dialogue. Plato in fact had a very high opinion of Epicharmus (*Theaet.* 152 e). His pieces are particularly rich in concise apophthegms: like Menander's, his were made into collections, and naturally this opened the door to large-scale forgery.

We can only understand this many-sidedness if we think of the dramas of Epicharmus, like the comedies of Aristophanes, as works that make many presuppositions of their audience. They borrowed a great deal from Doric popular farces, much also from the intellectual movements of their time. Above all, they were rich in that mimic element which had its especial home in the Greek west, certainly not without influence from Italy.

In their formal aspects too the fragments are very varied. Doric drama made use of the trimeter and trochaic tetrameter of the Ionian iambos. Here the fragments show a freedom which Attic comedy denied itself in this metre: dactyls are often found in the first five places. But two pieces, the *Dancers* (Χορεύοντεs) and the *Victory Celebration* (’Επινίκιοs), were entirely written in anapaests. This brings us to an old problem. We find the language of actors well developed in Epicharmus long before the Attic writers. Whether there were three actors is disputed, as we have seen. But did these plays have a chorus? Not normally, it would seem; but titles such as *The Dancers*, the use of anapaests, and the probability that in *The Sirens* these ladies served as a chorus playing opposite Odysseus have made scholars more cautious and less ready to deny that Sicilian comedy ever used a chorus.²

¹ KAIBEL, *RE* 6, 1907, 37. GENTILI, *Gnom.* 33, 1961, 334. WEBSTER, *Serta Philologica Aenipontana*. Innsbruck 1961, 88.

² Cf. HERTER (*v. inf.*), 57. 176. Titles suggesting use of a chorus: *Choreuontes, Epinicius, Sirenes, Musae, Bacchae, Comastae, Dionysi, Persae, Troiani.* Those who deny the chorus rest

We can only spare a glance at the continuation and development of the mimic elements in Epicharmus in the hands of Sophron, whose mimes Plato kept under his pillow. Like Epicharmus, Sophron worked in Syracuse: he flourished about the middle of the fifth century. Of his 'mimes of men' and 'mimes of women' we can only mention *The Women who Said They would Drive out the Goddess* (Γυναῖκες αἳ τὰν θεὸν φαντὶ ἐξελᾶν).[1] We shall meet Sophron again as a model for Theocritus, and in other connections we shall be able to speak of the very long-lasting influence of these realistic prose portrayals of everyday life.

A. KÖRTE, *RE* 11, 1921, 1207. H. HERTER, *Vom dionysischen Tanz zum komischen Spiel.* Iserlohn 1947. M. POHLENZ, 'Die Entstehung der attischen Komödie'. *Nachr. Ak. Gött. Phil.-hist. Kl.* 1949, 31. L. RADERMACHER, *Aristophanes' Frösche.* 2nd ed., by W. KRAUS. *Sitzb. Oest. Ak. Phil.-hist. Kl.* 198-4, 1954. T. B. L. WEBSTER, *Greek Theatre Production.* London 1956. – The ancient treatises on comedy and the fragments of Epicharmus and Sophron: G. KAIBEL, *Com. Graec. Frag.* I/1. Berl. 1899 (repr. Berl. 1958). Epicharmus: VS 23. A. OLIVIERI, *Frammenti della comm. greca e del mimo nella Sicilia e nella Magna Grecia.* 1. *Framm. della comm. dorica siciliana.* 2nd ed. Naples 1946. 2 and 3: *Framm. della commedia fliacica. Framm. del mimo siciliano.* 2nd ed. Naples 1947. Pseudo-Epicharmus: J. U. POWELL, *Collectanea Alexandrina.* Oxf. 1925, 219. The new texts: *Pap. Ox.* 25, 1959, 2426-2429. 2428 is probably Doric comedy, but cannot be certainly assigned to Epicharmus. On these papyri see B. GENTILI in *Gnom.* 33, 1961, 332. T. B. L. WEBSTER, 'Some Notes on the New Epicharmus'. *Serta Philologica Aenipontana.* Innsbruck 1961, 85. E. SIEGMANN, *Lit. griech. Texte der Heidelberger Papyrussammlung.* Heidelb. 1956, ascribes Pap. Heidelb. 181 to a comedy *Heracles* by Epicharmus.

on an *argumentum ex silentio*: those who affirm it do so without evidence. In consequence certainty seems not likely to be attained. T. B. L. WEBSTER in his study of the new Epicharmus fragments (*v. inf.*) thinks it possible that the poet developed 'from the anapaestic recitative ballet to the spoken iambic dialogue'.

[1] A papyrus fragment with bibliog. in GOW, Theocritus 2. Cambr. 1950, 34. PAGE, *Greek Literary Papyri.* Lond. 1950, 328. A small fragment with Doric prose: *Pap. Soc. It.* 14, 1957, 1387.

CHAPTER V

The Flowering of the Greek City State

A Beginning and Culmination of the Classical Period

I AESCHYLUS

The great classical age of Athens is bounded by two wars. The Peloponnesian war did not only end the political supremacy of Athens; it brought the collapse of the inner sources of strength which had powered the Periclean age. And the unchaining of this strength, after a long period of gradual ripening, had been the work of the heroic struggle which the Greek people had to wage for its political and cultural existence.

Before the battle of Marathon – so the legend has it – the Athenian messenger sent to implore Spartan aid was returning unsuccessful. As he toiled through the lonely Parthenion range, Pan appeared to him, promising help and friendship to Athens. In the battle a figure in a peasant's smock was seen slaying Persians – the hero Echetlus, so named from the ploughtail which grew from the soil of his birthplace. When all was in the balance at Salamis, a supernatural light shone over Eleusis, home of the mysteries; and from Aegina armed and gigantic forms stretched out their hands over the Athenian ships. Herodotus (VIII 109) makes Themistocles express what was in every mind after the victory: 'It is not we who have wrought this, but the gods and heroes.'

This was the age that moulded Aeschylus. Pausanias first (I. 14, 5) and many since have noted how significantly the epitaph which Aeschylus wrote for himself makes no mention of his writings, but only of his having fought against the Persians. He was at Marathon, where his brother Cynegirus fell, at Salamis, and in other lesser battles of the Persian war.

In the same passage of Herodotus Themistocles goes on to say that the gods helped the Greeks because they were unwilling that one man should rule both Europe and Asia – a man of sinful ambition, who had set himself up against the gods and the elements. There are many connecting links between Herodotus and Aeschylus, and the words of the victor of Salamis chime in well with the spirit of the great dramatist. His work is not full of pride and jubilation over the victory, nor yet of delight in the clash of arms, but of the profound emotion of one who has seen the working of Justice in the historical process. There is evidence much earlier of the central position which the concept of justice occupied in Greek thought: Aeschylus comes at one of the climacterics of its development. Justice, which he had seen in action in the most violent scenes of his life, appeared to him as an ever-present divine power.

The attempt has repeatedly been made to contrast in Aeschylus the religious thinker and the poet, or the poet and the theologian. With Aeschylus as with Sophocles this procedure stems from a fundamental error: it destroys a unity, to understand which is to understand the works themselves.

Aeschylus was born in 525/4, the son of a well-do-to land-owner called Euphorion in Eleusis.[1] We have no evidence for the view that the great mysteries of his native place had any influence on his mental development. The sphere of the mysteries, in which, according to Aristotle (fr. 15), teaching was less stressed than self-surrender, is to be sharply distinguished from that of tragedy, whose object is ultimately λόγον διδόναι, to describe and explain the position of man in the universe. There is more reason to believe the story (fairly well attested) that Aeschylus was put on trial for impiety as having divulged the mysteries, but was acquitted as having given offence unwittingly, without in fact knowing them.

He began to compete in tragedy at an early age; we have already (p. 230) mentioned the contest of the 70th Olympiad (499/496) in which he competed against Pratinas and Choerilus. His first victory is given by the Marmor Parium as 484. Twelve more were to follow. The figure of 28 given by Suidas, assuming the transmission to be correct, may be explained by supposing posthumous presentations to be included.

We have no knowledge of the motives which impelled the poet in the prime of his life to go to Sicily and the court of King Hiero. The ancients amused themselves with suppositions, but in fact no special explanation is needed to tell why the most distinguished poet of his age should have accepted an invitation to the court of a great ruler.[2] Very probably he gave a second performance there of the Persae, which had brought him victory at Athens in 472. We may well think that this was a very suitable piece for the court of Hiero, who wielded the sword for the western Greeks. The king was particularly concerned for his new foundation, the city of Aetna, which was founded in 476–475; although it was not until final victory over his enemies in 470 that Hiero established his son Dinomenes there as king. It was then that Pindar lauded the young state in the poem which we now call the First Pythian, and that Aeschylus composed his Aetnae[3] to celebrate the occasion. A papyrus fragment (Oxyrh. 2257, 1) gives us the end of a hypothesis which has been very plausibly referred to this play. The possibility of its belonging to the spurious drama of this name, which we find in the manuscript catalogue, is very slight. It is very striking that the play is said to have been divided into five parts, each of which had a different setting, only the first and third being in Aetna. One of the most remarkable of the new Aeschylus fragments brings in Dike, coming among men at Zeus' command,

---

[1] Biographical material in WILAMOWITZ' larger ed. The MS. life probably goes back in essentials to the life by Chamaeleon, early 3rd cent. B.C.

[2] On Aeschylus' connections with Sicily: M. BOCK, 'Aischylos und Akragas'. Gymn. 65, 1948, 402.

[3] The transmission suggests either Αἶτναι or Αἰτναῖαι, but cf. POHLENZ 2,200. On the new papyri: E. FRAENKEL, 'Vermutungen zum Aetna-Festspiel des Aesch.'. Eranos 52, 1954, 61.

to lead them to wealth and happiness. It is difficult to resist Eduard Fraenkel's conjecture that this verse came from the *Aetnae*. If this is so, the *morceau d'occasion* must have been ennobled by Aeschylus' religious philosophy of Zeus and Dike.

Shortly after, Aeschylus was in Athens again, since in 468 he was beaten for first place by Sophocles. The next year, however, he was victorious with the Theban trilogy, and in 458 again with the *Oresteia*. We do not know why he returned again to Sicily. A passage in the *Frogs* of Aristophanes (v. 807) gives us at least a suggestion: he was disgusted with the Athenian public! He died in Gela in 456–455, where his tomb became a place of pious pilgrimage for the servants of the tragic Muse. The Athenians honoured his memory with a singular law which permitted anyone who so wished to enter for the dramatic contest with plays of Aeschylus. His finest monument, however, is the *Frogs* of Aristophanes. This comedy of literary criticism has all the fanciful bizarrerie of Aristophanic humour; but beneath the grotesque trappings we see the outlines of a great portrait, which is worth more to us in forming a picture of Aeschylus than any collection of anecdotes.

Greek art in its heyday never sought to deny that it was craftsmanship raised to its highest and noblest form. Artistic ability in Athens often ran in families, and the tragedians are no bad example. Both the sons of Aeschylus, Euaeon and Euphorion, wrote tragedies. The latter, according to the hypothesis of the *Medea*, defeated both Euripides and Sophocles in 431. A nephew named Philocles was also a tragedian: according to the hypothesis to the *Oedipus Rex* his play was preferred to this masterpiece. From him the inheritance of genius fell on Morsimus and Astydamas, and on their sons Astydamas II and Philocles II, all four tragic writers.

The manuscript catalogue of Aeschylus' plays gives us 73 titles, from which we must exclude the spurious *Women of Etna*. We know of seven more, bringing the number to 79. Suidas speaks of 90. From all this profusion we have only seven tragedies, which we may reasonably assume to be those which found refuge in the schools of the Antonine period, when living interest in classical tragedy was no more.

It has been long known that the transmission has grudged us any early work of Sophocles and Euripides. With Aeschylus, it was thought, we were better off: the *Supplices* took us back before Salamis; perhaps we could even put it before Marathon. This confident theory has been badly shaken by a new papyrus text (*Oxyrh. Pap.* 2256, 3) – the remains of a didascalia in which the trilogy containing the *Supplices* is mentioned together with plays of Sophocles.[1] Now we know that Sophocles' first victory was in 468, and was also his first presentation. The papyrus says that Aeschylus was victorious; thus the *Supplices* cannot have been presented in 468 or earlier, nor yet in the next year, in which Aeschylus won with the Theban trilogy. Hence we are brought down very late:

[1] A. LESKY, 'Die Datierung der Hiketiden und der Tragiker Mesatos'. *Herm.* 82, 1954, 1. Bibliog.: *AfdA* 7, 1954, 135 and 12, 1959, 10, where one can gain an idea of the controversy. See also E. A. WOLFF, 'The date of Aeschylus' Danaid Tetralogy'. *Eranos* 56, 1958, 119; 57, 1959, 6.

indeed, if we can accept that it is necessary to complete the existing traces of letters by filling in the name of Archedemides, archon in 463, we must date the play in that year. Naturally, so late a dating was not immediately acceptable. The *Supplices* seemed too archaic for 463, and the period for developing to the masterly *Oresteia* of 458 far too short. But the supposition that this was a second presentation of the piece does not agree with the wording of the didascalia; while the alternative supposition that Aeschylus let the piece lie and did not present it until long after its composition, is an extension of modern literary practice to antiquity. Hence there is a growing willingness to accept the express testimony of the papyrus rather than pay so high a price to maintain a date which rests on the doubtful assumption that artistic development proceeds uniformly in a straight line. In any case, a glance at the *Seven against Thebes* of 467 will destroy the doubts about accepting the new date of the *Supplices*. The seven pairs of set speeches in the Theban drama are as archaic as anything in the surviving tragedies.

The consequences of the new dating are far-reaching. If we set aside the doubtful dating of the *Prometheus*, the oldest surviving play is the *Persae* of 472. Since we know that Aeschylus began to compete in the early 490's, it follows that his early work is a closed book to us, and we first meet him when he is over fifty. Hence we must suppose his early tragedies to have been very simple, and the extent of his development from the early to the mature period to have been far wider than was supposed when the *Supplices* was dated very early. 'The creator of tragedy' is the title given to him by Gilbert Murray in his fine work on Aeschylus; and our new knowledge underlines it. At the outset of his career Aeschylus had only one actor at his disposal, and it was a great advance when he added a second. This innovation is attributed to him by Aristotle (*Poet.* 1449 a 16), who says that he lessened the role of the chorus and made dialogue the dominating element. It was a long road that led from the choric song with speeches here and there to the marvellous trilogy-structure of the *Oresteia*. The new discovery allows us to be more confident in declaring that the thematic relationship of the components of a trilogy was not an original feature, but was the crowning touch of the new artistry that Aeschylus put into the shaping of tragedy.[1] The evidence for this view is found in the play which now has to rank as the oldest of those surviving.

In 472 Aeschylus was victorious with a tetralogy made up of the tragedies *Persae*, *Phineus* and *Glaucus Potnieus* and the satyr-play *Prometheus Pyrcaeus*. We must suppose the *Phineus* to have had as its theme the episode in the Argonautica in which the blind king is rescued from the persecution of the Harpies. The *Glaucus Potnieus*, like the *Glaucus Pontius* (a quite different play), is one of those for which we now have some fragments recently discovered; but they do not take us beyond the barest outline of the subject matter – the death of Glaucus, torn apart by his own horses. For the *Prometheus Pyrcaeus*, which shows the fire-bringer among the satyrs, we have a valuable access of knowledge.

---

[1] On the problem as it used to be: P. WIESMANN, *Das Problem der tragischen Tetralogie*. Zürich 1929.

There can be little doubt that a papyrus fragment[1] with parts of a song sung by satyrs in praise of fire comes from this piece.

It is palpably vain to try to establish any unity of subject matter between this satyr play and the rest of the tetralogy; and the attempts to find a thematic connection between the three tragedies are so at variance one with another that they only underline the absence of any such link. The other surviving plays were all parts of trilogies linked by a common theme: many of these[2] are known to us by name as the work of Aeschylus. Can it be pure accident that the tragedies with the earliest known date should refuse to be linked by any such unity? It would be rash to conclude that by 472 Aeschylus had not invented the thematic trilogy; but we can at least feel sure that the lack of any connection between these plays points to a time when no thematic link was demanded.

We have already spoken of the *Phoenissae* of Phrynichus, presented in 476. We proceed now from the assumption there made that the Persian defeat at Salamis was the theme of the earlier drama also. At once a considerable advance in dramatic technique is visible: in Phrynichus the defeat is narrated by the eunuch who appears as prologue, but in Aeschylus the news of disaster is brought in the course of the action. Not only does this impart more movement to the play, but it also enables Aeschylus to present scenes full of gloomy foreboding under an ever more threatening and stormy sky – a technique of which the fullest mastery was to be shown in the *Agamemnon*.

On the other hand, the influence of the earlier drama can be seen here and there. Aeschylus begins with the entry of the chorus, made up of Persian royal councillors. At the end of the parodos a council is proposed, but is delayed by the entry of the queen mother, and never takes place. Further, the nature of the 'old building' (v. 141 στέγος ἀρχαῖον) in which the discussion will take place is quite uncertain. Probably these anomalies come from the influence of Phrynichus' *Phoenissae*, in which the eunuch at the beginning sets out stools for the councillors. Such survivals are not significant: what is important is that we recognize in the structure an extended climax, beginning with the gloomy hints of the opening chorus, going through the Atossa scene with the account of her dream, the messenger's speech describing the battle (the finest description of Salamis) and the raising of Darius' ghost, to the closing scene which brings the wounded Xerxes in person onto the stage and brings the whole play to an end in wild oriental lamentations. It is this climactic composition which must defend the poet against the charge of having written the play in three unconnected acts.[3]

What is new in this play is not merely the advanced dramatic treatment of what in Phrynichus was a long-drawn series of lamentations. Aeschylus has often been commended for the fact that he celebrates for all time his country's

---

[1] *Ox. Pap.* nr. 2245 (fr. 343 M.). For a bowl in the Ashmolean Museum showing Prometheus among satyrs, with fire in a narthex-cane: J. D. BEAZLEY, *Am. Journ. Arch.* 43, 1939, 618.　　　　　　　　　[2] SCHMID 2, 188, 8.

[3] WILAMOWITZ, *Aisch. Interp.* 42. K. DEICHGRÄBER, 'Die Perser des Aisch'. *Nachr. Gött. Phil.-hist. Kl.* 1/4, 1941, 155.

finest hour without any trace of narrow national hatred. This is the natural consequence of the fact that the poet's mind passed beyond the concrete historical event to its significance in the totality of a universe ruled by divine justice.

In the anapaestic parodos and the first stasimon we find such just a collocation of themes as recurs in the opening of the *Oresteia*. We are given an overwhelming picture of the Persian power that set out to destroy Greek freedom. The technique of presentation is archaic: name after outlandish name of cities, countries and generals sounds in our ears, making by sheer repetition the impression of size and strength. Yet everything is overshadowed by the anxiety expressed in the opening verses. The obvious first purpose of this catalogue is to delay the arrival of news; but as the stasimon continues a deeper purpose becomes visible: in this very excess of power and ambition which the expedition embodies lies the greatest possible danger. Just as the hymn to Zeus in the first stasimon of the *Agamemnon* seeks the ultimate significance of human fortunes in a region far above the visible and sensible, so here Aeschylus speaks dark and difficult words of the deception and infatuation sent by God, which no mortal can escape. We are told of Ate; and here we meet a conception which in tragedy, particularly Aeschylean tragedy, is a basic feature of the philosophy of life. We have no single word for it: there are really two aspects, which the Greeks of that time saw as a unity. From the gods' point of view, Ate is the doom that they pronounce on mortals: to man it is the spiritual blindness which at first flatters and encourages him, but gradually deludes his senses, and finally sets him on the path to his own destruction.

What is merely hinted at in the opening chorus is made explicit in the scene by the grave of Darius. This scene shows us two sides of Aeschylus' creative genius. The ancient sepulchre on whose summit the dead king appears, the chorus that sinks trembling to the ground, Atossa who in this terrible hour tries to speak with her husband across the gulf of the grave – all this combines to produce a stage scene of extraordinary power and effectiveness. We cannot know precisely what stage-effects were at the poet's disposal, but his skill in deploying the available means is obvious. Sophocles worked quite differently, relying on the spoken word and its content, while Aeschylus and Euripides, although in different ways, allowed great importance to the stage-effect as such. On one side this scene displays Aeschylus as master of the stage; on the other as a religious thinker. The words of the Great King make clear to us the significance of what we are witnessing. The description of the Greek victory reveals itself as a reflection of God's power. This is not the self-praise of a jubilant victor: enquiry into the cause of the catastrophe finds the solution in a conception deeply rooted in Greek thought, but which finds peculiar expression in Aeschylus. The disaster which has overtaken the Persian kingdom is shown as the result of that basic sin which the Greeks called *hybris*. The man upon whom Ate is come crosses over the bounds laid down for him; disturbs the ordering of the world, and must fall at last, the victim of his own blindness. So had the Persian empire passed the measure allotted to it, and the hybris of this expedition found visible form in the sin of Xerxes, who reversed the order of the elements, turned sea into land, and chained the Hellespont in the fetters of his floating bridge. Salamis was the first part of the penalty, and Plataeae, to which Darius prophetically alludes, is to be the second.

The notion that Zeus punishes overweening ambition is one which Aeschylus shared with most of his people. But in this scene a different and darker conception is sustained; when a man is inflamed with ambition, Zeus goads him on (v. 742). On the path to his own destruction man finds in God a ready helper. The singular notion of a god who helps men to sin is left here in relative obscurity: not until the *Oresteia* is it to be fully expounded.[1]

Aeschylus' reported words have often been quoted – that his tragedies were scraps from Homer's banquet.[2] It is the subject matter to which he alluded, but meaning it in a wider context than that of our *Iliad* and *Odyssey*. In the fifth century many more poems were credited to Homer, among others the *Thebaid*: and it was no doubt to this that Aeschylus felt himself indebted when he wrote his Theban trilogy, which he presented in 467.

Here a close thematic unity between the three tragedies and the satyr play is declared in their titles: *Laius, Oedipus, Seven against Thebes* and *Sphinx*. But there our knowledge of the lost parts virtually ends. The main lines of the myth cycle may be supposed to have provided the plots – Oedipus killing his father and marrying his mother, bringing sorrow on himself and the world in his ignorance, Oedipus from his incestuous couch laying the curse on his sons, that they would divide their kingdom by the sword.[3] Here, as often elsewhere, attempts to establish more precise details of the content and structure of the lost plays are quite fruitless.[4]

There is, however, a passage in the *Seven* which gives at least the main theme of the lost plays: everything that happens in them arises ultimately from the curse laid upon the royal house of Thebes. This curse, as we are told in a decisive passage (v. 742), grew out of an ancient, inexorable punishment for guilt – a punishment which has now reached the third generation. Three times did the Delphic god warn Laius against begetting a son: but man disregarded God's law, and fell into sin which reproduces itself in each succeeding generation. The verses which bear so much stress at the end of the trilogy reveal Aeschylus' view of the family curse as self-perpetuating sin.

The opening of the *Seven against Thebes* allows such problems to stay in the background, and transports us at once into the agitated city awaiting the decisive onset. The opening speech of Eteocles speaks eloquently of the seriousness of the hour, and his words are powerfully reinforced by the report of a scout on the enemy's preparations. In considerable sections of the play Eteocles

---

[1] It will be plain that I do not share the low opinion of Aeschylus as a religious thinker which one finds in D. L. PAGE (his edition, Oxf. 1957, p. xv.) and H. LLOYD-JONES, 'Zeus in Aeschylus'. *Journ. Hell. Stud.* 76, 1956, 55.

[2] Athenaeus 8. 347 e.

[3] On the legend: F. DIRLMEIER, *Der Mythos von König Oedipus*. Mainz 1948.

[4] F. STOESSL, *Die Trilogie des Aisch.* Baden b. W. 1937. On the *Oedipus*: L. DEUBNER, *Sitzb. Berl. Phil.-hist. Kl.* 1942, 40.

is set before us as the prince responsible for the defence of his own city. His first words are of the duties of the man who stands at the helm of the state – a familiar image which we meet again in the development of the drama. In this metaphor of the ship of state we have a particularly clear specimen of Aeschylus' use of leading themes in his imagery.[1]

The chorus of Theban women rushes wildly onto the stage to seek refuge at a common altar (or group of altars) of the city's tutelary gods. Eteocles rebukes the extravagance of their anxiety; as a man he reproves women who panic, as the ruler those who endanger his work. More subdued, but still in passionate entreaty the chorus pours out its prayers in song. Then follows the middle part of the play, a long dialogue (over 300 lines) in archaic style between Eteocles and the scout, who has returned with fresh news. This great structure includes seven pairs of speeches, in which the scout describes the champions who are to assault each gate, while Eteocles gives instructions for counter-measures. Attack and defence take shape before our eyes. The poet deliberately leaves us uncertain how far Eteocles had posted defenders for each gate in the period after his first entrance.[2]

When the Theban trilogy was shown, the Persian wars were fresh in Athenian memory; and beleaguered Thebes must have seemed a symbol of Athenian danger. This may explain the unusual fact that the attackers are called 'foreign speaking men' (170, cf. 72), contrary to the legend.[3]

The judgment of Gorgias on the *Seven*, that it is 'full of Ares',[4] is well known, and Aristophanes makes it clear that this was the common opinion. But this judgment does not penetrate below the surface. Neither Aeschylus nor any other great writer of his nation was a lover of war for its own sake. This fact is witnessed by the great distance to which the Trojan war is relegated in the *Agamemnon*. That man fulfils one of the highest potentialities of his being when he defends his native land was a theme that Aeschylus knew how to adorn; and it is thus that he depicts Eteocles. But this is only one side of the character: the other comes terribly into view in the last pair of speeches. At the seventh of the gates which the scout describes Polynices is to deliver his assault. He prays the gods of Thebes for the fall of the city; a boastful device on his shield proclaims his coming return to power. Eteocles is at first seized with despair over the race accursed of the gods, in whom the curse of Oedipus is now to find its fulfilment. Then he takes his decision: at the seventh gate he himself will meet the attacker – prince against prince, enemy against enemy, brother against brother. This battle also will be a battle for his city's freedom, but it has another and a frightful aspect. It must be a battle of blood-relations, in which

---

[1] J. DUMORTIER, *Les Images dans la poésie d'Eschyle*. Paris 1935. O. HILTBRUNNER, *Wiederholungs- und Motivtechnik bei Aisch*. Bern 1950.

[2] Thus A. LESKY, *Wien. Stud.* 74, 1961, 7, against E. WOLFF, *Harv. Stud.* 63, 1958 (Festschrift Jaeger), 89. Wolff is also opposed by K. V. FRITZ, *Antike und moderne Tragödie*. Berlin 1962, 201.

[3] H. LLOYD-JONES, however, *Class. Quart.* 1959, 85, 3, thinks that this refers to their speaking a different dialect.

[4] Plut. *Quaest. Conv.* 715 e. Aristoph. *Ran.* 1021.

victory will be fratricide. In this double aspect a basic feature of Aeschylean tragedy presents itself forcibly. Human actions involve danger, and lead constantly to the way from which there is no return, in which the action dictated by necessity, obligation and duty at the same time involves the deepest guilt. The scenes which now follow between Eteocles and the chorus, in which, for all the inner movement, the sung verses of the women and the spoken lines of Eteocles are bound into a strong antiphony, reveal in full the problems of the central character. Behind the patriotic defender of his city we see the son of Oedipus, driven by his father's curse to set out to kill his brother.

There is another element visible in this scene which will be of importance in interpreting the *Oresteia*. Man is under the appalling necessity of acting, and knows that his action must involve destruction. But once he accepts the necessity, he surrenders his own will to it: he does not merely accept the need for action, he rushes upon it. Compared with the opening of the play, Eteocles and the chorus have now exchanged roles. The chorus persuades and advises – 'child' (τέκνον) is its form of address to the ruler – while Eteocles defends his rigid determination. The chorus declares (686. 692): 'In you yourself lies the impulse towards that which comes upon you as fate; by your own will you rush on what you fear'. The attempt has recently been made to set aside as irrelevant the words of the chorus,[1] to whom Eteocles' character and motives are unknown; but it is wrong thus to close one's eyes to the contradiction seen by Aeschylus in human actions.

Earlier we understood Homeric psychology as being the inseparable weaving of human motivation and divine direction. The problems of fate, responsibility and action in Aeschylus are far deeper rooted, but they root in the same ground.

Another feature, not peculiar to Aeschylus, but common to all true tragedy, is that Eteocles knows well that he is treading the path to his own destruction. He speaks powerfully of the darkness that encompasses a man whom the gods have abandoned: to the suggestions of the chorus that he should pray and sacrifice, he replies: 'The gods do not trouble with me any longer. Gifts from me, the condemned to die, cause them only surprise'.[2] His last words, before he goes to his death, are: 'Such evils as the gods send, man cannot escape'.

The following choral song, as so often, covers a great interval of time. We may suppose that this device, so useful in tragic composition, survives from the time when the intervening speech of the single actor served only the purpose of setting the scene for a new choral ode.

A striking feature of Aeschylean composition, which is found likewise in the *Oresteia*, is the contrast between the expansive opening sections, which set the tone of the drama, and the dramatic, quickly moving latter sections, speedily coming to their goal. Thus we have here a short messenger's speech telling of the deaths of the brothers at each other's hand, leading to the final *kommos* over their bodies.

[1] Thus H. PATZER, *Harv. Stud.* 63, 1958 (Festschr. Jaeger), 114. K. V. FRITZ, *op. cit.* 214.
[2] The interpretation of v. 703 is difficult. It is taken quite differently by (e.g.) H. J. METTE, *Glotta* 39, 1960, 59.

The end of the play, as we have it, is dramatically developed by the introduction of Antigone and Ismene. There also appears a herald from an assembly of *probouloi*, forbidding the burial of Polynices as traitor to his country. Antigone declares her opposition, and so prepares the way for new grief.

This ending has been the subject of much dispute.[1] To me it seems impossible that it should be genuine. To say nothing of particular difficulties, it seems unthinkable that Aeschylus should have ended his trilogy with the opening of a new conflict. We know that his plays were re-staged later, and it would be quite understandable if the plot were thus amplified by thematic elements derived from Sophocles' *Antigone*. Murray[2] supposes the true text to end at v. 1005. It remains an open question whether Antigone and Ismene as mourners are an invention of the redactor or not.

The *Suppliant Women* (*Supplices*, *Hiketides*) is the first play of the Danaid trilogy. We have already seen why, despite earlier datings, it should now be placed after the Theban trilogy. The most important actor is here the chorus of daughters of Danaus, who under their father's guidance have fled from the pursuit of their suitors, the sons of Aegyptus, and are now seeking protection in Argos. The large role of the chorus is conditioned by the story: it is not, as so long thought, a proof of extremely early date. We must also bear in mind that we have here the first part of a trilogy, as in the *Agamemnon*. Both there and here we notice the asymmetry of construction which we saw in the *Seven*. Here it is heightened further: the majestic choral odes of the first part set forth the themes not only of the play, but of the whole trilogy.

The legend speaks of fifty Danaids – the same number as that of the dithyrambic chorus, which Pollux (4, 110) gives as the number of the primitive tragic chorus. While the *Supplices* was being reckoned as an early work, it was natural to assume a chorus fifty strong, although this did indeed presuppose a very well filled stage. The chorus of Danaids, each of whom in the closing scenes has her attendant handmaiden, the king's suite, the Egyptians in sufficient strength to carry off the Danaids – all this makes a chorus of fifty seem improbable. All this overloading of the stage can be forgotten with the new dating: for the *Supplices*, as for the rest of Aeschylus, we have to reckon with a chorus of twelve. This number is discernible in the first part of the *Oresteia*, where the old men argue and hesitate before the fatal doors. The increase of the chorus to fifteen is ascribed to Sophocles, and we know that Aeschylus, although he followed the younger writer's lead in using a third actor, made no use – or could make no use – of the enlarged chorus.

We know a little more about the staging of this play than of the others. The stage had a raised section containing a common altar with symbols or representations of several gods. It can hardly be by coincidence that in the plays before the *Oresteia* we find a simple podium type of structure at the edge of the orchestra or of that part of it which was away from the spectators. This structure

---

[1] Bibliography in SCHMID 2, 215, 5. POHLENZ 2, 46. For recent work see the appendix to this section under the *Septem*.

[2] Anticipated by BERGK and WILAMOWITZ.

can represent the acropolis of Thebes with sculptures of the gods, or the grave of Darius, or even the background for the staging of the Prometheus story.[1]

It is this altar – to be imagined as outside Argos – that the chorus makes for on its first entry. They relate in sweeping and majestic strains the sorrows of Io,[2] the ancestress of their line, who came from that Argos where they now seek refuge; they sing of their own fears and troubles, and of their hope of divine help. In the middle of this great ode they sing the praises of Zeus, the god who brings all things to their appointed ending, brings vain ambition to nothing, and accomplishes all his purposes without effort.

Urged by Danaus, the chorus mounts the elevated altar area, and from there carries on the long and animated conversation with the king of Argos, who has learned of the arrival of the foreign ships. The conversation lasts a long time, giving both sides opportunities for question and answer, and leads steadily up to a dramatic climax. The heightening of tension is reflected in the formal aspects: the entreaties of the chorus turn into a choral ode, while the doubts and hesitations of the king are still in dialogue metre, thus producing the type of alternation known as epirrhematic structure.

The role of the king provides a further example of that tragic compulsion which we have found to be Aeschylus' basic problem in human life. To receive the Danaids means war with their Egyptian pursuers, sacrificing the lives of his citizens: but to reject them would be to offend Zeus who jealously guards the rights of suppliants. The decision must be made, but either course involves evil – this is the theme of the king's complaint, conveyed with the greatest richness of illustration. It is hard to reach a decision, until one is forced by the Danaids' threatening to hang themselves on the images of the gods, and thus to bring an irremovable reproach upon the city. The king yields; but his will must be confirmed by a decree of the citizens – prehistoric Argos was run on democratic lines! This passage, in which the king's decision must be ratified by a popular vote, is a particularly striking example of the way in which tragedy sees the heroic age through the spectacles of the city-state.

The text enables us to infer the stage-management. Before leaving, the king asks the maidens to descend from the altar onto the ground, or in other words the chorus comes down now into the orchestra, so that it can dance to its following choral ode. Danaus has favourable news of the meeting, and the chorus expresses its thanks in a song of benediction on Argos. But soon new troubles arise: from his high position the old man sees the Egyptian ships landing, and runs into the city for help. This provides an adequate motive for the maidens' being left alone; but in fact the dramatist had no choice. Aeschylus was still restricted to two actors, and both are needed in the following scene between the Egyptian

---

[1] H. KENNER, *Das Theater und der Realismus in der griech. Kunst.* Vienna 1954, supposes a more elaborate stage equipment. The stage building (skene), he thinks, was brought in fairly early. See his bibliography.

[2] R. D. MURRAY JR., *The Motif of Io in Aesch. Suppliants.* Princeton 1958, not without some rather forced interpretation of the text, points out the relevance of the Io-story to the situation of the Danaids.

herald, who with his men-at-arms seeks to drag the maidens from the altar, and the king, who sends him back to his ship after strong condemnation of his actions and threats of the consequences. Now nothing hinders the reception of the Danaids into the city. They form a procession with their handmaidens, and leave the stage singing antiphonally with them.[1]

It is easy enough to trace the outline of the action; but difficult to evaluate the content of this play. It is not merely that this is the first part of a trilogy whose continuation we do not know; the text itself has sufficient problems for us. Why do the maidens flee so fearfully from the pursuit of their suitors? The king, in his long conversation with them, elicits no good reason. What is the meaning of the verse (admittedly corrupt, but restored with tolerable certainty) in which the Danaids sing of their 'self-begotten shunning of men' ($αὐτογενὴς$ $φυξανορία$)? The old interpretation that they mean an inborn fear of men is exposed to grave doubts. If the words mean nothing more than that the decision to flee came from their own hearts, our understanding of the whole is not appreciably advanced. It is the final scene which is most instructive in this respect. The importance attached to its content by the poet is shown by his elevating the handmaidens, hitherto silent, to the status of a second chorus. We hear again the pleas of the Danaids that they may escape forced wedlock, and that the virgin Artemis may look on them with a kindly eye. But the chorus of handmaidens dwells on a different theme: they pay due honour to Aphrodite, who shares with Hera, the goddess of marriage, the place in heaven immediately below Zeus himself. The Danaids seek to know what is right: the handmaidens already know – to submit oneself to the will of god.

The play first shows us the fate of the Danaids, their desperate plight and the insolence of their pursuers. Then we are shown another side: the flight of the maidens is at the same time a revolt against a great law that runs through the divinely ordained world, bidding man and woman come together. Again human actions are shown in an obscurity that only the divine grace can illuminate.

We can know very little of the way in which Aeschylus managed the problems of this play in the remaining parts of the trilogy, the *Egyptians* and the *Danaids*.[2] In the second part, despite their being received into Argos, the Danaids are in a position where they must at least appear to consent to a union with their hated suitors. We may suppose that this situation is the outcome of a battle in which the tragic role of the king of Argos ends in his death. This play must also have contained the plot of the Danaids to murder their husbands on their bridal night. This would make it impossible for the sons of Aegyptus to

---

[1] There must then have been a subsidiary chorus. C. VAN DER GRAAF, *Mnem.* 10, 1942, 281 (now followed by R. D. MURRAY op. cit.), supposes that in the last scene the chorus divided itself into Danaids and attendants: but even for an audience so ready to suspend disbelief this would have been rather too much.

[2] K. V. FRITZ, 'Die Danaidentrilogie des Aeschylus'. *Phil.* 91, 1936, 121. 249; now in *Antike und moderne Tragödie.* Berlin 1962, 160. KRAUS (*v. inf.*), 117. POHLENZ I, 49. 2, 21. M. L. CUNNINGHAM, 'A Fragment of Aesch. Aigyptioi?' *Rhein. Mus.* 96, 1953, 223, takes *Ox. Pap.* 20, nr. 2251 as referring to the death of the Argive king.

be the main chorus despite the title.[1] Presumably the Danaids themselves were again the main chorus, with the sons of Aegyptus as sub-chorus – the role sustained by the serving-maids in the first play.

The third play, the *Danaids*, began with the morning after the fatal marriage-night. The surviving information suggests two possible themes for the development. One is the story of Hypermestra, briefly related by Aeschylus in the *Prometheus* (865 sqq.). She alone of her sisters opened her heart to compassion and love, and spared her bridegroom. Her action was severely censured, but she became the mother of a line of Argive kings. It has been supposed that the guilt of this Danaid in disobeying her father's advice and betraying the common plan caused her to be put upon a formal trial. This would square very well with the appearance of Aphrodite herself in the play (fr. 44 N.), making an elaborate speech declaring her power as being that of the cosmic Eros which brings about the sacred wedlock of heaven and earth. It may however be objected that at this stage Aeschylus did not have the machinery necessary for staging a formal trial-scene like that in the *Eumenides*. But at all events it cannot be doubted that Hypermestra's action was discussed and harshly judged. The speech of Aphrodite could very well serve to defend her even without a formal trial: equally well it could fit into the alternative theme which could have ended the trilogy – the purification of the Danaids and the overcoming of their aversion from marriage. Their punishment in the underworld – carrying water in a leaky vessel – belongs to a different context and to a later stage of mythology. It is noticeable that this trilogy, full of wrongs and suffering, ends with the reconciliation of conflicting elements in the great divine ordering of the universe. The same we know to have been true of the trilogy to which the surviving *Prometheus Vinctus* belonged, and a similar reconciliation distinguishes the *Oresteia*. Some of the lost trilogies also may be suspected to have had endings in reconciliation. We shall return again to the question of the significance that this feature has for Aeschylus's view of the world and of the nature of tragedy.

If we next choose the *Prometheus Vinctus* for consideration, this must be because the *Oresteia* marks the supreme height of Aeschylus' achievement in his surviving work: it does not presuppose anything about the date of the play, about which we have no reliable information. The description of Etna is not an accurate indication, since this celebrated natural phenomenon could perfectly well have been known to Aeschylus before he ever set foot in Sicily. But in many respects a later date would be acceptable, and recent attempts[2] to date it after the *Oresteia* cannot be lightly dismissed.

The nature of the subject produces a striking and novel stage effect. The Titan Prometheus is the friend of man, to whom he taught the use of fire and saved him from perishing – a traditional theme which in this play is overlaid with a picture of Prometheus as a universal culture-hero. Zeus' plans are thwarted, and he has the offending Titan fettered to a rock on a solitary mountain at the

---

[1] We cannot be sure that the individual titles in the trilogy were given by Aeschylus.

[2] E. C. YORKE, *Class. Quart.* 30, 1936, 153. H. J. ROSE, *Eranos* 45, 1947, 99 thinks differently.

world's edge. The piece opens with the discharge of these commands by Hephaestus with his attendants Kratos and Bia (Power and Violence). In their dialogue the compassion felt by the god is strongly contrasted with the ferocity of the demon Kratos. Prometheus remains silent, and does not open his lips to bewail his lot until the others have left. All the rest of the play is a series of scenes in which the chained Titan shares the dialogue with various personages who visit him. The chorus of Oceanids comes to him on winged cars,[1] full of tender compassion for the victim of such cruelty; Oceanus himself arrives on a flying creature, and gives worldly-wise advice, which shatters on the rock of Prometheus' resistance. The next scene sees Io rush frenziedly upon the stage, driven abroad in wandering anguish by Zeus' love and Hera's hate. Prometheus tells her what awaits her in the future, and in so doing shows the bond that unites them both, as those who have suffered the most as Zeus' victims. On the banks of the Nile Zeus will touch her with his finger and restore her to peace, and make her the mother of the race which at some time through the flight of the Danaids will come to Argos. From this race Heracles will be born, who will end the sufferings of the Titan. As Io departs, Prometheus tells the chorus his secret – that in his direst need he yet has power over Zeus. He knows of a marriage – with Thetis – that the king of gods will contract to his own destruction. From this union will be born a son more powerful, who will do to Zeus what he did to his father Cronos. The Titan's words have been heard in Olympus: Hermes comes down at Zeus' command to wrest Prometheus' secret from him. He threatens and inveighs in vain: the Titan defies even the thunderbolt, and at the end of the play he and the chorus which refuses to leave him sink together into the depths.

In 1856 Westphal drew attention to certain peculiarities of the choral parts of the *Prometheus*, and the problems which he raised are yet far from settled. The progress of research has revealed numerous features occurring only in this one play among all those of Aeschylus – the most obvious being the simplicity of the language. The overall impression is reinforced by a large number of particular observations[2] in the field of vocabulary, thought and management of themes. Hence there is more than the classic *delirium delens* in the view that the play either is not by Aeschylus or has been extensively rewritten. Wilhelm Schmid showed the courage of his convictions in treating the *Prometheus* (in his *Geschichte der griechischen Literatur*) as an anonymous drama written under the influence of the sophistic movement. This may, however, seem undue confidence, if we reflect how little we possess of Aeschylus' output, and how slender our basis of comparison is. Under the surprising and novel elements there is an undeniable grandeur of conception, and beside all that seems unlike Aeschylus

---

[1] That the Oceanids had not a winged chariot but winged seats is maintained by E. FRAENKEL, 'Der Einzug des Chores im Prometheus'. *Ann. Scuola Norm. di Pisa* 1954, 269. W. BUCHWALD, in the excellent introduction to his edition (Bamberg 1962) thinks that each of the girls had her own little winged chariot. The wings no doubt served to conceal the machinery that made them move.

[2] See e.g. *Gnom.* 19, 1943, 198, and F. HEINIMANN, *Nomos und Physis.* Basel 1945, 44. 92, n. 5. O. HILTBRUNNER, *Wiederholungs- und Motivtechnik bei Aisch.* Berne 1950, 75.

we recognize much that is entirely characteristic of him. The prevailing modern view is that the piece is genuine. The writer himself shares this view, but with a protest against the attitude of mind shown by many modern scholars, who refuse to admit that there is a *Prometheus* problem at all, and pass over in silence so many arguments which deserve the most careful consideration.

The most difficult question is that of the representation of Zeus in this play. How can the newly established tyrant of Olympus, holding sway by pure force, inflicting sufferings such as Io's, be reconciled with the just ruler of the universe depicted in the *Agamemnon*, to whom the name of Zeus is doubtfully and hesitatingly given by the prayers of the pious? Is a reconciliation possible? Jacob Burckhardt thought not.[1] If it is, then it must have been effected in the other two parts of the trilogy, now lost. It is time that scholars stopped applying to the *Prometheus* F. T. Vischer's words on the Old Testament – 'At that time God himself was still young' – even if Wilamowitz did set the example.[2] Nothing justifies our dragging in the notion of an evolving deity. There is no evolution in the Erinyes of the *Oresteia*: at the end of the trilogy they show only the other side of their double aspect. What the end of the *Oresteia* does show is that Aeschylus considered the sensible world as the reconciliation of originally opposing forces; and there is some reason to believe that the Promethean trilogy also ended in reconciliation between the Titan and the Olympians.

We know of three other Prometheus-dramas from Aeschylus' pen. If we set on one side the *Prometheus Pyrcaeus* (which we know to have been a satyr-play from the *Persae* trilogy) we are left with the *Lyomenos* and the *Pyrphoros*. The former, by its title, must have represented the loosing of the Titan; indeed we have express witness that it did from the scholion on v. 511 of the surviving play. This fact gives rise to a strong argument against the generally accepted theory that Prometheus on the rock was represented on the stage by a huge lay figure. The theory has certain advantages. It enables the opening scene to be staged with only two actors (Bia being a *muta persona*), and the sinking and disappearance in the last scene seems a well contrived way to get over the difficulties involved. We do not know whether the poet could have expected the stage illusion to be accepted by his audience; but the freeing of Prometheus at the end of the trilogy speaks decisively against the supposition.

The remaining Prometheus-play, the *Pyrphoros* (Firebringer), raises a difficult question. Where did it belong in the trilogy? Was it the first play, describing the theft of fire from heaven, or the last, bringing reconciliation of the opposing forces and the establishment of a Prometheus-cult? It is attractive to suppose parallelism with the *Eumenides*, but this is not a powerful argument. The content of the play is unknown to us, and we must not try to transcend the limits of our knowledge. It would be quite wrong to equate this play with the *Pyrcaeus* and to suppose a dilogy made up of the other two. Assuming then that the *Pyrphoros*

---

[1] *Griech. Kulturgeschichte* I, 319 (KRÖNER).

[2] J. A. DAVISON, *Ant. Class.* 1958, 445, with some justification, speaks of this theory of an evolving Zeus as a monstrous perversion of Aeschylus' theology. If anything evolves, it is Prometheus' understanding of Zeus.

belonged to a trilogy, we may imagine that there were greater possibilities of dramatic effect in making it the first play than if it were put at the end. Thus much and no more we may concede to Pohlenz[1] in his onslaught on Reinhardt.

In his very fine book on Aeschylus, Gilbert Murray quotes approvingly Swinburne's judgment that the *Oresteia* is probably 'the greatest achievement of the human mind'. It is now fashionable to shrink with horror from unseasonable expressions of sentiment, and all such enthusiasm is automatically suspect. But even today it may be permissible to speak of this trilogy as one of the highpoints of human artistic achievement. There is nothing to compare with it, except perhaps the sculpture of Michelangelo. Yet in its form the *Oresteia* by no means reaches the utmost fulfilment of the classic ideal. This great poem, with its cosmic scale, still has many features of the archaic style: but they are not worn as shackles – rather as badges of a gradually achieved mastery. The sculptures of the temple of Zeus at Olympia are nearly contemporary with the *Oresteia*; and the Apollo of the west pediment is closely akin to the Apollo of the *Eumenides*.

When Aeschylus in 458 brought out this trilogy, together with the lost satyr-play *Proteus*, the story already had a long history. We have glimpses of it here and there from Homer onward: a loss that must be particularly regretted is that of the choral lyric into which Stesichorus put the legend. The little that we know of his *Oresteia* indicates elements that were used to good effect in the drama. On the other hand there is force in Wilamowitz' observation that the cardinal importance of Apollo in the story is attributable to older epics under Delphian influence. However this may be, Aeschylus' achievement in the *Oresteia* is not principally in the invention of the story. Older versions represent Aegisthus as being the prime mover in the murder, and the importance given to Clytemnestra, who is so dominating a figure in the *Agamemnon*, has been taken as an innovation on Aeschylus' part. But the role that she plays in the reports in the *Odyssey* needs careful reconsideration, and the eleventh Pythian Ode of Pindar shows that earlier versions also had made Clytemnestra commit the murder with her own hand. It is in the *Eumenides* that Aeschylus handles the traditional plot with the greatest freedom; and indeed his most characteristic contribution is the new form that he gives to the old material and the new thought and feeling with which he loads it.

The stage presentation of the trilogy shows an advance in freedom and complexity on the earlier pieces. Effective use is made of the third actor, although we are still a long way from real three-part dialogues. As regards the set, the front wall of the *skene* is here for the first time used to represent the front of a palace, with a large central door and side entrances onto the stage.

All three plays begin with prologue-speeches. If we were right in our previous supposition (p. 228) that the prologue was in its origins a device to prepare the audience for the following choral ode, we have here a striking example of the art with which Aeschylus used it to set the different tone required by different plays.

[1] 2. 41.

The action of the *Agamemnon* opens at night, a little before sunrise. A watchman is on the roof of the palace, set there by Clytemnestra's order, to watch for the signal fire that is to bring from height to height the news of Troy's destruction to Argos. His complaints of the endlessness of his task are broken off by his sudden exultant cry on seeing the beacon flash out. But almost at once his joy is damped by his knowledge of the guilt and danger that lurk in the palace below him. So in thirty-nine verses Aeschylus draws the contrast that makes the whole play, and strikes what is to be the keynote of the drama. The spacious writing of the first half, before the meeting of Agamemnon and Clytemnestra, has a suffocating intensity of foreboding behind the rejoicing. The poet's genius goes on thickening and darkening the clouds until the lightning-bolt itself is a relief from the sustained tension.

The spaciousness of the introductory sections, especially of the choral odes which follow the prologue and the anapaestic parodos of the chorus of Argive elders, can be understood if we remember that we have here the exposition not only of the *Agamemnon*, but of the whole trilogy. In this connection we can see some significance in the respective lengths of the plays (1673, 1076 and 1047 lines respectively).

The lengthy parodos takes our minds back to the sailing of the Greek fleet. In Aulis Agamemnon was under the fearful necessity of sacrificing his child Iphigenia to appease the anger of Artemis and to buy a favourable wind. Here again is man groaning under the yoke of *Ananke*; here again he has to choose between two alternatives: neither seems endurable, yet one must be chosen. The Atridae, throwing their sceptre to the ground, with tears starting from their eyes, become the symbol of man confronted with a fateful but inevitable decision. And here again the human being who under the harshest compulsion has taken his decision, surrenders his own will to it. Agamemnon is now wholly decided (v. 221): he sacrifices his child and thus sets the great fleet free to sail. But in his wife's heart he has kindled a flame of hatred that is never to be quenched. Nevertheless, it would be a false simplification to ascribe Clytemnestra's action to this motive alone. It is her own passions, as much as her hatred of Agamemnon, that drives her into the arms of the lesser man, and makes her kill her husband. It is left for the later development of the action to show how all this is ultimately bound up indissolubly in a far wider web.

The choric part of the parodos is elaborately subdivided: in the middle of it comes the hymn to Zeus. The form of the primitive song of invocation, which tried to reach the god by using all his cult-names (cf. *Il.* 1.37) here becomes the vehicle of a religious sentiment that cannot be content with names: 'Zeus, whoever he may be, if it please him so be be called. . . .' There are few passages in which we catch so clearly the tone of the poet's own voice. The figure of Zeus, which had long ceased to be comparable with the Homeric 'father of gods and men' out of whom he had grown, is for Aeschylus the personification and the guarantee of a universal and intelligible world-order. Be the ways of God never so entangled, yet at the last they can be understood; and in this hymn Aeschylus proclaims their meaning. Man's path through guilt and sorrow is his path towards insight into God's law. The proverb, 'Suffering is learning', which at first meant no more than that adversity sharpened the wits, here becomes the key expression of a profound religious cosmology.[1] The same holds good of another proverb, to be put beside the former – 'The doer must be the sufferer'.[2] In this chain of action, guilt, expiation, recognition we encounter again the motif of the *Persae* – the notion of a god who helps man to sin. This is the god of Aeschylus, and this the hard road by which he leads us to recognition of him.

The *Agamemnon* shows in its composition that same inequality in dramatic tempo which we saw earlier: a long and slow preparation is followed by a rapid resolution of the tragic conflict. Clytemnestra has a long speech describing the course of the beaconlight over the mountain-tops; the first stasimon[3] of the chorus, in a series of leisurely transitions, sings of Zeus' punishment of Paris, who violated the laws of hospitality and stole the wife of his host, and of the curse that fell upon the war that was fought over a woman. All is gloom and foreboding. Aeschylus here does with great effect what he was to do again in the *Choephori*: into this atmosphere of anxiety and tension he brings an ordinary man who has no share in the drama and is free of the fears of those who know the circumstances. Onto the stage comes a herald to announce the landing of the king: his heart is full of joy at the homecoming, and he delightedly contrasts the happiness and safety of the moment with the hardships of campaigning.

Aeschylus' bold handling of time is well shown in the fact that we hear Clytemnestra's speech about the beacon fires before the first stasimon, and immediately after it Agamemnon's landing is announced. It has been commonly observed that a choral ode in tragedy can be taken as indicating a great lapse of time. Here, however, such an explanation is not enough: the arrival of the herald is explicitly connected with the confirmation of the tidings which the beacon has brought earlier (v. 489).

The second stasimon begins by dwelling on Helen as the great bringer of grief to the Achaeans, but then becomes more general. We hear the poet's own avowal (v. 750), that he does not share the popular view of the 'envy' of the gods: it is not a grudging attitude towards excessive human fortune, but the decrees of justice that direct God's hand when he punishes sin. Guilt is the root of all suffering. Such is the burden of the song up to the entrance of the victor. Agamemnon enters in a chariot: behind him cowers Cassandra, the Trojan princess whom he is bringing under Clytemnestra's roof as his concubine. The tension that pervades all the first half of the *Agamemnon* is marvellously sustained here. Agamemnon's cold reserve is met with feigned rejoicing from his wife, whose dissimulation is almost carried away with its own virtuosity. The scene ends in a verbal battle, in which Clytemnestra finally prevails upon her husband

---

[1] On the history of the term see H. DÖRRIE, *Leid und Erfahrung. Abh. Ak. Mainz, Geistes- und sozialwiss. Kl.* 1956/5.

[2] Cf. *inter al.* Hesiod fr. 174 Rz.

[3] The term denotes a song in a quiet or standing-still measure, not in a marching rhythm like the entrances and exits: cf. W. KRANZ, *Stasimon.* Berl. 1933, 114.

to walk over a purple carpet into the house. This victory foreshadows another that she hopes for within doors.[1]

Before the catastrophe Aeschylus has inserted a scene which suddenly widens the play's horizon. Clytemnestra comes forth to lure a second prey into the house: the Trojan princess remains silent where she is. Then the god comes upon her – Apollo who had decreed that she must prophecy the truth in vain. In a rapid interchange of wild, visionary song and clear intelligible speech she brings before our eyes the previous history of the house of Atreus: the defiling of a brother's marriage-bed, the hideous banquet of Thyestes, finally, bodily present to her inspired vision, a troop of furies, singing and revelling like drunkards in the house from which they can never be driven out. A new link is now welded onto the chain of guilt. Indoors Clytemnestra makes ready to slay her victorious husband and king like a sacrificial victim. Cassandra must share his fate, and after a last flicker of her will to live, she goes resignedly into the house to her death. Soon afterwards Agamemnon's death-cry comes from the house. The chorus argues and hesitates: the great door opens,[2] and Clytemnestra is seen with the fatal axe in her hand, standing over the bodies of her two victims. The frenzy of the deed is still upon her, and she likens the drops of blood that have bespattered her to the rain that falls on thirsty seeds. Then follows a long dispute with the chorus, who meet her exultation with a reminder of the heaviness of her sin and the certainty of expiation. Clytemnestra now sees the truth: not that she repents or abandons the attempt to defend her action – but she learns that she herself is now tied in the chain of sin and expiation which stretched from the earliest history of her house and will extend yet into the future, no man can say how far. She would gladly now make a pact with the ancestral daemon, that this might at last be enough. But, as if in answer, Aegisthus now enters – her paramour, who left her to do the deed and now plays the master. The old men's anger takes fire, and open battle would break out but for Clytemnestra, pleading with a woman's voice against any further bloodshed. She goes with Aegisthus into the palace where the two are now to reign.

The second play, the *Choephori*, shows in its structure a striking similarity to the first – a similarity that is particularly obvious at the climacterics of the action. Again a man is led by his guilty deed into the fatal circle that has now closed around the house of Atreus, again, despite all his unwillingness, he is forced to see the reality of this chain of guilt. As in the *Agamemnon*, so here also there are four scenes leading up to the confrontation of the main actors. The prologue, which has survived in fragmentary condition, is spoken by Orestes at the grave of his father. The innocent young man and his prayer are in violent and effective

---

[1] The scene is rather similarly interpreted by H. GUNDERT, Θεωρία, *Festschr. Schuchhardt*. Baden-Baden 1960, 69, who also discusses other views.

[2] In this and similar scenes there is no need to posit an eccyclema – a revolving stage which came at a later period; cf. E. BETHE, 'Ekkyklema und Thyroma'. *Rhein. Mus.* 83, 1934, 21. A. PICKARD-CAMBRIDGE, *The Theatre of Dionysus in Athens.* Oxf. 1946, is also against the eccyclema for the classical stage; see, however, T. B. L. WEBSTER, 'Staging and Scenery in the Ancient Greek Theatre'. *Bull. Rylands Libr.* 42/2, 1960, 493.

contrast with the stormclouds in which the *Agamemnon* ended. Next we hear the song of women approaching the grave, Electra among them: Orestes conceals himself, with his companion Pylades, to see what is the meaning of this procession. Clytemnestra, frightened by an evil dream, has sent her daughter with expiatory offerings to the tomb of the murdered king; but the prayer with which Electra accompanies the gifts is for the return of Orestes and for vengeance. She sees the lock of hair which her brother has left on the grave, recognizes his footprint,[1] and guesses that he is at hand. A third scene shows the mutual recognition of brother and sister – a scene technically simple, but appealing in the intimacy of its sentiment. Orestes and Electra join with the chorus in a long choric ode over the tomb, after which Orestes outlines his plan, thus leading through the fourth of our scenes to his first meeting with his mother. She still does not recognize him, as he feigns to be a messenger of Orestes' death. She takes him and his companion Pylades into the house, and sends a message to Aegisthus, who is away from home. The messenger is Orestes' old nurse – another example of the 'uninvolved' character, expressing the purely human in the most unadorned words. She also believes the story of Orestes' death, and finds the tears for him that his own mother does not shed. Her tender memories of taking care of his helpless infancy come well from the poet whose understanding of the dumb creation is so moving in the parodos to the *Agamemnon*.

All true works of art are made up of elements effective in several aspects at once. Thus the scene with the old nurse is not only good theatre in itself, but is significant in the plot as a whole. She was to have summoned Aegisthus to come with an armed retinue; but the chorus, letting her suspect the true facts, persuades her to modify the message in this vital point. After a choral ode which covers the time necessary for the message to be taken, Aegisthus arrives, and falls to Orestes' sword in the palace. A servant of Clytemnestra's calls her out from the women's quarters: his words, 'The dead slay the living', tell her all. Her old spirit flames up: she calls for the axe, but Orestes is there to confront her. There is a short battle of words. 'My child', she repeatedly calls Orestes, as if the word had power to save her; but her attempts to avoid her fate are in vain, and Orestes drives her into the palace to her death. Again the great door opens after a choral ode; again the slayer stands over the bodies of his two victims. Like Clytemnestra in the *Agamemnon*, Orestes tries at first to justify his action: he calls Helios to witness the rightness of his cause, and commands the servants to bring out the net in which Agamemnon was slain unarmed. But all his self-justification is of no avail: the darkness of horror settles upon his senses. The spirits of revenge for his mother's blood rise from the ground before his eyes, and in madness he rushes from the stage to seek purification at Delphi.

In the first half of the play a great deal of space (306–478) is given to a lyrical

---

[1] Vv. 205-211 and 228 f. (about the footprint), together with the hostile allusion to this theme in Euripides *El*. 518-544, have been called in question: E. FRAENKEL, *Aesch. Agam.* Oxf. 1950, 3, p. 815. But see H. LLOYD-JONES in *Class. Quart. N.S.* 11, 1961, 171 and H.-J. NEWIGER, *Herm.* 89, 1961, 427.

section – the *kommos* over the grave of Agamemnon, in which Orestes, Electra and the chorus all take part. The structure is elaborate, partly triadic: the significance is not confined to the *Choephori*, but extends to the whole trilogy.[1] It is not that Orestes here takes the determination to kill his mother – he came home with that resolve already made – but that there is a remarkable shift in the accentuation of the motive. Before the *kommos* Orestes makes a long speech declaring the necessity of his action, supporting it by appealing to the clear command of the Delphian Apollo, who threatened the severest penalty for disobedience.[2] But in the *kommos* itself, Apollo's command is suffered to slip wholly into the background – so much that it is not even mentioned. That Orestes who ended his account of the guilt of the house of Atreus and his own compulsion to act with the declaration, 'She shall rue the deed', is now no longer thinking of Apollo or of Aegisthus: he has made the dreadful resolution to kill his mother part of his own will, and acts now on his own responsibility. The basic feature here is that double motivation – divine decree and human will – which we saw to be a characteristic element of Homeric psychology; but what in Homer was a simple unity has here become the field of a deep tragic conflict. Here is a particularly clear example of that typically Aeschylean feeling that human actions are liable suddenly to show a fatal ambiguity. Orestes, the model of piety, who obeys the god and avenges his father, at the same time becomes the murderer of his mother, and thus is entangled in the chain of guilt and expiation that binds his house.

It is not only here that the double aspect of Orestes' motive comes out clearly. When Orestes, confronted with his mother, loses the power to act, Pylades speaks – the only speech he has in the play – to remind Orestes of the Delphic god, whose will has now to be brought to bear when Orestes' own will fails him. And at the end of the play, where the horror of the act embodies itself for Orestes in the *Eumenides*, he flees to the god who commanded him to do that which his own strength cannot bear.

The end of the *Choephori* with the madness of Orestes is one of the most overwhelming scenes in Aeschylus. In contrast, the last play of the trilogy, the *Eumenides*, opens quietly as morning comes to the peace of the Delphic sanctuary. The priestess utters a pious prayer before entering the temple, from which she comes tottering out, overwhelmed with horror. The sight that has terrified her is soon revealed by the opening of the great gate in the front of the temple. Orestes sits there at the sacred centre of the earth: around him are the dreadful figures of the Erinyes, his pursuers, who have fallen for the moment asleep after the exertion of the chase. Apollo has appeared to their quarry, and now promises him his support. Hermes is to guide him to Athens, to the old statue of the city

---

[1] The opposite positions: W. SCHADEWALDT, 'Der Kommos in Aisch. Choephoren'. *Herm.* 67, 1932, 312 (now *Hellas und Hesperien*. Zürich 1960, 106). A. LESKY, 'Der Kommos der Choephoren'. *Sitzb. Ak. Wien. Phil.-hist. Kl.* 221/3, 1943; id., 'Göttliche und menschliche Motivation im hom. Epos'. *Sitzb. Ak. Heidelb. Phil.-hist. Kl.* 1961/4, 52.

[2] If vv. 297-305 are genuine, which serve as a kind of appendix to Orestes' speech, they must be taken as a transition to the *kommos*.

goddess: there he will find judges to decide his case. The god sees Orestes safely on his way, and then turns out the Erinyes from his temple – the bright Olympian turning out the goddesses of an older and darker world.

Orestes' journey to Athens (in which the Delphic god sends him, as it were, out of his own province) shows us Aeschylus handling the traditional material more boldly than elsewhere in the trilogy. The power of Apollo as it was understood in the older sagas – freeing Orestes from guilt by rites of purification, or giving him the bow that was to defend him against the Erinyes – could not satisfy Aeschylus' ways of thought. The laws of Dike had been utterly violated and despised in the house of Atreus, and no mere outward forms, no washing away of guilt with the blood of animals, could make good the damage. The change of scene in this play symbolizes the entry on the scene of another and a greater purifying power than that of Apollo.

After a change of scene, probably effected by no more than the closing of the temple door and the setting up of a statue of Pallas (if indeed there was not one in the orchestra from the beginning), we are shown Orestes on the acropolis of Athens, in the protection of the goddess's statue. The chorus of Erinyes finds him there, bursts furiously into the orchestra, and seeks to bind him with dance and incantation. But gradually the rhythm of the dance becomes more peaceful, and the song of the goddesses tells us that they too have their place in the great plan of Zeus. These sleepless, unforgetting children of Night personify the inevitability of atonement for the shedding of blood. Athene, goddess of the world of light, is herself to say later (v. 698): 'Do not wholly drive out from your city that which gives you to fear. What man remains righteous, who fears nothing?'

After this song from the chorus, the goddess herself comes to her citadel, sees the strange assembly round her statue, and asks what is afoot. The role of the goddess is comparable to that of the king in the *Supplices*: she is confronted with pursuer and pursued, and neither can be easily dismissed. But the daughter of Zeus is not at a loss: she will set up for all time a court of justice to pronounce the law when human life has been taken.

The scene which follows the next choral song must be imagined as taking place on the Areopagus, another part of the acropolis; but it is not necessary, or even possible, to assume any external indication of the change of place. Here we see assembled the citizens whom Athene has chosen as judges. Apollo himself comes to speak for Orestes against the Erinyes before these judges. In the presentation of their cases by the leader of the chorus and by the god we breathe the atmosphere of an Athenian lawcourt: but behind all the advocacy is a conflict of gigantic forces. Apollo, the son of Zeus, stands for a younger world of gods, a world in which the father is supreme. In consequence the slaying of Agamemnon and the command to avenge him outweigh the killing of a mother. The Erinyes represent that powerful, primitive world-order of conception and birth in which the mother is all-important. Aeschylus shows unparalleled poetic power in his presentation of the two basic forces embodied in the religion of his people.

The two sides have presented their case. Athene now, at the very outset of her first speech, proclaims the founding of the court which is to be named from the hill of Ares, and which is for ever to judge those who have spilt human blood. The *Oresteia*, whose action now has the very universe for its stage, finds room for a piece of contemporary history. Four years before the play was performed Ephialtes had brought in a reform which stripped the Areopagus – traditionally dominated by aristocrats – of its political powers, leaving it only the right to try homicide and certain powers to supervise ceremonies. In the *Eumenides* Aeschylus avoids taking a side in the issue: through the mouth of Athene he only promises to the court those powers which the reform had left it. It is as the repository of the power to absolve from blood-guilt that the Areopagus is to remain in honour among a people who, in Athene's impressive words, 'loves neither licence nor to hear a lord's command' (v. 696).

The jurors cast their votes, and that of Athene is in Orestes' favour. The votes are thus equally divided; and according to the rule she has laid down, this result means acquittal.

It has often been remarked, and not without justice, that in the trial scene Aeschylus lays very great stress on the state as the repository of justice. But at the same time he lets his audience see the limitations of human justice. This equal division of votes expresses the impossibility of resolving by human wits the conflict of the *Oresteia*, which extends into the world of the gods. It is only the divine clemency that can rescue Orestes and break the chain of sin and punishment – the divine clemency operating through Athene, the beloved daughter of Zeus and thus the exponent of his will. It is then Zeus himself who favours the principle of clemency in the rule that an equal division of votes means acquittal.

Orestes' gratitude now flows from a full heart. He promises always to be true to the city where he found salvation. Never will an Argive spear be levelled against Athens. Again we hear the voice of the Athenian, well knowing the importance that Argive power had for his city in the conflicts of his day.

It still remains to complete the work of reconciliation where the gods are concerned. The goddesses of revenge rage and threaten in defeat; but Athene – the very personification in this scene of all the subtlety of Attic genius – is able to win them over. The powers of the underworld have as their province not only death, but budding life: they can curse, but also bless. Under the name of 'Eumenides' – the wise, the holy ones – the goddesses of revenge will have their shrine in Athens and bestow the blessing of which they now sing, placated by Athene's promise. The play ends with the forming of the procession that is to escort the divinities to their new seat of worship. Thus among the gods also the conflict has reached a happy resolution, and at the same time we have seen the accomplishment of the will of the supreme deity. In the words of the escorting chorus, 'All-seeing Zeus and Fate have together come to their goal'. The poet's religious philosophy has thus arrived at the reconciliation of the conflict between impersonal fate and a personal world-ruler, a reconciliation embodied in the person of Zeus.

Modern attempts to define tragedy commonly stem from the words of Goethe in a letter to Friedrich von Müller of 6th June 1824: 'The tragic flows entirely from an irreconcilable conflict. From the moment that reconciliation enters, or becomes possible, the truly tragic disappears.' The 'pantragism' of Hebbel together with Scheler's doctrine that the world of tragedy necessarily involves a destruction of values as a basic element, form intermediate steps from Goethe to current philosophies of tragedy. The *Oresteia* poses in an acute form the following question: How, in the light of modern views on tragedy, can we give that name to a trilogy which ends with the reconciliation of the conflicting forces? Is it a tragedy only in the sense of belonging to a recognized ancient literary genre, and does it in fact not contain true tragedy? This is a view that few would willingly adopt. It is hard to imagine a more tragic figure than Orestes, who by one and the same act becomes the righteous avenger and the devoted prey of the Furies. Yet the trilogy ends with that reconciliation which, as Goethe thought, was the negation of tragedy!

The question thus posed leads us straight into the central arena of the problem, 'What is tragedy?' – an arena much trodden in our day. It is a question that we cannot answer here. I shall merely suggest, where Aeschylus is concerned, a distinction which may perhaps have a wider application. There is a fundamentally tragic world-view, involving necessarily ultimate destruction: there is also another, which finds room for solution and reconciliation, but without excluding tragic situations in their sharpest form. On this view Aeschylus in the *Oresteia* shows that he is a master of tragic situations in their utmost breadth and depth, but has a philosophy of human existence which is not tragic in the modern application of the word. The end comes not in destruction and the mutual annihilation of values, but in the confirmation of those values within the framework of a world powerfully directed by the wisdom of God.[1]

Among the lost trilogies of Aeschylus we may mention, for the interest of their subject matter, that which dealt with the fortunes of Ajax (*Judgment of Arms, Women of Thrace, Women of Salamis*), and the *Lycurgeia*, made up of the tragedies *Edonoi, Bassarai, and Neaniskoi* and the satyr play *Lycurgus*.[2] The latter was based on one of the Dionysiac sagas of the conflicts between the god of ecstasy and mortal men – in this case Lycurgus, king of Thrace. This trilogy also seems to have ended in reconciliation of the conflicting forces. Other tragedies on Dionysiac themes were *Bacchae, Semele*[3] (Σεμέλη ἢ Ὑδροφόροι) – the latter probably forming a trilogy with *Pentheus* and *Xantriai* – and the satyr-play *The Nurses of Dionysus* (Διονύσου τροφοί).

Wilamowitz complained in his *Aischylos-Interpretationen* (1914) that the sands of Egypt had given us so far not a shred of Aeschylus. The situation was

---

[1] A fuller discussion of these problems: A. LESKY, *Die griech. Tragödie.* 2nd ed. Stuttgart 1958, 11: p. 269 gives a bibliography on the problem of tragedy.

[2] K. DEICHGRÄBER, 'Die Lykurgie des Aisch.' *Nachr. Gött. Phil.-hist. Kl.* 1/3, 1938/39, 231. K. VYSOKÝ, 'Aischylova Lykurgeia'. *Listy Filologické* 82, 1959, 177.

[3] *Ox. Pap.* 18, 1941, nr. 2164 (fr. 355 M.) is assigned to this play by K. LATTE, *Phil.* 97, 1948, 47.

dramatically altered in 1932 when Breccia excavated a rubbish heap at Oxyrhynchus which had long been protected by the grave of an Arab saint. His valuable discoveries, published by Girolamo Vitelli and Medea Norsa in *Pap. Soc. It.* 1 (1935), were followed shortly by an English publication containing new fragments of Aeschylus. As early as 1902-3 the same site at Kôm had been partly excavated by Grenfell and Hunt (who had to avoid disturbing the grave), and a good many fragments of papyrus were discovered. These included fragments of Aeschylus, mostly very small, which were published by Edgar Lobel in the 18th and 20th volumes of *Oxyrhynchus Papyri* (1941, 1952).

The Italian discoveries included 22 verses of the *Niobe*, describing the suffering of the bereaved mother and urging human beings to remember the limitations of their status. The passage is so damaged that it is hard to know who is the speaker. That it is part of a prologue spoken by a god or goddess (e.g. Leto) seems unlikely: it would suit better a nurse or someone else closely connected with Niobe. The possibility that Niobe herself is the speaker is rejected in the most recent discussion of the fragments: if it had been so, the verses would be from the second half of the play; for in Aristophanes' *Frogs* and in the manuscript life of Aeschylus Niobe and Achilles are cited as examples of Aeschylus' trick of keeping a character silent on the stage for a long time, only allowing him to speak when the play is more than half over. In this fragment we find the words that were previously known to us from a quotation in Plato (*Republic* 2, 380 a): 'God permits an αἰτία to grow up among men when he wishes utterly to destroy a house.' The Greek word is untranslateable, meaning both 'cause' and 'guilt'. Such an expression fits easily into the picture we have formed of Aeschylus' religious philosophy. We may set beside it frag. 301 N.: 'God is not above rightful deception.'[1]

The other important piece from the 1932 discoveries was 36 much damaged verses from the *Myrmidons*. This play formed part of the Achilles trilogy, together with the *Nereids* – so named from the chorus of sea-nymphs who bring Achilles his new arms – and the *Phrygians* or the *Ransoming of Hector*. In this play Achilles was characteristically shown as long sunk in silence in his grief for Patroclus. The fragments of the *Myrmidons* allow us to discern parts of a dispute in which Achilles' bitter resentment is carried to its ultimate consequence. *Ox. Pap.* 20, 2253 may very well come from the prologue of the play.

The judgment of antiquity (Diog. Laert. 2, 133; Pausan. 2. 13, 6) that Aeschylus took first place among writers of satyr-plays, is one which until recently we were unable to check. In consequence we are particularly glad to find among the new discoveries some that show us this other side of the poet of the *Oresteia*. The same service has been done for Aeschylus in this way as the *Ichneutai*-fragments did for Sophocles. One of the fragments discovered by the Italians and a larger one found by Grenfell and Hunt give us a tolerably good picture[2] of the *Dictyulkoi* ('The Drawers of Nets'), since the two fragments come from widely separated parts of the play. It formed part of a tetralogy on Perseus, the other

[1] Cf. κ. DEICHGRÄBER, *Der Listensinnende Trug des Gottes*. Göttingen 1952, 108 (*GGN* 1940). [2] Reconstruction essentially by PFEIFFER and SIEGMANN (*v. inf.*).

pieces being the *Phorkides*, featuring the adventure with the Gorgons, and the *Polydectes*, telling how Perseus after his adventure returned to Seriphos and protected Danae from the king of that island.

The fragment found by Breccia comes from the opening of the play, and represents two fishermen – one of them is Dictys, the king's brother – struggling with a catch of inexplicable weight.[1] This is in fact the chest containing Danae and her child, which has been washed up against the cliffs of Seriphos. Being unable to land it by themselves, they call for help. This is as far as the fragment goes: we may naturally suppose that the chorus of satyrs came on to help land the chest. There must have been a striking scene in which a woman is suddenly revealed as the contents: very possibly the cowardice of the satyrs made them take to their heels at the first surprise of the discovery. The larger fragment in Ox. Pap. 18 comes from a much later part of the play, since a verse-number in the margin appears as 800 – a surprisingly high number, for the play cannot have ended with the scene in question, and we must suppose a quite extraordinary length by the standards of satyr plays. The suggestion of Siegmann's, that the characters in this scene are Danae and Silenus, the lecherous and reprobate sire of all the satyrs, was the first to bring this fragment to dramatic life. Dictys has gone into the city to obtain a decision about Danae; and Silenus takes the opportunity to woo the fair piece of flotsam. He praises his services to her and promises her a happy life together. Danae in terror calls on the gods to deliver her from this lecherous demon of the woods. The poet handles most charmingly Silenus' attempts to win the heart of the mother by a thousand tricks to amuse the infant Perseus; and there is great humour in the anapaests of the chorus of satyrs, who urge a speedy consummation of the wedding, and interpret Danae's signs of reluctance as really betokening a warm passion for Silenus. Throughout the piece there is a fresh and natural flavour that enables us to understand the judgment of the ancient critics.

The *Spectators at the Festival* or *Visitors to the Isthmus* (Θεωροὶ ἤ Ἰσθμιασταί) must have been equally amusing, so far as the miserable remnants permit us to judge. The satyrs bring masks depicting their somewhat questionable good looks to hang up as adornments to the temple of Poseidon on the Isthmus. We gather also that they propose to take part in the games, and that for this purpose they are going to run away from their master Dionysus. Their athletic zeal presumably produced unexpected results, and at the end they returned to servitude as before.

A few tiny scraps of other plays such as *Glaucus Pontius* (or *Glaucus Potnieus*) and of unknown plays give us no clue to their contents. The *Aetna* has been already discussed.

The content of Aeschylean drama is matched by the weight of its language and expression. Aristophanes, himself a master of language, gave characteristic expression to this fact when he made Aeschylus in the *Frogs* declare that great thought must find correspondingly great language (v. 1059). It is in this connection that the most obvious features of Aeschylean language occur: even

---

[1] On the text see R. STARK, *Rhein. Mus.* 102, 1959, 3.

where Aristophanes is burlesquing him, we can read between the lines the very real respect which the comic poet had for the 'Bacchic prince' (Βακχεῖος ἄναξ) as the chorus calls Aeschylus (v. 1259).

There is no 'linguistic adornment' in Aeschylus. With him we are still in a realm where the name belongs to the named as part of its essential being, in which word-magic is still strongly alive. Three consequences flow from this fact. Firstly there are the etymologies which Aeschylus so loves. To us they seem odd and contrived; but in fact they are rooted in the notion that the name is the key to the nature of the thing. Secondly there is the repetition of particular words, often running as a sort of *leitmotiv* through whole sections[1] – not as a literary adornment, but as the expression of its significance. Thirdly there is Aeschylus' verbal imagery, which again belongs to this class. It is not often that he contents himself with setting the two things compared side-by-side, with a simple particle of comparison (an example is *Choe.* 501, where the children who preserve the memory of the murdered man are likened to the corks that keep a fisherman's net from sinking): more often the native force of his language extorts from a single point of contact the whole correspondence which Homer would have conveyed in an elaborate simile. Thus Agamemnon (*Choe.* 501) might pity the young birds that cower down upon his grave; thus Eteocles (*Septem* 371) stands as helmsman at the poop of the state. This kind of language sometimes goes as far as can be borne, as in *Septem* 371, when a man rapidly approaching 'plies the oars of his feet'.

Aeschylus' range of expression is extraordinary. We notice this most easily if we compare the clearly articulated language of his dialogue, marked by obvious antitheses and sparing use of adjectives, with the flowing majesty of the choruses, devoid of clearly marked subdivisions. But even within these two main divisions the variation in linguistic expression is very remarkable. In the dialogue we find passages where Aeschylus' language 'towers up' (*Frogs* 1004), and others where the greatest effects are achieved by extreme simplicity. But always his style is the outward expression of that greatness (μεγαλοπρέπεια) which ancient critics admired in him, even while they sometimes felt themselves oppressed or repelled by the peculiar character of this greatness.[2]

The transmission of the text of Aeschylus fits into the general pattern of transmission of classical texts as outlined in our first section. But there are special problems connected with the tragedians. Revivals of Aeschylus' tragedies were staged very shortly after his death: after 386 such revivals of the older writers become more and more common. Obviously some rewriting might be done on such occasions: we have the statement of pseudo-Plutarch (*Vit. Dec. Orat.* 7.841) that the orator Lycurgus, who in the last thirty years of the fourth century regulated public worship at Athens, introduces a law for the provision of an

---

[1] See HILTBRUNNER's work cited above (p. 254, n. 2).
[2] A. DE PROPRIS, *Eschilo nella critica dei Greci*. Turin 1941.

official copy of the tragic texts, and forbade any alterations by the actors. Certainly such alterations or interpolations have to be reckoned with: what is uncertain is their extent. The question is ably discussed by D. L. PAGE, *Actors' Interpolations in Greek Tragedy*, Oxford 1934.

This official copy is probably the manuscript which Ptolemy Euergetes acquired from the Athenians by rather dubious methods (Galen in *CMGV* 10, 2. 1, 79). The definitive work on Attic tragedy was that done by Aristophanes of Byzantium in Alexandria, which laid the foundations of all subsequent editions and commentaries. The Alexandrian scholars received the works of Aeschylus more or less intact. Losses first began to be suffered in the declining years of the Roman empire, ultimately leaving only the seven plays which we now have. The most general supposition, dating from Wilamowitz' edition of the *Heracles*, has been that these represent a selection made for school use in the Antonine period. But in the light of new papyrus discoveries, this date may be too early.[1]

For the present manuscript situation H. W. SMYTH's 'Catalogue of the Manuscripts of Aeschylus' (*Harv. Stud. Class. Phil.* 44, 1933) needs to be supplemented by A. TURYN's *The Manuscript Tradition of the Tragedies of Aeschylus* (N.Y. 1943).

The variants in the manuscripts do not allow us to suppose that one of those now existing is the archetype; but agreements in error are so numerous as to suggest that they are all derived from one exemplar. Apparently in late antiquity there was an uncial manuscript containing the seven surviving tragedies, which survived the dark ages and became the basis of several Byzantine copies when letters revived in the ninth century. It seems – as we see in papyri – to have had variant readings added which satisfactorily explains the differences between the surviving manuscript groups. The principal authority for the text is the Mediceus (Laurentianus) 32, 9 which contains the seven tragedies, the best scholia on them, and the *Argonautica* of Apollonius Rhodius. At a later date it was bound up with the seven plays of Sophocles. Several leaves are lost, affecting large parts of the *Agamemnon* (311-1066 and 1160-end) and the beginning of the *Choephoroe*. This important manuscript was written about 1000 and was brought from Constantinople to Italy by George Aurispa in 1423. It came into the Laurentiana in the latter half of the fifteenth century.

The seven selected plays of late antiquity were reduced to an even narrower selection of three by the Byzantines – *Prometheus*, *Persae* and *Seven*. The manuscripts of this class come from a single exemplar, which seems to be independent of the Mediceus. Another manuscript group includes these three and the *Agamemnon* and *Eumenides*. A member of this group is the Neapolitanus (II F 31) written by Triclinius himself about 1320. The importance of papyri in giving us new material has already been discussed.

Bibliographical works: M. UNTERSTEINER, *Guida bibliografica ad Eschilo*. Arona 1947; also my reports on current work in *AfdA* 1948 etc. (last in 1961); H. J.

---

[1] Cf. R. STARK, *Annales Univ. Saraviensis. Philos.-Lettres* 8, 1959, 35.

METTE, *Gymn*. 62, 1955, 393. Editions: one must still mention GODFREY HER-
MANN's (Leipz. 1852, 2nd ed. 1859), which was very important in the establishing of the text. The leading editions nowadays are: U. V. WILAMOWITZ, Berl.
1914 (ed. min. 1915, repr. 1958); P. MAZON, *Coll. des Un. de Fr.*, 7th ed. 1958;
G. MURRAY, 2nd ed. Oxf. 1955; M. UNTERSTEINER, Milan 1946; with Eng. trans.
in the Loeb Library by H. W. SMYTH, 2nd ed. Lond. 1957; with Germ. trans. in
the *Tusculum-Bücherei* by O. WERNER, Munich 1959, with the fragments and a
good appendix. Interpretation: U. V. WILAMOWITZ, *Aischylos-Interpretationen*.
Berl. 1914. H. J. ROSE, *A Commentary to the Surviving Plays of Aeschylus*. 2 vols.
Verh. Nederl. Ak. Afd. Letterkunde, N. R. 64. 1 and 2. Amsterdam 1957–58.
Individual plays (editions and studies): *Persae*: ed. P. GROENEBOOM, Groningen
1930 (com. trans. into German, in two parts, Göttingen 1960, as *Studientexte*
III-1). M. PONTANI, Rome 1951. G. ITALIE, Leyden 1953. H. D. BROADHEAD,
Cambr. 1960, with detailed commentary. L. ROUSSEL, Presses Univ. de France
1960 (original but rather problematical). (Stud.): K. DEICHGRÄBER, V. sup. p.
245, n. 2. – *Septem*: (ed.): P. GROENEBOOM, Groningen 1938. G. ITALIE, Leyden
1950. (stud.) E. FRAENKEL, *Sitzb. Münch.* 1957-3, with a very fine analysis of the
pairs of speeches. On the filling of a lacuna after v. 676: W. SCHADEWALDT, 'Die
Wappnung des Eteokles'. *Eranion. Festschr. Hommel.* Tübingen 1961, 105. The
spuriousness of the ending is maintained by W. PÖTSCHER, *Eranos* 56, 1958, 140.
The arguments against its being genuine are critically examined by H. LLOYD-
JONES, *Class. Quart.* 53, 1959, 80. The significance of the figure of Eteocles has
been the subject of several articles: E. WOLFF, 'Die Entscheidung des E. in den
Sieben gegen Theben'. *Harv. Stud.* 63, 1958 (Festchr. Jaeger), 89. H. PATZER,
'Die dramatische Handlung der Sieben gegen Theben'. ibid. 97. A. LESKY,
'Eteokles in den Sieben gegen Theben'. *Wien. Stud.* 74, 1961, 5. K. V. FRITZ,
'Die Gestalt des Eteokles in Aesch. "Sieben gegen Theben"'. *Antike und moderne
Tragödie*. Berl. 1962, 193. – *Supplices*: (ed.): J. VÜRTHEIM, Amsterdam 1928. M.
UNTERSTEINER, Naples 1935. W. KRAUS, Frankfurt a. M. 1948. (stud.): R. P.
WINNINGTON-INGRAM, 'The Danaid-Trilogy of Aeschylus'. *Journ. Hell. Stud.*
81, 1961, 141. *Prometheus*: (ed.): P. GROENEBOOM, Groningen 1928. E. RAPISARDA,
Turin 1936. O. LONGO, Rome 1959. (stud.): J. COMAN, 'L'Authenticité du Prom.
enchaîné'. Bucharest 1943. W. KRAUS, *RE* 23, 1957, 666. B. H. FOWLER, 'The
Imagery of Prometheus Bound'. *Am. Journ. Phil.* 78, 1957, 173. H. S. LONG,
'Notes on Aesch. Prom. Bound.' *Proc. Am. Philos. Soc.* 102-3, 1958, 229. G.
MÉAUTIS, *L'Authenticité et la date du Prom. enchaîné d'Esch.* Geneva 1960.– *Oresteia*
(ed.): W. G. HEADLAM – G. THOMSON, Cambr. 1938. (stud.): E. R. DODDS, 'Morals
and Politics in the Oresteia'. *Proc. Camb. Phil. Soc.* 186, 1960, 19. K. V. FRITZ,
'Die Orestessage bei den drei grossen griech. Tragikern'. *Antike und moderne
Tragödie*. Berl. 1962, 113. One mentions only under protest the perverse attempt
of R. BÖHME to represent our *Oresteia* as a concoction for the stage in 408–405:
Bühnenbearbeitung Aesch. Tragödien. Basel 1956; part 2, Basel 1959; also Ἀρκύ-
στατα. *Die Sprache* 7, 1961, 199. – *Agamemnon*: (ed.): P. GROENEBOOM, Groningen 1944. E. FRAENKEL, 3 vols. Oxf. 1950, a monumental edition with an
English translation, useful for the whole field of tragedy. G. AMMENDOLA,

Florence 1956. J. D. DENNISTON and D. PAGE. Oxf. 1957. (stud.): E. FRAENKEL, *Der Ag. des Aisch.* Zürich 1957 (lecture). *Choephori*: (ed.): P. GROENEBOOM, Groningen 1949. – *Eumenides*: (ed.): P. GROENEBOOM, Groningen 1952. (stud.): S. J. LURJA, *Die politische Tendenz der Trag. 'Die Eum.' Bibl. Class. Or.* 1960, 295. Fragments: (ed.): A. NAUCK, *Trag. Graec. Fragm.* 2nd ed. Leipz. 1889. H. J. METTE, *Suppl. Aeschyl.* Berl. 1939; with supplement Berl. 1949. B. CANTARELLA, *I nuovi frammenti eschilei di Ossirinco.* Naples 1948. Selection in D. L. PAGE, *Literary Papyri.* Loeb Class. Lib. 1950. H. J. METTE, *Die Fragmente der Tragödien des Aisch.* Berlin 1959 (a very full edition, to which a second volume is promised containing a translation, and a commentary tying the fragments together). LLOYD-JONES's appendix to the edition of H. W. SMYTH is very valuable for its textual suggestions on the larger papyrus fragments and its detailed bibliographies. On various fragments see also W. STEFFEN, *Studia Aeschylea.* Breslau 1958. (stud.): *Niobe*: bibliography in PAGE (v. sup.). *Myrmidones*: W. SCHADEWALDT, *Hermes* 71, 1936, 25. K. VYSOKÝ, 'Aischylova Achilleis'. *Listy Filologické* 81, 1958, 147. A bowl in Vienna relevant to the trilogy: H. KENNER, *Oest. Jahrh.* 33, 1941, 1; on the *Dictyulci*: R. PFEIFFER, 'Die Netzfischer des Aisch. und der Inachos des Soph.'. *Sitzb. Münch.* 1938, 12. E. SIEGMANN, 'Die neuen Aischylos-Bruchstücke'. *Phil.* 97, 1948, 71 (deals also with the smaller papyrus fragments). A. SETTI, 'Eschilo Satirico'. *Ann. Scuola Norm. di Pisa* 1948, 1 and 1952, 3 (deals also with the *Isthmiastae*). M. WERRE-DE HAAS, *Aeschylus' Dictyulci.* An Attempt at Reconstruction of a Satyric Drama. Leyden 1961. *Isthmiastae*: B. SNELL, 'Aischylos' Isthmiastai'. *Herm.* 84, 1956, 1. K. REINHARDT, ibid. 85, 1957, 1 (now in *Tradition und Geist.* Göttingen 1960, 167). The Heidelberg papyrus 185 is tentatively attibuted to the *Prom. Lyom.* by E. SIEGMANN, *Lit. griech. Texte der Heidelberg. Pap. Sammlung.* Heidelb. 1956, 21. See also K. REINHARDT, *Herm.* 85, 1957, 12 (now in *Tradition und Geist.* Gött. 1960, 182), who supposes that Pandora emerges to the accompaniment of blows from a hammer. N. TERZAGHI, 'Il Prom. di Heidelberg'. *Athenaeum* N.S. 39, 1961, 3. *Pap. Heidelb.* 186 may come from the opening of the *Danae*, according to M. GIGANTE, *Parola del pass.* 51, 1956, 449. *Pap. Ox.* nr. 2253 is attributed by R. STARK, *Herm.* 82, 1954, 372, to the prologue of the *Iphigenia*, with Calchas speaking.– Scholia: W. DINDORF, Oxf. 1851; on the *Persae*: O. DÄHNHARDT, Leipz. 1894.– Lexica: W. DINDORF. *Lexicon Aeschyleum.* Leipz. 1873. G. ITALIE, *Index Aeschyleus.* Leyden 1955. Translations: Droysen's German trans. has been reprinted by W. NESTLE, 4th ed. Stuttgart 1957, and by W. FRIEDRICH in his *Tragici Graeci.* Munich 1958. Eng. trans. in vol. 1 of *The Complete Greek Tragedies*, by D. GRENE and R. LATTIMORE, Univ. of Chicago Press 1959. Italian by C. CARENA, Einaudi 1956. WILAMOWITZ's translation of the *Oresteia* had enormous influence in its time. – Language: C. F. KUMANIECKI, *De elocutionis Aeschyleae natura. Archivum Filologiczne* 12. Kraków 1935. W. B. STANFORD, *Aeschylus in his Style.* Dublin 1942. F. R. EARP, *The Style of Aeschylus.* Cambr. 1948. DOROTHY M. CLAY, *A Formal Analysis of the Vocabularies of Aeschylus, Sophocles and Euripides.* 2 parts. American School in Athens 1958 and Minneap. 1960. LEIF BERGSON, *L'Épithète ornamentale dans Esch., Soph. et Eurip.* Uppsala (Lund) 1956. FR. JOHANSEN, *General Reflections in Tragic Rhesis.* Copenhagen 1959. Monographs: WALTER NESTLE, *Menschliche Existenz und politische Erziehung in der Tragödie des Aisch.* Tüb. Beitr. 23, 1934. G. MURRAY, *Aeschylus, the Creator of Tragedy.* Oxf. 1940. R. CANTARELLA, *Eschilo.* Florence 1941. G. THOMSON, *Aeschylus and Athens.* 2nd ed. Lond. 1946. K. REINHARDT, *Aischylos als Regisseur und Theologe.* Berne 1949. F. SOLMSEN, *Hesiod and Aeschylus.* New York 1949. A. MADDALENA, *Interpretazioni eschilee.* Turin 1951. E. T. OWEN, *The Harmony of Aeschylus.* Toronto 1952. M. UNTERSTEINER, *Le Origini della trag.* 2nd ed. Einaudi 1955. J. H. FINLEY, JR., *Pindar and Aeschylus.* Harvard Univ. Press 1955. D. KAUFMANN-BÜHLER, *Begriff und Funktion der Dike in den Trag. des Aisch.* Bonn 1955. G. J. M. J. TE RIELE, *Les femmes chez Eschyle.* Groningen 1955. W. KRAUS, *Strophengestaltung in der griech. Tragödie. I. Aisch. u. Soph.* Sitzb. Oest. Ak. Phil.-hist. Kl. 231-4, 1957. J. DE ROMILLY, *La Crainte et l'angoisse dans le théâtre d'Eschyle.* Paris 1958, a book which, starting from the words, penetrates deep into the spirit of Aeschylean tragedy. Ead., *L'Évolution du pathétique d'Esch. à Euripide.* Paris 1961. J. KELLER, *Struktur und dram. Funktion der Botenberichte bei Aisch. u. Soph.* Diss. Tübingen 1959 (typewritten). W. KIEFNER, *Der religiöse Allbegriff des Aisch.* Diss. Tübingen 1959 (typewritten). E. MOUTSOPOULOS, 'Une Philosophie de la musique chez Esch.' *Rev. Ét. Gr.* 72, 1959, 18. H. D. F. KITTO, *Form and Meaning in Drama.* 2nd ed. Lond. 1960. See also the sections in POHLENZ, HARSH, LESKY, KITTO and D. W. LUCAS, *Greek Tragic Poets.* 2nd ed. Lond. 1959.

2 SOPHOCLES

In ancient tradition the names of the three great tragedians are strikingly linked with the decisive battle of the Persian wars. Aeschylus fought at Salamis; Sophocles was one of a chorus of beautiful boys who danced to celebrate the victory; Euripides was born on the very day of the battle. The first two statements may be believed. The whole tradition, however, can be given a deeper meaning as symbolizing the significance to each man of those days when Athens burned and freedom was won. For Aeschylus those happenings were the ultimate attestation of divine justice; they shed a bright lustre over the life of Sophocles; Euripides could only hear of them from the generation before his own.

We may look upon the story in this way if we wish, but it arose simply from the passion for striking synchronisms which prevailed among ancient historians. It was permissible for such a purpose to adjust or even to invent dates. The date of Sophocles' birth is one which has been involved in uncertainty through constructions of this kind.[1] Of the various reports which we have, that of the Marmor Parium, dating it in 497-496, seems the most plausible.

His death, however, can be dated accurately enough. There is no reason to doubt the touching story in the ancient life of Euripides, that on the news of his rival's death Sophocles dressed his chorus and actors in mourning at the proagon of the Dionysia in 406. But when Aristophanes produced the *Frogs* at the Lenaea of 405 Sophocles was already dead.

[1] F. JACOBY, *F Gr Hist* on 239 *Marm. Par. ep.* 56 and 64 and on Apollodorus F 35.

In the comic literary criticism of that play Aristophanes brings out the contrast between Aeschylus and Euripides – a contrast between two epochs. This duel left no room for Sophocles, but Aristophanes made a virtue of necessity and removed him from the contest with a neat piece of characterization (82) which pleasingly attests the tragedian's tranquil and peace-loving temper. This was how the Athenians had known him while he lived. The manuscript *Life* which sometimes accompanies his tragedies, a late Hellenistic production, attests the charm of his personality, which won all hearts. The poet who knew the tragedy of human life and the very depths of sorrow as no other did, lived his outward life in a warm and peaceful light, and served his fellows as an example of a happy man.

His father was Sophillus, who gained his wealth from the manufactures of his slaves. The family was a distinguished one in Athens. The stress laid by the *Life* on his education in gymnastics and music accords well with his receiving the honour of appearing in the celebrations for Salamis. If his music-teacher really was Lamprus, he was following a good academic tradition, since the Pseudo-Plutarch *De Musica* groups Lamprus together with Pindar and Pratinas (1142 b).

The *Life* declares that it was Sophocles' love of Athens (φιλαθηναιότατος) that made him refuse invitations to the courts of kings. There may be a grain of truth here: certainly, so far as we know, Sophocles never left his city except upon its service. There is another respect in which he differs sharply from the other two tragedians: he signalized his participation in the life of the city by undertaking high public office. The Athenians were struck by his being chosen strategus in the Samian War together with Pericles (441-440). The hypothesis of the *Antigone* says that the appointment was a recognition of his poetic genius. In Athens at that time such a thing is conceivable. However that may be, Sophocles saw no fighting when he was one of the ten strategi. The soul of the college of generals was of course Pericles. Athenaeus[1] has preserved a contemporary story from the *Epidemiae* of Ion of Chios concerning the poet's stay on that island. The Athenian proxenus on Chios entertained the distinguished guest, who most engagingly displayed his wit and wide reading over the dinner-table. When he succeeded in snatching a kiss from a beautiful boy who poured out the wine, he remarked that he was not half such a bad strategist as Pericles imagined. The justice of this ironic self-criticism is borne out by Ion's own statement, that in the service of the state Sophocles displayed no particular ability or energy; in fact he behaved very much like any man in the Athenian street. All the reports fit together: those depths from which Sophocles' poetry of human fragility and suffering was born underlay a surface of peace and happiness, of light and animation.

Rather unreliable reports[2] make it just possible that Sophocles became strategus once again. His work in the principal financial commission of the state may well have been more important than his service in the field. Since the tribute-lists

---

[1] 13. 603 E = Ion fr. 8 Blumenthal.
[2] *Vita* 9. Plutarch *Nic.* 15. 2. Cf. EHRENBERG (*v. inf.*), 117, I. H. D. WESTLAKE, 'Sophocles and Nicias'. *Herm.* 84, 1956, 110.

for the year 443–442 name only him as Hellenotamias, he must have held a special place – probably the presidency – in that body.[1] This is the first occasion that a Hellenotamias is named in this way – an indication of the particular importance of that year of office, in which the Hellenotamiae made important innovations concerning the tribute from the maritime league.

The balance and sanity which Sophocles displayed to the world was probably the reason for his election in old age to that college of *probouloi* which after the Sicilian catastrophe had to face the oligarchical determination to have a tighter discipline in the state. Aristotle tells us this in *Rhet.* 1419 a 26, and goes on to report that Sophocles said to Pisander, referring to the putsch of 411, that he could not favour it, but there was no other way.

What we hear of Sophocles' various official posts is quite extraneous to the understanding of his poetry. It is interesting only as adding to his portrait a few strokes that do not come from the central qualities of his genius. What we hear of his activity in the worship of the gods is much more relevant. It was only recently that a clear picture could first be drawn.[2] In 420 the Athenians took up the cult of Asclepius, the great healer-god of Epidaurus, and Sophocles was given official duties in the establishment of the cult. A paean which he composed for the god was still sung in Philostratus' time (*Vita Apollon. Tyan.* 3. 17), and remains of it survived on fragments of inscriptions from the Empire (cf. D. *Anth. Lyr. Suppl.* 4 and 56). In return for such services Sophocles himself was posthumously honoured as a hero under the name of Dexion. His special connection with Asclepius is explained by the statement in the *Life* that he was priest of a healer-hero called Halon. When the excavations on the western slope of the Acropolis disclosed the shrine of a healer-god Amynus dating back to the sixth century including inscriptions naming Asclepius and Dexion, it was thought that for the Halon of the *Life* we should read Amynus. But O. Walter has now shown that the two inscriptions IG 22, 1252 f. refer unmistakably to two shrines – one of Amynus and Asclepius, the other of Dexion. The reason for Körte's proposed emendation thus vanishes. We follow the *Life* in connecting Sophocles with Halon, although we cannot say very much about this hero, except that he is reckoned to have studied with Asclepius under Chiron.

In very sharp contrast to Euripides, Sophocles quickly won and long maintained a favourable public. In his youth he is said to have followed the ancient practice of appearing in person on the stage: his lyre-playing as Thamyris and ball-playing as Nausicaa in plays of those titles were long remembered in Athens. He is said to have given up this practice because of the weakness of his voice. Sophocles must have begun to produce about the time when the actor-playwright tradition was dying out. The explanation offered by the *Life* is most likely an aetiological invention: in reality the increasing demands on the actor's technique enforced this separation of function.

---

[1] EHRENBERG (*v. inf.*), 120.

[2] O. WALTER, 'Das Priestertum des Sophokles'. *Festschr. Keramopullos.* Athens 1953, 469. Reception of Asclepius: WILAMOWITZ, *Glaube der Hellenen.* 2, 1932, 224. Attribution of an anonymous paean to Sophocles: J. H. OLIVER, *Hesperia* 5, 1936, 91.

It was in 468 that Sophocles produced his first play. We read in Plutarch's life of Cimon that on this occasion the leader of the aristocratic party together with his nine fellow-generals took on the duties of judges at the request of the archon presiding over the games, and that they awarded the prize to Sophocles. From Pliny, *Nat. Hist.* 18. 65 Lessing inferred that the victorious tetralogy probably included the *Triptolemus*. The story of the Eleusinian hero who on his winged chariot carried the gifts of Demeter and thereby the blessings of civilization all over the world must have been a subject very near to the hearts of the Athenians.

The inscription listing the victors at the Dionysia (IG 22. 2325) gives Sophocles eighteen victories. Suidas gives twenty-four, the *Life* twenty. The larger numbers are more probably right, and include victories at the Lenaea.[1] The *Life* gives some other valuable notices, such as that Sophocles was never beaten into third place in the competition and that Aristophanes of Byzantium had texts of 130 of his plays at Alexandria, of which, however, seven[2] were reckoned spurious. The knowledge that the Alexandrians – assuredly not without reason – excluded so many plays as spurious ought to give pause to those who seek to dismiss the problem of the genuineness of particular plays (e.g. the *Rhesus* of Euripides) simply by declaring how improbable it seems that spurious plays should have crept into a corpus of pieces attributed to any author.

According to Suidas Sophocles also wrote paeans and elegies. We spoke of paeans in connection with Asclepius, and an ode to Herodotus (D. *Anth. Lyr.* fasc. 1, p. 79), which the poet says he wrote at the age of fifty-five, is attested by a considerable fragment. We are a little doubtful when the same Suidas tells us that Sophocles also wrote a prose treatise *On the Chorus*, in which he contrasted himself with Thespis and Choerilus. We do, however, know that in Sophocles' day such men as Ictinus, architect of the Parthenon, and the sculptor Polyclitus wrote technical treatises on their art, and it is possible that Sophocles may have expressed his views similarly on questions connected with the chorus. Its numerical strength may have been one of the things discussed. The *Life* and Suidas are good evidence for his having increased the number from twelve to fifteen. This innovation either came later than the *Oresteia* of Aeschylus or was not adopted by him. Where the third actor was concerned, on the other hand, Aeschylus followed the younger poet's lead.[3] Aristotle's statement in the fourth chapter of the *Poetics*, that Sophocles introduced scene-painting, is difficult for us to interpret in the development of stage painting in antiquity, since we know so little about it. But fortunately we can form a clear idea of one innovation which was of great importance for the structure of tragedy. Sophocles gave up the trilogy unified by subject in favour of separate, independent pieces. He gave

---

[1] Cf. C. F. RUSSO, *Mus. Helv.* 17, 1960, 166, 2. On production dates see H. HOFFMANN, *Chronologie der attischen Tragödie*. Diss. Hamb. 1951 (typewritten).

[2] The *Vita* names 17, but the emendation proposed by T. BERGK brings this up to a reasonable figure which can be reconciled with Suidas' figure of 123 plays.

[3] Cf. PICKARD-CAMBRIDGE, *Dram. Festivals* 1953, 131.

up thereby a great compositional form, which had probably been the personal creation of Aeschylus; but this loss was compensated by increased tautness of structure in the separate plays. In the last resort this development expresses the tendency in Sophocles to make his tragedies more and more concerned with the fate of the individual as a central theme. But to break up the thematic trilogy was not a thing that Sophocles always did. The didascalic inscription from Aixona[1] speaks of a *Telephia* which may be plausibly assumed to have centred on the fortunes of Telephus, Heracles' son who later became king of the Mysians.

Our fragmentary tradition makes us see the great figures of classical antiquity in isolation, and we forget how lively their relations must have been with the intellectual movements of the time. We have to bear this in mind in considering the rather difficult statement of the *Life*, that Sophocles formed a 'θίασος to the Muses from the circle of the cultivated'. A *thiasos* to the Muses is mentioned also in Aristophanes (*Thesm.* 41), and in connection with Sophocles we must think of a circle which combined sociability with wit and learning. The tone of such a gathering is probably illustrated by the conversation on Chios which we mentioned earlier. The consecration to the Muses is of course in keeping with the period.

Our biographical tradition contains so much pure anecdote that it is often hard to say where fable ends and usable history begins. Thus the tale of family discord's having darkened Sophocles' later years has been and will be variously estimated. Iophon, the poet's son by Nicostrate, is said to have brought an action against his father before the *phratores* because he had unduly preferred a grandson in a collateral line. This grandson was also called Sophocles, and was the son of one Ariston, who was Sophocles' son by the Sicyonian Theoris.[2] Sophocles certainly did have a son Ariston and other descendants by that line, but the story of the action to have the old man put under his son's tutelage – which in any case could not have been presented before the *phratores* – is the more open to doubt since the name of Satyrus appears in connection with it in the *Life*. We shall need to consider the qualities of this writer in discussing the biography of Euripides.

The poet's death afforded particular scope for fables of this kind. To indicate once for all the character of these fables we give an example from the *Life*. First Sophocles choked while eating a grape. Secondly he overstrained himself reading a long section of the *Antigone* (note in passing the testimony to reading of the plays aloud). Thirdly, he died of joy at a victory! On the other hand, the inventions of the biographers can be as pleasing as the following: during the siege of Athens, being twice warned by Dionysus in a dream, Lysander allowed free passage to Sophocles on his last journey to the family grave that lay by the road to Decelea.

[1] PICKARD-CAMBRIDGE, op. cit. 53. On the content of the individual pieces *Aleads*, *Mysians*, and *Assembly of the Achaeans* see A. SZANTYR, 'Die Telephostrilogie des Soph.'. *Phil.* 93, 1938, 287. S. SREBRNY, *Studia scaenica*. Breslau 1960.
[2] Cf. the family tree in *RE* 3 A 1927, 1042.

Of the various portraits[1] of the poet the statue in the Lateran is the best known. It must be remembered, however, that the head is the result of a classicistic retouching by Tenerani. The plaster cast in the Villa Medici is older. It shows a countenance which breathes at once the fullness and freshness of life and a profoundly serious mind.

We are not too badly informed about the chronology of Sophocles' plays, although we cannot date them very precisely. We have only two exact dates, both for plays of the last period. The *Philoctetes* was produced in 409, the *Oedipus Coloneus* not until 401, after his death. There is less certainty about the dating of the *Antigone* in 442. But since the hypothesis tells us that Sophocles was chosen strategus in the Samian war in recognition of this play, we can most easily understand this as a *post hoc, propter hoc*. Certainly we cannot suppose long to have elapsed between the *Antigone* and Sophocles' command.

Thus we have a few fixed points around which the rest can be arranged with fair probability. It is a view commonly held, and based on archaic features in language and composition, that the *Ajax* is the oldest of the surviving pieces, and was probably written between 460 and 450.

The opening of this play is the only one in Greek drama (as we possess it) which brings a great Olympian deity onto the stage. Unseen to Odysseus, but hardly to the audience, Athene has followed her protégé on his solitary walk. In the adjudging of the arms of Achilles Ajax had been placed second to Odysseus. In the night he rushed forth to avenge himself with the sword upon his opponent; but the goddess struck him with madness, so that he fell upon the Greek flocks and slaughtered them. A confused report of this has reached Odysseus, and he goes to find the truth at Ajax's own tent. He now hears it from the goddess, who also tells him that Ajax is now sitting crazed in his tent, tormenting sheep which he imagines to be Greeks. The Athene here portrayed has two aspects. First she appears as the Homeric deity, dispensing favour according to her whim to those she loves; in this character she calls Ajax out from the tent, to afford Odysseus that delight which she calls the highest – triumph over a fallen enemy. But the poet here provides a most beautiful antithesis. The Odysseus of the closing scenes is here foreshadowed, and he is given traits of humanity which here and elsewhere raise Sophocles' poetry above his own age.[2] Odysseus wants none of this pleasure that Athene credits him with; he steels himself for the spectacle that awaits him; when he cannot escape it, he has only words of deepest compassion. Even more, in the fate of his enemy he recognizes his own lot as a mortal, and his words of deep insight into the darkling life of human beings make him the very type of a spectator of Sophoclean tragedy.

Yet this same Athene, who plays her cruel game with the defeated Ajax, is elevated at the end of the prologue scene into a grave moral adviser. The gods,

---

[1] On portraits of ancient writers in general: L. LAURENZI, *Ritratti greci*. Florence 1941. A. HEKLER, *Bildnisse berühmter Griechen*. 2nd ed. Berl. 1942. K. SCHEFOLD, *Die Bildnisse der antiken Dichter, Redner und Denker*. Basel 1943. The head of Sophocles in W. SCHADEWALDT, *Soph. u. das Leid*. Potsdam 1948 (now in *Hellas und Hesperien*. Zürich 1960, plate 3).

[2] Cf. *Sophokles und das Humane* (*v. inf.*).

she says, love reverence and self-restraint in men: overweening arrogance they can punish terribly. The voice is the voice of Athene, but the sentiments are those of her Delphic brother.

After the prologue, in which the central problems of the piece are presented, the chorus of Salaminian sailors comes on. Tecmessa, Ajax's slave-wife, tells them of the dreadful events of the night; then she opens the tent, and we see Ajax, his mind now recovered, sitting amid the slaughtered sheep. He had thought himself injured in his honour by the judgment of the arms: now he realizes that through his frantic action honour is wholly lost. With lofty resolution he draws the conclusion which his character makes inevitable: to live in honour or to die in honour becomes the noble soul (479). Inaccessible to the prayers of his wife and of the chorus, he says goodbye to his little son. As he goes to die – the only road now open to Ajax – there is a strange interlude, which has occasioned the most various misunderstandings.[1] After a choral ode, full of gloom and foreboding, Ajax comes out of the tent again and declares that he has learned to understand a law of the universe which is based on perpetual change and demands subjection even from him. Accordingly he is going to purify himself by bathing in the sea, bury the fatal sword which Hector once gave him, and make his peace with the Atridae. It used to be thought that Ajax cannot lie, and the speech was taken as an expression of his true intention. Others, however, correctly understood the final words about the journey that he must take and the redemption that he hopes to find, but gave a peculiar sense to the speech as a whole: Ajax is as determined on death as before, but he is a changed man, with insight into a moral law which he was wrong to break. Against such interpretations we must make the sober observation that this dissembling speech, more than any other in the play, has a necessary dramatic function. It takes Ajax away from the protective care of his friends, and leaves him an open road to death. This is, of course, not all that is to be said. The emphasis with which Ajax speaks of change and reconciliation as laws of existence has a particular significance. But Ajax does not recognize here that he has made a mistake: he recognizes only one thing, that his whole character has no place in a world of this kind. Taken in this sense, the passage reveals the inner tragedy of this piece at its deepest level.[2]

There is another respect in which this speech is significant in the articulation of the drama. The chorus believes Ajax, and sings an ode of relief and jubilation. We find similar odes before the catastrophe in the *Antigone* and the *Oedipus Tyrannus*. This feature of Sophocles' technique was so well known in antiquity that it was referred to by a technical term as 'stretching' or 'intensification' of tragedy.[3] But this device is not just a trick of the trade to make the following

---

[1] A selection of misunderstandings in R. EBELING, 'Misverständnisse um den Aias des Sophokles'. *Herm.* 76, 1941, 283. He adds to them.

[2] Chilon of Sparta, among many other proverbs, was credited with the one οὕτως φιλεῖν ὡς μισήσοντα (Favorinus, Περὶ φυγῆς 18). This is a worldly wisdom to which Ajax feels himself in irreconcilable conflict. Odysseus' policy, on the other hand, is μισεῖν ὡς φιλήσοντα.

[3] DONATUS on Ter. *Andr.* 297: *Haec omnis* παρέκτασις (coni. R. STEPHANUS, περίστασις codd.) *tragica est: gaudiorum introductio ante funestissimum nuntium.*

catastrophe plunge into an even deeper abyss: it serves also to underline the fallibility of human reasoning – a favourite theme of Sophoclean tragedy.

The rejoicing of the chorus quickly dies away when a messenger brings a warning from the seer Calchas; today Ajax must be guarded with all care, for the anger of Athene threatens to destroy him. If he survive this day, he can be saved. In the deepest anxiety the chorus and Tecmessa go off to look for their friend.

The scene now changes. We find Ajax on the seashore. The change of scene could very easily be contrived by playing the scene of Ajax's death before one of the *parascenia*, the lateral projections of the stage structure. Some bushes would easily provide the necessary cover for his falling on the sword and the exit of the actor, who is required in another part for the next scene. In a soliloquy before his death Ajax gives vent once again to his anger against the Atridae; then with profound and intimate feeling he casts a look at the world that he is leaving: the light of day, the meadows of his own country and the rivers of Troy.

This soliloquy of Ajax's comes not much more than halfway through the play: the drama of the hero's death is followed by a dispute over his posthumous honour. Tecmessa and the chorus find the body, and in their mourning they are soon joined by Teucer, the hero's half-brother, It is he who now leads the struggle against Menelaus and Agamemnon whose implacable hatred wishes to leave the corpse to dogs and vultures. In this contest he would be doomed to failure if he did not find an ally in Odysseus, who obtains honourable burial for the dead man.

This second part of the *Ajax* prefigures in a remarkable way the *Antigone*. In both conflict rages over the forbidding of burial, and humanity raises its voice against the revengeful will of an authority that does not know its own limits. Here the protest is voiced by Odysseus, who in the prologue saw Ajax only as an enemy. In his narrow hatred that extends even beyond the grave, Agamemnon cannot understand Odysseus, The latter knows what it is to hate an enemy, but he knows also the limits of that destructive passion (1347), and he knows the dead man's rights, which cannot suffer wilful infringement. When Odysseus says to Teucer (1376) that he wishes now to be his friend just as much as he was once his enemy, and makes himself willing to assist in obtaining honourable burial for the man who had been his bitterest foe, the narrow confines of hatred are left behind for that love which distinguishes the poet's noblest character.

Already in antiquity critics found fault (cf. schol. ad 1193) with the structure of the play, and in modern times it has been blamed for having a second and not much shorter part of the drama after the hero's death. But is the fate of Ajax in fact decided by his throwing himself on his own sword? Is not the fate of his corpse to ancient notions just as much a part of his history as what he did or suffered in his life? The inner unity of the play is undeniable, and it is visibly brought out by the presence of the corpse on the stage, with little Eurysaces kneeling beside it. But, on the other hand, it would be paradoxical to maintain that it has that admirable compactness of structure which characterizes high classical plays such as the *Oedipus*. The play has been well described as being in diptych form, and we shall find a similar structure recurring in the plays which immediately follow.

The difficult problem of interpretation here lies in the question: How far is the catastrophe to be considered as arising from the hero's own fault? One constantly finds the simple view stated that the hero's *hybris* is atoned for by his sufferings. Does not Athene at the end of the prologue speak of the anger of the gods against the overweening? Does not Calchas in his warning say that Ajax has twice injured the goddess by rebellious words? We are rather diffident nowadays of such simple estimates of ancient tragedy, especially Sophoclean tragedy,[1] and the *Ajax* has features which heighten that diffidence. The *hybris* of Ajax is not to be denied, but how strikingly marginal it is as a theme! It occurs in quite general terms in Athene's warning at the end of the prologue, and it is not made specific until the prophecy of Calchas in v. 762. What a striking limitation in time it is, that Athene's anger threatens the hero for this one day only: if he can be kept safe so long, he can be saved. In this context Franz Dirlmeier's observation[2] is very important, that the *hybris* of Ajax was a theme already supplied from epic poetry: Sophocles simply took it over and included it in his *Ajax*. The play, however, is not simply a drama of crime and punishment: it is the tragedy of the great man, whose excessive strength draws down lightning on his head and feels the full force of its deadly fires. Friedrich Welcker[3] perceived this better than many more recent critics when he said: 'It seems to me that Ajax fulfils his dramatic role more through what he is than through what he has done'.

It is also a tenable view that the Sophocles of the 'fifties, taking up the theme of guilt without giving it a central importance, had freed himself largely but not wholly from the influence of Aeschylus. This theory runs parallel to an expression of the poet's which is preserved by respectable tradition:[4] to reach self-fulfilment he had to free himself first from the grandiose style of Aeschylus, then from his own tendency to harshness and artificiality.

With some reservations to be made when we discuss the *Trachiniae* we can reckon it likely that the *Antigone* is the second oldest of the surviving plays.[5] We considered earlier how reliable the date 442 is.

There is no other play in which Sophocles brings out the leading themes so forcibly. Equally there is no other that has been so long and so determinedly misunderstood. The cause was the authority of Hegel, who highly praised the play in his *Ästhetik* (II 2. 1) while interpreting Creon and Antigone as representing state and family respectively. These are two opposing worlds of equal

---

[1] K. V. FRITZ, 'Tragische Schuld und poetische Gerechtigkeit in der griech. Tragödie'. *Studium Generale* 8, 1955, 194 and 219; now in *Antike und moderne Tragödie*. Berlin 1962, 1.

[2] 'Der Aias des Soph.' (*v. inf.*), 308.

[3] *Rhein. Mus.* 3, 1829, 68.

[4] Plut. *De Prof. in Virt.* 7, 79 B; cf. C. M. BOWRA, 'Sophocles on his own Development'. *Am. Journ. Phil.* 61, 1940, 385.

[5] On the previous history of the theme, which seems to go back to the epics, see H. LLOYD-JONES, *Class. Quart.* 1959, 96.

moral validity, whose representatives must needs come into a conflict that destroys both. What Hegel sketches out is a tragic theme of great potentiality - one which was developed in philosophy by Schopenhauer and in literature by Hebbel, and which has played its part in modern discussions of tragedy. But as applied to the *Antigone* the theory of equal but opposed schemes of values is a misinterpretation.

Polynices, who has organized the expedition of the seven against his native city, has died before her walls, an enemy of his country. Burial in his native soil might justly be refused him according to Greek notions of law, provided he was laid to his last rest somewhere outside the confines. But Creon, who has become master of Thebes after the mutual killing of the brothers, goes far beyond this. He sets guards over the corpse to ensure that it is torn by dogs and vultures and that the remains rot in the sun. The Athenians who heard this Creon speaking could not but recall the curse which a priest from the family of the Buzyges had pronounced among them on anyone who left a corpse unburied. Sophocles' Creon is not the spokesman of a state which knows its rights and also its limitations. He is driven on by that arrogance which only recognizes itself: a *hybris* which is doubly dangerous, doubly culpable when it claims to speak with the voice of authority. The *Antigone* is not a propaganda-play, but in the actions and sufferings of its characters the question is clearly posed whether the state can lay claim to ultimate validity and authority, or whether it has to obey laws which have their origin elsewhere and which remain always beyond its reach.

The play runs its course as a drama of developing resistance to Creon and his gradual condemnation on all hands. The resistance is led by Antigone, and the poet makes her perform two acts of rebellion. On the first occasion she contrives unnoticed to throw a light coating of dust over her brother's corpse; then when the guards have again uncovered the rotting body, she comes back and is caught while trying to renew this symbolic burial. The repetition of the theme serves the single purpose of making her rebellion against Creon appear as forcibly as the difficult circumstances of the attempted burial permit. In addition we are allowed to see Antigone momentarily triumphant, before we share the sorrow of her defeat.

Scarcely has Creon pronounced sentence of death upon Antigone when the process begins which is to lead to his destruction. His son Haemon, who loves Antigone, is the first to reject him. After a long dispute, beginning with mild filial expostulation and ending with a cry of despair, Haemon leaves his father's presence. From his lips Creon has had to learn that the city is unanimous in condemning his judgment (692. 733); but he stands firmly on what he takes to be his and the state's rights. Creon is not a vulgar tyrant who knowingly does what is wrong. His belief that his own power and that of the state (he equates them in v. 738) has no limits so inextricably ensnares him that his progress from *hybris* to disaster is not merely a moral paradigm but a piece of true tragedy.

The gods also abandon Creon. They do so first through the mouth of the seer Tiresias, who speaks of the ominous signs which show that the city is polluted by the presence of the unburied corpse. By now Creon is full of rash and hasty thoughts; the gods have made him mad. He suspects that the seer has been suborned; in a last access of arrogance he declares that the dead man shall not be buried even if the eagles of Zeus carry the remnants of the corpse to the throne of the most high. But when Tiresias has gone after pronouncing a terrible curse, that Creon will pay in his own flesh and blood for his impiety against the dead, Creon's blindness, pride and folly suddenly collapse, and he determines to save what can yet be saved.

But the gods will not take his change of heart as expiation. In the underground chamber from which he resolves to free Antigone he finds her hanged. Haemon, after a wild outburst of hatred against his father, kills himself upon her body. A messenger reports the event to Eurydice, Creon's wife, who goes without a word into the palace, where she curses her husband and dies. Broken and abandoned, Creon remains, spared only to recognize his mistake too late.

The play is a drama of two characters. Without being able to lay stress on either one, we can speak of a tragedy of Antigone and a tragedy of Creon. Hegel's influence has caused long-lasting doubt whether we can speak of 'tragic guilt' in connection with Creon. Victor Ehrenberg's splendid book might have been designed to put an end once for all to this false interpretation. What Antigone stands for is made clear in the great scene of conflict with Creon. She stands for the eternal, immutable divine law, which cannot be disturbed by any human pretensions to power. The whole feeling of the passage tells us that she is expressing the poet's own convictions, and the feeling is supported by the unequivocal testimony of the *Oedipus Tyrannus* (865), where Sophocles praises the law of heaven, which has its origin with the gods and not in the nature of man.

Ehrenberg has shown that the common opinion which makes Sophocles and Pericles representatives of a basically unitary epoch at the summit of the classical period conceals in fact a very significant difference. The poet and the statesman were respectively representatives of a theonomic and an anthroponomic view of the world – not indeed in open conflict, but in a state of tension which foreshadowed the battle of giants (Plat. *Soph.* 246 a) which a later age fought concerning man and existence. Sophocles witnessed with deep anxiety the stormy developments of his age. In political life these developments displayed themselves in the beginnings of Athenian imperialism, in the spiritual world in the iconoclastic ideas of the sophists. That very period in which Sophocles wrote the *Antigone* seemed ready to break all bounds. Then it was that he penned that ode which we find as the first stasimon in the play, which has echoed as no other has over the centuries down to our own day. Man is a great and powerful, but also strange and uncanny creature (both senses are borne by δεινός): he can bend nature to his will in all fields, and treads every path with the utmost boldness. But still the one decisive question remains: Does he know of the absolute to which the gods have made him subject, or does he despise the eternal order and bring himself and his society to destruction?

In the first draft of his *Empedocles* Hölderlin has a beautiful passage in which Rhea speaks of the questions that Athenian maidens are asking: which of them did Sophocles have in his mind when he created Antigone, the brave yet tender heroine. In recent interpretations the figure is often grotesquely travestied:[1] Hölderlin here grasped it in all that complete humanity with which the poet endued it. This is the whole person who says (523): 'My destiny was not mutual hate, but mutual love'. No effort has been spared by scholars to strip these words, the basic expression of western humanism, of their full and true meaning, and to exclude from them a notion of love which Sophocles has been thought incapable of entertaining.[2] It has also occasioned surprise that on her way to her death Antigone weeps for the life which she is to lose. Yet the primary reason why this drama has retained its validity over the centuries is that Antigone is no superhuman figure, but one of us, with our hopes and desires, but also with the great courage to follow God's command against all contradictions. But the loving Antigone, like all Sophocles' great tragic figures, must tread her road in total isolation. At the beginning of the play she asks her sister Ismene to help her. It is in vain: with a contrast that recurs in Sophocles, the great soul of Antigone, inaccessible to fear and coercion, is displayed against the human type that is ready to compromise and to turn away from the moral law under the stress of hardship.

The chorus of Theban elders also refuses to help, and its attitude has been accordingly condemned. But if we read on and see how after the scene with Tiresias this same chorus condemns Creon right down to the impressive closing words, we shall easily see that in the first section the poet makes the chorus hold back so that he can present Antigone in complete isolation. Fear of Creon is a simple and satisfactory motivation.

In one passage we are out of sympathy with Antigone, as Goethe was.[3] It is in her last speech (905), where she justifies her action by saying that she could make good the loss of husband or child, but, since her parents are dead, she cannot replace her only brother. This is the expression of a basic trait of Greek character: some intellectual reason has to be found for the feelings of the heart. At the same time the passage is an interesting demonstration of the poet's familiarity with Herodotus, who makes effective use of the same idea in the story of Intaphernes' wife (3. 119).

After the foregoing observations it can hardly be necessary to defend the inner unity of the play against those who find that the third part of it is too much an independent tragedy of Creon. This is not to deny, of course, that the compactness of the composition is not – we might well say not yet – at the level of perfection which Sophocles reached in the plays of his maturity.

The diptych form is visible in the *Trachiniae* also, but its themes will be seen to show a kinship with those of the first *Oedipus*. Consequently we may place it between these two plays. Appropriately enough, Reinhardt has pointed out in it various features of archaic drama: the isolation of the individual character,

---

[1] E.g. the inhuman figure destroyed by demonic forces, as she is seen by G. NEBEL, *Weltangst und Götterzorn*. Stuttg. 1951, 192.

[2] Cf. A. LESKY, *Herm.* 80, 1952, 95.

[3] Conversation with Eckermann, 28th March 1827.

whose reaction to his fate produces the tragic pathos, and its tendency to static scenes instead of the later dynamic handling. Yet we can hardly follow him in dating the piece before the *Antigone*. Despite all the caution to be exercised in comparing different scenes, it is hard to think of the report of Deianira's farewell to her husband's bed (920) and the comparable farewell of Alcestis as being wholly independent one of another. Since the context and treatment suggest that Euripides was first, and since his *Alcestis* appeared in 438, we have a *terminus post quem* of as much reliability as such cases permit.[1]

Whereas the plays hitherto discussed begin with dialogue, the *Trachiniae* begins with a long speech from Deianira by way of prologue, setting out what the audience needs to know in advance. This reminds us of the practice which became a mannerism with Euripides; and other Euripidean features have been described in the play, particularly in the erotic motivation of Deianira's behaviour. A Sophocles under the influence of his younger rival is not unthinkable, and the prologue may certainly be so interpreted, even though Sophocles does it in his own way. But in some other respects the influence of Euripides has been absurdly overstated. There is very little similarity between the quiet devotion of Deianira and the overwhelming outbursts of female passion which we see on the stage of Euripides, and the basic theme on which the *Trachiniae* is built is quite different and in the truest sense Sophoclean.

Deianira is in Trachis with her son Hyllus, awaiting the return of her husband: the many adventures of his roving life have led him she knows not where. At last he sends a messenger to say that he will soon come home; but with the messenger comes the beautiful young princess Iole to live in the house. The way in which Deianira learns why she is to have the stranger under her roof is highly affecting. The herald Lichas spares her the truth out of pity for her: it is a later messenger who demolishes the pious falsehood. She knows now that Heracles' heart has turned from her; he is sending his concubine into the house. She does not flame into hatred and fury: Sophocles depicts this Deianira, no longer young, and grieving for her husband's lost affections, with the greatest tenderness. She remembers a love-charm that she has in the house. The dying centaur Nessus gave her some of his blood, with which she could recapture at any time the love of Heracles. For the proper understanding of the play it is imperative that we do not drag in a guilt-theme in Deianira's behaviour, contrary to the poet's intention. Love-philtres might be variously judged among the Greeks, but Deianira, believing the assertion of the dying centaur, is endowed here with all the innocence of a loving heart. To make her husband love her as she loves him is her one purpose, and she accepts the means unquestioningly. So she steeps the festal robe which she is sending to Heracles as a thankoffering for his safe return in the blood of Nessus. This, however, had been permeated with the poison of the Hydra from the arrow of Heracles which mortally wounded Nessus, and Deianira is horrified to see how the wool which she used to smear

---

[1] There is, of course, always a subjective element in opinions of this kind. E. R. SCHWINGE, *Die Stellung der Trach. im Werke des Soph. Hypomnemata* I. Göttingen 1962, 63, thinks the *Trachiniae* was written first.

the garment crumbles and disintegrates in the light. The next moment Hyllus arrives and relates how his father, as soon as he put on the fatal robe to make sacrifice, was seized with unendurable agony, how he cried and screamed, and was now being carried dying to Trachis. Like Eurydice in the *Antigone*, Deianira leaves the stage without a word. We are told by a nurse of her miserable death, her last words being of the bed for which she suffered and dared and to which she now bids farewell.

After the report of her death – the scenes are separated, as always, by a choral ode – Heracles is brought in. After his terrible sufferings he has fallen into unconsciousness, but awakes to renewed anguish. His sufferings and outcries and his last instructions fill up the rest of the play. Again we find the destinies of two people who are fatally linked together worked out to the end in separate sequences, and we recognize again the two-part composition of the earlier plays.

After waking up Heracles breaks out into wild laments. This is the same Heracles who at the sacrifice had dashed against the rocks the bringer of the fatal robe. But when he hears of the poison of Nessus, he gives in to his fate. Old prophecies are now, he sees, being fulfilled: his death is certain. He tells his son to prepare his pyre on mount Oeta and to marry Iole; then the cortège that takes the hero to his death leaves the stage.

A prominent place is taken by oracles in this piece, and thus again it shows a kinship with the *Oedipus*. These prophecies, ambiguous and obscure, yet certain to be accomplished in their true interpretation, bear witness before men to the power of the gods. But they only inform: they leave wide scope to the thoughts and plans of man. It is in this sphere that the action unfolds itself, as in the *Oedipus*. Man is not a passive sacrifice to his destiny; he takes an active part. But the gods have so arranged it that every step which he takes in the hope of avoiding his fate brings him nearer to it. A woman who in the innocence of her heart tries to renew the bonds of her husband's love brings him down to suffering and death. The hero who has freed so many countries from their plagues dies helplessly in appalling anguish. No formulation like the Aeschylean 'learning through suffering' helps us to interpret this event. The power of the gods, working from an unapproachable distance and with undiscoverable intent, acts thus and not otherwise in this world. The great piety with which Sophocles honours the divine force, even where it exerts itself most unpityingly, is strikingly exemplified at the end of the play. In the last words of Hyllus (1264) – the only such occasion in all the extant plays – man raises his hands in reproach against heaven: 'this is how the gods forget one whom they themselves begot. They should be ashamed to let such things happen.' But these frantic words are repudiated in the closing verses of the chorus. Here, at the end of the play, we hear a sentiment that characterizes all Sophocles' work: 'In all this has nothing happened that was not Zeus'.

A passage from the *Oedipus Tyrannus* is parodied in the *Acharnians* of Aristophanes (27). Consequently the play must have come out before 425. The description of the plague with which the action opens, but which is given no importance in the rest of the play, has been taken as reflecting the plague of 429, but this is uncertain. What is described is not a particular disease, but a general withering away of men, beasts and crops, such as that with which the Erinyes threatened the Athenians at the end of the *Oresteia*. If there is any connection with that dreadful year, it is only very loose. For all that, a date between 429 and 425 remains highly probable.

We begin our analysis with the form, to make it clear that here we meet a strength and compactness of composition which is alien to the older plays. Not merely is Oedipus the central figure in the plot: with the exception of the messenger's speeches and some very short introductory sections, there is no single scene in which he is not present. We shall find the like in the *Electra*. In both plays the importance which the central figure has in the plot gives him a corresponding position in the structure as a whole. We may take the completeness of this correspondence as one of the marks of what is truly classic.

The *Oedipus* has been called an analytic tragedy, since the decisive events have all occurred before the play opens and the toils of fate have already been drawn round Oedipus. His attempts to shake and tug at the net, only to entangle himself more and more in its meshes and finally to encompass his own destruction, are depicted in this play with a mastery of concentration and compactness that has not its like in dramatic writing. The devices with which the poet achieves this effect are very simple. Laius, king of Thebes, being alarmed by an oracle, had his newly born son exposed in the wastes of Cithaeron. The servant who had this order to obey gave the child to a Corinthian shepherd, who took it back to Corinth to his king Polybus. Both persons, the shepherd and the servant, have other important functions in the course of the action. Such economy of force as this makes possible the extremely close texture of the dramatic structure. The servant who should have exposed the child is the only one who later came back from the fatal encounter at the Phocian crossroad. It was there that Oedipus, fleeing from the Delphic oracle that he should kill his father and marry his mother, slew the aged Laius in an angry quarrel. The Corinthian shepherd reappears in the piece as the messenger who at a significant moment brings the news of Polybus' death.

It is the critic's right and duty to recognize such poetic devices as these. The book which Tycho von Wilamowitz has written on Sophocles does so to the full, and draws attention to several difficulties in the plays which present themselves when we think them over afterwards. Much can be learned from such analysis, but it should never make its rules absolute and deny to works of dramatic art the right to be a law to themselves.

With a deadly logic Oedipus' road leads him into darkness and desolation. At the beginning he answers the complaints of the city with kindness and sympathy. At any moment Creon is expected, having gone to Delphi to ask why the plague is thus devastating Thebes. He reports the god's reply, demanding expiation for the murder of Laius. With eager energy Oedipus seizes on the Delphic pronouncement, which refers to himself. The blind seer Tiresias is summoned, but will not speak. Finally, irritated beyond endurance by Oedipus' false suspicions, he denounces the king: he, the blind man, denounces the reputedly sharp-sighted king with being himself the murderer and living in fearful incest. So sudden and so contrary to all appearances is this revelation that no one takes it seriously, least of all Oedipus. His quick brain follows another and a devious path. He suspects a plot hatched by Creon to make himself king. He is soon ready to pronounce sentence of death, and Jocasta has to come between them to prevent a fatal issue. She comforts her husband by deriding oracles and the craft of seers. Did not Apollo prophecy that Laius would be killed by his own son? Yet the son died on Cithaeron, and Laius was slain by robbers at a crossroad. In this play every attempt to find comfort is a step towards catastrophe. Oedipus recalls in terror his sudden act at the Phocian crossroad: but Jocasta spoke of robbers, or more than one man. That is now his hope, and the servant who alone survived that meeting and is now living in the country will be able to give confirmation. Meanwhile a messenger comes from Corinth to announce the death of Polybus, whom Oedipus still reckons as his father. Again Jocasta feels able to laugh at Apollo's prophecies, and Oedipus also thinks that he has escaped the destiny of being his father's murderer. But there is still the second part of the prophecy, that he should marry his mother; and his mother is still alive in Corinth. Now comes another fatal attempt to set Oedipus's mind at rest. The messenger tells what he knows of Oedipus' birth. He was only stepson to Polybus and Merope; he was found exposed on Cithaeron, where one of Laius' servants gave him to the Corinthian. The veil is now torn from Jocasta's eyes. She tries to stop Oedipus enquiring further, but her efforts to halt the wheel of fate are in vain. She goes back into the palace in despair. Once again the hasty mind of Oedipus rushes to a false conclusion: Jocasta is probably afraid that he may be of low birth, but he is proud (what a height of tragic irony!) to call himself a child of fortune. This expression gives the chorus its theme for an ode which once again strikes a note of rejoicing before the catastrophe. How many are the gods who sweep over the mountains! One of them may have fathered their beloved king. Then comes the servant, the survivor of the Phocian encounter, the same who was to have exposed the child. It is not easy to make him speak, but at last all the awful truth is revealed to Oedipus. He rushes into the palace, finds Jocasta hanged, and blinds himself with the pins of her brooches so as to close for ever the fountain of sight. He staggers back onto the stage, takes a moving farewell of his daughters and prepares to go into poverty and exile.

To understand this great work we must first clarify a question which is hardly a question nowadays. Is Oedipus atoning for guilt? Aristotle (*Poet.* 13. 1453 a 10) traces his overthrow to a mistake ($\dot{\alpha}\mu\alpha\rho\tau\dot{\iota}\alpha$ $\tau\iota\varsigma$). Since immediately before this he expressly excludes moral obliquity ($\kappa\alpha\kappa\dot{\iota}\alpha$ $\kappa\alpha\dot{\iota}$ $\mu o\chi\theta\eta\rho\dot{\iota}\alpha$), it is clear that this mistake was not one involving wickedness. This condemns all the unworthy attempts that have been made to turn this drama into one of sin and atonement and to reduce the unparalleled intensity of its tragic feeling to a mere story with a moral. The action at the cross-road, where Oedipus in sudden fury killed an old man who was unknown to him, could not be reckoned a terrible crime, certainly not in Greek eyes. Oedipus' quick brain also, which so often outruns itself, is not in its nature blameworthy: its significance consists only in its contrast with the frightful power of the gods which goes its way inexorably for all the wit and will of men. The gods are so very much the more powerful, they shatter human fortune with such deadly certainty, that some scholars have seen nothing else in the play, and have called it a drama of destiny. Many have gone further and have said the same of Greek drama as a whole. There is no point in discussing such mistaken notions here: even of the *Oedipus* they express only half the truth. The king of Thebes is not a fainéant, who awaits his fate passively; he goes boldly to meet it and grapples it with a burning passion for the truth and a readiness to suffer that make him one of the greatest figures of the tragic stage. The old servant hesitates before the final appalling disclosure: 'God help me, but I am about to tell you dreadful tidings'. Oedipus answers: 'And I about to hear them: but hear them I must'. The verse declares both his fate and the greatness of his soul. Tycho von Wilamowitz and others have disputed Sophocles' ability to draw 'complete characters'. Now it is true that the way in which the dramatist puts his figures before us is different from the individual character-drawing of modern drama. (We cannot consider the question whether the dominance of the psychological element in this kind of art is an unmixed advantage.) Nor can we deny that there are particular passages in which the management of the scenes took precedence in the minds of ancient dramatists over consistency in the presentation of individual character. But it is far more important to remember that Sophocles drew his characters from the pre-existing realm of myth, characters not in the modern psychological sense, but great personal figures whose traits are attached to one central feature. Free of all purely accidental and individual elements, they stand before us in their great essential qualities, an imperishable heritage. Oedipus is one of these.

In this drama also the noble soul with its unqualified determination is set off by the type that is ready always to weaken and compromise; to 'take life as it comes' is Jocasta's great maxim (979): the strongest possible contrast to the path that Oedipus treads.

In the *Oedipus* also the gods play a very large part. But what kind of gods are they who bring men to the depths of ruin without knowing why it all happens? Are we to understand the gods as cruel beings to whom man is a plaything? This is the view embodied in Hofmannsthal's treatment of *Oedipus and the Sphinx*, but it has nothing to do with Sophocles. It will be noticed that in this play, which depicts the extremity of suffering without offering any inter- pretation of human fate such as Aeschylus gives, we find a choral ode (864) which sings of the eternal divine laws that originate in the highest heaven. At the end of this play also we might say, 'Here is nothing that was not Zeus'. The divine governance, inaccessible to mortal thought, fulfils itself in an appal- ling manner, but remains always valid and deserving of reverence. When Sophocles wrote this drama, the sophists were already in full cry after everything that tradition held sacred. He expressed his rejection of the new iconoclasm as clearly here as in the first stasimon of the *Antigone*.

The *Oedipus* does not merely express the tragic with greater purity than any other play in European literature; it enables us to recognize in a special way that phenomenon of tragic pleasure which Hölderlin embodied in his famous epigram to Sophocles:

> Manche versuchen umsonst, das Freudigste freudig zu sagen,
> Hier spricht endlich es mir, hier in der Trauer sich aus.

The undeniable fact that we go home from a performance of the *Oedipus* with a feeling of elevation, even of pleasure, is very hard to explain. But part of the explanation is that in all the grief and horror the poet never for a moment leaves out of sight a great cosmic order, which remains eternally valid through all changes and all individual suffering.

We can certainly reckon the *Electra* as one of the late plays, without venturing to assign a more definite date. The title is well justified, since the character of Electra, who in the *Choephori* of Aeschylus takes no part after the recognition-scene and the *kommos*, is dominant here from the parodos of the chorus to the very end. Unlike the *Choephori*, this is not a drama of Orestes, and consistently with this the ethical problem of matricide remains firmly in the background.[1] It is his treatment of Clytemnestra that enables Sophocles to avoid the problems involved and merely to allude to the killing once (1425). He makes her wholly evil, without that daemonic force with which Aeschylus endows her. In Sophocles she stands outside the fatal bond of the family curse: she is a depraved wretch whose removal we feel to be justified. We are not called upon to consider the son's feelings in taking her life. For this reason Clytemnestra is killed before Aegisthus, and it is on his killing that Sophocles has laid the principal stress in the closing scene.

In old tradition Electra saved Orestes as a boy and stood by his side when he returned home a young man. From these two facts Sophocles created the character which remains one of his masterpieces. In the prologue-scene, which is by way of a prelude to the drama of Electra, Orestes comes with his aged tutor before the palace of the Atridae in Mycenae and prepares the device which is to pave the way to his revenge. His speech is significantly interspersed with cries of lamentation from Electra within. Orestes goes to his father's grave: Electra herself now enters and pours out her sorrows first in a monody, then in alternation with the chorus of Mycenaean women. Her father shamefully murdered, her brother far away, she herself is treated like the vilest maid-servant. But what she finds hardest to bear is the wickedness of which she is conscious in the rulers of the house. She must cease to be Electra if she is to reconcile herself to it, as her sister Chrysothemis has done. Chrysothemis here plays the Ismene to her Antigone. Clytemnestra has had a warning dream, and has sent her compliant daughter to the grave of Agamemnon, but Electra has persuaded her sister to pray, as she makes the libation, not for her mother but for Orestes and the destiny of their house.

---

[1] This has been denied by many writers. A. WASSERSTEIN, *Gnom.* 32, 1960, 178, is certainly right in opposing the view that Sophocles does not condemn the matricide. The real point is that it was no part of his purpose to make it a central issue of the play.

Clytemnestra's threatening dream can be traced back through the *Choephori* to the choral lyric *Oresteia* of Stesichorus, but its detailed execution is different here. The idea of the tree that grows from Agamemnon's sceptre and over-shadows all the land is a further token of the poet's familiarity with Herodotus: it comes from the dream of Astyages before the birth of Cyrus (1. 108).

The middle section of the drama is composed of two scenes which embrace Electra's confident hope and her deepest despair. In a lengthy *agon* she tears the mask of hypocrisy from her mother's face, and despite her own sufferings asserts the place of righteousness in the world. The thoughts of both women are centred on Orestes. On his homecoming Electra builds all her hope: Clytem-nestra ends the scene with a veiled prayer to Apollo for protection from his vengeance. The old tutor then enters and tells of Orestes' death in a chariot-race at Delphi. There is such an immediacy in this report, in which the poet's art shows itself equal to the epic mastery of the messengers' speeches in Euripides, that we seem to change places with the women and to feel what they feel. Clytemnestra sighs deeply with relief: Electra, her last hope gone, is plunged into seemingly irremediable sorrow.

The *kommos*, re-echoing the report of Orestes' death, is followed by a scene which corresponds to the first between the two sisters and forms a frame round the central pair of scenes. Chrysothemis comes back full of excitement from her father's grave: she has seen there flowers and a lock of hair, with traces of a libation. It can only be that Orestes has returned home, and has offered libation and prayer on his father's grave. Electra is now placed between illusion and reality, and the tragedy of her situation is that at first she chooses wrongly. What Chrysothemis tells her, what is in fact true, would mean the fulfilment of all her prayers. But she is caught up in self-delusion, and cannot recognize the truth; on the basis of her own mistaken belief she overbears and persuades her sister into error. Her reaction to the situation as she sees it is to take action herself. With her own hand she will be revenged; Chrysothemis shall help her. Hence she demands from her sister a support, which her timid and temporizing character will not let her give. If the two were sharply contrasted in the first dialogue, the difference between them comes out no less sharply here. Electra is as much alone as Antigone going to her death. Orestes now enters with an urn which he says contains the ashes of Orestes. He does not recognize his sister. She believes the story and pathetically speaks to all that now remains of her brother. Now Orestes realizes who it is that is thus lamenting, and discloses himself. We might perhaps comment on the lateness of this recognition. Elec-tra's rejoicing knows no bounds, corresponding to her utter dejection in her first scene. The masterly construction of the play then permits a final broad correspondence between the opening and the closing scene. In the former the young man returns from abroad to the house of his ancestors to pass judgment: in the latter we have the fulfilment of his vengeance which restores him to his rights.

The *Electra* shows the style of Sophocles' old age, a style which has been best characterized by Karl Reinhardt. Instead of the isolation of the individual personages and the 'static expression of emotion' which mark the older plays, we now find a new relevance of the actors one to another. At the same time the management of the scenes is more dominated by the spiritual factor and is more diversified, while the dialogue has a new animation that comes from a heightened tension and adroit transitions.

These phenomena may be interpreted as symptoms of a very important development. One could most briefly formulate it by saying that in such plays as the *Electra* or *Philoctetes* the human being comes into the middle of the action in a new way. This does not imply a secularizing of the old ritual tragedy, such as we see in Euripides in those plays where he brings gods onto the stage. We have not the slightest reason to suppose that there had been any change in the profoundly religious world-view of Sophocles. It is rather that there is a change of emphasis bringing certain consequences in its train. Men are still ruled by the same gods, but they have withdrawn from the foreground of the action. In plays like the *Ajax*, *Antigone* or *Oedipus* man is in continuous converse with the gods: how far this is true of the *Oedipus Tyrannus* we shall see in the last of the plays, which contains the marvellous echo of their conversation. In all these plays the voice of the gods is heard through oracles or seers, and plays a forceful part in the action. In contrast Apollo's injunction to Orestes that he must revenge himself is left as a very marginal theme, and it is very much subordinated to the single figure of Electra with her sorrows and her hopes and her fearless resistance. The new light in which man is placed in the later dramas of Sophocles also allows us to see a new realm of the soul. As Electra addresses the urn which she imagines to contain the ashes of her brother, she finds language of the deepest and most intimate tenderness, such as we scarcely find elsewhere in Attic drama. This same Electra flares up into wild hatred against her mother, and when Orestes is killing them within, she utters the almost unendurable words: 'Strike her again, if you are capable'. Electra has the great and unflinching determination of Antigone, but we need only to compare the two characters to see how much richer Sophocles' portrayal of personality has become.

In the *Electra* the theme is no longer, as in the *Trachiniae* or the *Oedipus*, the irresoluble conflict between human plans and divine ordinance: the play is not a tragedy in the same sense as the older dramas. The poet is not concerned with demonstrating a great world-order, unfathomable to the human mind, which is attested in the destruction of the individual man. We see a human soul meeting grief with courage and rejoicing at deliverance. We are recurring to what we said before if we venture to say that the *Electra*, while it depicts tragic situations of great depth and intensity, is not as a whole the expression of a tragic world-view as the *Oedipus Tyrannus* is.

Much of what we have said applies equally well to the *Philoctetes*, which Sophocles presented in 409. It was a part of epic tradition, incorporated in the *Cypria* and the *Little Iliad*, that the Greeks on their way to Troy marooned Philoctetes on the island of Lemnos: the suppurating and evil-smelling wound resulting from a snake-bite made his presence intolerable to the others. But towards the end of the siege they had to go and fetch him, since a prophecy had warned them that Troy could not be taken unless he helped in the fighting with his miraculous bow – a weapon which had once belonged to Heracles. According to a scholium on ł ind. *Pyth.* 1.100, Bacchylides composed a dithyramb dealing with the fate of Philoctetes, and Pindar alludes to it in the *First Pythian*. All three great Attic tragedians used this theme, and the 52nd oration of Dio of Prusa contains a comparison of the plays, incomplete, however, and very rhetorical in its treatment. We cannot now tell by what means Odysseus in the *Philoctetes* of Aeschylus persuaded the hero to help those who had once abandoned him. The remains of a hypothesis to this drama (*Pap. Ox.* 20, 1952, nr. 2256 fr. 5) contain the names Neoptolemus, Philoctetes, Odysseus. It is an easy assumption that these are the personages of Aeschylus' play, but St. G. Kossyphopoulou (*Hellenica* 14, 1955/6, 449) has shown that the remaining letters can be so supplemented as to make the hypothesis refer to the play of Sophocles. The *Philoctetes* of Euripides was produced together with the *Medea* in 431. The myth here was made to carry a problem in Greek patriotism. Ambassadors of Greeks and Trojans pay court to the bearer of the miraculous bow; he hesitates between revenge and Hellenic sentiment, but finally the latter wins the day.

Sophocles' two predecessors in this field had a chorus of Lemnians. He introduced an innovation by making Lemnos an uninhabited island – a very important change. Not only is his Philoctetes shut out from the community of the Greeks, he is in great suffering, a sick man in awful isolation, living a miserable life on what he can shoot with the bow. Inevitably bitterness has eaten deeply into this great and proud heart, yet he declares his feelings with a touching confidence to the young Neoptolemus and sees in him such another as himself when he promises that the castaway shall be taken home. The contriver of the intrigue is Odysseus, and one cannot say that his character has traits of Sophoclean humanity. In this drama, with its unique association in an involved plot of three men widely differing in age and character, if we see things onesidedly through the eyes of Neoptolemus, Odysseus cannot but appear as a deceiver and betrayer. Yet it is impossible to see him as purely evil and to make an Iago of him. What he does is under orders from the Greek council of war, and he is responsible for the success of a plan on which the whole outcome of the war depends.

It has been justly remarked that we are never made quite clear about Odysseus' instructions. Is Philoctetes with the bow, or is the bow by itself to be brought to Troy? In several passages this is left obscure, while in others it is stressed that there are two alternatives.[1] This fact has caused some critics to essay an interpretation[2] which would make the play akin to the *Oedipus Tyrannus*. On this view the oracle which meant that Philoctetes was to be persuaded to come to Troy was misunderstood by Odysseus, who sought treacherously to gain possession of the bow alone: in consequence all his plans come to grief. If this was in fact the poet's intention, we can only wonder at the care he took to conceal it. It is advisable not to give exaggerated importance to these

[1] Vv. 68. 77. 101. 112. 612. 839. 1055.   [2] BOWRA (*v. inf.*), 261.

inconsistencies, many of which are detected only by the critic in the closet. It is certainly permissible to examine the devices by which the poet secures a lively and animated development of the story, but the only thing that is important is the gain in dramatic power and psychological appeal that results from them.

If Odysseus in the course of the intrigue appears in sharp contrast to Neoptolemus, this is a repetition of the contrast in the *Iliad* between him and Neoptolemus' father Achilles. Replying to the embassy (9. 312) he says that he hates like the gates of hell the man who says one thing and has another in his heart. His son is no less a hater of lies, and when he has to make himself the instrument of them, his whole soul is troubled to a perilous degree.

Odysseus has persuaded him – with great difficulty – to win over Philoctetes by a false story. From the very beginning Neoptolemus is struck by the appalling sufferings of the man whom he has to betray. But he yields to the authority of his older and more experienced companion. Now he has to hear the poor wretch's cries of joy at the thought of seeing human beings and hearing the Greek tongue once again, since he believes the promises of Neoptolemus and the chorus of Greek sailors that they will take him home to Greece. They have made ready to go, when Philoctetes has a frightful access of his infirmity. Neoptolemus cannot but see the extremity of his suffering: his pathetic attempts to dissemble his anguish, his wild cries and final sinking into a coma. Before this, the sick man had given into his hand the ultimate token of his trust – the bow which had preserved his life, such as it was, on the desert island. Drama at that day had no means of showing what goes on in a man's soul stage by stage, but the beginnings of such a technique are visible here. Neoptolemus, who at first was so ready of tongue in playing his part, but found himself more and more at a loss for words before Philoctetes' suffering, now says (806): 'For a long time I have been pitying your plight'. This pity makes him decide to expiate his treachery, and he holds to this decision through all the many difficulties arising from the opposition of Odysseus and the obstinacy of Philoctetes. Recognition of his guilt is the first step, giving back the bow (and thus driving Odysseus to the most frenzied threats) the second, and when Philoctetes resists all persuasion to come willingly to Troy, he forms the ultimate resolution: their promise to take the sick man back to Greece, previously a piece of heartless trickery, must now be carried out in truth. The glory to be gained before Troy no longer matters; if the Greeks threaten revenge, let them threaten. Supported by Neoptolemus, Philoctetes hobbles towards the ship.

Properly this should be the end of the play, but it cannot end in this way. While the tragic poet has much freedom in treating the traditional stories, and can please himself especially in the psychological motivation of events, he cannot alter firmly accepted cardinal points in a myth. Philoctetes did go to Troy and his bow decisively contributed to victory. Consequently, on their way to the ship, Neoptolemus and Philoctetes are stopped by an epiphany of Heracles. The Olympian hero speaks to Philoctetes and ends his obstinate resistance, thus putting the myth back on the rails very much in the manner of a Euripidean *deus ex machina.* But his connection with the plot is much closer.[1] That the bow of Heracles has been in Philoctetes' hands since the former died on Oeta is a superficial connection; what is more important is that he changes his friend's mind not by peremptory exercise of his divinity, but by referring to his own destiny, which led through suffering to apotheosis. Heracles' injunction to reverence the gods is in the voice of Sophocles himself, who kept the same pious convictions all through his life.

The self-contained perfection of Sophoclean art made impossible such topical allusions as Euripides sometimes makes. But we have seen – in the *Antigone* above all – that he reacted strongly to the sophistic movement, which during his maturity was busy undermining all traditional values. Men were at variance then, especially over education. Some still clung to the old aristocratic doctrine that inherited qualities (φύσις) were decisive for a man's character and actions; others shared the view expressed by the sophist Antiphon (VS 87 60): 'The greatest thing in human life to my mind is education.' We cannot go into this fascinating debate[2] with which Euripides characteristically concerned himself. But the *Philoctetes* is Sophocles' avowal of that old Hellenic conviction which is strikingly evident in Pindar: 'It is by inborn greatness of soul that a man is worthy. He who has only what he has learnt is a man in darkness.' (*Nem.* 3. 40). Another quotation from Pindar might sum up the *Philoctetes*: 'Neither the red-glimmering fox nor the roaring lion can ever change its nature.' (*Ol.* 11, 19). Thus Neoptolemus finds himself in a deeply tragic situation, where in serving Odysseus he does violence to his own nature. He has to withdraw from a task which he can only carry through at the cost of destroying his own native qualities. He voices this view himself (902): 'Everything becomes hateful when a man abandons his own nature (φύσις) and acts at variance with it'. And after he has given the bow back to Philoctetes, the latter says (1310): 'My son, you have let us see those qualities which were born in you'. As with every great work of art, there are various possible approaches to the *Philoctetes*: one of them is to consider it as a drama of the inextinguishable natural worth of man.

There is another and more important characteristic of Sophocles that appears in this play. When Philoctetes finds that he has been cruelly tricked by Neoptolemus, he calls aloud in his misery upon the bays, the cliffs, the wild creatures that shared his life on the island. And when he leaves the island after all is well, he bids a moving farewell to the scene of his sufferings, with its whispering sea, its echo from the mountains and its springs which gave him water. We are reminded of Ajax's last farewell, and we notice particularly here how the poet makes his characters strive to bridge that isolation to which destiny or their own greatness has condemned them.

In extreme old age Sophocles wrote his second *Oedipus.* His grandson, also called Sophocles, produced it after the poet's death in 401. There can be few

---

[1] The special features of this Sophoclean *deus ex machina* are well brought out by A. SPIRA, *Untersuchungen zum deus ex machina bei Soph. und Eurip.* Diss. Frankf. Kallmünz 1960.

[2] W. HAEDICKE, *Die Gedanken der Griechen über Familienherkunft und Vererbung.* Diss. Halle 1936. A. LESKY, 'Erbe und Erziehung im griech. Denken des 5. Jh.s'. *N. Jahrb.* 1939, 361.

comparable instances of a poet's writing a sequel after twenty years to his greatest work, so that the two formed together a unity of a new and special kind. In the *Oedipus Tyrannus* we see the tragically stricken man, cast down by the gods into the deepest misery that can be conceived. Now, in the *Oedipus Coloneus*, we have a sublime paradox: the same man whom the gods have so terribly struck down is at the same time one of their elect. Because they wanted to make an example of him, his fall was also his exaltation. Thus at the end of his painful pilgrimage he is called by them to assume the status of a hero, to rule from the grave as the 'blesser and protector of a land that deserved its own service of sacrifice'.[1] The chorus expressly says in an important passage (1565) that the sufferer is being exalted; and they speak of the justice of God. But we must guard against hastily importing Christian elements into the drama and thinking of Oedipus as receiving absolution as the reward for patient endurance of suffering. In fact every attempt at a rational formulation of the relation between man and god as it is shown in the two Oedipus-plays is doomed to failure. When we are told at the end of the *Oedipus Coloneus* that the gods call Oedipus to themselves as one who belongs to them, one for whom they have long been waiting, we detect a tone of intimacy with these awful beings.[2] In his *Empedokles* Hölderlin makes Panthea speak of the relations between gods and men in terms of a lovers' quarrel. Perhaps this expression takes us somewhere near what Sophocles is conveying in the image of these two great plays.

When Sophocles wrote this story of the old man's death, he himself stood before the gloomy portals which his Oedipus was entering, and he himself was destined to be a hero to his people after his death. The poet's nearness to death, which is echoed in many passages, particularly in the ode on the sorrows of old age and on death the comforter, gives the work an affecting undertone of gentle melancholy.

It was an Athenian local legend that Oedipus at last found peace in the grove of the Eumenides at Colonus Hippius, the hill of Poseidon near Athens. Euripides alludes to it in some verses of the *Phoenissae* (1703), although their authenticity has been suspected.

At the opening of the piece Oedipus, a blind beggar on his miserable journey, enters the grove of the dread, unearthly goddesses. When a man dwelling near by tries to turn him out, he realizes where he is, and recalls the Delphic prophecy which promised him peace here after all his sorrows. The chorus of old men of Attica hears with wonder who the stranger is that has come to their land. They speedily send for Theseus to decide what is to be done. Meanwhile Oedipus obeys the suggestion of the chorus that he should placate the goddesses into whose sanctuary he has forced his way. He cannot see to fetch a libation, and so he sends Ismene, who has joined her father and sister to share their grief and privation. It is here that we find the verses (498) on the possibility of vicarious sacrifice, in which the amiable piety of the poet might again seem

---

[1] GOETHE, *Nachlese zu Aristoteles' Poetik*. Jubilee edition vol. 38, p. 93.

[2] Cf. A. LESKY, *Rhein. Mus.* 103, 1960, 376, where Reinhardt's detailed treatment of the passage is cited.

to foreshadow Christian doctrine: 'Sufficient, I think, for thousands is a single soul for such atonement, if it comes with a pure heart'.

Theseus, the king of the country, now enters. He is the pet figure of Attic mythology: to him national pride had ascribed a series of adventures that put him by the side of Heracles. Attic tragedy had invested him in a new humanity, and he was enlarged into an ideal of Athenian manhood. We shall find this exemplified in the *Suppliants* and *Heracles* of Euripides. The Theseus of those plays is a noble and lofty figure, but also a little didactic, like Euripides himself. Sophocles' Theseus is a warmer and richer personality. He radiates that magical quality of Atticism which charms us on the vases of the period, in the figures of the Parthenon frieze, in those of funeral carvings, which makes the characters of Menander so attractive, even though they have lost the nobility of the classical period. The entry of Theseus is preceded by an unusual sung scene between Oedipus and the chorus – a *kommos*. With unashamed curiosity the chorus asks Oedipus about his dark secrets and drags from him the unhappy story of some part of his past. This section, like two others (266. 960 ff.) serves the purpose of underlining Oedipus' subjective innocence and his knowledge of it; but this is not its only purpose. It also acts as an effective foil to the meeting of Theseus with the blind beggar. He asks no questions about his past sufferings: but alluding to his own past adversities and to the transitoriness of all that is human he sympathizes with Oedipus' present plight and shows himself ready to help and protect. He proves his readiness in the tribulations which still await Oedipus, and thus at the end of the piece he is the only one who may accompany him as he goes to meet his death. A narrative speech without its peer anywhere in literature allows us to be witnesses – at a proper distance – of the mystery of that death, which signifies a passing over to a higher plane of existence. Theseus with the dead man's daughters, giving them kindness and consolation and assuring them of his help – that is the group that is before us at the end of the drama.

The opening and the closing sections of the play are taken up with Oedipus on his way to burial as a hero. In between lies a group of scenes of a different nature and of powerful animation. Ismene on her arrival relates that Oedipus' sons have fallen out, that a struggle for mastery in Thebes is impending and that according to an oracle the victor will be he who secures the person of the old man. Truly enough they arrive: first Creon, who shares with Eteocles the defence of Thebes. This Creon has none of the weight and dignity of the Creon in the *Tyrannus*: to the brutal autocracy of the king in the *Antigone* is now added a new feature – calculating hypocrisy. When this avails him nothing and Oedipus resists all persuasion, he seizes the daughters as hostages. But the voice and arm of Theseus are there to support the right, and they are speedily restored to their father. The violent behaviour of Creon is in effective contrast to the scene with Polynices. The son who is leading a foreign army against his city and already bears the mark of Cain upon his brow, is profoundly moved at the sight of the father whom he himself has driven into exile. Conscious of his guilt, he beseeches the old man to help him and assure his restoration and victory. Oedipus is long silent: then he bursts out in the sudden fury which had long ago flamed forth at the Phocian crossroad. With a curse he sends his son to his ruin: himself a fratricide, he shall die by his brother's hand. Polynices leaves the stage brokenly: burial and obsequies – the Athenians must here have remembered the *Antigone* – are all that he asks of his sisters. After this scene a thunderbolt calls Oedipus to his last journey.

The question of unity of composition comes up here once again. We do not have to speak of 'diptych-form': rather the question is how the middle sections which we have just analysed – the scenes with Creon and Polynices – fit in with the opening and closing scenes which show Oedipus finding peace at last. An older generation of scholars, steeped in Homeric analysis, thought it could find layers in the composition. Wilamowitz, writing in his son Tycho's book on Sophocles, explains the middle section as a later addition with the intention of adding lively dramatic scenes. The theory has deservedly failed to gain acceptance. One would rather believe that the poet from the outset expanded the rather undramatic story of Oedipus' death with scenes intended to secure greater animation for the whole. Such a theory of course admits to a large extent the unity of the play. Nowadays, however, we think we can do better justice to the poet's art. Externally considered, the unity of the piece is largely secured by the fact that Oedipus dominates the stage from the opening scene onwards, even in the narrative of his death and in the lamentation of his daughters. In its inner structure we see the play thus: the old man, tried by suffering, before he finds peace must elude all those forces which yet throng upon him to perplex his existence. He faces them not as a victim, but armed already with the power to curse and to bless which he will exercise from his hero's grave. There is another way in which the middle section is in effective contrast with the flanking sections: in the two daughters of the exile the poet enshrines unforgettable pictures of filial love, while the scenes with Creon and Polynices are filled with hatred and fury. The curse upon the sons and the departure of the daughters with a last word of love bring out the contrast especially strongly through the nearness of the two themes.

All these considerations must be borne in mind when assessing this play, the last of Sophocles' extant dramas. Nevertheless, it cannot be contended that the connection of the various parts achieves the same closeness that we find in the plays of his maturity; nor does it have the same continuity and ease in the unfolding of the action. One result of the generally lyrical tone that pervades this work of his old age is that it contains some of his most wonderful choral passages. The ode in praise of his native Colonos was the poet's swansong to the beauty and greatness of Athens. It was a merciful gift of the gods that one who had so piously sung of their greatness did not live to see the overthrow of his city.

Apart from the seven extant, we know that Sophocles wrote a hundred and twenty-three plays.[1] That is to say, we have some information about all those which were known to the Alexandrians. On the other hand, there are not many

---

[1] According to BLUMENTHAL's list, *RE* 3·A 1927, 1051, which is not wholly certain.

fragments to help us on the lost plays, and the papyri also have given us comparatively little – with one exception, for which we cannot be too grateful. In 1912, in the ninth volume of *Oxyrhynchus Papyri*, Hunt and Wilamowitz published considerable pieces of a Sophoclean satyr-play, the *Ichneutae*. Its date is uncertain, but it may be plausibly assigned to Sophocles' early period. Small supplements followed in *Ox. Pap.* 17, 1927 (nr. 1153 P.).

Until this discovery the *Cyclops* of Euripides was our only example of the Attic satyr-play. Now that we can compare Sophocles and more recently Aeschylus, we can enjoy the very much greater liveliness, when compared with Euripides, which these two poets display in satyric drama. These satyrs are nature-spirits, a hypostasis of lechery and fertility. In the *Dictyulci* and the *Ichneutae* alike their vigorous and lusty life, quite unhindered by any notion of morality, yet oddly attractive and likeable, is conveyed with a wonderful immediacy. In Sophocles as in Aeschylus this carefree and delightful kind of poetry rubs shoulders with tragedies in which the sufferings of our human condition are given immortal expression.

Among the Homeric hymns we find that hymn to Hermes which describes the god's thievish childhood with Rabelaisian humour. The theft of Apollo's cattle and the invention of the lyre provide Sophocles with the theme of his drama, but probably the sequel to these actions was given a different twist from that in the hymn. Apollo has summoned a hue and cry after the stolen cattle, and the satyrs, led by their father Silenus, are acting as bloodhounds on the wooded slopes of Cyllene in hope of the reward. The situation has become critical, when from the cave in which Maia nursed her remarkable child an uncanny and unknown sound is heard – the music of the first lyre on earth. We now have a delightful dialogue between the satyrs – torn between cowardice and curiosity – and the nymph Cyllene who is helping to guard the infant Hermes. The end, which has not survived, must have dealt with the reconciliation of the brothers and the rewarding of the satyrs with money and freedom. It seems to have been a standard element in satyr-drama that the satyrs were in some kind of servitude. Who their master is in this play cannot be determined from the remains. Siegmann thought it was Pan: Page in his edition (*Lit. Pap.*) prefers Dionysus, in which case we have to suppose a lacuna before v. 171.

Sixty-eight much mutilated verses from a cartonnage coffin (*Tebt. Pap.* 3/1, 1933, nr. 692) probably belong to another satyr-play, the *Inachus*. R. Pfeiffer[1] has reconstructed a scene in which the cowardly satyrs are confronted with Hermes, who has come protected by the helmet of Hades to slay Argus.

We now have also the fragment *Ox. Pap.* 23, 1956, 2369, in which we can recognize a speech by Inachus, describing Io's transformation by a remarkable visitor, who can hardly be other than Zeus.

---

[1] *Sitzb. Ak. Münch. Phil.-hist. Kl.* 1938/2, 23. The new papyrus: *ibid.* 1958/6. J. T. KAKRIDIS in *Wiss. Jahrb. d. Philos. Fak. Thessalonike* 1960, 101. Both authors conclude very plausibly from the fragments that it was a satyr-play. W. M. CALDER in his attempted reconstruction ('The Dramaturgy of Sophocles' Inachus'. *Greek and Byz. Studies.* 1, 1958, 137) makes it into a tragedy.

At the same time as the *Ichneutae* the remains of a tragedy *Eurypylus* were found. Eurypylus was the son of Astyoche, Priam's sister. At Priam's request his mother sent him to Troy, where he fell by the hand of Neoptolemus. What survives is part of a messenger's speech telling of Priam's lamentation.

Remains of tragic trimeters on a papyrus (nr. 1157 P.) have been assigned by R. Pfeiffer[1] to the *Scyrii*. We may suppose that this play dealt with the carrying off of Neoptolemus by Odysseus and the opposition of his mother Deidamia.

Recent discoveries and researches have shown that one was mistaken in referring *Pap. Berol.* 9908 to the *Gathering of the Achaeans* ('Αχαιῶν σύλλογος). It is more likely to come from the *Telephus* of Euripides.

We should be very glad to know something about Sophocles' *Phaedra*, in which he embodied the sort of erotic theme which Euripides brought onto the stage. It is a likely guess that he wrote it as a counterblast to Euripides' first *Hippolytus* (the *Calyptomenus*). In a fragment (619 N.), probably from a speech by Phaedra, love is described as a grief sent by the gods.

We should mention the *Tereus* for its great influence. It related the grim story of Procne, who slew her son Itys to punish her husband Tereus for violating her sister Philomela. We may well suppose,[2] though it cannot be proved, that Euripides created his *Medea* under the influence of this tragedy.

In discussing the *Ajax* we quoted Sophocles' own description of his three-stage development. We have also several times spoken of differences in construction, use of dialogue and management of scenes between the older plays and the *Oedipus Tyrannus*, *Electra*, and *Philoctetes*. A closely related question is whether we can discern any development in the language of Sophocles, so far as we know it. In fact the older pieces, the *Ajax* above all, show features which tend to disappear later: a closer affinity to epic and lyric, many turns of phrase that are Aeschylean or at least recall Aeschylus, occasional pleonasms, here and there a trimeter made up of two or three heavy polysyllables (cf. *Aj.* 17). The same applies to the frequency of compound adjectives in the spoken parts. The development of his language is towards a simplicity which does not signalize itself, as so often in Euripides, by a lowering of tragic tone and an approach to the language of every day. To a large extent he gives up the heavy pomp of Aeschylean style, he limits his indulgence in imagery, he uses language in a new way, so that it dresses the thought like a well fitting garment, but maintains its grip on us through frequent short clauses with much use of antithesis. But the guiding spirit is different. The language of Sophocles, with its measured restraint which yet reveals to nearer inspection a rich wealth of movement and vigorous life, is as much an expression of the classic art of Athens as the sculptures of the Parthenon, in which the figures combine the perfection of art and the reality of life in a unity which has never since been attained.

[1] *Phil.* 88, 1933, 1.

[2] W. BUCHWALD, *Stud. z. Chronologie der att. Trag. 455 bis 431.* Diss. Königsberg 1939, 35, with discussion of the fragments.

The plays of Sophocles have had much the same transmission as those of Aeschylus. The decisive factor was the work of the Alexandrians, particularly of Aristophanes of Byzantium. The explanations found in our scholia were preserved by the industry of Didymus: we can sometimes detect his polemic against older commentators. With Sophocles also the requirements of schools in or about the second century of our era called forth a selection of seven plays. (On the date the reader should compare what was said earlier on the transmission of Aeschylus.) One Salustius, to whom we owe hypotheses to the *Antigone*, the *Oedipus Coloneus* and probably other plays as well, revised the editions of these seven plays in the late fourth century. It has been supposed that they survived the dark ages until the Byzantine renaissance in a single manuscript; but of recent years this view has been called in question. TURYN, however, whose knowledge of the transmission is unrivalled, has defended in his most recent work the theory of a single-strand transmission. The evaluation of the manuscripts has entered a new stage through various studies of which the most important are: A. TURYN, 'The Manuscripts of Sophocles'. *Traditio* 2. New York 1944; 'The Sophocles Recension of Manual Moschopulus'. *Trans. of the Am. Phil. Ass.* 80, 1949, 94; *Studies in the Manuscript Tradition of the Tragedies of Sophocles. Illinois Studies* 36/1-2. Urbana 1952 (on which see P. MAAS, *Gnom.* 25, 1953, 441); V. DE MARCO, 'Intorno al testo di Edipo a Colono in un manoscritto Romano'. *Rendiconti Accad. Napoli* 26, 1951 (1952), 260. R. AUBRETON, *Démétrius Triclinius et les récensions médiévales de Sophocle.* Paris 1949.

The main result of these researches has been to define the part played by learned Byzantines – particularly Planudes, Moschopulus, Thomas Magister and Triclinius – in the formation of the corpus of variant readings that we now have. It is not always easy to decide: as we shall see with Par. 2712, in many instances opinions differ on what is genuine tradition and what is Byzantine conjecture. The object of these studies is to unburden our critical apparatus of all that can be considered secondary. and thus to determine more accurately what the ancient tradition really is. For this purpose the most important MS. is that same Mediceus which we saw to be the most valuable for Aeschylus. Its text of Sophocles – written in the eleventh century and later bound up with the texts of Aeschylus and Apollonius – is often referred to as Laurentianus 32. 9. A close relative of this MS. is the Leyden palimpsest 60 A, but it does not go very far (see J. IRIGOIN, *Rev. Ét. Gr.* 64, 1951, 443). The Parisinus 2712 was long considered a second pillar of the text, but its credit has been impaired by TURYN's thesis that its variants in the *Ajax, Electra* and *Oedipus Rex* are Byzantine conjectures. Ideas here are now in flux. J. C. KAMERBEEK, 'De Sophoclis memoria'. *Mnem.* S. 4, 11, 1958, 25, has brought detailed evidence for his view that Par. 2712 does in fact give genuine ancient variants in these three plays, and that it is not fathered solely by MANUEL MOSCHOPULUS. We must also mention P. E. EASTERLING, 'The Manuscript A of Sophocles and its Relation to the Moschopulean Recension'. *Class. Quart.* N.S. 10, 1960, 51. TURYN, following de Marco, attaches particular importance to a 'Roman family' comprising the following MSS.: Laur. Conv. Soppr. 152; Par. suppl. Gr. 109; Vat. 2291; Moden. T. 9. 4. This view has not won the support of P. MAAS, *Gnom.* 25, 1953, 441, or of H. LLOYD-JONES, *Gnom.* 31, 1959, 478. A good many manuscripts only contain the three plays selected by the Byzantines: *Ajax, Electra, Oedipus Rex.*

Bibliography 1936–38: A. V. BLUMENTHAL, *Bursians Jahresber.* 277, 1942 (id. *RE* 3 A 1927, 1040). Later work: my reports in *AfdA* from 1949 onwards, last in 1961; H. J. METTE, *Gymn.* 63, 1956, 547; G. M. KIRKWOOD, *Class. Weekly* 50, 1956/57, 157. Recent editions: A. C. PEARSON, Oxf. 1924. P. MASQUERAY, *Coll. des Un. de Fr.* 2nd ed. 1929; now A. DAIN–P. MAZON, 3 vols. ibid. 1955–60. An edition with Spanish translation in the *Colección hispánica de autores griegos y latinos* by I. ERRANDONEA, S.J., has begun with the first volume, containing the two Oedipus plays, Barcelona 1959. Two old editions with commentary are still valuable for the text: R. C. JEBB, Cambr. 1883–96 (repr. unaltered 1902–1908, again 1962), text only Cambr. 1897; three more volumes containing the fragments by A. C. PEARSON, Cambr. 1917. SCHNEIDEWIN-NAUCK in the revised edition by E. BRUHN (*O.T.* 1910; *El.* 1912; *Ant.* 1913) and L. RADERMACHER (*O.C.* 1909; *Phil.* 1911; *Aj.* 1913; *Trach.* 1914).

Annotated editions and special studies upon individual plays: *Ajax*: (ed.): M. UNTERSTEINER, Milan 1934. V. DE FALCO, 3rd ed. Naples 1950. A. COLONNA, 2nd ed. Turin 1951. G. AMMENDOLA, Turin 1953. J. C. KAMERBEEK, Leyden 1953 (commentary only). (stud.): F. DIRLMEIER, 'Der Aias des Soph.' *N. Jahrb.* 1938, 297. R. CAMERER, 'Zu Soph. Aias'. *Gymn.* 60, 1953, 289. J. M. LINFORTH, *Three Scenes in Sophocles' 'Ajax'.* Un. of Cal. Press. 1954. K. V. FRITZ, 'Zur Interpretation des Aias'. *Rhein. Mus.* 83, 1934, 113; now *Antike und moderne Tragödie.* Berlin 1962, 241. – *Ant.*: CHR. DE VLEMINCK and R. VAN COMPERNOLLE, 'Bibliographie analytique de l'Antigone de Soph.', *Phoibos* 2, 1947/48, 85. (ed.): A. COLONNA, Turin 1941. J. C. KAMERBEEK, Leyden 1945. E. ANANIA, Florence 1957. (stud.): R. F. GOHEEN, *The Imagery of Sophocles' Antigone.* Princeton 1951. H. LLOYD-JONES, 'Notes on Soph. Ant.'. *Class. Quart.* N.S. 7, 1957, 12. J. M. LINFORTH, 'Antigone and Creon'. *Univ. of Cal. Publ. in Class. Phil.* 15/5, 1961, 183. G. MÜLLER, 'Ueberlegungen zum Chor der Ant.'. *Herm.* 89, 1961, 398. K. V. FRITZ, 'Haimons Liebe zu Antigone'. *Phil.* 89, 1934, 19; now *Antike und moderne Tragödie.* Berl. 1962, 227. *Trachiniae*: (ed.): J. C. KAMERBEEK, Leyden 1946; ibid. 1959 without text. G. SCHIASSI, Florence 1953. (stud.): H. D. F. KITTO, 'Sophocles, Statistics and the Trachiniae'. *Am. Journ. Phil.* 60, 1939, 178. G. CARLSSON, 'Le Personnage de Déianire chez Sénèque et chez Sophocle'. *Eranos* 45, 1947, 68. – *Oedipus Tyrannus*: F. DIRLMEIER, *Der Mythos vom König Oedipus.* Mainz 1948. (ed.): L. ROUSSEL, Paris 1940. D. PIERACCIONI, Florence 1949. O. REGENBOGEN, Heidelb. 1949 (text). (stud.): E. SCHLESINGER, *El Edipo Rey de Sof.* La Plata 1950. W. SCHADEWALDT. 'Der König Oed. des Soph. in neuer Deutung'. *Schweiz. Monatsh.* 36, 1956, 21. B. M. W. KNOX, 'The Date of the Oed. Tyr. of Soph.'. *Am. Journ. Phil.* 77, 1956, 133. Id., *Oedipus at Thebes.* New Haven 1957. M. OSTWALD, 'Aristotle on ἁμαρτία and Sophocles' Oedipus Tyr.'. *Festschr.* Kapp 1958, 93.–*Electra*: (ed.): G. KAIBEL, Leipz. 1896

(1911). N. CATONE, Florence 1959. (stud.): W. WUHRMANN, *Strukturelle Unter-suchungen zu den beiden El. und zum eurip. Orestes.* Winterthur 1940. R. P. WIN-NINGTON-INGRAM, 'The Electra of Sophocles. Prolegomena to an Interpretation'. *Proc. Cambr. Phil. Soc.* 1954/55, 20, which concentrates on the matricide and the Erinyes. K. V. FRITZ, 'Die Orestessage bei den drei grossen griechischen Tragikern'. *Antike und moderne Tragödie.* Berl. 1962, 113. *Philoctetes*: (ed.): J. C. KAMERBEEK, Leyden 1946. A. TACCONE, Florence 1948. (stud.): J. M. LINFORTH, *Philoctetes. The Play and the Man.* Un. Cal. Press 1956. R. MUTH, 'Gottheit und Mensch im Phil. des Soph.'. *Studi Castiglioni.* Florence 1959, 641. K. ALT, 'Schicksal und Physis im Phil. des Soph.'. *Herm.* 89, 1961, 141 (developing the view propounded by BOWRA, *v. sup.* p. 291, n. 2). P. W. HARSH, 'The Rôle of the Bow in the Phil. of Soph.'. *Am. Journ. Phil.* 81, 1960, 408.

Oedipus Coloneus: (ed.): G. AMMENDOLA, Turin 1953. D. PIERACCIONI, Florence 1956. (stud.): G. MÉAUTIS, *L'Oedipe à Colone et le culte des héros.* Neuchâtel 1940. J. M. LINFORTH, *Religion and Drama in 'Oedipus at Colonus'.* Un. Cal. Press 1951. Fragments: NAUCK, *Trag. Graec. Frag.* 2nd ed. Leipzig 1889. A. C. PEARSON (see above on Jebb's edition). E. DIEHL, *Supplementum Sophocleum.* Bonn 1913. Papyri in Pack; *Ichneutae* and some other fragments in D. L. PAGE, *Literary Papyri.* Loeb. Lib. 1950. D. FERRANTE, Naples 1958 (with trans.). V. STEFFEN, Warsaw 1960. E. SIEGMANN, *Untersuchungen zu Soph. Ichn.* Hamb. 1941. Scholia: W. DINDORF, Oxf. 1852. P. N. PAPAGEORGIOS, Leipz. 1888. V. DE MARCO, *Scholia in Soph. Oed. Col.* Rome 1952. Lexica: F. ELLENDT, 2nd ed. by H. GENTHE, Leipz. Berl. 1872, repr. Hildesheim 1958. Translations: English: prose trans. in JEBB's ed. (*supra*); verse trans. by GILBERT MURRAY have achieved wide popularity. D. GRENE and others, *The Complete Greek Tragedies (v. sup.* under Aeschylus). German: W. SCHILDKNECHT, *Deutscher Sophokles.* Bonn 1935. Complete trans. by H. WEINSTOCK, Stuttg. 1941. E. STAIGER, Zürich 1944. French: P. MAZON, 2 vols. Paris 1950; now in the *Coll. des Univ. de France (v. sup.).* Italian: E. BIGNONE, 4 vols. Florence 1937/38. Language: an important study in the 8th volume of SCHNEIDEWIN-NAUCK, rev. E. BRUHN, Berl. 1899. F. R. EARP, *The Style of Sophocles.* Cambr. 1944. J. C. F. NUCHELMANNS, *Die nomina des soph. Wortschatzes.* Utrecht 1949 (with bibliog.) LEIF BERGSON, D. M. CLAY, F. JOHANSEN *v. sup.* under the language of Aeschylus. Monographs: WILAMOWITZ, *Dramatische Technik des Sophokles,* Berl. 1917, still cannot be ignored. G. PERROTTA, *Sofocle.* Messina 1935. M. UNTERSTEINER, *Sofocle.* Florence 1935. T. B. L. WEBSTER, *Introduction to Sophocles.* Oxf. 1936. C. M. BOWRA, *Sophoclean Tragedy.* Oxf. 1944. K. REINHARDT, *Sophokles.* 3rd ed. Frankf. a. M. 1947. H. WEINSTOCK, *Sophokles.* 3rd ed. Wuppertal 1948. A. J. A. WALDOCK, *Sophocles the Dramatist.* Cambr. 1951. C. H. WHITMAN, *Sophocles.* Harvard Un. Press 1951. J. C. OPSTELTEN, *S. and Greek Pessimism.* Amsterdam 1952. Id., 'Humanistisch en religieus Standpunt in de moderne Beschouwing van Soph.'. *Nederl. Akad.* 1954. F. EGERMANN, *Vom attischen Menschenbild.* Munich 1952. Id., 'Arete und tragische Bewusstheit bei Soph. und Herodot'. *Vom Menschen in der Antike.* Klass. Reihe II. Munich 1957, 5 in forced opposition to the interpretation followed by REINHARDT and others, among them the author of this book. F. J. H. LETTERS, *The*

Life and Work of S. Lond. 1953. V. EHRENBERG, *S. and Pericles.* Oxf. 1954.
H. D. F. KITTO, 'The Idea of God in Aeschylus and S.'. Fondation Hardt (see p.
65 n. 3), 169. H. DILLER, 'Ueber das Selbstbewusstsein der soph. Personen'. *Wien.*
Stud. 69, 1956, 70. Id., 'Menschendarstellung und Handlungsführung bei Soph.'.
Ant. u. Abendl. 6, 1957, 157. H. D. F. KITTO, *Form and Meaning in Drama.* Lond.
1956. Id., *Sophocles, Dramatist and Philosopher.* Lond. 1958. S. M. ADAMS, *Sophocles*
the Playwright. Toronto 1957. M. IMHOF, *Bemerkungen zu den Prologen der soph.*
und eurip. Tragödien. Winterthur 1957. W. KRAUS, *Strophengestaltung in der griech.*
Tragödie. I. Aisch. u. Soph. Sitzb. Oest. Ak. Phil.-hist. Kl. 231/4, 1957. G.
MÉAUTIS, *Sophocle. Essai sur le héros tragique.* Paris 1957. I. ERRANDONEA, S.J.,
Sofocle. Investigaciones sobre la estructura dramática de sus 7 trag. y sobre la personalidad
de sus coros. Madrid 1958. G. M. KIRKWOOD, *A Study of Soph. Drama.* Cornell
Studies in Class. Phil. 31, 1958. J. KELLER, *Struktur und dram. Funktion des Boten-*
berichtes bei Aisch. und Soph. Diss. Tübingen (typewritten). A. MADDALENA,
Sofocle. Turin 1959. J. DE ROMILLY, *L'Évolution du pathétique d'Eschyle à Euripide.*
Paris 1961. See also the relevant sections in POHLENZ, HARSH, LESKY, KITTO and
D. W. LUCAS, *Greek Tragic Poets.* 2nd ed. Lond. 1959. Three short studies presenting the poet from different points of view: W. SCHADEWALDT, *Soph. und*
das Leid. 4th ed. Potsdam 1948. H. DILLER, *Göttliches und menschl. Wissen bei*
Soph. Kiel 1950. A. LESKY, 'Soph. und das Humane'. *Alman. Oest. Akad.* 1951
(1952), 222.

3   OTHER FORMS OF POETRY

Attic tragedy offers an example unique in history of a work of universal art
arising from a city community, an art in which words and music, dancing and
painting combined to give the old mythology new life and to connect it with
the spiritual problems of the age. It is not surprising if we find it hard to give
any account of the other forms of poetry that existed at the same time.

The old choral ode achieved a new flowering in the drama,[1] and it was an
action of great significance when the young democracy assigned a definite place
to choral lyric in the Great Dionysia and thus ensured its independent existence.
We infer this from the statement of the Marmor Parium (ep. 46) that Hypo-
dicus of Chalcis in 508 was the first to present a dithyramb with a male chorus.
From that time onwards the performance of dithyrambs, on the eighth of
Elaphebolion, preceded the days on which tragedies were presented. Five of the
ten tribes provided each a chorus of men, the others choruses of boys. These
were called cyclic choruses, since the fifty members performed their dance
around the altar in the middle of the orchestra. The accompanying instrument
was the flute. Here also victory was shared by the choregus who bore the cost,
and he was permitted to set up his tripod in public.[2] The costly monument of
Lysicrates was intended to carry one of these tripods. We do not know when
the dithyrambic contest stopped being held: it was probably under the Empire.

[1] W. KRANZ, *Stasimon.* Berlin 1933.
[2] Details in PICKARD-CAMBRIDGE, *Dramatic Festivals of Athens.* Oxf. 1953, 74 ff.

Out of all the choral poetry that was called for by the Dionysia, the Panathenaea and other festivals year by year, almost nothing survives. The poems of Bacchylides give us some idea of the classical dithyramb: the considerable changes in the genre during the second half of the fifth century will have to be discussed later.

Just as in the archaic period, a considerable part of a man's life centred on the jovial companionship of the symposium. This is very prettily illustrated in vase-painting. But now it was not only the nobility who organized their drinking habits in this way: the old forms were taken over by less select circles. This was the usual pattern in the best period of Athenian democracy: the inheritance of the aristocracy still survived to a large extent and was cultivated in a different milieu. Song naturally still remained the normal entertainment of such social occasions, and we may suppose that the scolion and the elegy were in high favour. Contemporary politics, no doubt, were often the theme, but such pieces were naturally fugitive. All that we have is a few verses by one Dionysius, who was given the cognomen Chalcus from his having contributed to the introduction of copper money: they express a harmless pleasure in companionable drinking,[1] and allude also to the game of *kottabos*, which we find represented in vase-painting. A metal disc, balanced on a rod, was sprinkled with the remains of the wine from one's glass so that it fell off. The love of games was highly developed among the Greeks of all periods. Dionysius amused himself by standing the elegiac couplet on its head and making it begin with the pentameter – an interesting sign that the old forms were losing their rigidity. The man is dated roughly by his participation in the founding of Thurii in 444. The pleasure that he takes in nautical metaphors shows him to have been a true child of the great age of Attic hegemony.

Elegy was extensively written at that time: Sophocles and Euripides were among the exponents. Leading statesmen were happy to be celebrated in this form, and we read in Plutarch's *Cimon* that the tragedian Melanthius and the philosopher Archelaus wrote in his honour.

We are better able to judge the epigrammatic poetry of the period. A trend that was strong before the Persian wars (*v. sup.* p. 172) reached a splendid maturity in the classical age. Poets from Simonides to Euripides and innumerable anonymi composed epigrams for graves, monuments and dedications. It was inevitable that many were forged in the name of distinguished authors: Simonides above all, as the acknowledged master of the epigram, had many foundlings left at his door.[2] Both literary and epigraphic[3] tradition have preserved enough for us to appreciate the perfection of form and the power of expression which this genre attained in the fifth century. The far-reaching influence of the Persian wars is discernible in this field also. Scarcely anywhere do

---

[1] Fasc. 1. 88 D.   [2] Genuine and supposititious 2, 107 D.

[3] T. PREGER, *Inscriptiones Graecae metricae ex scriptoribus praeter anthologiam collectae*. Leipz. 1891. G. KAIBEL, *Epigrammata Graeca ex lapidibus collecta*. Berl. 1878. W. PEEK, *Griech. Vers-Inschriften. I. Grab-Epigramme*. Berl. 1955; id., *Griech. Grabgedichte*. Berl. 1960 (with literal and metrical translations). U. V. WILAMOWITZ, *Hellenistische Dichtung*. 1. Berl. 1924, 124. H. BENGTSON, *Griech. Gesch.* 2nd ed. Munich 1960, 181.

we find the individual's sacrifice for his people expressed with greater depth and dignity than in the Attic epigrams on the fallen in the fifth century. The distich form is by far the most common: the language is Attic with a more or less strong tendency to borrow from epic.

The iambos probably had no independent development during this period, as appears from the vigour with which comedy trod in its footsteps. We have, however, some remains of the iambi of the comic writer Hermippus (*Anth. Lyr.* fasc. 3, 64 D), which he wrote side by side with his dramatic production.

Considering how little has been preserved of all the forms which were overshadowed by tragedy, we have to be glad that we can form a rather more definite picture of epic poetry of the period. This does not apply to the epic on Theseus, which probably existed in Attica at the time.[1] All that we can say, and that not with much certainty, about a Diphilus who wrote a *Theseid* and of whom two choliambic lines survive (*Anth. Lyr.* fasc. 3. 138 D), is that he lived in the fifth century.

We are better informed about Choerilus of Samos and his work. Plutarch in his life of Lysander (18) tells us that the latter had Choerilus constantly about him in the expectation of a poetical panegyric on his achievements. At this time Choerilus already had a reputation and was presumably no longer young. From Suidas' fabulous account of him we may mention the report that he fled from slavery in Samos and became a friend of Herodotus. This is literary anecdote reflecting the relation between the work of the epic poet and that of the historian. Ancient tradition[2] gives the title of his poem as *Persica* or *Perseis*. A papyrus (nr. 159 P.) gives the title (placed at the end after the ancient fashion) in the form: Χοιρίλου ποιήματα βαρβαρικά. μηδικά. περσ(ικά). We should not too hurriedly infer three poems from this, dealing with barbarians, Medes and Persians respectively. The subscription looks more like a rough table of contents. It is an attractive supposition that *Barbarica* refers to the wars of the Persians before their expedition against Greece. If this is so, the construction would resemble that used by Herodotus. Thematic connections with Herodotus are visible in the surviving fragments. A striking example is fr. 4, where at a military review, as in Herodotus (7. 70), exotic warriors appear wearing as helmets the flayed skin from the heads of horses. There are several other indications that Choerilus may have taken Herodotus for his model, but the passages concerned show variations which make it necessary to admit that they may both be following the same source, but making different use of it.

The surviving verses (fr. 1 and 1a) from the beginning of the poem are very illuminating. The poet complains that the servants of the Muses were lucky who lived in olden times when the meadows were yet untrodden.[3] Now everything has suffered a decline, the arts have become narrowly defined and the poets of the time fall in line with the latest fashion. Thus, while trying to harness Homeric techniques to the narration of history, Choerilus admits that poetry of

---

[1] L. RADERMACHER, *Mythos und Sage bei den Griechen.* 2nd ed. Vienna 1943, 252.

[2] G. KINKEL, *Epic. Graec. Fragm.* Leipz. 1877, 265.

[3] ἀκήρατος λειμών = Eur. *Hipp.* 73.

this kind has had its day. His life largely coincided with that of Antimachus of Colophon, who followed a new and different line in his epics. The merits of the two were frequently compared in the age that followed. In general the view that favoured Antimachus prevailed: it finds vigorous expression in an epigram of Crates (*Anth. Pal.* 11, 218). Choerilus represents the end of epic poetry in the Homeric manner, and was aware that he did.

4 DAMON AND THE THEORY OF MUSIC

The loss of ancient music is on two counts to be regretted where the classical period is concerned. First, we are prevented from grasping tragedy as an artistic whole; secondly, there was scarcely any time in which the effect and educative possibilities of music were examined with such enthusiasm and with such far-reaching influence.

Towards the close of the sixth century all creative impulses in the arts came to centre more and more on Athens. One indication among many is that the next great reformer of the dithyramb after Arion, Lasus of Hermione, worked at the court of the tyrant Hipparchus. Suidas says that he introduced competitive performance of dithyrambs, and that this became part of the regular programme of the Dionysia under the democracy. Apart from his changes in the dithyramb (we do not know what they were, only that they were considerable), he discussed various musical problems. According to Suidas he wrote a book on the subject: whether he did or not, he can certainly be reckoned as the founder of Greek musicology.

Pindar's instructor Agathocles, and probably also Lamprocles, who wrote dithyrambs and an ode to Athens which we have already mentioned, were the teachers of a man who became very influential not as a poet but as a musical theorist. Damon,[1] from the Attic deme of Oa, was close to Pericles in two ways – as his teacher in music and his adviser in politics; although it is possible that the introduction of payment for jurors was suggested not by Damon, but by his father Damonides. But certainly Damon took an active part in politics, and in so doing suffered ridicule from the comic writers and ostracism from the citizens (Plut. *Per.* 4). He went very deeply into the question of the effect that music has on the nature and behaviour of man. A fragment of Philodemus (*Mus.* 1. 13) tells us that he faced the question whether music conduced to virtue as a whole or only to particular virtues, and expressed himself decidedly for the former. So highly did he rate the effect of music on society that he maintained that changes in music led necessarily to constitutional changes in the state (Plat. *Rep.* 424 C). These views he expressed in a treatise purporting to be a speech to the Areopagus. The choice of this form is understandable, since, in dealing with questions of musical education, it was handling matters which at one time were

---

[1] U. V. WILAMOWITZ, *Griechische Verskunst*. Berl. 1921, 59 ff. with the passages cited. VS 37. H. RYFFEL, 'Eukosmia. Ein Beitrag zur Wiederherstellung des Aeropagitikos des Damon'. *Mus. Helv.* 4, 1947, 23. H. KOLLER, *Mimesis in der Antike*. Berne 1954, 21. V. EHRENBERG, *Sophocles and Pericles*. Oxf. 1954, 92. A. E. RAUBITSCHEK, 'Damon'. *Classica et Mediaevalia* 16, 1955, 78.

the immediate concern of that ancient court. There is no reason, however, to suppose that the treatise was written before the wings of the Areopagus were clipped in 462. The way in which Aeschylus speaks of it in the *Eumenides* shows that the form which Damon chose would be perfectly conceivable at a later date. Even much later the *Areopagiticus* of Isocrates attests the strong survival of the Areopagus as a conception.

Damon's treatise is most fully discussed in Plato's *Republic* (400 B). We learn there that he dealt with rhythms and the analysis of particular metres. But the book was far from being a handbook of metric: its main subject was undoubtedly the effect of music on morals and therewith the whole question of musical education. In the fragment of Philodemus which we have already mentioned Damon was speaking of singing and the lyre; it is a likely supposition that he took sides in the old 'battle of the instruments' and opposed the flute. It is a pity that we cannot say how far Pythagorean doctrines appear in Damon's work. He can hardly have escaped their influence. The musician Pythoclides, who taught Agathocles and Lamprocles and was thus Damon's academic grandfather, is referred to as a Pythagorean (schol. Plat. *Alc.* I 118 C).[1]

The influence of Damon is particularly apparent in Plato, who studied music under his pupil Draco. The questions which he raised were vigorously debated, as we see from the Hibeh Papyrus with fragments of a speech to the Athenians (nr. 1896 P. probably early fourth century), totally denying that music influences human character.

5 HERODOTUS

In Sophoclean tragedy and in the Parthenon Greek classical art reached its culmination.[2] It achieved maturity on Attic soil, and the combination of Ionic and Doric elements in the great temple on the Acropolis is an eloquent symbol of the special conditions under which this development was completed.

In Greece more strongly than anywhere else the different arts traditionally had a life of their own, and it is wholly understandable that they reached maturity at different times. Beside the mature drama of Sophocles we find the historical work of Herodotus, with its many archaic features and a patchwork quality about its component parts which has not yet arrived at organic unity. Yet in this quality lies the peculiar charm of Herodotus' narrative.

We know as little about his life as we usually do about classical authors, but it is enough to establish a connection between the multiplicity of separate elements in his work and the circumstances of his intellectual development.

Herodotus was born shortly before the expedition of Xerxes, in Halicarnassus on the south-west coast of Asia Minor. This was a colony sent out from Troezen, and thus essentially Doric. Earlier it had belonged to the Dorian league of six cities, but in Herodotus' time it had withdrawn. Ionian elements must have come

---

[1] W. BURKERT, *Weisheit und Wissenschaft*. Nuremberg 1962, 270, 79, cites passages supporting the view that the notion of music as a moral agent came from the Pythagoreans. He himself, however, remains sceptical.

[2] On the classic as a historical phenomenon: *Das Problem des Klassischen in der Antike* (by various hands). Leipzig 1931.

into the city fairly early, since we find fifth-century inscriptions from it in Ionic. But Herodotus' native city was predominantly Dorian, and at all times he had a certain sympathy for the Dorian character, which was displayed at its purest in Sparta. He also soon became acquainted with the qualities of Ionians, without being attracted by them.[1] His father was called Lyxes – a Carian name, like that of Panyassis, whom we met as an epic poet, and who was a close kinsman of Herodotus', probably his father's brother. Thus Herodotus' pedigree takes us back to the Carian hinterland of the city and suggests cultural influences from the near east.

While Herodotus was growing up, Halicarnassus was ruled by Carian despots, of whom the most outstanding was Artemisia. This remarkable woman, who showed the greatest loyalty to Xerxes in his expedition against Greece, is spoken of by the historian with obvious respect. When Greek power in the Aegean was strengthened by success against the Persians, Halicarnassus also rose against her foreign rulers. In the attempt to overthrow Lygdamis, a son of Artemisia's, Panyassis seems to have lost his life, while Herodotus had to go into exile. He lived for a time in Samos, where he was brought again into contact, closer now than before, with the Ionian way of life. From Samos he returned home to take his part in the overthrow of Lygdamis. This event cannot have occurred long before 454, since in that year Halicarnassus appears as an ally in the Athenian tribute-lists.

The next fixed point in his chronology is the founding of Thurii in 444/3. This pan-Hellenic colony was founded through the policy of Pericles near the ruins of Sybaris: the colonists included such well-known figures as the architect Hippodamus of Miletus, a great innovator in town-planning, and the sophist Protagoras. Even Empedocles is named among them. We do not know whether Herodotus went out with the original colonists or settled there later. At all events he was given full citizenship in the new colony: in good manuscripts of the *Histories* he describes himself in the opening words as Herodotus of Thurii, not of Halicarnassus (Aristot. *Rhet.* 3, 9. 1409 a 29).

Some time after the overthrow of Lygdamis and before settling in Thurii he undertook those travels which did much to influence his development and the composition of his history. We can distinguish two principal ventures. The first took him to Egypt, where he stayed for about four months, and thence to Phoenicia and Mesopotamia. A second journey led to Scythia, where he seems to have made Olbia the headquarters of his researches. Attempts to establish the relative chronology of these travels have led to no certain results. But from 3. 12 it seems likely that Herodotus was in Egypt for some time after the battle of Papremis (460).

The object of these travels was to learn about distant countries: they exemplified the same curiosity that caused the first steps in European science to be taken on Ionian soil. Herodotus himself gives 'having a look' ($\theta\epsilon\omega\rho\iota\eta$) as the motive for the travels of such men as Solon (1. 30) and Anacharsis (4. 76), which confirms the construction we have put on his own journeys.

[1] Cf. JACOBY (*v. inf.*), 211.

It was during the first period of travels that Herodotus stayed in Athens, which enriched his experience no less than his long journeys did. We may suppose this stay to have been in the years before, or perhaps shortly after, the foundation of Thurii. If so, it was the Athens of Pericles, with all its storm and stress, that took a decisive part in moulding the man and the writer. The sophists were already producing their revolutionary effect on intellectual life, and Herodotus must surely have made the acquaintance of Protagoras in connection with Thurii. Yet when we consider his attitude towards *nomos*, we shall see that sophistic ideas by no means went to his head. By a natural contrast – here again we must anticipate – tragedy affected him the more deeply. In many passages he shows a very great familiarity with epic and lyric poetry.[1] Presumably he brought this knowledge with him from home: now he had before him the full achievement of that branch of poetry in which all the power of many different traditions worked together to produce a greater emotional effect than had been seen before. He was particularly closely connected with Sophocles: in discussing the *Antigone* and *Electra* we have found indications of this affinity in thematic correspondences, and we mentioned (p. 274) the poem which the poet, as he himself attests, wrote at the age of fifty-five to his friend. Since Sophocles' birth is credibly dated in 497, we may suppose that the poem was connected with Herodotus departure for Thurii.

The question whether Herodotus should be described as an honorary Athenian subject will have to be discussed in connection with his work. In any case, the fact that a man from Halicarnassus should have spent a great part of his life in Athens shows strikingly how soon after the Persian wars that city had become the intellectual centre of Hellenism. In his treatise *De Herodoti malignitate* (26) Plutarch says that on the proposal of one Anytus, Herodotus was given a reward of ten talents. Eusebius puts this in his chronicle as having happened in 445/44, and says it was occasioned by a public reading given by Herodotus. This is uncertain: the sum of ten talents is quite incredible, but there is no reason to doubt some material recognition in Athens of the historian's work.

We know virtually nothing about Herodotus' later years, not even whether he came back from Thurii to Athens. He was still alive when the Peloponnesian war broke out. Several passages, of which some (e.g. 6, 91. 7, 137; 233. 9, 73) are beyond all doubt, refer to the first years of the war. If we are right in assuming that he worked on his history right up to his last days, then his death must have occurred about this time. Such passages as we have mentioned do not, of course, give us any certain information about the chronology of composition, since we must always reckon with the possibility of later additions.

The length and variety of Herodotus' work makes it hard to summarize and still harder to evaluate. He has sometimes been represented as a cheerful and rather shallow raconteur, sometimes as a profound thinker about human destiny, sometimes again as an historian who knew exactly what he wanted to achieve. The foreground will always be occupied with the question: How far was Cicero right in describing him as *pater historiae* (*De legg.* 1. 5)? To give

[1] SCHMID 2. 553 f.

some basis for the discussion of individual points, we give a synopsis of the work as a whole. It cannot, of course, be more than a bare outline.

He begins with a sentence avowing his purpose, and thus serving much the same function as a modern title-page. We are given the name and birthplace of the author and his intention to preserve the memory of the past and of great human actions:[1] finally he states his immediate purpose, which is to explain the causes of the war between the Greeks and the barbarians. At the outset he refers expressly to Persian writers – a fact which will be important in discussing his sources. According to these authorities the long feud between east and west began over the stealing of each other's women. The Phoenicians carried off Io from Argos; then some Greeks carried off Europa from Tyre. At this point they could have cried each other quit, but the Greeks sailed to Aea in Colchis and kidnapped Medea. It was now up to the Asiatics to level the score, and one generation later – corresponding to the relative chronology of the myths – Paris set out to capture Helen. So far it had been the tit for tat of gang warfare, but now the Greeks became really guilty: they began a war between nations over a runaway wife.

These first five chapters are remarkable in many ways. The old opposition between Europe and Asia, which for Herodotus reached its culmination in the expedition of Xerxes, is here tied up with mythology, but a mythology stripped of the glamour of the heroic age, forced into a pseudo-historical reconstruction and trivialized in the process. But Herodotus keeps up a critical aloofness. At the end of the Persian account of the rape of Io he quotes a Phoenician variant, but says that he has no means of deciding which is true. What he does is rather to put all these tales on one side and declare his own intention of starting the history with a description of the man who in his opinion was first guilty of aggression against the Greeks.

The name of Croesus introduces the section devoted to the Lydians (1. 6–94). After declaring that this king was the first to reduce Greek cities to subjection and payment of tribute, Herodotus characteristically casts his eyes back from the present scene to remote antiquity. Croesus was one of the Mermnad clan, who had ended the domination of the Heraclidae under such tragic circumstances. There follows the story of Candaules and Gyges, a story of double guilt which introduces us to the founder of the Mermnad dynasty. From Gyges he passes briefly over Ardys and Sadyattes to speak of Alyattes and his expedition against Miletus, with which the story of Arion is loosely connected. Alyattes was succeeded by Croesus: thus the long digression has come back to its starting-point. This archaic style of composition is characteristic of the work.

Once again (1. 26; cf. 1. 6) we are concerned with Croesus and his aggression against Greek cities, and we hear how his power grew. At the height of his fortunes he was visited by Solon, when that conversation took place between the rich Asiatic and the Athenian sage (1. 30–33) which turned on human value-judgments in relation to the divine governance. Croesus, who had reckoned himself the most fortunate of men, was punished by God and reduced to

<hr />

[1] On this sentence see p. 316.

extremity by two successive calamities. He lost a son in a hunting accident at the hands of that same Adrastus whom he himself had protected and purified from bloodguilt (1. 34-45). Then he took up arms for a campaign against the increasing might of the Persians: a campaign which was to cost him his empire. The preliminaries are related in detail – consulting of oracles, attempts to find powerful allies in Greece – and Herodotus finds room for an excursus on Pisistratus and on the early history of Sparta. Next comes Croesus' expedition into Cappadocia: he is shut up in Sardes, the city falls, and we have the striking tale of his last-minute rescue from being burnt alive. Some remarks on curiosities in Lydia are loosely tacked on to this section, which ends emphatically with the sentence: 'Thus the Lydians were now subjects of the Persians'.

It is the Persians now who occupy the foreground, and once again we have a long flash-back. We must stop here for a moment to see how true the observation is that the structure of the work follows archaic notions of art, that is, it goes by association of thought. It used to be considered a leading principle in the composition that the various nations received attention as and when the Persian expansion came up against them. If this were so, the first book would have begun with the earliest advances of Persian power, and the section on the Lydians would have taken a correspondingly later place. In fact the narrative is quite different; it is associative. For the sake of completeness, Herodotus has traced back all kinds of stories beyond the beginning of the hostilities that sprang from east-west opposition. All that he can say on his own authority is that Croesus was the first to enslave Greek cities. This leads him to the history of the Lydians, which ends with the overthrow of Croesus by the Persians. This gives him occasion to speak at greater length of the latter, which necessitates another beginning *ab ovo*. All this works out very smoothly and spontaneously; but at the same time it secures one advantage which can hardly be accidental: the edifying story of Croesus and Solon comes in this way at the beginning of the work and thus a note is struck which is to echo again and again in what follows.

A constructional principle which Herodotus often follows can be seen in the sequence of the Persian kings. Before dealing with the reign of Cyrus, Herodotus goes back to the Medish kings, then relates the miraculous story of the childhood of Cyrus with its eastern trappings, and adds on to it the overthrow of the Medish kingdom. The rise of the Persians to a dominant position gives occasion for a digression on Persian customs (1. 131-140).

During the reign of Cyrus the westward expansion of the Persians soon made the Greek cities of Asia Minor realize their growing danger. They sent ambassadors to wait on the king, and when he made no satisfactory reply they sought help from Sparta. Again we find a feature of archaic technique in composition, in that a long section follows (1. 142-151), describing the Greek settlements in Asia Minor, before we are told of the request to Sparta and the Spartan embassy to Cyrus.

The remainder of the first book consists of two long sections describing the rapid growth of Persian power. The first tells of the subjugation of western

Asia Minor and the Greek states by Harpagus: the second relates the expedition against Babylonia, which Herodotus calls Assyria. Here we find the 'Babylonian logos' (1. 178-200) describing the city and country and some parts of their history. The narrative that follows deals with Cyrus' expedition against the Massagetae and his death in the course of it (1. 201-216), and again there is a description of the lands and settlements of the people concerned.

The second book brings us to the reign of Cambyses. At the outset we are told that the new king regarded the Ionians and Aeolians as slaves whom he had inherited from his father, and accordingly he conscripted them into his expedition against Egypt. The third book begins with the same statement, thus marking the end of the largest of all those parentheses which in Herodotus have a life of their own outside the historical narrative. The 'Egyptian logos' which makes up the second book begins with a detailed account of the nature of the country, its curiosities, its religion and the diverse customs of its people (2. 5-98). Then comes a sketch of Egyptian history (2. 99-182) down to Amasis, Cambyses' opponent, where he picks up the thread of his story about the Persian expedition against Egypt.

The third book very strikingly illustrates how Herodotus, no matter how deeply involved in ethnography, never lets the historical dimension out of his sight. Thus the Egyptian logos in its second part is turned into a history of Egypt. We should also observe how carefully Herodotus tells us of the change in his sources when he passes (2. 99) from one section to the other. Until then he had gone on his own observation and enquiries: now, for the historical section, he has to follow Egyptian tradition.

The third book starts with the preparations for the expedition and the conquest of Egypt by Cambyses (3. 1-16). Then follow his hazardous expeditions from the newly won country (3. 17-26) and the description of his behaviour (3. 27-38) which branded him as a wanton persecutor of the native religion and a crazed tyrant.

It is a pure synchronism which effects the next transition: while Cambyses was marching against Egypt, the Spartans went to war against Samos and its ruler Polycrates (3. 39). The technique now familiar to us sandwiches in between here and 3. 44 the story of the rise of Polycrates[1] and the ominous return of his ring. The part played in this tale by Amasis affords a loose bond with the expedition of Cambyses.

The motives and the course of the Spartan campaign are described in detail (3. 39-59), and Herodotus brings into his narrative the enmity between Corinth and Samos as well. This gives him the opportunity to relate some dark episodes from the family history of Periander, tyrant of Corinth.

Book 3. 60 strikingly illustrates how all is grist for Herodotus' mill. He assures us that his reason for dealing with the Samians in such detail is that they were responsible for three feats unrivalled among the Greeks: their aqueduct bored through a mountain, the breakwater of their harbour, and the temple of Hera.

---

[1] H.-J. DIESNER, 'Die Gestalt des Tyrannen Polykrates bei Herodot'. *Acta Antiqua Acad. Scient. Hungaricae* 7, 1959, 211.

We should hardly be doing him an injustice if we saw the matter the other way round: the excuse is put there simply because he could not bear to pass over these great wonders in silence. This is very understandable if we consider his special connections with Samos.

In 3. 61, we come to the reign of Darius, which is prefaced by an account of preceding events, the death of Cambyses and the overthrow of the false Smerdis. Here we find those chapters (80-83) in which the conspirators argue about the type of constitution they propose.[1] The claims of democracy, oligarchy and monarchy are put forward: monarchy wins, and Darius, not without some adroit management, becomes sole ruler. An account of the satrapies and the tribute that each paid (3. 89-96) gives us a picture of Persian resources at the time. Herodotus next lists the peoples who were not tributary, but sent gifts: thus he is enabled to describe the wealth of the neighbouring territories (3. 106-116), and even to include a brief account of India.

After an episode describing the fall of Intaphernes, one of the conspirators against the Magians (3. 118 f.), comes an event of great significance in the Persian drive to the west – the conquest of Samos (3. 120-149). In this connection we are told of the downfall of Polycrates: thus the earlier narrative is continued and concluded. The book ends with the crushing of the Babylonian revolt.

The fourth book up to c. 144 is concerned with Darius' expedition against the Scythians. Again we find the characteristic manner of composition. The causes of the war are set out in the first four chapters, but it is not until c. 83 that he takes up the thread again with a description of the preparations. The intervening space is taken up with an account of the country, its people and their customs, which in its turn incorporates the story of Aristeas, a description of the Hyperboreans and numerous bits of geography. The chapters on the shape of the earth (4. 36-45) are particularly interesting, with their obvious polemic against the over-simplified map of Hecataeus. The account of warlike preparations on both sides (4. 83-121) incorporates an excursus on Zalmoxis – of great interest for the history of religion – and some information about the geography of Scythia and its neighbouring countries. The next section (4. 122-144) relates the course of the war up to Darius' return.

The narrative of the Libyan expedition, which takes up the rest of the fourth book (145-205), is rather differently composed. Herodotus explicitly defers any discussion of the causes of hostility and begins with the history of Cyrene and its rulers. Only then do we find the now familiar triadic composition – causes of the war; description of Libya; course of the campaign.

The fifth book begins with the reduction of Thrace by the Persians (1-27). In two passages Herodotus neatly brings in an account of Histiaeus, who was highly rewarded by Darius for his services in the Scythian expedition, but was later suspected and recalled to Susa. This serves as prelude to the narrative of the Ionian revolt, which carries over into the next book (5. 28-6. 32). Once again we have at first a relatively short section describing the motives of the Ionian revolt, the deliberations in Miletus and the first preparations, including

---

[1] H. APFFEL, *Die Verfassungsdebatte bei Herodot*. Diss. Erlangen 1957.

the dispatch of Aristagoras to Greece (5. 28-38). The narrative of this mission, which miscarried in Sparta, but met with some response in Athens, is interrupted by accounts of Spartan and Athenian history, which form – although on a more modest scale – a counterpart to the descriptions of foreign nations. We may also remember that another piece of diplomacy, Croesus' attempt to secure Greek support, as told in the first book, also provided the cue for some historical information about Athens and Sparta.

The course of the revolt, spreading to Phrygia, Caria, Cyprus and the Hellespont, is carried on without appreciable interruption down to the catastrophe of Lade, the fall of Miletus and the death of Histiaeus.

Before starting on the narrative of the great Persian expedition which threatened the liberty of Greece, as a kind of *entr'acte* between that and the Ionian revolt, Herodotus relates various hostile undertakings against Greek cities in the northwest Aegean and the expedition of Mardonius against Macedonia (6. 33-47). In the course of this narrative he has the opportunity to tell the story of Miltiades and to prepare us for his coming role at the decisive hour.

The greater part of the sixth book (48-140) is taken up with the expedition ordered by Darius and the great deliverance of the Athenians at Marathon. The techniques of composition are those that we know well. Darius demands tokens of subjection from the Greeks: when Aegina is one of the islands to give these tokens – earth and water – this leads to Athenian resentment and Spartan intervention under Cleomenes. This operation gives an opportunity to expound all the complex story of Athenian relations with the island on their doorstep; and the Aeginetan excursus in turn serves to enclose some passages of Spartan history. In this Herodotean sandwich the slices of bread are of very different thickness. A very brief statement of the beginning of the action is followed at once by the digression, and the important events are related at greater length afterwards. This technique often recurs. Here the mention of the Spartan king Cleomenes gives the cue for relating the conflict between him and Demaratus and the fate of the two men. This excursus is useful also as a significant prelude to the vital part played by Demaratus and his desertion to Darius in the following narrative.

The account of the expedition, leading to the defeat and withdrawal of the Persians, is followed by two appendices. The refutation of the rumour that the Alcmeonidae had tried to help the Persians by a treacherous signal leads to an excursus on the Alcmeonidae and their important part in Athenian history (6. 121-131). At the end is the story of Agariste, who dreamt that she gave birth to a lion. A few days later she became the mother of Pericles.

The second of these appendices deals with the death of Miltiades. This is Herodotus' way: when he mentions a famous man in the course of the narrative, he traces his destiny right to the end. He did this before, in the section on Sparta, dealing with Leotychides and Cleomenes.

The seventh book begins with the death of Darius and the succession of Xerxes (1-4). The description of his expedition against Greece occupies the remaining three books. The scale and significance of the invasion is matched by a broadening and heightening of the treatment. A lengthy prelude (5-19) gives an account of Xerxes' decision to make war, with a dramatic and circumstantial description of the council-meeting, speeches and counter-speeches of the generals, and miraculous dreams. The next two chapters, in distinctly elevated language, stress the uniqueness of the enormous undertaking, and set the tone for the following narrative of the preparations and advance of the Persian armies. The climactic points in the composition are the crossing of the Hellespont (44-57), with the conversation between Xerxes and Artabanus, and the great review at Doriscus (59-104) with the catalogue of contingents and the king's conversation with Demaratus. Both these conversations serve the purpose of warnings to a mortal who is priding himself on his power.

The war has necessarily to be described in narratives proceeding in parallel. This practice begins in the 58th chapter, where the sailing of the fleet is followed by the corresponding advance of the army. On a larger scale the part describing Persian preparations is paralleled by those which deal with Greek reactions and military precautions (138-178: the passage has a clearly marked introduction). Greek preparations are largely concerned with the sending of embassies. Since one of these was to Gelon of Syracuse, Herodotus characteristically takes the opportunity of describing him and his position in the Greek-speaking west. This is not done in the manner of those lengthy *logoi* that came in the earlier books: we have rather a predominantly historical survey, in which the struggle against Carthage makes a significant parallel to the main theme.

The section on Greek military measures ends with the deployment of their forces at Thermopylae and Artemisium. The Persians are now once more the theme, and the progress of their fleet is traced as far as Aphetae (179-195). In all that follows Herodotus sticks closely to the course of events, so that a brief summary is all we need give. The battle of Thermopylae (7. 196-206) has its counterpart at sea in the battle of Artemisium (8. 1-21). Next comes the Persian advance, with their ill-starred attempt on Delphi (8. 23-39), and the approach to the battle of Salamis (8. 40-82), with a detailed account of the councils of war on both sides, particularly the threefold discussions among the Greek leaders. The battle is described on a scale commensurate with its importance (8, 83-95), and its consequences and the movement of forces on both sides after the battle are described in detail.

The narrative of the second year of the war begins with movements of the rival fleets (8. 130-132), but soon passes to developments on land, leading to the decisive battle at Plataeae. The negotiations which went before this stage in the campaign, the deployment of the armies in the battle, the course of the fighting, the booty, the burial of the dead, are all described impressively and in great detail (8. 133-9. 89). A shorter narrative style is used for the last great event of this year, the storming of the Persian naval encampment at Mycale (90-113).

The conclusion of the whole work is in many ways remarkable. While the defeated Persians were retiring on Sardes, Masistes, one of Xerxes' brothers, scornfully condemned the general Artayntes for his mismanagement of the campaign. Artayntes drew his sword to cut Masistes down, but a third party intervened and prevented bloodshed. This leads at once to the story (108-113) that in Sardes Xerxes fell in love with his brother's wife, and that this guilty passion brought in its train many calamities, ending in the destruction of Masistes and his family. Is it simply that Herodotus, having occasion to mention Masistes just once, drags in a piece of Persian history purely for the interest that it may have in itself? Or has he something more in mind? He stresses that the man who saved Masistes from the sword of the infuriated Artayntes did so not only out of affection for Masistes, but for Xerxes also, whom he saved from losing a brother. This is the same Xerxes who in his infatuation prepares to dishonour his brother's bed, and causes the death of him and his family. Does Herodotus intend to impress us forcibly once more with the extraordinary vagaries of human destiny? Does he end with yet another example of that tyrannical caprice which had mortally threatened the freedom of Greece? We may think so, but we must remain aware of the danger of dragging in to such a long and varied work themes which were not intended by the author. Herodotus makes it more difficult for us, since he does not normally give any commentary on coincidences of this kind.[1] The uncertainties that thus arise are inherent in the largely archaic nature of his work.

A similar problem comes up in the last chapter of the work. After the story of Masistes Herodotus returns to the Greeks, and makes his last narrative that of their expedition to the Hellespont and the capture of Sestus by the Athenians. Here Artayctes, who had robbed a sanctuary of Protesilaus, suffered his punishment. Immediately after, at the very end of the book, we are told that an ancestor of this Artayctes was the author of a proposal submitted to Cyrus by the Persian nobles. Now that the Persians were powerful, he suggested, they should quit their small and barren country and take possession of a better. But Cyrus pointed out that strength and courage throve on a hard soil, while soft countries bred only soft men who were unable to maintain their freedom. The Persians yielded to his better judgment.

These are the last words that Herodotus has for us. It has been and still is keenly disputed whether we have to reckon this as the end or to suppose that the work was left unfinished.[2] The latter view has been supported by promises that Herodotus makes here and there in the Histories without ever carrying them out. Thus in 7. 213 he says that the death of Ephialtes will be told later, and it has struck many people that in 1. 184 he promises an account of the kings of Babylon in the Assyrian logoi, but never gives one. But these arguments are not decisive. Herodotus spent many years on his work, and there are indications of later additions.[3] It may be purely an oversight if Herodotus promises something and fails to do it. Herodotus has as good a right to nod as Homer. To decide the question whether 9. 122 is the end we have only the chapter itself. The mention of Cyrus, the founder of Persian power, and the basic

---

[1] A good example in H. STRASBURGER, 'Herodot und das perikleische Athen'. *Historia* 4, 1955, 1.   [2] POHLENZ (*v. inf.*), 163 with bibliography.
[3] E.g. in 4. 99 the reference to Iapygia – an addition made in the west.

political maxim put into his mouth are capable of two different interpretations. The passage looks back antithetically to the speech of Xerxes to his councillors (7. 8) in which he expressly assigns the traditional Persian claim to power as the reason for coveting ever new dominions: in both passages the key word is ἡγεμονίη. Thus we have the last three books, with their narrative of the decisive events, framed round by expressions pregnant with significance for the whole story. Or alternatively we might find the relevance of the chapter concerned in the very beginning of the work, where Herodotus makes healthy moderation the guarantee in one place of the individual's happiness, in another of the freedom of nations. We cannot deny that the judgment given by Cyrus could have had great relevance in the period of Atenian military and political expansion. This argument loses some of its weight when we reflect that the closing chapter is concerned with one specialized form of expansionist policy, namely the occupation of a foreign country in order to live there oneself. In addition, the relevance of the thought to a problem being discussed at the time could well have led Herodotus to include this section. Hard soil: hard men, and vice versa – this was akin to the theory that we find later in the Hippocratic *Airs, Waters and Places.*[1]

If nevertheless we find reasons in the subject matter for accepting 9. 122 as an appropriate ending, we certainly cannot find it so on formal grounds. It is hard to be content with such a haphazard ending to a work of such archaic elaboration and length, especially if we bear in mind the careful composition of the opening. But there is cogency in the arguments brought forward by van Groningen[2] in a wider context: that archaic and early classical compositions often show a fairly elaborate beginning, but an abrupt end. Thus there is something to be said for taking the conversation with Cyrus as the true ending of the work.

In considering the various constituent elements of this many-sided work we can best begin with the opening sentence. In the first words of a complex piece of syntax that is of basic importance for his philosophy of history he promises 'the exposition of his discoveries' – ἱστορίης ἀπόδεξις. This might serve as a mot.o for the work, so well does it show the soil from which it sprang: it is an expression of that constant and lively curiosity which accompanied the Ionian colonists on their distant travels, and which was most perfectly embodied in those voyages of exploration which took men far afield purely to increase knowledge. With these words Herodotus puts himself in the tradition of Ionian ethnography,[3] and thus continues in one (but only one) aspect of his work a tendency which was exemplified by Hecataeus. This aspect finds its purest expression in the large ethnographical *logoi*, such as the Egyptian, Scythian and Libyan, whose place in the work was apparent in our synopsis. To these may be added a number of smaller ethnographical digressions, like

---

[1] On differences of viewpoint see F. HEINIMANN, *Nomos und Physis.* Basel 1945, 24.

[2] *La Composition littéraire archaïque grecque. Verh. Nederl. Ak. N.R.* 65/2. Amsterd. 1958, 70.

[3] K. TRÜDINGER, *Studien zur Geschichte der griech.-röm. Ethnographie.* Diss. Basel 1918,

that on the Massagetae at the end of the first book. In fact an interest in ethno-graphy permeates the work down to its smallest details, and is constantly revealed in particular observations.

We can thus establish a line of descent from Hecataeus; but we must make an important distinction. The attitude of Herodotus is defined in that opening sentence from which we have been discussing the first words. The object of this 'exposition of his discoveries' is 'that what has happened among men should not be destroyed by time, and that great and remarkable achievements both of Greeks and of barbarians, should not lose their due fame, both generally and, in particular, how they came first to make war on each other'. In this sentence – a rather laborious formulation, as has been noticed – it is not easy to see the connection of thought between one part and another. In order to arrive at an interpretation partly satisfying the demands of more modern notions, some scholars have proposed that the 'great and remarkable achievements' (ἔργα) should be taken as referring to building works only, and that this conception is enlarged by the addition 'what has happened among men'.[1] Certainly we can reckon such things as the Pyramids among the 'achievements', but we ought not to restrict the latter in a way that is justified neither by the sentence itself nor by the course of the narrative. Rather, the last member of this somewhat ill-organized *tricolon* seems intended to define the theme of the work rather more closely. The author intends to deal with human history, more especially with great achievements of Hellenes and barbarians; finally – this being the main theme – he will relate the hostilities between them, meaning the course of the Persian wars.

Two things clearly emerge from this introductory sentence: how strongly Herodotus felt himself to be following Homer in preserving fame from oblivion, and how much his interests centre round men and what they do and suffer. Here again we see a difference from Hecataeus. Certainly there is much geographical information in Herodotus – to mention only his exposition of the parts of the inhabited world (4. 36) – but normally it is directly related to human life, as in the description of the Nile or of the rivers of Scythia. Man occupies a central place in the *Histories* as he cannot be supposed to have done in Hecataeus. The infrequency with which we find details of flora and fauna chimes in well with the observation made earlier, that the ethnographical *logoi* never lose sight of the historical dimension.

If we lay a particular stress on man as the object of Herodotus' curiosity, it is not with the intention of making a philosopher out of a teller of tales. We shall have occasion later to consider what Herodotus thought about the world in general, and how deep his thoughts were. But he was above all a child of the Ionian spirit, impelled by an insatiable curiosity to enquire into anything outside normal, everyday experience. Hence comes his delight in digressions on men and manners, their ways and circumstances of life; hence also the importance of a second constituent element in his work. The romance or novel, which declares by its very name that it is concerned with something new or unheard

[1] JACOBY (*v. inf.*), 334. Cf. also H. ERBSE, *Festschr. Snell*. Munich 1956, 209.

of, differs from saga or fairytale in that the remarkable element in it is confined to the human sphere and proceeds without any element of the supernatural. We remarked earlier that this kind of narrative must have had a vigorous life in Ionia from an early date, although we only catch sight of it here and there. Herodotus incorporates a great many such narratives into his work: he scatters them loosely, or sometimes makes a whole skein of them around some important individual. In this he was building on a rich, principally Ionian tradition, of which his work enables us to form some conception. One of the reasons for the large role played by the romance in Herodotus is his love of the unusual in human fate or behaviour: the other is his sheer joy in telling a story – a joy which came from his supreme skill.

Herodotus is equally valuable and equally delightful when he describes strange peoples and when he displays his mastery of anecdote. Sometimes these are the only elements in his work that have been recognized: it has been forgotten that we are dealing with a man whom the ancients themselves reckoned as the father of history. The reputation of Herodotus in this respect has suffered from his having Thucydides as his successor. Thucydides, who must have met him in Athens, whom legend represents as among his audience at a reading at Olympia, far excelled Herodotus as an historian in his critical survey of early Greek history and as a thinker in his physiology and pathology of power. But it is only by false and exaggerated application of the comparative method that Herodotus has been judged by Thucydides' standards and characterized by what he lacks in the comparison. Taken by himself, he has claims to genuine historical method which are good enough to deserve the title that Cicero gives him.

Any just evaluation of Herodotus as an historian must start from the sources that were available to him. In this connection scholars have mostly thought in terms of written sources, which they have pursued with great zeal. Unfortunately, firm ground has not been reached. Works such as the *Persian History* of Charon of Lampsacus or the *Lydian History* of Xanthus are not firmly enough dated to make it certain that Herodotus was the borrower. In the scanty remains there is no striking resemblance, and consequently we must treat the statement of Ephorus (ap. Ath. 12. 515e), that Xanthus was Herodotus' basic authority, with considerable caution. It is quite wrong to try to make Dionysius of Miletus the prime source for Herodotus and thus the real father of history. We know very little about his work, and what we do know contradicts the supposition that Herodotus was particularly in his debt. Thus the only predecessor established with certainty is still Hecataeus, and we see at once that Herodotus was keenly critical of him. He rejects very decidedly his explanation of the flooding of the Nile (2. 21) and his theory that the Nile flowed from the outer ocean: the latter he dismisses to the realm of fable. His ridicule of people who draw schematized diagrams of the earth and call them maps is aimed especially at Hecataeus. In these two places he refrains from giving the name, but he feels free to do so where he is not attacking the views expressed. Among such passages is 6. 137: an important example of Herodotus' respect for the truth. The Pelasgians were driven out of Attica by the Athenians, and he enquires whether this expulsion was just or unjust. He stresses that he can do no more than relate the tradition, which here is twofold. Hecataeus thought that justice was on the Pelasgian side: the opposite view is held by the 'the Athenians themselves'. This is an essential point in discussing Herodotus' use of sources. Who are the 'Athenians themselves' in this context? Is Herodotus using a written Athenian source, or did he hear an account orally during his stay in the city? This passage is typical of a number of others, where no certain result can be obtained.

We should not assume that the written sources available to Herodotus were as scanty as our knowledge of them. We have to think of him as using various collections, particularly collections of oracles, which he valued highly and quoted with corresponding care. There is occasional use of documents in the modern sense. The account of Persian satrapies in the third book can only come from an official list. Inscriptions are occasionally quoted: the best example is the use in 8. 82 of the inscription on the tripod dedicated at Delphi by those who took part in the fight for freedom.[1]

All that we have said about Herodotus' sources cannot conceal the fact that he himself regarded personal enquiry as the best means of finding out the truth. He does not mean enquiry into the books of his predecessors, but his own enquiries carried out as far as possible on the actual site. What is very important is his own assessment of his critical tools and of the degree of certainty that he can attain, expressed in 2. 99, where he changes his sources. In the preceding chapters he has given us the information about Egypt and her people which he acquired while living there. Up till now, he says, he has spoken from his own inspection ($\check{o}\psi\iota\varsigma$), his own judgment ($\gamma\nu\acute{\omega}\mu\eta$) and his own enquiries ($\iota\sigma\tau\rho\acute{\iota}\eta$): from now on he can only give Egyptian tradition ($\lambda\acute{o}\gamma\upsilon\iota$) as it was told to him. There follows an outline of Egyptian history beginning with Min. Thus Herodotus clearly differentiates between the results of his own enquiries and what he repeats as pure tradition. It is obvious that the order reflects the relative value; and the same holds good for the three components of the first group. Personal inspection is the most reliable source; then comes information drawn from the questioning of witnesses. There is another important feature. Only in the first group – inspection, judgment, enquiries – does personal judgment appear as a decisive element. One's own eyes and the testimony of others provide the material which cannot give useful results for the 'exposition of one's researches' until they have been critically evaluated. Such evaluation is scarcely possible when dealing with tradition: it must simply be accepted as it stands. This is what Herodotus explicitly does in the instance already quoted concerning the expulsion of the Pelasgi. Herodotus did not always have an easy task in prosecuting his enquiries, especially in foreign countries where he had to rely on an interpreter. It is very likely that a good deal of uncertainty came from this source, and much of the information that he received was probably made up on the prompting of his questions. He tells us himself in one passage how the Egyptians tried to dupe him. In Sais he was told a grim story about some statues

---

[1] Cf. SCHMID, 2, 629, 4.

which were said to commemorate some women whose hands had been cut off. But he observed that the hands had in fact fallen off in the passage of time and were still lying in front of the statues: consequently he rejected the whole story. Despite all difficulties, Herodotus acquired a great deal of useful knowledge on his journeys, and passed it on to us. We may cite in this connection the researches of K. Meuli,[1] which have surprisingly confirmed the historical value of some important statements in the Scythian *logos*.

Herodotus knew very well that by admitting tradition which he was unable to check he was bringing an element of uncertainty into his work. He roundly declares in 7. 152 – dealing with reports not wholly favourable to the Argives: 'I am obliged to report what people say, but I feel no obligation to believe it always. This holds good for my work as a whole.' But he is not always content with a *relata refero*. If he cannot select in the tradition what really happened, he can at least apply his scepticism to what seems unlikely. In this connection his attitude towards myth is very significant: he takes up an intermediate position which we shall find in other fields also.

We should first notice the very decided manner in which at the outset he excludes the epic world from his purview. He refuses to commit himself on the truth or falsehood of the various tales of the carrying off of women, and stresses that he can start to give historically sound information. There is also a formal distinction, in that the part on ancient history is preceded and followed by the reference to Persian tradition. This reference has to be taken seriously: Karl Reinhardt[2] has shown how much Herodotus is indebted to Persian tales from palace or harem both in the themes and in the intellectual attitudes of his work.

Herodotus is moving in a different world from that of Thucydides: he comes face to face with myth at every turn. His manner of dealing with it is not consistent. He does not rationalize it throughout, nor is he a thoroughgoing sceptic: yet at the same time he does not swallow the mythical tradition whole, and he is always ready with a critical objection. Between these limits his treatment constantly varies. The pretty story of the ugly duckling that received the blessing of Helen in her shrine and grew up to be the most beautiful woman in Sparta is given by Herodotus (6. 61) just as a current story, without any criticism. On the other hand he dismisses as nonsense the story (2. 45) of the Egyptians who sought to sacrifice Heracles. In the first place human sacrifice was forbidden in Egypt: in the second, how could Heracles, for all his strength, kill so many thousands? He does indeed add immediately that he hopes gods and heroes will not take his words amiss. This is one indication of the deep piety that underlay his ready criticism: his declaration (2. 65), that he particularly wishes to avoid any discussion of religion, is another.

Sometimes he suspends judgment, as when he tells us how the Athenians called on Boreas to help them. He is not able to say whether the north wind did

---

[1] 'Scythica.' *Herm.* 70, 1935, 121.

[2] 'Herodots Persergeschichten.' *Von Werken und Formen.* Godesberg 1948, 163; now in *Vermächtnis der Antike.* Göttingen 1960, 133. W. BURKERT, *Gymn.* 67, 1960, 549, is sceptical.

destroy the Persian fleet for this reason; but it is Athenian tradition anyway. It is sometimes interesting to see how he makes an old myth of the gods come to terms with a rational and natural explanation. The gorge of the Peneus is obviously the result of an earthquake. But at the same time one might indeed say that it was the work of Poseidon, since he is taken to be the god responsible for earthquakes (7. 129). Sometimes the supernatural rubs shoulders with rationalistic interpretation, without any reconciliation. The seven Persian nobles had agreed to settle which should be king when they took horse in the morning. He whose horse should first whinny to greet the dawn was to be king. Darius' cunning squire assured his master's victory by a stratagem, and the whinnying of the horse is thus naturally explained. But at the same time there is thunder and lightning from a cloudless sky.

What we have said about myth applies to Herodotus' methods in general. We cannot deny him critical powers: he displays them in many passages, and we recall that we spoke of him above as the first to give critical treatment to the epic cycle. But it is a critical method which applies itself to individual features; it does not go to the heart of the matter.

To say how far Herodotus was an historian we must first be sure what we mean by the term. Nowadays philosophy[1] has given us the conception of a science of history that may be called an exact science, and which wears a very different aspect from historiography based on ancient models. We demand of it that, when faced with fragmentary materials, it should have the courage of resignation, and should not deploy the resources of art to make a pleasing picture. It should not resemble an historical film-set, rather a ruined city with a few broken walls.

Herodotus certainly did not write history in this sense. Indeed the *pater historiae* can rather be taken as one of the reasons why western historiography did not content itself with inventories of remains. If we refrain from demanding its adherence to a set of standards outside itself, and consider it by itself as an intellectual entity, we can see that it is primarily aimed throughout at the establishment of factual truth, while at the same time it tries to understand and to point to the individual as a key to the universal.[2] This was the attitude of mind with which Herodotus wrote, and in this sense there is every reason to reckon him as the first name in European historiography.

The unity of his work must be considered first from the point of view of its contents: we can then consider whether it has an intellectual unity.

The introductory sentence refers to the conflict between Europe and Asia, which reached its climax (and, in Herodotus' eyes, its conclusion) in the Persian wars, as being the central theme. The work is not an assemblage of anecdote and ethnography about a loosely strung narrative, nor does it aim to give a general picture of the world: its primary object is to tell of the war in which Greece defended herself against the Persian menace. There are two important inferences to be made here. First, we see how highly freedom is rated in Herodotus'

---

[1] V. KRAFT, 'Geschichtsforschung als exakte Wissenschaft'. *Anz. Oest. Ak.* 1955, 239.

[2] Cf. K. V. FRITZ, *Philosophia naturalis* 2, 1952, 217.

scheme of values.[1] It is sharply contrasted with oriental systems as being the Greek way of life, the only one which allows individual and community to attain their full spiritual development (7. 135). That such liberty is only possible under the rule of law emerges clearly in the conversation between Xerxes and Demaratus at the parade (7. 104) where Sparta is taken as an example.

Secondly, given the theme of the work and Herodotus' personal relations with the city, it was inevitable that Athens should play a leading part in the narrative. He praises the Athenian contribution as having been decisive – a passage (7. 139)[2] which must have been written when there was obvious resentment of Athenian power-politics among many Greek cities. Since Eduard Meyer Herodotus' bias towards Athens has been much over-stressed: sometimes it has been seen as a tendency that dominates the work. This is overdone: what he says about Athens is much better assigned to a desire to reach a true assessment than to partisan spirit pure and simple.[3]

The individual parts of the work are subordinated to the leading theme by the device of adding the long ethnographical digressions where the peoples in question first came into contact with the expansion of Persia. This latter, of course, is immediately relevant to the main theme, and so the digressions are significantly linked with it. But we should be mistaking the archaic character of the work if we tried to tie every individual section firmly in to the basic narrative. In his Ionian fashion Herodotus has added a good deal out of pure pleasure in telling a story. He himself says that additions ($\pi\rho o\sigma\theta\hat{\eta}\kappa\alpha\iota$) are in the very nature of his work; he describes a section as being an insertion (7. 171 $\pi\alpha\rho\epsilon\nu\theta\acute{\eta}\kappa\eta$); and he often (e.g. 4. 82) calls himself back to the main theme. All this shows that he is sure enough of his route, but will not deny himself the pleasure of picking flowers at the roadside.

From our synopsis of the contents it is easy to see that the historical subject does not impose a rigid discipline on the work as a whole, but that it decisively influences its composition. The last three books, full of great and decisive events, are noticeably tighter in construction than the first six. Digressions are much shorter and fewer. In this connection it is striking that some peculiar customs of Halus are described in the form of a report to Xerxes (7. 197). If we take a general view of the composition, we see an exposition on the most generous scale, into which Herodotus has packed an amazing mixture of information, followed by a narrative which becomes more concentrated as the work progresses, until in the last three books he tells all the decisive events, not without harking back a good deal, but substantially as a complete narrative. We made the acquaintance of this kind of composition in Aeschylus: the first half of the Agamemnon, with its great choral odes, is followed by the later section in which the dramatic events are more closely packed. This again is an archaic feature.

Now that we have seen the loose but unmistakable order in which the individual elements – ethnography, romance and history – appear in Herodotus,

---

[1] M. POHLENZ, Griech. Freiheit. Leipz. 1955, 17.

[2] On this and other passages such as 8, 143 f.: H. KLEINKNECHT, 'Herodot und Athen'. Herm. 75, 1940, 241.   [3] Cf. H. STRASBURGER (v. p. 315, n. 1).

we can consider a view which seeks to bring them within the scope of an evolutionary theory. In his article on Herodotus (330) Jacoby propounds the theory that the great ethnographical *logoi* were originally independent works and date back to a time when Herodotus was a traveller interested in men and manners, not yet an historian. There is no convincing proof that the *logoi* once had a separate existence, indeed it is scarcely even probable. But the closer-knit structure and the concentration on historical essentials which we see in the later books may very well represent a later level in Herodotus' creative activity. Thus to some extent we can trace a development in his work.[1]

What gives its inner unity to the work is that everything which Herodotus relates is coloured with his profound conviction that the course of events is ruled by fate. He nowhere asserts this as a doctrine, but it finds expression both in individual episodes and in the treatment as a whole. Everything that happens is ordained, and cannot happen otherwise – that is Herodotus' firm belief, and we are twice told[2] that suffering haunts a man ineluctably and takes one or another occasion to seize upon him. This conviction forms the background to the whole work, although it never attains such rigid dogmatism as to lessen the importance of human decisions or the burden of human responsibility. This also is an archaic feature: we can trace back to Homer the notion that everything that happens, whether in the divine or the human world, takes its impetus and direction from this power. The various elements in the belief cannot be rationally sorted out. At the beginning of the seventh book, in the long and highly wrought passage where Xerxes decides on war, we find a combination of these two realms of motivation which reminds us of Aeschylus. His own ambition drives Xerxes to take arms, but the warning voices might have spoken louder if the gods had not sent a vision in a dream which pushed the wavering monarch to the fatal decision.

This belief in predestination is connected with the other belief in signs and prophecies by which fate is declared. This explains the large part which oracles play in Herodotus: they are firmly rooted in his conception of the world.[3] His kinsman, the poet Panyassis, is described in Suidas as an interpreter of signs, and thus Herodotus would have been very early acquainted with such things.

The irony which displays itself so powerfully in the tragedies of Sophocles is to be seen also in the contrast which we find in Herodotus between the certainty with which divine oracles reach their fulfilment and the vain reasoning and planning of men who try to elude them. The story of Croesus and Adrastus and that of Astyages are striking examples. If ever the individual knows what

---

[1] K. LATTE, 'Die Anfänge der griechischen Geschichtsschreibung' in *Entretiens sur l'antiquité. class.* 4. VANDŒUVRES-GENÈVE 1956, 3, also assumes a spiritual development by which H, under Athenian influence, moved from pure pleasure in the detail and reality of the logoi to the intellectual mastering of the past. However that may be, H.'s work can be seen as a unity embracing diverse elements, particularly the digressions. This view is insisted upon by H. ERBSE, 'Tradition und Form im Werke Herodots'. *Gymn.* 68, 1961, 239.

[2] 1. 8; 2. 61; cf. 5. 33; 9. 24.

[3] R. CRAHAY, *La Littérature oraculaire chez Hérodote.* Paris 1956, goes rather too far in assuming forgeries and in minimizing the political influence of Delphi.

is coming, his situation becomes deeply tragic, as it did for the Persian in the banqueting scene before Plataeae (9. 16): 'The worst sorrow for a man is to have knowledge of many things and power over none'.

Fate for Herodotus is not a blind force, but one determined by the will of heaven. His pantheon is not much like Homer's. The god most often mentioned is Apollo: this is linked with the great importance of oracles, particularly the Delphic oracle. For the rest, there are some passages, particularly in the Egyptian *logos* (2. 3 and 49 ff.), which make one think that he believed in a basic knowledge of the power and working of the gods which was common to all humanity and independent of individual titles and cults. His view of the Greek pantheon as a relatively recent creation by Homer and Hesiod, incorporating many Egyptian elements, is of a piece with the impressions which he received from the age-old cults of Egypt and the tales of her priests. The influence of Ionian thought and the results of his researches combined to make him speak by preference of God and the divine without any differentiation of person.[1]

This god or divinity works through fate in a particular way, which here and there in the narrative is expressly characterized. Evidently Herodotus took ideas which were deeply rooted in Greek thought and raised them to a level at which they served to interpret history. Sometimes the sequence of events seems to be morally determined: sin is followed by expiation. The most striking example is the story of Glaucus (6. 86), whose whole family died out because he asked the Delphic god whether a man might keep for himself a thing entrusted to him. Herodotus often raises the question, Who was first in the wrong? But such examples only give a partial notion of the operation of the divine will, which is not always determined by moral notions in our sense. According to the very characteristic story of Solon (1. 34) it appears that Croesus drew *nemesis* down upon himself from God, apparently by considering himself as the most fortunate of men. *Nemesis* must here be taken in its basic meaning of 'blame', 'reproach', and this is the quality of the divine power which appears most strongly in Herodotus. Anything that goes beyond measure, anything that threatens the norms of this world incurs the blame of the gods and thus certain destruction. The story of Polycrates is an example. The theme also recurs where Themistocles, in a very important passage (8. 109), expresses Herodotus' own pious conviction that not men, but gods and heroes wrought the salvation of Hellas: the gods grudged (ἐφθόνησαν) sole rule over Europe and Asia to a single man, one who burned temples, destroyed images and had the sea flogged and shackled. One immediately sees the kinship with the significant speech of Darius in the *Persae* of Aeschylus (747). The association here of the 'grudge' which the gods bear towards excessive power and the punishment of moral guilt is characteristic of Herodotus. The scene with Solon in the first book carries great weight in this connection. The Athenian sage speaks (1. 32) of the divine displeasure and the destruction which is always at hand when fortune seems assured.

---

[1] G. FRANÇOIS, *Le Polythéisme et l'emploi au singulier des mots* θεός, δαίμων. *Bibl. de la Fac. de Philos. et Lettres Liège* 147. Paris 1957, 201. W. PÖTSCHER, 'Götter und Gottheit bei Herodot'. *Wien. Stud.* 71, 1958, 5.

The central importance of moderation leads to a notion of compensation in human acts and destinies, which is one of the leading ideas of the work. Thus Oroetes has to pay for the treatment he accorded to Polycrates (3. 126 ff.), and Cleomenes atones for his behaviour towards Damaratus: here Herodotus expressly gives this as his interpretation (6. 84).[1] In history he sees the same processes that Anaximander saw in the cosmos – a mutual atonement of elements in their coming-to-be and in their passing away.

Herodotus was contemporary with the sophists, but the attempts to find traces in him of influence from any individual sophist have led to no certain result.[2] What is important is that in his attitude towards tradition he is wholly opposed to them. This comes to light very well in a story in the third book (38). Darius asks some Greeks, who burn their dead, and some members of an Indian tribe who eat theirs, how much they would each have to be paid to do what the others do. A horrified refusal is the answer of both. Herodotus, however, does not conclude, as the sophists would, that law and custom are purely relative. On the contrary, he takes the story as illustrating the compelling force of custom, and he ends the story by quoting Pindar's saying that custom is the ruler of all.

The style and language of the work are a faithful reflection of its richness and variety in content. This very quality ($\pi o\iota \kappa\iota\lambda\iota\alpha$) was particularly remarked upon by ancient literary critics.[3]

Herodotus sometimes tips out his information untidily and speaks in a tone whose unpretentiousness points clearly to its origin in popular story telling. But short sentences in parataxis are not his universal form of expression. We often find long periods with many subordinate clauses preceding or following the main clause.[4] The essential feature is that the individual elements are thus put together without producing that 'toothed' style in which the artificially constructed period emphasizes the logical relationship of the component parts. With this bricklaying type of construction Herodotus sometimes achieves remarkably effective scenes: no reader is likely to forget the sentence which ends the story of Atys and Adrastus (1. 45). But a comfortable expansiveness is the feeling more usually conveyed by this style of narration. Sometimes his weight of information is too much for the sentence structure: the passage on the sources of the Maeander (7. 26), with its pile of relative clauses, is a frightful example.

An important part is played by speeches, which do not, like those of Thucydides, bring out the unseen forces at work in a situation, nor yet serve to delineate individual character. Rather, they underline universal human patterns of behaviour and bring out points of view that transcend the purely personal and local. The warning friend[5] is a recurrent figure, and the admonitory speech

---

[1] Other exx. in SCHMID 2. 571. 5.

[2] W. NESTLE, *Vom Mythos zum Logos*. Stuttgart 1940, 509.

[3] Dion. Hal. *ad Pomp.* 3. 11; *de Thuc.* 23.

[4] F. ZUCKER effectively characterizes this type of sentence structure in his study 'Der Stil des Gorgias nach seiner inneren Form'. *Sitzb. Ak. Berl. Kl. f. Sprachen. Lit. u. Kunst.* 1956/1, 10. He suspects that ancient literary critics classed it with the $\lambda\epsilon\xi\iota s$ $\epsilon\iota\rho o\mu\epsilon\nu\eta$ of which Herodotus is cited as the representative (Arist. *Rhet.* 1409 a 27).

[5] H. BISCHOFF, *Der Warner bei Herodot.* Diss. Marburg 1932.

is an important and frequent feature in the work. Sometimes it is cast in the form of an illustrative parable (e.g. 6. 86). It is an indication of the broad area in which Herodotus draws for his component elements that in reading these stories we are as likely to be reminded of the tale of Meleager in Homer as of the popular moralizing fable (αἶνος). The same may be said of the speeches in general: they are akin at once to the epic and the romance.

Dialogue is not less effective than single speeches in setting the tone of some sections. It may range from long speeches on each side to rapid altercation. In the manner of his narrative Herodotus shows a particular kinship with epic, and the ancients themselves[1] were led by numerous observations tending that way to describe him as 'exceedingly Homeric' (ὁμηρικώτατος). At the same time there are features already noted which speak of the influence exerted on him by contemporary drama. When a papyrus came to light with the remains of a seemingly Hellenistic tragedy of *Gyges*,[2] modelled on Herodotus, it was possible to think that the boot might be on the other foot and that Herodotus' prose narrative might have been based on a precursor of that drama. A specially striking example is the tragic story of Adrastus, in which scene follows scene and dialogue dialogue, and there is even an *agon*-scene between father and son. But in his historical narrative and particularly in the decisive episodes Herodotus always aims at dramatic concentration, as we saw very clearly in the description of Salamis.[3]

It was observed in antiquity[4] that the dialect of Herodotus is mixed when compared with the pure Ionic of Hecataeus. This impression is given mostly by the admixture of poetic, especially Homeric, elements.[5] When prose first set up in rivalry to poetry, it was natural that many elements of poetic vocabulary were borrowed. Herodotus of course was particularly close to the spirit of epic, and he was receptive to many other influences as well. His long sojourn in Attica also may well have left its traces in his language.[6]

In forming a judgment of Herodotus' dialect we find that the transmission poses a special problem. Very probably the schoolmasters were responsible for thrusting false archaisms into the text – for example, uncontracted forms where we should expect contracted. Contrariwise, late vulgarisms crept into the text. A violent normalizing of Herodotus' language on the basis of the few Ionic inscriptions of his time is out of the question, and the problem of its original form can never be fully solved.

Herodotus kept his high reputation down to very late antiquity. His country-man Dionysius of Halicarnassus exemplifies the value set on him by early

---

[1] *De Sublim.* 13, 3. [2] *Herm.* 81, 1953, 1.
[3] Cf. w. MARG, 'Herodot über die Folgen von Salamis'. *Herm.* 81, 1953, 196.
[4] Hermogenes, Περὶ ἰδ. 423. 25 Sp. 411. 12 Rabe.
[5] See M. LEUMANN, *Homerische Wörter*. Basel 1950, 303.
[6] Atticisms in Schmid 2. 594. 8.

Imperial literary theorists. In addition to the passages already mentioned we may cite his comparison of Herodotus and Thucydides (*de imit.* 207 Us.-Rad.), from which Herodotus comes off well. We find here the notable judgment that Thucydides' strength lies in *pathos*, that of Herodotus in *ethos*. It was a rather dubious compliment to him when in the course of the Ionic revival he was credited with one of the biographies of Homer which have come down to us. Naturally he did not escape criticism, and Thucydides has several passages of polemic against his predecessor, although he does not name him. Quite understandably several Greek cities were not best pleased with the figure they cut in Herodotus, and Plutarch's pamphlet *Examples of Prejudice in Herodotus* (Περὶ τῆς Ἡροδότου κακοηθείας), animated by Boeotian local patriotism, gives us a specimen of such polemical literature.

The most striking proof of Herodotus' reputation is that the Alexandrians took him under their protection – an honour which they paid to very few writers of prose. We have a papyrus (nr. 357 P.) containing scraps of a commentary which Aristarchus wrote on him. Presumably then the same scholar issued an edition of the text. The division into nine books most probably took place at Alexandria: it is first attested in Diodorus (11. 37, 6). We cannot say whether the names of the Muses, which appear at the heads of the books, were attached to them from the beginning or not. They appear as early as Lucian (*Herodot.* 1). We know that commentaries were written on Herodotus in the first century of our era by Hero and Irenaeus, two savants of the Alexandrian school. Abridged editions were soon in circulation: one such was made by Theopompus (*F Gr Hist* 115 F 1-4). A papyrus leaf from c. A.D. 350 shows that the excursuses were sometimes left out.

The division of the manuscripts into two groups, proposed by H. STEIN in his fundamental edition of 1869/72, has held its ground. There is a Florentine family and a younger Roman family: the latter shows traces of normalization and is suspected in places of interpolation more than the Florentine. A synopsis of the extant MSS. and their relative values is given by A. COLONNA, 'De Herodoti memoria'. *Boll. del Comitato per la preparazione della ediz. nazion. dei Classici greci e latini*. N.S. fasc. 1, 1945, 41. In another article ('Note alla trad. manoscritta di Erodoto'. ibid. fasc. 2, 1953, 13) Colonna opposes the theory of B. HEMMERDINGER ('Eliminatio codicum Herodoteorum'. *Class. Quart. N.S.* 2, 1952, 97) that within the Roman group certain MSS. (URSV) are mediately derived from Vat. Gr. 2369 saec. XI (D) and can therefore be discounted. The transmission has been re-examined by G. B. ALBERTI, 'Note ad alcuni manoscritti di Erodoto' *Maia* 12, 1960, 331.

The 21 papyri known to us are discussed by A. H. R. E. PAAP, *De Herodoti reliquiis in papyris et membranis Aegyptiis servatis*. Leyden 1948. Significant errors common to some papyri and the MSS. point to an ultimately common origin. But on the other hand we find papyri of the first three centuries A.D. which have true readings against all the MSS., so that the common archetype of the others is to be dated after this time. A short account of the tradition is given by UNTERSTEINER (see below).

Editions: H. R. DEITSCH–H. KALLENBERG, 2 vols., 2nd ed. Leipz. 1924–33 (needs to be brought up to date). C. HUDE, 2 vols. Oxf. 1927. PH. E. LEGRAND, 11 vols. (intro., I-IX, index). *Coll. des Un. de Fr.* 1932–54 (often repr.). A. D. GODLEY, 4 vols., *Loeb Library*. L. ANNIBALETTO, *Le storie*. 2 vols. Milan 1956. The seventh book with critical study and commentary: G. AMMENDOLA, Turin 1956. Selection with notes by M. I. FINLEY, *The Essence of Herodotus, Thuc. Xen. Polyb.* Lond. 1959. With commentary: C. W. W. HOW–J. WELLS, 2 vols. 2nd ed. Oxf. 1928 (historical). B. A. VAN GRONINGEN, repr. Leyden 1949–59 (excellent school edition). Lexicon: J. E. POWELL, Cambr. 1938 (repr. 1960). Translations: J. E. POWELL, Oxford Library of Translations, 2 vols. 1949 (with account of previous translations into English). TH. BRAUN, Leipzig 1927; Wiesbaden 1958. AUG. IZZO D'ACCINNI, Florence 1951. Language: M. UNTERSTEINER, *La lingua di Erodoto*. Bari 1949. CARLA SCHICK, *Appunti per una storia della prosa greca 3: la lingua di Erodoto. Acc. dei Lincei. Memorie Cl. sc. mor. stor. fil.* 8/7/7, 1956, 344. H. FRÄNKEL, *Wege und Formen frühgr. Denkens.* 2nd ed. Munich 1960, 65. 83. Light is thrown on the question 'Ionisms or epic elements?' in VITTORE PISANI's excellent *Storia della lingua greca* in *Encicl. Class.* 2/5/1, Turin 1960, 100. (C. FAVRE, *Thesaurus verborum quae in titulis Ionicis leguntur cum Herodoteo sermone comparatus.* Heidelb. 1914, is still useful here.) He gives good syntactical examples and rightly protests against the normalizing of the text to agree with the inscriptions. HAIIM B. ROSÉN, *Eine Laut- und Formenlehre der herodotischen Sprachform.* Heidelberg 1961. Monographs: F. JACOBY, *RE* S2 1913, 205 (now reprinted with others of his Pauly articles as *Griechische Historiker*. Stuttg. 1956). M. POHLENZ, *Herodot*. Leipz. 1937. J. E. POWELL, *The History of Herodotus*. Cambr. 1939. J. L. MYRES, *Herodotus: Father of History*. Oxf. 1953. Discussions: O. REGENBOGEN, 'H. und sein Werk'. *Die Antike* 6, 1930, 202 (now in his *Kleine Schriften*. Munich 1961, 57). F. HELLMAN, 'Herodot'. *Das neue Bild der Antike* I. Leipz. 1942, 237 (with bibliog.). A. MADDALENA, 'L' umano e il divino in Erodoto'. *Studi di filos. greca*. Bari 1950, 57. H. STRASBURGER, 'Herodots Zeitrechnung'. *Historia* 5, 1956, 129. H. R. IMMERWAHR, 'Aspects o Historical Causation in H.'. *Trans. Am. Phil. Ass.* 87, 1956, 241; id., 'Ergon: History as a Monument in H. and Thuc.'. *Am. Journ. Phil.* 81, 1960, 261. M. MILLER, 'The earlier Persian Dates in H.'. *Klio* 37, 1959, 29. H. T. WALLINGA, 'The structure of Herod. 2. 99-142'. *Mnem. s.* 4, 12, 1959, 204. T. SINKO, 'L'Historiosophie dans le prologue et l'épilogue de l'œuvre d'H. d'Halicarnasse'. *Eos* 50, 1959/60, 3. A. E. RAUBITSCHEK, 'H. and the Inscriptions'. *Univ. of Lond. Bull. of the Inst. of Class. Stud.* 8, 1961, 59. A work by K. LATTE in *Entretiens sur l'antiquité classique, v. supra.* P. 323, n. 1. Detailed bibliography in *Fifty Years of Classical Scholarship*. Oxf. 1954, 178, and see now *Herodot. Eine Auswahl aus der neueren Forschung, hrsg. von W. Marg.* Munich 1962.

6 OTHER HISTORIANS

Herodotus' work is built on Ionian and archaic foundations, but from these beginnings he advanced to new realms of historical thought which created the assumptions that underlay later development. Of his successors we can form a clear enough idea to know that they represent the continuation of the old Ionian tradition up to and beyond the turn of the century. Some of them cannot be dated certainly, but the racial origin, as one would expect, is in most cases Ionian.

The remains of these writers show us how far the attitude towards mythology was a central question of the age. The movement began in philosophy, and Xenophanes – not of course alone – is a striking example of the radicalism some-times shown in facing the great stories of Greek tradition. Among the intellectual instruments used to tackle the problem were the rationalizing[1] and the alle-gorizing approach. The latter, so far as we know, began with Theagenes of Rhegium, and in this period it was continued by Stesimbrotus of Thasos.[2] He wrote a book on Homer and also lectured on the subject. His treatise *On Sacred Offices* (Περὶ τελετῶν) is a piece of Orphic literature, and seems to have dealt with the sacred stories of the mysteries in the same spirit as with the epics. He was probably in Athens in the 'thirties, but he afterwards attacked Athenian power-politics in his pamphlet *On Themistocles, Thucydides and Pericles*. This work, which is shown by a fragment (F. 11) to have been written after 430/29, was an expression of the deep dissatisfaction of the allies at the *hybris* of the Athenian democracy.

In Plato's *Ion* (530 c) Metrodorus of Lampsacus[3] and one Glaucon are mentioned in the same breath with Stesimbrotus as Homeric exegetes. What we know of Metrodorus confirms Tatian's judgment that he showed great folly in his treatment of Homer. He made the gods and heroes of epic represent allegorically not merely natural phenomena, but even the parts of the human body. Xenophon (*Symp.* 3. 6) mentions the younger Anaximander of Miletus[4] together with Stesimbrotus; but he has to be dated a little later – under Arta-xerxes II (404–358), according to Suidas. His *Heroologia* included allegorical interpretation, and with his *Explanation of Pythagorean Symbols* he inaugurated a series of books on the remarkable rules of the order, in which a good deal of popular superstition left its mark.

Allegorical interpretation, which sought a deeper meaning in the tales as they were told, had its last fling in the nineteenth century, when the myths were interpreted as symbolizing natural forces; the rationalizing school, which tried to extract historical facts from fabulous accretions, began with Hecataeus; and his methods, which placed Cerberus, for example, among early Greek fauna as a poisonous snake, also found countless imitators.

One of these was Herodorus of Heraclea Pontica,[5] whose literary work must be dated in the late fifth century. In addition to his lengthy *Story of Heracles* ('Ο καθ' 'Ηρακλέα λόγος) we hear of an *Argonautica* and a *Pelopea*. The golden

---

[1] Cf. WEHRLI, *Allegorische Deutung Homers*. Diss. Basel 1928. F. WIPPRECHT, *Die Entwick-lung der rationalistischen Mythendeutung bei den Griechen*. 1, 1902. 2, 1908. F. BUFFIÈRE, *Les Mythes d' Homère et la pensée grecque*. Paris 1956.

[2] *F Gr Hist* nr. 107.

[3] VS 61.   [4] *F Gr Hist* nr. 9.   [5] *F Gr Hist* nr. 31.

lamb over which Atreus and Thyestes fought was for him a golden image in the middle of a silver bowl (F. 57). This heavy-handed attempt to secularize and trivialize a myth is typical of many. But Herodorus also resorted to allegory, if we are to believe a later compilation. It is, after all, basically credible that he made Heracles a moral philosopher, scotching the passions with the club of the spirit, in the age which saw Prodicus' allegory of the choice of Heracles. But features like this are rare in Herodorus: he seems rather, judging from what survives, to have enlivened his explanations of the myths with pieces of Ionian science and ethnography.

Concerning Simonides of Ceos[1] – a grandson of the poet, according to Suidas – all that we can tell from his treatment of the story of Athene and Iodama (F. 1) is that he was a horse from the same stable. He wrote a work called *Genealogiae* in three books, in which we suppose that he imitated the methods of Hecataeus. He also wrote three books of *Discoveries* (Εὑρήματα).

The tradition that began in Ionia was carried on by an Aeolian who wrote a great deal and had a wide influence – Hellanicus of Mytilene in Lesbos.[2] Such help as the fragments give us in dating him points to the last quarter of the fifth century. A few scattered indications[3] show that he was acquainted with Herodotus' work, but there is nothing to show that he was greatly influenced by him. The line of tradition seems rather to go back to Hecataeus and to pass Herodotus by.

Hellanicus is the first of the great scribblers in Greek literature. We know of twenty-three works that he wrote, most of them in two books each. This is an important fact. However much Hellanicus may remind us of his Ionian predecessors, his methods were wholly different. Instead of personal travel and investigation we find now a pilgrimage over other men's books. This is a literature which is wholly based on *litterae*.

Unlike Herodotus, Hellanicus opens his pages wide to myth. In reducing his material to order his principal tool was genealogy. He reckoned three generations to a century, which became standard practice. The titles of his works – probably given by the author himself – resemble those of epic poems, or are indeed taken from epics: e.g. the *Phoronis*, in which various Peloponnesian families were traced back to the supposed first of men, one Phoroneus. In this work Homer was made a descendant of Orpheus in the tenth generation. Other works of the same kidney were entitled *Atlantis*, *Asopis*, *Deucalionea* and *Troïca*. There are instances of rationalization (F. 28 et al.), but it seems to have played a much smaller part than in Hecataeus. He seems to approach closest to Ionian ethnography in his works *On the foundings of cities and peoples* (Κτίσεις ἐθνῶν καὶ πόλεων), *On Peoples* (Περὶ ἐθνῶν) and *On the Names of Peoples* ('Εθνῶν ὀνομασίαι). These are probably different titles for the same work. The *Founding of Chios* (Χίου κτίσις) was probably an independent treatise. Ion also wrote a book with this title. Hellanicus wrote on a subject dear to Herodotus' heart in the *Foreign*

---

[1] Ibid. nr. 8.
[2] Ibid. nr. 4. F. JACOBY, *Atthis*. Oxf. 1949. K. V. FRITZ, *Gnom.* 22, 1950, 220.
[3] Jacoby on F. 166 f.

Customs (Βαρβαρικὰ νόμιμα). To many of these foreigners he devoted separate books: we hear of *Aegyptiaca, Cypriaca, Lydiaca, Persica* and *Scythica*. In addition to manners and customs, history and mythology found their place in these books, particularly in those which dealt with regions of Greece, such as the *Aeolica, Lesbiaca, Argolica, Boeotica* and *Thessalica*.

This last group included also the *Atthis*, in two books, with which the Aeolian Hellanicus inaugurated a particular genre of Attic historical writings. The line of Athenian local historians, sometimes called Atthidographers, reaches from Hellanicus down to Philochorus, who wrote his work of seventeen books in the third century. For a long time a theory was accepted which Wilamowitz put forward in his book on Aristotle and Athens – namely that these writings essentially derived from notes written up in the manner of chronicles by the *exegetae*. Jacoby, however, demonstrated in his *Atthis* that the activity of the *exegetae* was confined to ritual observances,[1] and that in Attica, as elsewhere in Greece, there is no ground for postulating an annalistic tradition as a precursor of true historiography. Surviving laws, lists of archons, oral tradition probably linked with the great families – these are the basic sources of the *Atthis* so far as we can now infer them.

Hellanicus constructed, by rather arbitrary methods, a list of Athenian kings, and he apparently extended the lists of archons backwards far enough to reach the kingly period. In this he was impelled by the wish to close the gap between myth and the historical tradition in the modern sense, and to bring the whole course of events from the beginning into a chronological sequence. This desire is fairly plain in the *Atthis*, and we may suppose that a similar notion underlay his other work.

There is not much in the fragments that can be called scientific history; yet in one important department Hellanicus took a great step forward. His books on the *Victors at the Carnea* (Καρνεονῖκαι) and the *Priestesses of Hera* (Ἰέρειαι τῆς Ἥρας) undertook the important task of establishing a firm chronological frame-work for the writing of history, using to this end the records of the Spartan games and the Argive priestesses. Later, however, reckoning by Olympiads became normal: Hippias paved the way with his *List of Olympic Victors*.

Hellanicus is said to have been the teacher of Damastes of Sigeum[2] who wrote in the late fifth century a mythographical and genealogical work on the ancestry of the heroes who fought against Troy. He also wrote on Greek history and on ethnographical topics. What we should most like to know is something about the contents of his book *On Poets and Sophists* (Περὶ ποιητῶν καὶ σοφι-στῶν). It is impossible to know exactly whom he meant by sophists in this juxta-position. At all events, the title points to the first beginnings of literary history in Greek. The same may be said of the treatise written by Glaucus of Rhegium *On the old Poets and Musicians* (Περὶ τῶν ἀρχαίων ποιητῶν καὶ μουσικῶν), which was written about the same time.

---

[1] Cf. also J. H. OLIVER, *The Athenian Expounders of the Sacred and Ancestral Law*. Baltimore 1950, and P. NILSSON, *Gesch. d. griech. Religion* I, 2nd ed. Munich 1955, 636.

[2] *F Gr Hist* nr. 5.

Local antiquarianism can be seen already in the genealogical epics. Hellanicus shows the continuation of such interests in prose. This was the budding of local history, which afterwards became such a vigorous growth. Representatives in Ceos and the Argolid were Xenomedes and Demetrius respectively, who may, however, have lived later than the fifth century.

Just as with poetry, philosophy and medicine, so with the writing of history the decisive impulse came to western Hellas from the Ionian east. In Suidas we find Hippys of Rhegium given as the first west Greek historian: he is said to have written *Chronica* and *Argolica* and works on Italian and Sicilian history. Jacoby[1] has taken grave exception to Hippys and Myres (the supposed epitomator of his *Sicelica*): he thinks that these are fictional adornments of a work written in fact about 300 B.C. If he is right, then Antiochus of Syracuse[2] becomes the first known historian of Sicily. He was much influenced by Herodotus, and aimed at supplementing his work where western Hellas was concerned. To this end he wrote the nine books of his *Sicilian History* (Τῶν Σικελικῶν ἱστορία), which went from the mythical king Cocalus to the peace congress in Gela in 424/23, and a treatise on Italy (Περὶ Ἰταλίας). He probably wrote in the last quarter of the fifth century.

7 PHILOSOPHY

The centripetal movement which gained momentum throughout the fifth century and brought men from all the areas of Greek colonization to Athens, making her 'an education for all Greece' (Thuc. 2. 41), brought it about that the last and much altered expression of Ionian science took place on Attic soil. Clazomenae, the Ionian city whose name is nowadays associated with elaborately painted clay sarcophagi, was the birthplace of Anaxagoras, who practised philosophy in Athens for thirty years. He was the friend of Pericles, and attracted a good deal of notice, not always sympathetic. It is hard to date the events of his life. The year of his death (428/27) and the Olympiad in which he was born (500/497) are attested by such a good witness as the chronicle of Apollodorus *F Gr Hist* 244 F. 331) but the date of the proceedings against him for impiety and of his flight to Lampsacus, which afforded him refuge until his death, cannot be certainly established. He seems to have come to Athens at the time of Xerxes' expedition, and this agrees with the statement in the archon-lists of Demetrius of Phalerum (fr. 150 W.) that he began to study philosophy at the age of twenty when Callias was archon. Demetrius speaks also of his thirty years' sojourn in Athens, which would date his trial about 450. Others, considering the general situation then, have preferred to put it in Pericles' last years, but the trial could quite conceivably have taken place earlier.[3]

Anaximenes, the last of the Milesian scientists, died only about a generation before the birth of Anaxagoras, but we find now the Milesian tradition carried on by a thinker whose most powerful influence was Anaximander. Like Parmenides, he begins with the maxim that there is neither any coming-to-be out

---

[1] In his commentary on *F Gr Hist* nr. 554.   [2] *F Gr Hist* nr. 555. *Atthis* 352, 2.
[3] A. E. TAYLOR, *Class. Quart.* 11, 1917, 81.

of nothing nor any passing away into nothing. Coming-to-be and passing away he considered simply as the mixing and unmixing of everlasting substances (B 10. 17. A 43. 45), processes which he depicted as wholly mechanical, unlike the physiological notion of mixture entertained by the Hippocratics.[1] Anaxagoras supposed an original mixture in which all substances and the qualities associated with them were contained in innumerable tiny particles. The mutual relation of substance and quality in his world-picture is much debated, but we can hardly suppose them to have been very sharply distinguished in thought.[2] From this original mixture – a distant cousin of Anaximander's *apeiron* – by processes of decomposition and recomposition individual things make their appearance. The separation of air and aether seems to have been the beginning (B 1. 2). The observation that semen ultimately is the origin of such diverse things as flesh and hair (B 10), and that the same may be said of food (A 45), led Anaxagoras to the doctrine that even in the individual things produced by decomposition and recomposition particles of every kind are to be found at any given time. It is the quantitative superiority of a given substance that determines the behaviour of individual things, and we recognize them by the correspondence with a related substance in ourselves. The infinitesimal material vehicles of the various qualities were called by Anaxagoras 'seeds' (σπέρματα): the expression *homoeomeria* probably was the first devised by the Aristotelians in their account of his theories.[3]

The indebtedness of this system to Ionian science is undeniable. Yet what is new is no less important. The power to move and form now no longer resides in the basic stuff itself, which in the hands of some of the Milesians acquired almost divine powers, but is a separate immaterial principle. Only *nus* exists by itself and unmixed: infinite and subject to nothing, it initiates that whirling motion which brings all things into being, and its ability to conceive their separation is at the same time the power to bring that separation about. *Nus* has power over all animate beings, and although we have no specific assertion of it, it seems likely that Anaxagoras conceived the human soul as part of this great spirit that informs the universe. Its guiding activity extends even to political society and to the rise of civilization. Its appearance in these connections is a new philosophical theme of great significance.[4] In none of the surviving fragments is *Nus* referred to as god or as divine. But the adjectives which Anaxagoras applies to it and the hymn-like strains in which he speaks of it, leave[5] little doubt that he felt it to be the divine power in the world. Yet his *Nus* is not pure spirit: it is only the finest and purest of all substances. This clearly anticipates to some extent the equally sublime material Logos of the Stoics. At the same time one may compare, though more remotely, the activities ascribed to the soul-atoms by Democritus and his followers.

---

[1] W. MÜRI, *Gymn.* 57, 1950, 198.　　　　[2] F. HEINIMANN, *Gnom.* 24, 1952, 272.

[3] On this important series of problems: H. CHERNISS, *Aristotle's Criticism of Presocratic Philosophy.* Baltimore 1935.

[4] H. FRÄNKEL, *Wege und Formen frühgriech. Denkens.* 2nd ed. Munich 1960, 285.

[5] B 12, cf. K. DEICHGRÄBER, *Phil.* 88, 1933, 347.

M

Anaxagoras was far from going the whole way to a consistent dualistic view of the world. Socrates in the *Phaedo* (97 b) professes dissatisfaction with the *Nus* of Anaxagoras, and Aristotle (*Metaph.* 985 a 18) reproaches him with invoking this power only where he is at a loss to explain things otherwise.

The Athenians could not but be suspicious of a man who set before their eyes the hitherto unknown spectacle of a life wholly devoted to contemplation. We do not know of any attack on traditional religion in his book (written in Ionic and naturally referred to later as Περὶ φύσεως); but it was impossible for a man to conceal his opposition to tradition when he declared the sun to be a red-hot stone, much larger than the Peloponnese (A 72), and favoured rational explanations of natural phenomena in general. Seeing tradition threatened, the Athenians reacted with the prosecution which deprived Pericles of his friend.

One of Anaxagoras' pupils was Archelaus of Miletus (or of Athens: presumably he was a Milesian who moved to Athens). He became associated with Cimon, for whom he wrote poems (Plut. *Cim.* 4), and with Sophocles, from whom we possess one pentameter of an elegy on the philosopher. He was known in antiquity above all as the teacher of Socrates: Ion of Chios (fr. 11 B 1) talks of their going to Samos together. In this context we should dearly love to know more about the alleged inclusion of ethics in Archelaus' teaching. But we know no more about this than about his development of Anaxagoras' theory, in which apparently heat and cold played some part as formative principles.

Some of the themes of Ionian natural philosophy were rehandled also by such men as Hippo of Samos and Idaeus of Himera, but none of these followers achieved real significance apart from Diogenes of Apollonia (either the Cretan or the Phrygian Apollonia). He also adopted the conceptions of the Milesians and took up energetically the old doctrine of an original basic substance. Otherwise he thought it impossible to explain the reciprocal influence and mixing of the different elements (B 2). His view of the basic substance as being air marks him as a follower of Anaximenes. On the other hand he took over and developed the theory of Anaxagoras that a spiritual force was at work in the forming and continuance of the universe. He thought that this world was the best of all possible worlds, on the ground that its phenomena like the seasons, day and night, rain, wind and sunshine are kept in due measure by law (B 3). To establish and maintain such a law an intellectual power (νόησις) is required: this Diogenes equates with the air (B 5). Thus this basic substance acquires high spiritual values, is spoken of as God, and is described in no less exalted strains than the *Nus* of Anaxagoras. Diogenes also had a high reputation as a physician. His importance is in the strong teleological tendency of his thought:[1] he infers the divine government of the universe from the order which results from it. We may suppose that detailed expositions such as we find in the long fragment (B 6) that deals with the veins of the human body played their part in his teleological arguments.

Diogenes also seems to have spent a long time in Athens. His influence there

[1] W. THEILER, *Zur Geschichte der teleologischen Naturbetrachtung.* Zürich 1925.

was particularly strong. Both comic and tragic writers allude to him, especially Euripides.

In our age we easily tend to look upon the atomic theory in cosmology as a unique achievement of the Greek genius, surpassing all else that it arrived at in the natural sciences. But the atomic theory is integral with the general development, that is to say, with the context of Ionian science.

We shall always associate atomism with the name of Democritus of Abdera, the first of a line which led through Epicurus, Lucretius and Gassendi to the physicists of today.[1] He came from the same city as Protagoras – an Ionian colony in Thrace. On his own statement (B 5) he was young when Anaxagoras was old, which sets his birth somewhere around 460. In antiquity he was one of the stock examples of longevity: he was said to have lived a hundred years or more. However that may be, his lifetime reached far into the fourth century. He was born about the same time as Socrates, but outlived him by many years. He was a great traveller, and according to Diodorus (1. 98, 3: doubtfully in fr. B 299) he spent five years in Egypt studying astronomy. What we know of his writings shows that his purpose there was very different from that of Hecataeus or Herodotus. He himself says (B 116) that he came to Athens, adding that no one knew him. Unlike Anaxagoras and Protagoras, he never became prominent in the life of the city.

All in all, we could associate the beginnings of atomic theory with a fairly distinct personality, if only there were not a difficult problem in the way. In several places Aristotle names Leucippus and Democritus as representatives of atomism: in one place Leucippus is said to have been a friend, in another the teacher of Democritus (VS 67 A 6; A 2). He was so overshadowed by the wide range and success of his follower's writings that his birthplace is unknown; Abdera, Elea and Miletus are given, but these are palpable guesses. Epicurus indeed denied that such a philosopher had ever existed (A 2). This may well have been a joking paradox rather than an historical statement, since, if a papyrus from Herculaneum has been correctly supplemented and dated (VS 75 A 7), the name of Leucippus was fairly familiar to Epicurus. But what makes it impossible to dispute his importance as a founder of the atomic theory is the fact that Theophrastus and his pupils ascribed to Leucippus a treatise called *The Great World-Order* (Μέγας διάκοσμος) which occurs in the list of Democritus' writings (VS 68 A 33. B 4 b). Another work, *On the Mind* (Περὶ νοῦ), was also ascribed to him, and no doubt the contact with Anaxagoras' views on *Nus* was of great importance to nascent atomism. If this interpretation of the work is correct, we have to date it after Anaxagoras, and Leucippus can probably be put between him and Democritus.

What we know of his teaching accords so closely with that of Democritus that it is hard to draw a clear distinction between their respective cosmologies. We ought probably to think of Democritus as the borrower in most cases. From all the foregoing we conclude that atomism as a physical theory should be credited to them jointly, without separating its various strands.

[1] For a more complete and continuous list see SCHMID 5, 347.

This theory seeks to explain the world in all its parts as arising from two things: tiny indivisible particles, called atoms (ἄτομα, sc. μέρη), and the void in which they move. The whole universe is made up of infinitesimal particles: this seems at first to be a variant on the *panspermia* of Anaxagoras. One cannot exclude the possibility of influence, but the very name of atom forbids its being confused with the endlessly divisible *spermata* of Anaxagoras. There are other, even more important, differences. Unlike Anaxagoras, the atomists thought that the qualities perceived by our senses were subjective and quite distinct from the world of the atom – the only true world (VS 68 B 9. 125). They recognized as real only the shapes of the atoms, which might be greater or smaller, round or angular, smooth or rough on the surface, and could be grouped together in different patterns. It has been rightly stressed[1] that the referring of our sense-impressions to mathematically expressible magnitudes marks an important step towards the methods of modern science. We find in fact Aristotle (*de Caelo* 3. 4. 303 a 4) making the striking statement that the atomists in their own fashion referred all natural phenomena to number. Democritus wrote several mathematical treatises: he also wrote a book on Pythagoras and is said to have been acquainted with various individual Pythagoreans.

The deepest rift between the atomists and Anaxagoras concerned the explanation of that motion which is necessarily involved in the building up and breaking down of bodies, and consequently in all apparent coming-to-be and passing away. *Nus* as the mover was distinguished by Anaxagoras, despite its material nature, from all other matter, and he made it act upon the latter from outside. The atomists, on the other hand, posited an eternal whirling movement, not traceable back to any cause, but associated with the atoms from the very beginning. In addition there is a kind of upward thrust on the lighter atoms and a centripetal tendency in the heavier. These, together with the rebound when atoms strike each other, are the constituent elements of that motion which produces all changes in the grouping of the unalterable atoms.

We can reckon these atoms, homogeneous in material and only varied in shape and surface, as a last metamorphosis of the primary material postulated by the Milesians. In the other direction we can trace a line of connection to the Eleans. The atoms and void constituted a basically unalterable existent, to which human knowledge could only have access when the veil of the sensible had been pierced. The atomists shared with the Eleatics a profound distrust of the senses. On their theory our perception of things arises from tiny images (εἴδωλα) formed of groups of atoms, which detach themselves from the object and find their way into the body through minute apertures. But one cannot gain knowledge of true being in this way (B 6. 7).[2] From the fallibility of sense-perception the Eleatics drew the conclusion that the world thus perceived was to be rejected as a world of appearances, separated by a deep gulf from the real world. The atomists reasoned another way. Sense-data, they thought, were the raw material, in itself admittedly inadequate, from which the reasoning and testing

---

[1] B. SNELL, *Die Entdeckung des Geistes.* 3rd ed. Hamburg 1955, 311 (cf. Eng. ed. p. 238).
[2] On δόξις ἐπιρυσμίη : H. LANGERBECK, *N. Phil. Unters.* 10, 1935.

intellect could gain a truer knowledge. Thus in his logical treatise *Rules of Thought* (Κάνονες B 11) Democritus distinguishes between 'dark' (σκοτίη) perception given by the senses and 'true' (γνησίη) perception, gained by the understanding. The latter begins where the first leaves off. But Democritus did not stop to consider how fragile the premises are in his epistemology. We find him often complaining of human ignorance – as for example his dictum about truth's lying hidden in the deep (B 117) – and in one passage he brings out dramatically the fundamental fault. The senses are depicted as saying to the reason: 'Poor Reason! You take your information from us, and will you use it to overthrow us?' (B 125).

The closed system of the atomists has one decided break in it. The soul is always explained as being made up of atoms, and the limits of the system are not exceeded by making these atoms round and therefore highly mobile. But it is quite inconsistent to ascribe a fiery quality to them (VS A 101-107). Atoms of this kind are found also in the universe, and they are drawn in out of the air with the breath. What underlies this whole conception is manifestly the old idea of the breath-soul, which has become tied up with Heraclitus' glorification of fire. In the cosmos atoms of this kind are present in large numbers, but they exert no mechanical influence on material things. In the body, however, they form an aggregate of atoms which is dissolved on death. Thus immortality of the soul is excluded, but in the living organism there is, as it were, a second, more refined body maintained by the drawing in of new soul-atoms in breathing. This spiritual body performs the most remarkable functions: it is the vehicle of independent impulses to movement, the vehicle of thought and sense; so that man, planning and judging, stands alone amidst a material world that is otherwise inanimate and is moved purely mechanically. In the way in which it comes to be and passes away this soul is within the framework of the atomistic cosmology; but it transcends the latter in its spontaneous movement which it imparts to the body and in those functions which make it approximate to the soul as conceived in a dualistic system.

The special problems and potentialities of man took a large place in Democritus' philosophy. He devoted to the subject his *Little World Order* (Μικρὸς διάκοσμος), presumably the counterpart of Leucippus' treatise. Thus there is some reason to believe that the psychology is mainly the work of Democritus, while the essentials of the system, if the tradition (A 28. 34) is true, were already found in Leucippus.

It was through his psychology that the materialist Democritus developed into a moralist. In the midst of the treatises that he wrote on such topics we find one entitled *On Cheerfulness* (Περὶ εὐθυμίης), which begins with a warning (B 3) against the evils of restless activity and shows a kinship with traditional Greek thought by its praise of moderation. But we also find here for the first time a new conception of the purpose of human life, before which the old aristocratic ethics and the ideal of the polis begin to appear rather faded. The individual is now seen as a world in himself, truly a little cosmos, in which the great duty is to maintain peace and order. This sounds at once individualistic and utilitarian.

But it is the picture that matters, not the frame, and we are amazed at the profound wisdom of the ethical notions, far ahead of their time, which grew on this soil. What we possess is a wealth of aphorisms, mainly in Stobaeus (B 169-217) and in a collection going under the name of Democrates (B 35-115), which seem like a continuation of the old literature of *hypothecae*. Yet the larger fragments forbid us to suppose that Democritus wrote in an endless sequence of detached aphorisms; and at the same time the attempts to construct a consistent ethical system out of what survives have been unsuccessful. It must be confessed that we have no means of knowing what Democritus' manner of composition was. This makes his individual utterances all the more impressive. To be ashamed of oneself he holds to be a corrective (B 84); it is the will, not the execution, that matters (B 62. 68: one remembers Herodotus' story of Glaucus); he speaks of regret at the preservation of life by dishonourable expedients (B 43), and we find also the opinion that Plato repeats in the *Gorgias*, that it is better to suffer injustice than to practise it (B 45). Human happiness he considers as the total of all pleasurable feelings: not just the vulgar pleasures, but pleasure in the beautiful (B 207). We are startled to hear the materialist saying (B 189) that the man who finds his pleasure elsewhere than in mortal things will achieve the highest happiness. Here we catch sight of the new ideal of a life wholly given up to intellectual work. This is truly the voice of the man who is reputed to have said that to find out the cause of any one thing was worth more to him than the whole kingdom of the Persians.[1]

Democritus' ethics are founded on understanding as far as men can attain it, and in consequence education takes a prominent place in his thought. We can again see new ground being broken when he says (B 242) that more men become virtuous through training than through native qualities. This contrasts with the unqualified enthusiasm for *physis* that we found still vigorous in the *Philoctetes* of Sophocles as an inheritance from aristocratic ethics.

Democritus' call to a moral life did not rest upon threats of punishment hereafter. Rather, in such books as his *On Hell* (Περὶ τῶν ἐν Ἅιδου) he strove to remove these terrors from the human soul. Nor did he base it on any moral law laid down by the gods. How far there were gods in his cosmos and what they did there is hard to say. In one passage (B 175) the gods are plainly spoken of as the providers of all that is good to men; but we do not know the context. Then again (B 166) we hear of great and scarcely approachable images (εἴδωλα) which come near to man to give knowledge of the future and awaken in him the notion of the divine. Cicero was probably right when he complained of Democritus' lack of clarity in this department (*de Nat. Deor.* I. 29; 120). We may venture to interpret it as the expression of an antinomy which several times threatens the consistency and unity of his atomistic cosmology.

Where Democritus found room for universal binding values in this cosmology, or how he accounted for them, is impossible to say. But we can confidently assume that he did recognize such values and constructed his ethics upon them. We saw him above (B 125) explaining such notions as colour, sweetness and

[1] B 118. A like view is expressed by Socrates in Plat. *Euthyd.* 274 a.

bitterness as purely conventional expressions, while in reality there was nothing but atoms and void; but this sceptical attitude towards sense-data cannot have been carried over into his ethics. On the contrary, far from espousing relativism in morals, he vigorously opposed it. A passage in Plutarch *In Colotem* (4 p. 1108 F=156 B) is very significant here. The writer defends Democritus against the charge of having thrown human life into disorder by his doctrine that nothing really possesses more of any one quality than of any other. Quite the reverse, says Plutarch: in several persuasive passages Democritus has spoken against Protagoras for holding such a doctrine. There is no explicit reference here to ethics, although such an application seems very likely: what puts the matter beyond doubt is a sentence (B 69) which we find among the sayings of Democrates:[1] *The same things are good and true for all men; but different things please different men.*

The literary activity of Democritus extended to every field of human activity. In the Μικρὸς διάκοσμος he expressed views on the evolution of mankind from a primitive condition which recur in similar form in Protagoras.[2] In the debate over the origin of speech he took the side of those who considered it not as a natural endowment (φύσις) but as a result of human ordinance (θέσις). He took an interest also in the arts, in poetry above all, and in his treatise on Homer he studied the linguistic usages in a way that makes him an early forerunner of Homeric philology.

Our review of the content and direction of Democritus' researches can give no idea of the enormous extent of his literary work, which finds no parallel in the older philosophers. We have a catalogue of his writings which was prepared by the Pythagorean Thrasyllus (Tiberius' court astronomer) on the basis of Alexandrian work (A 33). He classified the works into thirteen tetralogies, divided according to subject matter into five groups: works on ethics, physics, mathematics, music and technical treatises. He left out of his tetralogies nine works, of which eight, characteristically of Democritus, were called *Causes* (Αἰτίαι) and dealt with the most diverse questions. The ninth, entitled Περὶ λίθου, dealt with the lodestone. Thrasyllus lists separately some *Hypomnemata*, now reckoned not to have been genuine.

We cannot nowadays form any detailed impression of Democritus' style, but he was undoubtedly a man of high artistic gifts, and what we can still see of the colour and clarity of his writing tends to confirm the praises bestowed by ancient critics. The main feature of his style – terse but elevated, with a tendency towards parallelism in clauses and great care in word-order – can still be clearly seen in the fragments. We are quite unable to judge how pure his Ionic dialect

---

[1] For the basic genuineness of these sayings, despite the attribution to 'Democrates', cf. H. Diels on B 35.

[2] K. REINHARDT in *Herm.* 47, 1912, 492 (now in *Vermächtnis der Antike*. Göttingen 1960, 114) thinks that the cosmological and historical introductory chapter in Diodorus on the *Aegyptiaca* of Hecataeus of Abdera goes back to Democritus. But this thesis is disproved by W. SPOERRI, *Späthellenistische Berichte über Welt, Kultur und Götter. Schw. Beitr.* 9. Basel 1959, who thinks it is a late Hellenistic commonplace on the origin of the world and of culture.

was, since we only have fragments preserved through the mediacy of later authors.

Democritus' influence was very wide indeed, and sometimes it showed itself in strange forms. While as a philosopher of nature he left an inheritance that has yielded a richer and richer harvest over the centuries, he was represented by the Pythagorean Bolus of Mendes, who lived under Ptolemy II, as a disciple of Persian mages, a possessor of secret wisdom; and in this character Bolus turned him into the vehicle of his own cloudy philosophy (B 300). This work in turn had important influence, and was further developed in the alchemical writings of late antiquity. The great sage with magical powers is the picture of Democritus that we find in the spurious letters of Hippocrates from the early empire (C 2-6).

For bibliography see above, p. 167. Anaxagoras: VS 59. D. CIURNELLI, *La filosofia di Anasagora*. Padua 1947. J. ZAFIROPULO, *Anaxagore de Clazomène*. Paris 1948. F. M. CLEVE, *The Philosophy of Anaxagoras*. New York 1949; cf. F. HEINIMANN, *Gnom.* 24, 1952, 271, with recent literature. J. E. RAVEN, 'The Basis of Anaxagoras' Cosmology'. *Class. Quart.* 48, 1954, 123. CH. MUGLER, 'Le Problème d'Anaxagore'. *Rev. Ét. Gr.* 69, 1956, 314. D. BARGROVE-WEAVER, 'The Cosmogony of Anaxagoras'. *Phronesis* 4, 1959, 77. K. BLOCH, 'Anaxagoras und die Atomistik'. *Class. et Mediaev.* 20, 1959, 1. – Archelaus: VS 60. – Diogenes: VS 64. J. ZAFIROPULO, *Diogène d'Apollonie*. Paris 1956. – Leucippus: J. KERCHENSTEINER, 'Zu Leukippos A 1'. *Herm.* 87, 1959, 441. – Democritus: VS 68. K. V. FRITZ, *Philosophie und sprachlicher Ausdruck bei Demokrit, Plato und Aristoteles*. New York 1940. Id., 'Democritus' Theory of Vision'. *Festschr. Singer* 1. 1953, 83. G. VLASTOS, 'Ethics and Physics in Democritus'. *Philosophical Rev.* 54, 1945, 578; 55, 1946, 53. F. ENRIQUES – M. MAZZIOTTI, *Le dottrine di Democrito d'Abdera*. Bologna 1948. I. LANA, 'Le dottrine di Protagora e di Democrito'. *Acc. d. Lincei. Rend.* 1950. vol. 5, 185. W. KRANZ, 'Die Entstehung des Atomismus'. *Convivium. Festgabe f. Ziegler*. Stuttg. 1954, 14. CH. MUGLER, 'Les Théories de la vie et de la conscience chez Démocrite'. *Rev. Phil.* 33, 1959, 7. In the treatise of Aš-Šakrastānī we find 15 ethical fragments of Democritus: F. ALTHEIM and R. STIEHL, *Die aramäische Sprache unter den Achaimeniden*. 2nd impr. 1960, 187.

B The Enlightenment and its Opponents

I THE SOPHISTS AND THE BEGINNINGS OF RHETORIC

About the middle of the fifth century, amid the manifold intellectual excitements of the rich period between the Persian and Peloponnesian wars, there came a dramatic altering of intellectual horizons. Since Hegel it has been usual to compare the sophistic movement with the 'enlightenment' of the eighteenth century, and there are many similar features which justify the comparison. We should only remember that the influence of the sophists was largely confined to the intellectual and economic élite to whom it was directed. The delightful scenes at the beginning of Plato's *Protagoras*, in which the lions of the movement are being fêted at the house of the wealthy and enthusiastic Callias, give a good idea of the social level of the movement. But some of its exponents nevertheless appealed to a wider public at the national festivals.

The sophistic movement had its antecedents, going a long way back. The obsolescence of aristocratic ideals in an age when trade and the use of money had revolutionized Greek economy; the great widening of horizons that came with colonization; the awakened consciousness of the individual which expressed itself in lyric poetry; the penetrating criticism which various thinkers had levelled against traditional beliefs; the severing of the unity of human perception and reasoning through such philosophers as Heraclitus and Parmenides – all these factors contributed powerfully. One might pose here the question which is inevitable in all history of ideas, namely how far the movement changed the spiritual life of the age by a new dynamic, or how far it merely brought to fulfilment tendencies already existing. As almost always in such cases, an extreme position would be false on either side. Bruno Snell[1] amusingly compares a similar problem with the classical conundrum: 'Which came first – the chicken or the egg?'

No other intellectual movement can be compared with the sophistic in the permanence of its results. It is not that the sophists at one blow revolutionized Greek ways of thought: we had indeed to remark on the narrowness of the circles in which they were at first effective. But what they broke up was never put together again in Greek life, and the questions which they posed have never been suffered to lapse in the history of western thought down to our own day.

The Greek view of the world had been considerably enlarged and altered since the archaic period, and its certainty had been thus threatened. But essentially it continued without a decisive break down to classical times. Man still lived between known horizons; the storm-winds might blow around his well shuttered house, but in essentials things were as they had been in his father's and grandfather's day. The world was full of gods – the great deities of the epic and all the lesser ones who were dear to local belief. This was particularly true of Attica, which in many ways up to the beginning of the *pentecontaetia* had lagged behind the other areas of Greece in her intellectual development. The teaching of a Xenophanes or a Heraclitus about the old gods was unable to shake Attic traditional belief: in fact it was hardly known in Athens. The whole framework of human life, which had been their own creation, the gods now held under their protection: the law which was declared in their holy places, the family and education of children, growing up in a settled scheme of values, relations with citizens and strangers – in a word, the whole ordering of the *polis*, over which the goddess of the country stretched out her hand in protection from the acropolis, as Solon so vividly imagined and expressed it. There were

[1] In his very stimulating book *Poetry and Society*. Indiana Un. Pr. Bloomington 1961, 2.

indeed a good many internal political struggles, but on other fronts the unity of the city was not in question. Knowledge and education were not yet forces that opened a gulf between man and man. When the ancient myths found new expression on the tragic stage, the great semi-circle of the theatre on the southern slope of the Acropolis brought together all the free members of the city, to find in the religious drama a unity that transcended all conflict and disagreement.

It has been necessary to touch briefly on Greek tradition, the *nomos* inherited from their forefathers, in order to appreciate the powers against which the sophists pitted themselves and which they destroyed – not indeed all or at once, but a great many over a long time. Our judgment of this movement is made more difficult since our most detailed source for its history, Plato, was at the same time its bitterest opponent, and inevitably men's opinions have differed widely. According to their individual standpoint, some have seen it as the beginning of the break-up of Hellas, a mortal threat to the basic needs of human life, while others view it as the bold breaking out of the human spirit from the stronghold of tradition, a necessary shaking up of something in danger of ossification. The world of Greek thought here sets us a challenge to which each must reply as well as he can: what none can deny is that the sophistic movement was a decisive passage in the history of that people who, in Hölderlin's words, were unable to stand still in any place.

The basic assumptions of the sophistic movement had their origin in Ionia. At the price of some simplification and over-emphasis we might say that it represents the victory of Ionian curiosity over Attic conservatism. The greatest of the sophists, Protagoras, came from an Ionian area – Abdera, the birthplace of Democritus. Born about 485, he was a good deal older than Democritus, although ancient tradition made him the latter's pupil. The story that he received instruction from Magians accompanying the army of Xerxes does not deserve to be taken seriously, as it recently has been.[1]

The sophists were mostly men without a country of their own, and thus they had no strong ties. Plato makes this a reproach against them in the *Timaeus* (19e). Thus we have to think of Protagoras as spending most of his life travelling, although the course of his travels is unknown to us. He visited Sicily, and stayed in Athens several times and for long periods. We may suppose him to have been there in the mid-fifth century: then it was that he established close relations with Pericles, which led to the latter's entrusting him with making laws for Thurii (founded 444/43). We find him again in Athens in the second year of the Peloponnesian war, when he saw Pericles beside the bodies of his two sons – they had perished in the terrible epidemic of that year – and was struck with the greatness and dignity of his bearing. Protagoras' stays in Athens were probably more frequent than we know. At all events, it was there that he was threatened by Pythodorus with an action for impiety, which he escaped by timely flight. His books were publicly burnt, and he himself is said to have lost his life in a shipwreck while sailing to Sicily: a fact which seems to be unknown

[1] Greek-Magian connections: J. BIDEZ - F. CUMONT, *Les Mages hellénisés*. Paris 1938.

to Plato (*Meno* 91 e). Pythodorus represents the reaction of Athenian conservatives to the sophists. He belonged to the oligarchical circles which planned the putsch of 411, and it was about this time that the attack on Protagoras was made.

In Plato's dialogue Protagoras expressly and emphatically describes his activities as being those of a sophist (317 b). But, he says, the name is somewhat invidious: all his predecessors, from Homer onwards, who tried to form men by instruction, prudently chose another name. The passage shows that the word σοφιστής, which had formerly been used more widely and without such connotations, was now used very differently and in a pejorative sense.[1] This change of meaning, reflecting the sharp opposition between sophists and philosophers, had come about particularly in Socratic circles, which fought against the new movement.

The characteristic features of the sophist are well exemplified in Protagoras. He goes from city to city teaching, to impart his skills to those who become his pupils. He does not impart a philosophical system: rather he purveys knowledge and abilities which will put the pupil into a position to achieve by his skill in counsel (εὐβουλία was a witch-word of the age) the best possible place in the struggles of life and the pursuit of politics.[2] The skills thus imparted, technical knowledge as well as ability in rhetoric and dialectic, seemed so valuable to the sophist and his audience that he usually demanded payment, which might reach a considerable sum. Teaching was oral in private courses, although public lectures were sometimes given. The sophist gave notice of his intentions in a kind of programme (ἐπάγγελμα). His powers were displayed both in carefully prepared speeches and in improvisations: thus a practice was initiated which was never abandoned in antiquity, and which led to the gradual decline of the place that poetry held in national life.

The importance of the spoken word in sophistic teaching did not prevent the publishing of their doctrine in books. Unfortunately such works have almost entirely perished – largely through the activities of their opponents. We can gain some notion of sophistical display-speeches from the *Helena* and *Palamedes* of Gorgias: for their didactic works we are reduced to such miserable productions as the *Dialexeis* (see below) or the more valuable *Anonymus Iamblichi*. In addition, the lecture *On the Art of Healing* (Περὶ τέχνης) which is preserved in the Hippocratic corpus may be taken as a specimen of sophistic writing, although its attribution to Protagoras is now a thing of the past.

Diogenes Laertius gives us a long list of the works of Protagoras, including various technical treatises as well as those that we shall discuss later. The

---

[1] On the development of the meaning VS 79. W. NESTLE (*v. inf.*), 249. UNTERSTEINER'S edition 1, 2.

[2] F. HEINIMANN in *Mus. Helv.* 18, 1961, 105 plausibly suggests that Protagoras had developed a theory of τέχνη in which he demanded that a τέχνη should have a defined purpose connected with the advancement of human life, should be distinguishable from other τέχναι, and should have an end attainable by instruction. This theory, he thinks, influenced the Hippocratics (Περὶ τέχνης and Περὶ ἀρχαίας ἰητρικῆς), the Platonic Socrates, and the Hellenistic schools of philosophy with their rival claims.

catalogue may go back to the Alexandrian library: if so, the Alexandrians must have taken an interest in Protagoras. It is not easy to form a judgment on the titles, since there are good grounds for supposing that some refer to the separate parts of longer works. Untersteiner's theory[1] that the titles are all of subsections of the *Antilogiae*, and that even the title *On the Gods* is to be taken thus, is too sweeping to be fully demonstrable.

It is Diogenes again who tells us distinctly (9. 54) that the Περὶ θεῶν was the first of his works that Protagoras read in public: the house of Euripides (*inter alia*) is mentioned as the scene of this memorable reading. Despite its early date, this book may have been the main basis of the later action against Protagoras. It begins: 'Of the gods I can know nothing, neither that they are nor that they are not, nor how they are shaped if at all. Many things prevent such knowledge: the uncertainty of the question and the shortness of human life.' There could be no clearer expression of an agnosticism which at a single stroke wiped the glowing pictures of mythology off the slate of Greek life. We cannot say whether a thorough-going atheism lurked behind the words. Sometimes (A 12) Protagoras is spoken of as an atheist; but Cicero (*de Nat. Deor.* 1. 2; 117) says he was not. From what we know otherwise of this thinker, he may well have shrunk from the ultimate conclusion. Diogenes of Oenoanda in the large Epicurean inscription[2] says that Protagoras shared in effect the belief of Diagoras of Melos, but was more guarded in his expressions.

If Protagoras wrote the book *On Hell* (Περὶ τῶν ἐν ᾍδου) which the catalogue ascribes to him, it was no doubt akin to the work *On the Gods* and was intended to demolish the traditional horrors.

The principles of his activity in the education of political man were laid down by Protagoras in a book under the provocative title of *Truth, or Refutations* (᾽Αλήθεια ἢ καταβάλλοντες). At the beginning stood the sentence which constitutes one of the two opposing positions in the 'war of giants', as Plato once calls it (*Soph.* 246 a), about the nature of existence: 'Man is the measure of all things: of things that are, that they are, and of things that are not, that they are not'. We have given a simple translation, which does not burden the sentence with the weight of modern theorizing.[3] We may well think that the questions how far this statement is purely one of epistemology or how far it is ethical in its implications, whether the 'things' (χρήματα) are objects or qualities or values, whether 'Man' is used generally or individually, and so forth postulate differences in meaning which the words never had. In the history of philosophy the sequence of action and reaction dominates, and this sentence is to be taken above all as an attack. It expresses a protest against the Eleatic distinction between existence as perceived and existence as it really is, against the postulate of an

[1] 'Le "Antilogie" di Protagora'. *Antiquitas* 2/3. 1947/48, 34; *I sofisti* (*v. inf.*), 17.
[2] Fr. 12 c. 2, 1, p. 19 William = VS 80 A 23.
[3] Cf. E. KAPP, *Gnom.* 12, 1936, 71. M. UNTERSTEINER (*I sofisti: v. inf.*) gives one of his many wilful interpretations: he thinks it means 'l' uomo è dominatore di tutte le esperienze'! Cf. also E. SCHWARTZ, *Ethik der Griechen*. Stuttg. 1959, 77. E. WOLF, *Griech. Rechtsdenken*. 2. Frankf. a. M. 1952, 21. Some bibliog. in B. M. W. KNOX, *Oedipus at Thebes*. New Haven 1957, 208.

absolute, immutable Being, accessible only to the reason. This interpretation is strongly supported by an observation of Porphyry's on a work that Protagoras wrote On Being (Περὶ τοῦ ὄντος B 4), which we may take as identical with his Truth. It was directed against those who introduced the notion of Being as unique and therefore as an absolute. Thus Protagoras' thought stood in opposition to that of Parmenides, while in another aspect it was closely akin to it. It is, after all, permissible to see in homo mensura omnium the Parmenidean unity of thinking and being, which is now boldly transferred to the perceiving and thinking individual.[1] For certainly the sentence refers to the individual. Anyone who doubts it must hold that Plato is lying or mistaken when he interprets (Theaet. 152 a) the sentence thus: What he means is something like this: as things appear to me, so they are for me, and as they appear to you, so they are for you: you are a man and I am a man. A similar interpretation is given in Crat. 386 a. If we are determined to disbelieve Plato, we have still to reckon with other authors[2] whose use of the word ἕκαστος shows that they also took the sentence as referring to the individual.

There can be no possible doubt that the sentence in question expresses the most determined relativism where all human judgments of value are concerned. It is quite another question whether Protagoras, having started with the desire to destroy a hostile position, followed all the logical consequences of this relativism when he put forward his own. In this respect he is in sharp contrast with the more radical of his followers, for whom he nevertheless provided their basic tenets. In the Theaetetus of Plato (166 d) we find a defence of Protagoras' teachings which starts from the dictum 'man is the measure'. It is quite in Protagoras' manner when the sense of taste of a sick and a healthy man are considered in every case as being equally true and valid. Nevertheless – and here Protagoras takes us by the hand and vaults with us over an abyss – the situation of the healthy man is better than that of the sick, and it is consequently the duty of the physician to bring the latter back to health and to the sensations associated with it, just as in the same sense the teacher has to bring his pupil and the statesman his people into a 'better' condition. Now at the beginning of this section we were told that each individual is the measure of things, which manifest themselves to individuals in countless diversity and exist for them only in this appearance. This raises the question whence man derives standards for 'better' and 'worse' which transcend individual judgment. It is hardly possible to reply, if we follow consistently the implications of homo mensura omnium. The best we can arrive at is a naïve utilitarianism. We shall be better able to appreciate the attempts of Protagoras at a solution when we turn to his own views on the nature and origin of the state.

These questions were discussed by Protagoras in a treatise On the Original Condition of Mankind (Περὶ τῆς ἐν ἀρχῇ καταστάσεως), and we can feel fairly sure

---

[1] O. GIGON, Herm. 71, 1936, 206. F. HEINIMANN, Nomos und Physis. Schweiz. Beitr. 1, Basel 1945, 117.

[2] Aristot. Metaph. 1062 b 14. Sext. Emp. Pyrrh. Hyp. 1. 216 (= VS 80 A 14); Plato also uses the word in the 'apology of Protagoras' in Theaet. 166 d.

that the main lines of his teaching are given in a section of the Platonic dialogue that bears his name. In a '*mythos*', which he explicitly distinguishes from a treatment of the subject by reasoning (*logos*), he conveys a theory of the origin of civilization, beginning with a primitive condition of life. Man is less strongly armed for battle than the beasts, and despite the Promethean gift of fire he cannot make head against them in isolation. Attempts to form societies miscarry, because certain essential concepts are lacking, and a fight of each against all is the result. Zeus then sends by Hermes morality and a sense of justice (αἰδώς and δίκη), which make political life and cultural development possible.

The picture of human development that we find in this tale is in the sharpest possible contrast to the pessimistic picture which Hesiod draws in the *Erga* of the steady degeneration that accompanies the passage of ages. An unqualified optimism and belief in progress was as much part of the sophistic movement as it was of the eighteenth-century enlightenment.

When we remove the mythical trappings, we find ourselves faced with Protagoras' belief that in every man morality and a sense of justice are implanted by nature. Exceptions to this rule – men who cannot fit into a social pattern – are removed from the community by being put to death. But the normal innate tendency towards political virtue is not enough in itself: it needs to be developed by education. The importance of education – a basic element of sophistic doctrine – emerges very clearly from this elaborate context. In a valuable fragment (B 3) we find the thesis that learning requires both talent (φύσις) and training (ἄσκησις). Here again Protagoras is no radical: he does not totally reject the archaic and early classical doctrine of the decisive value of *physis*. What he does is to lay equal stress on the effects of education.[1] Recalling Pindar's jibes at self-made men, we may see this faith in education as a new element and one which was to Protagoras the basic justification of his activities. We are probably hearing the views of the historical Protagoras when Plato's character makes punishment purely an educative measure.

Protagoras thus avoided the danger of destroying the basis of political life by his relativism. He made his peace with *nomos*, whether we take it in the sense of traditional custom or of the law of the state. In his doctrine this human *nomos* does not have a powerful opponent in the person of unwritten natural law, claiming sole validity for itself. But we cannot fail to see that the line of thought leading from *homo mensura* to pure relativism is broken at an important place, and that the introduction of absolute qualities like morality and justice into a world in which man is the only standard brings about great difficulties. Protagoras had recourse to an intellectual construction when he ascribed a special authority to the *nomos* of the state as that of a collective. It is not that he derives principles of unqualified validity from the common nature of man: the *nomoi* of individual cities and states varied widely, as the Ionian enquirers had found long before, and in the *Theaetetus* (167 c) it is expressly given as Protagoras' opinion that for any given state the just and the beautiful are what that state considers such, and only so long as she continues to do so. This remarkable

---

[1] In Plato (*Prot.* 323 d) Protagoras gives this pedagogic trinity as ἐπιμέλεια, ἄσκησις, διδαχή.

mixture of heterogeneous elements enables him to maintain his relativism without sacrificing the authority of the state and with it the object of sophistic education.

The longest of Protagoras' works was probably the *Antilogiae*, which is the only one described as being in two books. We can gain no clear idea of its contents, and we are not helped by the declaration of Aristoxenus (VS 80 B 5) that most of Plato's *Republic* is contained in the *Antilogiae*. We have some indication, though a very general one, of its contents in Diogenes Laertius (9. 51), who says that on each topic there were two speeches, one for and one against. It was probably the object of the book to prosecute these methods through the various departments of human life. It would be natural for problems of justice and political society to be prominent in such a work, and this may explain the exaggerated statement of Aristoxenus. The invention of the 'speech both ways' (δισσοὶ λόγοι) can itself be explained in two ways. It may express a serious conviction that man lives in a world of antinomies; or it may reflect a clever speaker's temptation to put whatever view he espouses into the best possible light. It is in the latter sense that the ancients interpreted Protagoras' words in his prospectus (ἐπάγγελμα): 'to make the worse appear the better cause' (τὸν ἥττω λόγον κρείττω ποιεῖν). For Protagoras this was a possibility inherent in the idea of the δισσοὶ λόγοι, and he certainly had no intention of teaching a barren rhetorical artifice. But we cannot deny that he did provide the theoretical basis for such practices.

Protagoras exemplifies to a high degree what Prodicus (B 6) says about the sophists: they are a creature half-way between philosopher and politician (referring especially to the oratorical side of a politician's life). Thus the work of Protagoras finds reflections far and wide among the very different individuals who were called sophists, and was given a very personal colouring in the hands of Gorgias. Any classification is bound to break some of the threads, but we may profitably rank after Protagoras two men who were to some extent independent of him and show no trace of Gorgianic influence. One of them, Prodicus, is referred to as the pupil of Protagoras, but ancient tradition was so ready with these literary connections that such statements do not need to be taken very seriously.

Prodicus came from an Ionian area, from Iulis on Ceos, where he was probably born between 470 and 460. We know that he once or twice represented his people's interests in Athens, which no doubt gave him the opportunity to deliver lectures. We generally think of him as he is shown in Plato's *Protagoras*, where he is carefully wrapped up in numerous blankets and is conducting a class from his bed – a savant who did not seek publicity so determinedly as his colleagues. It is consistent with this picture of him that his voice did not carry well (A 1 a), and we hear only of his prepared speeches, never of improvisations. At the time when Socrates was prosecuted, Prodicus, Gorgias and Hippias all seem to have been still alive (Plat. *Apol.* 19 e).

His lecture-courses were expensive, and linguistic studies seem to have played a large part in them. Similar interests appear in Democritus and

Protagoras: Prodicus specialized in the differentiation of synonyms, in which he displayed an often exaggerated zeal. At the same time he tried to differentiate between the ideas expressed. It is significant that we find the word διαιρεῖν used in this connection (A 17. 19), since in effect Prodicus' methods of work looked forward to the 'diaeresis' which became a valuable tool in the methodology of the Platonic academy.

His work on synonyms was conveyed by oral instruction, and we do not know whether it was ever put into writing. There is very little that we know about his other works. The Alexandrians catalogued them under treatises on rhetoric, while the scholiast to Aristophanes' Birds 692 makes them philosophical: a further indication of his midway position. There is some doubt about an alleged book of his entitled On Nature or On the Nature of Man (Περὶ φύσεως ἀνθρώπου), but thanks to W. Nestle's researches[1] we know rather more about the Horae (Ὧραι). We do not know when it was written: possibly at a fairly late date, so that the title might have been given by the author himself. It is likely that the Horae were taken as goddesses of fertility, since agriculture as the basis of human civilization played an important part in the work. We can see some affinity to the questions posed in Protagoras' On the Primitive Condition of Mankind, although the treatment is wholly different and the main stress is laid on cultivation of the soil. We can be rather more confident in supposing the Horae to have expressed Prodicus' view that religion arose as man's reaction to the natural circumstances of his life. At an early stage he regarded the forces and gifts of nature as being themselves divine; later, by analogous reasoning, he raised to divine honours the inventors of various techniques that benefited humanity. This kind of rationalism has its forerunners in Ionian thought: in the other direction it anticipates the theory of Euhemerus. It was not without reason that Prodicus was sometimes[2] reckoned in antiquity as an atheist.

The purple passage of the Horae was the allegory of the choice of Heracles, who was met by Virtue and Vice in the form of two women of different appearance and attire. The story had its antecedents in Hesiod's description of the two ways of life (Erga 286) and the myth of the choice and judgment of Paris as Sophocles presented it with moral overtones[3] in his satyr-play Crisis. But Prodicus' story is neither poetry nor myth: it is the first of a long line of intellectual allegories which no longer have that feeling for a divine power which informs many archaic allegories of an apparently similar content. It is symptomatic that Xenophon (Mem. 2. 1. 21) should be the author who has retold the story at the greatest length. Its influence was very great: its most singular expression was in the symbolism of the letter Y, which first appears in the first century of our era, when it is ascribed to Pythagoras. The letter was considered as symbolizing the dividing of the ways, where Heracles and everyone else has to make up his mind.

[1] 'Die Horen des Prodikos'. Herm. 71, 1936, 151. Griech. Studien. Stuttgart 1948, 403.
[2] Sext. Emp. Adv. Math. 9. 51. Cicero, de Natura Deor. 1. 118.
[3] B. SNELL, Die Entdeckung des Geistes. 3rd ed. Hamb. 1955, 327 (cf. Eng. ed. p. 268).

In the Platonic dialogue that bears his name Protagoras attacks those sophists who made their pupils learn all kinds of technical disciplines such as mathematics, astronomy and music; and he does so with a side-long glance at Hippias (318 e). Hippias was the most determined exponent of that school among the sophists which aimed at mastering all arts and sciences. He was the representative of the Peloponnese in sophistic circles, having been born in Elis. Like his contemporaries, he travelled widely in the Greek world, went on various embassies for his city and earned a great deal of money by his lectures. To appear at Olympia was no great undertaking for an Elean, and he displayed himself there with great pomp, wearing a purple mantle like the most celebrated sophists of the Empire. He boasted that everything he had on his person, starting from the ring on his finger, was made by his own hand (Plat. *Hipp. min.* 368 b). His abilities with the pen were no less varied. According to the passage in Plato just quoted, he tried his hand at epic, tragedy, dithyramb and many kinds of prose literature. Of the last we possess a few titles – not very informative – such as *Names of Peoples* (Ἐθνῶν ὀνομασίαι) and *Collection* (Συναγωγή). Of what this was a collection we do not know, but from scattered references it must have had very varied subject matter. Hippias concerned himself with most of the branches of learning then recognized; and when we find arithmetic, geometry, grammar, rhetoric, dialectic and music among the contents, we may perhaps see here the elements, not yet reduced to system, which were later brought together in the notion of encyclopaedic education.[1]

It is probable that, under the influence of Plato's two dialogues, we underrate the work of Hippias, but at all events one of his works, the *List of Victors at the Olympics*, performed a considerable service in laying a firm foundation for Greek chronology. We should be glad to know more about his interpretation of poets, in which he and other sophists with similar interests provided the first studies in Greek literary history. In order to retain all his wide and varied knowledge, Hippias used a system of mnemonics which he had devised himself.

His work called *Troicus* (Τρωϊκός) was closer to the usual run of sophistic writing with its strong pedagogic tendency. In it Neoptolemus after the capture of Troy asks Nestor to advise him what pursuits will gain fame for a young man. Since the conversation is set at the end of a long war, presumably Nestor spoke of the tasks of peace. On war the sophists no doubt held much the same views as Gorgias.[2]

Among our bits of information about Hippias there is one in Plato's *Protagoras* that catches our attention. Hippias addresses the company (337 c) as 'kinsmen, men of like feelings, fellow-citizens, by nature [φύσει] rather than by law and custom [νόμῳ]'. He goes on to say that nature binds like and like together, while *nomos* like a tyrant (τύραννος: obviously a deliberate variant on Pindar's 'custom is king of all') often exerts a compulsion contrary to nature. The context and tone leave no doubt that Plato is repeating actual teachings of

---

[1] See R. MEISTER's judicious article in *Wien. Stud.* 69, 1956, 258.

[2] Cf. WILHELM NESTLE (*v. inf.*), 313, 34.

Hippias'. This is an antithesis unknown to Protagoras, but very influential later: *nomos* is set in opposition to *physis*, which alone can claim validity. We cannot trace this antithesis back before the middle 'twenties, when it finds vigorous expression in Antiphon. At this time Hippias may well have been active in Athens. Having virtually no philosophical interests of his own, Antiphon was probably the borrower, as has been plausibly argued.[1]

It was in the 'twenties, a period when new doctrines made rapid headway after the death of Pericles and under the influence of the war, that Gorgias came to Athens. He was already old when he came in 427 as ambassador from his native Sicilian city of Leontini and made the greatest impression by his elaborate rhetoric. He was probably born in the first decade of the fifth century and lived on until a few years after the death of Socrates. We know very little of his travels – he seems to have had good connections in Thessaly – and even less about his development. He is said to have been a pupil of Empedocles': he avowed this himself, according to Satyrus (A 3) – not of course the best of authorities. Influence from the west Greek philosophers is much more certainly attested by his book *On Not-being, or On Nature* (Περὶ τοῦ μὴ ὄντος ἢ περὶ φύσεως). We gain some notion of its contents from the reference in Sextus Empiricus (B 3) and the anonymous treatise *On Melissus, Xenophanes and Gorgias*[2] (*v. sup.* p. 209). It is said to have advanced the three theses: Nothing exists; if it did, it could not be perceived: if it could be conceived, it could not be communicated. This work was not a pure *jeu d'esprit*, nor was it serious philosophy, for as such it would have cut the ground from beneath the feet of all the sophists' work. Gigon rightly compares it with expressions of men like Protagoras or Xeniades (VS 81) which ultimately derive from Parmenides and pursue particular points of epistemology to extreme and sometimes paradoxical conclusions. We can see that Gorgias here used the same indirect argumentation that we find in his surviving epideictic speeches. A number of possibilities is brought down to one by a repeated *reductio ad absurdum*.

Another interpretation of the treatise is possible. We might take it as a turning-point in a career in which Gorgias was at first a physical scientist under the influence of Empedocles, then a philosopher under that of the Eleatics, finally, when he became dissatisfied with philosophy altogether, a teacher of rhetoric. But we have not the slightest evidence for such a development. Very likely he was the same in his earlier years as we find him in old age: an expert teacher and practitioner of persuasion by the spoken word.

The power of oratory was not a discovery of Gorgias' generation: it was known already to Homer. We read in the *Iliad* (9. 443) of the objects of a young noble's education – to be a speaker of words and a doer of deeds. Since time out of mind the law-court and the council chamber had been the scenes of the speaker's activity. It is obvious that his role became much more important with the rise of democracy and the introduction of people's courts. We cannot date the

---

[1] F. HEINIMANN (*v.* p. 345, n. 1), 142.

[2] Not in VS, but cf. 82 B 3. On the value of the quotation see O. GIGON, 'Gorgias "Ueber das Nichtsein"'. *Herm.* 71, 1936, 186.

important change by which the sung lament over the dead was replaced by a ceremonial funeral speech.[1] That it should have come about under sophistic influence is very unlikely: on the other hand the sophists were certainly responsible for the introduction of show-speeches (ἐπιδείξεις) at the great national festivals. This example shows particularly well how the orator was now disputing pride of place with the poet – with the choral lyrist above all.

Rhetoric as an art to be taught was not creative: it was a codification of features which had long existed in the practice of poetry and speech-making. What came now was that extraordinary increase in the use and the estimation of rhetorical methods and devices which contained in itself already the seed of over-cultivation and decay. We should not underrate the great and truly artistic achievements of fourth-century rhetoric, no matter how alien this side of the Greek genius may be to us. On the other hand, it cannot be denied that a concern with rhetoric in the later centuries played no small part in the decline of intellectual life.

Gorgias came to central Greece with his system already developed. In Sicily Corax and his pupil Tisias had written the first manual of rhetoric of which we have any knowledge.[2] We can certainly assume that Gorgias was influenced from this direction: certainly Tisias accompanied him to Athens in 427.

While the power of the spoken word played a more or less important part in every sophist's programme, it was the very core of Gorgias' teaching. The 'mistress of persuasion', as the Sicilians had probably already christened rhetoric, was for him a weapon of unlimited possibilities, a way of taking the soul captive, to which in the *Helen* he ascribes almost magical qualities. In order to make the worse appear the better cause, Protagoras had mostly had recourse to subtle argumentation, i.e. to the use of *logos* in the sense of reason. In Gorgias also we find the probable (τὰ εἰκότα: Plat. *Phaedr.* 267 a) taking the place of the indiscoverable and perhaps inexpressible truth. This 'probable' he seeks to establish mostly by the exclusion of other possibilities. He also laid particular emphasis on the adroit use of the favourable moment (καιρός): this was the subject of his first book (B 13).[3] But what was new in his speeches and gave them their particularly enthralling quality was *logos* in its other meaning – the word. Gorgias consciously used the sound of words as an instrument of rhetorical effect, often breaking through the barrier between poetry and prose. He does this not so much in his choice of words as in his untiring use of the figures of speech named after him (σχήματα Γοργίεια). Here again what we find is not the invention of something wholly new, but a reduction to system and a gross over-application of devices which poetry and emotive prose had used as they thought fit. Correspondence of clauses which are connected in thought by parallelism or antithesis is now heightened by isocola and parisa until even the number of syllables and relative position of words are balanced carefully. There are

---

[1] On this question see F. JACOBY, *Journ. Hell. Stud.* 64, 1944, 39, 8 and 57, 92.

[2] RADERMACHER (*v. inf.*), 28.

[3] An allied notion is the πρέπον, on which M. POHLENZ, GGN 1920, 170. 1933, 54.

frequent assonances between individual words, even where there is no basis for them in the sense, and our ears are repeatedly assailed with rhyming word-endings (ὁμοιοτέλευτα).[1]

We possess a large fragment of an *Epitaphios* which he wrote on Athenian dead in the Peloponnesian war. In it we find the dictum (B 5 b) that the victory of Greek over barbarian deserved to be celebrated, that of Greek over Greek to be lamented. This accords well with the appeal for Hellenic unity which is the tenor of his *Olympicus*. The anti-eastern theme was taken up by his pupil Isocrates. We also know of a *Panegyric on Elis* and a *Pythicus* which he delivered from the steps of the Delphic altar and which was connected with the dedication of a statue of him in solid gold (A 1. 7).

Two of his productions, the oldest rhetorical declamations that we possess, are preserved in their entirety. Both, like the rest of Gorgias' writings, are in a very ornate Attic dialect. In one, the *Helen*, he defends the much traduced heroine with every rhetorical device, without availing himself of Stesichorus' story of the phantom; the *Palamedes* is a similar defence against unjust condemnation. In both speeches the interpretations unfavourable for the defence are set aside on arguments of probability. In the last words of the *Helen* Gorgias admits that he is not serious.

Very probably the two speeches appeared as examples in Gorgias' treatise on rhetoric, about which we are very ill informed.[2] It is quite possible that it consisted wholly or mostly of examples like these. What part theoretical discussion played in it is not known.

Gorgias was well aware that his artistic prose hovered on the fringes of poetry, and he gave interesting expression to his views on the latter. The similarity between his kind of oratory and poetry (which he defined as oratory bound by metre) lay in the fact that both could exercise unrestricted mastery over the soul (*Hel.* 8 f.). Among the effects of poetry on the audience he enumerates 'fearful anxiety, tearful lamentation and grief-stricken yearning': an anticipation to some degree of Aristotle's famous words on the effects of tragedy.[3] In his views on tragedy Gorgias shows himself as a true sophist, for whom absolute being and absolute value have no meaning. He considers it (B 23) as an exchange or barter in which the deceiver is more just than the one who does not deceive and the one who is deceived is cleverer than he who is not deceived. In parts like these we find the beginnings of the theory of poetry; but we need not think that Gorgias had already planned a systematic treatment of it.[4]

---

[1] Some good analyses in V. PISANI, *Storia della lingua greca* in *Encicl. Class.* 2/4/1. Turin 1960, 107.

[2] Passages quoted before B 12; cf. SCHMID 3. 68. 12. NESTLE (*v. inf.*), 310, is too confident in his reconstruction; cf. RADERMACHER (*v. inf.*), 43.

[3] The interpretation of the passage of the *Poetics* in Schadewaldt, 'Furcht und Mitleid?'. *Herm.* 83, 1955, 129 (now in *Hellas und Hesperien*. Zürich 1960, 346), makes the connection even closer.

[4] Cf. M. POHLENZ, 'Die Anfänge der griech. Poetik'. GGN 1920, 142; also L. RADERMACHER-W. KRAUS, 'Aristophanes' Frösche'. *Sitzb. Ak. Wien.* 1954, 368. H. FLASHER, *Herm.* 84, 1956, 18.

Gorgias' influence appeared powerfully in his pupils. Among them were poets like the tragedian Agathon, who appropriately enough in Plato's *Symposium* composes his address to Love in a Gorgianic style, and the dithyrambic writer Licymnius, who wrote a textbook ($\tau \acute{\epsilon} \chi \nu \eta$) of rhetoric in which he dressed up the technical terms in metaphor.[1] Another *Techne* was written by Polus of Agrigentum,[2] who accompanied his teacher on his travels. Antisthenes[3] was for a long time one of Gorgias' pupils, until he attached himself to Socrates. The master himself probably was equally at home in prepared and extemporary speeches; but in two of his pupils these two abilities appeared sharply opposed. Isocrates raised the *epideixis* to the status of a respectable art-form, whereas Alcidamas, from the Aeolic city of Elaea in Asia Minor, wrote a polemical treatise *On the Sophists*[4] ($\Pi \epsilon \rho \grave{\iota} \tau \hat{\omega} \nu \tau o \grave{\upsilon} s \gamma \rho a \pi. \tau o \grave{\upsilon} s \lambda \acute{o} \gamma o \upsilon s \gamma \rho a \phi \acute{o} \nu \tau \omega \nu \mathring{\eta} \pi \epsilon \rho \grave{\iota} \sigma o \phi \iota \sigma \tau \hat{\omega} \nu$: e.g. Isocrates) in which he declared ᴁmprovisation was much more important. We also possess under his name a *Speech of Odysseus against Palamedes*, but its authenticity is doubtful. A miscellany of his entitled *Museion* has been lost: among its varied contents was a *Contest of Homer and Hesiod*.[5]

The history of the sophistic movement, which saw the most diverse developments of the ideas of Protagoras and Gorgias, is beset with difficult problems as soon as we speak of Antiphon. Under this name – a very common one in Attica – we possess quite a collection of writings, fragments and titles: various speeches (some actually delivered, some fictional), a party-pamphlet against Alcibiades, a *Politicus*, two books *On Truth*, one *On Common Sense* and one *On Dreams*. Didymus (quoted with some approval by Hermogenes: VS 87 A 2) was the first to distinguish two authors of the same name, ascribing the speeches to the one and the remaining works to the other. Modern critics have been divided: some follow Didymus (with variations), others cling to unity of authorship.[6] We are tolerably well informed about the orator Antiphon of Rhamnus, whose abilities are given generous recognition by Thucydides (8. 68): one of the best brains of his time, he kept himself mostly in the background, but his help was most valuable in court or in the assembly. He was the guiding spirit of the oligarchical putsch of 411, and after the overthrow of the Four Hundred he was condemned to death. He displayed a many-sided activity: he earned a great deal as a writer of speeches for others ($\lambda o \gamma o \gamma \rho \acute{a} \phi o s$) – in his speech in his own defence he speaks of attacks that he suffered on this score – and in Plato's *Menexenus* he appears as a distinguished teacher of rhetoric; Thucydides is sometimes described as his pupil. This versatility makes it impossible for us to be confident in separating the orator from the sophist Antiphon who figures

---

[1] RADERMACHER (*v. inf.*), 117.

[2] Ibid. 112.

[3] Ibid. 120.

[4] Ibid. 135. On the opposition of Alcidamas and Isocrates: G. WALBERER, *Isokrates und Alkidamas*. Diss. Hamburg 1938. W. STEIDLE, *Herm.* 80, 1952, 285. On stylistic peculiarities of Alc. cf. Arist. *Rhet.* III 3. 1405 b 34 and F. SOLMSEN, *Herm.* 67, 1932, 133.

[5] RADERMACHER (*v. inf.*), 134, who gives the older literature. Theories on the nature of the *Museion* in E. VOGT, *Rhein. Mus.* 102, 1959, 217, 68.

[6] Summary in UNTERSTEINER, *I sofisti* (*v. inf.*), 274.

as an opponent of Socrates in the *Memorabilia* of Xenophon.[1] The distinction would be permissible if we could be sure that Socrates' παρ' ἡμῖν (*Mem.* 1. 6, 13) implied that Antiphon was not an Athenian,[2] but this is uncertain. The question cannot be decided on stylistic grounds; Hermogenes is right in saying that differences of style could arise from the difference of literary genre. But Wilhelm Nestle's question still has to be squarely faced: Could the leader of the oligarchic *coup d'état* be the same man who declared his belief in the equality of all men (*On Truth*: B 4, fr. B, col. 2)? But we do not know the context or the area within which the principle was thought to be valid. Consequently, if in the next paragraphs we treat the orator and the sophist as two different men, we must confess how much doubt still remains.

The Alexandrians knew of sixty speeches of Antiphon's, but as early as the first century B.C. Caecilius of Cale Acte, who had made a special study of the orator, declared twenty-five of them to be spurious. We now possess a small *corpus orationum* under his name, of which three – delivered in a trial for homicide – are undoubtedly genuine. They are *Or.* 1, in which a stepson accuses his stepmother of poisoning, and *Orr.* 5 and 6, both for the defence, one against suspicion of murder, the other against a charge of the accidental killing of a youth. We have also on papyrus[3] some fragments of the speech which Antiphon made in his own defence. The surviving speeches, with their clear and neat construction and their unpretentious Attic language, are valuable examples of early oratory. F. Solmsen[4] has shown how in these speeches the old non-technical methods of proof – oath and examination of slaves under torture – were being replaced by a new method of argumentation directed towards the establishment of probabilities. The influence of sophistic teachings is obvious.

According to Plato (*Menex.* 236 a) Antiphon of Rhamnus was highly ranked as a teacher of rhetoric, and consequently we shall ascribe to him the technical treatises that we hear of under the name of Antiphon.[5] The *Technae* were indeed suspect even in antiquity (Pollux 6. 143), but we do know of a collection of commonplaces for beginnings and endings of speeches.

Rhetorical treatises at this time seem to have been mostly collections of examples. From one of these presumably came the three *Tetralogies* under Antiphon's name, each containing four speeches in trials of homicide, two for the prosecution, two for the defence. Considerations of style and subject matter compel us to leave it an open question whether the Antiphon of the extant speeches was the author of the *Tetralogies*.[6] But whoever wrote the speeches, they are no less valuable for the light they throw on the legal thought of the time.

[1] P. VON DER MÜHLL, 'Zur Unechtheit der antiphontischen Tetralogien'. *Mus. Helv.* 5, 1948, 1, thinks they are the same. On the part played by A. in Xenophon's dialogue see O. GIGON, *Schw. Beitr.* 5, 1933, 151.   [2] E. R. DODDS, *Class. Rev.* 68, 1954, 94.

[3] Nr. 46 P. Cf. W. FERGUSON, 'The condemnation of Antiphon'. *Mélanges Glotz* 1, 1932, 349.

[4] *Antiphonstudien.* Berl. 1931.   [5] RADERMACHER (*v. inf.*), 76.

[6] VON DER MÜHLL, cf. *sup.* n. 1. On the other side: G. ZUNTZ, 'Once again the Antiphontean Tetralogies'. *Mus. Helv.* 6, 1949, 100 (genuine: written about 444).

We shall discuss here the speeches of a man who takes us over into the next century, but whose fortunes and political activities were determined by events that took place before the Sicilian expedition. Andocides came from an old Athenian noble family; as a young man he joined the aristocratic political club of Euphiletus and took part in exploits which expressed the same combination of oligarchical principles and anti-religious freethought which we find in Critias. In consequence of the mutilation of the Hermae in 415 Andocides found himself in prison, and he was able to free himself only by betraying those who were guilty. This left an ugly stain on his character. In 407 he appeared before the *ecclesia* with the first of his extant speeches (Περὶ τῆς ἑαυτοῦ καθόδου), in which he sought unsuccessfully to be allowed to return to Athens. He did not in fact return until the amnesty of 403; but his enemies remained implacable, and in 399 they brought an action for impiety against him. Among the speeches of Lysias there is a spurious one purporting to be the accusation against Andocides: it is probably a product of the political pamphleteering of the early fourth century. Andocides' speech in defence is preserved (*De Mysteriis*: Περὶ τῶν μυστηρίων). This time he was lucky, and he attained some reputation in Athens, which is attested by a choregic monument to his victory with a chorus of boys at the Dionysia (IG II/III, 2nd ed. nr. 1138) and his participation in an embassy to Sparta (393/92). On this occasion he spoke before the people on peace with Sparta (Περὶ τῆς πρὸς Λακεδαιμονίους εἰρήνης). But the war went on; sentence of death was pronounced against the members of the legation, and Andocides had once more to seek safety abroad. A fourth speech ascribed to him under the title *Against Alcibiades* pretends to be an attack aiming at the latter's ostracism. It is spurious. His style has a simple and spontaneous flow, innocent of any conscious rhetorical effect.

Whereas Antiphon wrote speeches for others, Andocides spoke in his own cause, with less art than Antiphon, but with a strong expression of personality. A similar immediacy, with still less art, is found in the speech *For Polystratus*, which we find as the twentieth of Lysias' speeches. In it a son defends his father who has been deeply implicated in the activities of the Four Hundred. This also is a useful example of a rhetorical practice which we must assume to have been very widespread at the time.

After this brief summary we can return to the problem of Antiphon. With the reservations mentioned before we take it as the first fixed point that a sophist, distinct from the orator but otherwise unknown, wrote a treatise *On Truth* (᾿Αλήθεια). In addition to scattered fragments there are two fairly large pieces on papyrus (nr. 47 f. P.) coming from the second book, which give us an idea of the problems discussed. Ideas which were lightly touched upon by Hippias in the *Protagoras* are here forcefully developed. Protagoras tried to keep a place for *nomos*, but he could not prevent his own arguments from leading to its rejection. We can see that Gorgias' thought contained elements that pointed the same way: in a passage of the *Epitaphios* (VS 82 B 6, 15) he praised the dead for having often preferred mild equity to the harshness of the law. The latter had come to be called in question, as every truth that claims universal validity must be during a movement with 'man is the measure' as its starting-point. It is a process often seen in history: the secularization of law and custom, in an age which no longer believes in its gods, leads inevitably to their devaluation. The search for a new and reliable norm had already begun, and a development which had long been foreshadowed in Ionian science led to the installation of Nature in the vacant place as the highest and the universally valid sanction.

In the first book of the *Truth* Antiphon had discussed scientific questions in the manner of the Ionian physicists: in the second we find the *physis-nomos* antithesis very sharply brought out, the law of convention being condemned as an absurd restraint on nature. We cannot say precisely where this antithesis began nor who first had the idea of natural law; but mostly they came from the sophistic movement and were considerably developed in the hands of Antiphon.

It was in the light of natural law that Antiphon propounded his revolutionary doctrine of the equality of all men: first equality between noble and commoner in the same city, secondly between Greek and barbarian, on the ground that we all breathe through nose and mouth and use our hands in eating. The equality of freeman and slave is implicit in this theory: later Alcidamas (whom we met as the champion of improvisation) in his *Messenian Oration* was to declare explicitly[1] that God had made all men free and that Nature destined no man to slavery. The equating of God and Nature is obvious, and the passage in general echoes the tones of the Alcidamas who called philosophy a bulwark against laws and customs.

We are in difficulties with the treatise *On Working Together* (Περὶ ὁμονοίας). The surviving remains show a generally pessimistic attitude towards human life, and we may suspect that the work considered co-operation as the basis of human life, particularly of life in political communities. Since such co-operation is impossible without *nomos*, it is hard to recognize here the author of the *Truth*. The assumption that in his maturity he developed towards a Protagorean loyalty to the laws is pure hypothesis. In addition there are considerable stylistic differences between the dry reasoning of the *Truth* and the striking and lively manner of this treatise. On the other hand, one should not underrate the versatility of a sophist, and so we must be content to point out the differences without postulating plural authorship.[2] A characteristically sophistic feature is the praise of education as the best thing that mortals can have (B 60), with the metaphor, since worked to death, of seed planted in the soil. In view of the problems involved, there would be no profit in listing the various hypotheses concerning the authorship of the writings *Against Alcibiades*, *On Dreams* and the *Politicus*.

The antithesis between conventional and natural law appears clearly enough in Antiphon, but others took the doctrine to a radical extreme. Tradition was considered as a constraint laid on the gifted and able few by the prudence of

---

[1] Schol. Aristot. *Rhet.* I, 13. 1373 b 18. 'Bulwark': *Rhet.* 3, 3. 1406 b 11.
[2] An attempt to reconcile the differences is made by M. POHLENZ, *Griech. Freiheit.* Heidelberg 1955, 75.

the weak multitude, so as to keep them within the bounds of civil society. Natural law, on the contrary, is with those who break through such restraints and, like true supermen, make their own will the only law that binds them. This is the doctrine that Plato puts into the mouth of Callicles in the *Gorgias* and of Thrasymachus in the first book of the *Republic*. When Callicles in the first passage professes to see natural law exemplified in the man of iron who tramples on all laws, the moral notions of centuries were stood on their head, and only the total destruction of myth at the hands of the sophists made it possible to claim that Pindar's 'custom is ruler of all' supported this theory.

While we know so little of Callicles that even his historical existence has been doubted, we can say a little more about Thrasymachus. A metic from Calchedon on the Bosporus, he gained notice in Athens by his political writings. One of these, *On the Constitution*, protests against party strife during the crises of the war; the other, *For the People of Larissa*, defends their claim to freedom against Archelaus of Macedon.

Nothing in the surviving work hints at the enthusiastic advocate of the natural right of the strong. There is, however, the possibility of a reconciliation in a fragment (B 8) which complains to the gods of their neglect of human affairs: otherwise they would not have forgotten the greatest gift, righteousness, which is nowhere to be found among men. Certainly the fragments do not give us the picture of a man driven by bitter disillusion to the radicalism which he represents in the *Republic*.[1] We cannot of course neglect the part which Plato himself played in giving this impression of Thrasymachus.

A very influential work of Thrasymachus' was his textbook of rhetoric (Μεγάλη τέχνη), which played its part in the formation of Attic prose style. So far as we can see, the construction and articulation of speeches received most attention: the Gorgianic figures remained in the background, except that Thrasymachus laid stress on having a rhythmical close to sentences.[2]

Theoretical treatises on rhetoric were beginning to multiply. *Technae* were written by Theodore of Byzantium with special reference to the arrangement of material; and Euenus of Paros, who also wrote elegies, composed part of his didactic work in verse. The 'Oxyrhynchus Rhetoric'[3] is written in Doric.

No one so whole-heartedly practised the sophistic doctrines which he preached as Critias, Plato's uncle, a member of an old Athenian noble family. In his personality we find a union of all the impulses of the sophistic movement, whose period of *Sturm und Drang* reached a symbolic end in his dramatic death. The demand for individual freedom of action could now no longer be gainsaid, and in many respects Critias anticipates the strong men of the post-Alexandrine period, such as Demetrius Poliorcetes.

We may suppose that Critias, as a radical oligarch, very soon joined one of those aristocratic clubs which had sworn death to the democracy and welcomed the new teachings. Naturally he was involved in the mutilation of the Hermae, and he was later associated with Alcibiades, after whose overthrow he lived for

---

[1] WOLF (*v. inf.*), 106.   [2] RADERMACHER (*v. inf.*), 75.
[3] Nr. 1785 P.; RADERMACHER (*v. inf.*), 231.

some time in Thessaly. The defeat of Athens at last allowed him to indulge his taste for power. He quickly achieved pre-eminence among the Thirty, had the moderate Theramenes liquidated, and stained his own reputation by a reign of terror which we cannot forget despite Plato's favourable interpretation.[1] He died in 403 fighting against the democrats who were holding Munychia under Thrasybulus.

The many and varied talents of Critias and his active disposition led him to attempt many forms of literature. He was the last to write the kind of political elegy which addressed itself to an audience of kindred feelings and which came to an end with the passing of the old *polis*. Among the remains of these is part of one to Alcibiades. His constant pre-occupation with politics is attested by his *Political Constitutions*, partly in elegiacs (Πολιτεῖαι ἔμμετροι), partly in prose. We know that the latter dealt with Athens, Thessaly and Sparta: an elegiac fragment also survives that refers to Sparta. So far as we can see, customs and usage received most attention. It is interesting to find a fairly large fragment in hexameters containing an elegant tribute to Anacreon: it seems to have come from a work dealing with distinguished poets, comparable with the treatise of Glaucus of Rhegium *On the Old Poets and Musicians*.

Critias also wrote tragedies. In the biography of Euripides we read that the tragedies *Tennes, Rhadamanthys* and *Pirithous*[2] were considered not to be the work of the great tragedian. A notice in Athenaeus (11. 496 b) says that the authorship of the *Pirithous* was disputed between Euripides and Critias. On this basis the plays in question have been ascribed to Critias. One of the surviving fragments (B 22) is interesting: the able individual stands firmer than the law, which can only too easily be perverted by demagogues. Here again we find a depreciation of *nomos*. Critias also wrote a satyr-play *Sisyphus*, which scholars have supposed to have formed a tetralogy with the three tragedies. From this play we have a fragment (B 25), preserved by Sextus Empiricus, which is of great importance in the history of ideas. Like Protagoras, the writer supposes that a chaotic primitive condition of life was followed by the introduction of law and justice. But the final sanction of these ideas awaited the discovery of a subtle genius. He introduced the notion of gods who watched men even when they were secure from human observation. This explanation of the nature and origin of religion is the most radical consequence of sophistic thought.

Of Critias' prose writings we possess only a few titles, such as *Definitions* (Ἀφορισμοί) and *Conversations* (Ὁμιλίαι). We may amuse ourselves by supposing that they were like the Socratic dialogues, but it is better to admit that we do not know. It may be mentioned that Critias wrote *prooemia* to speeches meant for the assembly. While the main concern of the rhetoricians was the forensic speech, the politician Critias took an interest in persuasion of the masses.

The radicalism of Critias is by no means typical of the sophistic movement in the late fifth century. We must not see supermen everywhere in their notion

---

[1] Passages cited in NESTLE (*v. inf.*), 400. 5.

[2] A fragment on papyrus (nr. 165 P.) in D. L. PAGE, *Greek Lit. Pap.* 1950, 120. Ending of the hypothesis to the *Rhadamanthys: Pap. Soc. It.* 12/2. 1951, nr. 1286.

of natural law: with equal justice we might trace to this idea the whole ordering of society and the validity of the state and its laws. In its political application it meant that one did not have to be an oligarch to support the new order. Fortunately our picture is made more detailed by a treatise of which large sections have been preserved by the Neoplatonist Iamblichus in his *Protrepticus*. The writer is usually referred to as the *Anonymus Iamblichi*.[1] His world-view no longer turns on the crude antithesis of *physis* and *nomos*. Instead he treats law as a natural necessity, as an indispensable prerequisite to the forming of a community. Education – to which as a sophist he attaches great importance – is for him education to understand and obey the laws. The train of thought goes back to Protagoras.

A similar spirit is displayed by a work which has been imitated in various passages of the pseudo-Demosthenic speech *Against Aristogiton*.[2] Its author – not a distinguished intellect – piles up with disorderly enthusiasm the most diverse theories on the origin of law: a gift of the gods; the invention of clever individuals; the common consent of the citizen body.

We have a rather unsatisfactory piece of work in a treatise that survives in the manuscripts of Sextus Empiricus, called from its most important section Δισσοὶ λόγοι. It is written in Doric, refers to the Spartan victory of 404 as a recent event, and is probably a transcript of a sophist's lecture. In five chapters it supports the teaching of Protagoras in various departments by giving opposite examples to every custom or opinion that it mentions. The development of Ionian ethnography is strikingly apparent here. One of these antitheses deserves to survive as an illustration of Greek humanity: 'The Scythians hold it praiseworthy for a man who has slain another to hang the scalp on his saddle-bow, to set the skull in gold or silver and to drink from it or offer it to the gods: in Greece no man would go under the same roof with one who had done such a thing'. Four further chapters are devoted to the educational tasks of the sophists, to an attack on choice for political office by lot (written from a democratic standpoint) and to various questions of rhetoric, by which the sophists set such store.

Texts of the sophists: VS and in M. UNTERSTEINER, *Sofisti. Testimonianze e frammenti. Bibl. d. stud. sup.* vols. 4-6. Florence 1949 and 1954 (with bibliography and comm.). A. CAPIZZI, *Protagora. Ed. rivista e amplif. con un studio su la vita, le opere, il pensiero e la fortuna*. Florence 1955. – Text of the rhetors in L. RADERMACHER, *Artium scriptores. Sitzb. Oesterr. Ak.* 227/3, 1951. – Gorgias: W. VOLLGRAFF, *L'Oraison funèbre de Gorgias*. Leyden 1952. – Antiphon: L. GERNET, *Coll. des Un. de Fr.* 1923; repr. 1954. A. BARIGAZZI, Florence 1955 (nos. 1 and 6 with comm.). Index by F. L. VAN CLEEF, *Cornell Studies in Class. Philol.* 5, 1895. –

---

[1] VS 89. R. ROLLER, *Untersuchungen zum Anonymus Iamblichi*. Tübingen 1931.

[2] M. GIGANTE, Νόμος βασιλεύς. Naples 1956, thinks that the writer of the speech made the compilation himself.

Andocides: G. DALMEYDA, *Coll. des Un. de Fr.* 1930; repr. 1960. A. D. J. MAK-
KINK, Amsterdam 1932 (no. 1 with comm.). U. ALBINI, *Andocide, De reditu.*
Florence 1961 (with comm.). – Special studies: W. NESTLE, *Vom Mythos zum
Logos.* Stuttg. 1940. O. GIGON, *Sokrates.* Berne 1947, 240. M. UNTERSTEINER,
I sofisti. Einaudi 1949; Eng. tr. Oxf. 1954 (with good bibliogr.). E. WOLF,
Griechisches Rechtsdenken. 2 vols. Frankf. a. M. 1952. M. GIGANTE, Νόμος βασιλεύς,
Naples 1956. – G. M. SCIACCA, *Gli dei in Protagora.* Palermo 1958. – F. ZUCKER,
Der Stil des Gorgias nach seiner inneren Form. Sitzb. Ak. Berl. 1956/1. CARLA
SCHICK, 'Appunti per una storia della prosa greca'. *Paideia* 11, 1956, 161. W.
BRÖCKER, 'Gorgias contra Parmenidem'. *Herm.* 86, 1958, 424. V. BUCHHEIT,
Untersuchungen zur Theorie des Genos Epideiktikon von Gorgias bis Aristoteles.
Munich 1960. J. H. M. M. LOENEN, *Parmenides, Melissus, Gorgias. A Reinterpretation
of Eleatic Philosophy.* 1960. – U. ALBINI, 'Antifonte logografo I'. *Maia* N.S. 10,
1958, 38. – U. ALBINI, 'Rassegna di studi andocidei'. *Atene e Roma* 3, 1958, 129.
Id., 'Per un profilo di Andocide'. *Maia* N.S. 8, 1956, 163.

2 EURIPIDES

In connection with Sophocles we mentioned the synchronism which related
the three great men of tragedy in various ways with the battle of Salamis. The
story that Euripides should have been born on the day of the battle is certainly
fictitious, for other dates are also given. The one in the Marmor Parium (60),
giving 485/484, is perhaps equally doubtful, as it is synchronous with Aeschylus'
first victory,[1] but it is probably not far from correct. However this may be,
it is of special significance that Euripides belongs to a generation which knows
of the great years of the Persian wars only from their fathers' stories. Euripides
was approximately of the same age as Protagoras, and even though the difference
with Sophocles, born 497/496, is not very great, in the tempestuous development
which began in the middle of the 5th century a decade meant already a great
deal. It is decisive that Sophocles maintained his faith unshaken and remained
consistently averse to the revolutionizing process of the intellect by the sophistic
movement, whilst the attitude of his younger contemporary was different. But
the notion that Euripides was simply the poet of Greek enlightenment, as he
was occasionally called, must be rejected. Even ancient tradition assigned
Anaxagoras, Prodicus and Protagoras to him as teachers. Of course he knew
these men and also many other personalities of intellectual Athens, and in
individual cases there may have been closer ties, but Euripides was neither
simply a pupil of the sophists nor a propagandist of their ideas. He was open to
their influence, their problems were largely his, but he always preserved the
independence of his thought, while he frequently was outspokenly critical,[2] so
that there is no question of a pupil relationship with the sophists, but rather of
an incessant passionate altercation with the movement.

---

[1] On these chronological fancies F. JACOBY, *F Gr Hist*, Comm. on 239 A 50. 63 and 244
F 35. Ancient sources for the biography in the ed. of A. NAUCK, Leipz. 1871. The manuscript biography best in the ed. of the scholia of E. SCHWARTZ, Berl. 1887/91.

[2] Cf. *Hec.* 1187 against rhetorical artifices and fr. 439.

Great intellectual restlessness is generally the hallmark of Euripides and his work. This is movingly expressed by the bust of Euripides in Naples, and the hero of the tragedy *Bellerophon*, who wants to assault heaven on Pegasus to fathom the gods' secrets, becomes symbolic of the poet himself.

Hardly any figure in ancient literature is so hard to comprehend in his many aspects as Euripides. Many of the features of his work belong to the previous period; nevertheless the sublime compactness displayed in the Parthenon as well as in Sophocles' mature tragedies is beginning to break up. The fervour of blazing passion stands side by side with a rationalism alien to the plot; hymns are sung to the same gods who elsewhere are relegated to the realm of fables, and everywhere a great many more questions are asked than answered with certainty. Such a strong differentiation in Euripides' work, which is allied with an inequality of artistic value, forbids us to look for a uniform formula of explanation. All we are able to do is to group together related phenomena.

Both in his work and in the way he lived Euripides demonstrated that with him a new period was beginning. Aeschylus fought for his country as a soldier, Sophocles performed a number of high offices, but Euripides had no such ties with the *polis*. He repeatedly took a stand in his dramas on matters of public life, forcing arguments about such problems upon his artistic work with much greater unconcern than his predecessors; but in such cases he speaks as the inquiring thinker and not as the *polites* who is an immediate partner, like Aeschylus in the *Eumenides* or Sophocles in the first stasimon of the *Antigone*.

During the Hellenistic age and under the empire strangers were conducted to a cave in Salamis[1] in which Euripides was supposed to have contemplated the mysteries of life, far from men, his gaze directed at the sea. This sort of abode for great poets and thinkers is part and parcel of legendary tales, but the story is typical for the image which had been formed of Euripides. Creative genius now withdrew into an isolation which had previously been unknown and which opened up a wide, often fateful, gap between the great man and his people.

Such a position of the poet and the circumstance that many thoughts of the sophists were reflected in his verse combined to make him the chief object of the indignation and ridicule of the conservatives during that brief and exciting time. Comedy is full of it. The deplorable result for us is that the few available biographical details of this poet are even more cluttered up with anecdotal rubbish than usual. The *Lives* preserved in some manuscripts are a good example of this, but the Euripides biography of the Peripatetic Satyrus is an exceptional one. A papyrus (no. 1135 P) of the concluding portion of his 6th book of *Lives* gives us a vivid impression of this kind of scribbling, and it is distressing to find that he uses Aristophanes' *Thesmophoriazusae* as a historical source. He even has some literary pretensions, for he wrote the biography as a dialogue.

In view of such a tradition it would be unmethodical to claim at will that either one or another story is historical. We shall have to accept the fact that there is little that can be considered without suspicion.

---

[1] Life. Satyrus col. 9 Gellius 15. 20, 5. H. GERSTINGER, *Wien. Stud*, 38, 1916, 65.

The poet's father was the landowner Mnesarchus or Mnesarchides, his mother was called Clito; comedy turned her into a shopkeeper or greengrocer. The parents came from the Attic deme of Phlya, but the poet was born on his parents' property in Salamis. The story that his father first had him trained in gymnastics, because an oracle had promised him athletic victories, is one of the many tales of misinterpreted oracles. He is also supposed to have been a painter. The information in the biography that there had been pictures by him in Megara sounds quite definite, but in such cases the possibility of a similarity of names should be taken into account. The most reliable information is that Euripides, when young, was a dancer and torchbearer in the service of Apollo Zosterius, since the purpose of inventing this sort of thing would be hard to understand. The most evil libel, and one upon which comedy pounced with gusto, was levelled at the poet's home. First he married Melito, next Choerine; he had some unpleasant experiences in his married life, connected with a member of his household Cephisophon, who occasionally helped Euripides with his writing, but also assisted in other ways.

The profound difference between Sophocles, whose life was so solidly founded in the Athenian community, and Euripides, is also expressed in the different relationship of the two with their audience. Euripides was granted his first chorus in 455, but he was not successful. Among the plays performed was the *Peliades*, the poet's first Medea play. The theme of the drama was the cruel and crafty vengeance which Medea took on Pelias of Iolcus on behalf of Jason. Medea had promised that she would restore his youth by boiling him, and so the old king was killed by his own daughters.

According to the evidence of the Marmor Parium (60), Euripides did not win his first victory until 441.[1] Three more were added, which is little enough, for we know that he obtained a chorus for 22 tetralogies. Individual sources mention five victories, but these include the posthumous ones which his son of the same name or his nephew[2] won with the remaining plays *Iphigeneia in Aulis*, *Alcmeon in Corinth* and the *Bacchae*.

The public's opposition against Euripides is supposed to have resulted in an indictment for impiety by Cleon, but Satyrus is very suspect as a source. In spite of all distortion, however, some historical basis seems to be present here in the final analysis. Aristotle (*Rhet.* 3, 15. 1416 a 29) knows of a lawsuit of the poet's against a certain Hygiaenon about an exchange of property (antidosis) on the occasion of a public service (liturgy), in which aspersions against the poet's atheism are supposed to have also played a part.

An *Epinician Ode* on an Olympic victory in chariot racing, probably won by Alcibiades at Olympia in 416,[3] is attributed to Euripides; we have half a dozen lines of it (fr. 3 D.), but from Plutarch's *Demosthenes* we learn that in

---

[1] C. F. RUSSO, 'Eur. e i concorsi tragici lenaici'. *Mus. Helv.* 17, 1960, 165 gives the dates of performances which can still be ascertained, and attempts to prove with detailed arguments that it is extremely unlikely that the poet participated in the contests of the Lenaea.

[2] Son: Schol. Aristophanes' *Frogs* 67. Nephew: Suidas.

[3] C. M. BOWRA, 'Epinician for Alcibiades'. *Historia* 9, 1960, 68.

antiquity it was ascribed to others as well. A closer connection of the poet with Alcibiades is not very probable in view of the difference in character of the two men.

It is credible that the Athenians commissioned the poet of the *Troades* with the composition of the epitaph for those fallen at Syracuse. The epigram transmitted in Plutarch's *Nicias* (17) is extremely colourless, however.

Euripides, like Aeschylus, died abroad. In 408 he still staged his *Orestes* in Athens, but soon afterwards he moved to Archelaus' court in Pella. The manuscript biography makes the Macedonian sojourn follow upon one in Magnesia which is supposed to have honoured him with the proxeny and freedom from taxes. We do not even know which Magnesia is meant, and it is best to keep open the possibility that the report has been brought about by an inscription honouring the poet.

Archelaus, with whom Euripides passed the remaining years of his life, had the ambition to adorn his court, whose customs we must imagine as quite barbarian, with great names. Several are mentioned, among them the tragic poet Agathon and the dithyrambic poet Timotheus who, as a modernist, is supposed to have been very close to Euripides.

In Euripides' case it is demonstrated to what extent the death of great men is a theme irresistible to the anecdote-mongers. He is supposed to have been torn to pieces by Molossian hounds, offspring of a royal hound, for the killing of which the poet had obtained remission of punishment. The tearing up by dogs is probably meant as a punishment for the atheist, just as, according to the legend, Euripides' grave and his cenotaph were struck by lightning.

News of the poet's death reached Athens early in 406 before the great Dionysia. It sounds credible that in the proagon, a sort of introduction of the performers of the plays to be staged, Sophocles himself appeared in mourning and brought in the actors and chorus without wreaths. Archelaus is said to have buried the poet in Pella, but there are also reports of a tomb at Arethusa. The Athenian cenotaph on the way to the Piraeus has already been mentioned; it displayed the fine verses which are found in the biography with the bold indication of authorship 'Thucydides or Timotheus'.

The dates of performances handed down provide the first and most reliable basis for the chronology of the 18 surviving plays (we consider the *Rhesus* to be spurious); 438 *Alcestis*, 431 *Medea*, 428 *Hippolytus*, 415 *Troades*, 412 *Helen*, 408 *Orestes*; we also know that the *Iphigenia in Aulis* and the *Bacchae* were not performed until after the poet's death. Another important basis is supplied by comedy, whose allusions to Euripides are particularly frequent and cutting, and at times provide a definite *terminus ante quem*. Allusions to contemporary events, however, rarely yield reliable chronological support. Recently doubts have even been cast on the bearing which the lines spoken by the Dioscuri at the end of the *Electra* before their exit have on Athens' fleet in Sicilian waters. In recent years considerations of this nature have sometimes been carried a great deal too far and Euripides' tragedies have been interpreted as if they were history in disguise.[1] There is no doubt that the third of the great tragedians addresses his contemporaries from the stage more often than his predecessors, but tangible political allusions do not occur very frequently, and respect for his artistry should restrain one from seeking key figures in contemporary history among the persons of the drama. Style and metre are also chronological aids, though they should not be overestimated. But it is an undeniable fact that in Euripides' copious output related phenomena, especially with regard to themes, form groups which belong together in time.

The chronology of Euripides' tragedies, for which we have fairly firm foundations, reveals that none of the plays preserved is older than the *Alcestis* which was performed in 438. At the time Euripides had been writing for the stage for seventeen years, and so in this case also the possibility is denied to us of studying his early work.

We know from a hypothesis that the *Alcestis* was the fourth play in a tetralogy; it occurred in a position where we are accustomed to find a satyr-play. There is reason to believe that this is not the only case in which Euripides finished off his tetralogy with a play with a happy ending instead of a satyr-play. He was not gifted with the bright vivacity which still delights us in the *Ichneutae* and the *Dictyulci*; this is proved by the *Cyclops*, whose wit is of a different kind.

The position of the *Alcestis* in the tetralogy has been felt as a challenge to find as much of the comic or even burlesque in it as possible; in these attempts the character of this fine work, which has been so fertile in the literature of the world, has often been misunderstood.

Euripides took a legend which connects two widespread fairy-tale themes into an exciting whole. It is the story of the loving wife who offers her own life when death comes to claim her husband's. There is also the victorious struggle, used here as the dénouement, of the strong man with the demon of death, a theme which occurs frequently alone or in a different connection. Phrynichus had used the subject of *Alcestis* before, and his influence seems to have lingered in the scenes of Euripides' drama which deal with the arrival and the conquest of Thanatos, death personified. Without essentially altering the substance of the legend, Euripides created, in one stroke, spiritual conditions which were entirely new. In the old legend, and probably in Phrynichus too, the bride announced her willingness for the sacrifice on her wedding day, and already had to carry it out as well; but Euripides separated the two events by a period of several years, during which Alcestis fully experienced the happiness of being a wife and a mother. The question of cold reason, how Alcestis could have done this with the appointed day of death ahead of her, misunderstands the nature of the work. The poet was concerned with what he could gain by this bold stroke; his Alcestis sacrifices her life, as she once promised on her wedding day, but now in the full awareness of what she is leaving and giving up.

The play opens with the effective contrast between Apollo, the radiant god,

---

[1] E. DELEBECQUE, *Eur. et la guerre du Péloponnèse*. Paris 1951, goes farthest. Also contains further bibl.

and Thanatos, who has come to claim his victim. The Delphic temple scene of the *Eumenides* is influential in this confrontation of two gods from separate worlds. The chorus of old men of Pherae enters singing of care and grief; a servant informs them that inside the house Alcestis is bidding farewell to her home and family. This early messenger speech of Euripides' already demonstrates the epic mastery which he always maintained in the narrative portions of his plays. After a choral lyric, husband and wife enter and we witness the last words and lament of Alcestis, and her death. The very next episode brings Heracles, the saviour, who, on his way to one of his adventures, wants to call in on Admetus. The latter keeps silent about his bereavement in order to be able to entertain his guest-friend. The funeral procession is forming when Admetus' father enters with gifts for the dead woman. Here we become acquainted with the full development of an important element which recurs constantly; the scene of conflict, the agon; in a lucid, formal order, especially through a well-calculated alternation of long speech and stichomythia with its hard-hitting succession of lines, two parties settle the contest of words, using all arguments possible. The world of the διϭϭοί λόγοι opened up by the sophists has been given dramatic form. Pheres has refused to sacrifice his own life for his son's and is now blamed by him for his thirst for life, but Admetus has in turn to hear himself accused of letting his wife die through his unscrupulous egotism. After the agon, the funeral procession, and the chorus with it, leaves the stage, one of the rare cases of its being empty after the chorus's parodos. Heracles, who has meanwhile been merrily carousing inside, learns the true state of affairs from a servant. He sets out at once to fight Thanatos for his prey, and when Admetus returns from the tomb and is lamenting distractedly in front of the palace, Heracles brings him his wife, restored to life. Admetus has yet to stand up to a minor intrigue, when Heracles pretends that Alcestis, who is wearing a veil, is a strange woman and so tests his constancy, but then the happily reunited couple are allowed to cross the threshold of the palace to start a new life.

The *Alcestis* at once poses the basic problems of Euripidean tragedy with full sharpness. There is no need to waste many words over the fact that the gods have no longer the same meaning as for Aeschylus or for Sophocles in the *Oedipus* tragedies. Man with his troubles and fears, his hopes and plans, has taken up the centre of the stage. But how are they viewed by Euripides? No doubt psychological processes play a great part in his work, but is it therefore permissible to call him the discoverer of psychology in drama? And is it indeed psychology which is the motive power in his plays?

The *Alcestis* demonstrates in a special manner the difficulties into which modern notions and demands get us. There is Alcestis, the loving wife, who sacrifices herself for her husband. But where does she speak of her love? The poet shows her farewell to life twice, through the servant's message and in Alcestis' great scene. The accents in the two passages are different: in the messenger-speech it is one of tender lament; in the death-scene, after the lyrically expressed vision of fear, there occurs that lucid deliberation and summing up of the sacrifice which she is making which has astonished readers time and again. But

N 365

nowhere does Alcestis speak of the ardour which impels her to bring this sacrifice, nowhere do we hear the words which we expect from a loving wife. But it is the figure of Admetus which proves to be the greatest stumbling-block for moderns. How can a man be taken seriously who lets his wife die for him and then implores her, when she is dying, not to leave him, a man who fills his palace and the city with his lament over his fate and who would like to be pitied over what he got out of it!

The interpretations of the difficulties presented here deviate from each other in a way which is typical for the general criticism of Euripides.

The best way of acquiring a personal point of view is to establish first what are the most extreme positions taken with regard to these difficulties. For a long time present-day critics have sought between the lines the psychology not given directly by the text, and have made this part of their interpretation. Much of this sort of thing is found in Wilamowitz,[1] who claimed, for instance, that Alcestis had lost many an illusion and would not have repeated her promise to sacrifice herself. This method still has its representatives now and is particularly emphatic in Van Lennep's book on Euripides and his edition of the *Alcestis*. Of course Admetus comes off very badly, and the couple's future life does not bode well.

This kind of interpretation is rare now; the conviction has gained ground that such psychologizing completely misses the meaning of the ancient poet. So the pendulum has swung over to the other side, and Walter Zürcher could undertake, in his stimulating book *Darstellung des Menschen im Drama des Euripides*, the attempt to limit the psychological element in this poet considerably, and even to deny it altogether in important cases. Following the interpretation of Sophocles as defended by Tycho von Wilamowitz, Zürcher opposes the view that Euripides' characters are drawn completely. The dramatic character is rather secondary to the plot, and is merely a function of the dramatic fable. Presently we shall have to protest in cases where this view was pushed too far, even to the point of finally tearing great Euripidean characters to pieces. But something essential has been achieved; in Euripides' portrayal of man it is not so much a matter of character in the sense of modern individualism as of general human ways of reacting to hate and love, sorrow and joy. In this realm Euripides is a master; he unlocked great realms of the soul for the dramatic stage, and to this extent it is justifiable to speak of the importance of psychology in his work. Long ago J. Burckhardt aptly formulated his difference from Sophocles in this regard:[2] '*So whereas Sophocles is always preoccupied with the entirety of a character, Euripides has sometimes a way of exploiting the emotions of a single person in a certain scene down to the last detail . . .*'.

As to the offence which the *Alcestis* gives to our modern way of thinking, both the origin of the subject matter and the convention of ancient drama should be borne in mind. The heroine's reasoning, which often appears to be cold-blooded,

---

[1] *Griech. Trag.* 3, 87.

[2] *Griech. Kulturgesch.* 2,306 (Kröner). Nowadays we should prefer to say 'Ethos' in the case of Sophocles rather than 'Character'.

corresponds with the typically Greek craving to give an account of oneself, and suits this mature woman. Sophocles' Antigone does the same thing and she too has caused displeasure.

But the figure of Admetus presents any poet with almost unsurmountable difficulties. In a recent important paper[1] K. v. Fritz has made an acute appraisal of the way in which this character in Euripides offends our sensibilities. The view can hardly be accepted that this sort of criticism was beyond the possibilities of the fifth century, for in the agon Pheres (drawn to be utterly distasteful) voices reproaches which are like ours. K. v. Fritz has formulated a notion which is useful for large portions of Euripides' work; when Euripides' art converted ancient legendary subject matter and thus opened up new vision of the psyche, dissonances were bound to occur. There is no denying that these are found in the *Alcestis*. But the question remains whether they were called up by the poet's original intention or were the inevitable consequence of his creative method. We are not looking for a general answer which at any rate would not apply to part of Euripides' work, but are of the opinion that in the case of Admetus the poet has done a great deal to make the hospitable king, loved by Apollo and truly sorrowful, into a tolerable, if not lovable, figure. Does not Alcestis' parting from her marriage bed, as related by the servant, reflect upon the husband? But one has no right to deny meaning to her words that she would not have wanted to live without Admetus (v. 287), because she mentions the orphaned children in the same breath. The words which he utters on his return from the tomb (v. 940): '*Now I realize*', are important too; they may not indicate a reversal, they do imply understanding. Of course the poet could not motivate Admetus' acceptance of the sacrifice. He was therefore wise not to attempt to do this and to limit himself to the ancient legend. But he did show – and this was a new element – that the sacrifice turned against him with bitter sorrow when he had accepted it. But we can only take his grief seriously or rejoice in his redemption if we see more in Admetus than a deplorable egotist who avoids death by sacrificing his wife. We have no wish to evade the difficulty of these questions by taking cover behind Goethe's authority, but his farce *Götter, Helden und Wieland* is valid testimony that such a point of view is possible.

Of the three tragedies which preceded the *Alcestis* the first, the *Cretan Women*, deals with the story of Minos' granddaughter Aerope whom her father Catreus ordered to be drowned by Nauplius because of her unchastity. The latter, however, married her to Plisthenes. Correct utilization of the fragments of the *Alcmeon in Psophis*[2] has provided a better notion of the contents of this play. Its central theme is the faith which Arsinoe, who has a sisterly kinship with Alcestis, preserved for the exiled and inconstant Alcmeon. The third play, *Telephus*,[3]

---

[1] 'Euripides "Alkestis" und ihre modernen Nachahmer und Kritiker.' *Ant. u. Abendl.* 5, 1956, 27. Now *Antike und moderne Tragödie*. Berlin 1962, 256.

[2] W. SCHADEWALDT, 'Zu einem Florentiner Papyrusbruchstück aus dem "Alkmeon in Psophis" des Eur.'. *Herm.* 80, 1952, 46; now *Hellas und Hesperien*. Zürich 1960, 316.

[3] Important for the reconstruction: E. W. HANDLEY–J. REA, 'The Telephus of Eur.'. *Univ. of Lond. Bull. of Inst. of Class. Stud. Suppl.* 5, 1957, with new papyrus fragments and proof that *Pap. Berol.* 9908 (*Berl. Klass. Texte* 5/2, p. 64) belongs to this play and not to Sophocles'.

created quite a stir. The king of the Mysians obtained by force a cure of the wound inflicted by Achilles by stealthily entering the Greek camp in Argos in beggar's clothes and threatening the little Orestes. A king in rags was an unheard-of thing on the Attic stage of the time.

In the year 431 Euripides was allotted third place in the contest with the *Medea*, which nowadays we count among his masterpieces. In this case he once again penetrated more deeply into the ancient legend, giving it a turn which was of supreme importance for the depiction of the emotions. In Corinth a tomb of Medea's children was known, and there probably was also a version of the tale of her killing them by mistake when she attempted to make them immortal.[1] Out of this grew Euripides' murderess of her own children who in a violent passion exacted vengeance for Jason's infidelity. It is plausible that the children's murder as the revenge of a jilted woman was modelled after the myth of Procne and Tereus, but Sophocles' *Tereus* need not have had any influence. The information in the hypothesis that Euripides fashioned his play after a *Medea* of Neophron is unreliable; the remnants of this drama indicate that this playwright was rather the imitator who wanted to improve on Euripides.[2]

The plot of the *Medea* is contrived with an art which makes the final catastrophe appear inevitable. The Colchian princess, who followed Jason on all his wanderings as far as Corinth, sees herself betrayed and exposed to misery for the sake of the local ruler's daughter. At the beginning of the play, after an exposition in the prologue by the Nurse and a scene which shows the children, we hear the cries and curses of the deserted woman from inside the house. But then she appears composedly before the chorus of Corinthian women, speaking to them of the general lot of women and her personal fate. In Euripides rational statement maintained its right even in plays of the most violent passion; nor can it be denied that the poet manages to effect considerable contrasts through the alternation of emotion and reason, or effective climaxes by reversing this order.

Medea is bent on revenge, although she does not yet see her way clear. She advances step by step. She has to pledge the chorus to silence, a concession to the conventions of the stage. In itself it would be credible that women should support a woman, but that these Corinthians should aid a barbarian against their own royal house is something we have to accept for the sake of the play.

In a scene with Creon Medea makes sure that her impending exile is postponed for one day. Next there follows the great agon between her and Jason, which does not advance the plot – such verbal contests seldom do – but we get to know the man who excuses with smooth words his betrayal of the woman who once saved his life. In the next scene the Athenian king Aegeus, on his way home from the Delphic oracle, passes across the stage rather like a comet. The episodic

---

[1] *RE* 15, 1930, 42.

[2] On the *Tereus*: W. BUCHWALD, *Studien zur Chronologie der att. Trag. 455 bis 431*. Diss. Königsb. 1939, 35. Neophron: D. L. PAGE in his ed. of the play (*v. inf.*), xxx. K. V. FRITZ, *Antike und moderne Tragödie*. Berl. 1962, 334 considers Neophron's priority.

quality of this part has often been censured, but Aegeus' promise of a place of refuge for Medea supports the next part of the plot. It is possible that the *Aegeus* preceded the *Medea*, which showed Medea at the king's court in Athens and staged her assault upon Theseus' stepson. In this case this scene in the *Medea* would have been connected with a situation which the audience knew.

Now Medea's plan is ready: through her sons she will send presents to the young bride who will die miserably, and then she will kill her own children. She makes sure of Jason with a pretence of conciliation, and the fateful gifts find their way to Creusa. After a brief choral lyric, which, as often, covers a prolonged period of time, the children come back from the palace. Medea now knows that the boys, as the bringers of the lethal gifts, are lost, and even though her strength threatens to weaken, she now has to do under the coercion of the situation what she had planned initially as a deed of her own volition. Already the messenger arrives and reports the agonies of the deaths of Creon and Creusa; Medea strikes the mortal blow which she knows will strike at her own heart. Jason dashes up too late. He is only met with taunts of triumph over his misery.

No other Greek tragedy, except possibly the *Hippolytus*, is moved to such an extent by the forces which rise from man's soul to exert a demoniacal influence. This agrees with the fact that here, as nowhere else, Euripides displayed in the monologue the soul as the stage of opposing forces. This occurs in three speeches (364. 1021. 1236); these may be regarded as monologues, in spite of an occasional word addressed to the chorus (1043), since the purpose is not to impart information, but to reveal personal thought and struggle. The central one of these three is filled with the strongest emotion, and is exceptional in Greek tragedy. Four times Medea changes her mind: the violent yearning for revenge, the love of her children, the knowledge of the certain catastrophe in the palace and its consequences meet on the battlefield of her soul. The victory goes to the realisation that the children are lost in any case, but in her final words Medea reveals the forces whose conflict has produced all this: an ardent heart ($\theta\upsilon\mu\acute{o}s$) and consideration ($\beta o\upsilon\lambda\epsilon\acute{\upsilon}\mu\alpha\tau\alpha$); the latter's defeat is the cause of man's worst evils.

Some of the questions posed with regard to the *Alcestis* crop up again. Even ancient critics, whom we detect in the hypothesis and the scholia on line 922, have denied to a Medea who weeps over her children but kills them nevertheless the unity of her nature. Modern critics have followed this view and expressed the opinion that his figure is split up into its component parts. They misjudge the poet, who knew more of the human soul than his critics who would like to set their limits so narrowly. Extravagant hatred for the traitor and tender love for the children, and much else that is as distinct as fire from water, can very well find its place in *one* human soul. The influence of this figure in world literature, comparable with little else, is certain proof of the grandeur and rightness of its conception.

One fact, however, cannot be denied: our sympathy for Medea suffering in distress and guilt is extinguished when the magic chariot of her grandfather Helius comes to fetch her away. Here she is removed from the sphere of human understanding and pity, her demoniacal triumph separates her from our world. The dramatic poet gained an effective conclusion, but that is not all. In the words which she speaks from the magic vehicle (it must be imagined aloft, for instance on the roof of the skene), she founds the cult of her children, which actually existed in Corinth. This is a typical feature, for the endings of Euripides' tragedies refer quite often back to existing cults, in spite of all the freedom of presentation, as if the purpose had been none else but to explain their origin.

In 431 the *Medea* was followed by a performance of the *Philoctetes*, which was discussed in connection with Sophocles' use of the subject matter, and a third play, the *Dictys*, with the adventure of Danae in Seriphus, where she was oppressed by king Polydectes and rescued by her son Perseus when he returned from the adventure with the Gorgon.

In the *Hippolytus*, performed in 428, the scene in which Phaedra, ravaged by her passion, reveals her secret, is followed (373) in the true Euripidean manner by a quiet reflection on how man comes to sin. Phaedra opposes the dictum that guilt grows from defective awareness; rather do most people know what is right, but the temptation to evil pleasures is stronger. It has rightly been observed[1] that a polemic against Socrates' doctrine of knowledge of virtue is implied. But it also becomes clear that Phaedra's words point out that understanding and passion are the same opposites which Medea's great soliloquy mentioned as the guiding forces of her fate. In fact, with the *Hippolytus* we are not only very close to the *Medea* in time; the two tragedies, about which we shall have more to say, represent a part of Euripides' work in which the tragic conflict arises with particular intensity out of the elemental forces of human passion.

A few years earlier Euripides had already put on the stage in Athens the story of Minos' daughter Phaedra, Theseus' wife, whose consuming passion for her stepson destroys both him and herself. In this play Phaedra offered her love to her stepson without any restraint; he covered up his head in horror, from which the play was called *Hippolytus Calyptomenus*; we get some idea of it from parts of Seneca's *Phaedra*, Ovid's 4th *Epistula Heroidum* and some small fragments.[2] Until very recently modern man could hardly imagine narrative and dramatic literature without love as the central theme, and one seldom pauses to think how great a part Euripides played in the progress of this motif. The radical manner in which he showed on the stage things which were completely new there, greatly alarmed and shocked the Athenians. Frequent evidence of this is found in comedy. The first *Hippolytus* was rejected. The second, however, which was given the additional name of *Stephanephorus* or *Stephanias*, gained its author a victory in 428.

[1] BR. SNELL, 'Das früheste Zeugnis über Sokrates'. *Phil.* 97, 1948, 125.

[2] W. H. FRIEDRICH, *Unters. zu Sen. dram. Technik*. Leipz. 1933, 24; the same in the above-mentioned book, 118, in which he tries (148), to date the first *Hippolytus* in the Dionysia of the year 434 on the grounds of the lunar eclipse in Sen. *Phaedra* 788. On the modelling of the subject matter by Seneca cf. also FRIEDRICH and K. V. FRITZ in the papers mentioned in the bibl. of the play; also CL. ZINTZEN, *Analytisches Hypomnema zu Senecas Phaedra. Beitr. z. klass. Phil.* 1. Meisenheim 1960.

We can ascertain that the recasting was achieved by the figure of Phaedra. Now she is not the wanton Cretan who only recognizes the commands of her passion, here she is the noble woman who wishes to conceal her sinful desire deep in her soul, even if she should perish through it. The new version of the play possibly lost some of its elemental force; the contrast of the two main characters perhaps emerged more forcefully in the first conception, but it was a substantial deepening of the tragic contents that the chaste young man was now faced by a noble woman who was to be defeated in the struggle with the demon in her own breast and to ruin her whole house with herself.

The poet shows her sick and prepared for death, and in this condition she allows her secret to be wrested from her by the worried nurse. Euripides drew this figure with great subtlety, so that the transition from the initial horror of the simple woman to pandering helpfulness appears to be credible. But the Nurse's well-meaning services turn out to be harmful; Hippolytus feels only horror and loathing at her revelations, and Phaedra, who overhears him, knows that all is lost. Now she takes the way which from the very outset had appeared as the only one open to her, death. The letter which she leaves behind accusing Hippolytus of attempting to dishonour her and thus drawing him to ruin with her, was no doubt more plausible in the first version, since it corresponded with the characterization of Phaedra. But in the second *Hippolytus* it can be understood from the boundless bitterness of a woman spurned, threatened with humiliation in spite of her self-control and her pride of virtue. In the analysis we can separate the motives and observe that Phaedra goes to her death for the sake of her honour and leaves the fateful letter behind because of her longing for revenge, but the unity of her personality is called no more into question by this than Medea's was by the conflict of her emotions.

The position of the gods in this play, which is conceived entirely as arising out of human nature, is curious and difficult. Aphrodite opens it with her speech in the prologue, Artemis concludes it as the *dea ex machina*. Artemis has been fitted in more firmly and with more meaning. Through her, Hippolytus' nature is revealed with a directness which a poet of his time could only achieve in this way. The passages in which Euripides describes the relationship of the chaste young man with his goddess belong to the finest he ever wrote. This happens in the scene following Aphrodite's prologue, in which he honours Artemis with a wreath from a pure untrodden meadow. But this scene also reveals the one-sidedness of his nature which the Greeks called hybris. Hippolytus harshly dismisses the old servant who points to Aphrodite as a goddess worthy of veneration, thus renouncing a great force of real life which was divine to the Greeks.

Artemis has special significance in the construction of the ending. Returning from a long journey, Theseus has found Phaedra dead, with the letter of accusation next to her. So strong is its hold on him, that in the great agon he remains deaf to all his son's protestations; moreover, Hippolytus is bound by oath to preserve silence about Phaedra's motive. With one of the three wishes whose fulfilment his father Poseidon has granted him, Theseus calls down perdition on his son and banishes him from Troezen. The messenger-speech describes with terrible precision how the gigantic bull sent by Poseidon made Hippolytus' horses shy and caused his death. He is carried on to the stage as he is dying; Artemis appears and bids her huntsman goodbye in lines of incomparable tenderness, but then she reveals the truth to Theseus and founds the cult of Hippolytus which existed at Troezen and which formed the starting-point of the legend.

In the final scene just outlined, as well as in the prologue spoken by Aphrodite, there are passages which make the conflict appear to be a struggle between the two goddesses for honour and precedence. How are we to interpret this in this very drama which seems to be built so much on the human qualities of its characters? Euripides by no means believed in the existence of such goddesses, and the scenes in which they appear are removed from similar scenes in the *Oresteia* or the opening scene of the *Ajax* with Athena by a deep gulf, i.e. the influence of the sophists. Another extreme viewpoint must be rejected as well, the interpretation which, following Verrall's footsteps, sees in these divine figures nothing but the poet's protest against the tradition and an attempt to reduce them to absurdity. As in all Euripidean questions there is no simple formula by which to answer them; in the *Hippolytus*, however, Aphrodite and Artemis are symbols adapted from popular beliefs, leading swiftly and directly to an understanding of the basic forces which motivate the play.[1] The Athenian audience understood them, while the pious could accept them as reality. They must have contributed to the success of the surviving play, and it may be suspected that they did not appear in the first version.

Euripides liked to vary a treatment which had proved successful. The Potiphar theme was repeated in a tragedy which he wrote not long after, the *Stheneboea*,[2] in which, however, Bellerophon does not fall a victim to the sin of a woman in love, but punishes her with death by his own hand. We do not know what the contents of the *Peleus* was, but it may have been based on the same theme and portrayed the hero's temptation by Astydamea in Iolcus.

The *Phoenix* showed the man whom we met as Achilles' counsellor in the Embassy in the *Iliad*, imperilled by the snares of love during the years of his early manhood.

Other lost plays which are either earlier or whose date is uncertain follow here because the erotic element predominated in them. In the *Aeolus*, the fairy-tale from the *Odyssey* (10. 7) of the god of winds who married his sons with his daughters, was turned into a story of incest. In the *Cretan Men* the passion of Pasiphae, Minos' wife, for the bull sent by Poseidon motivated the plot.[3] The *Chrysippus*, performed together with the *Phoenissae*, is certainly of a late date; it owed its name to Pelops' handsome son. Laius carried off the son of his guest-

---

[1] Similarly NORWOOD, *Essays* (*v. inf.*), 108.

[2] B. ZÜHLKE, 'Eur. Stheneboia'. *Phil.* 105, 1961, 1.

[3] A. RIVIER, 'Eur. et Pasiphaé'. *Lettres d'Occident. Études offerts à A. Bonnard.* Neuchâtel 1958, 51, tries to find in the remnants an interpretation which shows Pasiphae not as the great sinner but as a tragic example.

friend and so became doubly guilty, for Euripides condemns pederasty. Euripides' *Antigone*, which was later than Sophocles', used Haemon's love as the motive which controlled the plot. In the *Meleager* the love of the hero of the Calydonian boar-hunt for Atalante guided his destiny; of the *Scyrians* we know that it contained Deïdamea's confinement and showed Achilles torn between love and heroic glory.

To this group formed around the *Medea* and the *Hippolytus* we may add the *Hecabe* because of the loftiness of its passion. It belongs in the twenties and is to be dated before the *Suppliant Women*.[1] In this play particularly the question of unity is raised which returns in other Euripidean tragedies. Those who like to take the plays to pieces seem to find it very easy to detect two loosely connected parts. The first could be called the Polyxena tragedy, in which Hecabe's daughter is sacrificed at the tomb of Achilles, approaching her bitter doom with noble dignity. In the view of these critics the second part to be separated off is the Polydorus tragedy. The unhappy queen of Troy has sent off her last son Polydorus with some treasure to the Thracian king Polymestor, when the city of Troy still stood. But the boy was murdered for the sake of the gold, and when the Greeks, held up by contrary winds after the fall of Troy, are staying in the Thracian Chersonnese, some Trojan women, fellow-prisoners of Hecabe, find the corpse. Her grief is as boundless as her vengeance. She obtains Agamemnon's promise not to interfere and destroys Polymestor with a terrible ruse. She entices him to come to her tent where the women kill the children and blind the king.

No one will deny that two parts have been combined in this tragedy, but it should not be disputed that the poet has succeeded in making them into a unity. This is already apparent in the skilful and discreet manner in which he never allows the spatial separation of the two scenes of action to become an intrusive element. It is only when the various passages are critically analysed that one is aware of the link between Achilles' appearance and Polyxena's sacrifice with the funeral mound in the Troad, while the history of Polydorus is placed in the environment of the Thracian Chersonnese.[2] At the end of the plot Euripides has connected the parts with well-considered devices. The play opens with a prologue spoken by Polydorus' shade, anticipating the second part which follows the Polyxena section. Misgivings about the boy's fate occur in the first part (429), and the dead body is found by the servant whom Hecabe sent to the shore for water to wash Polyxena's corpse. But the internal unity effected by means of a well-planned climax carries more weight than these connecting passages. Polyxena's sacrifice is a terrible blow to this *mater dolorosa* of the ancient myths, but as yet the girl's noble attitude, admired even by the enemy, alleviates her suffering to some extent (591). But Hecabe is overcome by a wild despair when the sight of Polydorus' corpse deprives her of her last

---

[1] Opposing the late date assigned by SCHMID (3. 464): POHLENZ 2, 116 and LESKY, *Trag. Dichtung der Hell.* Gött. 1956, 170, 2.

[2] Cf. KL. JOERDEN, *Hinterszenischer Raum und ausserszenische Zeit.* Diss. Tübingen 1960 (typescr.), 231.

hope. After following her a long way along her *via dolorosa* we can understand why this weary old woman, whom we saw tottering on to the stage after Polydorus' prologue, turns into an avenging demon who gloats over the impotent raging of her victim. The *Hecabe* is not dominated by the forces of the soul as completely as the *Medea* or the *Hippolytus*; external events have a stronger influence, but in the end the flame of passion blazes with the same sinister violence.

The *Hecabe* is well-suited to serve as an example of an important development in Euripides' tragedy. The chorus, made up of captured Trojan women, is given only relatively short passages between the episodes. But this does not imply a decline of the lyrical element, it is the actors rather who now take far more of the lyrical parts than in the older tragedy. After Polydorus' shade has spoken at the beginning, we hear Hecabe's plaintive anapaests, followed by those of the parodos in which the chorus announces Polyxena's fate. This information produces a lament first sung by Hecabe alone and then in alternation with her daughter. The latter's monody concludes the extensive lyrical structure.

It is characteristic of Euripides, however, that in this play, which abounds in expressions of passionate emotions, there should occur also the dispassionate reasonings of the reflecting mind. Even though there is a strong lyrical element in it, the dialectical agon has been extended considerably. In the first part Hecabe faces Odysseus who tears Polyxena away from her, in the second she confronts the blinded Polymestor in a formal law-court session presided over by Agamemnon.

Hecabe's reasoning in lines 592 ff. is particularly characteristic. She has just received the news of her daughter's heroic death, upon which she launches forth into reflections whose excursive nature she herself underlines powerfully by the conclusion (603): unlike the fields which yield now good, now bad fruit, the nature of a noble man is unchangingly firm. But here this aristocratic conviction appears to be put to the question in a new way. What is the origin of this constancy of nature? Is it determined by the parents, or a result of upbringing? Euripides, who clearly speaks through Hecabe's mouth, is still in doubt here, but he will soon express himself decisively in favour of the new educational optimism. Hardly anywhere else is it so conspicuous that the problems which motivate Euripides are forced out in places where they achieve a curious effect.

By the very nature of Euripides' work his interpretation moves between widely separated extremes. One group follows A. W. Schlegel's lectures and points out one fault after another in the poet, meanwhile forgetting what Goethe told Eckermann,[1] that modern man should do this only in a kneeling position. Others cannot bear any blemish on their tragedian, continuing, mostly unconsciously, the onesided view of the new humanism with its overestimation of the poet.

The *Andromache* cannot be considered a masterpiece when viewed without prejudice. This was already the opinion of ancient critics, for remnants of a

---

[1] 28th March 1827.

hypothesis, which probably goes back to Aristophanes of Byzantium, relegate the play to the second rate. According to the scholium on line 445 the *Andromache* was never performed in Athens. Modern commentators have had Argos or the country of the Molossians in mind, but all that is conjecture. The same notice dates the play in the first years of the Peloponnesian war.

In the beginning we see a tableau which returns in several Euripidean tragedies,[1] some suppliants who have taken refuge at an altar to escape from their oppressors. Such plays open with a set scene and it is not easy to see how this was enacted on the ancient stage. A curtain was not used until much later and so it can only be supposed that the group was formed with the audience looking on.

The opening of the play shows Andromache, who has sought sanctuary at the altar of the shrine of Thetis in Pharsalia. In accordance with Euripides' technique her distress does not stop her at all from giving a lengthy exposition of the very complicated previous history. After Hector's death she fell to Neoptolemus, Achilles' son, as his share of the booty; he took her home to Thessaly, where she bore him a son. But Neoptolemus married Hermione, Menelaus' daughter, who remained childless. While the master of the house is at Delphi to settle a quarrel with Apollo, Hermione, together with her father Menelaus who has come from Sparta, seeks to ruin Andromache and her child. Menelaus is a stage villain with whose deplorable qualities the poet makes quite unconcealed anti-Spartan propaganda. His sinister plans are close to success, for the chorus of Phthian women can commiserate with Andromache but are unable to help her. Menelaus, however, has not counted on the strength which still lives in old Peleus, Neoptolemus' grandfather. He comes and inflicts on the venal Spartan king, and his country into the bargain, such a moral defeat that Menelaus leaves Hermione in the lurch and departs miserably. Now Andromache has been saved and the plot, introduced by her prologue, is finished. But the play is not nearly finished. In this first part a lament in elegiac distichs by Andromache (103) is noteworthy as a formal feature unexampled in the other surviving plays.

A second part follows which is joined to the first to a certain extent by the figure of Hermione, although it would be impossible to claim that it is an organic connection.[2] Remembering what she had wanted to perpetrate, Hermione shudders to think of her husband's return. Then Orestes arrives; he has prior claims to her and is Neoptolemus' bitter enemy. He has been on the look-out for a long time and now avails himself of the opportunity to carry off Hermione. A new scene brings on a messenger who relates how Neoptolemus has fallen a victim to an attack instigated by Orestes. This message is interpreted by many as if Orestes were to be imagined present in Delphi himself at the moment of the deed. This would cause great inconsistency in the chronology of the plot and charge the poet with extreme carelessness. It can be shown, however,[3] that the fault is with the modern commentators. Orestes prepared the assault with great

---

[1] On the motif of taking refuge at an altar H. STROHM, *Euripides.* Zet. 15, Munich 1957, 17.   [2] Otherwise J. C. KAMERBEEK, *Mnem.* 3rd ser. 11, 1942, 54.

[3] A. LESKY, 'Der Ablauf der Handlung in der Andr. des Eur.'. *Anz. Öst. Ak.* 1947, 99.

care in Delphi, but has already left at the time of its execution in order to fetch Hermione. Here too Euripides is very careful in the motivation of the details, although of course he cannot avoid every objection. Such care in the portrayal of the probable (πιθανόν) reveals an element of the domestication of tragedy. To emphasize the contrast we recall the immediate succession of the fire beacon and the return of the fleet in Aeschylus' *Agamemnon*.

The dirge in the concluding part of the play is ended by the appearance of Thetis. She brings the play to a close with joyful promises. Andromache's son will found the ruling house of the Molossians, but Peleus, made divine, will live with her in her palace of the sea; he will also see Achilles again who, as a hero, is living in the island of Leuce. If the play was really written for the Molossians, they could be satisfied with the splendour which surrounded their ruling family.

The violently anti-Spartan sentiment expressed in the drawing of Menelaus agrees with the composition of the play in the first years of the Peloponnesian War. The mood of this period has been detected in other plays and it has been attempted to mark off a patriotic period in the poet's work, for which particularly the *Heraclidae* and the *Suppliant Women* are summoned as witnesses. This is correct in so far that thoughts and sentiments of those years are no doubt of significance for the works mentioned, but Günther Zuntz has rightly pointed out that the general human problems of these plays should not be overlooked and that their connection with their time should not be sought in key figures and a mass of political allusions.

Zuntz has put forward many arguments why the *Heraclidae* should be dated in 430; it is certainly before 427. Up to then the Athenian public could be expected to believe in Eurystheus' (1032) prophecy about the protection which his dead body would grant to the land of Attica against the offspring of the Heraclidae.

This play also begins with a tableau at an altar. Heracles' children are fleeing from Eurystheus, their father's mortal enemy, ·through many countries and have now sought sanctuary at the altar of Zeus at Marathon. Athenian generosity exemplified in the king of the country, Demophon, and in the chorus of ancients assures them of this protection. The herald of Eurystheus, who appears as the representative of brutal force, is dismissed in a verbal contest in which Iolaus pleads the cause of the Heraclidae before the king, and the latter decides to use Athens' arms on behalf of the persecuted. The battle, in which Heracles' son Hyllus intervenes with auxiliary forces, leads to the victory of the good cause. Eurystheus is captured and executed.

Euripides brought vigorous movement into the simple plot with individual characters and themes. The connection of the parts is not always particularly firm, but the antithesis of might and right, so important to Greek thought, maintains its dominant position and ensures the inner cohesion of this play.

Iolaus, Heracles' old comrade-at-arms, is an ardent defender of justice. He could have stayed quietly on his estate, as he says himself in the prologue, but he accompanies the hunted children as a protector on their path of sorrows. Before the decisive battle the frail old man has a servant arm him, a scene which has grotesque features in our eyes, contrary to the poet's purpose. But the messenger reports the miraculous rejuvenation of the old man, who manages to capture Eurystheus with his own hands. Iolaus as the vanquisher of the arch-enemy was part of the tradition,[1] and here, as in many other cases, Euripides left it to his spectators whether they wished to assume an enlightened or a pious attitude.

The unyielding, self-sacrificing devotion of the old man is matched by that of a young woman, which, blazing forth like a bright flame, provides an effective contrast and complement. Before the battle the seers have demanded the sacrifice of a life; however Athens may be ready to help, it cannot offer one from its own ranks. Then one of Heracles' daughters – the later tradition calls her Macaria – stands forth to protect her relatives, ensuring victory through her sacrifice.

The end of the play is curious. After his capture Eurystheus is brought before Alcmene, Heracles' mother, who is fleeing together with her grandchildren. The Athenians plead for indulgence towards the captive, but Alcmene demands his death in a paroxysm of hatred. The result is a peculiar bit of trafficking; Alcmene is to have the prisoner executed, but will give up the body for inter-ment. Eurystheus acquiesces and in gratitude announces to the Athenians an oracle of Apollo, according to which his tomb will safeguard the land of Attica. This ending is not satisfactory, but in accordance with the poet's aim it has to perform a variety of functions. The question of the fate of prisoners of war was a subject of lively interest to all in times of hostilities and its treatment on the stage was bound to create a stir. But the manner of stressing various aspects showed the humane quality of Athens in this dramatic panegyric of the city in radiant brightness. And perhaps we divine the poet's intention further by assuming that his ending implies a sort of ironical twist. Among the persecuted, on behalf of whom the justice of humanity had to intervene, a voice is raised, Alcmene's, which brutally denies this justice to the erstwhile persecutor.

With this play a problem is connected which nowadays is mostly pushed quickly to one side. The carrying-out of Macaria's sacrifice is not mentioned with as much as a word after her exit. Line 821 cannot very well be related to it,[2] and if this were the case, it would be very upsetting. Furthermore the hypothesis speaks of homage paid to the girl, and this can be extracted from the surviving work only with a great deal of dexterity.[3] Stobaeus preserves some lines of verse the tradition of which is not entirely unequivocal, but which can be rejected for the *Heraclidae* only under special conditions.[4] Finally this play, with its 1055 lines, is the shortest of all surviving Euripidean plays. Wilamowitz[5] has advanced the thesis that the present *Heraclidae* is an abbreviated version for a later per-formance. None of the arguments put forward is conclusive and in view of the

---

[1] PIND. *Pyth.* 9. 79.   [2] ZUNTZ (*v. inf.*), 153.
[3] SCHMID, 3. 422. 3. 7. On the revision D. L. PAGE, *Actors' interpolations*. Oxf. 1934, 38. Opp. this esp. G. ZUNTZ, 'Is the Heraclidae mutilated?'. *Class. Quart.* 41, 1947, 46.
[4] Thus POHLENZ, 2. 145.
[5] *Herm.* 17, 1882, 337; now *Kl. Schr.* I. 82; cf. *Glaube der Hellenen* I. Berl. 1931, 298, 3.

wide range of Euripides' creative activity we must recognize that wide variety is possible. But it should not be denied that this case remains open to doubt.

The extent to which our notion of Euripides still lacks a firm basis becomes painfully clear in two analyses of the *Suppliant Women*, which was written at about the same time. In his book which appeared in 1955, Günther Zuntz interpreted the play as praise of Athenian humanity as well as evidence for a new foundation, rational and basically untragic, of norms which once had a firm footing in religious tradition. But one year earlier Gilbert Norwood had declared that the *Suppliant Women* in its present form was an accumulation of débris thrown together by a dunce. His theory that this sorry creature had combined parts of a play by Euripides with one by Moschion into an artificial and logically impossible whole will hardly find any adherents, but it shows what is still possible in Euripidean studies.

Our interpretation largely agrees with Zuntz's. The story of how Theseus successfully intervened so that the seven fallen before Thebes might be buried had already been treated by Aeschylus in his *Eleusinii*. The general mood in the early stages of the Peloponnesian War and the poet's personal contribution to the ancient Greek quest after justice in this world make it understandable that he selected this subject. The negotiations carried on with the Thebans after the battle of Delium over the surrender of the fallen (424, Thuc. 4. 97), can only have enhanced the interest in this subject, even though no reflection of historical facts must be looked for in the play. This context is to be rejected, if Zuntz is right in his conjecture that it was performed as early as the beginning of 424; others have thought of 421, but it is inadvisable to go back further.[1]

The uneasiness of many of the interpreters can largely be explained by the fact that Euripides – we should like to know how Aeschylus went about this – divested the mothers of the seven heroes and the heroes themselves of their mythical individuality so as to emphasize in this way the general human problem in full clarity. So when, at the beginning of the play, we see the mothers of the dead heroes with their servants at the altar of Demeter of Eleusis, we must not focus on Jocaste or any one else, but we have to understand the group of fifteen choreutae as the expression of a collective grief and a collective supplication. In the prologue Aethra, Theseus' mother, explains the pathetic group. And when Theseus arrives and refuses his support to Adrastus, the vanquished king of Argos, Aethra turns his glance from the hybris of the Argive expedition to the misery of the mothers who are begging for their sons' corpses. The first of the passages referring to contemporary events, which are specially emphasized in the play, occurs in Theseus' speech abusing Adrastus. The optimistic praise of human intelligence and human genius is directly reminiscent of Protagoras' myth of the origin of human culture.

Theseus has to defend his decision to help the suppliants first against the Theban herald who demands the expulsion of Adrastus on behalf of his city, and an agon ensues which, before the actual contest, sparks off a great and

[1] Cf. H. DILLER, *Gnom.* 32, 1960, 232 on the question whether the alliance between Athens and Argos of 420 should be taken into account for the chronology.

fundamental debate; the herald asked for the tyrant of the country and on Theseus' reply that he has come to a free city they begin an argument about monarchy and democracy. It is a historical paradox that the king of Athens should act as the founder and champion of the latter form of government. But examples are not lacking that the Athenian Theseus legends connected their hero in various ways with the victory of democracy.[1]

It was not simply Euripides' purpose to place on the stage in this Theseus a Pericles dressed up like a hero, but it would be wrong to deny that this propagandist of Athenian democracy was largely fashioned upon ideas of the time and also bears some of the features of the great statesman. In the years after his death his image inevitably appeared in a brighter light.

Like Demophon in the *Heraclidae*, Theseus has to match the contest of words with one of weapons. A messenger-speech reports how he enforces by battle the surrender of the bodies. And now the Eleusinian scene turns at the end into the place for the funeral rites. Like so much in Euripides it is characterized by means of an alternation of lyrically solemn and rationally precise spoken passages. The dirge of the chorus is followed by a funeral oration by Adrastus, which reflects in the art of the drama the actual custom of the Athenian funeral oration of which Gorgias, Thucydides, Hyperides and the probably genuine *Epitaphios* by Demosthenes give us examples. Here too the image of the gigantic figures of the heroic age as drawn by Aeschylus has dimmed completely; the poet's age expresses itself through the words of the orators, especially when, unlike Hecabe in the play of the same name, he professes (911) a boundless educational optimism.

After a choral lyric with renewed lament follows a monody of great solemnity by Evadne, the wife of the dead Capaneus. She wishes to follow her husband and after frenzied lyrical utterances she affirms her resolution in the stichomythia with her father Iphis. Then she throws herself on the pyre. Those who bear in mind the great importance in Euripides of voluntary sacrificial death and the fervour of passionate love will not need to think of Indian customs in order to understand this melodramatic effect.

This harsh scene is followed by mourning of a different nature. A secondary chorus of boys enters; the children of the dead bring in the urns and unite their lament with that of the old women in a renewed dirge which rounds off the whole complex of scenes. Adrastus takes his leave with a promise of Argive loyalty to Athens, but then Athena as the provident patroness of the city intervenes from the machine and demands that the Argives corroborate their promise with a solemnly sworn treaty. This also reflects the historical situation, for the role of Argos was important for Athens in all times of hostility with Sparta. This detail does not give any special help for the date of the play.

Athenian self-sacrificing devotion was also celebrated in the *Erechtheus*, which has been conjecturally attributed to the same trilogy as the *Suppliant Women*. The Athenian offered his own daughter up to the goddesses to fulfil an oracle in

---

[1] NORWOOD (*v. inf.*), 136, compiles the evidence himself. Cf. now A. E. RAUBITSCHEK, 'Demokratia'. *Hesperia* 31, 1962, 238.

the distress of war and found his own wife on his side in the acceptance of this heavy sacrifice. The *Theseus*,[1] which no doubt glorified Athens's national hero with splendour, was performed before 422. The Evadne theme of the *Suppliant Women* has a kinship with the *Protesilaus* which cannot be dated precisely. In this play Laodamia treasured in her room an image of her husband who had fallen before Troy. Her father had it burned, but the widow threw herself into the flames, as Evadne had done.

The *Heracles* occupies a special position in the work of Euripides. Its date can only be approximately set between 421 and 415. When there is no recourse to other aids, metre provides a clue to some extent for the chronology of Euripides' plays. Those whose dates are certain indicate that resolution within the iambic trimeter increased fairly steadily.[2] According to this reckoning the *Heracles* is close to the *Trojan Women* of the year 415; this agrees with the fact that it is the first of the surviving plays to show trochaic tetrameters.[3] The return to the metre of early tragedy is part of the archaizing traits of later Euripidean drama.

It is incomprehensible that this play has been grouped with those dealing with patriotism and politics! Admittedly at the end we meet a truly Athenian Theseus, humanitarian and enlightened, but his only part is to contribute towards the solution of a conflict which is on an entirely different level.

The first part of the play deals with the rescue in the nick of time of people in distress. While Heracles descends to the underworld to perform his most difficult labour, the usurper Lycus wants to annihilate the hero's kith and kin. His aged father Amphitryon, his wife Megara and the children, have taken refuge at the altar of Zeus. But Lycus, who defends his action as the expedient of common sense in an agon with Amphitryon, threatens the suppliants with fire. The chorus of Theban elders cannot help and Megara prepares herself to face death with her children in a way worthy of Heracles' wife. The hero arrives at the right moment to save them and to destroy the tyrant. Of the final scenes of this section we do not forget the one of Heracles entering the palace with his wife and children, of the little ones clinging to their father's clothes so that it is of no avail to ask them to let go (627).

While within Heracles is sacrificing to the gods, a new plot is being prepared, clearly marked as such by the prologue. Up above, i.e. on the theologeum, which we imagine to be on the roof of the skene, Iris, the messenger of the gods, appears with Lyssa, the demon of insanity, whom she sends into the house at the behest of Hera. A messenger-speech which stresses the pathological details with sinister precision, describes the hero's attack of frenzy in the course of which he kills the very wife and children whom he has just saved from death. Athena stuns him with a rock hurled by her, to prevent at least parricide.

---

[1] Chronology: Schol. Aristoph. *Wasps* 313. Bibl. in HERTER, *Rhein. Mus.* 91, 1942, 234.

[2] E. B. CEADEL, 'Resolved Feet in the Trimeter of Eur. and the Chronology of the Plays'. *Class. Quart.* 35, 1941, 66.

[3] Tables in W. KRIEG, *Phil.* 91, 1936, 43. W. M. CALDER III, *Class. Phil.* 55, 1960, 128 correctly opposes the attempt to utilize *Ox. Pap.* 24, 1957, 2400 for the chronology of the play.

Then he can be tied to a column and thus we see the hero when the palace gate is opened. When he wakes up in the middle of the destruction which he has wrought, we think of the other awakening of a hero struck with madness, shown by Sophocles in the *Ajax*. The way in which the path of the two poets separates here characterizes the beginning of a new way of thought, the change of the heroic notion of honour to a domestic enlightened one. After the realisation of what he has done in his deranged condition, the only way open to Ajax was death, and we saw with what composure he went to meet it. Heracles too sees at first no other possible way in which to react to what has happened. But Theseus, his friend, who has also once been saved by Heracles when sorely oppressed, manages to guide him on to another course which is now considered to be the better. Heracles' heroism will not be proved by casting away his life, but by suffering it to continue in spite of all his misery and distress. Leaning on Theseus, he starts upon the way to Athens which will offer him asylum.

However strongly the two parts of the play may be contrasted, no one could call it a complete separation. The two parts are connected, rather, by an antithesis of very great impact: the hero, radiant in the splendour of his deeds, the saviour of his dependants, is shown in the second part as the wretched, broken man of sorrows, who now needs his strength only to drag himself through a life of the deepest misery.

Occasionally a misinterpretation which originated with Wilamowitz, but was subsequently withdrawn by him, still emerges.[1] According to this the insanity arose out of Heracles' own soul, from the greatness of his heroism; the rumbling of the impending thunderstorm had already been heard in the first part. But the hero's wrath at Lycus' attempt is understandable enough in itself and can never support an interpretation which puts complex psychological suppositions in the way of our understanding of the play. By irrational forces this Heracles is dashed from the height of his vital power into the depth of his misery. He may crown the deeds which he performed in the service of mankind with the rescue of his family, but all his strength, his security and his happiness are shattered in the one moment when the destructive blow from the realm of something totally alien strikes him. In no other play was Euripides so close to Sophocles as in this, which once more, in the spirit of the truly tragic, brings us face to face with the nakedness and weakness of human existence.

Heracles' insanity and the murder of his wife and children was part of the legend. Here too Euripides made the inner structure of his play possible with a stroke of genius. While in the legend these events occurred before the labours which Heracles had to perform in the service of Eurystheus, the poet now advanced these to the end of his heroic career. In this way everything was given a new interrelation. Whereas previously Heracles atoned for his insane deeds through his achievements, now, placed at the end, they point to the tragic problems of all human greatness.

But even here Euripides is not Sophocles. No faith, secure in tradition, stands above all the riddles and all the cruelty of life; here the call is not sounded, as at

---

[1] *D. Lit. Zeit.* 1926, 853; now *Kl. Schr.* 1. 466.

the end of the *Trachinian Women*: 'nothing of this which is not Zeus'. On the contrary, the poet speaks suddenly from the mask of his hero; in the attitude of a Xenophanes he denies the idle tales of bards about the immortals' adultery and hostility and raises before us an image of a god who has no wants outside himself (1345). The whole play was motivated by Hera's wrath and in perplexity we ask whether the poet does not invalidate the presuppositions of his own work by such criticism. It is understandable that the conclusion was reached that Euripides wanted to carry the subject of his play *ad absurdum*.[1] Actually we have to admit a paradox which necessarily arose from the constraint imposed on Euripides' work by his subject matter and its creator's intellect, which had outgrown the mythical tradition.

The grand form of the Aeschylean trilogy, covering one subject, had long been abandoned. This did not, however, stop the three tragedies performed together from being thematically connected on occasion, although we cannot examine the extent of this connection in any of the surviving examples. It cannot have been very close in the trilogy which Euripides staged in 415. The first play, the *Alexander*,[2] dealt with Paris. Because of evil prophecies his parents had exposed him on Mount Ida, where shepherds nourished him. He now comes to Troy and wins all the prizes in the games. His next-of-kin want to kill him, but recognition of Paris prevents the deed and he is received in the city whose destroyer he is to be. Considerable remnants, especially in some Strasbourg papyri, make it possible to reconstruct the play almost completely.

We know less about the second play, *Palamedes*. Earlier we learnt of the speech for the defence which Gorgias wrote for the inventive hero whom his rival Odysseus destroyed with an evil intrigue. All three of the great Attic tragedians wrote plays on Palamedes.

The *Trojan Women*, the third surviving play, is very close to the *Hecabe* in content. But whereas in the latter play the poet successfully attempted to dove-tail the pieces together, in the *Trojan Women* he made the succession of events into a principle of construction. And whereas in the *Hecabe* the outbreak of annihilating passion was being prepared and accomplished, the *Trojan Women* is wholly given over to suffering, the suffering brought upon people by war.

In this play Hecabe is also the central figure. In her lyrics and those of her fellow-captives the lament for their loss gushes forth in broad streams, but also fear of suffering yet to come. In comparison with the previous treatment of the theme in the *Hecabe*, Polyxena's sacrifice is only indicated, but otherwise almost everything that the tradition had to report of distress and misery has been included in the play. The herald of the Greeks, Talthybius, whose own heart is touched by the misery of the prisoners, comes and allots the women as slaves to their new masters. Cassandra, brandishing her torch, ecstatically sings her own bridal hymn. She has been assigned to Agamemnon and knows what is going to happen. Then little Astyanax is torn away from Andromache, who is Neoptolemus's share of the plunder, in order to be hurled from one of the

---

[1] Thus *inter alios* GREENWOOD (*v. inf.*).

[2] PAGE, *Greek Lit. Pap.* 1950, 54, with bibl. BR. SNELL, *Herm.* E 5, 1937, is still important.

towers of Troy. It was Odysseus' advice not to let the future avenger of Troy live. The poet has gathered all his resources in the final scene. Then the signal is given for setting sail and while in the background Troy goes up in flames, the women are led to the ships to serve as slaves in foreign lands.

But Euripides did not only depict the distress of the victims. We observe in this play how much he was concerned to proclaim the profound truth that the demon of war strikes the victor too with an even more frightful scourge. The prologue of the play is spoken by Poseidon, who is joined by Athena, and in the dialogue of the two gods the catastrophe is announced which is to destroy the Greek fleet on the homeward voyage and to strew the waves of the Aegean with corpses. And later there emerges from Cassandra's prophecy the image of future sufferings for the victors, who caused boundless misery for the sake of one adulteress. In the agon scene in the final part of the play the great war of Greek mythology which is sometimes celebrated elsewhere by Euripides as the greatest achievement of his nation, is shown in a curious light. Menelaus enters with Helen whom he is holding in a firm grip, like a prisoner. The faithless woman and Hecabe face each other in a kind of law-court scene in which both parties use all the tricks of forensic oratory. Particularly Helen's defence, which is based entirely on the myth of Paris' judgment and the influence of Aphrodite, gives a striking example of the sport with the mythical tradition which was inevitable when it was no longer taken seriously. Menelaus does proclaim that he will kill Helen when he is home, but the Athenians knew their Homer and were well aware that the weakling succumbed again to the charms of the beautiful woman, and held her, who was most guilty of the great evil, in honour in his palace in Sparta.

Before Hecabe enters into the debate, she pronounces a prayer which is one of the most impressive testimonies that the poet was seeking a new conception of the divine (884): 'You who bear the earth and are enthroned on the earth, whoever you may be, hard to reach for knowledge, Zeus, whether law of nature or man's intelligence, to you I pray: walking noiselessly you lead man's destiny to the just end.' The ancient form of the hymn of invocation is still there in its basic traits, we also hear the same formula of groping search as in the hymn to Zeus in Aeschylus' *Agamemnon*. But how the content has changed! Here, in these few lines, the intellectual labour of the Ionian thinkers is combined with the personal searching of the deeply stirred poet.

Euripides put his poem of the misery of war on the Athenian stage in 415. This was the time in which Athens' yearning for power reached far beyond the confines of the Aegean. In the summer of this year the fleet against Sicily put to sea. It has often been said with justice that in this year the poet, deeply concerned, placed before the eyes of the Athenians collected in the theatre of Dionysus an image of war in its full horror.

In later plays of Euripides', subjects from the myths concerning the Atridae are more frequent. According to Schol. Aristoph. *Ach.* 433 he wrote a *Thyestes* even before 425. The *Electra* has long been dated in the early part of 413. The Dioscuri, who appear as the *dei ex machina*, speak of their cares for the ships in the Sicilian waters, and it was the obvious thing to link this with the auxiliary fleet which at this time was sailing from Athens to Sicily. It still does not seem easy to exclude the possibility of a topical reference, but we cannot overlook the arguments, mainly derived from the metre, which Zuntz has advanced to defend an earlier date of the play between the *Hicetides* and the *Trojan Women*.[1]

The old question of the chronological relation of Sophocles' *Electra* with that of Euripides is still a desperate problem.[2] The extent of the controversies and the extreme subtlety of the arguments are evidence that no useful starting-points are available and that we shall have to be satisfied with the realisation that two great poets treated the same subject within a very short time in a totally different manner. Even if the early date of Euripides' *Electra* can be upheld, its priority is not assured, since there is considerable latitude for the dating of Sophocles' play.

Euripides' *Electra* is indeed completely different in conception. Just as in other cases links can be observed between Euripides and the oldest of the three tragedians, he agrees here also with Aeschylus in that the problem of matricide is stressed, whereas Sophocles had other aims. Of course, Euripides' notion of the conflict is as remote from that of Aeschylus as only the world of a veteran of Marathon can be from one who had learnt to doubt tradition under the influence of the sophists.

Aeschylus' *Choephoroe* was enacted in Argos, Sophocles' *Electra* in Mycenae, but Euripides makes Agamemnon's daughter await the day of vengeance on a farm at the borders of the Argive land. To prevent her giving birth to a dangerous avenger, Aegisthus has married her to a poor man, though of noble birth, who now has to earn his livelihood with the labour of his hands.

By this change of scene Euripides gained much for his plot, but in another direction he also made vigorous use of the new situation. The poor farmer, who does not touch Electra and attempts to soothe her suffering with deep understanding, is one of those figures in which the poet shows the break-through of new values. Ancient barriers have been pulled down and in Euripides we repeatedly[3] encounter the slave whose unfree body conceals a noble soul.

In comparison with Aeschylus, Euripides has artistically enhanced both the management of the recognition of brother and sister, and of the assault on the reigning couple, not least through the spatial separation of the individual characters. There are doubts[4] whether the lines with the notorious criticism of Aeschylus' recognition scene (518–544) are really by Euripides. The introduction of Agamemnon's old servant, who lives at some distance from Electra as a shepherd, is very effective. When Orestes and Pylades approach Electra's farm

---

[1] *The Political Plays of Eur.* Manchester 1955, 67; his objection against the use of 1278 ff. as an anticipation of the *Helen* is certainly correct. On the earlier date also K. MATTHIESSEN, *Aufbau und Datierung der El., der Taur. Iph. und der Hel. des Eur.* Diss. Hamb. 1961 (typescr.), 195, and H.-J. NEWIGER, *Herm.* 89, 1961, 427.

[2] Bibl. in POHLENZ, 2, 127, who himself gives precedence to Eur.

[3] Passages in WILH. NESTLE, *Eur., der Dichter der griech. Aufklärung.* Stuttg. 1901, 357.

[4] Cf. p. 260, n. 1.

and are examining the situation, she sends to the old man for some foodstuffs in order to give her guests some entertainment. He comes and brings about the recognition through unmistakable tokens – he himself once concealed Orestes. Now the plan is formed and carried out step by step. As in Aeschylus, Aegisthus falls first; Orestes kills him at a rural sacrifice. Clytemnestra, however, is lured to the farm with the pretence that Electra has borne a child. In the final analysis the agon between mother and daughter emerges from the same situation as in the corresponding scene in Sophocles, but a profound difference has been effected through the delineation of Clytemnestra. Her crime cannot be overlooked, but she has saved Electra from the death which Aegisthus had planned for her; she now has forbearance with her daughter's harsh words, she has learnt regret and in accents of unutterable weariness she affirms that her deeds have not given her much happiness. That is the woman whom Electra leads into the house to be slaughtered.

When the murder has been done, the fire of passion which blazed especially in Electra is extinguished in horror. In the kommos of brother and sister we hear two people break down under the burden of their deed, a deed which ought never to have been done. Already here Euripides has passed judgment on the myth of Orestes' matricide, and he does it once more in plain words through the lips of the Dioscuri, who at the end lead events into their traditional course. Electra will marry Pylades and Orestes will find redemption before the Areopagus. To this extent the Athenian audience had to be placated, but it was the poet's concern to state through the lips of the divine twins that Clytemnestra had paid the just penalty but that Orestes had not committed a just act. The wise god of Delphi had commanded unwisely. Where for Aeschylus the problem was profound, but completely contained in his religious thought, Euripides sees only the intolerable character of a myth which turns a son's murder weapons against his own mother. His *Electra* aims above all at being a dramatic work of art and not simply a manifesto of an enlightened protest, but it implies this protest and has made it part of the work. It is right that through this the presuppositions of the whole work are put to the question, and in this realization we recognize once again the profound antinomy which pervades the work of this tragedian.

In this play the chorus of Electra's neighbours is of little significance. An invitation to a feast is the motivation for their entrance, and what they sing is little more than an insertion to separate the episodes. This applies particularly to the lyric 432 ff. with the description of Achilles' armour forged by Hephaestus and the story of how the Nereids brought it to his home in Thessaly; it is an impressive example of the lyrics of the later plays with purely narrative contents which Walther Krantz[1] compared, as dithyrambic stasima, with Bacchylides' dithyrambs.

The *Helen* forms a strongpoint in the chronology of Euripides' plays. We know from two scholia on Aristoph. (*Thesm.* 1012 and 1060) that it was performed in 412 together with the *Andromeda*. This firm date is doubly

[1] *Stasimon*, Berl. 1933, 254.

valuable, since at the same time it fixes chronologically a whole group of Euripides' plays which belong together in form and content.

Already in the *Electra* the succession of recognition and intrigue (anagnorisis and mechanema) had formed the scaffolding of the plot. But while there a serious problem had been at the back of all this, now the elements mentioned become largely independent and dominate the whole play.[1]

In his *Palinode* Stesichorus had sung that only a phantom of Helen came to Troy, and Herodotus (2. 112) knew a story of her sojourn in Egypt. In Euripides' play we find Helen there, just at the time when Menelaus is wrecked on the coast of Egypt on the voyage home with the phantom image of his wife, for whose sake Troy had to fall. Helen's protector, old king Proteus, is dead, and his son Theoclymenus has driven her to his tomb with his violent wooing. There she speaks the prologue, which is especially necessary in view of the complex background of this play. Next Teucer enters, who is on his way to Cyprus; he thrusts her even deeper into misery. Together with other bad news he also brings the message that Menelaus is dead. After a lengthy lament, in which the women of the chorus participate, Helen goes with them to the palace to enquire from the king's sister, Theonoe, who has the gift of prophecy, about her husband's fate. This is one of the rare occasions when the stage becomes empty again after the chorus' parodos. This affords Menelaus, upon his entrance, the opportunity to explain his situation in a new prologue. When Helen, who has been made more hopeful by Theonoe, enters again with the chorus, the anagnorisis is developed, which, passing through various stages, removes the couple's suspicion and doubts.

But it is a reunion amidst distress and danger. The king threatens all strangers with death, and so the husband of Helen can least of all hope for consideration. Much depends on Theonoe; she is prevailed upon to keep silent in a long scene of persuasive reasoning which in form resembles the customary agon, and the way is open to plan for their rescue. As is the rule in plays of this nature, female guile finds the solution. Menelaus is to act before Theoclymenus as the messenger of his own death; then Helen will ask the king for permission to perform a sacrifice for her dead husband at sea and once they have a ship it will be used to flee home. The plan is successful and Theoclymenus has to learn from a messenger how Greek wit won the day over barbarian clumsiness. When in his rage he first wants to hit out at Theonoe to avenge himself, he is stopped by the Dioscuri. They explain to him that these things had been ordained by fate and so persuade him to acquiesce.

Is the *Helen* a tragedy? This question can easily give rise to confusion unless the various possibilities of limiting the idea are given consideration. A Greek from the poet's own time would not have understood it. To him a play with a subject from the myths, performed at the festival of Dionysus, was a tragedy as a matter of course. But things appear in a different light if we apply modern tenets of the tragic; now in the discussion of the *Oresteia* we defended the

[1] F. SOLMSEN, 'Zur Gestaltung des Intriguen-motivs in den Trag. des Soph. und Eur.'. *Phil.* 87, 1932, 1. Id. 'Eur. Ion im Vergleich mit anderen Trag.'. *Herm.* 69, 1934, 390.

conviction that the tragic in drama is not unconditionally connected with eventual death, but that it is rather tragic situations within the play which justify its definition as tragedy in our sense, if these situations are imbued with the truly tragic which penetrates to the roots of human existence. But this is no longer the case in a play like the *Helen*. Here man neither faces recognizable divine forces, nor has he to fulfil a destiny which comes to him from another world, nor does his remoteness from the divine, his being exposed to the irrational, become a tragic problem. The gods still act, and in the *Helen* we even hear that a quarrel between Hera and Aphrodite is very important for the fate of the couple, but all this has no bearing on the essence of the world in which these people plan and dare, struggle and win. A new controlling force is becoming visible behind all this, chance, which as Tyche dominates the plays of New Comedy. It has often been stated that with Euripides' later plays like the *Helen* we are on the way to the domestic drama, to the comedy of Menander. Earlier we characterized two elements as anagnorisis and mechanema, which here, as later, control the plot, and we shall later have an opportunity to point out parallel themes, among which such as Menander himself stresses with mischievous playfulness.

Of no less importance, however, is the similarity in another field. Menander would not have much meaning for us if the invention of complicated plots with seduced maidens, exposed children and cunningly executed intrigues were all that he had to offer. He still charms us in his plays especially with his portrayal of people who answer the whims of Tyche with their suffering, their hopes, their plans and their happiness. We have no wish to deny that in spite of the affinity of subject matter, the world of the later Euripidean tragedy is still something different from that of the lower middle-class Athens of New Comedy. But basically it is also in the latter that these rare events, these recognitions and rescues only occur to show us man and to let us hear a new wealth of accents of sorrow and yearning, despair and joy.

Nevertheless the *Helen* does claim a special place in Euripides' œuvre by virtue of the vivaciousness of this fairy-tale atmosphere and whimsical quality of this play, a quality which the poet achieved in none of his other works. Günther Zuntz[1] subtly remarked on its kinship with the *Tempest*, *The Magic Flute* or *Ariadne auf Naxos*. With the usual reservations to which such comparisons are subject, the operatic quality of presentation is excellently expressed.

Occasionally Euripides used the scheme of a plot which had proved to be effective once more within a short time. The plot of *Iphigenia in Tauris*[2] is mainly parallel with that of the *Helen*, although it is not possible to decide the relative chronology of the plays definitely.[3] In both two people find each other in a distant inhospitable land and have to bring off a rescue with guile and

---

[1] In the work mentioned in the bibl. on the play, p. 226.

[2] PLATNAUER states correctly in his ed. (V, 1) that *Iph. in Tauris* is a faulty rendering of the title 'Ἰφ. ἡ ἐν Ταύροις.

[3] W. LUDWIG, *Sapheneia*. Diss. Tübingen 1954, 120 argues in favour of the priority of the *Iphigenia*.

courage. The similarity goes even so far in one single passage, the song of joy of the reunited people, that in both plays the number of lines and several phrases agree.

Goethe's splendid creation was a reason for many to devaluate Euripides, and the Greeks generally with him at the same time, but this was the last thing the author had in mind. When such comparisons are made, Iphigenia, lying and cheating with consummate skill, cuts a poor figure beside the noble creation of the later writer. As if it were permissible to compare the value of two works which have nothing in common except the background of the subject! One Greek tragedian has also given impressive life to the noble man who cannot bear untruth, Sophocles in his *Philoctetes*. But Euripides' *Iphigenia* is a play about the rescue of two people of the same kin from a world full of· barbarian brutality.

A theme frequently used by Euripides is put into action before the recognition, so that its effect is enhanced: a hostile fate threatens to make people who are most closely linked by nature into one another's murderers. Carried off by Artemis from the sacrifice in Aulis, Iphigenia is living in the land of the Taurians as the goddess' priestess. A savage custom demands the blood of strangers for the goddess, and Iphigenia has to perform the consecration of the victims. Orestes is still being persecuted by some of the Erinyes even after the verdict of the Areopagus and is ordered by Apollo to bring the statue of Taurian Artemis to Attica. Pylades accompanies him also in this dangerous adventure. Iphigenia is introduced in her prologue, Orestes is shown first when the young men are approaching the temple to spy out the land. The chorus of captive Greek maidens is of little importance, but with their fine lyrics which sing of their yearning for home they provide a background to Iphigenia's longing for Argos and her kin. In the first of the two messenger-speeches of this play – both are masterpieces of Euripides' narrative art – a shepherd reports that an attack of frenzy of Orestes has led to the capture of the two friends. They will now die as victims at the goddess's altar. The anagnorisis, which won Aristotle's praise (*Poet.* 16. 1455 a) has been particularly skilfully contrived. One of the friends whom Iphigenia wants to save is to take a letter home for her. In an ingeniously entangled exchange of words the commission to deliver the message turns out to be the means of recognition. Their joy is followed by careful planning in a scene which very clearly demonstrates a new aspect of these plays. Iphigenia wants to bring about her brother's rescue even at the cost of her own. But Orestes can only think of joint rescue or death together with his sister. In the same way Helen advised her husband to flee from Egypt without her, and he too wanted to share either return home or death with her. The characters of these plays lack the grandly heroic attitude of the Sophoclean figures, but they win our sympathy through moving gestures of generosity, devotion and loyalty.

Feminine guile finds once again the saving plan; they pretend to Thoas, the barbarian king, that a purification of the goddess's statue and of the prisoners is necessary and must be done at the beach. The second messenger-speech relates the dramatic way in which they fight their way out in the ship which had brought Orestes and Pylades.

Athena is the *dea ex machina*, but she performs this function under peculiar circumstances. The three conspirators are already in the ship with the statue and under way when they are carried back to the land by a wave. This new peril, upon which Thoas pounces at once, has been inserted only to motivate Athena's appearance, which means that the function of the *deus ex machina* is not merely to untie the knot. The foundation of a cult by the god at the end of the play was at least of equal importance. However far Euripides may have followed his own course in the play, at its conclusion he sets it within the framework of the cults which his audience knew and loved. In the present case it is the worship of Artemis in Halae and Brauron which is founded by the goddess.[1]

While in the three plays just discussed Euripides employed recognition and intrigue with a regularity which threatened to become a pattern, in the *Ion* he produced an elaborately entangled play, probably the finest of his tyche-dramas. Nowhere is it made as clear how much the poet was concerned in dramas of this kind to strike the many notes with which he touches the human heart. It must also be admitted that this kind of emotion is worlds apart from the shock with which the *Oresteia* and the *Oedipus* send us home.

Once upon a time Apollo had enjoyed the love of Erechtheus' daughter Creusa on the Acropolis. Hermes, who speaks the prologue, was commissioned by him to take her child to Delphi, where the boy Ion grows up in the pious surroundings of temple service. Creusa, however, is given to Xuthus, who is the ruling king of Athens. Since the marriage remains childless, the couple go to Delphi, Creusa accompanied by her serving women, who form the chorus. Their first song, which follows upon a monody of Ion's, is noteworthy in that its subject is the works of art on the temple of Apollo. In a scene of the most subtle nuances mother and son meet and discuss their fates in veiled and allusive terms: the one who grew up without a mother and the woman whose child had been taken from her.

Xuthus asks the god about his childlessness, and the latter commences a subtly, or rather too subtly – as will soon appear – contrived deception. Through an oracle he passes Ion on to Xuthus as his son, and the king, full of joy, believes the oracle, for he can remember adventures of which Ion could well be a reminder. He is to go and live in the palace in Athens, but not at once as the king's son, to spare Creusa. Then she flies into the wildest passion. She had to lose her own child and now she is supposed to watch the bastard with title and honour in her house! From her bitterness grows the plan to murder Ion, which she discusses with her father's old pedagogue who is going to carry it out. But we learn from the messenger-speech which this time, contrary to the custom, is taken over by

---

[1] A. SPIRA, *Untersuchungen zum deus ex machina bei Soph. und Eur.* Diss. Frankfurt. Kall-münz, 1960, makes the noteworthy attempt to draw the *deus ex machina* back into the collective interpretation of the dramas. For Sophocles this is much more successful than for Euripides. In cases like the *Iph. Taur.* it should not be overlooked that the foundation of the cult is rather like an appendix.

the chorus, that the attempt to kill Ion at the banquet with poisoned wine has miscarried. Through the pedagogue's confession Creusa has been revealed as the originator and she is now to be executed. Threatened by Ion she flees to the altar; then the Pythia brings the little chest in which the child was once exposed with various objects and the mother and son recognize each other with the aid of these things which later in New Comedy are to play their typical role. At the end Athena comes on to make some arrangements which ensure a satisfactory finish to the further events.

It will not be wrong to date the *Ion* soon after the *Helen*. The tested procedures of the tyche-plays have been employed here with consummate skill. The poet's stroke of elevating Ion so high and moreover making Erechtheus' daughter the origin of all the Greek tribes should also be understood within this time when probably few people were thinking of the collapse of Athenian power, for according to Athena's prophecy she was yet to become through Xuthus the mother of Dorus and Achaeus.

This play once more raises the problem of how Euripides viewed the gods of the tradition. It has been pointed out that after all Apollo does put everything properly in order and therefore appears to be vindicated in his wisdom and providence. But this does not yet touch upon the poet's position with regard to these problems. Athena's speech especially appears in the twilight which lies over Euripides' world of gods. The pious Athenian could look with astonishment at the appearance of the patron goddess and be pleased with her prudence. But any one who looked more closely could not help noticing the blemishes on this splendour. How deplorably the great god of Delphi shows up who does not want to appear in person before mortals, because they might say all sorts of bitter things to him (1157)! But the most striking part is that the god has made a palpable miscalculation; it had been so well thought out that the deceived Xuthus was to take Ion into his house, who was not to find his mother until he was there. Creusa's passion spoiled the plan and the whole business narrowly escaped turning out badly. So gods also have to take the annoying tricks of Tyche into account – not a grand fate which can also bend their will, but the whims of peevish chance which cross their not quite honest plans. However, Athene industriously goes on elaborating her brother's projects; it will be better to leave Xuthus in the dark about the actual state of affairs.

In the *Ion* a number of themes has been combined which Euripides has frequently utilized elsewhere. In the *Aegeus*, which preceded the *Medea*, the machinations of the Colchian persuaded the king to plan the killing of Theseus on his return home, but then father and son recognize each other. In the *Alexander* it was a whim of chance which made Paris nearly die at the hands of his kinsmen. Similarly in the *Cresphontes* the hero was nearly killed by his own mother, because in the course of the plot he pretended to be his own murderer. The plot of the *Antiope*[1] is clear to a certain extent. The play is chronologically close to the *Ion*, for the scholium *Ran.* 53 numbers it with the *Hypsipyle* and the *Phoenician Women* as a play which was only a little earlier than the *Frogs* and it

---

[1] PAGE (cf. p. 382, n. 2), 60 with bibl.

has to be dated later than the *Andromeda* which was performed in 412. Here Antiope flees from the evil Dirce who wants to have her gored by a bull; she comes to Amphion and Zethus whom she once bore to Zeus. The recognition brought about Antiope's rescue and Dirce's just punishment. This play was noteworthy because it revealed a break between the two Theban Dioscuri, brought about by the sophistic movement; Amphion and Zethus opposed each other as the representatives of the contemplative and the active life, of the θεωρητικός and the πρακτικὸς βίος, like Epimetheus and Prometheus in Goethe's *Pandora*.

The murder of kinsmen became frightful reality in the *Ino*. Themisto wants to kill the children of Ino who, as the former wife of Athamas, used to have her position; she orders that her own children are to be given white covers, but those of Ino black ones. The opposite is done, and at night Themisto strikes her own children with a deadly blow.

With the proviso that in this sort of survey of lost plays we can only give some information about subject matter, and not of internal structure, we mention a few more plays which dealt with the carrying off of girls, secret birth and recognition of children, all of them themes on which New Comedy subsisted later.

There is Melanippe, who bore Poseidon twins. Euripides treated her fate in two plays. In the *Wise Melanippe* (M. ἡ σοφή) the heroine fights for the life of her children who had been concealed in a cowshed and were found there. The *Captive Melanippe* (M. ἡ δεσμῶτις) related how Melanippe, blinded and locked up by her father, was saved after many complications by her sons.[1] The *Alope*, which is again concerned with an exposed and found child of Poseidon's, presents thematic parallels with these two plays; so does the *Hypsipyle*,[2] whose late date we ascertained through the scholium to Aristoph. *Ran.* 53. Here the twin sons, whom Hypsipyle had conceived from Jason during his stay in Lemnos, rescue their mother from a distressing situation into which she had come through the death of a child of which she had to take care.

The *Danae* also dealt with the fate of a mortal woman over whom a god's love brought suffering. In the *Auge*, however, it was Heracles who at a nocturnal banquet (once more New Comedy presents itself for comparison) makes the priestess of Athena pregnant. The play contained (fr. 266) a protest, typical of the enlightenment, against the notion that a confinement could pollute the house of a goddess who was not unwilling to accept the armour of the fallen as dedicatory offerings.

The stepmother theme, which also played a part in the *Ion*, controlled the plot of the *Phrixus*. Here Ino invents an oracle demanding the sacrifice of her stepson for a failure of the crop, caused by Ino herself by baking the seed-corn. He showed his kinship with the devoted characters of other plays by being prepared to sacrifice his life when the deception came to light. Ino was to fall but then Dionysus appeared as the *deus ex machina* and saved her.

---

[1] On the two Melanippe plays PAGE (*v. sup.*), 108. 116.

[2] PAGE (*v. sup.*), 76.

The *Phoenissae* is among the plays which the scholium mentioned above relegates to 412. It was performed together with the *Oenomaus* and the *Chrysippus*. The mutilated hypothesis of Aristophanes of Byzantium appears to indicate a certain affinity of contents of the three plays, but its extent is uncertain.

If it is permissible to draw an inference from the few plays which survive from the poet's last Athenian period, he seems to have attempted to crowd an increasingly large quantity of subject matter into the framework of the plot, which he makes as exciting as possible. After Jocasta's introductory prologue the Homeric theme of watching the battle from the wall has been skilfully transferred to Antigone, who can thus carry on with the exposition and extend our understanding of the situation beyond the stage. The *Phoenissae* has an agon scene with particularly strong accents. At the call of his mother, Polynices comes into the city for the final negotiations about the sharing of the kingship. In spite of their names, which had been coined by the ancient legend, the nature of the two brothers has been altered in the sense of a 'salvation' of Polynices, who is ready for a conciliation, suffering as he does at being far from his country, which makes him bear the fate of an exile which was only too familiar to the poet's contemporaries; Eteocles, however, has a boundless lust for power, the sort of man whom the extremists among the sophists loved to depict as the true son of nature. The negotiations fail and Polynices goes to the Argive army to lead it against his native city. Eteocles, counselled by his uncle Creon, necessarily assumes the role of the defender of Thebes, but this does not imply a change of personality or the genuine tragedy of double motivation as in Aeschylus' *Seven Against Thebes*. Tiresias is also consulted and he advises Creon that Thebes can only be saved through the sacrifice of his son Menoeceus. Creon wants to save the boy and tells him to flee to Delphi. But Menoeceus is obedient to the oracle and voluntarily sacrifices his life. Two messenger-speeches conclude the threads of the plot with which the first part opened. The one describes how the assault of the Seven failed, but that the hostile brothers are preparing for the decisive combat. The second recounts how the brothers slew each other and Jocasta killed herself over their corpses. The dying Polynices asks to be buried in Thebes and this anticipates future events; his words of love for his brother are a piece of Euripidean stagecraft which is far removed from the harshness of the older tragedy.

But the play is not yet ended. Creon, as Thebes' new ruler, decrees Oedipus' exile and forbids Polynices to be buried in Theban soil. Then Antigone approaches. She refuses to accept the prohibition of burial and promises to bury her brother with her own hands. She declares that her betrothal to Haemon, Creon's son, is dissolved and wants to follow her father in his wretchedness.

The lyrics of the chorus which form a kind of cycle of the Theban myths, have been skilfully fitted into the *Phoenissae*. The chorus are Phoenician slave-women who are travelling to Delphi; this curious fact is possibly due to the tendency to gain effect by means of the unusual.

The assessment of this play, which is among those read most and which maintained its place in Byzantine schools alongside the *Hecabe* and the *Orestes*, has been a bone of violent contention. The hypothesis of a later date is evidence of the ancient critical opinion that it owed its effect on the stage to the range of themes it comprised, but that it contained parts which had been inserted without any organic connection. More recently this judgment has been opposed with an attempt[1] to interpret it as a play of the Theban *polis* and to assign to it a compact and organic composition around this centre. And the fate of Thebes must indeed be considered the framework within which everything happens, but it still makes a difference whether such a framework can only be recognized or whether the separate parts are as closely connected as is the case in Sophocles' best plays which are witnesses of the mature classical period. Much of the traditional criticism of Euripides indubitably requires reconsideration, but it would be a mistake to want to interpret away the lack of balance both in his work as a whole and in the individual plays.

Special problems are connected with the ending of the *Phoenissae*. Antigone's proclamation that she is going to bury Polynices in opposition to the prohibition, and her departure as the companion of her blind father in his hardship cannot be readily harmonized. It is at least permissible to enquire what really happened to Polynices. Consequently it has been attempted[2] to cut out the burial theme and to assign the relevant lines to a later revision. Nevertheless it is hazardous to remove from a play whose inclination towards abundance of subject matter was already observed by ancient criticism, a theme which contributes to this abundance in the concluding portion, even if it may upset the logical balance. Moreover, since Sophocles the burial theme had been so closely allied with Antigone that it is difficult to imagine Euripides giving up this feature. The last few lines, approximately from 1737 or 1742 onward, however, have justly been suspected as spurious. The Strasbourg papyrus of tragic lyrics[3] has not taken this passage into consideration.

Euripides' *Antigone* has been mentioned earlier (p. 373). He also wrote an *Oedipus*, probably at a later date to judge from the long trochaic lines. Its contents differed greatly from that of Sophocles, although we only know that some servants blinded Oedipus.[4]

The *Orestes*, of 408, is the last play which we know to have been performed in Athens before the poet's departure for Macedon. It is not a coincidence that the ancient criticism of the play, as it has been preserved in the hypothesis, is comparable with the one on the *Phoenissae*. The composition of the later play is more compact, but nevertheless the tendency towards animating the plot by means of repeated new twists can be clearly discerned. These twists made it a hit on the stage. We connect the relevant observations of the hypothesis with the repeat performances which occurred frequently of Euripides' plays; for the *Orestes* there is epigraphical evidence of such a performance in the year 341

[1] RIEMENSCHNEIDER and LUDWIG (both *v. inf.*).
[2] W. H. FRIEDRICH, 'Prolegomena zu den Phoin.'. *Herm.* 74, 1939, 265.
[3] BR. SNELL, *Herm.* E 5, 1937, 69.
[4] L. DEUBNER, 'Ödipusprobleme'. *Sitzb. Berl.* 1942/4, 19 is a doubtful attempt to derive the contents of the play from the Pisander scholium on *Phoen.* 1760.

(IG II/III 2nd ed. no. 2320). Beside this acknowledgment we read the opinion that this play shows only bad characters with the exception of Pylades. This had been repeated for a long time, until a fresh start was made with the attempt[1] to enquire into what the poet really had in mind here. It certainly was not possible for him to make Orestes into a hero whom we follow with sympathy, although the guilt for the matricide in the meaning of the *Electra* falls heavily on Apollo. Nor are the means with which the three people are fighting for their lives always of such a kind as to evoke the impression of lofty sentiments. But this battle, which is a matter of life and death, is directed against a world full of venal baseness and merciless malice. Because of this and the way in which these people unite into an indissoluble alliance in love and loyalty, they may claim our sympathy and gain it.

The play opens with an impressive tableau. In front of the palace of the Atridae, which is imagined to be in Argos,[2] Electra is nursing her brother who has been on the verge of death since the murder of his mother. She speaks the prologue to explain the situation; later she warns the chorus of Argive women to tread softly when they enter. In place of the customary parodos a joint lament over Orestes' suffering is sung. The scene after his awakening shows the disturbance of his darkened soul, but it also reveals the deep love which binds the two even closer in distress. Menelaus has now come back with Helen from his lengthy wanderings, and all the hopes of brother and sister hang on his intervention on behalf of Orestes against the roused city. The manner in which Menelaus approaches them leaves their hopes open, but then Tyndareus comes, the father of the murdered Clytemnestra; in a long verbal duel with Orestes he persuades Menelaus to back out, and this he does, trying laboriously to hide his cowardice behind fine words.

Aristotle (*Poet.* 15. 1454 a) has quoted this Menelaus as a model of a character needlessly depicted as evil. We are rather of the opinion that the poet showed so much wretchedness in order to make Orestes' will to resist increase at the sight of it. Wholly lethargic in the opening scenes, he is aroused to vigorous action in the next. He is greatly heartened by the arrival of his friend Pylades who wants to share every peril with the two. At his advice Orestes decides to conduct his own case in the Argive popular assembly. But this attempt also miscarries. Only one stout-hearted countryman stands up for the justice which, in spite of everything, was behind Orestes' deed. Once more, as in the *Electra*, we meet with one of those characters which put ancient class prejudices to shame. But demagogues have the upper hand; the result is that Orestes and Electra are convicted and are to take their own lives. Human nobility is enhanced to theatrical gesture in the true Euripidean manner when Pylades wants to die with his friends. But first they are going to revenge themselves on Menelaus. They will kill Helen who is guilty of all the evil; with this plan of vengeance is connected the idea that they may perhaps gain glory and work out their salvation. Electra contributes the advice to get hold of Hermione, Menelaus' daughter, as a hostage against him. The girl is captured when she comes back

[1] KRIEG (*v. inf.*) *inter alios.*   [2] Cf. p. 384.

from Clytemnestra's tomb. The poet brings the carrying-out of the attempt against Helen onto the stage in his most curious messenger-speech. A Phrygian slave, who has come from Troy with Helen, has fled from the palace in fear of his life and now reports in a lyric scene, surcharged with emotion and written in a strange style which resembles the muttering of barbarians and anticipates the baroque manner of Timotheus' *Persians*, how inside the friends tried to take Helen's life, but that she made a miraculous escape.

The final scene is composed in a more turbulent manner than in any other of Euripides' plays. The three conspirators appear on the roof, Orestes with Hermione against whom he has drawn his sword. Menelaus is raging impotently in front of the locked palace gate. Finally he has to capitulate to Orestes' demand for intervention on their behalf with the Argives; he gives in with the words: 'You have got me' (1617)! Now we quite understand that a dramatic poet cannot finish a play by making Orestes leave the stage with Menelaus after this forcible peace. But Euripides expects a bit too much when Orestes answers Menelaus' acceptance of his terms with the order to set fire to the palace. This astonishing reaction can be explained neither with psychology nor in any other way, it simply serves to carry the situation to its extreme. In the midst of this confusion which seems to be without remedy, Apollo appears as the *deus ex machina*, and if there was ever any need of someone to re-establish order, it is here. And he goes about it in a most efficient manner; he announces that Helen has been carried off, and she appears beside him; then, that Orestes will be acquitted by the Areopagus; he ratifies the union of Pylades with Electra, adding the promise that Orestes will take Hermione to wife, even if he did not approach her at first in a very loving manner. This ending, but not it alone, demonstrates that in these last Athenian years the poet's longing for fullness and effect began to have a dangerous influence on the quality of his art.

The *Ixion*, dealing with the great mythical criminal, the *Polyidus* in which the figure of this seer, and prophecy generally, must have played a part, and the *Phaëton*, belong to a later period. Of the latter large fragments survive in manuscript form,[1] but the restoration of the play is still a problem. Phaeton was supposed to become Aphrodite's husband, so much is clear; it is more difficult to find out in what way this caused him to proclaim his descent from the sun and to demand the fatal ride in the sun's chariot.

In 408 there was a Euripides performance in Athens and he probably was still there himself; in 406 he died at the court of Archelaus. The short sojourn in Macedon produced an extraordinary variety of works. It is more likely that he wrote the *Archelaus*[2] in Macedon, a play in which he created for his host a forefather with admirable qualities, than it is to assume that he wrote it earlier and that the invitation to come to Macedon was the result of this homage; it is likely that we shall not suffer much heartbreak over the loss of this play.

---

[1] Fr. 781 N.; H. VOLMER, *De Eur. fab. quae Φ. inscribitur restituenda*. Diss. Münster 1930.

[2] A new fragment turned up in the Hamburg Pap. no. 118: E. SIEGMANN, *Veröffentlichungen der Hamburger Staats- und Universitätsbibl.* 4, 1954, 1.

The poet deployed and enhanced the full wealth of his genius in the plays of the Macedonian period which his son of the same name (Schol. Aristoph. *Ran.* 67; Suidas knows of a nephew of this name) put on the stage after his father's death, and won the victory which his father so seldom did in his lifetime.

Two of these plays survive, the *Iphigenia in Aulis* and the *Bacchae*. The lost *Alcmeon in Corinth* seems to have had a close affinity with the plays of the time of the *Ion*. Tyche contrived that Alcmeon unwittingly bought his own daughter as a slave. Anagnorisis necessarily was the dominant theme of this play.

In many of the later plays of Euripides a new wealth and a new quickening of emotions is shown; this development has its peak in the *Iphigenia in Aulis*, one of his finest creations.

The opening of the play is unusual. The descriptive iambic prologue in the customary style has been fitted within an anapaestic scene between Agamemnon and a trusted servant. It is hardly possible to assume that this whole section was uniformly transmitted in view of the discrepancies in style of the two parts mentioned. The anapaests are partly of a lofty content, and a similar use in Ennius (*Iph.* fr. 1. 2 Kl.) and in Chrysippus (fr. 180 A) are evidence of their ancient lineage. It is quite possible to credit Euripides with such an opening, for he also began his *Andromeda* with the heroine's anapaests to which Echo responded. An obvious explanation of the striking composition of the opening passage of this play is that two of the poet's drafts were mixed up.[1]

The first scenes are extremely agitated and emotional. Agamemnon has ordered Clytemnestra to come to the army camp in Aulis with Iphigenia, ostensibly to marry the girl to Achilles, but actually to immolate her to Artemis so that the fleet may have a fair wind. He now thinks that he will be unable to commit this frightful deed and has despatched the old man with a second letter which revokes the instructions of the first.

The parodos of Chalcidian women has been particularly boldly conceived. Partly adopting the form of the epic catalogue in lyric metre, they give a picture of the assembled fleet and its heroes. Thereupon Menelaus comes dashing in. He has intercepted the old servant and does not spare any reproaches for his brother's vacillation. After a scene of violent quarrelling Clytemnestra's arrival is reported, and when Menelaus now sees his brother's despair, his mood changes. He proffers his hand to Agamemnon and is prepared to forgo the sacrifice. Their roles are now completely reversed, for Agamemnon declares that it is impossible to stop the course of things. The meeting with his wife and child, with a Clytemnestra who has not yet been estranged from him, and a tenderly loving Iphigenia, causes Agamemnon renewed distress and suffering. The two are still without misgivings, but then Clytemnestra meets Achilles, whom she joyfully greets as her daughter's future husband. The scene between the two unconscious victims of this deception contains, in spite of the tragic mood, the elements of comedy of situation, without which neither New Comedy nor its European offspring could be imagined.

[1] E. FRAENKEL, *Studi in onore U. E. Paoli.* Florence 1955, 302, allots the anapaests to Eur., the trimeters to a later author.

Iphigenia also learns now why she had to come to Aulis, and like Clytemnestra she resists. But while her mother hurls bitter reproaches at the man who
wants to sacrifice his child, Iphigenia, in youth's ardent desire to live, begs for
her life in the most touching tones. She denies the highest tenet of the ancient
aristocratic creed, when she concludes her great speech with the words:
better to live in shame than die in glory (1252). But this is not her last
word.

In Agamemnon's rejoinder a significant change of the aspect under which
the planned expedition against Troy is seen, becomes evident. What previously
appeared to be chiefly a private matter of the Atridae, the elopement of a wife
and her recapture, proves now to be a great national undertaking of the Greeks
as the decisive act in the struggle against Asiatic despotism. Soon the meaning
of the expedition which depends on her immolation is revealed to Iphigenia
from a different side. In the scene with Clytemnestra outlined earlier, Achilles
has at once joined the side of the women. He cannot tolerate any bandying
about of his name, and is going to protect Iphigenia under any circumstances.
But when he is ready to stand by his promise and prevent the sacrifice, the
army's wrath is roused against him, and it seems that he will have to sacrifice
his life for the pledge which he has given. Then Iphigenia intervenes, an
Iphigenia different from the one who begged for her life and assailed her
father's heart with tender memories. She restrains Clytemnestra's reproaches
against Agamemnon and also checks Achilles' preparedness for self-sacrifice.
She now sees her road clear and is ready to take it to ensure victory for the
Hellenic arms. She consoles her mother, sings a hymn to Artemis who demands
her sacrifice and then goes to meet her death.

The transmission of the ending is hopeless. A fragment in Aelian (*Hist. An.*
7. 39) seems to be from the genuine ending and to be related to a version, in
which Artemis as *dea ex machina* rescued Iphigenia by substituting a doe as the
victim and probably proclaimed that she had been carried off to enter the
goddess's service. The ending is lost (perhaps Euripides left it unfinished) and
was replaced by a messenger-speech to Clytemnestra describing the miracle
which occurred at the scene of the sacrifice. This speech, which was perhaps
written for the posthumous performance, must in turn have lost its ending, for
what we read at the end at present is probably a Byzantine restoration.

In this play Euripides has worked the frequently used theme of voluntary
sacrificial death into a particularly effective climax. In many plays it remained
an episode, but here it is the central theme and as such it has been related to a
new conception of the psychological processes which induce such an offer. In
some of the oldest plays there are already beginnings of the description of a
change of character, as for instance in the case of Admetus and Heracles, but
here we see for the first time, as a subject for a play, a change in the soul of a
young woman which leads from fear of death and passionate clinging to life
onto a firm and wholly voluntary readiness for sacrifice. We do not claim that
this change is described, i.e. traced through its separate phases. The *Iphigenia in
Aulis* represents a tremendous advance towards the new drama, but it is only a

o

beginning. The poet shows the starting- and finishing-point of a psychological process, both with great penetration.

In general the Greek demanded consistency of character in the figures of great poetry, chiefly those of tragedy.[1] Euripides stood isolated with his *Iphigenia in Aulis,* and the great judges of his art did not show any understanding for him. In the *Poetics* (15. 1454 a) Aristotle censured the play, because the Iphigenia who feared death cannot be considered to have anything in common with the one who made the supreme heroic sacrifice. We observe, without echoing it, that this judgment is typical of Greek thought.[2]

Euripides' work is largely controlled by the intermingling of elementary emotion and rational thought, which expresses his personality as well as that of the generality of his contemporaries, who saw everywhere the advance of a new age over the ruins of tradition. The *Bacchae* as the final creation is symbolic of these tensions within Euripides' work. The subject was taken from one of those legends which probably reflect the resistance of reason against Dionysian frenzy rather than historical events during the spreading of the cult. Here it is the Theban king Pentheus who opposes the god, thus encouraging him to take a cruel revenge. Pentheus is torn to pieces by the throng of Maenads led by his own mother and her sisters. Aeschylus had already treated the same subject in his *Pentheus.*

Hardly any other of Euripides' plays has been pulled so much hither and thither as this one. It has been interpreted as something like the poet's conversion; his scepticism had been silenced at the end of his life by the mighty call of the soul-redeeming god. The rationalism at the turn of the century, which is still finding followers, preferred the other extreme. Its adherents saw Pentheus as the man who carried on the struggle against madness and delusion on behalf of reason even though he might perish in the process. Only in this play was Euripides the true fighter against a tradition which produced gods like these.[3] The simplifying radicalism of these two interpretations has been abandoned now. There is no doubt that this play is the result of a genuine attempt of the poet to understand the Dionysiac phenomenon, and this means neither conversion nor rationalistic protest. It has been justly observed that in Euripides' later plays an increasing interest in mysticism and ecstasy is expressed which can well be reconciled with his renunciation of the universe of official myth dominated by epic poetry. Account should also be taken of impressions he received of foreign orgiastic cults like those of the Thracian Bendis or the Phrygian Sabazius when these invaded Athens during the Peloponnesian war; he also had an opportunity to see the cult of Dionysus much more directly in Macedon than anywhere else in Greece. During an important period of his creative activity Euripides had selected the irrational forces in man's soul as a basic

[1] Important passages on the demand for consistency of nature in Cicero, *De Off.* 1. 111. 114. 144. Also WOLF–H. FRIEDRICH, *Nachr. Ak. Gött. Phil.-hist. Kl.* 1960/4, 107.

[2] Otherwise ZÜRCHER (*v. inf.*), 184.

[3] In add. to the bibl. mentioned in R. NIHARD, *Mus. Belge* 16, 1912, 91, DILLER's work on the *Bacchae* (*v. inf.*) and LESKY, 199, 1 and 200, 2.

dramatic theme; once more he now gave it splendid shape in this play and so mastered the irrational which seemed to him to come from completely different spheres. The worship of Dionysus with its puzzling polarity has never been cast in a more impressive form. There are descriptions of the deep peace with which the god envelops man. When the women of the Dionysian thiasos are peacefully slumbering in the mountain forest, when they give suck to the young offspring of wild animals and strike the ground with their thyrsos to produce refreshing drink, all hostile separation of man from nature has been overcome and the bliss of union has been achieved of which Nietzsche spoke in dithyrambic words. But it is these same women who reply to any disturbance of their spell with a Maenadic frenzy, overrun the settlements in the valleys with elemental violence, tear deer to pieces and perform prodigies of savage strength. Euripides saw the Dionysiac element as a mirror of nature, perhaps even more as a mirror of all life in this polarity of peace and tumult, of smiling charm and demoniac destruction. He shows in the two messenger-speeches, the most perfect written, a picture which is overpowering in its contradictions. The first message of the doings of the Bacchae (677) puts the reality of Dionysiac worship before Pentheus, the second (1043) narrates the catastrophe. The women, goaded on by the god, espy Pentheus who is watching them from the top of a fir tree; they tear the tree out by its roots, and fall upon the unfortunate king in raging anger; his own mother, gloating over her quarry, tears his arm, together with the shoulder, out of his body.

The god's antagonist, Pentheus, king of Thebes, embodies that part of mankind which clings to what is closest at hand, tangible and directly intelligible, countering the seduction of the irrational with bitter opposition. In a scene which borders on the grotesque, he meets with the seer Tiresias and his grandfather Cadmus who bow to the new god like devoted servants. His resistance only increases at seeing them and hearing their admonitions. The god, as he proclaims himself in the prologue, has assumed a human shape and has come to Thebes, where the sisters of his mother Semele, among them Agave, Pentheus' mother, doubt his divinity. He wishes to punish them and to win the city over to his worship. In his human shape he allows himself to be caught by Pentheus' men and is led before the king. Through his double role he gains the upper hand at the hearing and escapes effortlessly from the prison to which Pentheus condemns him. The scene of his liberation is followed by the one of the messenger-speech about the doings of the rioting women, which increases the king's anger still further, while at the same time rousing his curiosity. The situation which follows is of a tragic irony differing from the one depicted by Sophocles. The opponent of deception and illusion falls through the very stirrings of the irrational which the god manages to evoke in his soul. The urge to watch what is concealed, coupled with feelings of lust, drives him, confused and oddly benumbed, to follow the god who is taking him to the mountain forest. There Dionysus makes him climb up to the top of the fir tree and leaves him to fall a victim to the Maenads.

In the scene in which Agave brings in the head of her dead son on the thyrsos and gloats over her prey, Euripides went to the greatest length to which a Greek tragedian ever dared to go. Her slow awakening to the horror of reality is depicted with consummate psychological skill. The concluding portion survives incomplete. Once more, as in the opening, Dionysus appeared as the god, drove Agave and probably her sisters as well into exile, but had the consoling promise for Cadmus, that after long suffering he was to win a dwelling in the land of the Blessed together with his wife Harmonia.

Here, where for us Greek tragedy ends, we experience once more the frightening miracle of Dionysiac frenzy which formed one of its beginnings. In many of Euripides' later plays we had reason to doubt whether they were compatible with our notion of tragedy; here, however, the tragic contrast between man who wants to cling to reason and the world of the irrational has been depicted with the utmost harshness.

The great inner force which pervades this work is matched by a compactness of form which is almost unexampled in Euripides' work. The chorus of Lydian Bacchantes who are following the god on his triumphant progress is more closely connected with the plot than anywhere else. The length of the choral lyric has been increased, so that the sung parts of the actors have become of secondary importance; the stichomythiae are numerous and of rigorous construction.

For a long time Euripides' *Cyclops* was the only play which gave us an idea of a Greek satyr play. But since we have come into the possession of large parts of Sophocles' *Ichneutae* and at least one intelligible scene from Aeschylus' *Dictyulci*, we know that this conception was quite onesided. The easy brightness, the sparkling fairyland freshness of these fictions were not within the scope of Euripides' art. In connection with the *Alcestis* we already remarked that in more than one case he concluded a tetralogy with a play ending happily rather than with a satyr-play.

This does not imply that there is no wit at all in the *Cyclops*, but it is of a different nature than in the plays of which we have now some fragments; it is more deeply controlled by the intellect.

Odysseus' adventure with the Cyclops, which was also on occasion a subject for comedy, necessarily had to be given a stage version which differed from the epic narrative. The plot could no longer be enacted inside a cave; it was visible in the background and, as has been recently demonstrated,[1] it was supposed to have a second exit at the rear for the final scene, like the cave in Sophocles' *Philoctetes*. The significance of the blinding changes with the scene; in Homer it led to the rescue of the prisoners, now it is Odysseus' revenge for the killing of his companions. It cannot always have been easy for the poets of satyr-plays to link the chorus of lewd woodland demons with the legendary subject chosen. A favourite expedient, which Euripides used here and probably also in the *Busiris*, *Sciron* and *Syleus*, was to let the satyrs become the slaves of a monster. This also offered an opportunity to extract some crude humour from their

---

[1] A. M. DALE, 'Seen and Unseen on the Greek Stage'. *Wien. Stud.* 69, 1956, 105. Cf. also P. D. ARNOTT, *An Introduction to the Greek Theatre*. Lond. 1959, 130.

cowardice and cunning. Thus in the *Cyclops* their leader and father Silenus is also the most humorous character. He serves the Cyclops as his cupbearer and even becomes the grotesque object of his amorous attention when he is drunk. Euripides put particular stress on the figure of the Cyclops, and he stresses him in the typical Euripidean manner. This giant spurns the law on principle, he only sacrifices to himself or to his stomach, without bothering about law or custom. He is thus made into an extremist adherent of natural justice, offering, according to the poet's purpose, an effective illustration of the doctrines which at the time were being championed by the most radical among the sophists.

There is no secure basis for dating the play, since we know too little of the development of the genre to be able to classify individual phenomena with any certainty. What we observed with regard to the drawing of the Cyclops recommends, together with the free form of the triple dialogue, a dating in the later period as the closest approximation.

We forgo an attempt to give a comprehensive characterisation of Euripides' work because of the antinomies inherent in it. A summary can therefore only mean a discussion of these. Some remarks about the formal elements may be useful as a starting-point.

It has long been observed that in Euripides individual parts, which are also present in the older tragedies, are marked off more sharply and tend to assume an existence of their own. This does not mean that the plays of our poet are broken up into their constituent parts, and recently it has been endeavoured, and rightly so, to do justice to Euripides' constructive skill in opposition to criticism of this kind.[1] The separate limbs do indeed form part of a living organism, but this does not exclude the fact that they stand out sharply as parts of the whole and are subject to their own laws of form.

The informative prologue of a single speaker forms an introduction typical of Euripides.[2] It was observed in connection with the *Iphigenia in Aulis* that later the poet sought other ways. It is not always the task of the prologue to anticipate the course of the plot in order to make possible a more complete enjoyment of the work by removing the suspense connected with the subject, as Lessing assumed in the *Hamburgische Dramaturgie*. Only prologues spoken by gods can achieve this, and they too leave open plenty of moments of tension. The Euripidean prologue served rather to explain the background of the plot; the poet's innovations in the subject matter easily found their place next to the tradition. Earlier (p. 228) we developed the notion that the explanatory prologue is one of the earliest manifestations of spoken verse. If this is correct, the Euripidean prologue appears to be an archaism. Since it has generally been cast as plain narrative, the possibility is left open of increased effect in the following scenes. The verbal argument shows a particularly vigorous independent life.[3] This fact has often been overlooked, so that attempts were made, as in the case

---

[1] Esp. LUDWIG, *Sapheneia* (*v. inf.*).

[2] M. IMHOF, *Bemerkungen zu den Prologen der soph. u. eurip. Tragödien.* Diss. Bern. Winterthur 1957.

[3] J. DUCHEMIN, L' ΑΓΩΝ *dans la trag. gr.* Paris 1945.

of the *Alcestis*, to derive the meaning of the play from the argumentation of the agon. In these passages Greek quarrelsomeness was given full rein, and they benefited extensively from the passionate delight of the Athenians in court proceedings. Any weapon will serve and the myths are also used in a manner which demonstrates once more that they are being undermined. The formal construction of the agon scenes is strictly observed, resting on the alternation of stichomythia, a kind of verbal fencing, and prolonged speeches.

Such rheseis of imposing size are often found in other positions in Euripidean tragedy as well. In this respect the question is urged upon us to what extent Euripides depends on the rhetoric of his age.[1] Its influence has long been exaggerated, but nobody now considers Euripides to have been the poet who worked according to the rules of rhetoric. Of course, in view of the well-planned and often clearly-marked construction of many speeches it cannot be denied that contemporary interest in speech cast into an artistic form also had its influence on Euripides.

It has become clear during the discussion of the individual plays, that the messenger-speeches, as epic achievements of the highest order, are special ornaments of Euripidean tragedy, consciously shaped as such by the poet.

Typical features are displayed in the form of the endings with the frequent use of the *deus ex machina*.[2] He does not have to sever the knot by any means, although he is a convenient expedient for putting things swiftly in order at the end. Sometimes, as in the *Iphigenia in Tauris*, a delay is purposely put into the plot which is speeding towards a smooth ending, in order to make it possible for the *deus ex machina* to put in an appearance. In such a case it is obvious that his most important function is to found the cult which is the result of the events. In this way Euripides stresses at the end of the play the return to the tradition of worship. There are reasons to assume that the Aeschylean trilogies also ended frequently with the founding of a cult and so we can establish a link between Euripides and the eldest of the great tragedians; this link also exists in other respects.[3] We recall in passing the utilization of special stage effects by the two tragedians mentioned, a usage in which they differed markedly from Sophocles.

Euripidean choral lyric must by no means be generally characterized as an insertion foreign to the plot. The late *Bacchae* especially shows an unusually close connection of the chorus with the happenings on the stage. But in this respect Euripides' work is also uneven and there is a whole series of songs which are independent lyrical narratives. Walther Kranz called them dithyrambic stasima.[4] With the exception of one lyric from the *Hecabe*, which is an earlier form, they belong to Euripides' later period in which the choral lyric was subjected to other profound changes as well. This New Lyric shows an overblown

---

[1] F. TIETZE, *Die eur. Reden und ihre Bedeutung*. Diss. Breslau 1933.

[2] SPIRA'S work, which attempts to prove a close link between the *deus ex machina* and the structure of the drama, is referred to on p. 389 n. 1.

[3] O. KRAUSSE, *De Eur. Aeschyli instauratore*. Diss. Jena 1905.

[4] *Hec.* 905, *Tro.* 511, *El.* 432. 699, *Hel.* 1301, *Iph. T.* 1234, *Phoen.* 638. 1019, *Iph. A.* 164. 751. 1036. KRANZ, *Stasimon*. Berl. 1933, 254.

richness of language which at times appears curiously incongruous with the contents. Aristophanes sharply parodied this sort of thing in the *Thesmophoriazusae* (49) and the *Frogs* (1309). Many of the texts of Euripides reveal that here and there the chorus is only incidental to the music. We know that it was the flamboyant, restless music, aiming at harsh effects, of the new Attic dithyramb,[1] which had a profound influence on Euripides. Among the tragedians it was used above all by Agathon; a strong influence was exerted by Timotheus, both of whom tradition allies with Euripides as friends.

Similar trends affected the actor's aria, which in Euripides gains ground at the expense of the choral lyric. This development, which we also observed in the older Sophocles, does not, of course, proceed in a straight line, and is later crossed to a certain extent by the New Lyric of the chorus,[2] but a play like the *Orestes* has only two strophic lyrics left in contrast with the boldly developed monodies.

It is part and parcel of the paradoxes in Euripides' work that the increasing flamboyance of the wording of the choral lyrics was contrasted in the dialogue by a simple and pure diction which, with certain reservations, approached colloquial speech. It is also contrasted by Aeschylus' impetus and the noble control, combined with a great capacity for modulation, of Sophocles.

Another contradiction in Euripides' work, apart from innovations which are particularly obvious in the choral lyric, are certain archaizing trends. One of these is the increase of trochaic passages in the later plays; in these he reverted to a tragic metre which was felt to be particularly ancient.[3]

In this discussion of the formal element it has already become increasingly clear to what extent Euripides' work is pervaded by contradictory forces. This applies in the same degree to his merit, and it is on this very point that any attempt to characterize this poet in general is bound to fail. He is not simply the philosopher of the stage or even the propagandist of the enlightenment. But to a large extent his intellect predominates. The thinker and the poet in him did not always blend so perfectly as in the songs of praise which the chorus in the *Medea* (824) sings to the Athens of Pericles.[4] A comparison with Sophocles' ode to his native land (*Oed. Col.* 668) reveals how much more intellectually inspired Euripides' verse is. The mythical figures and the forces raised to a divine level, the Muses and Harmony, the Erotes and Sophia, they also belong to this sphere. We hear the poet, to whom the exaggerated praise of athletes was a source of annoyance.[5] But when his verse praises the intellectual brightness and the light tread of people in the pure air of Attica we discern, through the poetical splendour of the words, the theories of the natural philosophers of his age, and all these elements have been combined in his verse into perfect unity. This is

---

[1] H. SCHÖNEWOLF, *Der jungattische Dithyrambos.* Diss. Giessen 1938.

[2] KRANZ (*v. sup.*), 229.

[3] W. KRIEG, 'Der trochäische Tetrameter bei Eur.'. *Phil.* 91, 1936, 42.

[4] On this theme H. R. BUTTS, *The Glorification of Athens in Greek Drama. Iowa Stud. in Class. Phil.* 11, 1947.

[5] It was already observed in antiquity that in this respect he followed Xenophanes (Athen. 10. 423 f.). Other passages in H. D. KEMPER, *Rat und Tat.* Diss. Bonn 1960, 107, 88.

not always so and sometimes Euripides presented his thoughts in a way which burst open the confines of the plays; nevertheless he is the greatest and most effective playwright who ever wrote for the stage. The trend of various recent studies,[1] vindicating the poet in him in contrast to the thinker, is sound and correct. Nor is Euripides the misogynist whom comedy called before the court of women at the festival of the Thesmophoriae. The demoniacal contrivers of evil are matched by noble figures of women with whom he is fond of connecting the theme of self-immolation. The least deserved of all was the designation of the poet as one who denied the divine. In the *Heracles* and the *Electra* we saw that at times his doubt of the tradition increased to violent criticism and rejection, but although he could not detect a divine nature in the figures of the official myths, he never stopped seeking for its manifestations in this world. Nor does the *Bacchae* imply that this search had come to an end, although we hear in this play some unexpected words about the wisdom of acquiescence. What is said of Tiresias (200) and the messenger (1150) can be interpreted as being part of their roles, but there is a much more personal tenor in the song of the chorus (386): a life of peace and of wise reflection makes homes secure; short is our road, idle the chasing after great things, τὸ σοφὸν δ' οὐ σοφία. Does the poet deny his own life here, he who had praised Athens in his *Medea*, because there the gods of love unite with wisdom? It would show an elementary misunderstanding to interpret the passage like that, but it remains a difficult task to ascertain its personal content. We would like to think that these lines make us the spectators of a gripping spectacle. At the end of a life full of intellectual struggling and the torment of eternally unsolved questions, the poet holds up before him the peaceful image of those secure in faith. But its peace can never be called his, for it was his task to bear the distress of incessant seeking and to give voice to the unrest of his age, which had not yet forgotten the old, but yet was striving along uncertain paths for the new.

According to the manuscript biography and Suidas, Euripides' total work comprised ninety-two plays. This number probably goes back to the research of the Alexandrians, who were already faced with a great deal of uncertainty. The biography states explicitly that of these seventy-eight survived, which means that they were present in the library at Alexandria. The number seventy-five also emerges (Varro in Gell. 17. 4, 3; variant in Suidas); the discrepancy is probably due to the deletion of the three plays attributed to Critias (*v. supra*). The spurious *Rhesus* has been included in the number of surviving plays.

Euripides, who fought so hard for recognition during his life, became the most popular tragedian as early as the 4th century and remained so until the end of antiquity. When the restaging of one old tragedy (παλαιά) became the custom in the dramatic agon, as we could ascertain for the year 386, it was especially Euripides' works which benefited.[2] This had its dangers for the text. Although

---

[1] RIVIER, GRUBE, MARTINAZZOLI *et alii*.　　　　[2] Proof in SCHMID 3. 824, 3.

the extent of actors' interpolations is difficult to mark off,[1] there can be no doubt that a good deal was altered in this manner. It is due to the later popularity of the poet that after Homer the greatest number of papyrus texts which we have are his. The older papyri, especially the Strasbourg papyrus of tragic lyrics (BR. SNELL, Herm. E 5, 1937, 69) reveal a similarity with those of Homer: the work of the Alexandrians was decisive in putting an end to the degeneration of the text. But this means, of course, that the form which they gave to them is the oldest accessible to us. Aristophanes of Byzantium produced the decisive edition with commentaries in independent books.

The principle of selection which is generally connected with the schools in the age of the Antonines also plays a part in the transmission of Euripides. It can be stated with certainty that this selection comprised the plays on which we have scholia: Alc., Andr., Hec., Hipp., Med., Or., (Rhes.), Tro., Phoen. It is likely, if not certain, that at one time the Bacchae was also included in this selection. Through a happy dispensation we are not dependent on this alone for Euripides, for in addition part of an alphabetically arranged edition has been preserved. This branch of the transmission is based upon a papyrus edition which contained one play each in one roll, combining five of them in containers, jars or boxes (BR. SNELL, Herm. 70, 1935, 119). The Hec., also belonging to the selection, further Hel., El., Heracl., Heracld. formed the contents of one, Cycl., Ion, Suppl. and the Iphigenia tragedies that of the other container.

J. A. SPRANGER, 'A Preliminary Skeleton List of the Manuscripts of Eur.'. Class. Quart. 33, 1939, 98, gives a survey of the manuscripts. The most important information is also found in the leading editions; fundamental for any further work on the text is also A. TURYN, The Byzantine Manuscript Tradition of the Tragedies of Eur. Univ. of Illinois Press. Urbana 1957, with an exact description of the main evidence and a wealth of important information, especially regarding Triclinius' activity. V. also P. G. MASON, 'A note on Euripidean Manuscripts'. Mnem. 1958, 123.

The most ancient manuscript is the Jerusalem palimpsest (Patriarch's Libr. 36) of the 10th century with more than 1600 lines from Hec., Or., Phoen., Andr., Med., Hipp. It has scholia and variants and does not form part of the other two known groups of manuscripts. Of the latter one contains only the plays of the selection with scholia. In point of value the Marcianus 471 (12th c.) with Hec., Or., Phoen., Andr., Hipp. (up to line 1234) is the best. The Parisinus 2712 (13th c.) has the same plays increased with the Med., the Vaticanus 909 (13th c.) all the nine comm. plays, the Parisinus 2713 (12th/13th c.) the same without Tro. and (Rhes.). The manuscripts of the other group also contain the plays of the alphabetical collective edition which was mentioned earlier. Here the most important manuscript is the Laurentianus 32, 2 (L, 13th/14th c.) with all the plays except the Tro. A further codex, written by one hand in the late 14th c., is a combination of the two parts Palatinus 287 and Laurentianus conv. sopr. 172 (P, 14th c.). It is of some positive value for the plays with the scholia, but for the plays without scholia there is some doubt as to its usefulness.

---

[1] D. L. PAGE, Actors' Interpolations. Oxf. 1934.

Many scholars, among them P. MAAS (*Gnom.* 1926, 156) dispute the opinion that the text of these plays originates eventually from Laur. 32, 2, and is consequently worthless. A. TURYN, to whom we owe the important discovery that the corrections in manuscript L originate from Demetrius Triclinius, defends (*v. supra*) the opinion that in the plays of the alphabetical arrangement P was not copied from L, but must be considered as a sister manuscript of the Laurentianus. Recently GÜNTHER ZUNTZ has re-examined the problem. He was good enough to permit the results to be stated here. According to him the plays in P without scholia were directly copied from L after the manuscript had been provisionally corrected by Triclinius. For the plays of the anthology it appears certain to him that P had a corrected copy of the common archetype which had also been corrected by Triclinius.

The upshot of all this is that our tradition has a better foundation for the plays with scholia than for the rest. An extreme example is afforded by the papyrus (no. 283 P.) discussed by E. R. DODDS in his edition of the *Bacchae*, containing lines 1070-1136, a passage which is missing from Laur. 32, 1. Variants, plus and minus lines demonstrate on what uncertain ground we are moving here. For the text reference is also made to J. JACKSON, *Marginalia Scaenica*. Oxf. 1955, since the suggestions for emendations of Greek authors collected in it refer chiefly to Euripides. In the style of dramatic criticism between Porson and Cobet he gives purely intuitively, without reference to the recensio, a wealth of mostly very worthwhile conjectures.

Research reports by the author in *AfdA* from 1949 onward, lastly 1961. H. W. MILLER, 'A Survey of recent Euripidean Scholarship 1940-1954'. *Class. Weekly* 49, 1956, 81. Recent editions: G. MURRAY, 3 vols. Oxf. 1902. 1904. 1910. Of the bilingual edition of the *Coll. des Un. de Fr.* by L. MÉRIDIER, L. PARMENTIER, H. GRÉGOIRE and F. CHAPOUTHIER vols. 1-6, Paris 1923-61 have appeared; *Iph. Aul.* (*Rhes.*) are still to come. A. S. WAY, 4 vols. biling. *Loeb Class. Libr.* Lond. 1912 repr. up to 1959. Of the Spanish biling. ed. of A. TOVAR (partly together with R. P. BINDA) 1, Barcelona 1955 (*Alc. Andr.*), 2, 1959 (*Bacch. Hec.*) have appeared in the Colección Hispánica de autores Griegos y Latinos par las universidades Españolas. Useful for the interpretation: H. WEIL, *Sept Tragédies d'Eur.* Paris 1868, 3rd ed. 1905 (*Hipp. Med. Hec. Iph. Aul. Iph. Taur. El. Or.*). Reference must be made particularly to the comm. Oxf. editions quoted hereafter with regard to the individual plays. E(ditions) with comm. and C(ommentaries) of the individual plays: *Alc.*: E: L. WEBER, Leipz. 1930. A. MAGGI, Naples 1935. D. W. F. VAN LENNEP, Leiden 1940. A. M. DALE, Oxf. 1954. AUG. MANCINI, Florence 1955. C: K. V. FRITZ, 'Euripides' Alkestis und ihre modernen Nachahmer und Kritiker'. *Ant. u. Abendl.* 5, 1956, 27; now *Antike und moderne Tragödie.* Berl. 1962, 256. W. D. SMITH, 'The Ironic Structure in Alc.' *Phoenix* 14, 1960, 127. O. VICENZI, 'Alkestis und Admetos'. *Gymn.* 67, 1960, 517. U. ALBINI, 'L'Alc. di Eur.'. *Maia* N.S. 13, 1961, 3. – *Med.*: E: D. L. PAGE, Oxf. 1938. U. BRELLA, Turin 1950. G. AMMENDOLA, Florence 1951. E. VALGIGLIO, Turin 1957. J. C. KAMERBEEK, Leiden 1962. C: O. REGENBOGEN, 'Randbemerkungen zur Med. des Eur.'. *Eranos* 48, 1950, 21. K. V. FRITZ, 'Die

Entwicklung der Iason-Medea-Sage und die Medea des Eur.'. *Ant. und Abendl.* 8, 1959, 33; now *Antike und moderne Tragödie.* Berl. 1962, 322. WOLF–H. FRIED-RICH, *Medeas Rache. Nachr. Ak. Gött. Phil.-hist. Kl.* 1960/4, 67. – *Hipp.*: E: A. TACCONE, Florence 1942. G. AMMENDOLA, Florence 1946. A. G. WESTER-BRINK, Leiden 1958. C: H. HERTER, 'Theseus und Hipp.'. *Rhein. Mus.* 89, 1940, 273. B. M. W. KNOX, 'The Hipp. of Eur.'. *Yale Class. Stud.* 13, 1952, 1. W. FAUTH, *Hippolytos und Phaidra. Abh. Ak. Mainz. Geistes- u. Sozialwiss. Kl.* 1958/9 and 1959/8 (enquires into the pre-history of the subject matter). R. P. WINNINGTON-INGRAM, 'Hippolytus: A Study of Causation'. *Entretiens sur l'antiquité class.* 6. Vandœuvres-Geneva 1960, 171. – *Hec.*: E: A. TACCONE, Turin 1937. M. TIERNEY, Dublin 1946. A. GARZYA, Rome 1955. C: D. J. CONACHER, 'Eur. Hecuba'. *Am. Journ. Phil.* 82, 1961, 1. – *Andr.*: E: J. C. KAMERBEEK, Leiden 1955. U. SCATENA, Rome 1956. A. GARZYA, Naples 1960. C: V. p. 375 n. 2 f. – *Heraclidae*: E: A. MAGGI, Turin 1943. C: G. Zuntz in his above-mentioned book; A. GARZYA, 'Studi sugli Eraclidi di Eur.'. *Dionisio* 19, 1956, 3. F. STOESSL, 'Die Her. des Eur.' *Phil.* 100, 1956, 207. V. also p. 377, nn. 2–5. – *Suppl.*: E: T. NICKLIN, Lond. 1936. G. ITALIE, Groningen 1951. G. AMMENDOLA and V. D'AGOSTINO, Turin 1956. C: G. ZUNTZ in the above-mentioned book. J. W. FRITTON, 'The Suppliant Women and the Herakleidai of Eur.'. *Herm.* 89, 1961, 430. – *Heracles*: E: WILAMOWITZ'S monumental ed. is still authoritative, Berl. 1889, 2nd ed. 1895. C: E. KROEKER, *Der Her. des Eur.* Diss. Leipz. 1938. Also H. DREXLER, *GGN phil.-hist. Kl.* 1934/9. – *Tro.*: E: A. TACCONE, Turin 1938. G. SCHIASSI, Florence 1953. C: G. PERROTTA, 'Le Troiane di Eur.'. *Studi sul teatro greco-rom. Dioniso.* 15, 1952, 237. A. PERTUSI, 'Il significato della trilogia troiana di Eur.'. Ib. 251. D. EBENER, 'Die Helenaszene der Troerinnen'. *Wiss. Zeitschr. Univ. Halle* 1954, 691. – *El.*: E: J. D. DENNISTON, Oxf. 1939. G. SCHIASSI, Bologna 1956. D. BACCINI, Naples 1959. C: W. WUHRMANN, *Strukturelle Untersuchungen zu den beiden El. und zum eur. Or.* Diss. Zürich 1940. F. STOESSL, 'Die El. des Eur.'. *Rhein. Mus.* 99, 1956, 47. – G. AMMENDOLA, Turin 1943. G. ITALIE, Groningen 1949. A. Y. CAMPBELL, Liverpool 1950. C: A. N. PIPPIN, 'Eur. Helen: a Comedy of Ideas'. *Class. Phil.* 55, 1960, 151. G. ZUNTZ, 'On Eur. Helena: Theology and Irony'. *Entretiens sur l'antiquité class.* 6. Vandœuvres-Geneva 1960, 201. Ib., 'The Papyrus of Eur. Hel. P. Ox. 2336'. *Mnem.* S 4, 14, 1961, 122 with following corrigendum. K. ALT, 'Zur Anagnorisis in der Hel.'. *Herm.* 90, 1962, 6. – *Iph. Taur.*: E: M. PLATNAUER, Oxf. 1938; repr. 1956. G. AMMENDOLA, Turin 1948. H. STROHM, Munich 1949. J. D. MEERWALDT, Leiden 1960. – *Ion*: E: U. V. WILAMOWITZ, Berl. 1926. A. S. OWEN, Oxf. 1939. G. ITALIE, Leiden 1948. G. AMMENDOLA, Florence 1951. C: M. F. WASSERMANN, 'Divine Violence and Providence in Eur. Ion'. *Trans. Am. Phil. Ass.* 1940, 587. D. J. CONACHER, 'The Paradoxon of Eur. Ion'. *Trans. Am. Phil. Ass.* 1959, 20. – *Phoen.*: E: C. H. BALMORI, Tucumán Argentina 1946. A. M. SCARCELLA, Rome 1957. C: W. RIEMENSCHNEIDER, *Held und Staat in Eur. Phön.* Diss. Berl. 1940. E. VALGIGLIO, *L'esodo delle 'Fenicie' di Eur. Univ. di Torino. Pubbl. della Fac. di Lett. e Filos.* 13/2. Turin 1961. – *Or.*: E: A. M. SCARCELLA, Rome 1958. C: W. KRIEG, *De Eur. Or.* Diss. Halle 1934. W. BIEHL, *Textprobleme in Eur. Or.* Diss.

Jena 1955. A. M. SCARCELLA, 'Letture euripidee: L' "Oreste" e il problema dell'unità'. *Dioniso*, 19, 1956, 3. D. D. FLAVER, 'The Musical Setting of Eur. Or.'. *Am. Journ. Phil.* 81, 1960, 1. V. DI BENEDETTO, 'Note critico-testuale all Or. di Eur.'. *Studi class. e orient.* 10, Pisa 1961, 122. K. V. FRITZ, 'Die Orestessage bei den drei grossen griech. Tragikern'. *Antike und moderne Tragödie*. Berl. 1962. – *Iph. Aul.* E: G. AMMENDOLA, 3rd ed. Turin 1959. C: BR. SNELL, *Aischylos*. Phil. Suppl. 20/1, 1928, 148. D. L. PAGE, *Actors' Interpolations*. Oxf. 1934, 130. V. FREY, 'Betrachtungen zu Eur. Aul. Iph.'. *Mus. Helv.* 4, 1947, 39. H. VRETSKA, 'Agamemnon in Eur. Iph. i. A.'. *Wien. Stud.* 74, 1961, 18. – *Bacch.*: E: G. AMMENDOLA, Turin 1941. E. R. DODDS, 2nd ed. Oxf. 1960. P. SCAZZOSO, Milan 1957. C: R. P. WINNINGTON-INGRAM, *Eur. and Dionysus*. Cambr. 1948. H. DILLER, 'Die Bakchen und ihre Stellung im Spätwerk des Eur.'. *Ak. Mainz. Geistes- u. sozialwiss. Kl.* 1955, no. 5. A.-J. FESTUGIÈRE, 'La Signification religieuse de la parodos des Bacch.'. *Eranos* 54, 1956, 72. Ib., 'Eur. dans les Bacch.'. *Eranos* 55, 1957, 127. – *Cycl.*: E: J. DUCHEMIN, Paris 1945. G. AMMENDOLA, Florence 1952. Fragments: NAUCK, *Trag. Graec. Fragm.*, 2nd ed. Leipz. 1889. H. V. ARNIM, *Suppl. Euripideum*. Bonn 1913. BR. SNELL, *Wien. Stud.* 69, 1956, 86. Pap.: P. nr. 276-329. H. HOMMEL, 'Eur. in Ostia'. *Rivista It. di Epigrafia* 19, 1959, 109 thinks that some lines on a bust of Hippocrates which stood in a graveyard in Ostia are a fragment of a choral lyric by Eur. – Scholia: E. SCHWARTZ, 2 vols. Berl. 1887/91. – Verbal index: J. T. ALLEN and G. ITALIE, *A Concordance to Eur.* Berkeley 1953. – In the American translation (cf. on Aeschylus) we single out particularly the two contributors R. LATTIMORE and D. GRENE. In Great Britain G. MURRAY's translations of numerous plays are excellent. In French *v. supra* the ed. of the *Coll. des Univ. de Fr.* Italian: M. FAGGELLA, *Eur. nuova trad. in versi.* 1-4, Milan 1935-37. – Language: W. BREITENBACH, *Unters. zur Sprache der eur. Lyrik.* Tüb. Beitr. 20, Stuttg. 1934. J. SMEREKA, *Studia Euripidea* I and II/1, Leopoli 1936/37. L. BERGSON, D. M. CLAY, FR. JOHANSEN v. appendix to Aeschylus under "language". – Metre: v. p. 380 n. 2 and 403 n. 3. Monographs and papers: D. F. W. VAN LENNEP, *Eur. ποιητὴς σοφός*. Amsterd. 1935. G. M. A. GRUBE, *The Drama of Eur.* Lond. 1941; 2nd ed. (with few alter.) New York 1961. A. RIVIER, *Essai sur le tragique d'Eur.* Lausanne 1944. F. MARTINAZZOLI, *Euripide.* Rome 1946. G. MURRAY, *Eur. and his Age.* 1913. 2nd ed. Oxf. 1946. W. ZÜRCHER, *Die Darstellung des Menschen im Drama des Eur.* Basel 1947. W. H. FRIEDRICH, *Eur. und Diphilos.* Munich 1953. L. H. G. GREENWOOD, *Aspects of Eur. Trag.* Cambr. 1953. G. NORWOOD, *Essays on Eur. Drama.* London 1954. W. LUDWIG. *Sapheneia. Ein Beitrag zur Formkunst im Spätwerk des Eur.* Diss. Tüb. 1954. F. CHAPOUTHIER, 'Eur. et l'accueil du divin'. *Fondation Hardt* (cf. p. 65, n. 3), 205. G. ZUNTZ, *The Political Plays of Eur.* Manchester 1955. C. PRATO, *Eur. nella critica di Aristofane.* Galatina 1955. H. STROHM, *Euripides.* Zet. 15. Munich 1957. K. REINHARDT, 'Die Sinneskrise bei Eur.'. *Die neue Rundschau* 68, 1957, 615; now *Tradition und Geist.* Göttingen 1960, 227 touches upon the centre of the problems of Euripides' work. The following works are preserved in the *Entretiens sur l'antiquité class.* 6. Vandœuvres-Geneva 1960, apart from those mentioned with the separate plays: J. C. KAMERBEEK, 'Mythe et réalité

dans l'œuvre d'Eur.'. A. RIVIER, L'Elément démonique chez Eur. jusqu'en 428'.
H. DILLER, 'Umwelt und Masse als dramatische Faktoren bei Eur.'. A. LESKY,
'Psychologie bei Eur.'. (Ib. 'Zur Problematik des Psychologischen in der
Tragödie des Eur.'. Gymn. 67, 1960, 10.) V. MARTIN, 'Eur. et Ménandre face à
leur public.' Many valuable observations in the book by J. DE ROMILLY, L'Évolution du pathétique d'Eschyle à Euripide. Paris 1961. Cf. POHLENZ, HARSH, LESKY
and KITTO.

3 OTHER TRAGIC WRITERS

Attic tragedy for us is linked indissolubly to the three great poets in whom
Greek art, fed from the springs of mythology and rooted deep in the life of the
community through its religious associations, reached its greatest height since
the epic. But we must not forget that what survives is only fragments of an
incredibly rich literary output. How good this output was we do not know; but
its almost total loss can probably be taken as reflecting a basically sound judgment of later ages. Its extent, however, can be fairly well known to us from
various sources. We have comedy, which loved to· direct its fire against minor
poets, and which gives us in the opening of the Frogs a striking impression of
the sense of decline which was felt after the death of Sophocles and Euripides.
Here and there in the Poetics Aristotle mentions names of poets who for us are
overshadowed by the great writers. But our best source is the remains of the
inscriptions which were put up by a drama-loving Athenian of the Hellenistic
period on the inner walls of a small building. The lists of plays performed at
the Great Dionysia and the Lenaea (IG II 2nd ed. 2318 and 2319-23) and the
lists of victors in tragedy and comedy at these festivals (ibid. 2325), even in their
fragmentary state, constitute a valuable chapter of Greek literary history, which
the skill and industry of Adolf Wilhelm[1] have enabled us to read.

Of all the many poets whose names and titles and fragments appear in
Nauck's collection, there are only a few of whom we receive a distinct impression. The classical period produced Ion of Chios, who was born between 490 and
480. He came to Athens in his early youth, and in his Epidemiae he embodied
reminiscences of a banquet distinguished by the presence of Cimon (Plut. Cim.
9). According to Suidas he presented his first tragedy in the 82nd Olympiad
(452-449). We must of course suppose him to have been in Athens then, and
presumably he often came later to see his plays produced. In the same passage
we read that after a tragic victory he gave a jar of Chian wine to every Athenian
citizen – an act of liberality only possible to a rich man. Certainly he was
closely associated with Athens and her intellectual leaders and he often lived
there for varying lengths of time. His acquaintance with Aeschylus is attested
by an anecdote that Plutarch tells about the Isthmia (Mor. 79 D.), and we have
previously noticed the story of Sophocles' stay with him in Chios.

This open-hearted Ionian took an active part in the intellectual life of his

---

[1] Urkunden dram. Aufführungen in Athen. Vienna 1906. A. PICKARD-CAMBRIDGE, The
Dramatic Festivals of Athens. Oxf. 1953, 103 (p. 105 on the relation between the inscr. and
the researches of Aristotle).

times, as the multiplicity of his writings attests. We are justified in dealing with him here, since in antiquity his tragedies were reckoned the most important part of his literary work.[1] Suidas gives three different numbers for the total of his plays: 12, 30 and 40. We can take this without difficulty as referring to ten trilogies, to which the satyr-plays were sometimes added in the reckoning. The number 12 was presumably the number of plays preserved at Alexandria, where Ion had the honour of being admitted into the canon of tragic poets. This is presumably why we have a relatively large number of fragments from him, which do not, however, enable us to form a soundly based judgment of his poetry. We have some assistance from the intelligent author of the Περὶ ὕψους, who makes the same kind of comparison between Ion and Sophocles as between Bacchylides and Pindar – a contrast between the smooth mastery of form and the fire of genius. The same critic, whose name we are sorry not to know, reckons the *Oedipus* of Sophocles as being worth more than Ion's whole dramatic output.

Among the known titles, all based on various mythical themes, the *Great Drama* (Μέγα δρᾶμα) singles itself out. It is an uncertain hypothesis of Blumenthal's[2] that the subject was the stealing of fire by Prometheus. We are best informed about the satyr-play *Omphale*, which depicted Heracles in bondage to the Lydian queen. Feasting played a large part, to judge from the fragments, and it is quite likely that the passage quoted in Pollux (2. 95) referring to Hercules' three rows of teeth comes from this context. A fragment on papyrus (60 Blum.) seems at first to show a change of scene, but Blumenthal has interpreted it so as to make such a supposition unnecessary. Aristarchus thought the piece worthy of his attention as a commentator.

According to ancient reports, Ion tried his hand at the most various fields of poetry. We have a large fragment of an elegy – a poem for the dinner-table, celebrating Bacchus and his gifts; dithyrambs and solo lyrics are well attested, and he also wrote a *Hymn to Opportunity*. This is remarkable, since some of the remains, like the elegiac fragment above, give the impression that Ion's poetry, with its mastery of form, came mostly from the intellect. Καιρός, the opportune, profitable, decisive moment, as the subject of a poem, points this way, since it was not a creation of living religious feeling, even if it did later have a cult in Olympia (Paus. 5. 14, 9), but of the realm of ideal concepts. It began to play a part in Greek thought in Ion's time, and in the age of Alexander it was pleasingly represented in plastic art as a running man with a bald head, having only one lock of hair on the front to grip him by, and balancing a pair of scales on a razor.

It has been thought that Ion's talents extended also to epic, and that his *Founding of Chios* was an example. But a verbal quotation (19 Blum.) is in prose. We are surprised to find that ancient sources[3] credited Ion with comedies also. None of the fragments can be so identified, and since at the end of Plato's *Symposium* it is stated purely as a theoretical possibility that the same man might

---

[1] Cf. SCHMID, 2. 515, 2.   [2] In his edition, fr. 59.
[3] Schol. on Aristoph. *Peace* 835; SUIDAS, s.v. διθυραμβοδιδάσκαλοι.

write comedy and tragedy, it seems unlikely that this should have been done by a well-known author some decades before.

Among Ion's writings in prose we have already mentioned the *Founding of Chios*. The quotations are concerned with mythology. As with Hellanicus, who also wrote a *Founding of Chios*, so here we find the continuation in prose of an originally epic form, as exemplified in Xenophanes' *Founding of Colophon*. This form later became popular. The most original of Ion's works seems to have been his *Epidemiae*, in which he gave a special embodiment of that Greek love of anecdote which was later to show itself so powerfully in Plutarch. The title refers to journeys: from what we previously noticed concerning Cimon, Aeschylus and Sophocles, it was as much concerned with visits of great men to Chios as with Ion's own travels. It is the personal element – the witty saying or the notable deed – that is always prominent. From the philosophical side we find Ion as the author of the *Triagmos* (also quoted as *Triagmoi*). But already we have said more about it than the evidence justifies. It was certainly concerned with the triad as a universal structural principle, as we see from the opening sentence: 'All things are three, neither more nor less than these three. Each man's usefulness is a trinity: reason, strength and luck.' An interesting light is cast on a field otherwise dark to us by a fragment (fr. 24 Blum. 2 D.) stating that Pythagoras used to attribute some of his doctrines to Orpheus. The influence on Ion of Pythagorean doctrines of the soul is attested by the elegant distichs which he wrote to Pherecydes of Syros (fr. 30 Blum.).

Apart from the three great names and Ion, the Alexandrians admitted only Achaeus of Eretria into the tragic canon. But we do not know what claim he had to this honour. His satyr-plays were well thought of, and the inscriptions credit him with a victory. Apart from a few titles of plays, this is all we know of him.

The plays ascribed to Critias were mentioned earlier in connection with his other literary work. We are indebted to comedy – though not to comedy alone – for giving us an impression, at least in its essential outline, of a tragic poet who flourished in Euripides' later years – the Athenian Agathon. In Plato's *Protagoras* (315 e) he appears as a young man of great talent and singular beauty of person. Since the dialogue is set around 430, we may assume that Agathon was born in the early 'forties. This agrees with the statement of Aelian (*Var. Hist.* 13. 4) that he was about forty years old when he accompanied Euripides to the Macedonian court.

We find the most diverse judgments of the man and his art in Aristophanes, Plato and Aristotle. The first-named chose Agathon's poetry as his particular target in the *Thesmophoriazusae*. His representation of the poet as an idle and effeminate aesthete presumably contains a good deal of comic licence, but certainly there must have been a kernel of truth to prompt the attack. The parodies of one of his monodies and of an astrophic choral ode are particularly valuable. We can see in the *Frogs* that, when Aristophanes is deriding Euripidean choral lyrics, despite all his exaggeration he sticks to the essential points. Thus the parodies in Aristophanes are a valuable indication that Agathon allowed himself to be greatly influenced by the later Attic dithyramb, whose contribution to the 'new song' of Euripides we had to discuss earlier. The overload of verbiage, reflected also in the music, seems to have attracted particular attention in Agathon. The symposium which Plato describes was supposed to celebrate the first tragic victory gained by Agathon at the Lenaea of 416, and the victor himself appears among those who sing the praises of Eros at the dinner-table. The encomium that he delivers, coming between the great but very differently conceived speeches of Aristophanes and Socrates, is so heavily laden with Gorgianic figures and assonances that Plato must have intended a parody of Agathon's manner. We clearly have here a convergence of different lines of development. Gorgias carried his artistic prose to a point where it almost crossed the borders of poetry, and the ancient critics[1] rightly remarked that he showed a particular affinity to the dithyramb. The development of the dithyramb showed the same tendency towards captivating the hearer by mere sound as we find in Gorgias' rhetorical teachings, and in Agathon we see the effect which had been produced on tragedy by both these tendencies. Taken together with other factors, it spelled the end of the unity that characterized classical art.

We can easily understand how a development of this kind led to the independence of the lyrical sections. This is in fact attested by Aristotle in a passage of the *Poetics* (18. 1456 a 30) where he says that Agathon began the practice of treating the choral odes as entr'actes.

Agathon's innovations in choral lyric were the most noticeable feature of his plays, and thus attracted most attention from comedy. But we see him, of course, in a distorting mirror, and we could easily forget that he was a dramatist of some note. Aristotle alludes to him frequently in the *Poetics*. Just before the passage last cited he tells us that Agathon went astray in only one point, but this caused him many failures. He made his plots too involved – a tendency which we can see in post-classical tragedy in general and which is exemplified in the *Phoenissae* of Euripides. The reservations with which Aristotle makes this criticism constitute high praise. Aristophanes himself in the *Frogs* of 405, when Agathon, like Euripides, had gone to the court of Archelaus in Pella – he died there not long after – speaks in friendly terms of the man he had so mightily ridiculed. 'A fine poet, much missed by his friends' – that is how Dionysus describes him in a passage (83 f.), from which we can very probably infer that Agathon had then given up writing plays.

A remarkable play of Agathon's is mentioned very favourably by Aristotle in another passage of the *Poetics* (9. 1451 b 21). The events and the names were freely invented by the playwright, who thus emancipated himself from mythology far more than Euripides ever did. The manuscripts give the title as either *Antheus* or *Anthos* (= flower). At all events, what Aristotle says excludes a subject within known mythology. We may perhaps wonder whether Alexander Aetolus gives us a reflection of this drama in his elegiac poem *Apollo*.[2] In that

---

[1] Dion. Hal. *Lysias* 10. 21 U.-R.

[2] Thus C. CORBATO, 'L'Anteo di Agatone'. *Dioniso* 11, 1948, 163. The *Apollo* in Powell, *Collectanea Alexandrina* 122. Lévèque is mistaken in supposing that *Anthos* was the title of a sentimental bourgeois comedy.

case the play would have been called *Antheus*, and its subject matter would have been the theme of Potiphar's wife in a rather individual treatment.

Fragments of the dramatists here mentioned in A. NAUCK, *Tragicorum Graecorum Fragmenta*, 2nd ed. Leipz. 1889. – A. V. BLUMENTHAL, *Ion von Chios. Die Reste seiner Werke.* Stuttg. 1939. The philosophical fragments: VS 36. Historical works: F. JACOBY, *F Gr Hist* no. 392 (with the usual exhaustive commentary). T. B. L. WEBSTER, 'Sophocles and Ion of Chios'. *Herm.* 71, 1936, 263. – P. LÉVÈQUE, *Agathon.* Paris 1955. J. WAERN, 'Zum Tragiker Agathon'. *Eranos* 54, 1956, 87.

4 OTHER POETRY

In the last decade of the fifth century dramatic production was so much to the fore and absorbed the general interest so exclusively that the other forms of poetry were quite overshadowed and are only dimly traceable. The only exception is choral lyric poetry, which nevertheless owed much of its influence to its close connection with drama, which justifies our mentioning it at this point. The activity of the poets with whom it brings us into contact extends a good way into the fourth century, but the formal innovations date from the second half of the fifth.

We examined above (p. 302) the significance of that development by which the young democracy gave the dithyramb its appointed place in the Dionysiac contests, and we spoke of the large-scale production required to meet the demands of the yearly festivals. The dithyramb was rooted in the same soil as tragedy, grew up beside it, and had an especially close connection with it at the Great Dionysia. Mutual influence was inevitable, and we have often had to take it into account. In particular the 'new song' of Euripides and the choral lyrics of Agathon could only be understood in reference to the later Attic dithyramb. We must now bear in mind that the latter could never have come into existence if it were not for the continuous competition, in which tragedy, with its more varied means of expression and greater intensity of effect, inevitably gained at the expense of the dithyramb. Thus it came about that the latter threw off the bonds of strophic response, abandoned the old lyric style of narrative (which in itself tended towards effective exposition only of single scenes) in favour of startling effects, and introduced mimetic elements as far as was possible. We have very little of the text of such poems, and no music at all. We have to rely on inferences from allusions in comedy and on the pseudo-Plutarch *De Musica*, which essentially follows Aristoxenus, but is in many ways influenced by Heraclides Ponticus. We are given the impression of a music directed strongly towards sensuous effect, with lively changes of rhythm and mode, treating the text like a poor relation instead of being subordinate to it in the manner of the old choral lyric. Naturally it aroused opposition among those who followed Pythagoras in considering music as an important instrument of education and closely linked to the formation of character. Plato also felt called to oppose it.[1]

Undoubtedly the revolution in the choral lyric and its music was intimately connected with the unrest which the sophists had brought to the spirit of the age. Their unsettling ideas, many features in the development of tragedy, the new tone of the dithyramb – all converged to one point: the replacing of tradition, of which men had grown tired, by something entirely new.

So far we have been speaking of the dithyramb. We must not forget that the old form of ritual song in honour of Apollo which Terpander raised to an art-form, namely the nomos, went through the same development and reached a stage very much like that of the new dithyramb. In consequence it will not be necessary in future to treat the two forms separately, since the solo song to Apollo with accompanying lyre and the Dionysiac choral song to the flute were often written by the same poet.

We are well enough supplied with names, but there are few to which we can attach a distinct personality. Phrynis of Mytilene is reckoned among those who helped the new movement on its way. His innovations in the nomos are said to have consisted chiefly in replacing the traditional hexameters by other rhythms and thus making greater variety possible. He had a victory in the Panathenaea about 450, but his greatest success was in being Timotheus' teacher.

Another citharode was Melanippides of Melos, who ended his life at the court of Perdiccas II in Macedonia. According to a fragment of the comedy *Chiron* (Pherecrates fr. 145 K.) he added further strings to the lyre.[2] But he also made innovations in the music of the dithyramb, according to Suidas, and the known titles and fragments point to dithyrambs. The *Danaides* shows that titles known from tragedy recur in this field, and a fragment from the *Marsyas* (2 D.) has Athene furiously rejecting the double flute because it distorts her features. This story was vigorously assailed by the dithyrambist Telestes of Selinus in an enthusiastic defence of the 'sweetly-blowing, sacred' flute (fr. 1. 2 D.). Diagoras of Melos was better known for his militant atheism[3] than as a writer of dithyrambs. We may add to the list Polyidus of Selymbria, whom Aristotle (*Poet.* 16. 1455 a 6) describes as a sophist and praises for the management of the recognition-scene in his *Iphigenia* (apparently a dithyramb), and Licymnius of Chios, whose pieces are said by Aristotle (*Rhet.* 3. 12. 1413 b 13) to be particularly effective when read. It will be seen that most of those who thus tried to overthrow tradition in music were not Athenians. One is immediately reminded of the sophists, most of whom came from abroad. If an Athenian like

---

[1] Particularly in the *Laws*, e.g. 3. 700 D.

[2] Details of this change in H. WEIL–T. REINACH, *Plutarque de la musique*. Paris 1900 (on 1141 A).

[3] The action for impiety, brought against Diagoras for blaspheming the Eleusinian mysteries, is mentioned by Melanthius in his treatise on the El. Mysteries (*F Gr Hist* III B 326 F 3). F. JACOBY, 'Diagoras ὁ ἄθεος'. *Abh. Ak. Berl.* 1959/3, tries to date the action in the 'thirties before 433–2, but F. WEHRLI, *Gnom.* 33, 1961, 123, has argued effectively against him. Diagoras' treatise under the title ἀποπυργίζοντες λόγοι is explained by Jacoby as 'arguments blockading the gods, or arguments fortifying mankind against the gods'. Wehrli attributes the work to an atheistic sophist. Since the work is in fact lost, neither conclusion can wholly convince.

Cinesias, son of the citharode Meles, composed dithyrambs and was also well known as a physical weakling, he could not escape the shafts of comedy; and thus the poor wretch cuts a pitiable figure in Aristophanes. The comic writer Strattis also made Cinesias the subject of a play when he took up politics in later life: in this piece he is attacked for atheism.

There are two poets of whom we can form something more than a vague impression: Philoxenus and Timotheus. Philoxenus of Cythera, if only half the stories of him are true, lived a very adventurous life. The dates of his birth and death are given by the Marmor Parium as 455/54 and 380/79. He left his native island as a child, enslaved by the Spartans, but he later attached himself to Melanippides, whom we mentioned as one of the innovators and from whom he received his training as an artist. According to Suidas he wrote 24 dithyrambs, while other sources refer to his nomes. One of his works achieved a resounding success, partly through its intrinsic merits, partly from the attendant circumstances. His dithyramb *Cyclops* dealt with the adventure of Odysseus (fr. 2. 3 D.), but its most striking theme was the love of the oafish monster for the Nereid Galatea, whose services Odysseus enlisted to deceive the Cyclops. Philoxenus had lived for some time at the court of Dionysius I in Syracuse, where he had had many distressing experiences. According to a widespread story the tyrant had him consigned to the quarries after he had expressed himself with too much freedom on his master's literary exploits. According to another account, rivalry with Dionysius over a hetaera brought him thither. Philoxenus may or may not have intended Polyphemus as a caricature of Dionysius:[1] at all events men saw or imagined a resemblance, which contributed to the success of the work. It was parodied by Aristophanes in the *Plutus* of 388 in a manner which justifies our assumption of dramatic elements in this poem. The most striking example of its influence is the eleventh idyll of Theocritus, which makes a charming theme out of Polyphemus' love for Galatea.

The traditional Ionian stronghold of Miletus was the native city of Timotheus, who was born about 450, lived to a ripe old age, and died about 360. He is traditionally represented as the friend of Euripides, and this well reflects the literary movement which both represented in differing degrees. It is said that Euripides encouraged him when he was cast down by early failures. Timotheus also is said to have visited Macedon, but this is not wholly certain. Reports of his work are very confused, but it appears that he wrote mostly dithyrambs and nomes. A choregic inscription from Aexonae on Hymettus (IG II/III, 2nd ed. 3091: early fourth century) refers to a tragic writer Timotheus. It may be the same, but the name is common enough.

In 1902 a fortunate discovery was made in a grave at Abusir in Lower Egypt, bringing to light a nome of Timotheus' entitled *The Persians*. In our opening chapter on the transmission we spoke of this papyrus (nr. 1206 P.) as the oldest Greek book. Here and here only do we receive a clear picture of this new art. That the poem is a nomos does not matter after what we said earlier about the

---

[1] SCHÖNEWOLF op. cit. 55 is over-confident; for a more general treatment see J. MEWALDT, 'Antike Polyphemgedichte'. *Anz. Oest. Ak. phil.-hist. Kl.* 1946, 269.

convergent tendency of the two genres. The old division into parts, made canonical by Terpander, is retained, all innovations notwithstanding. The surviving verses – several hundred in number – begin in the omphalos, the central narrative part. They depict the battle of Salamis, not as a single historical event, but in a series of separate pictures, which are conventional for all their startling colours and anticipate the battle-scenes of Hellenistic historians. Dramatic life is imparted by passages of passionate self-expression, such as the angry outburst of a drowning Persian against the sea, or the despairing cries of stranded barbarians for their homeland. In these places Timotheus represents foreign speech in a way that reminds us of the Phrygian in Euripides' *Orestes*.

The papyrus also includes the sphragis, in which the poet speaks in his own person. He defends himself with moderation and courtesy against the charges which had been made against him in Sparta, and vindicates his techniques, particularly his use of an eleven-stringed lyre. The epilogue consists of good wishes for the city's victory. Presumably the city intended is Miletus, which he has previously mentioned, and where we may suppose the nome to have been written shortly after 400.

It is reasonable to postulate choral performance of certain parts, such as the lamentations of the barbarians mentioned above. Now Clement of Alexandria (*Strom.* 1, 16. p. 51 St.) says that Timotheus was the first to use a chorus in a citharodic nome. If we bear in mind that there are good grounds[1] for supposing that the new dithyramb occasionally interspersed choral music with monodies, we can recognise two things: first, the mutual drawing together of the two forms; secondly their striving after dramatic effect. A grotesque example of the latter tendency is given by Aristotle (*Poet.* 26. 1461 b 31 with 15. 1454 a 30). In the production of the dithyramb *Scylla* the flute-player seized the chorus-leader by his clothing to bring home more forcibly the monster's attack.

The language of Timotheus, as attested by this fragment, shows a quick and restless movement in the battle-scene and a majestic tread in the sphragis. Copiousness of language is especially noticeable in attributive phrases, where far-fetched adjectives are piled up in the attempt to impress. There is a marked tendency to puzzle the reader with bold periphrases – a trait which looks forward to Hellenistic literature.

There is little to say about the other literature of the period. All we hear about epic writing is that great men like Lysander sought poets to sing their praises. We saw earlier (p. 304) that he hoped to find such a one in Choerilus; in the end one Niceratus of Heraclea obeyed his behest and wrote a eulogistic epic on him, with which he was victorious over Antimachus of Colophon at the Lysandreia in Samos (Plut. *Lys.* 8). The latter had begun to write in this period, but he essentially belongs to the fourth century, and so we shall discuss him later.

Religious ritual long demanded poetry, most of which did not rise above mediocrity and so has not been preserved. The *Hymn to Hygieia* of Ariphron of Sicyon, which is preserved in an inscription, was current well into imperial

---

[1] SCHÖNEWOLF op. cit. 22.

times. Licymnius of Chios, whom we noticed before as a choral lyrist, also wrote a hymn to Hygieia, of which we have a few verses.[1]

This period, like the rest of antiquity, showed a steady production of epigrams, which sometimes rose to real greatness when a community set up a monument to the fallen who had given their lives for it. The greatest writers were not too proud for this task. We mentioned that Euripides was commissioned by the state to write an epigram on those who had fallen before Syracuse. Ion of Samos composed the epigram for a votive gift that Lysander sent to Delphi after his victories in 405/04. The same man is credited with other poems, but this is uncertain.[2]

In these years the symposium still remained the true setting for table-poetry of every kind. We have already mentioned Critias and Ion of Chios. Evenus of Paros also, whose versified rhetoric we mentioned above (p. 357), wrote elegies with the symposium as their material, but we know them only through small fragments.

Parody achieved something like an independent life during this time. In the *Poetics* (2. 1448 a 12) Aristotle names Hegemon of Thasos, a contemporary of Alcibiades', as the first writer of parodies. Now parody in fact began much earlier, with the *Batrachomyomachia*, and it was an important element in Old Comedy. Aristotle's statement makes sense, however, if we suppose that Hegemon made an independent literary genre of it and entered for poetic competitions with work of this sort. Until the citharodes later became the object of parody, it was mostly epic that was the target. Thus in Athens the Panathenaea, which had long been associated with epic recitation, became the regular occasion for the performance of parodies. It was on such an occasion that Hegemon achieved a particular success with his *Gigantomachia*.

Remains of lyric poetry in *Anth. Lyr.* 2, 2nd ed., fasc. 5, with bibliography. On the papyrus of Timotheus we still need the edition of WILAMOWITZ, Berl. 1903. – History of the dithyramb: A. W. PICKARD-CAMBRIDGE, *Dithyramb, Tragedy and Comedy*. Oxf. 1927. H. SCHÖNEWOLF, *Der jungattische Dithyrambos*. Diss. Giessen, 1938. H. OELLACHER, *Pap. Erzh. Rainer*, N.S.1, 1932, 136. Epigram: see p. 174 and F. HILLER V. GÄRTRINGEN, *Hist. gr. Epigramme*. Berl. 1926. – Parody: P. BRANDT, *Corpusculum poesis Graecae epicae ludibundae*. Leipz. 1885/88.

5 POLITICAL COMEDY

If we were asked whether the Attic genius was most fully and characteristically shown in Sophocles or in Aristophanes, we should have to reply 'In both'. Either by himself is only half the picture: to see it whole we must view together the sublime poetry of human suffering and the colourful extravagance of a comic invention which has never known a rival.

[1] Both hymns discussed by P. MAAS, *Epidaurische Hymnen*. Königsb. Gel. Ges. 9/5. 1933.
[2] E. DIEHL, *RE* 9, 1916, 1868.

In an earlier chapter we discussed various popular usages, the Attic carnival and several other nuclei of primitive comedy in the attempt to trace at least the outlines of this rather complex picture. All these primitive elements are taken up into the supreme creations of Old Comedy; but how much else there is to make up the fascinating motley of these delightful plays! The manifold richness of life in Athens' proudest days, the heights and depths of her ambitious politics, her well-stocked markets, the foibles of her eccentrics (not all of them harmless), the inrush of new ideas and the revolution in art – all this is caught in a magical mirror in the hand of a genius who never allows us to lose sight, behind these thousand flickering lights, of the realities of life and the seriousness of his own convictions.

The Alexandrians were the first to divide the history of comedy into three stages: the Old Comedy, culminating in Aristophanes, the New, best represented by Menander, and a Middle Comedy in between. If we try to give figures and to date the change between 400 and 320, we must remember that the boundaries are in fact very fluid. We shall find in due course that Middle Comedy is a conception that is very hard to define.

While we can assume that the three great tragedians had no real rivals, the situation in Old Comedy is different. Here again there was a canon of three poets, which Horace has smoothly versified (serm. 1. 4, 1): Eupolis atque Cratinus Aristophanesque poetae. But in addition we know of a large number of other poets of Old Comedy who, if we judge by ancient reports and the extant fragments, claimed a respectable place beside the canonical three. All told, we know of some forty poets of the Old Comedy, although often it is a matter of a name and some titles. To give a complete list[1] would be alien to the purpose of this book: what we propose rather is to sketch in the salient features of the background against which Aristophanes stood.

A word must be said to justify the heading of this chapter. 'Political' comedy is not meant as comedy dealing with current politics, although Old Comedy does take much of its material from that source: the epithet rather refers to the intimate association of the genre with the common life of the *polis*, an association which in its closeness is unequalled anywhere else in Greek literature.

Aristophanes himself gives us an interesting light on the history of comedy in the parabasis of the *Knights* (517), where he proves how fickle the taste of the Athenian public is by citing examples of the rise and fall of earlier writers. He names first of all Magnes, whom we met before (p. 237) as one of the earliest writers of comedy. His eleven victories at the great Dionysia made him the most successful poet of Old Comedy, but all we have of him is a few titles. Among these the *Wasps* and *Frogs* are worthy of notice (he probably wrote a *Birds* as well) as illustrating the old practice of animal choruses which we found at the beginning of comedy. They also point out the general background to Aristophanes' work.

An older poet even than Magnes is the Chionides whom we mentioned in the same context, the first victor at the Dionysia in 486. The inscriptions enable

---

[1] As in SCHMID's fourth volume.

us to trace this competition as far down as 120 B.C. From the very beginning, probably, the number of comedies presented in one day was five. We know that at the Great Dionysia four days – the 10th to the 13th of Elaphebolion – were set apart for dramatic presentations, and it is widely believed, although we do not know for sure,[1] that the 10th was the day for comedy. In the darkest hours of the Peloponnesian war the number of comedies was reduced to three, and three days (probably the 10th, 11th and 13th) were celebrated by the performance on each of one tragic tetralogy and one comedy. At the Lenaea also five poets took part, each with one comedy, and here again the great war caused the number to be brought down to three.

Ancient tradition gives 24 as the number of the chorus in Old Comedy – twice the number of the old tragic chorus. We shall discuss the number of the actors when we deal with Cratinus.

Among the oldest comic writers known to us we must place Ecphantides. Two verses of his (fr. 2 K.) are worth notice, since they express a determined rejection of Megarian comedy. Thus we find here a feature that recurs in Aristophanes: an emphatic claim to a higher artistic level than the coarse jokes of Dorian comedy – although its slapstick element was of course indispensable. We are given some light on this early stage of Old Comedy by a late notice[2] which says that the plays of Chionides and Magnes never ran to more than 300 verses. Since most of these belonged to the chorus, we have to think rather of detached comic scenes than of a continuous plot.

The same section of the *Knights* gives a very individual picture of Cratinus,[3] one of the canonical three, as we saw. His production, which brought him six victories at the Dionysia and three at the Lenaea, can be traced from the mid-fifth century to about 423. We have 28 titles of his plays, and we know enough about them to see that his themes were as multifarious as those of Aristophanes: politics rubbed shoulder with fairy-tale, literary criticism with travesties of mythology. Pericles was his favourite target. In his *Nemesis* he took the story of Zeus' relations with that goddess and the engendering of Helen, and used it to attack Pericles, showing him dressed as Zeus trying to carry out his disastrous projects. We can form a clearer idea of the contents of the *Dionysalexandros*, since a papyrus from Oxyrhynchus (nr. 163 P.) has the greater part of the hypothesis. It must have been an extravagant burlesque of the judgment of Paris and its consequences, with Dionysus playing the part of Paris and trying to sneak off when things began to warm up. This mixture of parodied mythology and topical allusion, only possible in Old Comedy, must have been directed against Pericles as a wanton warmonger and simultaneously against Aspasia. The account of the contents shows us that we must suppose Cratinus to have had a great wealth of comic elements, but much looseness in construction. The hypothesis of the *Dionysalexandros* enables us to understand the judgment of an

---

[1] A. PICKARD-CAMBRIDGE, *The Dramatic Festivals of Athens*. Oxf. 1953, 64.

[2] *Corp. Gloss. Lat.* 5. 181; now in *Gloss. Lat. ed. Acad. Britann.*, I, 128.

[3] B. MARZULLO, 'Annotazioni critiche a Cratino'. *Stud. z. Textgesch. u. Textkritik.* Cologne 1959, 133.

ancient critic,[1] that Cratinus had a very happy invention where the main outline of a play was concerned, but he lacked the ability to carry his concepts into proper execution.

'Onion-headed Pericles with the Odeon on his skull' (fr. 71 K.) was severely handled also in the *Chirones*. The chorus of this piece consisted of wise old Centaurs who lamented the better times that were gone and deplored the corruption of Athens under Pericles and Aspasia. We have a fragment from the end of the play, which contains for once a reference to the poet's literary labours: this play, which seems to have been his favourite, cost him two years' hard work to complete.

The picture of Pericles in Old Comedy shows how rapidly the passage of time vindicates what has been condemned. When Eupolis produced his *Demoi* in 412, he was able to call up Pericles from Hades to bear witness to a happier past.

The attacks of Cratinus must have been exceedingly obscene. One is surprised to read[2] that Aristophanes fell far behind him in this respect. Cratinus has sometimes been hailed as having founded the drama of political satire, but in fact this kind of attack is found in the earliest Attic comedy. It is possible that Cratinus converted into topical political satire what had previously been attacks on neighbours and private citizens.

We should not exaggerate the importance of these political polemics, however obscene and offensive they may have been: they were all within the limits of a jester's licence and were not taken too seriously. There were, nevertheless, attempts from time to time to restrict the freedom of comedy, although many of the ancient stories in that connection are pure fable. A proposal of that nature in 440 must be considered historical, but it had little effect. The same may be said of the proposal of Syracusius in 415 which forbade attacks on named persons (ὀνομαστὶ κωμῳδεῖν). All these were attempts which lacked the means of execution.

Cratinus also took his age to task where religion and art were concerned. His comedy *The Thracian Women* was directed against foreign cults like that of Bendis, while his *Panoptae* attacked the know-all attitude of the sophists. The *Archilochoi* featured a contest between great poets of old, and it is significant that he brings in Archilochus in this connection, whose biting iambics were close in spirit to Old Comedy. We mention the *Satyroi* purely to show that these boon companions could be received as guests into comedy as well, and the *Odysseus* ('Οδυσσῆς) as being a parodied version of the adventure with the Cyclops, but apparently without any satirical purpose. The *Ploutoi* must have had a strong flavour of fairy-tale, to judge from the fragments on a papyrus from Oxyrhynchus.[3] The spirits of wealth rise up in this play to make a survey of deserved and undeserved prosperity in Athens.

Cratinus gained his last victory in the Great Dionysia in 423 with a comedy which scored a special success. The year before, Aristophanes in the parabasis

---

[1] Platonius in Kaibel, *Com. Gr. Fr.* 1. 6.   [2] Platonius *loc. laud.*

[3] Nr. 164 P.; D. L. PAGE, *Greek Literary Papyri*, 1950, 196.

of the *Knights* had spoken flatteringly of Cratinus' great comic power in his earlier years, but had painted a sorry picture of him in old age, a drunkard who had outlived his art. The object of this attack struck back: laughing at himself as only a genius can, he brought himself and his weaknesses onto the stage. He showed his wife, Comoedia, complaining bitterly of his relations with the idle slut Methe (drunkenness) and of his running after Oeniscus ('little wine': depicted as a pretty boy). The poet, however, defends the gifts of the god of comedy, being deeply convinced that the man who drinks only water will never create anything worth while (fr. 199). The Athenians agreed with him, and this play, the *Pytine*, was victorious over Aristophanes' *Clouds*.

In Tzetzes' *Prolegomena de comoedia* (Kaibel, *Com. Gr. Fr.* p. 18) we find the positive statement that Cratinus put an end to the previous freedom in the number of actors and limited it thenceforth to three. We are justified in doubting this statement, since Aristotle (*Poet.* 5. 1449 b 4) confesses that he does not know various details of early comedy, among which he includes the number of the players. We can believe Tzetzes' statement that the number of actors was at first not fixed, but the restriction to three is contradicted by the extant plays of Aristophanes, in which sometimes as many as five are needed.[1]

In the parabasis of the *Knights* Aristophanes also mentions Crates, whom he describes as entertaining the public with lenten fare and often having to endure their displeasure. Aristotle, who values plot above all else in drama, esteems him more highly. According to *Poet.* 5. 1449 b 7 Crates was among the first to give up personal invective ($\dot{\iota}\alpha\mu\beta\iota\kappa\dot{\eta}$ $\iota\delta\epsilon\alpha$) and to try to bring speeches and plot into a unity.[2] The two opinions can be reconciled. The disappearance of personal attacks made Crates' comedy more tame, but there was also more scope for a consistent plot and structure. We have some information about the *Beasts* ($\Theta\eta\rho\dot{\iota}\alpha$), in which the chorus of beasts, for understandable reasons, advocated the vegetarianism of Pythagoras.

The peaceful spirit of Crates seems to have been unique. Teleclides, we are told, often aimed his shafts at politicians of the day. Against the three victories of Crates he could boast of eight, five of them at the Lenaea. In his *Hesiodoi*, like Cratinus in the *Archilochoi*, he seems to have criticized the old poets. It is remarkable that a poet could have expected such a subject to have a wide appeal. But as yet there was no hard division into educated and uneducated: that came only as an effect and consequence of sophistic teaching.

One very hard-hitting poet was Hermippus, whose forty plays make him a remarkably prolific author. He pursued into the lawcourts the line that he took in his comedies. Plutarch (*Per.* 32) tells us that he brought an unsuccessful action against Aspasia for impiety and immorality. We mentioned earlier (p. 304) that he waged war in iambics as well as on the stage.

Hermippus was exceeded in acerbity (if that were possible) and certainly in directness by the comic writer Plato, who was younger than those named and roughly contemporary with Aristophanes. Here for the first time we find whole

---

[1] PICKARD-CAMBRIDGE, *Dram. Fest.* 148.

[2] The passage is not correctly interpreted by SCHMID 4. 90, 8.

comedies named after the politicians that they assailed: *Hyperbolus, Pisander, Cleophon*. The *Hellas* (also known as *The Islands*) went beyond the purely personal and dealt with general questions of Greek politics. Of all the thirty titles given in Suidas (some of them spurious) we need mention only the *Phaon*. This play came out in 391, and Plato at this time, like Aristophanes, allowed political satire to take a back seat. It is concerned with the fabled phallic demon after whom women run mad – the figure which appears so strangely metamorphosed in the story of Sappho's death.

Closer to the spirit of Crates than either of these was Pherecrates, in whose comedy *Chiron* Musica is brought on as a woman complaining of all the sufferings inflicted on her by the New Music. The Alexandrians had doubts about the authorship of this play, as of several others among those ascribed to Pherecrates. One thus doubted was *The Miners* (Μεταλλῆς), in which life in the underworld was depicted with those cuckoo-land qualities that we often find in Old Comedy. The Κραπαταλοί also included a descent to the underworld. The *Curmudgeons* (Ἄγριοι) had a chorus of misanthropes like Timon who had turned their backs on society. The comic writers loved to draw a contrast in various ways between primitive conditions of life and those of their own time. We should be most interested of all to know more about plays which, like the *Corianno*, *Petale* and *Thalatta*, were named after hetaerae. In these Pherecrates made central characters of personages who were to be dominant in Middle and New Comedy.

Although Old Comedy was so varied and so different from the comedy of stock characters, certain themes did recur. Thus Phrynichus also made play with the notion of a retreat from the age and its way of life in *The Solitary* (Μονότροπος). The title *Satyroi* has also appeared before. His *Muses* was produced in the same year as Aristophanes' *Frogs* and had a similar theme: for Phrynichus also the death of Sophocles and Euripides brought up the question of the relative merits of the great tragedians, and probably this play had, like the *Frogs*, a scene of contention among poets – this time under the presidency of the Muses. We have some pleasing verses (fr. 31) on the happy life and happy death of Sophocles, but we should not therefore leap to conclusions about the Muses' verdict.

Aristophanes' most serious rival, once his friend, later his enemy, was Eupolis. Born in 446, he was very nearly of the same age as Aristophanes. His first comedy was presented in 429, and in the next seventeen years (to 412) he won four victories at the Dionysia and three at the Lenaea. He died rather young in 412. Various stories, some of them rather romantic, are told about his death. If he really died fighting for Athens, for whose moral recovery he had so passionately fought in his plays, it was a striking and fitting end. But the tradition is not sound enough to earn our full belief.

The later reports and the fragments, which in one instance at least give us some impression of his art, convey the picture of a writer who brought a warm heart and a keen eye to bear on the life of his community, who directed his fire wherever he saw danger or degeneracy. In consequence that kind of Old Comedy which drifts away from reality into a free indulgence of fantasy –

which has been rather unhappily christened 'Märchenkomödie' in Germany[1] –
is noticeably absent in Eupolis. The only example seems to be the *Goats* (Αἶγες),
which had a beast-chorus. There is no evidence for personal attack in this play,
but that does not mean much in view of the scanty material.

We can gain a clear picture of Eupolis as a political fighter. In his earliest play,
the *Taxiarchoi*, produced in 427, he brought on the veteran warrior Phormio
trying to make a soldier out of the cowardly Dionysus. We may suppose that
it was Pericles whom the poet was attacking under the mask of Dionysus:
Cratinus also attacked him under that guise. A recently discovered papyrus
fragment (nr. 275 P.) has been assigned to the *Prospaltioi*, although the only
basis of the supposition is that the name of this Athenian deme occurs in it. In
any case the fragment is very hard to interpret, and it is only with great reservations[2] that we can suppose the theme to have been resistance by the Prospaltioi
to Pericles' warlike measures. In comparison with Aristophanes, whose writings
are largely a plea for peace, Eupolis seems to have had very martial sympathies.
His *Slackers* or *Hermaphrodites* ('Αστράτευτοι ἢ 'Ανδρογύναι), like the *Taxiarchoi*,
was a sign of his concern for the armed forces of Athens: here also Phormio was
the symbol of military virtues.

Cleon came under fire in the *Golden Age* (Χρυσοῦν γένος), which Eupolis
produced in 424 – the year of Aristophanes' *Knights*. There was no fairy-tale
fantasy in this piece: it poured bitter scorn on the politics of an age which let
Cleon rule. After Cleon came Hyperbolus, whom Eupolis attacked in the
Marikas: the word means a boy, or often a catamite. This play brought about the
break-up of the friendship between Eupolis and Aristophanes, who quarrelled
bitterly over a question of plagiarism. In a passage of the *Clouds* (553), put in
when the play was revised, Aristophanes accuses Eupolis of having shamelessly
rifled the *Knights* for material for his *Marikas*, and in the *Anagyros* (fr. 54 K.) we
are told that Eupolis made himself three ragged garments out of the mantle of
Aristophanes. But there was another side to the question: in the *Baptai* (fr. 78 K.)
Eupolis claimed that he collaborated with Aristophanes in writing the *Knights*,
and that he gave his contribution as a free gift. Collaboration between the two,
while they were still friends, is by no means incredible; but to search for verses
written by Eupolis in the *Knights* – as some critics in antiquity did – is a waste of
time.[3]

Aristophanic themes recur in the *Cities* (Πόλεις). Just like the *Babylonians*, the
play concerned itself with the basic problem of Athenian maritime empire – the
relation between the central power and the subject allies. It is remarkable that
the separate members of the chorus of cities were individually characterized.

Naturally Eupolis also was aware of the innovations that came with the
sophists. So far as we can judge, he seems to have directed his fire less at the
spirit of the movement itself than at the activities of particular groups under its
flag. Thus in 421 he produced the *Colaces* (*Flatterers*), set in the house of the

[1] T. ZIELINSKI, *Die Märchenkomödie in Athen*. St. Petersburg 1885 (much overstated).
[2] SCHMID 4. 114 is too confident; cf. D. L. PAGE, *Greek Lit. Pap.* Oxf. 1950, 216.
[3] M. POHLENZ (*v. inf.* on the *Knights*), 120.

wealthy Callias, who is very favourably depicted in Plato's *Protagoras* and the *Symposium* of Xenophon. Eupolis portrayed the swarm of parasites who buzzed around the rich man's table: Protagoras got his share of ridicule, and Alcibiades, the host's brother-in-law, was represented as a woman-chaser. Socrates was also portrayed: we should like to know how. If the biting words about chattering beggars and starvelings (fr. 352 K.) come from the *Colaces*, they were no doubt in character with a speaker, and must not be taken as expressing the poet's own views. In the next year he brought out the *Autolycus*, which he later revised. The principal figure was the Autolycus who won the pancration at the Panathenaea of 422, the beloved of Callias; and the play attacked the sexual licence of that circle. The *Baptai* must have been similar in tone: it was mainly taken up with ridiculing the followers of the Thracian goddess Cotytto with her ceremonies of baptism. This occupied only the foreground of the play, which was essentially an attack on the eccentric habits of Alcibiades, which set all rules at defiance. Thus much we learn from a scholium on Juvenal (2. 91), and it gave rise to the foolish tale that Alcibiades took his revenge by throwing Eupolis overboard (in 415!) on the voyage to Sicily, thus repaying the 'baptism'.

Eupolis' last play was *The Demes* (Δῆμοι) of 412. Of this we have remains on three papyrus leaves,[1] which combine with the other fragments and reports to give us a picture of the play that shows more clearly than anything else how serious this hearty, dirty, fanciful Old Comedy could become without denying its own nature. When Eupolis wrote this play, Athens had suffered the Sicilian disaster, which brought in its train the agonizing question whether Athens was on a road that led ever downwards to the end of the Athenian empire. So much had gone bad in the city, in her politics, her law-courts, her life as a community. But behind all these was the transfigured image of a past in which Athenians smote the Medes and sent their ships far over the sea to magnify their city's might. Then the way was pointed out by great and wise men, sure of their goal. Could these not be summoned up from the kingdom of the dead in this time of need? They could: it was within the power of poetry.

The part before the parabasis takes place in the underworld, where the leading men from the great days of Athens are conversing in tones of gravest concern. The best and ablest, it is decided, shall return to earth under the leadership of Myronides to see that everything is set in order. After a debate in order to choose the members of the mission, Solon, Miltiades, Aristides and Pericles are selected. The importance assigned to Myronides is quite baffling. The man referred to was the victor of Oenophyta (457), who is mentioned also by Aristophanes (*Lys.* 801) together with Phormio as examples of brave soldiers. If we assume that his death had been so recent that, compared with the others, he could pass as a representative of the present, we must certainly distinguish him from the Myronides of whom we hear at the time of the Persian wars. There is no certain answer.[2] It is doubtful whether the part before the parabasis had a chorus. If it

---

[1] Nr. 273 P.; D. L. PAGE, *Greek Lit. Pap.* 1950, 202.
[2] Confusion reigns in SCHMID, 4. 127, 6.

did, we must suppose that the demes figured in the underworld, as personified communities of the good old days. The demes of the present time appeared in the second part of the play, which took place in the Agora. The parabasis was followed by a series of separate scenes in the old style, in which the emissaries of the underworld confronted the representatives of the modern age, converting, rebuking or punishing them. The papyrus gives us parts of the first of these scenes, in which the just Aristides deals with a sycophant.

We know just enough of Eupolis to make us bitterly regret the loss of his plays. At least we have enough to see how just the judgment of the old critics was, as conveyed by Platonius.[1] They applauded him for the richness of his invention, the sublimity of his flight, the deadly accuracy of his satire and the charm of his style.

Aristophanes, from the urban deme of Cydathenaeum, was born in the happy days of the Periclean peace, in those years when the building of the Parthenon was begun. We know that he presented his first play in 427 when he was very young: thus we will not go far wrong if we suppose that he was born about 445. There is little known about his life. In the *Acharnians* (653) he says jokingly that the Spartans coveted Aegina because they wanted to rob him; so presumably he had possessions on the island. This may be connected with the expulsion of the Aeginetans in 431 and their replacement by Attic cleruchs. Every one of his plays attests his lively concern for the political and literary life of his day and his close familiarity with the great national poets. We have no ground for assigning him to any given political party. Political satire thrives in opposition to the régime of the day, whose weaknesses it always seeks to expose. In the service of the establishment it degenerates into pure propaganda. The comedies of Aristophanes were mostly written in a period when the structure of Athenian democracy was being undermined by the war and by its own internal deficiencies. It was on these that Aristophanes discharged the vessels of his satire. We shall not discuss the question whether he was basically an opponent of the democracy. What we have said must not be interpreted as if the poet's expressions on the questions of the day were dictated by a kind of mechanical opposition. He was only able to throw such a lurid light on all that seemed questionable or dangerous because amid all the headlong changes around him he retained a lively sense of the power of tradition and conservatism, which are as necessary for the life of men and countries as those forces which beckon forwards.

Aristophanes took part in public life, as we see from an inscription (IG II/III. 2nd ed. 1740) from the early fourth century, which speaks of Aristophanes of Cydathenaeum as a prytanis.

The last dateable play is the *Plutus* of 388. He wrote later the *Cocalus* and *Aeolosicon*, which were staged by his son Ararus, himself a writer of comedies like two other sons of Aristophanes. We may therefore say that the poet died in the 'eighties; but we cannot establish a more precise date.

The Alexandrians knew 44 plays of Aristophanes, but four were of uncertain

---

[1] Cf. p. 420, n. 1.

authenticity: Archippus also was mentioned as the author. These were the *Twice Shipwrecked* (Δὶς ναυαγός); the *Islands* (Νῆσοι), which we may suppose to have been a play of the type of Eupolis' *Cities*; a *Niobus*, which is sometimes cited under the strange double title of *The Dramas or Niobus* (it may have included parodies of mythology); finally the *Poetry* (Ποίησις), which may have represented the sufferings of poetry much as those of music were shown in the *Chiron* of Pherecrates. The Alexandrians also knew of a second play entitled *Peace*, but they had no text of it. Crates of Mallos, however, knew the play, if we can trust the third hypothesis to the extant *Peace*, and fragments of it survive (294-97 K.). Finally, some very plausible supplements to an inscription dealing with the Lenaea[1] give us the name of Aristophanes and the title *Odomanto-presbeis*. This play may have been connected with the embassy which the Athenians sent to the Odomantes in 422 (Thuc. 5. 6).

Our possession of eleven dramas from Aristophanes' output is due not to a proper appreciation of his merits, but to the Atticists who prized his comedies as the purest source of old Attic.

The first of Aristophanes' plays to be produced was the *Banqueters* (Δαιταλῆς) which won the second prize in 427.[2] A father has had his two sons brought up very differently: one in the good old school, the other under the modern rhetoricians. He now compares the results in the form of an agon[3] between the two sons in his presence, in which it is seen how the fashionable methods lead to the collapse of all true education and decent feeling. The view has been put forward that this play, unlike the *Clouds*, tilted at practical and forensic education rather than the contemporary philosophical and sophistic teachings. The later pieces show, however, that the boundaries are very hard to draw. At all events, the debate on education owed its sharpness and actuality to the impact of the sophists, and thus in his very first play we find Aristophanes called to grapple with them. The theme remained a living one down to the time of Terence's *Adelphi*.

In the fifth century it was normal for the poet himself to train the chorus and direct production. It was, however, possible for another to take over the task of chorodidascalus, in which case he was reckoned as the producer, and his name was entered in the official records. This was the situation when Aristophanes' first comedy was produced, and the same thing happened surprisingly often. Callistratus, who produced the Δαιταλῆς for him, did the same next year with the *Babylonians* and later with the *Acharnians*, *Birds* and *Lysistrata*; we know that Philonides was chorodidascalus for the *Wasps* and *Frogs* and for the lost *Proagon* and *Amphiaraus*. The production of the *Cocalus* by Aristophanes' son Ararus may well have been posthumous. All sorts of fabulous interpretations

---

[1] IG II/III 2nd ed., 2321; cf. PICKARD-CAMBRIDGE, *Dram. Festivals* 111.

[2] First presentation by Aristophanes: C. F. RUSSO, 'Cronologia del tirocinio Aristofaneo'. *Belfagor. Rassegna di varia umanità* 14, 1959, 2. He thinks the *Banqueters* came out at the Dionysia of 427; in 426 performances were given at both festivals – the *Babylonians* at the Dionysia, at the Lenaea not the *Dramata* or *Centaur*, as has commonly been thought, but some play which we can no longer determine.

[3] On this see W. SÜSS (*v. inf.*) 250.

were current in antiquity. Our brief survey shows at once that the appointment of a proxy had nothing to do with an age limit (thus schol. *Clouds* 510). Aristophanes himself in the parabasis of the *Knights* (512) speaks of the difficulty of producing a comedy, and gives the capriciousness of his audience as his reason for keeping in the background. The first of these reasons may well have been the true one: the producer's task was beyond his talents.

It was with youthful élan that Aristophanes in 426 launched his first attack on the policies of Cleon. He was taking no small risk. At the Great Dionysia, with representatives of all parts of the Athenian empire sitting in the theatre, the chorus of allied cities was seen and heard in the garb of slaves at a mill, bitterly complaining of the heavy yoke of their Athenian taskmasters. One year earlier the rebellious Mytilenians had been brought to heel with great severity, and we read in Thucydides (3. 36) that an appalling massacre, proposed and pertinaciously defended by Cleon, would have been carried out but for the last-minute intervention of wiser and better heads. To the latter Aristophanes looked for support when he brought out this play: the view formerly current, that he owed his victory to them, has recently been called in question.[1] Cleon retorted with the prosecution, which, according to the poet's own words in the *Acharnians* (377), was very critical for him; but we know no more about it than this.

The comedy *Dramata* or *The Centaur* has been thought, without very good grounds, to have been an early play. This view has been recently challenged: it is interesting if true, since in this early period Aristophanes uses mythological material much less than he did later, when he wrote such plays as *Daedalus*, *Danaids*, *Women of Lemnos* and the like.

The oldest of the extant plays is the *Acharnians*, which won against Cratinus and Eupolis at the Lenaea of 425. Scholars are divided here in a way which is symptomatic of our whole approach to Aristophanes. The question is put: Is the *Acharnians* a free play of fancy,[2] without any serious taking of sides, or is it a creation of the poet's deep convictions, part of his struggle against the war and the Athenian war-party? To us such a question seems to sunder a unity which is the secret of the great master of Old Comedy.

When Aristophanes wrote this play, Athens was sorely beset by epidemics and by the destruction of her crops and fields at the enemy's hands; the rural population above all, wretchedly housed between the Long Walls, had every reason to sigh for peace. Thus it is the peasant Dicaeopolis, his very name expressive of justice, who features here as the hero of peace. It is sheer comic fantasy when he procures a private truce of thirty years from Sparta – the truce is given bodily form as a skin of wine! – and leads a happy life in a little island of peace among all the hardships of war. But he has a hard task to defend his treasure against the chorus of brutal charcoal-burners from Acharnae, who will not give up the war until the ravaging of their homeland is avenged. But he is

---

[1] RUSSO op. cit. 10 thinks that an older competitor was the victor, and that Aristophanes was not victorious until the two festivals of 425; then in 424 came Eupolis' first success at the Dionysia.

[2] Thus RUSSO (*v. inf.* on *Acharnians*).

able to win them over and to enjoy the pleasures of the situation he has contrived, which stand in sharp contrast to the sufferings of the swaggering war-hero Lamachus.

Despite all their freedom and fantasy, the comedies of Aristophanes are made up of formally differing and separate scenes, which in earlier times had had a life of their own, as we saw in a previous chapter. The fairly clear articulation of the *Acharnians* will enable us to illustrate and characterize some of the more important of these constructional elements.

The piece begins with a prologue-speech in which Dicaeopolis vents his ill-humour over the hard times. This form of introduction may have been influenced by the type of prologue which Euripides had developed for tragedy, but underneath it lay the old and essentially popular form of the speech to the public. In comedy at that time the audience could be directly addressed and the dramatic illusion temporarily shelved: this contact with the spectators continued down to the time of New Comedy. The vigorous development of the aside comes largely from this root. It seldom occurs in Euripides; where it does, one must reckon on comic influence. A good example of this direct address to the public comes in the prologue-scene of the *Knights* (36 ff.), which has another interesting feature in its opening: the explanatory and introductory speech does not come until after a scene of dialogue. This feature recurs in others of Aristophanes' plays, and in Menander's hands became typical of New Comedy. In this close contact between comedy and its public we see again how intimately in this art-form the classical literature of Athens was associated with the whole population, and how it drew strength and life from this quarter.

In the *Acharnians* the prologue that gives us our bearings is followed by a sequence of scenes satirizing proceedings in the ecclesia and leading rapidly to the point where Dicaeopolis receives the wonderful drink that is his separate peace. Next comes the entry of the chorus – the parodos – here taking the form of a ferocious hunt for the bringer of peace. In discussing the origins of comedy, we saw that the original part played by the chorus was the parabasis (p. 235), which in this play does not come till later. The parabasis derives its name from the procession or parade of the chorus, which was once the first appearance that it made in the action. We now find it embedded in the play, as the result of a process of growth whose basic features we tried to understand earlier. In the fully developed form the chorus entered long before the parabasis, in a parodos like that of tragedy, and naturally we can suppose tragic influence. The same influence was no doubt at work in the development of scene-division in comedy.

After its parodos the chorus lies in ambush, and Dicaeopolis comes out of the house at the head of a little procession, which we may consider as the descendant of one of those phallic processions which Aristotle mentions as the beginning of comedy. The chorus jumps out upon Dicaeopolis, and after various preliminaries, of which we shall speak later, we come to the decisive battle of words, in which the advocate of peace has to plead his case with his head already on the block He succeeds in dividing the chorus – the ease with which it splits into two opposing halves is a traditional feature of the comic chorus. Those who still hanker for war call on Lamachus to help them and take the opposite part to Dicaeopolis. But he does no good, is laughed to scorn, and the chorus finally comes over completely to Dicaeopolis.

Thus in the part before the parabasis the agon shows itself as the decisive element. Its importance in the composition of comedy was pointed out by T. Zielinski,[1] but we must allow a considerably greater freedom to the comic writer than his theory does.[2] The *Acharnians* is put together with much more liberty than such an elaborately planned piece as the *Frogs* with its debate of two persons presided over by a third. It is dangerous to start imagining lines of development: we should do better to admit the wide range of what is possible.

Before Dicaeopolis can make his speech in self-defence, he has to force the chorus to hear him. To this end he seizes a bag of charcoal as a hostage and threatens to cut it to pieces unless they listen to him. This is a parody of the *Telephus* of Euripides, in which the hero extorts a hearing from the Greeks by threatening to kill the child Orestes. The vein of paratragedy continues. Dicaeopolis has to defend himself with his head on the block, and he dresses himself in pitiable mourning sackcloth for this precarious performance. He borrows these rags from Euripides: they are the same which he made Telephus wear on the stage – a novel and shocking piece of realism. The scene may be taken as typifying the free and fanciful manner in which Aristophanes constantly alludes to tragedy, particularly to the traegdy of Euripides. He has innumerable tragic verses either cited or parodied, and even single words do not escape his ridicule.

The agon-scene of the *Acharnians* is followed by the parabasis, which in the best period shows a regular sevenfold division. The entry of the chorus is marked by a short section, the commation, which dismisses the actors and announces what is to come. This section could only have been added after the once separate procession had been incorporated into the drama. Next come the anapaests, commonly felt to be the most important section, and often called 'parabasis' by themselves. It was here that the poet felt free to express personal views and concerns: thus in the *Acharnians* he speaks of his dealings with Cleon. Anapaestic metre is normal in this part of the play: it ends with the pnigos (also called μακρόν): the idea of choking was suggested by the breathless haste in which the short verses were gabbled out.

The three sections thus described make up the first part of the parabasis. This part has no strophic responsion, but it is followed by a second part with responsions in the form of an epirrhematic syzygy. Each sung section (ode and antode) has a corresponding spoken part (epirrhema and antepirrhema), normally in sixteen trochaic tetrameters each. The lyrical parts consist mostly of invocations of gods, and we often find here passages of great poetical beauty. The use of the antode for personal attack, as in the *Demoi* of Eupolis, is an exception. There is very little of the kind in Aristophanes (but cf. *Ach.* 692. *Peace* 781): the epirrhemata provide the normal place for obscene personal invective.

---

[1] *Die Gliederung der altattischen Komödie.* Leipz. 1885. T. GELZER, *Der epirrhematische Agon bei Aristophanes.* Zet. 23. Munich 1960.

[2] M. PÖHLENZ, *Nachr. Ak. Gött. Phil.-hist. Kl.* 1949, 40.

Thus we see that this elaborately articulated structure contains essentially two parts: one intended for the original marching entry of the chorus, written in lively anapaests, the other consisting of ritual song by the chorus followed by vigorous spoken passages.

We can clearly see from the extant dramas how the parabasis, the ancient core of comedy, degenerated in the course of time. Individual sections begin to be left out, as for example the parts without responsion in the *Frogs*; in the *Lysistrata* the parabasis is to some extent replaced by the lively agon between the two halves of the chorus; in the last plays (*Eccl.*, *Plut.*) the parabasis is missing altogether. In the older plays, however, up to and including the *Birds*, but excluding the *Clouds*, we find the responsional parts of the parabasis still present either wholly or largely. There seems no justification for speaking of a second parabasis, since precisely those elements are lacking which belong to the march past (παραβαίνειν) of the chorus. Only the *Acharnians* has in this passage an ode and antode preceded by a rather lengthy commation (1143).

As soon as we enquire how the parabasis was staged, we realize the paucity of our information on questions of this kind. We can be sure that lively dance-movements accompanied the anapaests, since the commation occasionally (*Ach.* 627. *Peace* 729) contains an injunction to lay aside (ἀποδύειν) something: we may take this something to be the chorus' stage properties or heavy robes – certainly not their masks. We may suppose that the anapaests were accompanied by the flute, but we cannot be sure of the epirrhemata. It is an attractive supposition that the ode and antode were performed by hemichori, in which case the epirrhemata would be spoken by the leaders of these.[1]

After the parabasis the *Acharnians* very well illustrates that sequence of scenes which we reckoned among the basic elements and which is also well preserved in the *Peace* and *Birds*. Dicaeopolis, making ready for the delights of festival, has proclaimed an open market. The first to come to it is a poor wretch from Megara, which had suffered severely from the war: he has his two daughters in a sack and seeks to sell them as piglets. Next comes the inevitable sycophant, and is smartly sent about his business. The third is a Boeotian with all manner of good things, including the prized Copaic eels. The Canephoria is then proclaimed, and Dicaeopolis prepares himself to celebrate it fittingly. But he has to keep off some unbidden guests, who try to cadge some of his peace-drink. In the last scene before the rudimentary second parabasis there is a scene of stichomythia which most amusingly contrasts Dicaeopolis, revelling in the feast, and Lamachus, who has just received his orders, arming himself for the battle and the camp.

The closing section again exemplifies a standard feature, although we must emphasize once for all that all the standard features in Old Comedy are merely the framework which the poet's genius fills with a unique life and gaiety. Dicaeopolis returns from a drinking contest victorious and in the highest spirits, while Lamachus, who has been most unheroically wounded while jumping over a ditch, is carried onto the stage groaning and howling. The

[1] PICKARD-CAMBRIDGE, *Dramatic Festivals of Athens*. Oxf. 1953, 162. 249.

contrast is further heightened. The tipsy Dicaeopolis is not alone: he has a girl on each arm, and he minces no words in describing the joys that await him. The play ends with an uninhibited komos, in which the erotic element is very pronounced. There is of course no lack of the erotic in Aristophanes, but it undoubtedly plays a specially prominent part in the end of the plays. We have only to consider how frankly the union of Trygaeus and Opora is spoken of at the end of the *Peace*: in the *Birds* greater decency is preserved, but again a marriage forms the end. The view advanced by Murray,[1] following a theory of Cornford's, that the gamos at the end of Old Comedy represents a survival of a ritual element in the Dionysiac komos, deserves serious consideration, although in this field one cannot bring convincing proof.

Cleon was not able to frighten Aristophanes by his action over the *Babylonians*. In the *Acharnians* (300), with an allusion to Cleon's work as a tanner, he promised to cut up Cleon into boot-soles for the knights. Thus he already had in his mind the plan for the comedy which brought him victory at the Lenaea in 424 – one of the greatest successes of his life. From the passage quoted we can infer that at the time of writing Aristophanes was already confident of the collaboration of the knights – members of a conservative *corps d'élite* – in the chorus of the play which bears their name. At a time when scholars did not pay overmuch attention to the monuments, it was fashionable to think of cavalry manœuvres executed by proud Athenian knights. Nowadays we prefer to follow the black-figure vases[2] which portray men with masks of horses, carrying others on their backs. This is another example in Aristophanes of the old and enduring tradition of the animal chorus.

As the play opens, two slaves, whom we recognize as the generals Nicias and Demosthenes, are deploring their lot in the service of their master Demos of the Pnyx. Life has been intolerable since a new slave, a Paphlagonian, has been practising his rascality in the house, getting round Demos by flattery and having his own way in everything. But they are able to lay hands on the Paphlagonian's collection of oracles, and they find the comforting assurance that he will meet his match in a sausage-seller who is an even baser wretch than he. The sausage-seller soon arrives and does full honour to the promise. From this point on the play consists for long stretches, both before and after the parabasis, in a series of agon-scenes, in which the two worthy contestants strive each to surpass the other in vulgarity and vilification, in speeches which they deliver before an ecclesia summoned for this purpose, in producing ludicrous oracles, and finally in entertaining their master Demos. The Paphlagonian's prospects grow steadily dimmer, until finally, on the strength of an oracle, he has to acknowledge in the sausage-seller his fated successor, and he yields to him.

While the two competitors are off the stage, preparing the entertainment for Demos, there is a sung scene between the latter and the chorus (1111) which is very important for the understanding of the whole. The old lord Demos shows himself in a new light, and makes it clear to the knights that he is not so stupid

---

[1] *Aristophanes*. Oxf. 1933, 6.

[2] M. BIEBER, *History of the Greek and Roman Theater*. Princeton 1939, fig. 79.

after all. He does in fact see through these rascals who are battening on him: he is deliberately letting them wax fat, but at the right moment he will take back all that they have stolen. We can see that Aristophanes is giving a charitable interpretation of Demos so as to avoid being reproached with a defamation that amounted to *lèse-majesté* But this section, which gives us a rest from the noisy altercation that has gone before, has another purpose also: it is to prepare us for the surprising *coup de théâtre* at the end. After the epirrhematic syzygy (1264–1315) – that repetition of part of the parabasis which is not uncommon in the older plays – the sausage-seller and Demos come on again. But what a sausage-seller, and what a Demos! The glib swindler of the early scenes comes on garlanded and in festal garments to give the glad tidings that he has boiled Demos young again. This is an old myth-motif, well known from the story of Pelias and its dramatization by Euripides. Then Demos himself enters – no longer the feeble old man, but in the prime of life, dressed in the style of the great days of Marathon and Salamis, the true embodiment of 'holy, violet-crowned Athens', and wildly acclaimed by the chorus as king of the Hellenes. Now everything will be different, everything will prosper. The new adviser takes Demos to task for his previous faults, but consoles him by saying that the blame really rests on the traitors around him. But from now on Demos will behave better in every way.

This startling reversal at the end has always puzzled scholars, and some have declared that it defies all logic and psychology. This is true by our own standards, but the thing looks different if we accept the 'logic' of Old Comedy, which was at liberty whenever it chose to flit from the thousand problems of reality to the bright world of dreams. We see the right of it only when we bear in mind that the poet had to consider the feelings of his own public, who could only accept a play like this if it gave a cheerful prospect of a better time to come – the ultimate consolation in times of adversity. If we choose to interpret the end as bitter irony, we may reach a conclusion that satisfies our own notions, but we go a long way from the free and fanciful world of Aristophanes.

The serious note struck at the end does not lessen the uninhibited merriment of the komos. There is no lack of obscenity, and the play ended with a dance of thirty pretty girls representing the thirty years of the truce. The scholiast says that prostitutes were enlisted for this purpose.

This was the first play that Aristophanes staged in person. It is said that he himself took the part of the Paphlagonian. Some doubt is justified here, since the tradition represented by the scholium on v. 230 seems to have been spun out of that particular passage. Aristophanes makes a slave say that the mask of the Paphlagonian is not true to life, since no one dared to make such a mask. We may take this as a fact, for portrait-masks did occur in comedy at this time (e.g. Cratinus in the *Pytine*, Socrates in the *Clouds*), although we do not know how true to life they were. But when the scholium goes on to tell us that Aristophanes daubed his face with vermilion or the lees of wine and played the part himself, we seem to hear the voice of a pedant airing his knowledge of ancient mumming and its devices.

Aristophanes went off in a different direction when he brought out the *Clouds* at the Dionysia of 423. What we have now is a fairly drastic revision of the play as then performed. It was a failure, which the author took greatly to heart. Cratinus came first with the *Pytine*, Amipsias second with the *Konnos*, which also concerned itself with Socrates. Aristophanes rewrote it later, but did not put the new version on the stage.

The play seems to begin as a bourgeois comedy of manners, but the fantasy of Old Comedy soon shows through. The peasant Strepsiades has defied the advice of Pittacus and taken himself a wife of higher social rank. His son Phidippides lives up to these origins and to his distinguished name, devotes himself to horses and brings the old man to the verge of ruin. After a sleepless night Strepsiades can see only one way out: the boy must go to the thinking-shop (phrontisterion) to learn the art of winning cases, just or unjust. But the youngster will not hear of these people, Socrates or Chaerephon, and so Strepsiades himself in his old age must try to learn the new art of perverting the truth. But the scenes where the length of a flea's hop is being measured, where the origin of a gnat's hum is discussed, and where Socrates observes the sun from a hanging basket, all these only enable Strepsiades to make himself a laughing-stock by his boundless stupidity. Now it is Phidippides' turn. For his instruction the dispute is staged between the dikaios logos and the adikos logos, the just and the unjust cause – the most brilliant of all the agon-scenes in Aristophanes, in which the representative of a new age, which knew how to take its pleasures unhindered by morality and justice, triumphs over the advocate of ancient piety and morals. Here is a school that suits Phidippides, and he makes such good progress that his father is delighted with his skill and is enabled to rid himself of two pressing creditors (the traditional sequence of encounters and dismissals). But over dinner inside the house he falls out with his son over the latter's infatuation with Euripides, and Phidippides commits the ultimate and inexpiable crime of beating his own father. Thanks to his schooling he is clever enough to justify his action as a requital of what he suffered from his father as a child. In a sudden revulsion of feeling, which gives no difficulty in comedy, Strepsiades regrets having associated with knaves to learn their knavery, and goes with his slaves to burn down the thinking-shop.

The play is named after the chorus of Clouds, a very complex poetical creation. At first these Clouds provide a vehicle for splendid poetry: their first song is one of the most beautiful in Greek literature; next, as the divinities worshipped by the dwellers in the phrontisterion, they serve as an example of 'enlightenment' and are associated with all sorts of metaphysical theorems. At the end, however, they underline the moral tone of the action and dress themselves in a kind of Aeschylean piety. When Strepsiades reproaches them with having led him into his perverse behaviour, they give a deeply meaningful reply: thus do they always when they see a man inclined towards evil, so that he may fall and learn through suffering to reverence the gods.

The central problem raised by the *Clouds* is the representation of Socrates. Scholars have long been content with the formulation that Aristophanes simply put all the sins of the sophists on Socrates' head without regard to his personal character and pursuits. An opposing school was started by Kierkegaard's seventh thesis in his doctoral dissertation: *Aristophanes in Socrate depingendo proxime ad verum accessit.* Both these views substitute part of the truth for the whole. Painstaking researches of recent years[1] have revealed in the Socrates of the *Clouds* many traits that are not sophistical, but Socratic. This is most obvious in the ascetic way of life attributed to the hardy old man, but it can be seen also in details of his methods and doctrine. Socrates the scientist is not so incredible either: in 423 undoubtedly his scientific days were behind him, but Plato makes him say in the *Phaedo* (97 c) that at one time he expected great things from studies of this sort. But there are other places where the contradiction is irreconcilable: above all the association of Socrates with the sophistic teaching which would make the worse appear the better cause. This difficulty is somewhat eased if we remember that Socrates himself is not shown teaching this art, but nevertheless it is in the phrontisterion that Phidippides acquires his lamentable proficiency, and v. 874 f. show that the association was intended by the playwright.

In essentials the facts are not hard to understand. In 423 Aristophanes knew enough of Socrates to represent many of his characteristics to the life. But at the same time he hastily brought him in to his general attack on the new ways of thought, of speech and of education which were destroying the good old ways, in short, into his attack on the sophists. This was possible because to the Athenians of that day Socrates inevitably appeared – without the distinctions obvious to us today – simply as a representative of suspect innovation, of a way of thought which called everything into question. How far Aristophanes shared the views of the many, how far he used them for his own purposes – these are questions which we cannot now answer. But the suggestion that his play had a double meaning, and that through all the ridicule one can perceive a serious representation of Socrates clearly set apart from the sophists, is one which ignores the nature of Old Comedy.

In Plato's *Apology* (19 c) Socrates attaches great significance to the attacks of comic writers upon him, and we must remember that what was comic licence in 423 bore a very different face after the Athenian catastrophe. Yet Plato understood the poet well enough, and in the unforgettable final scene of the *Symposium* he shows him in earnest conversation with Socrates. Aristophanes' speech in the same dialogue makes the characters of the poet and the philosopher appear so mutually congenial that we would be glad to assign to Socrates that epigram (14 D.) which says that the soul of Aristophanes is a temple of the Graces.

We know that the play was rewritten, but it is hard to say how extensively.[2]

---

[1] See under *Clouds* and v. EHRENBERG 273.

[2] For a moderate view see H. EMONDS, *Zweite Auflage im Altertum.* Leipz. 1941, 277. ERBSE (*v. inf.*) 396, 1 and H.-J. NEWIGER, *Zet.* 16, Munich 1957, 143, are sceptical. C. F. RUSSO, ' "Nuvole" non recitate e "nuvole" recitate'. *Stud. zur Textgesch. u. Textkritik.* Cologne/Opladen 1959, 231, thinks that there have been great changes, particularly where the agon of the logoi is concerned. For an account of the history of the problem see T. GELZER, *Zet.* 23, Munich 1960, 144, 1: he also follows the ancient notices and supposes considerable alterations.

Revision is obvious in the parabasis, where Aristophanes complains of the ill success of the first play. Ancient critics say that the agon and the final scene were revised: both probably were not inserted until the second version.

At the Lenaea of 422 Philonides presented two plays of Aristophanes', the *Wasps* and the *Proagon*. The subject of the lost play was the performance of actors before the tragic contest of the Dionysia,[1] into which Aristophanes no doubt brought much effective parody of contemporary tragedy.

In the *Wasps* we have the same conflict between father and son as before in the *Daitales* and the *Clouds*, but here the situation is reversed, and a son is plagued by the folly of his father. Here again they are at opposite poles politically. Their names, Philocleon and Bdelycleon, indicate that the father is as warm in his support of that controversial statesman as the son is in detesting him. Philocleon is the embodiment of a passion that was epidemic at the time. The Greeks of all ages loved litigation – a reflection perhaps of what has been called their competitive nature. It was a very fine thing for a man to enjoy the pleasure of feeling important as a juror and to be paid for it as well. Pericles had introduced payment of jurors: in 425 Cleon raised it from two to three obols. It was necessary to secure a large number, since the Heliaea consisted of six thousand lay judges chosen by lot, who had to divide into committees of several hundreds to deal with individual cases.

The struggles of Bdelycleon against his father's inordinate love of jury-service provide the stuff of the drama until the parabasis, which at v. 1009 is strikingly delayed. The form of the exposition is familiar: a dialogue between two slaves leads up to a continuous account given by one of them. They are guarding the father on the son's orders – Bdelycleon has shut him up in the house – to keep him away from the law-courts. Philocleon's amusing attempts to break out (one of them borrowed from the ruse of Odysseus in the cave of the Cyclops) provide scenes of rich comedy. The chorus now comes to find Philocleon – a chorus of jurors, dressed as wasps with long stings. They are gnarled old men, good old-fashioned Athenians, but possessed by the same passion. An agon follows in which Bdelycleon has a theoretical discussion of the question with his father and defends his own point of view. The chorus is convinced, but the young man then arranges a private court in which the old man decides a lawsuit between two dogs. The dog Labes of Aexonae has been accused of cheese-stealing by a dog from Cydathenaeum. In the latter we recognize Cleon, who brought an action for embezzlement in 425 against the general Laches of Aexonae (we know him from Plato's dialogue). It is a pretty point that the verdict of 'not guilty', which was given in the historical trial, is here arrived at only through an oversight on the part of the infatuated Philocleon.

It is nothing new to us to find Aristophanes ending his play along different lines from those which he has followed in the first part. Here again there is a change of theme in the parabasis, where Bdelycleon tries to bring his boorish old father into a better frame of mind and into more refined company. But once again Aristophanes is sceptical of experiments in education, and this one also

[1] PICKARD-CAMBRIDGE, *Dram. Festivals* 65.

brings unexpected fruits. The old man behaves abominably at the dinner-table, starts all sorts of quarrels, and steals a pretty flute-girl from his companions. Thus Aristophanes brings in that coarse erotic element which is typical of his closing scenes. The final komos here is particularly disorderly. The old man dances like one possessed, and challenges the bystanders to compete with him. This brings in the three dwarfish sons of Carcinus, and they all finally go dancing off the stage.

The part following the parabasis is effective enough in its slapstick comedy, but it is not very carefully constructed. Twice the rejuvenated Philocleon gets up to his mischief off-stage, and twice the slave Xanthias comes on to the stage to make an appropriate report (1292. 1474). On the first occasion the events coincide in time with the typical fragment of parabasis, on the second with a song from the chorus praising the conversion of Philocleon. After the old man's behaviour at the table this is rather hard to take, and everything would go more smoothly if we transposed the two strophes and the piece of parabasis. The latter would then be at a greater and more normal distance from the main parabasis. But in a piece composed like this one such conclusions cannot claim any certainty.

When Aristophanes wrote the *Peace* for the Dionysia of 421, he could be confident that the play was topical. After the death of Cleon and Brasidas, the peace parties on both sides gained ground, and in April 421, very nearly at the time of the Dionysia, the peace was concluded which was expected to last for fifty years. Despite the extreme topicality of the play, Aristophanes had to concede first place in the contest to Eupolis with the *Colaces*.

Again it is two slaves who begin the play, and one of them, directly addressing the audience as so often, expounds the situation. They are having a thin time, these slaves, in giving the necessary care and provender to a gigantic dung-beetle kept by their master, the vinegrower Trygaeus. This creature is to serve its enterprising owner as transport to heaven, where he will ask Zeus what he has in mind for the war-weary Hellenes. Again the fanciful invention has a specific target: the ride on the dung-beetle is a parody of the *Bellerophon* of Euripides, in which the hero tried to reach heaven on his winged steed. For this purpose some stage machinery was used which readily lent itself to ridicule. But in Aristophanes the enterprise has a happier issue than in the tragedy. Trygaeus reaches his goal and enters into discussions with Hermes. He notes with dis-approval that the gods have withdrawn into the highest aether to be away from the endless horrors of war, and that Polemos reigns unchecked. He has shut up the goddess of peace, Eirene, in a pit, and he is now about to take the cities of Greece and bray them in a gigantic mortar. Polemos is shown in person making his arrangements, while Trygaeus listens unnoticed. The scenes of eaves-dropping that are common in later comedy are foreshadowed here. Luckily Polemos' servant Kydoimos (the fear of battle personified) is unable to provide a pestle – Cleon and Brasidas are dead – and so Polemos has to go back into the house to make another. Trygaeus seizes the opportunity, calls on the Greeks, who appear as the chorus, gains the support of the anxious Hermes for his plan, and leads the rescue of Eirene, who is pulled up from her pit by ropes. At the same moment two goddesses appear – Opora, goddess of fruitfulness, and Theoria, who stands for joy at festivals. After a conversation with Hermes, in which the causes of the war are recalled in ludicrous travesty, they all return to earth, not by the dung-beetle on a stage flying-machine (Trygaeus and his three goddesses would have overloaded it), but by simply climbing down a route which is pointed out by Hermes with a light-hearted breaking of the dramatic illusion.

Here we must take the opportunity of saying that the notion of the stage that we can form purely from the text of the play is very problematical.[1] We can suppose that the scene in heaven was played on the roof of the skene; but then we shall have to suppose that Eirene's pit was at no great height above the stage, since the chorus which sets her free must have immediate access to the orchestra, where it sings and dances the parabasis.[2] When the chorus says goodbye to Trygaeus in the commation (729), he must go off with his womenfolk by another way, possibly to the part behind the skene.

After the parabasis, in which Aristophanes blows his own trumpet quite unashamedly, we find a sequence of loosely connected scenes, played out once more on the earth. Trygaeus generously bestows the naked Theoria on the members of the council, Eirene receives her due offering, at which a sponging interpreter of oracles is driven off complete with his fraudulent prophecies. The so-called second parabasis (in reality the second part of a parabasis proper) gives a delightful picture of peaceful country life. This is almost the only place where we find Aristophanes so near in spirit to the world of the peasant, but we should dismiss such notions as 'idyll' and 'pastoral' from our minds. At this time the life of the peasant was not so far removed from that of the town-dweller that it called for or underwent poetic transfiguration. Aristophanes' motive is political: the peasants, who were the worst sufferers in the war, were the obvious representatives of the desire for peace.

Further episodic scenes follow, contrasting peaceful industry with the activities of the warmongers, for whom hard times are coming. The piece ends with the joyous union of Trygaeus and Opora.

We mentioned earlier (p. 426) a second play entitled *Peace*. Whether it was a revised version of this one or a wholly different play we cannot tell. We do know that one of the characters in the lost play was Georgia (agriculture).

We have been able to follow Aristophanes' work through a number of years; but now it is not until 414 that we have another secure date. We know of various titles, but we cannot attach them to any clear notion of the plays. Apart from the comedies mentioned above (p. 426 f.), with subjects taken from mythology or at least connected with it, we may mention the *Georgoi* and *Horai*. Obviously the life and work of the countryside played a part in these plays, so that they must have been thematically akin to the *Acharnians* and the *Peace*.

---

[1] H. KENNER, *Das Theater und der Realismus in der griech. Kunst.* Vienna 1954 (on the *Peace* see p. 118).

[2] So one infers from v. 224, but it is not quite certain.

At the Lenaea of 414 Philonides produced for the author his *Amphiaraus*. Again it was a story of rejuvenation, taking place in the shrine of that hero in Thebes. If we are right in supposing that miraculous cures had their share of attention in the play, there was a thematic parallel to the later *Plutus*.

At the Dionysia of the same year Aristophanes brought out the most highly wrought of all his extant plays, the *Birds*. It features the flight of two human beings from the miseries of the world into a fairyland, and it combines the boldest flights of fantasy with the most delicate poetry in a way that gives perennial delight and constantly invites imitation. The scenes are more numerous and varied and at the same time more closely knit than in any other of his plays.

When Aristophanes was writing this play, the Sicilian expedition was already in hand – that venture which aroused such hopes and such forebodings. The most determined attempts have been made to find allusions in Aristophanes to this great event, but we must admit that Aristophanes does nothing to reward such determination. The two friends Pisthetaerus[1] and Euelpides, whom we find when the play opens walking through a wood led by crows and jackdaws, give as the reason for their flight the passion for litigation at Athens – nothing more. In this piece the free play of fantasy is overwhelmingly more important than any concrete political purpose.

Of these two friends Pisthetaerus (True Friend) shows himself as a man of action and sense, while Euelpides (Good Hopes) takes the part of a bomolochos or buffoon. They ask the hoopoe if it knows of a city where one can live quietly and enjoy oneself. This is a happy touch, since the hoopoe was once king Tereus, the son-in-law of Pandion, king of Athens. The outcome of their exploration is quite different, namely the founding of the bird-city, but we should not immediately declare that there are two different strands in the plot. In fact one theme leads naturally to the other. The hoopoe's suggestions are none of them satisfactory, and Pisthetaerus consequently comes to think that the birds themselves ought to found a city in mid-air from which they could starve out the gods and make them more obliging. The chorus of birds – a colourful troupe – is summoned up by a monody from the hoopoe, in which, as in other lyrical parts of the play, the sounds of nature and the artistry of words are so combined that the woods in springtime seem to be echoing with a hundred strains of birdsong.

The element of agon is brought in to the part before the parabasis by the chorus at first taking the two men for enemies and the hoopoe for a traitor. A long speech from Pisthetaerus is necessary before they will accept his plan for the establishment of a world empire run by birds. They did indeed have such dominion before the gods, as Pisthetaerus takes care to remind them. For any further measures it is necessary for the two men to become birds. The metamorphosis takes place during the parabasis, of which the anapaestic part is of particular interest. It gives a truly Aristophanic theogony from a bird's-eye view, which is probably freely adapted from Orphic tradition.

[1] Peisthetairos in the MSS. cannot be right: others read Peisetairos or Peithetairos.

After the parabasis comes the christening of the city, which received the memorable name of Cloudcuckooland[1] (Νεφελοκοκκυγία); the construction of the wall to cut off heaven from earth is begun, and the foundation-sacrifice is offered up. The inevitable mumpers appear – a poet, a pedlar of oracles, the astronomer Meton, an official observer from Athens, a seller of laws, all of whom are sent packing in the usual sequence of episodes. Next comes the epirrhematic partial parabasis, to which we are now accustomed, after which the gods come onto the stage. Iris is captured as she flies through the bird-kingdom, and is released to acquaint Zeus with the new posture of affairs. Before the gods do anything more, there is another series of dismissal-scenes. Various men come along and ask for feathers, to turn themselves into birds. A particularly striking passage is the arrival of the dithyrambist Cinesias, who wants to be a nightingale, and can only express himself in the exalted strains of his own dithyrambs. After a stasimon from the chorus, full of personal attacks, Prometheus comes in. A veteran plotter, he has prudently disguised himself and carries a large parasol so that he cannot be seen from above. He tells Pisthetaerus of the embarrassments in heaven caused by the birds' blockade, and encourages them to persevere. Thus Pisthetaerus knows how to act when a wildly heterogeneous embassy comes down from heaven. It is led by Poseidon, a rather incompetent diplomat; then comes Heracles, the coarse glutton of Dorian farce, and a barbarous Thracian as a representative of the foreign gods. The outcome of their negotiations is that Zeus has to give up Basileia (the personification of rule over the world), and the play ends (how else?) with the marriage of Pisthetaerus and Basileia. The tone of this ending is more solemn than we find elsewhere on a similar theme.

At the Dionysia of this year, however, it was not Aristophanes who won, but Amipsias with the *Revellers* (Κωμασταί). The third was Phrynichus with *The Solitary* (v. supra, p. 422), another play of escape.

Now comes another period of a few years in which we do not know what Aristophanes wrote, until in 411 he brought out two plays – the *Thesmophoriazusae* and the *Lysistrata* – both dealing with women, but with very different basic themes. We do not know which play came out at which festival, but the *Lysistrata*, with its panhellenic terms of reference, was most likely brought out at the Great Dionysia.

The Thesmophoria was a festival common to all Greece, celebrated by women at the time of sowing: men were rigidly excluded. In Athens it took place in the Pnyx, where the women spent the day of the festival in leafy bowers. Aristophanes' play is built upon the invention that the women of Athens at this feast are plotting serious measures against their incorrigible adversary Euripides. The writer of so many plays of intrigue has devised a stratagem for his defence against this threat: he proposes to smuggle a friend in woman's clothing into the secret festival. So he has arranged with Mnesilochus, a kinsman by marriage,[2] to

---

[1] On the name see MURRAY, *Aristophanes*. Oxf. 1933, 148.
[2] In the text only κηδεστής: the proper name appears in the list of persons in the Ravennas and in the scholia.

depute this part to Agathon, whose effeminate manners mark him out for it. Agathon is rolled out upon the stage from the very ecstasy of composition (like Euripides in the *Acharnians*),[1] but he refuses to undertake so hazardous an enterprise. Mnesilochus steps into the breach, but he has to be shaven and singed before he puts on the women's clothes from Agathon's wardrobe. The poet then makes us witnesses of the solemn assembly, in which eloquent complainants demand the death of Euripides for bringing their faults onto the stage and making men suspicious. The speech of Mnesilochus in defence is not exactly acclaimed, since he makes it a point in Euripides' favour that he has not revealed the worst of woman's character. The whole section is remarkable for its bringing in themes and stories in the manner of the Milesian tales or the Decameron. We must suppose that such stories were current and popular even then.

At last Mnesilochus is unmasked. He tries to save himself by Telephus' stratagem (previously parodied in the *Acharnians*). He snatches the child of the principal speaker and flees to an altar. But what the swaddling clothes contain is in fact a wineskin. That Athenian women greatly appreciated the gifts of Bacchus is a frequent theme in comedy, and is unlikely to have been a malicious invention.

Guarded by one of the women, Mnesilochus stays sitting on the altar while the chorus in its parabasis sings the praises of women and depreciates men. Thus the context of the play gives new life to the immemorial battle of words between the sexes which had been probably part of the amusement of the spring festival since the earliest times.

In his mortal danger Mnesilochus scribbles appeals for help on votive tablets and throws them outside, just as Palamedes in Euripides' play wrote of his sufferings on oar-blades and threw them into the sea. Euripides finds the appeal, and the sequence of episodes after the parabasis here takes the form of a series of attempts at rescue – brilliant and fantastic parodies of scenes in Euripides – separated by songs from the chorus. In the first Mnesilochus is Helen, and Euripides Menelaus, trying to free his wife as in the play of 412. But the only upshot is that Euripides is taken into custody by one of the Scythians who served as police in Athens at that time. Next comes the *Andromeda*, but Perseus-Euripides is no more successful. Mnesilochus is not freed until the third attempt, when the poet comes to terms with the women, promising a truce in future, and with their co-operation and that of a pretty street-walker gets the better of the stupid Scythian.

It can be seen from what we have said that this play battens on contemporary tragedy, but we cannot give any impression of the completeness with which tragic parody permeates it even in individual lines and words.

Aristophanes wrote another comedy under the title *Thesmophoriazusae*, which differed considerably from the extant play.

In the *Lysistrata* – again produced by Callistratus – the women have a quite different end in view. They aim at stopping the war, and thus this play takes its

---

[1] Against the use of a revolving stage: E. BETHE. *Rhein. Mus.* 83, 1934, 23. A different view is expressed by A. M. DALE, *Wien. Stud.* 69, 1956, 100.

place beside the *Acharnians* and *Peace*. But its tone is very different: in the earlier plays we heard much about the miseries of war, and there were many home thrusts against those who profited from the common calamity; but the *Lysistrata* breathes a spirit of forgiveness and conciliation. It is significant that in the middle of his city's struggle for existence Aristophanes could express so openly the conviction that there was a good deal·to be said for Sparta, and that Athens could do no better than extend the hand of friendship to her. Here Aristophanes looks far beyond the Athenian horizon and shows a true panhellenic feeling. In consequence the allusions to domestic politics are infrequent in this play, despite all the tension that must have preceded the oligarchical putsch. It is characteristic of Aristophanes that his obscenity is not abated one whit by his seriousness of purpose.

Like others of Aristophanes' plays (*Clouds, Wasps, Ecclesiazusae*), the comedy opens at the break of dawn. The heroine of the piece and inventor of the stratagem is Lysistrata, whose seriousness of character keeps her above the general obscenity, which here is very great indeed: she is waiting for her helpers whom she has summoned from Boeotia and the Peloponnese. One by one the conspirators arrive, but as soon as Lysistrata unfolds her plan – a sex-strike to compel the men to make peace – we see how hard such a sacrifice seems to them. The general tone of the play is well reflected in the fact that Lysistrata's best helper is the Spartan woman Lampito. The agreement is solemnized by a sacrifice (of a wineskin!), and the other measure prudently proposed by Lysistrata is carried out: the older women occupy the city to secure the state treasury, from which the men pay the expenses of the war.

From the very beginning of the *Lysistrata* there are two opposing choruses; but we cannot be sure whether they were two whole choruses or the halves of one. Certainly this was not an innovation: the use of two choruses disputing one with the other was an old feature.[1] First the chorus of old men comes on to storm the city and drive out the women. The chorus of women with ready tongues and buckets of water keeps the men in check. The dispute between the choruses is now followed in this beautifully constructed play by an agon of individuals. A high official arrives – a member of the college of probouloi which was set up with extensive powers in 413. A proboulos appears also in the *Demes* of Eupolis. In our play his authority avails him little; he has to hear a vigorous denunciation by Lysistrata of the faults of the men who aspire to rule, and he has to withdraw ·covered in confusion. There now follows, in obvious ring-composition, a further scene of conflict between the two choruses, singing one against the other. This would normally be the place where we should expect the parabasis. Did Aristophanes leave it out in order not to break the lively pace of the action, or was the old nucleus of comedy no longer felt in 411 to be an indispensable part? Both factors may have worked together.

It follows from the close texture of the play that episodic sequences play a smaller part in it than in the others. There is, however, one very fine sequence after the second conflict of the choruses. Three women one after another,

---

[1] Cf. J. LAMMER, *Die Doppel- und Halbchöre in der ant. Tragödie.* Paderborn 1931.

slaves of their own passions, try to sneak off. The series leads up to a good climax with the third woman, who uses a helmet to feign pregnancy. At the same time these attempts at desertion form an effective contrast to the stout-hearted behaviour of Myrrhine, who follows the spirit and letter of the plan. In a pro-tracted scene which could not be more explicit she drives her husband Cinesias to distraction and final frustration. The men of Sparta are no better off, as we hear from a Spartan herald and see in his own person. The great peace-treaty is preceded by a treaty between the two choruses, who now come together and form one. The Spartan ambassadors come to discuss terms, and Lysistrata appears accompanied by Forgiveness – another of those allegorical figures that come at the end of Aristophanes' comedies. She addresses both parties, and reminds the conflicting Greek nations of their common destiny in a speech which is one of the most noble and serious in Aristophanes. It is only natural that the spirit of the komos should now assert itself in feasting and dancing. The end is damaged, but not much appears to be missing.

We can well understand why this splendid play has been so often imitated, especially in times which have known the horrors of war. But we can also understand why all such attempts on stage or screen are doomed to failure. The incredible frankness with which sex is handled – yet without any prurience – is unacceptable to modern taste, while to Aristophanic comedy, its nature and origins being what they were, such frankness was quite indispensable. Here if anywhere we can see how necessary an historical sense is for full enjoyment of ancient literature.

At about the same time Aristophanes wrote plays in which he attacked Alcibiades. It seems that he did not display towards him the same hatred and detestation that he had for Cleon: he merely ridiculed some aspects of his behaviour. This attitude, basically not hostile, is reflected in the delicate equi-poise of his remarks on him in the Frogs (1422). The Tagenistai, which had a good deal to say about gluttony, was probably directed against Alcibiades: certainly the Triphales was, in which the erotic side of his life was handled in a way which the extant fragments show to have been highly Aristophanic.

The Gerytades seems to belong to this period of the author's work. It took as its theme the contrast between modern art and the old masters – almost a leit-motiv in the work of Aristophanes. The fragments point to a commission of modern artists being sent down by the ecclesia into the underworld, from which they probably brought back ancient art as an allegorical female figure. We are by now accustomed to the regular part played by such figures in Aristophanes.

The same problem was given a masterly handling in the Frogs, which Philo-nides produced for Aristophanes at the Lenaea of 405. In our high estimate of this play we agree with the Byzantines, although for different reasons. The judges also gave it the first place: the second went to the Muses of Phrynichus, on a kindred theme.

Up till now we have been able to see a certain uniformity in the construction of Aristophanes' plays: the element of agon is more prominent in the first half, the episodic element in the second half. In the Frogs the situation is reversed. It begins with a kind of prelude at the house of Heracles, to which Dionysus comes with his slave Xanthias to enquire the way to the underworld. Heracles has been there before to fetch up Cerberus, and Dionysus thinks it advantageous to go down in the costume of Heracles, with club and lion-skin, to make a good impression. The purpose of the venture is to bring back Euripides, who had died a little before: the god of the stage cannot endure his absence. He justifies his expedition in a conversation with Heracles on the pitiful state of the tragic stage in Athens.

With a lightning change of scene, as allowed by comedy, we find ourselves beside a lake in the underworld: Dionysus enters Charon's boat, where he has to row manfully himself. Here he is greatly troubled by the croaking of a subsidiary chorus of frogs, which gives the play its name. Xanthias is not allowed on board, and so he runs round the lake (i.e. round the orchestra) over which his master is rowing. In rather a similar way, although more ceremoniously, the god was borne through the city in his boat on wheels at the spring festival.

After going some little way on their journey, during which Dionysus gives several proofs of the most striking cowardice, the two meet a chorus of Eleusinian initiates, who are allowed to celebrate their festivals even in the underworld. (This is the first appearance of the chorus.) Their hymn of invocation to Iacchus is a pearl of Aristophanic poetry.

The value of the Heracles-costume becomes rather doubtful at this stage. At the sight of the supposed dog-stealer, Aeacus, the porter of hellgate, becomes furiously incensed and rushes off to fetch a policeman. Alehouse-women, whom Heracles has eaten out of house and home, fall upon the new arrival like maenads. But there is some consolation: a serving-maid of Persephone's comes with a charming invitation. In the course of these rapid episodes Dionysus makes Xanthias repeatedly change clothes with him so that he can pass off the slave as Heracles when it suits his book. In consequence, when Aeacus comes with the constables, it is impossible to establish which is the god. The matter is comically tested by flogging them both, but this leads to no certain result. In the end Aeacus sends the two heroes into the palace so that the gods of the underworld can decide.

The parabasis, the last that we have from Aristophanes, is shorn of its non-responsional parts, so that it shows the same form of epirrhematic syzygy that we have met in the second parts of the older plays. Its theme – an earnest and persuasive appeal to Athenians to heal the wounds within their city and to reach out the hand of forgiveness to political offenders – occasioned a second presentation of the play, according to Dicaearchus in the hypothesis. A pupil of Aristotle's deserves belief on such a point: but the date of the second presentation is uncertain. Most probably it was in the same year: perhaps even at the same festival.

After the parabasis Aeacus and Xanthias come on, having now struck up a friendship as between servants. From their conversation we hear of a dispute that has broken out in the underworld: Euripides is laying claim to the throne of tragedy, but the holder, Aeschylus, is defending it. It is now time for the two men's art to be examined and compared, and Dionysus is to be the umpire. It is obvious that the plot has here been changed. Dionysus originally went on this expedition in order to recover Euripides, but now there is to be a contest between the representatives of venerable tradition and of modern tragedy. But it would be wrong to talk of two plots side by side in the play, and to invent theories to account for the facts mentioned above. One such theory suggests that the contest was thought of while Sophocles was still alive, while the fetching back of Euripides was suggested by the parlous state of the stage after the former's death. We should be better employed in appreciating the art by which the poet twists the two themes together into an organic whole and gains the opportunity for an animated agon.[1] It is true, however, that Sophocles died while the play was in Aristophanes' mind, and this fact called for notice. The poet does this with a few light touches: we see this most clearly in those charming passages (78. 788) which express respect and admiration for the great tragedian.

The contest, which is inaugurated by a solemn sacrifice, divides itself into two formally distinct parts. This is of course no good ground for thinking that they were written at different times. The first of these parts (895–1098), like the dispute in the *Clouds*, is a good example of that strongly and symmetrically composed agon which Zielinski[2] considers to be the normal form. The individual elements are largely the same as we find in the parabasis. Ode, katakeleusmos ('encouragement'), epirrhema (in long verses) and pnigos are followed by their corresponding antode etc. The epirrhemata, of course, are not set speeches, but dialogues between the two contending poets. This section is concerned with general principles of tragic poetry. Here, as later, the weight and grandeur of Aeschylus, with its heavy pomp of words, is set in opposition to the lawyer-like rhetoric and realistic depiction of character found in Euripides. A question that receives particular attention is the value of poetry to the community, especially its value in education. Amid the deep and serious thought the cap and bells are not forgotten, since Dionysus punctuates the dialogue with interjections concerned with quite different aspects of life, which have the comic incongruity in which Aristophanes excels. The second section begins at 1119, and is in trimeters varied by occasional parodies of lyric. Twice the chorus has a short ode. In its subject matter the section may be said to end at 1414, where Pluto takes a part, having hitherto been a silent spectator. We are here concerned with the individual parts of tragedy – prologue, monody, choral ode –

---

[1] Ably treated by süss (*v. inf.*) 139. But see also H. DREXLER, *Die Komposition der Fr. des Arist.* Breslau 1928. SCHMID, 4, 345. KRAUS in RADERMACHER (*v. inf.*) 355. Drexler's analysis is opposed by H. ERBSE, *Gnom.* 28, 1956, 272 (with bibliog.). H.-J. NEWIGER, *Zet.* 16, Munich 1957, 67, 6. T. GELZER, *Zet.* 23, Munich 1960, speaks of two conceptions superimposed. This is certainly true, but whether a theory of the play's composition can be deduced from it is quite another thing. C. F. RUSSO, 'Per una storia delle "Rane" di Aristofane'. *Belfagor, Rassegna di varia umanità* 16, 1961, 1 (now *Storia delle Rane di Ar. Proagones* 2. Padua 1961), tries to prove rewriting in details after the death of Sophocles. See also his *Aristofane autore di teatro*. Florence 1962, 313. More moderation is shown by E. FRAENKEL, *Boobachtungen zu Ar.* Rome 1962.   [2] See p. 429, n. 1.

and each rather crudely travesties the other's verses in what is called a careful weighing of the several parts (βασανίζειν 1121). In the end they have recourse to a pair of scales, and, although the balance has tilted three times in favour of Aeschylus, Dionysus still cannot make up his mind: he admires the wisdom of the one, but takes pleasure in the other. Pluto prompts him to base his final decision on usefulness to the community: this brings us back to the subject matter of the epirrhematic part of the agon. Unfortunately the text is unsatisfactory here, and various passages are suspected of being interpolations; but it is certain that Dionysus does in fact make up his mind and takes Aeschylus back with him as a guardian of public morals. From a formal aspect Aeschylus here serves the turn of one of those allegorical figures which so often occur at the end of Aristophanes' comedies.

Two problems have to be faced here. What is Aristophanes' attitude towards the gods of popular belief, and what is his atttiude towards the poet whom he derides more than any other?

Aristophanes allows himself considerable liberties with the gods. One could hardly go further than to show Dionysus, frightened by Xanthias on his journey through the underworld, creeping in mortal dread behind the throne of his own priest. Such a scholar as Nilsson[1] explains this burlesque as betokening the downfall of religious belief: falsely, we think. There are kinds of ridicule which show a living proximity to their object more than distant respect can. The stories told by simple and primitive men about their beloved gods afford a good parallel, just as the destructive wit of a Lucian offers an illuminating contrast. In any case, it is not every god whom Aristophanes sees in this light. Such a treatment of Athene would be unthinkable: with Dionysus such jokes point to a very special intimacy.

It would be wrong to apply what we have just said without modification to Euripides, but the two questions do have a basic likeness. We should certainly miss the point of Aristophanic comedy if we supposed that deep animosity underlay the attacks on Euripides. The jokes of a comic writer must always be treated as jokes. Of course, behind all the fun and mockery there is a real concern to protect traditional values. But Aristophanes well knew that the target of his fire was a great spirit indeed; and as the master of paratragedy, he knew that the distorting mirror of parody is meaningful and effective only when it reflects something great. For lesser men he had the weapon of coarse abuse which the armoury of comedy supplied for use against Cleon and smaller fry, not against Euripides. The tragedian had a remarkable revenge: he made a pupil out of his determined opponent, not least where language and dialectics were concerned. This did not escape Cratinus, who coins the term *Euripidaristophanizon* (fr. 307).[2]

When the walls of Athens were razed by her enemies in 404, the only world in

---

[1] *Gesch. d. griech. Religion* I, 2nd ed. Munich 1955, 799. A. LESKY, 'Griechen lachen über ihre Götter'. *Wiener human. Blätter* 4, 1961, 30.

[2] Similarities in language are well brought out by C. PRATO, *Eur. nella critica di Aristof.* Galatina 1955, who also lists the passages where Euripidean influence may be suspected.

which Old Comedy could live collapsed into ruins. The work of Aristophanes, however, extends a good deal beyond this *débâcle*.

Of the late plays only two survive. If we can judge from them, common features were the reduction within narrow limits of topical references to men and affairs of the day, and the increased scope allowed to pure invention.

So we find it in the *Ecclesiazusae* ('Women in Parliament'), which was produced (according to the statement of Philochorus in the scholium to v. 293) two years after the treaty of alliance between Athens and Sparta, that is, in 392. Comparison with the *Lysistrata* is inevitable. In both plays women conspire in a revolution, in both it is one woman who holds the leading strings of the enterprise, and in both the play opens with a conspiratorial meeting at an early hour – here actually in darkness. But while the *Lysistrata* was concerned with the most burning of topical questions, namely the ending of the war, it is a comic Utopia that is depicted here. In the *Lysistrata*, behind all the fantasy, we felt an earnest hope and exhortation that reason might be suffered to prevail, but in the *Ecclesiazusae* the free play of fantasy leads light-heartedly to a *reductio ad absurdum*.

The women of Athens have had enough of the unsatisfactory government of men, and they propose to take over themselves. They sneak into the ecclesia in disguise to force through the necessary legislation: but first they listen enthralled to a speech from their leader Praxagora expounding her policy. They form themselves into a chorus, sing a song about what they are doing to do, and go into the ecclesia. Thus after the parodos the stage is empty, permitting a scene in which Blepyrus, the husband of Praxagora, is informed of the total revolution by Chremes, who has just come from the assembly. The chorus also comes back, and with it Praxagora, who outlines the programme of the new régime to her husband in a protracted agon in long verses. Basically it is simple: poverty is to be abolished, since all is to belong to all. We have seen before that Aristophanes often keeps his plots moving by entwining one sequence of themes with another. So here the original theme of the regiment of women drops out of sight, and the rest of the play turns on the enforcement of a primitive communism. While the play has no parabasis, in all other ways it keeps the old form of composition. The agon is followed by a series of episodic scenes throwing an ironical light on the new régime. A loyal citizen, all ready to give up his goods, is confronted with a sceptical smart-alec who is waiting to see how things turn out. There is a wholly mad and wholly Aristophanic scene – if that is not a tautology – concerned with the execution of an important point in the programme: women are to be assured of an equal share in the delights of love by making the old women mate before the young ones have their chance. Thus a young man who would fain fly to his love becomes the sorry victim of some Megarian hags like the daughters of Phorcys, who have all the allurements of a coven of witches.

Praxagora's revolution turns out differently in reality from what she intended. Here again she is unlike Lysistrata, and in the second half of the play she is seen no more on the stage. The end is negligently sketched. A serving-girl calls

Blepyrus to the communal feast which the other citizens have already enjoyed. This gives an excuse for the comastic ending that custom demanded, and Blepyrus comes on contentedly enough with some women of the town. How far the ironical tone of the previous scenes is maintained is difficult to say. At all events the invitation of the audience to go and have a good dinner – at their own houses (1148) – and the contrast between the description of the wonderful fare that is waiting (ending with a word of 168 letters!) and the pease-pudding that is served both point in this direction. The appeal to the judges is relegated to the closing section, since there is no parabasis in which to place it.

Plato in the *Republic* proposed complete community of goods among the Guardians, and treated the relations between the sexes in much the same way. Scholars have discussed untiringly the relation between the poet and the philosopher in this connection.[1] We should not take it too much to heart, for Aristophanes cannot be viewed as a serious theoretician of communism.[2] Coincidences between the two may well have arisen from the interest then taken in such questions. We know that Hippodamus of Miletus in the time of Pericles and Phaleas of Chalcedon at the beginning of the fourth century drew up schemes full of the spirit of enlightenment, the second calling for community of goods. Certainly Aristotle (*Pol.* 2, 7. 1266 a 34; 12. 1274 b 9) attributes these revolutionary proposals for family life expressly to Plato, but that does not mean that they were not discussed before. And it is always possible that Plato himself, some twenty years before the final appearance of the *Republic*, may have talked of these doctrines in one form or another.[3]

The last piece that we have from Aristophanes is the *Plutus*, which he produced in 388. He had brought out a play of the same name in 408. The little that we know about it suggests that the first *Plutus* was on the same theme as the extant play.

The age-old complaint of the unjust distribution of blessings is treated here in a kind of fairy-story which leaves out much of the personal invective and obscenity which were the stock-in-trade of Old Comedy.

Once again in late Aristophanes we find the theme of the *Daitales* and *Clouds*. The aged Chremylus has gone to Delphi to ask the god whether he would not do better for his son's career by training him to be a rascal. The god has answered with his favourite irrelevance that Chremylus is to take into his home the first man that he meets outside the temple. This turns out to be Plutus, whose blindness is responsible for the bad state of the world. He is to recover his sight by a miraculous cure in the temple of Aesculapius. This project is opposed by Penia, poverty personified, who stands up for herself in an agon of the old style with Chremylus. When Poverty praises her blessings, it is not the poverty of the beggar that is meant in this sociologically important section, but the poverty

[1] Bibliography in A. MEDER, *Der ath. Demos zur Zeit des peloponn. Krieges.* Diss. Munich 1938, 73.

[2] F. OERTEL in R. V. POHLMANN, *Gesch. d. soz. Frage u. des Sozialismus in der ant. Welt.* 3rd ed. Munich 1925, 566. Id., *Klassenkampf, Sozialismus und organischer Staat im alten Griechenland.* Bonn 1942, 42.   [3] Cf. MURRAY (*v. inf.*) 187.

which makes a man work for his daily bread, not for luxuries. Much that Poverty says is close in spirit to the closing chapter of Herodotus.

This play also shows a twining of different themes, leading in fact to considerable uncertainty.[1] Plutus is to have his sight when he distributes wealth to the good and just, but the notion is now slipped in that all men are to be both rich and good, which is contradicted by the scene with the sycophant in the later sequence of episodes.

The healing of the blind god is related in detail by the slave Carion, who with Aristophanic lack of inhibition tells in the same breath of the trickery of the priests and the wonders wrought by the god.

The new régime introduced (we know not how) by Plutus now that he can see is next illustrated in the familiar way by a series of episodes. In comes a good man to give thanks for his new prosperity; next a sycophant whose prospects are now blighted; then a hag, sister of those in the *Ecclesiazusae*, whose gigolo now no longer needs her money. Hermes comes to tell of the disorder in Olympus and asks for a new job; the priest of Zeus Soter goes over to Plutus. The latter is now conveyed to his seat in better days, the opisthodomus of the Parthenon. For the sake of a joke or two, the impassioned crone is enlisted into the procession, and thus the komos comes into its own (although very modestly) at the end of the play.

We have already remarked that the parabasis is missing in the later plays of Aristophanes. In addition it is obvious that the choral part lessens in importance, until finally it begins to disappear from our texts. In the *Ecclesiazusae* there are two choral lyric sections: in two other places (after 729 and 876) we find only the note χοροῦ. We find this once in the *Clouds* (after 888), where probably in the second revision no choral ode was written. The *Plutus*, which has no choral lyrics, has χοροῦ four times. In other words, we have reached the situation normal in New Comedy. The note simply indicates that a performance by the chorus took place: by now we could describe it as separating the acts. Some kind of dance was certainly involved: how far there was singing we cannot say with certainty.

It must now be apparent that in late Aristophanes Old Comedy has already lost many of its typical features. The jokes are fewer and less obscene, the chorus is unimportant; we may add that the Carion of the *Plutus* foreshadows in many ways the slaves who were stock figures of later comedy. The development in this direction engaged the attention of ancient critics. Platonius declares in his treatise Περὶ διαφορᾶς κωμῳδιῶν that such a piece as the *Aeolosicon*, a tragic parody without personal invective or choral odes, already showed the features of Middle Comedy. This may be true. But we must be more on our guard against a theory expounded in the ancient life of Aristophanes in reference to his last play, the *Cocalus*.[2] On this view Menander took some of his most important themes from this play, which had no invective, but a seduction and a recognition. This attempt to tie up New and Old Comedy in a neat line of development

---

[1] Cf. süss, *Inkongruenzen* (*v. inf.*), 298.
[2] On Cocalus see m. p. nilsson, *Opuscula selecta* 3, 1960, 505.

should be rejected as arbitrary; but we still face the question how comedy altered during the fourth century. Indications from Aristophanes' later plays are valuable, but they do not in themselves point the way to Menander. Nor must we think of Aristophanes as representing Old Comedy to its full extent. In the hands of other writers themes from bourgeois life may have played a larger part. In this connection we have already mentioned (p. 422) the plays of Pherecrates with the names of hetaerae as titles. Here may have been a starting-point for later developments.[1]

One observes with regret that amid all the critical work on the surviving plays there has been little attempt to bring out the elements of Aristophanes' humour. Despite his frequent use of comedy of situation, it is his language above all that carries his humour. In verbal point and wit, sometimes brilliant, sometimes overdone, he is inexhaustible. (This is another respect in which he may be compared with his Viennese counterpart.) He twists the meanings of words and makes use of similarities in sound – devices, in fact, which are common in popular speech in every age. From this quarter too comes his trick of exploiting every possibility of playing on form and meaning of proper names. He is very fond of compounds of three or more elements, which reach a monstrous complexity sometimes in the pnigos of parabasis or agon. A constant feature of his language is the appearance of heterogeneous elements side by side. Basically he uses the Attic of his own time; but just as he often sinks below it with coarse vulgarisms, so he frequently rises above it to the spacious realm of poetic language. His purpose in this case is usually to achieve a comic effect by parodying the stilted language of tragedy: sometimes, however, especially in lyrical passages, he uses poetical expressions with no such end in view. Thus the variety of his language mirrors the variety of content, which mingles the real and the fanciful in a manner that has never since been equalled.

Remains of Old Comedy apart from the surviving plays of Aristophanes: T. KOCK, *Comicorum Atticorum Fragmenta* I. Leipz. 1880. Supplemented now by J. DEMIAŃCZUK, *Supplementum Comicum.* Cracow 1912. M. F. PIETERS, *Cratinus.* Leyden 1946 (with comm.). D. L. PAGE, *Greek Literary Papyri.* Lond. 1950. J. M. EDMONDS, *The Fragments of Attic Comedy* I. Leyden 1957 (with trans.). List of papyri in Pack.

The textual transmission of Aristophanes falls into three main periods. The Alexandrians took a lively interest in Old Comedy. Eratosthenes wrote a detailed work on it, and so did the poet Lycophron; Aristophanes of Byzantium produced a critical edition of our poet, and other Alexandrians wrote exegetical works, or concerned themselves with Old Comedy in other ways. For a bibliography see T. GELZER, *Gnom.* 33, 1961, 26, 1. The great commentary of Didymus (1st cent. A.D.) was a compilation from a great mass of criticism and exegesis. A

[1] F. WEHRLI, *Motivstudien zur griech. Komödie.* Zürich 1936, 17. 27. T. B. L. WEBSTER, *Studies in Later Greek Comedy.* Manchester 1953.

second important factor in the transmission was that the Atticizing grammarians and litterateurs took Aristophanes as a source and model for their language. Commentaries pilfering from Alexandrian labours were compiled until the end of antiquity. Between Didymus and our present scholia we can detect a commentary by Symmachus (c. A.D. 100) and explanations of particular plays by Phaenus (between the second and fifth centuries). Thirdly, we have recently been able to form a better idea of the work done by learned Byzantines from the ninth century onward. It was laid down by WILAMOWITZ and commonly accepted that the eleven surviving plays came through the dark ages in a single majuscule codex with variant readings, and that this was the basis of all known manuscripts; but this view, like the corresponding views on transmission of other authors, has been seriously shaken by G. ZUNTZ, 'Die Aristophanes-Scholien der Papyri'. *Byzantion* 13, 1938, 635 and 14, 1939, 545, and by M. POHLENZ (cited below under *Knights*). The Byzantines copied out the majuscule into their own minuscule with consistent word-division and other aids to reading; but, as POHLENZ has shown, they had more than one MS. at hand, and recorded some of their readings as variants. According to a view developed by ZUNTZ, which is important for other authors as well, the Byzantines originated a new type of book in this process. Ancient commentaries (*hypomnemata*) were independent works, and comments were very seldom written in the margin: what came now was the MS. with generous margins to take the continuous exegesis in the form of scholia. The latter, where Aristophanes is concerned, came from various ancient sources, which still survived. W. J. W. KOSTER, *Autour d'un manuscrit d'Aristophane écrit par Démétrius Triclinius*. Groningen 1957, tries to prove from this autograph (Par. Suppl. Gr. 463) that Triclinius was responsible for other Aristophanes scholia as well.

List of the MSS.: J. W. WHITE, *Class. Phil.* 1, 1906, 1. 255; supplemented by T. GEIZER, *Gnom.* 33, 1961, 28, 9. The principal MSS. fall into three classes: 1. Ravennas 137 (eleventh century) with all eleven plays and scholia, although the latter are not so good as those in the Ven. 2. Marcianus Venetus 474 (twelfth century) with seven plays and valuable scholia; the missing plays (*Ach., Eccl., Thesm., Lys.*) are supplied by a MS. of the fourteenth century now in two pieces – Laurent. pl. 31. 15 and Voss. Leidensis 52. 3. A family of independent value comprises some MSS. of the fourteenth century (see COULON in his edition). List of papyri in Pack. On the indirect transmission: W. KRAUS, *Testimonia Aristophanea. Denkschr. Ak. Wien, phil.-hist. Kl.* 70/2, 1931.

Bibliography 1938–55 in K. J. DOVER, *Lustrum* 2, 1957, 52; see also SCHMID 4, 1946.

Old editions still valuable for the apparatus: A. V. VELSEN, Leipz. 1869–83 (incomplete, supplemented by K. ZACHER through his 2nd ed. of the *Knights*, Leipz. 1897 and the *Peace*, Leipz. 1909); J. VAN LEEUWEN, Leyden 1893–1906. The best currently available is that of V. COULON, with trans. by H. VAN DAELE, 1–5, *Coll. des Un. de France* 1923–30, often reprinted (vol. 1, 6th ed. 1958). See also COULON's *Essai sur la méthode de la critique conjecturale, appliquée au texte d'Aristophane.* Paris 1933. Criticism of Coulon's text is expressed by D. L. PAGE,

Wien. Stud. 69, 1956, 116, 1. Other editions: R. CANTARELLA, 1. (Proleg.) Milan 1949; 2. (*Ach., Equ.*) 1953; 3. (*Nub., Vesp., Pax*) 1954; 4. (*Av., Lys., Thesm.*) 1956. Individual plays: *Acharnians*: C. F. RUSSO, *Aristofane, Gli Acarnesi* (trans. with analysis). Bari. 1953. *Knights:* M. POHLENZ, 'Aristophanes' Ritter'. *Nachr. Ak. Gött. Phil.-hist. Kl.* 1952/5, 95. O. NAVARRE, *Les Cavaliers d'Aristophane. Étude et analyse.* Paris 1956. *Clouds:* ed. W. J. M. STARKIE, Lond. 1911. W. SCHMIDT, 'Das Sokratesbild der Wolken'. *Phil.* 97, 1948, 209. H. ERBSE, 'Sokrates im Schatten der arist. Wolken'. *Herm.* 82, 1954, 385. T. GELZER, 'Aristophanes und sein Sokrates'. *Mus. Helv.* 13, 1956, 65. C. F. RUSSO, ' "Nuvole" non recitate e "Nuvole" recitate'. *Stud. zur Textgeschichte und Textkritik.* Cologne 1959, 231. – *Wasps:* ed. W. J. M. STARKIE, Lond. 1897. – *Peace:* ed. P. MAZON, Paris 1904. – *Birds:* E. FRAENKEL, 'Zum Text der Vögel des Arist.'. *Stud. z. Textgesch. u. Textkritik.* Cologne 1959, 9. – *Thesmophoriazusae:* W. MITSDÖRFFER, 'Das Mnesilochoslied in Ar. Thesm.'. *Phil.* 98, 1954, 59. K. DEICHGRÄBER, 'Parabasenverse aus Thesm. II bei Galen'. *Sitzb. Ak. Berl.* 1956/2. – *Lysistrata:* ed. U. V. WILAMOWITZ, Berl. 1927, repr. 1958. – *Frogs:* ed. L. RADERMACHER, 2nd ed. by W. KRAUS, *Oest. Ak.* 1954. W. B. STANFORD, Lond. 1958 (with comm., no apparatus, good bibliography); cf. H.-J. NEWIGER, *Gnom.* 32, 1960, 751, with many critical observations. Edited by W. SÜSS with selected scholia, *Kl. Texte* 66, Bonn 1911, repr. 1959. H. DÖRRIE, 'Ar. Frösche 1433–1467'. *Herm.* 84, 1956, 296. B. MARZULLO, 'Aristophanes I'. *Acc. Naz. dei Lincei. Cl. di Sc. Mor. Stor. e Filol. s. VIII,* vol. 16. fasc. 7-12. 1961 (1962). See also the works cited on p. 444, n. 1. – *Plutus:* K. HOLZINGER, *Kritisch-exegetischer Kommentar.* Vienna 1940 (commentary without text). E. ROOS, 'De incubationis ritu per ludibrium apud Aristophanem detorto'. *Acta Instit. Atheniensis regni Sueciæ* 3, 1960, 55. – Fragments in KOCK and DEMIAŃCZUK and other works cited for Old Comedy. – Scholia: F. DÜBNER, Paris 1877. W. G. RUTHERFORD (only the more valuable scholia of the Ravennas), 3 vols. Lond. 1896–1903. J. W. WHITE, *The Scholia on the Aves of Arist.* Boston 1914. On Triclinius: K. HOLZINGER, *Sitzb. Ak. Wien.* 217/4, 1939. In the *Scholia in Aristophanem,* ed. W. J. W. KOSTER, of the projected part IV, *Joh. Tzetzae commentarii in Aristophanem,* two fascicules have now appeared: fasc. 1 with the prolegomena and commentary on the *Plutus,* ed. L. MASSA POSITANO, Groningen 1960, fasc. 2 with the comm. on the *Clouds.* ed. D. HOLWERDA, Gron. 1960. See also ZUNTZ op. cit. For a well-documented account of the editions of the Aristophanes scholia see T. GELZER, *Gnom.* 33, 1961, 26. – Verbal index: O. J. TODD, Cambr. Mass. 1932 (repr. by Olms of Hildesheim, 1963). Translations: B. B. ROGERS, Loeb Class. Lib. 1924. Also in *The Complete Greek Drama* (*v. supra* under Aeschylus). French tr. by H. VAN DAELE (*v. supra*). German by J. G. DROYSEN, 3rd ed. Berl. 1881. Italian, by various hands, ed. B. MARZULLO, in *La commedia classica.* Florence 1955 (includes all ancient comedy). Monographs: P. MAZON, *Essai sur la composition des comédies d'Aristophane.* Paris 1904. GILBERT MURRAY, *Aristophanes.* Oxf. 1933. V. EHRENBERG, *The People of Aristophanes.* 2nd ed. Oxf. 1951. W. SÜSS, 'Inkongruenzen bei Ar.'. *Rhein. Mus.* 97, 1954, 115. 229. 289. C. F. RUSSO, 'I due teatri di Ar.'. *Acc. d. Lincei. Rend. d. classe di scienze mor., stor. e filol.* 1956, 14 (attempts to distinguish by scenic technique the plays produced at the Dionysia from those at the Lenaea). C. PRATO, *Euripide nella critica di Ar.* Galatina 1955. W. W. GOLOWNJÁ, *Aristophanes.* Moscow Academy of Sciences, 1955; cf. *Gnom.* 29, 1957, 308. K. LEVER, *The Art of Greek Comedy.* London 1956. H.-J. NEWIGER, *Metapher und Allegorie. Stud. zu Aristophanes. Zet.* 16. Munich 1957. T. GELZER, 'Tradition und Neuschöpfung in der Dramaturgie des Ar.'. *Ant. u. Abendland* 8, 1959, 15. Id., *Der epirrhematische Agon bei Ar. Zet.* 23. Munich 1960. K. REINHARDT, 'Ar. und Athen'. *Eur. Revue* 14, 1938, 754; now in *Tradition und Geist.* Göttingen 1960, 257. O. SEEL, *Aristophanes oder Versuch über Komödie.* Stuttg. 1960. T. B. L. WEBSTER, 'Monuments illustrating Old and Middle Comedy'. *Univ. of London Inst. of Class. Studies. Bulletin Suppl.* 9, 1960. E. FRAENKEL, *Beobachtungen zu Aristophanes.* Rome 1962. C. F. RUSSO, *Aristofane autore di teatro.* Florence 1962. – Influence: W. SÜSS, *Ar. und die Nachwelt.* Leipz. 1911. F. QUADLBAUER, 'Die Dichter der griech. Komödie im literarischen Urteil der Antike'. *Wien. Stud.* 73, 1960, 40.

6 POLITICAL WRITINGS

The year 433 was a fateful one in Athenian domestic politics. Thucydides, the son of Melesias, leader of the conservative and oligarchic party, was ostracized, and thus victory finally declared for the democrats – that is, for Pericles. Thucydides' followers, however, who as landowners detested a policy based on strength at sea, remained in Athens in opposition, with their eyes always turned towards Sparta. The division was not hard and fast. Many admitted more or less openly their readiness to make peace with the demos and to secure a place in the political scene which had irrevocably changed: others withdrew into their political clubs and vowed war to the death against the democracy.

We have seen how far these tensions were reflected in comedy, and we must bear in mind that a mass of fugitive literature – scolia, elegies and epigrams – is now beyond our knowledge. In an age when Ionic prose had become an important instrument, and when speeches in the courts and the assembly had come to receive great attention, it is not surprising if political thought found new forms of expression. At first these were poetical, as before: when Timocreon of Ialysus was opposed to Themistocles, he wrote verses against him; but when Stesimbrotus of Thasus resented the policy of Athens in the first year of the Peloponnesian War, he expressed himself in a prose treatise On *Themistocles, Thucydides and Pericles.* This polemical tract, written from the viewpoint of the allies, has been credited with more influence than it had, since scholars have not remembered that we have in it one accidental survivor from a kind of writing which must have been much practised at the time.

We have a highly personal example of the political tracts of the period in the *Constitution of Athens* which a happy error has brought down to us among the works of Xenophon. 'The first constitutional and sociological essay in world literature', as Reinhardt has called it, poses some very difficult problems. We may first state what can be known. Obviously an oligarch wrote it for oligarchs: he hates the democracy as the rest of his party hate it, but he condemns as useless a war of words against it, and deprecates equally that foolish optimism which thought that the system could not last for long. He therefore shows that the demos has erected a wholly detestable domination of the 'bad' over the 'good', but that it has had sense enough to build skilfully on sure foundations.

The first of the three chapters, covering about twelve Teubner pages, devotes its first and longest section to the advantages which the demos derives in domestic politics. At section 14 he concentrates on relations with the allies, Athens' most serious problem; and at the end of the chapter he deals with questions of Athenian power at sea. This discussion takes up most of the second chapter as well, culminating in an analysis of the drawbacks which Athens suffered from not having an island situation – the ideal for a maritime empire. Here there is a certain contradiction in the writer's thought – one which he shared with most of his fellow oligarchs. He knows and declares what naval power means to Athens; but at the same time he realizes that it is bound up with the democratic constitution, which alone can man the fleets. What he says on Athenian strength at sea reflects the controversies of his time. We may thus explain his agreement with Thucydides (1. 143) who also stresses the advantages of an island site. At the end of c. 2 he returns to domestic politics. We see here, despite the closeness of the reasoning in general, that same 'ring-composition' which we met so often in archaic poetry.[1] It appears also in the beginning of the third chapter, which returns to the theme of total disapprobation of the democracy. In general this chapter has the look of an appendix, dealing with various abuses, particularly the tediousness of legal processes. At the end he raises the question whether the men who are unjustly defrauded of their civil rights by the democracy are numerous enough to overthrow it. He roundly declares that they are not. Far from calling for a *coup d'état*, he warns his fellow-oligarchs in these closing sections not to toy with notions of revolution without recognizing the difficulties in its way.

We may now consider the question of authorship. To assign it to a particular individual is quite impossible. Every possibility has been explored: the work has been attributed to Thucydides the politician, and with like confidence to Thucydides the historian. None of these attributions is worthy of being refuted. The political background of the author we have already stated. We may ask ourselves whether he lived in Athens or abroad, and to whom the work was directed. In this connection an important passage is 1. 11, where he says that one might well wonder at the freedoms permitted to slaves αὐτόθι (i.e. in Athens). The inference that this passage was written by someone away from Athens is not the only one possible, but it is the most likely. We can also profitably compare the way in which a speaker in a 'Socratic' dialogue[2] repeatedly uses ἐκεῖ and ἐνθάδε to signify Sparta and Athens respectively. This is one of the

---

[1] The importance of ring-composition in the work has been pointed out by two scholars simultaneously: R. KATIČIĆ, *Živa Antika*. Skoplje 1955, 267. H. HAFFTER, 'Die Komposition der pseudoxen. Schrift vom St. d. Ath.'. *Navicula Chiloniensis*. Leyden 1956, 79.
[2] *Pap. Soc. It.* 1215, cf. V. BARTOLETTI, 'Un frammento di dialogo socratico'. *Stud. It.* 31, 1959, 100.

reasons why Hohl's ingenious suggestion that the work is a private letter of an Athenian oligarch to a sympathizer in Sparta is not necessarily the right solution. This theory rests mainly on the words (1. 11): 'In Sparta my slave was afraid of you'. But if we take into account the preceding and the following sentences we shall see that the expression is purely general. The whole tendency of the work, with its scarcely concealed warning against rash attempts at revolution, seems to be aimed at those circles of émigré politicians in whom the Greek world was so wretchedly rich.

It is no less hard to say when the work was written, since we do not know who wrote it, and as the oldest piece of Attic prose it does not allow stylistic comparisons. The one clear token (pointed out over a century ago by Wilhelm Roscher) is in 2. 5, where we read that a land power cannot operate many days' march from its base. No one could have gone on thinking this after Brasidas had marched through the length of Greece to take Amphipolis.[1] At the other end scholars have tried to limit the possibilities by pointing to the references to the deliberations of the bule on the war (3. 2) and to what is said about hostile devastation in Attica (2. 14): these, they say, refer to the Peloponnesian War, and the work was written after it began. Thus we are reduced to the period between 431 and 424: if we try to narrow it still further, we do not succeed. But Instinsky has rejected the *terminus post quem* and has dated the treatise before the Peloponnesian War. In this Frisch and Hohl follow him. One must admit that 'the war' may simply mean hostilities in general, and that the devastation of Attica may have been discussed as a possibility in debates on Pericles' strategy before the war began. These considerations do not, of course, prove an early date. It may well have been written in the war, although naturally not published. That it was intended for a small circle of like-minded politicians seems beyond doubt.

The language of this piece, our earliest Attic prose, is very interesting. Sophistic influence is not detectable. A truly Attic striving towards clarity and actuality stands in attractive contrast with the artlessness of the periods and the sentence-connections. Catchwords at the beginnings of chapters are obviously used for articulation; antitheses are sought after, although the antithesis in form does not always correspond to one in sense; in driving home a point the writer often uses colloquial turns of phrase. We feel that we are witnessing the same progress that gives pleasure in some of the writings of the Hippocratic corpus: content and form are not yet perfectly matched. Classical Greek prose was to be an achievement of the fourth century.[2]

Editions: E. KALINKA, Leipz. 1913 (still fundamental). H. FRISCH, Copenhagen 1942 (both these with comm.). Kalinka's text with praef. and app. crit. was

[1] GIGANTE (*v. inf.*) unhappily gives this position up and will only allow the putsch of 411 as a *terminus ante quem*.

[2] V. PISANI, *Storia della lingua greca* in *Encicl. Class.* 2/5/1, 106, rightly stresses that this early Attic prose is much influenced by Ionian prose of the time.

reprinted Stuttg. 1961. Studies: H. U. INSTINSKY, *Die Abfassungszeit der Schrift vom Staate der Athener*. Diss. Freiburg 1932. K. I. GELZER, *Die Schrift vom St. d. Ath. Herm.* E 3, 1937. E. RUPPRECHT, *Die Schrift vom Staate d. Ath. Klio Beih.* 44, 1939 (tries to eject interpolations). M. VOLKENING, *Das Bild des att. Staates in der pseudoxen. Schrift vom St. d. Ath.* Diss. Münster 1940. E. HOHL, 'Zeit und Zweck der pseudoxen. Ath. Pol.'. *Class. Phil.* 45, 1950, 26. L. C. STECHINI, Ἀθηναίων πολιτεία. Glencoe, Illinois 1950. M. GIGANTE, *La costituzione degli Ateniesi*. Naples 1953.

7 THUCYDIDES

The external evidence for the life of the greatest historian of antiquity is no better than the general run of such traditions, in either extent or reliability. We have two manuscript lives, of which the more elaborate is a compilation from various sources, going under the name of Marcellinus. The opening shows that it is a lecture intended for the rhetorical schools, where Thucydides was studied after Demosthenes. To these can be added a fragment of a biographical collection on papyrus (1612 P.), the article in Suidas and a rhetorical encomium on Thucydides by Aphthonius. As often happens, the safest source of information s the work itself; and with an historian we are naturally better off than with a poet.

In the first sentence of his introduction Thucydides tells us something that will be important, when we consider the problem of compositional layers in the work – that he began to write the history of the war as soon as it broke out, realizing that it was greater and more fateful than any that had gone before. In the so-called 'second introduction' (5. 26) he tells us that during all the twenty-seven years of the war he was of an age to be able accurately to record the events; and in the same passage we learn that after his command at Amphipolis in 424 he was in exile for twenty years. The occasion of this banishment, from which he was not able to return until after the defeat of Athens, is related in an earlier section (4. 104 ff.). At the time when Thucydides became one of the ten strategi (424) and was charged, together with Eucles, with the safeguarding of Athenian interests in the northern Aegean, no one could have expected that this theatre of conflict could become a decisive one. Sparta, after the catastrophe of Sphacteria and the siege of Cythera by Nicias, was almost forced to her knees, when Brasidas, by a bold diversionary move, saved the situation. His march through the whole length of Greece and his action against Chalcidice threatened vital Athenian possessions. When he attacked Amphipolis on the estuary of the Strymon, Thucydides sailed from Thasos with a relieving force of seven ships. But he came too late, and he could do no more than secure the harbour of Eion. The brevity of the narrative does not conceal the fact that someone had blundered. Brasidas has already spent some time outside Amphipolis before he realised that his hopes of a speedy surrender were in vain. If Thucydides is right in saying that he responded immediately to the appeal for help, the blame must be laid on the man who sent for him too late. In Athens, however, judgment went against Thucydides, and he was banished.

In this same section Thucydides mentions the influence that he had in the area as the owner of some Thracian goldmines – which, no doubt, is why he was entrusted with command on that front.

Another scrap of information about Thucydides' life is his own statement (2. 48) that he suffered personally from that appalling visitation of the year 430 which we call the plague, although its identity, despite all investigations, remains obscure.[1]

If we try to add to the sparse details which Thucydides gives about himself, there is nothing that is certain, and little that is probable. If Thucydides was a young man in 431 when the war began, and on the other hand was at least thirty when he was chosen strategus in 424, we must place his birth about 460. The name of his father, Olorus (4. 104), is significant. The name is Thracian, and is the same as that of the Thracian king whose daughter was married to Miltiades, the victor of Marathon – a marriage of which Cimon was the offspring. Since this Thracian name is otherwise unattested at Athens, it is a plausible assumption that on his father's side Thucydides was related to Cimon's family in some way, although we do not know quite how. The Thracian goldmines, probably a family possession, fit well enough into such a context. Belonging to the Philaïd deme, the historian was very probably connected with Thucydides, the son of Melesias. This conservative statesman, Pericles' dangerous and persistent opponent until he was ostracized in 443, was according to Plutarch (*Per.* 11) a kinsman by marriage – probably a son-in-law, of Cimon. Thus we see that Thucydides was closely connected by birth with the leading conservative circle in Athens, which would hardly have predisposed him to appreciate and to record the greatness of Pericles. But Thucydides has well been described as a 'genius of objectivity', and the factual cast of his mind enabled him to assess the great potentialities of the democracy as well as to see the cracks in the fabric of Periclean Athens.

Thucydides is the exact opposite of the prejudiced or tendentious historian, and he has served all subsequent ages as an example of objectivity. Our own age, however, which has seen and read so much theoretical discussion of the unconscious working of prejudice, needs hardly to be told that Thucydides' earnest wish to be objective did not always save him from bias. When he says (2. 65) that the Athens of his day bore only the name of a democracy, being in fact under the rule of her first citizen, he may be right; but he is also showing how a man of the old nobility viewed the personality of Pericles. It says much for Thucydides' self-restraint where personal judgments are concerned that he warmly praises (8. 97) the constitution of the summer of 411, which lasted no more than eight months. It seemed to him to have effected that reconciliation of the interests of the many and the few, which was the goal of Aristotelian political thinking. Such a view cannot, of course, stamp Thucydides as an oligarch. It is idle to apply to such a man the political smear-words of his day. He is outspoken enough in condemning the oligarchic terror which preceded that moderate constitution.

---

[1] Most recently examined by D. L. PAGE, 'Thucydides' Description of the Great Plague at Athens'. *Class. Quart.* 47, 1953, 97.

After the disaster of Amphipolis Thucydides spent twenty years in exile, and we should like to know where he lived during that time. The life by Marcellinus shows us that even in antiquity many men thought many things, but nobody knew. The most credible tale is that he lived on the mainland opposite Thasos, on his estate of Skapte Hyle, although he can hardly have spent the whole time there. This was a place where he had ties both of birth and of property. In Skapte Hyle also a plane tree used to be pointed out under which he was supposed to have written. This is a typical local legend,[1] and reminds us of the cave of Euripides on Salamis. Marcellinus also says that the Peripatetic Praxiphanes listed Thucydides among that group of artists and writers whom Archelaus of Macedon gathered around him. On the same page we read that an epigram on the grave of Euripides (*Anth. Pal.* 7. 45) was ascribed to Thucydides. From such stories we should not accept that Thucydides was indeed connected with the circle in question: in fact what Praxiphanes says points rather the other way, and suggests that at the time Thucydides had acquired none of his later reputation.

Again we must turn to Thucydides himself to be on the safest ground. In the second introduction (5. 26) he says that his work benefited by the accident which gave him connections with both parties and with the Peloponnesians themselves. Presumably then in these twenty years he travelled considerably: precisely where, we cannot say.

The historian speaks of the military reforms of Archelaus of Macedon with evident approval (2. 100). This is a different view from Plato's, in whose *Gorgias* he appears as violent and unscrupulous. The passage does not give the impression of speaking of a man still living. Uncertain as it is, this is our one indication of the date of Thucydides' death, which we should then have to place after 399, when Archelaus died. If the supposition is correct, we can say that he was still working at his history after 399.

Thucydides' statement (5. 26) that he was in exile for twenty years after the loss of Amphipolis leaves no room for doubting that he returned to Athens after her defeat in 404. Pausanias (1. 23, 9) speaks of a proposal for the recall of Thucydides that was carried through the ecclesia by Oenobius. This proposal, one supposes, came a little before the peace treaty of 404 with its general amnesty; but we may put it after that date, if we imagine that Thucydides was at first unwilling to trust the amnesty. His return to Athens fits well with the account of his grave, bearing his name, and situated near the Melitan gate among those of Cimon's family. From Marcellinus we learn that a fierce controversy raged about this grave, which must have still existed. An obstinate tradition had it that Thucydides died in Thrace, and in consequence some took the grave in Athens to be a cenotaph, while others declared that his body had been brought home and secretly buried. Didymus, on the other hand, maintained that he died and was buried in Athens.[2] We cannot decide with certainty; but we can well believe that, after a visit to Athens, Thucydides might have returned to the northern districts which were his second home. In this case the cenotaph

---

[1] H. GERSTINGER, *Wien. Stud.* 38, 1916, 65.   [2] SCHMID is mistaken, 5. 15.

story would be the right one, and scholars have been wrong in dismissing it as pure invention.

We are told that Thucydides met a violent death,[1] some say in Athens, others in Thrace. The history ends suddenly in the middle of a sentence, which can be easiest explained by damage in the transmission. Possibly the violent death was invented to explain this sudden breaking off. An obscure tradition, which Marcellinus says is impossible, makes Thucydides' daughter the writer of the eighth book. Perhaps under this story may lie a fact: she played perhaps some part in preserving the text. To dismiss the account as mere fable is to be too sceptical.

There is no anciently attested title of Thucydides' work, and the division into eight books was not made by the author. We have evidence of other attempted divisions, which were finally dropped in favour of that which we now have.

Before considering the composition and inner form of the history, we should see briefly how the matter is laid out.

Dionysius of Halicarnassus (*ad Pomp.* p. 234 U.-R.) rather pedantically takes Thucydides to task for wilfully disarranging the natural sequence of events in his introduction, instead of telling what happened in an orderly manner. The introduction in fact shows us how much more Thucydides' heart was in research than in narration.

The first sentences declare that the war between Athens and Sparta had brought in its train, both for Greece and for most of the human race, a convulsion much greater than anything previously known. But Thucydides is not content with this unsupported statement: he at once brings an historical proof of it – the so-called 'archaeologia'[2] (chapters 2-19). Here we find a succinct account of Greek history from the earliest times up to his own day, dedicated to proving how important this war was when compared with earlier wars. The 'archaeologia' is like an overture in which themes and subjects which are to be of the greatest importance in the body of the work make their first appearance. In the foreground is always the question of concentration of power – a term which to Thucydides always means military potential. Hermann Strasburger[3] has recently pointed out that the preponderance of the political and military element in historical writing until recent times can be traced in a direct line from Thucydides. In this section also we meet the leading theme of the history – that in the Aegean world power meant always sea-power. Thus Thucydides begins with the setting up of a maritime empire by Minos, and gives a picture of it which we could not well judge until the large-scale excavations in Crete at the turn of the century. The naval factor is well to the fore all through this sketch of history, which goes up to the Persian wars and the rivalry between Athens and Sparta once the common danger was removed.

The archaeologia begins with a picture of the most primitive conditions of life in Greece, with no fixed settlements. It traces the development of a safer

---

[1] Marcellinus; Plut. *Cim.* 4; Paus. I. 23, 9.
[2] E. TÄUBLER, *Die Archäologie des Thuk.* Leipz. 1927.
[3] 'Die Entdeckung der politischen Gesch. durch Thuk.' *Saeculum* 5, 1954, 395.

and more ordered life through the putting down of piracy and the rise of large concentrations of power. In this he commits himself to the view of human history as a steady development from early primitive conditions – a view which contrasts with the Hesiodic conception of four ages, and which found its most active representative among the sophists in Protagoras. This progress is seen by the historian principally as the development of power-blocs, without any moral overtones.

Thucydides takes a scientific attitude in striving for complete accuracy (τὸ σαφές) in his reports. For contemporary events this may be achieved either by personal experience or by the witness of one who himself took part. To achieve such certainty about the past is more difficult, but here also a convincing indication (τεκμήριον) is the object sought after. It is significant that the word occurs in 1. 1 and 1. 19, as it were framing the archaeologia. Decisive documentary evidence, however, may not be forthcoming. Here the goal is harder to reach, and one must aim at the probable instead of the proven. To reach the probable (τὸ εἰκός) one uses a method (εἰκάζειν) which the sophists greatly developed in connection with forensic oratory. In the course of our treatment we shall see how impossible it is to imagine Thucydides without the background of the sophistic movement. But an important reservation has to be made: the sophistic speaker strove to attach the appearance of probability to whatever view suited his case; Thucydides uses the method of εἰκάζειν in order to approach as near as possible to the truth. An example is his treatment of the Trojan war. He does not simply take Homer as an historical source, but sets aside all the purely mythical elements in the attempt to extract historical data. In this he is on as slippery footing as we are today, and the questions that he puts are our questions.

Next come three chapters (20-22) which form a close unity. They are connected to the earlier chapters by a further demonstration of the importance of the Peloponnesian War; what is new here is that they set out the historian's objectives and the ways by which he hopes to reach them. The passage will be of great importance in considering other parts of the history.

The 23rd chapter makes a smooth transition. The unique scale of the Peloponnesian War is again stressed, with special reference to the Persian wars; then Thucydides passes to the outbreak of hostilities. Here we find a most interesting distinction between the particular motives (αἰτίαι) that led to the breaking of the Thirty Years' Peace in 446-5, and the underlying cause (ἀληθεστάτη πρόφασις), deeply rooted in the nature of things which compelled Sparta as if by a natural law to take up arms against the threat posed by growing Athenian strength.[1]

In the succeeding chapters (24-87) the causes are analysed and the narrative is taken up to the declaration of war. The first conflict arises from competition between Corinth and Corcyra; then come hostilities between Corinth and Athens, leading to Potidaea.

At length a conference is called of the Peloponnesian League at its headquarters, Sparta, where complaints are levelled against Athens. Thucydides here, going into greater detail than anywhere else in the work, gives us two antithetical

[1] A. ANDREWES, 'Thucydides on the Cause of the War'. *Class. Quart.* N.S. 9, 1959, 223.

pairs of speeches analysing the motives and the assumptions of the league in power politics. The Corinthian representative speaks to the League, and is opposed by one of the Athenian ambassadors who were in Sparta on other business. Then come speeches of the Spartans among themselves in council: Archidamus makes a thoughtful assessment of Athenian military resources, and is opposed by a wild and warlike speech from the ephor Sthenelaidas.

Chapter 88 also serves as a neat transition. The Spartans have decided on war, not so much for their allies' sake as in order to oppose the threatening growth of Athenian power while there is yet time. Thus we have at the same time a device of ring-composition, harking back to the underlying cause explained in c. 23, and a preparation for the following sketch of the 'pentekontaeteia'.

This outline (89-118)[1] of the almost fifty years between the victory over the Persians and the outbreak of the Peloponnesian War is recognized by Thucydides himself as breaking the thread of his narrative (97: ἐκβολὴ τοῦ λόγου). He justifies its insertion in two ways: firstly that this part of Greek history had been generally neglected, and had lately been treated very inaccurately by Hellanicus in his *Atthis*; secondly – this being the real reason – that he is thus enabled to trace the development of Athenian power.

The last section of the first book (119-146) is devoted to the last negotiations before the outbreak of hostilities; and here again the focal point is a pair of conflicting speeches. The Corinthian speaker enlarges on the necessity of the war and the prospects of victory to persuade his hearers to join in the war on Sparta's side, while Pericles, in the first of his three speeches,[2] sets out the prospects for the Athenians, and develops the basic features of his grand strategy, with which in Thucydides' view victory was indissolubly linked: full use of Athenian naval supremacy, but on land a purely defensive policy based on a strongly fortified Athens.

In describing the last negotiations between Athens and Sparta, Thucydides takes the opportunity of narrating the deaths of Pausanias and Themistocles. The relevance of these details lies in the important, although conflicting, roles which the two men played in the origins of the Athenian naval league.

In the second book the narrative of the war properly begins, the first event being the night attack of the Thebans on Plataeae in the spring of 431. Thucydides dates the outbreak by all the available systems, by the priestess of Hera at Argos, the eponymous ephor at Sparta, and the Athenian archon. Thus the starting-point is as firmly anchored as was then possible. Thereafter Thucydides dispenses with such chronological indications, and relates the events in yearly sequence, dividing each year into summer and winter. He attached such importance to this method for the clear overall view it gave of the course of the long war, that he accepted the many disadvantages of an annalistic treatment. Thus he is obliged to spread the account of the siege of Plataeae over three yearly sections. The division that he thus adheres to is underlined by a formal conclusion to each section, often giving the author's name. In 5. 20 Thucydides

[1] P. K. WALKER, 'The purpose and method of the Pentekontaetia in Thuc. book 1'. *Class. Quart.* N.S. 7, 1957, 27.   [2] H. HERTER (*v. sup.*).

deliberately defends his division into summers and winters preferring it to a division by archons or other officials.[1] Probably these reflections are aimed at Hellanicus, who divided up his *Atthis* according to the terms of office of archons.

The second book covers the first three years of the war, with the two Spartan inroads into Attica and the various attempts to neutralize each other's allies. At the end of the narrative of the first year Thucydides puts the highly wrought oration of Pericles over the fallen. Dionysius of Halicarnassus (*de Thuc.* 351 U.-R.) again misses the point when he says that the losses of that year were not heavy enough to justify such a highly wrought speech. He rightly observes that the occasion enabled Thucydides to give Pericles a speaking part; but this is not all. The epitaphios does not say much about the dead, but is eloquent about the city for which they had given their lives. Athenian power and national character were well illuminated in the speeches of the first book, from their very different standpoints: soon the historian will have to tell of the first heavy blows to the greatness and self-confidence of Athens. In the meantime he paints in this speech a picture of the Athenian state as Pericles wished to model it – a picture which to the speaker himself was more an ideal than an accomplished reality. In this context it would be vain to attempt any distinction between Thucydides' thought and that of Pericles. To the historian in his impressionable years the work of Pericles seemed to fulfil the ideal of political activity; and this agreement finds expression in the speeches that he puts into his mouth, most of all in the epitaphios. Like all great works of art, it is effective in several distinct ways. It offers the sharpest contrast to the Spartan way of life as that was variously viewed and depicted in the first book, while on the other hand it gives a self-contained picture of the spiritual inheritance which the state preserves for future ages. In this portrayal of the Athenian freedom of the individual in association with the whole, and in the exposition of Athens' destiny to be an example and an education to all Hellas, Thucydides richly compensates us for that determined reticence with which elsewhere he excludes all aesthetic and spiritual judgments from his study in the play of political power.[2]

Immediately following this portrayal of the city fulfilling itself in tempered freedom and spiritual values comes the painful description of the terrible plague which in the second year of the war dealt Athens her first real wound. We mentioned before that all the clinical accuracy of the description has not enabled us to identify the disease. The consequence of this affliction was a lowering of morale, which Pericles tried to counter in the third and last of the speeches that Thucydides gives to him (60-64). It is a renewed justification of that Periclean grand strategy, built upon naval supremacy, which the historian considered to be incontestably right.

[1] O. LENDLE, 'Zu Thukydides 5. 20. 2'. *Herm.* 88, 1960, 33.

[2] F. MÜLLER, 'Die blonde Bestie und Thukydides'. *Harv. 8tud.* 63, 1958 (Festschr. Jaeger), 171, brings out the ethical themes in the Funeral Speech. One does not sympathize, however, with his reading in 41. 4 of καλῶν τε καὶ ἀγαθῶν (instead of κακῶν τ. κ. ἀ.) with some recentiores. For a penetrating stylistic analysis of the speech see J. T. KAKRIDIS, *Der thukydideische Epitaphios*. *Zet.* 26. Munich 1961. He imagines the aged Thucydides, amid all his disillusion, penning this as a monument to his still enduring love for Athens.

This speech is followed at once by a lengthy chapter which has a special place in the history as a whole. In it Thucydides judges the statesman who was his political model, in all his clear foresight, the purity of his character and his gift for swaying the masses in the direction he chose. At the same time he assesses the permanence of his work, which was not wholly destroyed by the later catastrophes for which others were responsible. Not even the Sicilian expedition, in Thucydides' opinion, was an undertaking beyond Athenian strength: its failure was to be laid at the door of those leaders who were unfit to receive the legacy of Pericles. The generous estimate of Pericles' abilities is further heightened by the contrast with the incapacity of those who should have been his successors, who instead became the slaves of popular favour and of popular whims. The wide implications of this chapter embrace much of the future development of Athens, and introduce the second political leitmotiv of the work: just as Athenian power was the inevitable consequence of the national character and of the circumstances of the age, so in the core of the democratic structure were elements of danger, which were liable to lead to destruction when there was no strong man at the head of affairs.

In the narrative of the third year of warfare the Spartans made their début on the sea, while the Athenians, through their alliance with the Thracian king Sitalces, seek to enlist a major land power on their side. Thucydides takes the opportunity in this context of describing the kingdom of the Odrysae (97) and the dominance of Perdiccas in Macedonia (99). It is very instructive to compare this account, rigidly subordinated to the assessment of political power, with the lively detail and anecdote that marks Herodotus' excursions into ethnography.

The third book covers three years of the war, from the fourth to the sixth. In his account of the fourth and fifth year Thucydides lays stress on those incidents which show the heightening of hostile feeling and the frightening increase of barbarity. To allow this special emphasis he describes such things as the two Spartan inroads into Attica in the barest of chronicle styles (1; 26). The revolt and punishment of Mytilene is related at length (2-50), and again the important developments and the forces at work in them are brought out by the speeches which he inserts. The scene in which the Mytilenian ambassador, after his city has decided to revolt, comes to Olympia to ask for Peloponnesian help, underlines the internal problems of the maritime confederacy, in which Athenian supremacy leads inevitably to Athenian tyranny.

Such a form of empire had been considered by Pericles in his last speech (2. 63), in which he said that it would be wrong to seek such rule, but dangerous to abandon it. But now, when the Athenian people sits in judgment over the Mytilenians after their surrender, it is not Pericles who addresses them, but Cleon. It is he who gains the support of the popular assembly for the frightful decree that all adult males in Mytilene shall be put to death and the women and children enslaved, while the territory shall be divided up. Scarcely has the ship sailed with orders when the Athenian people regret their decision; another assembly the next day discusses the question anew. Thucydides has a powerful scene of debate (3, 37-40. 42-48),[1] in which Cleon angrily defends his first proposal, but is opposed by one Diodotus, who represents the senselessness of such brutality and substitutes a proposal which punishes only the guilty – albeit with extreme severity. A ship is hastily dispatched, and is just in time to prevent the carrying out of the first edict. It is characteristic of Thucydides and typically Greek that this impassioned debate is at the same time a general consideration of the value of deterrent punishments.

This picture of Athenian brutality is at once followed by its Spartan counterpart at Plataeae (52-86). After a siege of three years the city had been driven by hunger to surrender in 427. The case of the Plataeans was judged under Spartan presidency. Another of Thucydides' antithetical pairs of speeches sets forth the defence put forward by the vanquished and the complaints urged by Thebes against them. Here again a frightful revenge is taken. Plataeae had won glory in the defence of freedom against the Persian; but now two hundred of her citizens were put to death, the remaining women enslaved, and the city itself a little after razed to the ground.

Shortly before the trial of the Plataeans, in the summer of 427, the civil war in Corcyra had come to an end. For the third time we are given a picture of an inferno of political hatred. With Athenian help the oligarchs had been overthrown, and the demos was drinking their blood. Here we have those chapters (82 ff.) which give a complete pathology of the conflict, and reveal these bloody scenes as the working out of certain fatal laws of human behaviour. Thucydides here is like a physician at a bedside, making his diagnosis from the observable symptoms: he shows how war, which unchains the most violent human passions, leads from the inner tensions that are found in any state to a conflict of each against each. The fever of such conflicts is strikingly illustrated by the reversal of the meaning of words from that which they bear in time of peace. This keen observer may detect in the frightening change of usage of such terms as 'clever', 'brave', 'good' and the like. Like so many of the sections on which Thucydides lays particular stress, this passage has a double aspect. It focuses, as if in a burning-glass, the impressions we have received from the preceding narrative, while at the same time it looks forward to the later part of the work, in which a similar rake's progress brings even the great achievement of Pericles to destruction.

In contrast to the close texture of the main sections of the third book, its final chapters are taken up with scattered detail. The most important development here is the dispatch of a small fleet to Sicily in the spring of 427 to support the Ionian and Chalcidian cities against a Doric coalition centred on Syracuse.[2]

The fourth book again relates three years of war, the seventh, eighth and ninth. If Thucydides was obliged to relate disconnected detail at the end of the third, the fourth enables him to group his narrative around a focal point of the war. The Athenian general Demosthenes has occupied Pylos, on the west coast

---

[1] D. EBENER, 'Kleon und Diodotos'. Wi... Zeitschr. Halle 5, 1955/56, 1085.

[2] H. D. WESTLAKE, 'Athenian Aims in Sicily, 427-424 B.C. A Study in Thucydidean Motivation'. Historia 9, 1960, 385.

of the Peloponnese, with a true appreciation of its strategic possibilities. On the island of Sphacteria, lying a little offshore, a considerable number of Spartan elite troops have been cut off. The copious treatment (2-41) given by Thucydides to these operations shows his concern to represent them as one of the key points of the long conflict. Spartan feelings are deeply involved; she recalls her troops from Attica, concludes an armistice, and sends an embassy to Athens to discuss terms of peace. But Cleon brings these overtures to nothing. In a public debate, depicted with a masterly hand, he is manœuvred by Nicias into assuming command at Pylos; and in a very short time he forces the Spartan hoplites to surrender.

Among the events of the following year (424) Thucydides emphasizes those which point to a change in Athenian fortunes. The investment of Cythera was indeed a considerable reverse for Sparta, but in Sicily affairs took a turn unfavourable to Athens. Hermocrates in a meeting at Gela procured agreement among all the Sicilian Greeks, and the Athenians, thus cheated of an excuse for intervention, recalled their ships. Thucydides attached such importance to this action of Hermocrates' that he gives him a speech (4. 59-64) full of sound common sense, to which there is no answer.

From 4. 78 to 5. 11 the various episodes of the war are linked by the dominating presence of Brasidas, the saviour of Sparta, whom Thucydides treats throughout with unmistakable respect. His importance is shown by the historian's putting no less than three speeches into his mouth (4. 85-87 and 126; 5. 9). In the course of his campaigns around Chalcidice after his brilliant northward march came that successful swoop on Amphipolis which played so fateful a role in the career of Thucydides. In this first year of revived Spartan activity under Brasidas we read also of the heavy reverse which the Boeotian army inflicted on the Athenians at Delium: an action whose importance is stressed by the speeches given to the opposing generals before the battle (4. 92 and 95).

The fifth book covers a greater span of time than any other, extending from the tenth year to the winter of the sixteenth - accepting with Thucydides the year of the Peace of Nicias as part of the war as a whole. First comes the conclusion of Brasidas' operations: both he and Cleon meet their death before Amphipolis. On both sides the desire for peace now becomes effective, and in 421 Athens and Sparta make a peace and a defensive alliance to last for fifty years.

This treaty is recognized by Thucydides as a major event: as with the outbreak of hostilities, he dates it circumstantially, here by the ephor and the archon. Yet at the same time he shows that this peace at the very moment of its inception contained the seeds of future conflict. He treats the various phases of the long struggle as making up one Peloponnesian war, and devotes a special chapter (5. 26) to justifying this view. There is every reason for the term 'second prologue' which has been applied to this chapter, for it serves to introduce all that follows. Thucydides here looks forward to the intended conclusion of his work, which was to reach 404, and demonstrates that the years between the Peace of Nicias and the second outbreak of open hostilities does not represent a breaking off of the conflict between the two great powers. Each strove to injure the other where possible, and so these six years and ten months must be rightly understood as part of a great war of twenty-seven years. In discussing Thucydides' life we have dealt with the relevant data contained in this chapter.

The major part of the fifth book has the rather thankless task of relating this period of uncertain peace with its many small and devious campaigns. The book is less well written than the first four: few leading themes appear, and there is no analysis of events by means of speeches. It is very hard to say whether this fact arises from the nature of the material, its being taken up with so many detached incidents, its lack of dominant personalities, or whether the work did not receive the final touch of the master's hand. This is a question which will face us again in the eighth book.

It is hard to summarize such disconnected incidents; but what does emerge is the renewed strength of Sparta, which was decisive at the battle of Mantinea (418).

While much in the middle of this book is rather sketchy, the last section (84-116), dealing with the fate of the island of Melos, shows as finished workmanship and as serious content as anything in the history. A short account of the expeditionary force sent by Athens against the island in 416 is followed by the discussion between the Athenian representatives and the Melian councillors.[1] The dialogue form which Thucydides has chosen for it is highly unusual in an historical work: comparison with Socratic dialogues is unprofitable, and we should rather consider it as a heightening and concentration of the device of antithetical speeches which he uses elsewhere.

On one side stand the Melians, in the tragic position of small neutrals wishing to live at peace: on the other Athenian imperialism, refusing to tolerate such a position outside her dominion. It is to power alone that Athenian arguments appeal: as their first step they brutally thrust aside any appeal to right or honour. The Melians then have no alternative but to discuss the situation with purely rational arguments, and arguing on this level they are bound to fail. They urge that the hypertrophy of power must necessarily raise up opposing power on which it will shipwreck; they speak of the possibility of Spartan support. None of this will save them: what it does is to underline the problems of Athenian power-politics. Athens had now long cast aside the wise limitations of Periclean grand strategy; she knew now only the passion for ever-new acquisitions. The book ends with the frightful yet unemotional account of the punishment inflicted by the Athenians on the defeated island. The men, so far as they could be taken, were put to death, the women and children enslaved. The modern book-division obscures the immediate transition to the description of Athenian preparations during the same winter for the greatest exercise of their might – the Sicilian expedition. Thus, without any personal intervention of the writer, the link becomes visible which connects seemingly separate events within the framework of laws rooted deep in human life.

[1] G. DEININGER, Der Melierdialog. Diss. Erlangen 1939. H. HERTER, 'Pylos und Melos' (v. inf.), 317, n. 4-7 with full bibliography.

Thucydides is obviously concerned to present the Melian dialogue not merely as actual historical transaction but as a study in the physiology and pathology of power – indeed the whole work might be so described – and appropriately he leaves the speakers on each side anonymous. The theory that there had been a previous connection between Melos and the Athenian league, and that Thucydides deliberately suppresses it, cannot be sustained.[1]

The customary division into books is not original, as we have seen, but it is by no means clumsy. Particularly the beginning of the sixth and the end of the seventh book are well chosen boundaries between which the absorbing and almost separate drama of the Sicilian expedition is played out. This part of the history is given an introduction worthy of its importance. At his first touching upon the topic Thucydides points out (6. 1) that most Athenians had no notion of the size of Sicily or the density of its population. Five chapters later he briefly concludes: 'so many were the peoples, and so great the extent of Sicily', and framed in between comes an account of the settlement of Sicily, in which he acquaints us with the cities and tribes and draws a lively picture of the latest goal of Athenian ambition.

With the eighth chapter we enter on the seventeenth year of the war, which together with part of the summer campaigns of the eighteenth fills up the sixth book. This time it is Egesta's call for help against the threatening alliance of Selinus and Syracuse, that affords the excuse for Athenian intervention. The pan-Sicilian truce engineered by Hermocrates had been of short duration. Here again Thucydides distinguishes between the pretended and the real motive. In 6. 6 he repeats a phrase which he had used in 1. 23 (ἀληθεστάτη πρόφασις): the true purpose of the Athenians was to make themselves masters of all Sicily.

The importance of the undertaking and the vastness of its effects is matched by the elaboration of Thucydides' account, as shown both in its length and in the number of speeches inserted. The Athenians have decided (6. 8) on the dispatch of sixty ships. A few days later Nicias attempts, in the course of a debate ostensibly on the requirements of the task force, to reverse the whole decision. There follows a great scene of debate between him and Alcibiades (6. 9-25), which Thucydides characteristically uses not only to present the case for and against the invasion of Sicily, but to draw a striking picture of the two men who would have vital roles to play in what was to come. Alcibiades has indeed been on the stage before (5. 43), but there only a brief characterization is given of his position and his motives. Here, (6. 15), before his long speech, Thucydides shows the conflicting elements in his nature – his imposing presence, his brilliant flair for strategy, his passionate desire for recognition and his ruthless selfishness. The same scene presents with unmistakable clarity the tragedy of Nicias, on whom Thucydides' last words (7. 86) bestow profound sympathy and understanding. In the first of the three speeches he is warning the Athenians

---

[1] M. TREU, 'Athen und Melos und der Melierdialog des Thuk.'. *Historia* 2, 1954, 253 (further note 3, 1953, 58). On the other side: W. EBERHARDT, 'Der Melierdialog und die Inschriften ATL A 9 (IG I² 63) und IG I² 97. Betrachtungen zur historischen Glaubwürdigkeit des Thuk.' *Historia* 8, 1959, 284.

at the eleventh hour against the adventure; but all his moderating counsels are brushed aside by the counter-arguments of Alcibiades. He then speaks again: if the expedition is to take place, he demands the most extraordinary strength in men and ships and material. He still hopes by the magnitude of the expense to deter the Athenians from the project; he fails again, and thus it is he who has so largely contributed to the massive scale of the expedition.

After a description of the mutilation of the Hermae and the sailing of the fleet Thucydides returns to the Sicilian scene (32). Here he lets us witness a prelude to the battle which is obviously designed as a counterpart to the conflict in the ecclesia. Here again a clash of orators (33-41) reveals the dangers at the heart of the state; again there are three speeches (here allotted to three different speakers). First Hermocrates, the guiding spirit of Sicilian resistance, emphasizes the gravity of the situation and makes concrete proposals, which are opposed by the demagogue Athenagoras, to whom all this is simply a welcome opportunity to fan the fires of internal conflict and to declaim in favour of his extreme democratic programme. The debate is ended by a field commander who recalls the assembly to the claims of reason and necessity.

In the midst of the first operations of the Athenians, which begin under unhappy auspices, comes the recall of Alcibiades. He is summoned to defend himself on a charge of impiety, but escapes from the state galley and goes to Sparta. The extreme concern which the Athenians displayed to find those responsible for the mutilation of the Hermae and the betrayal of the mysteries is to be explained by their perpetual fear of a tyranny. Reference to this fear allows Thucydides to bring in his excursus on the Pisistratids (6. 54-59),[1] in which he gives the true version of the celebrated tyrannicide. He had mentioned earlier (1. 20) that Hipparchus was never tyrant, as an example of a mistaken Athenian tradition in their own history. Here he tells in more detail of the erotic intrigue that lay behind the deed of Harmodius and Aristogiton, and tries to evaluate more justly the services of the tyrants to Athens. The fact that he twice corrects the mistaken view of Hipparchus cannot be seized upon for analytical purposes, since the contexts in which they occur are so widely different.

It will already be apparent that the narrative of the Sicilian expedition is particularly rich in speeches. This is as true of the preliminaries as of the opening moves. At the first action against Syracuse we have a speech of Nicias to his troops (68), while a speech of Hermocrates on the necessary countermeasures is reported indirectly (72). A little later comes a lengthy interchange of speeches (76-87) in connection with the attempts of the Syracusans and the Athenians to enlist the support of the city of Camarina, which was standing neutral. Again it is Hermocrates who animates Sicilian resistance: on the Athenian side Euphemus stands for the same brand of power politics as we saw in the Melian dialogue.

During the rest of this year we hear of attempts on both sides to gain new

---

[1] SCHADEWALDT (v. inf.), 84. DEICHGRÄBER (v. inf.), 32. 144 with bibliog. H.-J. DIESNER, 'Peisistratidenexkurs und Peisistratenbild bei Thuk.'. *Historia* 8, 1959, 12.

allies. The decisive event, however, is the arrival of Alcibiades in Sparta. The Spartans still hesitate to join in, but he soon dispels their doubts. The decisive importance of his desertion comes out clearly in his long speech in c. 89-92. He urges the prompt dispatch of troops under a capable Spartan leader. This leader is to be Gylippus, with whose arrival in Sicily the hour will have struck for the Athenian forces, as book 7 will relate. It is Alcibiades also who advises the investment of Decelea to the north of Athens – another deadly blow to Athenian power, as the same book will show in a separate narrative (27 sqq.).

With the end of the sixth book we are in the eighteenth year of the war, which ends in 7. 18. Thus relatively little space has been allotted to this year – a decision reflecting the author's wisdom in the management of his material. The previous year, with the fitting-out and the first attack of the great fleet, was related in detail, with many speeches to let us understand the men, the circumstances and the realities of power. A similar breadth of treatment (although more sparing in speeches) is accorded to the nineteenth – the year of disaster. The eighteenth, on the contrary, standing between lofty expectations and unredeemed calamity, and not containing the decisive action, receives less space and less attention. In the middle of it comes the siege of Syracuse, which promises well after the seizure of the heights of Epipolae. But then the intervention of Gylippus alters the situation in a way which compels Nicias to send to Athens for reinforcements. The reading of his letter in the ecclesia (7. 11-15), serves the same purpose as a speech; and this year, as we saw, is treated in a way that omits speeches.

The seventh book, which Macaulay valued above any other prose writing he knew, relates the greater part of the events of the nineteenth year. That year is not, however, completed until the sixth chapter of the eighth book. The narrative begins ominously with the occupation of Decelea by the Peloponnesians, so that Athens loses her close contact with Euboea and her most important supply-line (19). Thucydides takes care afterwards that we do not lose sight of the difficulties under which this coup placed Athens. On the Syracusan front, where the Athenians are still masters of the sea, but have lost Cape Plemmyrium to Gylippus (22 sqq.), both sides try for reinforcements. Nicias receives them under Demosthenes, but the latter has not been able to bring with him 1300 mercenaries, who had arrived in Athens too late. Through shortage of money the Athenians have to send them home: this occasions a more detailed account of the military and economic difficulties under which Athens laboured after the seizure of Decelea (27 sqq.).[1] The attack of the returning Thracians on Mycalessus, and the massacre in which not even school-children were spared, give a frightful illustration of what was possible in this war (29). Having thus ensured that we do not lose sight of Attica as the second focal point of this phase of the war, Thucydides is able now to lay the main weight of his narrative once more on Sicily. The increasing naval strength of the Syracusans is endangering the position of the Athenian fleet, but still, in a manner reminiscent of Attic tragedy, before the catastrophe there are high hopes of a successful

---

[1] H. ERBSE (v. inf.), 38.

outcome. Demosthenes has sailed into the harbour of Syracuse with reinforcements (42); the Athenians are once more masters of the situation, but their decisive stroke intended to retake Epipolae miscarries (43 sqq.). Demosthenes himself now urges the abandonment of the whole campaign, but Nicias wavers; and no sooner has he decided on retreat than an eclipse of the moon terrifies the Athenians and causes them to wait for twenty-seven days. The Syracusans, now no longer content with self-defence, conceive the ambition of annihilating the enemy force. They have shown themselves superior even in naval strength, and they work out a plan for shutting the Athenian fleet up in the Great Harbour (56). Here, where the closing stages of this all-important campaign are to be depicted, Thucydides again reminds us of the magnitude of the conflict: two chapters (56-7) are given over to a comprehensive survey of the allies on either side. Then, by yet another example of his 'sandwich' technique he returns from this inserted section to the actual blocking of the harbour mouth. Next comes the battle in the harbour, with the unsuccessful attempt of the Athenians to break out – an action whose decisive importance in the Sicilian drama is underlined in two ways. First Thucydides puts a preliminary speech into the mouths of the opposing generals (Nicias 61-64, Gylippus 66-68); secondly, after the outcome of the battle he makes a signficant reference to Pylos. What the Athenians then inflicted on the Spartans in destroying their ships and cutting off their troops on Sphacteria, they now suffer themselves through the defeat of their fleet in Sicily.

All that remains is to march overland into friendly territory. Before this, the last march of the Athenian army, Nicias delivers a speech most skilfully framed by Thucydides to fit the character of a man so deeply traditional in his outlook. The whole expedition, he says, may have suffered the disfavour of the gods as being too great; but their present distresses may have been penance enough, and it may be hoped that fortune will now turn away from the enemy. But these reasonable hopes of a pious soul are falsified by events. After a march of frightful hardship the Athenians are overtaken by Syracusan forces. Losses are terrible: terrible also is the lot of the prisoners, who are taken to the quarries or otherwise reduced to slavery. Nicias and Demosthenes are put to death.

As we saw before, the narrative of the nineteenth year extends to the first six chapters of the eighth book. The last two of these chapters introduce elements which recur frequently in this book and are of decisive consequence for the closing stages of the war: the Persian satraps Tissaphernes and Pharnabazus take a hand in the game. The account of the twentieth year of the war (7-60) tells of three separate treaties between Spartans and Persians – Tissaphernes representing the latter – and gives the text of the documents verbally. Before the conclusion of the third treaty the Athenians also had sent an embassy to the Persian satrap. In this year Thucydides is mostly concerned with relating a series of small actions – largely the defection of Athenian allies in the islands and Asia Minor and attempts to recover them. The Spartans with their allies come more and more into prominence as a naval power to be reckoned with. Towards the end of this year developments occur which will come to fruition in the next. In the fleet before Samos oligarchical elements are working for the overthrow of the democracy in Athens, while Alcibiades, hoping thus to secure his return, is intriguing with Tissaphernes towards the same end.

The events of the 21st year impart a lively pace to the chapters (61-109) which deal with them. Athenian domestic politics necessarily take up a good deal of space. In the early summer of 411 the democracy was overthrown by an oligarchic putsch that placed all responsibility in the hands of a council of four hundred. A leading spirit in this movement was the orator Antiphon, of whom Thucydides writes a warm appreciation (68). But on the other hand he does not try to gloss over the reign of terror under this régime. Lack of support from the fleet at Samos compels a return to a more moderate constitution, based on the five thousand citizens who are capable of paying for their own military equipment. Thucydides highly praises (97) the moderation of this régime.

The defection of allies, particularly critical at Byzantium (80) and Euboea (95), assumes greater proportions, as does the dubious role played by Tissaphernes behind the scenes. But towards the end of the book and consequently of the whole work the entry of Alcibiades brings about a favourable turn for the Athenians. He is joyously received by army and fleet at Samos and chosen as commander. The Athenian naval victory at Cynossema and the recovery of Cyzicus introduces a new phase of the war. We hear of renewed activity on Tissaphernes' part; then the work ends, or, more accurately, it breaks off.

A question posed by the fifth book comes up again with the eighth. Direct speeches, which we have still to examine as one of Thucydides' particular devices in historical narrative, are lacking here as they were in the fifth – drawing our line, of course, before the Melian dialogue. We have to add another observation – that in both books we find documents quoted verbally; a species of historical raw material which admittedly recurs in the report of the one year's truce in 4. 118. Again, in books 5 and 8 the main lines of development seem to have been neglected in favour of unconnected incidents. From these facts the conclusion has often been drawn that Thucydides never put the finishing touches to these sections. The phenomena may, of course, be explained otherwise: we may point to the fragmentation of events themselves in the relevant years; we may explain the insertion of documents by a desire for particular exactness; but the most natural conclusion is that these parts were never brought by the author to a finished state.

The question which we have just broached leads us into a complex of problems which until recently almost exclusively occupied the attention of German researchers into Thucydides - so exclusively that one can speak of a Thucydidean question in much the same way as a Homeric question. The methods in both cases are the same. We must admit that in Thucydides 'stratum-analysis' finds quite a good deal to work on. He tells us in the first sentence that he began to write the story of the war from the moment of its outbreak, perceiving how important it would be. But since various passages prove conclusively that he was working on the history after 404, it must have come into existence over a long period.

Research into this question was begun and for more than a century dominated by Franz Wolfgang Ullrich, professor at the Hamburg Johanneum, with his *Beiträge zur Erklärung des Thukydides* (1, 1845; 2, 1846). He started with two observations. The early books contain no statement of the duration of the war as a whole, and references to it (ὅδε ὁ πόλεμος etc.) are so vague that we cannot infer a knowledge of the whole course of the conflict in all its various stages. Ullrich also laid particular weight on the so-called 'second introduction' (5. 26), which displays a knowledge of the war up to its conclusion and must therefore have been written after 404. These basic facts were supported by Ullrich with a number of smaller indications which led him to distinguish two main periods of composition. One lay in books 1–4, embraced only the first ten years, and was supposed to have been completed shortly after the Peace of Nicias. The other would have to be dated after the fall of Athens in 404, and would have been written with the whole course of the war in view. In addition to the books from the middle of 4 to the end of 8, Ullrich would ascribe to this phase of composition various references to the later parts of the war which he was compelled to recognize in the earlier books. Thus a hypothesis of later additions must be invoked to preserve the theory from overthrow.

For some time a new turn was given to this branch of study by Eduard Schwarz.[1] He attempted to refine the analysis still further, and as the Homeric analysts had done, he sought to prove contradictions and the existence of two versions in some places side by side. Thus the shade of the redactor, which had haunted the Homeric poems, was now invoked in Thucydides to explain inconsistencies. The stratification thus obtained was interpreted by Schwarz as corresponding to Thucydides' intellectual development. Others, like Schadewaldt, have pursued this path even further, so that it seems possible to distinguish a youthful Thucydides devoted to factual research from an elder Thucydides who wanted to understand history and to communicate his understanding to others.

In the most recent phase of Thucydidean research the separation into strata, arrived at with such self-confidence, has been examined to see whether it is really tenable. The position has been made clear best of all by Harald Patzer's careful evaluation of the arguments. As an appendix he prints a list of all the 'early' and 'late' indications, which affords us a rapid conspectus of the facts. Convincing indications of lateness are fairly frequent and are distributed throughout the work. 'Early' indications, on the other hand, so far as they can be taken seriously, are very rare, and Patzer shows that they have very unequal value as testimony.

Once again we must draw a parallel with Homeric studies. In both cases, after many indirections, research has enabled us to understand the form of literary works not just in the light of minute analysis by scholars, but in their own right as works of great creative power. Such a unitarian view as that represented by John H. Finley[2] fails to see what preceded the final form. In our chapter on Homer we strove to show the multitude of the hypotheses which throw light

---

[1] *Das Geschichtswerk des Thuk.* Bonn 1919; 2nd ed. 1929.
[2] *V. inf.* and 'The Unity of Thucydides' History'. *Harv. Stud.* Suppl. vol. 1, 1940, 225.

upon the form of the *Iliad* and *Odyssey*; and in assessing Thucydides we cannot close our eyes to his own declaration assigning several decades to the composition of the work. What we read today is not a mass of additions and insertions piled on top of a series of rough sketches widely differing in date and intellectual attitude, but a work of basic unity, conceived and executed on well defined principles. It certainly contains many passages of which the content or execution is a survival from an earlier period of the author's literary activity. That the work was never finished is shown by the ending and by the state of books 5 and 8, as we have interpreted them; but he was able to carry it far enough to be aiming at a unity which cannot justify our lightly dividing it up into ever smaller pieces. Thus in Thucydidean studies today we see a healthy attitude of restraint, not condemning the whole proceedings of the analyst, but regarding his results with a much greater scepticism and rejecting the headstrong theorizing of earlier years.

One pleasing result of this development is that in recent years increased attention has been given to the inner qualities of the work. When wishing to characterize the man in relation to his times, scholars have long been content to contrast him with Herodotus. This the author has himself invited by correcting Herodotus in several places[1] – admittedly without mentioning him by name – and by taking up arms against him in the chapter on historical method. One constantly finds Thucydides, as the inventor of political history, as the impeccable researcher and unswerving seeker after truth, contrasted with Herodotus as the representative of the Ionic love of a good story, as the uncritical accepter of unreliable traditions of every kind. There is a good deal of truth in this view, but the deep-rooted difference between the characters of the two historians cannot adequately be assessed along these lines. More truly we can speak of a difference in the degree to which certain definite principles are carried into practice. Herodotus also was well aware of the varying value of his sources, and if he does not always take the utmost pains to decide between them, he does repeatedly allude to their untrustworthiness; Herodotus also makes use of monuments and inscriptions for the purposes of history, and shows that he is at least no stranger to the use of documentary material. The difference admittedly is very considerable, and we should not try to minimize it. In Thucydides pleasure in narration for its own sake is rigorously excluded, and everything is subordinated to the one end of communicating what in fact happened. The techniques of historical method are here developed and applied to a quite different degree. Certainly Thucydides is writing contemporary history and has more detailed and reliable sources available than Herodotus had for the Persian War; but even in those parts where he deals with events long past he puts each foot on the hardest ground he can find. A typical example of Thucydides' methods of work is his excursus on the Pisistratids (6. 54–59), where he is concerned to prove that Hippias, not Hipparchus, was tyrant. He makes use of the dedicatory inscription of the Altar of the Twelve Gods, erected by the younger Pisistratus, grandson of the tyrant, in the Athenian Agora, together

---

[1] SCHMID, 2. 663. 7.

with an almost illegible dedication from Delphi and the stele that stood on the Acropolis to commemorate the expulsion of the tyrants. It is most instructive to see how he goes to work with this last piece of evidence. It affords him no direct support for his thesis, but the fact that the inscription mentions only the children of Hippias, not those of the other sons of Pisistratus, together with the order in which the names are given, confirms for him that Hippias was the eldest son of Pisistratus and therefore heir to the tyrannis. Thucydides is here working with the same conception of convincing probability ($\epsilon i\kappa\acute{a}\zeta\epsilon\iota\nu$) on which he remarked earlier in connection with the methods invented by the sophists for carrying conviction in courts of law. He has resource to such methods most of all when he tries to throw light on very early periods. Consequently the 'archaeologia' is the greatest field for employing this kind of argument, and we cannot fail to see the satisfaction with which Thucydides brought it to bear in this early stage of his work. The satisfaction is justified: the conclusion for example from the nature of early Delian graves and their furniture that the population of the island was originally Carian corresponds entirely to the methods of modern investigation.

We must stress again the decisive importance in Thucydides' historical writing of his unqualified determination to achieve objectivity. In this respect he goes far beyond Herodotus. But if we wish to see what basically distinguishes his work from that of his predecessor, we must go another way about it. Thucydides speaks of his purpose and his means of achieving it in chapters 1, 20–22. The last of these, the so-called 'chapter on method',[1] has received the most intense investigation in recent years, and too much has often been built on single words. But all the important results have been well established. What we find is first a manifesto of historical research made as accurate as can be. On this theme the writer has to show the untrustworthiness of oral tradition. Even events in the history of one's own country can be perverted by such a tradition, as he shows by reference to the supposed tyranny of Hipparchus and its overthrow by Harmodius and Aristogiton. It is to this question, as a particularly good example of his research methods, that he returns in greater detail in the excursus of the sixth book. Thucydides gives two further examples, this time from Sparta, to show the untrustworthiness of popular beliefs on matters of one's own day and therefore susceptible of verification, namely the supposed voting right of the kings, signified with two stones, and the imaginary lochos of Pitane. Both these things are mentioned in passing by Herodotus, and Thucydides' concern to be thought of differently from his predecessor becomes apparent. In the next chapter he contrasts his own careful work with those of the poets and of the logographers, two groups against whom he directs a powerful polemic – not wholly unjustified, but tending to over-simplification when he labels both as men who try to appeal to their readers by ornament and exaggeration. It goes without saying that the main targets of this attack are Homer and Herodotus.

[1] Bibliog. in H. HERTER, 'Zur ersten Periklesrede' (*v. inf.*), 613, 1. Cf. also H. ERBSE (*v. inf.*), 55.

The end of the 21st chapter provides one of those smooth transitions which we have often observed in Thucydides. The war that is to be his theme has been shown by the most exact researches into the past to be the greatest that Greece ever waged. An equal exactness will mark the principles that he follows in narration. The chapter on method (22) divides the subject in a manner immemorially current among the Greeks. In the *Iliad* (9. 443) Phoenix sums up the two ends of aristocratic education, which form in fact a unity: mastery of words and readiness for deeds. Thucydides here follows the same division in setting out the programme of his work. He deals with words first. Some speeches he heard himself (among the class thus attested we may well reckon those of Pericles), others at secondhand. Both for him and for his informants it was hard to piece together from memory the exact form of what was said (τὴν ἀκρίβειαν αὐτὴν τῶν λεχθέντων). With most modern students we take this as referring both to the wording and to the sequence of thought. After thus pointing out what he was unable to do and what the nature of his work rendered impossible even as an ideal, he explains his principles in the composition of speeches. He constructs them according to the needs of each situation (περὶ τῶν ἀεὶ παρόντων τὰ δέοντα), as he thinks they must have determined what the speaker said. Having admitted these freedoms, he adds an important reservation: the general sense (ξύμπασα γνώμη) of what was actually said (which in most instances was still accessible) is as far as possible preserved. We are not told here anything about the purpose of the insertion of speeches: that is a question which we must discuss later in a wider context.

In reporting actions, however, accuracy was the goal – accuracy unqualified and frequently attainable. With an obvious allusion to Herodotus Thucydides says that he was not satisfied with asking the first comer: a careful scrutiny of testimony was necessary, since even among eye-witnesses, through forgetfulness or partiality, reports varied widely.

Thucydides himself is well aware that the severity of his ideals will make it impossible for his work to be widely attractive. In considering its effect on the hearer he must have Herodotus in mind, who is known to have given public readings from his histories. If he cannot hope for success of this sort, Thucydides has his consolation: the people for whom he writes are of a different kind. He addresses himself to those who wish to obtain clear insight into what happened in the past and, by a basic uniformity in human nature, will happen again in the future in more or less the same way. He will be satisfied if his work is of use to men of such serious purpose, since it was not written as a show-piece for an occasion, but as a possession for all time (κτῆμα ἐς ἀεί). Here we are at the intellectual core of Thucydides' work, and at the point where the true difference between him and Herodotus begins to appear.

Behind the painstaking narrator of actual events we now see the writer of history, striving to impart political understanding that shall be of permanent value. The brief sentences in which Thucydides outlines this last purpose of his writing should not be taken as a simple application of the tag *historia vitae magistra*. Thucydides was concerned neither with imparting to his readers skill in political prognosis nor with giving them a book of rules which would enable them to take decisions in concrete instances. Rather, as he worked on his history, he gained an insight into certain patterns and forces which the trained eye will always recognize behind the endless and bewildering variety of actual events. Such a knowledge brings with it the clarification of pictures otherwise confused, and even if the particular situation is one scarcely likely to recur, the trained mind can see in it forces which belong to the realm of the timeless. One who possesses such knowledge has not of course been given hard and fast instruction in political behaviour, but he has gained the ability in any future case to throw light on a situation, to understand the basic laws of the interplay of forces, and use this knowledge and foresight in reaching his decisions. It is an example of Thucydides' historical purpose that, in describing so carefully the symptoms of the plague (2. 48), he says that his purpose is to save men from being wholly taken unawares if it should ever break out again.

The desire of Thucydides' to go beyond individual phenomena to something universally valid is characteristic of Greek thought in general. But undoubtedly it introduces an antinomy underlying his whole programme. To the researcher who is straining every nerve to achieve the maximum accuracy in narrating individual events, these events are not the true and ultimate goal: what he seeks is the universal that can be extracted from them. This antinomy cannot be resolved by assigning its elements to different periods of Thucydides' intellectual development: it is deeply rooted in his work and thought.

We shall try to attain a better understanding of the history with the help of two questions. By what methods does Thucydides undertake to impart to his readers the insight of which he speaks in c. 22, and in what sphere does he hope to find the universal and permanent which are to give the trained mind a deeper understanding of the concrete instance?

We must make a negative observation first. With very few exceptions Thucydides does not make personal appearances in his work to judge or to explain. The very fact that we hear his voice so seldom imparts to the whole that air of cool objectivity which has constantly been singled out as its especial characteristic. If he does ever speak in his own person, it is to say something of particular importance: the main lines of his methods and ideals (1. 22), his judgment on Pericles as man and statesman (2. 65) and his experience of the frightful upheaval of civil society occasioned by war (3. 83 sqq.). He is a little less reserved in the 8th book, where in 24 he praises the constitution of Chios, in 97 the moderate oligarchy established in Athens, and near the end of 96 discusses the various activities of Athenians, Spartans and Syracusans. It is very seldom that he expresses any personal view on events or individuals: exceptions are on Cleon (3. 36; 5. 16) and on the tragedy of Mycalessus (7. 30). His sympathetic verdict on Nicias (7. 86) will engage our attention again when we discuss his attitude towards religion.

These are all exceptions. Thucydides does not lecture, he narrates. But his narrative is not content to chronicle the particular facts: it probes deeply, detects connections, and in all the crucial situations of the long struggle gives us analyses in which all the presuppositions are clearly brought out, the possibilities are defined, and the men in charge of affairs, with all their thoughts and motives, are set before our eyes. It is by these analyses that the reader gains insight into the enduring behind the transient, the recurrent tendency behind the individual happening. On these elucidations of historical crises Thucydides has lavished a care which justifies the proud words in which he calls his work a possession for all time. In analysing situations his favourite device is the speech. In the passage already quoted he says that he was governed in their composition by the needs of the current situation – a sufficient indication of the role they have to play. There are over forty speeches in the whole work, of which about two-thirds occur in the first four books. A contributing factor here may be that some of the later sections never achieved their final form, but this is not a complete explanation. The especial frequency of analytical and interpretative speeches in the first half of the work arises from the purpose of these books, which is to bring out clearly the underlying causes of the war, the character and temper of the antagonists, and the possibilities which in the early stages were so wide and numerous.

This function of displaying the causes of events and the motives of the actors, thus enabling us to see through the purely factual to the real basis of things, is nowhere more clearly seen than in those places where opposing views are expressed in antithetical pairs of speeches. It is here, if anywhere, that we see the sophistic elements underlying Thucydides' work. It was from the sophists that he discovered the world of antinomies behind human action and passion, and learnt that opposite views may be expressed of any conceivable questions. Protagoras developed this line of thought in his *Antilogiae*, and the same word significantly appears immediately before the dispute between the Corcyraeans and the Corinthians in the Athenian assembly (1. 31). Nowhere, however, has Thucydides developed his technique of opposed speeches more elaborately than in that part of the first book which immediately precedes the Spartan declaration of war; and analysis has nowhere more signally miscarried than in wishing to separate these two pairs of speeches. In fact one speech complements the other, even where it attacks the opponent's views. By this means we are given a picture of the forces which inevitably led to this war and of the two great opponents Athens and Sparta, whose difference in character determined the course of events. Above all, these speeches contribute much to the depiction of Athenian national character with the dangers and the potentialities inherent in it. When the Corinthians (1. 70), with an almost clinical accuracy, describe the perpetual unrest of Athens, her dissatisfaction with all she had achieved, her inability either to be at peace herself or to suffer others to be so, a tragic element comes into the picture, and one thinks of the first stasimon of the *Antigone*, in which Sophocles sings of the fatal unrest of the human soul.

It has been justly remarked that in this tetrad of speeches that of king Archidamus, with its description of the Spartan character, is in some parts modelled as a counterpart to the funeral speech of Pericles. There are other examples of a like nature, in which correspondences may be detected between speeches delivered at widely varying times and places.

Towards the parties whom he thus opposes one to another Thucydides preserves an objectivity that can scarcely be rivalled in historical literature. Here he differs sharply from the sophists. He is not striving to give victory to one point of view, he is not supporting a *parti pris* through thick and thin: he gives us all the arguments for and against with such fullness that we have a wellnigh complete picture of the interplay of forces. A treatment of the situations from both sides is visible throughout: in summarizing the history we have already mentioned as exceptional those places where Thucydides puts a speech without any rejoinder, thus recognizing the cogency of its arguments. Pericles has no opponent, nor has Hermocrates when he calls for unity at the congress of Sicilian states (4. 59). Practically all the speeches are governed by the purpose of extracting from individual circumstances the basic and general elements.

The chapter on method lets us know how far we may speak of truth to history in the speeches. Certainly there are differences between those which Thucydides composed to embody his own appraisal of the situation and those which he either heard himself or received from reliable informants.[1] Very probably Thucydides personally listened to Pericles, and we may confidently assume a close correspondence between the stateman's political ideals and those which his generous admirer puts into his mouth in the history.[2]

In the multiplicity of political actions Thucydides seeks to find elements which regularly recur. In what sphere does he hope to find them? Here he treads a different path from that of Herodotus. Although the latter was a contemporary of the sophists, yet his world-view, as we saw when discussing him, is essentially presophistic, supposes a divine government, and thus is closely akin to the preconceptions of Attic tragedy. In Herodotus the gods of the old religion no longer take a personal share in the action, but nowhere does he show the slightest doubt that the destinies of men, while their free will has abundant opportunity to exercise itself, are ultimately determined in another world than ours. Expressions such as 'since it was ordained that he should come to grief' are an explicit avowal of a belief in a supernatural guidance of events.[3] Consequently ideas such as the displeasure of the gods, the preserving of a healthy moderation, the circle of good fortune and calamity assume a decisive importance. The ever-recurring figure of the warning friend is a special embodiment of this kind of belief.

Thucydides is wholly different. In his picture of history there are no metaphysical factors to account for events. In consequence his own views on religion can only be guessed at. In the Melian dialogue the Athenians make an allusion to the notion of deity with the greatest reserve, as a pure supposition – a view agreeing with that set out by Protagoras in the beginning of his treatise on the gods. We may well suspect that Thucydides' own views lay in that direction.

---

[1] On this question see K. ROHRER, 'Ueber die Authentizität der Reden bei Thuk.'. *Wien. Stud.* 72, 1959, 36.

[2] V. EHRENBERG, *Sophocles and Pericles.* Oxf. 1954, 41. J. T. KAKRIDIS, *Der thuk. Epitaphios. Zet.* 26, 1961, 112 is more reserved; see also M. H. CHAMBERS, 'Thucydides and Pericles'. *Harv. Stud.* 62, 1957, 79.　　　　[3] *V. sup.* p. 323.

According to Antyllus in Marcellinus' life he was a pupil of Anaxagoras and ἄθεος ἠρέμα. Yet he is no polemist against traditional belief. In the career of Nicias, a devout representative of the old creed, there was much to be related which would afford material for such attacks. We find in Thucydides nothing of the sort: indeed he shows an unusual warmth of feeling in an appreciation of his moral character (7. 86). The few other passages in which religious fraternities are mentioned (2. 53; 3. 82) give little reason to suppose that Thucydides belonged to one. The decisive fact is that in all the events that he relates he studiously avoids any metaphysical interpretation. He draws no sharp distinction between myth and history: the Trojan war, Hellen and his sons, Pandion, Itys, Procne and the like are treated as historical.[1]

Thucydides has himself indicated in what sphere within history he sees the roots of the recurrent, the regular and the largely calculable. In the chapter on method (1. 22) he speaks of human nature (τό ἀνθρώπινον) as the constant factor giving rise to similarities.[2] This same factor is mentioned repeatedly in other places, always the most highly wrought passages in the book. The Spartan king Archidamus is made to say in his great speech (1. 84) that it is wrong to suppose great differences among human beings, and in the study of party spirit (3. 82) he speaks of the deadly effects of domestic tension, which will recur as long as human nature remains the same. This basically unchanging nature displays itself for Thucydides above all in the struggle for power and personal advantage, in which the laws are resented as a hindrance.[3] This view again reminds us of the teaching of the sophists, which represented the right of the stronger as being the only genuine natural right; but again the difference is more important than the agreement. While the more extreme sophists spoke grandiloquently in favour of the right of the stronger, Thucydides refrains from all moral judgment, and makes his observations as dispassionately as the physician at a bedside or the scientist in a laboratory. The simile is not wholly fanciful. It has long since been observed[4] that correspondences, sometimes even verbal, have been found between Thucydides' ways of thought and those of contemporary natural science, especially medicine. We should probably think of this rather as the convergence of separate lines of development than as borrowing on Thucydides' part. It is a new manner of investigation, one which looks beyond the surface of phenomena for their underlying causes. The words of Anaxagoras (VS 59 B21a), 'that which appears is an earnest of what does not', may well be applied to the work of Thucydides.

We find in him that double motivation of actions, by divine contrivance and by human will, which can be traced through Homer into the classical period; but one half of it has been secularized. Nevertheless the confrontation of human

---

[1] Cf. such passages as 1. 3; 2. 15 and 29; 6. 2 and F. HAMPL, Serta Philol. Aenipontana. Innsbruck 1961, 42, 5.

[2] L. PEARSON, Gnom. 32, 1960, 15, totally mistakes the sense in rendering κατὰ τὸ ἀνθρώπινον as 'in all human probability'.

[3] 1. 76; 3. 45 and 84; 5. 105. Cf. TÖPITSCH (v. inf.).

[4] Most recently by K. WEIDAUER, Thuk. und die hippokratischen Schriften. Heidelb. 1954. Cf. H. DILLER, Gnom. 27, 1955, 9.

intelligence and courage with factors which cheat them of their ends is still part of the substructure. The human agent in Thucydides is by preference the statesman;[1] next to him the general. The function of the man at the top is intelligent planning, which alone can reach the desired goal, so far as human foresight can go. All the important characters in Thucydides are shown as planners and calculators, shrewdly assessing the future. The more effectively his intellect (γνώμη) formulates the situation and estimates the play of forces, the better are the prospects of success. A statesman of this kind must bring with him a deep understanding of those factors which he must accept as data, without hoping to alter them. By this Thucydides means the features of uniformity found in our common human nature, showing themselves, above all where power is concerned, in perpetual striving and unrest. The leader must also make every allowance for the particular characteristics of the society which he heads, as well as for those of the opponent. While Thucydides is convinced of the uniformity and homogeneity of human nature within certain limits, there is still room left for differences such as those so skilfully indicated between Spartans and Athenians.

Pericles is the archetype of the statesman in this developed sense. His grand strategy was so well adapted to all contingencies that only its faulty execution by his incompetent successors deprived Athens of victory. To produce such a statesman both talent and training are needed. From what he says, Thucydides seems to hope that his work may contribute to such an end. While the proposition that statesmanship can be taught must not be taken in too gross and palpable a sense, we may see in such hopes something of the sophistic spirit. The untutored genius, as Themistocles is portrayed (1. 138), is on this view a surprising exception.

When the responsible statesman has taken into account all the factors accessible to his intelligence, there still remains a realm from which his plans may suffer hindrance or total frustration. This incalculable element is called Tyche. By this word Thucydides does not mean some divine power: he does not make the irrational into a metaphysical entity. He only means in the simplest terms that human planning for the future has its limits, outside which is the unforeseen.[2] Thucydides knows the meaning of chance, but in his treatment of history he restricts its sphere of action in favour of rational calculation. In this he was a child of his time. We may again compare Democritus (VS 68 B 119), who was radical enough to say that Fortune (τύχη) was a bogey invented by men to excuse their own stupidity.

Any attempt to examine Thucydides' beliefs comes up at last against a question which the objectivity of his narratives and analyses renders extraordinarily difficult. Large sections of his work might give the impression that he writes with scientific detachment, studiously avoiding any ethical judgment of the events described. In other words: is human nature and the struggle for power

---

[1] Cf. H. HERTER (v. inf.).

[2] W. MÜRI, 'Bemerkungen zum Verständnis des Thuk.'. *Mus. Helv.* 4, 1947, 251. H. HERTER, 'Freiheit etc.'. (v. inf.), 135.

arising from it as by an inherent law of nature the only measure of all things that Thucydides possesses? Is the conscious rejection of right, honour and moral restraint expressed by the Athenians in the Melian debate to be taken as representing his own views? This type of enquiry has been only recently undertaken;[1] but it would appear that behind all Thucydides' reserve his personal conception of ethical values is recognizable enough. The intimation is often of the briefest, as in the tribute to Nicias, that in his life he had been second to none in the practice of every virtue,[2] or when he tells us that the crew of the Athenian trireme which had to bring the sentence of death to Mytilene (3. 49) made no haste to discharge their repugnant (ἀλλόκοτος) duty. More weight attaches to whole sections, such as the Epitaphios in a positive or the 'pathology of faction' in a negative sense: neither makes any sense without reference to some scheme of moral values.[3] Furthermore, in passages like the speech of Diodotus in Book 3 or the Melian Dialogue in Book 5 we can see a line of argument pointing out the dangers and uncertainties inherent in the misuse of power. The position still needs clarification; but Thucydides is far from being a propagandist for the will to rule: he is no extreme sophist in whose scheme all ethical values have been eliminated. He wrote what he saw as it presented itself to him. He might well think with Hesiod that Aidos and Nemesis had long since left the world and that Dike's situation in it was precarious; but he gives us no reason to believe that he was one who applauded their departure.

It is one of the antinomies of Thucydides' work that behind the cool and easy detachment that he maintains there is a great spiritual tumult, which finds corresponding expression in his manner of writing. Certainly there are great differences in style between different parts. In the purely narrative sections he uses mostly a plain, everyday chronicler's style. But in passages of particular stress, above all in the speeches, all the peculiarities of his ways of thought and expression come to light. The main lines emerge most clearly from a comparison with Gorgias. Both incline strongly towards antithesis: a tendency deeply rooted in the Greek genius, and exemplified in Thucydides often in an artificial and exaggerated degree. But whereas Gorgias underlines his antithetical structure by elaborate parallelism of clauses and an obtrusive use of assonance, often wearying the reader, the historian's antitheses are so cut up by constant syntactical variation that he never allows us the relaxation of seeing a construction move quietly to a foreseeable end. Hence comes that restless waywardness that often creates the greatest difficulties in understanding his meaning. Parallelism of thought is constantly in conflict with variation of expression. The general impression is well expressed by Isocrates, whose verdict Cicero thus renders (Or. 40): *praefractior nec satis, ut ita dicam, rotundus.*[4] When Dionysius of

---

[1] TOPITSCH (v. inf.), K. NAWRATIL, AfdA 6, 1953, 61 and 125. K. REINHARDT, 'Thuc. und Machiavelli'. Vermächtnis der Antike. Göttingen 1960, 184.

[2] This is the only possible meaning of ἀρετή (7, 86.)

[3] Cf. F. MÜLLER's study of the Funeral Speech (sup. p. 461, n. 2.).

[4] The text is rather doubtful. Nonius quoting the passage has Theodectes: Ernesti's conjecture Theodorus has been accepted by most editors.

Halicarnassus, in an elaborate study of Thucydides,[1] took up arms against the high esteem and wide influence that he enjoyed in late republican Rome, he remarked that very few men had read him all through, and even they needed a commentary in many places. Cicero (*Or.* 9. 30) describes his speeches as barely intelligible.

Another feature of Thucydides' language, closely linked to his individual ways of thought, is a tendency to abstract expressions. This tendency manifests itself in the preponderance of nominal elements in his language, including the constant use of abstract nouns and participles and infinitives used substantivally. The frequency of gnomic expressions[2] also plays its part here.

In recent years particular attention has been paid to the type of articulation used by Thucydides in linking the stages of his arguments. His technique here is developed from the old type of ring-composition.[3] The order 'statement – proof – statement' is found repeatedly, as also is a device by which, after an explanatory digression, he returns to the narrative not at the point where he left it, but a little later, as if the course of events had moved on during the interval.

WILAMOWITZ's thesis that work was done on Thucydides at Alexandria has often been rejected, but USENER thought that remains of Alexandrian exegesis could be detected, and the most recent study of the problem by O. LUSCHNAT, 'Die Thukydidesscholien'. *Phil.* 98, 1954, 14, tends to support him. LUSCHNAT gives a survey of ancient exegetical work – scholia, a papyrus with remains of a commentary on the second book (nr. 1205 P.), another on the archaeologia (nr. 1204 P.), not forgetting the help afforded by Dionysius of Halicarnassus (cf. n. 1). There is a good discussion of the problem and the material by R. STARK in his very useful study 'Textgeschichtliche und literarkritische Folgerungen aus neueren Papyri'. *Annales Univers. Saraviensis. Phil.-lett.* 8, 1959, 40.

We do not know how far Alexandrian work affected the text of Thucydides, but the transmission gives a fairly favourable impression. This is confirmed by the papyri, which are not plentiful, but which give us a text anterior to the present grouping of the manuscripts: nr. 1176-1203 P.; J. E. POWELL, 'The Papyri and the text of Thucydides'. *Actes V^e congr. int. de pap.* Brussels 1938, 344. E. G. TURNER, 'Two unrecognised Ptolemaic Papyri'. *Journ. Hell. Stud.* 76, 1956, 95. V. BARTOLETTI, 'Tucidide 2. 73, 1–74, 1 in un papiro dell' Università statale di Milano'. *Studi in onore di L. Castiglione.* Florence 1961, 61. For a survey of the MSS.: A. DAIN, 'Liste des manuscrits de Thuc.'. *Rev. Ét. Gr.* 46, 1933, 20; supplemented by J. E. POWELL, 'The archetype of Thuc.'. *Class.*

---

[1] Περὶ Θουκ., Περὶ τῶν Θουκ. ἰδιωμάτων. See also his second book Περὶ μιμήσεως and the treatise *ad Pompeium*.   [2] C. MEISTER (*v. inf.*).

[3] N. G. L. HAMMOND, 'The Arrangement of Thought in the Proem and in other Parts of Thucydides'. *Class. Quart.* 46, 1952, 127. H. ERBSE (*v. inf.*). R. KATIČIĆ, 'Die Ringkomposition im 1. Buch des Thuk. Geschichtswerkes'. *Wien. Stud.* 70, 1957, 179.

Quart. 30, 1936, 86. On the affiliation: V. BARTOLETTI, *Per la storia del testo di Tuc.* Florence 1937. J. E. POWELL, 'The archetype of Thucydides'. *Class. Quart.* 32, 1938, 75 and *Gnom.* 15, 1939, 281. See also the prefaces to the editions by J. DE ROMILLY and O. LUSCHNAT, the latter with a stemma codicum. B. HEMMERDINGER, *Essai sur l'histoire du texte de Th.* Paris 1955. G. B. ALBERTI, 'Questioni tucididee per la storia del testo'. *Bollettino del comitato per la preparazione della Ediz. Nazionale.* 1957, 19. 1958, 41. 1960, 81. 1961, 59. Two groups can be distinguished (CG and ABEFM); the oldest MS. is C (Laur. 69, 2) from the tenth century. Both groups go back to minuscule hyparchetypes, derived in turn from a minuscule archetype. But there are other strands of tradition, and two MSS. (B=Vat. 126 and the more recent H=Par. 1734) from 6. 92 onwards show readings going back to an uncial MS. of the fifth century. Since there is a good deal of contamination, eclectic methods have to be used in setting up the text. On the recentiores (how much is genuine, how much Byzantine conjecture): O. LUSCHNAT, *Gnom.* 26, 1954, 309. A. KLEINLOGEL, *Beobachtungen zu einigen 'recentiores' des Th. Abh. Ak. Heidelb. Phil.-hist. Kl.* 1957/1.

Summary of recent work: F. M. WASSERMANN, 'Thucydidean Scholarship 1942–56'. *Class. Weekly* 50, 1956, 65. 89. W. EBERHARD, 'Fachbericht Thuk.'. *Gymn.* 67, 1960, 209. 68, 1961, 329. For the older work see SCHMID 5, 1948.

Editions: H. S. JONES–J. E. POWELL, 2nd ed. Oxf. 1942. J. DE ROMILLY, book 1. *Coll. des un. de Fr.* 1953 (2nd ed. 1958); books 6–7 (with L. BODIN) 1955; book 2 1962. O. LUSCHNAT (an improved version of HUDE's edition) I (books 1–2) Leipz. 1954; 2nd ed. 1960. C. F. SMITH, 4 vols. Loeb Class. Lib., Lond. 1923. With commentary: the old edition of J. CLASSEN, 8 vols. Berlin 1862–76, reprinted to 1922 with the collaboration of J. STEUP, is still valuable. A. MADDALENA (book 1 in three parts), *Bibl. di studi sup.* Florence, vol. 15, 1951; 18, 1952; 20, 1952. Without text: A. W. GOMME, *A Historical Commentary on Thucydides* I (book 1), Oxf. 1945 (repr. with corr. 1950); II (books 2–3), III (books 4–5. 24), 1956. The commentary is to be completed by A. ANDREWES and K. J. DOVER. Selected parts in M. I. FINLEY, *The Greek Historians* 1959. – Scholia: C. HUDE, Leipz. 1927. – Lexicon: G. A. BÉTANT, 2 vols. Geneva 1843/47. Repr. by Olms of Hildesheim 1961. – Index: M. H. N. VON ESSEN, Berl. 1887. – Translations: English: THOMAS HOBBES, ed. by D. GRENE. Ann Arbor. Michigan Un. Pr. 1959. H. DALE, Lond. 1849. R. CRAWLEY, 1876 (repr. Everyman's Lib. 1910). B. JOWETT, 2nd ed. Oxf. 1900. R. WARNER (Penguin Classics), Lond. 1954. French: Romilly's edition (*v. supra*). German: A. HORNEFFER–H. STRASBURGER, Bremen 1957. Partial translations: H. M. WILKINS, *The Speeches from Thuc.* Lond. 1870. O. REGENBOGEN, *Thuk. politische Reden.* Leipz. 1949 (with good introd.). G. P. LANDMANN, *Die Totenrede des Thuk.* Berne 1945. C. TEN HOLDER, *Das Meliergespräch.* Düsseldorf 1956. – Language: J. ROS, *Die Μεταβολή (Variatio) als Stilprinzip des Thuk.* Paderborn 1938. – Monographs etc.: W. SCHADEWALDT, *Die Geschichtsschreibung des Thuk.* Berl. 1929. O. REGENBOGEN, 'Thuk. als politischer Denker'. *Das hum. Gymn.* 1933, 2. A. GROSSKINSKY, *Das Programm des Thuk.* Berl. 1936. H. PATZER, *Das Problem der Geschichtsschreibung des Thuk. und die thuk. Frage.* Berl. 1937. O. LUSCHNAT, *Die Feldherrnreden im Geschichtswerk des Thuk. Phil.*

S. 34/2, Leipz. 1942. J. H. FINLEY, Jr., *Thucydides*. Harv. Un. Pr. 1942 (1947). E. TÖPITSCH, 'Ανθρωπεία φύσις und Ethik bei Thukydides'. *Wien. Stud.* 61/62, 1943/47, 50. H. HERTER, 'Freiheit und Gebundenheit des Staatsmannes bei Thuk.'. *Rhein. Mus.* 93, 1950, 133. Id., 'Pylos und Melos'. *Rhein. Mus.* 97, 1954, 316. J. DE ROMILLY, *Thuc. et l'impérialisme athénien*. 2nd ed. Paris 1951. Ead., *Histoire et raison chez Thucydide*. Paris 1956. Ead., 'L'utilité de l'histoire selon Thuc.'. *Entretiens sur l'antiquité class.* 4. Vandœuvres-Genève 1956, 39. K. DEICHGRÄBER, *Der Listensinnende Trug des Gottes*. Göttingen 1952, 31. H. ERBSE, 'Ueber eine Eigenheit der thuk. Geschichtsbetrachtung'. *Rhein. Mus.* 96, 1953, 38. H. STRASBURGER, 'Die Entdeckung der politischen Geschichte durch Thuk.'. *Saeculum* 5, 1954, 395. Id., 'Thuk. und die politische Selbstdarstellung der Athener'. *Herm.* 86, 1958, 17. C. MEISTER, *Die Gnomik im Geschichtswerk des Thuk.* Diss. Basel 1955. C. MEYER, *Die Urkunden im Geschichtswerk des Thuk. Zet.* 10. Munich 1955. J. VOGT, 'Das Bild des Perikles bei Th.'. *Hist. Zeitschr.* 182/2, 1956, 249. H. J. DIESNER, *Wirtschaft u. Gesellschaft bei Thuk.* Halle 1956; cf. A. W. GOMME, *Gnom.* 30, 1958, 439 and DIESNER, 'Thukydidesprobleme'. *Wiss. Zeitschr. der Un. Halle. Ges.-Sprachwiss.* 8, 1959, 683. H. DILLER, 'Freiheit bei Thuk. als Schlagwort und Wirklichkeit'. *Gymn.* 69, 1962, 189. On biographical detail see O. LUSCHNAT, 'Der Vatersname des Historikers Thuk.'. *Phil.* 100, 1956, 134.

8 THE SCIENCES

Our discussion of the historians, philosophers and particularly the sophists of the second half of the 5th century suffices to give us a picture of a prose literature which developed vigorously in several directions. All the same a great deal is lacking for this picture to be completed in all its details. This age, which represents one of the most momentous revolutions in European intellectual life with its thrust toward rationalisation and individualisation, called forth in creative workers in the most varied fields the wish to justify or explain their activity by means of the written word. It should not be forgotten that, apart from their more easily remembered achievements, it was the Greeks who created the forms of scientific and technical literature which have henceforth remained standard.

In the discussion of Sophocles' treatise *On the Chorus* mention was made of the architect Ictinus and the sculptor Polycletus who wrote on the theory of their professions. It is a somewhat different matter when a technical paper is not concerned with a certain achievement whose understanding it seeks to facilitate, but itself contains and represents this achievement. This condition occurs nowhere so distinctly as in the case of the royal science of mathematics. Even ages which knew more about the Greek achievement than the present have hardly acquired a correct appreciation of the power and depth of vision which is evinced in the mathematical thought of the Greeks. It may be considered as certain that its beginnings can be looked for in Pythagorean circles, however poor our knowledge may be with regard to details.[1]

[1] But in chapter 6 of his important book *Weisheit und Wissenschaft*, Nuremberg 1962, W. BURKERT has sharply illuminated the problems of the *communis opinio*.

We discern three main problems: the squaring of the circle, the trisection of the angle, the doubling of the cube.[1] Hippocrates of Chios, who chose Athens as the scene of his labours and whose achievements are dated in the end of the 5th century, busied himself with the first and third of these. His 'lunes' have remained famous, since they represented a significant step toward the goal of establishing a rationally intelligible relation between the circle and the square. Its solution was carried further by the sophist Antiphon who sought to approach the circle by inscribing regular polygons with an increasing number of sides (VS 87 B 13), whereas Bryson of Heraclea, the son of Herodotus of the same city, attempted an approach through circumscribed polygons. Although these attempts were inconclusive, mathematics had started on the road along which Archimedes was to come to the expression of π by the limiting values 3.141 and 3.142. The versatile Hippias of Elis also occupied himself with mathematics, especially the trisection of angles; with his quadratrix he even approached the field of the higher curves. From Plato's *Theaetetus* we know of Theodorus of Cyrene who proved the irrationality of $\sqrt{3}$, $\sqrt{5}$ ... $\sqrt{17}$. The fact that Theodorus went up to exactly $\sqrt{17}$ is an excellent example of the use of geometrical figures to acquire this kind of knowledge.[2] It may be assumed that the Pythagorean Hippasus continued Theodorus' enquiries and that he was the discoverer of incommensurability.[3] It appears from some information in Iamblichus (VS 18) that Hippasus raised opposition within the Pythagorean circle and got into trouble. He was also politically active. It would probably be correct to put his date as the middle of the 5th century.

Oenopides of Chios, a younger contemporary of Anaxagoras, was another mathematician; his name is especially connected with an achievement in astronomy, the discovery of the ecliptic. Mathematics and astronomy also went hand in hand in other respects; the Athenian Meton, whom Aristophanes put on the stage in the *Birds*, determined the solstices, utilizing observations of the metic Phaënus, and collaborated with the Athenian Euctemon in improving the calendar by means of an intercalary cycle of nineteen years; he also had calendar tablets and a sundial put up in public places. It was characteristic of contemporary science that such empirical methods went side by side with the speculations of Philolaus, a Pythagorean of Croton. He was the teacher of Socrates' followers Simmias and Cebes whom we know from Plato's *Phaedo* and was the first, according to Demetrius of Magnesia,[4] to publish a book on Pythagoreanism. In Philolaus' cosmology the heavenly bodies circle round a central fire which is the source of power and movement. Together with the earth, which for the first time is moved from its central position, a counter-earth moves symmetrically though it cannot be seen from the inhabited world (VS 44 A 16 f.). Hicetas of Syracuse, whose date cannot be given with any precision,

[1] On the history of the problems in antiquity O. BECKER, *Das mathematische Denken der Antike*. Studienh. z. Altertumswiss. Göttingen 1957; in add. K. V. FRITZ, Gnom. 30, 1958, 81.

[2] Proved brilliantly by the 'commercial traveller' DR. J. G. ANDERHUB in *Joco-Seria*. Wiesbaden-Biebrich 1941, 161.

[3] K. V. FRITZ, 'The discovery of incommensurability by Hippasus of Metapontum'. *Ann. Math.* 46, 1945, 242.　　　　[4] Diog. Laert. 8. 85 = *VS* 44 A 1.

improved Philolaus' theory in one point, if Cicero can be trusted (*Acad. prior.* 2, 123). He makes the earth spin round its own axis, while the remaining heavenly bodies stand still. He apparently abandoned the peculiar counter-earth.

Agatharchus is considered to be the inventor of scene-painting, which probably means that he painted them in accordance with the laws of perspective. Vitruvius states (7 pr. 11) that he wrote a *commentarius* (ὑπόμνημα) on the subject and that Anaxagoras and Democritus followed him with treatises on perspective.

Although the splendid sweep of the older Ionian periegesis and ethnography ended as the century advanced, this genre was not discontinued. Phileas, probably an Athenian of the 5th century, was the author of a periegetical work which was used much later by Stephanus of Byzantium in his geographical lexicon.

The rich intellectual life which is revealed to us in the observations of this chapter speaks to us now only through some pitiful remnants. In numerous cases we can no longer indicate in what form the individual scientist expressed himself, and we even have to admit the possibility that a great deal was written down by pupils who based themselves on oral tradition. Only in the sphere of medicine are things entirely different; under the name of Hippocrates of Cos, the great physician, there exists a literature which fills many volumes. But it involves a number of very difficult problems; in spite of significant advances in the last few decades, philology and medical history are still far from solving them. On the one hand we have an undoubtedly historical personality of tremendous influence, on the other a voluminous corpus under his name whose composition shows the most disparate features. Is there a bridge solid enough to connect the two?

Biographical information about Hippocrates is found in Tzetzes (*Chil.* 7. 944), in Suidas, a Brussels manuscript of Priscian and a strongly idealized life under the name of Soranus. From this material very little can be learned. Hippocrates, the son of the physician Heraclides, was an Asclepiad of Cos. This means that he belonged to a guild of physicians who derived their origin from Asclepius after the example of the Homeric physicians Podalirius and Machaon, although we cannot tell whether such a genealogy was still taken very seriously at the time. His home was the island of Cos with its Dorian settlers off the southwest coast of Asia Minor. Opposite it lay Cnidos, likewise the seat of an important, perhaps even older, medical school.[1] That of Cos is indissolubly connected with the name of Hippocrates, but there had been medical activity there before him, and members of his family practised the art of healing in the island for generations before and after him. However untrustworthy it may be, yet the tradition that the treatise *On Fractures and Dislocations* was the work of his grandfather is characteristic. At present any conjectures which have sought to establish a close connection between Hippocrates and the cult of Asclepius are considered unfounded. The worship of the god, which acquired its Asclepieum, soon to become famous, in the island at the end of the 4th century, is of relatively late

[1] Cf. *Anonymus Londinensis* (no. 1820 P.) 4, 31.

date,[1] and at any rate the spirit of Hippocratic medicine shows the greatest contrast imaginable with the practices of the priests as we know them from Epidaurus. The close affinity of physician with priest which we may assume for an earlier age was brought to an end by Ionian science and the enlightenment of the 5th century.

It is certain that Hippocrates' influence reached its peak at the time of the Peloponnesian war, with which the date of his birth in 460 agrees. His teachers are supposed to have been first his father, then his gymnastics teacher and Herodicus of Selymbria (who later wrote on dietetics) and men like Gorgias, Prodicus and Democritus. As always in such cases, most of this has been squeezed from quotations in the writings and from real or supposed connections of individual passages. We can believe that he travelled far and also that he was buried in Thessaly, where his grave was shown in Larissa.

All this is little enough and its importance is far outweighed by some passages in Plato and Aristotle; in Plato these are *Protagoras* 311 b and *Phaedrus* 270 c, in Aristotle *Polit.* 7, 4. 1326 a 14 in which we find the additional information that Hippocrates was short of stature. But the second of the Platonic passages mentioned is far more important than any other piece of evidence. Socrates asks Phaedrus if he thinks it possible to comprehend the nature (φύσις) of the soul without knowing the nature of the whole. Phaedrus answers that, if one is to believe the Asclepiad Hippocrates one could not even learn anything about the body without this method. It is a difficult and controversial question what is meant here by this whole whose knowledge will bestow more profound knowledge of the body according to Hippocrates, and of the soul according to Plato. The majority of scholars have adopted the obvious interpretation that Plato had the universe in mind when speaking of *the whole*, thus offering invaluable evidence that Hippocrates derived his medical doctrines from a greater general knowledge of nature.[2] In the latest discussion of the question, however, Hans Diller is inclined to interpret the whole as 'the object of the treatment together with everything which stands in an active or passive connection of influence with it'. However this difficult passage may be interpreted, it is known for certain that the physician Hippocrates built up his doctrine on a theoretical basis and demanded that each detail should be derived from general principles. It is equally possible to defend with confidence the assertion that beside the empiricism of which the *Epidemics* gives us the most impressive evidence in the Hippocratic Corpus, the speculative element, the hypothesis, must have played a decisive role. But it also is important to realize the limitations of our knowledge, for although we may have found something of value with

---

[1] O. KERN, *Die Religion der Gr.* 3, Berl. 1938, 153. On the worship of the god: E. and L. EDELSTEIN, *Asclepius.* 2 vols. Baltimore 1945.

[2] EDELSTEIN, who understands by the *whole* the notion of the body and the soul, gives bibl. RE S 6, 1935, 1318. In add. DILLER, *Herm.* 80, 1952, 407, 1 and KÜHN (*v. inf.*), 88. Here we cannot discuss the matter of the parallel drawn in the *Phaedrus* between the Hippocratic method and a correct understanding of rhetoric. Opposite opinion in JAEGER, *Paideia* 2, 33 and KÜHN (*v. inf.*). On the problem of the 'whole' recently DILLER, *Jahrbuch der Akad. d. Wiss. u. d. Lit.* Mainz 1959, 275.

regard to Hippocrates' method, we have learnt hardly anything about his system. A clue to this system seemed to be offered when in 1892 a voluminous papyrus of the 2nd century A.D., the so-called *Anonymus Londinensis* (no. 1820 P.) became known, which contains excerpts from the history of medicine of Aristotle's pupil Menon. The remark is found here that Aristotle derived the aetiology of diseases from gases which form in the body during the process of digestion. The difficulty is that the *Corpus Hippocraticum* affords no basis (not in the writing *De flatibus* either) for the assumption that here we find Hippocrates' true doctrine handed down. The information mentioned may be the fruit of later interpretation and conjecture.

Can we find this Hippocrates, of whom we know something, though little, in the heterogeneous mass of writings which have been handed down in his name?

Some one hundred and thirty writings have come down to us in his name, a large part of which are rejected at the very outset as late forgeries. The books transmitted in the good manuscripts, written without exception in the Ionian dialect, constitute about half of the number mentioned, forming the so-called *Corpus Hippocraticum* as contained in Littré's monumental edition.[1] Fifty-eight writings have been collected in it in 73 books. The composition of the *Corpus* exhibits the same motley character in form and contents; prognostic, surgery, dietetics and gynaecology occur side by side with treatises in the physician's social position; finished books stand cheek by jowl with speeches, manuals and loosely connected notes. The *Corpus* also contains writings of the Cnidian school, whose most important physician was Euryphon; Ctesias, Artaxerxes Mnemon's physician-in-ordinary and writer of the *Persica* was also a member. This school laid the main stress on special pathology and it is a difficult, and as yet unfinished, task to single it out within the Corpus.[2] In this connection the polemic which the author of the writing *On Diet in Acute Diseases* (Περὶ διαίτης ὀξέων) directs against the Cnidian doctrines is particularly interesting.[3] Some very late parts can also be pointed out in the collection, the bulk of which belongs to the 5th and 4th centuries. Among these are the *Praecepta* (Παραγγελίαι), dated on good grounds in the 2nd century and written in an archaizing Ionian, and the treatise *On (the Physician's) Decorum* (Περὶ εὐσχημοσύνης), which must be dated in the same time or a little earlier.[4]

It has been impossible to come to a reliable conclusion about the manner in which the *Corpus* has been put together, which does not bode well for attempts

---

[1] Survey in LITTRÉ (*v. inf.*), I. 292. H. A. GOSSEN, *RE* 8, 1913, 1812; S 3, 1918, 1154. EDELSTEIN, περὶ ἀέρων (*v. inf.*), 160.

[2] J. ILBERG, 'Die Ärzteschule von Knidos'. *Sitzb. Sächs. Ak. Phil.-hist. Kl.* 76/3, 1924 attributes twelve writings to the school. EDELSTEIN (*v. inf.*), 154, is more critical. Cf. W. KAHLENBERG, *Herm.* 83, 1955, 252. JAEGER, *Paideia* 2. 19 is cautious.

[3] Cf. O. REGENBOGEN, *Studies presented to D. M. Robinson* II, 1953, 627.

[4] K. DEICHGRÄBER, *Herm.* 70, 1955, 106. U. FISCHER, *Untersuchungen zu den pseudo-hipp. Schriften παραγγελίαι περὶ ἰητροῦ und περὶ εὐσχημοσύνης. N. D. Forsch.* 240. Berl. 1939. H. DILLER, *Arch. f. Gesch. d. Med.* 29, 1936/7, 178 claimed that he detected Stoical-pneumatic elements in the treatise *On Nourishment* (Περὶ τροφῆς). Opposed by M. POHLENZ, *Die Stoa.* 2, 2nd ed. Gött. 1955, 177.

at separating the genuine Hippocratic writings from the rest. There is no secure evidence for anything written by Hippocrates before the age of the Alexandrians. In the 3rd century B.C. Baccheus of Tanagra composed a *Glossary* (Λέξεις Ἱπποκράτους) on a number of writings (about twenty?)[1] which he considered to be Hippocratic. This was the main source for a similar undertaking by Erotianus (Τῶν παρ' Ἱπποκράτει λέξεων συναγωγή),[2] who wrote in the 1st century A.D. He also has a catalogue of Hippocratic writings which comprises 38 books and in addition 2 non-medical writings (Πρεσβευτικός, Ἐπιβώμιος). The Brussels *Life* lists 53 books, Suidas a much admired collection of 60 books (Ἑξηκοντάβιβλος), apart from the oath, prognoses and aphorisms. Other combinations are found in the manuscript catalogues.[3] The most ancient commentary surviving, which was written by Apollonius of Cition about Περὶ ἄρθρων, must be dated in the 1st century B.C.[4] Thus there emerges a picture of a varying core with a certain tendency toward increase. When and how a Corpus Hippocraticum began to take shape at all it is impossible to say. There are plenty of conjectures, from the surmise that the library of the Coan school was preserved (Sarton), to the sceptical theory of Edelstein that the writings all came anonymously to Alexandria in the beginning of the 3rd century and that the name of Hippocrates was added to them later. There is no secure basis for any hypothesis, but in his oration to the Academy at Mainz (1959) Hans Diller demonstrated that there were good reasons for singling out from among these as the most probable that the bulk of Hippocratic writings does in fact originate from a library which was the tool of trade of the Coan school. It is understandable that in the course of time it was increased with various additions. Diller's strongest argument is his reference to the aphoristical instructions contained in the *Corpus*. These collections, the most celebrated of which are the Hippocratic aphorisms, were created in the period extending from the end of the 5th into the second half of the 4th century. They display such clear and extensive contacts with the didactic writings of the *Corpus*, that several of them must be considered to have been already closely connected with it at that time.[5] To account for this, the most obvious assumption is no doubt the existence of a medical library in Cos.

The question of the genuineness of the individual writings designated as Hippocratic is one which aroused a lively interest even in antiquity. Galen devoted a special book to it,[6] and it is still unanswered at present, even though the circle of what is held to be genuine has become considerably smaller.

Many scholars count the treatise On Ancient Medicine (Περὶ ἀρχαίης ἰητρικῆς)[7]

---

[1] Listed in DEICHGRÄBER, *Die Epidemien* (*v. inf.*), 146, 1.

[2] Ed. E. NACHMANSON, Uppsala 1918. The same, *Erotianstudien*. Ibid. 1917.

[3] J. L. HEIBERG, *Corp. Med. Graec.* I/1. 1.   [4] Ed. by H. SCHÖNE, Leipz. 1896.

[5] On the *Coan Prognoses*, probably the last of these collections, and presumably belonging to the 2nd half of the 4th century, O. POEPPEL, *Die hippokratische Schrift Κῳακαὶ προγνώσεις und ihre Überlieferung*. Diss. Kiel 1959 (typescr.).

[6] J. MEWALDT, 'Galenos ueber echte und unechte Hippocratica'. *Herm.* 44, 1909, 111.

[7] Bibl. in ERNA LESKY, *AfdA* 3, 1950, 99. Further H. DILLER, 'Hipp. Medizin und attische Philosophie'. *Herm.* 80, 1952, 385 with an attempt at late dating after Plato's *Philebus*. J.-H. KÜHN (*v. inf.*).

among the older books of the *Corpus Hippocraticum* which can be approximately assigned to the last thirty years of the 5th century. In this work, which bases itself on medicine concerned with the individual and centres on the effect of diet on the body in particular cases, war is declared on a modern school of thought which, as hypothetical medicine, starts from general principles and inclines towards speculations like those of the natural philosophers. This struggle about methods remains characteristic of science and philosophy in the following ages. The treatise which gives us this valuable understanding is certainly not of Hippocrates' hand. We can affirm, on the contrary, that, although he may not be the direct object of the attack, he starts from other premises, provided that the Platonic passage discussed earlier has been correctly evaluated.

We shall now cast a glance at a number of books which Pohlenz, in his monograph, grouped together as genuine. Two books stand out which, apart from any historical importance, are true treasures of Greek literature as evidence of archaic prose of the second half of the 5th century (prose reached its classical peak later than poetry) and through the pristine freshness with which the problems are broached.

The treatise *On Airs, Waters and Places* (Περὶ ἀέρων, ὑδάτων, τόπων) is often referred to nowadays as the treatise *On Environment*, a title which stresses the essential subject. In it aetiological thinking has taken up the question of the influence of natural conditions such as wind, weather, radiation of the sun, nature of the soil and water, on healthy and sick people and treated it in a way which founded a tradition lasting for more than a thousand years. It is impressive evidence of the keen interest of this circle in medical problems that while discussing macrocephalics they enquired into the problem of congenital properties (14). The sentence construction of this Ionian prose is as clumsy as the composition generally. It appears that the treatise consists of two parts, of which the first observes man under the influence of various environmental conditions, while the second, which is more closely allied with ancient Ionian ethnography, contrasts Asia and Europe with respect to composition of soil, climate and population. It has been strikingly observed that a travelling physician speaks in the first part, but an aetiologist[1] in the second, but that does not make it compulsory to assume two different writers for a treatise so uniform in composition.

The writing *On the Sacred Disease* (Περὶ ἱερῆς νούσου) has always been rightly considered a landmark of European science. Its writer proves in lucid and assured arguments that epilepsy is in no way more sacred than any other disease, and carries on his attack with splendid élan against the whole mess of demonology and other superstitions with which the conception of the universe of many of his contemporaries was disfigured. But his enlightened thinking was not irreligious. On the contrary, this very writing presents exquisite evidence of Greek devoutness, for the scientific enquiry after the natural causes of diseases is at the same time one after their divine origin, since in the final analysis everything came from the deity (2. 18). It is the same belief in the divine nature of

---

[1] H. DILLER, *Wanderarzt und Aitiologe. Phil.* Suppl. 26/3, 1934. More bibl. in NESTLE (*v. in*.), 217, 93, HEINIMANN and E. LESKY (both *v. inf.*).

the physis, which makes the writer of the treatise *On Environment* (22) ascribe to all that happens the same divine nature. In view of the great scientific significance of the treatise *On the Sacred Disease* it is of minor importance that the physiological explanation of epilepsy through mucous excretion from the brain and congestion of the passages through which air and blood flow, is far removed from modern medical knowledge.

Is it the same man who addresses us in the two works discussed? There is a far-reaching similarity in conception of the universe and scientific attitude, but F. Heinimann[1] wished to assume different authors on the ground of discrepancies in details and diction, dating *On Environment*, as being the older, shortly before 430, and *On the Sacred Disease* ten to twenty years later. But the question is still open whether the differences indicated necessarily imply different authorship; nor can the problem of relative chronology be considered as conclusively settled.

Do we hear Hippocrates himself in both treatises or at least in the one *On the Sacred Disease*? For some time it has almost become a dogma to affirm this and it is indeed attractive to equate the bold scientist with the great physician. But this does not imply certainty. What we said about the information regarding Hippocrates, about the history and the testimony of the *Corpus*, is sufficient indication that certainty cannot be attained.

Of another group of writings *no more can be said than that they may at least not have remained uninfluenced by the head of the school* (Deichgräber); Pohlenz assigns them also to Hippocrates, whereas Deichgräber[2] relegates the two writings just discussed outside this sphere on the ground of method and the formulation of the problem. In his penetrating study of the *Epidemics* (the title means visits to foreign cities), the scholar mentioned proved that Books 1 and 3 are the oldest parts and closest to Hippocrates; in addition to these the *Prognosticum* is the most important aid, used well into our modern age, which is supposed to make it possible for the physician to anticipate the course of a disease. From the older books written about 410, a later group can be separated (2, 4, 6); an epidemic in Perinthus between 399 and 395 gives a clue to their date. *Epidemics* 5 and 7 are later again and to be dated about the middle of the century. These case-histories from places in northern Greece with their painstaking casuistry are impressive evidence of the importance of conscientious and unprejudiced observation at the bedside, the empirical foundation of Hippocratic doctrine. But the urge to advance from the separate phenomenon to its cause and to derive it from general principles is indissolubly connected with it, as is expressed by the careful consideration of season and of weather conditions (doctrine of catastasis). All the books are guided by the same scientific spirit, and since the last group is certainly connected with Cos there is no doubt that the whole work may be attributed to the school of Hippocrates. There is no certainty in the matter of whether the older books contain notes from the master's own hand, but this is still possible.

In accordance with the time of composition and their scientific spirit we can join the main surgical work of the *Corpus* to the books mentioned. These are

[1] (*v. inf.*), 170.   [2] *Die Epidemien* (*v. inf.*), 170.

the two treatises *On Fractures* (Περὶ ἀγμῶν) and *On the Setting of Limbs* (Περὶ ἄρθρων ἐμβολῆς), by the same author, which at one time belonged together.

At least two more works from the rich stock of the Corpus must be mentioned which are somewhat remote from the ones dealt with so far. In the book *On the Nature of Man* (Περὶ φύσιος ἀνθρώπου) a theory of arteries is developed which Aristotle (*Hist. An.* 3, 3. 512 b 12) connects with the name of Polybus, Hippocrates' son-in-law, so that the work can most probably be attributed to him.[1] It may have been written in 400; it shows older theories elaborated into the doctrine of the four humours (blood, phlegm, choler and black choler) for which Empedocles' four elements served as a model. In this way Polybus prepared the way for the pathology of humours as well as the doctrine of the four temperaments. It would be particularly interesting to know to what extent he elaborated upon doctrines of his father-in-law's, but it is not possible to do so.

The four books *On Diet* (Περὶ διαίτης, an expression referring to the complete regimen), which are based on the notion that nourishment and work must be properly related, build up an eclectical system which utilizes various philosophical and medical sources. Although the work is usually dated at the end of the 5th century,[2] Jaeger argues in favour of dating it fifty years later.

The questions connected with the Hippocratic school are numerous and difficult. But in spite of the many unsolved problems the spirit of classical medicine stands forth clear and impressive. It is controlled by a strictly scientific attitude. Aetiology and prognosis precede therapy, whose possibilities were still very limited at the time, for in this respect the physician felt himself mainly to be the assistant of the force about which we read in the treatise *On Nourishment* (Περὶ τροφῆς 15): Nature suffices for all in all. Viewed as a whole, we can see that the main characteristic of all Hippocratic medicine is its intimate relation with the notion of *physis*. Nature, whom these physicians considered themselves to serve and from whom they drew their knowledge, was conceived as the great force which comprised everything and which also controlled all that was individual. In her are contained the forces which maintain health, restore what has been disturbed and which always aim at the right mean.[3]

Apart from the scientific attitude of classical medicine, which exerted an influence far beyond the scope of its activity, its lofty professional ethos remains an example for all times. Many passages in the separate writings attest to it, but it speaks to us most forcibly in the *Oath* which all Hippocratic physicians had to take before being admitted to their corporation. Even if the present version was not written until the 4th century, as was recently argued,[4] the moral

---

[1] Reservations in JAEGER, *Paideia* 2, 363, 20.

[2] A. PALM, *Studien zur hipp. Schrift* Περὶ διαίτης. Tüb. 1933. JAEGER, *Diokles von Karystos.* Berl. 1938, 167; *Paideia* 2, 45. H. DILLER, 'Der innere Zusammenhang der hipp. Schrift De Victu'. *Herm.* 87, 1959, 39.

[3] H. DILLER, 'Der griech. Naturbegriff'. *N. Jahrb.* 2, 1939, 241. D. HOLWERDA, *Commentatio de vocis quae est φύσις vi atque usu praesertim in Graecitate Aristotele anteriore.* Groningen 1955.

[4] L. EDELSTEIN, *The Hippocratic Oath. Text, Transl. a. Interpr.* Baltimore 1943. H. DILLER, *Gnom.* 22, 1950, 70.

seriousness which it expresses is appropriate to Hippocratic medicine as a great
intellectual movement from the very beginning.

On the problem of the genesis of the *Hippocratic Corpus v. supra*, two large
editions of Hippocrates are found in the 2nd century A.D., of which the one by
Artemidorus Capito was the source of the tradition of late antiquity and the
Middle Ages. Authoritative research in this field was done by E. PFAFF, 'Die nur
arabisch erhaltenen Teile der Epidemienkommentare des Galen und die Überlieferung des Corp. Hipp.'. *Sitzb. Ak. Berlin. Phil.-hist. Kl.* 1931, 558, and
'Die Überlieferung des Corp. Hipp. in der nachalexandrinischen Zeit.'. *Wien.
Stud.* 50, 1932, 67. The work of Galen, who tried to harmonize the medical
doctrines of the Hipp. school with Platonic philosophy, was of great importance
for the transmission of the Hipp. writings. Useful in this respect were his commentaries, and a glossary on Hippocrates. The commentaries were translated
into Syrian and Arabic, and from these into Hebrew and Latin. Along their way
they exerted considerable influence but at the same time they are an important
body of textual evidence which often leads to an edition deviating from the
direct tradition. H. DIELS, *Die Handschriften der antiken Ärzte. Abh. Ak. Berlin.
Phil.-hist. Kl.* 1, 1905; 2, 1906 has laid the foundation for the manuscript tradi-
ion; also cf. J. ILBERG in the edition of KÜHLEWEIN; HEIBERG in his praefatio.
Opposing a common archetype EDELSTEIN, *RE* S 6, 1935, 1313; ibid. about the
Syrian, Arabic and Latin translations. H. DILLER, *Die Überlieferung der hipp.
Schrift* Περὶ ἀέρων ὑδάτων τόπων. *Phil.* Suppl. 23/3, 1932 is still a model of textual
research; in add.: 'Nochmals: Überlieferung and Text der Schrift von der
Umwelt.' *Festschr. E. Kapp*, Hamburg 1958, 31. Important: A. RIVIER, *Recherches
sur la tradition manuscrite du traité hippocratique*, 'De morbo sacro'. Bern 1962.
Editions: Fundamental, and only partially superseded: F. LITTRÉ, 10 vols. Paris
1839–61 with introductions, notes and Fr. transl., at present being reprinted
by Hakkert, Amsterdam. The ed. of H. KÜHLEWEIN achieved only 2 vols.,
Leipzig 1894 and 1902. In the *Corp. Med. Graec.* only I/1 by J. L. HEIBERG 1927.
Selections: W. H. S. JONES–E. T. WITHINGTON, I–IV (*Loeb Class. Libr.*) Lond.
1923–31, with Engl. transl., reprinted 1959. Περὶ σαρκῶν: K. DEICHGRÄBER,
Leipz. 1935. Περὶ ἀρχαίης ἰητρικῆς: A.-J. FESTUGIÈRE, Paris 1948. Some writings
of the Corpus were dealt with in dissertations written in Kiel in the school of
HANS DILLER, and multiplied in typescript: G. PREISER, *Die hipp. Schriften De
Indicationibus und De Diebus indicatoriis. Ausgaben und krit. Bemerkungen.* 1957.
H. GRENSEMANN, *Die hipp. Schrift* Περὶ ὀκταμήνων (*De octimestri partu*). *Ausgabe
und krit. Bemerkungen.* 1960. The work of O. POEPPEL has been referred to on
p. 488, n. 5. W. MÜRI, *Der Arzt im Altertum*, 3rd rev. ed., Munich (Heimeran)
1962, offers an excellent survey of the texts of ancient medicine together with a
transl. – Translations: R. KAPFERER in 25 vols. Stuttg. 1933–40. W. CAPELLE,
Hipp. Fünf auserlesene Schriften. Zürich 1955; Fischer-Bücherei 255, 1959. *Hipp.
der wahre Arzt.* Zürich 1959 (with an essay by KARL JASPERS). K. DEICHGRÄBER,

Der hipp. Eid. Stuttg. 1955. J. CHADWICK–W. N. MANN, Oxf. 1950. L. UNTER-
STEINER CANDIA, Florence 1957 (Environment, oath etc.). R. MINGHETTI, *Hipp.
Aforismi (Prima e settima sezione). Trad. comm.* Rome 1959. – Monographs and
studies: L. EDELSTEIN, Περὶ ἀέρων *und die Sammlung der hipp. Schriften. Problemata*
4 Berl. 1931 (in add. J. MEWALDT, *D. Litt. Zeit,* 1932, 254). The same, *RE* S 6,
1935, 1290. K. DEICHGRÄBER, *Die Epidemien und das Corp. Hipp. Abh. d. Preuss.
Ak.* 1933/3. The same, 'Die Stellung des griech. Arztes zur Natur' in *Der
listensinnende Trug des Gottes.* Gött. 1952, 83. M. POHLENZ, *Hippokrates.* Berl.
1938. WILH. NESTLE, *Vom Mythos zum Logos.* Stuttg. 1940, 209. W. A. HEIDEL,
Hippocratic Medicine. New York 1941. F. HEINIMANN, *Nomos und Physis.* Basel
1945. W. H. S. JONES, *Philosophy and Medicine in Ancient Greece.* Baltimore 1946
(with ed. and tr. of Π. ἀρχ. ἰητρ.). ERNA LESKY, *Die Zeugungs- und Vererbungslehren der Antike.* Akad. Mainz 1950. W. MÜRI, 'Der Massgedanke bei den griech.
Arzten'. *Gymn.* 57, 1950, 183. F. WEHRLI, 'Ethik und Medizin. Der Arzte-
vergleich bei Platon'. *Mus. Helv.* 8, 1951, 36. 177. G. SARTON, *A History of
Science.* Lond. 1953, 331. L. BOURGEY, *Observation et expérience chez les médecins
de la coll. hippocr.* Paris 1953. O. TEMKIN, 'Greek Medicine as Science and Craft'.
Isis 44, 1953, 213. W. JAEGER, *Paideia* 2, 11. J.-H. KÜHN, *System- und Methoden-
probleme im Corp. Hipp. Herm.* E 11, 1956. H. HERTER–J. STEUDEL, 'Die Hippokr.
Medizin'. *Ciba-Zeitschrift* 8, 1957, 2814. H. DILLER, 'Stand und Aufgaben der
Hippokratesforschung'. *Jahrb. der Akad. d. Wiss. und Lit.* Mainz 1959, 271. CH.
LICHTENTHAELER, *La Médecine hippocratique. Études hippocratiques* 1-6. Lausanne
1948-1960. In his article 'Le "Miracle grec" en médecine'. *Méd. et Hyg.*
(Geneva) 19, 1961, 231, the same scholar aptly countered the principally mis-
taken opinions of G. EIS, 'Überschätzung der klass. Antike'. *Med. Monatsschr.*
1959, 725 by pointing out that it is not the sum total of positive knowledge
which matters so much as the foundation of the attitude from which European
medicine grew. F. HÜFFMEIER, 'Phronesis in den Schriften des Corp. Hipp.'.
Herm. 89, 1961, 51. R. JOLY, *Recherches sur le traité pseudo-hippocratique du
Régime. Bibl. de la Fac. de Phil. et Lettr. de Liège* 156, 1961. H. E. SIGERIST, *A
History of Medicine.* Vol. 2: *Early Greek, Hindu and Persian Medicine.* Ed. by L.
EDELSTEIN. Lond./New York 1961.

9 SOCRATES

In the last thirty years of the 5th century intellectual life in Athens displayed a
variety of form and an inner stirring as during no other period in Greek history.
In this epoch those contrasts came into the open which had been characterized
by Sophocles and Pericles during the peak of classical culture, but which had
then remained enclosed within one great harmony as a fertilizing tension. In
practically all departments of life adherence to tradition was opposed by radical
attack in the spirit of the sophists. The religious festivals bore witness to the
continuation of ancient piety, but at the same time circles formed round the
teachers of wisdom who rejected the myths or explained them in their own way.
For some the laws of the city remained the final norm, to others a new vision of
natural law had been opened up which in turn was interpreted in varying ways.

Problems of education were particularly subject to heated argument, while the position of women also began to arise as a problem. As in a magic mirror, comedy captured in its motley fantasy all this tugging at the old and searching after the new. As yet the whole range of the often opposing movements was enclosed within the framework of the polis, which at this very moment was engaged in the decisive struggle for its existence.

The picture of all these tensions and arguments would be incomplete if we were to forget the man who at this time was making his fellow-citizens uneasy in streets and public places with his unending questioning and probing, sometimes making them thoughtful but more often succeeding in annoying them. His questioning must have caught directly at the roots of this vexed time, or even at the very roots of human existence, for only in this way can the extent of the influence be understood which was achieved by a thinker who himself never put pen to paper. This influence developed in so many directions and inspired systems mutually so contrasting that later attempts to trace back all this to one uniform source, i.e. the life and work of that man, ended without success. The difficulties in forming an historical picture of Socrates are not due to a lack of information about him. Besides Plato, who makes Socrates play a part in all the dialogues except the *Laws*, and makes his fate the centre of individual dialogues (*Euthyphro, Apology, Crito, Phaedo*), we have Xenophon as our main witness. Firstly there are the *Memorabilia*, next the *Apology*, whose authenticity is still doubted by some,[1] then the *Symposium* and the *Oeconomicus*, whose fictitious character is beyond any doubt, so that they play no essential part in the argument. So we possess both a Platonic and a Xenophontic image of Socrates, displaying mutual differences generally as well as in detail.[2] These differences are roughly that Xenophon presents Socrates the virtuous citizen who, through his life, refutes all the reproaches which led to his death, while Plato shows us the thinker who struggles with the clarification of basic conceptions and – in the later dialogues – develops the theory of ideas. It was decisive for his image of Socrates that in his teacher he found the realization of the mode of living which for him counted as the perfection of the possibilities innate in man.[3] It is an essential factor in this unique process that actual memory and idealizing reflection affected each other constantly, but this should not be overlooked in its critical appraisal. The position taken by scholarship with respect to these two images presents a varied picture. Until recently the opinion prevailed that Xenophon, because of his very soberness and primitive quality, is the only reliable authority. Schmidt's chapter on Socrates was based on this conception of Xenophon's guileless fidelity. But generally this position has long since been given up. Personal relations between Socrates and Xenophon no doubt

---

[1] K. V. FRITZ, 'Zur Frage der Echtheit der xen. Apol.'. *Rhein. Mus.* 80, 1931, 36. JAEGER (*v. inf.*), 67, 13. On its authority: O. GIGON, 'Xen. Apol. des Sokr. I'. *Mus. Helv.* 3, 1946, 210.

[2] This material has been utilized by E. EDELSTEIN, *Xen. und platon. Bild des Sokr.* Diss. Heidelb. 1935.

[3] Impressive discussion about this by CARL KOCH, *Religio.* Nürnberg 1960, 237.

existed; evidence of this is supplied by the *Anabasis* (3. 1, 5) with the report of how Xenophon, before his departure for Cyrus' campaign, asked Socrates' advice and how the latter referred him to the Delphic oracle. This may stand as historically valid and is of some importance for Socrates; on the other hand Xenophon never was a pupil of Socrates' in the real sense of the word. In addition there is the important circumstance that Xenophon's Socratic writings were composed a long time after Socrates' death, hardly before the 'sixties. An attempt was made to prove that the first two chapters of the *Memorabilia* were an exception; according to a theory which attracted a great deal of attention[1] they were supposed to have been written substantially earlier as a *Defence* against an *Indictment* published in the 'nineties by the sophist Polycrates against Socrates and his defenders.[2] It has, however, become most dubious whether this division and antedating are tenable after Gigon's analysis. Nevertheless the late dating of Xenophon's Socratica presupposes an abundant literature centring on the figure of Socrates which preceded this work. And so the view has increasingly gained ground that in the *Memorabilia* Xenophon combines his personal memories to a large extent with extracts from the rich Socratic literature. This view was connected with a desire to determine Xenophon's sources. It was often thought that he depended mainly on Plato,[3] and points of contact do occur; but in view of the dissimilarity of the two authors, direct copying is not certain in every case. The influence of the same tradition from a third source should be taken into account. Others again were prepared to detect mainly Antisthenes in Xenophon,[4] though no such far-reaching dependence could be proved. Lately Gigon, in his book on Socrates, has strongly emphasized the thought that as an eclectic Xenophon has an extensive literature behind him, and holds out the prospect of reaching through him older Socratics who are independent of Plato and whose thought is simpler. It remains to be seen how far future research will succeed in singling out individual contributions.

Another group of scholars did not credit Xenophon from the outset with a real understanding of Socrates, though they assumed this wholly for Plato. Hardly anyone will wish to object to this, but it is another question whether

[1] H. MAIER (*v. inf.*), 22. O. GIGON, *Sokrates* (*v. inf.*), 50, cf. by the same *Komm. zum 1.* (*u. 2.*) *B. von Xen. Mem. Schw. Beitr.* 5, 7, 1953/6. On Polycrates: L. RADERMACHER (*v. inf.*), 128.

[2] E. GEBHARDT, *Polykrates' Anklage gegen Sokrates und Xenophons Erwiderung.* Diss. Frankfurt 1957 agrees with GIGON that Xenophon's work was purely of a literary nature, and shares his doubt about a separate early date of the *Defence*; on the other hand he would like to attribute to Xenophon generally more independence in inventiveness and composition. It seems to him that Plato takes a special position among his sources. A. H. CHROUST, 'Xenophon, Polykrates and the "Indictment of Socrates"'. *Class. et Mediaev.* 16, 1955, 1, like the books on Socrates mentioned at the end of the section, is extremely sceptical about the collective tradition (Plato and Xenophon), and tries to make a political figure out of Socrates. Older attempts at a reconstruction of Polycrates' indictment in J.-H. KÜHN, *Gnom.* 32, 1960, 99, 1.

[3] Thus GEFFCKEN (*v. inf.*), 11. 38 with bibl. w. WIMMEL, 'Zum Verhältnis einiger Stellen des xenoph. und des platon. Symposions', *Gymn.* 64, 1957, 230 wishes to invert the relationship.

[4] K. JOEL, *Der echte und der xenophontische S.* 3 vols. Berl. 1893-1901.

Plato wanted to present an historically true picture of the master based on his understanding of Socrates or rather an interpretation in the sense of his own philosophy. It is the Scottish school founded by J. Burnet and represented most emphatically by A. E. Taylor which has gone farthest in the full use of Plato for Socrates' image.[1] According to them the Socrates presented by the Platonic dialogues, the founder of the theory of ideas in all its parts, of the doctrine of the immortality of the soul and likewise the creator of the ideal state, is entirely historical. We shall soon become acquainted with the passages in Aristotle which offer the decisive obstacle to this view. The theory based on Plato exclusively belongs to the history of research. This does not imply that the earlier Platonic dialogues, in which the theory of ideas is not yet present and in which the conversation, carried on dialectically, circles round an attempt at finding definitions without a definite conclusion, do not reflect a good deal of the manner of Socratic conversation or at least carried it on in a straight line.[2]

At an early stage, i.e. as early as Schleiermacher,[3] the attempt was begun to make use of Plato and Xenophon for the historical image of Socrates, taking into consideration the nature of both sources and without preference to the one over the other. A large part of recent research has moved in this direction. Gigon's book on Socrates presents a necessary corrective to this by reminding of the considerable extent of lost Socratic literature which, apart from the two authors preserved, must indubitably have left significant traces in the mass of the tradition. This holds good for Phaedo, Euclides, Antisthenes, Aristippus and Aeschines. The critical sifting and ordering of the remnants of these Socratics, on whom we shall cast a glance at the end of this section, is a largely unexplored field in Socratic research.

Aristophanes must also be summoned as a witness. Some remarks about the problems of his image of Socrates will be found in the discussion of the *Clouds*. Presently, when we shall put the question of the purpose of Socrates' searching, we shall have to occupy ourselves with some passages from Aristophanes.

This brief survey demonstrates the multiplicity of the sources and the complexity of the problems in this field. It should also be constantly borne in mind that a large part of our information is derived not from work written for the purpose of historical truth but belonging to a literature which may be truly called Socratic fiction. But even when carefully weighing all these factors we need not wholly share Gigon's resignation, who roundly disputes the possibility of reaching any conclusion about the historical Socrates, his position in the intellectual life of his time and the causes of his vast influence. However much may remain unintelligible, some facts about the way in which he invaded the intellectual life of his time can be established, while others can be conjectured with some probability, apart from the external facts of his life which, in the case of Socrates, are not so scarce at all in comparison with other personalities of the ancient world.

[1] BURNET, *Greek Philosophy*. London 1914. TAYLOR, *Socrates*. Edinb. 1932.
[2] In this direction G. RUDBERG, 'Der plat. Sokr.'. *Symb. Osl.* 7, 1928, 1.
[3] Collected works, 3. 2. 297.

Socrates was born about 470 as the son of the sculptor Sophroniscus of the deme Alopece. For some time he may have followed his father's calling (as such it was considered then). Later three draped Charites at the entrance to the Acropolis were shown as his work,[1] but this can hardly be credited. The young Socrates witnessed the invasion of Ionian science in Athens and it is entirely beyond belief that this movement did not exert an influence upon him. In the Platonic Phaedo (96 a ff.) Socrates sketches his development leading to the theory of ideas. This is evidently Plato's own development, but since to a certain extent Socrates' questioning was a prerequisite to it, we may relate the first part of this significant section to Socrates himself. In the Phaedo he attests his initial interest in natural philosophy and in particular the great hopes which Anaxagoras' doctrine of the Nous roused in him. And this is quite credible in itself. In addition we have good evidence for his association with Anaxagoras' disciple Archelaus. In his Epidemiae (fr. 11 Blumenth.) Ion of Chios related that in his youth Socrates came to Samos with Archelaus. This could be connected with the Samian campaign (441/440) and Socrates could still be called rather young at this time. But the verb ἀποδημῆσαι actually points rather to a voyage. If we take it in this sense, we need to accept this one exception to the statement in Plato's Crito (52 b) that Socrates never undertook a journey and only left his native city on war service. In our discussion of Aristophanes' Clouds we already considered whether in this comedy a memory of Socrates' interest in natural philosophy had been preserved. In all this it should not be forgotten that Socrates has been fixed in the memory of mankind in the figure of the old man who directed all his searching and questioning at man. Earlier stages of his development necessarily had to recede into the background. In this connection later mention of Socrates in Aristophanes' comedies such as Frogs and Birds seems to aim more distinctly at the Socrates whom we know.[2] But this fact should not be considered an encouragement for more precise dating of Socrates' change of interest.

Socrates' participation in the battles of his years of manhood (Potidaea 431, Delium 424, Amphipolis 422) were often presented in detail in the tradition, as in Plato's Symposium. A complete denial of Socrates' share in these campaigns, as was proposed by Herodicus of Babylon in his bitter hostility to Plato in the second century B.C., goes rather beyond the mark.[3] Throughout his life Socrates was a loyal citizen of his city and no reason can be detected in him for Plato's later withdrawal from the political life of his city. In his Memorabilia Xenophon makes Socrates praise loyalty to the laws as the act of the just. This is in such striking agreement with the radical subjection to the laws of the state which Socrates defends in the Crito that we may recognize his actual attitude here. But this means that he has not included the conflict between enacted law and natural law in his questioning, a conflict which later caused so much stir among the

---

[1] Paus. 1. 22, 8; 9. 35, 7. Schol. Aristoph. Nubes 793. In the first passage also a Hermes Propylaeus.

[2] R. STARK, 'Sokratisches in den "Vögeln" des Aristoph.'. Rhein. Mus. 1953, 77.

[3] H. DÜRING, Herodicus. Stockholm 1941.

sophists, and to which he was very close. Protagoras' position in these questions is comparable in its results, though with an entirely different starting-point.

Socrates' attitude, as shown here, did not, of course, prevent him from criticizing obvious abuses such as appointment to office by means of the lot.[1] In the deplorable proceedings of the year 406, in which the popular assembly, after the victorious battle of Arginusae, condemned the generals en bloc to death because they had been unable to rescue their shipwrecked compatriots when a gale blew up, Socrates rose in public opposition to the mass, but not to the law, which he was actually defending. In his quality as prytanis, according to some sources as president of the Boule,[2] Socrates opposed the illegal and senseless proceedings without being able to prevail in any way. In the Apology (32 c) Plato makes Socrates mention his opposition against the illegal measures of the Thirty Tyrants; there is additional evidence for this tradition in Xenophon's Memorabilia (4. 4, 3). The Thirty were trying to implicate as many citizens as possible in their doings and ordered Socrates and four others to bring Leon up from Salamis for execution, but Socrates simply went home. It is difficult to evaluate the prohibition issued according to Xenophon (Mem. 1. 2, 31; 4. 4, 3) by the Thirty at Critias' urging to muzzle this troublesome fellow. We have to consider the possibility that measures of censorship of these terrorists were later placed in a particular relationship to Socrates. It is likely enough that on occasion he clashed with their rule of violence and people like Critias, who once followed him, must at that time have become his antagonists. Formerly Socrates had been listened to with approval in the circles of the oligarchical-aristocratic opposition and the man who stood so completely outside the framework of his own time exerted in his own way as great an influence as many a sophist. It cannot be doubted that Alcibiades and Critias stood in some kind of student relationship with Socrates, a fact which has caused the master's apologists some headaches. It is easy to understand that this relationship of Socrates and Alcibiades – it is hard to imagine two people more ill-matched – was presented in varying ways. In Plato's Symposium it became the subject for splendid fiction.

The role allotted traditionally to Socrates' wife Xanthippe, who gave him three sons, has been particularly bad. We can still partly trace how the image of the shrew who put the philosopher's equanimity to hard tests was a left-over from information of a very varied nature.[3] It is more difficult to evaluate the tradition of a second marriage of Socrates' with Myrto, a desperately poor daughter of Aristides the Just. Nor is the problem made any easier by the fact that this information is attributed to Aristotle's On Nobility (Περὶ εὐγενείας fr. 93 R.).

On evidential grounds two elements of Socratic biography are mostly considered to be historical, elements which are peculiar enough in a life whose background was the ordinary Athenian day in street and market-place. One is the saying of the Delphic oracle which, at the request of Chaerephon, singled out

[1] Xen. Mem. 1. 2, 9; 3. 1, 4; 3. 9, 10.
[2] Prytanis: Plat. Ap. 32 b. Xen. Hell. 1. 7, 15. President: Xen. Mem. 1. 1, 18.
[3] GIGON, Sokrates (v. inf.), 113.

Socrates as the most righteous and wisest among all men,[1] a distinction which is in agreement with Socrates' loyalty to the greatest Greek oracle. The other is his daemonion, and we may take this enigmatic warning inner voice, which would not permit him to deviate from his way, to be a factual reality of his life.[2] The irrational also claimed its place in this man who put himself with such passionate devotion in the service of the Logos.

All the information we have about his life recedes far into the background before his trial and death in the year 399. We may phrase this more precisely by saying that the Socrates on trial and in the hours before his death is the great figure from whom emanated the powerful influence on the intellectual tradition of the Western world. It is noteworthy, but by no means unparalleled, that the facts exerted this influence only in the special form into which tradition cast them.

Indictment and conviction were part of the reaction of the democracy whose first act in the course of its restoration was a sacrifice to Athene on the Acropolis (Xen. *Hell.* 2. 4, 39). To many people the man who interminably demanded justification of existing opinions would appear as a representative of the forces which undermined the old tradition and had brought in uneasiness and uncertainty. We are unable to tell to what extent the three accusers Meletus, Anytus and Lycon were impelled by personal motives. In the accusation lodged in writing with the Archon Basileus, Meletus was the initiator. But it was the politician Anytus who was the real instigator; at the time he was a strategos; we know of him from Aristotle's work *The Constitution of Athens* (34) as the representative of a moderate party of the centre which aimed at the 'constitution of the Fathers'. The accusation, formulated and sworn at the preliminary hearing, has been best preserved through Favorinus in Diogenes Laertius (2. 40). According to it, Socrates was accused of impiety because he did not accept the gods of the state and introduced new gods; secondly, he was charged with the corruption of youth. The accusers obviously used existing formulae, for this would explain the uncertainty of the tradition about the facts with which they wanted to prove the individual points of the charge.[3] Neither Plato's *Apology* nor the one attributed to Xenophon can be considered a reliable witness of Socrates' defence at the trial. They form the beginning of a whole literature of Socratic apologies, extending from the lost ones of Lysias, Theodectes of Phaselis, Demetrius of Phalerum, Theon of Antioch, Plutarch to Libanius' *Declamation* (5. 1 F.). It was a less happy idea to raise to the level of authentic information the whimsical versions of authors of the empire[4] who claimed that Socrates had remained quiet in court.

The jurors declared Socrates guilty with a modest majority (281 : 220) and

---

[1] WILH. NESTLE, 'Sokr. u. Delphi'. *Griech. Stud.* Stuttg. 1948, 173.

[2] H. GUNDERT, 'Platon und das Daimonion des Sokrates'. *Gymn.* 61, 1954, 513.

[3] GIGON, *Sokrates* (*v. inf.*), 69. A. MENZEL, 'Unters. zum Sokr.-Prozesse'. *Sitzb. Wien. Phil.-hist. Kl.* 145/2, 1902 (1903) is still important.

[4] Philostr. *Vit. Ap.* 8. 2. Maximus of Tyre, *Diss.* 3. H. GOMPERZ, 'Sokr. Haltung vor seinen Richtern'. *Wien. Stud.* 54, 1936, 32 with unfortunate reference to Plat. *Gorg.* 486 a, *Theaet.* 172 c.

condemned him to death with a somewhat larger number of votes (300 : 201).
An Athenian sacred embassy to Delos gave him a few days of respite and then
Socrates drank the cup of hemlock.

The great influence exerted by this man did not emanate from a consistent
doctrine. When Plato makes him state in the *Theaetetus* (150 c) 'the god compels
me to perform the duties of a midwife, but has prevented me from begetting',
the direction of his influence is caught with epigrammatical incisiveness.
Obviously this is not supposed to mean that his testing and questioning, the
whole intellectual uneasiness he knew how to arouse, was not aimed at a specific
end. Aristotle offers us the best testimony for this.[1] In his criticism of his
philosophical predecessors he no doubt fitted isolated phenomena into his
system and occasionally forced them into it as well, but nothing justifies the
assumption that Socrates' 'grandson-disciple' covered up his ignorance about
him with fiction. Of the greatest significance is the passage in the *Metaphysics*
(M 4. 1078 b 27), in which Aristotle describes Socrates' aim and method through
induction (ἐπακτικοὶ λόγοι) and the finding of definitions (τὸ ὁρίζεσθαι
καθόλου). The early Platonic dialogues give us a picture of this, though we
certainly must not interpret them as reports of Socratic conversation, but rather
as its continuation and elaboration. If this is correct, Socratic 'induction' appears
to be an approach to the object to be grasped with the aid of analogies from daily
life, particularly from that of craftsmen, and a step by step consolidation of the
ground gained against possible opposition. Xenophon (*Mem.* 1. 1, 16; 4. 6, 1)
also testifies that Socrates constantly searched for definitions, for τί ἕκαστον εἴη.

In order to place all this in the context in which the figure of the historical
Socrates in his greatness becomes visible through the chaos of a tradition bur-
dened with anecdotes, we shall go back a few lines from the passage in the
Metaphysics. There Aristotle states that Socrates' search belonged in the framework of his preoccupation with moral values: περὶ τὰς ἠθικὰς ἀρετὰς
πραγματευομένου. These, like Cicero's well-known words (*Tusc.* 5. 10; *Ac.
post.* 1. 15) that Socrates fetched philosophy from heaven and settled it in towns
and houses, characterizes the decisive era in which Socrates lived and of which he
himself formed part. We also read in an earlier passage of the *Metaphysics* (A 6.
987 b 1) that Socrates sought τὸ καθόλου in the province of ἠθικά, and in the
treatise *On the Parts of Animals* (642 a 28) Aristotle states directly that Socrates
finished with natural philosophy and ushered in an epoch of ethics. As he did
not hand on a formulated doctrine, his followers took different ways, but all
the systems which sprang from this soil are moulded into a unity as compared
with the past through one fact: philosophical enquiry turned wholly away from
cosmos and nature and henceforth was preoccupied with man, with the laws on
which his actions are based and with the road leading to the fulfilment of the
potentialities present in him. Socrates had this extreme concentration on man in

---

[1] W. D. ROSS, *Aristotle's Metaph.* Oxf. 1924, I, XXXIII. TH. DEMAN, *Le Témoignage d'Aris-
tote sur Soc.* Paris 1942. MAGELHÃES-VILHENA (*v. inf.*). At present especially O. GIGON,
'Die Sokratesdoxographie bei Aristoteles', *Mus. Helv.* 16, 1959, 174. Cf. also KRÄMER,
Arete bei Platon und Aristoteles. Abh. Ak. Heidelb. Phil.-hist. Kl. 1959/6, 520.

common with the sophists and it is from this very viewpoint that a superficial observer might fail to recognize the fundamental difference between the two schools of thought. In fact the sophists had no greater opponent than the man who sought to regain a firm foundation through ideas of general validity, while they surrendered a knowledge of reality and the norms of morality to the sport of debate. He did not pursue this course as a logician, for whom the work of the mind would have been a purpose in itself; his questions about the nature of piety, ustice or courage are asked throughout with the aim of establishing norms for the shaping of life, for individuals as well as for the community. In a fine chapter of his *Paideia* Werner Jaeger has shown that Socrates placed man's soul at the top of his table of values with a determination unheard of before then. In the greatest possible contrast with the aristocratic theory of life, man's value is now completely separated from power, property and outward recognition, and placed in the soul, which is his most precious possession and at the same time his greatest duty. This way of Socratic thinking leads to a radical opposition against the old aristocratic norm that being useful to one's friends and harming one's enemies makes a man. Doing wrong is now felt as a stain on one's own soul, and is no more permissible to an enemy as in any other case.

Socrates saw his search for the norms of morality and their realization in the practice of life as a complete unity. To him insight into the morally good is not only a prerequisite for acting rightly, but it is indissolubly connected with it. The often discussed doctrine of the knowledge of virtue culminated in the sentence that no one does wrong willingly. True knowledge of moral norms also guarantees acting according to them. The unconditional challenge of this phrase provoked opposition from the very beginning. It was already voiced on the contemporary stage, for the polemic of Phaedra (377) in the *Hippolytus* of the year 428 aimed plain words, in the true Euripidean reflection, against the equation of moral knowledge with moral action.[1] Aristotle (*Nic. Eth.* Z 13, 1144 b 17) also raised his voice in protest against the complete identification of moral soundness with moral insight.[2] Since then critics have not tired of stressing and reproving the onesidedness of Socrates' moral intellectuality. But Socrates' moral consciousness is founded on a more profound basis and is inadequately characterized as pure intellectuality, as demonstrated by the line of enquiry adopted by Richard Meister:[3] Socrates experienced moral value as the absolute and placed it as an unconditional demand in the centre of moral consciousness. The evidence of this experience of value is subject to neither logical nor

---

[1] BR. SNELL, 'Das früheste Zeugnis über Sokr.'. *Phil.* 97, 1948, 125, with more passages.

[2] O. GIGON, *Mus. Helv.* 16, 1959, 182 argues correctly that in view of the tension between λογικόν and ἄλογον there was no possibility for Socrates that the ἄλογον could challenge and vanquish the λογικόν. Consequently Aristotle inferred that Socrates had excluded the ἀκρασία from his conception. The tension between Socratic intellectualism and ethical optimism and pre- and post-Socratic thought is dealt with by P. RABBOW, *Paidagogia. Die Grundlegung der abendländischen Erziehungskunst im Kampf des Irrationalen und des Rationalen.* Gött. 1960.

[3] This appreciation of Socratic ethical knowledge was borrowed from RICHARD MEISTER'S lecture on ethics.

psychological objection, it falls within the scope of ideology. Criticism of this viewpoint could only note that Socrates erred in that he equated the values in which morality was experienced with a judgment of these values.[1]

Socrates' influence cannot be separated from his personality; its force is founded in the uncompromising spirit in which he not only made his demands, but also himself lived accordingly. Hardly any anecdote touches the centre of his being so profoundly as the one told by Diogenes Laertius 2, 33. Socrates is alleged to have left the theatre when Orestes, in Euripides' *Electra* (379), declared that it is best to leave certain obscurities in life undecided. Through his death Socrates gave to his disciples and posterity the final confirmation of his unconditional quest for morality to which the god had called him.

Plato, his greatest follower, lays claim to a separate place in a history of literature, because his completely preserved output proves him to be an artist with great powers of representation. A brief discussion of other Socratics follows to give an impression of the lost Socratic literature.[2]

In ancient tradition Euclides of Megara was considered to be the founder of the Megarian school. After Socrates' death his friends were supposed to have gathered round him, which does not mean that this was done from fear of further persecution. In his doctrine he stood very close to Parmenides' ontology and equated the absolute Being with the good as the only truly existing to which various wrong names are given by men (i.e. other philosophers). Among his dialogues, the *Crito* and the *Eroticus* recall Platonic works, if in the case of the latter we may think of the *Symposium*. The *Aeschines* belongs to the writings in which the Socratics referred to one another, while the *Alcibiades* had as its subject the personality whose relationship with Socrates particularly attracted and fascinated both his contemporaries and posterity. *Lamprias* and *Phoenix* are mere titles. Bryson, the son of Herodorus of Heraclea, was Euclides' disciple (*v.* p. 329). Ancient gossip (Athen, 508 c) made Plato dependent on him. The most distinguished representative of this school, Stilpo of Megara, also wrote dialogues like Euclides.

Antisthenes of Athens is believed to have had a Phrygian mother, and this agrees with the fact that he mostly gathered his followers around him at the Cynosarges gymnasium, where people of mixed descent exercised. The name of this place is connected with the Cynical school, whose spiritual founder was Antisthenes, though he was overshadowed by his most celebrated follower Diogenes of Sinope.[3] Before he became an enthusiastic adherent of Socrates, he had been a disciple of Gorgias'. The two declamations preserved, *Ajax* and *Odysseus*, fall within this period; they may be considered authentic. A *Defence of Orestes* is also attributed to him. It is more difficult to evaluate the information

[1] At this point R. REININGER'S division (*Wertphilosophie und Ethik*, Vienna 1939, 33) of the feeling of value, the statement of value and the criticism of value as the degrees of awareness of value becomes fruitful.

[2] Good survey in GIGON, *Sokrates* (*v. inf.*), 282.

[3] E. SCHWARTZ'S attempt, *Ethik der Gr.* Stuttg. 1951, 141, to separate the Cynics from Antisthenes is corrected by W. RICHTER in the relevant note. Information about rhetorical writings in L. RADERMACHER, *Artium Scriptores* (*v. inf.*), 120.

(Diog. Laert. 6. 1, 15) that he wrote Περὶ λέξεως ἢ περὶ χαρακτήρων. His attack on Gorgias in the *Archelaus* does not imply that the latter was not his teacher. He was not peaceable by nature and we learn that in his *Satho*, a work in three volumes, he treated Plato most maliciously. In his doctrine a strong aversion to speculation and a corresponding tendency to practical ethics is discernible. For him virtue does not depend on knowledge, and Plato's theory of ideas remained unintelligible to him. He very strongly emphasizes the ideal of autarky which aims at the greatest possible independence from passion and desire. It is especially on desire that he declared war and his maxim that he would prefer losing his mind to feeling desire has been preserved. Antisthenes' productivity as an author is comparable with Democritus'. We know the table of contents of an edition in ten volumes, amounting to about seventy titles. Among these the *Aspasia*, *Alcibiades* and *Menexenus* point to Socratic dialogues. The *Cyrus* may have been related to the *Cyropaedia* of Xenophon, who in that case probably drew on it. The *Alethea* has the same title as the work of Protagoras, which tells us very little about its contents; five books *On Education* and *On Names* may have touched upon Prodicus' researches; the *Heracles* is certain to have shown the ideal figure of the Cynics as the perfect master over all human weaknesses.

The enormous gap between the answers of the Socratics to the questions of the meaning and aim of life is demonstrated particularly plainly if we follow up Antisthenes with Aristippus of Cyrene. The Cyrenaic school is difficult to grasp, and though there are connected trends of thought, it must not be simply described as the predecessor of Epicureanism. Its criticism appears to be rendered more difficult because late information (Euseb. *Praep. Ev.* 14. 18, 31 f.) attributes the ethical doctrines of the Cyrenaics to the grandson of Aristippus who bears the same name,[1] but this tradition ought not to be thought to carry much weight. Aristippus' doctrine comprises a profound agnosticism regarding matters of the exterior world. For us, only our condition of desire and grief is perceptible. Between these there is a constant movement, so that a life of pure desire is unattainable for man. Here the beginning can be detected of the pessimism which under Ptolemy I secured for the Cyrenaic Hegesias the nickname of Pisithanatus, because he wished to prove that suicide was the most advisable solution to the problems of life. Aristippus, however, produced an ethical system which amounted to a correctly regulated balancing of attainable desire and avoidable grief, thus promising to the philosopher the superiority which Antisthenes tried to reach through ascetical self-control. There are numerous anecdotes about this. Two literary catalogues which we know offer a series of titles. It is difficult to tell what to make of a note that his Socratic writings were collected in one volume. In that case they cannot have been dialogues in the Platonic manner. A *Didactic Letter* to his daughter Arete, who is supposed to have carried on the tradition after him, is notable because one of the Socratic letters pretends to be addressed by Aristippus to this daughter of his.

---

[1] Approved by SCHWARTZ (*v. inf.*), 181; cf. G. B. L. COLIOSO, *Aristippo di Cirene*. Turin 1925. Rejected by GIGON, *Sokrates* (*v. inf.*), 300, and *Mus. Helv.* 16, 1959. 178, 3. Further information in the bibl. appendix to this section.

In contrast to the three men mentioned before, nothing can be affirmed of Aeschines of Sphettus, either with regard to doctrine or definite membership of a school. But he was particularly successful as a writer of Socratic dialogues, of which we can more or less make out some seven. The mimetic element, lively conversational tone and a wealth of scenic detail were strongly emphasized by him. His *Alcibiades*[1] and *Aspasia* are the most readily discernible. The contrast between the straightforward inexorable thinker and the radiant young aristocrat was presented in a very impressive manner in the first of these dialogues, while in the *Aspasia* the praise of this unusual woman was meant to prove the equality of her womanly ability. The unconcern for chronology which we know from Plato is made evident by the fact that Xenophon, his young wife and Aspasia are brought together here. The *Telauges* brought Socrates into conversation with a Pythagorean; as mere titles we add *Axiochus*, *Callias*, *Miltiades* and *Rhino*.

Phaedo of Elis, who gave his name to one of Plato's greatest creations, is not clearly tangible to us either as the founder of the Elean school or as a composer of Socratic dialogues. As such, a *Zopyrus* is attributed to him, as well as a *Simo*. The former owed its name to a Thracian who was supposed to be an inventor of physiognomical methods. From a study of Socrates' features he attributed to him dullness and evil passions, and Socrates admitted to these; but through his spiritual discipline he was supposed to have mastered his natural tendencies.[2] This anecdote could originally have come from Phaedo's dialogue.

Some elements of the rich tradition which we have traced here are reflected in the letters of Socrates and the Socratics,[3] products of the epistolography of the empire.

Bibliography: O. GIGON, *Bibliogr. Einführung in das Studium der Philosophie* 5, *Antike Philos.* Bern 1948, 23. Books on Socrates by H. MAIER, Tüb. 1913. H. KÜHN, Berl. 1934; repr. Munich 1959. A.-J. FESTUGIÈRE, Paris 1934. O. GIGON, Bern 1947 (Gigon's conception of Socrates opposed in: C. J. DE VOGEL, *Mnem.* 4, 1951, 30 and *Phronesis* 1, 1955, 26. J. H. KÜHN, *Gnom.* 26, 1954, 512; 29, 1957, 170). D. DE MAGELHÃES-VILHENA, *Le Problème de Socr. Le Socr. historique et le Socr. de Platon.* Paris 1952. In add. GIGON, *Gnom.* 27, 1955, 259. A. H. CHROUST, *Socrates, Man and Myth. The Two Socratic Apologies of Xenophon.* London 1957, cf. p. 494, n. 2. W. JAEGER's *Paideia* 2, 2nd ed. Berl. 1954 should also be consulted. – Much work remains to be done for the collection of fragments of the Socratics; MULLACH's *Fragm. Phil. Gr.*, Paris 1864 is obsolete and inadequate. On an important section of the subject now E. MANNEBACH, *Aristippi et Cyrenaicorum fragmenta*, Leiden 1961. C. J. CLASSEN, 'Aristippos'. *Herm.* 86, 1958, 182, and G. GIANNANTONI, *I Cirenaici. Raccolta delle fonte antiche. Traduzione e studio*

---

[1] On the reconstruction according to H. DITTMAR, *Phil. Unters.* 21, 1912, 97, now K. GAISER, *Protreptik und Paränese bei Platon. Tüb. Beitr.* 40, 1959, 77.

[2] Passages in WILH. NESTLE, *Vom Mythos zum Logos*, Stuttg. 1940, 490, 7.

[3] J. SYKUTRIS, *Die Briefe des Sokr. und der Sokratiker.* Paderborn 1933.

introduttivo. Florence 1958, try to oust Aristippus from the later tradition; the former tries to define the special approach to the subject by the Socratic, while the Italian scholar sees him as a talented hedonist without any philosophical object. Our material is too scanty for completely definite statements, but F. WEHRLI, *Gnom.* 31, 1959, 412, is correct when he rejects GIANNANTONI'S scepticism as too extreme. – Antisthenes' declamations in L. RADERMACHER, *Artium Scriptores. Sitzb. Österr. Akad.* 227/3, 1951, 122. – H. DITTMAR, *Aischines von Sphettos. Phil. Unters.* 21, Berl. 1912. Bibl. on Antisthenes: J. GEFFCKEN, *Griech. Lit. Gesch.* 2, Heidelb. 1934, note pp. 21, 30.

C The Fourth Century up to Alexander

I PLATO AND THE ACADEMY

When Athens' great age came to an end, its walls were destroyed and its fleets became a memory. The collapse of power and the terror of the Thirty had passed over the city, but in 403 Thrasybulus' action led to the restoration of the democracy, and a generously planned and executed amnesty offered the conditions for a peaceful internal development. So once more there was an Athens with a council and an assembly which, after the swift fiasco of the Spartan hegemony, could form a second naval league, exactly one hundred years after the first (377). In the Athens of this century there was a great deal of discussion about the constitution of the fathers and the splendid tradition of the city, and before the Macedonian military monarchy smashed everything and completely reshaped the Greek way of life in a period of violence, the enthusiasm for the old ideals once again flared up in a hot blaze.

This should not, however, be mistaken for a true restitution in contemporary Athens any more than at any other time in history. The old *polis* which had built the Parthenon could not rise again. The devastations of the Peloponnesian war had struck at the very heart of the property-owning class down to the small peasantry, and the new conditions, favouring speculations, promoted the rapid growth of new riches. The freedman Pasion who, as a banker and a shield-maker, came into a tremendous fortune and of whom we know through the orators, is a significant example of the new formation of capital. Only now did the heirs of the aristocratic era forfeit the importance which they had still commanded in most spheres of life in democratic Athens during the fifth century, while the emancipation from the bonds of the *polis.* prepared by the sophists, made irresistible progress.

The inscriptions tell us of the continued existence of the old festivals with their poetic contests until far past this time[1] and we know a great many poets' names and titles of works. It cannot be considered a coincidence that practically the whole output has been lost. To what extent the foundation for the great art of the classical period was removed with the fall of the old *polis* can be observed very clearly from the development of comedy.

In the fourth century the literary forms of prose, which only now reached its

[1] Some information in A. PICKARD-CAMBRIDGE, *Dramatic Festivals.* Oxf. 1953.

classical heights, dominate the foreground. The old myths, however, from which poetry drew its life during the fifth century, even though they had clashed grievously in Euripides, became a material mass of tradition from which inner life had fled. As in many other things, the preparation for the Hellenistic age was also active in this province long before the kingdoms of the Diadochi arose. Questions of a different nature now dominated the intellectual life of the time and the prominence of prose is only an external symptom of this tendency. The problem of education takes the forefront and is strong evidence of the legacy of the sophists, whether it is their opponent Plato or Gorgias' follower Isocrates who occupies himself with it. The controversy between these two men is the most important event in this period and in the history of ideas; they began the antagonism between philosophy and rhetoric in their claim on the education of the young. The very importance of this fact shows how much ground had been lost by politics as it was understood in the fifth century. The development against which Aristophanes had protested is irresistibly brought to its completion. The idealization of the old order in rhetorical panegyrics and the extremist attempts of philosophers to replace it with an entirely new construction both emphasize that in this century of transition Greek life was reaching out for new fields.[1]

Plato, the son of Ariston, son of Aristocles, was born during the archonship of Diotimus, which lasted from the summer of 428 until that of the next year. Nothing further is known of his family, but what we know of Plato's relatives on his mother's side forms an essential part of his biography. His mother Perictione was descended from old aristocratic stock, to which Solon was related in a manner which cannot be precisely ascertained. Her cousin was Critias, whom we know as the head of the Thirty and as a versatile author; her brother was Charmides, who became disastrously involved in the politics of the Thirty. Both appear, like Plato's brothers Adimantus and Glaucon, among the characters of his dialogues, one of which is called *Charmides*. Speusippus, Plato's successor as leader of the Academy, was the son of Potone, Plato's sister. After Ariston's death Perictione married the rich and distinguished Pyrilampes, who had been a member of Pericles' circle. From different sides we observe Plato's close ties with the world of the old Attic nobility, and even though this did not make him narrow-minded, he brought along certain basic attitudes which remain discernible in his work until the end.

Our knowledge of the profuse Platonic literature of the ancient world is only fragmentary. Already his most intimate students like Aristotle, Speusippus, Xenocrates and Philip of Opus wrote about him, their work being chiefly encomiastic. We may assume that even at that time the foundation was being laid for the conception of Plato as the 'divine man' which prevails in the later literature of Neoplatonic convention.[2] It is also the dominant element in the oldest extant biography of Plato, four short introductory chapters to Apuleius

---

[1] On the distinctive traits of the 4th century: V. EHRENBERG, 'Epochs of Greek History'. *Greece and Rome*. Sec. Ser. 7, 1960, 110.

[2] For biographical material WILAMOWITZ (*v. inf.*), 2. 1. The biography from Diog. Laert. in the *Festschrift Juvenes dum sumus*. Basel 1907. Additional in the ed. by G. F. HERMANN.

of Madaura's unfinished work *De Platone et eius Dogmate*. To the same stream of tradition belong the biography which occupies the third book of Diogenes Laertius, one by the Neoplatonic Olympiodorus, an anonymous one preceding the προλεγόμενα τῆς Πλάτωνος φιλοσοφίας in a Viennese manuscript and the articles in Suidas and Hesychius. Of other scattered source material mention must be made at least of the Herculanean papyrus (*Index acad. philos.*) with some notes on Plato's life. Various authors, especially Athenaeus (5, 217 a. 11, 504 c), reveal that there existed a literature which was hostile to Plato and which contributed gossip of the most diverse nature about the philosopher's person.

Little can be learned from the tradition recorded here, but of the thirteen *Letters* [1] which have been preserved under his name the seventh is of decisive importance for our image of Plato's life. Distrust against tradition of this nature has been roused since in 1699 Richard Bentley ushered in a new era in historical and literary criticism with his treatment of various letters, notably of those alleged to be of the Sicilian tyrant Phalaris. No doubt a large part of the letters attributed to Plato are also spurious. But the long struggle about the authenticity of this evidence has resulted in the conviction, nowadays shared by many scholars, that three of these letters are definitely Plato's. The *Third Letter* is a circular meant to establish a friendship between two former students of the Academy, Erastus and Coriscus, who were at that time in Scepsis in the Troad, and Hermias, the tyrant of Atarneus. This is the Hermias who became important in Aristotle's life and who gave him his niece Pythias as his wife. The *Seventh Letter* contains the answer to the Sicilian supporters of Dion who ask for advice after the latter's death and is devoted to an account which the old Plato gives of the three Sicilian voyages and the hopes and disappointments connected with them. Even if this letter should not be genuine,[2] it would still have great value as a source, since it was certainly written with a precise knowledge of the conditions. The *Eighth Letter* also contains advice to Dion's partisans, but presupposes a somewhat later situation.[3]

Plato received the careful musical and gymnastic education of an Athenian of a distinguished family, which gave him the intimate knowledge, even if it was to become a problem for him later, of the poetry of his people, as we know from his dialogues. We may trust the tradition that he who demonstrated his very high artistic skill in his writings and who also speaks to us in some epigrams,[4] turned to verse in his early years. Of special significance is the information about some tragedies which he wrote, but which he burnt when Socrates entered his life. Before this decisive period he became acquainted with Heraclitus' doctrine of the eternal flow of all things around us through the somewhat peculiar Cratylus after whom he named a dialogue.[5]

---

[1] E. HOWALDT, Zürich 1951, in Greek and German. Translated and introduced by I. IRMSCHER, Berlin 1960.   [2] So recently G. MÜLLER, *Arch. f. Philos.* 3, 1949/50, 251.

[3] EVA BAER, *Die historischen Aufgaben der Platonbriefe 7 und 8 im Urteil der modernen Forschung seit Ed. Meyer*. Diss. Humboldt-Univ. Berlin 1957.

[4] D. fasc. I, p. 102 with bibl. for separating out much spurious material.

[5] Diog. Laert., who 3. 6 dates the association with Cratylus after Socrates' death, merits no belief against Aristotle, *Met.* A 6. 987 a 32.

In his *Seventh Letter* (324 c) Plato speaks of his active participation in the political movements of his youth. When the collapse brought the Thirty into power, one of whom was his uncle Critias, certainly one of the most impressive figures of his adolescence, he hoped with the ready belief of youth for a new establishment of law and justice. What followed was worse, however, than anything before, and what caused him the deepest repugnance was the authorities' attempt to make Socrates the tool of their terror. When the tyrants fell and the democracy rose again, Plato was prepared, more than at any other time of his life, to come to terms with it and to co-operate in it. But he soon received the greatest shock from this quarter. Socrates, to whom he had been wholeheartedly attached for years, who meant for him the way of the good life, died in 399 through a verdict which made him the victim of reactionary resentment. At that time Plato saw the politics of his native town separated from his thought by an abyss which could no longer be bridged. In future his life belonged to philosophy and the search for a form of human society based upon it.

After Socrates' death Plato together with other of the Master's disciples spent some time at Megara with Euclides; this did not, however, mean that they had taken refuge there. He cannot have stayed there long. He is reported to have been engaged in military service twice and this can be related to the Corinthian war and the years 395 and 394.

In the ten years after Socrates' death Plato wrote his early dialogues including the *Gorgias*. Then follows an important break in his career, his voyage to the South of Italy and Sicily, upon which he embarked in the early part of 390 and 389 and from which he returned to Athens in the summer of 388. A much disputed problem of Plato's biography is connected with this voyage. Numerous ancient notices[1] make it into a kind of world tour and it is often clear that an attempt is made to link Platonic philosophy with the wisdom of the East. Much of this such as a sojourn in India or with the Magi is not now taken seriously by anybody. But even Wilamowitz, in his book on Plato, wanted to have a prolonged stay in Egypt and Cyrene considered as an historical fact. The evidence is well founded but it does not begin until Cicero (*De Rep.* 1. 16, *De Fin.* 5. 87). Plato's own silence and that of other sources such as the Herculanean Academic papyrus obtain some importance and one is inclined to believe that the stay in Egypt was invented for the sake of the old wisdom of its priests and some passages in the dialogues, and the one in Cyrene because of the mathematician Theodorus.

What is certain is that Plato went to Southern Italy before going to Sicily; there he made the acquaintance of Pythagoreanism in a process of rejuvenation mainly connected with the name of Archytas of Tarentum, who was important both as a statesman[2] and a scholar; through his mathematical studies he directed Pythagoreanism more firmly towards science. We can no longer tell how Plato's connections with Archytas and the inspiration he received from Pythagorean circles were distributed over the individual voyages. At all events the importance

Material and bibl. in J. KERSCHENSTEINER, *Pl. und der Orient.* Stuttg. 1945, 44.

[2] VS 47.

of these facts for Plato's development should be valued very highly. Looking back in his *Seventh Letter* (326 d) Plato wonders whether it was coincidence or divine providence which led him to Sicily. Actually his arrival at the island was the beginning of a tragedy which was to find its conclusion only some decades later. When Plato came to Syracuse Dionysius I (405–367) was at the height of his power. Elected strategos with full authority at the age of twenty-five, he had liberated the Sicilian Greeks from the deadly menace of Carthaginian oppression and ensured for them, as a political power, the leading position in the Hellenic world, of which his heavily fortified Syracuse had become the greatest city. In later times the character of his tyranny has obscured his great merits, and Plato will also have seen him mainly as a tyrant, for his experiences in Syracuse, about which there are a wealth of anecdotes, must no doubt have influenced the image of the tyrant which he draws in the *Republic*. But in Syracuse he also met Dion, the ruler's brother-in-law.[1] The *Seventh* Letter (327 a) tells how momentous this meeting was and what impression this young man, who was prepared to alter his whole life, made on Plato. Strained relations with the ruler were inevitable, and so he had Plato removed by ship and put ashore in Aegina. At that time the island was at war with Athens and served as the base of operations of a Spartan fleet. Plato was in danger of being sold as a prisoner of war, but an acquaintance from Cyrene, Anniceris by name, paid the ransom. The story was embroidered in many ways and it is subject to a great deal of suspicion.[2]

Upon his return Plato founded his school and with it a tradition which was to remain influential for nine centuries until the dissolution of the Academy by Justinian (529).[3] At no more than half an hour's walk northwest from Dipylon lay a gymnasium which, like the plain, was called Academea, apparently after the pre-Hellenic guardian spirit Academus or Hecademus. In the *Clouds* (1005) Aristophanes makes the Just Argument tell in beautiful verse how young men of good breeding trained there running under the sacred olive trees. Plato began to teach in this gymnasium, but he next bought a piece of land in the neighbourhood; from this the name of the Academy was immortalized. Presumably Plato lived there himself and gathered his scholars round him. Later, when the Academy had been considerably enlarged, many stories were told about an exedra, a semicircular seat. Basing himself on the topographical indications of Cicero in the impressive account (*De Fin.* 5. 1) of his visit to the Academy during his Athenian student days, and on those in Livy (31. 24), Pan. Aristophron has been digging for the remains of the Academy since 1930. The gymnasium has been uncovered and, although Plato's house has not been found, a stone with

---

[1] H. BERVE, *Dion. Abh. Akad. Mainz. Geistes- u. sozialw. Kl.* 1956/19. Id., 'Dion, der Versuch der Verwirklichung platonischer Staatsgedanken'. *Hist. Zeitschr.* 184, 1957, 1. H. BREITENBACH, *Platon und Dion. Skizze eines idealpolitischen Reformversuches im Altertum.* Zürich 1960.

[2] U. KAHRSTEDT, *Würzb. Jahrb.* 2, 1947, 295. GERTRUDE R. LEVY. *Pl. in. Sicily.* Lond. 1956.

[3] H. HERTER, *Pl.'s Akademie.* 2nd ed. Bonn 1952. C. B. ARMSTRONG, 'Pl.'s Academy'. *Proc. of the Leeds Philos. Soc.* 7, 1953, 89. O. SEEL, *Die plat. Akademie.* Stuttg. 1953.

four names (Charmides, Ariston, Axiochus, Crito) shows that we are within its precincts.

A shrine to the Muses[1] formed the sacred centre of the Academy which possibly occupied the legitimate position of a religious brotherhood. The older philosophers may already have established a tradition by gathering a group of students, and there was an association of Socrates' pupils, although Plato does not give much information about this for himself. His experience in Pythagorean circles must have been the strongest encouragement for the decision to found a school. Something will be said about the teaching at the Academy – of which we know very little – in connection with the philosophy of the later Plato.

The central work of Platonic literature, the *Republic*, is thought to have been produced in the 'seventies. It should not be simply called a utopia, for whilst Plato designed his plan for the ideal state, he was aware of the difficulties of its realization, though he did not fully renounce such a possibility. We do not know what to think of the various reports[2] that Greek cities wished to have Plato as a law-giver, but we do know of one serious attempt to imbue an actual state with the spirit of his philosophy. In 367 Dionysius I was succeeded by his son of the same name. His father had kept him far from politics, and when the talented young man took the reins no one could see where the journey would lead. It was under these conditions that Dion wrote to Plato, urgently suggesting that now was the time for him to fill the Syracusan realm with his spirit. Even if Plato has not himself written the words of the *Seventh Letter* in which he justifies the decision for the second voyage, they may yet be considered the correct expression of his purpose to match philosophical theory with political action and so to overcome the contrast between a theoretical and a practical mode of life which had arisen since the sophists. When he came to Syracuse in 366, the reception was festive and promising. So was the beginning, but soon those court-circles which were concerned about their influence regained the upper hand and succeeded in rousing Dionysius' suspicions of Dion to such a degree that the latter was exiled. Plato, however, remained the uneasy guest of the ruler until he could start on the voyage home in 365, but not without having to promise that he would return after the conclusion of the war which Dionysius had to wage just then. Dion was also to be permitted to return. During the next few years the tyrant urged Plato to come; meanwhile he had also attracted the Socratics Aeschines and Aristippus to his court. Dion himself was interested in this voyage, since he expected mediation from it for his return; the friends in Athens and the South of Italy demanded it point-blank and when Dion sent a trireme to Athens in the early part of 361 to fetch Plato, he decided with a heavy heart to 'venture for the third time into the narrows of Scylla in order to cross the evil Charybdis again' (*Ep.* 7. 345 d, after *Od.* 12. 428). This time things took an even worse course than before. The tyrant's philosophical interests proved to be a passing fancy and with Dion's fortune as a mortgage he played an evil game, finally forcing Plato to live outside the palace among the

---

[1] P. BOYANCÉ, *Le Culte des Muses chez les philosophes grecs*. Paris 1937, 261.
[2] Aelian, *Var. Hist.* 2. 42; 12. 30 Plut. *Mor.* 779 d. Diog. Laert. 3. 23.

mercenaries. It was with difficulty that in the early summer of 360 he was given an opportunity, through the intervention of Archytas, to return home. Dion, who saw all hopes of an agreement wrecked, prepared for a violent solution. Plato refused personal participation, but allowed him to recruit from among the members of the Academy. In 357 Dion occupied Syracuse and forced Dionysius to flee. For four years he carried on his rule under increasing difficulties, as his authoritarian plans involved him in opposition from the democratic camp. In 354 he fell a victim to a conspiracy backed by Callippus, the Academic who had gone to Syracuse as Dion's partisan. The moving distichs which Plato composed as his friend's epitaph are evidence of his deep grief over his death.[1]

The last part of Plato's life was given, without an interruption in his work, to the last dialogues, especially the *Laws*, and to his teaching in the Academy. He died at the age of 81 (348/47). According to Pausanias (1. 30, 3) he was buried in the vicinity of the Academy.

The systematic collection of Plato's writings in a complete edition did not take place until some time after his death. The intrusion of spurious works, inevitable in itself in view of the fame of his name, was considerably encouraged by this delay. Apart from a great deal that can be left out with certainty, there are dialogues on which the verdict is not yet definite.[2] The corpus contained in the manuscripts comprises in the first place nine tetralogies, in which the *Apology*, thirty-four dialogues and the collection of thirteen letters are contained. Then follow the Definitions (ὅροι) which were incorrectly attributed to Speusippus, but which remain for us as anonymous as the seven smaller dialogues which are next in the corpus and which were already rejected as spurious in antiquity: *On Justice, On Virtue, Demodocus, Sisyphus, Alcyon, Eryxias, Axiochus*. These writings are productions of little importance in the tradition of the Platonic school; they merely give recapitulations or dilate upon single questions. They represent an incidental selection from a much larger body of spurious material, as is proved by the titles of dialogues mentioned by Diog. Laert. 3. 62: *Midon or Hippotrophus, Phaeacians, Chelidon, Hebdome, Epimenides*, to which is added *Cimon* mentioned by Athenaeus (506 d).

The works mentioned are rejected at the very outset from the tetralogies transmitted as genuine, but they still contain a great deal which can be cut out with varying degrees of certainty. The *Letters* have already been discussed. With the exception of 6-8, there is not one whose authenticity can be defended with confidence, although the *Second* must be given serious consideration after Friedländer's exposition in the new edition of his work. In the last three places of the 4th tetrad and in the first of the following are four writings which can be erased from the ranks of the genuine with great probability: the *Second Alcibiades*, which is in complete linguistic discord with the rest; the *Hipparchus*, in which the notion of avarice is treated dialectically; the *Anterastae* with a

---

[1] 6 D.; C. M. BOWRA, *Problems in Greek poetry*. Oxf. 1953, no. 8.
[2] Bibl. in GEFFCKEN (*v. inf.*), 180 with the notes; LEISEGANG (*v. inf.*) 2365, with particular reference to the work done by J. PAVLU. O. GIGON, *Gnom.* 27, 1955, 15 authoritative on questions of Pl.'s authenticity.

polemic interesting for its theme, i.e. against sciolism and pure theorizing; and the *Theages*,[1] which borrows from the *Laches* and from other Platonic dialogues as well as such as the *Great Alcibiades*; it deals with Socrates the educator and raises his daimonion to the realm of the gods. In these and similar cases, when Platonic property is used with greater or smaller skill, it is difficult to reach a fairly exact dating. It is generally wrong to go far beyond the end of the 4th century; they are products of a time when the discussions at the Academy were still closely allied with the Master and ventured to imitate his manner of representation. The 4th triad opens with the (*Great*) *Alcibiades*. Its genuineness was first put to the question by Schleiermacher and it was subsequently generally accepted that this talk about justice and usefulness, self-knowledge and tending of the soul between Socrates and a politically inclined Alcibiades was not from Plato's hand. But a scholar who is as close to Plato as Paul Friedländer[2] has emphatically defended its genuineness; C. Vink[3] followed him up with a comprehensive investigation and A.-J. Festugière[4] gives the same verdict. In spite of these weighty opponents we remain in the ranks of the unbelievers, mainly on the ground of what Schleiermacher described as the cheapness of the dialogue, which contrasts it with the quality of thought in the genuine dialogues. Is this difference great enough to banish the danger of subjectivity? We should like to think so. Admittedly it was accepted as genuine in antiquity; the dialogue was even valued very highly well into Neoplatonism; Proclus, Olympiodorus and others wrote commentaries on it. The *Clitophon*[5] is a peculiar piece of work. The dialogue presupposes the *Republic*, in which Clitophon acts as Thrasymachus' companion, as well as the *Phaedrus*. The attack on Socrates' protreptic originates perhaps, as Wilamowitz[6] thought, from a scholar of Plato's who was a dissatisfied deserter. The dialogue *Minos*, a shabby attempt at a discussion about the law, stands close to the *Hipparchus*. Jaeger[7] suspects it to have been written by an Academic shortly after Plato's *Laws*.

The verdict on the *Epinomis* is difficult and not yet definite.[8] In our treatment we connect it with the *Laws*. In the course of time various Platonic writings, apart from the dialogues mentioned, have been suspected; only the *Greater Hippias* is at present subject to serious doubt. Since this doubt cannot be proved to be effective (*v. inf.*), the work is recorded here among the genuine ones.

Before giving an outline of the Platonic corpus as it now stands, a few

---

[1] G. KRÜGER, *Der Dialog Theages*. Greifswald 1935. Ed.: G. AMPLO. Rome 1957. P. FRIEDLÄNDER includes in his *Platon* the *Hipparchus* and the *Theages* among the genuine works and attributes them to the early period (vol. 3, 2nd ed. 419).

[2] FRIEDLÄNDER (*v. inf.*) and *Der grosse Alkibiades*. Bonn 1921 and 1923.

[3] *Platos eerste Alcibiades. Een onderzoek naar zijn authenticiteit*. Amsterdam 1939 (in chapter I a survey of the evaluation of the dialogue from antiquity up to FRIEDLÄNDER). A commentary by L. G. WESTERINK, Amsterdam 1954/56.

[4] *Contemplation et vie contemplative selon Platon*. Paris 1950.

[5] K. GAISER, *Protreptik und Paränese bei Platon*. Tüb. Beitr. 40, 1959, 141, 147 considers the authenticity. According to him the *Clitophon* 'was written over the *Thrasymachus*'.

[6] (*v. inf.*) I. 386, I.   [7] *Éloge de la loi*. Lettres d'*humanité* 8, 1949, 37.

[8] Cf. DODDS (*v. inf.*), 233.

preliminary remarks are called for on some problems concerning the origin and nature of his dialogues.

The dialogue, especially as it appears in the early and middle period of Plato's creative activity, displays a genius in its scenic structure, a directness and charm in its conversation, a love of life, of drama and of philosophy that make it a characteristic and inimitable work of art. One can readily sympathize with the opinion of such scholars as Jaeger and Wilamowitz that the Socratic dialogue is wholly Plato's creation. The author professes the same opinion to this extent, that the qualities of these works which have made them last for ever are Platonic and purely Platonic. But here also we are not excused from enquiring into the elements which they have utilized and embodied.

In the first place we have become acquainted in previous chapters, although through pitiful traces only, with a very extensive Socratic literature in which the dialogue form was certainly used in some cases, very probably in others.[1] We cannot prove direct dependence: all we can do is to look for any tendencies in earlier literature which can help us to understand how the Socratic dialogue arose.

We can make neither head nor tail of a notice preserved in Aristotle's dialogue *On the Poets* (fr. 72 R.), which tells us that one Alexamenus of Teos (otherwise wholly unknown) wrote dialogues before the Socratics. This must come from some piece of literary polemic, and we cannot tell what it is worth.

Gigon[2] has rightly traced a connection back to the sophists. It is clear that in their particular province of antinomy the technique of conveying one's own opinions through question and answer played an important part. There seems to be a core of truth in Diogenes Laertius' statement that Protagoras – of whom he quotes a book-title *Technique of Question and Answer* (τέχνη ἐριστικῶν) – created the form of the Socratic dialogue. Furthermore, the whole tendency of the Platonic dialogues is, to use Gaiser's words, protreptic and paraenetic, i.e. they urge the reader towards a definite form and conception of life; so that, despite the great difference in what they teach, the influence of sophistic propaganda techniques cannot be excluded. Gaiser[3] has gone into the question very thoroughly. Admittedly the tradition leaves us very much in the lurch when we look for early examples of the Platonic dialogue, and we have to be content with guesswork;[4] but he does a very good service in demonstrating the basic difference between the attitudes of sophistic and Platonic protreptic. The Platonic Socrates does not offer to pass on a definite knowledge or skill, but he brings about the intellectual change by showing his disciples what a wretched thing it is to be ignorant. In the same connection we should mention Zeno of Elea, of whom a title *Disputes* (Ἔριδες VS 29 A 2) has been transmitted, and whom Aristotle calls 'the inventor of eristics' (fr. 65 R.). A connection with the *Conversations of the Seven Sages* does not seem very likely.

---

[1] V. BARTOLETTI, 'Un frammento di dialogo socratico'. *Stud. It.* 31, 1959, 100, on an interesting fragment of political content which cannot be more precisely determined.

[2] *Sokrates.* Bern 1947, 202.

[3] K. GAISER, *Protreptik und Paränese bei Platon.* Tüb. Beitr. 40, 1959.

[4] Cf. E. DE STRYCKER, *Gnom.* 34, 1962, 13.

The dramatic element in the Platonic dialogues leads automatically to a further association. Many things, not the least his resistance against it, point to the influence which the stage had on Plato, who himself once used to write tragedies. It would be a mistake to call Plato's dialogues comedies, but there can be no doubt about the strong influence of comedy.[1] The verse of Epicharmus, who appears in the *Theaetetus* (152 e) as the great comic poet, shows great affinity with the game of question and answer of the Platonic dialogues.[2] Plato valued Sophron's prose mimes highly and used to keep a copy under his pillow. We need not think that communications between Athens and Sicily were so tenuous that Plato first had to travel there to come to know and value this poet. It should be noted that Aristotle, in his *Poetics* (1. 1447 d 9), ranks the mimes of Sophron and Xenarchus with the Socratic dialogues (λόγοι).

The lingering influence of Socrates' actual method of enquiry should be taken into serious consideration, though there is no need to accept direct copying or the use of written notes, as Rudolf Hirzel[3] does, or to give serious credit to the fiction in the introduction of the *Theaetetus*.

This creation with its rich ancestry, fashioned by Plato into such an independent form of art, occupies a peculiar position in the whole of his philosophy. We come up against the paradox that the man whose dialogues have not their equal in Greek literature, eloquently proclaims in a lengthy section of the *Phaedrus* (275 c ff.) that writing has little value and that the mute book is inferior to the live Logos which is astir in the soul of the student. This throws some light on the astounding statement of Plato in the *Seventh Letter* (341 c) that he has never written about the object of his aspirations and will never do so in the future. There are also the words about the spark which after a long life of common effort suddenly flashes across and kindles the light in the soul. So from another point of view these dialogues, which are filled with a profound moral seriousness and the true love of a scholar, are merely a decorative accessory to the essence of Plato's philosophy. The nature of these dialogues, which nowhere attempt to formulate a definite system, explains largely why individual problems are only touched upon superficially, why we are not infrequently duped by logical tricks, and why the borders between logos and myth become vague. Which does not, of course, mean to say that this varied work was without a definite purpose.[4] Presently, when we discuss the lecture *On the Good*, we shall have occasion to refer to the question which has lately dominated research on Plato, whether there is at the back of the dialogues a doctrine passed on orally, whose relation to the published writings could be elucidated.

---

[1] E. HOFFMANN, 'Die literarischen Voraussetzungen des Platonsverständnisses'. *Zeitschr. f. philos. Forsch.* 2, 1947, 472. Minimizing this K. GAISER (*v. sup.*) 22 f.

[2] *VS* 23 B 1 ff. with notes on the question of authenticity. A. THIERFELDER, 'Zu einem Bruchstück des Epicharmos'. *Festschr. Snell.* Munich 1956, 773. On Sophron KAIBEL, *Com. Gr. Fr.* 1, p. 152 f.

[3] *Der Dialog.* 1. Leipz. 1895.

[4] R. SCHAERER, *La Question platonicienne. Étude sur les rapports de la pensée et de l'expression dans les dialogues.* Neuchâtel 1938. Following Hegel J. STENZEL, *Kl. Schr.* 1957, 312 characterizes the movement of perception as the theme of the Platonic dialogues.

A characteristic of this sublime flight of fancy[1] is the art of the introduction, the listening to a story of what others have told, as well as the tendency to remove the scene far into the past without worrying about anachronisms. Thus in the *Symposium* they are celebrating the Lenaean victory which Agathon won in 416, in the *Parmenides* the grey-haired Eleatic meets with the young Socrates. The deliberate discord between content and setting is particularly exciting when the dialectic thrusts lead deep into the theory of ideas from situations placed in the distant past.

The chronology of Plato's writings presents a problem which is as difficult as it is methodologically attractive. It has a bearing on the sport with the background of time to which we just referred, so that hardly any assistance can be found within the dialogues for the purpose of dating; nor does the anecdotal tradition on Plato offer any help. Thus it is very hard to answer the very first question, that of the relation between Socrates' death and Plato's literary activity. Socrates promises in the *Apology* (39 c) that others, whom he had restrained so far, would continue the work of testing people. If we take this sharply as a *vaticinatio ex eventu*, this passage supports the view that Plato did not begin his Socratic writings until after 399, and the inference is that the shock of this year put his stylus into motion. But these arguments are not conclusive and those scholars who, like Wilamowitz, dated the first dialogues earlier, cannot be decisively refuted.[2]

For the task of determining the relative chronology of the Platonic writings, Schleiermacher's[3] attempt is still of fundamental importance. The principle of his research is the internal connection between the individual dialogues in which Plato methodically evolved the guiding thoughts which were present from the very beginning. Neither Schleiermacher's arrangement in its detail nor the extreme rejection of internal factors of development could be upheld; what does remain has been outlined by Jaeger (2. 152): the demand not to lose sight of the coherence of the whole, the movement towards a final goal which pervades the whole work. We shall presently have occasion to show how strong Schleiermacher's influence still is in the most recent literature on Plato (Krämer). Next, K. F. Hermann,[4] in contrast to Schleiermacher, placed the idea of an internal development of Plato's philosophy in the foreground. Although this principle was subsequently exaggerated to such a degree that it amounted to tearing up Plato's work to pieces, research can now no longer be imagined without it. The centre will always be taken by the evolution of the theory of ideas, as for instance in Ross. Whether this theory must be assumed to have been

---

[1] On the παιδία-character of the dialogues G. J. DE VRIES, *Spel bij Plato*. Amsterdam 1949. Cf. also H.-J. KRÄMER, *Arete bei Platon und Aristoteles. Abh. Akad. Heidelb. Phil.-hist. Kl.* 1959/6, 461 f. 468.

[2] P. FRIEDLÄNDER, *Platon*, 2nd ed. vol. 3. Berl. 1960, 423 tends to put the earliest writings in the 5th century; in the note he quotes the powerful opposition of ED. MEYER and JOH. GEFFCKEN, as well as the doubts of W. JAEGER, which are not, however, based on arguments. No importance can be attached to the anecdote in Diog. Laert. 3. 35, that Socrates read Plato's *Lysis* with surprise.

[3] *Pl.'s Werke* I/1/1804.   [4] *Geschichte und System der plat. Philosophie.* 1, 1839.

present in Platonic writings from the very beginning is a problem which will occupy us with the works of the middle period (*Symp.*, *Phaed.*).

A chronology based on the internal development would often have had to remain uncertain, if the statistical analysis of language had not come to the assistance. A start was made by L. Campbell in the introduction to his edition of the *Sophistes* and *Politicus* (1867), in which he combined these dialogues together with the *Timaeus*, *Critias*, *Philebus* and the *Laws* into a late group. Independently from him W. Dittenberger[1] opened up German research in this field. His successors, of whom at least C. Ritter and H. v. Arnim must be mentioned, made important progress, in which the statistical recording of certain forms of the affirmative played the most important part. Exaggerations were not lacking and the method was no doubt overworked when it was pushed into decimals. A linguistic scholar like P. Kretschmer[2] subjected it to basic criticism, but its merits are, within certain limits, undeniable.[3]

The prudent use of internal and external criteria has led to a view of the chronological order of the Platonic writings which may be largely considered as definitive. This means that large groups could be demarcated as works of the early, mature and late creative periods, and that there are no restless wanderers in this system. On the other hand it is peculiar to the nature of this method that a precise arrangement of the works inside the groups is difficult and has in most cases little prospect of success. This picture – definitive division into groups and uncertain arrangement in detail – can easily be observed when studying the inventory of the most important attempts at ordering which Gigon presents in his bibliographical introduction to Plato, and Ross in the preface to his book on the theory of ideas. In our arrangement, for which we, with others, select the Sicilian voyages as the caesurae, we follow Friedländer with regard to the late composition of the *Apology* and *Crito*, while we begin with *Laches* under the influence of Steidle's work on this dialogue;[4] all this is done, however, with the reservation that in this arrangement we cannot be perfectly certain of all the details. We refer particularly to the difficulty of allotting to the *Protagoras* a definite place among the earliest dialogues, and to the *Cratylus* in a later group.

Between Socrates' death and the first Sicilian voyage we place: *Laches*, *Charmides*, *Euthyphro*, *Lysis*, *Protagoras*, *Hippias Minor*, *Ion*, *Hippias Maior*, *Apology*, *Crito*, and the *Gorgias* as definitely the last. Those who believe the first book of the *Republic* to be a separate early dialogue with the hypothetical title *Thrasymachus* will have to insert it here in the vicinity of the *Lysis*. Between the first and the second voyages we place: *Meno*, *Cratylus*, *Euthydemus*, *Menexenus*, *Symposium*, *Phaedo*, *Republic*, *Phaedrus*, *Parmenides* and *Theaetetus*. This group displays evidence of the strains and stresses in Plato's life, as we would expect

---

[1] Herm. 16, 1881, 321.　　　　[2] *Glotta* 20, 1932, 232.

[3] Acceptable to P. FRIEDLÄNDER, (*v. sup.*) 415. The same line of research is followed in E. DE PLACES, *Études sur quelques particules de liaison chez Platon*. Paris 1929.

[4] R. BÖHME, *Von Sokrates zur Ideenlehre. Beobachtungen zur Chronologie des platonischen Frühwerks*. Diss. Bernenses 5. 1, 9. 1959 disagrees sharply with the dating defended here. He puts the *Gorgias* at the beginning together with the *Crito* and the *Apology* and makes one group of *Laches*, *Protagoras*, *Menon*, and *Phaedo*.

under the circumstances which we know of in his biography. The works from the *Symposium* to the *Phaedrus* represent the centre and peak; the preceding ones still form part of the dialogues of his ascent and the following ones belong to those of the later stages. The *Sophistes* and the *Politicus* are placed between the second and third voyages, after his last return *Philebus*, *Timaeus*, *Critias* and *Laws*, as well as the *Seventh Letter*.

The first three dialogues of our series form a particularly close unity in their purpose and the trend of the talk. In the *Laches*[1] the generals differ on the subject of fencing exercises in heavy armour; they begin to discuss it with Socrates, but the talk soon turns to the question of what the real nature of courage is. In the *Charmides*, in which Critias figures too, the scene is built up around Plato's uncle Charmides who appears here as a boy of greatly admired beauty. The subject is the nature of sophrosyne, common sense, which understands man's limits and adjusts its actions accordingly. In recent attempts to find an historical foundation for psychosomatic medicine an important part is being played by the remarks about Zalmoxis' doctrine that all the weal and woe of the body find their origin in the soul (P. Lain-Entralgo et al.). In the *Euthyphro*[2] Socrates is on his way to the court-house where he wants to enquire about the accusation lodged against him by Meletus, when he encounters the seer Euthyphro, a young man whose notion of justice is so fanatical that he is about to indict his own father for causing the death of a slave through negligence. The complex of problems connected with this action leads the debate on to the nature of piety. The *Lysis*[3] can be joined on to it, although many scholars put it later. In a conversation with two boys Socrates enquires about *philia*, the loving association of people in a variety of contexts, but particularly in friendship.

In these dialogues the direct relation with the Socrates shown by Aristotle's evidence is most obvious. He seeks a definition, passing during the process through several stages of attempt and rejection without achieving his object;[4] he aims at the practical, since the gaining of knowledge about things is supposed to be the guarantee for correct action. We are inclined to assume a similar origin for the constant – and very often far-fetched – analogies taken from the realm of artisans and professions. But these dialogues also display features which prepare the way for Plato's later philosophy. The purpose of the question $\tau\acute{\iota}$ $\acute{\epsilon}\sigma\tau\iota\nu$ is the understanding of something all-comprising (we should not be too ready to use an expression such as concept, borrowed from our logic) which is both a unity identical with itself and as such the archetype for separate phenomena. Already in the *Euthyphro* the words $\epsilon\tilde{\iota}\delta o\varsigma$ and $\iota\delta\acute{\epsilon}a$ (5 d. 6 d e)[5] are used,

[1] W. STEIDLE, 'Der Dialog L. und Pl.'s Verhältnis zu Athen in den Frühdialogen'. *Mus. Helv.* 7, 1950, 129.

[2] O. GIGON, 'Pl.'s Euth.'. *Westöstl. Abhandlungen R. Tschudi zum 70. Geburtstag*. Wiesbaden 1954, 6.

[3] A. W. BEGEMANN, *Plato's Lysis. Onderzoek naar de plaats van den dialoog in het oeuvre*. Diss. Amsterdam 1960.

[4] W. BRÖCKER, *Gnom*. 30, 1958, 512 is excellent on the elenctic of the early dialogues.

[5] On their history ROSS (*v. inf.*), 13.

but they do not as yet signify transcendental essences separated from the world of the senses; but the beginning of such a belief is unmistakable. The thought of the unity of all virtues becomes more and more prominent, which unity is expressed in the good as the final goal and final criterion.

The elements related to the mime prevail strongly in the introductory section of the *Protagoras*.[1] The studious Hippocrates urges Socrates at daybreak to introduce him to the sophist; the two have a preliminary discussion; there is the description of the dignified bearing of the great sophist at the house of the hospitable Callias; all this (presented together with the rest of the dialogue as Socrates' story) is done with the greatest liveliness. In the great rhetorical duel of Socrates versus Protagoras the question of the teachability of ἀρετή is placed in the centre. This word cannot be suitably translated, since the meaning of 'virtue' in its modern connotation is restricted to the province of ethics, whereas we should at least add the idea of usefulness or suitability, both ethical and technical. Such usefulness is connected with activity in the civic community; Socrates doubts its teachability, Protagoras answers with the myth of the origin of the state of which we learned (p. 345 f.) when dealing with the sophists, and, being able to turn his hand to anything, he follows it up with a logos. In the course of the dialogue Socrates energetically pushes into the foreground the enquiry into the unity of all separate virtues which is already in the background of the early aporetic dialogues. As an intermezzo there is an interpretation of a scolion of Simonides' (4 D.) on the hardship of true virtue,[2] done by both sides in a very arbitrary manner. Socrates subjects the separate virtues couple by couple to the evidence of their identity, opposes the thesis that in the final analysis virtue is knowledge of the good and thus arrives at the admission of its teachability, which meanwhile has become doubtful to Protagoras. The final statement that things have been turned upside down and that the enquiry after the nature of ἀρετή must be taken up again is to be taken as Plato's own to the effect that this dialogue wants to offer dialectic movement but no definite results. It shows, more than elsewhere, the urgency of the problem of the sudden transitions and mistakes in thinking which are either evidence of a logic which is still faulty,[3] or of an irony, a joking deception, which requires to be understood as such.

In the *Lesser Hippias* such a large part is played by dialectical brawling with logically contestable means that many critics of the dialogue want to consider it as a jest. The manner in which Socrates plays along with the smatterer Hippias in two passages of the debate must certainly be understood as a satire. The confusion of the notions 'better' in a technical sense and 'better' in a moral sense leads to quite unbelievable results in the course of an enquiry for a more

---

[1] O. GIGON, 'Stud. zu Pl.'s Protagoras'. *Phyllobolia für P. von der Mühll*. Basel 1945, 91, partly with dubious application of analytical and source-critical methods. F. DIRLMEIER and H. SCHAROLD, *Protagoras*. Munich 1959 (with comm.).

[2] H. GUNDERT, 'Die Simonides-Interpretation in Pl.'s Prot.': *Festschr. Regenbogen*. Heidelb. 1952, 71.

[3] On such elements in Plato: J. M. BOCHENSKY, *Ancient Formal Logic*. Amsterdam 1951. Also a great deal in LEISEGANG (*v. inf.*).

lofty appraisal of Achilles and Odysseus, of the truthful or the deceitful. The question why Plato allows the train to derail like this is a difficult problem, but the central question, whether there is a knowledge of the good commensurable with the technical knowledge of the artisan, the steersman or the general, can on the whole be followed.

The *Ion*[1] also ends up in two dialectical lines which are followed by fairly long discourses by Socrates. He points out to the self-confident rhapsode Ion that his claim to be able to say clever things about Homer's poetry is misplaced, since he is lacking in technical knowledge (τέχνη) and understanding (ἐπιστήμη) for this purpose. Significantly Plato's future arguments on the problems of poetry are anticipated in the parts in which the divinely inspired enthusiasm of the poet is contrasted with a knowledge based on technical ability as belonging in a totally different category.

Many reasons were advanced against the authenticity of the *Hippias Maior*, but none that are conclusive.[2] Linguistic statistics date it later than we do here, in the vicinity of the *Phaedo*. In terms of content it still belongs to the aporetic dialogues with their search for a definition. Hippias 'the beautiful' – the words significantly occur at the beginning – is shown in the splendour of his political and educational mission; by announcing a particularly 'beautiful' lecture he sets off the talk about the nature of the beautiful. Here too the search is for the one thing which, indivisible in itself, is the cause of the quality of beauty in all the separate phenomena which it approaches. Here too neither its ontological nature is clearly defined nor the nature of its relationship to the separate phenomena, but the determined enquiry after the beautiful in itself (286 d et al.) through which every individual beautiful thing has this quality, points to hardening of thought compared with the first aporetic dialogues. We are face to face with the formulation of the theory of ideas.

We mentioned earlier (p. 499)[3] that Plato's *Apology* is a free invention and forms part of a rich apologetic Socratic literature. E. Wolff[4] has shown that this form of Attic forensic rhetoric was so stimulated and reshaped under the influence of contemporary literature in its highest forms that it turned into the sage's self-portrait. Moreover, the inexorable search of the man who, conscious of his own ignorance, destroys the would-be knowledge of others was lifted into the realm of religious activity. The reply of Delphi to Chaerephon's question raised Socrates above the mass of those whose beliefs were without roots, and the daimonion in his breast also testifies to his vocation. Three speeches are united in the *Apology*: the actual speech for the defence which brings

---

[1] Ann. ed. by W. J. VERDENIUS, Zwolle 1953. H. DILLER, 'Probleme des plat. Ion'. *Herm.* 83, 1955, 171. X. FLASHAR, *Der Dialog Ion als Zeugnis plat. Philosophie*. Berlin 1959 (*Akad. Berl. Schr. d. Sekt. f. Altertumsw.* 14).

[2] On the defence by M. SORETH, *Der plat. Dialog H. maior. Zet.* 6. Munich 1953, cf. O. GIGON, *Gnom.* 27, 1955, 14.

[3] Comm. ed.: NILO CASINI, Florence 1957. A work by TH. MEYER will appear in the *Tüb. Beitr.*

[4] *Pl.'s Ap. N. phil. Untersuch.* 6, 1929. TH. MEYER, *Pl.'s Ap.* Diss. Tüb. 1956 on formal connections with Attic forensic oratory; cf. also K. GAISER, *Tüb. Beitr.* 40, 1959, 23.

in an element of dialogue in the argument with Meletus; the proposed penalty, first of free meals at the Prytaneum, then of a small fine, so that in each case he merely provokes the judges. The image of Socrates built up here by Plato is at the same time an outspoken piece of propaganda for the life of a philosopher.

The brief dialogue *Crito*[1] provides the reasons for Socrates' refusal to flee from prison with the aid of his friends. The motivation is difficult, since the point of view could be defended that Socrates' flight would have prevented rather than caused an injustice. Plato introduces the personified laws who speak to oppose Socrates' undermining the respect due to them; not the laws as such, but their abuse, has landed him in prison; they emphasize the contract into which a citizen who lives in a community enters with its laws. The modification of sophistic theories on the contractual nature of the state is clear. The great moral fervour of this dialogue must not lead us to overlook the fact that this legalism is far removed from the aloofness from the historical *polis* evident in the *Republic* (520 b) and even further in the *Seventh Letter* (326 a). The Socrates of the *Crito* is more closely allied with the champion of loyalty to the law of Xenophon's *Memorabilia* than any other representation of him by Plato.

The *Gorgias*[2] concludes and at the same time carries on the early dialogues. Three conversations, enlivened by the force of contrast, lead to results which are outlined with much greater clarity than in the aporetic dialogues. The argument with the sophists, which is carried on in this dialogue with considerably greater depth than in the related *Protagoras*, starts with an enquiry into the nature of their activity. Employing the method of dividing the leading ideas which is to be so important to Plato at a later stage, but which is not yet described as diaeresis here, Socrates determines in a conversation with Gorgias the sphere of action of rhetoric: in the realm of justice and injustice it provides the sort of persuasion which aims at credulous acceptance, not true knowledge. Gorgias defends himself by pointing to men like Themistocles and Pericles and stresses the actual power of rhetoric. He gets into difficulties in his enquiry into the importance of knowledge in the realm of justice, so that his student Polus intervenes. Once more the nature of rhetoric is sought through the separation of ideas and now the result is particularly unpleasant: rhetoric does not at all belong to those skills ($\tau\acute{\epsilon}\chi\nu\alpha\iota$) which tend the healthy and the sick body and the healthy and the sick soul; it is a phantom of the latter and like sophistry with which it is closely allied, it is only the practice of flattery ($\dot{\epsilon}\mu\pi\epsilon\iota\rho\acute{\iota}\alpha$ $\kappa o\lambda\alpha\kappa\epsilon\upsilon\tau\iota\kappa\acute{\eta}$) of the soul, as the practice of cleaning and cooking for the body. In the further course of the debate might and right are opposed in the sharpest conflict. Socrates contrasts the happiness of might with that of morality. His basically different valuation culminates in statements which were paradoxes at the time: to commit injustice is worse than suffering it, impunity is worse than right atonement. Then Callicles, the third and sharpest opponent, enters; adopting

---

[1] P. HARDER, *Pl.'s Kritik*. 1934. With a Spanish transl.: MARÍA RICO-GOMEZ, Madrid 1957. STEIDLE (*v.* p. 517, n. 1.), 138.

[2] Large comm. ed. by E. R. DODDS, Lond. 1959. V. ARANGIO-RUIZ, *Gorgia. Trad. introd. e comm.* Florence 1958.

the most extreme interpretation of natural law, he extols the superman who knows how to enforce his will to power against the mass of the weak and their laws. In the ensuing argument with Socrates the rhetorical-sophistic and the philosophical ideal of life enter into the sharpest conflict imaginable: the ideal of power as the highest value against morality, the technical instruction for mob-rule against education as the development of the best in man. Already at this stage we find that such an education is the task of the true statesman; compared with this ideal the great men of Athenian history are non-existent. Both in this respect and through the determination with which the relation of the individual to the community is put to the debate, the *Gorgias* can be recognized as the precursor of the *Republic*.

In the final eschatological myth the metaphysical background of the dialogue is revealed. The fate of the soul, which is the subject of the whole of Plato's work, is shown in a picture of the judgment of the dead which Plato's poetical skill has drawn with the aid of a variety of notions – especially of Orphic and Pythagorean origin.

Although at present the *Menon*[1] is no longer considered to be a prospectus for the foundation of the Academy, it is an important work for the shaping of the theory of ideas because it connects the question of the teachability of virtue raised in the *Protagoras* with problems of ontology and knowledge. Admittedly the ideas do not yet occur as metaphysical entities, but when the conversation with Menon bogs down in the attempt to comprehend the nature of virtue through definition, Socrates helps it along with the doctrine of anamnesis which was to become very important later. In its wanderings through the cycle of births, in this world and the other, the soul has seen all things and has retained the capacity of memory. The adoption of Orphic and Pythagorean elements here is very clear. Empedocles (VS 31 B 129) said of Pythagoras that he easily saw every detail of everything in existence during his twenty-seven life-times. In the *Meno* Socrates uses a slave to demonstrate anamnesis for the task of doubling the area of a square; the problem of *a priori* knowledge has entered the scope of Platonic philosophy. The end of the dialogue seems to be at a loss about the teachability of virtue. No certain proof has been found that 'virtue' can be imparted 'naturally' or through teaching. So it seems to come about only through divine providence (θείᾳ μοίρᾳ, 99 c), unless there should happen to be a statesman who could train another statesman. The present ἀπορία obviously anticipates the educational state of the *Republic*.

The *Cratylus*[2] deals firstly of the relation of words with things. The Heraclitean

---

[1] M. SORETH, 'Zur relativen Chronologie von Menon und Euthydemos'. *Herm.* 83, 1955, 377. R. G. HOERBER, 'Plato's Meno.'. *Phronesis* 5, 1960, 78. Large comm. ed. by R. S. BLUCK, Lond. 1961. With a Span. transl. A. RUIZ DE ELVIRA, Madrid 1958.

[2] E. HAAG, *Pl's Krat.* Tüb. Beitr. 19, 1933. J. DERBOLAV, *Der Dialog Krat.* Saarbr. 1953. C. J. CLASSEN, *Sprachliche Deutung als Triebkraft platonischen und sokratischen Philosophierens.* Zet. 22. Munich. 1959. (Deals in a wide scope with etymological interpretation of diction and with metaphors which can be condensed to terminology or parable.) On the effect of the *Cratylus* on the linguistic theory of the Stoics: K. BARWICK, *Probleme der stoischen Sprachlehre und Rhetorik. Abh. Akad. Leipz. Phil.-hist. Kl.* 49/3, 1957, ch. 5.

Cratylus, Plato's first teacher, sees this relation based in the nature of things; the Parmenidean Hermogenes believes that it is founded on convention. In the investigation which Socrates carries out, it is plainly shown that the derivation of names directly from the nature of things is very dubious, and with it the confidence that this nature can be ascertained from the words. The lengthy section on etymology which plays an important part in this argument is largely grotesque nonsense. The criticism of this section is difficult, because this etymological jest is linked with considerable knowledge of linguistic history and philosophy. The dialogue, which contains the largest number of problems of the whole Corpus, finally rejects the doctrine of constant flux, and strives towards the recognition of unchanging entities which alone render it possible to know and name things.

The *Euthydemus* goes closely with the *Cratylus*, and may have been written earlier. From a pedagogic situation – the boy Clinias in a gymnasium change-room among Socrates and the sophists – Plato develops the condemnation of sophistic methods of argument, represented here by Euthydemus and Dionysodorus. In the excellently constructed dialogue the series of sophisms refuted by Socrates is interrupted twice when the latter makes speeches urging them to aspire after true knowledge and true arete. The persuasive propaganda of the sophists is matched by Plato's.

The *Menexenus*[1] is a peculiar composition. During a meeting with this man, Socrates (399) delivers a fictional funeral oration supposedly meant for the national memorial celebration for the fallen of the year 386; it is even alleged to have originated from Aspasia. The praise of Athens is kept up right through it in the rhetorical style initiated by Gorgias, but it is carried off with such mastery and élan, that it is necessary to pay close attention to hints in the introductory dialogue, to Plato's attitude to the Athenian state as described in the *Seventh Letter* and the deprecation of the great statesmen in the *Gorgias*, if one is to see through this delightful irony. Later times failed to do this, for Cicero (*Orat.* 151) reports that the oration was declaimed annually at the ceremony for the dead. P. Friedländer's comparison with the central speech of the *Phaedrus* will be found very useful for its understanding; in this Socrates outdoes Lysias' speech without leaving the latter's pedestrian level. His confrontation of the encomium on Athens with the Atlantis myth in the *Critias*[2] is also valuable. This juxtaposition opens up a special understanding of the way in which in Plato's historical elements and overlapping norms are related. Recently increasing attention has been paid to Plato's treatment of history and the beginnings of a philosophy of history in his work.[3]

The *Symposium* and the *Phaedo* belong together, because poetically they are

[1] Bibl. in K. MEULI, *Westöstl. Abh.* (cf. p. 517, n. 2.), 64, 7. N. SCHOLL, *Der platonische Menexenos. Temi e testi* 5. Rome 1959. J. V. LÖWENCLAU, *Der platonische Menexenos, Tüb. Beitr.* 41. Stuttg. 1961.

[2] *Platon*, 2nd ed. vol. 3, Berl. 1960, 357.

[3] R. G. BURY, 'Pl. and History'. *Class. Quart.* 45, 1951, 86. R. WEIL, *L' 'Archéologie' de Pl. Ét. et Comm.* 32. Paris 1959, comparing the philosopher's method with the historian's. K. GAISER, *Pl. und die Geschichte*. Stuttg. 1961.

the most perfect of Plato's creations and because in them the central themes of the Platonic theory of ideas[1] break through most clearly. We must now determine our position with regard to a vexing question. Plato regards ideas as transcendental unities, separate from the things of the world of the senses and leading a permanent and unchanging existence, yet at the same time being the original form and the original cause of physical phenomena. Now is this doctrine at the back of Plato's dialogues, or was it developed only in the course of his philosophical activity? Basing ourselves upon the careful analysis of Plato's work by David Ross, we adopt the second position; in our discussion of the earlier dialogues we have already pointed to the various beginnings and preliminary elements.[2]

Aristotle (*Met.* A 6, 987 a 32; cf. M 9. 1086 a 37) gives a representation of the theory of ideas which probably simplifies construction but does not correctly single out the essential.[3] According to him the young Plato became acquainted, through the Heraclitean Cratylus, with the doctrine of the flux of all things comprehensible to the senses which do not permit true knowledge. Socrates, however, led him to the question of the general and the permanent in the realm of ethics. Thus he came to the separation of the sensory from the intelligible world; he settled the ideas in the latter, connecting things perceptible by the senses with them by means of 'participation' ($\mu\acute{\epsilon}\theta\epsilon\xi\iota\varsigma$). The Pythagorean conception of the nature of things as being analogous to numbers served for his model in this. The greatest difficulty of the Platonic theory of ideas is in this notion of 'participation'. This is also supported by the vagueness of expression in the *Phaedo* (100 d ff.), where the problematic relation between the idea and the individual thing appears as $\pi\alpha\rho o\upsilon\sigma\acute{\iota}\alpha$ or $\kappa o\iota\nu\omega\nu\acute{\iota}\alpha$, $\mu\epsilon\tau\acute{\alpha}\sigma\chi\epsilon\sigma\iota\varsigma$ or $\mu\epsilon\tau\alpha\lambda\alpha\mu$-$\beta\acute{\alpha}\nu\epsilon\iota\nu$. This is also the point of Aristotle's[4] rudest attack (*Met.* A 9. 991 a 20), when, though mentioning no names, he speaks of empty phrases and poetical metaphors. It is probably also the reason why the problem of the chorismos has remained the centre of Platonic criticism in a way which far outweighs its importance. In the face of it one is liable to forget what the Platonic idea has achieved. We should like to state this achievement in a phrase of Hermann

---

[1] It has become increasingly dubious whether one can speak of a theory of ideas. The ideas are an essential element of Plato's philosophy, but they cannot be considered as the whole of his ontological statement. In his book which will be mentioned presently, H. J. KRÄMER removes the ideas particularly far away from the centre of Plato's thought, which according to him is occupied by the One. This proviso should be made, but we do not think it necessary to speak of the theory of ideas only between quotation marks, as was done first by W. PATER in his book *Pl. and Platonism*, 1893, whose example was followed at times by A. E. TAYLOR and others.

[2] The Scottish school, who claim that Plato's doctrine is Socrates' up to the *Republic*, was mentioned in connection with it. Their tenets are echoed to a certain extent by R. C. LODGE, *The Philosophy of Pl.* Lond. 1956, but have no longer any influence.

[3] Cf. H. E. CHERNISS, *Aristotle's Criticism of Pl. and the Academy.* I. Baltimore 1944, who lays the basis for the view that Aristotle is no unconditional authority for our interpretation of Plato, but criticizes on the basis of his own system; on the other hand he goes too far in his devaluation of Aristotle's information. We also refer in this context to Gigon's essay in *Mus. Helv.* 16, 1959, 174 mentioned in the chapter on Socrates.

[4] CHERNISS (*v.* prev. n.), ROSS (*v. inf.*), 165.

Kleinknecht's:[1] '. . . to make the reality in which man exists recognisable and comprehensible in connection with what it truly is'. Since Plato, man has known an above and a below which is not spatial nature and which remains withdrawn from his individual perspective.

Aristotle's sketch must be at least completed with a reference to the fundamental importance of Parmenides' ontology for Plato;[2] there can be no doubt that he influenced Plato through his doctrine of a pure, intelligible and indivisible being. Recently H. J. Krämer[3] has developed a conception of Platonic philosophy in which the Parmenidean One as the ontological principle stands temporally at the beginning, but has a central position according to its importance. According to this conception the idea came in later between the One as the primary substance and the separate, individual things. Since Plato confronted, from the very beginning, the primary substance of the One with the dyadic principle of smallness-bigness and fitted the cosmos of the ideas in between primary substance and the world of sensory appearances, he managed to form a universal ontological conception of reality. In our discussion of the lecture *Of the Good* (p. 540) we shall have to refer to the related questions of the extent to which we can grasp an esoteric doctrine of Plato's and in how far we must assume a development in his thought. Aristotle points out another important factor in this section by stressing the significance of mathematics for Plato's path to the absolute.[4] Plato placed his mathematical structures between the ideas, with which they shared permanency, and matter, with which they shared plurality. It is difficult to express this doctrine more precisely or to trace it in the surviving writings. Against the scepticism of Cherniss, however, Ross[5] has advanced good arguments in favour of Aristotle's knowing that this view is actually Platonic.

In the *Symposium*[6] Plato presents one of his boldest narrative situations. Agathon's Lenaean victory and the banquet to celebrate it must be placed in the year 416. Plato's work, however, introduces it as the report told many years afterwards by a certain Apollodorus who did not take part in the symposium himself and who bases his story on that of a certain Aristodemus. This retrospect into the past removes the story, which is told with great vividness, from the actuality of every day and places it in the temporal remoteness which great poetry needs.

In this symposium, which does without flute-girls and buffoons, the power of Eros is celebrated in six speeches of incomparable variety and loftiness.

---

[1] 'Platonisches in Homer.' *Gymn.* 65, 1958, 73.

[2] Cf. A. BREUNIGER, *Parmenides und der frühe Pl.* Diss. Tüb. 1958 (typewr.).

[3] *Arete bei Platon und Aristoteles. Zum Wesen und zur Geschichte der platonischen Ontologie.* Abh. Akad. Heidelb. Phil.-hist. Kl. 1959/6.

[4] On this K. REIDEMEISTER, *Das exakte Denken der Griechen.* Hamb. 1949, 45.

[5] 59. 64 ff. The argument seems insoluble. A. WEDBERG, *Pl.'s Philosophy of Mathematics.* Stockholm 1955, and G. MARTIN, *Klassische Ontologie der Zahl.* Cologne 1956, side with ROSS; opposing him is E. M. MANASSE, *Philos. Rundschau.* Beih. 2, 1961, 96, 149.

[6] O. APELT, *Das Gastmahl. Mit griech. Text neubearbeitet von* A. CAPELLE. Bibl. survey by P. WILPERT, 2nd ed. Hamb. 1960 (*Philos. Bibl.* 81).

Phaedrus' speech sticks to the conventional pattern with its wealth of quotations from the poets; Pausanias adopts the manner of sophistical rhetoric to defend the love of boys in the meaning of the ancient aristocratic ideal; the physician Eryximachus singles out the scholar, especially the natural philosopher; Aristophanes follows with a brilliant speech which forms the first climax with its myth of the ball-shaped people who have been cut in halves and are longing to be made whole again. Agathon the host is next with an encomium decorated with Gorgianic tinsel; his speech serves as an interlude between those of Aristophanes and Socrates. Socrates reveals Eros as a daemon between god and man and interprets it as the desire to ensure lasting possession of the beautiful by creative activity in the realm of beauty. But significantly his words are at the same time lifted up above the Socratic sphere; it is not his own thought which he relates, but a conversation in which the seer Diotima[1] disclosed to him the nature of Eros. He uses the myth, his method of question and answer and finally the language of the mysteries not to ascend to the final peak, but to embrace it with a glance. As in the initiation of the mystics, the way leads in steps from corporeal to spiritual beauty, and in a final ascent to the beauty of knowledge in the realm of pure intellectual striving. From this point the everlasting, the absolute beautiful, beauty itself, can be perceived in one blessed moment (ἐξαίφνης, reminiscent of the kindling spark in the *Seventh Letter*). At the conclusion of Socrates' speech Alcibiades, drunk, bursts in on the symposium and depicts Socrates as the great man filled with Eros who can generate beauty in the soul of others through the beauty of the soul which rests within himself like the gold image of a god in a Silenus-shaped shrine.

The *Phaedo*[2] is also a narrative, this time an eye-witness report of Socrates' last hours. We are told that Plato was ill and therefore absent (59 b); the implication is obviously that we are not to expect a factual report but a philosophical fiction. The *Phaedo* is a dialogue *On the Soul*, which is the subtitle in the manuscripts. The talk, which unites Socrates with his friends for the last time, revolves round the proof of the soul's immortality. Two lines of argument are followed in which the doctrine of anamnesis and the association of the soul with the world of imperishable ideas play the major role. The objections of Simmias and Cebes, two Pythagoreans who used to be Philolaus' students, create a pause. In the third and last line of argumentation Socrates reaches far into the past to discuss in the passage which occupied us previously (p. 497) his development, which is really the development of Plato up to the theory of ideas. And this theory also gives decisive support to the third proof with the notion that the soul, which has a share in the idea of life, could not absorb that of death. The final

---

[1] On her historical authenticity: W. KRANZ, 'Diotima von Mantineia', *Herm.* 61, 1926, 437; cf. *Die Antike* 2, 1926, 320. H. KOLLER, 'Die Komposition des plat. Symp.'. *Diss.* Zürich 1948, thinks that the Diotima speech is the primary element of the *Symposium*; one can agree with this conception of the whole without having to think of a stratified growth.

[2] F. DIRLMEIER, bilingual ed., Munich 1949; 2nd ed. 1959. R. HACKFORTH, Pl.'s *Phaedo* (*surv. and comm.*). Cambr. 1955. Repr. New York 1960. R. S. BLUCK, Pl.'s *Phaedo*. Transl. with *Intro., Notes and Appendices*. Lond. 1955. NILO CASINI, *Il Fedone*. Florence 1958 (with comm.). W. J. VERDENIUS, 'Notes on Pl.'s Phaedo'. *Mnem.* 4, 11, 1958, 193.

climax of the discourse is another great eschatological myth. Outlining an unusual, but very graphic, global geography he argues that we humans live in the non-real world in large cave dwellings at the bottom of the air-sea; he then proceeds to tell the story of the fate of the soul before the judgment in the other world. In the *Phaedo* elements of Orphic and Pythagorean mysticism are closely interwoven with the dialectical struggle for positive knowledge. The enduring influence of the work, however, rests on the depth of feeling with which Plato has moulded into a unity the death of the sage and his unshakable belief in the immortality of the soul.

We date the completion of the work which represents the climax of Plato's creativity, the *Republic*,[1] in 347; various references place it between the *Symposium* and the *Phaedo* on the one hand, and the *Theaetetus* on the other; Plato himself (540 a) states that the philosopher only reaches his goal, the vision of the idea of the good, at the age of fifty. A construction like this presupposes a long time of growth. In the *Republic* all the impulses and themes of Platonic philosophy are united into one whole, and blended with such artistry that a short sketch can only trace the most important outlines of the structure.

The first book differs conspicuously from the following nine (although the division into ten books is not Plato's own); it performs the function of a vestibule, through which we are led into the actual realm of the problems. The whole work is presented as a single narrative by Socrates; nothing transpires about the place where the story is told or about the audience. At the day of the Bendis celebrations in Piraeus Socrates enters the house of the well-to-do Cephalus, whose old age is comforted by the consciousness that he has never cheated or lied to any one, so that he is able to undertake the journey to another world with an easy mind. The confession of the old man from which a thread runs to the final eschatological myth, provokes a discussion among the younger ones about the nature of justice. After several attempts to find a definition have failed Thrasymachus, whom we met earlier (p. 357) as an historical personality, introduces a sharper note into the conversation. Like Callicles in the *Gorgias*, he passionately argues the right of the stronger against the mass and their laws in the most extreme manner of the sophists. The similarity of this first book with the early aporetic dialogues is unmistakable and there were many supporters for the hypothesis that Plato had fitted an early dialogue about justice, called *Thrasymachus*, into the great work. It would no doubt have been an unfinished dialogue, but could have been an unused draft; a conscious return to the early manner[2] cannot be excluded as such, but the results of linguistic statistics favour an early date.[3]

[1] The transl. by K. VRETZKA, *Reclam*, 1958 offers good explanatory notes and bibl. For R. RUFENER'S transl. *v. inf.* in the bibl.

[2] F. DORNSEIFF, *Herm.* 76, 1941, 11; cf. JAEGER 2, 150. H.-J. KRÄMER, *Abh. Akad. Heidelb. Phil.-hist. Kl.* 1959/6, 42 determinedly argues in favour of an early date of a dialogue *Thrasymachus* on a basis of linguistical statistics.

[3] H. V. ARNIM, *Sitzber. Akad. Wien. Phil.-hist. Kl.* 169/3, 1912, 223. 230 ff. FRIEDLÄNDER too, and recently GAISER and KRÄMER firmly favour an early dialogue *Thrasymachus*.

In the first part of Book 2 the speeches of Glaucus and Adeimantus, Plato's two brothers, who henceforth dominate the conversation together with Socrates, lead to a precise wording of the problem. From the nature of justice and injustice the precedence of the former as the true blessing which brings happiness for itself by its very nature, should be proved. At this stage Socrates suggests (368 d) that the problem should be dealt with not within the context of individual life, but within the larger one of the state, which to Plato means the city-state. So the subject of the next part, including Book 4, is the conceptual experiment of developing a city from its primitive beginnings and of exploring in the course of its growth the place and role of justice in it. Although this theoretical political structure with its new, broadly planned establishment of an absolute order of values is in the sharpest possible contrast to the sophists' notions, it is founded on this movement in its non-historical rationale. It is not without its predecessors either; two of these can be mentioned:[1] Hippodamus of Miletus, who worked as an architect in Piraeus under Pericles, and Phaleas of Chalcedon, who in 400 formulated a plan demanding equality of property and education as well as nationalization of industry.

In the conception of the Platonic state the guardian class, which provides the rulers, is placed in the foreground. From the very beginning the central problem is that of education, which alone can offer to Plato the possibility of moulding the Greek notion of royalty as the harmony of power and justice (Solon 24, 16 D. Aeschylus fr. 381 N.) into a political structure in conformity with his theory of ideas. The third class, that of the employed, fades into the background behind the two classes of rulers and guardians; it is merely the object of statesmanship, and Plato has often been reproached for being destitute of social feeling because he did not care how the many lived. But he stated categorically in prominent places in his work (420 b. 466 a. 519 e) that his whole plan purposes to ensure to all parts of this state the highest happiness attainable for them. At this juncture we should also consider the unfair rashness with which in recent times Plato's designs have been abruptly made the equivalent of the abuses of totalitarian systems and have been condemned through a distorting transference into present-day conditions.[2] It is an irresponsible act of injustice

[1] WILH. NESTLE, Vom Mythos zum Logos. Stuttg. 1940, 492.

[2] The attacks on Plato were begun by J. DEWEY, Reconstruction in Philosophy, 1920 and The Quest for Certainty, 1929. They were continued by W. FITE, The Platonic Legend, 1934 and particularly K. R. POPPER, The Open Society. Lond. 1945, Germ. ed. Der Zauber Platons. Die offene Gesellschaft und ihre Feinde I. Bern 1957. R. H. S. CROSSMAN, Plato to-day. Lond. 1957; 2nd rev. ed. New York 1959 takes the same line. Profound refutation of Popper by R. B. LEVINSON, In Defence of Plato. Cambr. Mass. 1953. Also J. WILD, Pl.'s Modern Enemies and the Theory of Natural Law. Chicago 1953, although he reads teleological themes into Plato's notions of the physis. Considered opinions in these matters in E. M. MANASSE, Bücher über Pl. Philos. Rundschau. Beih. 2. Tübingen 1961, 162. F. M. CORNFORD, The Republic of Plato. New York 1954 (first pr. 1941), a transl. with introd. and comm., is still important for the criticism of the Republic. Also N. R. MURPHY, The Interpretation of Pl.'s Republic, Oxf. 1951 who claims that Plato's ethics and politics are in touch with reality. J. LUCCIONI, La Pensée politique de Pl. Paris 1958. R. W. HALL, 'Justice and the Individual in the Republic'. Phronesis 4, 1959, 149. T. A. SINCLAIR, A History of Greek Political Thought. Lond. 1952. W. C. GREENE, Harv. Stud. 61, 1953, 39.

to claim, as does W. Fite, that Plato's designs grew out of the ideology of a leisure class which held the masses in contempt. There is not a single line in Plato which describes the struggle for power as worthwhile for the sake of individual profit or the advantage of a specific social class; on the contrary, such aspirations are wholly rejected in the chapter on the tyrant. Plato has taken sufficient care to ensure that there can be no doubt about the goal of his ideal state, to lead people to the life which suits them and so to happiness by fitting them into a cosmos based on morality, i.e. on reason. It is equally clear that the three classes are not castes with rigid demarcations; they describe the place allotted to the individual on the ground of his abilities. F. M. Cornford[1] has aptly observed that Socrates began with the moral reform of the individual; the final aim of his reform must be a community consisting of such converts. Plato, on the other hand, takes into account the individual talents as facts and makes the best of them by fitting them into a permanent structure. One point is admittedly correct, but here we can touch upon it only briefly: Plato's ideal state, which is wholly pervaded by the idea of the good, which exists for the true happiness of its citizens and demands the greatest sacrifices from its rulers for the interests of others, is conceived for the development of human values in each of its members; but he cannot attain his high purpose without overstepping in various places the boundary which separates beneficial means from suffocating coercion. Here the inner law of politics is revealed as a sinister reality and Plato sensed this when he repeatedly laid stress on education and persuasion to prevent harsh compulsion. There is another difficulty connected with what has just been said, a difficulty which Plato's ideal state can avoid no more than any other. His conception is meant to be final, remaining permanently unchanged. But it cannot withstand the dynamic power of the constant stream of life and is bound to remain a utopia through its very claim to permanence. But in spite of all these objections the result which Cornford found in his commentaries still holds good: Plato's analysis proved for all times that a political system which aims at amassing riches or the gaining of more power is incompatible with one which aims at lofty ideals. Perhaps the sentiment voiced so often that politics is a dirty business is actually less close to reality than anything that Plato has written in his *Republic*; though of course it boils down to what one means by truth.

This design for a state starts off as a conceptual experiment to find justice, but gains more and more a life of its own; although Plato does not present it as a concrete proposal for an historical situation, he nevertheless leaves open the idea that it might possibly be realized, even if he only mentions it in a marginal note and stresses the difficulty (499 c d et al.).

The tripartite division of the state in classes is paralleled with the three parts of the soul in Platonic psychology. Then Plato allots here and there to each part its suitable virtue, so that the following system is the result:

rulers	intelligence	wisdom
ἄρχοντες	λογιστικόν	σοφία

[1] *The Unwritten Philosophy and Other Essays.* Cambr. 1950, 59.

guardians	high spirits	courage
φύλακες	θυμοειδές	ἀνδρεία
workers	desire	moderation
δημιουργοί	ἐπιθυμητικόν	σωφροσύνη

Now the place of the fourth cardinal virtue, justice, has been found. When things are in their proper order, it pervades the whole, since it allots to each part its correct place and binds together the whole with its harmony. Jaeger[1] showed that this picture of an order based on everyone doing his duty within his limits (τὰ ἑαυτοῦ πράττειν) originated in the medical notion of health being an equilibrium.

Book 5 develops the conditions of life necessary for the guardian class (not the workers); for these Plato takes the exclusion of private ownership a step further to the extreme of making wives and children common property. The complete equality of men and women in their work for the state was for Plato's time also a rationalistic hyperbole, which, by the way, is quietly withdrawn in the Laws (781 a).

In this Book 5, almost exactly in the centre of the whole work, there occurs the phrase which also forms the intellectual centre of the whole: a change for the good can only come about in politics when the philosophers seize power or when the rulers become philosophers. The same phrase made its appearance in the Seventh Letter (326 a) as an early statement of faith after his alienation from the state of Athens. The work which began as a quest for justice and was carried on as an attempt to build up a state, passes into the realm of pure philosophy as a matter of course without relinquishing any of the previous themes. Up to the end of Book 7 the subject is chiefly the nature and the education of the men who, as philosophers, are to rule in the ideal state; the philosophy meant is Platonic philosophy, and we have moved into the realm of the doctrine of true being. The rulers, who come from the guardian class, and are sometimes called guardians as well, have to undergo a long period of training. The old question of 'talent or education' is solved according to the meaning of these two factors. Those who show the greatest aptitude pass through a long course of study in arithmetic and geometry to which the newly created subject of solid geometry is added; they also study astronomy and harmonics, and the climax of the course is pure dialectic. Along the way another stricter selection takes place among the thirty-year-old which singles out the most suitable candidates for the final part of the course; it is only at the age of fifty that the final goal is attained with the vision of the idea of the good. In the light of this last and highest understanding the men who have been educated in this way will rule the true state.

In this part three successive sections are especially important for the development of the theory of ideas. Towards the end of Book 6 Plato compares the idea of the good as the source of spiritual existence, imparting truth to intelligible objects and the possibility of comprehending them to him who perceives

[1] 3. 48 and Eranos 44, 1946, 123, where also the medical origin of the expression θυμοειδές is explained.

them, with the sun which causes things to exist in the world of the visible, but creates for us the condition in which we see them with its light.[1] Similarly the idea of the good towers above all the other ideas in a way which assigns to it a place above the cosmos of ideas as the actual principle of being. This anticipates Neoplatonism in an essential point;[2] it is also obvious to equate the idea of the good with God.[3] This is followed up by the symbolization of the steps of perception with a line which is divided into two parts, representing the realm of the visible and that of the intellectual. Each part is again bisected in proportion to the main sections, so that now four steps are marked out: illusion, based on shadows and images (εἰκασία), belief in direct physical perception (πίστις), the processes of reason based on visible shapes (διάνοια, e.g. geometry) and as the final step insight into the world of the absolute (νόησις) achieved through dialectic. At the beginning of Book 7 follows the cave-simile, a splendid parable of man rising in his perception to the truth of being, which exerted a powerful influence in the ancient world and beyond it. The process can be divided into five steps,[4] the first four of which are obviously parallel to the degrees of perception mentioned just now. The people chained up in the cave with their backs towards the exit see only the shadows thrown on the wall by the objects carried past outside; they are imprisoned in the realm of illusion, of δόξα. When they have been set free of their bonds they are allowed to see the things themselves by the light of a fire, and also the fire itself. When they have climbed out of the cave, they stand in the bright daylight and see the things in sunlight. After much toil this third step is followed by the vision of this light itself, which means the idea of the good as the symbol of the highest. On the fifth step they return to the cave as the enlightened to influence others with their knowledge. This return is a harsh duty; it corresponds with the ethical necessity which forces the philosopher away from the happiness of the *vita contemplativa* to the *vita activa* of political life. These two notions were rigorously separated in the thought of the 5th century, but with Plato they enter into a new combination of a nature peculiarly their own.

Books 8 and 9 describe how the ideal form of society upheld by justice degenerates in a descending line via timocracy, oligarchy and democracy to tyranny. The parallel between the state and the individual soul is also continued in this description of decay; it shows a great depth of historical and psychological understanding.

The 10th Book[5] has often been taken for a supplement of some kind in which

---

[1] K. SCHMITZ-MOORMANN, *Die Ideenlehre Pl.'s im Lichte des Sonnengleichnisses des 6. Buches des Staates*. Diss. Munich 1957, Münster 1959.

[2] HERTER (*v.* p. 509, n. 3) with bibl. H. DÖRRIE, *Philos. Rundschau* 3, 1955, 20, about PH. MERLAN, *From Platonism to Neoplatonism*. The Hague 1953.

[3] Opposing this ROSS (*v. inf.*) 43. 235, otherwise JAEGER 3, 8 and W. J. VERDENIUS, 'Pl.'s Gottesbegriff' in *La Notion du divin*. Vandœuvres-Geneva 1954, 273.

[4] Cf. E. M. MANASSE, *Philos. Rundschau*. 5. Jahrg. 1. Beih. Tüb. 1957, 23 about M. HEIDEGGER, *Platons Lehre von der Wahrheit*, Bern 1947. M. ZEPF, *Der Mensch in der Hohle und das Pantheon*. Gymn. 65, 1958, 355.

[5] J. FERGUSON, *Plato's Republic*, Book 10. Lond. 1957.

Plato wished to add various afterthoughts. This may apply up to the splendid ending which crowns the work. An important section is the one in which the poetic criticism of the end of Book 2 and the beginning of Book 3 is resumed and placed on a firm foundation. Here we find the puzzling devaluation of art as a mere imitation of the objects of the physical world which themselves already imitate the ideas; we also find here the renunciation of the national poetry as posing a threat to the correct conditions for the mind through a stimulation of the passions. One thing is certain in Plato's complex and by no means homogeneous attitude to art:[1] the struggle between the artist and the philosopher took place in Plato's own breast. When we read (608 a) how hard Plato fights against Homer's spell, we will understand the inflexibility of his judgment as a measure of the trouble with which this thinker, himself a gifted poet, wrested it from himself.

The ending is formed by the third of Plato's great myths of the other world,[2] the narrative of the Armenian Er about the fate of the soul which wanders through births and shares in the decision of its density through the choice of its future life. Here it is necessary to put an extremely difficult question which also applies to other parts of Plato's work, such as the curious speculation on numbers in Book 8 of the *Republic* (546 b): What elements of his work came to Plato from the Orient? The agency of contemporaries such as Eudoxus of Cnidos is thought of in this connection; there is also mention of a Chaldean among the visitors to the Academy (*Ind. Acad.* p. 13 M.). In antiquity the supposition of such connections led to the invention of Plato's travels to the East; more recently it has become the subject of lively discussions[3] which still continue. This much can be stated that for individual elements which appear so alien in the work as the numerical speculation, origin from the Orient is very likely, but that the constitutive elements of the Platonic doctrine are entirely of Greek origin.

Some dialogues follow which form a closer group through the stronger stress upon dialectic.[4] The *Parmenides*[5] brings the grey-haired Eleatic and Zeno

---

[1] H. GUNDERT, 'Enthusiasmus und Logos bei Pl.'. *Lexis* 2, 1949, 34. P.-M. SCHUL, *Pl. et l'art de son temps (arts plastiques)*. 2nd ed. Paris 1952. B. SCHWEITZER, *Pl. und die bildende Kunst der Griechen*. Tüb. 1953. R. C. LODGE, *Pl.'s Theory of Art*. Lond. 1953. E. HUBER-ABRAHAMOWICZ, *Das Problem der Kunst bei Pl.* Winterthur 1954. P. VICAIRE, *Platon. Critique littéraire*. Paris 1960. L. RICHTER, *Zur Wissenschaftslehre von der Musik bei Pl. und Aristoteles*. Berl. 1960 (D. Akad. Schr. d. Sekt. f. Altertumsw. 23).

[2] K. REINHARDT, *Pl.'s Mythen*. Bonn 1927.

[3] J. KERSCHENSTEINER (cf. p. 508, n. 1) with excellent bibl. A.-J. FESTUGIÈRE, 'Pl. et l'Orient', *Rev. Phil.* 21, 1947, 1. W. J. W. KOSTER, *Le Mythe de Pl., de Zarathoustra et des Chaldéens*. Leiden 1951. W. BRANDENSTEIN, 'Iranische Einflüsse bei Pl.'. *Miscellanea G. Galbiati* 3, 1951, 83. SARTON (*v. inf.*), 435.

[4] On the change of meaning of 'dialectic'. A. WENZL, *Sitzb. Bayer. Akad. Phil.-hist. Kl.* 1959/8, 9.

[5] For these and the following dialogues in add. to the works mentioned in GIGON'S bibl. esp. ROSS (*v. inf.*). On *Parm.* and *Soph.*, with a different opinion: F. M. CORNFORD, *Pl. and Parmenides*. 3rd ed. Lond. 1951, repr. New York 1957; survey and comm. CORNFORD is of the opinion that the Platonic Parmenides, in contrast to the historical thinker, renewed the Pythagorean doctrine of evolution which led from unity to the plurality of observable objects. On this dialogue also: W. F. LYNCH, *An Approach to the Metaphysics of Plato through*

into conversation with Socrates as a young man; the elaborate disguise of the tale which retells a story told some time before underlines its fictitious nature once more. The dialogue is extremely difficult and is interpreted in various conflicting ways; its first part consists of a criticism of the theory of ideas by Parmenides, which is offered *inter alia* regarding the formulations of the 'participation' of physical objects in the ideas. The opinion is probably correct that Plato here attempted to face the difficulties in his doctrine which had occurred to himself and others. The second part with its complex and often vulnerable argumentation leads to a dialectical wrestling-match which is supposed to train the faculties to overcome the problems shown earlier. The most important problem of this part is the question how much of Plato's ontology looms up behind the eight hypotheses of the One. The answer may be that at the back of these attempts with their contradictory results there is Plato's basic dualism of unity and plurality which allows the One to develop into many other shapes and in this way promotes this One to the true being.[1]

The *Theaetetus* contains an important chapter of Plato's theory of knowledge. It is characteristic of Plato's high estimation of mathematics[2] as preparatory schooling for aspiring dialecticians on their path to true knowledge that the young Theaetetus appears here as Socrates' partner in the conversation together with his teacher Theodorus of Cyrene. Theaetetus is believed to have been the founder of solid geometry and the doctrine of the five regular solids; in 369 he fell, fighting bravely, in the war against the Thebans and his death was a severe loss to the Academy. The dialogue which preserves his memory seeks the nature and the categories of knowledge. The laborious separation of physical perception, true judgment and true knowledge does not lead to a valid definition of true knowledge, but it creates the epistemological prerequisites for the theory of ideas without any reference to its metaphysics. It is understandable that modern philosophers considered this very work to be important for the principles involved. The so-called 'Apology of Protagoras' is an important passage since it affords the possibility of a proper understanding of the doctrine of this sophist.

In the *Phaedrus*[3] Plato's artistic powers once more reach their full height before they begin to diminish in the later dialogues. The conversation between

the *Parmenides*. Georgetown Univ. Pr. 1959. A. SPEISER, *Ein Parmenideskommentar. Studien zur plat. Dialektik.* 2nd rev. ed. Stuttg. 1959. E. A. WYLLER, *Pl.'s Parmenides in seinem Zusammenhang mit Symposion und Politeia. Interpretationen zur plat. Xenologie.* Oslo 1960. Cf. also W. BRÖCKER, *Gnom.* 30, 1958, 517.

[1] So argues with great confidence H. J. KRÄMER, *Arete bei Pl. u. Aristoteles. Abh. Akad. Heidelb. Phil.-hist. Kl.* 1959/6, 262.

[2] CH. UNGLER, *Pl. et la recherche mathématique de son époque.* Strasbourg 1948. A. WEDBERG, *Pl.'s Philosophy of Mathematics.* Stockholm 1955. G. MARTIN. *Klassische Ontologie der Zahl.* Cologne 1956.

[3] R. HACKFORTH, *Pl.'s Phaedrus* (surv. and comm.) Cambr. 1952; repr. New York 1960. With Span. transl.: LUIS GIL FERNANDEZ. Madrid 1957. W. J. VERDENIUS, 'Notes on Pl.'s Ph.'. *Mnem.* s. 4, 8, 1955, 265. Cf. GUNDERT (*v.* p. 531, n. 1). Model speeches: W. STEIDLE, *Herm.* 80, 1952, 258, 4. On late dating of the dialogue: O. REGENBOGEN, *Miscellanea Academica Berolinensia.* 2/1, 1950, 201.

Socrates and Phaedrus takes place under a mighty plane-tree which spreads its branches over a spring near a shrine to the Muses outside the city. It falls into two parts whose unity depends on their relation to rhetoric. The first part comprises three speeches on the subject of Eros. First of all Phaedrus declaims an oration of Lysias', which Socrates at once surpasses with one of his own. It is kept in the same tenor and depicts Eros as a disastrous madness. In the third speech, however, follows the palinode when Socrates, himself one who is filled with Eros, extols it as a divine madness which is very closely related to a prophetic, cathartic and poetical enthusiasm. Here Plato fashioned his picture of the soul's chariot with its two winged steeds controlled by the 'best part' of the soul. It urges them up into eternity when it is strong enough to control the impure part of the soul.

If one thread leads from the Eros speeches of the first part back to the *Symposium*, the second with its enquiry into the nature of true rhetoric points back to the *Gorgias*. Only the philosopher can be a true orator, since he knows the real nature of the things about which he speaks. As the path to knowledge leads through dialectic, it is the only means to make rhetoric into a true techne. The two basic elements of Platonic dialectic, the division of the notions (diaeresis), and the meaningful union of the separated parts (synagoge), are clearly detectable in the *Phaedrus*.

The characters in the *Theaetetus* agreed, before they parted, to meet again the next morning, thus preparing the stage for the *Sophistes* and the *Politicus*.[1] In addition to Socrates, Theodorus and Theaetetus, a stranger from Elea turns up who represents symbolically the closer tie with the Eleatic school. Even if Plato had to reject Parmenides' extreme ontological monism as well as the radical separation of the intelligible One from the world of growth, the Parmenidean conception of Being had a considerable share in the preparation of the theory of ideas. In the *Sophistes* Socrates' complete withdrawal is of great importance. His influence is still present, but it no longer stimulates the whole. The subject is the nature of the sophists and the heuristic method is the diaeresis[2] which already played a part in previous dialogues, but which now is given greater stress. The problem of the relation between the individual ideas and the possibility of

---

[1] F. M. CORNFORD, *Plato's Theory of Knowledge. The Theaetetus and the Sophist of Pl. Translated with a Running Commentary*. Lond. 1935, 4th impr. 1951. New York 1957 (Libr. of Lib. Arts. 100), assumes that the two dialogues are complementary. The *Sophist* gives the theory of ideas its place in cognition and allots to the realm of being the essence of the intellect which is in motion. E. M. MANASSE, *Pl.'s Sophistes und Politikos. Das Problem der Wahrheit*. Berlin 1937, on the relation of the two dialogues to one another and to the *Theaetetus*. J. B. SKEMP, *Pl.'s Statesman. A Translation of the Politicus of Pl. with Introductory Essays and Footnotes*. Lond. 1952, which gives the wholly uncertain date of 362/1 for this dialogue because, after refusing to support Dion's expedition, Plato could not have approved of violence as a means of saving the state. H. HERTER, 'Gott und die Welt bei Pl. Eine Studie zum Mythos des Politikos'. *Bonner Jahrb*. 158, 106.

[2] On the method of diaeresis KARSTEN FRIIS JOHANSEN. *Class. et Mediaev*. 18, 1957, 23. H. KOLLER, 'Die dihäretische Methode'. *Glotta* 39, 1960, 6. Attempts to connect this method with Democritus' atomism are still doubtful; cf. J. STENZEL, 'Platon und Demokritos' in *Kl. Schr. zur griech. Philosophie*. Darmstadt 1956.

bringing them into a system which occupied the older Plato especially is also brought into relief.

The *Politicus*, which also uses diaeresis and gives an account of its methodology, concerns the nature of the statesman. Once again Plato uses a myth with a picture of the development of mankind to point out a prerequisite of all rulers. This ideal condition is fulfilled in the true statesman who possesses true knowledge and is of much greater importance than any code of law. In the *Republic* such a code also becomes superfluous through the proper education of the rulers. It has repeatedly been claimed that Plato was thinking of Dion in this sketch of the principles of the just politician, and the possibility cannot be denied. The *Sophistes* (217 a) announces a definition of the sophist, the politician and the philosopher, but the last definition is not given. There has been much puzzlement why Plato did not write a separate dialogue *Philosophus*, but the most likely explanation is that he was never serious about his promise.[1]

The formulation of the problem of the *Philebus*[2] stresses an entirely ethical matter: is pleasure or perception the highest goal which should be the object of our lives? And it turns out that to live the good life neither the one nor the other is adequate, but that a mixture of the two is needed. The subject, however, is dealt with entirely on the plane of ontological problems. Pleasure and perception as such are each divided into a plurality, and the elaboration of the notion leads to an extensive use of diaeresis. At the same time the basic problem of the theory of ideas emerges once more with the question of how the oneness of the idea can be reconciled with the plurality of the appearance of the things which share in it. The *Philebus* gives evidence of being a late work by the demand that in the diaeretic search for the structure of the world the number of the members obtained through division should at all times be taken into account. By the stress on this element the dialogue points to the work of Plato's old age which had the greatest influence in later periods, the *Timaeus*.[3]

This dialogue was conceived as the first of a trilogy which was to be continued with the *Critias*, which remained unfinished, and a *Hermocrates*, which was not committed to paper. As a whole it was meant to give a history of the world from the genesis of the cosmos up to the development and degeneration of political life, as well as a view of the restoration of the latter. At the beginning of the *Timaeus*, which owes its title to the main speaker, the Pythagorean

---

[1] So criticizes P. FRIEDLÄNDER, *Platon*. 2nd ed. vol. 3. Berl. 1960, 261 with bibl. in n. 5. H. J. KRÄMER (*v.* p. 524, n. 3), 317, considers it possible to reconstruct the plan of the contents, but comes to the conclusion that Pl. could not write the dialogue, because his philosophizing would have come to a stop through it; bibl. on p. 247, 7.

[2] A. E. TAYLOR, *Pl.'s Philebus and Epinomis. Transl. and Introd.* Ed. by R. KLIBANSKY with G. CALOGERO and A. G. LLOYD. Lond. 1956. R. HACKFORTH, *Pl.'s Examination of Pleasure.* Cambr. 1945. Repr. New York 1960. H.-D. VOIGTLÄNDER, *Die Lust und das Gute bei Pl.* Diss. Frankf. 1959; Würzb. 1960. H. P. HARDING, 'Zum Text des plat. Philebos'. *Herm.* 88, 1960, 40.

[3] F. M. CORNFORD, *Plato's Cosmology. The Timaeus of Plato. Translated with a Running Commentary.* Lond. 1937; 4th impr. Lond. 1956. New York 1957 (*Libr. of Lib. Arts* 101). H. CHERNISS, 'The Relation of the Timaeus to Plato's Later Dialogues'. *Am. Journ. Phil.* 78, 1957, 225. CH. MUGLER, *La Physique de Platon. Éd. et comm.* 35. Paris 1960.

Timaeus of Locri, the Atlantis theme is broached which will be discussed with the *Critias*. The first main section is taken up with Timaeus' lecture on cosmogony in the form of a myth which is plausibly presented in its main features. In this late work the abrupt turn to cosmology is a new feature; so are the form and the role of the divine world architect, the demiurge. This creator is by no means a free agent; the eternal ideas stand above him and with these in view he shapes the visible things into a realm of order, the cosmos.[1] And so the old problem of the participation of the physical world in the ideas has found a mythical, personal solution. The cosmos has the most perfect form, the sphere, and is a great rational being filled and guided by the world spirit. It is most clearly shown as being controlled by a soul in the regular orbits of the constellations, which are a race of gods. Another new feature is the meaning of space which is for the first time seen as a universal notion, since it is the place of genesis.

In the second part of the dialogue the teleological explanation of the universe is followed up by a causal-mechanistic one. Apart from the existence of the ideas in accordance with which the demiurge directs the generation of things, the dark realm of ananke also plays a part in the genesis of the universe. There is, however, no question of a dualism such as that of the Iranian religion; reason largely succeeds in persuading ananke to submit to the best order (48 a), but one part remains unredeemed, necessarily resulting in imperfection and evil. In this section Plato explains the construction of the universe out of the four elements which is built up entirely mathematically. Theaetetus had evolved solid geometry and developed the doctrine of the five only possible regular solids. Four of these (the dodecahedron is reserved for the universe, 55 c) are used for the explanation of the structure of fire, air, water and earth from solids of this shape, whose surfaces break up into triangles; with these the smallest constructional forms have been found. Their combinations may change, so that transition from one element into another is possible. It has been thought that it was especially this notion which meant to take issue with Democritus,[2] but it has connections with the whole of the earlier natural philosophy, both through its dependence on and opposition to it. The third part depicts in a similar speculatively constructive way the physical and psychical structure of man.

No other dialogue has had an influence as lasting as this one.[3] Plato should not be censured for the fact that in later times each word of this myth was accepted as scientific fact. The first commentary, that by Crantor of Soloe (*c.* 300 B.C.)

---

[1] On this concept W. FRANZ, *Kosmos*. Bonn 1956. On Platonic religiosity with particular reference to the belief in constellations: A.-J. FESTUGIÈRE, *Personal Religion among the Greeks*. Univ. of Cal. Pr 1954, 45.

[2] Bibl. in LEISEGANG (*v. inf.*), 2509. Important is A. E. TAYLOR's *Timaeus comm.* Oxf. 1928. An outline of the advance of a new conception of the universe through physics is drawn by W. SCHADEWALDT, 'Das Welt-Modell der Griechen'. *Neue Rundschau* 68, 1957, 2nd vol., 1. Similarly P. FRIEDLÄNDER in the excursus 'Platon als Physiker' in vol. 1 of his *Platon* (2nd ed. 1954); but E. M. MANASSE, *Philos. Rundschau*. 5. Beih. 1, 1957, 15 warns against too rash analogies.

[3] Evidence in SARTON (*v. inf.*), 428; cf. also G. S. CLAGHORN, *Aristotle's Criticism of Pl.'s Timaeus*. The Hague 1954.

was followed by several others; we find parts of the dialogue in Cicero's translation and the one by Chalcidius (4th cent. A.D.)[1] was the only Platonic text known in the Middle Ages until the translation of the *Meno* and the *Phaedo* in the twelfth century. The Arabic translation which began in the ninth century was no less important than the Latin one.

The *Critias* remained unfinished, but the fragment was enough to give birth to a piece of silliness which cannot be rooted out.[2] A prehistoric Athens, conceived as the ideal state, is shown being tested in a severe struggle which it had to fight 9000 years ago against the powerful land of Atlantis which sank down under the ocean. The creator of this myth, which is as fanciful and allusive as his other ones, could have had no idea that thousands of years later Atlantis would be searched for with the same grim seriousness with which Odysseus' voyages are plotted on maps.

Plato no doubt postponed this and other work for the sake of the most extensive of his writings, the *Laws*.[3] Socrates no longer takes part in the conversation; he is actually excluded because the scene is laid in Crete. Three old men, one an Athenian who leads the conversation and who remains unnamed, the Cretan Clinias and the Spartan Megillus are walking from Cnossos to the mountain cave in which Minos received the laws from Zeus. The first three of the twelve books contain basic and preliminary considerations; in the fourth the construction of the imagined state is begun; it is the second which Plato built. A fundamental change has taken place compared with the *Republic* and the *Politicus*. In these dialogues the role of the laws faded into the background behind the hopes which Plato placed in the philosophically trained ruler, or a group of such men; now the stress has shifted. The rule should be in the hands of a young talented τύραννος (709 e), who must combine with a suitable legislator, so that the right constitution will be the outcome of this meeting of power and wisdom; the 'nocturnal council', which has to maintain the spirit of the law and with it the proper hierarchy of values, is comparable with the group of guardians who are the ruling class of the *Republic*; Plato states categorically that the sole ruler over all this is the law which the ruling classes also serve like slaves (715 d). Another difference in this connection is that the *Republic* also seeks happiness for all but that it trusts that this happiness will be provided by

---

[1] J. C. M. VAN WINDEN, *Calcidius on Matter. His Doctrine and Sources. A Chapter in the History of Platonism.* Leiden 1959.

[2] Cf. H. HERTER, 'Altes und Neues zu Pl.'s Krit.'. *Rhein. Mus.* 92, 1944, 236. LEISEGANG (v. *inf.*) 2512. P. FRIEDLÄNDER, *Platon.* 2nd ed., vol. 1, Berl. 1954, 213. 272; Vol. 3, Berl. 1960, 357. More recent bibl. in H. CHERNISS, *Lustrum* 4, 1959 (1960), 70.

[3] G. MÜLLER, *Studien zu den plat. Nomoi.* Zet. 3, 1951. In add. H. CHERNISS, *Gnom.* 25, 1953, 367. M. VANHOUTTE, *La Philosophie politique de Platon dans les 'Lois'.* Louvain 1954. O. GIGON, 'Das Einleitungsgespräch der Gesetze Pl.'s'. *Mus. Helv.* 11, 1954, 201. R. MUTH, 'Studien zu Pl.'s Nomoi'. *Wien. Stud.* 69, 1956, 140. F. SOLMSEN, 'Textprobleme im 10. Buch der Nomoi', *Stud. z. Textgesch. u. Textkritik.* Cologne 1959, 265. G. R. MORROW, *Pl.'s Cretan City. A Historical Interpretation of the Laws.* Princeton Un. Pr. 1960; id., 'The Nocturnal Council in Pl.'s Laws'. *Arch. f. Gesch. d. Philos.* 42, 1960, H. 3. H. GÖRGEMANNS, *Beiträge zur Interpretation von Pl.'s Nomoi.* Zet. 25, Munich 1960, with abundant bibl. and a good survey of the criticism of the *Laws* up to now.

the right leadership of those who have had the right education, and that it does not trouble about codified legal norms for the life of the third class. In the *Laws*, however, he develops an abundance of rules which in their great breadth embrace and control the population as a whole. In this work Plato has become more empirical, not with respect to its method, which remains theoretical and speculative, but in the choice of objects; it is more inclined toward the descriptive, a feature which could also be observed in the *Timaeus* in its description of the cosmos.

The part played by the theory of ideas has been reduced to such an extent that individual interpreters have claimed that it is wholly absent in the *Laws*.[1] This will not do, for the guardians of the law are enjoined to look up to the 'one idea' (965 c), which cannot be anything but that of the good, the primary source of all values.[2] But belief in God as the supreme ruler and in the manifestations of the divine in the constellations are prominent as a combination of philosophical and theological thought. In obvious antithesis to Protagoras, God is now called the measure of all things (716 c). In Book 10 a lengthy exhortation on the belief in God introduces legislation in religious matters which does not shun rigorous coercion. In this part Plato's pen was moved by passionate zeal for his faith.[3]

In spite of all disparity, the two great works about the state are tied together by the one basic feature of education which in the *Laws* is also considered as a great, if not the only, power. This is borne out by Books 1, 2 and 7 with their wide coverage of educational problems, and also by the preambles with which Plato wants to introduce his laws to convince the citizens of their justness and efficiency, as physicians do at a sickbed[4] so as to replace blind obedience by understanding. But this design is also open to the dangerous tension between the education of free people who accept order, and harsh compulsion.[5] Thus we read (942 a b) that no one may individually decide on the smallest step without reference to, and supervision of, his superior.

The *Laws* deviates so much from the rest of Plato's work and shows so much roughness in composition and detail that Fr. Ast (*Platons Leben und Schriften*, 1818) and E. Zeller (*Platonische Studien*, 1839) denied that they were Plato's. Zeller withdrew his opinion in his *Philosophy of the Greeks*, but the latest analysis of the work by G. Müller points entirely in this direction. At the opposite end

---

[1] H. KUHN, *Gnom*. 28, 1956, 337; continuation or modification of the theory of ideas in the late Plato is still an open problem.

[2] Cf. CHERNISS (*v. sup.*), 375.

[3] F. SOLMSEN, *Plato's Theology. Cornell Studies in Class. Phil.* 27. Ithaca 1942, observed in the later works a peak of religious feeling as a preparation for the road which only few can take to reach the highest goal, the idea of the good. O. REVERDIN, *La Religion de la cité platonicienne*. Paris 1945. A.-J. FESTUGIÈRE, *La Révélation d'Hermès Trismégiste. 2. Le Dieu cosmique*. Paris 1949, 132. 153. 219. W. JAEGER, *Aristoteles*. 2nd ed. Berl. 1955, 140 ff. stresses that the cosmology of the *Timaeus* and the religious belief in the constellations of the *Laws* were important starting-points for the Hellenistic cosmic religion.

[4] Cf. F. WEHRLI, 'Der Arztvergleich bei Pl.'. *Mus. Helv.* 8, 1951, 179.

[5] W. KNOCH, *Die Strafbestimmungen in Pl.'s Nomoi. Klass. Phil. Stud.* 23. Wiesbaden 1960. Bibl. on the arguments about Pl.'s conception of the state *v.* p. 527, n. 2.

we find Friedländer and Jaeger who attempt in their study to do justice to the truly Platonic elements and the richness of thought of the work.[1] Apart from a great deal else, to deny that the *Nomoi* is Plato's work means to impute to Aristotle, who quotes them as being Plato's (*Pol.* 1266 b 5. 1271 b 1, cf. 1264 b 26) an 'astonishing negligence'. That has in fact been done. E. M. Manasse[2] found the finest expression for the element which separates the *Laws* from Plato's other work and also connects it with them: 'The *Laws* are, more than Plato's other writings, the human work of a spirit which once was a divine flame'.

Diogenes Laertius (cf. Suidas sub φιλόσοφος) reports that Plato's secretary Philip of Opus published the work from the rough draft ('from the wax', as he puts it), divided it into twelve books and added the *Epinomis*[3] from his own works. This treatise serves as an appendix to the *Laws*; the elements of an astronomical theory have been further elaborated in it, plainly under the influence of Pythagoreanism. It is difficult to judge how much there is of Platonic legacy in this little work. For the *Laws*, however, the evidence referred to leaves open the possibility of editing, displacement and faulty combination of individual sections by the editor, which, together with the fact that the work is the product of Plato's old age, may account for many of the peculiarities. Yet Gigon is right[4] in demanding a modern commentary on the work as a prerequisite for the decision of these difficult problems.

In style the *Laws* also deviates from the early dialogues, completing a development evident in the later works. The enchanting freshness and conversational quality of Plato's phrasing, which conceals a very high degree of stylistic art, lapses into rigidity and artificiality. This difficult and little enjoyable style of his old age trifles with word order and elaborate interweaving, and its playing about with sound effects (assonance[5]) demonstrates the renunciation of the simple charm, the true Attic charis, which makes Plato one of the great classics of Greek prose.[6]

We previously (p. 514) encountered Plato's statement that his writings do not contain the whole of his doctrine. What he wrote after his return from Sicily must be seen against the background of the work of the Academy. It was the place where Plato sought to lead talented students along his road, until the spark flashed across and finally cognition was opened up. We know so little about the scholastic activity of the Academy in Plato's time that sometimes there has been a tendency to deny its scientific character. Such a scepticism is unfounded; the course of training prescribed for the guardians of the *Republic* may be transferred with some confidence to the work of the Academy. Individual personalities of the Platonic circle point to the great significance of mathematics for the schooling in dialectic which was based on it and without doubt

---

[1] M. VANHOUTTE, *La Philosophie politique de Platon dans les 'Lois'*. Louvain 1954 is important for the place of the *Laws* in Plato's whole œuvre.

[2] *Philos. Rundschau*. Beiheft 2, Tüb. 1961, 117.

[3] F. NOVOTNY, *Platonis Epinomis commentariis illustrata*. Prague 1960.

[4] Cf. p. 536, n. 3.   [5] J. D. DENNISTON, *Greek Prose Style*. Oxf. 1952, 132.

[6] P. STÖCKLEIN, *Wege zum späten Goethe*. Hamb. 1949, 211, compares Plato's late style with that of Goethe.

there is substantial truth in the anecdote that a notice over the entrance to the Academy read: 'No one shall enter who knows no geometry'.[1] We know furthermore that the diaeretic method which we discussed in connection with the later dialogues, played an important part in the quest for an ordered conception of the universe and in reaching definitions through the division of concepts of a higher order. This was so well known that the mockery of Middle Comedy was provoked by it.[2]

In the *Phaedrus* (275 c ff.) Plato himself did not rate the value of written information very high compared with the educative worth of conversation, and in the *Seventh Letter* he assures that he never and nowhere wrote about the essence of his doctrine. There is also one single but very important non-Platonic piece of information, Aristotle's reference to Plato's λεγόμενα ἄγραφα δόγματα (*Phys.* 209 b 15). In spite of the unequivocal language of these witnesses the interest in Plato's esoteric doctrine was hampered for a considerable time by Schleiermacher's verdict. In the introduction to his translation of Plato he denied the existence of a doctrine which the philosopher had not developed in his dialogues, but had reserved for oral instruction. In opposition to this there has been an increasing interest during the last few decades in research into those elements of Platonic doctrine which are not contained in the dialogues or are only hinted at. In Hans Joachim Krämer's[3] book, which aims at introducing a new period of this research, there is a comprehensive survey of the efforts to detect Plato's esoteric doctrine. A report about this must necessarily be provisional, for only an exhaustive exchange of opinions together with new enquiries will be able to decide how many of these revolutionary theses will be lasting.

The image of Plato, developed by Krämer, partially accepts and partially rejects Schleiermacher. On the one hand he assumes emphatically, in contrast to the latter, the existence of an esoteric doctrine, reserved for oral teaching at the Academy; on the other he follows Schleiermacher explicitly in his acceptance of an original unity of Platonic thought. This implies rejection of the school who think that they can detect Plato's intellectual development in his dialogues and use them as an internal biographical source.[4] We are in doubt here. Does not Krämer see Plato as too static, and is it not probable that a thinker of such

[1] On this type of 'KEEP OUT' notice O. WEINREICH, *Arch. f. Rel.-Wiss.* 18, 1915, 16. Bibl. on Plato's mathematics, *v.* p. 532, n. 2.

[2] Epicrates fr. 11 K. In add. the Diogenes anecdote in Diog. Laert. 6. 40. Bibl. on diaeresis *v.* p. 533, n. 2.

[3] *Arete bei Platon und Aristoteles. Zum Wesen und zur Geschichte der platonischen Ontologie.* Abh. Akad. Heidelb. Phil.-hist. Kl. 1959/6. A survey of the progress of research with extensive bibl. 381-386; P. WILPERT, *Zwei aristotelische Frühschriften über die Ideenlehre.* Regensburg 1949 is particularly worth singling out. In his three lectures, *The Riddle of the Early Academy*, Berkeley 1945, H. CHERNISS diametrically opposed the existence of an esoteric doctrine of Plato's. A prospective 2nd vol. of his work *Aristotle's Criticism of Plato and the Academy*, Baltimore 1944, is to occupy itself with the indirect evidence of Plato's philosophy and the nature of the ideal numbers.

[4] Founded by K. F. HERMANN, *Geschichte und System der platonischen Philosophie.* Heidelb. 1839.

an unheard-of dynamism should display fairly clear phases of his development? This, of course, in spite of the fact that certain conceptions were present from the very beginning, which should not be denied.

Another decisive factor for Krämer is his doubtlessly correct conviction that Plato's esoteric doctrine was not something mysteriously separated from the sphere of the dialogues, but formed a unity with them.

It is natural that everything that we know of Plato's lecture *On the Good* is of cardinal importance in the questions raised by Krämer. According to the tradition the doctrine propounded by Plato in his λόγοι περὶ τἀγαθοῦ was taken down in writing by several of his students.[1] The lists in Diogenes Laertius[2] prove that a treatise Περὶ τἀγαθοῦ was written by Aristotle, by Xenocrates and by Heraclides. The most extensive report about these lectures are found in the *Harmonics* of Aristoxenus of Tarentum (44. 5 M.) who reproduces what he had heard Aristotle tell. The lecture (ἀκρόασις) had been attended by hearers who had expected to learn something about human goods such as riches, health and power. But when the whole thing turned out to be mathematical, they had turned away. The cause of this pedagogical failure had been the lack of a previous explanation of the theme.

Krämer was able to prove that nothing in this report shows that such a lecture was something unique, and has formulated, in the face of the accepted dogma, the thesis that these λόγοι περὶ τἀγαθοῦ were neither limited to a single course nor were public, but were rather a typical occurrence in Plato's school. For this he has to call in the report in Themistius (*Or.* 21. 245 c), which was already done by others. It is of course possible that his is a mere embroidery upon Aristoxenus' report.[3] It had been the custom to consider this lecture as one held by Plato in his old age, but Krämer has made it clear that there is no evidence for this dating in the ancient sources. He accounts for this general late dating in his history of the research, which again stresses, in opposition to Schleiermacher, an esoteric doctrine of Plato's, but separates this from the bulk of the dialogues as his mature philosophy.

Through his rejection of long-standing opinions Krämer came to a picture of the Platonic doctrine which was greatly different; the lectures *On the Good* were neither a unique occurrence nor one which took place in Plato's old age. In general it is by far preferable to assume a series of didactic conversations than a complete doctrine (though it must be pointed out that the most reliable of the reports mentioned speaks of ἀκρόασις). According to Krämer the λόγοι περὶ τἀγαθοῦ are only another expression for an esoteric Platonic philosophy which had existed side by side with the dialogues, or rather had formed the background which often became visible in them. Long passages of the book are occupied

[1] Bibl. in HERTER (*v.* p. 554, n. 2), also ROSS (*v. inf.*), 216. P. WILPERT, *Zwei aristotelische Frühschriften über die Ideenlehre*. Regensburg 1949. Some information in Simplicius, *Phys.* 151, 10 D.; *De An.* 28, 7 Hayd. Philoponus, *Phys.* 521, 10, 14; *De An.* 75. 34 ff.

[2] 5, 22. 4, 13. 5, 87, to which are added for Aristotle the catalogues of Hesychius and Ptolemy, as well as several references in Alexander Aphr.; the passages in KRÄMER are 412, n. 61 f.

[3] Cf. KRÄMER 404, n. 43. 404–409.

with proof that from an early stage the dialogues pointed to the esoteric doctrine. Its essence and centre is, according to Krämer, the One, which is at the same time the Good, as the absolute basis of Being. So he fixes Plato more firmly in the tradition of Parmenides and in the number of thinkers concerned with the ἀρχή. But Plato went beyond Parmenides by opposing the principle of the One to another, that of the duality (ἀόριστος δυάς) of opposites (μέγα-μικρόν) and explained the universe in its plurality through the pervasion of the two principles. Since the One has both ontological and axiological meaning, the Platonic notion of arete is firmly rooted in it as well. But for the Plato of Krämer's interpretation the ideas do not form a primary part of Plato's ontology; they enter only subsequently between the One as the principle of Being and the separate, individually existing things, and thus constitute the communication between the principles.

It was necessary to sketch this new picture of Plato in a broad outline. Research will have many relevant questions to consider. Can the basic ontological doctrine of the One as the principle of Being really be traced back so far? To what extent can we be sure of the identity of the functions of the One and the idea of the Good? Does the cosmos of ideas really rate a relatively second place in Plato's ontology? How much proof can be found for connections between the dialogues and the doctrine of the One as the principle of Being? And finally, even if it is no longer imperative to seek Plato's mature doctrine in the lectures *On the Good*, does this deny that it is still possible, or even likely, to do so?

We mention here one of the most important pieces of evidence given by Aristotle, with which he contrasts the conception of the number of the ideas with an earlier phase of the theory of ideas (*Metaph.* 4. 1078 b 9). In a considerable number of passages in the *Metaphysics*[1] Aristotle concludes that Plato accepted, apart from the mathematical ones, a number of ideas which originated both in the One and in the Opposite (μέγα-μικρόν). This doctrine of the numbers of ideas has become the subject of a lively controversy in the recent phase of Platonic research. Harold Cherniss especially has opposed its importance, and has tried to explain away Aristotle's observations as a misinterpretation of the dialogues.[2] We may take it that this scepticism is going too far and that Krämer has proved that the observations mentioned provide important evidence for Plato's esoteric doctrine.[3] Now in the passage of the *Metaphysics* referred to above Aristotle attributes the numbers of ideas to a later phase of Plato's philosophy, while on the other hand he connects these numbers with the two principles of the One and the Opposite; it may therefore be seriously considered whether all this taken together does not refer to the later Plato.

Now, since it is obvious to assume that the sense of these numbers of the ideas was to make the order of the ideas intelligible, a second question is raised. Can

---

[1] Quoted by KRÄMER 250 f.

[2] So in *Aristotle's Criticism of Plato and the Academy* I. Baltimore 1944, and especially in *The Riddle of the Early Academy*. Berkeley 1945.

[3] Opposing CHERNISS'S scepticism also E. M. MANASSE, *Bücher über Platon. Philos. Rundschau.* Beih. 2, 1961, 90, who supposes a doctrine of Plato's old age.

any connections be established from this point with the method of building up conceptions, i.e. diaeresis, which plays an increasingly important role in the dialogues after the *Theaetetus* and which, as we know, played such an important part in the teaching at the Academy? Julius Stenzel most strongly stimulated the attempts at establishing a relationship between the doctrine of the numbers of the ideas and their origin on the one hand, and the diaeretic search for structure on the other.[1] It will, however, hardly be possible to come to another conclusion from the sum total of the endeavours in this field up to now than the one of Kurt v. Fritz[2] who observes that with the means at our disposal it is impossible to achieve any certainty regarding Plato's notion of the origin of the numbers of the ideas or of the way in which he associated them with the ideas. But this does not by any means imply that such an association did not actually exist.

The Academy drew large crowds. There is a story of a peasant who came from his fields to enrol after reading the *Gorgias*, of a Chaldean and even of a woman in men's clothing. More important than such anecdotes are some names which give us a picture of the circle round Plato. Some were the pioneers in mathematics, of whom we have already met Theaetetus with his great merit in the realm of solid geometry. But the most important entrant was Eudoxus of Cnidos[3] who arrived in 367 with a group of students. He had been taught mathematics by Archytas; as a young man he had studied some time under Plato, but then he set out to travel, finally going to Egypt where he remained for a long time. Next he opened a school at Cyzicus and after more years of travel came his sojourn at the Academy, after which he finally returned home. His influence on the development of astronomy was as great as his services in mathematics, in which his outstanding achievements were the theory of proportion, that of the golden section and the method of exhaustion, which was a significant advance toward the infinitesimal calculus. In astronomy he founded the doctrine of the concentric celestial spheres with the earth as the centre. Through the movement of these spheres, which spin round partially within one another, partially together with one another, he explained the orbits of the planets. In the realm of ethics he replaced the Platonic idea of the good with desire which is founded in the human physis, but which is characterized by its relation to the divine.[4]

In his commentary on Euclid's *Elements* Proclus supplies some meagre information about the contemporary mathematicians who were connected with the

[1] *Zahl und Gestalt bei Platon und Aristoteles.* Leipz. 1924; 2nd ed. 1933; repr. Darmstadt 1958. Other works by O. TÖPLITZ and STENZEL in KRÄMER 256, 26; also O. BECKER, *Zwei Untersuchungen zur antiken Logik.* Wiesbaden 1957.

[2] *Gnom.* 33, 1961, 7; esp. 12. More positively KRÄMER 434. 437.

[3] SARTON (*v. inf.*), 441. 447. *Gnom.* 24, 1952, 39. W. SCHADEWALDT, *Eud. v. Knidos und die Lehre vom unbewegten Beweger. Satura,* O. WEINREICH dargebracht. Baden-Baden 1952, 103.

[4] E. FRANK, 'Die Begründung der mathematischen Naturwissenschaften durch Eudoxos'. *Wissen, Wollen, Glauben. Ges. Aufsätze.* Zürich 1955, 134. F. DIRLMEIER, *Aristoteles, Nik. Eth.* Berl. 1956, 574, argues that Eudoxus is dependent on Plato for his basic notions. On the connection of the quest for pleasure with the divine cf. SCHADEWALDT, prev. note.

Academy. We only know the names of a Leodamas, Neoclides and one Leon, although we learn of the first that he was a student of Plato's. Menaechmus, who was trained by Eudoxus, formulated the theory of the conic sections[1] in connection with the ancient problem of the doubling of the cube. His brother Dinostratus also worked on the old basic problems, while Theudius of Magnesia made a handy summary of the elements of geometry, presumably for the benefit of the Academy. Elsewhere there is mention of the Platonic scholar Hermodorus; we know of him that his treatise Περὶ μαθημάτων dealt with astrology.

During the lifetime of its founder, the men who were to be his first and his second successor to the headship of the school were also members of the Academy. Speusippus, the son of Plato's sister Potone, led the Academy after the Master's death until about 339.[2] The selection of his nephew was not a happy choice; for Aristotle and Xenocrates it must have been the cause for turning their backs upon Athens. In the collection of letters of the Socratics a letter of Speusippus to Philip II is preserved which is now considered to be genuine.[3] Its writer supports the claims of the king of Macedon to Amphipolis and Chalcidice with painstaking argumentation. As to his further development of Plato's doctrine, it has been made likely by Ross[4] that various passages in Aristotle point to his stressing numbers as the true entities and a disavowal of the forms in the Platonic sense. If we follow Ross's interpretation of the references in Aristotle, the result is that Xenocrates, who succeeded to the headship of the Academy, simply equated number and form. This puritanical, but rather insignificant man, whose writings are listed by Diogenes Laertius in Book 4, led the Academy for 25 years. He adhered to the doctrines of Plato's old age, appears to be strongly influenced by Pythagoreanism and influenced later times particularly by his doctrine of the realm of demons between God and man. Of the tripartite divisions which he applied to all the provinces of his thought, the one of philosophy found its way into physics, logic and ethics.

Another of Plato's students was Heraclides from Heraclea on the Pontus.[5] Plato is even believed to have entrusted the direction of the Academy to him during his third Sicilian voyage. His further development carried this versatile and restless spirit to the Peripatos. Diogenes (5. 86. fr. 22 Wehrli) gives an extensive list of his writings, which he classifies into works on ethics, physics, grammar, the musical arts, rhetoric and history. A considerable part of these writings was in the form of dialogues. In connection with the Oriental relations of the Academy it is interesting that he wrote a *Zoroaster*. On the other hand

---

[1] Some information about his controversy about basic assumptions with Speusippus in Proclus, Eucl. p. 77, 15-79. 2 FRIEDLÄNDER.

[2] TH. MERLAN, 'Zur Biographie des Speusippus'. *Phil.* 103, 1959, 128.

[3] E. BICKERMANN and J. SYKUTRIS, *Speusippus' Brief an König Philipp.* Sitzb. Sächs. Ak. 80, 1928/3. Fragments: P. LANG, Diss. Bonn 1911. Important for Speusippus' place and with a new fragment is PH. MERLAN's above-mentioned book. Also H. DÖRRIE, *Philos. Rundschau.* 3, 1955, 15. – Xenocrates: R. HEINZE, *Xen.* Leipz. 1892.   [4] (*v. inf.*), 151.

[5] The fragments with comm.: F. WEHRLI, *Schule des Aristoteles VII. Herakleides Pontikos* Basel 1953.

Wehrli's rational treatment of the text (fr. 104-117) has been largely responsible for casting serious doubt on Heraclides' fame for anticipating in essential points the heliocentrical system of the early Hellenistic astronomer Aristarchus of Samos.

For the difficult problem of the Platonic tradition we proceed from the established fact that the medieval manuscripts (survey in BURNET's edition, further in O. IMMISCH, *Philol. Studien zu Pl.* 2. Leipzig 1903, most important in J. GEFFCKEN, *Gr. Lt.-Gesch.* 2, Heidelb. 1934, note p. 26) exhibit without exception the arrangement in tetralogies mentioned above (p. 511) This dates back to antiquity and is often erroneously connected with Thrasyllus, Tiberius' Court astrologer, who produced an edition of Plato, but who found the tetralogies ready-made. Varro (*De L.L.* 7, 37) presupposes them at any rate. The question of a considerably earlier date is connected with another of the oldest editions. WILAMOWITZ (*Platon*, 2, 325) assumed that at about the time of Arcesilaus or Lacydes as heads of the school, i.e. in the 3rd century B.C., the Academy collected in 9 tetralogies whatever was supposed to be Platonic at that time. G. JACHMANN has energetically denied such an authoritative edition by the Athenian Academy (*Der Platontext. Nachr. Akad. Gött. Phil.-hist. Kl.* 1941/11. Fachgr. 1 N.F. 4/7, 1942; cf. H. LANGERBECK, *Gnom.* 22, 1950, 375). He derives our tradition from an ancient recension with variants whose author was Aristophanes of Byzantium or at least some competent Alexandrian. Recourse to an older, scholarly edition was no longer open to him; on the contrary, the only sources left to him were the strongly interpolated recensions which uncritical editors had produced for the book trade. On the other hand E. BICKEL (*Rhein. Mus.* 92, 1943, 94; id.: 'Geschichte und Recensio des Platontextes', ibid. p. 97) and M. POHLENZ (*Nachr. Akad. Gött. Phil.-hist. Kl.* 1952/5, 99, 7) have pointed out that the suggestions of Aristophanes of Byzantium (Diog. Laert. 3. 61) for a trilogical arrangement presupposes the tetralogical one. And so an edition by the Academy arranged in tetralogies is still probable; it admitted a great deal that was spurious and can certainly not have been the product of critical textual treatment. This assumption is quite compatible with the date of the Alexandrian editions, though we cannot demarcate Aristophanes' share. There is also evidence for an edition by Dercyllidas (2nd/1st century B.C.).

The theory has been abandoned now that one single copy, salvaged by the Byzantines, is the archetype of all our manuscripts. The indirect tradition (Neoplatonists, Stobaeus, etc.) as well as the papyri (nos. 1082-1117 P.); also *Pap. Soc. It.* 14, 1957, nr. 1392 f. Cf. also O. VINZENT, *Textkrit. Untersuchungen der Phaidros-Papyri.* Diss. Saarbrücken 1962, p. 153 on the Platonic tradition and bibl. attest so many readings of our manuscripts as ancient that acceptance of one single archetype with variant readings is inadmissible. JACHMANN has correctly pointed out (loc. cit.) that the task of the recension of our Platonic tradition is not yet complete. He has also emphatically brought it to our notice to what a great extent, especially in these texts, distortions and above all additions have to be taken into account. Apart from the diaskeuasts for the book trade the intrusion of interpreting glosses will have to be reckoned on. In view of this situation any hope of being able to reach Plato's original wording in all cases is very faint indeed. The first task is to establish what has survived; restoration of the original will by no means be always possible.

Editions and bibl. in o. GIGON, *Platon. Bibliogr. Einführungen in das Studium d. Philos.* 12. Bern 1950. A concise summary by D. ROSS in *Fifty Years of Class. Scholarship.* Oxf. 1954, 134. Abundant bibl. data in the works of CAMP and CANART mentioned below, and in FRIEDLÄNDER. Complete bibl. for 1950–57 in H. CHERNISS, *Lustrum* 4, 1960, 5 and 5, 1961, 323. E. M. MANASSE, 'Bücher über Pl. Werke in deutscher Sprache'. *Philos. Rundschau.* Beih. 1, 1957 and 'Bücher über Pl. Werke in englischer Sprache'. Ibid. Beih. 2, 1961 (with an excellent introduction on research in Britain from GROTE and JOWETT to TAYLOR and SHOREY) provides information on recent works in book form with profound and considered criticism.

Under the conditions indicated above the edition of J. BURNET, 5 vols. Oxf. 1899–1906 is still the standard work. In addition there is an edition in the *Coll. des Un. de Fr.*, 13 vols., 1920, reprinted many times up to 1961, by a staff of French scholars. The scholia appear partly in the 6th vol. of the ed. of C. F. HERMANN, Leipz. 1853. W. C. GREENE, *Scholia Platonica.* Haverford 1938. The editions of the commentaries of Proclus, Damascius, Hermias, Olympiodorus and Chalcidius in GIGON loc. cit., 15. In add. P. LOUIS, *Albinos Épitomé.* Paris 1945. L. G. WESTERINK, *Ausgaben der Kommentare des Proklos und Olympiodoros zum 1. Alkibiades.* Amsterdam 1956. Id., *Damascius, Lectures on Philebus wrongly attributed to Olympiodorus.* Amsterdam 1959 (with trans. and comm.). F. AST's *Lexicon Platonicum* (3 vols., Leipz. 1835–38), reprinted Bonn 1956 may be replaced by one in preparation in Hinterzarten. *Index Graecitatis Platon.* by T. MITCHELL, 2 vols., Oxf. 1852. – In addition to the translations mentioned by GIGON, op. cit., 11 and apart from those referred to in connection with the individual dialogues recent publications are: R. RUFENER, *Die Werke des Aufstiegs* with an introduction by G. Krüger. Zürich 1948; id.: *Der Staat.* Zürich 1950. E. HOWALD, *Die echten Briefe.* Zürich 1951 (Gr. and Germ.). R. RUFENER, *Meisterdialoge,* with an introduction by O. GIGON. Zürich 1958; by the latter, *Frühdialoge.* Zürich 1960 (all the vols. mentioned in the *Bibl. der Alten Welt*). Reprint of B. JOWETT, *The Dialogues of Plato.* 4 vols., Oxf. 1953 (transl. with introd. and analyses). Similarly SCHLEIERMACHER's translation in *Rowohlts Klassiker der Litt. u. Wiss.* Vol. 1-6, 1957–59. Good introductions by E. HOFF-MANN, *Platon.* Zürich 1950. R. C. LODGE, *The Philosophy of Plato.* Lond. 1956. G. J. DE VRIES, *Inleiding tot het denken van Pl.* 3rd ed. Assen-Amsterdam 1957.

Of leading critical works we also mention here U. V. WILAMOWITZ, *Platon, sein Leben und seine Werke.* 2 vols., Berl. 1919, 5th ed. of the 1st vol. by B. SNELL, Berl. 1959; 3rd ed. of the 2nd vol. by R. STARK, Berl. 1961. P. FRIED-LÄNDER, *Platon* I. Berl. 1928. 2nd ed. 1954. II (interpretation of the Platonic writings) 1930. 2nd ed. in 2 vols.: II 1957. III 1960. J. GEFFCKEN, *Griech. Lit.*

Gesch. 2, Heidelb. 1934, 35. To complete the bibliographies referred to above: G. J. DE VRIES, *Spel bij Pl.* Amsterd. 1949. H. LEISEGANG, *RE* 20, 1950, 2342. E. R. DODDS, *The Greeks and the Irrational.* Un. of Cal. Press 1951 (repr. 1956), 207. CLOYS DE MARIGNAC, *Imagination et dialectique. Essai sur l'expression du spirituel par l'image dans les dialogues de Pl.* Paris 1951. D. ROSS, *Pl's. Theory of Ideas,* 2nd ed. Oxf. 1953. G. SARTON, *A History of Science.* Lond. 1953, 395. JAEGER, vols. 2 and 3 (largely devoted to Plato). P. M. SCHUHL. *L'Œuvre de Pl.* Paris 1954 – Other recent works: R. ROBINSON, *Plato's Earlier Dialectic.* 2nd ed. Oxf. 1953 (Divides the development of Plato's logic into three periods on considerations of elenchos, hypothesis, diaeresis). J. DERBOLAV. *Erkenntnis und Entscheidung. Philosophie der geistigen Aneignung in ihrem Ursprung bei Pl.* Vienna-Stuttgart 1954. R. LORIAUX S.J., *L'Être et la forme selon Pl.* Bruges 1955 (on this K. W. MILLS, *Gnom.* 29, 1957, 325). J. GOULD, *The Development of Pl's Ethics.* Cambr. 1955 (with good bibl., but dubious in its interpretation of the development). J. V. CAMP and P. CANART, *Le Sens du mot* ΘΕΙΟΣ *chez Pl.* Louvain 1956. M. VANHOUTTE, *La Méthode ontologique de Pl.* Louvain 1956. A. D. WINDSPEAR, *The Genesis of Pl's Thought.* 2nd ed. New York 1956. A. RIGOBELLO, *L'intellettualismo in Pl.* Padua 1957. L. ROBIN, *Les Rapports de l'être et de la connaissance d'après Pl.* Paris 1957 (Lectures published posthumously 1932/33). L. SICHIROLLO, *Antropologia e dialettica nella filosofia di Pl.* Milan 1957. E. VOEGELIN, *Order and History III. Pl. and Aristotle.* Louisiana State Un. Pr. (Its guiding principle is an order whose antithesis is not freedom, but disorder.) R. E. CUSHMAN, *Therapeia. Pl's Conception of Philosophy.* Un. of N. Carolina Pr. 1958. H. J. KRÄMER, *Arete bei Pl. and Aristoteles. Zum Wesen und zur Geschichte der plat. Ontologie. Abh. Akad. Heidelb. Phil.-hist. Kl.* 1959/6 (About Krämer's new conception of Plato, centring round the lecture *On the Good, v. supra*). E. MOUTSOPOULOS, *La Musique dans l'œuvre de Pl.* Paris 1959. K. GAISER, *Protreptik und Paränese bei Pl. Tübinger Beiträge,* 40. Stuttgart 1959. H. GAUSS, *Philosophischer Handkommentar zu den Dialogen Pl.s* I 1. 2. II 1. 2 III. Bern 1952–60. P. M. SCHUHL, *Études platoniciennes.* Paris 1960. H. D. VOIGTLÄNDER, *Die Lust und das Gute bei Pl.* Würzburg 1960. J. STENZEL, *Pl. der Erzieher.* Leipz. 1928; repr. Hamburg 1961, with an introduction by K. Gaiser with a good account of Stenzel's work and its significance for Platonic research. – On the later history of Platonism: P. H. MERLAN, *From Platonism to Neoplatonism.* The Hague 1953. E. HOFFMANN, *Platonismus und Mittelalter. Vortr. Bibl. Warburg* 3, 1923/4, now in *Platonismus und christliche Philosophie,* Zürich 1960, 230. R. KLIBANSKY, *The continuity of the Platonic tradition during the Middle Ages* 1. Lond. 1950. On the published parts of the *Corpus Plat. Medii Aevi:* H. LANGERBECK, *Gnom.* 25, 1953, 258. Also *Pl. Arabus* 3, 1952 and *Pl. Latinus* 3, Lond. 1953 and 4, 1961, with the edition by J. WASZINK of the *Timaeus* transl. which was authoritative throughout the Middle Ages. Association Guillaume Budé. Congrès de Tours et de Poitiers 3-9 sept. 1953. *Actes du Congrès.* Paris 1954. *Recherches sur la tradition platonicienne. Sept exposés par* P. COURCELLE, O. GIGON, W. K. C. GUTHRIE, H. J. MARROU, W. THEILER, R. WALZER, J. H. WASZINK. *Entretiens sur l'ant. class.* 3. Fondation Hardt. Vandœuvres-Geneva 1955 (1957). J. C. M. VAN

WINDEN, *Calcidius on Matter. His Doctrine and Sources. A Chapter in the History of Platonism.* Leiden 1959. C. R. VAN PAASEN, *Platon in den Augen der Zeitgenossen. Veröff. d. Arbeitsgem. Nordrhein-Westfalen H.* 89 Cologne 1960.

2 ARISTOTLE AND THE PERIPATOS

In spite of his renunciation of the politics of his native city, Plato remained an Athenian at heart. The charis of his dialogues is only imaginable in these surroundings, as is the art of rhetoric of Isocrates or Demosthenes, inspired by the greatness of an Athens which had already become past history. Aristotle, however, came to Athens from the sphere of Ionian culture and in important sections of his work one can observe clear connections with the older Ionian philosophers. On the other hand, although he was never a pure positivist, his work begins to divorce the independent search for facts from the domination of philosophy and so started the development which leads to the science of Alexandria. The road upon which Aristotle set out connects large areas of Greek intellectual life, but it led through Athens and via Plato. The tensions which entered his work in this way pose innumerable problems, even if they constitute the secret charm of his books in spite of all the dryness of their form.

The Peripatos was naturally the first place to occupy itself with the tradition of Aristotle's life. The oldest biography of the philosopher was possibly the one by Ariston of Ceos. But it was inevitable that the extensive biographical literature of the Hellenistic age with its tendency towards anecdotes and fiction should have claimed the founder of the Peripatos. To some extent the activity of Hermippus can be detected here. There can be no doubt about the wide range and variety of form of this tradition, of which a great many, though largely late, witnesses have survived. They were edited and provided with an excellent commentary by Ingemar Düring;[1] his edition replaced J. Th. Buhle's[2] old collection, since whose appearance only occasional and inadequate publications had been available.

Apart from the school tradition and belles-lettres the biography in Book 5 of Diogenes Laertius stands on its own. In addition to other material it contains the chronology of Aristotle's life by Apollodorus (cf. *F Gr Hist* 244 F 38) which also occurs in the chapter of the letter to Ammaeus (cap. 5) devoted to Aristotle in Dionysius of Halicarnassus. The first part of the *vita Menagiana*, which was named after its author, agrees with the article on Aristotle in Suidas. The main ingredient of the life going under Hesychius' name is a catalogue of Aristotle's works, a parallel to the list of Diogenes Laertius (5, 22–27). A separate group is formed by three biographies under Neoplatonic influence: the *Marciana*, preserved only in the Codex Marc. Gr. 257 which contains a section from

---

[1] *Aristotle in the Ancient Biographical Tradition. Studia Graeca et Latina Gotoburgensia* 5· Göteborg 1957. Also O. GIGON, 'Interpretationen zu den antiken Aristoteles-Viten'. *Mus. Helv.* 15, 1958, 147. By the same the ed. of the *Vita Mariana* Berl. 2962 (Kl. Texte 181) with excellent comm. which covers the whole tradition. M. PLEZIA, 'Supplementary Remarks on Aristotle in the Ancient Biographical Tradition'. *Eos* 51, 1961, 241; id. *Gnom.* 34, 1962, 126.

[2] *Aristotelis opera omnia Graece.* Zweibrücken 1791, 3.

Philochorus (*F Gr Hist* 328 F 223), the *Ammoniana*, also called *Vulgata* and the *Latina*, whose manuscripts are older than those of the two Greek versions and which have a relatively important value as sources. Düring thinks that their author belonged to the generation of William de Moerbeke, but M. Plezia[1] goes a step further and proves that there is some likelihood that William translated it himself.

The Syrian and Arabic biographies which Düring presents in an English translation are derived for the largest part from the same source as the three Neoplatonic ones; this is the Πίναξ of a certain Ptolemy whom the Arabs nicknamed el-Garib (i.e. the unknown). Very little credit is given now to the ancient assumption that this was Ptolemy Chennus, but he is believed to be the Platonist who wrote at the turn of the third and fourth centuries.

In addition to the tradition mentioned there are a host of scattered references of the most varied origin which are also collected in Düring's work.[2] The nature of this material can best be illustrated by the fact that important detail was supplied by the remnants of a commentary by Didymus on Demosthenes (no. 241 P.).

Aristotle came from an old Greek colony; he was born in 384 in Stagirus (Stagira is the later form), in the eastern part of Chalcidice. His father Nicomachus was physician-in-ordinary to Amyntas II of Macedon. In his *Hist. Anim.* 497 a 32 Aristotle refers to his father's *Anatomy* (ἐν ταῖς ἀνατομαῖς), illuminated with diagrams, and much of his scientific interest may have been paternal legacy, although it did not extend to medical practice. After Nicomachus' death Proxenus of Artaneus, who was to play a significant role in his life, became his guardian.

Aristotle's first period of life came to an end with his migration to Athens when he was about 17 and his admission to the Academy. In the subsequent life of the philosopher three epochs are marked off by clear breaks and we mention here the question of the division of his works in accordance with these periods.

Aristotle came to Athens in 368/67. It was the time of Plato's second Sicilian voyage which aroused great expectations. The *Theaetetus* can most easily throw some light on the questions which preoccupied the Academy at that time. We may definitely assume that Eudoxus of Cnidos exercised a particular influence on the new arrival. Aristotle remained his student for fully twenty years until Plato's death in the year 348/47. During this time he no doubt looked round in many directions, but we have no reason to suppose that in these years there ever was a break in his relationship with Plato.

We have already indicated that Plato was not only Aristotle's great inspiration, but that he also became the problem which determined the course he

[1] *Gnom.* 34, 1962, 129.

[2] There (164) also a survey of the medieval Aristotle biographies, which possess little historical value. DURING has included the Aristotle biography of Leonardo Aretino which was written *c.* 1430 and which leads on to the humanistic biographies. On the fabulous tradition J. STOROST, 'Die Aristoteles-Sage im Mittelalter'. *Monumentum Bambergense. Festgabe für Benedikt Kraft.* Munich 1955, 298.

struck. Aristotle had to detach himself from Plato if he was to follow his own destiny, but he could not do this completely without destroying his own foundations. It is not worth while repeating the anecdotes which used to be told about the relationship of the two men; Aristotle's criticism of his teacher is obvious enough in his works and sometimes it is quite cutting, as in the *Anal. post.* (83 a 33) where he calls Plato's ideas 'twitterings'. But apart from such demonstrations of a lack of respect, he also shows deep affection, and however much the accent may have shifted in the course of time, Aristotle must have felt personal reverence while he was critically aloof through all the stages of his development, as shown for instance in *Nic. Ethics* 1, 4. 1096 a 12.[1] And we agree with Jaeger[2] that in the elegy which Aristotle wrote (D. fasc. 1. 115) on the founding of an altar and which he addressed to Eudemus (the Cyprian or the Rhodian?), the man whom the evil are not even entitled to praise is not Socrates, but Plato himself.

Aristotle and Xenocrates left for Assos in Mysia,[3] when Speusippus succeeded to the headship of the school after Plato's death. Earlier, two Platonic scholars, Erastus and Coriscus, had already settled there, and in Plato's *Sixth Letter* we have evidence of his efforts to bring about a lasting bond of friendship between these two and Hermias, the ruler of Atarneus. For a time Assos, which Hermias ceded to his new friends, was the seat of a brisk intellectual life. Callisthenes and Theophrastus also lived there. Hermias, under whose protection they prospered, succeeded long in availing himself of the weakness of the Persian régime and built up around Atarneus a small kingdom within the kingdom. In his last years he conspired with Philip II, since he obviously expected an attempt of the Macedonian power on Asia. His plans were betrayed, however; the Persian general Mentor besieged him in Atarneus and captured him finally through treachery. He was crucified in Susa after unflinchingly refusing to divulge his plans while under torture. Hermias' terrible end shocked Aristotle who was then already living in Macedon, the more so as he was married to his adoptive daughter and niece Pythias. He wrote the dedicatory epigram (3 D.) for his memorial in Delphi and honoured his memory in a hymn full of warm feeling (5 D.)

Aristotle stayed in Assos for three years; then, accompanied by his student and friend Theophrastus, he went to Mytilene in the latter's native island and spent two years there. Already at that time the close association with Theophrastus, which continued throughout his life, was of the greatest importance for Aristotle. In a prefatory notice to his translation of the *Historia Animalium*,[4]

---

[1] The verses found in the Aristotle-biography of the codex Marcianus are characteristic for the relationship of the two men; cf. W. KRANZ, 'Platonica'. *Phil.* 102, 1958, 80, and P. FRIEDLÄNDER in the Festschr. für Gadamer (*Die Gegenwart der Griechen im neueren Denken*). Tübingen 1960. H. CHERNISS, *Aristotle's Criticism of Plato and the Academy* 1. Baltimore 1944; 2nd ed. 1946, shows that Aristotle, like the other philosophers, formulates Plato's principles anew with the notions of his own system and treats them and criticizes them in this formulation.　　　　[2] *v. sup.*, 106. There also on the alleged altar inscription.

[3] PH. MERLAN, *Trans. Am. Phil. Ass.* 77, 1946, 103, shows, however, that later Aristotle was considered to be a member of the Academy.　　　　[4] Oxf. 1910.

D'Arcy Thompson pointed out that the biological works of Aristotle, especially the one mentioned, contain many references to the coasts of Asia Minor, to Lesbos and Macedon. This may not be decisive for the date of the surviving works, but these observations prove that Aristotle's interest and studies were even then directed actively towards the observation and explanation of natural historical phenomena. It is quite possible that in the joint work with Theophrastus the considerably younger scholar provided the stimulus in many respects.

Theophrastus accompanied Aristotle when he was called to Macedon in 343/2 to undertake the education of the heir to the throne. This summons cannot be explained with the epigrammatical formula that the king of science (which Aristotle was not at all then) was summoned to educate the king of the future. We have no way of knowing to what extent Aristotle's connections with Hermias and the tyrant's with Philip played a part, but they probably did.

In Mieza, some way inland from the royal residency Pella, Aristotle guided the education of the young Alexander. It is understandable that we wish to form a picture of its plan and of the association of these men who were as unusual as they were different.[1] Little is known, but two things can be stated: the years in Mieza gave Alexander a profound and direct knowledge of the culture of the Greeks, especially of their great poetry. We can believe the information that his teacher made the *Iliad* one of his assignments, for Aristotle was actively occupied with Homeric problems (fr. 142 ff. R.). But we have no reason to think that Aristotle had any influence on Alexander's political activity. The former's political thinking was confined by the proportions of the Hellenic city-state and did not look to Alexander's future empire, and when it was being formed, the philosopher addressed himself to his former scholar in a memorandum *Alexander or On Colonisation* (fr. 648 R.); this writing is lost, but a well-known passage from a letter (fr. 658 R.) survives in which Aristotle advises Alexander that he should be the leader of the Greeks and the lord of the barbarians; he should treat the ones as his friends and equals, the others as animals or plants. This passage shows that Aristotle's notions were in contrast not only with the ideas of individual sophists about the equality of men, but also with his royal scholar's plans for the unity of nations. Several reports show (Ath. 9. 398 e. Plin. *Nat. Hist.* 8. 44; cf. 10. 185) that Alexander later generously supported his teacher's scientific studies, but the fate of Callisthenes necessarily led to an estrangement. This man, a nephew of Aristotle's, was already his scholar in Assos and later helped him to draw up the lists of Delphic victors. He accompanied Alexander on his expedition as the recorder of his deeds,[2] but his conduct was recalcitrant and it was especially through his refusal to prostrate himself that he fell under the suspicion of being involved in a conspiracy and in 327 he was executed without a trial. The view of Alexander among the Peripatetics was influenced by this act of violence, but it was reserved for a later time to invent the malicious tale that Aristotle had the king poisoned.

---

[1] Cf. F. SCHACHERMEYR's description: *Alexander d. Gr.* Graz 1949, 66.
[2] The remnants F Gr Hist. no. 124.

It is not possible to tell exactly how long Aristotle remained the prince's teacher; it probably went on for two or three years. He remained in Macedon for a considerable time, but we have no details about his position or what he did. We hear that he is promised that his native town of Stagirus, which was destroyed by Philip, will be restored, but also that this promise was not carried out (fr. 657 R.). Meanwhile Speusippus, Plato's successor as head of the Academy, had died. In connection with his succession the Herculanean index of Academics (p. 38 Mekler) has preserved the interesting information that the young members of the Academy elected Xenocrates, because Aristotle stayed on in Macedon.[1] This means that at that time his ties with Plato's school were still felt to be strong enough for him to be considered as its leader.

Aristotle did not return to Athens until 335/34. Just at this time Alexander's verdict against Thebes robbed the anti-Macedonian circles in Athens of all hope of successful resistance, and when Aristotle set about establishing his own school, he knew that he could rely on the protection which Antipater, his friend from Pella and now Alexander's representative, loyally accorded him. He began his teaching in the gymnasium Lyceum which was situated in the neighbourhood of a shrine to Apollo Lyceus. The covered walk in the grounds (περίπατος) gave its name to the school of the Peripatetics. It may be presumed that suitable accommodation was soon found on a piece of land in the vicinity because of the large numbers which the school drew. Its position in the eastern part of the city separated Aristotle from the Academy in the north-east. This distance symbolized the absence of communication between the two seats of intellectual activity. Xenocrates, who headed the Academy, used to be Aristotle's associate in Assos, but their intellectual attitude had now removed them far from one another. Aristotle's writings give a good idea of the teaching at the Peripatos, since his lectures were the basis for them. We also know a good deal about the external arrangements. The difficult lectures took place in the forenoon, those for a wider circle of students were programmed for the afternoon (ἑωθινός and δειλινὸς περίπατος). It has been attempted to relate this system with the doctores de mane and de sero at the medieval universities.[2] Common meals and common drinking (syssities and symposia) provided an internal bond for the community which, like the Academy, was a thiasos with a shrine sacred to the Muses for its centre; the founder himself had worked out the formalities for such occasions.

Aristotle led his school for close on thirteen years, and then politics once more sinned against science. Alexander's death in 323 provoked a new anti-Macedonian movement which also hit Aristotle. The attack was the result of the resentment which later speaks out in the fragments of a speech of Demochares[3] in which this nephew of Demosthenes' defended the psephisma of Sophocles (307/6), which was an assault on the freedom of the philosophers' schools in Athens. In such times the silliest pretext is good enough and so the philosopher

---

[1] Cf. PH. MERLAN, in the work quoted p. 549, n. 3.
[2] O. IMMISCH, Academia. Freib. i. Br. 1942, 10.
[3] BAITER-SAUPPE, Or. Att. 2, 341.

was threatened with a charge of impiety, because his hymn to Hermias was a paean and therefore represented the profanation of a religious song. Aristotle avoided the attack and went to Chalcis where his late mother had owned a property. There, soon afterwards, in the year 322, he succumbed to a gastric complaint. Two reports show him in the last period of his life. One is a passage in a letter (fr. 668 R.) in which he himself admits that, grown so lonely and depending entirely on himself, he finds an increasing delight in the myths; the other is his will, whose text was preserved by Diogenes Laertius (5. 11) together with the last dispositions of his three successors as leaders of the school – Theophrastus, Straton and Lycon.[1] Aristotle's old friend Antipater was appointed executor; Herpyllis, who lived with him after Pythias' death, the children – his daughter Pythias of his first wife and Nicomachus, his son by Herpyllis – the other dependants of the household down to the slaves were all taken care of with paternal kindness.

There are two ancient judgments on Aristotle's style which at first sight seem to be strikingly contradictory. Cicero (*Acad.* 2. 119) praises the *aureum flumen* of the philosopher's language, while Philodemus (*De Rhet.* 2 p. 51, 36, 11 S.) claims that he stammered (ψελλίζειν). The reason why these opinions vary so much is that they are based on different writings. In several places which can easily be found by consulting Bonitz' index, Aristotle mentions exoteric books (ἐξωτερικοὶ λόγοι). Nowadays it is no longer seriously disputed that this refers to writings which were mainly produced in the early period and which were meant to have some influence beyond a rather limited circle and so had some literary pretensions. They are identical with the 'published' (ἐκδεδομένοι λόγοι[2]) books which Aristotle mentions in the *Poetics* (15, 1454 b 18). This group stands apart from the works which were the product of Aristotle's teaching and were planned for this purpose, which is why no attention was paid to their form and style; and in many cases the long and complex history of the growth of the surviving works also had an adverse effect on their form. Modern scholars now habitually refer to the esoteric books in contrast to the term used by Aristotle for the literary writings, whereas we find that Aristotle himself (*Eud. Eth.* 1217 b 22) contrasts the λόγοι κατὰ φιλοσοφίαν with the ἐξωτερικοί. The esoteric works are often called pragmatiae, and in Aristotle there is a beginning of this usage. These are the only surviving works, but the attempts of scholarship to trace remnants of the exoteric works (*v. infra*) are well founded, for they belong mainly to the young Aristotle of the time when his early work overlapped Platonic philosophy in its later form. The comparison with the twofold sphere of Plato's activity, i.e. the dialogues and the doctrine taught orally only to a

---

[1] The biographical sketch of Ptolemy which is the source of the Neoplatonic biographies and the Arabic tradition, also contained Aristotle's will. Its text now also in M. PLEZIA, *Aristotelis epistularum fragmenta cum testamento.* Warsaw 1961. The Arabic sources only have an Athenian decree of proxeny for Aristotle with the story of its passing, its withdrawal and its restitution. Whereas DÜRING (cf. p.547, n. 1) thinks the whole story a fiction, M. PLEZIA, *Gnom.* 34, 1962, 131, believes that the tradition has some historical value.

[2] Comparable with Isocrates' (5. 11) ὁ ἐκδοθεὶς λόγος, and Plato's (*Soph.* 232 d) δεδημοσιωμένα.

very limited circle of scholars as upheld by Dirlmeier,[1] reveals immediately the basic difference: Aristotle put down the whole of his internal doctrine in his esoteric writings.

We possess three catalogues of Aristotle's writings which date back to antiquity: one in Diogenes Laertius (5. 22); one appended to the above-mentioned *Vita Menagiana* and one by Ptolemy which can be restored from Arabic sources. Recently Paul Moraux has devoted a scholarly book[2] to these catalogues, in which he plausibly traces Diogenes' list back to Ariston of Ceos[3] who led the Peripatetic school after Lycon in the last quarter of the third century B.C. The register, which gains in importance through these considerations, begins with nineteen titles; on the ground of individual testimony and general considerations it seems to be practically certain[4] that they are dialogues written in the beginning of Aristotle's career. The only late-comer is the work mentioned above, *Alexander or On Colonisation*. While individual titles like *Sophistes*, *Menexenus* or *Symposium* are already reminiscent of Plato's dialogues, the fragments of several of these writings also show how close the affinity is with the intellectual world of the Master.[5] The dialogue *Eudemus*[6] was named after a friend of Aristotle's, the Cypriot exile Eudemus who followed Dion to Sicily and died there. Five years before, when he fell ill in Thessaly, a vision had promised him that he would return home at the end of that period. This homecoming was now revealed to his friends at the Academy as the return to eternity. So, like Plato's *Phaedo*, the *Eudemus* is a discourse about the soul, and under this title (Περὶ ψυχῆς) it appears in Diogenes' catalogue. Aristotle opposes the view of the soul as a harmony between the parts of the body and argues its preexistence and immortality. This is a long way removed from the considerably later treatise *On the Soul* in which body and soul are thought of as the two sides of one single substance and are understood to be matter and form in their mutual relation.

The *Protrepticus* is also a work of the years during which Aristotle was a member of the Academy; it is an exhortation in the Platonic tradition to a spiritual life, praising philosophical cognition, φρόνησις[7] as the highest man can achieve. It is still an open question whether the *Protrepticus* was a dialogue. Jaeger thinks that it was a propaganda speech; its form goes back to the teaching methods of

---

[1] *Sitzb. Ak. Heidelb. Phil.-hist. Kl.* 1962/2, 9.

[2] *Les Listes anciennes des ouvrages d'A.* Louvain 1951. I. DÜRING (*v.* p. 547, n. 1) also to be consulted now. Cf. also V. MASELLIS, 'Tradizione e cataloghi delle opere arist.'. *Riv. Fil.* 34, 1956, 337.

[3] F. WEHRLI, *Die Schule des A.* 6. Basel 1952.

[4] W. D. ROSS in the Praefatio to *A. Fragmenta selecta.* Oxf. 1955.

[5] In his book *Aristoteles. Einführungsschriften. Eingel. und neu übertr.* Zürich 1961 (*Bibl. d. Alten Welt*) O. GIGON made the noteworthy attempt to enrich by using various sources our knowledge of the writings which were meant to be introductions to philosophy.

[6] O. GIGON, 'Prolegomena to an Edition of the Eudemus'. In: *Aristotle and Plato in the Mid-fourth Century. Papers of the Symposium Aristotelicum held at Oxford in August 1957. Studia Graeca et Latina Gothoburgensia* 11. Göteborg 1960, 19. The work is important for the problems of the reconstruction of these writings.

[7] On the development of this notion JAEGER (*v. inf.*), 82.

the sophists. Others like D. J. Allen and H. Langerbeck[1] stress the fact that in his *Hortensius* Cicero imitated the *Protrepticus* in the form of a dialogue and they also assume that this was the form of Aristotle's work. In order to account for the insertion of the address to the Cypriot prince Themison it could be argued that Aristotle pretended to have written a dialogue about the meaning of philosophy at the former's request.

In 1869 Ingram Bywater substantially increased the fragments of the *Protrepticus*[2] by pointing out that Iamblichus' book of the same title contained numerous excerpts from the Aristotelian work. Jaeger made an important contribution in his book on Aristotle by increasing their number and defining them. It is preferable to attribute any inconsistencies in these excerpts to Iamblichus, who confuses what is Aristotelian with Platonic work, than to an Aristotle, supposedly freeing himself from Plato's influence.[3]

It is impossible to doubt that the *Protrepticus* is largely Platonic in spirit, but this does not solve one of the fundamental problems of present-day Aristotelian scholarship: Was the Platonic theory of ideas as such accepted in this work as was done in the *Eudemus*? Jaeger thinks it was and he draws his strongest support from the passage in Iamblichus (fr. 13 Ross) with the separation of true reality from images, but lately it has been legitimately doubted[4] whether Aristotle ever defended, as his own conviction, the Platonic theory of ideas which separates a transcendental reality from the things of the material world which exist only through participation. According to the present interpretation the important fr.13 (Ross) shows that Aristotle meant by true reality the normative Physis which is accessible to man through theoretical knowledge.

The *Protrepticus* exerted a wide-spread influence. Its propaganda for the philosophical way of life alarmed the followers of Isocrates with their rhetorical teaching programme. P. Von der Mühll[5] has shown that in his *Antidosis* oration of 353 Isocrates probably made allusions to the *Protrepticus*. If this should be correct, a probable date would become a certainty. The *Admonition to Demonicus*, a product of Isocrates' school, seeks to counter the *Protrepticus* by the most feeble

---

[1] *Gnom.* 26, 1954, 3.

[2] W. GERSON RABINOWITZ, *Aristotle's Protrepticus and the Sources of its Reconstruction. Univ. of Calif. Publ. in Class. Phil.* 16/1, 1957, is rather too sceptical of previous attempts. He doubts the utilization of the *Protrepticus* in the *Hortensius*. On the connection between these two writings A. GIGON, 'Cicero und Aristoteles'. *Herm.* 87, 1959, 154. – I. DÜRING, *Aristotle's Protrepticus. An Attempt at Reconstruction. Stud. Graeca et Latina Gothob.* 12, 1961. Bibl. of earlier attempts in F. DIRLMEIER, *Gnom.* 28, 1956, 343, I and W. SPOERRI, *Gnom.* 32, 1960, 18, 4.

[3] On this question G. MÜLLER, *Mus. Helv.* 17, 1960, 134, who formulates on p. 134 as follows: 'not a Platonizing Aristotle, but a contaminating Iamblichus'.

[4] I. DÜRING, 'Problems in A.'s Prot.'. *Eranos* 52, 1954, 139; 'A. in the Prot.' in *Autour d'Aristote.* Louvain 1955, 81. Id. 'A. the Scholar' (p. 576, n. 2), 75. R. STARK (*v.* p. 576, n. 3), 9. F. DIRLMEIER, *Gnom.* 28, 1956, 343. Cf. also the bibl. in the two previous notes.

[5] 'Isokrates und der Prot. des A.'. *Phil.* 94, 1941, 259. On the *Demonicea*: C. J. DE VOGEL, *Greek Philosophy. A Collection of Texts* 2. Leiden 1953, 24.

methods. It enjoyed particular esteem with the Neoplatonists and the work had a deciding influence on Augustine via Cicero's *Hortensius*.

We confidently date the dialogue *On Philosophy*, which comprised three volumes in antiquity, in the Assos period[1] soon after Plato's death; it had an equally great influence, as we can observe, for instance, in Cicero's *De Natura Deorum*. Fr. 9 (Ross) proves that Aristotle turned away from Plato's doctrine of ideal numbers and it may be assumed that this criticism was only part of a refutation of the theory of ideas as a whole as we know it from *Met.* A 9 and M 4 f. The survey which Book 1 gave of the historical development of philosophy is a significant new element, and at the same time a basic feature of Aristotle's scientific work. The fragments show that Aristotle reached far beyond Greek philosophy and included the wisdom of the East in his observations side by side with Hellenic theology. In this he had a direct association with the interests of the older Plato and the Academy. It is also clear that after the criticism of the theory of ideas in Book 2 Aristotle introduced his own cosmology and theology in the next book; judging from the fragments he struck a bold line which had a subsequent effect both in his own later work and in other authors. Here Aristotle produced the proofs for the existence of God, using for his argumentation in one of these the cyclical motion of the constellations which he conceived as divine beings with a soul. There is a connection here with the role of the astral gods in Plato's later work and in another direction with the dominance of astrology in the Hellenistic age. There is no need to stress the fact that at the back of all this there arises the question of the extent and weight of Oriental influences. The loss of this work is the more regrettable as Aristotle also searched for the foundations of the subjective knowledge of God and so laid the basis for the religious philosophy of the West. The adaptation of the Platonic cave-simile belongs in this same context; it was probably told by Plato himself as a partner in the conversation.

As to the form of the dialogue just dealt with, we know that an introduction was prefixed to each of the three books and that then the individual themes were dealt with separately in speeches in the manner of lectures. There is proof (fr. 8. 9. 78 R.) that Aristotle himself was one of the lecturers. The difference with Plato is as clear as the connection with Cicero, which the latter confirms himself (*Ad Fam.* 1. 9, 23); Jaeger, however, is justified when he warns that we must not think that Aristotle's dialogues were wholly uniform.[2] Individual ones like the *Eudemus* or the *Gryllus* with the subtitle *On Rhetoric* may have been closer to the Platonic manner.

We add here two writings of Aristotle's early career which, though they do not belong to the exoteric group, are yet of some significance for his relationship

[1] Acc. to JAEGER (129), H. LANGERBECK, *Gnom.* 26, 1954, 5. H. D. SAFFREY, *Le Περὶ φιλ. d'A. et la théorie platonicienne des idées nombres.* Leiden 1955 (p. 13, 3). Objections in H. CHERNISS, *Gnom.* 31, 1959, 36. M. UNTERSTEINER, 'Περὶ φιλοσοφίας di A.'. *Riv. Fil.* N.S. 38, 1960, 337; 39, 1961, 121.

[2] F. DIRLMEIER, *Sitzb. Ak. Heidelb. Phil.-hist. Kl.* 1962/2. 13 stresses that in the pragmatiae there is something like an internal dialogue style, which is evident from the exchange of question and answer.

with Plato.[1] The book *On the Good* (Περὶ τἀγαθοῦ) contained a copy of the lecture of the older Plato which was discussed above (p. 540). The treatise *On Ideas* (Περὶ ἰδεῶν) is later and belongs perhaps to the Assos period. Fragments of this work in the commentary of Alexander of Aphrodisias show that, in opposition to Plato's theory of ideas, Aristotle defended the notions which form the basis of his criticism in the *Metaphysics*.[2]

The extensive Corpus Aristotelicum which has been transmitted comprises the books, often called pragmatiae, which are the products of Aristotle's research and teaching. Scholarship has made a clean sweep of the earlier belief that this Corpus represents the complete educational system of the second Athenian period and was completely written at that time. A mass of problems was raised at the same time and in most cases only the merest start has been made in dealing with these. It was particularly Werner Jaeger who showed for the most important works that they were composed of parts which were written in different periods and which are only loosely connected. Furthermore it may be assumed that, in view of the repeated use of these books for teaching purposes, Aristotle made individual additions which could not always be fitted in smoothly; and finally, with regard to the manuscript tradition (*v. infra*), the vexing question arises to what extent it is possible to trace additions and interpolations made by editors.[3] The uncertainty in this field was recently demonstrated in a striking manner when an attempt was made to attribute the greater part of the Corpus Aristotelicum in its present form to Theophrastus.[4] We hope that this episode will soon be forgotten, but a series of difficult tasks is waiting to be undertaken and it would be in the interest of scholars to realize the limits of what can be achieved when they deal with these questions. Emendations intended to smooth out the style of the pragmatiae are completely senseless in any case.

It will be understood from the above that the brief summary, which is all that can be given here, cannot present the wealth of material in chronological order. So we start, like the Corpus, with the writings on logic and dialectic which the Peripatos considered as its tools; next in importance we place the works in which Aristotle developed his conception of the universe; then follow the works which deal with man's soul and his activity in the realm of ethics, politics and art. The scientific works form the conclusion.

While other systems of antiquity divided philosophy into logic, physics and

---

[1] P. WILPERT, 'Reste verlorener Aristotelesschriften bei Alexander von Aphrodisias'. *Herm.* 75, 1940, 369, and *Zwei arist. Frühschriften über die Ideenlehre*. Regensburg 1949. Following JAEGER an earlier period is assumed here, during which A. based himself on the theory of ideas.

[2] On this now F. DIRLMEIER, *v. sup.* 25.

[3] On the methodological problems O. GIGON's discussion of *De Caelo*: 'A.-Studien I'. *Mus. Helv.* 9, 1952, 113; cf. also STARK (*v.* p. 576, n. 3), 61.

[4] J. ZÜRCHER, *A.'s Werk und Geist*. Paderborn 1952. E. J. SCHÄCHER, *Platon-A.* I, Salzburg 1957 deals with the thesis elaborately and disapprovingly. ZÜRCHER dealt with Plato no less radically: *Das Corpus Academicum*. Paderborn 1954. Cf. DIRLMEIER's bold opinion: *Nik. Ethik* (*v. inf.*), 249.

ethics, Aristotle, like his school, allocated to logic[1] only a place in the forecourt of his philosophical building. The Peripatos described the logical works as the *Organon*;[2] they considered that these were the instruments needed for intellectual work. The two brief treatises at the beginning of the *Organon* immediately demonstrate the complexity of the problems which confront the critic of Aristotle. The *Categories*[3] with the ten basic forms of the statements on Being were already suspected in antiquity. The present position of scholarship can be described as accepting the contents as a whole as Aristotelian, while objections to the form seem to recommend to some the rejection of parts, to others of the whole work.[4] The same applies to the treatise *De Interpretatione* ($\Pi\epsilon\rho\grave{\iota}$ $\dot{\epsilon}\rho\mu\eta\nu\epsilon\acute{\iota}\alpha s$) which deals with the parts and forms of the sentence. Andronicus rejected it while Alexander of Aphrodisias considered it to be genuine; at any rate it fits into the framework of Aristotle's works on logic in so far as these take to a large extent the actuality of the living language as the starting-point. The main work in this realm are the four books *Analytics* ($Ἀναλυτικ\grave{α}$ $\pi\rho\acute{o}\tau\epsilon\rho\alpha$ and $\H{υ}\sigma\tau\epsilon\rho\alpha$).[5] The first two (*An. priora*)[6] deal with the general theory of inductive inference; the last two (*An. posteriora*) with the acquisition of knowledge through proof and definition, with which the statement of the figures of deductive inference is connected. One wing, vast indeed, of this building is formed by the eight books of the *Topics* ($Τοπικ\acute{α}$),[7] whose completion is dated before that of the *Analytics*. They grew out of dialectic as it was practised both at the Academy and in the disputes of the sophists' circles. The author proclaims his aim at the start: he will teach how in any question probable statements can be reached by way of dialectic and how these can be successfully defended without getting into contradictions. The *Sophistical Refutations* ($Σοφιστικο\grave{ι}$ $\H{ε}λεγχοι$), which oppose the deceptive inferences of the arguments used by the sophists, are a sort of sequel to the *Topics*.

Aristotle's logic is most probably the result of his endeavours to work out a method for scientific discussion; in this way he came to the analysis of the syllogism and his doctrine of deductive inference. Modern logic takes another way, but this does not detract by any means from the importance of his

---

[1] J. M. BOCHENSKI, *Ancient Formal Logic*. Amsterdam 1951. J. LUCASIEWICZ, *A.'s Syllogistic from the Standpoint of Modern Logic*. Oxf. 1951; 2nd ed. enlarged 1957. J. LOHMANN, 'Vom ursprünglichen Sinn der arist. Syllogistik'. *Lexis* 2, 1950/51, 205. C. A. VIANO, *La logica di A*. Turin 1955.

[2] G. COLLI, *A. Organon. Introd., trad. e note*. Turin 1955. Important discussion by I. DÜRING, *Gnom.* 28, 1956, 204. Transl. by EUGEN ROLFES in 2 vols. Leipz. 1925, repr. Hamb. 1958. *Nouvelle Trad. et notes* by J. TRICOT, 6 vols. Paris 1946–50, 1 and 2 in new ed. 1959.

[3] Ed. by L. MINIO-PALUELLO, Oxf. 1949 (with *De interpretatione*).

[4] On its authenticity: MINIO-PALUELLO in his ed. Oxf. 1949. DE RIJK, *Mnem.* 4, ser. 4, 1951, 129. M. WUNDT, *Untersuchungen zur Metaphysik des A*. Stuttgart 1953. Further bibl. on the question of authenticity in G. VERBEKE, *Gnom.* 28, 1956, 230.

[5] Ed. with Comm. by W. D. ROSS, Oxf. 1958.

[6] G. PATZIG, 'Die aristotelische Syllogistik. Logisch-philologische Untersuchungen über das Buch A der "Ersten Analytiken"'. *Abh. Ak. Göttingen. Phil.-hist. Kl.* 3. Ser. 42, 1959.

[7] Ed. with comm. of the *Topica et Soph. Elenchi* by W. D. ROSS, Oxf. 1958.

achievement which, indeed, does not derive from a method of scientific operation, but from the formal analysis of certain mental operations.[1]

For a long time Aristotle's name was allied with an inflexible system; this
idea is the result of medieval Aristotelianism. Only the work of the last few
decades has shown us the dynamic force and sweep of his investigations which
moved between the two poles of empiricism and the speculative method which
was permanently influenced by Plato. Therefore the two works, the *Physics* and
the *Metaphysics*, which dominate Aristotelian philosophy, do not represent for us
the record of a system, but the evidence of a seeking which had its origin as
much in Greek thought as in the personality of Aristotle.

The title of *Physics* (Φυσικὴ ἀκρόασις, 8 books)[2] must be understood to
comprise the wide scope of meaning which the word physis had in Greek.[3] The
objects of Aristotle's extensive enquiries are nature as the scene of all spontaneous
movement and change, the aetiology of these occurrences and their goal, and
this work lays the foundation for this undertaking. So on the one hand it
represents the prerequisite to all scientific studies, but on the other it is continued so obviously in the *Metaphysics*, that in our arrangement this tie seemed
more important.

The first two books develop the leading principles (ἀρχαί) of the Aristotelian
account of nature. Here are developed the correlative notions of matter (ὕλη)
and form (εἶδος), by means of which Aristotle overcame the Platonic separation of a purely intelligible reality and the world of the senses. He replaced the
ideas as transcendental essences by the Eidos, which realized itself in matter and
so restored to the things of our world their validity and substance.[4] With this
notion as a starting-point Aristotle could formulate the requirement which was
the guiding principle of all his investigations and which he expressed as follows
in Book Z of the *Metaphysics*: Always start from what the observations of the
senses present as certain and proceed from there to the objects of pure thought.

A third principle, that of movement, is needed in order to make hyle and
eidos enter into the relation which enables the form to realize itself in matter.
For this purpose the meaning of the Greek word κίνησις has been broadened
to include, apart from local movement, quantitative growth and qualitative
change. The process of movement, or preferably change (e.g. seed-growth-
plant), represents the transition of the potentiality of the form to its actuality,

---

[1] On a lost work Περὶ διαιρέσεων cf. F. DIRLMEIER, *Sitzb. Ak. Heidelb. Phil.-hist. Kl.*
1962/2, 29.

[2] Ed. with comm. by W. D. ROSS, Oxf. (1936) 1955, Text Oxf. 1950. W. WIELAND, *Die
aristotelische Physik. Untersuchungen über die Grundlegung der Naturwissenschaften und die sprach-
lichen Bedingungen der Prinzipienforschung bei Aristoteles.* Göttingen 1962. The works of F.
SOLMSEN: 'A. and Presocratic Cosmogony'. *Harv. Stud.* 63, 1958 (*Festschr. Jaeger*) 265. *A.'s
System of the Physical World. A Comparison with his Predecessors.* Cornell Un. Press 1960 are
important for Aristotle's challenge of his predecessors' notions of the physical universe.

[3] M. HEIDEGGER, 'Vom Wesen und Begriff der φύσις. Aristotles Physik. B. 1'. *Il Pensiero.*
(Milan) 3, 1958, 131 and 265.

[4] N. HARTMANN, 'Zur Lehre vom Eidos bei Platon und Aristoteles'. *Abh. Preuss. Ak.
Phil.-hist. Kl.* 1941/8 showed that it is also possible to think that Aristotle's εἶδος implied a
retrograde step towards the Platonic idea.

two notions (δύναμις and ἐνέργεια) which dominate Aristotle's thought. In addition to matter, form and movement there is the fourth principle of goal or purpose, the final cause in addition to the material, formal and efficient causes. In the development which proceeds from the obscure power of Anaxagoras' *nous* via Diogenes of Apollonia's perception of divine authority derived from the orderly arrangement of the universe (p. 334) and by way of the prototype character of the Platonic ideas, Aristotle is the staunchest representative of teleological thought. For him nature is an impersonal but at the same time wholly purposeful force which, as we can observe, does nothing without intention (μάτην) (*De Respir.* 10. 476 a 12. *De Caelo* 14. 271 a 33). The movement towards the form is at the same time a movement towards a naturally given end. This holds good both for the genesis of the plant and for the development of a literary genre to its perfect form (*Poet.* 4. 1449 a 15). What this doctrine meant for the foundation of the theory of evolution is obvious. It was to honour the ancient thinker that H. Driesch used the Aristotelian term entelechy to give a name to his 'completing factor'.[1] Aristotle's work on space, time and infinity cannot be dealt with here, but a word must be added about the genesis of the *Physics*. Jaeger has made considerable advance in the analysis of this work, as he has done with other major works of Aristotle's, and he has presented a whole range of problems for discussion. He dates the general intellectual contents of the *Physics* in Aristotle's earliest period, even earlier than the oldest parts of the *Metaphysics*. On the other hand he thinks that our present version was made up at a fairly late date by the combination of old and new pieces. Book 7 occupies a special position; so does Book 8 which the *Physics* quotes as being earlier and which was probably the product of his mature years. Here, as elsewhere, many questions still have to go unanswered, but basically the genesis of the pragmatiae has no doubt been correctly grasped. It is important in this connection that Jaeger has pointed out that in the *Metaphysics* the writings On the Heaven and On Generation and Corruption are referred to as *Physics*. This means that at that time this term described a group of individual lines of research; the combination of different parts into our present *Physics* followed later. When this happened and by whom is one of the most important and difficult problems of scholarship.

Two works must be mentioned in close connection with the *Physics*. The four books On the Heaven (Περὶ οὐρανοῦ)[2] present a cosmology in which the theory of the aether plays a decisive role. Aether is added as a fifth to the four simple substances fire, air, earth and water with their natural tendency to a rising and falling movement; to this element a circular rotation is natural. This theory, which is directly related to Anaxagoras (VS 59 A 42. 71) is meant to help to prove that the cosmos is finite, spherical and eternal. It is closely connected with the discovery of Eudoxus of Cnidos that the orbits of the planets can be explained by the motions of spheres which rotate round the earth in a

---

[1] *Philosophie des Organischen.* Leipz. 1907, 145.

[2] Ed. by D. J. ALLAN, Oxf. 1936. Transl. by J. TRICOT, Paris 1949 (together with the spurious work *On the Universe*). O. GIGON, *Vom Himmel. Von der Seele. Von der Dichtkunst.* Zürich 1950 (Bibl. d. Alten Welt).

concentrical order. Chapter 8 of Book Λ of the *Metaphysics*, whose late date has been proved likely by Jaeger (372), shows that Aristotle worked continuously at these questions. Of great importance to him was the stimulus he received from Eudoxus' pupil Callippus of Cyzicus, the reformer of the Athenian calendar. The beginning of the era introduced by Callippus falls in the year 330/29; so his association with Aristotle belongs to the latter's second Athenian period. Eudoxus believed that he needed twenty-six spheres to account for the planetary orbits (including the sun and the moon); Callipus increased their number to thirty-three, while Aristotle came to fifty-five. The writing *On the Heaven* occupies an intermediate position in his efforts for a rational explanation of the orbits of the heavenly bodies; his development of the theory of aether advanced towards it, but the conception of the planets as divine reasonable beings was retained.

The second book ends with the expositions of the spherical shape of the earth which rests motionless in the centre of the cosmos.[1] Here Aristotle also records the conclusion that observations of the stars made at different places north and south of each other show that the sphere of the earth is of a moderate size, a significant prelude to Eratosthenes' calculation of the circumference of the earth. On the other hand it cannot be denied that it was Aristotle's very authority which supported the geocentric system with its planetary spheres so effectively that the progress made by Aristarchus of Samos towards a correct understanding had no influence.

The treatise *On Generation and Corruption* (Περὶ γενέσεως καὶ φθορᾶς, 2 books)[2] also belongs within the scope of the *Physics*; it puts forward a theory of the two processes mentioned in the title, and adopts a particularly sharp attitude against the Eleatics.

In any discussion of Aristotle the *Metaphysics* (Τὰ μετὰ τὰ φυσικά, 13, with α 14 books)[3] must occupy an important position. Its author called its subject 'First philosophy'; the description *Metaphysics* originated perhaps with Andronicus, in whose edition the work was placed after the *Physics*. The work does not offer a complete presentation of a system; it is a Corpus composed of different parts; Jaeger has also successfully analysed this work in his book on Aristotle.[4] Bonitz

---

[1] This means rejection of the theories of Philolaus, Hicetas, Ecphantides who assumed a spontaneous motion of the earth round a central fire or its own axis, cf. WEHRLI on Heraclides Ponticus fr. 104-108.

[2] Ed. by H. H. JOACHIM, Oxf. 1922. Transl. by J. TRICOT, Paris 1951.

[3] A. SCHWEGLER, *Die Metaphysik des A. Grundtext, Übersetzung und Kommentar nebst Erläuterungen und Abhandlungen*. 4 vols. Tübingen 1847, Repr. in 2 vols. Frankf. a. M. 1960. Ed. and comm. by W. D. ROSS, 2 vols. Oxf. 1924, repr. with corr. 1958. Ed. by W. JAEGER, Oxf. 1957. J. WARRINGTON, *Metaphysics. Ed. and Transl. Introd. by* W. D. ROSS. Lond. 1956. L. ELDERS, *A.'s Theory of the One. A Commentary on Book X of the Met.* Wijsg. teksten en stud. 5, 1961. Transl. by J. TRICOT, 2 vols. Paris 1948. A. CARLINI, *A., La metafisica*. Bari 1950 (traduz. e comm.) BONITZ's comm. on the Met. (1849) was reprinted in 1960.

[4] Critical arguments on J.'s thesis in ROSS' ed. (*v. inf.*) and H. V. ARNIM, *Wien. Stud.* 46, 1927/28, 1. Recent bibl. in PH. MERLAN, 'Metaphysik: Name und Gegenstand'. *Journ. Hell. Stud.* 77, 1957, 87. Also W. THEILER, 'Die Entstehung der Metaphysik des A. mit einem Anhang über Theophrasts Metaphysik'. *Mus. Helv.* 15, 1958, 85. On the elements used in

had already preceded him when he separated out those parts which can be marked as later additions. The appendix to the first book, designated as small α, comes from a copy of a lecture delivered by Pasicles, a nephew of Eudemus of Rhodes. Book Δ was interpolated by the editors; it is an independent treatise by Aristotle on the various meanings of some terms important to the philosopher. It is quite evident that Book Λ stands on its own; it is a summary of Aristotle's thoughts on the highest Being, usually designated as 'Theology'. What remains after these obvious skimmings have been removed? The composition planned by Aristotle is still a many-layered structure. Book I, for instance, is a treatise complete in itself, on the Being and the One, of which Jaeger (209) assumes that Aristotle incorporated it only during the work on the final form of the *Metaphysics*. The difference in the position of the proposition and the asymmetrical treatment of the notion of substance decisively prove the distance in time separating the research projects combined by Aristotle, as shown by Jaeger. We cannot go into the details of later additions and revisions, but two areas can be marked off. One is the introduction A-Eɪ (without Δ), which belongs to the early period and to a large extent to the years of Assos. It is in accordance with the methodology invented by Aristotle for posterity that A contains a historical survey of the efforts of his predecessors regarding the causes of Being. Aristotle's criticism in this realm produces some problems of a particular nature.[1] The chronology is determined by the fact that in these books, especially in B, the cognition of the transcendental Being, which is beyond the world intelligible to our senses, is emphasized as the goal of the new science. Contrary to this we find in the so-called substance books Z H Θ another notion of Being which comprises the things of the senses and the immaterial, both the transient and the eternal. In their present arrangement these books with the wide scope of treatment of substance (οὐσία) form a sort of preliminary enquiry to the discussion of the immaterial Being. As regards the books not yet discussed we merely refer to Jaeger's opinion that in K 1-8, M 9; 10 and N we have parts of the older conception of the *Metaphysics* which at that early stage was concerned only with the immaterial Being.[2]

In Book Λ of the *Metaphysics* especially Aristotle made some statements about his difficult notion of the divine, in which his metaphysical thought found its completion. As the unmoved first mover his God is the highest form without any material admixture. As the perfect thought-force he can only direct himself to the most perfect, himself. This divinity did not create the universe, does not pervade it like the Logos of the Stoics and does not rule in the sense of the providence which forms the main point of doctrine of that school. It has been

the construction of *Met.* A, O. GIGON, *Mus. Helv.* 16, 1959, 185. M. WUNDT, *Untersuchungen zur Metaphysik des A.* Stuttgart 1953, follows his own, very dubious course, in the analysis of the strata.

[1] H. E. CHERNISS, *A.'s Criticism of Presocratic Philosophy.* Baltimore 1935. Id.: *A.'s Criticism of Plato and the Academy* 1. Baltimore 1944, 2nd ed. 1946.

[2] H. WAGNER, 'Zum Problem des aristotelischen Metaphysik-Begriffes'. Postscript by PH. MERLAN, *Philos. Rundschau* 7, 1959, 129. L. ELDERS, *A.'s Theory of the One. A Commentary on Book X of the Met.* Assen 1961.

argued that, compared with Plato, Aristotle has only shifted the chorismos which now separates God and the world.[1] Perhaps one could wonder if Aristotle wholly escapes the reproach which the Platonic Socrates (*Phaed.* 98 b) levels at Anaxagoras that he placed mind (*nous*, as in Aristotle) at the head of the universe, but fails to utilize this doctrine for an explanation of the internal events of this universe. Even if Aristotle does not assume a divine creative activity which influences it, yet the motion of the universe is directed towards him. Each movement has its entelechy in the form which it wants to realize. The highest of all entelechies is necessarily the highest of all the forms, God, towards whom the motion of the whole universe tends. Unmoved himself, he is its cause, just as the object of desire rouses desire and keeps it in motion. This brief outline is not, however, meant to conceal copious individual problems. The variety of the notions proposed is proof of Aristotle's unceasing struggle of the thinker with these problems. To what extent can a deity who is pure thought-force influence the movement of the fixed stars? Or is the ultimate explanation that the outer heaven, conceived like the planets as a divine soul-endowed being, seeks its perfection in eternal regular movement in its longing for the deity as the ever-active (but unmoved) intelligence? Chapter 8 of Book Λ (cf. *supra*), proved by Jaeger to be a later insertion, introduces a new line of thought. While in the previous sections the movement of the outer heaven is the cause of motion in the world of things, Aristotle here adds individual movers to the spheres, corresponding in number with these spheres, in order to account for the planetary orbits.[2] It would also be difficult to mark off the realm of nature as the purposeful creator from that of the divine influence in the various phases of Aristotle's thought. In a phrase of Aristotle's quoted earlier (*De Caelo* 1, 4. 271 a 33) some difficult questions cross one another: 'The deity and (?) nature do (?) nothing without a plan'.

In the *Eudemus* Aristotle argued the pre-existence and immortality of the soul in the Platonic sense. Through stages which are difficult to trace separately,[3] he came to the convictions which he confirms in his treatise On the Soul (Περὶ ψυχῆς, 3 books).[4] Since the subject is not the human soul alone, but all the stages of animate life, the work can be considered as an introduction to

---

[1] H. LANGERBECK, *Gnom.* 26, 1954, 7. On A.'s notion of the divine: W. THEILER, 'Ein vergessenes Aristoteleszeugnis'. *Journ. Hell. Stud.* 77, 1957, 127. W. J. VERDENIUS, 'Traditional and Personal Elements in A.'s Religion'. *Phronesis* 5, 1960, 56.

[2] But cf. ALLAN (*v. inf.*). On the question of the transcendental cause of motion in the partially contradictory passages in W. K. GUTHRIE's bilingual ed. of On the Heavens. Loeb Class. Libr. 1939. KL. OEHLER, 'Der Beweis für den unbewegten Beweger bei A.'. *Phil.* 99, 1955, 70. PH. MERLAN, 'Aristotle's Unmoved Mover'. *Traditio* 4, 1946, 1. H. A. WOLFSON, 'The Plurality of Immovable Movers in A. and Averroës'. *Harv. Stud.* 63, 1958 (*Festschr. Jaeger*), 233.

[3] *v.* p. 575 on NUYEN's book.

[4] Ed. by W. D. ROSS (rec. brevique adnot. instr.), Oxf. 1956. The comm. ed. of FR. A. TRENDELENBURG, Berl. 1877, was photomechanically reprinted in Graz 1957. A Cura di A. BARBIERI, Bari 1957. Transl. and comm. W. THEILER, Berl. 1959. Transl. by O. GIGON, *Vom Himmel, Von der Seele. Von der Dichtkunst.* Zürich 1950 (*Bibl. d. Alten Welt*). J. TRICOT, Paris 1959.

Aristotle's scientific works. On the other hand it contains such essential statements on man that we place it before the works dealing with his existence and activity.

The leading idea is now derived from the relationship of body and soul. These represent two aspects of one single substance; they stand in a mutual relationship of matter and form, of ὕλη and εἶδος. As a form of the essence of life the soul is at the same time its entelechy according to Aristotle's doctrine. The soul's action manifests itself in five different soul forces whose influence in the realm of the animate presupposes a hierarchy, but this should by no means be associated with the modern conception of the evolution of one species from another. The simplest species of soul, that possessed by plants, only has the power of nourishment (θρεπτικόν), to which that of propagation is added. Animals possess the faculty of sense perception (αἰσθητικόν) which varies greatly in individuals; in the highest species desire (ὀρεκτικόν) and locomotion (κινητικόν) is added. But man alone has the power of thought (διανοητικόν). Aristotle again gives an historical survey in Book 1; then he deals more elaborately, after the separation of the various powers of the soul[1] with perception through the five senses; to these is added the 'combining sense' which can relate the various sense observations to one uniform object. The *nous*, to which the concluding part is devoted, is alone capable of forming general notions and of proving regular occurrences. It alone remains free of the union with the corporeal; it apparently enters the embryo from outside and is, at this stage of Aristotelian thought, the only part of the soul which lives on. It is hard to say how Aristotle envisaged this after-life; but since there was definitely no question of the preservation of the whole soul, he cannot have meant immortality in the form of the Orphic-Pythagorean belief in the hereafter and of Platonic myths.

A series of small works follow here which turned up as a compilation under the title *Parva Naturalia*[2] in Aegidius Romanus (Gilles de Rome) at the end of the thirteenth century. Aristotle's own comments on the phenomena which are of common interest to body and soul (436 a 7) most aptly characterize the nature of these writings. The titles which also indicate their contents are: *On Perception and the Perceptible* (Περὶ αἰσθήσεως καὶ αἰσθητῶν), *On Memory and Recollection* (Περὶ μνήμης καὶ ἀναμνήσεως), *On Sleeping and Waking* (Περὶ ὕπνου καὶ ἐγρηγόρσεως), *On Dreams* (Περὶ ἐνυπνίων), *On Divination in Dreams* (Περὶ τῆς καθ' ὕπνον μαντικῆς),[3] *On the Long and the Short Life* (Περὶ μακρηβιότητος καὶ βραχυβιότητος); three works followed which probably constituted a uniform whole: *On Youth and Old Age* (Περὶ νεότητος καὶ γήρως), *On Life and Death* (Περὶ ζωῆς καὶ θανάτου), *On Breathing* (Περὶ ἀναπνοῆς).

These writings correspond in many respects with the biological works in

---

[1] On the two parts of the soul (ἄλογον: τὸ λόγον ἔχον within which φρόνησις: νοῦς) G. MÜLLER. *Mus. Helv.* 17, 1960, 129.

[2] Ed. and comm. by W. D. ROSS, Oxf. 1955. Transl. J. TRICOT, Paris 1951.

[3] *Ar. De insomniis et De divinatione per somnum. A New Edition of the Greek Text with the Latin Translations*, by H. J. DROSSAART LULOFS. 2 vols. Leiden 1947.

their considerations of the conditions and termination of animal life. It is important that Aristotle consistently takes the heart as the seat of the functions of the soul, a momentous retrogression after Alcmeon's findings. In the introduction to his authoritative edition, W. D. Ross has proved that it is likely that the writings mentioned belong to Aristotle's middle creative period (Assos, Mytilene, Macedon), and largely before the work *On the Soul*.

In the Corpus Aristotelicum three works have been preserved which deal with the forms and conditions of moral excellence: the *Nicomachean Ethics* ('Hθικὰ Νικομάχεια, 10 books),[1] the *Eudemean Ethics* ('Hθικὰ Εὐδήμεια, 7 books) and the *Great Ethics* ('Hθικὰ μεγάλα, 2 books).[2] At present hardly any one will doubt the authenticity of the first of these three didactic works, and only few the late date of the last. The *Great Ethics*, which bears this title in spite of the fact that it has the smallest size of the three works, belongs to the late-Hellenistic tradition of the Peripatetic school. We follow Dirlmeier's dating[3] who in his commentary attempts to prove that the unknown Peripatetic is not the composer of the *Great Ethics*, but the editor of the earliest outline of the ethics of the Master himself. The little treatise *On Virtues and Baseness* (Περὶ ἀρετῶν καὶ κακιῶν) must have been written considerably later.

A problem which has not yet been solved by any scholar on Aristotle is posed by the *Eudemean Ethics*, although the voices in favour of its genuineness are increasing. An explanation of its title, like that of the *Nicomachean Ethics*, as a dedication to the person concerned, cannot be upheld, since such a dedication of a didactic work does not agree with the usage of the time. The assumption is probable, but not certain, that the two works were named after their editors. In the one case this would be Nicomachus, Aristotle's son who was named after his grandfather, in the other Eudemus of Rhodes, who must not be confused with the title role of the early dialogue. This pupil of Aristotle's and friend of Theophrastus' is also notable as the first historian of mathematics and astronomy of whom we know.

Contrary to the opinion that Eudemus was the editor of Aristotle's work, it has been claimed that he wrote the ethics called after him. This was propounded by L. Spengel more than a century ago and found a great following. It is of importance in this problem that, in contrast with the principles of the *Nic. Ethics*, the moral demands of the former work have a theological basis. After P. Von der Mühll (Gött. 1909) and E. Kapp (Freib. 1912) had already attempted

---

[1] A cura di A. PLEBE, Bari 1957. Comm. by H. H. JOACHIM, Oxf. 1951. Transl. with penetrating comm. by F. DIRLMEIER, Berl. 1956, 2nd ed. 1960. Transl. by O. GIGON, Zürich 1951 (*Bibl. d. Alten Welt*). J. TRICOT, Paris 1959. R. A. GAUTHIER and J. Y. JOLIF, *Nik. Eth. Introd., trad. et comm.* 2 vols. Louvain 1958/59.

[2] Transl. and extensive comm. by F. DIRLMEIER, Berl. 1958.

[3] 'Die Zeit der Gr. Ethik.' *Rhein. Mus.* 88, 1939, 214. There bibl. 214, 1. Now also extensively discussed by F. DIRLMEIER in the introduction to his translation (*v.* prev. n.). I. DÜRING, *Gnom.* 33, 1961, 557, agrees with his opinion after some objections. On this question also D. J. ALLAN, *Journ. Hell. Stud.* 77, 1957, 7. O. GIGON, *Mus. Helv.* 16, 1959, 209 again devaluates the *Great Ethics* as a poorly compiled handbook. Survey of the older bibl. in E. J. SCHÄCHER, *Studien zu den Ethiken des Corpus Aristot. I. Stud. zur Geschichte und Kultur des Altertums* 22, 1940.

in their dissertations to restore the work to Aristotle, Jaeger showed that the difference between the two ethics just indicated corresponded with Aristotle's development as he sketched it in his book. A further complication in solving the troublesome problem of whether this is the work of one of Aristotle's scholars who echoes the Master's thoughts here or who edited the result of his research, is the fact that Books 5-7 of the *Nic. Ethics* are similar to Books 4-6 of the *Eud. Ethics* and are no longer transcribed in the manuscripts of the latter work. But it is altogether likely that they primarily belong to the work called after Nicomachus.[1]

The *Nic. Ethics*, which is dated with some confidence, after the tenor of the work, in the last period of Aristotle's creative activity, reveals the contrast with Plato more clearly than any other work excepting the *Politics*. No longer does man's morality depend on his looking up to the world of eternal essences in which the idea of the good sheds its light over everything; in a disproportionately higher degree than Plato, Aristotle takes the *hic et nunc* of man's actions into account. The *Nic. Ethics* is not an urgent appeal to reshape one's life; it presents an analysis of morality as it appears under the various conditions of reality; and consequently the critical considerations are varied with a series of portrayals of types, whose force of description and sharpness of observation is later carried on in a different manner by Theophrastus in his *Characters*.

It is not with Plato's educational zeal, but rather with the attitude of the analysing scientist that Aristotle enquires into the nature of happiness ($\epsilon\vec{v}\delta\alpha\iota\mu o\nu\acute{\iota}\alpha$), indisputably the highest good which our actions can acquire. He finds it in an activity of the soul in the meaning of its essential excellence ($\dot{\alpha}\rho\epsilon\tau\acute{\eta}$, 1, 13. 1002 a 5). It is the task of the following books (2-6) to define the forms of this excellence. The system of the four Platonic cardinal virtues is abandoned and replaced by one of rich variety. It is of decisive importance that the virtues of character, such as courage, high-mindedness, gentleness, are contrasted with the virtues of intelligence. Of these latter sophia, which leads to the enduring truths, is attainable by few only, while phronesis is indispensable for any moral action. The development of the notion of phronesis is significant in the history of ideas; it has now lost the Platonic sense of the transcending vision and has become practical intelligence.[2] The tension between the virtues of character and phronesis which controls them is of fundamental importance for Aristotle's ethics. The Socratic moral knowledge has been abolished in the twofold meaning of the word. Since the virtues of character are not based on knowledge, but on a constant directing of the will, this realm of man's soul has been granted its due importance. On the other hand, the essentially Greek Socratic line of thought is continued in the indispensable control by phronesis. Essentially Greek also is another leading thought in these ethics, the idea of proportion on the basis of

---

[1] Recently it was attempted by G. LIEBERG, *Zet.* 19, 1958, 14, to attribute the three books to the *Eud. Eth.* and to account for the appearance of these books in both places with the hypothesis that books 5-7 of the *Nic. Eth.* had been lost and were replaced by 4-6 of the *Eud. Eth.* – On the style: R. HALL, 'The special vocabulary of the Eudemian Ethics'. *Class. Quart.* 9, 1959, 197.   [2] Cf. JAEGER (*v. inf.*), 249.

which various ways of behaviour appear as the right mean between extremes.[1] The very significance of 'mesotes' shows that the descriptive tendency of Aristotle's ethics by no means excludes a normative nature of the knowledge gained.

The following books[2] do not form the same strict unity; of their contents we can only single out for special mention the elaborate essay on friendship and the twofold discussion of the problem of desire.[3] When Aristotle has presented in this way a phenomenology of morality with his deep sympathy for the whole breadth of life, he makes his personal confession in Book 10 where he describes scientific endeavour as the highest attainable form of living. But the praise of the purest happiness fulfilled in enquiry[4] is at the same time a Platonic legacy; for Aristotle, the philosopher's road also comes to its perfect end with the vision of the divine. In his *Republic* (9. 582 c; 585 e) Plato connected true and highest desire with the philosopher's striving after knowledge of the Highest. In Aristotle's work the phrase occurs which the older Greeks would have considered hybris: man should not be satisfied with what is human only but follow the highest given to him and so aspire to immortality. For: 'If, compared with man, the spirit is something divine, then a life in the spiritual is something divine compared with human life'. This is the way in which the ὁμοίωσις θεῷ opens up, in Aristotle's opinion, the possibility for man to reach the divine.

The end of the *Nic. Ethics* forms a transition to the subject of the *Politics*, a feature which shows that Aristotle thought that these two fields were closely allied parts of a science which applied to the individual as well as to society. Aristotle would not have been Plato's student if the problems of politics had not stirred him at an early stage. Among the exoteric works appear a *Politicus* (2 books), a treatise *On Justice* (Περὶ δικαιοσύνης, 4 books)[5] and an *On Royalty*

---

[1] This does not mean formalism, cf. ALLAN (*v. inf.*), 168. H. J. KRÄMER, *Arete bei Platon und Aristoteles. Abh. Ak. Heidelb. Phil. hist. Kl.* 1959/6, 342 and further *passim*, argues with great emphasis that the μεσότης-doctrine must be derived from Plato. He attacks KALCHREUTER, JAEGER and WEHRLI who think that it was derived from medical thought; essentially conveyed in W. JAEGER, 'Medizin als methodisches Vorbild in der Ethik des A.'. *Zeitschr. für phil. Forschung* 13, 1959, 513. G. LIEBERG, *Zet.* 19, 1958, 59 thinks that Aristotle owed the doctrine to Speusippus. Probably none of these assumptions is tenable and account should be taken of this doctrine being anticipated in ancient Greek thinking, not in the last place in the religion. – General: R.-A. GAUTHIER, *La Morale d'A.* Paris 1958. M. S. SHELLENS, *Das sittliche Verhalten zum Mitmenschen im Anschluss an A.* Hamburg 1958.

[2] M. VAN STRAATEN and G. J. DE VRIES, 'Notes on the VIIth and the IXth Books of A.'s *Nic. Ethics*'. *Mnem.* S. 4, vol. 13, 1960, 193. JAN VAN DER MEULEN, *A. Die Mitte in seinem Denken.* Meisenheim/Glan 1951.

[3] GODO LIEBERG, *Die Lehre von der Lust in den Ethiken des A. Zet.* 19, Munich 1958; 'Die Stellung der griech. Philosophie zur Lust von den Pythagoreern bis auf A.'. *Gymn.* 66, 1959, 128. A.-J. FESTUGIÈRE, *A. Le Plaisir (Eth. Nic. VII 11-14. X 1-5). Introd., trad. et notes.* Paris 1960 (first 1937). G. MÜLLER in his excellent essay, 'Probleme der aristotelischen Eudaimonielehre'. *Mus. Helv.* 17, 1960, 121, stresses that A. returns to pre-Platonic philosophy (Empedocles, Anaxagoras, Democritus) by placing happiness in intellectual enquiry.

[4] On θεωρία ANTONIE WLOSOK, *Laktanz und die philosophische Gnosis. Abh. Ak. Heidelb. Phil.-hist. Kl.* 1960/2, 17.

[5] P. MORAUX, *A la recherche de l'Aristote perdu. Le dialogue 'Sur la justice'.* Louvain-Paris 1957, a circumspect, though not necessarily hypothetical reconstruction, which places the dialogue in a certain proximity to Plato's *Republic*.

(Περὶ βασιλείας, 1 book). The last treatise was probably written when he held his teaching post in Macedon.

We know that his interests in questions of this nature moved Aristotle to collect facts on a large scale; the results are lost to us with one gratifying exception. There were the *Customs of the Barbarians* (Νόμιμα βαρβαρικά), a title which recalls early Ionian enquiries; the *Pleas of the Greek Cities* (Δικαιώματα Ἑλληνίδων πόλεων) and especially the *Constitutions* (Πολιτεῖαι), a collection of 158 Greek constitutions of a wide scope which were no doubt compiled with the aid of many assistants. A papyrus find of the year 1891 (nr. 98 P.) yielded the greater part of the *Athenian Constitution* (Ἀθηναίων πολιτεία),[1] of which smaller pieces had come to light before. It forms the first book of the complete work and was written by Aristotle himself. The first part, which describes the early historical development, is followed by a concise account of the political institutions of Athens. The mixture of irregularities and a generally fluent style reflects its contents. However gratifying certain valuable new views may be, there is some disappointment over many mistakes and a certain aristocratical prejudice, as, for instance, in his criticism of the coup of 411. It is apparent that Aristotle worked in a hurry and was dependent on sources which were not always reliable; in such a difficult task this was an almost inevitable condition, and the treatise was only a small part of his gigantic work. On one occasion Olof Gigon[2] remarked that we would be surprised at the contrast between his credulity in this realm and his enormous discernment in biological matters, if Aristotle's complete works on cultural history had been preserved. It probably is no accident that his historical works perished in antiquity.

It seems tempting to say, as has often been done, that Aristotle collected material on such a large scale in order to build up his theoretical structure of the best state on the broadest empirical basis. But it does not simply go without saying that the *Constitutions* were a preliminary work to the *Politics*. In the first place it is obvious that collecting on such a large scale, dependent as it was on assistants, could not have been carried out until Aristotle's last, i.e. his second Athenian, period. The mention of the expedition to southern Italy which was undertaken by Alexander of Epirus, fixes 330 as the upper time limit for the completion of the *Dicaeomata*; the *Athenian Constitution* was not published before 329/28.[3] On the other hand, the history of the genesis of the *Politics* (Πολιτικά, 8 books)[4] goes back a long way. It was outlined by Jaeger, disputed by v. Arnim,

---

[1] Of particular importance: K. V. FRITZ-E. KAPP, *Aristotle's Constitution of Athens*. New York 1950. Ed. by H. OPPERMANN, repr. Leipz. 1961.

[2] *Der Bund*. Bern 26. 9. 1958. The work of K. V. FRITZ, 'Die Bedeutung des A. für die Geschichtsschreibung'. *Entretiens sur l'antiquité classique (Fondation Hardt)* 4, Vandœuvres-Geneva 1956 (1958), 85, has a different point of view. E. RIONDATO, *Storia e metafisica nel pensiero di A*. Padua 1961.

[3] JAEGER (*v. inf.*), 350. Bibl. on Ἀθ. πολ. in G. T. GRIFFITH, *Fifty Years of Class. Scholarship*. Oxf. 1954, 162, esp. n. 62.

[4] Ed. by W. D. ROSS, Oxf. 1957. Transl. by O. GIGON together with *The Athenian Constitution*. Zürich 1955 (*Bibl. d. Alten Welt*).

but recently Theiler has corroborated its major points in a penetrating study.[1] We shall first briefly survey its structure.

Book 1 deals with the general conditions of social life, considered to be the characteristic form of existence for man, in Aristotle's famous phrase ζῷον πολιτικόν. He also discusses the question of slavery; he adopts the conservative attitude in his defence of the dominion of the free over those who are born in servitude, or of Greeks over barbarians, which he considers to be a condition based upon nature. A few years later the Stoa and its theory of life would tear down the barriers which Greek thinkers had been shaking since the days of the sophists; I need only to recall the passage from Alcidamas' *Messeniacus* (p. 356). But it should not be overlooked that even though in the *Nic. Ethics* Aristotle considers the slave to be a living tool, he thinks that friendship is possible for him because he is a human being. It is typical for Aristotle's thought that he cannot allot a place to physical work in his scheme of values, since for him human happiness finds its completion in intellectual activity. Book 2 gives the historical survey which we expect to find in an Aristotelian didactic work with such a lofty purpose. Here he discusses his predecessors in theoretical constitutional models, examines various legislators, and especially the constitutions of Sparta, Crete and Carthage. His criticism deals very extensively with Plato's political thought, and also refers to the *Laws*, though not always correctly. In Book 3 Aristotle deals with some basic principles of political engineering and in one of the best-known parts of the work he discusses healthy and degenerate constitutions. The continuance of Plato's criticism of various types of constitution in his *Republic* is quite clear here. Monarchy, aristocracy and constitutional democracy are contrasted with the degenerate forms tyranny, oligarchy and unbridled democracy.[2] In the following parts of the work Books 4 to 6 form a distinctive group dealing with the historical reality of political life in its various forms and transitions, the defects incidental to them and the possibilities of eliminating them. This is followed up with the plan for the best state in Books 7 and 8. It may lack the consistency and completeness of the Platonic models, but it is also free of the extreme demands made in these. Generally, however, Aristotle followed his teacher in that he attached the greatest significance to education as the most important prerequisite for a healthy development of a state. Education is to make possible the growth of a society in which the purpose of the state is fulfilled: to offer to human nature the possibility to develop its characteristic talents. The model of the best state remained incomplete, but Aristotle hardly intended to give detailed instructions for its administration. His planning did not go beyond the boundaries of the old Greek city-state. In the matter of the distribution of authority, which he considers to be fundamental, he weighs in an undogmatic way the possibilities actually

---

[1] JAEGER (*v. inf.*), 271 ff. v. ARNIM, *Zur Entstehungsgesch. d. arist. Pol. Sitzb. Ak. Wien. Phil.-hist. Kl.* 200, 1924; *Wien. Stud.* 46, 1928, 45. w. THEILER, 'Bau und Zeit der arist. Pol.'. *Mus. Helv.* 9, 1952, 65. H. HOMMEL, *Festschrift f. Zucker.* Berl. 1954, 205 thinks of an edition by a pupil.

[2] A. does not yet use the expression ochlocracy and simply says δημοκρατία.

obtaining, but as a thinker of moderation he is inclined to entrust the maintenance of balance in the state to those who, because of their talent or education, are suitable to form a class which stands between the two extremes.[1]

It cannot be denied that the *Politics*, as we have it, shows in broad outlines that
the author worked according to a definite plan. The analysis has demonstrated,
however, that this structure was built up by combining parts which were
written at different times. Here, too, a great deal of detail remains dubious,
although some large sections have been marked off and dated authoritatively.
Jaeger places the discussion on the best state in Books 7 and 8 at the beginning.
Books 2 and 3 were prefixed to these as an introduction, so that we may
recognize in these four books the original *Politics* composed in Assos. Of course,
some difficult problems remain to be solved,[2] especially with regard to the
chronological classification of Book 2. On the whole, however, there is agreement that Books 4 to 6 must be allotted to the second Athenian period. Therefore a substructure from a collection of the various constitutions in the Πολιτεῖαι
is seriously questioned for these parts of the *Politics*, with which, according to
Jaeger, Book 1 must also be included as a preface of a later date.

Among Aristotle's numerous works none can be compared in influence with
one small treatise, which is, moreover, incompletely preserved. A history of the
criticism of the *Poetics* (Περὶ ποιητικῆς)[3] would have to review an important
part of the intellectual life of the western world; at the same time it would be a
history of widespread and influential errors and absurdities. In the last category
the most momentous was the adoption of the *Poetics* as a binding book of rules,
which it is no more than 'an apology for the national Greek poets and directions
for correctly understanding them' (Christ-Schmid). The great observer of all
living things, from the plants to the soul-endowed stars, also drew poetry
within the circle of the things which he wanted to investigate on the laws of
their nature and growth. Early indications of such a trend are already observable
in the sophists, of whom Gorgias was the most active in this respect.[4] It was also
observed long ago that Plato's criticism of the national poetry was one of the
most important starting points for Aristotle.[5] He did not sally forth to save

---

[1] E. BARKER, *The Political Thought of Plato and Aristotle*. New York 1959. R. WEIL, *Aristote
et l'histoire. Essai sur la 'Politique'. Étude et comm.* 36. Paris 1960.

[2] THEILER (*v.* p. 568, n. 1), 78.

[3] F. L. LUCAS, *Tragedy in Relation to A.'s Poetics*. Lond. 1928. 6th impr. 1949. S. H. BUTCHER,
A.'s Theory of Poetry and Fine Art. With a prefatory essay by John Gassner. 4th ed. New York
(Dover Publications) 1951. DANIEL DE MONTMALLIN, *La Poétique d'A. Texte primitif et
additions ultérieures.* Neuchâtel 1951. L. COOPER, *The Poetics of A., its Meaning and Influence.*
Cornell Un. Pr. 1956. H. HOUSE, *A.'s Poetics. A Course of Eight Lectures.* Lond. 1956. Scholarship will have to take a stand particularly with regard to the erudite, witty, but often
dubious book by G. F. ELSE, *A.'s Poetics, The Argument.* Leiden 1957. Recent transl. by O.
GIGON, *Vom Himmel, Von der Seele. Von der Dichtkunst.* Zürich 1950. (*Bibl. d. Alten Welt.*)
Reference must also be made to L. RICHTER, *Zur Wissenschaftslehre von der Musik bei Platon
und A. Deutsche Ak. d. Wiss. Berlin. Schriften der Sektion f. Altertumsw.* 23, 1960. For bibl.
on the *Poetics* cf. p. 570, n. 1.

[4] M. POHLENZ, 'Die Anfänge der gr. Poetik'. *GGN* 1920.

[5] G. FINSLER, *Platon und die arist. Poetik.* Leipz. 1900.

Homer and tragedy; his aim was to evaluate the form and the effect of great poetry without the educational and political objects of Plato.

The title of one of the lost dialogues, On the Poets (Περὶ ποιητῶν, 3 books) shows that Aristotle was interested in literary questions at an early stage. The date of the composition of the Poetics cannot be accurately determined; it belongs to the later rather than the middle period of Aristotle's creative activity. Book 1, the only surviving part, deals with tragedy and the epic. It may be regarded as certain that the subject of Book 2 was the iambos and comedy. In the preserved book the part on tragedy is far more extensive than the one on epic. The starting-point is formed by a definition which is extraordinarily characteristic for the tendency and purpose of the Poetics and which contains a problem which has sparked off a controversy of principles lasting for centuries: 'A tragedy is the imitation of an action which is serious and also, as having magnitude, complete in itself; in language with pleasurable accessories, each kind brought in separately in the parts of the work; in a dramatic, not in a narrative form, δι' ἐλέου καὶ φόβου περαίνουσα τὴν τῶν τοιούτων παθημάτων κάθαρσιν'. The problem of Aristotelian catharsis is in the interpretation of the last clause. This is not the place for relating the history of this interpretation[1] and we can forgo it, the more so as it has been cleared up by a line of scholarly research which led from J. Bernays[2] via F. Dirlmeier[3] to W. Schadewaldt.[4] According to this interpretation the Aristotelian catharsis means neither the purging of the emotions mentioned by Aristotle in the sense that they are ennobled (as especially Lessing, Hamb. Dram. 78. Stück), nor the betterment of the man who is freed from an excess of such emotions or their harmful residue. Two things decided the correct solution; first the understanding that the term catharsis originates in the field of medicine where it means a relieving secretion; in the second place a reference to what Aristotle says on catharsis in Book 8 of the Politics (1341 a 21-24 with 1342 a 1-18). Interpreted along these lines the result is that in the Poetics Aristotle, always aiming at the functional in his study of phenomena, understood the effect of tragedy as the relief from the emotions aroused in it, combined with pleasure. The specific pleasure in tragedy, pleasure in the excitement of 'horror and misery' (rather than 'fear and pity') and in the relief at the disappearance of these feelings, is harmless for man as a cathartic pleasure,

[1] L. COOPER and A. GUDEMAN, A Bibliography of the Poetics of A. New Haven 1928 (supplement by M. T. HERRICK, Am. Journ. Phil. 52, 1931, 168) records some 150 statements on this question. A good deal about the history of the problem in M. KOMMERELL, Lessing und A. Frankf. 1940, 268. A good survey of the arguments in H. FLASHAR, 'Die medizinischen Grundlagen der Lehre von der Wirkung der Dichtung in der gr. Poetik'. Herm. 84, 1956, 12; more bibl. by the same in Gnom. 31, 1959, 210. C. W. VAN BOEKEL, Katharsis. Een filologische reconstructie van de psychologie van A. omtrent het gevoelsleven. Diss. Nijmegen. Utrecht 1957 (with bibl. up to 1955).

[2] Zwei Abhandlungen über die arist. Theorie des Dramas. Berl. 1880. Previously Grundzüge der verlorenen Abhandlung des A. über Wirkung der Trag. Breslau 1857. But it must not be forgotten that H. WEIL, Verh. der 10. Vers. deutscher Philologen. Basel 1848, 131 had led the way with the correct interpretation of catharsis.

[3] 'Κάθαρσις παθημάτων', Herm. 75, 1940, 81.

[4] 'Furcht und Mitleid', Herm. 83, 1955, 129.

according to Aristotle. In this way he arrives at a view which rejects Plato's radical banishment of the tragic play from society.

It is not Aristotle's fault that his important statement about ἁμαρτία (13. 1453 a 10) was long mistaken for moral guilt and so had a fatal influence on the interpretation of Greek tragedy. Aristotle was definite enough in his exclusion of moral defect (κακία καὶ μοχθηρία) from his notion of ἁμαρτία as the failure of the righteous man.[1]

The plot and the dialogue, which are its vehicle of expression, are given the greatest prominence by Aristotle. This emphasis relegates the chorus as a constituent element of the tragic work of art to the background and we see that in this way the original unity is dissolved and that tragedy is on its way to becoming a literary work to be read rather than to be seen.[2]

Two more remarks seem to be called for. What Aristotle understands as the effect of pleasure proper to tragedy has no connection whatever with the joyfulness which Hölderlin praises in his epigram on Sophocles' works. There is at most a faint indication in Aristotle's *Poetics* of the modern view of the tragic as a very special way of looking at the world. Nor should our admiration for the acuteness with which this form of literature is analysed and described in many essential features blind us to the many surprising opinions which are quite alien to ours. To call Oedipus a 'middle' character between good and evil seems an inadequate description to us, and one of Euripides' finest plays, *Iphigenia in Aulis*, is censured because the heroine shows a lack of consistency in her nature by her change from fear of death to readiness for sacrifice.

It has now been correctly decided that Aristotle did not mean his cathartic effect to be an ethical one. But this does not imply that he denied it such a nature. It did not suit him to express an opinion on this question, and any attempt to interpret his observations about its nature and function as an ideological statement of principles is doomed to failure, whether it adopts one ideology or another. Therefore Aristotle cannot be used as a witness in the controversy about the educational influence of a work of art, which is so important in the history of ideas. This problem sprang up in antiquity;[3] it was solved by Goethe, when he wrote in *Dichtung und Wahrheit* (12, Jub.-Ausg. 24. 111): 'Of course a work of art can and will have moral consequences, but to demand moral aims from the artist means to corrupt his art'. In his *Archaischer Torso Apollos* Rilke also had these 'moral consequences' in mind: '... for there is no place which does not see you. You must change your life'. But Aristotle did not express himself on these questions, because he had no call to do so.

His bent for documentation and for penetrating poetic criticism, to which the *Poetics* bear witness, also put its stamp on some of the lost works. The *Homeric*

---

[1] Important for the elucidation of these questions: K. V. FRITZ, 'Tragische Schuld und poetische Gerechtigkeit in der griech. Trag.'. *Studium Generale* 8, 1955, 194 and 219; now in *Antike und moderne Tragödie*. Berlin 1962, 1. Important material on ἁμαρτάνω in G. ZUNTZ, *Gnom.* 30, 1958, 23.

[2] Passages on this subject in H. SCHRECKENBERG, *Drama*. Würzburg 1960, 132.

[3] Cf. W. KRAUS, 'Die Auffassung des Dichterberufes im frühen Griechentum'. *Wien. Stud.*. 68, 1955, 65.

Problems ('Ἀπορήματα Ὁμηρικά) deals with the answering of single questions. The book belongs to a literary genre which had begun to develop since the sophists. Homer, still the teacher of the Greeks, inevitably became the subject of critical controversies as literary-historical interest developed. A witness to its lively spirit is Zoïlus of Amphipolis (F Gr Hist 71), a fourth-century orator and sophist, opponent of Isocrates, who in his writings criticized Homer in a way which earned him the nickname of 'Homer's Scourge' (Ὁμηρομάστιξ).

Among the elaborate civic programmes which Aristotle undertook as the head of the Athenian school – the earliest of this nature of which we know – also belonged the systematic arrangement of material important for the history of culture and literature. In 355 Aristotle and his grand-nephew Callisthenes compiled the *List of Pythian Victors* (Πυθιονῖκαι). We have the inscription[1] with the decree of the Delphians to wreathe him and Callisthenes as an expression of their gratitude. But a renewed outbreak of anti-Macedonian feeling after Alexander's death deprived him of this honour. A passage is extant from a letter (fr. 666) in which he mentions these reversals with composure. A *List of Olympian Victors* (Ὀλυμπιονῖκαι) is mentioned among his works. With the *Didascaliae* (Διδασκαλίαι) and thᵊ *Victories in the Town-Dionysia and the Lenaea* (Νῖκαι Διονυσιακαὶ καὶ Ληναϊκαί) Aristotle used the archons' archives to prepare material which was the indispensable basis for later scholarship, especially for the Alexandrians.

When Aristotle compiled his didactic works, rhetoric had already become an educational force with an important tradition. In his early dialogue *Gryllus* (Γρῦλλος ἢ περὶ ῥητορικῆς) he had already taken his stand with regard to this form of intellectual activity; now, in the years of his maturity, he produced the three books of the *Rhetoric* (Τέχνη ῥητορικῆς),[2] which opposes the works of the professional teachers of rhetoric Theodectes and Anaximenes, while siding with them at the same time. For on the one hand Aristotle propounds the doctrine of a rhetoric in the spirit of science, guided by the attempts to examine this realm also for the laws behind the phenomena and to develop these logically; on the other, he writes for the practice of the orator, so that in many parts, especially in Book 3, he approaches to a certain extent the scholastic rhetoric initiated by Isocrates. There are many obscurities and irregularities of arrangement, caused by this twofold purpose and by the fact that the work is a collection of lecture notes. This arrangement can only be traced here in broad outlines. Book 1, divided according to the three genres (συμβουλευτικόν, ἐπιδεικτικόν, δικανικόν), deals with the various kinds of proofs. Part of Book 2 takes this subject up again and gives the general means of proof, applicable to all genres; the treatment of the enthymemes is important here, by which Aristotle means rhetorical deductions without the conclusive force of those of dialectic. The first part (1-11) of Book 2 deals with the emotions (πάθη), and then with the ἤθη (12-17). Aristotle introduced an innovation by adding to the technical means of

---

[1] *Fouilles de Delphes* III/1. Paris, 1929, no. 400. DITTENBERGER, *Sylloge* 3rd ed. 1, no. 275.

[2] New ed. A. TOVAR, Madrid 1953. W. D. ROSS, Oxf. 1959. Good analysis in W. KROLL, *RE* S 7, 1940, 1057. Cf. F. SOLMSEN, *Die Entwicklung der arist. Logik und Rhetorik*. Berl. 1929.

proof the possibilities which are gained from the character of the speakers. Book 3, whose genuineness can no longer be doubted, deals first (1-12) with style (λέξις) from the point of view of clarity, the selection of the correct lofty tone and of propriety, and then (13-19) with the correct arrangement (τάξις), from there he passes on to the separate parts of speech, paying more attention generally in the rest of this book to practical instruction.

Rhetoric constantly had Aristotle's attention. It is significant for the place which he allotted to it as a δύναμις, as a formal techne, outside pure science (ἐπιστήμη, cf. 1359 b 13), that the lectures dealing with it took place in the afternoon, which was reserved for lighter subjects. Rhetoric also came under the large-scale collecting activity of the later period; the Collection of Rhetorical Textbooks (Τεχνῶν συναγωγή) surveyed the entire previous development of this literature. It is difficult to determine the contents of the Theodectes, which is also lost. Its title in the catalogue of writings in Hesychius and Diogenes, Τέχνης τῆς Θεοδέκτου συναγωγή, indicates that Aristotle collected and published a Techne of Isocrates' scholar Theodectes of Phaselis, who also made a name for himself as a tragedian.[1]

In accordance with the purpose of this study, the various scientific works will now be briefly enumerated, but this brevity should not give a distorted picture of the importance of this side of Aristotle's creativity. The Meteorology (Μετεωρολογικά, 4 books), translated by J. Tricot, Paris, 1955, is related with the treatise On the Heaven in that here he deals with the phenomena underneath the aether-filled astral spheres, i.e. from the moon down to the interior of the earth. Heat and cold are the controlling forces for the aetiology of the events which occur in the realm of the four elements inferior to the aether. The work is important because it asks and answers numerous questions about the wide scope of nature. Book 4, which is of doubtful authenticity,[2] occupies a special position; it leads up to the threshold of modern chemistry with its treatment of matter. The writing On the Rising of the Nile (Περὶ τῆς τοῦ Νείλου ἀναβάσεως) was handed down in a Latin translation only and was long considered to be spurious. Lately it has found advocates[3] who can point out that the final explanation of the rising of the Nile through rainfall is preceded by a historical discussion of the problem in the typical Aristotelian manner.

As part of a project planned on a broad scale, Aristotle assigned to Theophrastus the description of the vegetable kingdom, while he himself undertook the zoological part of the gigantic work which, according to his plan, was to span the whole realm of nature. The imposing work of the Zoology (Αἱ περὶ τὰ ζῷα ἱστορίαι, 10 books)[4] was built up by Aristotle from a tremendous wealth of observations, both his own and others', into a description containing, apart from a great deal which is erroneous, excellent information about the anatomy,

---

[1] Cf. F. SOLMSEN, RE 5 A, 1934, 1730.

[2] Cf. GEFFCKEN, Griech. Lit.-Gesch. 2, 2nd part, 208, n. 36. On its genuineness I. DÜRING, A.'s Chemical Treatise. Göteborgs Högskolas Årsskrift. 1944, 2. Otherwise F. SOLMSEN, Gnom. 29, 1957, 132.

[3] GEFFCKEN (v. sup.), 209, n. 47.

[4] Transl. by J. TRICOT, 2 vols. Paris 1957.

physiology and habits of numerous animals. The description of the reproduction of the smooth-skinned shark, which anticipated the discoveries of the middle of the last century, was called 'almost uncanny' by the science-historian George Sarton. Joseph Wiesner[1] gave an impressive demonstration of how ancient skill at observation was preserved in Aristotle with his example of the 'squid's wedding'. We have to take interpolations of others into account in this work, even more than in any other. Jaeger attributed the last books generally to minor members of the school. The *Problems* ($\Pi\rho\circ\beta\lambda\dot{\eta}\mu\alpha\tau\alpha$)[2] is completely different; it deals largely with scientific questions and contains, apart from Aristotle's own, so much foreign matter that it can no longer be numbered among the genuine works.

A row of spurious works are related with this one, which claim legitimacy for their scientific compilations in the Master's name; such are *On Breathing* ($\Pi\epsilon\rho\grave{\iota}\ \pi\nu\epsilon\dot{\nu}\mu\alpha\tau\circ\varsigma$), *On Colours* ($\Pi\epsilon\rho\grave{\iota}\ \chi\rho\omega\mu\dot{\alpha}\tau\omega\nu$), *On Hearing* ($\Pi\epsilon\rho\grave{\iota}\ \dot{\alpha}\kappa\circ\upsilon\sigma\tau\hat{\omega}\nu$), *On Plants* ($\Pi\epsilon\rho\grave{\iota}\ \phi\upsilon\tau\hat{\omega}\nu$), *Mechanics* ($M\eta\chi\alpha\nu\iota\kappa\dot{\alpha}$), *Physiognomy* ($\Phi\upsilon\sigma\iota\circ\gamma\nu\omega\mu\iota\kappa\dot{\alpha}$), *Estate Management* ($O\grave{\iota}\kappa\circ\nu\circ\mu\iota\kappa\dot{\alpha}$).[3]

The *Zoology* is a great descriptive and also illustrated (510 a 29) collection,[4] comparable with similar comprehensive works in other fields; in a series of other works, however, Aristotle tackled the aetiology of the phenomena he had described, which in his opinion largely coincides with their teleology: *On the Parts of Animals* ($\Pi\epsilon\rho\grave{\iota}\ \zeta\dot{\omega}\omega\nu\ \mu\circ\rho\dot{\iota}\omega\nu$, 4 books),[5] the first book of which contains a loftily written statement of principles as an introduction to Aristotelian scientific research; *On the Generation of Animals* ($\Pi\epsilon\rho\grave{\iota}\ \zeta\dot{\omega}\omega\nu\ \gamma\epsilon\nu\dot{\epsilon}\sigma\epsilon\omega\varsigma$, 5 books);[6] *On the Gait of Animals* ($\Pi\epsilon\rho\grave{\iota}\ \pi\circ\rho\epsilon\dot{\iota}\alpha\varsigma\ \zeta\dot{\omega}\omega\nu$) and the unjustly suspected treatise *On the Movement of Animals* ($\Pi\epsilon\rho\grave{\iota}\ \zeta\dot{\omega}\omega\nu\ \kappa\iota\nu\dot{\eta}\sigma\epsilon\omega\varsigma$),[7] which soars from a discussion of the mechanism of animal movement to the question of the unmoved mover.

In the course of this study we had to point now and then to spurious parts in the Corpus Aristotelicum. Another three should be mentioned. The treatise *On the Universe* ($\Pi\epsilon\rho\grave{\iota}\ \kappa\dot{\circ}\sigma\mu\circ\upsilon$) has been the subject of a great deal of critical interest because of its curious position among the systems and because of its religious spirit.[8] It is no longer assumed that it is closely connected with Posidonius; the work, which dates from A.D. 100, belongs to a Peripatetic tradition with a strong Platonic tendency. The writing *On Indivisible Lines* ($\Pi\epsilon\rho\grave{\iota}\ \dot{\alpha}\tau\dot{\circ}\mu\omega\nu\ \gamma\rho\alpha\mu\mu\hat{\omega}\nu$),

---

[1] *Arch. Jahrb.* 74, 1959, 38. Cf. also L. BOURGEY, *Observation et expérience chez A.* Paris 1953.

[2] G. MARENGHI, 'La tradizione manoscritta dei Problemata physica aristotelici'. *Boll. del comitato per la preparazione della Ed. Naz. dei class. Greci e Lat.* Fasc. 9, 1961, 47.

[3] Transl. by J. TRICOT, Paris 1958.

[4] About its special character as a textbook now F. DIRLMEIER, *Sitzb. Ak. Heidelb. Phil.-hist. Kl.* 1962/2, 20.

[5] Comm.: I. DÜRING, Göteborg 1943.

[6] On A.'s doctrine of generation and heredity, ERNA LESKY in the book mentioned on p. 493. There (1377) also on a break in A.'s system.

[7] L. TORRACA, *De motu animalium. Testo, trad., comm.* Naples 1958 (*Coll. di studi greci*).

[8] A.-J. FESTUGIÈRE, *La Révélation d'Hermès Trismégiste. II. Le dieu cosmique.* Paris 1949, 460. H. STROHM, 'Studien zur Schrift von der Welt'. *Mus. Helv.* 9, 1952, 137.

which belongs to the late Platonic tradition, was also attributed to Theophrastus.[1] The *Peplos* is alleged to be Aristotle's (fr. 637 ff. Ross); it is a mythological work of a mixed content from which sixty-three epigrams have been preserved, mainly on the fallen in the Trojan war.

The study which has been made of Aristotle's work is founded on the notion of Aristotle which is the result of the last few decades of scholarship, but it seems to be imperative to stress, in conclusion, the main problem. The important point is that Aristotle has been dismissed from his isolated position of an authoritarian headmaster, and returned to history, and that his work is no longer regarded as a dogmatical system complete in itself, but as the expression of an intellectual movement of very great dynamic power. Aristotle was a product of Plato's teaching, and he left behind pupils who passed his legacy on to the Hellenistic age and so evoked a new form of science. The enormous distance between the two ends of the time-span just referred to is the result of a profound change whose decisive epoch coincided with Aristotle's labours. The following example will serve to illustrate this point. The emancipation of individual branches of science from the primacy of philosophy, which is complete in Alexandria, is still unthinkable with Plato, but it is being anticipated in some of Aristotle's works, though it is by no means certain that he had such a drastic course in mind.

In 1923 Werner Jaeger blazed a new trail for scholarship with his book on Aristotle. In it the notion of the historical development of thought, which Aristotle created, was decisively brought to bear on the philosopher's work itself. The picture sketched by Jaeger was chiefly a picture of a development which more and more led away from Plato. During a first period, to which the majority of the dialogues belong, Aristotle must have been a Platonist with the theory of ideas as a foundation; in the middle period of Assos, Lesbos and Macedon, during which *inter alia* the older strata of the *Physics*, *Metaphysics* and *Politics* were written, he freed himself of his belief in the transcendence of the ideas and turned, during a third period, in his quality as leader of the school, to the empirical investigation of isolated phenomena and founded a new type of science. Since Jaeger's book appeared, the study of Aristotle has been mainly occupied with the task of testing this first great sketch on its reliability in detail, and altering it where needed. F. Nuyens[2] attempted to utilize the change in Aristotle's conception of the soul for a chronology which deviated in many respects from Jaeger's. In his opinion the road led from the dialogues with their adoption of Platonic notions to an extension of the idea of the soul over all the forms of life in the biological works of a middle period, and finally to the conception of the soul as the entelechy of the individual in the late work *On the Soul*. In his excellent book on Aristotle (15) D. J. Allan proposed to replace the long and steady development of the philosopher by one which was brought about by a crisis. We may now think that this interpretation was a sudden whim.

---

[1] O. REGENBOGEN, *RE* S 7, 1940, 1542, with a list of pseudo-Aristotelica possibly by Theophrastus.

[2] *L'Évolution de la psychologie d'A.* Louvain 1948 (Dutch 1939).

Scholarly research into this complex of questions is still in a state of flux, as is demonstrated by the opposition offered to Jaeger's sketch of the development by a group of scholars. F. Dirlmeier,[1] I. Düring[2] and R. Stark[3] concur, though they vary in detail, in the opinion that Aristotle did not pass through a development from being a pure Platonist to empiricist, but that these two sides remained observable in him, and controlled his work, all the time.[4] They argue that Aristotle never accepted the theory of ideas but that he remained a Platonist in aiming his empiricism at the cognition of the permanently valid and in his appreciation of the intellect. The battle still goes on, but the basic idea of a continued development of Aristotle's thought will, no doubt, make good its claim. On the other hand, the scope of the opposition to Jaeger's conception has been substantially reduced and there is a stronger stress on a certain constancy in the basic factors which, apart from many variations, stimulated Aristotle's research in detail. The dating of individual works and parts of them still poses many problems. Thompson's indication (p. 550) that Aristotle's biological research was already off to a brisk start in Assos will have to play an important part. He opposes an extremely late date of the biological writings and recommends Nuyen's estimate at least for their older parts.

Aristotle's research took place in an environment of a richly developed scientific life, which had been called forth largely by the Master himself. Here we can only afford a brief glance at some of its representatives. Aristotle's undertaking to collect systematically the achievements and conjectures of his predecessors in all fields of knowledge – and this must have demanded considerable library resources, precursors to the great libraries of Alexandria and Pergamum – set many hands and minds in motion. Theophrastus's great work *History of Physics* (Φυσικῶν δόξαι, 18 books) falls within the scope of the great plan; our knowledge of this field is largely derived from it in spite of many breaks and gaps. Eudemus of Rhodes, a pupil of Aristotle's and a friend of Theophrastus', was the first, as far as we know, to write a history of arithmetic, geometry and astronomy; the little information we have about pre-Euclidean mathematics may be attributed to him. We add here the two mathematicians Aristaeus and Autolycus of Pitane who were active at the end of the fourth century and who represent the transition to Euclid. Two mathematical works

[1] *Jahrb. f. d. Bistum Mainz* 5, 1950, 161; *Gnom.* 28, 1956, 344.

[2] *A.'s De part. anim.* Göteborg 1943, 36; 'A. the Scholar'. *Commentationes in hon. E. Linkomies.* (*Arctos* Nov. Ser. 1) Helsinki 1954, 61, esp. 75 f.; 65, n. 4 gives bibl. Cf. also bibl. quoted on p. 554, n. 4.

[3] *Aristotelesstudien. Zet.* 8. Munich 1954, esp. 91 f. Opposing a steady development leading away from Plato, also M. WUNDT, *Untersuchungen zur Metaphysik des A.* Stuttgart 1953. Survey of the recent history of the problem in G. VERBEKE in: *Autour d'Aristote.* Louvain 1955, 18.

[4] Doubt of JAEGER's notion of Aristotle's development is also voiced by K. OEHLER, 'Thomas von Aquin als Interpret der aristotelischen Ethik'. *Philos. Rundschau* 5, 1957, 135, and G. MÜLLER, 'Probleme der aristotelischen Eudaimonielehre'. *Mus. Helv.* 17, 1960, 127; but MÜLLER's reference to fr. 78 R. must not be overlooked; it loses its force as support for JAEGER's theory only if one thinks that A. offered an opposing view in his dialogue.

of the latter,[1] dealing with spherical geometry, have been preserved; a third, which is lost, criticized the theory of the homocentric spheres.

Meno was commissioned by Aristotle to write a history of medicine. A voluminous papyrus of the second century A.D., the so-called *Anonymus Londinensis* (nr. 1820 P.), contains an extract of it which is also our main source for one of the most important physicians of the Sicilian school, Philistion of Locri, who started from Empedocles' four elements and explained the facts of physiology mainly with the aid of his pneuma theory. In other respects the connections of Aristotle and his school with medicine have also been exceedingly active. Recent research[2] has especially related the teaching at the Peripatos with Diocles of Carystus, the only physician of whom we have any knowledge between Hippocrates and the Hellenistic era. It has been proved that Diocles' date in the early fourth century is erroneous, but his floruit should not be placed later than the decades 340–320. He was the first physician to write Attic Greek, which proves that he set a high standard for the form of his publications. Among his main works we know of a *Hygiene* (῾Υγιεινὰ πρὸς Πλείσταρχον) and a therapeutical work *Pain, Cause and Cure* (Πάθος αἰτία θεραπεία). Jaeger wanted to prove that the *Prophylactic Letter to King Antigonus* (᾽Επιστολὴ προφυλακτική) was genuine, but recently F. Heinimann[3] has raised serious objections to this. To characterize Diocles as one of the leaders of the dogmatic school, as was done in antiquity, is inadequate; the pneuma-doctrine of the Sicilian school had a very strong influence on him and it is from this centre that connections with Aristotle can be traced. Among the followers of Diocles is Praxagoras,[4] the head of the Coan school of medicine. The connections of the Peripatos with medicine acquired a domestic note when Pythias, Aristotle's daughter, married Metrodorus, a physician of the Cnidian school. Erasistratus, the great Hellenistic physician, worked with him after his initial training in Cos.

We add here two of Aristotle's pupils who, like Theophrastus, followed their master's example in the versatility and span of their works. Aristoxenus of Tarentum is supposed to have filled 453 book rolls and the fragments bear witness to a variety of themes. He is of importance to us as a theoretician in music. In the three books of his *Harmonics* (᾽Αρμονικὰ στοιχεῖα[5]) he portrayed a tradition reaching back to the Pythagoreans, with which he dealt in the spirit of the Peripatos. His *Rhythmics* (῾Ρυθμικὰ στοιχεῖα) is known to us from several

---

[1] After the ed. of F. HULTSCH, Leipz. 1885, J. MOGENET, Louvain 1950. In add. we refer to T. HEATH, *Mathematics in A.* Oxf. 1949 (the texts in transl.). The fragments of Eudemus: F. WEHRLI, *Die Schule des Aristoteles* 8. Basel 1955.

[2] W. JAEGER, *D. von Karystos.* Berl. 1938. Id. *Festschr. f. Regenbogen.* Heidelb. 1952, 94; cf. also *Paideia* 2. 49. The fragments in M. WELLMANN, *Die Fragm. der sikelischen Ärzte.* Berl. 1901.

[3] 'D. von Karystos und der prophylaktische Brief an König Antigonos.' *Mus. Helv.* 12, 1955, 158.

[4] F. STECKERL, *The Fragments of Praxagoras of Cos and his School. Collected, edited and translated.* Leiden 1958.

[5] Editions: H. S. MACRAN, Oxf. 1902. ROSETTA DA RIOS, Rome 1954. Survey of the editions since Meursius: *Gnom.* 28, 1956, 279. The fragments of the remaining works: F. WEHRLI, *Die Schule des Aristoteles* 2. Basel 1945.

fragments, one of which, probably from Book 2, is fairly large. He took a very lively interest in Pythagoreanism. He wrote a biography of Archytas, and also a βίος πυθαγορικός by which he meant a way of life according to Pythagorean ideals. Biographies of Pythagoras and his scholars, and of Socrates and Plato were also among his works. In Cicero (Ad Att. 2. 16, 3) we find Theophrastus described as one who favoured a life devoted to speculative thinking in contrast to Dicaearchus of Messene[1] who attached more importance to the practical side of life. Dicaearchus also wrote about a great variety of subjects, such as philosophy, politics and literature, but he interests us chiefly for two of his fields of enquiry. With his works in the history of culture he opened a new territory for scientific work and in his Life in Greece (Βίος 'Ελλάδος, 3 books) he applied his methods of observation to his own people. His other achievement is in geography, in which, with his Description of the Earth (Γῆς περίοδος) he paved the way for a line of research which led via Eratosthenes to Strabo. Next to Theophrastus he was Aristotle's most important pupil and in his case we are particularly sorry to possess only some scraps.

Geographical research, as represented by Dicaearchus, a revival of ancient Ionian ἱστορίη, is closely allied with the great voyages of discovery of that time. One of these was undertaken by Pytheas of Massalia with such a boldness that its results were disbelieved; at the time of the expedition of Alexander the Great he travelled all over north-western and northern Europe up to the fringes of the Arctic; we do not know how far he went, especially as regards his Thule (Iceland or Norway?). The effect of his work On the Ocean (Περὶ 'Ωκεανοῦ) can be traced in many places.[2] At about the same time (325/24) Alexander's admiral Nearchus undertook his voyage from the Indus to Persia, and so repeated, after nearly two centuries, the bold enterprise of Scylax, to whom a survey of the Mediterranean coast was attributed at the time of Philip II (cf. p. 219). We can form a picture of the vividness with which Nearchus related his observations from the parts which Arrian utilized in his book on India ('Ινδική.)[3]

A decisive chapter in the history of the Aristotelian tradition is preserved in Strabo (13. 54, p. 608, also Plut. Sulla 26). It sounds like fiction and has often been dismissed as such, but it is in such striking agreement with Aristotle's connections with north-western Asia Minor that there is no room for doubt. It claims that the master's legacy of didactic writings passed first to Theophrastus, from him to Neleus of Scepsis, a son of the above-mentioned Coriscus,

---

[1] Fragments: F. WEHRLI, Die Schule des Aristoteles I. Basel 1944.

[2] R. GUNGERICH, Die Küstenbeschreibungen in der griech. Lit. Münster 1950, 16. H. J. METTE, Pytheas von Massalia. Kl. Texte 173. Berl. 1952. D. STICHTENOTH, Pytheas von Marseille, Über das Weltmeer. Aus dem Lateinischen übersetzt und erläutert. Weimar-Cologne 1959. R. KNAPOWSKI, Zagadnienia chronologii . . . Poznań 1958, discusses questions of chronology and extent of the voyages of discovery.

[3] GUNGERICH (v. n. 2), 14, subject matter in JACOBY, F Gr Hist no. 133. Transl. and interpretation in O. SEEL, Antike Entdeckerfahrten. Zürich 1961 (Lebendige Antike).

who heard Aristotle in Assos and is often mentioned in the didactic works. Fearing the Attalids' mania for collecting books – they were building up their large library in Pergamum – his heirs stored the books in a subterranean room, which did not have a good effect on the rolls. In the first century B.C. Neleus' heirs sold them together with Theophrastus' works to a certain Apellicon of Teos, who, according to Strabo, was a bibliophile rather than a philosopher. Soon after his death his library came into the possession of Sulla and moved to Rome with him. Tyrannion first occupied himself with Aristotle's works, without notable results; the Peripatetic Andronicus of Rhodes produced, still in the first century B.C., the edition on which the entire subsequent tradition rests. The exoteric works did not lead a subterranean life, after Aristotle's death, like the didactic ones, but they were lost late in antiquity. However, it can hardly be assumed that before the treasure of Scepsis became known, the didactic works had been altogether forgotten. We can no longer make out how much new material was contributed by it.

The utilization of the complete manuscript tradition for Aristotle is a remote goal. The best information about the foundations, which vary from work to work, can at present be found in the relevant chapters of the second volume of J. GEFFCKEN's *Griech. Literaturgeschichte* (Heidelberg 1934). Also E. MIONI, *A.'s codd. graeci qui in bibliothecis Venetis adservantur*. Padua 1958. On the independence of Vat. 1339 as compared with Laur. 81. 1 recently I. DÜRING, *Gnom*. 31, 1959, 416, with bibl. On one special work E. LOBEL, *The Greek Manuscripts of A.'s Poetics*. Oxf. 1933 (Suppl. to the Biographical Society's Transactions 9). Apart from the find of the Ἀθηναίων πολιτεία, the papyri do not yield a great deal. On the gain from the point of view of textual criticism R. STARK, *Annal. Univers. Saraviensis. Philos. – Lettres* 8, 1/2, 1959, 36. There (38) also about a dubious attribution. The *Ox. Pap*. 24, 1957 have added fragments to *Nic. Ethics* 6 in no. 2402 and to the *Categories* in no. 2403. Aristotle was translated into Syrian, Arabic, Hebrew and Latin; A. JOURDAIN, *Recherches critiques sur l'âge et l'origine des traductions latines d'A. et sur les commentaires grecs et arabes employés par les docteurs scolastiques*. Nouv. éd. revue et augm. par CH. JOURDAIN 1843, repr. New York 1960. Much remains to be done for the utilization of this type of transmission. An example of its importance, and equally of the problems involved, is J. TKATSCH's work *Die arabische Übersetzung der Poetik des A. und die Grundlage der Kritik des griech. Textes. Akad. Wien* 1, 1928. 2, 1932. A. GUDEMAN's edition of the *Poetics*, Berl. 1934, gives an example of an exaggeration of its importance. The work of R. WALZER, 'On the Arabic Versions of Books A, α and Λ of A.'s Metaph.'. *Harv. Stud*. 63, 1958 (*Festschrift W. Jaeger*), 217 is important for its methodology. The exemplary collection of the scattered material carried out by the Union Acad. Internationale laid the basis for the utilization of the Latin translations which begin with Boethius and reach their climax with William de Moerbeke. The plan upon which was decided in 1930 proposes the edition of the translations before 1280 in an *Aristoteles Latinus* as the first part of a comprehensive *Corpus Philosophorum Medii Aevi*. The establishment of the manuscript tradition was substantially completed in 1939; its results are available in *Aristoteles Latinus: Pars prior*. Rome 1939, repr. Bruges-Paris 1957, edited by G. LACOMBE et al. *Pars posterior* (which also contains Supplementa to I) Cambr. 1955. *Suppl. Alterum*. Ed. L. MINIO-PALUELLO. Cambr. 1962 – The *Prolegomena in Aristotelem Latinum* are also part of the preliminary work for this plan; two fascicules of these have appeared in the Polish Acad. of Sciences: I: A. BIRKENMAJER, *Classement des ouvrages attribués à Aristote par le moyen âge latin*. Cracow 1932. II: W. L. LORIMER, *The Text Tradition of the Interpretation anonyma of Pseudo-Aristotle De Mundo*. Cracow 1934. The continuation of the series is planned with L. MINIO-PALUELLO, *Collected Papers on Some Translators and Translations of Aristotle in the Middle Ages*. – At present the publication is in the hands of L. MINIO-PALUELLO, R. A. B. MYNORS, O. GIGON, H. J. DROSSAART LULOFS and J. H. WASZINK. Published so far (in Bruges-Paris, unless otherwise indicated): I/1-5 *Categoriae vel Praedicamenta, translatio Boethii, recensio composita, translatio Gu. de Moerb., lemmata Simplicii Gu. de Moerb. interprete, paraphrasis Themistiana (Pseudo-Augustini Categoriae Decem)*. Ed. L. MINIO-PALUELLO 1962. IV/2 *Analytica post., translatio anonyma*. Ed. L. MINIO-PALUELLO 1953. IV/3 *Analytica post., Gerardo Cremonensi interprete*. Ed. L. MINIO-PALUELLO 1954. VII/2 *Physica, translatio Vaticana*. Ed. A. MANSION 1957. XI/1-2 *De Mundo, translatio anonyma et translatio Nicolai*. Ed. W. L. LORIMER. Rome 1951. XXIX/1 *Politica (libri I-II), translatio anonyma*. Ed. P. MICHAUD-QUANTIN 1962. XXXIII *De Arte Poetica, Gu. de Moerb. interprete*. Ed. E. VALGIMIGLI; reviserunt, praefatione indicibusque instruxerunt AE. FRANCESCHINI et L. MINIO-PALUELLO 1953. Printing: II *De Interpretatione, translatio Boethii, Gu. de Moerb.* Ed. L. MINIO-PALUELLO and G. VERBEKE. II/1-2 *Analytica priora, translationis Boethianae recensiones duae et translatio anonyma; Appendix scholia antiqua a Graeco translata continens*. Ed. L. MINIO-PALUELLO. – A good survey and history of the programme by L. MINIO-PALUELLO, *Studi Medievali* 3. ser. 1, 1960, 304. On this basis a bulletin, *Programme and Progress*, will be published in the near future. On the relevant questions of a philosophical historical nature I. DÜRING, 'Von A. bis Leibniz'. *Ant. u. Abendl.* 4, 1954, 118. F. VAN STEENBERGEN, *A. in the West*. Louvain 1955. *A. and Plato in the Mid-Fourth Century. Papers presented at the Symposium Aristotelicum held at Oxford, August 1957*. Ed. by I. DÜRING and G. E. L. OWEN. Stockholm 1960. 12. *Congr. int. di filosofia Venezia 1958. Atti Vol IX; Aristotelismo padovano e filosofia aristotelica*. Florence 1960. The numerous surviving commentaries and paraphrases are important for criticism and interpretation. The exegesis of Aristotle begins with Andronicus and has continued since him as a process of the greatest importance in the history of the West. The foundation was laid by the programme of the Preuss. Akademie *Commentaria in A. Graeca*, 23 vols. with 3 suppl. vols. Berl. 1882–1909. Reprints have begun with 2. 2 (Alex. Aphrod. in A. Topic.) and 4. 2 (Dexippus in A. Categ.) Berl. 1959. – G. VERBEKE, *Themistios: Comm. sur le traité de l'âme d'A. Trad. de Guillaume de Moerbeke. Éd. critique et étude sur l'utilisation du comm. dans l'œuvre de saint Thomas. Corpus Lat. Commentariorum in A. Graecorum* 1. Louvain 1957. Id.: *Comm. sur le Peri Herméneias d'A. Trad. de Guillaume de Moerbeke. Corpus Lat. Commentariorum in A. Graecorum* 2. Louvain 1961. K. GIOCARINIS, 'An unpublished late thirteenth-century comm. on the Nic. Eth. of A.'. *Traditio* 15, 1959, 299. LYMAN W. RILEY, *A. Texts and Commentaries to 1700 in the Univ. of Pennsylvania Library.* Philadelphia 1960. Selected commentaries of Averroes are published by the Mediaeval Society of America, Cambr. Mass. under the leadership of H. A. WOLFSON. I *Epitome of Parva Naturalia. Latin Text.* Ed. EMILY L. SHIELDS 1949. *Hebrew Text.* Ed. H. BLUMBERG 1954. Id.: *English Transl. and Comm.* 1961. II *Long Commentary on De Anima. Latin Text.* Ed. F. S. CRAWFORD 1953. III *Middle Commentary and Epitome of De Generatione et Corruptione. Latin Text.* Ed. F. H. FOBES 1956. *Hebrew Text.* Ed. S. KURLAND 1958. Id.: *English Transl. and Comm.* 1958. *De Substantia Orbis* and other vols. are due to follow. A reprint of *A. Opera cum Averrois commentariis.* Venetis apud Iuntas 1562–74 in 11 vols. and 3 suppl. vols. is being prepared by Minerva G.m.b.H. Frankfurt a. M.

The older bibl. on A. by K. PRAECHTER in F. UEBERWEG'S *Grundriss d. Gesch. d. Philos.* I, 12th ed. Berl. 1926. For the scholarship of the last ten years a number of surveys is available: P. WILPERT, 'Die Lage der Aristotelesforschung'. *Zeitschr. f. philos. Forsch.* I, 1946, 123. M. D. PHILIPPE, *Bibl. Einf. i. d. Stud. d. Philos.* 8. *Aristoteles.* Bern, 1948. W. JAEGER, 'Die Entwicklung des Studiums der griech. Philos. seit dem Erwachen des hist. Bewusstseins'. *Zeitschr. f. philos. Forsch.* 6, 1925, 200. W. D. ROSS in *Fifty Years of Classical Scholarship.* Oxf. 1954, 136. E. J. SCHÄCHER, *Platon-Aristoteles* I. Salzburg 1957, 10. *Aristotele nella critica e negli studi contemporanei* (contributions of It. scholars). Milan 1957. H. S. LONG, 'A Bibliographical Survey of Recent works on Aristotle.' *The Class. World* 51, 1957, 47. 57. 69; 52, 1958, 96. 117. 193. 204. G. VERBEKE, 'Bulletin de littérature aristotélicienne'. *Rev. philos. de Louvain* 56, 1958, 605. The bibliogr. notes (also on the separate works) in the *Lexicon d. Gesch. d. Naturwiss.*, sub Aristotle, edited by J. MAYERHÖFER are useful. The books by MORAUX and NUYENS mentioned p. 553, n. 2 and p. 575, n. 2 give a good bibliogr. On the exoteric works bibl. in W. D. ROSS, *Works of A.* 12, Oxf. 1952; also L. ALFONSI, *Herm.* 81, 1953, 45, 2. The most important texts from this now in W. D. ROSS, *A. Fragmenta selecta.* Oxf. 1955.

Modern scholarship on Aristotle was begun with the complete edition of the Preuss. Akademie in 5 vols. 1831–70, from which we quote; Book 5 contains H. BONITZ's indispensable *Index Aristotelicus.* Of the 2nd ed., by GIGON, I and II have appeared Berl. 1960 (with register of the most important editions since BEKKER), IV (reprint of the most important parts of the commentaries on A. and a concordance with the *Commentaria in A. Graeca,* as well as a new edition of the *Vita Marciana)* and V *(Index)* Berl. 1961 (the *Index* was already reprinted in 1955). III will comprise the collection of fragments brought up to date; the Latin translation of A.'s works is not included. – Most texts in the *Loeb Classical Library;* in the *Coll. des Univ. de Fr.:* Phys., On the Heaven, Parva Nat., Ath. Const., Polit., Poet., Rhet. 1-2, On the Parts of Animals, On the Generation of Animals (both series bilingual). The Teubner texts and those of the *Bibl. Oxoniensis* can always be profitably consulted. In general we refer for editions, commentaries and translations to the bibliographical aids mentioned, but stress as particularly important the Oxford editions (with comm.) by W. D. ROSS, to which reference was made in connection with separate works. Some information on recent editions in A. COLONNA, 'Note a recenti edizioni di A.'. *Boll. del comitato per la preparazione della ed. naz.* 5, Rome 1957, 13. There is also a survey in GIGON's new edition of the Berlin publication (*v. supra*). To complete the bibliographies mentioned we refer to the recent works in the notes. Particularly suitable introductions are: W. D. ROSS, *Aristotle*. Lond. 1923 (5th ed. repr. 1960, also Meridian Books, New York 1960). Id.: *The Development of A.'s Thought*. Lond. 1957. L. ROBIN, *Aristote*, Paris 1944. D. J. ALLAN, *The Philosophy of A.* Oxf. 1952. W. JAEGER's *Aristoteles*, a book whose importance was repeatedly mentioned in this study, appeared in Berl. 1955, 2nd ed. A brief introduction by J. H. RANDALL JR., *Aristotle*. New York 1960. Important contributions in: *Autour d'Aristote. Recueil d'études de philos. anc. et médiév. offert à A. Mansion*. Louvain 1955. W. BRÖCKER, *Aristoteles*. Philos. Abhandlungen I. 2nd ed. Frankf. a. M. 1957. TH. MERLAN, *Studies in Epicurus and A.* Wiesbaden 1960 (Kl. phil. Stud. 22). A selection of individual works has been published in translation. Of particular value is the comprehensive monumental transl.: *The Works of A. Transl. into English under the Editorship of* W. D. ROSS. 12 vols. Oxf. 1908–52. The transl. of the didactic works by P. GOHLKE has progressed to vol. 9: *Problemes*. Paderborn 1961.

3 THE ART OF RHETORIC

The influence of Plato's and Aristotle's works extends far beyond the boundaries of the century in which they created them. The founder of the Peripatos had stronger links with contemporary life than his teacher, but he also regarded education as the means of forming man as an individual; his political ideal also soars from broad empirical foundations into the realm of the timeless patterns in which the structure of the Platonic *Republic* had found its origin. But the full picture of the intellectual history of the fourth century cannot be completed with Plato and Aristotle only, for this century was an epoch of irreconcilable contrasts and hesitating transitions, until in the last part the beginnings of a new world emerged. The old hegemonic themes continued to be played for some more time, in the Spartan, Athenian and, for a change, in the Boeotian mode, but above all the restless change the call for general security and a general peace (κοινὴ εἰρήνη)[1] was heard more and more clearly, while in Asia, and later in the Macedonian north, powerful neighbours were interestedly following the attempts of Greek states to call up the shade of the Athenian maritime empire. At no time had there been so much and such loud talk of Athenian greatness, but it was the greatness of the past which paraded with museum exhibits. Different voices were also being raised, which prepared for an association of nations in the spirit of the Hellenistic age when cultural influences reached far beyond the frontiers of the city-states. Tradition and transition also jostle one another in the realm of literature. Many of the old forms of poetry were still being cultivated, as we shall soon be able to show with tragedy as an example. But rhetoric,

---

[1] Bibl. on this concept in H. BENGTSON, *Griech. Gesch.* 2nd ed. Munich, 1960, 250.

which had made an early start in the previous century, developed into a force which contested poetry's title to its own subject-matter, and it largely made good its claim in the course of its development. At Isocrates' school this same rhetoric also challenged philosophy and with its claim on the education of the young[1] initiated a struggle which was to go on for centuries. It will be clear from this that we consider the rise of rhetoric a characteristic feature of the fourth century and accordingly single out Isocrates as the typical representative of this epoch.

It is difficult to judge this man, and critics waver between extremes.[2] His intellectual mediocrity, lack of originality and of strong creative impulses contrast sharply with the quite unprecedented influence of his school. Statesmen, orators, historians and poets emerged from it in such quantity that Cicero once compared it (De Or. 2. 94) with the Trojan horse which contained only hand-picked heroes.[3] This influence, which lasted well after the end of antiquity, is a historical fact, and any description of Isocrates and his work will have to try to account for it.

Isocrates lived from 436, the time at which Athens was at the height of its power and was anticipating the quarrel with Sparta, until the year 338, when Philip of Macedon won his victory at Chaeronea and ushered in an era which started off an entirely new development. Isocrates was a native of Erchia, a deme in the eastern part of Athens, where his father ran a workshop[4] which produced flutes. His origin from a well-to-do home ensured for him a careful education; the usual conjectural biography of antiquity associates him with men like Prodicus, and this may well be correct. A sojourn in Thessaly had a decisive influence on him, for there he was taught by Gorgias, whose doctrine he wished to continue in its most important points. The time and extent of this study are matters of dispute; it may have occurred in the last decade of the fifth century or the years immediately beforehand. The Hellenistic periegete Heliodorus of Athens (in Pseudo-Plut. Vita dec. or. 838 d) saw on Isocrates' tomb a representation of his teachers and pupils, which showed him next to Gorgias and so preserved the memory of a relationship which guided his development.

It must have been the financial collapse of the paternal home in the confusion of war (cf. Antid. 161) which compelled him to earn a living and led him to the profession of logographer, or writer of forensic orations. Because in later years Isocrates denied this occupation, it became the subject of a controversy of which we hear the echo in Dionysius of Halicarnassus. His Isocrates, an important

[1] The history of the pedagogical battle between philosophy and rhetoric in H. V. ARNIM, Leben und Werke des Dion von Prusa. Berl. 1898. Cf. also H.-I. MARROU, Histoire de l'éducation dans l'antiquité. Paris 1955; Engl. tr. London 1956.

[2] Some apt observations and ref. on this in H.-J. NEWIGER, Gnom. 33, 1961, 761.

[3] The Callimachean Hermippus wrote Περὶ τῶν Ἰσοκράτους μαθητῶν. On his influence: H. M. HUBBELL, The Influence of I. on Cicero, Dionysius and Aristides. Diss. Yale Univ. 1913. R. JOHNSON, 'A note on the number of Isocrates' pupils'. Am. Journ. Phil. 78, 1957, 297. Mikkola (v. sup. on Isocrates), 272, 3, records the detail that Elizabeth I translated To Nicocles and Nicocles at the age of fourteen.

[4] We avoid the expression 'factory'; cf. F. OERTEL in R. V. POHLMANN, Geschichte der sozialen Frage und des Sozialismus in der antiken Welt. 2nd vol. 3rd ed. Munich 1925, 525.

source for us besides Pseudo-Plutarch, Suidas and an anonymous *Life*, reports (18) that Aphareus, Isocrates' adoptive son, denies any activity of his father for the law courts in a speech which he wrote against Megaclides on the *Antidosis*. This implies that this activity had been alleged and according to Dionysius' evidence, Aristotle made the same claim, mentioning whole bundles of Isocrates' forensic speeches circulating at the booksellers'. This, however, is not the only demonstration of ill-feeling which is reported of Aristotle (cf. Cic. *De Or.* 3. 141); but the orator also seems to be attacking the philosopher in the *Antidosis* (258). Relations between the two rival schools will hardly have improved, when Aristotle placed rhetoric on his syllabus. Dionysius correctly seeks the truth somewhere between the extremes and follows Cephisodorus, a faithful pupil of Isocrates', who defended his master against Aristotle in his publications. This witness confirms a small number of forensic speeches by Isocrates. But this occupation, which was closely connected with a trade, did not offer any expectations which might satisfy his ambition, while according to Isocrates' own admission he lacked a powerful voice and the personal courage to embark upon a career as a political orator. His desire and his talents pointed out another course to him. He wished to influence his contemporaries with the written word, whether recited by others or read by readers, and to form pupils into successful men by evoking and fostering rhetorical ability. In this way he followed the aims of the sophists, though no longer as a wandering teacher; he became the head of a school which he opened in 399 or soon afterwards and which was flourishing in a short time. Until his death, for more than fifty years, he lived in Athens and achieved the widespread influence which we mentioned earlier.

The humanist, Hieronymus Wolf of Augsburg, a friend of Melanchthon's, who translated and edited Isocrates, forced the speeches into the pedantic division of paraenetic, symbuleutic, epideictic and forensic and arranged them in the order which our editions retain. Nowadays chronological considerations would be taken into account and the six speeches which Wolf placed at the end would come at the beginning as products of Isocrates' occupation as a logographer. The *Aegineticus*, a speech before an Aeginetan court of law on a matter of inheritance, and the *Trapeziticus* on behalf of a metic who was reclaiming a deposit from the banker Pasion, should be put shortly before the foundation of the school. The speech *On the Team* (Περὶ τοῦ ζεύγους) should be dated somewhat earlier; it was written for the son of Alcibiades of the same name and in places it turns into an encomium for the father. In addition there are three forensic speeches *Against Callimachus*, *Against Lochites* and *Against Euthynous*; of the last of these only the torso has been preserved. This suit won some notoriety because neither party in the case could produce any witnesses (λόγος ἀμάρτυρος). Lysias wrote the speech for the opposition and Antisthenes availed himself of the opportunity to attack Isocrates.[1]

The speeches written after the foundation of the school are models and showpieces of what Isocrates wished to offer with his rhetoric. The epideictic

[1] L. RADERMACHER, *Artium Scriptores*. Sitzb. Öst. Ak. Phil.-hist. Kl. 227/3, 1951, 120.

character which is peculiar to all of them must have been most effective when solemnly declaimed; they were also published to be distributed in larger circles and served at the same time as examples of the school's business. *Against the Sophists* (Κατὰ τῶν σοφιστῶν), written in the 'eighties, is a propaganda speech; in it Isocrates defends his objectives against many attacks, against the philosophers, against political-technical rhetoric based principally on improvisation and against the teachers of forensic oratory. We add here at the same time the *Antidosis* (Περὶ ἀντιδόσεως), which Isocrates, according to his own statement (9), wrote when he was 82; we mention it here because this juxtaposition readily demonstrates the consistency of his programme. Of this, the longest of the Isocratic speeches, only the beginning and the ending were known, until in 1812 A. Mystoxides discovered the middle part (73-309) in an Ambrosianus. The speech, which purports to give a kind of autobiography (7)[1] takes a lawsuit finished long ago for its starting-point. In accordance with Attic law Lysimachus had availed himself of the possibility of removing the costly performance of the trierarchy on to a more affluent citizen by proposing an exchange of property in case of refusal (ἀντίδοσις). Now Isocrates pretends that he was compelled by public attacks to defend his life and his work. And he does so at great length; he copies Socrates' situation before his judges; passages from previous speeches are supposed to play the part of evidence.

Isocrates' first great epideictic achievement with a political background was the *Panegyricus*[2] which he completed in 380 after many years of work.[3] In form it is an address to the Hellenic nation, who are imagined to have come together in an assembly; this follows a tradition initiated by Gorgias with his *Olympicus*, while there is also some connection with Lysias' *Epitaphios*. Both these features were already noticed in antiquity (Theon. *Progymn*. 1. 4. p. 63 Sp.),[4] but the relatively small number of commonplaces which necessarily occurred in these speeches, should be taken into account.[5] In his book *Aristoteles und Athen* (1893) Wilamowitz suggested the interpretation of the *Panegyricus* as a propaganda pamphlet for the Second Naval League, and W. Jaeger took this interpretation even further.[6] This statement has proved to be untenable in this positive form; it was reduced to correct proportions especially by Edmund Buchner. The composition of the *Panegyricus* adroitly combines two logoi, an epideictic and a symbuleutic one. The opening, epideictic, part draws a picture of Athens's great achievements for Greece in peaceful cultural occupations and in the wars fought for the existence of Greece, an idealized picture which since then has been copied

---

[1] Cf. G. MISCH, *Gesch. der Autobiogr.* 1, 3rd ed. Bern 1949, 158.

[2] E. BUCHNER, *Der Panegyrikos des Isokrates*. Wiesbaden 1958 (*Historia*, Einzelschriften 2). O. SCHNEIDER'S comm. (1860) was not yet available to the author.

[3] Ten years after Anon. Περὶ ὕψους, 4, 2.

[4] H.-J. NEWIGER, *Gnom*. 33, 1961, 761, opposes with an elaborate discussion Buchner's overemphasis of the relations with Lysias. Cf. also on this question J. WALZ, *Der lys. Epitaphios. Phil. Suppl.* 29/4. 1936.

[5] Cf. H. LL. HUDSON-WILLIAMS, 'Thucydides, Isocrates and the rhetorical method of Composition'. *Class. Quart*. 42, 1948, 76. On the praise of Athens in tragedy cf. H. R. BUTTS, *The Glorification of Athens in Gr. Drama. Iowa Stud*. 11, 1947.

[6] Cf. *Paideia* 3, 142 and *Demosthenes*. Berl. 1939, 197. 207, 31.

time and again. The symbuleutic part, which opens with 133, counsels the Greeks to unite, for only in this way will they be able to prevail over the barbarians. Sparta and Athens will have to share in the leadership. The epideictic logos is subordinate to the symbuleutic part in that it elaborates upon Athens's historical title to the hegemony in order to ensure full justification of her claim to partnership with Sparta in the supreme command.

The *Busiris*[1] and the *Helen* are school speeches, which are linked directly with the sophistical tradition and were probably written soon after teaching was begun. Isocrates uses the prefaces for personal purposes; in the *Busiris* he takes issue with Polycrates, who had written a defence of Busiris and an indictment against Socrates (cf. p. 495); in the *Helen* he attacks writers of dialogues, with whom he ranges Plato and the other Socratics.

Three speeches which show that Isocrates had some connection with the reigning house of Cyprus must be dated a good many years after the *Panegyricus*. The one *To Nicocles* (Πρὸς Νικοκλέα) addresses a lengthy lecture on kingship to the young prince who, in about 374, after the death of his father Euagoras, took over the reign of Cyprus; he had previously been a pupil of Isocrates', though the nature of the association cannot be determined; in the *Nicocles* the prince speaks to his subjects. In the *Euagoras*, however, the praise of the deceased ruler is made into a general mirror of princes.

The *Plataïcus*, probably belonging in the year 373, continues the political speeches. A Plataean is cast as the speaker who brings an action against the Thebans after their brutal destruction of his city.

The *Archidamus* also attacks Theban pretensions to power. Here Isocrates casts the Spartan pretender as the spokesman in the struggle against Messene, the new city which had arisen on the site of Ithome in the 'sixties under Theban influence.

Even when Isocrates criticizes Athenian domestic politics and in times of crisis constantly expresses his recurring desire for authoritarian government, he shows a penchant for the past, not for new forms. The form of constitution which he believes to be desirable is a moderate oligarchy and a political trend as adhered to by men like Cimon, Thucydides the son of Melesias, or Theramenes. Solon and Clisthenes are models taken from Athens' domestic history. The *Areopagiticus*[2] advocates a restitution of this venerable body which would ensure for it adequate authority for the education and spiritual guidance of the citizens. This speech has often been dated in the period immediately after the War of the Allies (357–355) which broke up the Second Naval League, but Jaeger[3] argued in favour of an interpretation of this speech as a warning against this crisis. Recently, however, serious doubts have been cast on the political actuality of Isocrates' speeches, so that a definite decision about the date of the *Areopagiticus* has not yet been reached.

---

[1] L. GIOVANACCI, *Isocrate, Il Busiride*. Con introd. e comm. Florence 1955.

[2] C. COPPOLA, *Areopagitico. Con appendice su la prosa greca d' arte*. Milan 1956.

[3] 'The Date of I.'s Areopagiticus and the Athenian Opposition'. *Harv. Stud.* Suppl. vol. 1, 1940, 409; now *Scripta minora* 2. Rome 1960, 267.

On the Peace (Περὶ Εἰρήνης) is a product of the mood prevailing immediately after the catastrophe, as is proved by the resignation with which Isocrates recommended renunciation of seapower and the peace of Antalcidas (386) as the basis of Athenian politics. New hopes for the deployment of Greek power, even though under foreign leadership, were roused by the rise of Philip of Macedon. When the peace of Philocrates seemed to open up the possibility of an agreement with the new power, Isocrates sent forth an open letter to Philip,[1] an invitation to the king of the Macedonians to unite the Greeks as their benefactor (εὐεργέτης) and to lead them in their great national struggle against the Persians.

Isocrates, one of the μακρόβιοι of antiquity, began his last work, the *Panathenaïcus*, when he was ninety-four (3) and completed it at the age of ninety-seven (270). His power of composition has noticeably decreased. He has not succeeded in making an organic unity of his praise of the city, to which he was so devoted in his own way, with the review of his own work and the search for the best constitution, which he found in a compromise between the three main forms.

Together with the speeches, nine *Letters* of Isocrates' have been handed down. The well-founded distrust with which the epistolographical tradition has been regarded since Richard Bentley's classical criticism (1699) also makes it difficult to decide on individual letters by Isocrates; but it is more probable that genuine letters have been preserved of the great publicist than in other cases. The parts which fit into Isocrates' political programme as we know it from the speeches are of particular importance. In *Phil.* 81 there is mention of an open letter to Dionysius I of Syracuse and it is possible that the preface to this letter has been preserved as *Ep.* 1; it is supposed to win the tyrant over to a combined Greek enterprise.[2] The letter to Philip (*Ep.* 2) is definitely considered as genuine. It is datable to 344, because mention is made of a wound received by the king. In this letter Isocrates hopefully seeks to bring about good relations between his city and Philip. *Ep.* 3 is also addressed to Philip and the genuineness of the letter is defended by influential scholars.[3] Directly after Chaeronea Philip is invited to undertake the leadership of the Greeks against the Persians. *Ep.* 4 to Antipater may be considered as genuine, while *Ep.* 5, a short letter to Alexander, is subject to serious doubt.[4] Of two letters, *Ep.* 6 to the children of Jason of Pherae and *Ep.* 9 to Archidamus, only some fragments have been preserved; the latter especially is of doubtful genuineness.[5]

Of the surviving works the *Speech to Demonicus* is rejected as spurious; it loosely combines some exhortatory maxims into a sort of pragmatism. It belongs to the fourth century and shows Isocratic features. Its connection with

---

[1] S. PERLMANN, 'Isocrates' *Philippus* – a Reinterpretation'. *Historia* 6, 1957, 306.

[2] Thus cautiously JAEGER, *Dem.* (v. p. 585, n. 6).

[3] Bibl. in BENGTSON, *Griech. Gesch.* 2nd ed. Munich 1960, 315, 4.

[4] JAEGER (v. sup.), 247.

[5] Opposing the authenticity of Ep. 6, though not convincingly, MIKKOLA (v. inf. on Isocrates), 290. Ep. 9 athetized by SCHMITZ-KAHLMANN (v. inf. on Isocrates), 123 and by others, but cf. STEIDLE (v. inf. on Isocrates), 284. 5.

Aristotle's *Protrepticus* was mentioned earlier (p. 554). Parts of the speech *To Nicocles* are missing in the portions quoted in the *Antidosis*, but this is not decisive evidence against its genuineness.[1] Many details of Isocrates' rhetorical teaching have been handed down,[2] but a proper textbook (τέχνη) by him did not exist.

Isocrates' influence was as variegated as the epoch in which he lived. We shall attempt to trace it in three spheres which are variously interrelated, those of the educator, the political publicist and the literary artist.

Isocrates stressed the special nature and what he considered the special value of his teaching by drawing clear boundary lines between it and philosophy as Plato understood it and the purely practical rhetoric of law-court and assembly. The last-mentioned circumstance brought him close to Plato; and the latter could hardly fail to be pleased (cf. *Phaedo* 96 a ff.) at the rejection of natural-philosophical speculation (Ant. 285 τῶν παλαιῶν σοφιστῶν τερατολογίαι). There were other points on which they were in agreement, such as an appreciation of talent and education as factors in the training of the good orator. So to some extent we can understand the praise which the Platonic Socrates bestows upon the young Isocrates at the end of the *Phaedrus* (279 a), that his intellectual physiognomy showed a philosophical trait and that there were great expectations for his future. But it must also be borne in mind at once that the *Phaedrus* is not an early work of Plato's and that Isocrates had already crossed the threshold of old age when this passage was written. This fact puts the praise in a curious light, and it has been interpreted as being more like cutting sarcasm.[3] This is going too far and it would be more justified to stress the retrospective nature of this statement, by which Plato wanted to show his appreciation for certain possibilities of rhetoric as he saw it.[4]

In spite of such expressions of mutual esteem, however, they were separated by something far more important. Isocrates did not take a stand against the speculations of the natural philosophers alone. In his speech *Against the Sophists* and in the preface to the *Helen* he attacks the eristics, and though Plato is not mentioned, the Academy is included. And even when in some of the works of his old age (*Antid.* 261 ff. *Panath.* 27) he grants, with some readiness for concessions, a certain value for a formal education to mathematical and philosophical studies, his attitude is as radically separated from Plato's unconditional way to the Absolute as Callicles' opinion in Plato's *Gorgias* (484 c) that philosophy is a praiseworthy thing for a young man, but should be stopped at the right time. In both cases he reproached philosophy, as Plato understood it, with being divorced from life. Isocrates, however, wishes (*Antid.* 285) to train in his school people who know how to run their own homes properly and to take a successful

---

[1] Otherwise MIKKOLA (*v. inf.* on Isocrates), 285 with bibl.
[2] Collected by RADERMACHER (*v.* p. 584, n. 1), 153.
[3] Thus H. RAEDER, 'Platon und die Rhetoren'. *Filos. Medd. Dan. Vid. Selsk.* 2/6, 1956, 15.
[4] KL. RIES, *I. und Platon im Ringen um die Philosophie*, Diss. Munich 1959, is of the same opinion in his exhaustive interpretation of the passage of the PHAEDRUS. This diss. also has a collection of the bibl. of this theme, completed by W. BURKERT, *Gnom.* 33, 1961, 349.

part in political life. In principle it is the old tenet of the sophists, good counsel (εὐβουλία), which turns up again.[1]

How serious a competitor of the Academy Isocrates was with his educational claims is shown by the very fact that he states that he represents true philosophy (*Antid.* 270). For him it is based on the anti-Platonic conviction that absolute knowledge (ἐπιστήμη) is denied to man because of his very nature and that therefore the proper thing to do is to ensure success in each single case on the basis of correct opinion (δόξα), or, speaking Isocratically, to seize the καιρός.[2] According to Isocrates' repeatedly stated conviction, rhetorical schooling provides the training for such worldly wisdom, for in his opinion the right word is found in the same way as proper counsel and action. It has been rightly observed[3] that in accordance with Greek linguistic usage the ethical element is retained in these notions, but this should not conceal the fundamental difference with Plato which appears here too; while Plato demands that every expression of human life should aim at the metaphysical idea of the good, Isocrates claims that one should intelligently consider the best way to face the realities of life, of which ethical postulates are a part.

Isocrates' programme was not ideally elevated by transcendental values and least of all by his religious impulses, for he combined a hearty streak of agnosticism with a friendly benevolence towards tradition. Isocrates was very much the spokesman for his age in that education was the leading idea which provided the stimulus for his entire activity and doctrine. For Isocrates education means above all else the ability to speak, for man is distinguished from animals, and the Greek from barbarians, by the power of speech. It has been correctly observed that these are the elements of a humanism, based on eloquence, which Cicero passed on to Petrarch.[4] Education of this nature flourished in Athens more than in any other Greek city. Pericles' words (Thuc. 2. 41) describing Athens as an education for Greece, are echoed with an effective extension of meaning (*Paneg.* 50): the students of this city are the teachers of other people. Here we also find the significant statement that the name of Greek describes partnership in Greek culture rather than racial kinship.[5] Of course, this remark does not yet propose a general idea of humanity, nor is it an outline of Hellenistic culture, but the changing emphasis implied is an indispensable condition for the loosening of old bonds by new ones. At the same time a development is completed which began with the sophists; educated man as envisaged by Isocrates is separated from his fellow-citizens by a deep chasm.

A considerable number of Isocrates' speeches deal with political questions of great moment. He is vividly interested in the old problem of reshaping the

---

[1] W. BURKERT, *Gnom.* 33, 1961, 353, raises the question of how Plato and Isocrates would react to the reality of our time. The question is interesting and can yield a great deal for a criticism of our era but little for that of the men compared.

[2] Contrast between ἐπιστήμη and καιρός, e.g. *Hel.* 5. *Antid.* 184. 271. On the καιρός-notion in I.: WERSDÖRFER (*v. inf.* on Isocrates), 54.

[3] STEIDLE (*v. inf.* on Isocrates), 268. 270.

[4] Cf. B. SNELL, *The Discovery of Mind*, Oxf. 1953, 247.

[5] On the passage J. JÜTHNER, 'I. und die Menschheitsidee'. *Wien. Stud.* 47, 1929, 26.

Athenian constitution on authoritarian principles and the very assiduous emphasis on good democratic principles shows that basically old oligarchic tendencies are active here. But the demands of foreign politics matter most to him and the thought that a union of Greek states could enable a new deployment of power aimed against Persia, occupied him from an early stage until his death. In the *Panegyricus* he still hopes that a sort of Athenian-Spartan dyarchy could bring about the end he desired (17), with the Athenians regaining their former naval supremacy; later he became more and more convinced that only a strong personality could carry through this fusion of the Hellenic powers. For a time Jason of Pherae roused these hopes (*Phil.* 199 f.), then Dionysius I, until Philip of Macedon stepped forth as the candidate for this position. The open letter to him and the earlier mentioned letters are the clearest expression of this line of thought.

Isocrates' political publications were criticized in many different ways.[1] In the *Antidosis* (276) he contrasts the subjects of his own speeches with those of practical rhetoric as great, beautiful, mankind-loving (φιλανθρώπους) and concerned with the common weal. Were these themes, as many believed, merely a momentous and dignified opportunity for the exhibition of his rhetorical art? Or are the defenders of the opposite view right who, as Beloch does, assigned to Isocrates' publications great importance for the historical development and even assumed, with extreme exaggeration, that the orator had influenced Philip's policies? This is out of the question, but it should not be overlooked that many of the speeches dealt with questions of decisive and immediate importance. Isocrates certainly was not the first to put them, nor did he express them in original terms,[2] but his speeches were broadcast all over the Greek world in the form of pamphlets and they must have exerted some influence on public opinion, even if we can no longer assess its extent. Nor should it be overlooked in this connection that renowned politicians, notably Conon's son Timotheus, the strongest personality of the second naval league, were pupils of Isocrates' and remained in close touch with him.

Isocrates achieved his strongest influence in the realm of Greek literature through his perfection of Attic literary prose. In this respect he was, of course, the pupil of Gorgias, who discovered the magic of words as embodied sound, but he learned to employ with a wise moderation what his teacher lavishly squandered for the sake of emotional effect. He himself declared (*Phil.* 27. *Panath.* 2) that he even increased this economy in his old age. For the restless play of antitheses with the flashing lights of piled-on sound figures he substituted the broad flow of the period. Careful avoidance of hiatus and sustained rhythm raise it to the level of a rationally calculated work of verbal art. Isocrates always knows how beautifully he speaks. It is obvious that in his work an event with

---

[1] Bibl. in Bengtson (*v.* p. 587, n. 3), 292. J. E. BUCHNER strongly reduces the political actuality of the speeches, *v.* p. 585, n. 2. Bibl. on the question also in H.-J. NEWIGER, *Gnom.* 33, 1961, 761.

[2] Renunciation of originality (*Paneg.* 10) is to a certain extent generally Greek, but particularly characteristic of I.

fateful consequences for the future is taking place. Literary prose, sure of its influence, begins to drive out poetry with imperious self-assurance. In the speech *To Nicocles* (43) Hesiod, Theognis and Phocylides appear as counsellors and admonishers, which function is now taken over by the orator; and in the *Euagoras* (9 ff.) he himself stresses the competition with poetry with regard to the encomium.

We just spoke of a fateful event. An objective observation of the widespread influence which Isocrates exerted through his school, an appreciation of a certain importance as a political publicist, the broad construction of his periods cannot conceal the fact that in his speeches the beginnings of the depletion and torpidity become perceptible which in the course of the centuries affected the whole of Greek literature and finally let it go to ruin in the name of rhetoric. This skill, which vaunts (*Paneg.* 8) that it can make the great insignificant and bestow greatness on the petty[1] ousts the unity of form and contents. Perhaps our judgment of Isocrates may appear to be harsh; it was, however, said by Hermogenes (π. ἰδ. 397. 24 R.) not by modern critics, that his style smacks of senility and pedantry.[2]

It should be borne in mind that Isocrates' rhetorical occupation was part of a very lively activity in this field. In connection with the sophists we have already met a number of teachers of rhetoric: Antisthenes (p. 353), Polus (p. 353), Thrasymachus (p. 357), Alcidamas (p. 356);[3] to these we may probably add as improvising rhetoricians Lycophron,[4] Theodorus (p. 357), Licymnius (p. 353), Evenus (p. 357) and Polycrates (p. 495). Anaximenes of Lampsacus was a pupil of the orator and Homeric critic Zoelus,[5] whom we also mentioned earlier. We shall presently meet him as an historian, but here we must mention his *Rhetorica ad Alexandrum* ('Ρητορικὴ πρὸς 'Αλέξανδρον), which finished up among Aristotle's works. P. Victorius correctly suggested that it should be attributed to Anaximenes in view of Quintilian 3. 4, 9. This is corroborated by a very early Hibeh papyrus (no. 43 P., first half 3rd cent. B.C.), which contains considerable parts of the work. It owes its name to the spurious dedicatory letter to Alexander. Since we have to date it before Aristotle's *Rhetoric* in about 340, it is our oldest surviving textbook in this field. Recently Manfred Fuhrmann[6] showed in an excellent analysis that in spite of the use of important principles of classification the work does not present a true system of rhetorical theory, but sticks to individual precepts and that its composition is largely controlled by

---

[1] In Plat. *Phaedr.* 267 a, this appears as the project of Tisias and Gorgias; cf. also Ps.-Demetr., *De Eloc.* 120. Cic. *Brut.* 47.

[2] This judgment was felt to be 'more than a little unfair', so we shall summon another witness from antiquity, Philonicus the dialectician who in Dion. Hal. *de Isocr.* c. 13 reproaches Isocrates with κενότης.

[3] On the contrast between Isocrates and Alcidamas, cf. P. FRIEDLÄNDER, *Platon* I, 2nd ed. Berl. 1954, 117.

[4] VS 83. RADERMACHER (p. 584, n. 1), 189.

[5] *v.* p. 572, also RADERMACHER, *v. sup.* 198. Anaximenes ibid. 200.

[6] *Das systematische Lehrbuch*, Göttingen 1960. Comm. ed.: L. SPENGEL, *Anaximenes, Ars Rhetorica*. Leipz. 1844. Text in SPENGEL-HAMMER, *Rhetores Graeci* I/2. 1894. Transl. W. D. ROSS, *Works of Aristotle* 11. Oxf. 1952.

association and antithesis. An oration written in Doric, of which we find fragments in an Oxyrhynchus papyrus,[1] may also belong to this epoch; its author is unknown.

Of the ten masters of Attic rhetoric who were collected in one canon in the Hellenistic age we already discussed Antiphon and Andocides in connection with the problems posed by the former's name. Isocrates, who was also classed with the great models, demanded a separate discussion. We shall now survey the remaining seven.

During the second half of the last century and close to the First World War the Attic orators attracted the attention of scholars, especially in Germany, to such a degree that later they had to pay the penalty for this favoured position. During the past few decades little work has been done in this field in comparison with other authors. Rhetoric had come to be distrusted; only what was true to life and absolutely genuine was wanted from antiquity. It may be expected, however, that in the not too distant future the Attic orators will be appreciated for what they undoubtedly still are, important witnesses of the cultural and intellectual life of the fourth century and representatives of Attic prose at its classical height.

The great discussion of the Platonic *Republic* is staged at the house of Cephalus, who is shown at the opening of the work in the peace of a sunny old age. This Cephalus had migrated from his native Syracuse to Athens as a metic and had amassed a considerable fortune manufacturing shields with 120 slaves. His sons were Polemarchus, who takes part in the conversation in Book 1 of the *Republic*, Euthydemus and Lysias, who are both mentioned as being present. The latter became the most successful writer of forensic speeches and a much-admired model of style for later times whom the Atticists in particular chose as their guide. Besides his speech *Against Eratosthenes*, the writings of Dionysius of Halicarnassus (*Lysias*) and Ps.-Plutarch (*Vita dec. or.*) help us to form a picture of his life.

His father lived in Athens for thirty years; he had come there at the invitation of Pericles, who had probably already reached a leading position at that time. This establishes 460 as the earliest date for the migration from Syracuse and 430 for Cephalus' death. After his father's death Lysias, then fifteen years old, went to the new colony of Thurii in southern Italy with his elder brother Polemarchus. This gives 445 or a short time later as the date for Lysias' birth; the ancient indication of the year 459 is based on the erroneous assumption that Lysias came to Thurii in the year of its settlement (444).

In southern Italy the young Lysias received his rhetorical training. The pseudo-Plutarch mentions Tisias as his teacher. When conditions became difficult for Athenian sympathizers in Thurii after the Sicilian débâcle, he returned to Athens with his brother. There he lived in very comfortable circumstances, which, however, became his misfortune when the Thirty seized his wealth. The tyrants had his brother Polemarchus killed and he himself escaped to Megara. From there he supported the movement for the democratic restitution with money, weapons and men. Directly after the return of the

---

[1] No. 410=no. 1785 P. W. KROLL, *RE* S 7, 1940, 1052. RADERMACHER, *v. sup.* 231.

democrats to the city, which took place in September 403, Thrasybulus put a motion for citizenship for Lysias together with other metics, but Archinus, who was a moderate like Theramenes, lodged an indictment for illegality (παρανόμων); Thrasybulus' motion had not been submitted to the council for approval (προβούλευμα) and so the objection brought about the annulment of the decree. Lysias remained a metic all his life, though he belonged to the group favoured by isotely, which meant classification with the citizens in respect of financial payments. His activity can be traced up to his speech for Pherenicus (c. 380); we do not know how long he lived after that.

A passage in Cicero's Brutus (48), which refers back to Aristotle, contains a notice that Lysias at first taught the technique of rhetoric, but he was so far over-shadowed by Theodorus that he preferred to turn to the business of speech-writing and wrote forensic orations for others. So his development was the reverse of Isocrates'. In fact, we have several testimonies to writings of Lysias'[1] which do not suit the speechwriter but the teacher of rhetoric and the composer of models. We hear of a speech for the defence For Nicias, though Dionysius wants to deny him this; of one For Socrates and of Letters, which were largely of erotic content. Here Lysias appears as the originator of a genre which had representatives well into the Byzantine era. The Eroticus which Plato reproduced in his Phaedrus is of this genre, though it is hard to say how accurate his repro-duction is. In the typical sophistical manner the non-lover is compared with the lover as the more profitable partner of a liaison. Mention is also made of Technical Writings (Τέχναι ῥητορικαί), which were probably similar to the Parasceuae, to which is also referred.

It is difficult to say how early this tendency in Lysias' development is to be dated. His rhetorical activity may have begun soon after his return from Thurii. Nor can two sharply separated periods in Lysias' creative work be inferred from the Cicero passage quoted; the speechwriter may occasionally have returned to working as an orator and sophist.

Lysias was extraordinarily prolific and this productivity inspired the forgers who placed their products under his celebrated name. Ps.-Plutarch reports 425 speeches which circulated as Lysias', and adds that in the circle of Dionysius and Caecilius 233 of these were recognized as genuine. Blass compiled the titles of 172 speeches; of these thirty-four have been preserved without the Eroticus. It becomes clear at once that Lysias wrote only for parties to a lawsuit. His few surviving speeches also show exceptions, of course. A fragment (34 in our editions) which Dionysius preserved in his Lysias comes from a political speech delivered against a motion of Phormisius' in the situation of 403. The speaker, who advocates a radical restoration of the democracy, opposes the return of the exiles and the restriction of citizenship to landowners. Joseph Walz[2] has shown

---

[1] References in RADERMACHER, v. sup. 147.

[2] Der lys. Epitaphios. Phil. Suppl. 29/4/1936. Otherwise P. TREVES, Riv. Fil. N.S. 15, 1937, 113. 278. The authenticity vigorously defended by E. BUCHNER, Der Panegyrikos des Iso-krates. Wiesbaden 1958 (Historia Einzelschr. 2). On this question also J. KLOWSKI, Zur Echtheitsfrage des lysianischen Epitaphios. Diss. Hamb. 1959 (typescr.).

that it probably was Lysias who wrote the much suspected *Epitaphios* (2) on the fallen in the Corinthian War, and that he did so before Isocrates' *Panegyricus*, with which it has some similarity. But it remains unbelievable that Lysias as a metic should have delivered this speech; it must be considered as a purely literary work. The *Olympiacus* (33) was actually read out at the Olympic celebrations of 388; once again Dionysius has preserved part of it. This call for Greek unity accompanied with violent attacks on Dionysius I of Syracuse had a very drastic result; the ostentatious marquee of the Syracusan embassy to the festival was looted by the mob.

Everything discussed so far seems to be only accessory to the picture of Lysias the speechwriter, who in his speeches for others put on so many masks. But once he himself also appeared in the lawcourt, when in 403 in his speech *Against Eratosthenes* (12) he accused the latter of having caused, as a member of the Thirty, the execution of his brother Polemarchus. The legal premises are not quite clear, but it seems to have been a matter of an indictment at the occasion of the account which Eratosthenes had to give of his actions in order to rehabilitate himself according to the law of amnesty of 403. A few years later Lysias wrote the speech *Against Agoratus* (13) who had caused the death of democratic politicians while he was in the pay of the oligarchs. One of the papyrus finds which have increased our knowledge of Lysias contains fragments of a speech *Against Hippotherses* (no. 1015 P.); they show that for years after the restitution of the democracy Lysias was still involved in lawsuits about his lost fortune.[1]

An important part of the value of these and other speeches is that they give a direct insight into the internal conditions of Athens. This also comprises economic history in the speech *Against the Wheat traders* (22, Κατὰ τῶν σιτοπώλων) which indicts, obviously in the interest of the wholesalers, some metics who as middle men had bought up wheat over the legally permissible quantity. The reproach has been levelled at Lysias that in his speeches he readily changed opinions according to the customer of the moment; Ferckel in particular has zealously drawn him as an unprincipled opportunist. Now it is correct that Lysias, the sworn democrat, occasionally wrote for oligarchs as well (16; 25); that he, as each occasion demanded, took the viewpoint of the current law of amnesty or carelessly ignored it; that in the years of renewed Athenian power politics he lent his voice in the speeches *Against Ergocles* (28) and *Against Philocrates* (29) to an extravagant radicalism and that he dealt with the questions of the fortunes of the highly placed in a way which wholly contradicted his speech *On the Fortune of Aristophanes* (19). But instead of turning Lysias into a scoundrel without a country, of whom nothing better can be expected, it is more useful to understand, as a historical fact, the position of a speechwriter who lived and wrote in an era which was dominated by the sophists. No one will wish to argue that his adaptability – is it typical of Lysias only or of his age? – is a morally elevating spectacle, but in his work it has a bearing on something much more gratifying, his great ability to shape his speeches according to the

---

[1] On the difficult individual questions Ferckel (*v. sup.* on Lysias), 63.

character and condition of the people for whom he writes.[1] Lysias proved his artistry, in which nobody equalled him, especially in his speeches for private persons. His masterpiece is the speech *For the Cripple* (24, Ὑπὲρ τοῦ ἀδυνάτου),[2] in which a little man battles cunningly and humorously for the continuance of his pension. The speech *On the Olive-tree* (7, Περὶ τοῦ σηκοῦ, which refers to the enclosure of a sacred olive tree) has an entirely different background, but it is equally sharply and accurately understood. Here a member of the property-owning class defends himself before the Areopagus with dignity and indignation against the accusation that he had offended against one of the holy trees or its fencing.

The faithful portrayal of character in these forensic speeches imposed narrow limits on the use of rhetorical ornamentation, which Lysias was very well able to apply in the epideictic speeches. He succeeded in turning this enforced simplicity into a special merit which was greatly admired by a later age. These speeches also show great narrative power. When in the speech for the defence of Euphilus *On the Murder of Eratosthenes* (1, Ὑπὲρ τοῦ Ἐρατοσθένους φόνου)[3] he tells the story of the wanton who locks her husband up in his room when she is making love, and of his well-planned revenge, it is indeed hardly possible not to think of Boccaccio. Though little more than the title is known, we also mention his speech *On his Own Services* (Περὶ τῶν ἑαυτοῦ εὐεργεσιῶν or. deperd. 47. fr. 36 Th.) because it must have contained autobiographical information.

Since we know of numerous forgeries which circulated in antiquity, the question cannot be avoided whether any such can be detected among the preserved speeches. The decision is so difficult that Hude in his excellent edition attributed everything to Lysias, even when it is of doubtful genuineness. As stated earlier (p. 355), the sixth speech with the indictment of Andocides and the twentieth with the defence of Polystratus are spurious. For the rest we content ourselves with pointing out the particularly strong grounds for suspicion against the eighth speech[4] and the need for a new treatment of the whole complex of questions.

Isaeus, the son of Diagoras from Euboean Chalcis, was also a metic. He, too, worked as a teacher of rhetoric and[5] composed speeches for others, though there

---

[1] It is, of course, no longer possible to refer what Dionysius of Halicarnassus, *Lys.* c. 8, praises as the orator's ἠθοποιία simply to his skill in characterizing individuals. In his penetrating work Ἀνηθοποίητος. *Eine semasiologische Untersuchung aus der antiken Rhetorik und Ethik* (Sitzb. Deutsche Akad. Kl. f. Spr., Lit. u. Kunst 1952/4, 1953) FRIEDRICH ZUCKER has shown that Dionysius does not imply with ἠθοποιία a differentiation of the speakers' characters. They should rather appear as honest, right-thinking men of integrity, who express themselves in this way.　　　[2] Comm.: U. ALBINI, Florence 1956.

[3] Excellent discussion by U. E. PAOLI, *Die Geschichte der Neaira*. Bern 1953, 28 (the Ital. original: *Uomini e cose del mondo antico*. Florence 1947). He correctly denies that in the case of Eratosthenes' death it was a matter of the man to whom L. in the 12th speech imputed guilt for the killing of Polemarchus.

[4] P. A. MÜLLER, *Oratio quae inter Lysiacas fertur octava*. Munster 1926. Several atheteses in CHRIST-SCHMID, *Gesch. d. gr. Lit.* 1, 6th ed. Munich 1912, 559, 5.

[5] The scanty evidence in RADERMACHER (*v.* p. 384, n. 1), 190.

is no evidence that these two activities succeeded one another as in the case of Lysias. Dionysius of Halicarnassus, who also wrote an *Isaeus*, admits in the introduction that he knows little of the date and course of his life. But he was Demosthenes' teacher and Hermippus, who wrote a treatise about Isocrates' pupils, says that he was one of these. Isaeus' care in avoiding hiatus agrees with this statement without proving its truth. For the date of his work as a speech-writer only the first half of the fourth century can be roughly indicated.

According to the notice of Ps.-Plutarch in the *Vitae or.* he left sixty-four speeches; the authenticity of fourteen of these was dubious. We possess eleven speeches on legacy cases, of the last one the torso only. In Dionysius' treatise there is also a fairly large fragment from the speech *For Euphiletus*, who brought an action against the deme Erchia for his deletion from the citizen-list.

According to Dionysius Isaeus' style had some affinity with Lysias', but he also shows subtle understanding in his analysis of the difference between them. It is well put that the forensic speeches of Lysias (and Isocrates) create an impression of simple honesty even in notorious cases, while those of Isaeus (and Demosthenes) rouse suspicion through the abundance of artifices, even when the case in point is a good one. In fact, Isaeus is lacking in the natural simplicity which in Lysias is the result of an extreme refinement. Not only is his argumentation more subtle, due to the requirements of difficult legacy cases, but his language also displays a greater richness in figures of speech than Lysias'.

In the same way in which the Greeks meant Homer when speaking of 'the poet', so Demosthenes was simply 'the orator' for later antiquity. At that time his fame had been an established fact for a long time, and it remained associated with his name until in this century modern scholarship made him a controversial problem. As a result of the fame which Demosthenes enjoyed in antiquity, there are fairly abundant sources available for him. Apart from Ps.-Plutarch's *Vitae or.* and the two treatises of Dionysius of Halicarnassus (Περὶ τῆς Δημοσθένους λέξεως and Ἐπιστολὴ πρὸς Ἀμμαῖον) there is Plutarch's biography of Demosthenes which also contains polemical features; another of the same kind by the orator Libanius, with hypotheses to the individual speeches; one by Zosimus; an anonymous one; and finally three articles in Suidas. The remains of ancient commentaries will be discussed with the tradition. Since most of Demosthenes' speeches provided a great deal of biographical information, they are of great importance, like the speeches of his opponents Aeschines, Hyperides and Dinarchus, for our knowledge of his life.

Demosthenes, the son of Demosthenes of the deme Paeania, born in Athens in 384, belonged, like Isocrates and the metic Lysias, to the class of the well-to-do entrepreneurs. His father had a weapon-workshop and also possessed other property. His mother Cleobule is supposed to have had Scythian blood, which caused his opponents (Dinarchus, *Against Dem.* 15. cf. Aeschines, 3. 172) to turn him derisively into a Scythian. Still it may be fairly asked if the sombre passion which, together with a very acute feeling for form, moulded him into the greatest orator of antiquity, should not be understood as a maternal legacy.

When the boy was 7 years old he lost his father. The three guardians, Aphobus, Demophon and Therippides, proved to be untrustworthy trustees of the
property, and immediately upon reaching manhood Demosthenes was involved
in important lawsuits to save at least something of his previous wealth. So at an
early stage he had to test in earnest what he had learned from Isaeus, whom
tradition mentions as his teacher. Already during his training he gave evidence
of the rigour of his will-power which later ensured his influence over the masses,
when he successfully struggled with several physical handicaps. He formed his
mind with the same care. According to Cicero[1] he read and even heard Plato.
Thucydides had a particularly strong influence on him[2] and the picture of
Athenian greatness which he found there remained a controlling influence in
his life; Plutarch's story of how he became interested in rhetoric (*Dem.* 5) sounds
like an anecdote; his pedagogue smuggled him into the session of the law-court
at which Callimachus defended himself brilliantly against the accusation that the
loss of the frontier place Oropus was his fault, and there the young Demosthenes
received the decisive impression of the power of speech. The veracity of the
story cannot be proved, but it should not be rejected out of hand.

Demosthenes' speech of indictment in the legal battle he had to wage against
his dishonest guardians, *Against Aphobus*, and his answer to the latter's defence,
have been preserved. A third speech, *Against Aphobus*, in which Demosthenes
defended the witness against the accusation of perjury, was often suspected, but
increasingly serious grounds for its authenticity have been produced.[3] At first
Demosthenes had some success in his action, which lasted for years and was held
up for various reasons, such as his service as an ephebe. But Onetor, the brother
of Aphobus' divorced wife, disputed this success by laying hands on a piece of
land which Demosthenes wanted to mortgage. And so the battle was carried
on, of which two speeches *Against Onetor* provide us with evidence. We do not
know its result but suspect that Demosthenes incurred heavy losses.

The art which he had practised for his own ends was now put at the disposal
of others against payment. He is supposed to have given classes in rhetoric as
well,[4] but there is nothing to tell of the extent of this activity; he certainly did
not run a school.

Our tradition offers an imposing number of speeches in private lawsuits
(27-59). But it is in this very part that the uncertainty of our tradition becomes
apparent, for much that is spurious is no doubt hidden under the name of
Demosthenes. Even the most conservative critic must surrender unconditionally
in the face of a piece like the speech *Against Theocrines* (58), since Demosthenes
himself is violently attacked here. But not all the cases are so clear-cut and it is
to be expected that a new treatment of these questions will move the limits

---

[1] *Brut.* 121; also *Or.* 15 with the doubtful appeal to letters of D. Cf. F. EGERMANN, *Vom
attischen Menschenbild*. Munich 1952, 59 with n. 86 f.

[2] Dionysius, *Thuc.* 53. Plut. *Dem.* 6 and others.

[3] Already by BLASS, *Die att. Beredsamkeit*. 2nd ed. 3/1, 232. Then by G. M. CALHOUN, 'A
problem of Authenticity (Dem. 29)'. *Trans. Am. Phil. Ass.* 65, 1934, 80. GERNET assumes
in his edition that an editor combined various parts written by Demosthenes.

[4] Aeschines I, 117; 170 ff.

somewhat in favour of authenticity. Blass was prepared to recognize only fifteen speeches[1] as definitely genuine, including those dealing with the legacy lawsuit. In these speeches Demosthenes rarely reaches the power of description and the subtlety of calculated argumentation which we value in Lysias. But the speech *Against Conon* (54) deserves to be singled out for the manner in which it depicts a violent brawl with adequate directness.[2] Eight among the speeches preserved concern lawsuits in which a certain Apollodorus appears. The speech *For Phormio* (36) which was read by an advocate (συνήγορος), is without doubt Demosthenes'. Whether this reader was Demosthenes himself is dubious. Interesting is the insight which we are given into the structure of a certain class of Athenian society about 350.[3] Phormio was first a slave, then an assistant, finally through tenure the successor in business of the great financier Pasion (*v.* p. 505). When the latter died, Phormio married his widow, as the will stipulated. But since there were two sons – the elder was Apollodorus, who was of age by now – a situation arose which hardly ever comes to a conclusion without recourse to law. The trouble arose from some sums of money which Phormio was alleged to have kept for himself after the woman's death and when the business seemed to have been settled by agreement, Apollodorus appeared after a long time with a new complaint against Phormio. The latter retorted with an objection for which the grounds are given in Demosthenes' speech and which achieved its purpose. But Apollodorus was not satisfied and soon afterwards preferred charges of perjury against Stephanus, the witness for the defence. There is no denying the deplorable fact that Demosthenes wrote the speech *Against Stephanus* (45) and, as a witticism preserved in Plutarch (*Dem.* 15) states, sold in fact daggers from his weapons shop to both parties in the dispute. But there is a conjecture which may make his conduct easier to explain. Apollodorus was proving useful to the anti-Macedonian party and was determined to oppose payment of the theoric money. This made him Demosthenes' ally and so he could claim his support.

This Apollodorus was a litigious man in other respects, of which six other speeches (46, likewise *Against Stephanus*, 49, 50, 53, 59) give evidence. They are one and all spurious. Their appearance in the corpus of Demosthenes' speeches is instructive, for here we observe for once how a mass of spurious material entered the tradition from private archives which were justifiably assumed to contain genuine Demosthenes. The last speech in this series is the one *Against Neaera*,[4] a one-time hetaera whom a political adventurer of the worst kind had smuggled into middle-class Athenian society, together with her daughter. Apollodorus was the speaker of the complaint on behalf of his son-in-law.

The speech *Against Zenothemis* (32)[5] belongs already in the reign of Alexander;

---

[1] Cf. p. 597, n. 3. It concerns speeches 27-31, 36-39, 41, 45, 51, 54, 55, 57.

[2] Paoli has discussed the speech in an excellent manner, cf. p. 595, n. 3. There (22) also about the dating.

[3] On the dating Paoli *v. sup.* 93. Comm. E. ZIEBARTH, Heidelb. 1936.

[4] In detail on this PAOLI, (*v. sup.*), 65. A collection of this sort of tradition in WILA-MOWITZ, *Herm.* 58, 1923, 68; now *Kl. Schr.* 4, 324.

[5] The authenticity remains subject to doubt. On the speech PAOLI *v. sup.* 113.

it deals with the fantastic adventures of a ship's cargo. The speaker is Demon, a relative of Demosthenes'. In the concluding part, unfortunately truncated, he tells that he had asked Demosthenes for legal assistance but that the latter had pointed out his position in politics and his consequent abstinence from private cases. If this is an actual statement of Demosthenes', it proves that he had ceased to perform the function of an attorney (συνήγορος) since he had been playing an active part in public affairs as an orator. This does not contradict the fact that at this time he still wrote forensic speeches for others.

Items 25 and 26 of our collection are two speeches *Against Aristogiton*, forensic speeches with an historical background, since they opposed the action of an evil demagogue who was also being sued by Dinarchus and Lycurgus. Dionysius (*Dem.* 57) already declared them to be spurious. Earlier (p. 359) we mentioned the first of them, because of its statements about the origin of enacted law.[1]

Demosthenes' entry into Athenian politics is announced by four of his speeches, three of them in lawsuits concerning domestic politics (*Against Androtion, Against Timocrates, Against Leptines*), while the speech *On the Symmories* was his first policy speech. It is important that we can date the first of the speeches mentioned with sufficient confidence at 355/354.[2] At the time the War of the Allies (357–355) and with it the dream of the restoration of Athenian naval power had just come to its conclusion. The prevailing mood was one of resignation, as reflected in the peace oration of the ageing Isocrates. But Demosthenes was of a different opinion; for him the failure of the naval alliance could not mean the end of a glowing faith, nourished by tradition, in the greatness of Athens. In those years an opposition had formed which wanted to make a clean sweep of the leaders of the régime that had failed, in order to raise up Athens again economically through prudent limitation to what was feasible and with a careful maintenance of peace. The faction which advocated this sober economic programme, which is also reflected in Xenophon's *Poroe*, was headed by Eubulus, who since 354 had held a key-position as the administrator of the fund for theatre moneys (theoricon). Recent research[3] has brought to light the important information that Demosthenes, though his later path inevitably deviated from Eubulus', took his first steps in politics as the latter's follower.

The speech *Against Androtion* is directed against the pupil of Isocrates who is known as the compiler of an *Atthis* which is often referred to and who played a political role in the circles against which the representatives of the new political trend had declared war. Formally it deals with an indictment for illegal motion (γραφὴ παρανόμων); Androtion had moved the crowning of the council, although they had not completed the construction of new ships to the number prescribed. Its actual aim, however, was the political elimination of Androtion,

---

[1] Opposed by M. POHLENZ, 'Anonymus περὶ νόμων'. GGN 1924, 19 trying to prove its authenticity. C. H. KRAMER, *De priore D. adv. Aristogeitonem oratione.* Diss. Leipz. 1930. We have left the controversial 51st speech *On the Trierarchical Crown* out of consideration.

[2] JAEGER, *Dem.* (*v. inf.*), 215, 21.

[3] Bibl. in BENGTSON, *Griech. Gesch.* 2nd ed. Munich 1960, 305, 2 and JAEGER, *Dem.* (*v. inf.*), 220, 16.

who had also made himself unpopular through the collection of taxes. The speech *Against Timocrates* points in the same direction. It attacks a law which had helped state debtors, amongst them Androtion, to escape impending imprisonment for debt. An extensive section of the *Timocratea* (160-168 and 172-186) has been lifted almost verbally from the speech *Against Androtion* (47-56 and 65-78), a circumstance which strongly stresses the similar direction of the attack just indicated. Occasionally doublets of this kind are also found elsewhere in Demosthenes.

While the two speeches just mentioned were written for personally insignificant speakers who were to lead the way for the attack, Demosthenes himself is supposed by the tradition (Dion. *Ep. ad Amm.* 1. 4) to have spoken the speech *Against Leptines* as Ctesippus' attorney. The latter was a son of Chabrias' who fell in 357 off Chios as trierarch and who had been one of the greatest hopes for Athens' new rise. The speech opposed Leptines' motion to repeal all freedom from taxes (ἀτέλεια) and to permit exceptions only for descendants of the tyrant-slayers. If Demosthenes really wrote it to be read by himself, the precise solemn tone, which stands in strong contrast with the vehemence of the later political speeches, deserves special attention.

Demosthenes' first political speech, *On the Symmories*,[1] is of the same time as the three forensic speeches just discussed. The expression symmories means tax-fellowships which had to equip naval units. Demosthenes appeared before the popular assembly in order to increase the number of citizens liable to this duty from 1200 to 2000. The proposal for the increase in armament is connected with the Persian question in that it opposes all frivolous warmongering against the old enemy with the consideration that at the time Athens did not command the resources for such an undertaking.

Conjointly with this oration there are two political speeches which each deal with a current problem of foreign policy. The speech *For the Megalopolites* of the year 352 throws a light on the unutterable confusion of Greek politics. While Thebes held its position of hegemony, it had taken under its protection the federal state of the Arcadians founded in 370 and Messene which gained its independence in 369 as a bastion against Sparta. But when Thebes was past its heyday and got into difficulties through its troubles with the Phocians, the position of the new Peloponnesian states with relation to Sparta became highly critical. At the time the Arcadians asked Athens for an alliance and although they were still tied to Sparta by treaty, Demosthenes favoured this request. We emphasized the confusion of the situation to make it understandable that a criticism of the correctness of this attitude is not easy. At any rate, according to Eubulus' interpretation, Athenian intervention in the Peloponnesus meant re-embarking upon the adventure of power politics, and so the paths of the two politicians separated. In the speech *For the Liberty of the Rhodians*,[2] which possibly

---

[1] E. LINK, *Unters. zur Symmorienrede des D.* Diss. Frankf. 1940. A. KÖRTE, *Gnom.* 19, 1943, 34. Further bibl. in BENGTSON (*v. sup.*), 305, 3. On the dating at 354/53 and the often confirmed datings of Dionysius, JAEGER, *Dem.* (*v. inf.*) 215, 21; 218, 6.

[2] FOCKE (*v. inf.*), 18; cf. JAEGER, *Dem.* (*v. inf.*), 224, 41.

dates from the same year 352, Demosthenes recommended support for the democrats whom the Carian despot Mausolus had ejected. Such a recommendation was neither easy nor promising, since the same democrats had allowed themselves to be persuaded by Mausolus to defect from Athens and so bore a share of the guilt in the failure of the second naval league.

Against Aristocrates, though delivered before the law-court, is also one of the speeches on foreign politics. Demosthenes wrote it for Euthycles of Thria, with whom he had been trierarch at the Hellespont. The speech deals with conditions in the Thracian region, which was so important for Athens. At the time – the speech was delivered in 352 or 351 – Philip had already undertaken his first advance into Thrace, but as yet the danger which Philip meant to Athens is not emphasized. The indictment for illegality is directed against the motion of Aristocrates for a vote of special protection for the person of Charidemus, the brother-in-law and minister of the Thracian king Cersobleptes; whoever killed him was to be outlawed. In opposition to the group for whom Aristocrates spoke, Demosthenes favoured support for the Thracian joint ruler Amadocus, Cersobleptes' brother.

Very soon after this speech, Philip of Macedon decisively intervened in Thracian affairs. His intervention forced the Thracian kings to ally themselves to him by treaty and brought him before the walls of Heraeum Tichus north of the Propontis and in dangerous proximity to Byzantium. At the time the Athenians had been in a state of war with Philip for several years; he had provided the cause for this in the year 357 by occupying Amphipolis and there were enough other occurrences which indicated who was going to make history in the future. Pydna had been occupied by Philip, Potidaea destroyed; in the summer of 354 he took the Greek city of Methone on the Gulf of Therme opposite Chalcidice; then the 'sacred war' against the Phocians about the hegemony in the Delphian amphictyony, which divided all Greece in two camps, gave him an opportunity to intervene and to find a footing in Thessaly in 352. But beforehand he had had to accept two defeats at the hands of the Phocian Onomarchus, and in the summer of 352 he had been forced to retire by a demonstration of Greek power at Thermopylae. And finally Macedon did not possess a fleet which could constitute a real danger. So far there had been other worries to occupy the Athenians, but the siege of Heraeum Tichus, the attempt on the Black Sea approaches, was the storm-signal. In the *Third Olynthiac Speech* Demosthenes reminds the Athenians of the alarm and activity which the report of Philip's undertaking had evoked in the city, though this had soon abated again. It must also have been the moment of understanding for himself, for from now on we see his political leadership directed only against one single country and enemy: Macedon and Philip.

The earliest evidence of this understanding and its consequences is the *First Philippic*,[1] a vigorous call to the Athenian citizenry, which links criticism of past failures with cheering encouragement. He makes a concrete proposal for equipping two battle-groups in order to harass Philip incessantly on land and to

---

[1] A. RONCONI, *Dem. La prima Filippica. Con introd. e note.* Florence 1956.

be able to attack him with a naval force in his territory. Demosthenes also gave a detailed plan for the procurement of the means for these forces, but in our text we read only the key-word 'indication of financial measures' ($\pi\acute{o}\rho ou\ \grave{a}\pi\acute{o}\delta\epsilon\iota\xi\iota s$), valuable evidence that the speeches, which were actually delivered, were meant to exert their influence also as pamphlets in which some details had been altered by the author.

The dating of the speech poses a difficult problem. Dionysius (*Ep. ad Amm.* 4) indicates the archontic year of 352/1. The time immediately after the attack on Heraeum Tichus and the relief caused by Philip's illness would provide an excellent background to the speech. But it mentions an attempt by Philip against Olynthus (17), and this can hardly refer to any other but the one of 349. On this basis Eduard Schwartz[1] established the date in this year and this has found general acceptance.

Wilamowitz and others wanted to deny that the speech *On the Reorganisation* ($\Pi\epsilon\rho\grave{\iota}\ \sigma u\nu\tau\acute{a}\xi\epsilon\omega s$)[2] was by Demosthenes, taking into account the correspondence of numerous passages with other speeches, but recently there has been a tendency to admit it as genuine. The tenor of the speech, which demands financial reforms and calls for exertion in the interest of the city, indicates the year 350.

An illness had deprived Philip of success before Heraeum Tichus; for Athens it only meant a pause for breath. The next Macedonian thrust was aimed at the Greek cities in Chalcidice, especially Olynthus.[3] In the year 348 the city fell and was completely destroyed; Chalcidice was in Philip's hands. At the last minute Athens had concluded an alliance with the Chalcidians and sent auxiliary forces, but everything came too late. Demosthenes' three *Olynthiac Speeches*[4] occurred in the period of the impending catastrophe, i.e. between the spring of 349 and the early part of 348. It is no longer possible to connect them in detail with concrete causes and especially in this case it is difficult to decide what part belongs to the spoken oration and what was originally political publication. The first of the speeches generally continues the tone and suggestions of the *First Philippic*. This applies also to the second which attacks the habits of making Philip into a bogyman in order to overawe the people; he argues that what is required is rather the strengthening of their inner attitude. Philip's power is shown to be a structure erected on falsehood and deceit; this moral fervour is nourished by the ancient Greek conviction that hybris cannot escape its 'dike'. The *Third Olynthiac* goes particularly far; though taking the existing laws

[1] *Festschr. f. Th. Mommsen.* Marburg 1893. Otherwise JAEGER, *Dem.* (*v. inf.*) 121, but it remains difficult to attribute the mention of Olynthus to a revision. Edition: U. E. PAOLI, Milan 1939.

[2] F. W. LENZ, *De Dem. II. συντ. oratione.* Diss. Berl. 1919. FOCKE (*v. inf.*), 12. JAEGER, *Dem.* (*v. inf.*), 234, 24 is dubious about its authenticity.

[3] This strong settlement of the fourth century was revealed by American excavations: D. M. ROBINSON, *Die Antike.* 11, 1935, 274, and *RE* 18, 1939, 325.

[4] P. TREVES, 'Le Olintiache di D.'. *Nuova Riv. Stor.* 22, 1938, 1. On the question 'Speech or pamphlet?' JAEGER, *Dem.* (*v. inf.*), 237, 46. H. ERBSE, 'Zu den Olynthischen Reden des Dem.'. *Rhein. Mus.* 99, 1956, 364.

into consideration, it moots the subject of utilizing the theoric fund for munitions. What a *crimen laesae maiestatis* – Demades called the theoric fund the glue
of democracy (Plut. *Plat. Quaest.* 1011 b) – any attempt on these moneys was
considered is demonstrated by the reaction to a motion of Apollodorus, whom
we met earlier in connection with several private law-suits (Ps.-Dem. *Against
Neaera* 3-5).

The speech *Against Midias*[1] also falls in the period of the battle of Olynthus.
Midias, one of the wealthiest Athenians, had long pursued Demosthenes with
his enmity until, at a festival of Dionysus, this unpredictable bully attacked the
orator openly. Demosthenes reacted immediately with a provisional complaint
(προβολή), but probably did not proceed to sue him, powerful as he was. Since
Midias belonged to Eubulus' party which Demosthenes was opposing more and
more vigorously with his policy of action, this affair, which originally was
entirely a private matter, now also acquired political colouring.

Philip's successes had created a situation in which only a united Greece could
have any chance of effective action. But this was still a very remote goal, and
so Demosthenes joined the Athenian embassy which went to Pella in 346 for
negotiations with Philip. In the same year the peace of Philocrates was concluded which forced the Athenians to abandon the Phocians and permitted
Philip to find a firm footing in central Greece. It was evident that this situation
would produce a host of new conflicts, but also that at the time Athens had no
prospect of success and so Demosthenes advocated the preservation of peace in
his speech *On the Peace*. It was the time in which Isocrates in his *Philip* called on
the Macedonian to be the leader of Greece.

In the following years of a hollow truce Demosthenes succeeded in gaining
control of Athenian politics in an increasing degree. In foreign affairs it was
necessary to win allies in order to form the most united possible Greek front
against Philip; at home the pro-Macedonian party had to be suppressed. The
Second Philippic[2] of the year 344 warns against Philip, deals with Argos and
Messene, which complain about Athens's pro-Spartan policy, and in its final
section sharply attacks Aeschines. Demosthenes had had the latter indicted for
bribery and fraud soon after the return of the embassy of 346. But Timarchus
was an unfortunate choice as the formal accuser and Aeschines managed to make
him impossible with a morals action of which his speech has been preserved.
Not until 343 did matters come to a head between Aeschines and Demosthenes,
who this time had to conduct his own prosecution. The two speeches *On
the Fraudulent Embassy* (Περὶ τῆς παραπρεσβείας) have been preserved, the
one by Demosthenes in a revised form meant for publication; consequently
Aeschines' defence does not correspond in individual points with the accusation
preserved. Aeschines was acquitted with a slight majority. The party of the

[1] H. ERBSE, 'Über die Midiana des D.'. *Herm.* 84, 1956, 135, tries to refute the opinion
that D. neither delivered this speech nor published it himself. He conjectures the late spring
of 349 as the time of the trial. HUMBERT-GERNET retain in their ed. the opinion defended
by him, and F. ZUCKER, *Gnom.* 32, 1960, 608, agrees with them.

[2] G. M. CALHOUN, 'D.'s Second Philippic'. *Trans. Am. Phil. Ass.* 64, 1933, 1.

pro-Macedonians lost ground, but Hyperides managed to have Philocrates sentenced to death, whereupon he fled abroad.

To this period (342) belongs the speech *On Halonnesus*, which defends Athens' title to the little island south of Lemnos. In antiquity, however, some authors such as Libanius in his *Hypotheses* thought that Hegesippus of Sunium rather than Demosthenes was the writer.

When in 342 Philip had firmly incorporated Thrace in his realm and the direction of his thrust to the sea approaches began again to become distinct, tension, and with it Demosthenes' activity, rose to its highest pitch. Three speeches of the year 341 bear this out. In the one *On the Affairs in the Chersonese* (Περὶ τῶν ἐν Χερρονήσῳ)[1] he adopts a protective attitude against Philip's complaints about Diopithes, the mercenary commander whose operations from this territory had become an annoyance to Philip. Demosthenes reached the climax in his career as a political orator with the *Third Philippic*. It blazes with the passion which Eratosthenes compares with the emotion of one possessed by Bacchus (Plut. *Dem.* 9). He stresses that the need of the moment is to speed up the manufacture of munitions and to work towards the union of all Greeks against Philip; nothing else counts more than this. The speech is preserved both in a shorter and a longer form. It is difficult to determine whether Demosthenes wrote them both or the second has been interpolated.[2] The authenticity of the *Fourth Philippic* used to be disputed, but Alfred Körte restored it to Demosthenes.[3] The speech strongly stresses that attempts were being made to reach agreement in domestic politics; in public opposition to Isocrates, Demosthenes (32-34) underlines the hope of collaboration with Persia more strongly than elsewhere.

These years were the climax of Demosthenes' career. Philip's attacks on Perinthus and Byzantium were unsuccessful, but under the impression of this danger the greater part of the Greek states united in one league under Athens's leadership. Thebes, which still held aloof, did not join until directly before the decision. At home the new law of the symmories demonstrated an increased readiness to sacrifice self-interest. Twice, in the years 340 and 339, the people, who now recognized Demosthenes as their political leader, honoured him with a golden wreath.

In the Corpus Demosthenicum a letter of Philip of the year 340 has been preserved (12)[4] in which he complains of Athens' help for Perinthus and Byzantium. The commentary on Demosthenes by Didymus (no. 241 P.) has proved that a section of Book 7 of the *Philippics* of Anaximenes of Lampsacus is Demosthenes' address in reply (11) to this letter.

Since 340 Athens had again been in open warfare with Philip. Battles in the north of his realm caused a delay of the decision, which fell eventually in the year 338 at Chaeronea. It meant the end of Greek freedom, but at the same time

---

[1] A. MORPURGO, *Orazione per gli affari di Chersoneso. Con introd. e comm.* Florence 1956.

[2] P. TREVES, 'La Composition de la 3e Philippique'. *Mélange Radet* 1940, 354.

[3] 'Zu Didymos' D.-Commentar'. *Rhein. Mus.* 60, 1905, 388. Recent discussion in C. D. ADAMS, 'Speeches VIII and X of the Dem. Corpus'. *Class. Phil.* 33, 1938, 129.

[4] Bibl. in BENGTSON (*v. sup.*), 291.

604

the beginning of a new era, for the Philip who in the very year of Chaeronea united the Greek states except Sparta under one 'general peace' and in one alliance under his leadership, proved himself to be one of the few men in history who can think of peace after winning a war.

The Athenians did not make Demosthenes suffer for the defeat; he was commissioned to deliver the funeral oration for the fallen. The preserved *Epitaphios* is quite remote both in style and emotion from the assembly speeches, but the difference of the situation and the genre should be borne in mind. Those who defend its authenticity are probably right.[1] Years later Demosthenes delivered the real and lofty *Epitaphios* to Athens' fight for freedom under unusual conditions. In 336 Ctesiphon moved his solemn crowning in the theatre during the Great Dionysia for his merits in improving the walls and for his sacrifices of personal property in the service of the state. Aeschines objected with a complaint of illegality, but the trial was postponed and the case was not tried until 330. Aeschines' formal objection merely offered a pretext to fight once more, in a way typically Greek and typically Athenian, the great battle of the years before Chaeronea whose outcome had long ago been decided by history, this time on the field of rhetoric. We possess both speeches, Aeschines' *Against Ctesiphon* and Demosthenes' *On the Crown* (Περὶ στεφάνου) in which he elaborated his defence of Ctesiphon into a tremendous retrospect of the ends aimed at and a justification of the course taken at the time. Demosthenes was victorious, Aeschines did not even obtain a fifth of the votes and had to leave Athens.

It is not difficult to imagine that Demosthenes shared the hope of Athens which blazed up at Philip's death (336), but the speech *On the Treaties with Alexander* (17, Περὶ τῶν πρὸς Ἀλέξανδρον συνθηκῶν) handed down under his name, which opposes the Macedonians, is not his.

A dark shadow fell over his old age when he became involved in the Harpalus affair. This faithless treasurer had deposited in Athens some money with which he had defected from Alexander and had passed part of it on to Athenian politicians. Demosthenes was one of them; we do not know the motives which made him accept the money. The court imposed (324) a fine of fifty talents on him; he avoided imprisonment for debt by fleeing to Troezen. When Athens rose together with Argos and Corinth at the death of Alexander, he returned home in triumph. But the rebels' dream of freedom soon ended with the defeat of the fleet at Amorgos and of the army at Crannon. Again Demosthenes had to flee; in the late autumn of 322 he committed suicide with poison on the island of Calauria when he saw himself surrounded by Antipater's myrmidons.

Demosthenes' work was surveyed in connection with his life and political

---

[1] J. SYKUTRIS, 'Der dem. Epitaphios'. *Herm.* 63, 1928, 241, and M. POHLENZ, 'Zu den att. Reden auf die Gefallenen'. *Symb. Osl.* 26, 1948, 46. Against the authenticity P. TREVES, 'Apocrifi demosthenici'. *Athenaeum* 14, 1936, 153 and 233. Other bibl. in JAEGER, *Dem.* (*v. inf.*), 253, 24, who doubts the authenticity. The speech *On the Crown*: P. TREVES, Milan 1933 (with comm.).

activity. It has become clear that the collection of sixty-one speeches is interspersed with an abundance of spurious material. Among the latter is also the *Eroticus* (61), a letter which praises a beautiful boy. Another six letters have been preserved, all of which, except the fifth, have his exile as a background.[1] For the second and the third the question of authenticity may be considered, but is by no means settled. On the other hand many of the fifty-six prefaces to political speeches are genuine, for several of them reappear in the surviving speeches. It may be supposed that a collection of Demosthenes' works was later enriched with imitations.

The changes to which the image of Demosthenes was subject in the course of time form in themselves a chapter of history.[2] Cardinal Bessarion published in 1470 the *First Olynthiac Speech* in Latin in order to incite enthusiasm for the struggle against the Turks; Friedrich Jacob translated Demosthenes in the days of Napoleon; time and again attempts were made to kindle new flames with the glow of his ardour. The latest member in this series is Clemenceau's *Démosthène*[3] of the period after the first world war. During the same war appeared Engelbert Drerup's book *Aus einem alten Advokatenrepublik*[4] which represents an extreme opposite viewpoint. Since our picture of Greek history has tremendously changed through Droysen's discovery of the Hellenistic era, judgment of Demosthenes' political activity has been made from a different aspect. The Greeks' last struggle for freedom became a period without interest compared with the world-wide influence which Alexander's deeds opened up for the Hellenes, and Demosthenes withdrew in the shadows of those who welcomed Philip as the bringer of a new development. He necessarily fared badly by such a judgment passed *ex eventu* and he had to pay heavily for the classical halo which he still wears in Arnold Schäfer's great work. At present the pendulum may have stopped swinging between the two extremes and the time may be ripe for a formulation of questions which result from another point of view. We have some comprehension of the interplay of the forces which prepared for the end of the polis of the classical era and which blazed a trail for new developments and we can evaluate what was lost and what gained. As for Demosthenes, our questions are whether his life and struggles are of a truly tragic character or were a mere shadow-play. Our answer will depend on two further questions: did the issues for which he fought belong to the rank of great historical reality or were they illusions? did he fight his battle for these issues for the sake of a conviction or did he use legal quibbles for personal renown and gain? These two questions answer themselves in the asking. And this means that Demosthenes, whose task it was to bear witness to the proud tradition of his polis in the very hour of its downfall, becomes a great tragic figure in the history of the Greek people.

[1] H. SACHSENWEGER, *De D. Epistulis*. Diss. Leipz. 1935. A section from *Ep.* 3 in a London papyrus of the 1st c. B.C. (no. 239 P.).

[2] E. DRERUP, *D. im Urteil des Altertums*.Würzb. 1923. For more recent times: G. D. ADAMS, *D. and his influence*. Lond. 1927.

[3] Paris 1924.   [4] Paderborn 1916.

The art of his rhetoric endures independent of the appreciation of his political activity. Especially in Britain, but in other European countries as well, he has long been esteemed and utilized as the unrivalled teacher of political eloquence. Earlier, in connection with Isocrates, we spoke of the dangers of rhetoric for Greek intellect and Greek art. Therefore it should be emphasized all the more strongly that in Demosthenes true passion and power of conviction pervade the perfected form to such an extent that his strongest speeches are inspired with real life. In the beginning of his rhetorical career Demosthenes still shows here and there that he is influenced by the example of the Isocratic period with its calculated balance and cool smoothness, but he soon acquires a personal style which draws even in the most elaborate sentence constructions on the actuality of situations and permeates them with the temperament of the speaker. The uniformity of Isocratic speech is contrasted in Demosthenes by an incomparably greater richness of variety,[1] just as the broad sweep of the political speeches is in clear contrast with the simpler period construction of the forensic speeches. He is moderate in the use of figures of speech and sound; he avoids hiatus, though not with the same strictness as Isocrates, and in his choice of words he exerts the same discipline, although occasionally he does not shrink from using a strong expression. Already in antiquity it was noticed that the effect of Demosthenes' speeches depended largely on their rhythm. It is difficult to ascertain the laws of this rhythmical construction. Blass discovered one important detail when he observed that Demosthenes avoids the sequence of more than two short syllables.[2] The effect of Demosthenes' style rests largely on the moderate utilization, controlled by a very subtle sense of rhythm, of the freedom of word-order which gave to writers of Greek such an abundance of possibilities to create an effect. Like other masters of prose, Demosthenes devoted careful attention to the rhythmical structure of his sentence conclusions. The study of this technique of clause construction has not yet achieved any definite results and has lately stagnated somewhat.[3]

We single out two from among the ancient critics of Demosthenes' style: the syncrisis of the orator with Thucydides in the historian's biography (56 f.) transmitted under the name of Marcellinus, which stresses Demosthenes' vigorous use of metaphor avoided by Thucydides. Recently Friedrich Zucker[4] has shown that it is very probable that this criticism comes from the works by Caecilius of Calacte Περὶ τοῦ χαρακτῆρος τῶν δέκα ῥητόρων. The confrontation

---

[1] Dionysius, Dem. 43-52 already observed the essential points.

[2] L. DISSEN laid the foundation for the analysis of D.'s period structure in the introduction to his edition of On the Crown (1837). F. BLASS, Att. Beredsamkeit, 2nd ed. Leipz. 1893, vol. 3/1, is still of importance. Rhythmical analyses in E. NORDEN's Die antike Kunstprosa 2, Leipz. 1898, 911. On the avoidance of accumulated short syllables: C. D. ADAMS, 'D.'s avoidance of breves'. Class. Phil. 12, 1917, 271.

[3] The theory defended by NORDEN (v. sup.), 914 ff. that the final rhythm is based principally on the cretic is opposed by A. W. DE GROOT, A Handbook of Antique Prose-rhythm. Groningen 1918, who finds a preference for dactyl and choriamb.

[4] 'Ἀνηθοποίητος. Eine semasiologische Untersuchung aus der antiken Rhetorik und Ethik (Sitzb. Deutsche Akad. Kl. f. Spr., Lit. u. Kunst 1952/4 1953), with excellent interpretation of the two passages referred to herc.

of Hyperides and Demosthenes by the author of the treatise *On the Sublime* (34) is particularly impressive: in spite of all his splendid qualities, in spite of his wit and elegance, Hyperides is separated by an abyss from the passionate greatness of Demosthenes.

Aeschines, who as the henchman of Eubulus and the Macedonian king was Demosthenes' most violent opponent, was borne into history in the latter's wake; otherwise this politician and orator would not have caused much of a stir. About Aeschines we have the article in Suidas and two biographies (one signed by a certain Apollonius), apart from the sections in the Ps.-Plutarch's *Orators* and Philostratus' *Lives of the Sophists*. At the time of the controversial embassy he was 44 years old (1. 49), which puts the year of his birth in 389. In contrast to Demosthenes he was of humble origin, his parents being the schoolmaster Atrometus and Glaucothea, who, as often happened at that time, earned some money in the obscure mystery cults. She was helped by Aeschines when he was a boy, and Demosthenes flung this fact in his face in an exceedingly malicious way in a passage from *De Corona* (259), which is of some importance for the history of religion. When he grew up, Aeschines tried the stage, but got no further than being a poor tritagonist, if we are to believe Demosthenes (*De Cor.* 265, 267). We find him in the subordinate civil service position of ὑπογραμματεύς, but he succeeded at last in gaining the confidence of Eubulus, the head of the peace party. We know little else about his entry into politics. It is peculiar that we possess three speeches of his which are of a routine nature, but are unable to find any further indications of his oratorical activity. One speech which he is supposed to have held in Delos on behalf of Athens, was already correctly denied to be his in antiquity, since he never represented his city there as we know from Hyperides (fr. 1 Burtt).

Aeschines' part in the negotiations of the Delphic Amphictyony in the year 339 is particularly dubious; these negotiations led to the Sacred War against the Locrians of Amphissa, and Aeschines, Athens' envoy at the time, contributed to this war and with it to Philip's intervention, whatever his motives may have been.[1] We already discussed the three speeches preserved and the relevant circumstances in connection with Demosthenes. Aeschines spoke *Against Timarchus* in order to convict the accuser in the embassy trial of immorality and to have him deprived of his citizen's rights; in the speech *On the Fraudulent Embassy* he successfully defended himself against Demosthenes, but suffered a decisive defeat at his hands in 330 in the case of the crown with his speech *Against Ctesiphon*. When he had to leave Athens he went to Asia Minor and is supposed to have taught rhetoric in Rhodes. According to the information in the *Life* by Apollonius, which is completely unreliable, he died in 314.

Twelve *Letters* preserved under his name are spurious; partly they presuppose, quite unhistorically, his formal exile and represent him requesting his recall. The *Tenth Letter* merits literary interest, since it is in effect a Milesian tale with a shameless story of seduction.[2]

---

[1] For this epoch: F. R. WÜST, *Philipp II v. Maked. u. Griechenland in den Jahren von 346–338.* Munich 1938, 146. [2] Cf. A. LESKY, *Aristainetos.* Zürich 1951, 40.

Dinarchus was another opponent of Demosthenes to be mentioned, although since he was born in Corinth in 360 a great part of his activity belongs to a later epoch. In spite of his mediocrity, Dionysius of Halicarnassus devoted a treatise to him (Περὶ Δεινάρχου) and this also provided the material for the *Life* in Ps.-Plutarch. He came to Athens in 342, studied under Theophrastus and became a confidential friend of Demetrius of Phalerum. From 336 onward he wrote speeches and acquired some importance when the great orators had retired from the stage of Athenian life. But when in 307 the Macedonian-supported régime of his patron, Demetrius of Phalerum, had to give way to Demetrius Poliorcetes, he extricated himself from the threatening situation and fled to Chalcis in Euboea. He was not allowed to return until 292, probably through Theophrastus' intercession. At an advanced age he appeared for the first time legally in a trial against his one-time friend Proxenus[1] whom he indicted in connection with an affair of property. How long he lived after that is unknown.

The number of his speeches according to the tradition varies considerably, but most figures seem to be unbelievably high. Dionysius reports sixty genuine and twenty-seven spurious ones. Some more titles turn up in other authors. We possess six of the speeches mentioned by Dionysius and it well shows how confused the tradition of the orators is when we observe that three of these are in the Corpus Demosthenicum (39. 40. 58) and that only the first of them is by Demosthenes. Three of Dinarchus' speeches in the Harpalus trials survive. The first of these was read by an unknown speaker as the second speech for the prosecution (deuterology) *Against Demosthenes*. Dionysius reports (1) the doubts which Polyhistor Demetrius Magnes had of its authenticity. This critic of style compared Dinarchus with Hyperides in charm and found that the speech *Against Demosthenes* deviated too strongly in style from the others. The first opinion is obviously invalid; and when we compare it with the other preserved speeches, we observe the same haphazard composition, the same predominance of abuse over argumentation and the same dependence of a degenerating rhetoric on great models, so that we can ignore Demetrius' doubts. The second speech is *Against Aristogiton*, that dubious demagogue who is the subject of two spurious speeches in the Corpus Demosthenicum (25 f.). He, too, had accepted money from Harpalus. In the third speech *Against Philocles*, this representative of the anti-Macedonian party, who had served Athens in high positions, is charged with the same offence. The two last-mentioned speeches are mutilated in the final sections.

Demosthenes, however, also had a few followers among the orators of his time. The most interesting profile among them is that of the Athenian Hyperides. He was born in 390, studied under Isocrates and heard Plato, if we may believe the biography by Ps.-Plutarch. In his private life he was fond of the good things of the earth, and although there is a great deal of fiction in the mockery which comedy levelled at his enjoyment of the pleasures of the table and of

---

[1] Bibl. on the question of whether this was possible for the metic in Ferckel (*v. inf.* on Lysias), 76.

hetaerae,[1] there must have been some reason for these inventions. One anecdote became celebrated. When he delivered his speech for the defence of Phryne – Messala Corvinus translated it into Latin – he impressed the jurors by baring the beauty's bosom. This same Hyperides faithfully and energetically stuck to the line of anti-Macedonian policy up to his terrible end. In 343 he obtained the conviction of Philocrates who gave his name to the peace of 346 and soon afterwards successfully represented Athenian interests in Delos. Like Demosthenes he recruited allies for Athens and served his city in naval expeditions as a trierarch, as, for instance, at Byzantium in 340. After Chaeronea he was active as a distinguished legal orator, appearing in 324 as accuser against his old party friend Demosthenes. But he was reconciled with him, and when Alexander died he was at his side in the revolt of which he was one of the leaders together with the strategos Leosthenes. And like Demosthenes he fled after the disaster of 322, under the threat of execution; in the same year he was captured in Aegina and cruelly executed at the order of Antipater.

Hyperides is one of the authors of whom we have acquired a thorough knowledge only through the papyri and so scholarship has done more for him in the last few decades than for the other authors. Finds in the second half of the last century produced extensive remains of six speeches. The best preserved are the speech *Against Athenogenes*[2] in a private suit about a contract of sale, and *For Euxenippus*, charged with incorrect division of land at Oropus. A vision in the Amphiareum played an interesting part in the affair. The speech *Against Demosthenes*[3] in the Harpalus trial has come to us in a very fragmentary condition. The one *For Lycophron* featured in a law-suit in which the orator Lycurgus, as one of the accusers, attempted to use an εἰσαγγελία in order to turn a charge of adultery with a background of property rights into a matter of state. The speech *Against Philippides* attacks an advocate of pro-Macedonian measures. After the bitter end of the rebellion Hyperides spoke the *Epitaphios*[4] over the fallen in the Lamian War. The extensive remains show that Hyperides had reached the limits of his linguistic ability along his way to the grand style. He was not gifted with the eruptive violence of Demosthenes' oratory which broke forth from a profound emotion. The composer of the work *On the Sublime* (34) gave an excellent characterization of him when he stressed the richness of his tones and called him a sound jack-of-all-trades who performed skilfully in all the aspects of his art without being first in a single one. It was also rightly observed that next to Demosthenes he owed much to the naturalness and charm of Lysias. In his speech we discern the linguistic laxity by which the transition of Attic to Koine, the Hellenistic common speech, begins to be marked out.[5]

[1] Ath. 8, 341 e. 13, 590 c. Cf. т. в. l. WEBSTER, *Studies in Later Gr. Com.* Manchester 1953, 46.

[2] Comm. ed. of this and the following speech: v. DE FALCO, Naples 1947.

[3] G. COLIN, *Le Discours d'H. contre Dém. sur l'argent d'Harpale.* Paris 1934.

[4] G. COLIN, 'L'Oraison funèbre d'H.' *Rev. Ét. Gr.* 51, 1938, 209. 305. H. HESS. *Textkr. u. erkl. Beiträge zum Epitaphios des H.* Leipz. 1938 (with bibl. on Gr. funeral orations).

[5] D. GROMSKA, *De Sermone Hyperidis. Studia Leopolitana* 3, 1927. U. POHLE, *Die Sprache des Redners H. in ihren Beziehungen zur Koine.* Leipz. 1928.

Lycurgus, of the venerable family of the Eteobutadidae, the only Attic orator from the ranks of the nobility, was the soul of the restoration policy after 338. Born in 390, he entered the ranks of the anti-Macedonian patriots in the forties and administered Athenian finances, partly himself, partly through his friends, in an exemplary way in the years 338–327. But this man, whose consistent strictness against himself and others had almost un-Athenian traits, exerted an influence beyond the limits of public financial administration. His family was connected with high priesthoods, such as that of Poseidon in the Erechtheum, and that of Athena Polias, and he himself devoted particular care to the public cult of Dionysus. It was as a service to the god that Lycurgus restored the theatre of Dionysus in stone; he had the statues of the three great tragedians placed there and attempted to stem the degeneration of the tradition by means of a state copy of the tragic texts (v. p. 267). He died not long after his term of office, probably in 324.

In antiquity fifteen of his speeches were extant, all forensic and all for the prosecution, except two, which he delivered for his own defence in trials on matters of audit. We have only his speech *Against Leocrates*, an Athenian who had fled from the city in a panic in 338 and wanted to settle there again in 331. His strict prosecutor charged him with high treason, basing himself on the general conception of civic duty rather than on specific laws. Numerous poetic quotations, among which is a speech from Euripides' *Erechtheus*, demonstrate the speaker's yearning for the great past.

The one specimen which we have bears out Dionysius' opinion (*De imit.* 5. 3) that his strength lay in powerful emphasis and unreserved expression of the truth, not in wit and charm. The smoothness of the period of Isocrates, his teacher according to the tradition, is as alien to him as the sweeping solemnity of Demosthenes' mighty sentence-constructions.

The ten Attic orators collected in the canon represent a selection from a considerably larger number. We have various names, but they remain almost completely shadowy to us. In connection with Demosthenes we already met Hegesippus as the probable composer of the speech *On Halonnesus*, and Aristo-giton who has little to charm us; Stratocles can be added as Demosthenes' chief prosecutor in the Harpalus case. Occasionally talent remains a family property as with the tragedians. The orator Glaucippus was a son of Hyperides', and Demochares, Demosthenes' nephew, attempted to revive his uncle's patriotic fervour in a time when it must have sounded hollow. He took diligent care of his relative's memory; thus he erected a statue for him in the market place in 280. In the year 306 he supported in a speech for Sophocles the latter's motion that the teaching activities of the undemocratic philosophers should be restricted. He also wrote contemporary history.

We are best informed about Demades of the deme Paeana. With wit and adaptability he worked his way up from humble conditions – he is supposed to have even been an oarsman – to a leading position in Athenian politics. He was also involved in the Harpalus affair and at this time he had to accept many a set-back, but in 322, after the defeat of the rebels, he took over the helm, together with Phocion, and put the motion which led to the conviction and death of Demosthenes and Hyperides. Then his good fortune left him. When he went to Macedon with his son in 319 to work for the withdrawal of the Macedonian garrison from Munychia, Craterus accused him of double-dealing and had him executed.

As an orator Demades had a natural talent and was much esteemed for his ready wit. Choice examples have been preserved of the 'Demadea'.[1] According to Cicero (*Brut.* 36; cf. Quint. 12. 10, 49) no speeches were extant. This is one of the arguments against the authenticity of the excerpts from a speech *On the Twelve Years* ('Υπὲρ τῆς δωδεκαετίας) preserved in a Palatinus, which contains a defence of Demades' policy after Chaeronea.

Isocrates:

There is no evidence that the Alexandrians occupied themselves with Isocrates, but he meant a great deal to the Atticists, and the considerable number of papyri (nos. 970-1005 P.) shows that he was diligently read in imperial times. Forgeries occurred, too; out of sixty speeches in circulation, Caecilius of Calacte marked twenty-eight, Dionysius of Halicarnassus only twenty-five as genuine (Ps.-Plut. *Dec. Or. Vitae* 838 d). In the manuscript tradition we have, besides a fairly good stemma represented by the valuable Urbinas 111 (9th/10th c.), the vulgate within which the Laurentianus 87. 14 (13th c.) is again separated from the group of the remaining manuscripts.

Editions: G. E. BENSELER – F. BLASS, 2 vols. Leipz. 1878/9; repr. of the ed. Leipz. 1887-98 (3 parts in 4 vols.) in prep. by Olms/Hildesheim, is still the standard ed. E. DRERUP (I. only) Leipz. 1906 with elaborate details on the tradition. G. MATHIEU–E. BRÉMOND, *Coll. des Un. de Fr.* (bilingual) 1, 2nd ed. 1956. 2, 3rd ed. 1956. 3, 2nd ed. 1950. Vol. 4 with *Panath.* has not yet appeared. The ed. of the *Loeb Class. Libr.* (bilingual) in 3 vols. (1954, 1956, 1945) by G. B. NORLIN and V. HOOK. R. FLACELIÈRE, *Isocrate. Cinq discours* (*Hel. Bus. Contre les soph. Sur l'attelage. Contre Callim.*) Ed. introd. et comm. Paris 1961. – *Scholia Graeca in Aeschinem et Is.* Ed. W. Dindorf Oxf. 1852. – S. PREUSS, *Index Isocrateus.* Leipz. 1904. On all the orators the extensive work by F. BLASS is still indispensable, *Die Attische Beredsamkeit.* 3 vols. 2nd ed. Leipz. 1887-98 (repr. in prep. by Olms/Hildesheim). R. C. JEBB, *The Attic Orators from Antiphon to Isaeus.* 1875; repr. in 2 vols. New York 1962. On history and theory of rhetoric R. VOLKMANN, *Die Rhetorik der Griechen und Römer.* 2nd ed. Leipz. 1885 (repr. in prep. by Olms/Hildesheim) has not yet been improved upon. Good, brief survey by W. RHYS ROBERTS, *Greek Rhetoric and Literary Criticism.* New York 1928. W. KROLL, *Rhetorik RE* S 7, 1940, 1039. D. L. CLARK, *Rhetoric in Greco-Roman Education.* New York 1957. M. DELAUNOIS, *Le Plan rhétorique dans l'éloquence grecque d'Homère à Démosthène. Acad. royale de Belgique. Cl. de lettres. Mémoires. Sér.* 2, 12, 2. 1959. With a wide coverage H. LANSBERG, *Handbuch der*

---

[1] Ps.-Demetr., *De eloc.* 282 ff. Also H. DIELS, *Rhein. Mus.* 29, 1874, 107.

literarischen Rhetorik. Eine Grundlegung der Literaturwissenschaft. Mit Registerband. Munich 1960. For terminology we still largely depend on J. CHR. G. ERNESTI, *Lexicon Rhetoricum.* Leipz. 1795. repr. Olms/Hildesheim 1962. – Studies: G. MATHIEU, *Les Idées politiques d'Isocrate.* Paris 1925. G. WALBERER, *Isokrates u. Alkidamas.* Diss. Hamb. 1938. G. SCHMITZ-KAHLMANN, *Das Beispiel der Geschichte im pol. Denken des I. Phil.* Suppl. vol. 31/4. 1939. H. WERSDÖRFER, *Die φιλοσοφία des I. im Spiegel seiner Terminologie.* Leipz. 1940. S. WILCOX, 'Criticism of I. and his φιλοσοφία'. *Trans. Am. Phil. Ass.* 74, 1943, 113; 'I.'s fellow-rhetoricians'. *Am. Journ. Phil.* 66, 1945, 171. H. L. HUDSON–WILLIAMS, 'Thuc., I. and the rhetorical method of composition'. *Class. Quart.* 42, 1948, 76; 'I. and recitations'. *Ibid.* 43, 1949, 65. W. STEIDLE, 'Redekunst und Bildung bei I.' *Herm.* 80, 1952, 257. EINO MIKKOLA, *Isokrates.* Helsinki 1954 with ext. bibl. F. ZUCKER, *I.' Panathen.* Berl. 1954. M. A. LEVI, *Isocrate.* Milan 1959 (with special attention to the political ideas). E. BUCHNER, *v.* p. 585, n. 2. – In L. RADERMACHER'S *Artium scriptores* (*v.* p. 584, n. 1), 163, the section *Isocratis doctrina ex ipsius orationibus petita* with index of subjects is very useful.

Lysias:

Our tradition of speeches 3-31 is based on a Heidelberg manuscript damaged in several places, the Palatinus 88 of the 12th c. Among the manuscripts which depend on Pal. 88 the Laur. plut. 57, 4 is noteworthy because of a number of remarkable emendations which anticipated later philological work. Only for the first two speeches there is an additional second stemma, best represented for 1 in the Marcianus 422 (15th c.) and for 2 in the Parisinus (Coislinianus 249; 11th c.). Dionysius preserved the fragments of speeches 32-34 in his *Lysias.* The papyri (nos. 1012-1016) produced a series of new fragments, e.g. from the above-mentioned speech *Against Hippotherses* and *Against Theozotides* (no. 1016 P., a papyrus of the 3rd c. B.C.; cf. A. WILHELM, *Wien. Stud.* 52, 1934, 52). – Editions: Th. Thalheim, 2nd ed. Leipz. 1913. K. HUDE, Oxf. (1912) 1952. L. GERNET–M. BIZOS, 2 vols. *Coll. des Univ. de Fr.* 1924/26, 3rd ed. rev. and corr. Paris 1955 (bilingual). R. S. SHUCKBURGH, *L. orationes XVI with analysis, notes, appendix & indices.* Lond. 1939. U. ALBINI, *Testo crit. introd. trad. e note,* Florence 1955. M. HOMBERT, *Lysias, Choix de discours.* 3rd ed. Brussels 1960. I. C. SABBADINI, *Lysias. Contro Alcibiade. Con introd. e note.* Florence 1958. M. GIGANTE, *Lysias. Contro Epicrate.* Naples 1960. – Index: D. H. HOLMES, Bonn 1895, repr. Amsterdam (Servio) 1962. – Studies: On forensic speeches generally the basic work is still J. H. LIPSIUS, *Das attische Recht und Rechtverfahren.* 1, Leipz. 1905. 2, 1908. 3, 1915. Also: R. J. BONNER and G. SMITH, *The Administration of Justice from Homer to Aristotle 1.* Chicago 1930. F. LÄMMLI, *Das att. Prozessverfahren in seiner Wirkung auf die Gerichtsrede.* Paderborn 1938. L. GERNET, *Droit et société dans la Grèce ancienne.* Paris 1955 (Transactions of the period 1909-53). On Lysias: F. FERCKEL, *Lysias und Athen.* Würzb. 1937 (very subjective with a good survey of the appreciation of L. in recent works). W. VOEGELIN, *Die Diabole bei Lysias.* Basel 1943. H. ERBSE, 'Lysias-Interpretationen'. *Festschr. Kapp.* Hamb. 1958, 51. M. GIGANTE, 'Il discorso olimpico di L.'. *Studi L. Castiglioni* 1, 1960, 375,

E. HEITSCH, 'Recht und Taktik in der 7. Rede des Lysias'. *Mus. Helv.* 18, 1961, 204, with valuable study on the structure of legal procedure and the logographers' importance depending on it.

Isaeus:

The Cod. Crippsianus of the 13th c. in the Brit. Mus. is the basis of the tradition. For the first two speeches there is in add. an Ambrosianus of the 13th or 14th c. Papyri: no. 968 f. P. Editions: TH. THALHEIM, Leipz. 1903. T. C. W. WYSE, Cambr. 1904, with ext. comm. P. ROUSSEL, *Coll. des Univ. de Fr.* (1922) 1960 (bilingual). In the *Loeb Class. Libr.* E. S. FORSTER 1957 (bilingual). U. E. PAOLI, *Iseo, Per l' eredità di Pirro.* Florence 1935 (with comm.) – Transl. with introd. and notes: K. MÜNSCHER, 'Isaios'. *Zeitschr. f. vergl. Rechtswiss.* 37, 1919, 32–328.

Demosthenes:

The Alexandrians had no scholarly interest in Demosthenes or any of the other orators, but they did have him in their library; Callimachus catalogued him. In imperial times a more intensive study of Demosthenes was begun, marked for us by the names of Didymus, Dionysius of Halicarnassus (*v. supra* p. 596) and Caecilius of Calacte. A fairly large piece of Didymus' collective commentary on the *Philippics* is preserved in a Berlin papyrus (no. 241 P.). The more strictly conventional Atticists, who preferred Lysias, did not prevail and from the 1st century A.D. we see Demosthenes in the undisputed position of the greatest orator of antiquity. Papyri of the 2nd century A.D. are fairly abundant (nos. 166-239 P.); a recent addition is presented in *Pap. Soc. It.* 14, 1957, no. 1349 f. Tradition of a varying nature attests to diligent endeavours to understand and linguistically interpret Demosthenes' speeches. Apart from the abundant scholia we only mention here Harpocration's *Lexicon of Orators* (2nd c. A.D.), a treatise by a certain Tiberius who cannot be accurately dated (Περὶ τῶν παρὰ Δημοσθένει σχημάτων. *Rhet. Graec.* 3. 59 Sp.) and the summaries of contents (hypotheses) of the orator Libanius.

The conjecture that an edition of Demosthenes by Atticus, of whom we know through the subscription to the tenth speech in manuscripts B and F, could have been of significance for our tradition, has proved to be untenable. Our manuscripts are divided into three classes (BUTCHER and RENNIE distinguish four, J. HUMBERT and L. GERNET follow them in their edition in the *Coll. des Univ. de Fr.*) of which the most important representatives are in each case: Parisinus 2934 (early 10th c.), Venetus Marcianus 416 (10th/11th c.) and Monacensis (Augustanus) 485 (11th c.). While otherwise Parisinus was considered of particular value, Gernet, in the introduction to his edition of the speeches in civil lawsuits, has just proved the special quality of Monacensis for these.

Editions: C. FUHR and J. SYKUTRIS planned to revise the old Teubner edition of F. BLASS (3 vols. 1888–92). Vol. 1 (1914) and 2/1 (1937) have been published. Further: S. H. BUTCHER and W. RENNIE, 4 vols. Oxf. 1903–31. In the *Coll. des Univ. de Fr.* (all bilingual): Harangues: M. CROISET, 2 vols. 1924/25 (several reprints; latest 1955 and 1946); Plaidoyers politiques: O. NAVARRE et P. ORSINI, tome 1 (speeches 22, 20, 24) 1954. J. HUMBERT and L. GERNET, tome 2 (speeches

21, 23); G. MATHIEU, tome 3 (speech 19) 1945, 2nd ed. 1956; tome 4 (speeches 18, 25, 26) 1947; 2nd ed. 1958; Plaidoyers civils: L. GERNET, tome 1 (speeches 27-38) 1954; tome 2 (speeches 39-48) 1957; tome 3 (speeches 49-56) 1959; tome 4 (speeches 57-59) with index by J. DE FOUCAULT and R. WEIL 1960. The bilingual ed. in the Loeb Class. Libr. by J. H. VINCE, A. T. MURRAY et alii comprises 7 vols. (latest 1956). – The scholia in the 2nd vol. of Oratores Attici by BAITER and SAUPPE (Zürich 1838-50) and in the Dem.-ed. of W. DINDORF, 9 vols. Oxf. 1846-51. Additional material from papyri (v. supra), firstly Didymus (no. 241 P.). – Index: S. PREUSS, Leipz. 1892. – General works and papers: still indispensable A. SCHAEFER, D. und seine Zeit. 3 vols. 2nd ed. Leipz. 1885-87 and vol. 3/1 of the above-mentioned work (p. 597) by F. BLASS. Recent: E. POKORNY, Studien zur griech. Gesch. im 6. und 5. Jahrzehnt des 4. Jh. Diss. Greifswald 1913. F. FOCKE, Demosthenesstudien. Tüb. Beitr. 5, 1929, I. P. TREVES, D. e la libertà greca. Bari 1933. A new point of view of the figure of Demosthenes in W. JAEGER, D. Origin and Growth of his Policy, Berkeley 1938; also Paideia 3, 345. M. POHLENZ, Gestalten aus Hellas. Munich 1950, 427. F. EGERMANN, Vom attischen Menschenbild. Munich 1952, 57. 110. P. CLOCHÉ, D. et la fin de la démocratie athénienne. Paris 1957. In two vols. written in modern Greek Nikon Kasimakos undertakes to represent Demosthenes' ethical tenets as outliving the political events: 1. Dem. as humanistic value. Athens 1951. 2. Dem.'s notions of gods, man and state. Athens 1959. J. LUCCIONI, Dém. et le panhellénisme. 1961. – Style: G. RONNET, Étude sur le style de D. dans les discours politiques. Paris 1951. D. KRÜGER, Die Bildersprache des Dem. Diss. Göttingen 1959 (typescr.). B. GAYA NUÑO, Sobre un giro de la lengua de Dem. Manuales y anejos de 'Emérita' 17. Madrid (examines the type verb + infinitive from which another infinitive depends). R. CHEVALLIER, 'L'Art oratoire de Dém. dans le discours sur la couronne'. Bull. Budé 4, 1960, 200. – Subsequent influence: E. DRERUP, Dem. im Urteile des Altertums. Würzburg 1923.

Aeschines:

Aeschines was diligently read in antiquity, as demonstrated by a handful of papyri (nos. 1-12 P.). In addition to these W. H. WILLIS, 'A new Papyrus of Aeschines'. Trans. Am. Phil. Ass. 86, 1955, 129, and Ox. Pap. 24, 1957, no. 2404 (in Ctesiph. 51-53). Cicero translated his speech Against Ctesiphon together with De Corona. Didymus and others wrote commentaries on him. The criticism of the transmission is based on the work of M. HEYSE, Die handschr. Überl. der Reden des Aisch. Ohlau 1912, but French editors suggest a different classification of the manuscripts. Editions: F. BLASS, Leipz. 1908. In the Loeb Class. Libr. bilingual by C. D. ADAMS 1919. G. DE BUDÉ-V. MARTIN, 2 vols. Coll. des Un. de Fr. 1927/28; latest 1952 (bilingual). M. DESSENNE, Eschine. Discours sur l'ambassade. Paris 1954 (polytypé). – The abundant scholia in the edition of F. SCHULTZ, Leipz. 1865. – Index: S. PREUSS, Leipz. 1896 (reprint. 1926).

Dinarchus:

As in the case of Antiphon, Andocides and Lycurgus, the tradition is based on a Crippsianus in the Brit. Mus. of the 13th c. and an Oxoniensis of the 14th c., both dependent on the same archetype. A fragment of an unknown speech of Dinarchus' in *Antinoopolis Pap. Part 2*. Lond. 1960, no. 62. – Editions: F. BLASS, 2nd ed. Leipz. 1888. A useful work is the *Minor Attic Orators* by J. O. BURTT in the *Loeb Class. Libr.* (1954) with the fragments and transl. L. L. FORMANN, *Index Andocideus, Lycurgeus, Dinarcheus*. Oxf. 1897 repr. Amsterd. 1963.

Hyperides:
Papyri: nos. 963–966 P. with the further references quoted there. – Editions: F. G. KENYON, Oxf. 1906. CHR. JENSEN, Leipz. 1917 (with authoritative revision of the text). G. COLIN, *Coll. des Univ. de Fr.* Paris, 1934. J. O. BURTT (*v.* on Dinarchus). – G. SCHIASSI, *Hyp. Epitaphios*. Florence 1959. – Index in Jensen.

Lycurgus:
Transmission: cf. on Dinarchus. Editions: F. BLASS, Leipz. 1899, brought up to date by F. DURRBACH, *Coll. des Univ. de Fr.* 2nd ed. 1956. J. O. BURTT (*v.* on Dinarchus). Comm.: C. REHDANTZ, Leipz. 1876. A. PETRIE, Cambr. 1922. P. TREVES, Milan 1934. – Index as for Dinarchus.

Demades:
Editions: V. DE FALCO, Pavia 1932; 2nd ed. Naples 1954. J. O. BURTT (*v.* on Dinarchus). – P. TREVES, 'Démade'. *Athenaeum* 11, 1933, 105.

4 HISTORIOGRAPHY

The strong influence exerted on historiography by rhetoric in the fourth century led us to arrange the material so that the former follows the latter. But we must first refer back to an author who had not yet been influenced by rhetoric and who aimed far beyond history in his literary work. This is also why we find Xenophon's biography in the writings of Diogenes Laertius, who is not the only ancient author to rank him seriously among the philosophers. There are some further notes in Suidas which do not, however, provide any essential addition.

Xenophon was a fellow-demesman of Isocrates for he was also born in the deme of Erchia[1] in 430 (the date is quite uncertain), as the son of well-to-do parents. Like other young Athenians of wealthy family he could devote himself whole-heartedly to horses and riding, which remained his great love; he also found time for many other things. It is not necessarily true, as Diogenes relates, that one day Socrates stopped the young man in the street with his stick and made him follow him, but this singular examiner and guide attracted him in no slight degree. He was not a pupil of Socrates like the others who never again escaped from philosophy in their lifetime, but the impressions received at the time were lasting ones, though they did not become forces which moulded his life. His completely untragical nature was not suited to this.

When in 401 his Boeotian friend Proxenus was recruiting for the expedition of the young Cyrus, who wanted to thrust his brother Artaxerxes II from the throne, he allowed himself to be persuaded to join the enterprise. The battle of Cunaxa, which lost its significance in the middle of its victorious course through

[1] On his biography: E. DELEBECQUE, *Essai sur la vie de Xénophon*. Paris 1957.

Cyrus' death, the difficult situation of the Greek contingent and the perilous return march through the Armenian highlands to the Black Sea, all this provided rich food for his yearning for adventure, and gave us his liveliest work. Participation in the undertaking which was supported by Sparta, had not been favoured by Athens, but soon Xenophon became an even stronger adherent of the ancient enemies of his native land. Agesilaus, who took the command of the fight against the Persians in 396, became his idol. When the king had to return to Greece with the Spartan troops to overthrow the coalition which had risen there against Sparta, Xenophon went with him and took part in the engagement of Coronea of 394. There is no possible excuse, not even the pro-Spartan sympathies of the circle from which he originated, for the fact that at that time he took up arms against his native city. It was for this action that Athens exiled him, and not, as stated by the ancient sources, for his participation in Cyrus' expedition. This did not hit him hard, for the Spartans first compensated him with the proxeny and a few years later (390 or soon afterwards) with a property in Scillus not far from Olympia. In a portion of the *Anabasis* (5. 3, 7) Xenophon described several details of the domain, to which he was obviously very attached. The farmer in him, vying for place with the soldier, could rejoice there in the splendid stand of timber and excellent grazing. But the huntsman also came into his own with game of all imaginable kinds. There the Ephesian priest of Artemis visited him to hand over his share of the booty which, after the expedition of the Ten Thousand, had been reserved for Ephesian Artemis, and been deposited in Ephesus. With the money Xenophon erected for the goddess an altar and a temple, a small-scale copy of the one in Ephesus, containing an image of the goddess in cypress-wood similar to the golden one in Ephesus.

The idyll of Scillus came to an end in 370, when the Eleans fell out with the Spartans and captured Scillus after the battle of Leuctra (371). Xenophon fled to Corinth. Here he probably spent a large part of the last period of his life, about which our information is scanty. Soon after Leuctra, Athens and Sparta came closer together under the increasing pressure which Thebes was capable of exerting. In this political atmosphere Xenophon's banishment was repealed. We do not know, however, how far he availed himself of the opportunity of living once more in the city of his birth. But he made his two sons serve in the Athenian cavalry and one of them, Gryllus, fell at Mantinea fighting bravely (362). The widespread respect which his father's name had already at that time is proved by the series of encomia and epitaphs[1] with which his death was solemnized.

In the *Hellenica* (6. 4, 36), Xenophon mentions the death of Alexander of Pherae, which gives 359 as the *terminus post quem* for the end of his own life. But since nowadays there is far-reaching agreement on the authenticity of the *Poroe* which presupposes the conditions of 355, the limit in question is moved on somewhat further.

Our information on the periods of this life is not uniformly scanty, however much it may vary. Contrariwise, there are great difficulties in fixing the

---

[1] Cf. the exaggerated statement of Aristotle in Diog. Laert. 2, 55.

chronology of Xenophon's literary activity with some accuracy. Nothing indicates an early start of his writing, which observation corresponds with the biographical data. One would like to imagine the years at Scillus as particularly productive, but noteworthy indications point to an even later date for several works[1] so that it is the very latest period of Xenophon's life which may have been his most fertile. Since a chronological arrangement would be a gamble, we shall introduce them grouped according to contents.

Among the historical works – the expression understood in the broadest sense – the *Anabasis* (Κύρου ἀνάβασις)[2] occupies a special place through the directness with which Xenophon reports his own experiences, through the abundance of geographical and ethnographical details and the good soldierly spirit of the whole. An anabasis, a march into the interior, is related only in the first six chapters of Book 1; then follows the description of the battle of Cunaxa, while the main part of the work is occupied by the narrative of the bold march back to the Black Sea right through hostile country and impassable mountains; also the subsequent fortunes of the force up to the union with the Spartan troops under Thibron are minutely described. We may condone the fact that Xenophon makes the share of the Spartan Chirisophus, who was commander-in-chief, recede into the background in favour of his own activity. A certain Sophaenetus of Stymphalos probably wrote an *Anabasis* before him;[3] he himself mentions (*Hell.* 3. 1, 2) a work by Themistogenes of Syracuse and describes its contents in words which agree accurately with his own *Anabasis*. Plutarch (*De Gloria Ath.* 345e) already correctly observed that this was the pseudonym under which he first published the work.[4] The division of the work into seven books is of a later date just as the summaries of previous events before the individual books.[5] The entire problem of Xenophon's chronology becomes obvious in the question of dating. If those who think that the *Anabasis* was utilized in Isocrates' *Panegyricus* are right[6] then we must place it before 380. But the supposed correspondence does not enforce this conclusion and the arguments for a later dating cannot be rejected; Xenophon speaks of the establishment in Scillus in the imperfect, and the passage 6. 6, 9 with the retrospect to a time in which Sparta ruled over all the Greeks, assumes at least the withdrawal of the Spartan garrison from the Theban Cadmea (379). It should be noted that in the *Hellenica* (5. 4) this very incident is

---

[1] *v. inf.*; a survey in JAEGER 3, 229. The extreme opinion that X. did not write at all before 370, advocated by E. SCHWARTZ, 'Quellenunters. zur griech. Gesch.'. *Rhein. Mus.* 44, 1889, 191; now *Ges. Schriften.* Vol. 2, Berlin 1956, 136. cf. e.g. TH. MARSCHALL, *Unters. zur Chronologie der Werke X.'s.* Diss. Munich 1928.

[2] Bilingual: W. MÜRI. Munich 1959 (Tusculum).

[3] FRANZ SCHRÖMER, *Der Bericht des Sophainetos über den Zug der Zehntausend.* Diss. Munich 1954 (typewr.).

[4] Otherwise, but not convincingly W. K. PRENTICE, 'Themistogenes of Syracuse, an error of a copyist'. *Am. Journ. Phil.* 68, 1947, 73; Cf. JACOBY's commentary on *F Gr Hist* 108.

[5] In Book 6 the summary occurs only before Ch. 3, which may indicate a different division into books.

[6] A. KEPPELMACHER, 'Zur Abfassungszeit von X.'s Anabasis'. *Anz. Ak. Wien. Phil. hist. Kl.* 60, 1923, 15. Recently P. MASQUERAY in his edition p. 8.

stressed as the turning-point of the Spartan hegemony. Of course, we remain aware of the fact that in this and every similar case, the possibility of sectional composition complicates the matter exceedingly.

The *Hellenica* relating Greek history from 411 to 362 in seven books, is Xenophon's main historical work. A work of this nature was hardly written down in one sitting and since indications for a syncretic growth are not lacking, various theories have been attempted to clarify it. These have yielded at least one fairly definite caesura in one passage. The work enters upon the events of the year 411 with μετὰ ταῦτα and in this way seeks direct connection with Thucydides. That it does not quite fit without a flaw need not be discussed here. To effect the attempted connection, a division of the material on annalistic principle as well as the most impersonal possible reporting has been observed. This is carried on up to 2, 3, 9 with the end of the Peloponnesian war, i.e. up to the point where a complement to Thucydides had its natural conclusion. In Book II follows the fairly continuous narrative of the rule of the Thirty, but in the further course of the story significant deviations from the first section of the work are evident in the negligence of chronology, unbalanced division of the material and a stronger emphasis on the personal element. This is also notable in the use of language; the frequent use of the otherwise rare future optative after 2. 3, 9 has been pointed out. Attempts to establish further subdivisions in the second greater section beyond this division have proved to be without prospects.[1] Xenophon continued to work on the second part for many years after Mantinea (362), as already proved by the earlier mentioned passage on the death of the tyrant Alexander of Pherae. We must definitely put the part directly joined to Thucydides earlier, though it is, of course, uncertain how far it should be separated in time.

The very material proximity of Xenophon's work to Thucydides only places him the more effectively in the latter's shadow. But Burckhardt bestowed overwhelming praise on the first two books of the *Hellenica*[2] and in more recent time much has happened, especially through Breitenbach's dissertation, for a fairer appreciation of Xenophon as an historian. A dominant feature is that the old soldier had a vivid understanding of all military matters and that he used it in his work. It must similarly be admitted that he often manages to depict effectively the leading personalities whom he places emphatically in the foreground. Thus an attempt at a characterization of Alcibiades from two different viewpoints (1. 4, 13) is quite noteworthy; Tacitus developed this sort of feature with great skill in the first book of the *Annals*. Xenophon proves to be the forerunner of Hellenistic historiography in the drawing of effective single scenes, such as Alcibiades' entry, Theramenes' death or the return of the exiled Thebans. He also understands the value of little highlights, as when he relates how ashamed the Oriental Pharnabazus is of the carpets he has brought along when he is face to face with the Spartans and sits down on the grass like them.

---

[1] Bibl. in J. HATZFELD's edition, p. 7. In add. *Bursians Jahresber.* 251, 1936, 1 (J. MESK) and 268, 1940, 1 (J. PENNDORF). Cf. *Fifty Years of Classical Scholarship.* Oxf. 1954, 185, 69.

[2] *Griech. Kulturgesch.* Kröner-Ausgabe 2, 472.

But an appreciation of what Xenophon can do should not lead to exaggeration and to an obliteration of the distance between him and Thucydides. He admittedly based his *Hellenica* on one leading idea which is prominent in the inserted preface 5. 4, 1; the rise of Sparta to be the ruler of Greece was necessarily followed by the decline of her power; in the spirit of ancient Greek piety, this was related to the wrath of the gods, for the Spartans had broken the oath that they would leave the autonomy of the Greek states unimpaired. But who would want to compare this with Thucydides' penetrating search for the forces which determine the course of history? When Xenophon develops series of causes, he always remains superficial compared with Thucydides' aetiology. His work has an abundance of speeches and displays skill in the characterization of the speakers without, however, sounding the interplay of forces in their very depths like Thucydides does. His limits also show in the finish and distribution of his material. He does not even mention such important events as the sea-battle of Cnidos, the second naval league, the founding of Megalopolis, while he often lingers extensively over subordinate matters. Thus Felix Jacoby's dictum remains justified, who called the combination of Herodotus, Thucydides and Xenophon the 'unnatural triad of our literary history'.[1]

From the material which he utilized in the *Hellenica*, Xenophon shaped his *Agesilaus*, an encomium on the greatly venerated Spartan king, which displays a stronger rhetorical tendency than the historical work.

Xenophon's friendship for Sparta also inspired his stylus in the composition of his writing on the state of the Lacedaemonians (Λακεδαιμονίων πολιτεία).[2] Lycurgus' constitution and the kingship based upon it are for him the historical foundations of Spartan power. Of course, he is aware of its decline, which is caused by the neglect of the old ways. The portion which used to be subject to unjustified suspicion[3] relegates this minor work to the final period of Xenophon's life. It performed for us the inestimable service of attracting into the Corpus Xenophonticum through an entirely external association, the valuable treatise of an anonymous oligarchical sympathizer on the constitution of Athens (v. p. 452).

The writing *On the Revenues* (Πόροι) deals with economic conditions in Athens; its authenticity is generally no longer disputed nowadays.[4] Its suggestions for a reorganization of Athenian finances are in line with the policy of peace advocated by Eubulus. The situation of Athens which is presupposed in the writing is the one after the unhappy result of the War of the Allies of 355; the observation in 5. 9 on the attempt of a power to establish itself in Delphi in place of the Phocians points to the second half of the 'fifties.

It is difficult to allot a place to the *Cyropaedia* (Κύρου παιδεία), a work in eight books; nor can it simply be called an historical work. Its title poses the same problem as that of the *Anabasis*; this story of the elder Cyrus' youth, rise

[1] *RE* S 2, 1913, 513.
[2] Edition: F. OLLIER, Lyon-Paris 1934. MARÍA R. GOMEZ-M. F. GALIANO, Madrid 1957 (bilingual).   [3] Cf. JAEGER, 3, 425, 53.
[4] A. WILHELM, 'Unters. zu X.'s Πόροι'. *Wien. Stud.* 52, 1934, 18. Comm. edition: J. H. THIEL, Diss. Amsterd. 1922.

and reign devotes only part of the first book to his education. The fact that this was considered important enough to give its title to the whole attests to the educational optimism founded by the sophists. Of course, Xenophon connects this estimation of education with ancient aristocratic thought in an association not otherwise rare, when in 1. 1, 6 he mentions origin and natural talent side by side with training as the causes which made his hero rise to such greatness.

The *Cyropaedia* deals very lightheartedly with historical facts. Thus Cyrus, who fell in the battle against the Massagetae,[1] here dies peacefully in bed; it concentrates various qualities in him and in this way it becomes the portrayal of the ideal king. This earliest historical novel is closely connected with the *Agesilaus* and the *State of the Lacedaemonians* and together with these works it is part of the intellectual preparation for monarchy, whose greatest hour was to start with the Hellenistic age. In this work, which is richly interspersed with moralizing speeches and a number of episodes, the story of Panthea is noteworthy, a noble woman who remains true to her husband Abradates unto death. It anticipates the lofty conception of love which occurs in Hellenistic literature so abruptly side by side with lasciviousness and frivolity.

Like the *State of the Lacedaemonians*, this work concludes with a melancholy glance at decline and degeneration. There is no solid foundation for suspecting this portion.[2] The completion of this work is also placed in the later years of Xenophon's life by the mention of the surrender of the rebellious Ariobarzanes by his son (8. 8, 4), an event of the year 360.

The influence of the *Cyropaedia* was greater than its literary value. It provoked many similar writings about the life of great rulers and Cicero translated part of the ending in his *Cato Maior*.

Xenophon, the soldier, country squire and hunter had a pronounced tendency toward the didactic which is observable in writings on the most important spheres of his life.

The *Hipparchicus* gives instructions for the cavalry-commander, the writing *On Riding* (Περὶ ἱππικῆς)[3] for the individual trooper and the treatment of his horse. Both works, particularly the first, presuppose Athenian conditions. The *Hipparchicus* alludes to the Boeotians (7. 3) as enemies and stresses (9. 4) good relations with the Spartans. This points to the time before the battle of Mantinea (362). *On Riding* is of a later date, since it refers to the *Hipparchicus* in the final sentence. Admittedly the genuineness of this sentence, which does not occur in Cod. A, is subject to doubt. The two references to the technical handbook of a certain Simon of Athens (1. 3; 11. 6) proves the existence of more literature of this kind, which could have been assumed even without this evidence.[4] The hunting book, the *Cynegeticus*, belongs in this class in respect of content. Its authenticity, however, has been the subject of lively argument. The linguistic form, deviating as it does in many respects from Xenophon's pleasant simplicity,

---

[1] Thus Herodotus 1, 214 who also knows of other variations.
[2] Cf. p. 620, n. 3.
[3] Comm. edition: E. DELEBECQUE, Paris 1950, with bibl. on Greek horsemanship.
[4] A piece from this in Delebecque: *v. sup.*

presents a considerable obstacle,[1] while its defenders would like to consider it a youthful work. A special position is occupied by the preface, which was at any rate inserted substantially later. The aim is to prove that hunting is an outstanding educational aid; this is in the best Xenophontic spirit, but certainly corresponded with general opinions.

For the sake of the practical didactic contents we here present a work which is usually mentioned together with the philosophical writings, since Socrates appears in it as taking part in the conversation. In the *Oeconomicus*, however, he is not the main figure, since it depicts an interview with Ischomachus in which he is chiefly the reporter. Ischomachus, a well-to-do property-owner who married recently, describes how he organizes his day and the work of his servants. In this context the work offers an abundance of facts of cultural-historical importance, while Ischomachus' report on how he introduces his very young wife to her domestic duties provides an invaluable insight into the life of an Athenian woman. There were many admirers of the work; Cicero translated it.

In the chapter on Socrates mention was already made of Xenophon as a Socratic author, so that a brief indication will suffice here. The main work is the *Memorabilia* (Ἀπομνημονεύματα Σωκράτους),[2] four books of Socratic discourses and episodes in motley variety. We refer to the section mentioned for a discussion of the late time of composition of this and the other Socratic writings, for its historical value and for the problem whether the first two chapters were composed substantially earlier as a defence against the pamphlet of the sophist Polycrates.[3] Gigon's radical attempt at resolving the *Memorabilia* into a number of groups of ideas originating in the extensive Socratic literature before Xenophon has greatly contributed to the clarification of this work in which so much is implicit. Xenophon no doubt utilized to a large extent the Socratic writings of others, but it is not possible to deny that he also had personal memories of the Master. In the criticism of the *Memorabilia* and of the related works, the Xenophontic element should especially be taken into account, the didactic tendency to discuss things from the point of view of a practical morality without too great a profundity of thought and to ensure for oneself in this way the correct behaviour with regard to state and gods. Hardly anyone would claim that the

[1] Bibl. in H. EMONDS, *Zweite Auflage im Altertum*. Leipz. 1941, 383. JAEGER, 3, 250, considers the writing genuine.

[2] O. GIGON, *Komm. zum 1. Buch von X.'s Mem. Schw. Beitr.* 5, Basel 1953. Id. on Book 2 *Schw. Beitr.* 7, 1956. In add. J. H. KÜHN, *Gnom.* 26, 1954, 512 and 29, 1957, 170. H. ERBSE, 'Die Architektonik im Aufbau von X.'s Memorabilien'. *Herm.* 89, 1961, 257.

[3] Important recent bibl.: A.-H. CHROUST, 'Xen. Polycrates and the "Indictment of Socrates".' *Class. et Mediaev.* 16, 1955, 1. E. GEBHARD, *Polykrates Anklage gegen Sokrates und Xen.'s Erwiderung*. Diss. Frankfurt 1957, which assumes that Xen. utilized Plato extensively. v. LONGO, Ἀνὴρ ὠφέλιμος. *Il problema della composizione dei 'Memorabili di Socrate' attraverso lo Scritto di difesa*. Genoa 1959, argues that the 'Defence' was written considerably earlier than the rest of the *Memorabilia* as an immediate reaction to Polycrates' pamphlet; he observes three strata in it. A justified protest in E. GEBHARD, *Gnom.* 34, 1962, 26, who also rejects the assumption that the 'Defence' was published separately. Older bibl. on Polycrates in J.-H. KÜHN, *Gnom.* 32, 1960, 99, 1.

combination of such heterogeneous elements has yielded a whole of convincing unity.

The *Apology of Socrates*[1] – this written defence is, of course, one of a number of similar works (cf. p. 499) – is in all respects of small format. Socrates' speeches before and after his conviction form only part of the work; they are flanked by reports about his conduct before and after the trial. This Socrates of Xenophontic proportions cannot forgo the opportunity of availing himself of the prophetic vision of one near to death and foretells a terrible end for the son of his accuser Anytus. The detail that he refused to move his own punishment at his trial may be historical in view of Plato's irony.

The most charming writing of this group is the *Symposium*,[2] the description of a banquet given by the rich Callias, whom we know from Plato's *Protagoras* as hostel-warden to the sophists (cf. pp. 424 and 518), on the occasion of a victory which his favourite Autolycus won in the pancratium during the Pan-athenaean festival. Socrates makes many edifying statements and also delivers an oration on sensual and spiritual eros. Of the symposiastic byplay the mime of the union of Dionysus and Ariadne is particularly noteworthy, since it gives us one of the few testimonies for such performances before the Hellenistic age.

The *Hiero* is a unique work; it is a dialogue representing the poet Simonides in a discussion with the Sicilian prince on the nature and the possibilities of a monarch. Its subject is that of the traditional novels about the relationship of these two men (*v.* p. 185); within the compass of Xenophon's writings it is another proof of the vivid interest with which the question of monarchy inspired him.

The Hellenistic age did not at first know what to make of Xenophon, but in its later period there arose an interest in this author which constantly increased throughout the empire[3] until by the end of the ancient world the seven forged *Letters of Xenophon* prove this in their own way. But Xenophon certainly was not the Attic bee as he is called by Suidas. His Attic Greek is not completely pure and in many ways it anticipates Koine. But the lucid simplicity of his language (ἀφέλεια) and the easy intelligibility of his thought gained him his readers and we can understand his light shining especially in late antiquity. No one will deny his considerable and versatile talent, but it was a talent without the spark of genius.

None of the many historians of the fourth century can claim to be a true heir of Herodotus or Thucydides, though many attempted to follow them in a variety of ways. Ctesias of Cnidos (*F Gr Hist* 688) depends on Herodotus,

---

[1] On the question of authenticity *v.* p. 494 with n. 1. On the chronological relation to Plato's *Apology v.* p. 495 with n. 2.

[2] G. J. WOLDINGA, *X.'s Symp.* Hilversum 1938/39 (prol. and comm.) W. WIMMEL, 'Zum Verhältnis einiger Stellen des xenoph. und des plat. "Symp."'. *Gymn.* 64, 1957, 230, attempts to prove Xen.'s priority, but the explanations of F. OLLIER in his edition in the *Coll. des Univ. de Fr.* prove that the arguments are not yet definite. Ollier's introduction may urge some caution also for other problems of relative chronology concerning Plato and Xen.

[3] K. MUNSCHER, *X. in der griech.-röm. Lit.* Phil. Suppl. 13/2, 1920.

although he constantly censures his model with the pretence of better knowledge. He was court physician to Queen Parysatis and is believed to have lived at the court of Artaxerxes II Mnemon for seventeen years. According to a later report (Xen. *Anab.* 1. 8, 26) he cured the wound which the king's brother had inflicted at Cunaxa. In the beginning of the fourth century he wrote the twenty-three books of his *Persica*, dealing first with Assyrian and Median, then with Persian history from the legendary King Ninos up to the year 398. In Nero's time the learned Pamphilia made an extract from it; an extract from this by the Patriarch Photius has been preserved. Obviously Ctesias was more important as a story-teller than as an historian; he is a valuable witness for conditions at the Persian Court. Athenaeus (2. 67 a 10, 442 b) attests to a work *On the Tribute of Asia* (Περὶ τῶν κατὰ τὴν ᾿Ασίαν φόρων) which was possibly part of the great work. He also wrote a book *Indica*, of which we likewise have an extract by Photius, and a geographical work called *Periplus* or *Periodos*. The fragment in *Ox. Pap.* no. 2330 displays a surprising Attic colouring. Dinon of Colophon, the father of Clitarchus, historian of Alexander, revised Ctesias' *Persica*, continuing this work until the end of the 'forties. He and Ctesias were utilized a great deal by later writers. Agathocles of Cyzicus (*F Gr Hist* 472), who wrote about this city in the Ionic dialect, should be dated about the middle of the third century, contrary to the long accepted early date.

The abrupt termination of Thucydides' work in the middle of the stream of events seemed to invite continuation. We saw Xenophon attempting it, but he was not the only one. The challenge was taken up amongst others by Theopompus of Chios (*F Gr Hist* 115), an author of manifold interests but filled with inner unrest. We possess no complete work of his, but enough fragments to be able to discern his character to some extent. He was born in 378/376 and was given abundant experience of the uncertainty of the times during his life. He was forced to go into exile with his father Damasistratus on account of the latter's pro-Spartan sentiments (T 2), an event which presumably took place in his youth. Not until 333/332 could he return to his country due to Alexander's intervention, but at the latter's death he had to go abroad again. He then went to Egypt, where friends had to protect the wanderer against a conviction by the king. In the early periods of his life he travelled far in the Greek world, spending some time at the court of Philip; he also lived in Athens, although the time of his sojourn there cannot be fixed. In antiquity it was an accepted fact that he was a pupil of Isocrates, and it is very doubtful whether modern critics have not pushed their scepticism too far with their contention that this pupil-relationship is a mere fiction derived from his literary dependence.[1] This dependence should not be minimized. Theopompus may have carried on the tradition of Ionian ἱστορίη but he accompanied it on its way to domination by rhetoric. With his *Epideictic Speeches* (e.g. a *Panathenaicus*), *Encomia* (on Philip, Alexander, Mausollus, with which he gained a victory in a contest organized by Artemisia) and *Open Letters* he developed an activity which makes it understandable that

---

[1] Thus Jacoby on T I with bibl. Isocrates' influence on historiography: G. MURRAY, *Greek Studies*. 3rd ed. Oxf. 1948, 149.

Suidas ranks him as an orator, and of which we now get an even better impression through the epigraphical evidence of the book lists of Rhodes (T 48). But his name was mainly connected with his historical works. In two books he gave an *Epitome of Herodutus*; he continued Thucydides with his *Hellenica* (12 books) carrying on up to the battle of Cnidos (394), a well-chosen conclusion, since Conon's victory put an end to Spartan hopes of a hegemony over the whole of Greece. His greatest work was the *Philippica* in fifty-eight books beginning with Philip II's enthronement and ending with his death (336). But although the work was guided by the conception that Philip introduced a new era, the description of his achievements was only the framework for a general contemporary history and numerous additions with special chapters about Persians, Greeks and Sicilians.[1] When Philip V had a compilation made of the parts which directly concerned his forefathers, a work of only sixteen books was the result (T 31). The title Θαυμάσια (F 64-77) designated part of Books 8 and 9, to which the story of the wonderland Meropis (F 75) also belongs; *On the Sacking of Delphi* (Περὶ τῶν συληθέντων ἐκ Δελφῶν χρημάτων F 247-249) was treated in a separate work.

Theopompus, who was very temperamental in his judgments – he also attacked Plato in a very malicious manner (F 259; 275) – was governed entirely by oligarchical and aristocratic ideals and later turned increasingly toward the principle of a patriarchal monarchy as the protection of a conservative social order.[2]

In Greek historiography, as it developed in the wake of the great authors of the fifth century, certain continuous tendencies stand out.[3] Rhetorical aids were soon used to ornament the language: in this respect it was Isocrates and his school who had a decisive influence. Another momentous development is connected with Gorgias, who had stated that the aim of poetry and epideictic oratory was delight and enchantment, an end which was now also being pursued by history. What we discern in Ctesias can be recognized as the beginning of a development which we shall find clearly marked by Duris and Phylarchus in the Hellenistic age. A form of historiography is developing which aims at a violent emotional effect (ἔκπληξις) as a rival of tragedy, seeking to realize this by casting the material in a theatrical form without respect for historical reality. In implacable opposition to this tendency are the historians, who considered the tracing and preservation of truth as their only business, as exemplified particularly by Polybius.

The picture briefly sketched here gains in diversity when we consider that

---

[1] H. D. WESTLAKE, 'The Sicilian Books of Th.'s Philippica'. *Historia* 2, 1953/4, 288. A. E. RAUBITSCHEK, 'Theopompos on Thucydides the Son of Melesias'. *Phoenix* 14, 1960, 81, attempts a reconstruction of the information about the activity of this Thucydides in Book 10 of the *Philippica*; bibl. on other attempts to trace Theopompus' treatment of Athenian statesmen is given 95, n. 19.

[2] K. V. FRITZ, 'Die politische Tendenz in Th.'s. Geschichtschreibung'. *Antike und Abendland* 4, 1954, 45.

[3] Important and illuminating F. WEHRLI, 'Die Geschichtschreibung im Lichte der antiken Theorie'. *Eumusia. Festgabe für E. Howald*. Zürich 1947, 54.

renunciation of Gorgias' brand of seductiveness does not imply the simultaneous renunciation of rhetorical usage. This describes the position of Theopompus. Following the footsteps of his teacher Isocrates he sought a moderate rhetorical transformation of his style without sacrificing the historical substance to dramatic effects. His benevolent critic Dionysius of Halicarnassus (*Ad Pomp.* 6) testifies to his sincere diligence in the search for facts; he stresses especially the wealth and great variety of didactic dicta, and also the careful testing from a moral standpoint of the motives of the various personalities.

We became acquainted with a follower of Thucydides of considerable importance through a papyrus find of the year 1906 which gave us twenty-one columns of an historical text[1] dealing with events of the year 396/395; a comparison of this material with Xenophon's reporting favours the new text. The *Hellenica Oxyrhynchia* was written after 387 and before the end (346), probably before the outbreak (356) of the Sacred War about Delphi. The annalistical division of the material according to summer and winter points to a close connection with Thucydides. Unless Ephorus was earlier, the *Hellenica* was his main source. A few more fragments[2] came to light in 1934, got lost and were rediscovered by V. Bartoletti in 1948. Scholars have vainly attempted to relieve the Oxyrhynchian historian of his anonymity. Solutions indicating Theopompus, Ephorus and many others can be ignored nowadays. Some thought that Cratippus of Athens (*F Gr Hist* 64) was a likely candidate, as, according to Dionysius' information (*De Thuc.* 16), he was a contemporary of Thucydides and carried on the latter's work. Schwartz and Jacoby[3] went too far by casting suspicion on this testimony and turning Cratippus into a Hellenistic author, but we know too little about him to guarantee that this conjectural ascription is correct. Jacoby hesitantly allotted the *Hellenica Oxyrhynchia* to Daemachus (*F Gr Hist* 65). Ephorus utilized him, and the circumstance that he was a Boeotian can be combined with the valuable information of the anonymous author about the Boeotian League. But the support is weak and the *Hellenica Oxyrhynchia* remains deprived of its author's name.

Like Theopompus, Ephorus of Cyme was a pupil of Isocrates (*F Gr Hist* 70).[4] The date of his birth is uncertain, but might be placed in the first quarter of the fourth century. He wrote at least the greater part of his main work, the thirty

---

[1] *F Gr Hist* 66. No 1711 P. Discussion and bibl. in G. T. GRIFFITH in *Fifty Years* (*v.* p. 619, n. 1), 160. Editions: M. GIGANTE, Rome 1949. V. BARTOLETTI, Leipz. 1959 on the basis of a new collation of the papyri. On the question of authorship esp. H. BLOCH, 'Studies in historical literature of the fourth century'. *Stud. pres. to W. S. Ferguson* (special vol. of *Harv. Stud.*) 1940, 303. F. JACOBY, 'The Authorship of the Hell. of Ox.'. *Class. Quart.* 44, 1950, 1.

[2] *Pap. Soc. It.* 13, 1949, no. 1304. Also printed by P. MAAS in the appendix to JACOBY's essay (*v.* prev. note). M. TREU, 'Zu den neuen Bruchstücken der Hell. von Ox.'. *Gymn.* 59, 1952, 302. R. STARK, *Annales Univ. Saraviensis. Philos.-Lettres* 8, 1/2, 1959, 47 n. 7 with bibl.

[3] Both in the comm. and in the work referred to above, n. 1; but cf. Griffith (*v.* p. 619, n. 1), 161. V. BARTOLETTI (by letter) is inclined to accept Cratippus as the author.

[4] G. L. BARBER, *The Historian Ephorus*. Cambr. 1935. A. MOMIGLIANO, 'La storia di Eforo e le Elleniche di Teopompo'. *Riv. Fil.* 13, 1935, 180.

books of the *Historiae*, after 350. Its important influence – Diodorus amongst others made extensive use of it, while Polybius honestly admired it – is based on its quality as the first universal history.[1] Ephorus began with the conquest of the Peloponnese by the Dorians, excluding the mythical era, and continued his work, extending its scope, until the beginnings of Philip. Since he did not achieve the conclusion which he had planned, his son Demophilus added the history of the Sacred War. The remnants prove that Ephorus was a compiler of great style who collected his sources without profound historical understanding and occasionally harmonized in an arbitrary manner. His work attained a peculiar quality through the moralizing didactic tenor which was particularly evident in the prefaces. This agrees with the rationalism with which he treated the myths. Much of this, such as the Delphian Python with the nickname Dracon, a dangerous monster who is shot by Apollo (F 31), is reminiscent of the finest 'explanations' of Hecataeus. As an Isocratic, he made certain demands upon his style, which was probably the subject of his treatise *On Style* (Περὶ λέξεως). He knew how to separate epideictic speech from historical narrative (F 111) and also remained aloof from Gorgianic seductiveness. It was considered that his style lacked vigour,[2] which agrees with his slow manner of working. Isocrates is alleged to have said that Theopompus needed reins, but Ephorus spurs (T 28). His *Local History* ('Επιχώριος λόγος), devoted to the tradition of his native town, and the work *On Inventions* (Περὶ εὑρημάτων) in at least two books, stand as independent works beside the *Historiae*.

Ephorus could already use the ten books of the *Hellenica* of Callisthenes of Olynthus (*F Gr Hist* 124), which covered the period from the peace of Antalcidas up to the beginning of the Sacred War (356), which was dealt with in a separate treatise. Callisthenes, probably a great-nephew of Aristotle's, with whom he also compiled the *List of the Pythian Victors* (*v.* p. 572) was born about 370, accompanied Aristotle to Assos and to the Macedonian court and put his writing into the service of Macedonian ideas with a Panhellenic accent. In this sense he panegyrically extolled the deeds of Alexander, whom he accompanied on his expedition, in the 'Αλεξάνδρου πράξεις. But when he raised objections in the matter of the proscynesis, he was executed in 327. Of his other writings we mention a *Hermeas* and a *Periplus*. That his name was attached to the fabulous Alexander romance is due to the fanciful way in which he wrote history.

Anaximenes of Lampsacus (*F Gr Hist* 72), whom Ephorus also utilized and whom we already met as the writer of the *Rhetorica ad Alexandrum* (p. 591), was important as an orator and only briefly rubbed shoulders with history, according to Jacoby. But the connection was rather longer, for he wrote a *Hellenica*, extending from mythical pre-history to the battle of Mantinea; furthermore, *Philippica* (Αἱ περὶ Φίλιππον ἱστορίαι), from which a letter of Philip and a fictitious speech by Demosthenes have been preserved,[3] and a *History of Alexander*

---

[1] On one of the problems, AUR. PERETTI, *Eforo e Ps.-Scilace. Studi Class. e Orient.* 10. Pisa 1961.

[2] Evidence in WEHRLI (*v.* p. 625, n. 3).

[3] 12 and 11 in the Demosthenes Corpus; *v.* p. 605. The speech also *F Gr Hist* 72 F 11.

(Τὰ περὶ ᾽Αλέξανδρον), which fixes the second half of the fourth century as his creative period. On Theopompus he played the trick of fathering upon him a *Tricaranus* (F 20 f.) in which Athens, Sparta and Thebes appeared as the cause of the political misery of Greece.

Of historians of the fourth century who are hardly more than names to us we mention Heraclides of Cyme with a *Persica* (*F Gr Hist* 689), then Cephisodorus of Thebes (*F Gr Hist* 112) and Leon of Byzantium (*F Gr Hist* 132), who both wrote about the Sacred War. Of the last mentioned, a pupil of Aristotle's, there were also works on the history of Philip and Alexander. Andron of Halicarnassus (*F Gr Hist* 10) moved into the field of genealogy with his enquiries into the kinship of Greek states.

The first Athenian in the series of Atthidographers led by the Aeolian Hellanicus (*v.* p. 330) was Clidemus (*F Gr Hist* 323). Inscriptions testify to this version of his name against the form Clitodemus, also handed down and also correct. We know of four books of his *Atthis*, which is also referred to occasionally as *Protogonia* and which had some literary pretensions. It was probably written in the middle of the fourth century. Clidemus, who himself was an exegete (perhaps of the group of the Pythochresti), demonstrated his interest in matters of worship also with the composition of an *Exegeticus*.

Among the Atthidographers Androtion (*F Gr Hist* 324)[1] occupies a special position because he wrote Athenian history as an active politician. We already met him as an opponent of Demosthenes' (p. 599), who directed two speeches against him in the beginning of his political career. He came from a distinguished family, was born in Athens in the last decade of the fifth century and studied under Isocrates. After a turbulent political career he went to Megara as an exile in the late 'forties. There he wrote the eight books of his *Atthis*, which extended up to at least 344/343.

A short span of time separates Androtion's *Atthis* from the one by Phanodemus (*F Gr Hist* 325), who is identified, with a fair degree of probability, as the father of Diyllus, the partisan of Lycurgus' restoration policy. In 343/342 he was a member of the Council and may have begun writing his *Atthis*, of which we identify nine books, soon after 340. He is characterized by the particular interest in cult and mythical tradition evinced by the fragments. He also wrote a book *On the Island of Icos* (᾽Ικιακά) with which personal memories must have connected him. The most important representative of Sicilian historiography, whose beginnings were mentioned earlier (p. 332), was at this time Philistus of Syracuse (*F Gr Hist* 556). He was born in 430; his death can be definitely fixed at 356/355. He was a faithful adherent of the policy of the tyrants, which did not prevent him from being exiled for a time by Dionysius I. His historical work consists of two parts conceived as a unity and later combined into the *Sicelica*. The seven books of the first part (Περὶ Σικελίας) deal with the history of the island up to 406/405, the second part in six books (four on the elder, two on the younger Dionysius) gave contemporary history. Philistus' report on the younger Dionysius remained a torso and it was at this point that Athanis (or Athanus) of

---

[1] JACOBY'S comm. gives an exhaustive monograph. In add. his *Atthis*, Oxf. 1949.

Syracuse (*F Gr Hist* 562) began his twelve books of contemporary history leading up to at least the retirement of Timoleon (337/336).

Other authors of Sicilian history of this time are Timonides of Leucas (*F Gr Hist* 561), who was a member of the Academy, and Hermeas of Methymna (*F Gr Hist* 558), who was the first foreigner to occupy himself with Sicilian history. There is a creditable report (*F Gr Hist* 557) that Dionysius I also wrote history.

The first technical manual on warfare of which we know is a *Treatise on the Defence of a Besieged City*, written by Aeneas Tacticus in the middle of the century.[1] The possibility may be considered that the writer is identical with the Arcadian general Aeneas of Stymphalos (Xen. *Hell.* 7. 3, 1). At any rate, he was a man of the sword, not of the pen. The historical examples and the glimpses of conditions in the fourth century are valuable; the Greek is artless and displays elements of Koine. What has been preserved was once part of a larger work quoted by Polybius (10. 44: Τὰ περὶ τῶν στρατηγικῶν ὑπομνήματα).

Ephorus showed that the line of rational interpretation of myths, initited by Hecataeus and Herodotus, continued in the fourth century (though not ending with him). Palaephatus' writing *On Incredible Stories* (Περὶ ἀπίστων))[2] cannot be dated more precisely, but belongs in the same century. The writer's name is perhaps a pseudonym, but he clearly demonstrates his mettle in the consistency with which he squeezes his own brand of 'truth' from the myths down to the last detail. Of the five books of this work an epitome with fifty-two stories has been preserved.

Finally we add a curious writer who should otherwise remain unnoticed. Antiphanes of Berge, an author of incredible stories (perhaps the title was Ἄπιστα) managed to make 'Bergaïc speech' (βεργαΐζειν) into the technical term for unadulterated humbug. O. Weinreich[3] has proved that he belonged to the fourth century and has shown that the fairy-tale of the frozen notes goes back to this man.

The Xenophontic manuscript tradition varies with regard to the different works; it is copious, but contains fairly late codices. F. G. DEL RIO, *Manuscritos de Jenofonte en bibliotecas espanõlas.* Émérita 26, 1958, 319. H. ERBSE, 'Textkritische Bemerkungen zu X.' *Rhein. Mus.* 103, 1960, 144 (with numerous conjectures which presuppose minuscule corruptions on the basis of the history of the transmission). The quite numerous papyri (nos 1210–1233 P.), especially *Pap. Ox.* 463 (no 1211 P.), have led to a more careful assessment of the less

---

[1] Edition: Illinois Greek Club (with Asclepiodotus and Onasander). *Loeb Class. Libr.* 1923. L. W. HUNTER and S. A. HANDFORD, *Aineiu Poliorketika.* Oxf. 1927, with elaborate discussion of the style. Lexicon: D. BARENDS, Utrecht 1955.

[2] Edition: N. FESTA. Leipzig 1902; cf. WILH. NESTLE, *Vom Mythos zum Logos.* Stuttg. 1940, 148 with bibl.

[3] *Antiphanes und Münchhausen. Sitzb. Ak. Wien. Phil.-hist. Kl.* 220/4, 1942. Correct date already in WILAMOWITZ, *Herm.* 40, 1905, 150 = *Kl. Schr.* 4. Berl. 1962, 203.

valued manuscripts. A Ptolemaic papyrus in E. SIEGMANN, *Lit. griech. Texte der Heidelberger Pap. Sammlung.* Heidelberg 1956, no 206 with Xen. *Mem.* 1.3, 7-13; *v.* R. MERKELBACH, *Stud. zur Textgesch. u. Textkritik.* Cologne and Opladen 1959, 157. Details in the editions mentioned below, also *v.* Delebecque in his ed. mentioned p. 621, n. 3 of the work *On Riding.* In his ed. of the *Symp.* and *Apol.* in the *Coll. des Univ. de Fr.* F. OLLIER rejects the possibility of a manuscript-stemma; he believes that only an eclectic approach is feasible.

Editions: TEUBNER: C. HUDE, *Anab.* 1931. *Hellen.* 1930. *Memor.* 1934. TH. THALHEIM, *Opuscula* 2 vols 1910/12. Bibliotheca Oxoniensis: E.C. MARCHANT, 5 vols, 1900–1920 (all vols repeatedly reprinted). Id. bilingual in the *Loeb Class. Libr.* 2 vols with *Mem.*, *Oecon.* and *Scripta Minora*, 1956. *Coll. des Univ. de Fr.* (bilingual): P. MASQUERAY, *Anab.* 2 vols 1930 (3rd impr. 1952). J. HATZ-FELD, *Hellen.* 2 vols 1936/39 (2nd impr. 1949/48). P. CHANTRAINE, *Oecon.* 1949 F. OLLIER, *Symp.*, *Apol.* 1961. – G. PIERLEONI, *X. opuscula.* Rome 1937. M. I. FINLEY, *The Greek Historians, The Essence of Herod, Thuc. Xen. Polyb.* New York 1959 (Selected passages with notes and introductions). Individual editions mentioned in the notes. – F. W. STURZ, *Lexicon Xenophonteum*, 4 vols. Leipz. 1801–1804. – Recent transl.: W. H. D. DOUSE, *The March up country.* Michigan 1958.

Language: L. GAUTIER, *La Langue de X.* Geneva 1911. M. SACHSENHAUSER, 'Untersuchungen über die Sperrungen von Substantiv und Attribut in X.s Anabasis.' *Wien. Stud.* 72, 1959, 54. – Studies: A. MOMIGLIANO, 'L' egemonia tebena in Senof. e in Eforo.' *Atene e Roma* 37, 1935, 101. E. DELEBECQUE, 'X., Athènes et Lacédémone.' *Rev. Ét. Gr.* 69, 1946, 71. A. DELATTE, 'La Formation humaniste selon X.' *Bull. de l'Ass. Budé* 35, 1949, 505. H. R. BREITEN-BACH, *Historiographische Anschauungsformen X.s.* Diss. Basel 1950. M. SORDI, 'I caratteri dell' opera storiografica di Senof. nelle Elleniche'. *Athenaeum* N.S. 28, 1950, 1; 29, 1951, 273. J. LUCCIONI, *X. et le socratisme.* Paris 1953.

The other historians:

Bibl. on individual authors given in the notes. On the whole section: G. DE SANCTIS, *Studi di storia della storiografia greca.* Florence 1951. – The first continuous piece of Ctesias' *Persica*, surprisingly in the Attic dialect, was supplied by *Ox. Pap.* 22, 1954, no. 2330; cf. K. LATTE, *Gnom.* 27, 1955, 497. R. MERKEL-BACH, *Arch. f. Pap. Forsch.* 16, 1956, 109. D. DEL CORNO, 'La lingua di Ctesia (*P. Ox.* 2330)'. *Athenaeum* N.S. 40, 1962, 12b.

5 DRAMA

In the field of dramatic poetry the fourth century also produced a great many works.[1] Wherever the Greek migrated, his theatre came with him and found appreciation. Pottery gives apt evidence of the extent to which at the time tragedy conquered the Greek west. In the course of this development the great tragedy of the fifth century came gradually to be regarded as classical compared

---

[1] T. B. L. WEBSTER, *Art and Literature in Fourth Century Athens.* Lond. 1956. Id. 'Fourth Century Tragedy and Poetics', *Herm.* 82, 1954, 294. Theatrical production: id. *Greek Theatre Production.* Lond. 1956. A. PICKARD-CAMBRIDGE, *The Dramatic Festivals of Athens.* Oxf. 1953. On comedy *v.* p. 632, n. 4.

with the new trend. Starting presumably in 386, the restaging of an old tragedy had been inserted in the festival programme of the Dionysia. The fragment of the epigraphical Didascaliae for 341–339[1] shows that Euripides was selected in each of the three years. The young Astydamas, a descendant of Aeschylus, who was victorious in 341 and 340, complained in some lines (1, p. 113 D.), meant for his statue in the theatre, that he could not compete directly with the greatest men in his art. Lycurgus had the statues of the three classic tragedians placed in the new stone structure and established the text by means of a state-copy; this meant the acknowledgment and the conclusion of a development which condemned later work to ruin.

But we believe that we have an example of the production of the fourth century in the *Rhesus*, which has been handed down to us under the name of Euripides. Recent attempts to prove its authenticity have remained inconclusive;[2] the essential features of the play indicate the post-classical era. The dramatization of the Dolonea (*Iliad* 10) with many a charming lyrical note as in the morning song of the guards (*v.* 527), and the picture of life in camp, beginning with the anapaestic scene of the prologue, has been vividly drawn. The story how Odysseus and Diomedes first kill the Trojan counterspy Dolon and then the Thracian king Rhesus, who had just boastfully arrived to support the Trojans, has been shaped with obvious pains to achieve dramatic effect. But it is right here that the contrast with Euripides appears; through all kinds of insinuations and accusations minor secondary conflicts are kindled which die out rapidly and without effect; the play as a whole does not gain dramatic life or even the aspect of true tragedy. In this sphere the writer of the *Rhesus* remains far distant even from Euripides' weaker plays. Gottfried Hermann[3] already thought that the almost complete absence of the gnomic element in the play was a valid argument for its rejection.

The abundance of poets' names and tragedy-titles which Nauck's collection of fragments provides for this period gives us an idea of how much has been lost. We must be satisfied with being able to make some observations of basic importance. With regard to subject-matter, Agathon's experiment of free invention (*v.* p. 412) was obviously not carried on. Again and again we come upon the old subjects with their assured effect, and an unmistakable tendency toward the blatant, the theatrical, the τραγικόν as this time understood it. Meletus (the father of the accuser of 399?) wrote an *Oedipodea* and presumably was not the only one to take up the old trilogy combination again on occasion. Carcinus, a grandson of the bearer of this name who was jeered at by Aristophanes, for a time a guest at the court of the younger Dionysius, wrote an

---

[1] PICKARD (*v. sup.*), 110.

[2] Lately C. B. SNELLER, *De Rheso tragoedia*. Diss. Utrecht. Amsterd. 1949. Against it A., LESKY, *Gnom*. 23, 1951, 141. Cf. G. BJÖRCK, *Arktos* N.S. 1, 1954, 16; *Eranos* 55, 1957, 7. LESKY, 1218. H. STROHM, 'Beobachtungen zum Rhesos'. *Herm*. 87, 1959, 257, shows how single Euripidean themes are embroidered upon in the play. Its spuriousness is derived by him especially from the manner in which, contrary to Euripides, events are brought on the stage which should take place behind the scenes. Parts of the hypothesis: *Pap. Soc. It.* 12/2, 1951, no. 1286.   [3] *De Rheso tragoedia*. Diss. 1828.

Orestes in which he made his hero speak in riddles. Aristotle refers in various passages[1] to his plays *Amphiaraus, Alope, Oedipus, Medea*. Of the earlier mentioned Astydamas we know the titles *Antigone, Alcmeon* and *Hector*; Antiphon is supposed to have concluded the series of models of old subjects approved in classical tragedy with his *Andromache*, to which Aristotle refers on occasion (*Eth. Eud.* 7, 4. 1239 a 37), his *Meleager* and *Philoctetes*. We can discern that this new form of tragedy was largely shaped after the model of the later Euripidean tragedy with its whims of Tyche, its ingenious intrigues and recognitions. Thus Hyginus *fab.* 72 produced a modification of the Antigone theme, perhaps after Astydamas' play,[2] in which Haemon conceals his bride with shepherds and in which, years afterwards, a son of the two comes to Thebes for the games and so brings about the dramatic complication. It is dangerous to venture a comprehensive judgment in a field of which so little is known, but it seems most probable that these epigonic tragedies subsisted of technical refinement and had no longer any bearing on the religious issue; in that spirit the fifth century had conserved the myths as a great manifestation of the spiritual.

The poets of the time who selected historical subjects could claim Aeschylus as their model. Besides many plays on mythical subjects, Theodectes of Phaselis also wrote a *Mausolus*, and of Moschion, who possibly belongs to the third century, there was a *Themistocles* and *Pheraeans*, probably a play about the murder of the tyrant Alexander of Pherae. Only rarely do more remote subjects appear, as when Dionysius I, a dilettante of the drama, bestowed upon his age a *Leda* and an *Adonis*. For the satyr-play it is interesting that we know of a play *Agen*,[3] whose author is alleged to have been a certain Python, if not even Alexander himself. In it the renegade Harpalus is mocked with his hetaerae. This may have been an isolated occurrence, but at any rate we see that the borders between satyr-play and comedy begin to give way.

In the *Poetics* (6. 1450 b 7), Aristotle supplies valuable evidence of the phenomenon that the tragedy of the time was no less subject to the influence of rhetoric than history, when he connects the speeches of the older tragedy with politics, and those of the younger with rhetoric. Theodectes of Phaselis whom we already met as an orator (p. 572), Astydamas and a certain Aphareus, who appears in the Didascaliae of 341 as third with *Peliades, Orestes* and *Auge*, were pupils of Isocrates; Chaeremon is compared with a speech-writer by Aristotle (*Rhet.* 3. 12. 1413 b 12).

The musical element became very independent in comparison with the rhetorical. We already observed, in discussing Agathon (p. 411 f.), that Aristotle makes him the starting-point of the degeneration to a mere appendix of the choral song, which once was the essential carrier of the meaning. A papyrus of the early third century[4] containing a fragment of a post-classical tragedy has

---

[1] These in NAUCK and in WEBSTER'S essay (*v.* p. 630, n. 7), 300.

[2] WEBSTER (*v.* prev. note), 305.

[3] W. SÜSS, *Herm.* 74, 1939, 210. A. V. BLUMENTHAL, ibid. 216. H. HOMMEL, ibid. 75, 1940, 237, 335.

[4] No. 1348 P. = PAGE, *Greek Lit. Pap.* Lond. 1950, no. 28, cf. A. KÖRTE, *Arch. Pap. Forsch.* 5, 1913, 570.

between two scenes only the note 'Song of the Chorus' (χοροῦ μέλος). From the symptoms in Euripides it may be supposed that this choral lyric, having become independent, developed in the style of the new dithyramb.

The disintegration of that perfect blending of the arts in classical tragedy, a unity which was achieved at no time or place in the same way, also betrays itself otherwise. There is evidence that, in the period of post-classical tragedy, an exaggerated importance was attached to production and to the performance of the actors, then, as now, symptoms of decadence. A celebrated producer, restaging Euripides' *Orestes*, turned it into a 'musical' by making Helen appear at the beginning, marching on speechlessly with the rich plunder from Troy (Schol. *Or.* 57). For an appreciation of the actors we shall leave aside individual anecdotes and names[1] and content ourselves with Aristotle's complaint (*Rhet.* 3, 1. 1403 b 33) that in his time mimes had preference over the poets. On the other hand, the same Aristotle (*Rhet.* 3, 12. 1413 b 12) attests the occurrence of dramas meant to be read and mentions Chaerephon, to whom he referred before, as a poet of this genre.

While our slight knowledge of the tragedy of the fourth century means that from that time onward this form of art is lost in relative obscurity until the Romans renewed it, things are different with regard to comedy. We know a good deal about it in the time of Alexander, but it is extremely difficult for us to restore the bridge between the old comedy of Aristophanes and the new of Menander. The Hellenistic era had already introduced the tripartition of comedy into Old (*Archaia*), Middle (*Mese*) and New (*Nea*) (cf. p. 418),[2] but the boundaries between the three phases can only be approximated with the years 400 and 320. Already the late plays of Aristophanes reveal the gradual change of form of the comic play; the parabasis is left out, the choral passages become more independent, the political element recedes and personal ridicule is silenced.

We can supplement the history of Middle Comedy[3] with authors' names and titles of plays. The anonymous *On Comedy* mentions fifty-seven poets and 607 plays and it can be argued with good reason that this number is far too low.[4] As in the case of tragedy, we find here, too, an artistic family tradition; thus, Aristophanes' sons Ararus, Nicostratus and Philetaerus[5] wrote comedies. From the abundance of other names we single out three particularly prolific and successful authors. Antiphanes, born at the very end of the fifth century, lived and worked until deep into the second half of the following. According to Suidas he wrote 280 or even 365 plays; we still know 134 titles.[6] He does not leave his younger contemporary Alexis of Thurii far behind; Suidas mentions

---

[1] Cf. LESKY, 221.

[2] On the unsuccessful attempt to place this division in the Hadrianic era A. KÖRTE, *RE* 11, 1921, 1256.

[3] KÖRTE, *v. sup.*; T. B. L. WEBSTER, *Studies in Later Greek Comedy*. Manchester Un. Pr. 1953 (with chronol. table). In add. Webster's two books mentioned p. 630, n. 7).

[4] Evidence and discussion in KÖRTE (*v. sup.*), 1265, 56.

[5] Some confusion remains with regard to the third name, cf. SCHMID 4, 222.

[6] Confusion with a younger poet of that name should be taken into account.

the number of 245 for him, while we record 130 titles. A modest exception compared with these is Anaxandrides of Camiros in Rhodes (or Colophon according to others) with a legacy of sixty-five plays. His activity, which brought him his first victory in the Dionysia of 376, continues even into the first few years of the second half of the century.[1] One thing is at once evident from these figures; this production was no longer concerned with Athens only. It still remained the centre of dramatic art to which poets of foreign origin migrated, but its plays went out into the entire Greek world with its vast number of theatres.

The numerous remnants of Middle Comedy delight us with their abundance of cultured wit, but in no case do they give an idea of the structure and form of the plays. Therefore we would be all the more grateful, if we could with some certainty allot to this period of the history of comedy one of the originals of the Latin comic plays. This attempt has been made for three plays of Plautus', the *Persa*, the *Menaechmi* and the *Amphitruo*,[2] but all attempts to find a firm footing are unsuccessful. In the case of the *Persa* the probability of origin from Middle Comedy is greatest; in it a resourceful slave tricks a girl from a procurer's hands with the aid of a fellow-slave and a parasite. Nevertheless, the fragments permit some of the features of Middle Comedy to be ascertained. They enable us to discern gradual transitions, since we can observe that many of the elements of Old Comedy were retained and not a few of the New anticipated.

The Middle Comedy is no longer political in the sense that it grew wholly out of the soil of the *polis* and was directly connected with its life, as is most clearly demonstrated by the omission of the parabasis. This implies by no means that comedy had renounced all reference to contemporary events and in particular to Athenian politics. The comic poet Theopompus, whose work overlaps the end of the Old and the beginning of the New, attacked (fr. 30 K.) Callistratus, one of the engineers of the Second Naval League and in the *Peace*, which repeats an Aristophanic title, as does a play by Eubulus, he probably selected as his subject one of the peace-conferences of the 'seventies. The Sicilian tyrants were the butt of Eubulus in his *Dionysius*, and of Ephippus in his *Homoeoe* (fr. 16 K.). The fragments referring to Demosthenes[3] are numerous and Philip came in for his share as well. One of the few fragments whose force and fancy are reminiscent of Old Comedy – it is from Mnesimachus' *Philippus* (fr. 7 K.) – depicts the Macedonian as a savage iron-eater. Timocles turned this into an ironic variation on Demosthenes in his *Heroes* (fr. 12 K.).

Of the philosophers, the adherents of Pythagoras and Plato[4] particularly attracted the attention of comedy. Earlier (p. 539) we came upon the large anapaestic fragment of an unknown play by Epicrates which we considered an important piece of evidence for the teaching activity of the Academy (fr. 11 K.).

---

[1] An inscription with numerous details in PICKARD (*v.* p. 630, n. 1), 122.

[2] In great detail WEBSTER (*v.* p. 633, n. 3), 67, 78, 86. For this attribution of the model for the *Persa* also K. J. DOVER in *Fifty Years of Classical Scholarship* Oxf. 1954, 118, with bibl. On late dating of the *Amphitruo* recently W. H. FRIEDRICH, *Euripides und Diphilos*. Zet. 5, 1953, 263.

[3] WEBSTER (*v.* p. 633, n. 3), 44.   [4] WEBSTER (*v. sup.*), 53.

Finally we should at least mention the passage from Ephippus' *Nauagus* (fr. 14 K.) in which a foppish Academic is depicted.

Nor did personal ridicule against individual citizens, the ὀνομαστὶ κωμῳδεῖν, in vain objected to in classical times, come to an end in any way with the exit of Old Comedy.[1] But all this should not let us lose sight of the fact that the aspects referred to were (at least as a rule) of secondary importance, no longer concerned with the innermost essence of a wholly political play.

Ancient criticism[2] stressed the preference in Middle Comedy for the travesty of myths. This holds good only with certain reservations. Old Comedy was already quite familiar with this tendency, of which a series of titles of Aristophanes' later period (p. 427) gives adequate evidence. On the other hand, the travesty of myths may play an important part in the Middle Comedy, but it is by no means dominant. The parody can be directly aimed at the myth or at its representation by tragedy. The first is the case in most comedies which have the story of a divine birth for their subject. Here, too, the line becomes evident which leads down from Old Comedy, for Hermippus' *Birth of Athena* falls still within its scope. In Middle Comedy the theme was continued in a series of plays. Philiscus had a marked preference for it, using it for Zeus, Aphrodite, Apollo and Artemis, Hermes and even Pan. In many other cases the effect of such a *Comodotragoedia* (a title of a play by Alcaeus, who belongs to the Old Comedy, and by Anaxandrides) was attempted by parodying well-known tragedies. It was no doubt a capital joke when Orestes for once did not run his sword through Aegisthus' breast and the two left the stage as thick as thieves,[3] or when in a topsy-turvy world Odysseus was working at the loom instead of Penelope (Alexis, *Odysseus the Weaver*) and Ajax, wild with fear of Cassandra, fled to Athena's statue.[4] Comedies, such as Antiphanes' *Aeolus*, Anaxandrides' *Helen*, Eubulus' *Auge*, *Ion*, *Medea* and *Phoenix*, point at Euripidean tragedies. The latter had already achieved the greatest popularity in the fourth century and a title like Axionicus' *Phileuripides* epitomizes a whole chapter of literary history. A noteworthy phenomenon is the receding of myth travesty from the middle of the century onward. This is principally connected with the growing alienation from the myths, for as a rule it is the things with which an internal relation exists which are parodied. On the other hand impudent jesting with the old myths seems to have maintained its place in the phlyax-farce of the Greek west, especially according to the evidence of pottery.

We can only guess at the stages of a development which took place in Middle Comedy, leading gradually to Menander's domestic comedy. This is clearly expressed in Aristotle's criticism (*Poet.* 9. 1451 b 13) of contemporary comedy that it built up the action according to the laws of probability, adding names as they happened to come to mind. In addition, Antiphanes complains in his prologue to the *Poesis* how much worse off comedy is than tragedy; while the

---

[1] A good list in WEBSTER (*v. sup.*), 29.
[2] Platonius, Περὶ διαφορὰς κωμῳδιῶν, 11 in KAIBEL, *Com. Graec. Fragm.* I, 1899, 5.
[3] Aristot. *Poet.* 13. 1453 a 37.
[4] Vase picture in M. BIEBER, *History of Gr. and Rom. Theatre*, Princeton 1939, fig. 366 f.

latter needs only one single mythical name to have its plot ready made, the former has to use free invention for everything, action and names.

We observed earlier (p. 448) that the elements of middle-class comedy were already present in Old Comedy; it was, however, the later tragedies of Euripides and his period which were decisive for this development. Comedy was connected with them in two ways. It continued parodying them while also borrowing themes and compositional forms. Love themes are adopted freely now and the significance of intrigue and anagnorisis clearly demonstrates the influence of Euripidean models. When we review Eubulus' *Wreath-dealers* (Στεφανοπώλιδες) with the aid of the fragments from Naevius' *Corollaria*, we find a procuress who does not want her daughter to marry, but wishes to keep her for her profitable trade of shame, a timid suitor and another one who knows how to act. Slave parts also begin to stand out and their relations with one another could equally well belong to the New Comedy. In this connection it is important that already in Middle Comedy we meet with all the stock-figures which from now on people the comic stage of the ancient world and, in an often only slight disguise, that of the modern western world: the hetaera,[1] the comic old woman,[2] the procurer (the latter for the first time in Eubulus' Πορνοβοσκός), the young man in love, the braggart[3] typified in Aristophanes' *Acharnians* by Lamachus, the parasite,[4] the cook[5] and the slave, already shown playing an important part in Aristophanes' *Plutus*.

Although we are able to describe a certain range of subjects of Middle Comedy with sufficient accuracy, a great deal remains obscure such as the numerous titles taken from trades and professions.

Two more important facts can, however, be gleaned from the remnants. The obscene joke, which from the earliest beginning of Old Comedy had claimed the right to be as broad as it liked, gave way before a greater decency of language, and the separation of the choral parts from the body of the play, already marked in the late Aristophanes, continued.[6] There were still some intermediate stages, for some sparse remnants seem to prove cases in which the choral lyrics were already insertions foreign to the plot, while the chorus remained on stage during the play and occasionally took part in the dialogue. Many transitional forms must have occurred, but the complete separation of the choral part as shown in the New Comedy had certainly already been completed in Middle Comedy.

The disappearance of the choral lyrics meant, of course, that we find nothing like Aristophanes' polymetry, but a certain variety is found in the metre of the dialogue.[7] Longer anapaestic systems are not rare.

[1] H. HAUSCHILD, *Die Gestalt der Hetäre in der griech. Kom.* Diss. Leipz. 1933.

[2] H. G. OERI, *Der Typ. der kom. Alten in der griech. Kom.* Diss. Basel 1948.

[3] O. RIBBECK, *Alazon*, Leipz. 1882; ἀλαζών in Anaxandrides fr. 49 K.

[4] Title of a play by Alexis. The ancestors of this type go back to Epicharmus.

[5] A. GIANNINI, 'La figura del cuoco nella commedia greca'. *Acme* 13, 1960, 135.

[6] On the question of the chorus: K. J. MAIDMENT, 'The Later Comic Chorus'. *Class. Quart.* 29, 1935, 1. A. PICKARD-CAMBRIDGE, *The Theatre of Dionysus*. Oxf. 1946, 160. T. B. L. WEBSTER, *Studies in Menander*. Manchester Un. Pr. 1950, 182. Cf. Papyrus no. 1239 P.

[7] Survey in KÖRTE (*v.* p. 632, n. 2), 1265, 17.

The Attic oenochoe[1] in Leningrad with actors and masks proves that the old comic dress with patched shirt and phallus continued into fourth century. But we may assume that the costumes of New Comedy which approximated to those of the middle class were being prepared for during the later stages of Middle Comedy.

A. WILHELM's research is still fundamental for the drama of this period; *Urkunden dram. Aufführungen in Athen*. Vienna 1906. In addition the books by Pickard and Webster mentioned p. 636, n. 1. The texts for tragedy in NAUCK, *Trag. Graec. Fragm.* 2nd ed. Leipzig 1889, for comedy in TH. KOCK, *Com. Att. Fragm.*, 2, Leipzig 1884, but his sometimes arbitrary treatment of the text invites references to A. MEINEKE, *Com. Graec. Fragm.* (5 vols.) 1839 ff. J. M. EDMONDS, *The Fragments of Attic Comedy. II Middle Comedy*, Leiden 1959. Cf. B. MARZULLO, *Gnom.* 34, 1962, 543. Anonymous fragments of Middle Comedy also in III A. Leiden 1961. Pictorial studies: T. B. L. WEBSTER, *Monuments illustrating Old and Middle Comedy, Univ. of London Inst. of Class. Stud. Bull. Suppl.* 9, 1960. Remnants of the phlyaces farce: A. OLIVIERI, *Frammenti della commedia greca e del mimo nella Sicilia e nella Magna Grecia. II. Framm. della comm. fliacica*. 2nd ed. Naples 1947.

6 OTHER FORMS OF POETRY

Earlier we mentioned (p. 305) that the old epic came to an end with Choerilus and that he was aware of this. But that this did not mean the end of epic poetry, is shown at about the same time by Antimachus of Colophon.[2] Plato esteemed this poet highly; since we know from Philodemus that the Stoic Ariston of Chios praised the educational ideas in Antimachus' poems[3] we also understand that Plato was not, at least not only, impelled by aesthetic considerations. At any rate he appointed Heraclides Ponticus to go to Colophon to collect Antimachus' poems.[4] This dates Antimachus' death prior to Plato's (348/347), one of the few indications which we can give of this poet's life. Plutarch (*Lys.* 18) relates that at the festival of the Lysandrea, as the Samian Heraea had been servilely renamed, Lysander himself allotted the victory to a poet Niceratus over Antimachus, and that the latter destroyed his poem in a fit of passion. This gesture of bad temper may be a decorative invention, but there is no reason to doubt the contest, and so we can date some of Antimachus' poems before Lysander's death; the latter fell before the walls of Haliartos in 395. The dates mentioned leave a wide margin; Apollodorus of Athens places Antimachus' floruit in 404,[5] and this will be approximately correct. Chronologically it is impossible that he was a pupil of Panyassis and so we shall not give much credit to Suidas' other statement that

[1] BIEBER (*v.* p. 635, n. 4), fig. 121. PICKARD (*v.* p. 632, n. 4), fig. 80. Photo in E. BETHE, *Griech. Dichtung*, Plate 8. Other material in PICKARD (*v. sup.*), 234; WEBSTER, *Production* (*v.* p. 635, n. 4), 55; DOVER (*v.* p. 634, n. 2), 121.

[2] B. WYSS, *Antimachi Colophonii Reliquiae*. Berl. 1936, with an extensive introduction.

[3] Test. 16 W.; praef. 41.

[4] Test. 1 W. Heracl. Pont. fr. 6 Wehrli.   [5] Test. 4 W.

Stesimbrotus was his teacher. Of his two main works one, the *Thebaïd*, was an epic. From the quotations five books can be distinguished with certainty, but it is probable that the work comprised twenty-four. With erudite thoroughness (the series of *poetae docti* begins with Antimachus) he begins with Zeus' love for Europa, and so arrives at the foundation of Thebes. The fragments are too scanty for us to be able to discern anything substantial about the structure of the whole; that Statius' *Thebaid* should be largely dependent on Antimachus has proved to be a heresy.[1] We have no way of knowing how much Antimachus still knew of the old cyclic *Thebaïd* (cf. p. 80) or whether he utilized it, but it certainly was his ambition to enter the lists with Homer's *Iliad*: not, of course – and this denotes the hiatus between Antimachus and all preceding epic poetry – in the sense of direct continuation and imitation, but through learned absorption of Homeric artifices and their conscious revival and enhancement. For the poet of the *Thebaïd* was at the same time a Homeric philologist. We have already (p. 75) mentioned an edition of Homer, and individual bits of evidence[2] point to studies in the poet though we cannot indicate, where Antimachus has reported their results.

His second great poetical work, the *Lyde*, narrated in elegiac metre stories of unhappy love as presented by the myths. According to the tradition the poetical expression of mythical sorrow of love would bring the poet solace after the death of his beloved Lyde.[3] What we can still grasp points to elegiac narrative. The story of the Argonauts was dealt with elaborately, possibly in Book I. In the admittedly scanty remnants a personal note does not sound anywhere. It certainly cannot have been entirely absent and may have found its place in the introduction to the whole work. In the same way in which Antimachus revived Homer in his *Thebaïd* according to his own ideas, he renewed elegiac poetry in the style of Mimnermus' *Nanno*. But while there we cannot establish a cohesion of the parts and at most think of separate elegies, Antimachus combined in his *Lyde* the various stories into one whole. No doubt catalogue poetry in the manner of Hesiod was an important model for him. We regret that on this very point we cannot go beyond general observations, for Antimachus shows in these achievements of his, the shaping of elegiac narrative and of 'collective poetry', that he was a precursor of Hellenistic art.

One quotation (fr. 72 W.) points to Book II, but the *Lyde* must have been of considerably larger size. Callimachus,[4] who simply could not stand big books, also ridiculed this poetry for its popularity.

Other works of this poet such as the *Delti* and the *Artemis* are mere titles for us.

The literary-historical importance of Antimachus is proved by the exceedingly lively controversy over him in the following era. The judgments, as Wyss has

---

[1] In his preface WYSS correctly criticizes the scholium on Statius' *Thebaïd* 3, 466 (in KASPAR VON BARTH). There (5) also on the problem connected with Porphyry's scholium on Horace, *Ars Poet.* 146. The confusion has been cleared up and it has been proved that for the *Thebaïd* only the size of 24 Books can be made probable from the notice.

[2] Wyss, praef. 30.

[3] Hardly the poet's wife (thus Test. 7). The name points to servile origin.

[4] Fr. 398 Pf.; Antim. Test. 19 W.

collected them, are extremely divergent. We heard of Callimachus' ill-will which is still echoed by the Neoteric Catullus (95). This is contrasted with such warm recognition as that uttered in the epigrams of Asclepiades and Posidippus (*Anth. Pal.* 9. 63; 12. 168). Earlier (p. 305) we heard that in this battle of the critics – Choerilus on the one side, Antimachus on the other – Crates of Mallos resolutely took position for the Colophonian. This discord of opinions and not in the last place the reserve of his contemporaries (Test. 3) indicates that Antimachus' poetry meant a radical change. For that reason we regret its loss all the more. Nevertheless we can, on the basis of various features, understand him to be the precursor of Hellenistic poetry and already mentioned some that point in this direction. The most important and momentous is that in Antimachus we recognize a poet who consciously combined the work of the scholar with that of the artist. This means that poetry now withdraws from the association which in classical times bound artist and community into a firm unity. Only for the educated is it possible to follow the learned poet on his laborious way and something like 'l'art pour l'art' announces itself. A gap which began to open with the sophists, now also becomes visible in the literary sphere.

The direction indicated reveals itself to us both in the delight in remote factual detail and in the linguistic form. The few verses which we know abound with Homeric forms; it does not now indicate a rhapsodic tradition but the result of careful research and painstaking consideration. Also in the choral language numerous borrowings are made. The rare word, 'select' in the true sense, the gloss, is now considered the special ornament of speech, a tacked-on ornament which only the connoisseur can appreciate. The search for this sort of thing begins at the time of Antimachus and we think that in Antidorus of Cyme who wrote *On Homer and Hesiod* and compiled a *Lexis* we can recognize a precursor of the later glossographers who perhaps still belongs in the fifth century.

But art of this nature does not live only on the results of such collecting and sifting; it aims at gaining new recognition for the material by means of skilful variation and we can find examples of this in Antimachus' fragments. But we cannot tell if behind all this there was a real poet, as was, for instance, the case with Callimachus. From the criticism of the ancients we can conclude that Antimachus had none of the former's charm, for this is the very quality they denied him, characterizing his poetry as austere, flat and laborious.[1] Perhaps the judgment of the time which allowed his work to perish was not unjustified, however regrettable it may be for us.

There were other epics written in the fourth century, but names in odd notices such as Dinarchus of Delos or Persinus of Ephesus tell us little or nothing.[2] We get somewhat further with Archestratus of Gela who was roughly contemporary with Alexander and good-humouredly taught gastronomical lore in the hexameters of his *Hedypathea*. Athenaeus has preserved extensive fragments,[3]

---

[1] Dionysius of Halicarnassus, *De compos. verb.* 22; *De imit.* 2, 2. Plutarch, *Timol.* 36; *De garrul.* 21. Quintilian, *Instit.* 10. 1, 53.

[2] Some detail in WILAMOWITZ, *Hellenistische Dichtung.* 1, Berl. 1924, 104.

[3] In P. BRANDT, *Corpusculum poesis epicae Graecae ludibundae.* 1. Leipz. 1888, 114.

and Ennius passed this breviary for gluttons on to the Romans with his *Hedyphagetica*. With the fourth century we have already entered a time of growing polygraphy and so we see that Archestratus, too, was a representative of a genre in which mention must be made at least of Matro of Pitane with his *Attic Meal* (Δεῖπνον 'Αττικόν) and of Philoxenus of Leucas with his *Deipnon*. These writings must not be simply termed Homer-parodies; the real stimulus was the endeavour to test the old epic verse on subjects for which it was not really created.

Chares' trivial *Maxims* can give us an impression of some lower forms of the literature of this time. His iambic aphorisms have even been found in an early Ptolemaic papyrus (nr. 155 P.; D. Suppl. 13; Powell, *Coll. Alex.* 223). These moral precepts in one-line verse have a certain affinity, in point of content, to the prose-paraenesis of the Pseudo-Isocrates in the *Address to Demonicus* (*v.* p. 554).

This stroll through the poetry of these decades was not over-enjoyable; we did not catch anywhere the sound of true poetry which might touch our hearts over the centuries, and the impression is forced upon us that this has not been caused merely by the unkindness of the tradition. And so we listen with the greater delight when we hear the pure voice of a young woman, a voice of a sad sweetness which knows how to express sorrow with a directness reminiscent of Sappho. Only scanty pieces have been preserved of a poetess whose life itself remained only a fragment. Erinna of Telos, a small island belonging to Rhodes, while still a young girl, lost her friend Baucis, who had followed a man in marriage. The nineteen-year-old wrote to her friend a poem of sorrow and reminiscence and died soon afterwards. We are indebted for this knowledge to a poet, Asclepiades, of Samos, who paid homage to her in an epigram (*Anth. Pal.* 7. 11). Of the poem, the *Distaff* ('Ηλακάτη) we only had some slight fragments, until a papyrus of the first century B.C.[1] gave us a somewhat longer piece. The verses are badly mutilated, and most of the modern emendations are, as is usual in such cases, evidence of linguistic ability rather than reliable restoration. All the same the remnants are sufficient for us to recognize the tenderness and vividness of the art with which Erinna, thinking of her dead friend, evokes the images of their games, work[2] and childish sorrows. It is difficult to associate this poem, which is written in the Doric dialect with epic elements and comprises 300 hexameters, with a definite genre. It would be called an elegy, if it had been written in distichs; the use of hexameters suggest a description as epyllion. There is no need to attach too great an importance to questions of this nature when discussing true poetry, but it is of some significance that in the remnants of the *Distaff* we find an anticipation of the delight of Hellenistic epyllia in depicting little scenes. This agrees with the impression – it can hardly be more in view of the paucity of the material preserved – that, in spite of the lyrical tone, the narrative is

[1] No. 263 P. and D. 1, fasc. 4, 207. Further bibl.: K. LATTE, 'Erinna'. *Nachr. Ak. Gött. Phil.-hist. Kl.* 1953, 79. F. SCHEIDWEILER, 'Erinnas Klage um Baukis'. *Phil.* 100, 1956, 40. P. MAAS' attribution of *Pap. Soc. It.* 14, 1957, no. 1385 to Antimachus is still hypothetical.
[2] This may be connected with the title of the poem, which cannot be Erinna's.

removed from older Greek lyrical poetry with its personal association. The metre with its frequent use of bucolic diaeresis and dominant dactylic construction anticipates Hellenistic versification.

The *Distaff* established for the girl who died so young the name which she deserved. Thus Meleager of Gadara inserted three poems by Erinna, when he wove his garland of epigrams; one of these (*Anth. Pal.* 6. 352) praises the successful painting of a girl, while the other two (*Anth. Pal.* 710. 712) are funeral epigrams on her friend Baucis. A notice of the elder Pliny (34. 57) refers to a poem which Erinna wrote, when a friend's cicada and grasshopper had perished. Later times were fond of many varieties of this sort of poetry.[1]

The *Propempticon* for Baucis, of which verses have been preserved (fr. 2 D.) is a forgery and according to Athenaeus (7. 283d) was recognized as such already in antiquity.

What we have of Erinna also provides evidence of the cultivation and spreading of the epigram; this is frequently corroborated by epigraphical evidence.[2] Epigrams were composed for inscriptions as before, but in addition they were current as a form of intimate literary art or as a means of polemic. Thus, for instance, the pugnacious Theocritus of Chios, Theopompus' opponent, aired in this way his rancour against Hermeas and Aristotle. Poets of rank, philosophers like Plato, and dilettanti, every one wrote epigrams. The cultivation of this genre reached its peak in the Hellenistic age; it will be discussed further in the relevant section. The same applies to the writing of hymns, which led a vigorous existence in the service of the various forms of worship. We shall presently encounter some characteristic examples of it.[3]

[1] Cf. G. HERLINGER, *Totenklage um Tiere in antiker Dichtung. Tüb. Beitr.* 8, 1930. On the misconception which is the basis of the notice in Pliny, WILAMOWITZ (*v.* p. 639, n. 2), 110.

[2] Some detail in WILAMOWITZ *v. sup.*, 132. Cf. R. LAQUEUR, *RE* A 5, 1934, 2025.

[3] Here it is enough to mention the survey in ALLEN-HALLIDAY-SIKES, *The Homeric Hymns.* 2nd ed. Oxf. 1936, 89 f. of the introduction.

CHAPTER VI

The Hellenistic Age

A Athens

I NEW COMEDY

In the last century an event occurred of momentous influence in the history of ideas. The idealized image of antiquity, as the new humanism had shaped it, was challenged by the desire to grasp it historically in all its dimensions. One of the most important stages in this development was the opening up of the Hellenistic age by Johann Gustav Droysen (1808–84). One year after Goethe's death he demanded, in his first lecture, a treatment of antiquity as an historical phenomenon, and in the same year appeared his *Geschichte Alexanders des Grossen*. With two more volumes on the diadochi and the epigoni Droysen combined the work into one *Geschichte des Hellenismus*.[1] It has long since been established that the choice of this description for the time after Alexander is based on an error. Droysen understood the Ἑλληνισταί of the Acts of the Apostles (6. 1) to be orientalized Greeks and accordingly called the time which for him was characterized by the blending of Greek with Oriental, the Hellenistic age. The interpretation of the passage mentioned is not defensible, but it matters little in view of the significance and range of Droysen's achievement. Through this achievement the road was opened to an understanding of an epoch which unlocked for the Greeks new spaces and influences and which had a decisive effect on the development of the West.

This mighty leap beyond the old frontiers of Greek life, this swift growth of new economic and cultural centres will always be considered as the main feature of the picture of the Hellenistic era. But in the homeland they still dreamed the old dream of the splendour of the autonomous polis; though historical reality belonged to the new kingdoms, plays were still performed for the old gods, there were still poets and philosophers. It was a culture of a personal nature which, remote from the great new cities, lived a quiet life but one which in the first few decades after Alexander was still a very intensive one. While we reserve the characteristics of the new world with its large proportions for a later section, we shall first consider the achievements of the city which the Pericles of Thucydides' Funeral Oration had praised as an education for all Greece.

Our study has frequently offered an opportunity to speak of the slackening of the ties which had controlled the structure of the classical polis. We need only

---

[1] This was already the title of the two volumes on Diadochi and Epigoni (1836–43)' which Droysen combined with the extensively revised first work under the same title in 1877.

to recall the sophists and the decline of political comedy. The process which permitted individualism steadily to gain ground in the fourth century is connected with this slackening, as is the dim realization among the best people of the time of other, richer relationships. The individual suffered hardships, for the struggle for life had increased in sharpness. The time of compensations allotted by the state for attendance in assembly and court of law was past. This was now considered to be the characteristic of an extreme democracy which was no longer highly rated. Social contrasts sharpened. The poor wretch whose ideals still were redemption of burdens and redistribution of land had difficulty in ensuring a minimal existence in the face of falling wages and strong slave-competition. On the other hand, there existed in the city a fairly large moneyed class. The unlocking of the Orient brought with it considerable openings for commerce, as in those territories the demand for Greek commodities was great and in this manner much of the treasure of the East found its way to the West. Industry succeeded in increasing its output through more rational techniques with a larger number of slaves; bottomry loans and banking promised large profits. Until about 280 the factors which promoted capital-formation remained effective, but then it began to be seriously felt in the homeland that the centres of economic life had definitely moved eastward. The money made in the decades of the boom was largely invested in land as the best guarantee of steady value. This circle of property-owners controlled what remained of the public life of the polis in festivals, building activity and other local tasks. It is a middle-class world with narrow limits. Gain and the security of gain dominate; the great political decisions are made elsewhere and people are pleased when they do not notice their effect. For who would hope for pleasure from the sport of the great? Each individual with his circle created a world for himself with its own wants, desires and passions. The picture which Athens in the time of the diadochi presents is not an elevating one, and yet in this soil there grew a conception of humanity and its dignity which we would not like to be without for the very reason that it became of the greatest importance for the development of humanism and with it for the culture of the West. It speaks to us most clearly through Menander, the only poet of New Comedy of whom we have some knowledge and who was its most important representative at the same time.

A Roman stone (*Inscr. Gr.* 14. 1184; now lost), which is our most important source for Menander's life besides the information of Suidas and the anonymous Περὶ κωμῳδίας, fixes the poet's birth and death in the years 342/341 and 293/392, according to the archon mentioned in the inscription. It is annoying that this inscription, which also mentions his father Diopeithes and the deme Cephisia, indicates the age reached by the poet as fifty-two. Körte[1] has given an explanation of this statement which is worth mentioning; according to him the number of years is correct, while the year of his death was confused with that of the last performance as stated by the Didascaliae. Menander would then have died in 291/290.

The poet's life coincides with one of the most troubled periods of ancient

[1] *RE* (*v. inf.*). 709.

history. In his youth he witnessed the victories of Alexander which swept away frontier after frontier. The information about his first performance is not uniform, but he probably began his poetical career with the *Orge* in 321. At that time the great conqueror had been dead for two years; in the previous year Athens' reach for freedom and power had ended with the defeat of her navy at Amorgos; Munichia had had to accept a Macedonian garrison and Demosthenes had taken poison in Calauria. When Cassander gained the upper hand in the confused wars of the diadochi in the subsequent years, Athens also fell under his sway. He appointed Demetrius of Phalerum, a pupil of Theophrastus', as epimeletes of the city; during his ten years of philosopher's rule (317–307) he ensured order and internal peace. It is significant for the shifting of the intellectual centres that this man whom we shall meet again as a versatile writer, went to Egypt some time after his fall and participated in the first Ptolemies' constructive cultural programme. Menander's intimacy with Demetrius was almost fatal for him after his exile, but he was saved through personal connections (Diog. Laert. 5. 79). Demetrius Poliorcetes was now lord of Athens and the apparent freedom which he permitted, was celebrated by the Athenians with extravagant rapture as the restoration of the old greatness. The revival of the pan–Hellenic League of Corinth, which Demetrius brought about at the Isthmian games of 302, proved to be illusory in the next year, when on the battle-field of Ipsus the idea of maintaining the realm of Alexander undivided came to an end. Athens could preserve its sovereignty for another two years, but when Demetrius had dispatched his business in Asia, he marched against the rebellious city which had once erected gilt statues and sung odes to him. At that time Athens, ruled by the energetical tyrant Lachares, resisted to the best of its ability, but it had to capitulate early in 294. Thereupon, a few years before Menander's death, Athens was given garrisons on the Museum hill, in Munichia and the Piraeus, which pulled a tight rein on the restless city.

It is of profound significance for the nature of the new comedy that so little can be noticed in Menander's plays of the endless chaos of the time. They have been called a mirror of life, but unlike in Aristophanes' comedies this life is not political. Throughout the alternation of dreams of liberty and servility, during the motley procession of rulers, Athens remained intellectually unchanged and unimpregnable; at the time it did not yet administer its inexhaustible legacy like a museum collection, but preserved it alive in its best citizens. Here Menander took root. We already mentioned his friendship with Demetrius of Phalerum; we may believe that both had been pupils of Theophrastus'. This raises at once the question of the connection between Menander's portrayal of people and the Peripatetic's *Characters*. If the charming opuscule with its lifelike mosaics was written in 319, which can hardly be guaranteed,[1] it precedes the greater part of Menander's comedies; it also seems tempting that four titles (*Agroecus, Apistus, Disidaemon, Colax*) correspond with characters of Theophrastus'. But closer observation reveals Menander's independence and warns against accepting him as Theophrastus' pupil in this sphere. The latter is more strongly inclined

[1] Cf. O. REGENBOGEN, *RE* S 7, 1940, 1510.

toward the typical, adding individual features and especially recording deviations from the norm. Nor should it be forgotten that delight and interest in human peculiarity belong to the period and not to the individual poet.

Epicurus was born in the same year as Menander and there is evidence that they went through their military service as ephebes together. It is therefore natural to look for traces of Epicurean doctrine in the poet's plays.[1] It was specially believed that this could be detected in the wisdom of Onesimus (*Epitr.* 653=729 Kö.) who denies the gods' individual providence for man. But Epicurus did not found his school in Athens until 306 and lived in Asia Minor after his return from his year as ephebe. The ephebes may have exchanged many ideas, but a lasting influence of Epicurus on Menander can hardly be credited. Where connections between his ethical notions and contemporary philosophy can be discerned, they lead to the Peripatos.[2]

Contemporary Athens with its immeasurable treasures in tradition and its already somewhat over-ripe culture fascinated people of wit and sentiment in the same way as the old European capitals do in our day. Thus Menander ignored the tempting call of royal courts, whether it came from Egypt or Macedon (Plin. *Nat. Hist.* 7. 111). In later times his loyalty to Athens found a most charming expression in Alciphron's two letters (4. 18 f.) in which this epistolographer of the Antonine period makes the poet and his beloved Glycera exchange ideas about Ptolemy's offer and the impossibility of an Athens without Menander. His love for Glycera, also known to Martial and Athenaeus, has long been considered as a genuine part of the poet's biography. Körte[3] has correctly stressed the slight reliability of this evidence. Since Menander wrote a *Glycera* and also used the name elsewhere (*Peric.*), the basis for this invention may be sought there. The information that the poet lost his life while bathing at Piraeus does not sound fictitious.

We possess only a scant supply of dates of his poetical career. We do believe that we can fix his first performance, the one of the *Orge*, with some confidence at 321, but otherwise we have a firm date only for the *Imbrii* (301) through the archon's name in the *Periochae*,[4] and possibly also for the *Heniochus* (312) through the emendation of A. Wilhelm in a passage of the inscription of the Didascalia.[5] For an appreciation of Menander's development it is particularly important that its didascalia revealed that the newly found *Dyscolos* was an early play of the year 316. Allusions to contemporary events are rare as is typical of New Comedy and even when they do occur they are not always as useful as the one in the *Periceiromene*; the reference to the Corinthian troubles and the allusion to the murder of Alexander, the son of Polyperchon (*v.* 89 ff.), point to a date soon

---

[1] M. POHLENZ, 'M. und Epikur'. *Herm.* 78, 1943, 270. Rejected by N. W. DE WITT, 'Epicurus and M.'. *Stud. Norwood* (*Phœnix* Suppl. 1). Toronto 1952, 116. Otherwise P. W. HARSH, *Gnom.* 25, 1953, 44, 1.

[2] WEBSTER, *Stud. in M.* (*v. inf.*), 195; connection with *Poetics*: 175.

[3] *RE* (*v. inf.*), 712 and *Herm.* 54, 1919, 87. On the comedy *Glycera* KÖRTE's Menander-edition 2, 42; the evidence for M.'s life and poetry ibid. 2, 1.

[4] *Pap. Ox.* no. 1235=no. 1039 P. In KÖRTE's edition 1. 149. v. q105.

[5] *IG* II III, 2nd ed. 2323 a = Test. 27 Kö.

after 314 for the performance of this play. Only internal evidence can give further help, but this does not produce irrefutable proof. There are many indications that in the course of his career Menander's art became more refined and that he rejected grotesquely comic elements. Ancient literary criticism also observed a development of the poet, as we learn from Plutarch (*Aristoph. et Men. compar.* 853 f.); when one compares Menander's early plays with his middle and late ones, it can be estimated what the poet might have achieved if he had been granted a longer life. Where we find similar subjects utilized it seems still possible to observe parts of this development, for instance from the *Perinthia* to the *Andria*, from the *Colax* to the *Eunuchus*. It agrees with what we said that personal ridicule on a particularly large scale can be demonstrated from the fragments of the very earliest play, the *Orge* of 321. Of course, it is no longer the bitter attack of Old Comedy on leading politicians, but only fops and parasites get an occasional cut. In this respect the custom of Middle Comedy is obviously carried on; as in the latter, we also find occasional ridicule of philosophers. In Menander's time it was especially the Cynics who invited mockery; and so he has a little romp with Crates in the *Didymae* (fr. 104 Kö.) and with Monimus in the *Hippocomes* (fr. 215 Kö.). Middle Comedy had already become quite mannerly compared with Old, and this goes even further in New Comedy. But a blunt word or an obscene allusion in a servant's mouth has not wholly disappeared and it corresponds once more with the development indicated earlier that this sort of thing occurs in the *Periceiromene*, which belongs to the first decade of Menander's career. In general, however, we shall not be able to proceed beyond mere possibilities with chronological aids of this nature.[1] But the *Epitrepontes*, with its lack of burlesque scenes, the decency of its speech and the strong intensification of the action may be allotted to Menander's last year. The striking contrast with the more newly found play of Menander's early years will be shown presently.

We derive our knowledge of the poet from a variety of sources. Before the beginning of the papyrus-finds we only possessed fragments from grammarians, lexicographers and anthologies in Greek texts, quite a few in number, in the most favourable cases groups of verse revealing a speech with a complete train of thought, but never large enough to afford an insight into the dramatic construction. Yet this stock was sufficient to enable Goethe to discern the charm of this poet. He called it unattainable.[2] A peculiar tradition, largely pseudo-tradition, is represented by *Menander's Maxims* (Γνῶμαι Μενάνδρου), collections of single lines which have a long history. This kind of literature, which must have flourished especially in the schools, came to the fore in the fourth century, where Chares (*v.* p. 640) gives us a sample of it. Such collections, which consisted of a motley mixture of lines of various poets combined with new work, were continued into the Byzantine era. Heretofore, Euripides had supplied a great deal for this purpose; later Menander proved to be a fertile

---

[1] This also applies to WEBSTER's chronological survey (*Stud. in M.* 107 of the 1st ed.), which utilizes all accessible aids for the dating.

[2] To Eckermann 12 May 1825, cf. 28 May 1827.

source. So it happened that such collections were put under his name as *Menander's Maxims*. In his collection of comic fragments Meineke has gathered 758 of such μονόστιχα. There is some genuine Menander among these, as is proved by the occurrence of individual lines in other contexts. When such corroboration is missing, the extraction of the genuine parts is a doubtful business.

Besides the fragments from the originals there were imitations of Menander in Latin comedy. Of these Terence is the most fruitful, the *dimidiatus Menander*, as Caesar called him. Of the six plays preserved the *Andria*, *Heautontimorumenos*, *Eunuchus* and *Adelphoe* were modelled upon our poet. The figure of the father who regrets his harshness towards his son and wishes to do penance through a life of privation in the *Heautontimorumenos*, and the witty treatment of the problem of education in the *Adelphoe* provide us with particularly valuable samples of Menander's portrayal of people. Since Terence replaced the informative prologue of the originals with introductory speeches to defend himself, he could give us the information that he contaminated his originals with the insertion of parts of other comedies. Thus the *Andria* contains a bit from the *Perinthia*, in the *Eunuchus* there is one from the *Colax* and in the *Adelphoe* a scene from the *Synapothnescontes* of Diphilus. He was impelled to do this by the desire to increase the dramatic vigour. Now that we know something of the originals, we can observe how much of Menander's art Terence managed to conceal in the Latin words. This largely holds good of the noble humanity and balance, free from gloomy seriousness and tasteless hackwork, which so delighted the Scipionic circle. How much was lost of linguistic artistry in the Latin imitation is shown by Statius Caecilius, another poet of Latin Comedy who modelled himself on Menander. Aulus Gellius (*Noctes Att.* 2. 23) has preserved for us a portion of the comedy *Plocion* (fr. 333 Kö.) with the Latin translation.

That Plautus borrowed far less frequently from Menander's plays is connected with the sturdier nature of his humour. All the same we can establish, as the precursor of his *Stichus*, the first *Adelphoe* (Terence's comedy was made after the second play of this title) and as the one of the *Bacchides* the *Double Cheater* (Δὶς ἐξαπατῶν); we know that the *Cistellaria* goes back to an original of Menander, but we cannot ascertain its title.[1] With great confidence, founded especially on the splendid portrayal of people, we also recognize Menander in the *Aulularia*, the comedy of a poor devil driven half crazy through finding a treasure-trove.[2] Finally it may be supposed that Menander's *Carchedonius* was the original for *Poenulus*.

[1] WEBSTER, *Stud. in M.* (*v. inf.*), 91 of the 1st ed. thinks with FRAENKEL of the *Synaristosae*.

[2] Conjectures on the original in WEBSTER (*v. sup.*), 120. On the Menandrian character of the play G. JACHMANN, *Plautinisches und Attisches. Problemata* 3. Berl. 1931, 128. On the thematic relationship with the *Dyscolos*: W. KRAUS, 'Menanders Dyskolos und das Original der Aulularia'. *Serta Philologica Aenipontana*. Innsbruck 1962, 185. Kraus emphasizes that it is impossible to be sure of a Greek original, but that it was probably Menander's *Hydria*. A penetrating study of the structure of the Greek original by W. LUDWIG, 'Aulularia-Probleme'. *Phil.* 105, 1961, 44. 247. He concludes that Plautus generally adheres to the sequence of scenes of the original. He also holds for certain that this was by Menander, as corroborated strongly by the *Dyscolos* find. He rejects the *Hydria* as the title of the Greek play and reckons with a supposed second *Thesaurus* and the *Apistus* (considered by Webster), but especially

It is far more difficult to detect traces of the original in the Plautine plays than in Terence. Plautus' recasting goes much deeper; he made the spoken plays of New Comedy into musical comedies which aim at powerful farcical effects by means of the most varied changes and additions. Also there is the question of how far contamination spread in Plautus. Terence (*Andr.* 18) states expressly that he did contaminate; but does this refer to the borrowing of single scenes or did he combine whole plays? Certain German scholars, who laboriously endeavoured to untie the Plautine knot, proceeded upon the latter assumption. Nowadays a reaction, brought about chiefly by British scholars,[1] prefers to trace the inconsistencies in the dramatic structure, which led to the hypotheses of contamination, back to the Greek originals themselves. We deem ourselves lucky in not having to engage in this struggle, but we believe that the reaction is tending towards an extreme viewpoint. A structure like the Plautinian *Stichus* cannot be properly considered to be a completely genuine translation of a work of Menander's, even assuming a great breadth of variety; the ending of the *Dyscolos* should warn us to be extremely cautious in our criticism of the final scene with the carousing slaves.

It was through the papyri (nos. 1019-1040 P.)[2] that we first acquired this correct knowledge of Menander. The first was the Cairensis which Gustave Lefèbre found in Aphroditopolis, the modern Kōm Esqawh, in 1905. Flavius Dioscorus, an Egyptian lawyer and minor poet, had preserved a number of deeds in a jar by plugging it with scrap paper. This was part of a papyrus-codex, written in the fifth century A.D., and consisting of quires. The remnants of five comedies can still be gleaned from the badly mixed-up tatters. Some belong to a play of which we do not know the title;[3] others to the *Heros*, the *Epitrepontes*, the *Periceiromene* and the *Samia*. Further papyrus-finds have brought remnants of some other plays. These permit us to recognize, at least for the *Georgus*, essential features of the plot which in many of its motives resembles that of the *Heros*, though it carried them through quite differently. Of one comedy without a known title,[4] mostly called the *Comoedia Florentina* after the place of storage of the papyrus, enough is available for a reconstruction to be attempted. We also mention the *Theophorumene*[5] because of its rare subject; a girl is thrown into

---

with a *Philargyrus*. There is no corroboration for this title and so the whole matter is still undecided. WEBSTER, *Later Com.* (*v. inf.*), 196 also considers originals by Menander for the *Pseudolus* and *Curculio.*

[1] Thus W. BEARE, *The Roman Stage.* London 1950; WEBSTER, *Stud. in M.* (*v. inf.*); G. E. DUCKWORTH, *The Nature of Roman Comedy.* Princeton 1952. W. H. FRIEDRICH, *Euripides und Diphilos.* Zet. 5. Munich. 1953, inclines to this conception.

[2] There is also a largish fragment from a parchment codex of the 4th c. *Antinoopolis Pap.* 2nd ed. J. W. B. BARNS and H. ZILLIACUS. Lond. 1960, 8, printed with apparatus by H. J. METTE in the end of his *Dyscolos*-ed. Gött. 1961, 60. It is likely that the lines are Menander's, but K. LATTE, *Gnom.* 34, 1962, 152 has rejected the attempt to attribute them to the *Misogynes.*

[3] A. KÖRTE, 'M.'s fabula incerta'. *Herm.* 72, 1937, 50.

[4] WEBSTER, *Stud. in M.* (*v. inf.*), 146 (1st ed.) thinks of the Ἑαυτὸν πενθῶν. E. ULBRICHT, *Krit. u. exeg. Studien zu M.* Diss. Leipz. 1933, 1, deals extensively with the *Com. Florentina.*

[5] A. KÖRTE, 'Zu M.'s Theoph.'. *Herm.* 70, 1935, 431. A. LESKY, 'Die Theoph. und die Bühne M.'s'. *Herm.* 72, 1937, 123.

a frenzy by the Great Mother, is suspected of pretence, but must have been united with her lover in the happy ending. The scene in which the young man's father watches, together with a friend, the orgiastic dance of the ecstatic girl is distinguishable from the remnants. Apart from this series of finds there is the oldest literary papyrus to come to Europe, the Didot papyrus, which was found in the Serapeum of Memphis as long ago as 1820. Further mention will be made of it presently. Finally reference should be made to the *Periochae* of Menander's plays, of which in one papyrus (no. 1039 P.) considerable remnants of two columns have been preserved. For the individual plays the contents followed after the opening line together with Didascalian information; an appreciation was added. The preserved section refers to the *Hiereia* and the *Imbrii*. According to Suidas a certain Homerus Sellius wrote such *Periochae*. Our papyrus could be from his book.

This was all that had survived, until the year 1959 produced the most important addition to the poet's work since the Cairensis with Victor Martin's publication of a papyrus of the Bibliotheca Bodmeriana of Cologny near Geneva.[1] Ten leaves written on both sides and one recto of a papyrus codex of the third century A.D.[2] contain Menander's *Dyscolos*, from the hypothesis in twelve trimeters, which pose as lines by Aristophanes of Byzantium, up to the end, which proved to be identical with the adespoton fr. 616 K.[3] The text, marred by mistakes and hiatuses, is a copy of a model which was not always completely understood. Some pages bear the ancient page numbering, the first

[1] In his meritorious pioneering edition (*Papyrus Bodmer* IV. Cologny-Geneva. Bibl. Bodm. 1958; published March 1959) V. MARTIN immediately indicated the extensive philological labour which the bad transmission of the text was to demand. It started off directly in such abundance that here only a selection of editions and studies can be given, and that further reference must be made to bibliographies. One such is given by J. T. MCDONOUGH, *The Class. World* (formerly *The Class. Weekly*) 53, 1960, 277; more *Paideia* 15, 1960, 327; the collective work of the Univ. di Genova, Fac. di Lett.; *Menandrea Miscellanea Philologica* (1960) contains G. BARABINO, 'Saggio di bibliografia sul Dyscolos'; cf. further the special report by F. STOESSL, *Gymn.* 67, 1960, 204 and *Gnom.* 33, 1961, bibl. app. I. 7. Many references in the ed. of J. MARTIN (*v. inf.*). We mention specially the comment. edition of W. KRAUS, *Sitzb. Öst. Ak. Phil.-hist. Kl.* 234/4, 1960. B. A. VAN GRONINGEN, Leiden 1960. J. MARTIN, Paris 1961 (*Erasmus. Coll. de textes grecs comm.*); critical edition of the text: H. LLOYD-JONES, Oxf. Class. Texts 1960. J. BINGEN, Leiden 1960. H. J. METTE, Gött. 1960 (with verbal index); bilingual: W. KRAUS, Zürich 1960 (*Lebendige Antike*). M. TREU, Munich 1960 (*Tusculum*). The following translations are mentioned: R. CANTARELLA, Urbino 1959. B. WYSS, *Neue Rundschau* 71, 1960, 39. PH. VELLACOTT, Lond. 1960. Special mention must be made of the criticism of the play by FR. ZUCKER, 'Ein neugefundenes griech. Drama'. *Sitzb. D. Ak. Berl. Kl. f. Spr. Lit. u. Kunst.* 1960/5. A summary of the criticism by B. A. VAN GRONINGEN, 'Le Dysc. de Mén. Étude crit. du texte.' *Verh. Nederl. Ak. Afd. Lett. N.R.* 67/3. Amsterdam 1960. Best ed. now: E. W. HANDLEY, Lond. 1965.

[2] V. MARTIN thought the first half of the 3rd c., while ZUCKER (*v. sup.* 3), follows E. G. TURNER, *Bull. Inst. Class. Stud. Univ. Lond.* 6, 1959, 64 with a date in the 4th c., W. KRAUS (p. 10 of his critical ed.) bases his dating in the 3rd c. on records in the Öst. Nationalbibliothek of the period 250–260 which were pointed out to him by H. HUNGER; they show correspondence with the writing on one side of the codex which is of a different hand though it is contemporary with the rest of the text, and compares extremely well with datable records.

[3] On this E. VOGT, 'Ein typischer Dramenschluss der Néa'. *Rhein. Mus.* 102, 1959, 192.

the number IΘ. We are used to great many surprises from Tyche, but it seemed too much to expect to find a play by Menander complete from the first to the last letter. It is at least permissible for scholars to hope that in the course of time something will turn up of what was on the preceding pages of the manuscript; and their curiosity to know what is on the reverse side of the last leaf is quite understandable.[1]

The hypothesis is followed by the didascalia, which, owing to the certain alteration of the transmitted archontic name of Didymogenes into Demogenes, gives the year 316 at whose Lenaea the play was performed. As the play opens, Pan emerges from his shrine, a nymphs' cave, and informs us that we are in Phyle, a hill area in Attica. In the house on the right, the god tells us, lives Cnemon, a veritable misanthrope. Once upon a time he married a widow who had a son from her previous marriage, and who next gave birth to a baby girl. But she could not bear to go on living with the insufferable fellow and now shares a house with her son Gorgias and a faithful slave at the other side of the shrine, while Cnemon lives with his daughter and an old maidservant, and wrestles with the poor soil. The god feels pity for the girl who has grown up in these uncongenial surroundings into a gentle and artless young woman, and so he has arranged that Sostratus, the son of a well-to-do landowner, has seen the girl while he was hunting and, as is the custom in such tales, immediately fell in love with her.

After this informative prologue, which has not the usual place in Menander's plays following the first scene, the play begins with the entrance of Sostratus and his parasite. It soon becomes clear that the latter's boasting is not going to be of much use to Sostratus in his love affair, when Sostratus' huntsman, whom he had sent out to reconnoitre, bursts in upon them and tells them of Cnemon's harsh reception; the parasite goes off on hearing this. It is going to be very difficult to approach Cnemon, unless circumstances come to his assistance. And this soon happens. Cnemon's maid has dropped a pitcher into the well and now the daughter goes to fetch water from the nymphs' cave. This gives the enamoured Sostratus the desired opportunity to approach the girl with the greatest circumspection. Gorgias' slave notices this with displeasure, for he is suspicious of the fine young gentleman's motives. After an interval with a dance by worshippers of Pan, and probably with a song as well, the slave tells Gorgias at the beginning of Act 2 what has happened. He suspects the worst of Sostratus, but is soon persuaded of the latter's honourable intentions and concludes a friendship with him in anticipation of future family ties. Sostratus will find it easier to approach Cnemon if he works on the field side by side with Gorgias and takes his share in the digging. After the exit of the two allies some servants of Sostratus' family enter; they are going to prepare a sacrificial banquet in the cave. The cook dominates the scene; pompous and inquisitive, as is characteristic of the part, he finds out from one of the servants that a dream of the mother's is the cause of the sacrifice; she has dreamed that Pan chained her

---

[1] An indication of the beginning of the following play without title, hypothesis or didascalia in V. MARTIN, *Scriptorium* 14, 1960, 3, 2.

son and made him dig up a field in working clothes. The third act brings first
the dramatic meeting of Cnemon with the cook and the servant, who wish to
borrow some utensils for the banquet in the cave, but they are sent away with a
snarl. We then learn that Sostratus' trouble has been in vain, for he has not met
Cnemon in the field. Meanwhile matters are getting worse at the well; the old
maid has now also let fall in the pickaxe with which she wanted to get out the
pitcher, and Cnemon is in a rage. Now he has to go down the well himself.
How will this end? At the beginning of Act 4 we hear, of course, that he has
had an ugly fall and is badly injured. He is rescued by Gorgias, his stepson, with
whom he has never wanted to have anything to do. Sostratus relates how the
brave young man descended down the well-shaft while he himself held on to
the rope, more occupied with the crying girl than with the rescue. Then Cnemon
enters supported by his daughter and Gorgias and we hear his speech full of
profound understanding and noble decisions; man cannot go through life on his
own, he depends on those around; this has been shown him by Gorgias and his
action and he is now going to be his adopted son; he will take charge of the
small property and as his sister's guardian he will find her a husband. This is
easily and quickly done, for Sostratus is already on the spot as a suitor. As it
turns out, he did not get sunburnt for nothing working in the field, for it even
evokes a word of approval from Cnemon. At the end of the act Callippides,
Sostratus' father, enters and is sent into the cave to have something to eat first.
In Cnemon's great scene and the betrothal following it the iambic trimeters are
replaced by trochaic tetrameters (708-763) which impart some pomp and
solemnity. This is in contrast with the *Periceiromene* (77-163) and the *Samia*
(202-270) where liveliness is aimed at.[1]

The fifth act is somewhat like an appendix. It appears that one wedding is
not enough. Sostratus manages to persuade his father to betroth his daughter,
Sostratus' sister, to Gorgias. The latter's opposition, caused by his pride, is overcome, too. Then comes the most surprising aspect of this find, a burlesque
closing scene in which the cook and the slave who had been previously treated
so cavalierly by Cnemon, vent their anger on him now that he is defenceless.
They carry him out in front of the house, annoy him with questions which they
think up, but finally their vengeance does not go beyond dragging the old man
to join in the festive delights of the banquet. We had hardly expected such a
conclusion from Menander. His robust humour may have contributed to the
success of the play; Menander won one of his eight victories with the *Dyscolos*.
As we already indicated, no one can any longer deny with any confidence that
the slave's carousal in the closing scene of Plautus' *Stichus* corresponds with
Menander's first *Adelphoe*, since this, too, like the *Dyscolos*, has the address to the
flute player. Walter Kraus[2] has shown that the elated atmosphere of the ending
of the *Dyscolos* with a wedding and a banquet belongs to a tradition which
goes back to the early days of comedy. The form of this closing scene is also

---

[1] FR. ZUCKER (*v. sup.*), 9 has pointed out that in Euripides the trochaic tetrameter has the
same twofold character. Cf. FRANCA PERUSINO, 'Tecnica e stile nel tetrametro trocaico di
Menandro'. *Riv. di cult. class. e med.* 4, 1962, 3.   [2] Crit. ed. p. 21.

a surprise. Lines 880 to 958 are iambic catalectic tetrameters, recited melo-dramatically to the accompaniment of the flute. This metre is frequent in Old Comedy, can be traced occasionally in Middle Comedy, but was so far unknown in Menander.

This survey of the contents showed the simple structure of plot developing in a straight line and beginning without a complex pre-history. If we compare this with all that is supposed to have happened before the opening of the *Epitrepontes*, and the suspense in the course of its plot, we observe some stages of a develop-ment which illustrates Plutarch's earlier-mentioned remark that from a com-parison of Menander's early with his later plays it can be estimated what he might have achieved yet if he had lived longer. The construction of the *Peri-ceiromene* is also considerably more artistic than that of the *Dyscolos*. So if the dating of the former play in the period soon after 314 is correct, as we argued earlier, we may observe that the development of this poet also did not follow a straight course. But that was to be expected.

Though the dramatic structure of the *Dyscolos* may be simpler than that of other plays, in the acute but loving observer of human foolishness and misery the complete Menander can already be recognized. The figure of the mis-anthropic, surly, lonely crank who makes life a burden for himself and others, has literary ancestors. Even in Old Comedy we meet the *Hermit* (Μονότροπος), a play staged by Phrynichus in 414. In the *Agrii* by Pherecrates of 420 mis-anthropy also played a part. In Middle Comedy there was a *Dyscolos* by Mnesi-machus, but little is known about it. The figure of Cnemon is also an important part of the tradition connected with Timon the misanthrope,[1] who already appears with typical features in Old Comedy (in Phrynichus' *Monotropos* and in *Birds*, 1549). But in spite of his obligations to predecessors this Cnemon is Menander's own creation and still an impressive figure for moderns. Neither a fool nor a criminal, experience has made him suspicious of the world and of people. The social factor also plays an important part in this play, as it does elsewhere in Menander. One figure in the play characterizes Cnemon in a phrase which makes him a representative of a whole class (604): 'He is a typical Attic peasant. He struggles with the rocky soil which bears only thyme and sage. He can sing a song of trouble and he reaps no good from it.' Menander does not, however, see Cnemon as a mere product of circumstance, for his stepson Gorgias grew up in the same misery into a completely different man. The poet is aware of the importance of man's predisposition, which was ancient Greek knowledge. And so, through Gorgias' bearing, Cnemon comes to the awareness that people need one another, but he is not going to alter his nature for that reason any more than Sophocles' Ajax – and this comparison is quite legitimate – can cast off his own in spite of his awareness of the way of the world. And so, even after his accident, he wants to remain alone; even the old maid must go, and Sostratus gives way before his unyielding character (τρόπος ἄμαχος). But this character could finally not cause evil: differences in social background break

---

[1] Shown by W. SCHMID, 'Menanders Dyskolos und die Timonlegende'. *Rhein. Mus.* 102, 1959, 157.

down before the young people's happiness and these aspects reflect Menander's humane conception of the community of mankind, which was rooted strongly in the Peripatos.[1]

The superior, but inoffensive, irony with which he observes mankind is also a facet of Menander's humanity. He puts Sostratus on the stage ready to tackle his unaccustomed labours and ardently singing the praises of the girl whom he has discovered here in the country; and then suddenly breaks down (390): 'But this mattock weighs four talents, it will kill me beforehand'. Thus emotion and reality clash. And during the dramatic rescue it was the same Sostratus who, according to his own speech, nearly dropped the old man into the well again three times, because he had only eyes for the girl.[2] Although Menander knows man's passions, he never turns into a morose zealot, but he always retains the indulgent smile of the φιλάνθρωπος. He did this already when he was only 25 years old.

In order to show the dramatist's development, as far as we know it, we shall begin with the later of the two best preserved plays of the Cairensis. The beginning of the *Epitrepontes* (suitably translated as the *Arbitrators*) shows us an apparently hopeless situation. A young man called Charisius has married a middle-class girl called Pamphile and has come to love her dearly. But when he comes home from a voyage he had to undertake soon after the wedding (voyages play an important part in the plot-mechanism of New Comedy), he has to learn from the slave Onesimus that Pamphile has meanwhile given birth to a child which has been exposed. Deeply hurt, he leaves his wife, retires to the house of his friend Chaerestratus in the vicinity where he tries to forget his grief. It is one of the finest features of the play that we are shown the uselessness of his attempt and that thus the depth of his love in spite of his unhappiness is demonstrated. He hires a harp-girl Habrotonon (if only Pamphile finds out!), but in the course of the play we learn that he did not touch her. Here and elsewhere Menander had grown beyond the carelessly masculine notion of sexual matters which generally governed Greek life. Outwardly, however, Charisius' goings-on have to give the impression of regular debauchery. Little wonder that his father-in-law, old Smicrines, hurries along, a great deal more concerned about the fine dowry than his daughter's happiness. But before he can interfere to establish order in his own way, he is stopped by an extraordinary incident. Two slaves, the shepherd Daos and the charcoal-burner Syriscus, have fallen out over a foundling. Daos has handed over the child, which was found exposed in the forest, to Syriscus at the latter's request, but wishes to keep for himself a few objects which had been left as a means of recognition. Syriscus, however, as the child's representative, wants these, since it may be possible to find its parents with the aid of these things. In accordance with ancient usage, the two want to end their quarrel by means of arbitration. So, when they see old Smicrines

---

[1] W. SCHMID (*v. sup.*), 170 and 'Menanders Dyskolos, Timonlegende und Peripatos'. *Rhein. Mus.* 102., 1959, 263.

[2] L. STRZELECKI, 'De Dyskolo Plautina'. *Giorn. Ital. d. filol.* 12, 1959, 305 has shown that in his version Plautus made the scene into a canticum. The only definite fragment *virgo sum; nondum didici nupta verba dicere* appears to indicate a duet, unless it must be assumed that Sostratus is reporting what the girl said.

approaching, they think that he is the right man for this purpose and present their case to him in a quarrel-scene which is obviously inspired by the Euripidean agon. Smicrines decides in favour of the foundling with whom the objects are to remain, and so makes possible the solution of all the conflicts although he does not realize this. For the baby who is the subject of the argument is his own grandson, born of Pamphile and exposed by her because she was afraid. She conceived it at the Tauropoliae, a nocturnal festival, when a young man in his cups violated her. With the exposed child she left a ring which she had pulled off the young man's finger, all she could do in her distress. When Onesimus enters, Syriscus is making a sort of inventory of the objects found and he recognizes the ring as his master's property. He is in a quandary, for Charisius had hardly been grateful for his revelations and now he is to burn his fingers again! Then the harp-girl Habrotonon, who remembers an incident at last year's Tauropoliae, comes to the assistance. If the ring is really his, Charisius could be the young man who at the time raped the girl. So she takes the baby and the ring to pretend to Charisius that she is the mother and thus to test her suspicion. This trick is so successful that at first the confusion is considerably increased. When Smicrines finds out that Habrotonon has a child of Charisius, he is quite certain that in spite of all opposition he has to get Pamphile away from this husband, while Charisius realizes the blame he has incurred. But Pamphile and Habrotonon, who is holding the child, only have to meet once in order to effect a recognition so that all troubles change into the greatest happiness; the girl whom Charisius had wronged at the festival was no one but Pamphile, who later became his wife. The child will now only strengthen the tie between the two, though even at the worst moment it was never quite broken.

In the case of the *Epitrepontes* other finds came to the aid besides the Cairensis, particularly a page from a parchment-codex of the fourth century A.D. which Tischendorf discovered in the Catharine convent on Sinaï in 1844, and which Uspenski brought to St Petersburg in 1855. A second page of this manuscript gave us a piece of the comedy *Phasma*. Before her marriage, a certain woman gave birth to a girl who is now being reared in the neighbouring house. A wall has been pierced and camouflaged as a shrine, permitting meetings of the daughter with her mother, while the latter's stepson believes he is seeing an apparition (phasma) and falls violently in love. Donatus gives the contents in his commentary to the prologue to Terence's *Eunuchus* (9. 3). We know of repeat-performances of the play in the years 250 and 167 B.C.; generally Menander's comedies were often replayed.

D. S. Robertson[1] wished to insert the forty-four trimeters of the earlier-mentioned Didot papyrus in the *Epitrepontes*.[2] A. Körte[3] has rendered it probable

---

[1] *Class. Rev.* 36, 1922, 106; *Herm.* 61, 1926, 348.

[2] CHR. JENSEN, *Rhein. Mus.* 76, 1927, 10 and ed. (*v. inf.*) XXVI is reserved on this question, gives bibl. inform. in the passage quoted of his ed., but reveals his doubt. H. OPPERMANN inserted the lines of the Didot manuscript in his ed. of the *Epitrepontes*, Frankf. a. M. 1953.

[3] *Herm.* 61, 1926, 134. 350. D. L. PAGE, *Lit. Pap.* Lond. 1950, 180 (with bibl.) wishes to keep open the possibility of attribution to a tragedy of the fourth century.; cf. also A. BARIGAZZI, 'Studi menandrei'. *Athenaeum* n.s. 33, 1955, 267.

that the lines given to Euripides by the papyrus belong actually to New Comedy and to Menander. The speech of a woman who opposes her father and refuses to leave her husband in misfortune corresponds in its general features with Pamphile's situation and with the words overheard by Charisius, but details like her claim that her husband has always been of one mind with her, make the ascription impossible.

The *Periceiromene* – one could translate this as the *Shorn Woman* – also starts off with a situation in the worst possible confusion. The preliminary history of the play, which takes place in Corinth, is even more complex than that of the *Epitrepontes*. A poor woman has found exposed twins. Of these she left the boy to the rich Myrrhine who wanted a child, while she reared the girl herself. When Glycera had grown up, the old woman gave her to a high-ranking officer, the chiliarch Polemon, to be his concubine. Before her death she revealed everything to Glycera, also that Moschion in Myrrhine's house was her brother. Glycera keeps the secret in order not to distress her brother, who is enjoying the life of a pampered young man of a rich family. But when Moschion, who lives in the house next to hers, once kisses her on a rash impulse of love, she permits him to do it because he is her brother. Unfortunately Polemon comes upon them and cuts off her hair in a fit of wild jealousy. This was then considered to be a humiliation. Glycera seeks refuge in Myrrhine's house, to whom she now reveals her secret. Polemon, deeply hurt, has retired to the country. Toward the end of the plot there are all kinds of complications, as when the slave Daos lies to his master Moschion that Myrrhine has taken Glycera into her house to please him or when in a regular siege-scene, not the only one of its kind in New Comedy, the refugee is to be taken from Myrrhine's house. In the dénouement Pataecus, a neighbour of Polemon and Myrrhine (so the stage shows three houses[1]), plays a decisive part. It is difficult to place him in the plot, but he definitely was not Myrrhine's husband. At any rate he turns out to be the father of the exposed twins. Now Glycera, who has forgiven her hot-tempered Polemon, can marry him, but the lovelorn Moschion has acquired a sister.

The preserved plays are only a small section of an uncommonly rich output. The numbers handed down vary, but are without exception above 100; according to Gellius (17. 4, 4, who also gives other information), Suidas and the anonymous Περὶ κωμῳδίας, Menander wrote 108 comedies. We must repeat what we observed for the poets of Middle Comedy, that an output of this volume was no longer merely intended for the Athenian festivals but for the whole world of Greek culture. We possess little of it, but it is enough to permit us to understand Menander's art.

New Comedy is a structure with a rich and varied background, in which two centuries of dramatic genres have been preserved. It has appropriated the legacy of Euripidean tragedy while on the other hand it is part of a tradition of comic drama which leads via the classics of Old Comedy and Middle to the Hellenistic

[1] Bibl. on the question of houses on the comedy stage in T. B. L. WEBSTER, *Greek Theatre Production*, Lond. 1956, 24.

age. Over and above all this, the personality of individual poets should be borne in mind; in the case of Menander we can still find out to a certain extent.

Let us begin with the external features, the themes and their technical construction. Menander's comedy is without exception middle-class comedy. We know that other poets of New Comedy like Diphilus and Philemon occasionally selected mythical subjects. Parody of myths had been a feature of Middle Comedy, but obviously Menander did not find clowning of this nature to his taste.[1] The samples of plots which we discussed showed us stock themes of which we could add an extraordinary number of additional examples; violation of a girl, exposure of children, recognition, often after many years, and cleverly devised plots to overcome the difficult situations. It was already observed in antiquity that most of this was prepared for in Euripides; Satyrus expresses it clearly in his Euripides biography (nr. 1135 P.). The *Epitrepontes* offers a fine example of how Euripidean themes, transferred into Menander's middle-class world, develop a new life of their own. If we may accept Hyginus' 187th *fabula* as the contents of Euripides' *Alope*, which is extremely probable, this means that the tragic poet already connected the story of an exposed child with a controversy about the accompanying objects. Furthermore, in his account the arbitrator was also the child's grandfather, King Cercyon, Alope's father. But while in the tragedy the child was exposed a second time, Menander made the arbitration the decisive instrument for a satisfactory solution. With the superior freedom which is the hallmark of genius the poet himself points at these connections; in the judgment-scene he makes the glib Syriscus parade examples from tragedy which show how important such trinkets are for a foundling and in one of the last scenes (*v.* 767 Kö.) the nurse Sophrone threatens the sluggish Smicrines, who still refuses to understand, that she will declaim a speech from Euripides' *Auge*. In this play, too, the violation of a girl by a drunk plays a portentous part.

Menander was by no means the first to avail himself of themes tested in tragedy. We can still distinguish this usage in Middle Comedy[2] and we learnt (p. 448) that seduction and recognition occurred as themes in one of Aristophanes' last plays, the Cocalus.

How the legacy of tragedy was fused with that of comedy becomes clear in a series of technical details.

The complex situation of Menander's comedies demands a preparation of the audience by means of an informative prologue. Figures like Tyche in the *Florentine Comedy*, or Agnoia, personified unawareness, in the *Periceiromene* are, of course, particularly suited for tasks of this nature, but it is by no means the rule for Menander to use them, for the *Phasma* had no divine prologue and it is quite improbable that the *Epitrepontes* had one. The affinity with the prologue-

---

[1] T. IVANOV, *Une Mosaïque romaine de Ulpia Oescus*. Sofia 1954, publishes a mosaic of the 2nd/3rd century A.D. with a theatre scene which according to the note is supposed to be from Menander's *Achaeans*. This is questionable evidence which hardly enforces a revision of the opinion that M. did not write travesties of myths.

[2] WEBSTER, *Later Com. (v. inf.)*, 74.

speeches of Euripidean tragedy is directly observable and becomes so even more, when here and there we find indications of the future course of events. Besides this we should not overlook the history of the form of comedy. Though the material does not permit us to state this as a general rule, Menander is fond of letting his prologues follow upon brisk opening-scenes which already show some of the characters of the play and pique the interest. The *Periceiromene* offers a good example, while the position of the prologue, spoken by Auxilium in Plautus' *Cistellaria*, must reflect the construction of the original. Such a late position of the prologue, however, has its precursors in Aristophanes' comedies. We need only refer to the opening of the *Equites* in which, after a dialogue of the two slaves, one asks (36), if he is now to tell the story to the audience and then follows up with the complete tale. A further essential feature which is a legacy of the comic play stands out clearly in the example mentioned. We mean the direct address to the audience, the ever-present contact with the spectator which reaches back to the early stages of literary comedy with its cheerful abuse of individual and community. This contact with the audience was maintained throughout in New Comedy. Apart from many other instances, we have splendid evidence of this in the prologue which the Didot papyrus (*v. supra*) presents as the second text. In this an enthusiastic young man speaks in ardent words of his awakening through philosophy. (Presumably love spoilt this notion for him in the further course of events.) He begins with the assurance that he is entirely on his own and that no one can hear him. But then he addresses the audience as a matter of course in the usual manner (ἄνδρες).

The address to the audience is by no means restricted to the prologue alone, it returns also in the numerous monologues within the play with which people enter and leave the stage. In the majority of cases the monologue of New Comedy, through its address to the audience, proves itself to be a descendant of the technique which permitted the actor of Old Comedy to speak directly to the audience at any moment. Of course, Menander's monologues have a kinship with tragedy as well. Here fine nuances can be detected. Charisius' monologue in the *Epitrepontes*, in which he remorsefully recognizes his wife's love, would be unthinkable, in view of its style, as an address to the audience. It is immediately preceded by the monologue of the slave Onesimus, who fearfully reports the excited behaviour of his master inside the house. This is a message for the audience, who are addressed with ἄνδρες (567 K.).

Once more this example demonstrates that in New Comedy various trends of development converge. The servant who reports the peculiar behaviour of someone inside the house, then making way for the latter, can be compared both with the indignant slave in the *Alcestis* and Heracles' action following this story, and with Aristophanes' *Wasps*, where Xanthias first describes the mad goings-on of Philocleon, followed by the latter's appearance in full splendour.

The audience-contact of the comic play is closely connected with the important role of the aside which has remained a significant element of comedy ever after.[1] These glosses directed at the spectators are particularly favoured in scenes in

---

[1] Asides are rare in Euripides. There may be some influence of comedy.

which a concealed listener accompanies a monologue or dialogue with his remarks. New Comedy made this into a frequently used device for a lively connection of scenes.

If we take the citizens' chorus of both tragedy and comedy as the representatives of the collective community, we understand why it lost its meaning under the altered circumstances. This could be clearly traced in the last few comedies of Aristophanes, while, on the other hand, tragedy had already allowed the choral lyric to recede in favour of a more and more elaborately developed plot. We mentioned earlier Aristotle's observation (p. 412) that in Agathon the choral songs were only insertions. Middle Comedy already revealed in what forms this development came to its conclusion. New Comedy shows the same condition. The chorus has been completely separated from the action, its song and dance are a fill-in between acts, and in our texts[1] its rule is merely indicated by the notice χοροῦ which we already found in Aristophanes' *Ecclesiazusae* and *Plutus*. In two cases (*Epitr.* 33, *Per.* 71, *Dysc.* 230. Comedy fragments in Antinoopolis Pap. 2. 1960, 8. An example already in Alexis fr. 107 K.) its appearance is announced as the entrance of a crowd of drunks. This must have been typical, just as the masking of the chorus as a band of revellers, as a komos, which recalls the Dionysian origin.

This regular division by the chorus justifies our speaking of acts. It is another question whether we may accept for Menander the division into five acts which Horace sets up as the norm (*Ars poet.* 189). Of the fragments preserved only those of the *Epitrepontes* reveal the number of five acts. Now the completely preserved *Dyscolus* displays this division. W. Kraus[2] has pointed out that the number of five acts already appears to be conventional here, as in this play the stage is also emptied in other places which suit the end of an act. So even if we cannot with certainty accept Horace's rule for New Comedy, the likelihood of such an assumption has been considerably increased.[3] Though it is probable, it also remains a conjecture that the poet had more than three actors at his disposal.[4]

Menander is a clever and careful dramatic constructor. An anecdote often told has been handed down by Plutarch (*De Gloria Athen.* 4. 347 f.). The poet is reminded of the fact that the Dionysia are near and that he has not yet written the play due. But he answers that he has already organized the material, and only has to write the verses for it. For all the excellence of his dramatic technique we would certainly not agree with his admirer Aristophanes of Byzantium who wanted to allot to him the second place among all the Greek

---

[1] The passages in the verbal index in vol. 2 of KÖRTE's ed. under χοροῦ; cf. also K. J. DOVER, *Fifty Years of Class. Scholarship*, Oxf. 1954, 116. Added are now the four interludes of the *Dyscolos* (232, 426, 619, 783) and one in the comedy fragm. *Antinoopolis Pap.* 2, 1960, 8.   [2] P. 13 of his ed.

[3] Opinions varied: KÖRTE, RE (*v. inf.*), 755 and WEBSTER, *Stud. in M.* (*v. inf.*) 181., assumed five acts in New Comedy; opposition from W. BEARE, *The Roman Stage.* Lond. 1950, 188 and G. E. DUCKWORTH (cf. p. 648, n. 1), 99. The older arguments in G. BURCKHARDT, *Die Akteinteilung in der neuen griech. und der röm. Kom.* Diss. Basel 1927. R. T. WEISSINGER, *A Study of Act Divisions in Class. Drama.* Iowa Stud. 9, 1940.

[4] KÖRTE (*v. prev. n.* 3). On the scene of the *Misumenus* important for this question: WEBSTER, *Stud. in M.* (*v. inf.*), 19, 3 of the 1st ed.

poets.[1] Menander maintains his high rank as an artist rather through his style and portrayal of people.

Hardly ever at any time were verses written which remained so completely free of any trace of metrical coercion. The extraordinary richness in nuance of this style, of which Quintilian with full justice admired the adaptability to age, position and mood of the speaker (10. 1, 69; 71), which is deployed with a fascinating natural ease. He combines an extreme conciseness with the greatest possible effect; each word has its special place. With all its directness and actuality this style has a suppressed quality which we appreciate as an expression of the resignation with which Menander observed the world and mankind. It is the exception, and done for the sake of the effect, that in the recognition scene in the *Periceiromene* the colloquial tone gives way to the tragic style.[2] Menander's diction is full of the inimitable Attic charis, which in no way means purism in the sense of the Atticists of imperial times. In many details, of which we only refer to the disappearance of the difference between aorist and perfect, Koine announces itself. The fact that Menander could not be considered a reliable example of pure Attic, was harmful for his preservation in times when schools set the fashion.

The image of life as drawn by Menander is a tissue of manifold threads. It is the middle-class world of Athens with its narrow confines which we already attempted to sketch in a few lines. It is controlled by a convention which allots to people and things their fixed places. Young people's marriages are arranged by their parents, calculation playing an important part. Money is throughout the great controlling agent. When one is past the tempests of youth, one clings to one's piece of property, unwilling to share the miserable fate of the poor, of which much is heard in Menander's verse. Some commotion is brought into this life by the hetaera, but she, too, has her fixed place in the order of things. Many of those who belong to her class aspire to escape from it into freedom, and gain is here, too, mostly the goal. The soldier moves through this company in an easier manner. He is always a mercenary and although he is fond of surrounding himself with the splendour of great adventure, he, too, is mostly impelled by considerations of a material nature, for booty provides the way to easy circumstances. But the citizen protects his world from being disturbed by the warrior by unmasking him as a braggart whenever he can.

The lives of these people who have home, hearth and food could pass in comfortable peace, if there were not a power which likes to throw people and things into confusion and plays the oddest games with the fate of the individual. The old faith has been challenged, the traditional forms remain on the surface, superstition is rampant and avenges, as it does at all times, the past in the rationalism of the present. Above all this hovers Tyche,[3] the quasi-religious

---

[1] Epigram on a Herme *IG* 14, 1183 = Test. 61 c Kö.

[2] The same stylisation in the anagnorisis of an anonymous comedy: no. 1304 P.; PAGE, *Lit. Pap.* Lond. 1950, 310. Hardly to be understood as a parody.

[3] On representations and cult M. P. NILSSON, *Gesch. d. griech. Rel.* 2, 2nd ed. Munich, 1961, 200.

power of the Hellenistic age. She no longer embodies a great destiny, filled with divine forces, though lofty in its final unintelligibility, such as people face in tragedy; it is the whimsical power which we find active in some of Euripides' last dramas in which it would be idle to look for a meaning. We need only to recall the *Epitrepontes* to illustrate the meaning of Tyche for the plot of New Comedy. It is not related to a well-defined concept. As characteristic for this time as the belief in its control is the indefinite, fleeting character of the ideas connected with her. Menander calls her blind (fr. 463 Kö.)[1] agreeing with his friend Demetrius of Phalerum who wrote *On Tyche* (fr. 79-81. 121 Wehrli). On the other hand, it does not mean a great deal when someone, who has been successful in every respect, wants to level this reproach at Tyche (*Coneiaz.* 13). But at the end of the *Comoedia Florentina* Tyche presents herself as power in whose hands is the control of things and indeed the happy ending of complex stories does not agree with the government of a hopelessly blind power. Thus there is one mention (fr. 417 Kö.) of Tyche's intelligence, compared with which human wit has no importance. Such contradictions may depend on the situation of the speakers, but they testify in any case to the indistinctness of the notions. When in the *Epitrepontes* (554 Kö.) Habrotonon says to Pamphile that one of the gods has taken pity on the couple, and in the *Periceiromene* Agnoia, a close relation of Tyche herself (49 Kö.) speaks of god who turns evil into good, it becomes clear that the old faith maintains its title beside and within new ideas. Nor are attempts lacking to dissolve Tyche into nothingness. We are reminded of Zeus' complaint at the beginning of the *Odyssey*, when one speaker reproaches another for his accusations against Tyche (fr. 486 Kö.); man himself is guilty of his misfortune. Another again denies Tyche as a person (fr. 486 Kö.); he who cannot bear what happens to him according to nature, calls his own character (τρόπος) Tyche.

With this last passage we enter the sphere in which Menander's art is displayed at its purest. When his admirer Aristophanes of Byzantium[2] praised him with the witty question, who had really imitated the other, Menander life or life the poet, he did not mean the faithful depictor of middle-class convention or the inventor of complex plots, but above all else the great portrayer of people. Menander received from the comic tradition many stock characters, as enumerated, for instance, in the *Florida* (16) by Apuleius, but he made his figures into more than types by giving them the richness of individual life and so rose above Theophrastus, who gives in his *Characters* most subtly differentiated types, but types all the same. It is, however, not only the acuteness of observation and the faithfulness of the portrayal which brings Menander's characters so close to us. The best of its effect comes from the conciliatory mildness of this clairvoyant observer and his genuine faith in the possibility of goodness in people. To make a type into a living individual does not mean a mere elaboration

---

[1] Passages on her capriciousness in A. KÖRTE, 'Die Menschen M.'s'. Ber. *Sächs. Ak. Phil.-hist. Kl.* 89/3. 1937, 14, 1.

[2] Syrianus on Hermogenes 2, 23 RABE = Test. 32 Kö.: ὦ Μένανδρε καὶ Βίε, πότερος ἄρ ὑμῶν πότερον ἀπεμιμήσατο.

of the former, but a far-reaching innovation. For all his rash nature, Polemon in the *Periceiromene* has changed from a braggart soldier into an upright and lovable person. His closest kinsman is Thrasonides (the name still has the old typical ring) in the *Misumenus* who loves a captive girl without touching her and through such generosity he earns her hand when she has been freed. A figure like Habrotonon in the *Epitrepontes*, who in spite of her trade has her head and heart in the right place, is the property of Menander.

In all the motley sport of Tyche, man's nature remains an important and often decisive factor. It has been correctly observed[1] that the events taking place inside people often anticipate the outward happenings and thus create the basis for the happy ending before this is brought about by external circumstances. Thus Charisius in the *Epitrepontes* has earned the reunion with his wife through the awareness of how small he is in his pride compared with his wife, who sticks to him in spite of all her father's urging. Polemon in the *Periceiromene* can obtain the forgiveness and the hand of his Glycera, because he truly regrets his hot temper. And how lovable Demeas in the *Samia* is in all his erring! In the course of an extremely complex sequence of events and mistakes he has to believe that his stepson Moschion has deceived him with the Samian Chrysis, his life's companion. His first anger has hardly passed away when he thinks up all reasons imaginable to excuse the young man. Of course, Chrysis then has to experience his anger, until everything turns out well. A humanity which does not shock the world with great deeds but proves itself true to a noble conviction is now considered to be the true manifestation of Greek nature. Thus in the *Periceiromene* Pataecus says of Glycera that she has proved herself to be a true Greek with her willingness to forgive (430 Kö.).[2] Greek nature is the subtlest flower of humanity; the old pride toward the barbarians has found a new expression based on civilization and inner culture. But Menander is also aware of a humanism which reaches beyond these borders. In fragment 612 Kö. we hear words which were certainly not contradicted in the course of the play. In a conversation with his mother a son opposes ancestral pride and class-prejudice; not the place of one's birth is what matters, but the natural inclination toward the good, which the Aethiopian or Scythian can also have. Similarly it is said (fr. 475 Kö.): no one is foreign to me if he is upright. All men are naturally equal, only character creates individual differences. The first part of this is reminiscent of the revolutionary statement made by Antiphon as an exponent of natural law (*v.* p. 356), but is also closely akin to Menander's best-known phrase (Ter. *Heaut.* 77): *homo sum: humani nil a me alienum puto.*[3] In the passage concerned this fine phrase is supposed to serve as the justification of an inquisitive person. It was not a new find, but a thought which readily sprang to mind. We rate even higher the line with which Menander ennobled his work by the confession

---

[1] R. HARDER, *Die Antike* 15, 1939, 71; now *Kl. Schr.* Munich 1960, 247. K. BÜCHNER, 'Die Neue Kom.'. *Lexis* 2, 1949, 67; *Röm. Lit. Gesch.* Stuttg. 1957, 90.

[2] More in WEBSTER, *Stud. in M.* (*v. inf.*), 21. 205, 5 of the 1st ed.

[3] An argument on the possibility of determining the original verse is recorded in POHLENZ, *Herm.* 78, 1943, 270. In add. F. DORNSEIFF, *Herm.* 78, 1943, 110. Neither fr. 475 Kö. nor the monostich in Meineke *FCG* 4, 340, 1 are of account.

that the image of true humanity, held up to us as the finest and highest task, stands above all misery, confusion and passion. It is the fragment (484 Kö.) which speaks of the magic of the man who is truly human. No translation can do justice to the Greek: ὡς χαρίεν ἔστ᾿ ἄνθρωπος, ἂν ἄνθρωπος ᾖ.

For New Comedy, too, we know a considerable number of poets' names – sixty-four have been counted – but only in few cases can we get some idea of their plays through Latin imitations. It is self-evident that Latin elements in the transformation, especially in Plautus, make our judgment more difficult.

Ancient opinion ranked Philemon closest to Menander, *fortasse impar, certe aemulus*, as Apuleius (*Florida* 16; cf. Quintil. 10. 1, 72) puts it. He was born in Syracuse between 365 and 360, but acquired Athenian citizenship in 307/306 and belongs with his art at least to the tradition of the New Comedy which had grown in Athens and was filled with the spirit of the city.[1] He left his adoptive city for a time and stayed at the Ptolemaic court. There he seems to have written his comedy *Panegyris*. Many stories were told (Plut. *De ira* 9. 458 a; *De virt.* 10. 449 e) of his return voyage during which he was supposed to have been driven on to the shore by a gale which put him into the hands of King Magas of Cyrene. This was unfortunate, since Philemon had held this man's lack of culture up to ridicule (fr. 144 Kö.), but according to the story the insulted party proved his magnanimity. The *Marmor Parium* is evidence for his first victory at the Dionysia of 327, and the list of victors (IG II/III, 2nd ed. 2325), in which he directly follows Menander, testifies to his threefold success at the Lenaea. The above-mentioned Latin authors state that his contemporaries often preferred him to Menander. Apuleius also knows a touching story of the poet's death (264/263); he died over a book while his audience was waiting for him.

The elements of New Comedy with which we became acquainted in Menander, are practically all found in him; but his comedies also have titles like *Myrmidons* and *Palamedes*, which indicate mythological subject-matter. As an apt variant of the divine prologue he once (fr. 91 K.) casts in this role the air, which is everywhere and sees everything. Of Plautine plays the *Mercator* was modelled on Philemon's *Emporus* and the *Trinummus* on the *Thesaurus*, as Plautus himself states in the prologues. We can with near certainty infer that Philemon's *Phasma* was the original for the *Mostellaria*.[2] As far as we can see, Philemon had excellent control of dramatic technique and knew how to make sure of a thrilling and surprising ending. This is contrasted by an inclination towards a broadly moralizing tone. Philolaches' entrance-monologue in the *Phasma*, which we can derive from the corresponding canticum of the *Mostellaria*, is as excellent an example of this as the *Trinummus* is as a whole.

Diphilus was not a native Athenian either; he was born at Sinope on the Pontus between 360 and 350. He must have come to Athens early, in 340, if

---

[1] The Philemon of Soloe in Cyprus (Strabo 671 c) is another comic poet of this name.

[2] A number of other ascriptions (the early papyrus no 64 in PAGE, *Lit. Pap.* Lond. 1950, *Captivi, Truculentus* et al.) is still quite doubtful; cf. WEBSTER, *Later Com.* (*v. inf.*), 142. On the evaluation of the *Thesauros-Trinummus:* F. ZUCKER, *Freundschaftsbewährung in der Neuen attischen Komödie. Ber. Sächs. Ak. Phil.-hist. Kl.* 98/1. 1950.

we are permitted to believe that the stories told about his connections with the hetaera Gnathaena are historical fact. He died early in the third century in Smyrna, but had, together with his father Dion and his brother Diodorus, a tomb in Athens of which we know the inscription (IG II/III, 2nd ed. 10321). In his case, too, we find, besides many titles which indicate middle-class comedy, some from the sphere of mythology as *Danaids* or *Peliads*. The names of a *Heracles*, *Theseus* and *Hecate* we must, of course, attribute to the speakers of the prologue, as this is certain after Menander's example in the case of the *Heros*. Diphilus also wrote one of the six comedies on Sappho which we know by title.[1] Untroubled by chronology, he makes Archilochus and Hipponax appear in it as the lovers of the poetess. Plautus recast the *Clerumenoe* in his *Casina*, a play with an unknown title (*Pera?*) in the *Rudens*, and the *Schedia* in the *Vidularia*.[2] Terence informs us in his prologue to the *Adelphoe* that Plautus also used Diphilus' *Synapothnescontes* in his *Commorientes*, but left a scene from the beginning of the play unused which Terence inserted in his comedy. It is a scene both roughly comic and at the same time wittily constructed, in which a procurer abducts a girl and he himself is given a sound cuffing. Boisterous comedy with disguises and thrashings is also found in the *Casina*, a play otherwise not very enjoyable, in which father and son pursue the same girl, pretending to be her servants. On the other hand, the *Rudens* has justly found its admirers. This does not mean that the plot with its lovers, procurers and the girl recognized as a middle-class daughter is unusually original, but its austere structure is given a particular charm by the locale of the plot at the coast of the sea which, formally one of the actors, causes the proper shipwreck, washes the proper trunk ashore and wafts a piquant, salty breeze over the scenes. The fragments of the *Vidularia*, also a trunk-comedy, show that it dealt with similar material.

It is not accidental that Terence translated, besides four plays by Menander, two by Apollodorus of Carystus, the *Epidicazomenus* into *Phormio* and the *Hecyra* with the same title. His affinity to Menander led him to a poet who continued Menander's way in essential features, in the motivation from within the characters, in the description of middle-class milieu and the utilization of family-relations, though he could not compare with him. This Apollodorus is to be distinguished from the comic poet Apollodorus of Gela, a contemporary of Menander's; he succeeds the latter by about a generation and is presumably identical with the Apollodorus of Athens who, according to Suidas, wrote forty-seven plays and won five victories. His style can be discerned especially in the *Hecyra*, which deals with the material of Menander's *Epitrepontes*, but opens up new aspects of the theme in the parts played by the parents of the young couple. Taking the reunuciation of comic effect in addition, one observes the development of the middle-class play at its end.

In the prologue of his *Asinaria* Plautus mentions as his original the *Onagus* of a certain Demophilus who must not be forced into oblivion by being altered into

---

[1] Cf. the index in KOCK's *CAF*.

[2] WEBSTER, *Later Com.* (*v. inf.*), 173, considers ascription of the original of the *Miles Gloriosus* to Diphilus.

Diphilus.[1] The mediocre play in which money is cheated out of someone for a girl and the lover's father helps to further his own obscene purposes, belongs in the third century, probably even to the second half.

A certain Posidippus of Cassandrea in Macedon – once more we observe the wide area of penetration of Attic comic poetry of the time – was very successful in Athens after Menander's death and appears in Gellius (2. 23, 1) among the sources of the Roman comic poets.[2] Philippides, an Attic author of the deme Cephale, ventured to insert a political element into his plays and revealed the undignified adulation with which many Athenians humiliated themselves.[3]

For bibl. on the political and economic relations of the Hellenistic era we refer to section VI B 1. For Athens: A. H. M. JONES, 'The Social Structure of Athens in the fourth century B.C.' Econ. Hist. Rev. 8, 1955, 141. Bibl. on Menander listed in the editions of JENSEN and KÖRTE (until 1938) as well as of ZUCKER, Der Hellenismus in der deutschen Forschung 1938–1948. Wiesbaden 1956, 1, and in CLAIRE PRÉAUX's essay (v. infra). On the tradition: R. CANTARELLA, 'Fata Menandri'. Dioniso 17, 1954, 3. The papyri are elaborately described in JENSEN and KÖRTE – Editions: CHR. JENSEN, Berl. 1929 on the basis of a new collation of the Cairensis. A. KÖRTE 3rd ed. 1 (papyri), Leipz. 1938; new impression with additions by A. THIERFELDER, Leipz. 1957; 2nd ed. 1959, 2 (fragments with authors) published by A. THIERFELDER, Leipz. 1953; 2nd ed. aucta et corr. 1959. J. M. EDMONDS, The Fragments of Attic Comedy. III. A. New Comedy, except Menander. Anonymous Fragments of the Middle and New Comedies. Leiden 1961. III. B. New Comedy, Menander. Leiden 1961. Both volumes with translation into English verse. It is very painful to have to state that this work cannot be credited. In one work, 'The Cairensis of M. by infra-red', Stud. Norwood (Phoenix Suppl. 1) Toronto 1952, 127, EDMONDS had already published a group of new readings which he claimed to have derived from the Cairensis by means of infra-red. These were paginations, titles, stage directions, scholia and marginal as well as interlinear paraphrases. Similar additions are now made to Menander in EDMONDS's Fragments. While much of this information is already incredible per se, B. MARZULLO, 'Il Cairense di M. agli infrarossi', Rhein. Mus. 104, 1961, 224, has had to declare, after carrying out the most careful technical tests (226):

[1] On the problems of chronology T. B. L. WEBSTER, Studies in Later Comedy. Manchester Un. Pr. 1953, 237.
[2] E. SIEGMANN, Lit. gr. Texte aus der Heidelb. Papyrussammlung. Heidelb. 1956, published parts of the six last lines of Posidippus' Ἀποκλειομένη as Pap. Heidelb. 183. They correspond nearly verbatim with the two lines of the Menander fragment 616 K. which WILAMOWITZ and, hesitantly, KÖRTE added at the end of the Epitrepontes, whereas now they have proved to be the concluding lines of the Dyscolos. E. VOGT, 'Ein stereotyper Dramenschluss der Néa'. Rhein. Mus. 102, 1959, 192, recognizes here a τόπος which has its parallel in some of the endings in Euripides. – We also mention Pap. Heidelb. 184 with 10 new fragments of the unknown comedy, of which G. A. GERHARD, Griech. Pap. Diss. Heidelb. 1933, 40, had already published five fragments.
[3] Plut. Demetr. 12, 26.

Il risultato di ogni fotografia era totalmente negativo. Separate editions: *Epitr.* WILAMOWITZ, Berl. 1925, with a section on Menander's art. New impression 1958. *Samia*: J. M. EDMONDS, Cambr. 1951 (questionable). *Dysc, v.* p. 649, n. 1. – A translation of the *Epitr.* by A. KÖRTE in the Inselverlag 1947. *Samia* – Fragments transl. by W. MOREL: *Gymn.* 65, 1958, 492. The translation of the fragments by G. GOLDSCHMIDT, Zürich 1949, is not satisfactory. With English translation F. G. ALLINSON, *Loeb Class. Libr.* 1951. The translation *La commedia classica.* Florence 1955, carried out by B. MARZULLO, extends from Epicharmus to Menander. French translations in PRÉAUX (*v. infra*) 85, 2. – Verbal index in KÖRTE's edition. – General works and discussions: E. FRAENKEL, *Plautinisches im Plautus.* Berl. 1922, 374. A. KÖRTE, *RE* 15, 1931, 707. T. B. L. WEBSTER, *Studies in Menander.* Manchester Un. Press. 1950. 2nd ed. 1960. Id., *Studies in Later Greek Comedy.* Manchester Un. Press 1953, 184. L. A. POST, *From Homer to Menander.* Un. of Calif. Press 1951, 214. G. MÉAUTIS, *Le Crépuscule d'Athènes et Ménandre.* Paris 1954. JULIANE STRAUS, *Terenz und Menander. Beitrag zu einer Stilvergleichung.* Diss. Bern 1955. CLAIRE PRÉAUX, 'Menandre et la société athénienne'. *Chronique d'Égypte* 32, no. 63, 1957, 84. In add. to the works mentioned there (p. 91, 2) on M.'s style: H. TEYKOWSKI, *Der Präpositionsgebrauch bei M.* Diss. Bonn 1940. – Works on Attic law in PRÉAUX, 93, 2. – On Diphilus: F. MARX, Comm. edition of the *Rudens. Abh. Sächs. Ak. Phil. – hist. Kl.* 38/5, 1928. G. JACHMANN, *Plautinisches und Attisches. Problemata* 3. Berl. 1931, 3. W. H. FRIEDRICH, *Euripides und Diphilos. Zet.* 5. Munich. 1953. On Philemon, Diphilus and Apollodorus: WEBSTER, *Later Com.* (*v. supra*) – The fragments of New Comedy in TH. KOCK, *Com. Att. Fragm.* Vol. 2 and 3, Leipz. 1884 and 1888 (cf. on the work p. 637). In add. J. DEMIAŃCZUK, *Suppl. comicum.* Kraków 1912. O. SCHROEDER *Novae com. fragm. in papyris reperta exceptis Menandreis.* Bonn 1915. Some information with translation and comm. in D. L. PAGE, *Lit. Pap.* Lond. 1950. On EDMONDS *v. supra* – T. B. L. WEBSTER, *Monuments illustrating New Comedy. Univ. of London. Inst. of Class. Stud. Bull.* Suppl. 11, 1961. – On the types of New Comedy cf. the bibl. quoted for Middle Comedy (p. 637).

2 ATTIC PROSE

To an age when Athens was reduced to a place outside the sphere of great politics, the mythical and historical past of the city must have appeared necessarily all the more glamorous. On the other hand, contemporary history up to the consolidation of the new balance of power was so rich in strong personalities, crises and hopes that it claimed a record of its own. This marks out the two great fields to which the Atthidographers devoted their labour; the distribution of importance and stress varied, of course. The first Atthidographer to be mentioned after Phanodemus, with whom we concluded the earlier series (p. 628) is the quite shadowy Melanthius (*F Gr Hist* 326). His date is uncertain, but he may have been a contemporary of Philochorus. In addition to his *Atthis* in at least two books he also wrote *On the Eleusinian Mysteries*; thus, like many of his literary colleagues, he was particularly interested in religious matters.

For Demon (*F Gr Hist* 327) the year of the appearance of his *Atthis*, which was, at any rate, quite a voluminous work, can also be only approximately indicated. All the same we know that Philochorus wrote against him, so that his date may be estimated at about 300. The frequency of this and similar names among Demosthenes' kinsmen permits the conjecture that he was a relative of the orator; Jacoby thinks of a son of the Demon who acted as speaker in the oration *Against Zenothemis* (cf. p. 598). Besides his *Atthis* Demon also wrote *On Sacrifices* and *On Proverbs*; so he seems to evince the antiquarian interest which subsequently called forth such a vast literature.

The most important and to us most intelligible figure among the Atthido-graphers is Philochorus of Athens (*F Gr Hist* 328), though we do not know a very great deal about his life. We may possibly place the date of his birth after the middle of the fourth century. According to the evidence (T. 1. 2) he was a seer, interpreter of sacrifices and exegete. Interests of this nature can also be detected in titles of works and in fragments (F 67. 135).[1] Combined with the observations which the fragments of his *Atthis* allow us to make, this indicates that he had a conservative turn of mind. Without doubt he was inspired by the ancient Athenian ideals which governed his attitude during the last attempts to regain freedom and influence for the city. When Ptolemy II Philadelphus, in alliance with Sparta and Athens, tried to break the Macedonian influence in the Aegean, it was Philochorus who led the anti-Macedonian party. In 267 the Chremonidean War broke out, which owes its name to a popular decree moved by Chremonides.[2] Athens' capitulation to the Macedonian besiegers was its bitter conclusion (263/262). Suidas reports that Philochorus, suspected of anti-Macedonian sentiments, fell a victim of an ambush (ἐνεδρευθείς) by Antigonus Gonatas. This sounds quite vague and, if we may attach so much importance to the wording, points to political murder rather than execution. Nor can Philochorus' end be with any success closely related with the events of the war; in any case it occurred in the 'sixties and probably at the end of that period.

Suidas gives a list of twenty-one titles of works; other information increases the number to twenty-seven.[3] Among them a large number of specialized studies can be detected and it is most probably that these works preceded Philochorus' main work, the *Atthis*. There are monographs *On the Tetrapolis*, *On the Foundation of Salamis* and *On Delos*. Individual titles like *On Contests in Athens*, *On the Mysteries in Athens* testify to the bearing of these books on the city and consequently we will be permitted to consider the writings *On Divination, Sacrifices, Festivals, Days,*[4] *Purifications* as having particular reference to Athens. This tendency of his work is revealed especially in the *Attic Inscriptions*

[1] JACOBY, *F Gr Hist* 3b (suppl.), Vol. 1, 1954, 235, has justly taken position against LAQUEUR'S construction (*RE* 19, 1938, 2436) of an internal development which led Philochorus to scepticism at a more advanced age. [2] *IG* II/III 2nd ed. no. 687.

[3] Conveniently arranged list in Jacoby (*v. sup.*), 242.

[4] The fragments of the work (85-88) which comprised at least two books, indicate the religious importance of the separate days. But also calendars in the meaning of the appendix to Hesiod's *Works* and the Orphic Ἡμέραι ἢ Ἐφημερίδες probably occurred.

('Ἐπιγράμματα Ἀττικά), the first collection of this kind that we know of. Something of the spirit of the Peripatos can be detected in this undertaking; the treatise *On Inventions* (Περὶ εὑρημάτων), also dealt with a theme favoured in that circle.

In some other books Philochorus contributed his share to the already extensive literature about the tragedians. Heraclides Ponticus (Περὶ τῶν τριῶν τρα-γῳδοποιῶν) and Aristoxenus (Περὶ τραγῳδοποιῶν) occupied themselves with this subject; of Philochorus we know the title *Treatise on Tragedies* (Περὶ τραγῳδιῶν σύγγραμμα), *On the Themes of Sophocles* ((Περὶ τῶν Σοφοκλέους μύθων, 5 books) and *On Euripides*. The *Letter to Asclepiades* ('Ἐπιστολὴ πρὸς Ἀσκληπιάδην) belongs with these, since Philochorus in this way makes a public attack against Asclepiades of Tragilus (F Gr Hist 12), the pupil of Isocrates, who had been the first to discuss tragic themes in his *Tragodumena*. In accordance with his general attitude the works of Philochorus mentioned should be considered as having less of a grammatical bias than a historical and antiquarian one. The form of the learned letter recurs in the *Letter to Alypus*.

Philochorus' interests, however, were by no means restricted to Attica. Evidence of this are two Pythagorean treatises, his contribution to the rich Pythagorean literature of the time: *On Symbola* and *Collection of Heroines or Pythagorean Women*. He also wrote *On Alcman*.

His main work was the *Atthis* in seventeen books, believed to have been written in the late 'nineties and 'eighties. The different distribution of the material in his treatment of the theme is significant of Philochorus' interests. Books 1-6 certainly covered the period up to Chaeronea (338), possibly even as far as the beginning of the rule of Demetrius of Phalerum (317). In this section he followed the *Atthis* of Androtion, whom he esteemed as greatly as he disliked Demon (T 1). The other eleven books dealt with the whole scope of contemporary history up to Antiochus of Syria (T 1), though it cannot be decided whether the second or the third Seleucid is meant. There is no foundation for the confidence with which 262/261 is frequently stated as the final year of the work.[1] The work was cast in the annalistic form. What we can still observe of his style points to simplicity and clarity with an absence of rhetorical ornamentation and stylistic pretence. Admittedly our verbal quotations come almost wholly from narrative sections written in a chronicler's manner.

In opposition to the romantic conception of the 'last of the Attics', Jacoby placed the criticism of Philochorus on a new basis in his monumental study of the Atthidographers. He has taught us to understand that the Athenian priest and patriot was at the same time a scholar who should be taken seriously.

The man who conceals himself behind the obviously fictitious[2] name of Amelesagoras (F Gr Hist 330) falls in a different category. The author of this *Atthis* stepped forth with the claim that he had been inspired by the nymphs and appears to anticipate a development which was already evident in

---

[1] When Suidas mentions an epitome of his own *Atthis*, this is probably a slip. JACOBY (v. p. 666, n. 1), 256 dates the epitome at the end of the 1st century B.C.

[2] JACOBY, F Gr Hist 3 b (suppl.) Vol. 2, 1954, 488, n. 7.

Phanodemus (p. 628) and which under such titles as Ἀττικά, Ἱστορίαι Ἀττικαί led to a fictional presentation of the sparse tradition of ancient time.

We add here Ister the Callimachean (F Gr Hist 334) even though this pupil of the great Cyrenaean was not an Athenian. In his Ἀττικά (at least fourteen books), for which also the title Συναγωγὴ τῶν Ἀτθίδων has been handed down, he presented a critical collection of the tradition of Attica's pre-history, perhaps up to Codrus. From the titles we can still trace a prolific literary production with antiquarian interests by this writer, who found subjects from practically all parts of the oecumene. Scholarship had become international. The cyclical collection of large ranges of subjects – Ister also wrote Argolica and Eliaca – is as typical as the collective Atacta, Symmicta, Hypomnemata, which are beginning to become fashionable.

Jacoby justly opposed the opinion that Ister cut off the life-line of Atthidography with his collection. It ended as historiography with Philochorus and it did end with him because the Chremonidean war put a period to Athens' active participation in contemporary events. But there was by no means a decrease in interest in the religious and political institutions, for this interest had also been quite active in Atthidography and had produced at its fringe such works as On the Demes and On (Tomb-) Memorials by an otherwise unknown Diodorus (F Gr Hist 372) who is dated in the time of Philochorus. Nicander of Thyatira (F Gr Hist 343) also wrote on the demes but considerably later, not before the end of the third century. The collections of decrees of Aristotle and his circle also found imitators. Thus Demetrius of Phalerum wrote on Athenian constitutions and his own legislation (fr. 139-147 Wehrli). An increasing number of non-Athenians also began to devote interest and work to these subjects. A significant example of this is the Collection of Decrees (Συναγωγὴ τῶν ψηφισμάτων) which Craterus the Macedonian (F Gr Hist 342) published on the basis of archive research, perhaps still in the time of the Peripatos.

One of the characteristics of the Hellenistic age is its lively interest in the organisations of the cults, an interest, however, that was antiquarian and historical rather than religious. In Athens there were particularly diligent practitioners of this kind of literature, as is proved by a series of late-Hellenistic authors: Ammonius (F Gr Hist 361) wrote On Altars and Sacrifices (Περὶ βωμῶν καὶ θυσιῶν), Crates (F Gr Hist 362) likewise On Athenian Sacrifices, Habron (F Gr Hist 359) wrote a book On Festivals and Sacrifices, Apollonius (F Gr Hist 365) one On the Athenian Festivals (Περὶ τῶν Ἀθήνησιν ἑορτῶν).

But the antiquarian interest was not restricted to cults; the great families, people ridiculed by comedy and not in the last place celebrated hetaerae were subjects for writers. The desire to contribute to the interpretation of authors had, of course, an important share in products of this sort. Entirely in the same line of interest is the periegesis which could join on to the geographically oriented periplus and periodos literature of the Ionians (v. p. 219), which in the Hellenistic age also developed a variant with historical interests. An early example of such a travel-guide, obviously chiefly geographically oriented, is offered by the Papyrus of Hawara (F Gr Hist 369; nr. 1708 P.). In the fragment preserved the port of Athens is discussed; this does not, however, guarantee that the whole work is concerned with Athens. Of course, there did exist a periegesis which dealt exclusively with Athens. We know of a travel-book of this kind under the double name of Callicrates-Menecles[1] (F Gr Hist 370). The share of Athenians in such literature is slight; only the periegete Heliodorus (F Gr Hist 373) is incontestably a son of Athens.

In Hellenistic Athens little was done in the way of historiography which went beyond the city, but two names at least can be mentioned. Demochares (F Gr Hist 75), a nephew of Demosthenes, whose vicissitudes were caused by his participation in the city's politics (he was exiled in the first decade of the third century) wrote Historiae.[2] Diyllus (F Gr Hist 73), probably a son of the Atthidographer Phanodemus, continued Ephorus' work up to the year 297 in his Hellenica.

Jacoby has discussed the Atthidographers within the framework of his F Gr Hist, and especially thoroughly in 3 b Suppl. In add. his Atthis, Oxf. 1949.

3 THE PHILOSOPHICAL SYSTEMS

Although its political importance continued to dwindle, Athens could at least maintain its central position in one region of intellectual life. No doubt philosophy was also cultivated in other places at the time, no doubt not a few of the most important philosophers who were working in Athens had come from abroad, but Socrates' city remained the centre in which the lines of force converged and from which new ones went out.

Philosophy tended to move away from literature as belles-lettres to a much greater extent than in the time of the first generation of Socratics. In comparison with Plato and Aristotle the development of thought took a turn which was characteristic of the Hellenistic age. The aim of philosophy is no longer an elevation to the vision of final and eternal things, nor knowledge gained for its own sake; in this epoch of profound change and constant uncertainty, man should rather be shown the way to individual happiness. All other themes of thought are subordinated to the one goal. In accordance with this development traditional literary forms are only occasionally used for teaching this type of philosophy, and they are even more rarely the expression of genuine emotion. The result is that a history of literature has to limit itself to surveying concisely the main features of the period's intellectual background.

We begin with the Cynics, because their critical attitude to the world – we may by no means speak of a school – continued from Socraticism directly into the Hellenistic age and gave a strong impetus to the most important of the new systems, the Stoa. The most striking Cynic, the hero of numerous world-spurning anecdotes, is Diogenes of Sinope, the Socrates gone mad (Diog. Laert.

---

[1] Perhaps a certain Menecles revised the older periegesis of a Callicrates.

[2] We should like to know more about him, especially whether he influenced Duris of Samos. Some interesting observations by A. MOMIGLIANO and K. V. FRITZ in: Histoire et historiens dans l'antiquité. Fondation Hardt. Vandœuvres-Geneva (1956) 1958, 140, 142. His style seems to have been passionate, excited and aggressive.

6. 54), the snapping dog who thought it his vocation to revise all prevailing values and to point the way back from the aberrations of a civilization over-loaded with pretence to a healthy and unpretentious naturalness. He did not spurn the written word and among his works there were also some tragedies which were, of course, meant to be read rather than performed. His pupil, Crates of Thebes, also wrote, but he was a much milder critic of society who donated a considerable fortune to his city and went off on his Cynical wander-ings. There was much amazement at the fact that Hipparchia, a girl of a dis-tinguished family, the sister of his pupil Metrocles, became a companion on his beggar's journey. He wrote little satirical poems (παίγνια), and there were also tragedies of his hand as of his master Diogenes. It almost goes without saying that letters were forged under their names.

The most successful literary achievement of Cynic popular philosophy, however, is the diatribe, the propaganda speech declaimed with sharp wit and aggressive satire and enlivened with polemic in fictional dialogues. It is connected with the name of Bion of Borysthenes, a freedman whose experience in Athens decided his development. For some time he stayed at the court of the Stoically-minded Macedonian king Antigonus Gonatas, who died before him (239). Unfortunately a few titles and notes reveal to us no more than that his diatribes attacked various kinds of passions and prejudices. To illustrate how widespread their influence was it will be sufficient to recall that Horace (*Ep.* 2. 2, 60) speaks of satires with sharp wit as *Bionei sermones*. To stress the signi-ficance of the Cynical diatribe as an important precursor of satire does not imply a denial of the Romans' original achievement in this realm. The spirit of this aggressive protreptic can be traced somewhat better in the remnants of the diatribes of Teles who was active in the middle of the third century. Stobaeus has preserved them for us. Besides other Cynic commonplaces the fragments reveal also an indifference to all ties with country and native town. A papyrus published by Victor Martin[1] who dates it about the middle of the second century A.D. gives a good idea of this widespread literature. It contains the report about a conversation of Alexander the Great with the Indian sage Dandamis, which is found as an insertion in Book 3, version A of the Alexander Romance imputed to Callisthenes. According to Martin the passage contained in the papyrus comes from a version which was closer to the original. It is followed by the 7th letter[2] forged under Heraclitus' name which has here been expanded considerably. Both writings display the style of the diatribe, brisk and inclined to brevity, both rail against the corruption of an over-refined civilization which they contrast with the ideal of primitive naturalness. This genre was given a special development, in which wit and fancy dominated over the didactic tendency, by Menippus of Syrian Gadara, a former slave who became a well-to-do Theban citizen. His writings filled thirteen books and attacked under the most varying guises man's foolishness as well as the systems of philosophers.

---

[1] 'Un Recueil de diatribes cyniques. Pap. Gen. inv. 271'. *Mus. Helv.* 16, 1959, 77. Also PÉNÉLOPE PHOTIADÈS, ibid. 116 and J. TH. KAKRIDIS, ibid. 17, 1960, 34.

[2] HERCHER, *Epistolographi Gr.* Paris 1873, 283.

His *Arcesilaus* ridiculed the good cheer at the Academy, his *Birth of Epicurus* the personality-cult in the Garden. The *Necyia* assaulted the foolishness of the traditional representations of life after death. Much of the spirit of this satire recurred in Lucian touched up in the Atticist manner.[1] Menippus introduced variety of form into his work by alternating prose and verse. The Romans adopted this and developed the specific variety of their *satura*, in which connection mention must be made of Varro's *Saturae Menippeae*, Petronius' romance and Seneca's *Apocolocyntosis*.

Cynic criticism of the ways of the world and society also found its way into various forms of a contemporary poetry with its commonplaces. In the third century Phoenix of Colophon carried on an Ionian tradition with choliambs; we met Hipponax of Ephesus as its early, one might almost say classic, representative. In addition to smaller fragments like those from the *Ninos*, a poem on the mythical glutton, we have a Heidelberg papyrus (no. 1265 P.) in choliambs against the perversity of the rich.[2] Of Phoenix there survives a treasure of folklore; it is a begging song which was sung going round with a crow (κορωνισταί), a fine example of this widespread genre.[3]

An iambic fragment (fr. 11 D) attacking gluttony has been preserved of Cercidas of Megalopolis, who may possibly be identified with the statesman and general in Polybius (2; 48. 65). Many scholars[4] also wished to assign to Cercidas the choliambs against greed which we find in a London papyrus (no. 153 P. and no. 154) and in the Heidelberg papyrus mentioned in connection with Phoenix, but this is unwarranted. We become acquainted with Cercidas in his meliambs as a hearty sermonizer; he also stands out from the chorus of these Cynical zealots by his powerful, Doric-tinted language. In an original mixture of various metres he scolds the gods for the unjust distribution of earthly goods, while in another poem he tells of the friendly or ruinous wind which Eros can blow from his cheeks.

Here we can add Timon of Phlius, whose thought is influenced by Pyrrhon of Elis, the prophet of scepticism.[5] The quest for complete inner rest by conquering all false beliefs and idle attempts to gain knowledge affords many points of contact with Cynical criticism of the world. Timon, who lived about 320–230, described in a prose-work *Python* his career as an adherent of Pyrrhon; in another, *Arcesilaus' Funeral Banquet* ('Αρκεσιλάου περίδειπνον) he deemed the Academic, whom he had opposed earlier, worthy of honourable memory. He wrote various kinds of dramas to be read, not for the stage. He was most influential with his *Silloi*, satirical poems in which he followed the example of

---

[1] The principal work is still R. HELM, *Lukian und Menipp*. Leipz. 1906.

[2] For this and similar material G. A. GERHARD, *Ph. von Kolophon*. Leipz. 1909; the poem mentioned in POWELL (see below, n. 4), 235, 6 and fasc. 3, 124 D.

[3] L. RADERMACHER, *Aristophanes' Frösche*. 2nd ed. Sitzb. Öst. Ak. Phil.-hist. Kl. 198/4, 1954, 7.

[4] Thus J. U. POWELL, *Collectanea Alexandrina*. Oxf. 1925, 213; 216. A. D. KNOX, *The Firs Greek Anthologist* interpreted the Heidelberg papyrus as the remnant of an anthology edited by Cercidas. The choliambs also fasc. 3, 131 D.

[5] V. BROCHARD, *Les Sceptiques grecs*. 2nd ed. Paris 1923.

Xenophanes (*v.* p. 217). In three books in hexameters he told the story of a tremendous battle of philosophers and then again of a journey into the underworld in which the philosophers got their proper share of abuse. The *Indalmoe*[1] in elegiac verse presumably dealt with Pyrrhon's doctrine. Of course, poetry of this nature could no longer address the people as a whole, but the interest in the philosophers' promises and their bitter quarrel was yet so great that there was no lack of a fairly large audience.

The spirit of Cynicism proved to be considerably influential in the system which was to acquire its greatest effect in the following centuries and to become the ideological background for many Greeks and Romans. Zeno, the founder of the Stoa, was born in 333/332[2] in Cition in Cyprus as the son of the merchant Mnaseas; Cition was a Phoenician settlement and his father's name is interpreted as the Hellenization of Phoenician Manasse or Menahem. These few biographical observations indicate a controversial problem. To what extent are Semitic elements influential in the doctrine of Zeno, who came to Athens in 312/311 and began to teach there in the Stoa Poikile in 301/300? Contrary to Pohlenz[3] it is now assumed that the importance of such elements is slight; Zeno received his intellectual training substantially from Greek thinkers; he heard the Megarian Stilpon and the Academic Polemon, and especially the Cynic Crates: with Diodorus, likewise a Megarian, and his pupil Philo,[4] he studied dialectic and occupied himself thoroughly with the older philosophers.

The wide influence of the Stoa in future times was indicated by the large number of pupils which flocked to it from the most different places and classes. Among them was the last freedom-fighter Chremonides, as well as Antigonus Gonatas, the later ruler of Macedon. This fact will have been taken into consideration when the demos honoured the memory of Zeno, who died in the autumn of 262, with the gold wreath and a state tomb in the Ceramicus, although the psephisma (SCF 1. 7[5]), which has been preserved, expresses genuine reverence.

Zeno wrote early and a great deal. When he was still Crates' student he composed his *Politeia*.[6] He also wrote about the poets, presumably according

[1] 'images' in the sense of 'illusions' with reference to philosophical opinions of the schools?
[2] On the biographical chronology: F. JACOBY, *F Gr Hist* 2 D. Comm. on F 244, p. 737. M. POHLENZ, *Die Stoa* 2, 2nd ed. Gött. 1955, 14.
[3] Besides his book on the Stoa (v. *inf.*) POHLENZ esp. 'Stoa und Semitismus'. *N. Jahrb.* 1926, 257. Against him E. SCHWARTZ, *Ethik der Griechen*, Stuttg. 1951, 161 and 249, 13. W. SCHMID, *Der Hellenismus in der deutschen Forschung*. 1938–1948. Wiesbaden 1956, 83. Yet basically Pohlenz' formulation of the problem is still correct; with some critical caution, W. THEILER, *Gnom.* 23, 1951, 225, indicates that it is possible to explain the exaggerated consistency of the Stoic doctrine from the origin of many Stoics.
[4] Some clever paradoxes are attributed to him, but presumably only the more precise version is his at the most. On the so-called λόγος κυριεύων (deductions from the tenet that nothing impossible could result from the possible): A. N. PRIOR, *Philos. Quart.* 5, 1955, 205. P.-M. SCHUHL, *Le Dominateur et les possibles.* Paris 1960. O. BECKER, 'Zur Rekonstruktion des Kyrieuon Logos des Diodoros'. *Festschrift Litt.* 1960. (id. previously *Rhein. Mus.* 99, 1956, 289). K. V. FRITZ, *Gnom.* 34, 1962, 138.
[5] The quotations according to the fragment-numbers in V. ARNIM (*v. inf.*).
[6] Cf. POHLENZ, *Stoa* 2, 2nd ed. Gött. 1955, 75.

to his philosophy; the register of his works (fr. 41) with which we have to be satisfied apart from small remnants, mentions five books of Homeric problems. Latterly it seemed as if the tradition of Zeno might be increased from two other sources, but the yield is modest at best. A medieval philosopher Šakrastānī, who wrote in Arabic, copied in a passage on ancient philosophy dicta of various authors like Homer, Solon, Hippocrates, and among these there are also some of a certain Zeno. Since immediately before Zeno the Elder (i.e. the Eleatic) is mentioned, he is probably also the author of the sayings. F. Altheim and R. Stiehl[1] showed that it could also be the Stoic. But recently E. G. Schmidt[2] examined the dicta attributed to Zeno critically; his criticism shows that the relation with the Stoa is often very slight and in some cases completely absent. Though he does not exclude the possibility of Stoic tradition in some cases, Schmidt thinks that the Arabic sayings were put under Zeno's name in late antiquity or the early Middle Ages.

Other hopes, also realized in small measure only, were raised by four manuscripts in the government Matenadaran (manuscript-archives) in Jerewan.[3] They contained one Old Armenian treatise of a philosophical content attributed by two of these sources to a philosopher Zeno. It was first believed that Zeno's treatise On Nature (Περὶ φύσεως) had been found in translation. A more precise analysis[4] demonstrated, however, that it was a late tractate, worked up from many sources (Neoplatonic inter alia) which has only little bearing on Stoicism. The most interesting part is the concluding passage with the tetrad void-matter-motion-infinity. According to Dörrie the only Zeno who might be considered would be Zeno of Pergamum, the pupil of Proclus. But it is more likely that this cento was given the philosophical authority of the Stoic. With this writing an excerpt from an Old Armenian doxography came to light, containing doctrines of Plato, Aristotle and the Stoics. Some were attributed to Zeno and this is genuine Stoic material, though it does not give us anything new.

We know many names of pupils of Zeno's. Persaeus, from his native town Cition, was particularly close to him. When Antigonus Gonatas called Zeno to Macedon, he sent as his representatives Persaeus and Philonides of Thebes. Persaeus became the prince's teacher and later commander of Corinth. There he died when Aratus of Sicyon took the city in 243. Being a man who enjoyed life, he wrote symposia (Συμποτικά ὑπομνήματά), but also about the worship of the gods and about the state of the Laconians. This was also an interest of Sphaerus of Borysthenes, who was called to Sparta by Cleomenes in connection with educational problems.

---

[1] Forsch. U. Fortschr. 36, 1962, 12 with reference to earlier work by the scholars mentioned. They first drew attention to these dicta of ZENO's in Porphyrios und Empedokles. Tübingen 1954, 10, n. 12. [2] Forsch. U. Fortschr. 36, 1962, 372.

[3] L. S. KHATSCHIKIAN, Der Bote aus dem Matenadaran 2, Jerewan, Publ. of the Acad. of Science of the Armenian SSR 1950, 65. A Russian translation by S. AREFSCHATIAN, ibid. 3. 1936, 315.

[4] H. DÖRRIE, Gnom. 29, 1957, 445. E. G. SCHMIDT, Die altarmenische 'Zenon'-Schrift. Abh. D. Ak. Wiss. Berlin. Kl. f. Spr. Lit. u. Kunst 1960/2. 1961.

Cleanthes of Assos, the place which at another time also had played its part in the history of philosophy, was Zeno's successor in the direction of the school. Being a man of an upright character, he also gained the respect of his opponents in the Academy. With great vigour of feeling he made Zeno's doctrine his own and found the finest expression for Stoic piety in his *Hymn to Zeus*.[1] Aeschylus' splendid prayer in the *Agamemnon* (160), Euripides' intense intellectual struggle (*Troad.* 884) and this hymn praising, under the name of the father of the gods, the Stoic universal god, the bearer of order and cosmic intelligence, impressively represent three ways of Greek religious perception, all bound to Zeus' name, yet basically different.

Although he was the most winning personality among the older Stoics, Cleanthes was not the man to give the school a solid centre and to carry Zeno's doctrine through against the attacks of the competing systems. Some serious events occurred. Dionysius of Heraclea, who at home had also been a student of Heraclides, turned his back upon the Stoa; Ariston of Chios who had a strong influence as a lecturer, opposed any attempt at a positive evaluation of the 'natural things' such as health and prosperity and set himself up as an independent lecturer in the Cynosarges. Under his influence Herillus of Carthage also detached himself from the main body of the school. In this situation Chrysippus of Soloe in Cilicia, who was considered the new founder of the Stoa in antiquity (Diog. Laert. 7. 183), intervened. Both for his birth and his death we can only indicate the Olympiad: 281/277 and 208/204. Galen states that he learned proper Greek in Athens, but he did not appreciate him (SVF 2. 24. 894). He first attended the Academy, where he found a suitable cultivation of his intellectual talents in dialectic. This schooling enabled him to write his six books *Against Customary Views* (Κατὰ τῆς συνηθείας) in which he denied the validity of our sense perceptions. It also enabled him, after his conversion to the Stoa, to write seven books on the same subject (Περὶ τῆς συνηθείας) from a different point of view. But it was particularly this dialectical schooling which placed Chrysippus in a position to set the Stoic doctrine on a new basis by means of logical proofs, and to protect it from ruin through a carefully thought-out development of the system. His lectures drew large crowds, so that he read in the Lyceum in the open air. He is alleged to have written more than 705 works (SVF 2. 1) but we should bear in mind the unreliability of such numbers.[2] We have some idea of his work *On the Soul* (Περὶ ψυχῆς) and the *Therapeuticus* which summarized his doctrine of the emotions. He dealt particularly with two central notions of the Stoa: *On Providence* (Περὶ προνοίας) and *On Fate* (Περὶ εἱμαρμένης).

To characterize the Stoa in a very general way, it may be stated that it combined into one system various elements of a rich philosophical tradition; it was neither consistent nor did it cover all details, but it supplied an excellent framework for the rigorous ethical demands of the school. To no other of the older

---

[1] G. ZUNTZ, 'Zum Kleanthes-Hymnus'. *Harv. Stud.* 63, 1958. (Jaeger-Festschr.), 289.

[2] A. MARIA COLOMBO, 'Un nuovo frammento di Crisippo?' *La parola del passato* 9, 1954, 376.

philosophers does the Stoa owe so much as to Heraclitus. This becomes at once evident, when we glance at the central idea of its system, the Logos,[1] from which all else receives meaning and life. This Logos is the universal intelligence which has created everything from itself and preserves everything; it is the Pronoia, the controlling providence, but it is also the Heimarmene, the indestructible chain of causes and effects which determines the course of things. Furthermore, this Logos is the Physis, nature as the creative force and the eternal law active in it. Above all this Logos is God. Beside it the anthropomorphism of the old religion has no longer a place, but the Stoa concluded a clever peace with popular religion by systematizing the old method of allegorical explanation[2] and thus leaving a reservation for the multiplicity of the gods. We get a good impression of such Stoic allegory from the *Homeric Allegories* ('Ομηρικὰ προβλήματα) of a certain Heraclitus who probably wrote in the first century A.D. But the Stoic Logos is not pure spirit, but substance consisting of the most refined form of the fiery aether. As Pneuma, as a warm breath, it pervades the world and is present wherever there is form and life. Man has the most important share in it, and so remains separated from the animals by a wide abyss. The controlling part of the soul, the hegemonikon as bearer of the intelligence, is pure Logos, part of the divine universal fire. The old analogy, equally significant in Greek as in Oriental thought, between macrocosmos and microcosmos[3] was now expressed in its most lucid form: the cosmos as a whole is a living being endowed with intelligence, a ζῷον λογικόν, and so is the individual human through his share in divine universal intelligence. Therefore the upward glance at the macrocosmos, which displays the laws of its nature in the most impressive form in the stars is a special theme of Stoic religiosity. In connection with this the erect posture of the human body was considered to be a teleological proof of God's existence. In this way the Stoa with the wide scope and elasticity of its thought absorbed also a little of Hellenistic astrology into its texture.

Zeno taught that Logos pervades the universe as the building material, as honey the honeycomb (SVF 1, 155).[4] *Materiam mundialem a deo separat*, says our source and thus describes a dualistic factor in the properly speaking monistic system which only knows of matter. Here appear the difficulties to which Lactantius points in his criticism (SVF 2, 1041); the Stoics divided the universe into one part which plans and executes and another which experiences the effect; but both are matter and are supposed to form a unity. *Quomodo potest idem esse quod tractat et tractatur?* Would it not be madness to call cask and cooper the same things? The difficulties, upon which we can only touch here, are outweighed by rich gains. Antinomies which most profoundly moved Greek

[1] On Heraclitus' Logos cf. p. 212.

[2] Cf. p. 209; 329 and BUFFIÈRE, *Les Mythes d'Homère et la pensée grecque*. Paris 1956. Heraclitus' work was published by the Bonner Philol. Gesellschaft. Leipz. 1910.

[3] G. P. CONGER, *Theories of Macrocosmos and Microcosmos in the History of Philosophy*. New York 1922..H. HOMMEL, 'Mikrokosmos', *Rhein Mus.* 92, 1943, 56.

[4] Heraclitus VS 22 B 67 is remotely comparable: God is in all opposites, but he changes like fire which, when mixed with incense, is called after the scent of each.

thought are dissolved by the coincidence of the opposites. Nomos and Physis are no longer opposed, for in nature and law the same Logos reigns. Positive law and natural law cannot be truly contradictory, since positive law which can lay claim to validity can only be initiated by legislators who act from their understanding of the great universal law and on the basis of their share in the divine universal intelligence.[1] But, above all, this conception of the universe produces for the individual an ethical system without conflict, one which knows of no compromise. It is man's task to contribute to the firm rule of Logos in the world by bringing his own moral actions into correspondence with the great universal law which controls the cosmos, by repressing the irrational impulses of passion. This is the meaning of the Stoic telos-formula of the natural life: ὁμολογουμένως (τῇ φύσει) ζῆν.[2] Man acquires the standards of value given by Logos through Oikeiosis.[3] This difficult term, which is only imperfectly rendered by 'inclination' or 'sympathy', means that every living being places the things in his surroundings in a relationship to his own existence, which is either useful or injurious. But for the man whose logos develops in the time of his maturity, oikeiosis can only mean the correct appreciation of Logos and submission to its law. The Stoics were inevitably faced with a problem whose complete difficulty had not been grasped until then and could no longer be put to rest; if everything that happens in the universe is decided by an unbroken chain of causes, by the Heimarmene in which the Logos operates, where is then the scope for man's free will, which is the condition of all moral action and for all challenges involved?[4] Chrysippus, in particular, struggled with this problem; he illustrates his conception by means of a simile (SVF 2. 974, 1000) which specifies rather than removes the difficulties: a roller needs a first push to roll while the actual cause of this movement is due to its cylindrical form; in the same way the true cause for our decisions is not in the external stimulus, but in our own freely chosen position. The notion of synkatathesis is adduced here; as bearer of the Logos man is able to accept or reject the impulses which are roused in him by the perception of his senses and the images evoked by them. In *Epist.* 113. 18 Seneca represents the mechanism of Stoic philosophy with Latin terseness; we take the liberty of inserting the Greek terms in the text: *Omne rationale animal nihil agit, nisi primum specie alicuius rei inritatum est (φαντασία), deinde impetum cepit (ὁρμή), deinde adsensio (συγκατάθεσις) confirmavit hunc impetum.*

Even though he tends to simplify somewhat in chapter 32 of his *Life of Coriolanus,* Plutarch shows here how at that time Homer's epics were also examined from such points of view regarding the possibilities of human

[1] A. LESKY, 'Zum Gesetzbegriff der Stoa'. *Österr. Zeitschr. f. öff. Recht.* 2, 1950, 587.

[2] The addition τῇ φύσει originated by Cleanthes. On the changes of the telos-formula Pohlenz in *Die Stoa* (v. sup.). Cf. O. RIETH, *Gnom.* 16, 1940, 109.

[3] In opposition to F. Dirlmeier's attribution of the oikeiosis-doctrine to Theophrastus (*Phil. Suppl.* 30, 1937) POHLENZ, *Stoa* 2, 65, with bibl. In add. H. LEISEGANG, *Phil. Wochenschr.* 62, 1942, 424. In agreement with this O. REGENBOGEN, *RE* S 7, 1940, 1555, 63.

[4] Max Pohlenz dealt with these questions in his work about the Stoa (*v. inf.*), and in his book *Griechische Freiheit.* Heidelberg 1955, 131.

free will and how Homer was defended with the assistance of Stoic categories.[1] Every human being, Greek or barbarian, free or slave, is endowed with senses. This fact removed age-old barriers for the Stoic. When the cosmopolitanism of the Stoics, for whom the whole world now means home, enters into such radical opposition to the polis-bound thought of the past, the parallel of this change of thought with the historical event of the forming of the great kingdoms cannot be overlooked. Stoic cosmopolitanism, however, does not lead to the renunciation of the individual state, which under the prevailing historical conditions offers the most suitable framework for a demonstration of public spirit, for justice and for the love of mankind, without imposing strict limits on them.

Its ethics[2] are no doubt the main point of the Stoic doctrine. It is not possible to go into its logic[3] and physics here, but mention should be made of two things at least. Zeno rightly included linguistic expression in the realm of logic and to that extent made a substantial contribution to the foundation of western grammar.[4] A great many terms still in use go back to the Stoics. They established a tradition which passed via the school of Antiochus of Ascalon finally to Varro and from him to Augustine. The other endeavours of the Stoics, especially of Chrysippus, who were mainly concerned with hypothetical conclusions, remained comparatively in the background.

Of Stoic physics[5] we single out the doctrine of ecpyrosis. The universe, which the divine Logos has created from itself, returns, after the expiration of a cosmic period, to the unity of the original condition of fire. From there it once more begins its way to the separation of the elements and the multiplicity of things. Since this expiration is always accomplished according to the same universal law of Heimarmene, the eternal return of the same things is guaranteed by this law down to the last detail.

After Chrysippus there followed in the Stoa a time of traditionalism and defence against attacks, which emanated particularly from the Academy. In the second century B.C. we can trace a collection of essays of the Stoic Hecaton in which Zeno was also represented.[6] A revival is connected with the person of

[1] A. LESKY, Göttliche und menschliche Motivation im homerischen Epos. Sitzb. Ak. Heidelberg· Phil.-hist. Kl. 1961/4, 18.

[2] O. LUSCHNAT, 'Das Problem des ethischen Fortschrittes in der alten Stoa'. Phil. 102, 1958, 178, with bibl. on Stoic ethics.

[3] O. BECKER, Zwei Untersuchungen zur antiken Logik. Wiesbaden 1957 (in the 2nd part on the Stoa; the so-called θέματα, i.e. secondary rules, are also dealt with here). J. MAU, 'Stoische Logik', Herm. 85, 1957, 147. BENSON MATES, Stoic Logic. Lond. 1961.

[4] M. POHLENZ, 'Die Begründung der abendländischen Sprachlehre durch die Stoa'. GGN Phil.-hist. Kl. Fachgr. 1 NF 3/6. 1939. K. BARWICK, Probleme der stoischen Sprachlehre und Rhetorik. Abh. Ak. Leipzig. Phil.-hist. Kl. 49/3, 1957 (with contribution about the Stoic part in the development of the doctrine of tropes and figures). H. DAHLMANN, Varro und die hellenistische Sprachtheorie. Problemata 5. Berl. 1932.

[5] S. SAMBURSKY, Physics of the Stoics. Lond. 1959, restores Stoic physics to a place of some honour.

[6] Cf. Diog. Laert. 7. 1, 26. On the importance of the information of Persaeus and Hecaton for our knowledge of Zeno: U. V. WILAMOWITZ, Antigonos von Karystos. Phil. Unt. 4, 1881, 108.

Panaetius of Rhodes. The impetus which went out from him was so strong that some moderns have made him the initiator of the 'middle Stoa'.[1] This is neither an ancient expression nor a complete school of thought; nevertheless an important epoch in the history of the Stoa can be defined in this manner.

Panaetius, a descendant of old Rhodian nobility, was born in Lindos in 185. He had a chequered career which took him from Rhodes to Rome and Athens, where, in his fifties, he joined the Stoa under Diogenes of Babylon.[2] In 129, after the death of Antipater of Tarsus he undertook the direction of the school, ending his life in the beginning of the first century. In Rome the young Rhodian aristocrat was admitted to the leading circle; he won the friendship of Scipio and Laelius and it was largely due to his contribution that the new rulers of the world adopted the Stoic notion of life. It is significant that Panaetius' main work which he wrote with one eye on Rome, bears the title *On Duty* (Περὶ τοῦ καθήκοντος). According to his own evidence Cicero largely followed Panaetius in his work *De Officiis* (3. 7).

The great influence which Panaetius exerted is due to the fact that he largely broke down the rigorous and doctrinaire attitude of the older Stoa; more open to the world, he took into account its realities and those of human nature. Under him a new stream of students flocked in from all parts of the inhabited world. Among these was also the Rhodian Stratocles who wrote a history of the Stoa,[3] a work which was repeated some time after him by Apollonius of Tyre. But the most important pupil of Panaetius was Posidonius of Apamea. As a young man he left the Syrian city in which he was born in 135, to study in Athens where Panaetius opened the intellectual world of the Stoa to him. Like his teacher he visited Rome and like him he gained access to the houses of the old nobility. The long journeys which he undertook in the tradition of ancient Ionian ἱστορίη must have taken place in the years of his manhood. His knowledge of Asia Minor may be partly due to his origin; that of the western world he acquired entirely as a discoverer. We can still sense the vivid interest with which he roamed through Gaul from Massalia and through Spain. Everything came within the scope of his enquiries, Celtic ways of life, the tides of the ocean, Spanish silver mines, their rich yield but also the outrages committed upon slave labour there, troops of apes on the north coast of Africa. He then turned teacher and settled in Rhodes, which at the time combined economic activity with a rich intellectual life. He maintained an active connection with Rome which sent him many students. Cicero became familiar with him during his Rhodian sojourn (77). When Pompey established order in the East he visited Posidonius on the way out and on his victorious return home. There were many edifying anecdotes about the veneration for intellect of those in power. The fact that Posidonius devoted a monograph to Pompey obviously inspired Cicero's desire for a similar memorial. He sent the philosopher a record of his political

---

[1] A. SCHMEKEL, *Die Philosophie der Mittleren Stoa.* Berl. 1892.

[2] In 155 Diogenes took part in the Philosophers' Embassy to Rome, in which Carneades represented the Academy, and Critolaus the Peripatos.

[3] Extract in the *Index Stoicorum*, Pap. Herc. 1018.

achievements with the request to have the material cast in an artistic form. But Posidonius declined; the bulkiness of the consignment did not encourage but deterred him from writing. In this homage we detect the subtle irony of the man who also in other respects knew how to make his point. Rhodes, which granted him citizenship, sent him to Rome in 86 where he negotiated with Marius, who was dangerously ill. Suidas knows of another voyage to Rome in the year 51 in which Rhodes and Rome renewed their treaty. He died in the same year.

We know more than two dozen book titles of Posidonius,[1] which show that he was a scientist as well as a philosopher (Περὶ ὠκεανοῦ καὶ τῶν κατ' αὐτόν, Περὶ μετεώρων, Περὶ τοῦ ἡλίου μεγέθους) and a historian. Besides the History of Pompey already mentioned, he dealt with the period of 145/144 until some time after the conclusion of peace between Sulla and Mithridates (85) in a gigantic work of fifty-two books (Ἱστορία ἡ μετὰ Πολύβιον).

Posidonius had an important, although sometimes exaggerated, influence on ancient intellectual life. The endeavour to comprehend him as an investigator and thinker has become a major problem of classical scholarship, whose history Karl Reinhardt has traced with admirable objectivity.[2] For a long time the image of Posidonius developed in P. Corssen's dissertation[3] was current; it was mainly based on Cicero, Tusc. I, and on Somnium Scipionis; its elaboration by A. Schmekel[4] and others made of Posidonius a mystic follower of Pythagorean and Platonic ideas. In an entirely new approach Reinhardt[5] questioned the reliability of this assumption and examined Posidonius' 'inner form', basing himself on the larger fragments. Since his formulation there have been an old and a new Posidonius, but the discussion of the philosopher in Pohlenz's book on the Stoa has led to a gratifying mutual approach of the two views. Work on Posidonius is not nearly finished. Olof Gigon[6] even argues that it should be started afresh. He thinks that Reinhardt's selection of Strabo as a starting-point was very useful, but that he left the basis of what could be achieved with some certainty too rashly for the sake of building up hypotheses. This basis is provided, apart from Strabo, by Galen, Cleomedes, Seneca's Nat. Quaest. and Diodorus 33-37.[7] Careful corroboration must provide a basis for all future work. We exclude the controversial points (usefulness of Tusc. I, Posidonian

[1] In REINHARDT, RE 22, 1953, 567.　　[2] V. sup., 570.

[3] De P. Rhodio Ciceronis in primo libro Tusc. et in Somnio Scipionis auctore. Bonn 1878. Cf. id. Rhein. Mus. 36, 1881, 506.　　[4] Cf. p. 768, n. 1.

[5] Poseidonios. Munich 1921. Kosmos und Sympathie. Munich 1926. P. über Ursprung und Entartung. Orient u. Antike 6. Heidelb. 1928. Now the great RE article.

[6] Arch. f. Gesch. d. Philos. 44, 1962, 92.

[7] A lively controversy has sprung up around the question whether the account of the pre-history of the world and of human civilization in Diodorus 1, 7f. goes back to Posidonius. G. PFLIGERSDORFFER, Studien zu Poseidonios. Sitzb. Öst. Ak. Phil.-hist. Kl. 232/5, 1959, argues that it does. A different line is taken by w. SPOERRI, Späthellenistische Berichte über Welt, Kultur und Götter. Schw. Beitr. z. Altertumswiss. 9. Basel 1959; he opposes Pfligersdorffer in Mus. Helv. 18, 1961, 63. O. GIGON (v. sup. 97) may have called a temporary halt to the argument; he argues that there is no definite proof, but that attribution to Posidonius is most likely.

origin of the syndesmos-representation of man as the link between the sphere of the celestial and that of the earthly, Panaetius or Posidonius in Cicero, *De nat. deor.* 2. 115 ff.) and restrict ourselves to some few basic features. In spite of all his independence of thought Posidonius retained the foundation of the Stoic Logos-doctrine, but as an ethnologist,[1] geographer and historian, as a scientist whose interests embraced all the stages of existence, he drew the most diverse branches of knowledge into the scope of this doctrine. Less stress is placed on ethics and even less on logic in our sources, which is probably no coincidence, since they are fairly representative. What gives him his special significance is that he overcame a long-established separation and combined once more philosophy into a unity with the scientific disciplines. He had secured the rich legacy of Greek thought and met the unending variety of the phenomena of culture and nature with an open mind, but through the idea of sympathy this Stoic combined everything into a unity with himself; heaven and earth and generally all parts of the cosmos are seen in relations which pass influences from one to the other. Divination could also maintain itself on this basis.

Posidonius was a vitalist who found a profusion of variously graded forces active in the universe, from rocks to the animate stars and who, as an aetiologist, enquired in all fields after the impact and effect of the dynamically conceived Logos. Along the same line Posidonius believed – following Panaetius in this – that there was a compulsion active in man which is not a degeneration, but a natural condition. His high duty, wholly Stoically seen, is to be always guided by the Logos.

Posidonius took over the ancient telos-formula of the Stoics and elaborated it at the same time significantly.[2] It seems likely, though it is not certain that we read the text in Clement of Alexandria (*Strom.* 2. 129, 4): τὸ ζῆν θεωροῦντα τὴν τῶν ὅλων ἀλήθειαν καὶ τάξιν καὶ συγκατασκευάζοντα αὐτὴν κατὰ τὸ δυνατόν. It is a Stoic axiom that as bearer of the Logos man has access to the truth and order manifested in the universe; but here the synthesis of the *vita contemplativa* and *activa* is remarkable; it is still a majestic conception that man should be participating in the realization of the great order according to his powers. The further phrase κατὰ μηδὲν ἀγόμενος ὑπὸ τοῦ ἀλόγου μέρους τῆς ψυχῆς contains both a recognition of the Alogon in the soul as a fact and a demand for its subordination to the Logos.

Posidonius' eschatology should at least be briefly touched upon. For him the soul is an emanation of the sun which he considered as the heart of the cosmos, although not its centre in the meaning of Aristarchus. As the soul descends to earth by way of the moon, so it returns there along the same way. All details here are difficult and uncertain, but we can at least observe that Posidonius has abandoned the position of the older Stoa and also of Panaetius. The soul comes neither into being only at the birth of man, nor does it perish at his death; it is of a sunlike origin and maintains, within certain limits, an existence of its own.

---

[1] J. J. TIRNEY, *The Celtic Ethnography of Poseidonios. Proc. of the Royal Irish Acad.* 60/C/5, 1960.

[2] Valuable indication for the interpretation in Gigon, *v. sup.* 96.

Neither Panaetius nor Posidonius decided the character of the Stoa for the future; their thought had followed too individual a course. Plenty of names of Stoics for this epoch have been handed down, but little can be said of men like Mnesarchus and Dardanus who undertook the direction of the school after Panaetius. We can distinguish a number of Stoics who lived in Rome as teachers or in the houses of the leading men. Thus we find Diodotus with Cicero; with Cato Uticensis, who himself became a great model of the Stoic attitude, Antipater of Tyre and Athenodorus of Tarsus, while with Areus Didymus we have already arrived in the time of Augustus whose court-philosopher he was.

No less momentous and powerful an influence than that of the Porch was achieved, over wide spaces of time, by the system which was brought to new life by Lucretius in his poem *De Rerum Natura*, and by Pierre Gassendi through his work. Its founder Epicurus was born in Samos as the son of the Athenian Neocles in 341. Since his father lived in the island as an Athenian migrant, he was a citizen of Athens; and so he performed his military service there in 323. We met him earlier as a fellow-ephebe of Menander's. At the time he had already completed some years of philosophical study which he mainly passed in Teos with Nausiphanes (VS 75). The latter revealed to him Democritus' atomic theory which was later to become the foundation of his own system. After his training as ephebe Epicurus did not return to Samos since meanwhile the Athenian settlers had been expelled. Years of a wandering life followed which led him to Colophon, Mytilene and Lampsacus. At an early stage the strong influence of his personality proved itself, which obviously combined delight in his doctrine with the training of people. He made friends in the cities mentioned, beginning his philosophical teaching in Mytilene in 310 and continuing it in Lampsacus. In the summer of 306 he returned to Athens, the ancient home of his family. There he acquired the garden in which he taught and after which his followers were called 'philosophers of the garden'. He died in Athens in 270, revered by his followers as a divine being.

This man whose influence rested to a large extent on the charm of his personality, also put the written word with great diligence into the service of his teaching. His literary legacy comprised about three hundred rolls, of which thirty-seven belonged to his work *On Nature* (Περὶ φύσεως). Only brief reference can be made to some of the numerous other titles; the work on a theory of knowledge *On Criteria* with the sub-title *Norm* (Περὶ κριτηρίου ἢ κανών), the ethical writings *On the Highest Good* (Περὶ τέλους), *On Just Action* (Περὶ δικαιοπραγίας), *On Living* (Περὶ βίου) and the book *On Rhetoric* (Περὶ ῥητορικῆς), which banned this educational system from the realm of philosophy.

None of the works mentioned has been preserved, and what we possess by Epicurus himself is little enough. For the sake of their contents Diogenes Laertius inserted three of his letters, of which there were collections, in the tenth book of his work. The *Letter to Herodotus* deals with physics in the broadest sense; the one *To Pythocles*, which we may probably leave to Epicurus in spite of earlier doubts, is concerned with meteorology while the one *To Menoeceus* examines ethical and theological questions.

Epicurus tried to facilitate access to his doctrine by means of extracts from his own works and the coining of aphorisms. A collection of forty such maxims (Κύριαι δόξαι) has also been preserved by Diogenes. While Epicurus renounced artistic form in continuous writing, his skill at expressive terseness is proved in these sayings. It is understandable that there were collections of Epicurean maxims besides the *Kyriai Doxai*; such a one (*Gnomologium Vaticanum*) with eighty-one maxims about ethics and conduct was found in a Vatican manuscript (Vat. Gr. 1950, 14th c.) in the last century. What we have at our disposal is scanty enough in comparison with Epicurus' work, even when we add his last will, preserved by Diogenes. But in the case of Epicurus, a source-situation both original and bristling with problems permits a completion of the picture of his doctrine in many ways. Of Greek texts we have, in addition to Diogenes Laertius' contributions, first of all the papyri of Herculaneum. Inside a villa which probably belonged to Piso, the carbonized rolls of a library with mainly Epicurean texts have been found; the author of the greater part of these is Philodemus of Gadara. This Epicurean, in Athens a pupil of Zeno of Sidon, came to Italy in the seventh decade of the first century B.C. and there became the friend and personal philosopher of the L. Calpurnius Piso whom we know as Caesar's father-in-law and Cicero's opponent. In his younger years Philodemus wrote epigrams which were excellent in form, but largely frivolous in content; we have several of them.[1] They also had some influence on Latin love-poetry. Next to Siron, the teacher of Vergil, Philodemus became the leader of the Epicurean circle in Italy which had its centre in Naples. We may assume that he personally knew Vergil and Horace, who mentions him in *Serm.* I. 2, 120. Cicero had a genuine appreciation of him, however little he may have liked Piso.

Philodemus was a prolific author, although the Herculanean rolls give us only a limited impression of his numerous works.[2] Besides writings on logic and rhetoric which defend philosophy in the spirit of Epicureanism against the pretensions of the teachers of rhetoric, there are treatises on poetry and music.[3] Ethics and theology claim their place; in addition there are works on the history of philosophy, diatribes and dialogues written for a wider audience.[4]

Not all the rolls have yet been read, but even those which have been laboriously processed yield only sparse remnants of the writings which they once contained. The work on the Herculanensia is one of the most difficult tasks of classical scholarship. It is, however, worth while because of the very fact that

---

[1] G. KAIBEL, *Ind. lect. Greifsw.* 1885, is still authoritative. Texts: *Anth. Pal.* B. 5-7, 9-12 and 16.

[2] W. LIEBICH, *Aufbau, Absicht und Form der Pragmateiae Philodems.* Berlin-Steglitz 1960.

[3] A. J. NEUBECKER, *Die Bewertung der Musik bei Stoikern und Epikureern. Eine Analyse von Philodems Schrift De musica.* Berlin 1956 (D. Ak. Inst. f. gr.-röm. Altertumskunde. Arbeitsgruppe f. hellenistisch-röm. Philos. 5).

[4] The title (Philodemus is not always mentioned as the author) and the editions in Philippson's article *RE* 19, 2444. In add. the editions of Schmid and Diano listed *inf.*

Philodemus was not an independent philosophical thinker and is therefore quite useful as a witness for the tradition of the system of the school. The remnants are, of course, particularly valuable, when they use Epicurus' own words. Thus we owe to them the fragment on the problem of free will from the work *On Nature*, the most significant fragment we have of it.[1] For Epicurus' ethics another papyrus from Herculaneum[2] is important since it contains general outlines. Characteristic for the problems connected with the texts is the argument in which sometimes Epicurus is called the author, then again Philodemus or some older Epicurean.

The lengthy inscription which Diogenes of Oenoanda in Lycia had inscribed for the citizens of his city in A.D. 200[3] is a curious witness of the extent of Epicurus' following. It combines sections of Epicurus' doctrine with aphorisms and two letters, one of which was composed by the originator of the inscription. Plutarch's polemics against Epicurus and Colotes should also be added to the Greek sources. Of the Romans Lucretius has given us the most elaborate representation of the Epicurean doctrine. Friedrich Klingner[4] admirably demonstrates that in this great poem a passionate temperament has pervaded the doctrine of the soul at peace with a pugnacious spirit. Cicero's philosophical writings are also important, especially *De Natura Deorum*, and it may be assumed that Seneca utilized a collection of Epicurean maxims.

Epicurus' doctrine demonstrates particularly clearly how great a change had come over Greek philosophical thought since Socrates. The aim is no longer knowledge sought for its own sake; the final purpose of this philosophy is a form of living which ensures man of the greatest share of attainable happiness. Only from the aim itself can it be understood how utterly Epicurus' whole system is directed toward it. This aim is the complete peace of soul secure both from threat and temptation – Epicureans are fond of comparing it with the quiet of the sea. In this Epicureanism meets its arch-enemy, the Stoa, half-way. For Epicurus also uncontrolled passions are the great adversaries of human happiness. He declared war especially against fear which with its wrathful and vindictive gods, its superstitious interpretations of the phenomena of nature and threatening notions of life after death, never permits man to draw a quiet breath. For the sake of this battle Lucretius praised him as the great hero and conqueror.

It is only in this context that Epicurus' physics and theology become important; they are not investigations for their own sake but instruments in the battle against traditional religion. Democritus' doctrine which admitted nothing but empty space and atoms was the appropriate foundation for an interpretation of the universe without fear of the irrational. Epicurus altered Democritus' doctrine

[1] Pap. Herc. 1056. 967. 1191. Now in Diano's edition (*v. inf.*); cf. WOLFG. SCHMID, *Gnom.* 27, 1955, 406. Addenda to Book 14 of Περὶ φύσεως. WOLFG. SCHMID, *Rhein. Mus.* 92, 1944, 44.

[2] Pap. Herc. 1251. SCHMID's edition *v. inf.* Id., *Der Hellenismus* (*v.* p. 672, n. 3), 78 with bibl. and survey of the suggestions on the problem of authorship.

[3] A. GRILLI, *Diogenis Oenoandensis fragmenta.* Milan-Varese 1960 (*Testi e documenti per lo studio dell' antichità* 2).

[4] *Röm. Geisteswelt* 4th ed. Munich 1961, 191.

in that he set certain limits to the number of the forms of atoms and the direction of their movement. The atoms cannot be beyond a size which excludes their visibility, and they move through space in a perpendicular direction of fall. In order to explain the origin of universes, Epicurus needed the fatal parenclisis, a slight deviation of individual atoms from their direction which led to combinations and forming of clusters. The cause of this phenomenon is not looked for.

The soul is an atomic structure like everything else and perishes at death, which need not be feared as it is an absolute disintegration. The gods are also atomic structures; in the spaces between the worlds (metacosmia, intermundia) they lead a blissful life without any share in events within the cosmos or in the actions of mankind. How these gods remained unaffected by the perishable nature of all other atomic structures, how they are recognized by man and appear to him in images released from their surfaces, all these questions are connected with problems of interpretation with which scholarship is actively occupied at present.[1] It has also been proved that the claim that Epicurus, basically an atheist, made a hollow truce with tradition by means of his doctrine of the gods, is a misrepresentation. It has rather been recognized that there is an Epicurean piety which is realized in the contemplation of the peaceful bliss of the divine.[2]

Apart from fear, man must master desire and grief if he is to achieve peace for his soul. On the other hand, Epicurus took pleasure from the rank of the emotions and made this the final purpose of all aspirations by equating it with secure inner peace. Such a high valuation of pleasure is reminiscent of Aristippus, but while for the latter pleasure meant movement in a particularly profitable form, it is for Epicurus something which is tranquil within itself, removed from movement. There is hardly any need to mention that for Epicurus pleasure does not mean the greatest possible sensual satisfaction, although many challenging formulations by the Epicureans themselves may have led to the idea of the *porcus de grege Epicuri*.[3]

It is self-evident that for Epicurus the foundation of a doctrine of ethical values was a great deal more difficult than for Plato or the Stoa. This is shown quite clearly by his troubles with the notion of justice. It is based neither in the idea nor in physis, but the wise man will uphold it, since transgression cannot remain concealed and is followed up with punishment. The laws of the state which have come about through treaties demand respect for practical reasons. But the Epicurean turns his back upon politics on the guiding principle of

[1] G. FREYMUTH, *Zur Lehre von den Götterbildern in der ep. Philosophie*. Berl. (D. Ak. d. Wiss. Inst. f. hellenist.-röm. Philos. 2) 1953, with incorporation of the abundant bibl. Id. 'Eine Anwendung von Epikurs Isonomiegesetz'. *Phil.* 98, 1954, 101; 'Methodisches zur ep. Götterlehre'. *Phil.* 99, 1955, 234. G. PFLIGERSDORFFER, 'Cicero über Epikurs Lehre vom Wesen der Götter'. *Wien. Stud.* 70, 1957, 235.

[2] Cf. the outstanding work of WOLFG. SCHMID, 'Götter und Menschen in der Theologie E.s'. *Rhein. Mus.* 94, 1951, 97, who meets Klingner in his criticism of Lucretius (*v.* p. 683, n. 4).

[3] Against such an opinion Seneca, *De Vita beata*, 12, 4.

Live Unobserved (Λάθε βιώσας). The most suitable relationship for this purpose is friendship between congenial people; their genuine cultivation of this bond gave to the garden its special character.

The succession after the founder is of much less importance for Epicureanism than for the Stoa. There was no question of elaboration or modification of the doctrine which seemed inviolable to its adherents through the very person of its founder. Metrodorus of Lampsacus,[1] a particularly loyal follower of his master, died before him; the direction of the school passed on to Hermarchus[2] and after him to Polystratus. Both also defended their doctrine in written works. So did Colotes, who attacked Plato and of whom we get some impression from the Herculanean rolls. We earlier met some Epicureans of Cicero's time in connection with Philodemus. Behind all these names an extensive literature is at the service of the doctrine which had to protect itself against numerous attacks, especially by the Stoics.

Polemon and Crates were no more able to give a new impetus to the Platonic Academy than their predecessors Speusippus and Xenocrates. A change occurred with Arcesilaus of Pitane in Aeolia, who undertook the direction of the school in 268. According to an ancient classification the Middle Academy began with him.[3] His doctrine, which he passed on by word of mouth, was based on Socratic ignorance, denying the possibility of giving definite judgments on the basis of our perception. Opponents of the Academy claimed that with this reserve (ἐποχή) Arcesilaus copied the scepticism of Pyrrhon of Elis, and moderns have mostly followed suit. But Arcesilaus' primary motive was to oppose the Stoic theory of knowledge which, based on the senses, adopted as the foundation of all knowledge the images of sense-perception; these were rather dubiously divided into convincing and non-convincing images.[4] In his devaluation of perception Arcesilaus remained wholly Platonic; it is difficult to ascertain to what extent he also defended the Platonic theory of ideas for a smaller circle of pupils.[5] Under Carneades of Cyrene (214–129) the war against the Stoa widened into a polemic against all conceivable schools of philosophy. Carneades, who went to Rome as a member of the philosophers' embassy in 155, directed the Academy from that date to 137. He did not leave any writings; pupils, especially Clitomachus, recorded his doctrine.

The realization that in such a general polemic the Academy was losing its footing, led under Philo of Larissa to a reaction. He restricted his battle to the Stoic notion of truth and restored the Platonic one to its rightful position. During the Mithradatic war he fled to Rome, where as a teacher he gained a

---

[1] The fragments in A. KÖRTE, *N. Jahrb. Suppl.* 17, 1890, 531, with the notes in WOLFG. SCHMID, *Reallex. f. Ant. u. Chr.* 5, 1961, 703.

[2] The fragments in K. KROHN, Diss. Berl. 1921.

[3] On the various ancient divisions of the Academy O. GIGON, 'Zur Gesch. der sog. Neuen Akademie'. *Mus. Helv.* 1, 1944, 62.

[4] Gigon lays the basis for this opinion in the important essay mentioned in the previous note. On Arcesilaus' poems: P. VON DER MÜHLL, *Studi in onore di U. Paoli.* Florence 1955, 717.

[5] Material in GIGON, *v. sup.* 55.

determining influence over Cicero.[1] Antiochus of Ascalon,[2] whom Cicero heard in Rome, went much further than Philo. He wanted to bridge the gap to as many systems as possible and sought the way to true Platonism through a conspectus of the early Academic, Stoic and Peripatetic tradition. Cicero (*Ac.* 1. 132) characterized him with his observation that he was called *Academicus*, but that he needed to change only a little to become *germanissimus Stoicus*. Through such an exaggerated eclecticism he got into opposition to Philo and so into a controversy which is an example of the claims of various schools that they possessed the true Plato. The possibility of such a dispute is deeply rooted in the aspects of Platonic philosophy. The one of the mystic vision remains far in the background during this period; in a later epoch of Platonism it will come to the fore with greater force.

Among important Peripatetics of the early time of the school we have already met Eudemus, Aristoxenus and Dicaearchus in connection with Aristotle. There we also learned of Theophrastus of Eresus in Lesbos as his student, collaborator and friend since Assos. When Aristotle died in 322, he could find no better successor than this companion of his investigations. Theophrastus headed the school until he died in 288/287 or 287/286 at the age of 85. The prosperity of the Peripatos in this period – the tradition mentions a total number of 2000 students – is indicative of his personal popularity. Even though he was a metic, he managed to acquire property through the intermediacy of Demetrius of Phalerum, and an action for impiety, brought against him by Hagnonides between 319 and 315, miscarried completely, and so concluded this inglorious chapter in the history of Athens. To a large extent it was the momentum of Theophrastus' protest which strengthened the resistance to the attack against the freedom of teaching by philosophers, undertaken by a certain Sophocles (*v.* p. 551). When he was carried to his grave, the city showed by its mourning how important he had been there. His will was preserved by Diogenes Laertius in Book 5 of his history of philosophy, which, with its biography and register of works, is our most important source for Theophrastus.

His tremendous work shows the same universality as that of his master. The conformity of the subject-matter with which they dealt is plainly discernible from the recurrence of such titles as *Analytica*,[3] *Topics*, *Poetics* and themes like physics, meteorology or zoology. His scientific publications are, like those of Aristotle, closely connected with his lecturing activity; of this we have valuable testimony in a letter to Phaenias in Diog. Laert. (5. 37).[4]

Even the little that has been preserved of Theophrastus attest to the breadth of his interests. Entirely within the scope of Aristotelian scientific research are

---

[1] A. WEISCHE, *Cicero und die Neue Akademie. Untersuchungen zu Entstehung und Geschichte des Antiken Skeptizismus.* Munster 1961 (Orbis antiquus H. 18).

[2] A. LUEDER, *Die philos. Persönlichkeit des Antiochos von Askalon.* Diss. Gött. 1940. G. LUCK, *Der Akademiker Antiochos. Noctes Romanae* 7. 1953. Further ref. in A. WLOSOK, *Laktanz und die philos. Gnosis. Abh. Ak. Heidelb. Phil.-hist. Kl.* 1960/2, 50, n. 2. On Philo: K. V. FRITZ, *RE* 19, 1938, 2535.

[3] J. M. BOCHENSKI, *La Logique de Théophraste.* Fribourg 1947.

[4] On the interpretation Regenbogen, *RE* S 7, 1940, 1359, 36.

the two botanical works: *Botany* in nine books (Περὶ φυτικῶν ἱστοριῶν α'-θ') and the six books *On the Causes of Plants* (Φυτικῶν αἰτιῶν α'-ς'). The mutual relation of these works is similar to that of Aristotle's *Zoology* to the aetiological works in the province of zoology, although differences can be detected which have a bearing on Theophrastus' personality generally. His stronger inclination toward empiricism is connected with a reserve with regard to speculative solutions and constructive synthesis. Instead of firmly defined demarcations we often find gradual transitions. But the scientific worker is by far predominant in him over the philosopher in that he develops a problem in all its dimensions while renouncing a definite solution. Whole series of problems, like those in the works on plants, but also in the fragments of other works, are characteristic of this attitude. In the authoritative monograph of his *RE*-article, Regenbogen shows that we must not overrate either Theophrastus' personal fieldwork or the importance of Alexander's expedition, but rather that these works owe a great deal to a well-established tradition and various channels of information. It is important for the history of botany[1] that Theophrastus is the first author whose botanical scientific interests are not dominated by medicine.

Besides these two works there are the *Characters* ('Ηθικοὶ χαρακτῆρες) with totally different subject-matter; we mentioned this work earlier in connection with Menander (p. 644). Here Theophrastus brings together thirty sketches of personalities, types which have been portrayed in a life-like manner and differentiated with great subtlety, whose generally human weaknesses are presented in motley Athenian dress. The preface and the moralizing epilogues are spurious additions. The question of the purpose of the opuscule has not yet been satisfactorily answered, a fact which should not detract from our delight in so much striking observation. It should be borne in mind, however, that Theophrastus was not the only one to write such sketches. In his treatise Περὶ κακιῶν Philodemus preserved samples of character-sketches by Ariston of Ceos. This seems to be a work about dietetics for the soul. Does this permit us to draw conclusions with respect to Theophrastus?[2]

[1] A survey of the history of Greek botany is found in the introduction to MARGARET H. THOMPSON, *Textes grecs inédits relatifs aux plantes*. Paris 1935, with bibl. It is difficult to date these texts, but they are generally of a late date; of course this does not apply to the tradition passed on in them. V. R. STROMBERG, *Griech. Pflanzennamen*. Göteborgs högskolas årsskrift 46/1, 1940.

[2] Recent editions: *I caratteri* a cura di E. Levi. Milan 1956. M. F. GALIANO, *Los caracteres* Ed. biling. Madrid 1956. G. PASQUALI, *I caratteri*. Testo, introd., trad. e comm. 2nd ed. Florence 1956 (prod. by V. DE FALCO. Abundant bibl. references). P. STEINMETZ, *Th.s Charaktere herausg. u. erkl.* Wort der Antike 7, 2 vols. Munich 1960, 1962. R. GLENN USSHER. *Th. The Characters with introd. comm. and index.* Lond. 1960. – REGENBOGEN, *v. sup.* 1507 ff. on its purpose. Doubt expressed by WOLFG. SCHMID, *Der Hellenismus* (v. p. 672 n. 3), 77, 1. Useful on Peripatetic depiction of character. W. BÜCHNER, 'Über den Begriff der Eironeia'. *Herm.* 76, 1941, 339. D. J. FURLEY, 'The Purpose of Th.s Characters'. *Symb. Osl.* 30, 1950, 56, again takes up the theory propounded by O. IMMISCH, *Phil.* 57, 1898, 193, that it is a parergon to Theophrastus' rhetorical works in order to illuminate theoretical instruction with practical examples. Otherwise P. STEINMETZ, 'Der Zweck der Charaktere Th.s'. *Ann. Univ. Saraviensis. Phil. Lettres* 8/3, 1959, 209, with good survey of the history of the problem; id., 'Menander u. Th.'. *Rhein. Mus.* 103, 1960, 185. He considers the *Characters*

From among Theophrastus' remaining works mention was made in the section on Aristotle (p. 576) of his fundamental doxography Φυσικῶν δόξαι. The attribution of the fragment De Sensibus to the great work, which was long confidently defended, has become dubious,[1] but the combination of a discussion with excellent criticism, which can be detected in this fragment, was no doubt the structural principle of this doxography.

Brief mention will be made of only two more of Theophrastus' many spheres of activity. In addition to his numerous investigations into ethical problems, there are those on religion and cult. From excerpts in the second book of Porphyry's De Abstinentia we get some idea of the treatise On Piety (Περὶ εὐσεβείας). Theophrastus was led to reject many follies, especially blood-thirsty sacrifices, by a belief that worship should be profoundly serious; he assumed that such practices had developed from an innocuous origin and was also convinced that all living beings were connected by a natural kinship.

Theophrastus occupied himself exhaustively with rhetoric, and in this respect it was especially his doctrine of the four virtutes dicendi (ἑλληνισμός, σαφήνεια, πρέπον, κατασκευή) which had further influence. J. Stroux[2] extracted these from Cicero, Orat. 75 ff.[3] Unfortunately, it is impossible to make any positive statements about the treatise Περὶ ἱστορίας, but it is likely that Theophrastus dealt with theoretical questions of historiography.[4]

For a long time scholarship was preoccupied with Aristotle at the expense of Theophrastus, but some present-day scholars, especially Regenbogen, have done him more justice and have shown in how many points he was independent, as, for instance, in his doctrine of judgments, the conception of the soul,[5] his criticism of Aristotle's notion of space, to mention only a few. In general he is the great continuator of Aristotle's work: he was also responsible for carrying further the emancipation of individual branches of science from philosophy, which was to be completed in Alexandria.

The scientific spirit of the Peripatos was also maintained by Theophrastus' successor Straton of Lampsacus who, under Democritus' influence, inclined toward a purely physical explanation of phenomena and a monistic image of the universe. He was particularly interested in physiological functions; as such he

to be a polemic in the meaning of the Aristotelian θεωρία against an ethically directed philosophy, by showing the unchanging nature of average people. In the face of these varying opinions it seems permissible to wonder whether these splendid παίγνια have indeed a sharply definable purpose.

[1] REGENBOGEN, v. sup. 1399, 56 and 1537, 26.

[2] De Theophrasti virtutibus dicendi. Leipz. 1912. Also F. WEHRLI, Phyllobolia für Peter von der Mühll. Basel 1946, 29.

[3] There is some reason to conjecture that Hamb. Pap. 128 (Griech. Pap. der Hamburger Staats- u. Univ. Bibl. Hamb. 1954, 36), written before 250 B.C. (cf. Arch. Pap. Forsch. 16, 1959, 108), originated from Theophrastus' Περὶ λέξεως. On fragments of Theophrastus' treatise On Music in the works of the medieval philosopher Sakrastani, who wrote in Arabic: FR. ALTHEIM and R. STIEHL, Gesch. d. Hunnen 3, Berl. 1961, 131.

[4] Cf. F. W. WALBANK, Gnom. 29, 1957, 418.

[5] Cf. also E. BARBOTIN, La Théorie aristotélicienne de l'intellect d'après Théophraste. Louvain 1954 (with abundant bibl.).

also understood spiritual life, and so he denied that there was any immortal part of the soul. He also saw all zoological phenomena in this context, whether it was procreation, embryology or monster-births. Lycon, who directed the school for forty-four years, devoted his attention to its outside influence; nor did Ariston of Ceos manage to inspire it with new life. His successor Critolaus is known as a member of the philosophers' embassy, which caused so much admiration and opposition in Rome in 155. He also contributed to the altercation with rhetoric. But it was not until Andronicus of Rhodes, who led the school from about 70–50, that its work once more provided a stimulus through its publication of Aristotle's textbooks (v. p. 579).

The broad scope of the literature which flourished in this soil is connected with Peripatetic interests, which from the beginning extended beyond purely philosophical problems. The most impressive example of this is Demetrius of Phalerum, Theophrastus' pupil and, as Cassander's trusty, regent of the city in the quality of Epimeletes from 317–307. His sensible and moderate rule during which he did not disavow his interest in philosophy[1] was cut short by Demetrius Poliorcetes. He first fled to Thebes and then went on to the court of Ptolemy I, perhaps after a sojourn in Macedon. It is not possible to assess precisely his share in the cultural policy of Ptolemy and in the founding of the Museum and the Library, but it must have been considerable. At his advice Ptolemy called to Egypt Straton, the Peripatetic and later director of the school, as a teacher for his children; the connection of the Peripatos with Alexandria can be observed in this as well. The succession to the throne of Ptolemy Philadelphus was fateful for Demetrius; he was expelled from court and died in Upper Egypt.

We already met Demetrius as the editor of a collection of Aesop's fables (p. 155) and of maxims of the seven sages (p. 157). This characterized the interests of this ruler, who organized readings of Homer's poems at the Thymelian Games and wrote commentaries on the *Iliad*, the *Odyssey* and on *Homericus*. The numerous titles known testify to a literary activity which covered philosophy, rhetoric, history and politics. In a systematic study of Athenian political organization (Περὶ τῆς ᾿Αθήνησι νομοθεσίας) and a description of the constitutions of the city and their chronology (Περὶ τῶν ᾿Αθήνησι πολιτειῶν) we see him following Aristotle's footsteps. The *Record of Archons* was in the nature of a chronicle; in the works *On the Ten Years* (Περὶ δεκαετίας) and *On the Constitution* (Περὶ πολιτείας) he gave an account of his régime. Sometimes he used the form of the dialogue. Diogenes Laertius (5. 76) also contains evidence[2] of paeans to Serapis, who cured his eyes.

The treatise *On Style* (Περὶ ἑρμηνείας),[3] a work of the first century A.D. and probably of Peripatetic origin, dealing with rhetorical expression and its aids, is not of Demetrius' hand. The treatise *On Kinds of Letters* (Τύποι ἐπιστολικοί), a dull schematical tractate, is also spurious. Its similarity with a late work imputed to Libanius according to one interpretation, to Proclus in another

---

[1] Cf. E. BAYER's monograph *D. Phalereus der Athener. Tüb. Beitr.* 36, 1942.

[2] Doubts in WEHRLI on fr. 200.

[3] Edition by L. RADERMACHER, Leipz. 1901. Cf. F. SOLMSEN, *Herm.* 66, 1931, 241.

(ἐπιστολιμαῖοι χαρακτῆρες) justifies Wehrli's[1] dating in the early empire against the considerably earlier date of others.

Of the numerous other Peripatetic authors Praxiphanes rouses our curiosity through the information that he undertook the construction of a scientific grammar and was the teacher of Callimachus and Aratus. Callimachus (v. infra) attacked some of his dicta in On Poets and On Poems. In his treatise Περὶ ἱστορίας he probably dealt with theoretical questions, as Theophrastus had done. Clearchus of Soloe was a diligent scribbler, whose work On Forms of Life (Περὶ βίων, 8 books; there is evidence of a similar title for Theophrastus) is as much under Peripatetic influence as an Osteology (Περὶ σκελετῶν). He is of some interest as a representative of the group of Peripatetics who inclined towards the Academy. He praised Plato in an encomium and wrote a commentary on the Republic and possibly another on the Timaeus. He was in opposition to the contemporary rationalism of scientific research, and in this respect he was akin to Heraclides Ponticus, who wrote On Piety and reveals his belief in miracles repeatedly in the surviving fragments. In his treatise Περὶ ὕπνου Praxiphanes introduces Aristotle as one of the speakers in the dialogue, in the course of which he tells of his wonderful experiences in the other world and so converts the scientist to a belief in the immortality of the soul.

Peripatetic writers were particularly active in history and biography and created depositories of tradition which remained influential until the end of antiquity through manifold ramifications. It is curious to note in this field that those who held themselves to be the intellectual successors of Aristotle were wholly devoid of critical awareness in their treatment of this tradition.

More credit is due to those who stayed close to home and initiated the history of the schools of philosophy: Antisthenes of Rhodes and Sotion of Alexandria, who both wrote their Diadochae in the second century B.C. Under Ptolemy VI Philometor, a certain Heraclides Lembos, who also wrote history, excerpted Sotion's voluminous work in six books. The form created by Sotion remained influential up to Diogenes Laertius, who himself is an exponent of the continued Peripatetic tradition.

Peripatetic biography became particularly productive[2] after Aristoxenus, of whom we heard as a theoretician of music (p. 577), had preceded with his biographies. There were various early beginnings of biographical writing in Greek literature. Plato's Apology is often quoted as an example and it may be conjectured that such elements also occurred in the writings of the other

---

[1] On Demetrius fr. 203.

[2] F. LEO, Die griech.-röm. Biographie nach ihrer litt. Form. Leipz. 1901 is still the starting-point. Yet W. STEIDLE, Sueton und die antike Biographie. Zet. 1. Munich 1951 (esp. 166), has justifiably objected against the separation of a Peripatetic biography which describes chronologically while using an artistic form, from a pattern which arranges according to subjects, supposedly originating from the Alexandrian grammarians. Important for the origins of Greek biography, for its difference from the modern version and especially for the ethical-psychological notions of the Peripatos in its tradition: A. DIHLE, Studien zur griech. Biographie. Abh. Ak. Gött. Phil.-hist. Kl. 3. 37, 1956. On Herodotus HELENE HOMEYER, 'Zu den Anfängen der griech. Biographie'. Phil. 106, 1962, 75.

Socratics. Xenophon provides an example of the educational romance with his *Cyropaedia*, and his *Agesilaus* is a sample of encomiastic literature which necessarily contains a great deal of biographical information. Going back even further, scholars have lately quoted biographical elements in Herodotus as examples, especially his stories about Cyrus and Cambyses, and to a less extent those about Miltiades and Themistocles. But these are all mere beginnings and there is no doubt about the vigorous encouragement which biographical writing received from the Peripatos. Two factors especially were influential: in the first place there was an interest in the great thinkers, particularly the founders of the schools, whose lives they wished to interpret as the confirmation of the principles for which they stood; and then, in his ethical writings, Aristotle had shown his interest in the various patterns of behaviour. The Peripatos had also produced a rich literature περὶ βίων, on the choice of life, in which a wealth of examples was an unavoidable element. It was equally inevitable that the anecdotes and the romance tended to occupy considerable room in this sort of literature.

There is evidence that Aristoxenus wrote biographies of Pythagoras, Archytas, Socrates, Plato and Telestes the dithyrambic poet (*v.* p. 414); he also wrote *On the Tragic Poets* and *On Fluteplayers*, but it is doubtful whether these monographs appeared in a collection.[1] A fertile author in this field was Chamaeleon, who wrote on poets of all genres and times in a large number of biographies and also produced numerous other works, such as one *On the Satyr-play* (Περὶ σατύρων). Even authors in whose work biography does not occupy such a large place reveal the delight in anecdotes and legendary material, as, for instance, Phaenias of Eresus in Lesbos, who wrote *On the Sicilian Tyrants* (Περὶ τῶν ἐν Σικελίᾳ τυράννων) and *The Removal of Tyrants as Revenge* (Τυράννων ἀναίρεσις ἐκ τιμωρίας).[2] Hieronymus of Rhodes was involved in a philosophical polemic with Lycon and Arcesilaus for which he also utilized biographical material, though apparently not doing any better than the others. Of biographical writing of this kind we have acquired a shocking example in a papyrus (no. 1135 P.) which is from the sixth book of Satyrus' biographical work and contains parts of the life of Euripides. The dialogue-form of these biographies, which were written in the second century B.C., was new to us; but in their contents we observe an uncritical attitude which was satisfied with any sort of tradition. The biographical material thus produced was passed on by numerous authors – we only mention the Callimachean Hermippus of Smyrna and Ister of Cyrene with their collections and it did not improve in the process. When we complain of the sorry state of ancient biography which had its origin here, and of the decline of the critical spirit, we must not forget one extenuating circumstance: ancient biographers were faced with a poverty of sources which cannot be compared with modern conditions. Therefore any information was welcome, but in particular they squeezed more out of

[1] WEHRLI on fr. 10.

[2] On Phaenias, Theophrastus and the tyranny in Eresus cf. REGENBOGEN (*v.* p. 686 n. 4), 1359, 20.

the works of the poets themselves than these could yield. And the pleasure in romancing which so fertilized the growth of the novel in Ionian soil was a great encouragement for a rich crop of anecdotes.

As a rule only works have been referred to which can complete O. GIGON's bibliography (v. p. 167). Particular attention is directed to *Fifty Years of Class. Scholarship*, Oxf. 1954, 141 ff. and WOLFG. SCHMID's survey in *Der Hellenismus in der deutschen Forschung 1938–1948*. Wiesbaden 1956, 72. For this section: C. J. DE VOGEL, *Greek Philosophy. A Coll. of Texts with Notes and Explanations.* 3: *The Hellenistic-Roman Period.* Leiden 1959. For its subsequent history: H. HAGENDAHL: *Latin Fathers and the Classics*. Göteborg 1958. Further bibl. in the notes.

Cynics: Introduction to the Cynical diatribe in the translation by W. CAPELLE, *Epiktet, Teles und Musonios*. Zürich 1948 (*Bibl. d. alten Welt*). Teles: O. HENSE, *Teletis reliquiae*. 2nd ed. Tüb. 1909 (also important for Bion). Menippus: cf. p. 671, n. 1. Phoenix and Cercidas: A. D. KNOX: *Herodes, Cercidas and the Greek choliambic poets*. London 1929. J. U. POWELL, *Collectanea Alexandrina*, Oxf. 1925, 201. 231. *Anth. Lyr.* D. fasc. 3, p. 124 and 141 with bibl. A. PENNACINI, *Cercida e il secondo cinismo*. Atti di Acad. d. Scienze di Torino, 90, 1955. Cf. p. 671, n. 2. – Timon: H. DIELS, *Poetarum philos. fragmenta*. Berl. 1901, 173.

Stoa: the texts: H. V. ARNIM, *Stoicorum veterum fragmenta*. 4 vols. (Vol. 4 contains indices). Leipz. 1903–1924. M. HADAS, *Essential Works of Stoicism*, New York 1961. The most important study by M. POHLENZ, *Die Stoa, Geschichte einer geistigen Bewegung*. 2 vols. Gött. 1948–49, the 2nd vol. in 2nd ed. 1955. Contains abundant bibl., as well as the important detailed studies by POHLENZ on problems of the Stoa. By the same a translation of the most important evidence with introduction and connecting text: *Stoa und Stoiker*. Zürich 1950 (*Bibl. d. Alten Welt*). Further: F. BARTH – A. GOEDECKEMEYER, *Die Stoa*. 6th ed. Stuttg. 1945. E. HOFFMANN, *Leben und Tod in der stoischen Philosophie*. Heidelb. 1946. R. BULTMANN, *Das Urchristentum im Rahmen der antiken Religionen*. Zürich 1949 (in chap. 4 the ideal of the Stoic sage). G. NEBEL, *Griech. Ursprung*. Wuppertal 1948, 319. E. SCHWARTZ, *Ethik der Griechen*. Stuttg. 1951, 149. Individual Stoics: G. VERBEKE, *Kleanthes von Assos*. Brussels 1949. M. VAN STRAATEN, *Panaetii Rhodii fragmenta*. Leiden 1952; 2nd ed. amplificata 1962. G. PICHT, *Die Grundlagen der Ethik des Panaitios*. Diss. Freib. i. Br. 1942 (not printed). A. GRILLI, 'Studi panezziani'. *Stud. It.* 29, 1957, 31. K. REINHARDT, *RE* 22, 1953, 558–826 gives a large-scale synopsis of Posidonius. His three books on Posidonius are mentioned p. 679, n. 5. A contribution to the collection of fragments of P. announced by L. Edelstein in F. KUDLIEN, 'P. und die Ärzteschule der Pneumatiker'. *Herm.* 90, 1962, 419.

Epicureanism: PH. DE LACY, 'Some recent publications on E. and Epicureanism (1937–54)'. *Class. Weekly* 48, 1954–55, 167. 232. Bibl. also in Gigon's survey (*v. infra*). The best information now supplied by the long Epicurus-article by

WOLFG. SCHMID in the *Reallex. f. Ant. u. Christent.* 5, 1961, 681, which also (816) contains good bibl. and a reference to a complete bibl. prepared by B. HÄSLER. The texts: H. USENER, *Epicurea.* Leipz. 1887. C. BAILEY, *Epicurus.* Oxf. 1926. G. ARRIGHETTI. *Epicuro, Opere.* Turin 1960, especially important for the remnants of the lost works. P. VON DER MÜHLL, *Epicuri epistulae tres et Ratae sententiae.* Leipz. 1922. EMILIE BOER, *Epikur, Briefe an Pythokles.* Berl. (D. Ak. d. Wiss. Inst. f. hellenist. röm. Philos. 3) 1954. C. DIANO, *Epicuri Ethica.* Florence 1946. Herculanean rolls: A. VOGLIANO, *Epicuri et Epicureorum scripta in Herculanensibus papyris servata.* Berl. 1928. In add. K. V. FRITZ, *Gnom.* 8, 1932, 65. An important ethical fragment (*v.* p. 683 n. 1): WOLFG. SCHMID, *Ethical Epicurea. Pap. Herc.* 1251. Leipz. 1939. The letters in Philodemus' πραγματεῖαι: C. DIANO, *Lettere di Epicuro e dei suoi.* Florence 1946. Id., 'Lettere di E. agli amici de Lampsaco a Pitocle e a Mitre.' *Stud. It.* 23, 1948, 59. A. VOGLIANO, 'I resti dell' XV. libro del Περὶ φύσεως di E. Aus dem Nachlass herausg. von B. Häsler'. *Phil.* 100, 1956, 253. The numerous separate editions of Philodemus' writings in R. PHILIPPSON's authoritative article on this Epicurean, *RE* 19, 1938, 2444. On Epicurea in Egyptian papyri *v.* P. under Epicurus. In add. the Heidelberger. pap. (Inv. 1740); cf. WOLFG. SCHMID, *Der Hellenismus in der deutschen Forschung 1938–1948.* Wiesbaden 1956, 79. The inscription of Oenoanda: J. WILLIAM, Leipz. 1907. A. GRILLI, *Diogenis Oenoandensis fragmenta.* Milan-Varese 1960 (*Testi e documenti per lo studio dell' antichità* 2). Papers: Leading work in WOLFG. SCHMID's abovementioned Epicurus-article with excellent treatment of the related problems. The following represents only a limited selection: E. BIGNONE, *L'Aristotele perduto e la formazione filosofica di Epicuro.* 2 vols., Florence 1936. A. J. FESTUGIÈRE, *Épicure et ses dieux.* Paris 1946 (Engl. Oxf. 1955). Important essays on this theme: p. 684, n. 1 f. E. SCHWARTZ (*v.* on Stoa). ROMANO AMERIO, *L'epicureismo.* Turin 1953. N. W. DE WITT. *E. and his philosophy.* Minneapolis 1954 (problematical; cf. PH. MERLAN, *Philos. Rev.* 64, 1955, 140. G. FREYMUTH, *Deutsch. Lit. Zeit.* 78, 1957, H.I. W. KULLMANN, *Gymn.* 64, 1957, 271 with bibl.). Important comprehensive criticism by WOLFG. SCHMID, *Gnom.* 27, 1955, 405. A. CRESSON, *Épicure, sa vie, son œuvre.* 3rd ed. Paris 1958. Univ. of Genoa, Fac. of Arts. *Epicurea in memoriam Hectoris Bignone. Miscellanea Philologica.* Ist. di Filol. Class. 1959 (numerous contrib. of Ital. scholars, of WOLFG. SCHMID and R. FLACELIÈRE). PH. MERLAN, *Studies in Epicurus and Aristotle.* Wiesbaden 1960 (*Klass.-phil. Stud.* 22). Vogliano's work on the Herculanensia in the two vols. *Prolegomena,* Rome 1952/3. The same 'Gli studi fil. epicurei nell' ultimo cinquantennio'. *Mus. Helv.* 11, 1954, 188. Excellent information in WOLFG. SCHMID's 'Zur Geschichte der herkulanischen Studien'. *Parola del passato* 45, 1955, 478. On the technical aspect of the edition: O. LUSCHNAT, *Zum Text von Philodems Schrift De musica.* Berl. (D. Ak. d. Wiss. Inst. f. hellenist.-röm. Philos. 1) 1953. An analysis of this work by A. Jeanette Neubecker in no. 6, 1956 of this series. On the language: H. WIDMANN, *Beiträge zur Syntax E's.* Tüb. Beitr. 24, 1935. C. BRESCIA, *Ricerche sulla lingua e sullo stilo di E.* Naples 1955.

Translations: O. GIGON, *E. von der Überwindung der Furcht.* Zürich 1949 (*Bibl. d. Alten Welt,* with valuable introduction.) J. MEWALDT, *E. Philosophie der*

Freude. Stuttg. 1949. Ital.: E. BIGNONE, Bari 1924. R. SAMMARTANO, *Epicuro, Etica. Opere e framm. In app. la vita di Epicuro di Diogene Laerzio.* Trad. e note. Bologna 1959. – *Lexicon Philodemeum* by C. J. VOOYS and D. A. KREVELEN, Purmerend 1934–41.

Academy: Besides the works mentioned in p. 685 n. 3 and p. 686 n. 2. Pohlenz in his *Stoa* (*v. supra*) I, 174 and 187. S. MEKLER, *Academicorum philosophorum index Herculanensis* 1902 in photo-reprint Berl. 1958.

Peripatos: For Theophrastus O. REGENBOGEN's article *RE* 7, 1940, 1353–1562 is still the authoritative monograph, containing editions and collections of fragments. The *Botany*, biling. by A. F. HORT, 2 vols. *Loeb Class. Libr.* 1916. Editions of *Characters* and bibl. p. 687 n. 2.

On the bibl. in Regenbogen and the above-mentioned bibls.: G. M. A. GRUBE, 'Th. as a literary Critic'. *Trans. a. Proc. of the Am. Phil. Ass.* 83, 1952, 172. J. H. H. A. INDEMANS, *Studiën over Th.* Diss. Amsterd. 1953; cf. F. DIRLMEIER, *Gnom.* 26, 1954, 508. H. STROHM, 'Th. und Poseidonios'. *Herm.* 81, 1953, 278. G. SENN, *Die Pflanzenkunde des Th. von Eresos, seine Schrift über die Unterscheidungsmerkmale der Pflanzen und seine Kunstprosa.* Basel 1956. On the metaphysics: J. TRICOT, *Théophraste. La Métaphysique.* Trad. et notes. Paris 1948. W. THEILER, *Mus. Helv.* 15, 1958, 102. The remaining Peripatetics of some importance have now been made accessible through F. Wehrli's great collection of fragments with comm.: *Die Schule des Aristoteles:* 1. *Dikaiarchos.* Basel 1944. 2. *Aristoxenos.* 1945. 3. *Klearchos.* 1948. 4. *Demetrios von Phaleron.* 1949. 5. *Straton von Lampsakos.* 1950. 6. *Lykon und Ariston von Keos.* 1952. 7. *Herakleides Pontikos.* 1953. 8. *Eudemos von Rhodos.* 1955. 9. *Phainias von Eresos. Chamaileon. Praxiphanes.* 1957. 10. *Hieronymos von Rhodos. Kritolaos und seine Schule. Rückblick, Der Peripatos in vorchristlicher Zeit. Register.* 1959, with an excellent exposition of the swift disintegration of the Peripatos; although its ontology and ethics made it unsuitable for either exclusiveness or for recruiting new members, the very versatility of its empiricism provided a good deal of incentive for Alexandrian science.

B The New Centres

I GENERAL CHARACTERISTICS

In the image of the Hellenistic age Athens, the Porch and the Garden are overshadowed by the great kingdoms which assumed Alexander's legacy and developed new forms of political, economic and intellectual life. This epoch, like any other, is not marked off by clearly drawn boundaries, either with regard to its beginning or its end. In previous sections we have time and again pointed out that the Hellenistic era was anticipated in various fields and it is understandable that many authors place its beginning a good while before Alexander.[1] But it was the Macedonian conqueror who first burst open the gate to all the new roads, so that it is still sensible to date its beginning in the time when the effects

[1] R. LAQUEUR, *Hellenismus.* Giessen 1925, makes the period begin with the 4th century, H. BENGTSON, *Griech. Gesch.* 2nd ed. Munich 1960, 285, in 360.

of his achievements became apparent. On the other hand, it can be shown with good reason that the culture of the Empire also forms part of this period. There is no need to overestimate the Hellenistic elements which remained effective up to the decline of antiquity; and profound changes, such as the extension of the Roman political organization or the Atticist reaction in literature, indicate the need for a break. A significant date for this is the year 30, in which the last of the Hellenistic kingdoms came under the rule of Rome with the fall of Alexandria.

The Hellenistic age is historically important in that it conclusively overthrew the narrow limits of the polis and opened up the whole inhabited world for the Greeks to settle and spread their civilization. The tremendous influence of Greek culture on that of Rome is part of this movement; it did not lead to its Hellenization, but the clash of ideas was fruitful and produced the first humanism of the western world. It affected the West in a different way from the East, where in turn its development showed considerable varieties according to countries and peoples. Sociologically the most important question is that concerned with the nature, extent and depth of the mingling of the immigrant Greeks with the indigenous population. With regard to the Ptolemies and the Seleucids it may be stated that initially they did not think of adopting Alexander's policy of fusion which found such tangible expression in the mass-wedding at Susa. In Egypt as in Syria powerful regents were supported by a class in which the Macedonians, numerically too weak, were supplemented by numerous Greeks. In this first period, aptly called 'Hochhellenismus' by R. Pfeiffer,[1] which lasted until about 250, this top class, which formed the prop of the government, cannot be said to have fused to any great extent with the foreign nations. As for Egypt, it has been correctly pointed out that the extensive correspondence of the Zenonpapyri of the middle of the third century does not produce any combination of Greek and Egyptian names. This corresponds with the tight coherence within the Greek stratum. It is vouched for by the educational system and especially by the gymnasium,[2] while the influence of the theatre should not be underestimated either, since every town of any importance possessed one. The uncommonly active and varied club-life of the time[3] attests the feelings of solidarity which united the Greeks abroad.

All these things are important. They support and explain the observation which we derive directly from the evidence preserved that the intellectual culture of the Hellenistic age in the time of its most significant achievements was utterly Greek. At most an indication of some religious fusion can be observed. It is well known that Ptolemy I created and propagated the Sarapis-cult; Osiris-Apis was brought to Alexandria from Memphis, where he was Hellenized to a certain extent by means of a temple and statue.[4] Later this cult,

---

[1] *Deutsche Lit. Zeit.* 1925, 2136.

[2] H. J. MARROU, *Histoire de l'éducation dans l'antiquité*, 3rd ed. Paris 1955. M. P. NILSSON, *Die hellenistische Schule.* Munich 1955. Good survey in W. SCHUBART, *Die Griechen in Ägypten Beih. z. Alten Orient* 10, Leipz. 1927.

[3] M. SAN NICOLÒ, *Ägypt. Vereinswesen zur Zeit der Ptolemäer und Römer.* 1, Munich 1913; 2/1, 1915. Other bibl. in Bengtson (*v.* p. 694 n. 1), 444.

[4] This particular in NILSSON, *Gesch. d. gr. Rel.* 2, 2nd ed. Munich 1961, 156.

together with that of Isis, spread far and wide, but in the world of Callimachus and Apollonius Rhodius these gods have practically no meaning. It is still dominated by the ancient Olympians, and though they may no longer inspire faith, they are still indispensable elements of their poetry.

Hellenistic art and science is mainly connected with Alexandria, the great conqueror's foundation on the western arm of the Nile-delta. Even if the proportions of the tradition – in Egypt alone the dry desert-sand provided the conditions for the preservation of papyri – tend to make the differences appear greater, there can still be no doubt that the Egypt of the Ptolemies was far superior to the great realm of the Seleucids in activity and productivity of its intellectual life. Two reasons suggest themselves directly, of which we place the generous provisions of the Ptolemies first. We already made mention of the founding of the Museum, a scientific workshop which permitted scholars in all fields to carry on research far from daily worries and political upheavals (p. 3), when we discussed the gigantic library of this institute and its vicissitudes. In addition the varying conditions of settlement should be borne in mind. While the Greek population of Egypt settled mainly in some density on the lower course of the Nile, in a relatively restricted area, they spread in the realm of the Seleucids from the Aegean on to the Hindu Kush over enormous areas. A simple calculation shows that even in the big cities of this realm, such as Antioch on the Orontes, Seleucia on the Tigris and the city of the same name in Pieria, the Greek stratum cannot have been very strong.

The Macedonian kingdom of the Antigonids did not have a direct share in the intellectual activity of the period which demands special mention. When Athens was occasionally occupied by the Macedonians, life, as we saw, went on as usual. Besides Alexandria, Pergamum should at least be seriously considered, although it did not begin to flourish until a good deal later. The defeat of Antiochus III near Magnesia on the Sipylus (190) enabled the small state of Pergamum to become a large power which ruled almost all of Asia Minor, though of course this was largely due to its friendship with Rome. Under the ambitious Attalids this political rise went hand in hand with a splendid development of the arts and sciences. The new role of Pergamum demonstrates clearly how the emphasis had shifted in the time following the peak of the Hellenistic era.[1] No longer did Alexandria predominate as before: the coastal and island fortresses developed and maintained by the Ptolemies could no longer be protected by a strong navy, financial strength declined, pressure on the other Successor-kingdoms decreased. Under Antiochus III Antioch rose to a high cultural peak, even if the fall of Seleucid power was not far off. The town reached the top of its development later under the Roman empire. But Rhodes, which managed to maintain its freedom even in periods of the heaviest pressure of the

[1] P. PÉDECH, *Erasmus* 1960, 47, makes some stimulating observations about the periods of the Hellenistic age. He describes the period of 250–168 as *moyen hellénisme*, characterized by a new susceptibility, emotional and realistic, occasionally inclined toward the baroque; he considers the years 168–30 as the last section, a time of intellectual reaction, of consolidation of earlier results and of synthesis in various fields.

Ptolemies, took a leading position with a vigorous intellectual life. We shall come across the island in connection with the names of poets, thinkers and orators; great Romans visited it to study there.

From the foregoing it will have become clear that the Hellenistic age displays a great variety of aspects. Its characterization defies any formula, but a number of essential features can be inferred from the historical fact that now the polis as the fixed centre which controlled people's ideas and mode of living definitely belongs to the past. Many Greek cities, especially the ones in Asia Minor, managed to maintain various degrees of independence at various times within the kingdoms of the Successors; but this does not alter the fact that in the centres of Hellenistic culture itself forces of a totally different nature were at work.

The lack of a fixed centre corresponds with the broadening of strong contrasts in the new proportions and forms of life. One of the most striking features of the Hellenistic age is its tendency towards large dimensions in which there seems to be some legacy of the spirit of Alexander. The newly founded cities were of gigantic proportions and their Hippodamian method of construction (v. p. 527) made long rows of streets cross one another at right angles; Alexandria exceeds everything with its artificial port-installations, the lighthouse on the island of Pharos, a work by Sostratus of Cnidos, which was later counted among the wonders of the world, and the royal quarter which with the buildings for the court, the barracks, the chancelleries, the museum and a theatre formed a city within the big city. In Achilles Tatius' description of Alexandria (5. 1) the greatness of the impression which the visitor received can still be detected in spite of the rhetoric. The architect Dinocrates had a dominant share in the planning and building of the city; his name is connected with a project which is characteristic like none other for the megalomaniac characteristics of the Hellenistic age; Mount Athos was to be carved into one huge statue of Alexander; in the one hand he was to carry a city, while he would let the waters of the mountain flow from the other. The same tendency is expressed in many other instances, such as the Helios-colossus of Rhodes, the gigantic procession of Ptolemy Philadelphus,[1] in Hiero II's huge freight-vessel, in the tremendous siege-engines. And yet this same time developed a playful delight in the diminutive and the dainty; it was the first to discover the individuality of the child in body and nature,[2] and created products of the art of the miniature.

The Hellenistic era is the time in which Greek science reaches its climax in the conception of the heliocentrical system by Aristarchus of Samos. At the same time, however, we see superstition rife, although it prevailed in the other stratum, which fused together a great variety of elements, to a large extent of non-Greek origin. In Theocritus' *Pharmaceutria* we have impressive proof that at that time its subsequent widespread occurrence was being anticipated. But in one case the two contrasting aspects just mentioned met to produce an illegitimate

---

[1] In honour of the θεοὶ σωτῆρες Ptolemy I and Berenice, instituted in 279 or 270. On the dating Nilsson (*v. sup.*), 159, 4. Elaborate description by Callixinus in Ath. 5, 196 ff.

[2] H. HERTER, 'Das Kind im Zeitalter des Hellenismus'. *Bonner Jahrb.* 132, 1927, 250.

child of sinister vitality. Nilsson[1] justifiably claimed in explanation of the rise of astrology as a well-organized pseudo-science that the ancient Chaldaean belief in stars in Hellenistic Egypt was elaborated by the Greeks into the detailed system which has maintained its power over people's minds up to the present day.[2] In the time of the Ptolemies an astrological work, a regular Domesday book of this ineradicable pseudo-science, was written, which appeared under the twin-name of Nechepso-Petosiris[3] and which found a great following, just as the book ascribed to Hermes Trismegistus.[4]

Another paradox which seems to us to be characteristic of the Hellenistic era is that to an even greater extent than in the fourth century the individual has freed himself from the ties of tradition; generally all he asks of the state (it can hardly be called the community any longer) is that it guarantees him peace and personal security. But at the same time, in spite of individualism, a certain external uniformity begins to become apparent. However splendid the Hellenistic architecture of Pergamum or Miletus may appear to us, in the numerous little Greek cities of the time temples, colonnades, theatres, gymnasiums and baths came out of the same mould of a classicism which had come to a standstill. Thus in the later Hellenistic era we see an anticipation of the uniformity which passed on to Roman provincial building generally only little variety of style.

In the sphere of language the tension between various directions also becomes evident. The Hellenistic age completed a development which left to the individual dialects only a restricted local usage or an occasional literary role, while Koine[5] assumes a dominant position as the means of intercourse throughout the new kingdoms. The era of Athenian hegemony had already given to Attic Greek a corresponding dominance and expansion, in which the close contacts with the Ionian territories of Asia Minor were not without influence. The decisive fact was that the Macedonian overlords or a new era made 'the Ionized Great-Attic dialect, stripped of some striking peculiarities' (Schwyzer) into the official language and guaranteed its diffusion in the states of the Diadochi. In this time social differentiation is still, of course, an important factor.

---

[1] (v. sup.), 268 with bibl. A. J. FESTUGIÈRE, La Révélation d'Hermès Trismégiste I. L'astrologie et les sciences occultes. Paris 1950. A good introduction by BOLL-BEZOLD-GUNDEL, Sternglaube und Sterndeutung. 4th ed. Leipz. 1931. A good deal also in F. H. CRAMER, Astrology in Roman Law and Politics. Memoirs of the Am. Philos. Soc. 37. Philadelphia 1954.

[2] The part played by Egyptian elements is difficult to assess, cf. H. G. GUNDEL, Gnom. 28, 1956, 371.

[3] On a dating immediately before 150 B.C. now W. BURKERT, Phil. 105, 1961, 30. On contents and evaluation A. WLOSOK, Laktanz und die philosophische Gnosis. Abh. Ak. Heidelb. Phil.-hist. Kl. 1960/2, 35. According to a fragment in the prooemium of Book 6 of VETTIUS VALENS' Anthologiae Nechepso was carried off by a divine being and taken for a heavenly ride through the astral universe.

[4] The sorry mass of tradition of later times is made accessible by the Catalogus codicum astrologorum Graecorum. Brussels since 1898. Latest St. Weinstock 9/1, 1951; 9/2 1953: Codices Britannici. The vols. of the Catalogus also contain selected texts.

[5] Best survey in E. SCHWYZER, Griech. Gramm. 1, Munich 1939, 116. In add. L. RADERMACHER, Koine. Sitzber. Ak. Wien. Phil.-hist. Kl. 224/5, 1947. J. PALM, Über Sprache und Stil des Diodoros von Sizilien. Lund 1955, 194 (general points of view). V. PISANI in: Encicl. Class. Ser. II. Vol. 5, T. 1. Soc. Ed. Int. 1960, 113.

There is a difference between popular Koine and standard Hellenistic prose; in authors of the late fourth century its beginnings are already apparent and its development is completed by 250. Our most important sources of evidence are Polybius and Diodorus, apart from some scientific authors such as Apollonius of Perga or Philo of Byzantium and historical papyri.

While in this way a certain standardization of the linguistic forms was carried through in everyday Hellenistic life, including the activity of a considerable administrative organization, we find in another sphere of linguistic life a tendency toward the extraordinary, exaggerated, almost baroque. Early in the third century a reaction arose against Isocrates' period with its symmetrical construction and ready intelligibility. Attempts were made to avoid these qualities of the Attic school and to replace these by the new style, mainly elaborated in Asia Minor; it affected a conscious restlessness of style by means of a rapid succession of brief clauses and, in imitation of Gorgias, through an unnatural accumulation of words that excited with sense or sound. The new style is supposed to have been originated by Hegesias of Magnesia of whom Cicero (Or. 226) says uncharitably that once you knew him, there was no need to look any further for a man of bad taste. Hegesias also made an attempt at writing a history of Alexander and thus contributed to the infection of historiography with this abstruse style. Cicero, who witnessed the flourishing in Rome of Asianism in Hortensius Hortalus, divides (Brutus 325) it into two forms, one of which aimed at daintiness without depth of thought, the other at a grand loftiness. The long inscription of Antiochus I of Commagene on the Nemrud Dagh in Taurus[1] gives an impressive example of the latter.

Our brief survey served to bring out the diversity of phenomena and the great internal unrest of this age. Particularly in the initial period the Hellenistic era was a time of great independent achievements in many fields. But in later antiquity it failed to carry on in the same way to elaborate these achievements. Much of the gain fell into oblivion or its growth was arrested; from this point of view this time appears to be one of transition which brought important developments to conclusion, at the same time breaking ground for the entirely new and different growth which came into the world with Christianity.

Good survey in w. w. TARN, Hellenistic Civilisation, 3rd ed. (by G. Th. Griffith), London 1952. M. ROSTOVTZEFF, Social and Economic History of the Hellenistic World. 3 vols. Oxf. 1941, is the standard work. V. EHRENBERG, Der Staat der Griechen II. Der hellenistische Staat. Leipz. 1958. Id., The Greek State, Oxf. 1960. A. B. RANOWITSCH, Der Hellenismus und seine geschichtliche Rolle. (transl. from the Russian) Berlin 1958. A. J. TOYNBEE, Hellenism. The History of a Civilisation. Lond. 1959. (The Home Univ. Libr. vol. 238); also V. EHRENBERG, Historia 8, 1959, 491. F. SCHACHERMEYR, Griech. Geschichte. Stuttg. 1960, 323.

[1] Orientis Graec. Inscr. I, 383. JALABERT ET MOUTERDE, Inscr. gr. et lat. de la Syrie I, no. I. Stylistic analysis: E. NORDEN, Die antike Kunstprosa I, 1898, 141.

On Alexander's intellectual influence A. HEUSS, *Ant. u. Abendl.* 4, 1954, 65. Very useful bibl. in H. BENGTSON, *Griech. Gesch.* 2nd ed. Munich 1960, 415 and 443, and in the collective work *Der Hellenismus in der deutschen Forschung 1938–1948.* Wiesbaden 1956. Vol. 4 of the *Historia Mundi,* Bern 1956, contains a stimulating synopsis by A. AYMARD and F. GSCHNITZER. – On religion: M. P. NILSSON, *Gesch. d. gr. Rel.* 2nd ed. Munich 1961. V. GRÖNBECH, *Der Hellenismus. Lebensbestimmung. Weltmacht.* Gött. 1953 (abbreviated transl. of the Danish work *Hellenismen*) stands alone. In this book the Empire is projected on to one surface with what we call the Hellenistic age and in a most one-sided manner the individual's care of his soul is made into the guiding principle. F. SUSEMIHL, *Gesch. der griech. Lit. in der Alexanderzeit.* 2 vols. Leipz. 1891/2 is still important for the whole literature of this period because of its copious material.

2 CALLIMACHUS

What we learned in the preceding section about the Asianic reaction against the classical prose of Isocrates may be in itself not very attractive, but it did reveal one definite fact; there was no inclination to be satisfied with an imitation of approved models of an unnecessary classicism. The era had enough individual vitality to develop new trends of style. The same process took place in the province of poetry, but the new style, achieved and perfected by poets like Callimachus and Theocritus, was strong enough to escape being overwhelmed by subsequent classicist coatings.

The poets mentioned belonged to a circle whose activity falls within a very limited period of the Hellenistic era. It is not a coincidence that it corresponds largely with the reign of Ptolemy II Philadelphus (285 co-regent, 283 sole regent until 247). This king did not only take care of the library and the museum as his father before him; he tied the leading figures more closely to the court and made this the centre of a cultural life with an Alexandrian character which maintained its independence within the Hellenistic civilization while still forming part of it. His sister-consort Arsinoe II had a decisive influence on this development. But the share which the court played was only one strand in the rich texture of this art. Its close affinity with learning was more important, and this is most clearly evident when science and poetry meet in one person. This literature does not address itself to the many, it postulates a great deal which is disclosed only to the expert, its language both avoids adopting traditional formulae without alteration and removes itself from the scene of every day. Grandiose loftiness and unreserved emotionality are forbidden. The poet is in a private circle and the exquisite things he has to relate do not bear loud sounds.

In the prologue to his *Aetia* Callimachus points to Philitas of Cos as the model of an art[1] which has mastered subtlety of expression; the Latin elegiac poets considered him to be their leader[2] and to us he is also the originator of the new poetry. For the literature of the Hellenistic era we are badly provided with

---

[1] On the problems of the passage *v.* p. 711 on the *Aetia.*

[2] Passages in M. PUELMA, *Mus. Helv.* 11, 1954, 103, 6; there p. 114 on the restoration *Philetae* in Catullus 95, 9 which is still doubtful.

precise dates. We can only state of Philitas[1] that he lived at the time of Alexander and Ptolemy I. It was a step of great moment when the latter invited him to be the educator of the later Philadelphus. We do not know how long the Coan remained in Alexandria, but no doubt he exerted a strong influence there. The librarian Zenodotus, Hermesianax the poet of the Leontion, and Theocritus are mentioned as his pupils. Even if *Id.* 7. 40 should be the source of a fiction in the case of Theocritus we must at any rate reckon with a lasting influence of Philitas on the growth of a new literature. What we glimpse of his work is scanty enough.[2] But it is important to know that he selected rare words, hardly or no longer intelligible, from old poems and that in his publication of the collection as *Unarranged Glosses* ("Ατακτοι γλῶσσαι) he expressly renounced a systematic treatment. The interest of the scholar and the desire of the littérateur (he was called ποιητὴς ἅμα καὶ κριτικός) to avoid the ordinary were blended in a manner which remained influential in Alexandrian poetry and led to deliberate ornamentation as well as baffling rococo complexity. The very scanty remnants of Philitas' poetry rather suggest that he knew how to be moderate in the application of the 'selected' material. Hermesianax (fr. 2. 77 D.) and Ovid (*Trist.* 1. 6, 2; *Ex Ponto* 3. 1, 57) allude to poems, probably elegies which he addressed to Bittis (or Battis), a lover or wife, not a playful fiction, as was thought.[3] We possess nothing of this poetry, but here we find ourselves face to face with the much discussed question whether Hellenistic literature already developed the personal love elegy which we find in its complete form in Latin poetry. There will always be some uncertainty attached to this problem, since we only possess a fraction of the work produced, but it may be stated that no fragment and no information of Hellenistic poetry points to elegies in the manner of Tibullus or Propertius. Nor does the material preserved recommend this assumption by any means. Thus Aug. Rostagni[4] may have understood the development correctly when he spoke of a 'rovesciamento degli elementi'; mythology predominated in the Hellenistic volumes of elegies, although the author's personality put its stamp on it. In Latin elegy, however, it is only an item of decoration (the necessity of which could be argued about) in a world of personal experience and passions. But it should be borne in mind that a clear line runs, in point of themes, from the Hellenistic epigram to the elegy, though the depth of perception may have been different with the Romans.

[1] Many write Philetas, we follow the inscriptions, cf. s. f. GOW, *Theocritus* 1950, 2, 141. Otherwise *v.* BLUMENTHAL, *RE* 19, 1938, 2165.

[2] The fragments in G. KUCHENMÜLLER, Diss. Berl. 1928; those from the poems: J. U. POWELL, *Collectanea Alexandrina.* Oxf. 1925, 90. *Anth. Lyr.* fasc. 6, 49 D. with bibl.

[3] KUCHENMÜLLER (*v. sup.*), 25 also reads Βαττίδα in Hermesianax in accordance with the Ovid-tradition and takes βαττίς as γλῶσσα who thus would be Philitas' beloved. The jest is imaginable in Hermesianax, but one will have to be careful about explaining the Ovid-passages from a misunderstanding.

[4] ' L' influenza greca sulle origini dell' elegia erotica latina ' in *Entretiens sur l'antiquité class.* 2. Vandœuvres-Geneva 1953 (with discussion). Further A. A. DAY, *The Origins of Latin Love Elegy.* Oxf. 1938 with older bibl., which also in CHRIST-SCHMID, *Gesch. d. gr. Lit.* 6th ed. 2/1, Munich 1920, 118, 3, to which should be added that F. LEO, *Plautin. Forsch.* Berl. 1895 started the ball rolling; cf. also HERTER, *Bursian* (*v. sup.*), 77.

We know of Philitas that he wrote a *Demeter*[1] in the elegiac metre. The epyllion *Hermes* was composed in hexameters; its content is reproduced by Parthenius. It is interesting to observe how the love theme is introduced into the old story of Odysseus and the wind-god by means of an adventure of the much-travelled hero with Polymele, Aeolus' daughter. Hellenistic poetry is fond of picking up remote aspects from mythology or of inventing ingenious new ones. So we must not ask why the poem was called *Hermes*. Of a *Telephus* we only know the title and a notice referring to the legend of the Argonauts. The fact that the poet's father was called Telephus should not be brought into relation with the poem. Of Philitas' *Trifles* (Παίγνια) and *Epigrams* only traces have been preserved.

We are in a much better position with regard to Callimachus; although many questions have to remain unanswered, we can still grasp the main traits of his work and understand that it is the climax of Alexandrian poetry. Callimachus was born in Cyrene a few years before 300 – we have no precise dates either for his birth or death. According to the article in Suidas, our main source for his life, his father was called Battus, the name of the city's founder. According to Strabo (17. 837) the family traced its origin back to this illustrious ancestor. No doubt this is what Callimachus means when he calls himself Battiad (*Ep.* 35). In *Epigram* 21 he states that his grandfather, who had the same name as the poet, won fame as strategos. His distinguished origin could not shield him from want. When he went to Alexandria as a young man, he had to earn a living as a primary schoolteacher in the suburb of Eleusis. From his subsequent success we may conclude that in this condition he also worked at his education with stubborn industry. The grammarian Hermocrates of Iasus is mentioned as his teacher; we cannot determine in what period. We do not know when he had the good fortune to draw Philadelphus' attention; nor of what nature his first connection with the court was. Little sense can be made of Tzetze's remark[2] which described him as νεανίσκος τῆς αὐλῆς. And so we adhere to the fact that, under Ptolemy II, Callimachus was entrusted with the formidable task of making the possessions of the Alexandrian library usable. The start of this undertaking should not be dated too late.[3] Only if Callimachus began it in his early manhood can we understand that he completed the 120 books of his *Pinaces* (Πίνακες τῶν ἐν πάσῃ παιδείᾳ διαλαμψάντων καὶ ὧν συνέγραψαν, fr. 429-253 Pf.). Although Zenodotus with a few assistants like Alexander of Pleuron and Lycophron had done some preliminary arranging, the task as Callimachus set about it made tremendous demands. First he had to make a division according to the main realms of literature such as epic, lyric, drama, oratory, etc.; within each of these all authors had to be arranged, in alphabetical order, separating the different genres in the work of an individual author which in turn were probably also arranged alphabetically. Since the works were by no means clearly titled, Callimachus also listed the initial words and the number of lines. When we observe furthermore that he added in each case a brief

---

[1] New mention in the schol. *Ox. Pap.* 2258 on *Hymn* 2, 33, cf. Pfeiffer 2, LIII and 47.
[2] *De com. gr.* 31, 13 K. = test. 14 c Pf.   [3] S. HERTER, *Bursian* (*v. inf.*), 87.

biography of the author, and necessarily had to express an opinion on questions of authorship in numerous cases, we understand that a considerable piece of literary-historical research went into the writing of this catalogue. The fragment of a commentary on Bacchylides, *Ox. Pap.* 23. 1956, No. 2368, shows that this research was also subject to criticism. Aristarchus censored Callimachus because he had included the dithyramb *Cassandra* among the paeans. We also learn that a certain Dionysius of Phaselis agreed with Aristarchus' characterization of the poem as a dithyramb. The importance of the *Pinaces* as a basis for all further research can be seen, for instance, from Aristophanes of Byzantium's treatise *On the Pinaces of Callimachus* (fr. 453 Pf.) which purported to complete and correct it. Athenaeus' quotations from it show (9. 408 f.) that genuinely difficult questions of semantics could crop up. The importance and complexity of special fields induced Callimachus to treat them separately. We can still trace his work on Democritus (Πίναξ τῶν Δημοκρίτου γλωσσῶν καί συνταγμάτων) and on drama (Πίναξ καὶ ἀναγραφὴ τῶν κατὰ χρόνους καὶ ἀπ' ἀρχῆς γενομένων διδασκάλων), for which work Aristotle prepared the ground with his *Didascaliae* (cf. p. 572).

However closely Callimachus may have been connected with the library of Alexandria, he never was its head. We do not know why it was not he, but his pupil Apollonius of Rhodes, who was Zenodotus' successor. But it may be assumed that the prolonged argument about Callimachus' librarianship[1] has been settled by *Ox. Pap.* no. 1241 (no. 1611 P.), in which the list of librarians begins with Apollonius Rhodius and is continued with Eratosthenes, Aristophanes of Byzantium, Apollonius the idographer[2] and Aristarchus. Now since Tzetzes (p. 25, 13; 32, 38 Kaibel) in two places calls Aristarchus the fourth or fifth librarian after Zenodotus, there is no room left for Callimachus. The fact that the papyrus mentions a second Apollonius in this series has made it possible to explain misunderstandings about which we shall have to speak in connection with the biography and work of the Rhodian. It is difficult to form an opinion on his relationship with Callimachus and this question will be dealt with when the prologue to the *Aetia* is discussed.

Callimachus was still alive when Euergetes came to the throne. The only poem which we can date with precision is the one on *Berenice's Locks*; it is based on events of the year 246/245 and its composition falls within this time. That Berenice, Ptolemy Euergetes' consort, is the ruler meant in the epilogue of the *Aetia* (fr. 112, 2 Pf.) seems more likely now that the assumption that Arsinoe was referred to in the prologue has lost ground.[3] *Epigram* 51 also extols the wife of Euergetes. We do not know for how long Callimachus lived under this ruler, but the traditional date of his death in 240 will not be very far wrong.

The work of this scholar and poet was tremendous, even if we do not altogether credit Suidas' assertion that he wrote 800 volumes. We already spoke of his great catalogue and some related aspects. We possess a considerable

---

[1] Bibl. in HERTER (*v. sup.*).
[2] On confusion in the text, which makes it possible to date the idographer before Aristophanes: HERTER, *Rhein. Mus.* 91, 1942, 315.   [3] Cf. Pfeiffer 2, XL.

number of other titles of prose-works which remind us of the broad span of interests in Peripatetic circles, but which at the same time suggest the collector of curiosa. The book *On Contests* may have had some connection with the catalogue work; the title *Customs of Foreign Peoples* (Βαρβαρικὰ νόμιμα) which we met already with Hellanicus (p. 330) has the ring of ancient Ionian ἱστορίη. *Ethnically Varying Names* ('Εθνικαὶ ὀνομασίαι) collecting the descriptions of similar objects in different areas was a work of a glossographical nature. It is the first example we have of a lexicon arranged in groups of subjects. It seems to be fairly certain that a treatise mentioned by Suidas *On the Changes of Names of Fishes* (Περὶ μετονομασίας[1] ἰχθύων) is part of this work; there is no such proof for the writings *Names of Months according to Peoples and Cities* (Μηνῶν προσηγορίαι κατὰ ἔθνος[2] καὶ πόλεις), *On Winds* (Περὶ ἀνέμων), *On Birds* (Περὶ ὀρνέων). A work *On the Rivers of the World* (Περὶ τῶν ἐν τῇ οἰκουμένῃ ποταμῶν) points to geographical interests, one *On the Founding of Islands and Cities and Changes of Names* (Κτίσεις νήσων καὶ πόλεων καὶ μετονομασίαι) to both historical and glossographical interests; behind the title *Curiosities Collected all over the World according to Place* (Θαυμάτων τῶν εἰς ἅπασαν τὴν γῆν κατὰ τόπους συναγωγή), however, we recognize the classifying collector of all that is odd. In this way Callimachus founded paradoxography, which was cultivated long after antiquity and the Middle Ages, until the earth became small and the spell of remoteness disappeared. Antigonus of Carystus utilized Callimachus' work for part[3] of his *Book of Marvels* ('Ιστοριῶν παραδόξων συναγωγή), changing the arrangement according to place into one according to subject. The title *On the Nymphs* points to mythology, while Περὶ λογάδων remains unintelligible. The report of a work *Against Praxiphanes*, however, is of some interest. This interpretation of the title Πρὸς Πραξιφάνην is proved to be correct by the Florentine scholium on the beginning of the *Aetia*, in which Praxiphanes appears among Callimachus' opponents. This Peripatetic no doubt wrote *On Poets* and *On Poems* in the spirit of Aristotle, challenging Callimachus to defend the foundations of the new poetry. The titles of *Museum*, also used by Alcidamas (p. 353) and *Hypomnemata* presumably point to scholarly collections.

We have somewhat elaborated on this subject not only for the sake of Callimachus, but because this series of titles illustrates the interests of a literature which has a scope in the Hellenistic age whose breadth is unparalleled.

We have so little reliable support for the dates of Callimachus' poems that we proceed to discuss them according to the various conditions of preservation and tradition and will deal with their chronology in each case. The great variety in the transmission also makes it desirable to discuss it in connection with the individual works rather than at the end in the customary way.

The *Hymns* and *Epigrams* have come down through manuscript tradition. For the former it was decisive that an unknown collector combined them in one corpus together with the Homeric *Hymns*, those of Orpheus, the Orphic

---

[1] Daub conjectured κατονομασίας.
[2] Pfeiffer, 1, 339 takes κατὰ ἔθνη into consideration.
[3] Chap. 129-end, text in Pfeiffer fr. 407.

Argonautica and Proclus' *Hymns*. One epigram, copied together with the hymns, which also enumerates other works of Callimachus' (Test. 23 Pf.), was not written before the sixth century and probably even considerably later. This fixes the upper limit for the insertion of the *Hymns* in the collection. Remnants of all the hymns, except the fifth, have come to light in papyri.[1] These give rise to the suspicion that our manuscript-tradition has suffered more than was so far assumed. This tradition is copious and permits a number of hyparchetypes to be derived which in turn all go back to the collector who gathered the books of hymns just mentioned in one corpus.

The *Book of Hymns*, which we possess entire, begins, of course, with one dedicated to Zeus. As we shall see, it was written earlier than the others and already displays all the traits of this poetry which abounds in assumptions and substrata. The question asked in the first stanza, to whom else but Zeus one should sing when pouring the libation, sets the scene of a symposium. Not a cult-celebration, but the company of congenial friends receptive to erudite subtlety, is the frame-work of these poems. The whole hymn is constructed on the traditional plan of composition of religious hymns; the opening with the legend of the birth must be followed by the praise of divine achievements (the γοναί followed by the ἀρεταί of the god). The very opening shows what Callimachus has made of the old elements. Where actually was Zeus born? Arcadians and Cretans put forward their claims, but it is known, of course, that all Cretans are liars at all times, for they have fathered a tomb on the immortal god! All this is not presented with the seriousness of the critic or the solemnity of the inspired singer; it is a sport with the tradition although it never tries to devaluate or scorn it as a rationalist might, but rather savours its treasure, its venerableness, and its poetry, and imparts this to others. The fact that the learned Callimachus stands far above the mythical tradition while at the same time sensing the power and beauty it possesses constitutes the peculiar charm of his creations, which are equally remote from assured prophecy as from rational criticism. Adorning his story with odd bits of knowledge of Arcadian streams and nymphs, he tells how Zeus was born in the Arcadian province of Parrhasia, how Rhea struck water from a mountain in the dry country and handed over the child to the nymph Neda. But the poet always succeeds in harmonizing with the charm of his verse what the scholar cannot forbear putting in. The *Hymn to Zeus* brings out another feature of Callimachean poetry; the selective element is obvious in the unequal compactness of the narrative. The rearing of the child in Crete is already dealt with much more briefly than the Arcadian birth, and Callimachus does not think at all of lingering over the god's deeds. It is more important for him to inveigh against a piece of tradition, in this case Homeric (*Il.* 15. 187); it is a foolish invention that Zeus had drawn lots with his brothers for shares in the rule of the world. Actually the brothers ceded sovereign authority to the younger, because they recognized his superiority. It is true that Hesiod's variant (*Theog.* 881) is played off against Homer's and that the poet

[1] The only authoritative synopsis in Pfeiffer, 2, LI; there also LXXXIII the manuscript stemma.

does not point with one word to a special context of the passage.[1] Yet we can hardly help suspecting that the renunciation of Zeus' brothers was brought in, because he had to serve as a model for the elder half-brother of Philadelphus, Ceraunus.

The final passage pays homage to the king as him whose might inspires his thoughts with perfection. The greeting to the god, typical of the end of a hymn, follows. The poet begs for virtue and riches; we hear in this the poet who hopes for promotion from his king, the earthly Zeus, in his straitened circumstances. In other ways the manner in which Philadelphus appears in the hymn also indicates a period during which Callimachus was not so close to the court as at the zenith of his fame.

We next add the fourth and the fifth hymns, since the other three form a group with common characteristics. The *Third Hymn*, dedicated to Artemis, strongly brings out the blending of different elements of subject-matter and style. The second part (v. 183) begins with a question about the islands, mountains, ports, cities, nymphs and heroines which are particularly dear to the goddess's heart and so introduces a passage which has almost the character of a manual, although the calculated art of variety turns even such an enumeration into poetry. The first part also contains erudite information. When we are told that the Cyclops' island Lipara was still called Meligunis when young Artemis visited it, we listen to the scholar who wrote on the changing of the names of islands and cities, as in the first hymn we remembered the writer of treatises on rivers and nymphs. But this first part of the hymn draws three unforgettable pictures full of a humour which is never coarse and never offends, the humour which constitutes the intimate charm of Callimachean poetry as the subtlest expression of intellectual superiority. The little goddess is sitting on the knees of her father Zeus, wheedling everything out of him that she has set her heart on; then again we see her in a similar position with the Cyclops as she pulls the hair by the handfuls out of the chest of the benevolent giant Brontes; finally Heracles is brought in, who even in Olympus has not lost his appetite. He is always waiting at the gate when Artemis returns home with her bag and cunningly teaches her to kill pigs, which harm the crops, instead of hares and does. And since roast beef is a tasty dish, cattle have to be harmful too. It is useful to place this beside the coarse effect of humour of the Homeric Hermes-hymn to appreciate the distance between two totally different spheres of poetry.

The *Fourth Hymn*, celebrating Delos as Apollo's birthplace, is a purely literary creation like the others. Attempts to establish a connection between the hymn and a specific Delian festival led to mistakes. It is clear that in the portrayal of Leto's wanderings and her confinement in Delos, the island which until then had been restlessly floating about, Callimachus had in mind the Homeric hymn to Delian Apollo. But it would be erroneous to call it an imitation, since the many changes, additions and the altered emphasis stresses the original character of the new artistic trend – and we may speak of a most deliberate trend – forcibly enough. As a story the hymn is more complete than the two discussed

---

[1] Stressed by HERTER, *RE* S 5, 1931, 437, 62.

before; Callimachus achieves a special effect when he makes cities, countries and rivers run away for fear of Hera at Leto's request for a refuge. We must not attempt a concrete interpretation here; the ancient Greek unity of location and divinity has here been utilized for a peculiar effect in a manner which Ovid knew well how to handle. The same device is employed when in our hymn (264) Delos takes the child Apollo to her breast while at the same time she speaks as the island.

In the very middle of the hymn Callimachus has inserted a homage to Philadelphus which combined humour with praise. When still in the womb, Apollo is already skilled in prophecy, and when Leto is approaching the island of Cos he asks her not to bring him into the world where one day another god is to be born, a Ptolemy to whom the earth will be subject. Since Philadelphus appears here as a god, the deification which followed Arsinoe's death in 270 is presumed. On the other hand, the lines are founded on Egypt's imperious claims to world-power which could no longer be checked after the end of the Chremonidean war,[1] especially after the fall of Athens (263–262). These facts produce relatively narrow limits for the date of writing. It can merely be conjectured that the third was written in the same period.

A brief glance at contents and structure are needed to give reasons why the *Second, Fifth* and *Sixth Hymns* should be combined more closely. The *Second*, addressed to Apollo, differs even more from the continuous narrative epic style than the hymns discussed. With the very first few lines we are flung into the excitement of a crowd in front of a temple, impatiently waiting for the epiphany of its god. As in the case of the *Fourth* and *Fifth Hymns*, we must throughout assume a speaker who clearly reveals himself as a man from Cyrene, in other words the poet himself. His words capture the festive mood and the marvel of the epiphany;[2] they show us a boys' choir and extol the god's beauty and the well-known spheres of his power, and then abruptly and surprisingly he tells the story of how he founded the city. This provides an opportunity to relate the rise of Cyrene where the god had the most splendid ceremonies at the Carnean festival. We can understand that Callimachus is fond of talking of his native town, but there is an additional factor; the king placed next to Apollo in line 26 is Ptolemy III Euergetes, as stated by the scholium. Now the alliance of this ruler with the Cyrenaic princess Berenice, the daughter of Magas, which took place immediately before his accession, returned Cyrene to Egypt. The reference to Ptolemy III dates the hymn in the poet's old age and we may appreciate the special dramatization of the style, the increased vividness of representation, coupled with a close sympathy for religious feelings as the perfection of his

---

[1] On the dating of the battle of Cos H. BENGTSON, *Griech. Gesch.* 2nd ed. Munich 1960, 397, 1. On the date of the *Fourth Hymn* also P. VON DER MÜHLL, 'Die Zeit des Apollonhymnos des Kall'. *Mus. Helv.* 15, 1958, 8.

[2] O. WEINREICH, *Gebet und Wunder. Tüb. Beitr.* 5, 1929, 231, 59, and generally on the introit of the hymn; cf. also J. KROLL, *Gott und Hölle.* Leipz. 1932, 480. Ext. bibl. in HERTER, *Bursian (v. sup.)*, 196. In add. HOWALD, *Der Dichter K. (v. sup.)*, 86. H. ERBSE, 'Zum Apollonhymnos des K.' *Herm.* 83, 1955, 411. P. VON DER MÜHLL, 'Die Zeit des Apollonhymnos des K.' *Mus. Helv.* 15, 1958, 1, attempts to call the late date in question.

endeavours in this province. It is quite typical of Callimachus that the arbitrary compositional form, which often leaves the sequence and connection of individual details vague, is contrasted by an arrangement in almost stanza-like paragraphs.

True to the Callimachean manner, the praise of Cyrene is followed by an aetion; the worshippers' shout *hie paieon* is explained from the shots (ἱέναι) taken at the dragon Python. The manner in which the final passage abruptly passes over into the personal is reminiscent of the sphragis of ancient citharodic poetry (cf. p. 129); with a kick Apollo chases away Phthonos, the daemon of envy, because the latter wanted to convince him that only lengthy poetry, large like the sea, was important. But the god knows that the mighty Euphrates carries along mud and refuse, while pure water as used for ritual is fetched from a trickling spring. The poet finishes with the wish that Momus, censure, may follow Phthonos. The question of the opponents whom he wards off in this way will be dealt with in the discussion of the prologue to the *Aetia*.

The *Fifth Hymn*, the bath of Pallas, firstly surprises us with its form. Like the sixth it is written in Doric, which is not simply the poet's native dialect, but a literary language which varies epic diction with Dorisms. The fifth is the only hymn to display elegiac metre. Wilamowitz[1] has pointed out that the use of anaphorae and the segmentation of cola and commata is unlike that of epic; but the composition and the method of narrative do not differ in considerable detail from the related hexameter poems. Again we have a speaker – we can think of him as the master of ceremonies – who gives orders, explains and reports the proceedings of a cult-celebration and very vividly passes on the religious atmosphere of the festival, the tension rather than the emotion.[2] We are in front of the temple of Athena of Argos at a festival which features the ritual bath of the goddess's statue; this does not, of course, imply that this Alexandrian poem was written for the Argive festival. The poem is especially fascinating because the progress of the goddess's image to the Inachus has been combined with the bath of the goddess herself in a way which does not permit rational analysis, diffusing over the whole the splendour of a divine epiphany. The festival themes include the story of Tiresias, told at some length, who loses his sight on glimpsing the goddess in her bath.

The composition of the *Sixth Hymn* is done along the same line; ritual proceedings are reported with thrilling directness through the mouth of a speaker who also tells the myth behind the cult. We are eagerly anticipating the procession which in the service of Demeter is going to pass by with the sacred objects of her mystery. The procession probably takes place in Cyrene, where Demeter was worshipped[3] or in Alexandria, where the suburb Eleusis provided such excitements, but such a search for precise detail is of little importance for the atmosphere of this poem. Here, too, the speaker tells of the dreadful violence with which the goddess can punish when she has been offended. The story of

---

[1] *Hellenist. Dicht.* 2, Berl. 1924; reprinted 1961, 15.

[2] K. J. MCKAY, *The poet at play, Kallimachos. The Bath of Pallas.* Leiden 1962.

[3] Cf. HERTER, *Bursian (v. inf.),* 209.

Erysichthon serves as an example; he felled some trees in the sacred grove of the goddess and was punished with an unsatiably voracious appetite. The story of the white-tailed terror of mice who is also forced to go to the kitchen in the end brightens up this edifying tale of crime and punishment with a gaily ironical light – a genuine and lovable Callimachean touch.[1]

There are no positive aids available for dating these last two hymns, but perhaps their structural affinity with the *Second Hymn* justifies the conclusion that L. Deubner[2] was correct in assuming a late date. The same scholar has tried to account for the peculiar form of these three hymns, with their strong flavour of mimetic elements, through Theocritus' influence. Now it is correct that the latter's poetry often has a mimetic character, as in the *Pharmaceutria* and the *Gorgo and Praxinoe*, to mention two; it is also correct that there are various points of mutual contact between him and Callimachus,[3] but nevertheless the independent, typically Callimachean quality of this impressive poem should not be overlooked.

The *Epigrams* form the second group of surviving poems. There is sufficient evidence[4] that they were collected in one book in the ancient Callimachus editions. We even know of a commentary by Archibius (perhaps also Hedylus; test. 44 f. Pf.). We cannot tell whether Callimachus himself compiled this book of epigrams. At any rate a selection from it reached the *Anthologia Palatina* via Meleager and Constantine Cephalas; this transmission will be discussed in the next chapter. If we agree with Pfeiffer and others to reject *Ep.* 3, 36 and 63 (probably the last word has not yet been said about 63[5]), the *Anthology* has preserved for us fifty-eight indubitably genuine items, to which are added another two from other authors (5 f.). When Maximus Planudes compiled his *Anthology* in 1299, he copied twenty-two genuine epigrams by Callimachus from the Palatinus. Unlike the *Palatina* this *Planudea* never lapsed into oblivion. So it happened that the epigrams preserved in the latter precede in our editions the ones which were added from the rediscovered *Palatina*, the result being that the order is very confused. Some very scanty fragments (393-402 Pf.) indicate that we possess only one, possibly quite restricted, selection of the epigrams of our poet.

The Alexandrian art of the miniature finds its perfect expression in Callimachus' *Epigrams*. At this stage we shall only consider it briefly, since the Hellenistic epigram will be discussed later. Epitaph and dedication, the original forms, return with a variety of wit and emphasis; newer themes appear in erotic poems, mainly about the beauty of boys, and in those about literary principles. A large part of the lighter epigrams can be allotted to the poet's youth, when friendship and love helped him to bear his poverty, but already at an early stage

---

[1] K. J. MCKAY stresses particularly the elements of humour: *Erysichthon. A Callimachean Comedy.* Leiden 1962 (*Suppl. to Mnem.* 7).   [2] *N. Jahrb.* 1921, 376 ff.

[3] G. SCHLATTER, *Theokrit und K.* Diss. Zürich 1941; in add. HERTER, *Gnom.* 19, 1943, 325; cf. also A. S. F. GOW, *Theocritus*, Cambr. 1952, XXIII. In F. DORNSEIFF, *Echtheitsfragen.* Berl. 1939, 25, a series of ancestors, reaching back into the Orient, of mimetic poems with a fictional situation.

[4] PFEIFFER 2, XCII.   [5] Cf. F. ZUCKER, *Phil.* 98, 1954, 94.

he also gave them a more serious content and no doubt this poetry accompanied him into his old age. His mastery of great conciseness and of a style which couples supreme art with simplicity, imparts to most of these creations a cool and smooth surface. *Epigram 2* is the finest example of how real feeling can penetrate; basically it is a brief elegy remembering his dead friend, the poet Heraclitus of Halicarnassus.[1]

In the epigram Callimachus also occasionally toys with dialect and form; five poems show Doric colouring (14. 46. 51. 55. 59) and four (37-40) were written in lyric metre.

Callimachus' main work, the *Aetia*, is lost, but some lucky finds and scholarly work have revealed the essential features of this poem. When Rudolph Pfeiffer published his *Callimachi fragmenta nuper reperta* in 1923, he was able to utilize ten papyri one of which (*Pap. Gen.* 97) has since been rejected. In the prolegomena to the second volume of his monumental edition he presents seventy-three papyrus texts from the first century B.C. up to the sixth/seventh century A.D., a considerable part of which is useful for the *Aetia*. Before we enter into details of content and structure of this work, we must discuss its prologue (fr. 1 Pf.), the most valuable find which has been made with regard to Callimachus and the one with the most problems. This prologue is presented as the poet's revenge upon his opponents, who are introduced as *telchines*, malicious goblins. They abuse him because he did not know how to celebrate the deeds of kings and heroes in an epic of many thousands of lines with continuous action (διηνεκές). But he loves thrifty, subtle poetry, for Demeter's nourishing gift weighs much more than the mighty oak tree (on whose fruit mankind had to feed in the crude days of pre-history).[2] Here the same poet speaks who in *Hymn 2* preferred the slight trickle of the spring to the muddy Euphrates and who announced in *Epigram 28* his abhorrence of the cyclic poem (ποίημα κυκλικόν). We also recall *Epigram 21*, the epitaph for the poet's father, in which Callimachus speaks of his poetic victory over squinting envy (βασκανίη).[3] On the other hand, we have no support for relating the famous condemnation of big books (τὸ μέγα βιβλίον ἴσον . . . τῷ μεγάλῳ κακῷ fr. 465 Pf.) to poetry in particular. Though he may differ from him in other respects, Callimachus, in his rejection of continuous narrative, follows Aristotle's criticism (*Poet.* 23. 1459 a 27) which contrasted Homer's happy choice of part of an occurrence with comprehensive epics like the *Cypria*. The difficult distich in the prologue to the *Aetia* (11 f.), which also mentions the name of Mimnermus, attests his preference of the small subtle poem over the long. The learned Florentine scholium (*Pap. Soc. It.* 1219 fr. 1; no. 24 Pf.) notes on this passage that Philitas was also mentioned and that Callimachus separated the small poems of these two from their larger works as being more valuable. Numerous modern scholars have made this opinion the basis for their attempts at restoration. All the same,

---

[1] Cf. HOWALD, *Der Dichter K.* (*v. inf.*), 63.

[2] The paraphrase makes it clear that I consider the reference of the lines to definite titles of works superfluous.

[3] PFEIFFER rightly struck out the last distich (cf. fr. 1, 37 f.).

it is surprising that Callimachus should have subjected these two highly esteemed masters of narrative elegy to a criticism which was essentially denigratory. Therefore it will be necessary to consider an interpretation and restoration of the passage which contrasts Mimnermus and Philitas with the uncouth poetry of others. In that case the *Large Woman* (v. 12) could refer to Antimachus' *Lyde*, which Callimachus mocked in an epigram (fr. 398 Pf.) as a fat poem.[1]

The Florentine scholium just mentioned also gives concrete indications about the identity of the malicious imps. Besides unknown and only partially preserved names there appear Praxiphanes against whom Callimachus wrote (*v. supra*) and, surprisingly, Asclepiades and Posidippus, themselves two masters of the epigrammatic art, the first of whom was no doubt friendly with Callimachus at some time. But they must have disagreed on matters of criticism, for we know that both voiced the greatest appreciation for Antimachus' *Lyde* (*Anth. Pal.* 9, 63. 12, 168). But there is no mention of Apollonius Rhodius, who was especially assumed to be among the Telchines (who are, after all, mostly Rhodian!), and there is little hope of fitting him into a hiatus in the scholium.[2] On the other hand, we do not know to what extent the scholiast is only making learned conjectures and his importance is overrated if a conflict between Callimachus and Apollonius and any reference to the matter in the various polemical passages and in the *Ibis*[3] is completely denied. The biography of Apollonius will give us an opportunity to take up this question again.

In the Aetia-prologue Callimachus speaks of the burden of old age which lies upon him like Sicily on Enceladus (cf. Eur. *Heracles* 638): so he wrote these lines in the last period of his life. But this is disputed by the fact that Apollonius used the *Aetia* in various places of his epic,[4] and that it becomes difficult or, if Berenice is recognized in the epilogue of the *Aetia* (fr. 112. 2 Pf.), impossible, to date the latter's work so much later.

Pfeiffer solves the difficulties by conjecturing[5] that the *Aetia*, written considerably earlier, were published by Callimachus in his old age, in a new edition, and that he prefixed the Telchines-prologue to it. According to this theory, the originally independent *Lock of Berenice* was fitted into this new edition with some alterations at the end; at the same time an epilogue was added which formed the transition to the *Iambs* which followed in the edition.

The *Aetia* was a fairly voluminous work in four books, but Callimachus maintained his artistic principle by combining in this collective poem a large number of brief stories in elegiac metre; the work owes its name to the causes

---

[1] On the controversy HERTER, *Bursian* (*v. inf.*), 100, who himself inclines toward the second opinion which is defended by M. PUELMA, 'Die Vorbilder der Elegiendichtung in Alexandrien und Rom', *Mus. Helv.* 11, 1954, 101; 'K. – Interpretationen.' *Phil.* 101, 1957, 90. Cf. also w. WIMMEL, 'Philitas im Aitienprolog des Kall.' *Herm.* 86, 1958, 346.

[2] Cf. PFEIFFER, on line 11 of the Schol. Flor.

[3] Bibl. in HERTER, *Bursian* (*v. sup.*) 89. 110. 200, further ibid. Vol. 285, 1944/55, 225, and *Rhein. Mus.* 91, 1942, 310.

[4] Cf. PFEIFFER 2, XLI. HERTER, *Bursians Jahresber.* 285, 1944/55, 232.

[5] *Herm.* 63, 1928, 339; now 2, XXXVI. HERTER, *Gnom.* 26, 1954, 77 f., discusses the scanty possibilities of success without this assumption.

(αἴτια) which it gives of festivals, customs, institutions and names. The idio-syncrasy of its creator made all attempts to reconstruct the work seem fruitless, until new finds provided extensive help. Callimachus' poems were industriously commented upon; we know, for instance, of commentaries by Theon in the Augustan age and of Epaphroditus in the Flavian era; we also possess in papyri considerable remnants of commentaries by authors whom we do not know. A somewhat simple aid, but of invaluable help for an understanding of the poet, are the extensive tables of contents which we call Diegeses after the subscriptio of the Milanese papyrus (no. 8 Pf.). We possess remnants of a rather solid treatise which approximates to a commentary (Pap. no. 24. 26 Pf.) on parts of the first book of the Aetia, and also of a rather flimsy one, probably excerpted from the papyrus just mentioned (no. 8 Pf.), on the two last books of this work, on the Iambs, lyrical poems, the Hecale and the first two Hymns.

At present the subject-matter and sequence of large parts of the Aetia are known to us; the variety aimed at in the length and presentation of the various passages is clearly recognizable. After the Telchines-prologue the roundelay of the Aetia is opened with the story of how the poet dreamed that he was as a young man (ἀρτιγένειος) on Mount Helicon where the Muses met him; it may be conjectured that Arsinoe accompanied them as the tenth. Of course, Hesiod's consecration as a poet is the background of the story of this dream and the fragments reveal that Callimachus mentioned this and so indicated his original. The Muses conversed with him more informally than with Hesiod, for we observe that a brisk exchange of question and answer took place, during which the inquisitive poet received information about all sorts of unusual matters of culture and legend. The very first question is typical: Why do the Parians sacrifice to the Graces without flute music and wreaths? The Aetia contained an abundance of such problems: Why is the sacrifice to Apollo in Anaphe accompanied by obscenities, and that to Heracles in Lindos with invective? Why is there a month called the Sheep's month (Ἄρνειος) in Argos? Why does the statue of Artemis in Leucadia carry a mortar on its head?[1] Why do not the inhabitants of Zancle invoke their foundation-heroes by their names at the festival? and much else of this nature. They are not great subjects, and there is nowhere in the remnants a question which penetrates to greater depths than can be reached by learned curiosity. But all the time we observe the hand of a consummate artist who never tires because he always knows how to bring variety, and who reveals with subtle irony how little seriously all this should be taken.

The finds have shown that in the last two books the dialogue of the Muses was discontinued and that the individual Aetia followed each other without transition, in so far as we may infer from the intelligible examples. Stories continued to be told, and while they occasionally are subservient to the purpose of the aetiology, it could also recede into the background and permit the story to do full justice to itself. The finest example of this is the story of Acontius and Cydippe in the third book. The boy from Iulis fell in love at first sight at the

[1] Probably a mistaken κάλαθος.

Apollo festival in Delos – poetry of this kind only knows of love at first sight – with the girl from Naxos. Eros suggests to him the stratagem of rolling an apple with an inscription on it in front of his beauty's feet; unsuspectingly she reads out from the fruit the oath on Artemis that she will marry Acontius. It should be borne in mind that in antiquity reading was done aloud. An oath must be kept, and in spite of her virginity the goddess sees to it that this is done. We knew the outlines of the story from Aristaenetus, who (1. 10) repeats the story fairly faithfully; in sections 20 and 21 of his *Heroides* Ovid artfully toys with the theme.[1] Larger fragments in papyri have given us samples of Callimachus' narrative style. Again the surpassing objectivity with which he tells the story is striking; but small fragments show that the expressive monologue of the enamoured boy, as given by Aristaenetus, occurred in a similar form in the *Aetia*. The poet can hardly have taken such despair too seriously. The feigned solemnity with which he refers to the Cean chronicler Xenomedes as the source of his history fits this picture completely.

The largest of the fragments (75 Pf.) contains a detail in which we recognize an oft-repeated trick of Callimachus' technique, the characterization of a situation by one single stroke paraphrased in choice language. Callimachus does not say: 'In the morning the festive sacrifices are to be brought in', while 'The animals are ready to be slaughtered' would be too flat. 'The oxen fearfully watch in the reflecting water the knife plunged into their backs.' With this stroke the complete picture is presented.

It has also been established from papyrus evidence that the story of the worthy Pieria, who manages to turn a love affair into the reconciliation of two quarrelling cities, belonged to the third book of the *Aetia* and the old conjecture of R. Reitzenstein that Aristaenetus also paraphrased Callimachus in 1. 15 has been splendidly confirmed.[2] We have also become acquainted with other themes, such as the explanation of the Athenian Thesmophoriae, Simonides' tomb, the Cabiri, the Hyperboreans and the statue of Delian Apollo. In a vivid dialogue an explanation is found of the god's attributes, which the god supplies himself; he holds the bow in his left hand to punish the presumptuous, but he has the three graces on his right hand, because he is swifter with gifts for the good than with punishment for the evil.[3]

The *Lock of Berenice*, which was probably inserted in the fourth book of the *Aetia*, requires some brief remarks. Berenice, the consort of Ptolemy III Euergetes and Callimachus' compatriot, had pledged to dedicate her locks for the happy return of her husband from the Syrian expedition. But the precious hair disappeared from the temple and Conon, the court-astronomer, discovered them in the sky as a constellation. The tresses themselves relate that they were first carried off by Zephyrus into the shrine of Arsinoe-Aphrodite. Here homage for the dead queen was combined with one for the living. This poem by the old

---

[1] Cf. A. LESKY, *Aristaenetus*. Zürich 1951, 144. [2] *Index lect. Rostock* 1892/3, 15.

[3] Fr. 114 PFEIFFER; cf. his splendid essay: 'The Image of the Delian Apollo and Apolline Ethics'. *Journ. of the Warburg and the Courtauld Institutes* 15, 1952, 20. There, p. 27, the indication that here the miniature dialogue of epigram has been transferred to an aetion.

Callimachus, which we can date in 246–245, is court poetry, but even in this the poet does not relinquish his exquisite superiority, showing us that homage of this nature can still be tasteful. Catullus translated it into Latin (66), and the twenty-one stanzas of the original which we can now read coherently (Pap. no. 1 Pf.) show us what pains he took to be accurate.[1]

In the last line of the *Aetia* the poet announces that he is going to enter the domain of the pedestrian Muse,[2] i.e. the realm of prose. Now Horace speaks of his satirical poetry as *Musa pedestris* (*Serm.* 2. 6, 17; cf. 2. 1, 251), and it was thought that in the epilogue of the new edition Callimachus used these words as a transition to the *Iambs* which followed the *Aetia*. It seems preferable to assume simply that the aged Callimachus was thinking of turning back to scholarly work.

In any case the *Iambs* come next in the edition which can be recognized from the remnants. In this book with its thirteen poems the principle of variety has been adhered to throughout. The first four and the thirteenth have been written in choliambs; in between there are epodic forms as well as pure and brachy-catalectic iambic trimeters beside trochaic verse. The dialect pretends to be Ionic, while Doric occurs as well. We can form some impression of the diversity of the contents from the new fragments and the *Diegeses*. *Iamb* 1 provides a good beginning; it brings up Hipponax, the initiator of the choliamb, from the underworld who with an edifying tale exhorts the race of scholars to be modest. The Arcadian Bathycles has donated a gold cup for the cleverest man, but none of the seven sages deems himself worthy and finally the cup is dedicated to Apollo.

The largest fragment which we possess is of *Iamb* 4. It presents the old agon theme in a struggle between the laurel and the olive tree. The point is in the blunt snubbing of a third who wants to join in; the *Diegesis* gives evidence that some literary dispute was behind this. The other iambs contain fables, aetio-logical themes, polemics and occasional poetry, such as congratulations to a friend to whom a daughter had been born.

There is no dependable evidence for the date of the *Iambs*. Special account should be taken of the possibility that in this book individual poems have been collected which Callimachus wrote during different periods of his life. Its diversity made the book into a true *satura lanx* as the Romans called the sacrificial dish filled with various gifts.

Understandably a direct line has been traced from Callimachus' *Iambs* to early Latin satire.[3] Such an observation is quite compatible with a recognition of the

---

[1] In one papyrus (no 37 Pf.) Catullus' lines 79–88 seem to be lacking, while at the end there is a distich which is absent in the Latin. PFEIFFER 2, XXXVII, explains this intelligibly by alterations effected in the transfer to the *Aetia*.

[2] πεζόν (enallage) to be read rather than πεζός. On the controversy of interpretation HERTER, *Bursian* (*v. sup.*), 144 and PFEIFFER on this passage. M. PUELMA, 'Kall.-Interpreta-tionen 2: Der Epilog zu den Aitien.' *Phil.* 101, 1957, 247. The future ἔπειμι indicating an action in the future is important.

[3] M. PUELMA PIWONKA, *Lucilius und K.* Frankf. a. M. 1949. L. DEUBNER, 'Die Saturae des Ennius und die Jamben des K.'. *Rhein. Mus.* 96, 1953, 289.

original achievements of Latin poetry and only means a restriction, not a denial, of Quintilian's: *satura quidem tota nostra est* (10. 1, 93).

In the edition which was the basis for the *Diegeses* there followed lyrical poems in selected metres which reveal the poet's delight in metrical experiment. They are *Exhortation to a Beautiful Boy*, in phalaecean metre; a *Pannychis*, a poem for a festival at which the Dioscuri and Helen were invoked, in Euripidean fourteen-syllable verse (iambic dimeter and ithyphallic verse); the *Apotheosis of Arsinoe* in the rare archebulean which we know better than the others through a fairly large fragment. An uncommon theme shows that here, too, Callimachus did not choose the broad paved road; Philotera, the sister of the royal couple who died young and was carried off to the service of Demeter, comes from Sicily to visit Charis, Hephaestus' wife, and requests her to spy out from Mount Athos what the meaning is of the smoke which is wafted over the sea in the south. Then she learns of Arsinoe's death. The event fixes the earliest date of the poem in 270. The fourth song in choriambic pentameters, the *Branchus*, was addressed to Apollo's favourite, the ancestor of the Branchidae of Didyma.

The miniature epic *Hecale* was of great importance for the principles underlying Alexandrian poetry and its sequence. Owing to the peculiar character of Callimachean poetry it is not possible to reconstruct this poem with some precision either, but the remnants, among which the tablet in the Viennese papyrus collection occupies a special position, reveal a picture of the nature of the whole and of numerous details.[1] A. Hecker's ingenious thesis,[2] confirmed by the papyrus finds, that the dactylic fragments in Suidas are from the *Hecale* and from no other work has also proved useful.

Thanks to the *Diegeses* the plot can be given in rough outline. Theseus has avoided Medea's snares and is recognized by Aegeus, who keeps him carefully protected. But the young man secretly sets out to subdue the evil bull of Marathon. On the way he is forced by a rainstorm to take shelter with old dame Hecale, who entertains him with the modest means of her poverty. Theseus vanquishes the bull, but on his return he finds the old woman dead. He laments her, names the newly founded deme Hecale in her honour and establishes a shrine of Zeus Hecalius. Thus the story ends in an aetion.

This brief outline should not give the mistaken impression that the narrative flowed smoothly. By calling the *Hecale* an epyllion[3] we do not only indicate its small size, but also a specific method of narrative different from the larger epic. Certain episodes, mostly not the central ones, are taken from the context of old

---

[1] On individual papyrus fragments: A. BARIGAZZI, 'Il dolore materno di Ecale (P. Ox. 2376 e 2377)'. Herm. 86, 1958, 453. F. KRAFFT, 'Die neuen Funde zur Hekale des Kall.'. Herm. 86, 1958, 471. – Ox. Pap. no 2376 f. have also made it possible, apart from facilitating the reading of fragments already known, to attribute fr. 629 (in PFEIFFER still incertae sedis) to the *Hecale*; also C. GALLAVOTTI, Gnom. 29, 1957, 423. Fragment Ox. Pap. 24, 1957, no. 2398, is also important; together with Ox. Pap. 25, 1959, no. 2437 and no. 2217 it contributes considerably to a passage of the crow's speech between cols. III and IV of the Viennese tablet (fr. 260 Pf.). Also BR. GENTILI, Gnom. 33, 1961, 342.

[2] *Commentationes Callim.* Groningen 1842. Bibl. on the attempts at reconstruction PFEIFFER on fr. 230 and HOWALD-STAIGER (v. inf.), 385.

[3] This description of short poems in antiquity only Athen. 2, 65 a.

legends and are lovingly reshaped, while the remaining themes are left at the fringe. Thus in this case it is not the story of the battle with the Marathonian bull which stands in the centre, but his stay with the old woman, whom Callimachus had discovered in the atthidographical tradition. To what extent we have to reckon with surprises in this form of art, especially in Callimachus, is shown by the Viennese tablet with a dialogue of birds,[1] in which one of the characters, the crow, relates all kinds of old stories. The old theme of the evil reward meted out to the bringer of bad news is also brought up. It can still be observed that this passage followed on to the conquest over the bull, but how it fitted into the context of the poem remains obscure.

The *Hecale* had an extraordinary influence; poems of the Roman neoterici, such as the *Io* of Licinius Calvus or the *Smyrna* of Helvius Cinna are modelled upon it; Catullus' poem on the *Marriage of Peleus and Thetis* and the *Ciris* from the Appendix Vergiliana also bear testimony to this influence. The Hecale subject was given a completely new form in the spirit of true poetry and rich humanity in Inez Wiesinger-Maggi's *Theseus der Jüngling* (1953).

In the fourth of the *Iambs* (fr. 194. 77 Pf.) the 'girl-diver' Olive, whom Theseus enjoys, is clearly from the *Hecale*; this could provide a relative chronology, but it is not very helpful since the *Iambs* cannot be dated. What makes the chronology of the epyllion more difficult is the fact that we are still far from a trustworthy picture of the development of Callimachus' art. Therefore the assumption that the *Hecale* is chronologically close to the *Aetia* must be tentative.

The *Hecale* offers an opportunity to make some few remarks about the subtle structure of the hexameter in Callimachus.[2] Certain arrangements of the verse, already developed in Homer, are increasingly preferred, deviations more strictly avoided. Caesura is subjected to narrower limits so that the structural forms stand out more clearly. There is an organic connection between this development and the greater conciseness of language, the large-scale rejection of conventionally epithetical ornament and of fixed formulae, and bright diversion by means of occasional brief cola.

Of other poems in epic or elegiac metre of which traces survive only the *Victory Ode to Sosibius*[3] has become partially known; it celebrated victories in chariot races at the Isthmian and Nemean games. The few distichs are of

---

[1] The two birds fall asleep at last. PFEIFFER, 'Morgendämmerung'. *Thesaurismata. Festschr. f. I. Kapp.* Munich 1954, 95, elegantly rectified the conjectures of WILAMOWITZ, *Hellenist. Dicht.* 1. 189, of a third bird who wakes them early. A conjecture of the insertion of the bird-scene in A. BARIGAZZI, 'Sull' Ecale di Callimaco'. *Herm.* 82, 1954, 308. Otherwise B. GENTILI, *Gnom.* 33, 1961, 342. V. BARTOLETTI, 'L'episodio degli uccelli parlanti nell' Ecale di Call.'. *Stud. It.* 33, 1961, 154, thinks that the birds' dialogue happens in Athens after the message of the conquest over the bull and of Theseus' impending arrival has been received.

[2] Of fundamental importance H. FRÄNKEL, 'Der kallim. und der hom. Hexameter'. *GGN* 1926, 197; revised in *Wege und Formen frühgr. Denkens.* Munich 1955, 100. A. WIFSTRAND, *Von K. zu Nonnos.* Lund 1933.

[3] On the desperate problem of the person celebrated HERTER, *Bursian* (v. inf.), 154 and PFEIFFER on fr. 384. Influence of Pindar in poems on Nemean victories of the period 200–150 B.C.: W. PEEK, 'Zwei agonistische Gedichte aus Rhodos'. *Herm.* 77, 1942, 206.

importance, since in these we see the choral-lyrical epinicion translated into the style of the elegy. Fr. 383 Pf. shows that this ode was not the only one of its kind. We know desperately little of the lampooning poem *Ibis*. Ovid, who relieves his personal rancour under the same title, is of little help. At any rate Callimachus wrote a moderately sized poem (probably elegiac), in which, introducing various remotely connected stories, he hurled imprecations at an enemy whom he compares with the unclean ibis. According to ancient notices[1] this opponent was Apollonius; we shall have to accept this as a possibility, although there can never be any certainty that such observations are not conjectural.

To conclude from the title of the *Grapheum* and from one distich that it dealt with the history of literature is pure guess-work. A hexameter poem *Galatea* may have dealt with the Nereid. With regard to an *Elegy to Magas and Berenice* Pfeiffer (cf. on fr. 388) has shown that it is possible that Hyginus *Astr.* 2. 24 has a bearing upon it; an *Ode to Arsinoe's Wedding* remains entirely obscure. Suidas has another series of titles which mean nothing to us; some of them might refer to parts of the *Aetia*. He also knows of tragedies, but any possibility of checking ends here.

Callimachus' art reflected the intellectual ferment of the young metropolis; by combining ancient tradition with entirely new aspirations it produced patterns of a greatly varying texture. It is an art which bears the imprint of its scholarly origin and of true poetry; its peculiar nature has been brought out in the foregoing evaluation of separate works, so that a summary would be superfluous.

In each case the most necessary details with regard to the tradition of individual works have been given; we add here merely the hardly credible fact that much of Callimachus was not lost until the Middle Ages, after having survived the perils of the dark ages. There is no proof that this preservation was in an edition published by Salustius the expositor of Sophocles (*v*. p. 299) and Callimachus. PFEIFFER, Prol. 2. 29, has correctly stressed this in opposition to Wilamowitz. But it is a fact that Michael Choniates, the pupil of Eustathius, still counted the *Aetia* and the *Hecale* among his favourite reading. The fatal year 1204 also destroyed these together with other tradition.

The basis for all work on Callimachus was laid by R. PFEIFFER's monumental edition: 1. (Fragments) Oxf. 1949; 2. (Hymni et Epigrammata) 1953. This work has been made into an unparalleled tool by the extensive prolegomena in the second volume on the textual evidence and its history, the precise apparatus criticus, the useful addition of the scholia, the substantial commentaries on the fragments and the complete verbal index; but this was brought about above all by the exemplary scholarly disposition which produced it. Bilingual: in the *Coll. des Un. de Fr.*: E. CAHEN, 4th ed. 1953. *Hymns, Epigrams* and the fragments

---

[1] Suidas *s.* Callimachus; Epigr. adesp. text. 23 Pf.; Schol. Patav. on Ovid, *Ibis* v. 447.

of importance with good introductions: E. HOWALD-E. STAIGER, *Kallimachos.*
Zürich 1955 (*Bibl. d. Alten Welt*). In the *Loeb Class. Libr.* C. A. TRYPANIS 1958
(Fragments); A. W. MAIN 1955 (Hymns and Epigrams). Comm. editions of the
Iambs C. GALLAVOTTI, Naples 1946. CH. M. DAWSON, *Yale Class. Stud.* 11,
1950. U. V. WILAMOWITZ, *Call. hymni et epigrammata.* 6th ed. Berlin 1962, is an
unaltered reprint of the 4th ed. of 1925. Cf. Puelma's book p. 714, n. 3. Comm.
on the *Hymns*: E. CAHEN, *Les Hymnes de C.* Paris 1930. – An invaluable aid for
work on Callimachus in the years 1921–35 is the report of H. HERTER, *Bursians
Jahresber.* 255, 1937. By the same the *RE*-article S 5, 1931, 386. For 1938–48
F. ZUCKER, *Der Hellenismus in der deutschen Forschung*, Wiesbaden 1956, 3. Still
indispensable R. PFEIFFER's *Kallimachosstudien.* Munich 1922 and U. V. WILAMO-
WITZ-MOELLENDORFF, *Hellenistische Dichtung in der Zeit des K.* 2 vols. Berlin
1924, reprinted 1961. A rapid, excellent introduction to the whole field: A.
KÖRTE, *Die hellenistische Dichtung*, 2nd completely revised ed. by P. HÄNDEL,
Stuttg. 1960 (Kröners Taschenausg. 47). Monographs: E. CAHEN, *Callimaque et
son œuvre politique.* Paris 1929. E. HOWALD, *Der Dichter K. von Kyrene.* Erlenbach-
Zürich 1943. A study '*On Art and Play in C.*' in BR. SNELL, *The Discovery of the
Mind.* Oxf. 1953, 264. W. WIMMEL's book *Kallimachos in Rom. Die Nachfolge
seines apologetischen Dichtens in der Augusteerzeit. Herm.* E. 16. 1961 contains a
section on the apologetic form in Callimachus. Also K. J. MCKAY, *The Poet at
Play. Kallimachos. The Bath of Pallas*, Brill. Leiden 1962 contains an analysis of
Hymns 5 and 6.

3 THEOCRITUS

If directness of influence is taken as a criterion – in so far as it is permissible
to speak of influence with regard to Alexandrian poetry – Theocritus takes
precedence over Callimachus. However slight the volume of his work may have
been, yet it was able to establish a genre in antiquity and exert a wide influence in
the modern era, even if it took on the dubious form of pastoral poetry.

We are poorly off for data on the life of this poet, and once more it becomes
clear that our sources[1] largely work with conjectures from internal evidence.
We can only state that Theocritus' life roughly coincided with the golden age
of Alexandrian poetry, i.e. the years 300–260. He may have been born a little
earlier, and there are no indications of poetic activity after the period mentioned;
if he did live longer he must have been silent in his old age. In its summary of
Id. 4 the scholium places Theocritus' floruit in the 124th Olympiad (284/284 –
281–280). If this were credible, the poet's birth would have to be fixed much
earlier. But this is obviously a clumsy simplification of the chronology, since
the Olympiad mentioned is the first to be held during Philadelphus' reign
and Theocritus no doubt reached the climax of his creativity under this
ruler.

Three places in the Mediterranean world played an important role in the
poet's life. He was born in Sicily as the son of Praxagoras and Philina. If we may

---

[1] Suidas, a biography in the scholia and notes in these. Everything in GOW, I, XV.

trust the epigram[1] meant for a portrait or an edition of the works of Theocritus, he was of humble origin, 'one of the many Syracusans'. Because the poet introduces himself in *Id.* 7 under the disguise of Simichidas, he was provided with a father called Simichus or Simichidas, a fine example of the origin of ancient biographical tradition. Theocritus' poetry is connected with his home-land through the Sicilian colouring of many of the bucolic *Idylls*, but especially by the sixteenth, in which he is searching for a patron for his muse and addresses Hiero of Syracuse, who after Pyrrhus' departure from Sicily was elected to be the leader of the expedition planned against Carthage. The situation which can be inferred from the poem makes 275–274 a very likely date. Theocritus possibly was in Sicily at this time, although we cannot be sure of this.[2]

Alexandria played an important part in his career; in his *Adoniazusae* he gives a splendid portrayal of its metropolitan bustle and its petty bourgeoisie. The proud claim of Theocritus-Simichidas in *Id.* 7 (93) that the fame of his poems has penetrated to Zeus can only mean that they drew the attention of Philadelphus. *Id.* 18 is also addressed to him, the *Encomium to Ptolemy*, a eulogy in epic metre, i.e. the kind of encomium which took the place of the old lyric form from the time of Lysander onward. Earlier (p. 637) mention was made of the poetic contest of the Lysandrea in which Antimachus was defeated by Niceratus. Theocritus' encomium presupposes that Arsinoe is still alive and describes the power of Ptolemy II in a manner which was hardly possible before 274. Perhaps we can arrive at a more precise date, since Ulrich Wilcken[3] is probably right in arguing that the poem was composed for the Ptolemea of the year 270,[4] the festival with the gigantic procession (cf. p. 697). It is worth while comparing Theocritus' praise of princes with that which Callimachus blended with his hymns to Zeus and Delos. The Sicilian is flatter, more conventional, less free; the superior intellect with which the other also masters the courtly gesture is not his; on the other hand, his emotional effect is stronger in his best poems.

At the time of the *Encomium to Ptolemy* Theocritus must have been in Alex-andria. It is obvious to assume that he approached the Ptolemies when Hiero II did not fulfil his expectations. The *Adoniazusae* may also possibly be placed in this period. At any rate he met Callimachus in Alexandria[5] and wholeheartedly endorsed the latter's poetic principles. This is given forceful expression in *Id.* 7, the *Thalysia*; it rejects (45) builders who wish to build houses tall like mountains and jeers at the Muses' birds whose cackle wants to vie with the singer from Chios. He shows his reverence for Homer, but rejects imitations of him as an impossible undertaking. The compliment for Asclepiades of Samos[6] and

---

[1] *Anth. Pal.* 9, 434; (27) in GOW. Ἄλλος ὁ Χῖος probably does not refer to Homer, but to the sophist Theocritus of Chios who attacked Aristotle and Theopompus *int. al.* and under Antigonus Monophthalmus expiated his sarcasm with his death.

[2] Cf. GOW I, XXV, 2.2, 324. The interpretation of 107 does not offer a firm basis.

[3] *Sitzb. Ak. Berl.* 1938, 311, 5; otherwise WILAMOWITZ, *Hellenist. Dichtung* 2, Berl. 1924, reprinted 1961; 130.

[4] On the chronology v. p. 697, n. 1.   [5] On their mutual influence, cf. p. 709.

[6] His connection with Callimachus does not indeed appear to have remained untroubled. cf. p. 711.

Philitas (40) is in the same tenor. Predictably these two appear in ancient tradition as Theocritus' teachers.

With no place does Theocritus show such close connections as with the island of Cos. There he made a circle of friends, of which we hear some detail in the *Thalysia*.[1] The physician Nicias of Miletus, remembered in *Id.* 11, 13, and 28 and *Epigram* 8, who himself wrote epigrams, may have become friendly with Theocritus in Cos, for the hypothesis to *Id.* 11 mentions him as a fellow-student of Erasistratus', probably during his stay in the island. Interpretation of the poem has revealed many relations with Cos and its circle;[2] the special emphasis on Cos as the island of birth of the ruler in the *Encomium to Ptolemy* may also be connected with the poet's personal liking for the island.

Syracuse, Alexandria and Cos: the three names indicate the essential background to Theocritus' life. There are many hypotheses on the distribution of the various epochs of his life and of the separate poems over these three places. We do not propose to increase these, since we consider it wrong to obliterate the limits imposed on our knowledge by conjecture at any price. But we do not wish to neglect the second hypothesis of the *Thalysia*, according to which Theocritus stopped at Cos on his way to Alexandria. If we may trust this report we have to assume a sojourn in the island between the Sicilian years and the period in Alexandria without being able to indicate the time limits for it. At any rate we think that after Alexandria Theocritus went back to Cos.

In *Id.* 16 (105) Theocritus mentions Orchomenos as the cult centre of the Graces. Misunderstanding of the passage led to attempts at establishing a connection between the Boeotian place and the poet or his ancestors.[3] We may consider these endeavours as finished now.

We are accustomed to call Theocritus' poems *idylls*,[4] using an expression which appears in Greek in the scholia on Theocritus and was first used in Latin, as far as we know, by the younger Pliny (4. 14, 9) to denote smaller poems. The origin of the term is obscure; the scholiasts were already racking their brains over it, but it is certain that the expression itself has nothing to do with bucolic poetry or with idyllic in our sense. It also appears that it can be applied to poems of greatly varying content. It acquired the connotation in which we use it now because it was connected with the sort of poems which were held to be typical of Theocritus and which produced a following of a definite character. Special titles have been handed down for individual poems, but it is doubtful whether we may attribute any of these to the poet himself. The very circumstance that in a few cases two and more titles have reached us must raise doubts.

---

[1] The names of Lycopeus' sons Phrasidamus and Antigenes must probably not be thought of as pseudonyms.

[2] Various details in A. V. BLUMENTHAL, *RE*, 5 A, 1934, 2004.

[3] CHRIST-SCHMID's Lit. History, 2, 6th ed. Munich 1920, 186 f., goes particularly far; in its Theocritus chapter it is also in other respects very unfortunate. Nothing can be done with the corrupt scholium 7, 21, cf. GOW 2, 128.

[4] On the term GOW 1, LXXI. E. BICKEL, 'Genus, εἶδος und εἰδύλλιον in der Bedeutung "Einzellied" und "Gedicht". *Glotta* 19, 1941, 29.'

The most complete representative of our manuscript tradition, the Ambrosianus 104 (15th/16th c.), contains thirty *Idylls* and the *Epigrams*. Remnants of an *Id.* 31 have only been preserved in a papyrus from Antinoë (no. 1163 P.). There is another fragment of a poem *Berenice* (almost certainly Philadelphus' mother) preserved by Athenaeus (7. 284 a), and the *Syrinx*, one of those technopaignia which playfully imitate objects by means of varying length of lines. It still remains to be demonstrated that the body of tradition contains much that is spurious.

The division into groups adopted in the following survey of the poet's genuine work does not necessarily imply that precise boundary lines can be drawn to separate them. We commence with the bucolic poems with which Theocritus established the tradition of pastoral poetry. They should by no means be considered as the earliest for that reason. It is not even certain whether chronologically they belong close together. Attention should be paid to the attempt to demonstrate that in the portrayal of nature in these poems elements proper to the eastern Mediterranean are prevalent.[1] This corresponds with various references to Cos which are apparent in individual poems.

In the *Thyrsis* (*Id.* 1) a goatherd asks Thyrsis for the melancholy song of Daphnis' death. There were many versions of this traditional Sicilian song about the passing away of the beautiful youth who is the mythical archetype of bucolic poetry. It occurs as early as Stesichorus. Among the presents with which the goatherd loosens Thyrsis' tongue is a carved wooden cup, decorated with exquisite figures.[2] Its description, especially the one of the coquettish beauty and her two lovers, is a fine example of the typical Greek ecphrasis which fills the figures described with life and movement.[3] Sicilian themes also occur in the *Bucoliastae* (*Id.* 6),[4] in which two shepherds sing of Polyphemus and Galatea. In a witty reversal of the story as told by Philoxenus (*v.* p. 415) Polyphemus is here the coy one. In the *Cyclops* he is the wooer, but learns to appreciate that song, of which we are given a sample, is a cure against the pangs of love. In the *Comus* (*Id.* 3) the singer entrusts his goats to Tityrus while he serenades Amaryllis. A jewel of a special nature is the *Thalysia* (*Id.* 7), the poet's walk to the harvest-home at the farm of distinguished Coan friends and the gay rustic festival, all permeated with the warm light of a summer's day in the southern scenery. We already referred to the fact that the Simichidas who tells the tale is the poet himself. This poses the question whether any other figures of the poem, perhaps also from other bucolic idylls, are masks. This has sometimes been pushed too far and there has been talk of a Coan poet's club with a religious background. At present there is more caution; the possibility of various masks is not denied, but there is some reserve about mentioning names. The nearest conjecture we

---

[1] A. LINDSELL, 'Was Th. a botanist?' *Greece and Rome* 6, 1937, 78.

[2] A deep cup with three scenes applied on the outside: A. M. DALE, Κισσύβιον. *Class. Rev.* 66, 1952, 129, against GOW's interpretation. On the poem W. C. HELMBOLDT, 'Theocritus I'. *Class. Weekly* 41, 1955, 59.

[3] Cf. A. LESKY, 'Bildwerk und Deutung bei Philostrat und Homer'. *Herm.* 75, 1940, 38.

[4] R. MERKELBACH, 'Βουκολιασταί (Der Wettgesang der Hirten)'. *Rhein. Mus.* 99, 1956, 97.

can make is that the goatherd Lycidas whom Simichidas meets on the way and with whom he successfully vies in love songs was a contemporary poet. Wilamowitz thought of Dosiadas of Crete, others had different fancies.[1] On no account can the Aratus of Simichidas' song, to whom *Id.* 6 is also devoted, be the poet of the *Phaenomena.*

While Virgil depicts an idealized shepherds' life in an Arcadian landscape,[2] Theocritus draws the shepherds of his homeland with greater realism. This is especially demonstrated in *Idylls* 4, 5 and 10; in the latter (*Theristae*) reapers appear at harvest. From these three poems with their lively dialogue form, it becomes clear that one of Theocritus' literary ancestors was the mime, with which he became acquainted in his Sicilian homeland through the miniature dramas of Sophron, but also through the purely traditional forms. Theocritus dressed it up in the more distinguished garb of the hexameter.

This legacy proved to be influential, especially in three poems which we can simply describe as mimes and of which the first two show this element in the art of Theocritus at the height of perfection. In the *Pharmaceutria* (*Id.* 2) a girl is trying to draw her unfaithful lover back to her with a magic wheel and all kinds of other spells. The model was given in Sophron's witches (*v.* p. 240). Here, in particular, the delight of the Hellenistic age in the lower forms of popular customs is noticeable; it is not a coincidence that much can be corroborated from papyri on magical subjects.[3] In the second part of this nocturnal poem Simaetha tells the tale of her passion. Theocritus' mastery is demonstrated by the fact that only by paying very close attention do we notice how much skill has been applied to the thrilling presentation of an everyday occurrence. An effect like that of comedy is achieved with the *Adoniazusae* (*Id.* 15), the chattering middle-class women in Alexandria who are going out to gasp at the splendid performance of the Adonis-celebration of Arsinoe at the palace and to listen to the singing of a girl. The narrow horizon of these women – Theocritus depicts them with the realism of a Herodas – is timeless. The vivid dialogue of *Idyll* 14 (*Aeschinas and Thyonichus*) is set among the heataerae with themes typical

[1] Survey by QU. CATAUDELLA, 'Lycidas'. *Studi in onore di U. E. Paoli.* Florence 1955, 159, who indeed sees Lycidas merely as a poetry-writing shepherd. J. H. KÜHN, 'Die Thalysien Theokrits'. *Herm.* 86, 1958, 40 presents on page 66 a devastating collection of all interpretations of Lycidas; he himself rejects any identification but regards Lycidas as an aspect of the poet himself. Recent contributions: F. LASSERRE, 'Aux origines de l'anthologie: 2. Les Thalysies de Th.'. *Rhein. Mus.* 102, 1959, 307. M. PUELMA, 'Die Dichterbegegnung in Th.s "Talysien"'. *Mus. Helv.* 17, 1960, 144, who rejects an historical identification, but discerns in this encounter the reflection of Theocritus' introduction to the poets' circle of Cos. On the technique of the portrayal of the bucolic agonal element in the poem: B. A. VAN GRONINGEN, 'Quelques Problèmes de la poésie bucolique grecque: le sujet des Thalysies'. *Mnem.* S. 4, 12, 1959, 24.

[2] Idealization already in Theocritus' Hellenistic imitators: K. LATTE, 'Vergil'. *Antik eund Abendland* 4, 1954, 157. Why Virgil made Arcadia into the bucolic landscape is a difficult question: BR. SNELL, 'Arcadia. The discovery of a spiritual landscape' in *The Discovery of the Mind.* Oxf. 1953, 281 ff. G. JACHMANN, 'L' Arcadia come paesaggio bucolico'. *Maia* N.S. 5, 1952, 161.

[3] Edited by K. PREISENDANZ, *Papyri Graecae magicae* 1, Leipz. 1922; 2, 1931. E. HEITSCH, 'Zu den Zauberhymnen'. *Phil.* 103, 1959, 215.

of the milieu. The desperate lover relates how he found someone else in the favour of his Cynisca and like his fellow-sufferers in comedy wishes to go soldiering. This provides an opportunity for his partner in the dialogue to advise him to take service under Ptolemy and to sing the ruler's praise.

The two poems 16 and 17, which are addressed to reigning monarchs, were mentioned earlier because they provide important chronological evidence. Theocritus also included subject matter from the great heroic legends in his wide range of themes, and he proved that he was able to carry on the narrative manner of the Homeric hymns in the style of the new epyllion. In the *Hylas* (*Id.* 13) he uses the form of an erotic paraenesis to clothe the story of how Heracles loses his lover to the enamoured nymphs of the spring. In the *Dioscuri* (*Id.* 22), on the other hand, the longest of the poems, the hymn-form has been maintained. The contents of this poem, which is composed like a diptych, is the boxing victory of Polydeuces over Amycus, the uncouth king of the Bebrycians, and Castor's battle with Lynceus when carrying off the Leucippides. Hylas and Amycus represent episodes which were also incorporated in the *Argonautica* by Apollonius. Here we are again faced with one of those vexing questions of priority for which we have only arguments of style at our disposal. In this case, too, they are not sufficient for a definitive judgment.[1] At any rate the confidence with which Theocritus was represented as the poet who corrected the Rhodian is unjustified in this instance. The most charming poem in this group is the *Heracliscus* (*Id.* 24).[2] The remnants of the final passage in the Antinoë papyrus (no. 1163 P.) show that one essential feature of the hymn, the request for a blessing at the end, was used. The story of the little Heracles, who thinks it is a capital joke to strangle the evil snakes sent by Hera, is told in an enchanting manner, illuminated with details from the nursery which are reminiscent of Callimachus. Tiresias prophesies the future greatness of the boy. The added biographical details make an impression of being appended; the end portion is lost.

The *Epithalamium for Helen* (*Id.* 18),[3] sustained by delicate sentiment, is only loosely connected with mythology. Its tone and theme is reminiscent of Sappho's wedding songs, but it is Hellenistic in that the action for the wreathing and anointing of a Helen-plane tree by the young women of Sparta has been unobtrusively woven into the poem.

A number of poems form a separate group in that they have a common theme the ἔρως παιδικός. The *Aïtes* (*Id.* 12) celebrates the return of the beloved and once again we are conscious of the warmth of feeling which is mostly concealed by Callimachus. The two *Paedica* (*Id.* 29 f.), written in the Aeolian dialect and in lyric metres, are also both addressed to beautiful boys. Some scanty fragments of a third (*Id.* 31) are preserved in the papyrus just mentioned. Aeolic is also

---

[1] Ext. bibl. in H. HERTER, *Bursians Jahresber.* 285, 1944/55, 352. Thematic and stylistic analysis in D. HAGOPIAN, *Pollux' Faustkampf mit Amykos.* Vienna 1955.

[2] H. HERTER, 'Ein neues Türwunder'. *Rhein. Mus.* 89, 1940, 152. S. G. KAPSOMENOS, 'Zu Th.s Herakliskos'. *Phil.* 94, 1941, 234.

[3] Cf. R. MERKELBACH, *Phil.* 101, 1957, 19.

used in the *Distaff* (*Id.* 28), the charming poem accompanying the ebony implement of Syracusan workmanship with which Theocritus paid homage to the wife of his Milesian friend, the physician Nicias.

The Theocritus tradition has twenty-two epigrams in common with the *Anthologia Palatina*; a few others from the *Anthology*, which could be considered Theocritean, are still quite doubtful.[1] The smallest part of the *Epigrams* have bucolic themes; *Epigr.* 4, a description of a shrine of Priapus and a supplication in a love affair, is more of an elegy with its nine distichs. Besides various dedicatory inscriptions and epitaphs there is a separate group of epigrams on famous poets (17-22). Their various metres are often recognizable as literary homage; the fictional epitaph for Hipponax, for instance, is written in four delightful choliambs. There is the least doubt about the authenticity of this group.

The fragments of the *Berenice* have already been mentioned. There are two more poems to be discussed whose genuineness is subject to serious doubts though they cannot be definitely athetized. In the *Lenae* or *Bacchae* (*Id.* 26) Pentheus' death is related in the same way as in Euripides. The hexameters are of very uniform structure through the complete absence of enjambement; in spite of all attempts the meaning of line 29 with the mention of the childish age of 9 or 10 years remains wholly obscure. The poem has now come to light in Theocritus papyri (no. 1263 f. P.), which is no slight support for its authenticity,[2] but the papyri are so late that the assumption that these editions already contained spurious material is still permitted.

The *Syrinx* imitates the form of a shepherd's pipe in ten dactylic couplets decreasing from hexameter to catalectic dimeter. The text, written in riddling language,[3] is a dedication of the pipe to Pan; the lines are apparently addressed to the instrument. The wording provides no valid argument against the authenticity, although Simichidas instead of Theocritus in 12 could be understood as an imitator's reminiscence of the *Thalysia*. Gow probably passed the capital sentence when he rightly stated in his commentary that syrinxes with decreasing lengths of pipe cannot be proved to have occurred before the first century B.C. We are now waiting for the decisive word from the archaeologists.[4]

The *Syrinx* belongs to a collection of technopaegnia which probably used to constitute an independent book, since scholia have been preserved. Nowadays we find the poems in Book 15 of the *Anthologia Palatina* (21 f. 24-27) and scattered in the bucolic tradition.[5] In its riddle character and in the use of mythological figures the *Syrinx* is particularly closely related to the *Altar of*

---

[1] GOW 2, 523, 527 detailed on the question of authenticity and on the individual epigrams. He defends the correct point of view that also for the group of 22 doubt is often possible and that neither authenticity nor spuriousness can be definitely proved.

[2] WILAMOWITZ, *Glaube der Hell.* Berl. 1932, 72, 2, forcefully presents the precarious situation with regard to this poem.

[3] Illuminating paraphrase in WILAMOWITZ , *Bucolici* (*v. inf.*) GOW gives excerpts from the scholia in his *Bucolici* (*v. inf.*).

[4] Note 554, 3 in GOW, shows that the last word has not yet been said.

[5] The texts in the *Bucolici* of WILAMOWITZ and GOW (*v. inf.*) and fasc. 6, 142, 181. 183 D.; cf. also the following notes.

Dosiadas, whom many conjecture to be hidden behind the Lycidas of the *Thalysia*. The historian, belonging to the early Hellenistic age, who wrote the first known *Cretica* is presumably the Simias of Rhodes,[1] to whom Suidas attributes a collection of glosses (3 books) and four books of miscellaneous poetry, We have beginnings of songs for the gods in lyric metres, although they were probably already meant to be recited, some epic fragments (*Apollo, Gorgo*) and a few epigrams. The technopaegnia *Axe*, *Wing* and *Egg* have been preserved. As a late-comer to this Hellenistic sport for virtuosi, Besantinus turns up in the Hadrianic era with his *Altar*.

Theocritus' poetry bears the imprint of Hellenistic art, especially in the well-considered neatness of form. The word ἐκπονεῖν makes itself heard; it occurs in *Id.* 7. 51 in a passage which is important because of the principle embodied. He proves that he is a true artist in that we find so little evidence in his poems of this painstaking work. The subtlety with which he manages to vary the hexa-meter, the main metre of his poems, is shown by the following observation:[2] in the mimic section of the *Adoniazusae* (1-99) the caesura after the fourth foot with monosyllabic thesis, avoided elsewhere, occurs twelve times, in some cases even marked by punctuation. Another striking feature in this passage is the considerably freer use of monosyllabic words at the end of lines.

In Theocritus we observe the same delight in linguistic and metrical experiment as in Callimachus. Most of his poems display a powerful Doric colouring which came to him easily from his native dialect. It is joined with elements of epic language into a combination without any discordance; the *Dioscuri*, on the other hand, are in the epic tradition and avoid Dorisms.[3] *Id.* 12 is written in Ionic, 28-30 in Aeolic, 31 probably as well. Attic is missing – it is the speech of drama. In the poems written in Aeolic Lesbian lyric metres occur which are here used stichically for recitation. Theocritus' delight in polymetry runs riot in the epigrams on poets which were discussed before. But apart from the artificial dialect and the metre used his work is characterized by an incomparably tender lyrical quality which is at the same time the cause of its lasting influence. Theocritus' poems are composed with a mimetic skill which is rarely equalled in ancient literature. In his bucolic idylls especially he does not merely portray this world but is part of it himself. The notion of fruitful alienation[4] introduced by the new theory of literature can be profitably applied to his poems.

The spurious works preserved under the poet's name are a very motley collection. In no single case can we give the poet's name; most of it has little value, but it gives a glimpse of a literature whose bulk is lost. *Idylls* 8 and 9 are bucolic singing contests between Daphnis and Menalcas. In the former elegiac distichs

---

[1] The fragments: H. FRÄNKEL, *De Simia Rhodio.* Diss. Gött. 1915. Fasc. 6, 140 D. J. U. POWELL, *Collectanea Alex.* Oxf. 1925, 109; Dosiadas ibid. 175.

[2] P. MAAS, *Griech. Metrik* (in Gercke-Norden), Leipz. 1929, 34. He correctly reminds us of the varying role of Porson's bridge in the tragic and the comic trimeter.

[3] We must add 'almost completely', if we accept some Dorisms of the tradition as original.

[4] Cf. M. LÜTHI, *Volksmärchen und Literaturwissenschaft* 1960, p. 11 of the special edition of *Die Freundesgabe* 1960/II.

(33-60) have been interposed between the hexameters; in the latter the umpire, a figure familiar from Virgil's *Eclogues*, himself attends with a song. There is an odd mixture of milieux in *Id.* 20 in which a shepherd laments his vain wooing of a city hetaera. Three other poems have love themes. *Eros* (*Id.* 19), who has been stealing honey, complains of a bee sting; he is given a pointed reminder which recurs in the *Anacreontea* (33) of the bad sting which he can inflict himself. The *Erastes* (*Id.* 23) uses an old novella theme: an Eros statue slays a boy who has driven a lover to suicide with his hardheartedness. The *Oaristys* (*Id.* 27),[1] whose lasciviousness, masking as naïveté, is reminiscent of scenes in Longus' novel, presents lovers' talk of a shepherd and his shepherdess in stichomythia. The lengthy poem (281 lines) of *Heracles the Lionkiller* (*Id.* 25) belongs to the same category as the Hellenistic epyllion. It consists of three individually unimportant episodes from the Heracles-Augeas story, the third comprising the story of the Nemean lion, which is given as an insertion. The most interesting item is *The Fisherman* (*Id.* 21), whose relentless realism goes far beyond Theocritus. Two poor wretches are leading a lonely life of the bitterest poverty on the sea coast. A dream conjures up to one of them a happy catch of a fish of gold, but the other calls him back to harsh reality which threatens with starvation. In ancient literature this portrayal of grinding poverty is only comparable with the pseudo-Virgilian *Moretum*, which contrasts so sharply with the ideal Arcadian world of the *Eclogues*.

We know a little about two Hellenistic poets who were among those who followed Theocritus' lead. Moschus of Syracuse appears in Suidas as a pupil of Aristarchus, and since the latter is probably the great grammarian we can date his activity in the second century B.C. His epyllion *Europa* with the well-known story of Zeus as the bull has been preserved. Moschus puts in the description of Europa's golden basket and its figured adornment with that Hellenistic technique whose perfection was reached in Catullus' poem of the *Wedding of Peleus and Thetis*. It is not an important poet who expresses himself in these lines which are quite plain for a Hellenistic writer. But what is really charming is the description of how the Zeus–bull swimming across the sea with his spoil is accompanied by its natural and mythical inhabitants, and how they celebrate the wedding procession with a *trionfo del mare*. The same may be said of the first of the three *Bucolica* preserved by Stobaeus. The bright sea, and then again the security on land when gales are raging, are evoked by the intimate susceptibility to nature,[2] for which the Hellenistic age found new ways of expression. The poetical warrant with which Aphrodite is looking for the runaway Eros ("Ερως δραπέτης) is not bad either. The hexameter poem *Megara*, on the other hand, has nothing to do with Moschus. It is insignificant as a poem, but is notable for its theme. The other side of Heracles' great heroism is shown in the sorrow

---

[1] W. THEILER, *Studien zur Textgeschichte u. Textkritik*. Cologne and Opladen 1959, 279, maintains it should be athetized, in spite of attempts to rescue it by M. SANCHEZ-WILDBERGER in her diss. *Theokrit-Interpretationen*. Zürich 1955.

[2] Bibl. in LESKY, *Thalatta*. Vienna 1947, 316, n. 214 and H. HERTER, *Bursians Jahresber.* 285, 1944/55, 296.

and fear of the two women, his wife and his mother, who are closest to him.

One poem which we should not like to miss as typically Hellenistic we owe to Bion of Smyrna. We possess the poem on his death ('Ἐπιτάφιος Βίωνος)[1] by a pupil and friend, which celebrates him in the style of bucolic poetry, and indicates that he was the victim of murder by poison. He was younger than Moschus and could be dated two generations later. His *Adonis* ('Ἀδώνιδος Ἐπιτάφιος) is a complex composition of great fascination. Though written for recitation, this hexameter poem achieves the effect of passionate song, by means of its lively movement of syntactically simple cola, its sound-effects and the refrain-like repetition of the lament. Theocritus already made copious use of the refrain line for a similar purpose, especially in *Idyll* 2. The *Adonis* is particularly noteworthy, because in the lament for the beautiful beloved of Aphrodite, with whose death nature dies, we see oriental themes penetrate Hellenistic poetry. Only the later Hellenistic era opened itself to this influence. The subject matter evokes a lofty fervour which stands in strong contrast to Callimachean control and is typical for this epoch of the Hellenistic era. Latin poetry followed this trend in a large measure. A charming trait is added to this picture of grief by the Erotes who are busily occupying themselves with Adonis' corpse. In Hellenistic art Erotes in the plural appear without conceptual difference beside the one boy Eros, who, in some of Bion's shorter poems which we also find in Stobaeus, plays a part which has been strikingly compared with the dallyings in Pompeian murals. There are also bucolic poems among the fragments, but none bears comparison with the *Adonis*. The fragment which goes by the unapt name of *Epithalamium to Achilles and Deidamea* is not Bion's. It is a poem on an epic subject in a bucolic framework in which shepherds tell each other the story of Achilles' love adventures in Scyros.

A specimen of the history of tradition as founded by him is the *Textgeschichte der griech. Bukoliker*, Berl. 1906, by U. V. WILAMOWITZ-MOELLENDORFF. He postulates an edition of the collected poems by Theocritus and attributes the first collection of bucolic poems to the grammarian Artemidorus, who lived in the first half of the first c. B.C. While this collection combined various Bucolica, Artemidorus' son Theon published Theocritus' poems with a commentary. At about the same time the poet was expounded by Asclepiades of Myrlea. From the second century A.D. onward we see literary men take a particularly lively interest in the poet and for the later centuries we even know the names of expounders like Munatius, Theaetetus (both also feature in the scholia) and Amarantus. With the Byzantine renaissance there came a final stage in the interest in Theocritus. The imposing erudition of Wilamowitz' book must not cover the hypothetical character of individual conclusions, cf. GOW I, LX. The papyri (no. 1163-1170 P.; GOW in the pref.) among which pre-Christian ones are lacking, have much to offer for the text through many new variant readings,

[1] Transl. in WILAMOWITZ, *Reden und Vorträge*. I. Berl. 1925, 292.

but hardly anything essential for its tradition. Gallavotti's edition, upon which Gow builds, is important for the knowledge of the manuscripts. The extensive manuscript evidence which begins in the end of the thirteenth century can be divided into an Ambrosianus and a Laurentianus group between which there is one Vaticanus. Since all codices containing *Id.* 14 and 25 show a lacuna between these it may be assumed that they go back to one single manuscript accessible to the Byzantines.

K. LATTE, 'Zur Textkritik Theokrits'. *GGN Phil.-hist.* Kl. 1949, 225, with methodologically important notes on the difficulty of arriving at Theocritus' dialect form. On a collation of the lost codex Patavinus which may be reconstructed from the printed editions of Zacharias Kallierges and the Juntine, by F. NUÑEZ, cf. A. TOVAR, *Anales de Filología Clásica* 4, 1949, 15; cf. W. BÜHLER in his edition of *Europa* (*v. infra*), 13. For the epigrams we have the bucolic tradition and that of the *Anthologia Palatina*; R. J. SMUTNY, *The Text History of the Epigrams of Th.* Univ. of Calif. 1955.

Among the new editions the one by C. GALLAVOTTI, *Theocritus quique ferentur Bucolici Graeci.* Rome 1946 (new impression with addenda 1955) deserves emphasis, since it puts the recensio to a large extent on a new basis. It was due to chronological circumstances that K. LATTE, *Th. Carmina,* Iserlohn 1948 could not yet utilize its material. This was done by A. S. F. GOW in his *Theocritus.* Oxf. 1950, 2nd ed. 1952, in two volumes with an extensive introduction and a thorough commentary which is particularly informative in technical questions. It also offers an abundant bibl. – Of older collective editions of the bucolic poets we mention:

WILAMOWITZ, 2nd ed. Oxf. 1910 (often reprinted), now A. S. F. GOW, Oxf. 1952; by the same *Greek Bucolic Poets transl. with brief notes.* Cambr. 1953. J. M. EDMONDS in the *Loeb Class. Libr.* 1950. PH. E. LEGRAND, 2 vols. *Coll. des Un. de Fr.* 1925/27 (new edition 1946/53). – Scholia: C. N. WENDEL, Leipz. 1914. Id., *Überlieferung und Entstehung der Th.-Scholien. Abh. Gött. Ges. d. Wiss.* 17/2, 1920. – Lexicon: J. RUMPEL, Leipz. 1879; repr. Hildesheim 1961. Language: C. GALLAVOTTI, *Lingua, tecnica e poesia negli idilli di T.* Rome 1952. Interpretations: WILAMOWITZ, *Hellenist. Dichtung.* 2, 1924, 130. M. SANCHEZ-WILDBERGER, *Theokrit-Interpretationen* Diss. Zürich 1955. Recent bibl. in J. H. KÜHN, *Herm.* 86, 1958, 41, 5. – On Moschus: W. BÜHLER, *Die Europa des M. Text, Übers. u. Komm. Herm.* E. 13, 1960, also valuable for stylistic problem of Hellenistic poetry.

4 APOLLONIUS

Of the many epic poems written between Homer and Nonnus one single great epic has been preserved, the *Argonautica* by Apollonius Rhodius. By calling the poet after this island we are at once in the middle of the problems connected with the sparse and uncertain information about his life. Apollonius became a Rhodian, because he passed part of his life in the island and perhaps was granted honorary citizenship there, but he was the only important Hellenistic poet to be born in Alexandria. He is occasionally called Naucratites, which may be connected with his epic poem on the founding of Naucratis unless there is a somewhat contemptuous allusion to his Egyptian origin concealed in the expression.

Our main sources, Suidas and two brief biographies,[1] call him a pupil of Callimachus. Now in such cases we cannot rid ourselves of the fundamental doubt that literary connections could have been made into a pupil-relationship, but in this case a personal relation of this nature between the two men both working in Alexandria has a great deal of probability in its favour. If Apollonius may be thought to be the younger man, his birth will have to be dated between 295 and 290.

Earlier (p. 703) we had occasion to discuss the papyrus which establishes Apollonius' librarianship between Zenodotus and Eratosthenes as the most important fact in his life. Since in this function he also was the governor of Ptolemy III Euergetes, we can place the beginning of his administration in the 'sixties.

The questions of his relationship with Callimachus, his residence at Rhodes and the writing of the *Argonautica* are extremely difficult through the poverty and confusion of ancient information and they have produced a tremendous quantity of literature.[2] We shall first outline as briefly as possible the position of the problems. Callimachus' utterances against the voluminous cyclical epic with a continuous plot (p. 710) seem to hit at Apollonius' work; on the other hand, we have only scanty information about any ill-feeling between the two poets; what there is connects Callimachus' *Ibis* with Apollonius,[3] while he is missing among the Telchines' names in the Florentine scholium on the Aetia prologue. Furthermore, in the first of the two biographies we find data which cannot be made to agree. According to one, Apollonius was first with his teacher Calli-machus and turned to poetry only at a late date. The other states that as an ephebe he had already publicized his *Argonautica* by means of an epideixis, which may be taken to mean a recitation, but this had turned out to be a failure. Thereupon he went to Rhodes, ashamed and hurt, revised the work there and was successful when he recited this new version. The second biography tells the same story and, appealing to 'some people', makes an addition; Apollonius returned to Alexandria, where he gained such distinction that he was deemed worthy of the library and the museum. He was even buried together with Callimachus. Finally we find repeated reference in the scholia to a previous edition (προέκδοσις) of the *Argonautica*, of which variants are given as well.

It is difficult to separate out what can be known from this chaos of partly contradictory information, more difficult at least than covering up lacunae and discrepancies with all sorts of conjectures. In spite of all reserve we may rely on the following facts: Apollonius was librarian at Alexandria, he went from Alex-andria to Rhodes – obviously at a decisive turning-point in his life – and there were two editions of the *Argonautica*, the second of which was written or

---

[1] In Wendel's edition of the scholia.
[2] Abundant evidence in HERTER (*v. inf.*), 223.
[3] Cf. p. 717, n. 1 in add. HERTER, *Bursians Jahresber.* 255, 1937, 89.

completed in Rhodes. Individual scholars[1] wanted to relegate the conflict with Callimachus to the realm of fables since in fact Apollonius is not at all at variance with his teacher's principles. But as there is no denying that the *Argonautica* is a continuous (διηνεκές) narrative poem of heroic deeds as demanded by the Telchines in the prologue of the *Aetia* and that Callimachus rejects this, the conflict of the two men may also be considered to be an historical fact; and similarly a connection with Apollonius' departure for Rhodes may be thought likely.

We proceed a step further when we remind ourselves that the papyrus just mentioned produced a second Apollonius, the idographer, as librarian after Aristophanes of Byzantium.[2] Confusion was inevitable and it is very likely that the variant of the biography which makes Apollonius return to Alexandria after the Rhodes period and only then become librarian owes its origin to the incorrect identification of the Rhodian with the idographer.[3] If this is so, the report which knows of a return of Apollonius to Alexandria and inserts his librarianship in a late period of his life, but the writing of the *Argonautica* in an early one, is unmasked as a conjecture. But then the conception based on the first variant of the first biography, i.e. on a late start of Apollonius' poetic activity, becomes more likely. This start should be allotted to the period of the librarianship, the duration of which can be determined to some extent. The office of librarian was connected with that of tutor to the prince. Since Euergetes (b. about 280) was his charge, we arrive, as has been stated, in the 'sixties. On the other hand, we have the valuable information in Suidas (*v.* Eratosthenes) that Eratosthenes, Apollonius' successor, was called upon to undertake the direction of the library by Ptolemy Euergetes. In 246 this ruler mounted the Lagides' throne, but we have to keep open the possibility that he had Eratosthenes appointed when he was still heir apparent, so that we shall have to go back a few years for Apollonius' departure. There is no simple proof, but it remains by far the most likely assumption that this departure of Apollonius was connected with Callimachus' opposition, which in turn was influenced or given impetus by the direction which Apollonius' poetry had taken. But then we may place some confidence in the tradition which testifies to a twofold edition of the *Argonautica* and believe that the first was written in Alexandria, the second in Rhodes. And the possibility cannot even be excluded that the report of the unfortunate epideixis in Alexandria contains some truth, even though we shall have to imagine this as taking place not in the poet's youth, but during his time as librarian. It is natural enough to bring together this Alexandrian epideixis with the first provisional edition mentioned by the scholia. It is not known how long Apollonius, writing poetry and teaching grammar, lived in Rhodes after he settled there.

It is not until the Hellenistic age that, with Apollonius' *Argonautica*, we dis-

---

[1] Cf. with p. 711 n. 2. It is entirely uncertain if the epigram *Ant. Pal.* 11, 275 implies an attack by Apollonius on Callimachus, cf. HERTER, *Bursians Jahresber.* 285, 1944/55, 224.

[2] On the possibility that he should be dated prior to Aristophanes, *v.* p. 703, n. 2.

[3] So also H. HERTER in his recent sensible discussion 'Zur Lebensgeschichte des A. v. R.'. *Rhein. Mus.* 91, 1942, 315.

cover a complete epic presentation of this circle of legends, one of the oldest in Greek mythology. In the *Odyssey* we could identify the echo of ancient poetry which related the story of the voyage to the sunland Aea on the great stream of Ocean (cf. p. 43), but in Apollonius' time this had long been lost. But poetry in all its forms had time and again turned to the legend of the Argonauts and the local history of many places connected with it. Thus Apollonius was faced with a rich tradition with many, partly contradictory, variants. We cannot imagine his source studies extensive enough; the thoroughness with which he proceeded and the pains he took are especially perceptible in the first two books of the *Argonautica*.[1]

The composition exhibits generally a systematic arrangement as the subject matter presented itself. The first two books describe the voyage to the land of Colchis, the third the adventures leading to the winning of the Fleece, while the fourth tells of the dangers of the flight and the return home. The stress on details, however, is variedly distributed; beside rapid transitions there are passages over which he has lingered lovingly, so that we observe the same rejection of symmetry, the same tendency to variety as elsewhere in Hellenistic poetry.

While a prooemium with prayer formula is merely indicated and much of the preceding history is saved for later, the introductory passage offers an elaborate catalogue of the Argonauts, geographically arranged in the manner of a periplus and leading from the north of Greece via east and west back to north. The catalogue tradition of ancient epic served as its model. The scenes of departure in Iolcus and on the beach of Pagasae are spun out in detail; then follows the long series of stopping places and adventures on the way out, which is made along the usual route to Colchis. For the part up to the passage through the Symplegades, which are thought to be at the entrance to the Pontus, the tradition had a number of effective episodes ready-made which he elaborated successfully. There is in the first place the landing in Lemnos, whose women, under a curse of Aphrodite, had killed their husbands. But now they are glad to put up the Argonauts. The result is a delectable sojourn from which Heracles has to call his companions to action. Then follow the initiation in the mysteries at Samothrace and the adventures in Cyzicus where the Argonauts give the Doliones effective help against the evil giants, only to get into a bitterly regretted nocturnal battle with their friends through a misunderstanding, when they are driven back to Cyzicus by unfavourable winds. The next stop on the coast of the Propontis brings the Hylas episode. Nymphs seize the beautiful boy, Heracles seeks him in the woods and the Argonauts continue their voyage without him, since the sea-god Glaucus announces that the hero is destined to perform other deeds. In this way the greatest of the companions is eliminated beside whom Jason would have been unthinkable as the main hero in Colchis.

The story passes without a stop from Book 1 to Book 2, which begins with

---

[1] The mythology in L. RADERMACHER, *Mythos und Sage bei den Griechen*. 2nd ed. Vienna 1938, 154. On the original fairyland object of the voyage A. LESKY, 'Aia'. *Wien. Stud.* 63, 1948, 22.

Pollux' boxing match against Amycus, the barbarian king of the Bebryces. This story as well as that of Hylas was also the subject of poems by Theocritus. When we discussed these, we also touched upon the vexing question of priority. In Bithynia the Argonauts come upon the blind king Phineus who, in deep misery, is doing penance for some ancient offence. The Boreades liberate him from the Harpies, predatory storm spirits who rob him of every meal or defile it. As a reward he gives them good advice for the rest of their voyage. The compositional significance of this preview is that the various minor episodes of the second half of the voyage are summed up in it. The passage through the Symplegades after the pigeon's test flight is depicted with dramatic power; then there follow up to Colchis a number of stops of minor importance, of which only the island of Ares rates a mention. There the Argonauts drive out the Stymphalian birds, and there they meet the sons of Phrixus, who want to go to their father's native land. Their mother is Chalciope, Aeetes' daughter and sister of Medea. She is going to play her part in the events in Colchis and so the meeting in the island of Ares forms a link between the description of the voyage and the winning of the Golden Fleece.

Book 3 starts with a new prooemium and portrays the events in Colchis by means of a technique which often resolves the happenings into parallel strands of action. Medea's decisive intervention is first motivated in a scene in which the goddesses Hera and Athene enjoin Aphrodite to have Eros do his work. Independent from this motivation, however, Medea's awakening love, her hard struggle between loyalty to her father's house and passion for the handsome stranger is presented to us as a drama full of tension with the girl's soul for a stage. Another plot concerning Chalciope, which leads to the intervention of Phrixus' widow and the decisive talk between the sisters, runs alongside it. The plot is split up further in that the council in the Argonauts' camp and in that of the Colchians is depicted separately. The composition of this book is particularly careful; developing through several stages, it comes to the meeting of Medea and Jason, when he receives the magic ointment; then follows the yoking of the fire-breathing bulls and the defeat of the armed men who spring out of the sown dragons' teeth (a theme taken from the Cadmus legend), and finally, when treason threatens from Aeetes' side, Jason carries off the Fleece and escapes with Medea.

The last two events, however, already belong in Book 4, which begins with a brief invocation to the Muse, in which the poet asks the question whether Medea's action is fate or a responsible deed, without giving an answer.

The return differs completely in aspect from the voyage to Colchis. When the fabulous land Aea on the bank of Ocean used to be the Argonauts' goal, they sailed back on the mighty circling river and came from it into the Mediterranean. One of the most enchanting chapters of mythical geography is the way in which it modified the return of the Argonauts as the knowledge of foreign countries and seas increased, newly discovered facts and ancient mythical elements forming various and often grotesque combinations.[1] In Apollonius this

[1] Survey in A. LESKY, *Thalatta*, Vienna 1947, 61.

return voyage has developed a particularly complex and rich background, individual phases achieving a vivid dramatic life through the pursuing Colchians. Apollonius could no longer let the Argonauts reach the Ocean through the Phasis, so he makes them sail up the Ister for which he followed a rare version of Timagetus, one of the Hellenistic writers of works *On Ports* (Περὶ λιμένων). In the voyage through the Ister, Eridanus and Rhodanus into the Tyrrhenian sea the unusual description of river branches plays a great part which fits quite well into this phantastical geography. The mouth of one of the branches of the Ister is thought to be in the Gulf of Fiume; there the group of pursuers which took a different route under Apsyrtus overtakes the fugitives and there Medea's brother falls a victim to her ruse. In the Tyrrhenian sea the Argonauts go to see Circe, Aeetes' sister, who purifies Jason and Medea from blood guilt in a series of scenes elaborated with psychological effect, but who nevertheless turns the guilty couple out of her house. On the next leg of the voyage to the island of the Phaeacians the Argonauts pass by mythical places from the *Odyssey* which Apollonius, in accordance with the widely accepted contemporary theory, thought to be in the western part of the Mediterranean, like the island of the Sirens and the Planctae. This danger spot was negotiated with the aid and large-scale participation of benevolent gods. When they are with the Phaeacians, who live in Corcyra, the fugitives meet the second group of Colchians. Since Alcinous only wants to surrender Medea if they are not married, a quick wedding is celebrated in Corcyra.

From Corcyra the Argonauts do not yet reach home; there follows a passage, rather like an appendix, into which the various traditional stories have been fitted. A gale of nine days – we know the number on such an occasion from the *Odyssey* – sweeps the Argonauts to Libya. Here there are still all sorts of encounters and dangers. As in Pindar (*Pyth.* 4), the Argonauts have to carry their ship over land for twelve days. In one situation in which there seems to be no way that leads any farther, Triton turns up as a helper. The vanquishing of the bronze Cretan giant Talos has been inserted in the last leg of the homeward voyage. Also two aetia, one of a sacrificial custom in Anape, the other for an agon in Aegina, have been put in. Callimachus (fr. 7, 19. 198 Pf.) dealt with these as well. A brief and entirely unadorned report on the voyage to Pagasae is joined on to the poet's wish for a blessing for his work, a prayer which has a formal kinship with the conclusion of hymns to the gods.

Apollonius' epic has numerous aspects which depend largely on the literary-historical background of the work. Consequently it has been very variedly appreciated in the course of time. To one it seems unpoetical, dry, pedantic, while others – and especially in recent times such a judgment is increasing – stress the truly poetical qualities in the *Argonautica*.

In the first place it should be clearly understood that the intellectual world out of which this epic originated was separated from that of Homer by an immeasurable distance. When the older poets moulded for their people the history of the heroic past, they claimed that their verses imbued true events with splendour and permanence. And in these events gods were active everywhere, great spirits inspiring faith who helpfully allied themselves with man or wrathfully struck out at him. This sort of reality had not existed for Apollonius for a long time. The living myth had already become mythology for people like him or it was proceeding toward this condition. Hardly anything can be said about Apollonius' personal religious feelings, but his attitude to tradition cannot have been very different from Callimachus'. His pen was guided by an erudite interest in mythical tradition and at the same time a delight in the unfading beauty of its creations. Both can be discerned in his verse.

The tremendous distance from Homer's world is in exciting contrast with the fact that numerous and essential elements of ancient epic remained preserved. In Apollonius also the gods act, but the very nature of the great Olympian scene at the opening of Book 3 reveals the ornamental character of such passages. With Hera, Athene and Eros a complete divine apparatus is developed, but Medea's love and its consequences are also imaginable without it. And in the portrayal of the girl's emotional struggles we recognize this poet much more directly than in the conversations of the Olympians. While in Homer man's actions were determined by his own impulses and the influence of the gods simultaneously, this duality of motivation has now resulted in separate spheres of action. The divine plot takes place on an upper stage; its connection with earthly happenings is neither indissoluble nor irrevocably necessary.

Apollonius retains important formal elements of Homeric epic. While he is sparing with metaphors, he uses similes with great frequency. But their free spontaneity as we know it in Homer has been restricted in favour of a more direct bearing on the action, though the subject matter has been expanded in many directions. Illustration of emotions by means of similes, found in Homer only in an initial stage,[1] has been developed by him with great skill. Thus Medea's agitation and irresolution are elucidated by the image of the sun's ray (3. 756), which is reflected on to a wall by the ruffled surface of water.[2] This rare simile returns in Virgil (Aen. 8. 22) and Aristaenetus (2. 5), a good example of the ramifications of Hellenistic tradition. Apollonius also uses stock scenes, but he restricts – and this is characteristic for the limits of his formal imitation of Homer – completely recurrent formulae to a minimum. This is connected with another, fundamentally important, observation. Apollonius' language is largely based on Homer. But this does not mean that he accepted the tradition without due reflection or that he imitated it naïvely. It is rather a repetition of what we already observed in the case of Antimachus of Colophon; the linguistic resources borrowed are given new effectiveness through constant, well-planned variation, sometimes even by means of a shifting of the meaning. Added to this Apollonius was widely read, which circumstance admitted an influx of elements from post-Homeric poetry up to his own time.[3]

[1] W. SCHADEWALDT, Iliasstudien. Abh. Sächs. Ak. Phil.-hist. Kl. 43/6, 1938, 120, 4.

[2] A surmise about Stoic origin of this image in H. FRÄNKEL, Mus. Helv. 14, 1957, 17.

[3] G. MARXER, Die Sprache des A. Rh. in ihrer Beziehung zu Homer. Diss. Zürich 1935. H. ERBSE, 'Homerscholien und hellenistische Glossare bei A. Rh.'. Herm. 81, 1953, 163 in which it is demonstrated that A. utilizes the most diverse linguistic elements but not the grammatical scholarship of his time.

The Homeric legacy which functions as a sort of framework for this epic with regard to themes and style, is contrasted by what we have to consider as its Hellenistic element. In the first place he was a realist, the expression to be taken in its broadest sense; this realism is in the final analysis connected with the altered attitude toward the myths, with the awareness of their illusory nature. What we mean is most closely akin to what H. Fränkel lately summarized under the catchword of fixation. Apollonius may be granted important poetic ability, there may be much that is praiseworthy in his work, but he was not truly a poet filled with the god; time and agə'n we are struck by the factual coolness with which his glance takes in things. And this also entails the great care taken in motivation and establishment of cohesion. It is only one, though a very important, aspect of this attitude that Apollonius, unlike Homer, put his story on the basis of a continuous and verifiable period of time.

The poet frequently accounts for contemporary customs by seeking explanations in early history, and in this way he links his own time with the mythical past. Apollonius is a true Hellenist in that he devotes a large part of his poem to aetiological matters, interspersing the narrative of the voyage with a wealth of such stories.

As a portrayer of emotions, especially of those with which Eros visits the human soul, Apollonius belongs entirely in the sphere of Hellenistic poetry, which had its origin in Euripides' works. It has always been considered that his best achievement was his description of Medea's pangs and doubts until, following her own passion and at the same time moved by other impulses, she goes her fatal way. After the longwinded description of the outward voyage which at times sinks down to the level of a learned guide book in spite of effective episodes, we enter the realm of true poetry with the passages indicated. This is also attested by the tremendous subsequent influence of Book 3 in ancient literature. It is also comparable with Euripides in that the effective portrayal of an individual emotion is more important than a completely drawn picture of a character. The girl who is close to a breakdown in the tempest of her first passion, and the great sorceress who with supreme control applies her skills in the further course of things could not be readily combined in one description.

We also observe a Hellenistic element in many a description of nature which would be unthinkable in this way in the old epic. There are successful seascapes in which new colour effects are achieved, as the sailing of the Argo when the dark flood foams under the beat of the oars, the men's armour flashes like fire in the morning light and the long wake seems like a bright path in a green meadow. Apollonius also shares with the rest of Hellenistic art the discovery of children.[1] The Eros of the celestial scenes of Book 3 is a veritable model of the spoilt rascal who cheats his comrades at play and can only be induced by his divine mother to perform a service by means of an expensive present. It is hardly possible to imagine a greater contrast than that between this scene and that in Book 1 of the *Aeneid*, when Venus addresses the numen of her son Amor!

[1] H. HERTER, 'Das Kind im Zeitalter des Hellenismus'. *Bonner Jahrb.* 132, 1927, 250.

It will have become clear that Apollonius cannot be characterized concisely. He proves himself to be a poet of considerable importance in not a few passages of his work, but he was by no means completely successful in blending the rich tradition which attracted the scholar with his own creation without some annoying sediment. His fire was too weak to fuse all the heterogeneous elements into one whole.

The remnants which attest Apollonius' *Ctisis* poetry are exceedingly scanty. He wrote in hexameters about the founding of the cities of Alexandria, Naucratis, Cnidos, Rhodes and Caunus. Attribution of a *Founding of Lesbos* is doubtful. The poem *Canobus*, dealing with the city near Alexandria, a favourite pleasure resort, was written in choliambs. We also know of scholarly works on Homer (Πρὸς Ζηνόδοτον), on Hesiod, Archilochus and Antimachus.[1]

The appreciation of Hellenistic literature is strongly influenced by Callimachean literary principles. The *Argonautica* is practically the only surviving work which deviates from these. This should not lead to the wrong conclusion that voluminous epic poems had become a rarity in the Hellenistic era. Just as previously we saw Lysander (p. 304) in search of a poetic herald of his deeds, the Hellenistic rulers were also fond of having their praise proclaimed. There was Choerilus of Iasos,[2] who wrote for Alexander the Great, Simonides of Magnesia for Antiochus and Musaeus of Ephesus for the Attalids. Mythological epic poetry flourished alongside these. We can give only some names here and are not confident in every case that the author concerned does not belong in the imperial age. The tradition is at any rate the same. In the scholia on Apollonius mention is made of the *Argonautica* by Cleon of Curion and Theolytus; Menelaus of Aegae wrote a *Thebaïd*; Antagoras and Demosthenes dealt with the same subject. Heracles, for whom we mention Diotimus of Adramyttion, and Dionysus, connected with the name of Neoptolemus of Parium, were also favourite themes of this late epic. Nicaenetus of Samos or Abdera wrote of the adventures of Lyrcus with which the founding of Caunos (*v. supra* Apollonius' ctisis-poetry) is connected; a *Catalogue of Women* is mentioned and some epigrams have been preserved; local history was also treated, in epic form. While generally we have hardly any reason to deplore the loss of all these products, such as the voluminous *Bithyniaca* of Demosthenes of Bithynia, we encounter in Rhianus of Crete a poet of greater importance and wider influence. He wrote his poems in the second half of the third century and was also active as a dramatist. The readings preserved in the scholia give us a favourable impression of his edition of Homer. As an epic poet he wrote a *Heraclea* in fourteen books and some poems named after districts: *Thessalica, Achaica, Eliaca* and *Messeniaca*. In general we do not know how the elements of mythical and historical tradition were distributed, but we can say a little more of the *Messeniaca* which Pausanias utilized in Book 4 alongside the historian Myron of Priene.[3] Here (6. 3) we learn that Aristomenes, the hero of

[1] On an epigram attributed to Apollonius v. p. 730 n. 1.

[2] WILL RICHTER, *Nachr. Ak. Gött. Phil-hist. Kl.* 1960/3, 41, 3, calls Choerilus 'the courtly flatterer of Alexander, the notorious caricature of a pseudo-poet'.

[3] J. KROYMANN, *Pausanias und Rhianos.* Berlin 1943.

the second Messenian war, played a no less important part in Rhianus than Achilles in the *Iliad*. A fragment of unknown origin preserved by Stobaeus (1 Powell) contains twenty-one plainly and firmly constructed hexameters about the blindness of mankind. A series of *Epigrams* (66–76 Powell; fasc. 6, 64 D.) displays conventional love themes.

The main textual source for Apollonius is the Laurentianus 32. 9 of the beginning of the eleventh century which we mentioned in connection with Aeschylus and Sophocles. In addition there is some other noteworthy tradition; H. FRÄNKEL (*v. infra*) distinguished three families. The papyri (no. 52–65 P.) yield little. P. KINGSTON, 'A papyrus of Ap. Rhod.'. *Univ. of London. Bulletin of the Inst. of Class. Stud.* 7, 1960. H. FRÄNKEL, 'Die Handschriften der Argon. des A. v. Rh.'. *GGN Phil.-hist. Kl.* 1929, 164 has clarified the foundations of the recensio. Standard text H. FRÄNKEL, Oxf. 1961 (*Oxf. Class. T.*) which has replaced older editions by A. WELLAUER (Leipz. 1828), R. MERKEL (Leipz. 1854) and R. C. SEATON, Oxf. 1900. Comm. eds. of Book 3: M. M. GILLIES, Cambr. 1928. A. ARDIZZONI, Bari 1958. F. VIAN, Paris 1961. The abundant scholia in which material from several ancient comm. (Theon under Augustus, Lucillus of Tarrha, 1st or 2nd c. A.D., Sophocles in the 2nd c. A.D.) has been incorporated, in the excellent edition of C. WENDEL, Berl. 1935; 2nd unrev. ed. 1958; id.: *Die Überlieferung der Scholien zu A. v. Rh. Abh. d. Gött. Ges. d. Wiss.* 1932. – Verbal index in WELLAUER's edition. – Translation: German, *Th. v. Scheffer*. Leipz. 1940; English, E. V. RIEU, Penguin Class. 1959. For the bibl. on Apollonius we possess a unique aid: H. HERTER, *Bursians Jahresber.* 285, 1944/55, 213. In add. the important essay by H. FRÄNKEL, 'Das Argonautenepos des A.'. *Mus. Helv.* 14, 1957, 1. On the characteristics of individual personages, id. 'Ein Don Quijote unter den Argonauten des Apollonios'. *Mus. Helv.* 17, 1960, 1. Some details in A. Ardazzoni, 'Note crit. ed. eseg. sul testo di Ap. Rhod.'. *Riv. Fil.* 34, 1956, 364. – The fragments of Apollonius as well as of other epic poets in J. U. POWELL, *Collectanea Alexandrina.* Oxf. 1925, 4. 9. For Rhianus also D. fasc. 6, 64 *F Gr Hist* 265 – K. ZIEGLER, *Das Hellenistische Epos.* Leipz. 1934.

5 EPIGRAM

The epigrams of Callimachus and Theocritus were discussed in a previous chapter; both these poets made their contributions to raising a form which had a long history behind it[1] to the degree of perfection which it reached in the Hellenistic age. As we said before (p. 641), the final phase of this development had already become evident in the fourth century. The old inscription on funeral stele and sacrificial object began to be separated from its vehicle and to live a life of its own. But it would be wrong to think that this divorce was

---

[1] *v. sup.* p. 172; 303; 417; 641. On the theory of the epigram, LESSING, *Zerstreute Anmerkungen über das Epigramm und einige der vornehmsten Epigrammatisten* (1771) and HERDER in the *Anmerkungen über die Anthologie der Griechen* (Vol. 15, 344. 372 of the ed. by B. SUPHAN).

complete.[1] In the Hellenistic period and the time following it, epigrams still appeared as actual inscriptions on stone. Epigraphical works overwhelm us with examples, and it is enough to open, for instance, Heberdey's Termessus-volume of the *Tituli Asiae Minoris* (III/1) to see what artistic ambition still achieved with varying success even under the empire. But this does not alter the fact that the epigram freed itself from its original subjection to its purpose and could appear as independent literature.

The tremendously increased scope of themes now cast in the form of epigrams was the result of this newly gained freedom. It may be stated without exaggeration that this form, like none other, became the faithful mirror of the diversity and at the same time of the narrowness of Hellenistic life. For Alexandria and its literary domains it achieved about the same as Menander's comedy for Athens, which means that the lofty note of self-sacrificing devotion and proved bravery which rings from the funeral inscriptions in the times of Greek freedom have fallen silent. In their stead a rich stream of themes from everyday life flows in. A peculiar development is evident from the first themes which we wish to introduce, the pleasures of the banquet and those of love (and its attendant sorrows). Earlier (p. 172) we said that it was worth while considering the possibility that in the early history of the epigram elegy as a lament for the dead and as a hymn had influenced epitaphs and dedications. In the era under discussion the epigram approached elegy again and one might well wonder whether Callimachus' *Ep.* 1 or Leonidas, *Anth. Pal.* 10. 1 should be called a short elegy or an epigram. But also the older monodic lyric was still thriving, so that it could be said that only now the epigram actually became a lyric poem expressing the most varied shades of feeling. It is significant that Asclepiades, *Anth. Pal.* 12. 50 (this is also basically a short elegy) very emphatically quotes Alcaeus (346 LP). The Hellenistic poet, of course, combines the quotation with an artistic variation. Certainly we have to imagine that not a few of these epigrams were declaimed at a banquet of friends such as were held in Alexandria or Rhodes or in other places. The spoken epigram took the place of the sung scolion of earlier times, and this occurrence is symptomatic.

The range of subject matter of these epigrams extended far beyond the sphere of the symposium and of love; it comprised such varying themes as a description of primitive occupations, impressions received from nature, or a discussion of works of art. The form of the epigram also showed a variety of patterns; funeral and votive inscriptions continued to be composed mainly according to the old models, even when they were fictional, but the influence of the mime led to a vivid dramatization. An example of an epigram which was really a mime is *Anth. Pal.* 5. 181, in which Asclepiades abuses a servant who dares utter only a timid objection, and then sends him off to do some shopping on credit; or *Anth. Pal.* 5. 46, an epigram of Philodemus' with a bold accumulation of fragments of conversation. Here this development reaches its peak.

The motley diversity of the Hellenistic epigram is not only due to its subject

[1] In opposition to R. REITZENSTEIN, *Epigramm und Skolion*. Giessen 1893, WILAMOWITZ' treatment of the problem in *Hellenist. Dicht.* 1, Berl. 1924 (2nd unaltered ed. 1961), 119.

matter, it is expressed no less forcefully by the variety in the individual poets. Certain differences of style – they have been called schools – are noted. The artistic physiognomy of Leonidas of Tarentum shows interesting features. At an early stage he left his home in lower Italy, wrote for Neoptolemus in Epirus, then for Pyrrhus, and died in 260 after a restless wandering life. He likes to pretend that poor men like huntsmen and peasants dedicate their tools to the gods of the district in which they perform their labours. He was assiduously imitated up to a very late date, as shown by *Anth. Pal.* 6. 4, the fisherman's dedication.[1] In Leonidas the misery and realism of the theme stands in a peculiar and affected contrast to the language, which is of a baroque extravagance. Yet he can express himself more simply as well, as in *Anth. Pal.* 10. 1, in which Priapus, here as the god at the harbour, announces the beginning of sea travel in the midst of the delights of spring. He can also swing into a powerful attack on opponents, and we feel directly sympathetic when the homeless poet complains of his restless life and finds his only consolation in the gift of the Muses (*Anth. Pal.* 7. 715, probably the concluding poem of his collection).

Among the poets of mainland Greece Phalaecus, probably a Phocian, and Perses of Thebes wrote epigrams even before 300. What we have of the latter shows that they were plain inscriptions; the prosodists have called a verse Phalaecean after the former, like a Simiac after Simias of Rhodes (*v.* p. 725) and a Callimachean after the great Alexandrian. They all used a stichic metre borrowed from older lyric poetry which they developed further. The epigrammatist Mnasalces of Sicyon, who wrote in the middle of the third century, was obviously an imitator who, like so many after him, trifled with variations on the traditional themes. It is noteworthy that in this circle we meet poetesses of no inconsiderable merit. Nossis of Epizephyrian Locri wished to compete with Sappho in epigram *Anth. Pal.* 7. 718, which evidently concluded her book of poems; Anyte of Tegea shows her charm in delicate descriptions of nature (e.g. *Anth. Pal.* 9. 144), when she observes children at play (*Anth. Pal.* 6. 312) or writes an epitaph for a dead pet. Both these poetesses also tried writing hymns.

In the Greek Orient the art of the epigram shows a marked contrast with Leonidas' manner. Side by side with Callimachus, who proves his mastery in the rejection of all superfluous ornament, in rigid tension and controlled conciseness, there is Asclepiades of Samos, who wrote *circa* 320 to 290. We heard his praise sung in Theocritus' *Thalysia*, in which he appears as Sicelidas and we were surprised to encounter him in the Florentine scholium on the prologue to the *Aetia*, together with Posidippus among Callimachus' opponents, the Telchines. In his verse we recognize the pleasure-seeker who has a great deal to say about love, both of beautiful women and of boys. Many of his verses are quite *risqué* (cf. *Anth. Pal.* 5. 203. 207), but he never sinks to those depths of prurience which was a common feature of the later epigrams. The slightness of the majority of themes corresponds with the extreme simplicity of style. But he shows his skill in the compactness and directness of atmosphere which he calls

---

[1] Cf. *Anth. Pal.* 6. 5. 23. 25-30. 90. 192 f.

up and the honest feeling which he expresses. Although they had many points in common, he is far removed by his lively temperament from Callimachus' loftiness. Splendid proof of this is found in *Anth. Pal.* 5. 64, a prescription for a life full of pride and passion; Zeus, the god whose own ardour showed him the way through bronze walls, is not going to stop him from enjoying the pleasures of love with his snow and hail, thunder and lightning.

Asclepiades probably lived for some time in Alexandria where he became friendly with Posidippus of Macedonian Pella and Hedylus of Samos. Posidippus composed poetry for the Aeolians, who honoured him with their proxeny; he also took an interest in philosophy before he took up writing epigrams in the style of Asclepiades in Alexandria. Hedylus is a product of the Samian community whose zest for life still echoes in his verse and who played an important part in the development of his style. His family was favoured by the Muses. We have a fragment of an elegiac narrative *Scylla* (fasc. 6, 48 D.) by his mother Hedyle, a daughter of the Attic iambic poetess Moschine.

The names which we gave here represent a selection from a great abundance, but from among the many others Heraclitus of Halicarnassus should at least be mentioned; we have of him only one surviving epigram, a funeral poem on a young woman who died in childbed (*Anth. Pal.* 7. 465), which reveals a deep and strong emotion.

The flourishing of the epigram lasted through the most vigorous epoch of the Hellenistic age, and came to an end together with it soon after the middle of the century. When at the end of the third century the Greek desire for freedom was roused once more and the Aetolian league with Sparta at its side faced Macedon in the War of the Allies (220–217), epigrams resounded once again with the praise of Spartan ideals, steadfastness in battle and heroic death. Alcaeus of Messene was the leader of a not inconsiderable chorus. This period ended when Flamininus proclaimed to the Greeks their Roman-made freedom at the Isthmian games of the year 196. In Alexandria at this time Dioscorides also sang of ancient Spartan discipline. Here the political alignment played a part, since for the present Egypt was supporting Cleomenes. For the rest he wrote erotic epigrams in imitation of Asclepiades, but he is particularly interesting for a number of epigrams on literary personalities[1] such as Thespis, Aeschylus, Sophocles and Sositheus (*Anth. Pal.* 7. 410 f. 37. 707), which seem to have belonged to illustrations of a book.

At the end of the second and the beginning of the first century the Hellenistic epigram underwent a late revival in a group of poets collectively called the Phoenician School. Antipater of Sidon is not a poet of power and originality, but he exhibits greater seriousness than the other epigrammatists of the time by giving, for instance, profound interpretations of the symbols of funeral monuments (*Anth. Pal.* 7. 423-427; cf. Leonidas 7. 422).[2] Meleager of Gadara entirely follows the tradition of the Alexandrian epigram with his poems of wine and

---

[1] M. GABATHULER, *Hellenistische Epigramme auf Dichter*. St Gallen 1937.

[2] Epigraphical texts for Antipater given by W. PEEK, 'Delische Weihepigramme'. *Herm.* 76, 1941, 408.

love. Philodemus of the same city, the Epicurean of Herculaneum (*v.* p. 682), also belongs to this circle with his lewdly erotic epigrams. The most important observation about these productions is that rhetoric is gaining a greater hold on the writing of epigrams with its metaphors and sound-effects. The subject matter used by poets like Meleager and Philodemus had a great deal in common with the Latin love elegy, but they are clearly separated on the other hand by the decreased dominance of subjectivity and a greater realism.

It was not until the turn of the century that the epigram came to new life with poets like Crinagoras, but he marks the beginning of a development which it will be better to discuss in a later section.

The fact that we can read epigrams from a variety of periods and by so many writers is due to a much-stratified tradition whose history can be largely reconstructed.

The collecting of epigrams was begun early in the Hellenistic era if not earlier. When Philochorus made his collection of Attic inscriptions (*v.* p. 666), it also contained poetry as a matter of course. On the other hand, there are good grounds for assuming that several of the above-mentioned poets of epigrams published them in the form of books. In addition there were in the Hellenistic age collections of epigrams by different writers, as the papyri (no. 1256. 1258. 1263. 1393 P.) show. The one published by Meleager of Gadara in 70 B.C. under the title *Stephanus* was destined to have the greatest influence. Its introductory poem has been preserved (*Anth. Pal.* 4. 1). We may believe the lemmatist of the Palatinus (*v. infra*) that it was arranged in alphabetical order. Next came the collection of Philippus of Thessalonice, likewise a *Stephanus*, compiling in A.D. 40 the epigrams written since Meleager, once again alphabetically arranged. Again the introductory poem of this *Garland* with an enumeration of the poets it contained found its way into the collection preserved (*Anth. Pal.* 4. 2). Philippus' *Garland* showed the clearest indication of a literary school; attempts to outline such schools as the Peloponnesian, Alexandrian or Phoenician according to style and subject matter are of doubtful value. Information about collections in later times are mostly very vague; of great importance is the one which Agathias published in connection with the revival of epigrammatic poetry towards the end of antiquity in the middle of the sixth century. Suidas quotes it as *Cyclus*; we find the introductory poem in the *Anth. Pal.* (4. 3); it was arranged in subject-groups. When epigrams found renewed interest in the Byzantine Renaissance, and people even began to write them, various smaller collections, among which the earliest was the *Sylloge Euphemiana*, were made; in 900 Constantine Cephalas, the highest churchman (protopapas) at the court of Byzantium, compiled the largest. He took the three old ones mentioned as his basis and added individual poets from various editions. He attempted to combine corresponding subject-groups, but he was not entirely successful, so that groups in alphabetical order have been preserved. The evidence which we have is founded on Cephalas' collection. In the year 1299 (on the date cf. BECKBY in the introduction 70. 4) the monk Planudes finished in Constantinople the collection in seven books which we usually refer to as the *Anthologia Planudea* and which is preserved in the Marcianus 481 in his own copy. It was the only one to preserve the memory of the Greek epigram, until at the end of the sixteenth century a much more comprehensive collection emerged in the Heidelberg Codex Palatinus 23. The manuscript was mainly written by four scribes in 980; it has scholia and its first part has been checked by a corrector. Of importance are also the additions of the so-called lemmatist, a well-informed man who appended lemmata. The Heidelberg manuscript soon caused a sensation; it was donated to Pope Gregory XV (1623) by Maximilian of Bavaria and so came to the Vatican. It was then divided in two parts bound separately, and this was to prove disastrous. In the year 1797 Napoleon demanded the surrender of the manuscript which then came to the National Library in Paris. When after the conclusion of peace in 1815 its return to Germany was asked for and obtained, only the first larger part of the manuscript came back, while the second with the last two books of the anthology remained in France as Parisinus Suppl. Gr. 384. Both parts were collected in an excellent reproduction by K. PREISENDANZ, *Anthologia Palatina, codex Palatinus et codex Parisinus phototypice editi.* Leiden 1911.

The collection of the *Anth. Pal.* contains (according to the modern numbering) in Book 4 the introductory poems which Meleager, Philippus and Agathias prefixed to their collections. The anthologist copied them from Constantine Cephalas' work, the same applying substantially to Books 5-7, and 9-12, although actually there is no certainty with regard to all the parts, especially of Book 12. The ancient collection was extended in the *Anth. Pal.* with Books 1-3, 8, 13-15 (later poems, many of them Christian, but also older work which had not been included by Cephalas).

The most notable difference between *Palatina* and *Planudea* is that the latter has another 388 poems, although in other respects its volume is smaller than that of the *Palatina*. Modern editions of the anthology append this surplus as *Appendix Planudea*, or Book 16, to the *Palatina*. According to his own indications Planudes used two prototypes. One could have been the *Codex Palatinus* itself or a copy of it, the second, however, an independent abbreviated edition of Cephalas.

Editions: For a complete text of the *Anth. Pal.* we are still dependent on F. DÜBNER–E. COUGNY, 3 vols. Paris 1864–90 (with Latin translation). In the *Loeb Class. Libr.* the text was prepared without apparatus, with an English transl. by W. R. PATON, 5 vols. Lond. from 1917. The Teubneriana by H. STADT-MÜLLER, important because of its apparatus criticus, is unfinished; available are: I (Book 1-6) 1894; II/1 (Bk 7) 1899; III/1 (Bk 9, 1-563) 1906. G. LUCK, *Gnom.* 30, 1958, 274, draws attention to some manuscripts from Planudes' circle (Marc. XI/1) in Planudes' own hand which could be utilized. The bilingual edition of the *Coll. des Univ. de Fr.* by P. WALTZ and G. SOURY, frequently reprinted, has progressed to the seventh volume (9. 1-358) in the years 1928-60. All the 16 books with apparatus criticus, German transl. and notes are now available in the 4 vols. of the Tusculum-Bücherei, prepared by H. BECKBY, Munich 1957-58. The readings of Marcianus 481, unknown so far, have been included for Books 10-16. Vol. I has an extensive introduction with a history of the epigram, enumeration of the textual evidence and copious bibl. A. PRESTA, *Ant. Pal. con introd. di* G. PERROTTA. Rome 1957. – Since the discovery of the *Palatina* the *Anthologia Planudea* has only had some value as an aid for restoration. The latest edition is the one by H. DE BOSCH, 5 vols. Utrecht 1795-1822, with the splendid Latin transl. by H. GROTIUS. – Separate studies: J. GEFFCKEN, *Leonidas von Tarent.* Leipz. 1896. AUG. OEHLER, *Der Kranz des Meleagros.* Berl. 1920 (bilingual). G. LUCK, 'Die Dichterinnen der griech. Anthologie'. *Mus. Helv.* 11, 1954, 170. A. S. F. GOW, 'Leonidas of Tarentum'. *Class. Quart.* 8, 1958, 113. Id., *The Greek Anthology. Sources and Ascriptions.* Publ. by the Society for the Promotion of Hell. Studies. London 1958. C. GALLAVOTTI, 'Planudea (II)'. *Accad. d. Lincei. Comitato per la preparazione della Edizione Nazionale.* N. Ser. fasc. 8, 1960, 11. – Transl. into English verse with Greek text: Leonidas: E. BEVAN, Oxf. 1931. Callimachus: G. M. YOUNG, Oxf. 1934. Asclepiades: W. and M. WALLACE, Oxf. 1941. A useful selection from inscriptions and texts in J. GEFFCKEN, *Gr. Epigramme.* Heidelb. 1916. F. L. LUCAS, *A Greek Garland. A Selection from the Anth. Pal.* 2nd ed. Lond. 1949. Other material in Beckby (*v. supra*).

6 DRAMA

In the Hellenistic age comedies and tragedies were also written in large numbers, but there were local variations of emphasis. The flourishing of New Comedy in Athens has been discussed; it must be considered the exception that one of the poets of this genre, Machon of Sicyon or Corinth, worked in Alexandria. It is different with tragedy. Although at this time there were also tragic poets in Athens, like Astydamas, whom we add as the third in a family of tragedians (*v.* p. 243) to bear this name, the centre of this poetry was not Athens, but Alexandria. Philadelphus, the great patron of the Dionysian arts, who made the actors' guild (οἱ περὶ τὸν Διόνυσον τεχνῖται) take part in the famous gigantic procession,[1] organized dramatic contests in Alexandria and attracted a circle of poets to his city from whom a Pleiad was selected after the model of the classical canons. The following names appear to be definitive: Alexander Aetolus, Lycophron of Chalcis, Homer of Byzantium, the son of the poetess Moero,[2] Philicus of Corcyra, whom we shall meet later as the composer of a hymn to Demeter, and Sositheus, probably from the Troad.[3] Sosiphanes, Aeantiades, Dionysiades, who also wrote character-sketches of the comic poets, and Euphronius appear alternatively in various lists. In addition to these names there are another fifty from notices and inscriptions; we must not, of course, think that

---

[1] Cf. GOW in the comm. on Theocritus 17, 112.

[2] Fragments of a hexameter poem *Mnemosyne* and of elegies (these also fasc. 6, 69 D.), further mention of a hymn to Poseidon and of maledictory poetry in J. U. POWELL, *Coll. Alex.* Oxf. 1925, 21. The same on the name: Moero or Myro?

[3] Alexander and Sositheus are missing in Tzetze's introduction to the Lycophron scholia in which a Pleiad of poets of various genres is given.

all of these were connected with Alexandria; a large number came from all over the Greek world.

Out of all this profusion a total of nine fragments with twenty-two lines has been preserved. If Moschion, whose date is uncertain (*v.* p. 632), is put in the third century, the number indicated is slightly higher. Does this wholesale loss mean that these works were of little value? This much can be stated at any rate that we have not the least reason to think that any of them were great achievements. The titles present roughly the same picture as in the fourth century. The old groups of subjects also supply themes for the present time, but there are also new, far-fetched ones. Of the many unusual titles we only mention the *Adonis* of Philicus and of Ptolemy Philopator himself. Dionysius I had preceded him with the dramatization of this theme (*v.* p. 632). Historical drama, such as, for instance, Philicus' *Themistocles*, was also written, and themes were even borrowed from contemporary history, like the *Cassandreis* by Lycophron. It would be interesting if we could ascertain to what extent the Latin Praetexta linked up with these.

Two of the poets mentioned in connection with the Pleiad demand further discussion. Alexander Aetolus, so called after his native land, worked at the court of Gonatas and in Alexandria. There he arranged the standard texts of tragedies and satyr plays. Remnants of epyllia (*Halyeus, Circa*, doubted in Athen. 7. 283 a) and of elegies (*Apollo, Musae*)[1] have been preserved. Earlier (p. 412) it was conjectured that the subject of the *Apollo* is related to Agathon's *Antheus*.

Lycophron of Chalcis also came to Alexandria in the time of its great literature under Philadelphus. In the library he was in charge of comedy, the fruit of which work was a bulky volume Περὶ κωμῳδίας. His dramas, of which we already mentioned the *Cassandreis* with a subject from contemporary history, offer an opportunity to discuss the revival of the satyr play in this time. Some lines of the *Menedemus* have been preserved. This satyr play apparently subjected the philosopher from Eretria to some friendly chaff.[2] An epigram of Dioscorides (*Anth. Pal.* 7. 707) celebrates Sositheus as the renewer of the genuine old satyr play of Doric stamp; Sositheus was also a member of the Pleiad. His *Daphnis* or *Lityerses* dealt with the liberation of Daphnis, as far as we can make out, and the killing of the monster Lityerses; it was a mythological play with some new characters.

What is probably the most peculiar product of Alexandrian poetry, the *Alexandra* in 1474 iambic trimeters, is from Lycophron's hand. A messenger reports the prophecy of Cassandra which proclaims, after the recognition of Paris (which Euripides presented in his *Alexander*), the fall of Troy and the further fortunes of the Greeks. Many allusions in the poem refer to the poet's own time; the west was given special attention, for which Timaeus of Tauromenium was the main source. Alexander, 'the lion of the race of Aeacus and

---

[1] POWELL, (*v.* p. 743, n. 2), 121. Fasc. 6, 74 D. The Athenaeus tradition gives *Crica*.

[2] On the criticism of the contradictory information WILAMOWITZ, *Hellenist. Dichtung* 2, Berl. 1924, 2nd unaltered ed. 1961, 143. 1.

Dardanus' (1440), will finish the struggle between east and west. The most difficult passage (1446) promises that after the sixth generation a man of Cassandra's blood will fight the wolf of Gadara (personification of Macedon?), but will then be reconciled with him and share in the plunder. Wilamowitz' expedient[1] that Cassandra speaks at this moment only of a future which goes beyond the poet's time, is a desperate one, but none better has yet been found. On the other hand, it is clear that the part played by Rome's early history (1226) is proof of the impression which its rise made in the realm of the Ptolemies.

Riddling speech (γριφῶδες) had been customary in oracles from times immemorial, but profane poetry also had a predilection for it.[2] The techno-paegnia already showed us the delight found in this kind of thing in the Hellen-istic age. Lycophron outdid them all with his diction which makes a point of avoiding calling a spade a spade, operates with a host of unusual words partly found only in his work and conceals a vast store of scholarly knowledge behind subtly confusing appellations. Such poetry was meant exclusively for the entertainment of men of wide reading. It is not, of course, a tragedy, but nothing is gained by calling it an iambus. It is simply a tragic fictional messenger speech, which also in many a tragedy of Euripides' is a part which could stand on its own. It is understandable that in the presence of so much erudition there is little room for poetry. The *Alexandra* is mainly important for its mythological con-tents. The scholia are a great help in its interpretation; their older stratum goes back to Theon (under Tiberius), while an elaborate compilation of Isaac Tzetzes' was given its final revision by his brother Ioannes.

For Hellenistic tragedy two texts can be made serviceable, although both with considerable reservations. In Book 9 of his *Praeparatio Evangelica* Eusebius pre-served from the work *On the Jews* by Alexander Polyhistor (first century B.C.) 269 trimeters of the *Exagoge* by Ezechiel, who is mentioned by Clemens (*Stromat.* I. 23) as a writer of Jewish tragedies. In this Mosaic drama of the second century B.C. various episodes of the Jews' exodus from Egypt, chrono-logically far apart, had been brought together. This was made possible through a shifting of the scene, as we can ascertain in two cases. It was possibly divided into five acts and limited to three actors. Both these facts correspond with Horace's *Ars Poetica* (189. 192); there is, of course, generally a good basis for the assumption that in Horace there are important elements of the Hellenistic theory of art.[3] The fragments give no indication that a chorus is used in the *Exagoge*, but the *Ars Poetica* and Latin tragedy favour the assumption that it was

---

[1] *v.* prev. note, 146.

[2] Good enquiry by INGRID WAERN, Γῆς ὄστεα, *The Kenning in Pre-Christian poetry.* Uppsala 1951.

[3] E. BURCK in the epilogue to Kiessling-Heinze's edition of the *Epistolae*, Berl. 1957, 401 gives information on the related problems of how much earlier Neoptolemus is and whether Horace has Hellenistic or contemporary poetry in mind. K. ZIEGLER (*v. inf.*), 1972 makes great advances in the utilization of the *Ars Poetica* for Hellenistic drama. The careful con-sideration of the art of characterization which, in contrast to Aristotle, is stressed rather than the construction of the plot may indeed correspond with facets of Hellenistic drama in-fluenced by rhetoric.

also usual on the Hellenistic stage. Its task can hardly have been more than filling up the interval between acts. In view of the paucity of material available, the *Exagoge* is valuable – also linguistically, since in spite of its poor quality the verse reveals that Euripides is its model – but it must be borne in mind that it was written by a non-Greek and that it is doubtful whether it warrants any conclusions about the general picture of contemporary tragedy.

In 1950 E. Lobel[1] published a papyrus from Oxyrhynchus (end second or beginning of third century A.D.) with the remnants of three columns; the middle one contained sixteen trimeters, in a fair state of preservation, of a Gyges drama. From the queen's speech about the events in the bedroom it is clear that Herodotus was closely followed. On the grounds of the archaic terminology it was conjectured that the opposite was the case and that the historian followed an earlier tragedy – by Phrynichus, for instance – but these elements, which occur side by side with later usage, can be explained from a tendency to archaïze, while the versification also agrees with a later date, probably the third century, although the fourth must not be ruled out. If we assume that the whole play is equally dependent on Herodotus, a reconstruction without a change of scenery is not feasible, and this fits in quite well with what we found out about the *Exagoge*.

The development of New Comedy in the work of Menander, Philemon and Diphilus had made it into a genre of literature which could no longer satisfy the thirst for a variety of subjects of a wide audience in the Hellenistic cities, or provide sufficient food for their delight in shock-effects and coarse humour. The mime, the realistic portrayal of the actuality of everyday life, could do this in a different way. We can trace its beginning a long way back (*v.* p. 235 f.);[2] the form which Sophron gave it was mentioned on p. 240. In the Hellenistic age we must already reckon with an extensive development and differentiation of such mimetic presentations. They took the form of songs or the spoken word, prose and verse, monologue or scenic performance. It is difficult to separate the large number of descriptions; there is, however, a good case for assuming that hilarody or simody meant a more measured type of presentation, while magody or its close relation lysiody was of a lasciviously humorous nature, although the boundaries were probably not too rigid. We have an excellent example of a mime sung by a soloist in a papyrus of the second century B.C. with the *Maiden's Complaint*.[3] In agitated rhythms, mainly dochmiac, a girl who has been cast off by her lover after a quarrel is complaining in front of his door. According to

[1] 'A Greek Historical Drama.' *Proc. Brit. Ac.* 35, 1949, 207; now *Ox. Pap.* 23, 1956, no. 2382. Further bibl. in *AfdA* 5, 1952, 152 and 7, 1954, 150 and in A. E. RAUBITSCHEK, *Class. Weekly* 48, 1955, 48. Id. 'Die schamlose Ehefrau'. *Rhein. Mus.* 100, 1957, 139. E. BICKEL, 'Rekonstruktionsversuch einer hellenist. Gyges-Nysia-Tragödie'. *Rhein. Mus.* 100, 1957, 141.

[2] E. WÜST, *RE* 15, 1932, 1730 ff. has taken great pains to separate all sorts of actors and dancers of folk-lore such as the deikeliktai, ithyphalloi, phallophoroi, phylakes, autokabdaloi from the mime. But such a separation should not be too schematic, but admit that, although the groups mentioned cannot be classified with the mime, all this folk-lore contained elements of the mime.

[3] Easily accessible in POWELL (*v.* p. 743 n. 2), 177, who quotes related fragments.,

the theme this song, which is not without some power of passionate expression, is a paraclausithyron such as is otherwise sung by the male lover in front of the closed door. F. Leo's attempt[1] to link this type of song with Plautus' cantica has had no success.

The song, which was written on a temple door in Marissa (between Jerusalem and Gaza) in the middle of the second century B.C., is remarkable. A hetaera is conversing with a lover, who has been locked out, in a dialogue which was probably sung as a solo. The ditty and the locality where it was found bear out Athenaeus' statement (15. 697 b) that all Phoenicia was full of such songs. He described such light fare as Locrian and at the same time transmits the little aubade mentioned earlier (p. 108). Besides the descriptions of solo mimetic songs there is a series of expressions, such as mimologoi, ethologoi, biologoi, which indicate the spoken word in verse or prose. Names like ionicologoi and cinaidologoi show that they were Ionic in form and lewd in contents. Athenaeus mentions (14. 620 e) a number of poets of this genre, among them to our surprise Alexander Aetolus, who must have been very versatile. Next to names like Pyres of Miletus and Alexas the best-known is Sotades of Maronea.[2] He also levelled his impudent wit at Philadelphus and his marriage to his sister, for which he was punished by death at the hands of the king's nesiarch in Caunus. Suidas lists a large number of titles such as *Descent into Hades*, *Priapus*, in which connection we remember that this god of the district of Lampsacus on the Hellespont was gaining widespread popularity at this time as a hyperithyphallic garden god. He was permitted to appear in the festival procession beside Alexander and Ptolemy and inspired a special genre of poetry in the *Priapea*, the metre of which was created by Euphronius of Chersonnese. Other titles are *To Belestiche* (Philadelphus' mistress) and *Amazon*. The other ones in Suidas belong to the comic poet of the same name. The cinaedologue survives in some scanty fragments of a *Poem to Theodorus*, an *Iliad* and an *Adonis*. His name also lives on in the Sotadeum, a variation of the Ionic hexameter which he used stichically for spoken verse. The aphorisms (Sotadea) preserved by Stobaeus, must presumably be rated with those collections which, enriched with forgeries, appear under the names of Epicharmus and Menander (v. p. 239).

Plutarch (*Quaest. conv.* 7. 4. 712 e) mentions the division of mimes into paegnia and hypotheses, which we can only render imperfectly as 'toys' and 'plots'. The first term probably denotes solo performances. We refer here to the *Mimiambi* of Herodas,[3] a poet of whom we knew little more than his name until

---

[1] *Die plaut. Cantica und die hellenist. Lyrik.* Abh. Gött. Ges. N.F. 1/7, 1897.

[2] Fragments in POWELL (v. p. 743, n. 2), 238. Fasc. 6, 186 D. E. DIEHL's conjecture (*Anth. Lyr.* Suppl. 66) that G. A. GERHARD, *Gr. Pap.* Diss. Heidelberg 1938, no. 179, was from Sotades' epigrams, was refuted by 3 new fragments in E. SIEGMANN, *Lit. gr. Texte der Heidelb. Pap. Samml.* Heidelb. 1956, no. 190. They are fragments of satyrical prose, whose origin it is difficult to assess. H. LLOYD-JONES, *Gnom.* 29, 1957, 427 thinks that it was a manual of rhetoric.

[3] Herondas in Athen. 3, 86 b, Herodas in Stobaeus' quotations and Plin. *ep.* 4, 3, 4 (Herodes). The various versions were no doubt used at the same time; forms in -ondas are found in Boeotian, while in Cos the *v* was probably not pronounced.

a find in the year 1890 produced a roll with a considerable portion of his poems (no. 359 P.). Since Cos is definitely the background of two iambic mimes (2 and 4), we may assume a fairly close connection of the poet with the island whose intellectual life was mentioned in relation with Theocritus. It is unknown whether Herodas was born there. The securest support for his date is the reference to the shrine of the sister goddesses (1. 30), which gives us a period after 270; since furthermore it is most likely that the 'good king' in the same verse is Euergetes[1] we can limit the date to within his reign (246–221). To a certain extent the literary ancestors of these realistic miniature dramas with their relentlessly sharp focus are the mimes of Sophron's genre; but Herodas did not write prose, he appropriated Hipponax's choliambs, whom he also followed in the Ionic coloration of his diction. Within this traditional framework, however, it was still quite possible to achieve a very lifelike reality and a genuine atmosphere of milieu by drawing the characters sharply and by a skilful adaptation of style. His strength lies in the consistently effective use of the realistic components which mark the Hellenistic era, but his claim to the title of poet is dubious. The contents of these *Mimiambi* is as varied as life itself: the procuress who entices an honourable woman when she is a grass-widow; the greedy brothel-keeper, who in court tries to make capital out of an attack on his house; the schoolmaster who flogs a rascal at his mother's urging; women at sacrifice who admire the statues in the shrine of Asclepius of Cos (we are reminded of Theocritus' *Adoniazusae*); the cruel sport of a depraved woman with the slave who has let her have her will of him and almost meets his death through her jealousy; an obscenely lewd conversation between two women friends; a visit to a shoe shop and the haggling over a bargain. *Mimiambus* 8, *The Dream*, is unfortunately in such a bad state of preservation that only guesses can be made by way of restoration.[2] This is regrettable since in this poem the poet defended his own work against others. Of a few other *Mimiambi* only fragments have been preserved which do not give any clue of what they were about.

The idea of scenic performances of these *Mimiambi* has long since been abandoned; they probably were not meant to be merely read either, and so they were probably recited by a speaker who personified the various characters by means of skilfully executed nuances.

The question whether scenic performances of mimes with a continuous plot, such as were prevalent during the empire, already occurred during the peak of the Hellenistic era would have to go unanswered, were it not for an unpretentious object, a terracotta lamp from Athens (third century B.C.), which shows three actors and bears the legend: 'Mimologoi. Hypothesis: The mother-in-law.'[3] It must be assumed that plays without masks, in which actresses appeared, were staged as early as this period. There must have been a great deal of improvisation, for they simply took a subject from a successful comedy and gave an extempore

---

[1] Correctly WILAMOWITZ, *Hellenist. Dichtung* 2. Berl. 1924; 2nd unaltered ed. 1962, 318.

[2] O. CRUSIUS and R. HERZOG, 'Der Traum des H.'. *Phil.* 79, 1924, 370.

[3] ΜΙΜΟΛΩΓΟΙ Η ΥΠΟΘΕΣΙΣ ΕΙΚΥΡΑ. Picture in M. BIEBER, *The History of the Gr. and Roman Theatre.* Princeton 1939, fig. 290.

performance with the approved methods, as was obviously done by the mimologoi of Athens. But there is no doubt that there were written ones as well, as we know from the papyri under the empire. Some of these texts may even go back to the Hellenistic period. This is certain at least for the dialogue with a drunkard,[1] if the chronology of the ostracon in the second/first century is correct. Mention was made earlier (p. 236) of the phlyaces who have a certain kinship with the mimes, and of the development of their plays which resulted in the *Hilarotragodia* of Rhinthon of Syracuse in 300. Titles like *Heracles*, *Iphigenia in Aulis* and *in Tauris*, *Medea* and *Orestes* reveal that he was fond of borrowing from Euripides for his travesties of the myths, additional evidence for the latter's popularity in the Hellenistic age. Such plays were also performed in Alexandria, where Sopater of Paphus wrote dramatic parodies.

Although there is some affinity, the mime must be considered as a genre different from the pantomime,[2] in which a richly instrumented orchestra and a choir accompanied a single dancer; all he did was to represent by his movements (he wore a mask) the various characters of fables which were usually derived from the myths. The pantomime flourished during the empire. Its artists were the object of abuses to which parallels can be easily found. The notion that the Cilician Pylades was the creator of the pantomime in the Augustan era is stubbornly passed on, but as long ago as 1930[3] L. Roberts proved from epigraphical sources on the representation of tragic subjects through rhythmical movements that this kind of art can already be identified in Asia in the first half of the first century B.C.

Hellenistic tragedy: F. SCHRAMM, *Tragicorum Graec. hellenisticae quae dicitur aetatis fragmenta etc.* Diss. Munster 1931. K. ZIEGLER, *RE* 6 A 1937, 1967. V. STEFFEN, *Quaest. trag. capita tria.* Poznań 1939. P. VENINI, 'Note sulla trag. ellenistica'. *Dioniso* 16, 1953, 3 – Lycophron: C. V. HOLZINGER, *L.s Alexandra.* Leipz. 1895 (with transl. and comm.). Because of paraphrases, scholia and index E. SCHEER's edition in 2 vols. Berl. 1881 and 1908 is still important. Together with Callimachus, Lycophron was published in the bilingual edition of the *Loeb Class. Libr.* A. W. MAIR, 1921. Translation by G. W. MOONEY, *The Al. of L.* Lond. 1921. L. MASCALIANO. *L. Alejandra.* Barcelona 1956 (with Span. transl. and bibl.). ST. JOSIFOVIĆ, *Lykophron-Studien. Jahrbuch d. phil. Fak. Novi Sad* 2, 1957, 199. – J. WIENEKE, *Ezechielis Judaei poetae Alexandrini fabulae quae inscribitur* 'Εξαγωγή *fragmenta.* Münster 1931. The text now in the edition of the *Praep. Ev.* of Eusebius by K. MRAS I, Berl. 1954. – For the mime the scholarly but problematical work by H. REICH, *Der Mimos*, I. Berl. 1903 must still be taken into account. Also E. WÜST, *RE* 15, 1932, 1727. A. OLIVIERI, *Framm. della comm. greca e del mimo nella Sicilia e nella Magna Grecia.* 2: *Framm. della comm. fliacica.* 2nd ed.

---

[1] POWELL (*v.* p. 743, n. 2), 181. D. L. PAGE, *Greek Lit. Pap.* Lond. 1950, no. 74, p. 332.
[2] V. ROTOLO, *Il pantomimo. Studi e testi.* Palermo 1957.
[3] *Herm.* 65, 1930, 106.

Naples 1947. – Herodas: O. CRUSIUS, 5th ed. Leipz. 1914 (with related texts). Bilingual after Crusius with preface and notes. R. HERZOG, Leipz. 1926. W. HEADLAM and A. D. KNOX, Cambr. 1922 (with copious explanatory material); Knox also inserted Herodas in the bilingual ed. of the Choliambics *Loeb Class. Lib.* 1929. J. A. NAIRN et L. LALOY, *Coll. des Un. de Fr.* 1928, repr. 1960. QU. CATAUDELLA, Milan 1948 (with transl.). G. PUCCIONI, Florence 1950 (with comm.).

7 OTHER POETRY

In the preceding sections a number of names were mentioned, but there remains a great deal to be added to round off the picture.

Firstly, one more genre, the didactic poem, must be added to the ones which have been discussed, even if Aristotle (*Poet.* 1, 1447 b 16), who called Empedocles its representative, was not prepared to allot it a position in the realm of poetry. To a certain extent the ancients were justified in feeling that Hesiod was the creator of this genre, although to describe the *Days and Works* as a didactic poem does not cover everything and basically not much at all. Didactic poetry was written before the Hellenistic age; Euenus of Paros wrote his rules of rhetoric in verse (*v.* p. 357), but the Hellenistic Greeks were particularly devoted to it. We may assume in cases like Euenus that verse was chosen because it was more easily memorized, but now the contrast between erudition and artistic form gave special pleasure.

The most significant example and one of the most successful poems of antiquity was written by Aratus of Cilician Soloe, the city which sent Chrysippus the Stoic to Athens. It would be frivolous to attempt to indicate the dates of Aratus' birth and death, as Wilamowitz[1] correctly observed. We must be satisfied with fixing some important stages in his life. Reservation must be observed with regard both to the four detailed biographies and the spurious letters. Aratus went to Athens as a young man and there joined the Stoics. One of his close friends was Dionysius of Heraclea, who after his change-over from the Stoa to Hedonism was called ὁ μεταθέμενος (cf. p. 674). In the biographical tradition he appears now as Aratus' teacher, then again as his pupil in astronomy.[2] Firm support is given by the information that Aratus was called to Pella to Antigonus Gonatas' court (276–239), whose Stoic sentiments must have influenced this choice. His *Phaenomena* was probably written in Macedon at the urging of Antigonus. We may also believe that he spent some time with Antiochus I of Syria, for *Vita* III appeals for this fact to Dositheus of Pelusium who worked in Alexandria as an astronomer together with and after Conon. Antigonus of Carystus seems to be responsible for the information that he edited the *Iliad* in that city.[3]

Cicero (*De Orat.* 1. 69) records his firm opinion that Aratus, the author of such excellent verses about the stars, was a *homo ignarus astrologiae*. What we

---

[1] In an important section on Aratus in his *Hellenist. Dichtung* 2, Berlin 1924, 2nd unaltered ed. 1962, 276.

[2] Cf. MARTIN, *Hist.* (*v. inf.*), 165.   [3] MARTIN (*v. sup.*), 175.

know of his literary work shows that it covered a great variety of subjects. So much can at least be ascertained, although the details in Suidas and the *Vitae* contain contradictions and obscurities enough.[1] A *Hymn to Pan* was written for the wedding of Antigonus Gonatas to Phile, and the god must have appeared in a Stoic interpretation for which his name offered plenty of scope. We know further of *Epicedea* to friends, and of one to his brother Myris; of poems on medical subjects (was the *Ostologia* part of the *Iatrica?*) and of a collection of trifles under the title of Κατὰ λεπτόν which occur in the *Appendix Vergiliana*. We already heard of his philological activity with regard to Homer.

All this is lost; the only surviving poem is the one which kept Aratus' name alive even in ages which had little knowledge of Greek lore. He was by no means the first to undertake the teaching of astronomy by means of a poem. It is difficult to date Cleostratus of Tenedos, but it is quite likely that he wrote poems on the constellations before Eudoxus. An epigram of Ptolemy Euergetes' recognizes Aratus' precedence over the astronomical poets Hegesianax and Hermippus (fasc. 6. 93 D). The tradition enables us to compile whole lists of authors in this field;[2] there can be little doubt that the belief in the divine nature of the stars which we saw advancing from the fourth century onward, and the pseudo-scientific system of astrology developed in the Hellenistic age, contributed to literature of this nature.

Suidas mentions Menecrates of Ephesus, Menedemus and Timon as teachers of Aratus. For the last two this only implies that Aratus had friendly relations with them; Menecrates' didactic poems *Erga* and *Apiculture* (Μελισσουργικά) may also have given rise to this conjecture, but he could possibly have preceded and influenced Aratus.

The great success of the *Phaenomena* with its 1154 hexameters doomed all other poetry of this nature to oblivion; this is mainly due to Aratus' unique sense of form. His verse, constructed with less strictness than Callimachus', presents the subject intelligibly with its smooth flow, at the same time maintaining a certain loftiness. Callimachus' epigram[3] in praise of the Hesiodic element in the *Phaenomena* aptly identified its stylistic ancestor.

It was well known to experts in antiquity that Aratus was largely dependent for his subject on two works by Eudoxus, the *Phaenomena* and the *Enoptron*. Hipparchus proves this emphatically in his *Commentary on Aratus and Eudoxus* (Τῶν 'Αράτου καὶ Εὐδόξου Φαινομένων ἐξηγήσεις, 3 books[4]), since he had to protest against a tradition which was unwilling to acknowledge this in favour of Aratus. But Aratus' modest specialist knowledge also imposed strict limits on his use of Eudoxus; he does not venture to enlarge on the planets or on the appellation of the celestial spheres.[5] On the other hand, he only rarely brings

---

[1] Discussed very judiciously by MARTIN (*v. sup.*), 177.   [2] MARTIN (*v. sup.*), 182, 184.
[3] 27 = *Anth. Pal.* 9. 507. On its interpretation B. A. VAN GRONINGEN, *La Poésie verbale grecque*. Nederl. Akad. Afd. Letterk. N.R. 16, 4, 1953, 248 and H. HERTER, *Gnom.* 27, 1955, 256, 1.   [4] Edition K. MANITIUS, Leipz. 1894 (with Germ. transl.).
[5] On Aratus' conception of the firmament: R. BOKER, *Die Entstehung der Sternsphäre Arats*. Sächs. Akad. Math. -natw.Kl. 99/5, 1952. Böker raises valid objections against the assumption that Eudoxus was Aratus' main source.

in the myths to account for the constellations; others soon completely rectified this omission.[1] That is why large sections of the *Phaenomena* are rather dull reading and why we feel stirred by the poet in some passages only. This happens first of all in the opening with the hymn-like praise of Zeus. We recognize in him the universal god of the Stoics; in the utterance that man is of his race we hear Cleanthes, who used the same phrase[2] in his *Hymn to Zeus* (v. 4).

The fine section on the constellation of Virgo (96–136) is largely inspired by Hesiod's genius and subject matter. Aratus interprets her as Dike, the goddess of justice who in a previous age left the earth full of loathing and now lives among the stars. The passage which, after the conclusion of the description of the stars, passes over to the second part of the poem (758–772), also attests the poet's profound faith in the sway of divine wisdom in the universe.

The final part of the poem deals with meteorology; it is very similar to the treatise on this subject (Περὶ σημείων)[3] transmitted under Theophrastus' name, a collection of excerpts of the Alexandrian era which goes back, with Aratus, to a common source, possibly a book by Theophrastus.

Mention was made before of the tremendous success of the *Phaenomena*, of the praise bestowed on it by Callimachus and Ptolemy Euergetes. Leonidas of Tarentum (*Anth. Pal.* 9. 25) joined in the chorus of admirers with an epigram. We have fragments of a translation by Cicero; the translations of Germanicus and Avienus have been preserved; there is also one in barbarous Latin of the seventh century; Varro of Atax used the work at least for his meteorology. In some Vatican manuscripts (Gr. 191 and 381) there are registers of authors who wrote about Aratus. The number of twenty-seven commentators gives an impression of the whole literature. Some of these were of a polemical nature like the commentary of Hipparchus, who was mentioned earlier. We know numerous names; interpretations of Achilleus and Leontius have been transmitted and there are also numerous scholia.

A poem of 169 iambic trimeters ('Εμπεδοκλέους ἀπλανῶν ἄστρων σφαῖρα) with a description of the constellations in the manner of Aratus[4] has been fraudulently attributed to Empedocles, which shows how great the influence of the *Phaenomena* was. About 60 B.C. Alexander of Ephesus, nicknamed Lychnos, wrote astronomical and geographical didactic poems, of which large fragments survive describing the harmony of the spheres.[5] This probably includes him among the imitators of Eratosthenes' *Hermes*, which will be discussed presently.

However bad the state of preservation of Hellenistic literature may be, there is no cause for complaint about the transmission of didactic poetry. Colophon, which from Mimnermus onward gave many a poet to Greek literature, was the

---

[1] Contemporary narrative of Greek legends of the stars by w. SCHADEWALDT (Fischer Bücherei 1956).

[2] Aratus' notion is quoted in Paul's speech at the Areopagus, *Acts* 17, 28.

[3] On this O. REGENBOGEN, *RE* S 7, 1940, 1412. A papyrus of the 2nd century B.C. (no. 1574 P.) contains fragments of a treatise on weather indications.

[4] The tradition in J. MARTIN (*v. inf.*), 219.

[5] Cf. w. BURKERT, *Phil.* 105, 1961, 32, with bibl. on Alexander of Ephesus and on the attempts to link the distances separating the constellations and certain musical theories.

native city of Nicander. For his life we have, apart from some notices and the article in Suidas,[1] a biography in the scholia, but we are faced with a confusion which makes it hardly possible to come to any definite conclusions. In the first place the biography gives his father's name as Damaeus, whereas Suidas calls him Xenophanes. Has the old Xenophanes of Colophon come into the picture? What is worse is that our material does not permit a precise dating of his life. We have in the biography the positive information that Nicander devoted a hymn (fr. 104) to Attalus III of Pergamum (138–133), but other notices claim that he was a contemporary of Callimachus', while others again produce 200 as a date. With Gow we accept the facts of the biography; the date of Nicander's floruit in the middle of the second century is the most likely. He is at least later than Numenius of Heraclea, who wrote in the middle of the third century and who has a certain affinity with Nicander as author of *Theriaca*, *Halieutica* and a *Deipnon*.[2] Our chronology shows that we do not identify the epic poet Nicander of Colophon, the son of a certain Anaxagoras, who is honoured in a Delphic inscription[3] of the middle or the second half of the third century, with the writer of the didactic poems preserved. He may have been an ancestor, probably his grandfather. It is very likely that Nicander occupied an hereditary priesthood in the shrine of Apollo of Claros near Colophon, considerable parts of which have been revealed by recent French excavations. The biography mentions that he spent a long time in Aetolia; this would be acceptable if we could assume that the *Aetolica* (fr. 1–8) is the work of this Nicander. Apparently it was written in prose; quotations of hexameters from it are references rather than evidence of a mixed form. In this case as with many other writings under the name of Nicander the question crops up whether we should not assume that the older bearer of this name was the author.

Two hexameter poems have been transmitted, the *Theriaca* (958 lines) on remedies against the bite of poisonous animals, and the *Alexipharmaca* (630 lines) on aid in cases of food poisoning. Nicander is no more expert in his subject than Aratus in astronomy. His basis was the works of Apollodorus, who wrote in Alexandria on vegetable and animal poisons in the beginning of the third century. This sort of poetry was not so much concerned with the subject itself or the expansion of knowledge, but with the artistic representation of out-of-the-way learning in an exquisite form. The acrostic with his name (*Ther.* 345 ff.) is also characteristic of this tendency. It is obvious that Nicander took great pains over his writing, although not to its profit. His language is overloaded with curious glosses and difficult technical terms; these elements are not blended into true poetry, so that much of it is quite pedestrian.

Of the lost works the *Heteroeumena* is interesting. In five books he narrated legendary metamorphoses such as had occurred in the Greek myths from time immemorial, but which were now compiled in the form of a poetic collection. This form already appears in Hesiod's catalogue poetry (*v.* p. 103 f.), but whereas

---

[1] Conveniently accessible in GOW's edition, p. 3.

[2] Dependence on Numenius: Schol. *Ther.* 237.

[3] DITTENBERGER, *Syll.* 3rd ed. 452; bibl. on the chronology in GOW's edition, p. 6.

his principle of composition was a simple succession of stories, we find in the Hellenistic age a tendency towards artificial linkage and animating variety. Callimachus' *Aetia* already points in this direction and Ovid's *Metamorphoses* shows the perfection of this poetry in Latin. The remnants suggest that Nicander was a dull story-teller, but the excerpts which Antoninus Liberalis gives in his *Collection of Metamorphoses* indicate that he tried to link the individual stories by means of ingenious devices.[1] In the same Antoninus there is repeated mention of a poem evidently related to it, an *Ornithogonia*, which recounted transformations into birds; the author's name was Boeo or Boeus.

Through Athenaeus we have some fairly large fragments of the *Georgica*. It was often thought that the book about bees, the *Melissurgica*, used to be part of this, but it is worth while considering that Athenaeus gives only one reference (2. 68 c) under this title, but not a few others under that of the *Georgica*. These are mainly concerned with botanical matters and the vegetable garden, but this may have been due to Athenaeus' interests. The narrow didacticism which is also evident in this work is far removed from the incomparable ethos in which Virgil wrote his poem.

We have many more titles. The *Versification of the Hippocratic Prognostica* (Προγνωστικὰ δι' ἐπῶν) must have been genuine Nicander. The *Collection of Remedies* ('Ιάσεων συναγωγή) was probably also in verse, although some doubt remains, just as in the case of the *Colophoniaca*. The *Aetolica* must have been written in prose, while the references to the *Oetaïca*, *Thebaïca*, *Sicelia* and *Europia* indicate that they were in verse. Because of the affinity of its subject matter to the poems preserved we mention the *Ophiaca*, although we are quite in the dark about its contents. Collecting glosses was part of Nicander's business.

In this connection mention must be made of a curious piece in hexameters preserved in a Viennese papyrus (*Pap. Graec. Vind.* 29801=No. 1410 P.). Silenus mocks Pan, who has had his flute stolen by the Satyrs. The god is supposed to play at a Dionysian festival, makes himself a new instrument and tests it. It is difficult to be precise about its date and genre. Oellacher's attempt[2] to prove Nicander's authorship (possibly *Melissurgica*) has not been successful; he argues that it was written in the Hellenistic period, whilst Keydell relegates it to the empire; the latter also conjectures that the epic poet Nestor of Laranda (under Septimius Severus) could have been the author.

In connection with Nicander's didactic poem we mention Callimachus' pupil Philostephanus of Cyrene, who wrote, besides numerous historical, geographical

---

[1] On the poetic medley: E. MARTINI, 'Ovid und seine Bedeutung für die röm. Poesie', *Epitymbion H. Swoboda*. Reichenberg 1927, 165. On Anton. Lib. cf. also MARTINI's ed. Leipz. 1896 and E. CAZZANIGA. *Ant. Lib. Μεταμορφώσεων συναγωγή. Testi e documenti per lo studio dell' antichità* 3. Milan-Varese (in prep.). GOW, ed. p. 206 advises caution. *Orinthogonia*: POWELL, *Coll. Alex.* Oxf. 1925, 24.

[2] Πὰν συρίζων, *Studi It.* N.S. 18, 1941, 113. Id. 'Der Pap. Graec. Vind. 29801. Handlung und lit. Einordnung'. *Mnem.* S. 3, 12, 1944, 1. D. L. PAGE, *Lit. Pap.* Lond. 1950, 502, also holds that it is a Hellenistic poem; he appeals to COLLART. E. HEITSCH, *Die griech. Dichterfragmente der röm. Kaiserzeit. Abh. Ak. Gött. Phil.-hist. Kl.* 1961, 10, 1 resolutely defends KEYDELL'S dating in the empire. Bibl. in HEITSCH, 55.

and mythological works of a purely learned character, a poem in distichs *On Curious Rivers* (Περὶ παραδόξων ποταμῶν). In his choice of subject matter he probably followed his teacher, whose work *On the Rivers of the World* we mentioned earlier (p. 704). Towards the end of the second century a periegesis in iambic verse of the coasts of Europe and the Black Sea was written,[1] which was irresponsibly attributed to Scymnus of Chios. This author, who wrote a periegetical description of the three continents (Europe, Asia and Libya) is dated by a Delphic inscription of the year 185/184.[2] He did not, however, write the iambic poem mentioned, which is now usually referred to as the Pseudo-Scymnus.

Didactic poems written by Eratosthenes and Apollodorus of Athens will be discussed together with the other work of these scholars.

A few more titles and names complete the picture of Hellenistic catalogue-poetry. Phanocles, for whom we cannot give a precise date, sang of love for beautiful boys in his Ἔρωτες ἢ καλοί in elegiac metre. The story of Orpheus and Calais has been preserved in Stobaeus.[3] The love theme served as a prop for the narrative of the singer's death and the voyage of his head, and also to give an aetion for the tattooing of Thracian women. The stories were connected with the words 'or as' (ἢ ὡς). Nicaenetus of Samos also wrote[4] his *Catalogue of Women* (Κατάλογος γυναικῶν) in imitation of Hesiod's plain method of connecting stories. He probably lived in the second century; for Sosicrates or Sostratus of Phanagorea, who reveals Hesiod's structural principle in the very title of his *Ehoeae*, not even an attempt at chronology is possible.

What we know of Hermesianax of Colophon reveals more individual features. He is supposed to have been close to Philitas, and so he belongs in the early Hellenistic age. His elegiac poetic medley *Leontion* owes its title to its being addressed to his sweetheart of this name, but as in the case of the *Lyde* by his compatriot Antimachus, there is nothing to indicate that its theme is personal emotion. An extensive piece of Book 3[5] has the character of a catalogue which enumerates first the poets and then the philosophers vanquished by Eros. He sports with the tradition by representing Penelope as Homer's mistress and Ehoea as Hesiod's, but there is none of Callimachus' elegant irony. Excerpts in Antoninus Liberalis (39) and Parthenius (5) reveal that the *Leontion* also contained more elaborate elegiac narrative and that the individual parts were possibly more clearly varied; in the surviving section lines 79-84 between the catalogue of poets and the one of the philosophers also show his attempt to link the various sections with more artistry.

A late representative of the poetic medley who passed Hellenistic forms and themes on to the Romans was Parthenius of Nicaea. During the Third Mithridatic War he came (73) to Rome as a prisoner. He was among the spoils of a

---

[1] MÜLLER, *Geogr. Gr. min.* I, 196.   [2] DITTENBERGER, *Syll.* 3rd ed. no. 585, 197.
[3] 4, 461 HENSE. POWELL (*v.* p. 671, n. 4), 106. D. fasc. 6, 71.
[4] Lines from an epic poem *Lyrcus* which, like a poem of Apollonius (*v.* p. 736) related to the founding of Caunus, and some epigrams, in POWELL (*v. sup.*), I.
[5] POWELL (*v. sup.*), 98. D. fasc. 6, 56.

certain Cinna, probably a Helvius, for the Neoteric Helvius Cinna was greatly influenced by Parthenius. As a freedman he lived in Rome, then in Naples, exercising a significant influence on early Latin poetry. His *Metamorphoses* was probably written in elegiac metre.[1] W. Ehlers' well-founded arguments have upset the widespread belief that the *Ciris* in the *Appendix Vergiliana* was a revision of this work.[2] Various titles and small fragments attest to the great volume of his work. Apart from mythological poems like a *Heracles* or *Iphiclus* he wrote dirges and occasional poems for friends. Part of the *Epicedeum* on *Timander* was supplied by a London papyrus (no. 1051 P.). A papyrus fragment (no. 150 P.), ascribed to Parthenius after a prolonged controversy, has given a clearer notion of his *Arete*.

It was Parthenius' purpose to offer his Roman literary friends unusual subject matter in the easiest possible form. Thus he dedicated to Cornelius Gallus a collection of *Sorrowful Love Stories* ('Ερωτικὰ παθήματα) which has been preserved. It reveals the characteristics of Hellenistic love poetry in its tendency towards elevated sentiment, vivid dramatization and emotional appeal. Like Parthenius' collection, Conon's (*F Gr Hist* 26) is also only of interest to us because of its subject matter. This *Diegesis* with its fifty legends is dedicated to Archelaus of Cappadocia, who ruled from 36 B.C. until A.D. 17.

Euphorion of Chalcis was a particularly successful representative of another poetic form, the epyllion, which was called typically Hellenistic in connection with Callimachus and of which Theocritus, genuine as well as spurious, and Moschus, offered us examples. His birth in 276–275[3] falls still within the peak of the Hellenistic civilization, although his work already displays the degeneration of style developed in the period. He studied in Athens; as far as we know he did not go to Alexandria, which makes him one of the few contemporary poets who apparently had no relation of any kind with the Ptolemaic court, but at an advanced age he was called to the library of Antioch on the Orontes by Antiochus III. He also put his poetic talents in the service of palace propaganda.[4] His occasionally great success also provoked envy and we read all sorts of gossip about his ugliness and the questionable life which he was leading. Since he was extremist in his advocacy of the Hellenistic principles of art he had a strong influence on the young Romans, and for this reason Cicero aims a blow (*Tusc.* 3. 45) at this group when he describes them as *cantores Euphorionis*.

New papyrus finds enable us to form an opinion based on some specimens of

---

[1] MARTINI's objections in the work mentioned (*v.* p. 754, n. 1) (173, 23) against ROHDE offer no solution.

[2] 'Die Ciris und ihr Original.' *Mus. Helv.* 11, 1954, 65. Fragments of Parthenius in E. MARTINI, *Mythographi Graeci*, 2, 1 suppl. Leipz. 1902. Further *Anth. Lyr.* fasc. 6, 94 D.; also suppl. 54 with the *Epicedeum on Timander*. *Arete*: R. PFEIFFER. *Class. Quart.* 37, 1943, 23. A. MEINEKE, *Analecta Alexandrina*. Berl. 1843, 255 is still indispensable.

[3] Suidas gives the 126th Olympiad (276–272) and adds ὅτε καὶ Πύρρος ἡττήθη ὑπο 'Ρωμαίων. SKUTSCH, *RE* 6, 1907, 1175 records his doubts, which are not convincing.

[4] Cf. fr. 174 POWELL (Tertull. *De An.* 46): *Seleuco regnum Asiae Laodice mater nondum eum enixa providit; Euphorion provulgavit.*

his work. In the first place two fragments[1] came to light in a parchment manuscript of the fifth century A.D.; one of these describes how Heracles brings Cerberus to Tiryns. The other is from the *Curses* or the *Man Who Stole a Cup* ('Ἀραὶ ἢ Ποτηριοκλέπτης), in which a vast accumulation of mythologic examples is used to curse some one who has robbed the poet. We should like to interpret this display as irony, but fear that in this way we would not divine the learned poet's meaning. In addition, there are papyrus fragments[2] with a few dozen partly very badly preserved lines from the large find which Breccia made in the Kôm of Ali-el-Gammân (cf. p. 265) in 1932. The greater part of the material preserved belongs to a poem *Thrax*, which poses a difficult problem by its concise rendering of various legends. Some of it is quite recondite, such as the story of Apriate's flight from Trambelus' violent wooing and his death at the hands of Achilles. A note appended to Parthenius 26 proves that this theme occurs in Euphorion's *Thrax*. The conjecture that the poem was written around this legend as the main theme has proved to be untenable. Since one passage speaks in the Hesiodic manner of Dike's inexorable rule and the whole poem ends with a malediction against the murderer and a wish for a blessing for his sacrifice, there is much to say for Bartoletti's assumption that it is a maledictory poem with mythological examples, like the *Arae*. We shall leave the question open whether it was inspired by any concrete cause or was quite fictitious. If we place Callimachus' *Ibis* and Moero's (*v.* p. 743, no. 2) *Arae* next to it, we receive the impression that his impassioned cursing, which we know in its primitive condition from the maledictory tablets used in the Hellenistic age, is a cultivated literary form ornamented with baroque erudition. Euphorion's *Chiliades* seems to have had a similar content.

The *Thrax* is followed in the papyrus by the *Greater Hippomedon*, whose contents remain obscure.[3] There is no indication of a connection between the two poems and we receive no help for the solution of an old problem. Suidas mentions only three titles, *Hesiodus*, *Mopsopia* or *Atacta* and *Chiliades* in five books. The passage seems to be confused and has given rise to many emendations. But the question still is whether the titles mentioned earlier as well as quite a few others – among these many mythological ones such as *Inachus*, *Hyacinthus* and *Philoctetes* – should be considered to refer to parts of the works mentioned by Suidas or to independent poems. We can only guess which Alexander was the subject of his poems with this title. Treves[4] merely conjectured when he considered Craterus' son who ruled in Corinth for a time. In addition to the poetical works there are scholarly treatises in prose. Titles like *On the Aleudae*, *On the Isthmian Games* show his historical interest which is also evident in the

---

[1] No. 268 P.; POWELL (*v.* p. 671, n. 4), fr. 51 and 9; PAGE, *Greek Lit. Pap.* Lond. 1950, 488 (with bibl.).

[2] No. 269 P. Now excellent study by V. BARTOLETTI in *Pap. Soc. It.* 14, 1957, no. 1390, with bibl. With transl. PAGE (*v.* n. 1), 494. The papyrus is of the 2nd century A.D.

[3] P. TREVES, *Euforione e la storia ellenistica*, Milan 1955, 48, now assumes, after WILAMOWITZ, *Berl. Klass. T.* 5, 65, 1 (who adds, however, 'such possibilities are of no help'), that the poem is called after Ptolemy's agent in Thrace.

[4] *v.* foregoing note.

collective title Ἱστορικὰ ὑπομνήματα. It was doubted whether a *Hippocratic Lexicon* in six books was a work of this Euphorion; the name is not entirely rare.

The lines which survive do not inspire much grief for what was lost, but they make it intelligible why this style mixed with glosses and this self-imposed obscure narrative manner appeared to the adherents of an anti-classical modern trend to be the authentic embodiment of their principles. The steady shift of stress from the essential part of the story to far-fetched accessories, the avoidance of epic sweep and epic fluency, show that Euphorion expressly sought to contrast Homer and was at the same time an industrious, conscious follower of Callimachus. His struggle to achieve this can be detected in every line, whereas the amiable superiority of the Cyrenaean is completely absent. Recently B. A. van Groningen[1] has attempted to recognize in Euphorion's work special formal value as *poésie verbale*; he sees in it especially the fulfilment of a direction in the Hellenistic age which does not try to gain effects through contents and thought, but through the euphony of choice sound-effects. An opinion on these effects is purely subjective and this method could hardly lead to a higher evaluation of this poet who once exerted an influence which was strong even if short-lived. Nevertheless this presents an opportunity to point out that modern research into the sound-effects of ancient poetry and speech has long restricted itself to a hesitant groping. It is different with ancient theories in this field which, as far as we know, began with Democritus' Περὶ καλλοσύνης ἐπέων. Περὶ εὐφώνων καὶ δυσφώνων γραμμάτων. According to Aristotle (*Rhet.* 3, 2. 1405 b 6) the dithyrambic poet and orator Licymnius (*v.* p. 414) measured the aesthetic value of a word according to meaning and sound. Dionysius of Halicarnassus provides the clearest evidence for this tradition.

Some anonymous remnants also bear witness to the predilection of the Hellenistic age for the epyllion, although it is not always easy to ascribe these with certainty to a period and genre. A Berlin papyrus[2] has preserved a long but badly damaged passage from a *Diomedes*. The poem seems to form part of a cyclical *Alcmaeonis*; the lines preserved depict in idyllic features the environs of old Phidon, in whose hut Diomedes has left his little son with Argus. In an Oxyrhynchus papyrus[3] an old woman, in whom we should like to recognize a kinswoman of Callimachus' Hecale, portrays her poverty in verse. A London papyrus[4] contains remnants of a hexameter poem *Telephus*, which perhaps belongs to this period, and ten lines in a papyrus in the John Rylands Library[5] offer a piece from the oldest version of the legend of Hero and Leander which has been transmitted in the late poem by Musaeus.

The small fraction of epyllic poetry which we could identify agrees with what we know of lyric poetry. Of this we also have some odd remnants which are valuable as evidence of a brisk cultivation of various lyric forms (in the

---

[1] Cf. p. 751, n. 3. On Euphorion's characteristics K. LATTE, *Phil.* 90, 1935, 152.

[2] No. 1406 P.; POWELL (*v.* p. 671, n. 4), 72.

[3] No. 1409 P.; POWELL (*v. sup.*), 78; PAGE (*v.* p. 757, n. 1), 498.

[4] No. 1417 P.; POWELL (*v. sup.*), 76; PAGE (*v. sup.*), 534 with date in the late empire.

[5] No. 1411 P.; PAGE (*v. sup.*), 512. Other epic remnants in POWELL (*v. sup.*), 71, 79, ff., esp. 89.

broad meaning of the modern term). Some specimens of elegiac narrative are still closely related to the hexameter epyllion; Ox. Pap. I, 14[1] has remnants of a description of the golden age, while a Hamburg papyrus[2] of the third century B.C. contains the angry speech of a Hellenistic king at the report of an envoy. Mention is made of Medes and Galatians, but it is not possible to refer this to a definite historical occurrence. Some papyrus texts,[3] written in 100 B.C., are a very motley compilation; it is preferable to think that they are writing exercises rather than an anthology. A complaint of Helen in cretics introduces a theme unattested elsewhere that Menelaus left her after their return from Troy; a second piece depicts in ionics an early morning in the country, followed by two erotic paegnia. A Berlin papyrus,[4] written in the early third century, combines some scolia in various metres which probably date back to the fourth century. To emphasize the variety of subjects we refer also to some anapaests in a Berlin papyrus,[5] one passage of which contains praise of Homer, another an oracle of Cassandra's.

In our look round in various fields of poetry we must not forget the religious cults. The fact that for many people the old gods did not have the same meaning as in the time of the autonomous *polis* did not do any harm to the continued existence of the ancient sacrifices and festivals. As before, these provided a theme and a background for a rich crop of religious poems. The ancient ones long remained popular; as we mentioned before (p. 273), Sophocles' *Paean to Asclepius* was still sung in the empire,[6] New material was also added; the remnants give us an impression of its poetic value.

We saw in the case of Callimachus that Hellenistic hymn writing could pass completely from the realm of worship to that of literature. The same is shown by Philicus of Corcyra, whom we mentioned earlier (p. 743) as a member of the tragic Pleiad. He was the leader of the Dionysian technitae in Alexandria and played his part in the oft-mentioned pompous procession of Philadelphus. Protogenes painted him in the posture of a thinker (Plin. *Nat. Hist.* 35. 106) and an inscriptional epigram by a contemporary praises the deceased in lofty terms. A papyrus[7] produced part of a hymn to Demeter whose opening line (in Hephaestion) addresses the literary connoisseurs (γραμματικοί) on matters of literary principles. A poem in catalectic choriambic hexameters was a piece of metrical bravura of which its author was very proud. He chose Attic as his literary dialect, the obvious choice for a tragic poet. The hymns of Castorion of Soloe, an early Hellenistic poet, were probably also literary; Athenaeus has

[1] No. 1388 P.; POWELL (*v. sup.*), 130; *Anth. Lyr.* fasc. 6, 88 D.

[2] No. 1386 P.; POWELL (*v. sup.*), 131; *Anth. Lyr.* fasc. 6, 89 D.; PAGE (*v. sup.*), 462.

[3] No. 1266 f. P.; POWELL (*v. sup.*) 185; *Anth. Lyr.* fasc. 6, 201 f. D.; PAGE (*v. sup.*), 410.

[4] No. 1515 P.; POWELL (*v. sup.*), 190; *Anth. Lyr.* fasc. 25. 90 D.; PAGE (*v. sup.*), 386.

[5] No. 1516 P.; POWELL (*v. sup.*), 187; *Anth. Lyr.* fasc. 6, 204 D.; PAGE (*v. sup.*), 412. Most accessible survey of lyrical and other papyrus fragments of Hellenistic poetry in P(ack).

[6] Cf. also MAAS, *Epidaurische Hymnen. Schr. d. Königsberger Gel. Ges. Geistesw. Kl.* 9/5, 1933, 155.

[7] No. 1055 P.; *Anth. Lyr.* 6, 158 D.; PAGE (*v. sup.*), 402. (The epigram 452); C. GALLAVOTTI, *Pap. Soc. It.* 12/2, 1282; K. LATTE, 'Der Demeterhymnos des Ph.' *Mus. Helv.* 11, 1954, 1.

preserved (10. 455 a) an extremely artificial trimeter to Pan. The same applies to the *Hymn to Eros* by Antagoras[1] whom wc met (p. 736) as the epic poet of a *Thebaïs*. He spent part of his life in Macedon with Antigonus Gonatas. In Crantor's time and even later up to Arcesilaus' headship he had connections with the philosophers of the Academy. The seven lines of this hymn, preserved by Diogenes Laertius (4. 26), show that the old introduction with the birth of the god had changed into a learned enumeration of mythographical variants. This was done much more elegantly by Callimachus (*Hymn* 1. 5) with relation to a verse of Antagoras'.

Cleanthes shows how the philosopher could also avail himself of the ancient hymn form to state his creed. But besides literature of this nature there is a large number of poems which had to do with worship. The excavations at Epidaurus at the local shrine of Asclepius have shown that Isyllus was a poet of modest talent.[2] He can be approximately dated because the inscription indicates a time prior to 300, and he himself states that he was a boy when Philip marched across the Isthmus and menaced Sparta after the battle of Chaeronea. After a gnomic prologue in trochaic verse he tells in laborious hexameters how a procession in honour of Apollo Maleatas and Asclepius was founded and relates a message of benediction which, in a time of peril, he, Isyllus, was chosen by the god to pass on. In between them there is a *Paean to Apollo and Asclepius* in ionics.

A dactylic *Paean to Asclepius* in an inscription in Erythrae[3] is pre-Hellenistic, since it is a few decades older than Isyllus'. Other inscriptions of religious poems must be dated in approximately the same period: the *Paean* of one Macedonius *To Apollo and Asclepius*, found near the Athenian Asclepieum, a *Hymn to Zeus of Dicte* from Cretan Palaikastro, and a *Hymn to the Dictaean Dactyls* from Euboean Eretria.[4] Of the stones inscribed with religious texts yielded up by the earth of Delphi, the *Paean* of Philodamus of Scarphea[5] still belongs to this period. Twelve stanzas, in which choriambic trimeters and glyconics predominate, celebrate Dionysus with true Bacchic enthusiasm. The poem, which can with some probability be attributed to the year 325/324 from the archon's name in the subscriptio, is important evidence for the interpenetration of the worship of Apollo and Dionysus in Delphi. Some other Delphic texts are substantially younger. Aristonous' *Paean to Apollo*,[6] which shows metrical kinship with Philodamus' poem, belongs in the year 222 or near it, according to the archon's name. By the same poet a dactylo-epitrite *Hymn to Hestia* has been

---

[1] P. VON DER MÜHLL, 'Zu den Gedichten des Antagoras von Rhodos.' *Mus. Helv.* 19 1962, 28. The second of the poems printed in POWELL, *Anal. Alex.* 120 (= PEEK, *Gr. Versinschriften* I 1923) is an epitaph for Crates and Polemon.

[2] Text in POWELL (*v. sup.*), 132; *Anth. Lyr.* fasc. 6, 113 D. (with bibl.). WILAMOWITZ, *Isyllos von Ep. Phil. Unt.* 9. Berl. 1886 is still a classic in research. Other remnants of inscriptional Epidauric hymns in P. MAAS, *v.* p. 759, n. 6.

[3] POWELL (*v. sup.*), 136; *Anth. Lyr.* fasc. 6, 110 D.

[4] POWELL (*v. sup.*), 138. 160. 171; *Anth. Lyr.* fasc. 6, 127. 131 D. On the Cretan hymn WILAMOWITZ, *Griech. Verskunst.* Berl. 1921, 499.

[5] POWELL (*v. sup.*), 165; *Anth. Lyr.* fasc. 6, 119 D.

[6] POWELL (*v. sup.*), 162; *Anth. Lyr.* fasc. 6, 134 D.

preserved. Two Delphic *Paeans*,[1] the first of which written by an unknown Athenian, the second by Limenius, are about a century younger (128/127?). The quality of these poems, in which paeonic rhythm predominates, is not above the average poetry used for cult practices, but these texts are unusually important because the music is added. In this context it should be borne in mind how meagre our store of ancient music is; a few lines from Euripides' *Orestes* in papyrus no. 300 P.,[2] the short *Sicilus-song* in an inscription and three hymns by Mesomedes form the substance, together with the Delphic texts.[3] Among recent additions two items merit special interest. There is firstly the fragment in Oslo which is probably from a tragedy so far unknown. Its counterpart is *Ox. Pap.* no. 2436,[4] which is not likely to be from a satyr-play as conjectured by the editors. A. M. Dale ascribes it to a monody of Althea in Euripides' *Meleager*. What matters is that they are plain proof that it was the custom in Hellenistic-Roman times to set classical texts to music for concert performances. The plays were then sung by τραγῳδοί in public ἀκροάσεις.[5] Nero used to treat his contemporaries to such shows.

Greek songs were also sung in the worship of the new gods. An inscription in Delos[6] in prose reports the founding of the Serapeum by a certain Apollodorus, with an additional sixty-five hexameters of an *Aretalogy* of the god

[1] POWELL (*v. sup.*), 141 (with the notes and their modern transcription); *Anth. Lyr.* fasc. 6, 172 D.

[2] E. G. TURNER, 'Two unrecognized Ptolemaic papyri'. *Journ. of Hell. Stud.* 76, 1956, 59, dates the Orestes papyrus at *c.* 200 B.C.

[3] On an alleged Pindaric melody cf. p. 207. Other papyri with notation nos. 1512. 1897 P. New fragments in an Oslo papyrus: R. P. WINNINGTON-INGRAM in *Fragments of Unknown Greek Tragic Texts with Musical Notation*. Oslo 1955, and *Ox. Pap.* 25, 1959, no. 2436, discussed by R. P. WINNINGTON-INGRAM; also BR. GENTILI, *Gnom.* 33, 1961, 341. Survey and summarizing discussion of the musical fragments: C. DEL GRANDE, *Enciclopedia class. Sez.* 2/Vol. 5, Turin 1960 (*Cenni sulla musica greca* 401-476). E. PÖHLMANN, *Griech. Musikfragmente. Ein Weg zur altgriech. Musik.* Nuremberg 1960 (*Erlanger Beitr. zur Sprach- und Kunstwiss.* 8). Also R. P. WINNINGTON-INGRAM, *Gnom.* 33, 1961, 692. Id., research report, 'Ancient Greek Music 1932-1957.' *Lustrum* 1958/3, 5. Recently 6 small fragments in the papyrus collection of the Austrian National Library were added to the body of knowledge: H. HUNGER and E. PÖHLMANN, 'Neue griech. Musikfragmente aus ptolemäischer Zeit in der Pap. Samml. d. Öst. Nat. Bibl.'. *Wien. Stud* 75, 1962, 51. The fragments from tragedy could belong in the earlier discussed category of pieces for solo recitation. – Comm.: E. MARTIN, *Trois Documents de musique grecque. Transcriptions commentées* (hymne delph. à Apollon, Épitaphe de Seikelos, fragment d'un chœur d'Or. d'Eur.). Paris 1953 (Ét. et comm. 75). – We add some recent works on Greek music and remind of C. VON JAN, *Musici Scriptores Graeci.* 2 vols. Leipz. 1895/99; repr. by Olms/Hildesheim. In the *New Oxford History of Music.* Ed. E. WELLESZ, Vol. 1: *Ancient and Oriental Music.* Lond. 1957. ISOBEL HENDERSON wrote the section on Greek, E. SCOTT the one on Roman music. THR. GEORGIADES, *Musik und Rhythmus bei den Griechen.* Hamb. 1958. Frequent reference to Greek music by E. WERNER. *The Sacred Bridge. The Interdependence of Liturgy and Church in the first Millennium.* New York 1959. H. HUSMANN, *Grundlagen der antiken und orientalischen Musikkultur.* Berl. 1961. L.P. records with texts by F. A. KUTTNER. New York 1955 and *His Master's Voice* 1957.   [4] Cf. BR. GENTILI, *Gnom.* 33, 1961, 341.

[5] Epigraphical evidence: M. GUARDUCCI, *Atti Ac. Cl. Scienzi mor.* ser. 6, vol. 2, 1927/29, 629. K. LATTE, *Eranos* 52, 1954, 125.

[6] IG 15/4, 1299. POWELL (*v. sup.*), 68. On the founding of the cult M. P. NILSSON, *Gesch. d. griech. Rel.* 2, 2nd ed. Munich 1961, 121.

written by a certain Maeistas in the end of the third century. The *Isis aretalogies*[1] in praise of the goddess Isis form a special branch of literature; this goddess had a greater influence on the Greeks than any of the other foreign gods. It is significant in this context that the ancient formulae of praise of the divine power remained relatively pure in the Greek texts; this is demonstrated most impressively in the brief powerful sentences of the inscription of Cyme, apart from the hexameters of Andros and the trimeters of Cyrene. Late Hellenistic texts stress syncretically Isis' equality with the great goddesses of other religions.

We add here a papyrus from Chicago;[2] it contains some badly damaged remnants of hymnal poetry and there is some possibility that one of these is a poem on Arsinoe-Aphrodite. It leads on to the praise of mortals who were extolled with religious honours. At an earlier stage Hermocles of Cyzicus had set himself up as the spokesman for Athenian adulation. He won a closely contested victory (Athen. 15. 697 a) with *Paeans* on Antigonus and Demetrius Poliorcetes; a *Processional Song* by Duris in trimeters with alternately following ithyphallics has been preserved in Athenaeus (6. 253 d).[3] Its theme is Demetrius' return from Corcyra and the way in which it honours the god present by wiping all the others from the board (15 ff.) is as much a testimony to adulation as to frivolity in religious matters. The late Hellenistic age bowed before their Gods also. The Delphic poem of Limenius just mentioned ends with a wish for loyalty to Rome. In the last period of the Hellenistic age such devotion sometimes rose to turgid heights, as in an epigram by Alpheus of Mytilene (*Anth. Pal.* 9. 526), which warned Zeus that he should take care of his Olympus in the face of such irresistible conquerors. It is amusing that Stobaeus (*Ecl.* 3. 7, 12) preserved in a section περὶ ἀνδρείας a *Hymn* of Melinno on Rome, because he confused the name of the city with ῥώμη. The poem consists of five well-composed stanzas, but it is very difficult to fix a date for it within the Hellenistic age. Its latest interpreter[4] allots it to the first half of the second century, during which time the worship of the dea Roma was fast gaining ground. Plutarch gives the final portion of a *Paean*[5] on *Titus Flaminius* in his *Life* (16).

In order to round off this account a word should be added about prose-writing. The question how far the origin of the love novel goes back into the Hellenistic age is to be discussed in connection with the later flourishing of this genre; nevertheless the present context calls for a mention of the Ionian novella. In an earlier chapter (p. 317 f.) it was pointed out that from the earliest beginnings onward it had led a brisk life underneath the surface of great literature and that Herodotus' delight in telling a story revealed a great deal of this. Love themes

---

[1] W. PEEK, *Der Isishymnos von Andros und verwandte Texte.* Berl. 1930. In add. NILSSON (*v. sup.*), 626, 5.

[2] POWELL (*v. sup.*), 82; no. 1279 P.

[3] POWELL (*v. sup.*), 173; *Anth. Lyr.* fasc. 6, 104 D., with the remnants of a poem in the same metre, connected with the celebration of the Soteria by the technitae and written by a certain Theocles of uncertain date.

[4] C. M. BOWRA, 'Melinno's Hymn to Rome'. *Journ. of Rom. Stud.* 47, 1957, 21.

[5] POWELL (*v. sup.*), 173; *Anth. Lyr.* fasc. 6, 107 D. On the metre WILAMOWITZ, *Griech. Verskunst.* Berl. 1921, 439, 3.

always played a part in this field; the increasing importance which such themes were acquiring throughout Hellenistic literature also determined the character of the novella of this time. The genius of Ionia survived in it and its ancient birthplace Miletus gave its name to the Hellenistic variety of this genre: *Milesian Stories* (Μιλησιακά) was the title of the collection of novellae with which Aristides produced, in 100 B.C., a work of doubtful but not inconsiderable fame. L. Cornelius Sisenna translated it into Latin and according to Plutarch (*Crassus* 32) Roman officers carried it in their baggage. We do not know whether Aristides linked the stories, nor what was tradition or his own invention. Various sources can still give us an impression of what these stories were like; the love theme was treated with very little lofty sentiment and a strong dash of frivolity. An instance of this is given by the novelistic insertions in the novels of Petronius and Apuleius, among which the story of the matron of Ephesus could hardly be outdone as an example of disenchantment. The tenth of the alleged letters of Aeschines contains a rare admixture, a real *Milesia*, the story of the impudent rascal who uses the ancient sacrificial customs of brides in the Troad to assume the part of the river god Scamander and thereby pick the flower of maidenhood. Even the late-comer Aristaenetus[1] has many such stories in his letters. This does not mean that Aristides was responsible for all of them; the *Milesian Story* became a collective idea.

The textual history of Aratus, for which the Marcianus 476 (end 11th cent.) is the most important evidence, was recently described with great thoroughness by J. MARTIN: *Histoire du texte des Phénomènes d'Aratos*. Paris 1956. Also extensively R. KEYDELL, *Gnom*. 30, 1958, 575. The editions and studies of E. MAAS: *Arati Phaenomena*. Berl. 1893; 2nd unaltered ed. 1954. *Commentariorum in Aratum reliquiae*. Berl. 1898; 2nd unaltered ed. 1958. *Aratea. Phil. Unters*. 12, 1892, are still fundamental. Text with Engl. transl.: G. R. MAIR, *Loeb Class. Lib.* 1921 (with Callimachus and Lycophron); with French transl.: J. MARTIN, *Bibl. di studi sup*. 25. Florence 1956. A. SCHOTT–R. BÖKER–B. STICKER, *Aratea, Wort der Antike* 6. Munich 1958 (with survey, introd. and notes). Extensive bibl. in V. BUESCU, *Cicéron, Les Aratea*. Paris-Bucharest 1941. – A. S. F. GOW and A. F. SCHOLFIELD, *Nicander. The Poems and Poetical Fragments*. Cambr. 1953 with introd., comm., Engl. transl. and bibl., as well as the editions of the scholia. In add. I. CAZZANIGA, 'Nuovo frammento di Scholion a Nicandro, Ther. vv. 526–29'. *Stud. It.* 27/28, 1956, 83. JACOBY *F Gr Hist* 271 f. with comm. – Of most of the poets discussed in this section texts are in J. U. POWELL, *Collectanea Alexandrina*. Oxf. 1925. *Anth. Lyr.* fasc. 6 D. The notes give detailed references. For Euphorion also F. SCHEIDWEILER, *Euph. fragm*. Diss. Bonn 1908, cf. also p. 757, n. 1. P. TREVES, *Euforione e la storia ellenistica*. Milan 1955. On the novella: QU. CATAUDELLA. *La novella greca. Prolegomeni e testi in traduzioni originali*. Naples 1957. Sophie Trenkner, *The Greek Novella in the Class. Period*. Cambr. Univ.

___

[1] A. LESKY, *Aristainetos*. Zürich 1951, 43.

Press 1958 introduces the interesting argument that Athenian classical literature, especially Euripides and comedy writers, contains numerous novella themes, evidence that this form of narrative existed already in the classical period.

8 HISTORIOGRAPHY

The fourth century showed already the tremendous lateral development of Greek historiography. When during the Hellenistic age this tradition entered an era which itself made history to a degree unknown before, a profusion of works was inevitable; in a passage of major importance[1] Dionysius of Halicarnassus states that the day would not be long enough if one should want to enumerate all the authors. We do not wish to submerge our work in the mass of names which have been transmitted,[2] but we shall trace certain trends of development and restrict ourselves to the most important aspects.

In the passage just referred to Dionysius complains of the literary short-comings of post-classical historiography. He begins his series with Phylarchus, Duris and Polybius, but this synopsis conceals a profound contrast which becomes clearly visible elsewhere. Polybius (2. 56) levels violent reproaches at Phylarchus which are aimed at a whole trend in historiography; it has betrayed the true task of all writing of history, the observation and transmission of truth, by prostituting itself for the sake of effect at any price. Excitement and emotional effect (ἐκπλῆξαι καὶ ψυχαγωγῆσαι) are its only purpose, and this is also served by the demand for ἐνάργεια, vividness. This form of history is censured for speculating on the emotional participation (ἔλεος, συμπάθεια)) of the reader and because it deliberately jettisons the fundamental difference between the aims of historiography and tragedy. This obviously implies that writers in the manner of Phylarchus and Duris – Ctesias is their predecessor in the fourth century – attempted to dramatize their facts with the devices of tragedy and blotted out the distinction between fiction and historical writing to such a degree as to make them unrecognizable. Plutarch's criticism of Phylarchus (*Them.* 32) is along the same lines. The key-words ecplexis and psychagogy indicate that here the same development turns up which we previously connected with Gorgias and his principles (p. 625). In fact the conflict in historiography which is revealed in Polybius is part of the wider controversy in which the stylistic ideals of simplicity and lucidity were opposed by Gorgias' epideictic trend and its claim to poetic effect.[3]

E. Schwartz[4] claimed that the fanciful historiography stigmatized by Polybius was based on a Peripatetic theory,[5] supposed to be condensed in Theophrastus'

---

[1] *De comp. verb.* 4, 30; p. 21, 5 US.-RAD.

[2] Extensive enumeration in CHRIST-SCHMID's *Hist. of Lit.*, 6th ed. II/1, Munich 1920. The remnants in JACOBY's *F Gr Hist*.

[3] Important for the elucidation of this antinomy: F. WEHRLI's essay 'Der erhabene und der schlichte Stil in der poetisch-rhetorischen Theorie der Antike'. *Phyllobolia für P. Von der Mühll*. Basel 1946, 9 and 'Die Geschichtsschreibung im Lichte der antiken Theorie'. *Eumusia. Festgabe für E. Howald*. Zürich 1947, 54.

[4] Especially in the *RE* articles on Diodorus and Duris of Samos, which now also occur in the collection *Griech. Geschichtschreiber*. 2nd unaltered ed. Leipz. 1959.

[5] Bibl. in the second of the essays just-mentioned by WEHRLI, 69, 1.

statement of principles *On Writing History* (Περὶ ἱστορίας), and his opinion remained influential for a long time. Now Duris of Samos was a pupil of Theophrastus' and certain symptoms of degeneration in Peripatetic biography (cf. p. 691) show some similarity with the straining after effect of dramatized history. Fritz Wehrli, however, has disputed this relation with Peripatetic principles on a sound basis.[1] We are especially indebted to him for elucidating a finding which is as important for the complex rhetorical and aesthetic theories as for the practice of historiography. So far two pairs of opposites had stood out sharply – firstly, care of, as opposed to indifference to, the linguistic form; secondly, a strict sense of truth against writing for the sake of effect – but this did not by any means imply that the two antinomies were parallel. On the contrary, we already observed in the case of Theopompus (p. 625) that the use of rhetorical aids did fit in with the search for historical truth, just as, on the other hand, we saw that the historical dramatist Duris was rebuked for his linguistic inadequacy in the passage of Dionysius with which we opened this section.[2] So Wehrli comes to a conception of Theophrastus' historiographical principles which shows the Peripatetic in a certain rapport with the aim of the Isocrateans. Gorgianic 'psychagogy' is rejected, and faithful reporting of truth and substance is demanded, but on the other hand an elevation of style through a moderate use of rhetorical means is emphatically recommended.

K. von Fritz[3] has also broached these complex questions in an important paper which also contains an excellent survey of the complicated history of the problem. Without attempting to return to the notion of a Peripatetic historiography, he puts the case that Duris and others like him could have adopted certain principles under the influence of the *Poetics* in a way not intended by Aristotle. In a well-known passage (*Poet.* 1451 b 5 ff.) Aristotle gives philosophical precedence to poetry over history, because it is μᾶλλον τὰ καθόλου, while history is μᾶλλον τὰ καθ᾽ ἕκαστον; with some caution this may be interpreted that poetry with its capacity for concentration and emphasis can stress certain broad features of a 'case' more clearly. According to v. Fritz, this gave Duris' school the stimulus to make ἱστορίη compete with poetry for the quality of καθόλου by adopting its means of presentation. The same point of

---

[1] *v.* prev. note. Cautious criticism of Theophrastus' treatise by REGENBOGEN, *RE* S 7, 1940, 1526.

[2] Important indication by WEHRLI, *Eumusia* (*v.* p. 764, n. 3), 57 that Aristotle's theory (*Rhet.* 3, 12) in its separation of γραφική and ἀγωνιστικὴ λέξις shows a reservation against the use of rhetorical artifices in forensic and political orations.

[3] 'Die Bedeutung des Aristoteles für die Geschichtsschreibung' in *Histoire et historiens dans l'antiquité, Entretiens sur l'ant. class.* 4. Fondation Hardt, Vandoeuvres-Geneva 1956, 85. Mention of the question also in G. AVENARIUS. *Lukians Schrift zur Geschichtschreibung.* Diss. Frankf. 1954. Meisenheim a. Glan 1956. Like WEHRLI he does not derive tragic historiography from the Peripatos, but believes that the latter was responsible for a third style in addition to Polybius' tendency and Hegesias' Asianism. F. W. WALBANK, *Gnom.* 29, 1957, 417 has justifiable doubts about this; he has discussed this problem frequently: 'Tragic History. A Reconsideration.' *Bull. Inst. of Class. Stud. Univ. Lond.* 1955, 4, and 'History and Tragedy'. *Historia* 9, 1960, 216. WALBANK recommends that theories about the origin are abandoned and that tragic elements in Greek historiography are examined.

view would also make it inevitable that they should oppose the didactic tendency of the Isocrateans.

In all this it should be borne in mind that hardly enough survives of historians like Duris and Phylarchus to give a reliable impression,[1] while various factors may have affected their writing. Von Fritz' contention – and here he agrees with Wehrli – is still important in any case. He argues that the characteristics of style and language in the separate histories have no definite link with specific tendencies of literary expression, but that a variety of styles was prevalent. And this seems to be borne out by the meagre remnants.

The tradition is scanty and so it is possible to ascertain of only a few of the Hellenistic historians which of the various tendencies discussed was favoured by each of them. In the very first group, however, that of the historians of Alexander, contrasts such as were indicated are discernible in some cases.

Foremost in this group, in view of his position and reliability, not according to his period, is Ptolemy Lagu (*F Gr Hist* 138). He was already close to Alexander in Philip's reign, went to war with him as a cavalry officer and had been his personal aide (σωματοφύλαξ) from 330 onward. He wrote the history of his great king when he was the ruler of Egypt, obviously in his old age. It is quite conceivable that he was led by the desire to oppose would-be history of Alexander with his superior knowledge. When Arrian, himself a high-ranking administrator and military officer, wrote his *Anabasis* of Alexander, he used Ptolemy's work as a basis and attempted to separate this valuable material from the popular tradition (λεγόμενα). Thus Arrian is our main source for Ptolemy, giving us a picture of an unbiased work in spite of the strongly autobiographical elements in which military and political factors far outweighed geography and ethnography. Ptolemy, who was indeed able to write history in the original sense of personal investigation, also utilized the royal *Ephemerides* (*F Gr Hist* 117), written at the headquarters under the direction of Eumenes of Cardia and Diodotus of Erythrae.

Ptolemy's work, a factual report covering the wide range of his experience, is contrasted by that of a group of authors who willingly submitted to the lure of representing unusual subject matter in a romantic way. Callisthenes and Anaximenes have been mentioned before (p. 627); the orator Hegesias of Magnesia (*F Gr Hist* 142), whom we met as the founder of Asianism, is a historian of Alexander, whom we must consider as belonging to the extreme fringe of the rhetorical historians. The most lasting effect was achieved by the work of Clitarchus (*F Gr Hist* 137), who wrote in about 310, after Alexander's death but before the publication of Ptolemy's memoirs. According to Cicero he did this *rhetorice et tragice*. Following the conqueror's career from his accession until his death, he founded the popular tradition with its fictional features. Diodorus excerpted it in Book 17[2]; Curtius Rufus and Justin follow the tradition and so does much of the λεγόμενα in Arrian. Soon after Alexander's death

---

[1] The interesting arguments provoked by v. FRITZ and printed in the *Entretiens* bring out the complexity of the problem.

[2] W. W. TARN, *Alexander*. 2 vols. Cambr. 1948, 5 ff., tried to upset this opinion.

Onesicritus of Astypalaea (*F Gr Hist* 134), who also took part in the great expedition, wrote the king's history (πῶς ᾽Αλέξανδρος ἤχθη) [1] in which his hero's portrait was apparently provided with philosophical, especially Cynic, features. Chares of Mytilene (*F Gr Hist* 125) also wrote a history of Alexander. The remnants still show that he accompanied the expedition as chamberlain (εἰσαγγελεύς), but it is not possible to make sure how reliable his facts were. A distinguished Macedonian who grew up with Alexander, Marsyas of Pella (*F Gr Hist* 135), a brother of Antigonus Monophthalmus according to Suidas, also wrote about the king, but it is very difficult to ascertain the nature of the work with any precision. Did it form part of the framework of his *Macedonica*? This much can be observed, however, that he wrote from a Macedonian point of view and did not witness the cult of Alexander's person. Among the writings which appeared soon after 323 was also the one of Ephippus of Olynthus (*F Gr Hist* 126), who sharply attacked Alexander's personality on the basis of good information; it was probably not unique in this respect.

In this mixed chorus a special position is taken by Aristobulus of Cassandrea (*F Gr Hist* 139). He participated in Alexander's expedition, but did not begin to write his history, according to his own evidence (T 3), until the age of 84. This means that he wrote later than the authors mentioned so far and mixed his own memories with the abundant literature available at the time; but his capacities were up to neither effective criticism nor to writing an influential work on Alexander, and Eduard Schwartz,[2] justifiably made objections to Aristobulus' being mentioned in one breath with Ptolemy.

In a different context (p. 578) mention was made of the report of Alexander's admiral Nearchus of his voyage from the mouth of the Indus to the Persian Gulf.

We spoke of the fictional character of the history of Alexander in which numerous openings offered by the subject matter combined with a certain tendency of contemporary historiography. It is also useful to mention a product of historical writing which, in the form transmitted, is of late origin, but whose roots go back to the period under discussion. The Alexander–romance, attributed to Callisthenes, is accessible only in editions of the late empire. Various Greek revisions exist alongside the Vulgar Latin text of Iulius Valerius of the end of the third century. There are, in addition, some translations which are important as stemmata of the transmission; the Armenian one ranks first in importance among these.[3] Recently Reinhold Merkelbach has been successful in largely elucidating the growth of this abstruse and complex structure. Two new papyri were of great assistance (Pap. Soc. It. 1285, 2nd c. A.D. and Pap. Hamb. 129, 1st c. B.C.); they contain part of a fictitious correspondence of Alexander which in part turns up again in the romance. One of its main ingredients proves to be a

---

[1] Perhaps the opening words were used as a title, like the one of Xenophon's *Cyropaedia*. Monograph: T. S. BROWN, *Onesicritus*. Calif. Un. Pr. 1949.

[2] *RE* 2, 914 = *Griech. Geschichtsschreiber*. Leipz. 1957, 125.

[3] Swift survey provided by R. MERKELBACH, *Die Quellen des griech. Alexanderromans*. Zet. 9, Munich 1954, IX; extensive description of the transmission ibid. 61. H. VAN THIEL, *Die Rezension λ das Pseudo-Kallisthenes*. Bonn 1959.

quantity of letters, among which an epistolary romance[1] about Alexander can be distinguished (*circa* 100 B.C.). In addition there are letters of Alexander to Aristotle and Olympias about his adventures and two special writings about his talk with the gymnosophist and on the king's last days. This largely deplorable mass of tradition was compiled by Pseudo-Callisthenes together with a history of Alexander which dates from the Hellenistic age and bears the imprint of the fictional historiography which was characterized earlier. The compiler was a sorry fellow who, apart from the questionable quality of his material, often fitted the members wrongly into the body which he wanted to create and dislocated them into the bargain. His Alexander marches against the Persians through Asia Minor, Sicily, Italy and North Africa, to mention one thing only. This conglomeration was no doubt written in the third century A.D.; it corresponds to its intellectual level. The romance had an immense influence on the literature of times for which Greek thought was something alien. In numerous revisions and translations it fixed the image of Alexander up to the beginning of the modern era as a much coveted subject for entertainment.

In the following section we shall single out some historians from the profuse quantity of material of the third century, without adhering too closely to chronological limits. We are faced at once, as before, by the contrast between subject matter and effect. Modern scholarship has acknowledged the work of Hieronymus of Cardia (*F Gr Hist* 154) as an important and reliable source for the half century after Alexander's death.[2] Hieronymus, who took part in important events during the wars of the Successors on the side of Eumenes, Antigonus Monophthalmus and Demetrius Poliorcetes, wrote his contemporary history during the last few decades of his life, which fell roughly between 350 and 260. He covered the period from Alexander's death probably up to Pyrrhus' end (272) and became the standard source of this period for later authors (Diodorus, Arrian, Plutarch, etc.). His objectivity based on an extensive factual knowledge shows that he is of the same high integrity as his predecessor Ptolemy. If he really wrote his work to offset Duris' exuberance with responsible adherence to fact, this would offer new scope for comparison.

However this may be, the tenets of Duris of Samos (*F Gr Hist* 76), whose lifetime (*circa* 340–270) largely coincides with that of Hieronymus, put him in the opposite camp. In the opening of his *Histories*,[3] which probably began with the death of Philip's father Amyntas and went on to Pyrrhus, he rebukes Ephorus and Theopompus, because they fell behind with events; they lacked the talent for mimesis, the catch-word for poetry, and in a more limited sense, for

---

[1] About this genre in which the school of rhetoric participates, cf. SYKUTRIS, *RES* 5, 1931, 213.

[2] T. S. BROWN, 'Hieronymus of Cardia'. *Am. Hist. Rev.* 52, 1946/7, 684. Hieronymus was considered as the author of *Pap. Soc. It.* 1950, no 1284. We add a reference to an anonymous history of the Successors in the Heidelberg epitome (*F Gr Hist* 155) to give an idea of the frequency of this species.

[3] Perhaps the title was *Macedonica*, cf. JACOBY on T 3. E. G. TURNER considers attributing *Ox. Pap.* no. 2399 to Duris. WILLIAM M. CALDER III, *Class. Phil.* 55, 1960, 128 agrees enthusiastically.

dramatization. Concentrating only on the written word they did not know how to make their presentation enjoyable, to give ἡδονή (F 1).[1] An instructive example of Duris' method of uncritical adornment and heightening of effect is given by F 70 (Plut. *Alcib.* 32). When the victorious Alcibiades was sailing into the Piraeus, Chrysogonus, champion at the Pythian games, accompanied the rowing with the music of his flute, while Callippides, the tragic actor, gave the rhythm of the strokes, both, of course, fully dressed for their profession, while the flagship made its entry with a purple sail hoisted. Plutarch states that this is found neither in Theopompus, Ephorus nor Xenophon, and that it is quite unlikely to have happened. There was a curious contrast between his attempts to instruct and dramatize and the slight literary value of his style; this contrast is worthy of note in view of our previous remarks about this author.

Duris wrote a great deal; we mention his *Story of Agathocles* and his *Samian Chronicle*; his *On Painting* and *On Toreutics* are examples of the literature on art which was already fully developed at the time.

Phylarchus (*F Gr Hist* 81)[2] worked entirely in the manner of Duris. We found that both Polybius and Plutarch objected to him. His floruit falls in the second half of the third century; his work was the main source for later authors of the period from the death of Pyrrhus (272) to the beginning of Polybius' historical writing (220).[3]

Earlier (p. 669) we met, as Athenian writers of contemporary historical works, Demosthenes' nephew Demochares and Diyllus, probably the son of the Atthidographer Phanodemus. In one part of his work Diyllus completed Ephorus' contemporary history, carrying it on up to 297 in the second part. It was continued by Psaon of Plataea (*F Gr Hist* 78), whose work probably continued up to 220, and carried on in turn by Menodotus of Perinthus (*F Gr Hist* 82).

A problem is posed by Neanthes of Cyzicus (*F Gr Hist* 84), since there were two men of that name, one an orator in 300, the other an author, apparently very versatile, of the end of the third century. The most obvious solution would be to attribute to the latter the historical works *Hellenica*, *History of Attalus* and *Chronicle of Cyzicus*. Other works, like the one *On Famous Men*, are probably his as well.

Historiography was still intimately connected with geographical interests, just as it was in the early stages. This is clear in the case of Eudoxus of Rhodes (*F Gr Hist* 79), an author of the third century, who wrote a *Periplus* in addition to *Histories*.

Among the historians of the time of Alexander and the Successors we have met men who themselves witnessed a considerable part of the events which they described; Polybius will be another example. Another step led from this kind of

---

[1] We reproduce here this passage which is as important as it is concise: Ἔφορος δὲ καὶ Θεόπομπος τῶν γενομένων πλεῖστον ἀπελείφθησαν οὔτε γὰρ μιμήσεως μετέλαβον οὐδεμιᾶς οὔτ' ἡδονῆς ἐν τῷ φράσαι, αὐτοῦ δὲ τοῦ γράφειν μόνον ἐπεμελήθησαν.

[2] It is not certain whether Athens, Sicyon or Naucratis was his birthplace.

[3] T. W. AFRICA, *Phyllarchus and the Spartan Revolution.* Un. of Cal. Publ. on Hist. 68, 1961.

historiography to the writing of memoirs, although this did not become so frequent and important among the Greeks as it did among the Romans.[1] This agrees with the fact that the personal portrait was perfected in Rome. Two works by Demetrius of Phalerum about his own affairs, *On the Ten Years* and *On the Constitution*, were mentioned before (p. 689. F Gr Hist 228 – Fr. 131 ff. Wehrli). Memoirs (Ὑπομνήματα) were written by Aratus of Sicyon, the excellent statesman who had been leading the Achaean league with great skill since 245. The work covered the period up to the battle of Sellasia (222); its remnants reveal a strongly apologetic tendency and we observe that such writing is a descendant, at least to a large extent, of forensic oratory.

At this juncture we make special mention of Nymphis of Heraclea (*F Gr Hist* 432) from among the historians of the 3rd century who are of some importance. He dealt with the history of Alexander up to about the middle of the third century in a large work (twenty-four books) and wrote in addition a history of his native town in thirteen books (Περὶ Ἡρακλείας). With this he introduces us to the immense number of local monographs which was now growing to gigantic proportions through a tradition of an even earlier origin. Felix Jacoby, in the third part of his monumental work with its 345 numbers referring mainly to this period, has marshalled this profusion in an admirable manner, reminding us that we have a relatively small portion of the total output and that a find like that of the *Anagraphe of Lindus* (*F Gr Hist* 532) with a series of new names makes the limitations of our knowledge painfully clear.

It is self-evident that writing of this nature was often more antiquarian than historical in character, as shown by the example of Sosibius the Laconian (*F Gr Hist* 595), a grammarian who treated Spartan antiquities with the methods of Hellenistic psychagogy. In addition to a work on chronology (Χρόνων ἀναγραφή) there are works such as *On Spartan Sacrifices*.

The historical interests of the time found their expression in the publicly exhibited *Chronicles*, of which inscriptions like the *Marmor Parium* (*F Gr Hist* 239, up to the year 264/3) and the *Anagraphe of Lindus* (*F Gr Hist* 532, inscribed in 99 B.C.) give us invaluable samples.

Even districts which were somewhat remote from the ancient centres of Greek cultural life had their writers. Thus Xenophilus wrote about Lydia (*F Gr Hist* 767), Menecrates of Xanthus about Lycia (*F Gr Hist* 769). A continuation of this trend was the adoption of the Greek language by natives of non-Greek countries to write the history of their native land. Thus the *Aegyptiaca* was the work of Manetho of Sebennytus (*F Gr Hist* 609), an Egyptian priest in Heliopolis who took part in the introduction of the cult of Serapis under Ptolemy I; a *Babyloniaca* was produced by Berossus (*F Gr Hist* 680),[2] a priest of Marduk who also lived in the early part of the Hellenistic age. Phoenician

---

[1] Cf. F. JACOBY, F Gr Hist 2 C, p. 639. G. MISCH, *Gesch. d. Autobiographie.* 3rd ed. I/1 Bern 1949, 66.

[2] P. SCHNABEL, *Berossos und die babylonisch-hellenistische Lit.* Leipz. 1923 (with the fragments). W. HELCK, *Untersuchungen zu Manetho und die ägyptischen Königslisten. Unters. zur Gesch. und Altertumsk. Ägyptens* 18. Berl. 1956. A biling. ed. of Manetho with Ptolemy, *Tetrabiblos*, by W. G. WADDELL and F. E. ROBBINS. *Loeb Class. Libr.* 1940.

history was the subject matter of a work by Menander of Ephesus (*F Gr Hist* 783).

It goes without saying that the Far East, whose gates had been thrust open by Alexander, had strongly beckoned the Greeks, who delighted in exploration. Megasthenes (*F Gr Hist* 715), who in 300 travelled several times to the Indian king Chandragupta (called Sandrocottus by the Greeks) as an envoy in the service of Seleucus Nicator, wrote an *Indica* in four books which is more like the ethnographical writings with their wide scope, which were once the root of Ionian history. Another *Indica* was written by Daemachus[1] of Plataea (*F Gr Hist* 716), who came to know the country as the ambassador of Antiochus Soter; another author to be mentioned in this group is Patrocles (*F Gr Hist* 712), who served Seleucus Nicator and Antiochus Soter in important positions; he was the first to provide fairly precise information about the Caspian Sea which he had collected in a voyage of exploration.

While the new centres, especially Alexandria, dominated intellectual life throughout the main period of the Hellenistic age, the new great power in the Mediterranean area forcefully demanded attention from the end of the third century onward. The development of the west and Rome's conflict with Carthage inevitably evoked a lively echo in Greek literature, even before Polybius appeared as the great interpreter of this epoch. For the First Punic War he used the monograph of Philinus of Agrigentum (*F Gr Hist* 174), who had little love for the Romans. Side by side with an admiration for this swift rise to power whose poetical expression was mentioned before, there arose at an early stage an intellectual opposition against Rome.[2] It is not strange that the fascinating figure of Hannibal was also portrayed by a Greek. According to the convincing emendation of Athenaeus 12. 542 a, Silenus of Calacte probably wrote his history of Hannibal when his star had already sunk. Coelius Antipater owed a great deal to him. Polybius (3. 20, 5) dismissed another historian of Hannibal of this time, Sosylus of Lacedaemon (*F Gr Hist* 176) as a vulgar chatterbox, together with a certain Chaerias, of whom nothing further is known, but food for thought is given by a papyrus (no. 1162 P.; F 1 Jac.), which reveals Sosylus as a reporter to be reckoned with.

In earlier sections (pp. 332; 628) we observed the growth of Sicilian historiography; early in Hellenistic times it came to an end with a work of extraordinary influence. Its writer, Timaeus of Tauromenion (*F Gr Hist* 566), was born in the middle of the fourth century as the son of Andromachus, who brought about the resettlement of Tauromenion in 358–357, retaining his position of power through his political skill even when Timoleon established a new order in the island after 344. When, however, Agathocles brought the most important Greek cities of Sicily under his power, Timaeus was forced to go into exile. He lived in Athens for fifty years; there he first became a pupil of the Isocratean Philiscus. According to a treatise *On Octogenarians* going under Lucian's name,

---

[1] The form Δημίαχος has also been transmitted.

[2] Its history written by H. FUCHS, *Der geistige Widerstand gegen Rom in der ant. Welt.* Berl. 1938.

he reached the age of 96, but it is uncertain whether he ever returned to his native country.

His work, quoted under various titles, among which is *Historiae*, told the story of the Greek west from the beginning up to the outbreak of the First Punic War An introductory section (προκατασκευή) of probably five books can be distinguished, dealing with the geography of the west as far as the extreme north, a great deal of legendary material and probably also the most ancient colonization. The quotations extend up to book 38, for which Agathocles' death (289) provided a convenient conclusion. This bitterly hated tyrant was the subject of the last five books; in F 34 of book 34 a fragment of the preface to this, once probably independent, part of the work seems to have been preserved. The books *On Pyrrhus*, written later in life, were an addendum which probably led on to 264.

Timaeus became a historian not in the centres of political and military influence, but in the libraries of Athens; Polybius, who got into history by an entirely different way, reproached him for his theoretical book-learning (12. 25 h: βιβλιακὴ ἕξις). He levelled other malicious criticism at Timaeus, who himself had been nicknamed Epitimaeus (T 1. 11) because of his censoriousness which, as a pupil of an Isocratean, he directed, for instance, at the Peripatos. This an expression of a vice which is not exclusive to the Hellenistic age, of making criticism of one's predecessor the background of one's own glory. It is no slight merit that Timaeus composed a detailed history of the west from the viewpoint of the contrast between Greeks and barbarians, basing himself on a large number of foregoing works; probably he could already draw on the book *On Sicily* by Lycus of Rhegium (*F Gr Hist* 570), Lycophron's adoptive father. He early recognized Rome's significance; he enlarged upon its archaeology[1] as well as its development to a great power. He was careful in his chronology and made his contribution to the continued use of Olympiads for dating. The *Olympionicae* was presumably a preliminary work in this field. He had some stylistic pretensions and was so partial to the new fashion in writing that Cicero classed him (*Brut.* 325) with the Asianic writers who strove for effect through gracefulness. Timaeus' work became an important source; its traces are discernible in the most widely scattered fields and his critic Polybius showed his respect for him by joining his own work chronologically on to that of Timaeus.

Polybius' career as a historian passed through the chequered stages of a life closely connected with contemporary events. His works contain autobiographical material to an extent rare in any other historian. He was born in 200 in Megalopolis; this city was a bastion against Sparta, formed after Leuctra (371) by means of a comprehensive synoecism. For some decades it had been a member of the Achaean League which managed to extract many advantages out of the rivalry of the great powers and to maintain a certain amount of influence. Polybius' father Lycortas had several times performed the office of strategos of the League, and Philopoemen, who had brought the League to its eminence through his skilful diplomacy, was always his much-admired model; when he

[1] Timaeus had considerable influence on the shaping of the saga of Rome's origin.

died in hostile Messenia of poison in 183, Polybius carried the urn with his ashes in solemn procession to Megalopolis. These youthful experiences did not lose their significance when his career took him all over the world. In the year 169 he became hipparch, thus reaching one of the highest positions in the League, though it was not to his advantage. When the Romans had broken the Macedonian power at Pydna in 168, they deported, largely at the urging of the pro-Roman party in the League, 1000 eminent Achaeans to Rome where they were to be put to trial. It never came to this, but it was not until seventeen years later that the surviving 300 were permitted to go home. Although he stayed in Rome under coercion, Polybius' position was by no means that of a prisoner. The circle of the high nobility, which was friendly to the Greeks, was soon opened to him and he himself relates in an impressive passage of his work (32. 9 f.) how in the house of the victor of Pydna the younger Scipio became his friend for life.[1] After his return Polybius probably did not remain in his native land for long. As early as 149 he was apparently already called to the African theatre of war, where he participated in the campaign up to the fall of Carthage, evidently on Scipio's staff. His voyage of discovery westward along the African coast, for which Scipio provided the ships, probably also took place in this period.[2]

Before Carthage Polybius had been able to give advice as an expert in tactics and the art of siege-warfare; but he was soon charged with important diplomatic duties during the worst days for his native land. A senseless catastrophic policy had led, in 146, to war with Rome, which ended in a complete collapse. The destruction of Corinth by L. Mummius revealed the gravity of this fall in a fearful manner. By intervening Polybius could achieve some mitigation and in many places managed to help in collaboration with the senate committee which was charged with resettlement. He then went back to Rome where he could also achieve a great deal for his compatriots, and finally returned to his native land, where at the age of 82 he died as a result of falling from his horse. He may have left Greece in his old age several times more; it is very likely that he took part in Scipio's Spanish campaign and at least in the conquest of Numantia; a sojourn in Alexandria during the reign of Ptolemy Physcon may also have occurred in this period.

A number of Polybius' minor works, the *Biography of Philopoemen*, some of which is probably concealed in Plutarch, the *Tactica*,[3] On *Conditions of Habitation in the Equatorial Zone*, the monograph On *the Numantine War*, are lost. About a third of the great historical work which Polybius wrote in the conviction that the fate of Rome was decisive for the world has been preserved. We shall begin with a few remarks about its length, structure and state of preservation. Of the forty books of the whole work the first two are an introduction

---

[1] P. FRIEDLÄNDER, in the section *Sokrates in Rom* of his *Platon* I, 2nd ed. Berl. 1954 demonstrated the influence of Socrates' association with his followers as a model for this description.

[2] F. W. WALBANK and M. GELZER (*v. Gnom.* 29, 1957, 401) consider it likely that Polybius travelled to Spain and Africa with Scipio as early as 151.

[3] This sort of literature was abundant. There is therefore little reason for tracing Asclepiodotus' *Tactica* in the Florentine manuscript via Posidonius to Polybius.

(προκατασκευή) with a brief survey of the period 264–220, which represents the link with Timaeus' work. Books 3–5 depict events in Italy and Greece up to the year of Cannae. Book 6 follows with his theory of constitutions and his assessment of the constitution of Rome. In Book 7 the year 215 marks the beginning of an annalistic treatment compiling events in the east and the west year by year. This arrangement is abandoned only occasionally to prevent a distortion of the context. The material has been distributed in such a way that generally one whole or half an Olympiad fills a book unless particularly eventful years demand all of this space. Book 12 with the polemic against the older historiographers forms a caesura, like Book 6, so that at least for this part a composition in hexads seems to be marked off; the consistency of this structure, however, should not be exaggerated. With Book 26 the momentous year of Pydna (168) is reached. The rest of the work leads up to the year 144. At that time Carthage and Corinth had been destroyed, conditions in Greece resettled and the large realm of Rome had been placed on a broad foundation. Apart from minor gaps Books 1–5 have been entirely preserved; of the other ones we only have pieces in excerpts the size of which varies greatly for the individual books. The most important excerpt-manuscript, the Codex Vaticanus Urbinas Gr. 102 (11th/12th c.) has epitomes of Books 1–16 and 18, in which the order of the original has been maintained and whose attribution to individual books is certain. Is this a selection made in antiquity? A definite answer is not possible. In addition there are a large quantity of pieces from the comprehensive collection of manuscripts which Constantine VII Porphyrogennetus ordered to be compiled in the tenth century. Attribution to individual books poses a number of difficult problems in this case.

A work so extensive and of so rich a content is not written in one stroke, and there is evidence of its syncretic growth. The prooemium (1. 1, 5) announces the description of the fifty-three years (220–168) in which Rome achieved world-dominion[1] and a number of passages[2] still presupposes the existence of Carthage. Attempts to separate the various strata led to some excesses of analysis; scholars went so far, for instance, as to squeeze five layers from the work.[3] The inevitable reaction was to make Polybius write the whole work down in one stroke after the year 146.[4] It may be assumed that he conceived the main part of the work up to Pydna in Rome, presumably in the years after 160. Subsequent events, especially his participation in the Third Punic War, decided him to carry it on; this decision was given a theoretical foundation in chapter 3, 4, which was inserted later; it was not only the success (Pydna) but also the situation after the victory which demanded thoughtful analysis. On the question of syncresis in Book 6 some further remarks will have to be made. To record everything that can be stated with some certainty we add the theory of Matthias

---

[1] Other passages in W. THEILER, 'Schichten im 6. Buch des P.' Herm. 81, 1953, 302.

[2] In ZIEGLER (v. inf.) 1485, 39.

[3] R. LAQUEUR, Polybios. Leipz. 1913.

[4] H. ERBSE, 'Die Entstehung des polybianischen Geschichtswerkes'. Rhein. Mus. 94, 1951, 157. He defends his point of view in 'Polybios-Interpretationen'. Phil. 101, 1957, 269.

Gelzer[1] that the extensive passages about the history of the Achaeans are from a period preceding the writing of the universal historical work. It is difficult to ascertain whether parts were published separately and with what intervals, but there are also good grounds for assuming a posthumous edition of the whole.[2]

Polybius expressed himself very positively and elaborately on his principles of historiography. We are reminded in more than one aspect of Thucydides, but only with regard to the theoretical side; in the execution there is no common measure for Polybius' pragmatism and Thucydides' profundity.

In the question whether history should serve usefulness or delight ($\dot{\omega}\phi\acute{\epsilon}\lambda\epsilon\iota\alpha$ or $\tau\acute{\epsilon}\rho\psi\iota\varsigma$), a question over which minds were divided in Hellenistic times, he resolutely championed the cause of usefulness. On this principle we saw him attack Phylarchus and people like him; what mattered to him was to separate historiography as he understood it from the emotions of tragedy. In the introduction to Book 9 he discusses the austerity and uniformity of his own work with objective judgment (or in defence against outside criticism?). But he declares with conviction that he believes in a historiography which does not entertain with genealogies, stories of foundations and such like, but which hands on to the politically minded a knowledge of actions done by rulers and peoples. This is what he means by pragmatical history ($\pi\rho\alpha\gamma\mu\alpha\tau\iota\kappa\grave{o}\varsigma$ $\tau\rho\acute{o}\pi o\varsigma$). It imposes the unconditional duty of objective search for truth. Hardly any contemporary historian would have put the problem of this demand theoretically in the way in which Cicero did this later in the famous letter to Lucceius (*Ad fam.* 5. 12), but for Polybius it was a task which he took very seriously. In Book 12 (25 d ff.), in his criticism of Timaeus, he draws an interesting parallel between medicine and history, dividing each into three parts. For the pragmatical historian they are represented by work on written sources, geographical information gained through personal enquiry and insight into the practice of politics. In this respect the man who had acquired such insight to an unusual degree through his own activity stands out from the man of letters. It agrees with this background that in his criticism of Timaeus he also condemns the free invention of speeches. Whenever he inserts these himself, he demands that they should achieve the authentic idiom as much as possible. He must have been able to do this for the history of the Achaean League and occasional proceedings of the Senate. All the same it is characteristic that Thucydides' notion of inner truth and the imposing use of speeches for the revelation of the basic forces of political happenings were beyond Polybius' scope.

The form in which Polybius proposed to carry out his task is not that of the monograph, but of universal history. He felt himself to be a master in this sphere, giving only credit to Ephorus (5. 33) as his predecessor. In accordance with his principles he describes in detail in the early part of his work how events in separate areas had become interwoven into an organic whole ($\sigma\omega\mu\alpha\tau\omega\epsilon\iota\delta\acute{\epsilon}\varsigma$) since the 140th Olympiad, with which his discussion begins.

---

[1] 'Die Achaïca im Geschichtswerk des P.' *Abh. Akad. Berl. Phil.-hist. Kl.* 1940/2; cf. *Gnom.* 29, 1957, 406.

[2] Cf. ZIEGLER (*v. inf.*), 1487, 41.

Polybius took history literally as the *magistra vitae*, trusting that its mastery would lead to an understanding of political situations (e.g. 9,2, 12, 25 b). But in the second passage mentioned we are told that this useful effect is not produced by merely telling the story of the events, but by penetrating into their causes. This seems to have some affinity with Thucydides, but when Polybius begins to work with notions like αἰτία and πρόφασις (22, 22 a) which the great Athenian uses pregnantly (*v.* p. 459), the difference between them becomes clear. Nor does Polybius' aetiology attempt to penetrate to the common humanity which Thucydides reveals as the deepest level of motivation; his thinking rather moves among the categories of political life as he had come to know it in domestic and foreign politics. In this context he greatly stresses the idea, not new in itself, that there is a close correspondence between the fate of states and their constitutions. To this circumstance we owe the much-discussed expositions of Book 6, in which his criticism of Rome's constitution is placed within a broad framework of theoretical considerations. Others had preceded Polybius here, but his personality is revealed by the sweep of this passage, even if it is not quite free from contradictions. It has been observed for a long time that two theories were joined together here. The doctrine of the cyclic change (μεταβολή)) of constitutions through degeneration, for which Polybius himself mentions Plato and other philosophers (6. 5) as predecessors, was blended with the evaluation of the mixed constitution as the best and most lasting form. This great esteem for the mixed constitution had first been expressed by Aristotle's pupil Dicaearchus in his *Tripoliticus*.[1] A controversial question[2] is whether the two theories belong to different strata of the work or whether the author wished to combine them in the sense that the mixed constitution proves to possess the greatest resistance against degeneration and change. If this possibility is accepted, later additions are not necessarily rejected by implication. These can apparently be distinguished especially in the gloomy view of Rome's future (6. 9. 12 f.). Polybius had observed – so much is clear from a first stratum – that the essential basis of Rome's rise was its mixed constitution which reveals elements of monarchy, oligarchy and democracy in consuls, senate and people. But in the passage referred to he states that Rome, like everything else that has grown naturally, cannot escape from the law according to which growth and vigour are followed by decay. These must be the sentiments of the older Polybius, to whom the wrongs and dangers in a constitution whose unexampled successes had at one time made him its unreserved admirer were becoming apparent.

[1] F. WEHRLI, *Dikaiarchos*. Basel 1944, 28, 64. The opinion that Polybius borrowed his political convictions directly from Dicaearchus is opposed by K. V. FRITZ, most recently in *Entretiens sur l'antiquité class.* 4. Fondation Hardt, Vandoeuvres-Geneva 1956, 95.

[2] This passage is discussed in a broad context by H. RYFFEL, Μεταβολὴ πολιτειῶν. *Noctes Romanae* 2. Bern 1949. W. THEILER (*v.* p. 774, n. 1) advocates a division of thought groups according to layers in the work. The analysis of K. V. FRITZ, *The Theory of Mixed Constitutions in Antiquity*, New York 1954 is based on a broad historical and constitutional-historical background. In his analysis of the strata he adopts a cautious attitude without denying subsequent additions. In all the three passages referred to ext. bibl. Also H. ERBSE (*v.* p. 774, n. 4) and M. GELZER, *Gnom.* 28, 1956, 83, who fundamentally agrees with THEILER and is rather inclined to assume stages of composition in the work.

Polybius was no philosopher and least of all a religious thinker. He was familiar with philosophical doctrines, but he was neither a Stoic nor an adherent of any other philosophical sect. His appraisal of Roman religion discloses clearly (6. 56, 6) that his attitude was that of the enlightened Hellenist; he acknowledges its great importance, but for him it meant the guarantee of a social order on an ethical basis. This conception leaves religious worship inviolate. Tyche is often mentioned; it has frequently been observed[1] that various notions are confused: Tyche obviously as the providential ruler of the universe, Tyche as envious as the gods of old, Tyche as the irrational element whose domain is narrowed by intelligent historiography as best it can without denying her existence. This observation can neither be explained by assuming a development in Polybius' thought nor can the opposites be reconciled by means of logical construction. The fact is simply that in Polybius we find the multiplicity of notions which in the Hellenistic age had collected as the flotsam of religious thought.

It will be understood that Polybius' language is far remote from freshness and naturalness. Its grammar is largely Attic. It has been aptly stated that Polybius' attitude to Attic Greek is conservative, that of the Atticists reactionary.[2] This can be gathered from the use of the optative which Polybius, and later to a less extent also Diodorus, still retains, while in authors like Dionysius of Halicarnassus it was artificially revived. His style owes its peculiar character to a strong tendency towards the abstract. This is firstly clear in the vocabulary, which contains many noun-formations and compound verbs which have little in common with Attic Greek; then the structure of his periods lacks smoothness and balance through his attempts to force a maximum of thought content into a many-layered sentence construction by means of participles and substantival verbs. His careful avoidance of hiatus proves that he does not aim at formlessness. The background to Polybius' style is the language of the Hellenistic chancellery which, in the age of Koine, had developed into a vehicle for writing official documents which combined verbosity with precision.

Polybius' work was epoch-making in the historiography of the later Hellenistic age, as is illustrated by the fact that others took up where he left off. Posidonius' extensive history of the world (v. p. 679)[3] indicated this intention in its title; Strabo, whom we shall meet later as a geographer, wrote a *Historica Hypomnemata* (F Gr Hist 91), of which four books formed a comprehensive introduction followed by a voluminous main part (forty-three books?) with the sub-title *History of the Time after Polybius* (τὰ μετὰ Πολύβιον).

The latter part of the Hellenistic age did not produce a historian of importance. The special characteristic of this period was the tendency to make new compilations of material which had been assiduously extracted from the mass of older literature. The voluminous historical work of Agatharchides of Cnidos (F Gr

---

[1] K. V. FRITZ (*v. sup.*), 388. ZIEGLER (*v. inf.*), 1532.

[2] Cf. A. DEBRUNNER, *Gnom.* 28, 1956, 588.

[3] We possess only fragments; of great importance the careful arrangement by JACOBY F Gr Hist 87.

Hist 86)[1] was probably such a work; in ten books it dealt with Asian history and in another forty-nine with Europe. We know more about his work *On the Red Sea* (by which he means the Persian Gulf) through various remnants, among which an excerpt of Photius. It can only be called geography in the broad meaning of a literature which had a variety of interests apart from geography based on mathematics. Agatharchides, who lived in the second century and would hardly have written later than 160, was a Peripatetic philosopher and was a writer bitterly opposed to Asianism. Timagenes of Alexandria (*F Gr Hist* 88) was an orator. In 55 he was brought to Rome as a prisoner of Pompey's; there he gained some distinction, but gave offence because of his wicked tongue, finally finding a refuge for his old age with Asinius Pollio. His work *On Kings* started with pre-history and continued at least up to Caesar. His subsequent influence was strong, but nowadays it is an open question[2] to what extent Pompeius Trogus' *Philippica* is dependent on Timagenes.

Strictly speaking, the Hellenistic age ends in 30 B.C., although this date does not represent a rigid boundary. Timagenes lived beyond it, and so did some other compilers who are as yet untouched by the classicist reaction.

In spite of the volume of work preserved Diodorus Siculus of Agyrion has to be satisfied with a modest place in the history of literature. His life can be approximately dated by the mention of the removal of a Roman colony to Tauromenion (probably 36 B.C.) as the latest event. In the forty books of his *Bibliotheca* he presented to a broad public a synchronous account of Greek and Roman history based on a large number of different sources; the combination of Greek and Roman chronology caused him considerable difficulties. He could not resist inserting the history of his native island as well, mainly after Timaeus and Duris. The quality of Diodorus' public can be gauged by the retrograde step which he took in including mythical pre-history in his account. But in spite of all abuse of Diodorus we are glad to accept his donations. Thus in Book 3 from chapter 52 onward and in 4 he utilized, besides Dionysius Scytobrachion, a mythographical handbook, and since we have very little of this sort of thing, this passage is very important for its subject-matter. And this also applies to other aspects of the *Bibliotheca* which goes up to Caesar's conquest of Britain (54). Because Diodorus' work is entirely dependent on his sources, even when he makes a brave display in his prooemia, it is relatively easy to detect them, in many cases with certainty. For the classical period he largely uses Ephorus, for the next Duris and Phylarchus, and further Polybius. For Books 33-37 he took Posidonius' historical work as his basis. And so he is important for history because of the material he preserved and for historiography because of the recognizable sources, but with these his significance has been substantially summed up.

The origin of the introductory chapter 1. 7 f. which deals with cosmogony and cultural history has recently been the subject of a lively discussion. The

---

[1] Only the historical fragments. Those on the work *On the Red Sea* in MÜLLER, *Fragm. Hist. Graec.* Paris 1841 ff. and *Geogr. Gr. Min.* Paris 1855/61, I, III.

[2] Jacoby collects all the arguments for V. GUTSCHMIDT's old thesis which is violently opposed by O. SEEL, *Die Praefatio des Pompeius Trogus.* Erlangen 1955, 18 (19, 15 bibl.).

opinion of K. Reinhardt that in these passages Diodorus goes back to Democritus' *Diacosmus* via Hecataeus of Abdera, can at present be considered to have been refuted.[1] In an earlier section (p. 679, n. 7) the most recent arguments were reported; they still leave open the possibility of considering Posidonius in this context.

Books 1-5 and 11-20 (from Xerxes' expedition to the alliance against Antigonus Monophthalmus) have been completely preserved, and we possess a great deal of the lost parts in various excerpts. There are those in the collection of Constantine Porphyrogennetus mentioned in connection with Polybius, those by Photius and the ones in a lost manuscript published in 1603 by David Hoeschel in Augsburg as an appendix to the *Eclogae legationum*. Quotations from the *Bibliotheca* occur only late in ecclesiastical authors and the Byzantines.

Stylistically Diodorus is a pre-classicist Hellenist who, like Polybius, avoids hiatus in his Koine. Significant differences in the manner of narrative are connected with the sources; for instance the vivaciousness of the passages on Agathocles can very probably be traced back to Duris. On the other hand, a comparison of parts of Book 3 (11-48) with Photius' excerpts of Agatharchides' treatise *On the Red Sea* reveals that Diodorus avoids unevenness and writes more smoothly, but also less colourfully, than his original.

The universal history of Nicolaus of Damascus (*F Gr Hist* 90) was the largest in size. In the third decade we find him with Antony and Cleopatra as their children's educator; later he went to Herod's court where he remained until the king's death (4 B.C.). At the order of the son he represented his interests in Rome where he probably died. Occasionally he is called a philosopher (T 2), one of his works being *On Aristotle's Philosophy*. A collection of curious customs ('Εθῶν συναγωγή) was dedicated to Herod; Stobaeus has preserved some of it; it reveals the line which starts in Ionian ethnography, continues via the Peripatos (Aristotle's Νόμιμα βαρβαρικά) and winds up in the Hellenistic paradoxography. Nicolaus also wrote biographies, one of Augustus and his own. Constantine's excerpts have preserved a little of both; they also give epitomes of the main work *Historiae* in 144 books, starting with the great realms of the Orient, passing on to Greek pre-history and finishing off with the year of Herod's death. We also find here a compilation on a large scale which included Roman history; the increase in volume which is apparent for the period which Nicolaus witnessed himself lets us suppose that he added original work here.

The compilers mentioned are joined by one of royal rank. Juba II of Mauretania (*F Gr Hist* 275) passed his youth in Rome as a hostage; he used this time to study diligently, until in 25 he received from Augustus part of his paternal domain. According to the titles and some remnants he was an antiquarian with an insatiable appetite for material who made accumulations of excerpts. These referred to various countries; among them there was a *Roman History*. The *Similarities* ('Ομοιότητες, 15 books) must have been an exhaustive collection

---

[1] W. SPOERRI, *Späthellenistische Berichte über Welt, Kultur und Götter. Schweiz. Beitr. z. Altertumswiss.* 9. Basel 1959. According to him Diodorus' text has no longer any title to its position among the fragments of Democritus VS 68 B 5.

of details which in accordance with this kind of literature drew comparisons between all and sundry in the world. A pleasant surprise is his interest in art and the theatre. His work *On Painting* comprised at least nine, the *History of the Theatre* at least seventeen books.

The name of historian in the strict sense was no longer applicable to some of the last-mentioned authors, and to an even less extent to Alexander Polyhistor of Miletus (*F Gr Hist* 273). He came to Rome as a prisoner of war with Cornelius Lentulus and was granted his freedom in 82 in the course of the measures after Sulla's proscriptions.[1] Suidas characterizes his writings briefly as innumerable. A large number of ethnographical books can be distinguished which are not part of a collective work. Thus he wrote about Egypt, Libya, Syria, India, about Assyrians, Jews and Chaldaeans and even though titles like *On Rome* (5 books), *On the Oracle in Delphi*, *On Pythagorean Symbols* or *Collections of Marvels* attest to Polyhistor's manifold other interests, a large part of his work consisted in informing the Romans about the east.[2]

It is no rare occurrence to see the Greek stylus in the service of Romans in this period. Theophanes of Mytilene (*F Gr Hist* 188) can be quoted as an example; he accompanied Pompey and described the latter's eastern campaigns for propaganda purposes. Others like Metrodorus of Scepsis (*F Gr Hist* 184),[3] who wrote for Mithridates, took up a position in the camp of Rome's enemies.

The geographical-historical periegesis, assiduously cultivated as a form by Alexander Polyhistor, leads to the special literature of the periegetes, whose development was discussed earlier (p. 668 f.). In this field we meet Polemon of Ilium, who lived in the second century; he provides a contrast with the search for startling effect and the mere collector's industry of the compilers through his genuine scientific disposition and honest services to scholarship. He also paid tribute to the delight in the bizarre of the time in a treatise *On Marvels* (Περὶ θαυμασίων), but this means little in comparison with the vast output in which he recorded the results of careful personal investigations in nearly all Greek areas. He was nicknamed the 'hoarder of inscriptions'.[4] We can only selectively indicate the extent of his achievement. His periegeses concerned Athens' Acropolis, the sacred road to Eleusis, dedicatory offerings in Sparta, treasuries in Delphi, notable places like Ilium, Dodona, Samothrace. In the form of histories of foundations (Κτίσεις) he reported on cities of the Greek north and west. Occasionally he wrote treatises in epistolary form on learned questions like epithets of gods, an obscure proverb or semantic developments. A scholar who sought truth so honestly could not avoid polemic. He directed a particularly extensive treatise of this kind against Timaeus.

Demetrius of Scepsis also belongs to the second century; he wrote an elaborate periegesis of the Troad as a commentary on the Trojan catalogue in the *Iliad*

---

[1] Cf. APPIAN, *Bell. Civ.* 1, 469.

[2] A positive assessment of his writings in F. JACOBY, *F Gr Hist* 39, 253, 293.

[3] JACOBY has good reason for distinguishing an older Metrodorus of Scepsis, the Academic and mnemotechnic, from a younger one, Mithridates' favourite.

[4] στηλοκόπας can only be rendered approximately.

(2. 816-877). He also occupied himself with the position of ancient Ilium, although with the wrong assumption, which was only definitely removed by Schliemann. It shows the vigour of contemporary intellectual life that a work of ponderous erudition could be written in little Scepsis, although the place had already been something like an outpost of the Academy as far back as the fourth century (p. 507).

A few brief notes are added on pseudo-history, which cannot claim a section for itself. A border-case is Hecataeus of Abdera (*F Gr Hist* 164), who wrote under Ptolemy I. It was thought that his work *On the Egyptians* could be distinguished in Diodorus' Book 1 on Egyptian religion (11-13).[1] It reveals a peculiar form of 'ethnographical Utopia' (Jacoby), connecting historical–ethnographical material with mythology and free invention in a manner which makes the whole a lively expression of certain ideas about state and society. Ancient Egypt, for instance, which had been the land of venerable secrets for the Greeks from times immemorial appears as the place where civilization and an ideal constitution developed. The book *On the Hyperboreans* is staged entirely in the realm of fantasy. The excursus on the Jews in Diodorus 40. 3 has been assigned with great probability to Hecataeus' book on Egypt (F 6). This earliest known utterance was probably the reason for connecting the forgery of a book *On the Jews* and of an *Abraham* (Κατ᾽ Ἄβραμον καὶ τοὺς Αἰγυπτίους) with the name of Hecataeus.

It is not a long way from Hecataeus to the approximately contemporary Euhemerus of Messene (*F Gr Hist* 63), the friend of Cassander (317/316-298/297). His *Sacred Record* (Ἱερὰ ἀναγραφή) told the story of the island of the Pan-Achaeans in the Indian Ocean in which Euhemerus had found a golden stele with information about Uranus, Cronus and Zeus; on the basis of this 'document' he explained that the gods – in so far as they were not personified forces of nature – were nothing but highly meritorious people from the remote past. Euhemerus achieved some fame; Ennius made him known to the Romans and even nowadays Euhemerism is used as a term for interpreting religion in a certain manner. But the fact should not be overlooked that Euhemerus represents only one point, though a notable one, along the line of a rationalizing interpretation of mythology which we can follow from Hecataeus of Miletus and Stesimbrotus onward. A similar line runs from the sophists to Euhemerus.

We have often come upon Hellenistic authors who collected all kinds of marvels; such a paradoxography developed into a separate genre which had its roots in ancient Ionian ἱστορίη. Mention must also be made of Bolus of Mendes (VS 78) whom we met earlier (p. 340) as a doubtful Democritean. He introduced the tradition of occult medical and alchemical sciences which was still rampant in the Middle Ages. His χειρόκμητα was put under the name of Democritus. Antigonus of Carystus, under whose name a *Collection of Wonderful*

---

[1] SPOERRI (cf. p. 679, n. 7) has shown that this is by no means certain; he thinks that it could be late Hellenistic traditional material which is no longer within our grasp. Authoritatively on his sceptical attitude O. GIGON, *Gnom.* 33, 1961, 776.

Histories ('Ιστοριῶν παραδόξων συναγωγή)[1] has been preserved, also belongs in the third century. Since Wilamowitz' well-known investigation,[2] many scholars assume that this Antigonus is identical with the often-quoted writer of lives of philosophers,[3] and also with the Antigonus who wrote about toreutics and painting at the court of Attalus I. If this is correct, Antigonus must be counted among those artists who, through their reflections on the conditions and aims of their work, added a new dimension to the Greek theory of art early in the Hellenistic age.[4]

This paradoxography flourished in a rich soil. Pliny the Elder and an anonymous treatise on all kinds of marvels in the waters,[5] give some idea of the book by Isigonus of Nicaea on *Paradoxa* (first century B.C.). It shows the similarity between the various branches of the tradition.

The mythological handbook which presented the material in an easy way obviously belonged to this time as well. Dionysius of Samos (*F Gr Hist* 15) made claim to serious consideration; in about the first half of the second century he wrote his *Cyclus* in seven books. By way of contrast there is Dionysius with the nickname Scytobrachion (*F Gr Hist* 32) who sported with tradition according to his whims in his mythographical novels about the history of the gods, the Trojan War and the expedition of the Argonauts.

Since there are serious objections against including Asclepiodotus' *Tactics* (Τέχνη τακτική)[6] among the sciences, it is mentioned here. This treatise was written in the first century B.C., and therefore it is the first example of that scholastic treatment of an obsolete art of war, which was continued under the empire by such military writers as Aelian and Onasander. Polyaenus' *Strategemata*, too, are related to this genre.

JACOBY's *F Gr Hist*, which deserves the highest praise and respect, is an inexhaustible storehouse for the authors of this section. On many of those mentioned here there are valuable *RE* articles by E. SCHWARTZ, now conveniently collected in *Griech. Geschichtsschr.* 2nd unalt. ed. Leipz. 1959. – Bibl. on Alexander: H. BENGTSON, *Griech. Gesch.* 2nd ed. Munich 1960, 319 ff. Also F. SCHACHERMEYR, *Alexander d. Gr.* Graz 1949. C. A. ROBINSON JR., *The*

[1] Edition: O. KELLER, *Rerum Naturalium Scriptores* I. Leipz. 1877. Ibid. the Paradoxographus Vaticanus which Antigonus uses. [2] *A. V. Karystos. Phil. Unters.* 4, 1881.
[3] Vide K. V. FRITZ, *Gnom.* 28, 1956, 332. According to him these biographies were based on personal memories and inquiries without following a Peripatetic pattern of composition. They dealt with contemporaries and meant to illustrate their lives how to progress to happiness and moral uprightness.
[4] On the development of the theory of art in connection with Hellenistic and later philosophical systems B. SCHWEITZER, 'Der bildende Künstler und der Begriff des Künstlerischen in der Antike'. *Neue Heidelberg. Jahrb.* 1925, 28. *Xenokrates von Athen. Schr. d. Königsberg. Gel. Ges. Geistesw. Kl.* 9/1. 1932. 'Mimesis und Phantasia.' *Phil.* 89, 1935, 286.
[5] H. OEHLER, *Paradoxographi Florentini anonymi opusculum de aquis mirabilibus.* Tüb. 1913.
[6] H. KÖCHLI-W. RÜSTOW, *Griech. Kriegschriftst.* 2/I, Leipz. 1855. W. A. OLDFATHER, *Aeneas Tacticus, Asclepiodotus and Onasander.* London 1923. On this sort of literature KRÖMAYER-VEITH, *Heerwesen und Kriegsführung der Gr. u. R.* Munich 1928, 9 (bibl. 17).

History of A. the Great I. Brown Un. Pr. 1953. – Alexander-romance: Text: W. KROLL, I. *Recensio Vetusta.* 2nd unalt. ed. Berl. 1958. Analysis and bibl. in Merkelbach, *v.* p. 767, n. 2. Also A. MEDERER, *Die Alexanderlegenden. Würzb. Stud.* 8. Stuttg. 1936. – Bibl. on various authors of this period: *Fifty Years of Classical Scholarship.* Oxf. 1954, 186. Also L. PEARSON, *The Lost Histories of Alexander.* Baltimore 1959. – E. KORNEMANN, *Die Alexandergeschichte des Königs Ptolemaios I. von Ägypten.* Berl. 1935. – Phylarchus: J. KROYMANN, *RE* S 8, 1956, 471 ff. – Timaeus: T. S. BROWN, *Timaeus of Tauromenium. Univ. of Calif. Publ. in History* 55, 1958. GU. MANSUELLI, *Lo storico Timeo di Tauromenio.* Bologna 1958. – Polybius: A survey of the books preserved was given above. For Books 1-5, transmitted almost completely, the most important manuscript is the Vaticanus Gr. 124, written in 947. Critical editions: F. HULTSCH, 4 vols. (1 and 2 in 2nd ed.) Leipz. 1870-92. TH. BÜTTNER-WOBST, 5 vols. (1 in 2nd ed.) Leipz. 1889-1904. Commentaries: F. W. WALBANK, *A Historical Commentary on P. I (Comm. on 1-6).* Oxf. 1957. M. I. FINLEY, *The Greek Historians. The Essence of Herod. Thuc. Xen. Polyb.* New York 1959 (Selected passages with notes and introd.). P. PEDECH, *Pol. Histoire. Livre XII.* Texte établi, trad. et comm. Paris 1961. The old inadequate lexicon of J. SCHWEIGHÄUSER (Oxf. 1822) is now being replaced by A. MAUERSBERGER, *Pol.-Lex.* (1/1 and 2 (to ζ)), Berl. 1956 and 1961. Engl. transl. in the biling. ed. of the *Loeb Class. Libr.* by W. T. PATON, 6 vols. 1922-27. Italian transl. by C. SCHICK, 2 vols. Milan 1955. E. MIONI, *Polibio.* Padua 1949. K. ZIEGLER's great *RE* article (21, 1952, 1440) is a thoroughgoing monograph. M. GELZER, *Über die Arbeitsweise des P. Sitzb. Ak. Heidelb. Phil.-hist. Kl.* 1956/3. IRENA DEVROYE and LYSIANE KEMP, *Over de historische methode van Pol.* Brussels 1956 (Kon. Vlaamse Acad. Kl. d. Lett. 18/28). Further bibl. in the notes.

Diodorus: the transmission differs for individual parts, concise survey in CHRIST-SCHMID, *Gesch. d. gr. Lit.* part 2, 6th ed. Munich 1920, 409. Text: F. VOGEL – C. T. FISCHER, 5 vols. (Bks. 1-20). For the remaining books the old ed. by W. DINDORF, Leipz. 1867/68. With English translation C. H. OLDFATHER, R. M. GEER, F. R. WALTON, C. L. SHERMAN, C. B. WELLES, 12 vols. *Loeb Class. Libr.* 1933 ff. JOHN SKELTON's transl. edited by F. M. SALTER and H. L. R. EDWARDS. 1, Lond. 1956; 2, 1957. Of particular importance the great *RE* article by SCHWARTZ (coll. ed. v. *supra*), 189, 109. Also J. PALM, *Über Sprache und Stil des D. von Siz.* Lund 1955, who undertakes to establish Diodorus' share by comparing passages of Diodorus with available originals. G. PERL, *Kritische Untersuchungen zu Diodors römischer Jahreszählung.* Berl. 1957.

Polemon: Important article by D. DEICHGRÄBER, *RE,* 21, 1952, 1288. – Demetrius of Scepsis: good collection of the fragments R. GÄDE, *Dem. Scepsii quae supersunt.* Diss. Greifsw. 1880. – Euhemerus: G. VALLAURI, *Euemero di Messene.* Turin 1956 with introd. and comm.

9 THE SCIENCES

At the beginning of this book we observed that this history of Greek literature could not be at the same time one of Greek science. This applies particularly to the Hellenistic age during which the divisions, which were growing increasingly evident in the course of our study, finally became definite. In this context, too, the sophists' movement was the starting point and the Peripatos an important stage. During the latter the separation of the individual disciplines made rapid progress. Whereas Aristotle or Theophrastus had still been able to survey numerous fields, it was only a matter of time until the special subject demanded the specialized worker. The Hellenistic age allowed this development to run its full course and completed, in the realistic attitude which is also one of its fundamental features, the dissociation of the individual sciences from their ancient maternal soil of philosophy. A third phenomenon, part of the same development, is the technical treatise without any claim to literary merit. It was discussed in earlier sections, but since the fourth century its output increased until it became incalculable.[1] It increasingly took the form of controversies within a circle of scientists and scholars, limited from the very outset.

What we observed in the realm of poetry and other literary activity is repeated in a similar manner in that of science. Although something of importance was achieved for some time after the peak of the Hellenistic era, there was a strong decline after the first two centuries; parallel with the development of historiography, a period of industrious compilation succeeded that of productive progress. Against the larger background of the history of science, the Hellenistic age was of great importance, because it spurred science on quickly in many fields, once it had been liberated from *a priori* speculation. Increased specialization was an inevitable adjunct to this development. The Hellenistic age, and the following centuries even more so, were fated, however, to lack the strength to collect itself with new vigour, so that many intellectual structures remained standing in their scaffolding. It was to be a long time before other workers mounted these.

In the framework of our study those parts of Hellenistic science demand our attention whose subject is the literary tradition of the Greeks. In this respect we only have to recall what has been stated before. In the section on transmission (p. 3) the decisive importance was stressed of the Museum at Alexandria with its gigantic library for the preservation and scholarly treatment of Greek literature. Mention was also made of its links with the Peripatos. We add here the name of Straton of Lampsacus, Theophrastus' successor in the direction of the school, to that of Demetrius of Phalerum. He was the teacher of Ptolemy II and exerted a strong influence on Alexandrian science.[2] In this context it is not without interest that Straton opposed the theory of the immortality of the soul.

We have also already heard of Alexandrian criticisms of Homer (p. 74 f.), one of the most significant achievements of this circle of scholars.[3] Then Callimachus

---

[1] M. FUHRMANN, *Das systematische Lehrbuch. Ein Beitrag zur Geschichte der Wissenschaften in der Antike.* Göttingen 1960.

[2] F. WEHRLI, *Die Schule des Aristoteles.* 5. Basel 1950.

[3] On the connection between the origin of critical philology and the anti-traditional poetry there are some excellent notes in Pfeiffer, *Ausgew. Schriften.* Munich 1960, 159, and *Philologia Perennis.* Festrede Bayer. Ak. 1961, 5: philology is an institution of the poets. On the participation of Alexandrian literary research by the Peripatos *v.* F. WEHRLI, *Die Schule des Aristoteles.* 10. Basel 1959, 124.

gave us an opportunity (p. 703) to ascertain the succession of heads of the library with the help of an important papyrus find. The result was the series Zenodotus, Apollonius Rhodius, Eratosthenes, Aristophanes of Byzantium, Apollonius the idographer[1] and Aristarchus.

The latter died in Cyprus, which fact is no doubt connected with the expulsion of Greek scholars by Ptolemy Physcon (the Paunch) in the year 145. This ruler, who was neither without talent himself nor hostile to education, had come into opposition against the intellectual leaders of the Greeks in the confusion of the struggles for the throne. According to Athenaeus (4, 184 c), other parts of the Greek world received a considerable influx of important scholars, but for the operations of the Museum the intervention no doubt meant a severe setback. Work was resumed quite soon, but now it was the work of assiduous followers. Other centres of intellectual life such as Pergamum and Rhodes disputed Alexandria's hegemony. It receded to such an extent that it is difficult to tell how greatly the library fire of the year 47 influenced local scientific and scholarly work. It was not only Physcon's measure which had such consequences; the circumstance that the policy of the ruler rested predominantly on the non-Greek elements was far more important. Thus the crown yielded to the growing national consciousness of the indigenous population and there appeared a crack in the wall which had long safeguarded a splendid isolation for the Greeks in Hellenistic Egypt.

We have had to point repeatedly to the fundamental importance of Alexandrian scholars for the transmission. In this respect Aristophanes of Byzantium should be singled out because of the versatility and circumspection of his work, a distinction justified already by his achievement in the field of drama (v. pp. 268; 449).

The specialization which we mentioned at the opening of this section was not carried through in Alexandria as a rule without exception. It should be borne in mind that Callimachus was the author of a tremendous scientific work, even if, in our opinion, it is little more than a compilation. The versatility of his compatriot Eratosthenes of Cyrene is of a different nature, and therefore he deserves further mention. According to Jacoby[2] his birth must be dated earlier than was done so far, as early as the 'nineties. His work in Alexandria, which led to his being called to the Library by Ptolemy III Euergetes in 246, was preceded by a lengthy study period in Athens. Here he first attended Zeno's lectures, but then joined the opposition under Ariston of Chios (v. p. 674) and Arcesilaus of Pitane (v. p. 685). He also wrote philosophical works, but nothing is known of these. His important achievements are in other fields.

Of two of his poems[3] the contents can at least still be recognized. The hexameter poem Hermes passed from the story of the god's birth and youth to his

---

[1] As stated on p. 703, n. 2 the possibility of dating the idographer before Aristophanes remains open.

[2] On F Gr Hist 241 where the chronographical and geographical fragments are combined with various other ones.

[3] J. U. POWELL, Coll. Alex. Oxf. 1925, 58. Fasc. 6, 84 D. F. SOLMSEN, 'Eratosthenes' Erigone: A Reconstruction'. Trans. Am. Phil. Ass. 78, 1947, 252.

ascent to Heaven, which led to a survey of the arrangement of the cosmos. The god had invented the lyre and now heard in the planetary spheres the same tones as those given forth by his instrument. The *Erigone*, which told the story of the Attic peasant Icarius, was written in elegiac metre. Icarius had been given the vine at the occasion of a visit by the god Dionysus, but he was killed by the drunken peasants. His daughter Erigone hanged herself upon finding the corpse. As far as we can see, Eratosthenes followed the poetical footsteps of Callimachus. This agrees with the aetiological element; Erigone's hanging founded the Attic swinging festival (Aeora); the killing of a goat which had nibbled of the young vine leaves explained the custom from which, according to Hellenistic theory (p. 229), tragedy had originated.

Since in both poems mortals were placed among the stars – in the *Erigone* it was Icarius, his daughter and his dog – we add here the *Catasterismi*,[1] a prose work on the legendary origins of all the constellations. We possess an excerpt of it which has been changed in various ways. Friedrich Solmsen[2] has shown that a connection can be established between all the legends told by Eratosthenes and his Platonic belief in the origin of the soul from the astral spheres.

As a poet Eratosthenes followed the course set by Callimachus, but as a scholar he was far ahead of him. He described his scholarly position with the word φιλόλογος, not, of course, in the modern sense, but rather to convey that his purpose was to impart and explain a wide variety of facts. Thus in his work *On Old Comedy* he occupied himself with a great many subjects of the most varied nature, fertilizing the investigations of his successors like Euphronius (the teacher of Aristarchus), Aristophanes and Didymus. His sound basic tenet that the poet should above all affect the soul without wanting to teach (Strabo C.15) placed him in opposition to Stoic allegory. In the same spirit he voiced his splendid objection, ineffective up to the present day, against attempts to trace Odysseus' wanderings (*v.* p. 42).

Professional envy hung the epithet 'Beta' on Eratosthenes, because he remained in a secondary position in his numerous spheres of activity. The injustice of this criticism is revealed in two cases. In his *Chronographiae*, of which the *Olympionicae* was a subsidiary subject of enquiry, he created the basis of Greek chronology which Apollodorus could elaborate and which proved its efficiency in subsequent times. Even though he was not one of the great mathematicians,[3] it was his achievement to create mathematical geography by the successful application of exact knowledge. The three books of his *Geographica* were written in the new scientific spirit. With him ancient geography reached a level which it did not manage to maintain for long. Artemidorus of Ephesus, however, deserves to be mentioned, who *circa* 100 improved his work in geography by travelling.

---

[1] The reconstruction is still doubtful. C. ROBERT, *Eratosthenis Catasterismorum Reliquiae.* Berl. 1878. E. MAAS, *Analecta Eratosthenica.* Berl. 1883. A. OLIVIERI, *Mythographi Graeci* 3/1. Leipz. 1897. G. A. KELLER, *E. und die alexandrinische Sterndichtung* (Diss. Munich) Zürich 1946. On the transmission: J. MARTIN, *Histoire du texte des Phénomènes d'Aratos.* Paris 1956, 58.

[2] *v.* p. 785, n. 3. Also id. *Trans. Am. Phil. Ass.* 73, 1942, 192.

[3] VAN DER WAERDEN. *Science awakening.* Groningen 1954, 228.

Eratosthenes' most impressive achievement was his measuring of the sphere of the earth[1] about which he reported in a treatise Περὶ τῆς ἀναμετρήσεως τῆς γῆς). By measuring shadows with the aid of the gnomon (a peg in a hemisphere) in Alexandria and Syene, after first measuring the distance between the two places, he found a circumference of the earth of 250,000 stades. We cannot state precisely how correct this was, because we do not know on what stadion the calculation was based, but it remains an effort worthy of the highest praise.

The most important successor of the great Alexandrian librarians, in particular of Eratosthenes, was Apollodorus of Athens (F Gr Hist 244). He was born in 180; in Athens he attended Diogenes of Babylon, the pupil of Chrysippus; in Alexandria he worked for many years with Aristarchus. From there the expulsion of the scholars probably brought him to Pergamum in the year 145. He died in Athens between 120 and 110. Trained in the three great centres of contemporary intellectual life, he owed his greatest debt to the Alexandrian tradition of factual research founded on philosophy. This was the spirit in which he wrote the twelve books of his *Commentary on the Catalogue of Ships*, while in his *Chronica* (four books) he developed Eratosthenes' *Chronographiae* in a way which obscured the older work. Because it was the more readily memorized he used the fluent iambic trimeter, but this does not make it permissible to think that the work was didactic.[2] The chronology covered the period of the fall of Troy (1184/83) up to 120/119. There are few works of that time of which we should like to know more than the great *On the Gods* in twenty-four books. Jacoby, whose treatment of these fragments, like everything in his great work, is of outstanding value, has demonstrated the difficulties involved. Nevertheless, it cannot be doubted that Apollodorus started from a definite notion of the gods, on which his educational background must have had some influence. We may also assume that his study of Greek religion was guided by the notion of development. But we only get an impression of the 'Alexandrian' quality of his work, the philological-historical basis, which rested on the mastery of a huge quantity of material. The *Bibliotheca*, imputed to Apollodorus, has nothing to do with him. It will be discussed presently. Castor of Rhodes (F Gr Hist 250) continued work on the chronology of Eratosthenes and Apollodorus. He wrote a *Chronica* (six books) from the Assyrian Ninus up to the settlement of conditions in Asia Minor by Pompey (61/60).

Among the Alexandrians the study of language received the greatest attention. It is therefore significant that their school initiated works on the systematic approach to language which in turn contained, of course, Stoic, Peripatetic and even older legacy. Dionysius Thrax (circa 170–90) was a pupil of Aristarchus before he moved to Rhodes, probably on the occasion of the expulsion of the

---

[1] A. ELTER's lecture 'Das Altertum und die Entdeckung Amerikas'. *Rhein. Mus.* 75, 1926, 241 is still worth reading.

[2] G. NEUMANN, *Fragmente von Apollodors Kommentar zum hom. Schiffskatalog im Lexikon des Stephanos von Byzanz*. Diss. Gött. 1953 (typewr.). Earlier (p. 238) mention was made of remnants of a catalogue (*Ox. Pap.* 25, 1959, no. 2426), probably written in trimeters by Apollodorus.

scholars by Physcon. His short *Greek Grammar* (Τέχνη γραμματική),[1] the oldest known, has been preserved, 'a skeleton of divisions, definitions and enumerations' (Fuhrmann). An illuminating conjecture is that he linked up directly with the Stoa. During the War of Mithridates his pupil, the elder Tyrannion, came to Rome as a prisoner, where he gained great distinction as the representative of Alexandrian philology. The younger Tyrannion carried on his work there. Another pupil of Dionysius Thrax was Asclepiades of Myrlea, who produced a systematic study of philology in addition to commentaries on poets and historical work. The fact that he also worked in Rome for some time is another indication of the direction of the development.

As in other fields, here, too, the gigantic industry of compilers brings the Hellenistic age in a way to its conclusion. Didymus' activity in this sphere was quite astronomical, even if the 3500 books of the ancient tradition (Suidas *et al.*) should be exaggerated.[2] His importance for Homer has been assessed in an earlier chapter (p. 76), and this applies to the greater part of ancient literature, because he collected most of the Alexandrian commentaries in immense reservoirs, from which a variety of channels led to the later tradition. Parts of his commentary on Demosthenes in a papyrus were mentioned earlier (p. 604). Scholarly industry keeps a man healthy, and so Didymus, a contemporary of Cicero, also witnessed part of Augustus' reign.

Didymus' contemporary Tryphon of Alexandria rounded off the studies of dialects, diligently pursued by the Alexandrians, in treatises and lexicographical works. It is doubtful whether the final portion of a grammar in a London papyrus (no. 1208 P.) and a treatise *On Tropes* (Spengel Rhet. 3. 189) are his. *Ox. Pap.* 24, 1957, no. 2396 has now produced the title page of his treatise *On the Dialect of the Spartans.*

Alexandria, which in the peak of the Hellenistic age maintained its central position almost unrestrictedly apart from philosophy, had to tolerate important rivals at its side in the further course of the development.[3] One of these was especially Pergamum, which, through a skilful association with Rome and the utilization of the conflicts of the Diadochi in Asia Minor, managed to establish an important kingdom. The peace of Apamea (188) signified a considerable step in this evolution, connected especially with the name of Attalus I and Eumenes II. At this time the art of Pergamum reached the height of its splendour, which is gloriously represented by the memorial of the Gauls and the altar of Zeus. But the munificence of the Attalids also provided a well-appointed

---

[1] Edition: G. UHLIG. Leipz. 1883. Scholia: A. HILGARD, *Gramm. Graeci* 3, Leipz. 1901. V. DI BENEDETTO, 'Dionisio Trace e la techna a lui attributa.' *Annali Scuola Norm. Sup. di Pisa.* Ser. 2, 27, 1958, 169. 28. 1959, 87, who discerns in the surviving Τέχνη a compilation and dates its main part in the 3rd or 4th century. Excellent treatment of the writing in M. FUHRMANN, *Das systematische Lehrbuch.* Göttingen 1960, 29. 145. H. ROSENSTRAUCH, 'De Dionysii Thracis grammatices arte'. *Classica Wratislavensia* 1, 1961, 97.

[2] M. SCHMIDT, *Didymi Chalcenteri fragm.* Leipz. 1854.

[3] R. STARK, *Ann. Univ. Saraviensis. Philos.-Lettres* 8, 1959, 41, 47, points out that the direct tradition of Alexandrian grammarians' industry can be followed up to the 1st century A.D., and mentions in this context Irenaeus, Περὶ Ἀττικῆς συνηθείας.

centre for science and study, probably in rivalry with Alexandria. The most important figure among the Pergamenian librarians was Crates of Cilician Mallos. In 168 we find him in Rome as Attalus' envoy; here he gave a series of lectures while nursing a broken leg.

Strabo (c. 30) calls Crates the greatest grammarian next to the Alexandrian Aristarchus, but in spite of this similarity the two men were at the same time sharply opposed. Suidas calls Crates a Stoic philosopher, which we need not take too literally, but in his interpretation of the poets, especially of Homer, but also of Hesiod, Euripides and Aratus, he adopted the method of allegorical commentary which, though not a Stoic invention, was yet applied by them with great industry. Another point at which Crates differed in his work from the factual enquiry of the Alexandrians is that as a cosmologist[1] and geographer Crates has obviously a penchant for speculation, for instance when he assumes four continents distributed *more geometrico* over the surface of the earth. His attitude to linguistic phenomena is of the greatest importance.[2] In this context it is significant that Diogenes of Babylon (Seleucea), the writer of a Stoic grammar (Περὶ φωνῆς), was probably his teacher. In Aristarchus and Crates the contrast between analogy and anomaly appears which henceforth dominated in the ancient world not only grammar, but also such fields as medicine and juris- prudence. Whereas Aristarchus' school considered certain groups of forms as paradigmatic and observed these as the norm in their processing of texts, Crates conceded the anomalies which the observation of linguistic usage (συνήθεια) revealed to him. There were also mediators in this struggle such as Philoxenus of Alexandria, who wrote his numerous works in the first century B.C. The whole complex of problems was connected with the question, of the greatest practical importance, how best to put into practice the demand of writing pure Greek ('Ελληνισμός). We refer to the fact that among the *virtutes dicendi* taught by Theophrastus (v. p. 688) was 'Ελληνισμός. Inevitably the question of the importance of Attic Greek emerged in this quest after pure Greek. It is no coincidence that Crates wrote *On the Attic Dialect*. We are still a long way from the Atticist crystallization of the Greek literary language, but nevertheless some preliminaries for this fateful occurrence took place in the Hellenistic age.

We already saw that Rhodes was a centre of intellectual labour. Castor and Dionysius Thrax wrote there, the names of Panaetius and Posidonius are con- nected with the island; it numbered Cicero and Caesar among its students. We do not have a great deal of information about Hellenistic rhetoric,[3] but we can ascertain the important fact that in the second century Hermagoras of Temnos[4]

---

[1] H. J. METTE, *Sphairopoiia. Untersuchungen zur Kosmologie des Krates von Pergamon*. Munich 1936.

[2] H. J. METTE, *Parateresis*. Halle 1952 with the passages. Important for Hellenistic linguistic theory: H. DAHLMANN, *Varro und die hellenistische Sprachtheorie. Problemata* 5, 1935; the article *M. Terentius Varro* in the RE S 6 1935, 1172; *Varro de lingua Lat. VIII. Herm.* E 7 1940.

[3] Cf. R. GÜNGERICH, *Der Hellenismus in der deutschen Forschung 1938–48.* Wiesbaden 1956, 412

[4] Extensive bibl. in D. MATTHIES, *Hermagoras von Temnos 1904–1955*. Lustrum 1958 1959. 58. 262.

gave it a firmer logical foundation with his status-doctrine in which he combined into a system the essential points (στάσεις) which occurred in each individual case. The Rhodian school of rhetoric made common cause with Hermagoras, but it also included the question of style in its doctrine, and so offered increased opposition to Asianism. Its most important representative was Molon, whose teaching was of decisive influence on Cicero. The opposition to Asianism had a considerable number of representatives in this period, but, as in the case of Aeschylus of Cnidos, they are mere names.

The influence of the status-doctrine was extraordinarily persistent.[1] There were Hermagoreans until late in antiquity. Several Latin revisions can be observed. The subscriptio to Iulius Victor's *Ars Rhetorica* proves that he used Hermagoras. Codex Parisinus 7530 contains a mutilated excerpt of a Latin version.[2] The fragment *De Rhetorica* left by Augustine utilizes and quotes Hermagoras.

Rhetoric was taught everywhere. A certain Gorgias of Athens, the teacher of Cicero's son, wrote a compendium on figures of speech (Περὶ σχημάτων), which he illustrated with examples from classical and Asianic authors. P. Rutilius Rufus used it as a basis for his work *De figuris*.

At no other stage of their intellectual history did the Greeks progress so far in the field of exact science as during the Hellenistic age. Its precursor and warranty of this development was the royal science of mathematics, one of the noblest growths on Greek soil. Significantly there is, in the early Hellenistic age, a compilation of the rich material which had been acquired in the preceding period, especially within the circle of the Academy. Consequently the basis was laid for further progress, but also for its application in other branches of science. As early as the reign of Ptolemy I, Euclid (whose origin is unknown) compiled his thirteen books of *Elementa* (Στοιχεῖα) which have been preserved together with an abundance of commentaries.[3] The *Elementa*, which in its construction and classical method of proof is a didactic masterpiece, was used until very recently in Britain as a school textbook. While the Vaticanus Gr. 190 (10th c.) only represents the old tradition, the other textual evidence goes back to an edition by Theon of Alexandria, who belonged to the local Platonic school in the fourth century A.D. Euclid's *Data* (Δεδομένα) is contained in his edition as well as in an older one; this work is important for the development of algebra. The transmission of the *Optica* has a similar twofold distribution. Numerous other works are lost. Of the one *On Divisions* (of figures)[4] the propositions at least have been preserved in Arabic.

[1] K. BARWICK, 'Augustins Schrift de rhetorica und Hermagoras von Temnos'. *Phil.* 105, 1961, 97.   [2] HALM, *Rhet. Lat. Min.* 585.
[3] Edition of Euclid: J. L. HEIBERG and H. MENGE, 8 vols. Leipz. 1883–1916 (with Latin transl.). In vol. 5 books 14 and 15 of the *Elementa*, late appendices of Hypsicles of Alexandria (2nd century B.C.) and Isidorus of Miletus (6th century A.D.). Engl. transl. of the *Elem.* with notes: TH. L. HEATH, 3 vols. 2nd ed. Cambr. 1926; repr. 1956. P. VER EECKE, *Euclide: l'Optique et la Catoptrique*. Survey with introd. and notes, Bruges 1938; repr. Paris 1958. E. J. DIJKSTER-HUIS, *The First Book of Euclid. El. with Glossary*. Leiden 1955. M. STECK, 'Die geistige Tradition der frühen Euklid-Ausgaben.' *Forsch. u. Fortschr.* 31, 1975, 113.
[4] R. C. ARCHIBALD, *Euclid's Book on Divisions of Figures*. Cambr. 1915.

The greatest mathematician of antiquity, Archimedes of Syracuse (287–212), studied in Alexandria, but spent the rest of his life in his native city. His fame rests on a twofold foundation, firstly on his achievements as an engineer who constructed the waterscrew which was so important for irrigation-plants, machines for aimed missiles and for the moving of heavy loads, and supported the defence of his city against Marcellus· (212) with unusual war-machines. He was killed at the fall of Syracuse, according to the well-known anecdote – *noli turbare circulos meos* – in the middle of learned work. In the second place Archimedes lives on as a writer of mathematical works of fundamental importance, not a few of which have been preserved.[1] Here we shall merely refer to the *Psammites*, which solved the problem of large numbers, so difficult for the Greeks, by calculating the grains of sand which would fill up the cosmos, and the work on rotating bodies allied with the three conic sections (Περὶ κωνοειδέων καὶ σφαιροειδέων), which shows his complete mastery of the doctrine of conic section. Of particular importance is the treatise on methodology, extracted in 1907 from a Jerusalem palimpsest (Περὶ τῶν μηχανικῶν θεωρημάτων πρὸς 'Ερατοσθένην ἔφοδος), which proves that Archimedes anticipated the integral calculus.[2] This stubborn genius did not write in Koine, but in his native Doric dialect which, however, has become somewhat faded in the course of the transmission. Archimedes' own appreciation of the two sides of his activity, according to Plutarch (*Marcellus* 17) is of the greatest importance, not only for an evaluation of the scientist himself, but also for the whole of contemporary science. For him his skill at engineering was only a by-product of his work; he saw as its essence the intellectual mastery of the problems.

The doctrine of conic sections, which can be traced back to Menaechmus (p. 543), was given form and systematic presentation in the *Conica* in eight books by Apollonius of Perge in Pamphylia. His activity was divided between Alexandria and Pergamum, which proved its ambition in this field, too. The first four books are preserved in the Greek text in Eutocius' edition (6th c.); they are also linguistically interesting evidence for Koine. The three following books are in an Arabic translation.[3] Of the lost works a treatise on the foundations of geometry is of particular interest; remnants of it are preserved in Proclus' commentary on Euclid.

[1] Edition: J. L. HEIBERG, 2nd edition 3 vols. Leipz. 1910–15 (with Latin transl. and scholia). Engl. transl. with excellent introd.: TH. L. HEATH, *The Works of A.* Cambr. 1897 with suppl. 1912, now in the Dover Edition New York, 3 vols. 1956. HEATH transposed Archimedes into modern mathematical formulae. Best study with survey: E. J. DIJKSTERHUIS, *Archimedes*. Copenh. 1956. Id. *Archimedes. The Arenarius. The Greek Text with Glossary*. Leiden 1956. P. VER EECKE, *Les œuvres complètes d'Archimède. Trad. avec une introd. et des notes. Suivies des Commentaires d'Eutocius d'Ascalon*. 2 vols. Vienna 1961.

[2] Other works preserved: Περὶ σφαίρας καὶ κυλίνδρου. κύκλου μέτρησις· περὶ ἰσορροπιῶν. Περὶ ἑλίκων. τετραγωνισμὸς παραβολῆς. Περὶ τῶν ὀχουμένων. Στομάχιον. The πρόβλημα βοεικόν is a riddle in distichs. The Λήμματα (auxiliary propositions), preserved in Arabic transl., contains some fragments of Archimedes.

[3] Greek text in J. L. HEIBERG, 2 vols. Leipz. 1891/93 (with Latin transl.). Engl.: TH. L. HEATH, Cambr. 1896; repr. 1959. With a Latin transl. of the Arabic books (5–7): E. HALLEY, Oxf. 1710.

The cardinal problem of Hellenistic astronomy was accurately designated by Sosigenes, the teacher of Alexander of Aphrodisias,[1] of whose theory of the spheres we have excerpts in Simplicius. He argued that the assumption of Eudoxus and his numerous followers of homocentric spheres could not account for a whole series of phenomena which were already known then. The time was ripe for the bold step of Aristarchus of Samos. His work falls within the first half of the third century, the peak of the Hellenistic age. Straton of Lampsacus, the Peripatetic physicist (v. p. 688), was his teacher. Aristarchus conceived the heliocentric system in its entirety. The fact that it did not gain ground, that we only know of Seleucus of Seleucea (150 B.C.) as the champion of his doctrine, is connected with the deep roots which the geocentric system and spherical astronomy had in the religious thought of the age. The protest raised by the Stoic Cleanthes against Aristarchus is significant. Of the great astronomer's work only the small treatise On the Size and Distance of the Sun and the Moon (Περὶ μεγεθῶν καὶ ἀποστημάτων ἡλίου καὶ σελήνης)[2] has been preserved.

Important astronomers attempted to deal with the anomalies observed on the basis of the geocentric theory of spheres. The mathematician Apollonius was the originator of the theory of epicycles which assumed an additional circular movement round a centre located in the main sphere, Hipparchus of Nicaea (middle 2nd c.) tried to apply this theory combined with the eccentricity of the main circle. The exact knowledge which he obtained of the position and movement of stars, of precession and eclipse, in spite of incorrect basic hypotheses and inadequate instruments, merits the highest esteem. Only his early treatise with a polemic against Aratus (Τῶν Ἀράτου καὶ Εὐδόξου φαινομένων ἐξήγησις)[3] has been preserved. Hipparchus no doubt worked with material obtained from Babylonian astronomical observation. On the other hand, we see Babylonian astronomy flourish anew in the schools of Borsippa, Sippara and Uruk in the era of the Seleucids.[4] There was a brisk exchange of influence. Hipparchus' main geographical work was one in three books which critically challenged Eratosthenes. Much of this can be traced in Strabo, probably also the title Πρὸς τὴν Ἐρατοσθένους γεωγραφίαν.[5]

Numerous diligent workers rowed in the wake of the great ones. We mention Hypsicles of the first half of the second century, in whose treatise On the Rising of the Stars (Ἀναφορικός)[6] the division of the ecliptic into 360° is found for

---

[1] Another Sosigenes advised Caesar on his reform of the calendar, cf. A. REHM, RE A 3, 1927, 1157. On the problems indicated here: J. MITTELSTRASSE, Die Rettung der Phänomene. Berlin 1963.

[2] TH. L. HEATH, A. of Samos, the ancient Copernicus. A History of Greek Astronomy together with A.'s Treatise on the Sizes and Distances of the Sun and the Moon. A New Greek Text with Transl. and Notes. Oxf. 1913; repr. 1959.

[3] Edition: K. MANITIUS, Leipz. 1894. On Hipparchus' catalogue of stars: Ἐκ τῶν Ἱππάρχου περὶ τῶν ἀστέρων in Catal. Cod. Astrolog. Gr. 9/1, Brussels 1951, 189.

[4] J. BIDEZ, 'Les Écoles chaldéennes sous Alexandre et sous les Séleucides.' Annuaire de l'Institut de philol. et d'hist. orient. 3, 1935, 41. G. SARTON, 'Chaldaean Astronomy of the last three centuries B.C.'. Journ. Am. Or. Soc. 75, 1955, 166.

[5] D. R. DICKS, The Geographical Fragments of Hipparchus. Ed. and transl. with an introd. and comm. Lond. 1960.   [6] K. MANITIUS, Progr. Dresden 1888.

the first time. Next, at about the same time, Theodosius of Bithynia wrote his *Sphaerica*[1] and Geminus (first half of the first century B.C.) his *Introduction* (Εἰσαγωγὴ εἰς τὰ φαινόμενα),[2] in which the epitome of a commentary by this Rhodian Stoic on Posidonius' Περὶ μετεώρων has been preserved.

We spoke of the creation of mathematical geography as one of the greatest achievements of Eratosthenes. Posidonius' many-sided interests in the description of foreign countries were also mentioned before, while many references were made to geography in the chapter on Hellenistic historiography. We further recall that the Hellenistic Greeks gained access to a translation of Hanno's report of his bold voyage along the west coast of Africa[3] (*v.* p. 219). Mention is also made of the wholly unliterary *Periplus maris Erythraei*, which is valuable because of the anonymous writer's open mind, and of the travelling impressions, written like a kind of tourists' guide book, by a certain Heraclides Criticus (transmitted Creticus) which gives the most faithful reflection of conditions in the late third century.[4] Artemidorus of Ephesus, who wrote *circa* 100 B.C., was an independent geographer. His native city sent him to Rome as an ambassador and long journeys brought him to many places in the inhabited world. The results of his experiences and studies were collected in a work of eleven books which was probably entitled Γεωγραφούμενα.

The technical development for which in the Hellenistic era mathematics and mechanics opened up vast possibilities, proceeded in two different directions; on the one hand it was, as always, in the service of warfare, on the other it ended in all kinds of ingeniously contrived trifles. We see hardly any attempts to replace human labour with machines, to mechanize in the modern meaning, and when we do observe it, as in the case of Archimedes' screw, we know hardly anything about its application. Various factors prevented the realisation of a technical development which could have influenced the economy and changed the face of the era. The possibility of exploiting human labour to the utmost at the slightest cost removed any stimulus for the development of the machine. Moreover, the men who possessed this technically useful knowledge were fellow-travellers of Plato's, devoted to pure knowledge, as in the case of Archimedes.

Much of what the technology of the third century achieved in the two directions indicated, war and games, is connected with the name of Ctesibius, who worked under Philadelphus. Most of what we read in Hero must be date

---

[1] J. L. HEIBERG, *Abh. Gött. Ges. Phil.-hist. Kl.* N.F. 19, 1927; contains also Theodosius treatise Περὶ οἰκήσεων edited by E. RECHT. Περὶ νυκτῶν καὶ ἡμερῶν has now been published in a Latin transl. by G. AURIA, Rome 1951. The Fr. transl. of the *Sphaerica* by P. VER EECKE with introd. and notes. Bruges 1927; repr. Paris 1959.

[2] K. MANITIUS, Leipz. 1898 (with transl. and comm.). E. J. DIJKSTERHUIS, *Gemini elementorum astronomiae capita I. III-VI. VIII-XVI. With a Glossary.* Leiden 1957.

[3] *Geogr. Graeci Min.* I, I. W. ALY, *Herm.* 62, 1927, 321. R. GÜNGERICH, *Die Küstenbeschreibung in der gr. Lit.* Münster 1950, 17. L. DEL TURCO, *Periplus Hannonis.* Florence 1958. Transl.: O. SEEL, *Antike Entdeckerfahrten.* Zürich 1961 (Lebendige Antike).

[4] Comm. ed. of the Periplus, also comprising the Koine of the treatise, by H. FRISK, *Göteborgs Högskolas Årsskrift* 33/1, 1927. GÜNGERICH (*v.* prev. note), 18. – F. PFISTER, *Die Reisebilder des Herakleides. Sitzber. Öst. Ak. Phil.-hist. Kl.* 227/2, 1951 (with comm.).

in the same epoch. At the time torsion artillery with its bundles of twisted ligaments began to supplant the primitive bow-projector. Improvements in many details were also effected in the technique of siege-warfare and defence, which had already been highly developed during the fourth century. Athenaeus, the mechanical engineer, whose date wavers between the Hellenistic era and the empire, gives some information in his treatise Περὶ μηχανημάτων; likewise Biton, who dedicated his work on war machines and catapults to Attalus I or II.[1] Fire-engines and water-organs are considered to be Ctesibius' special achievements; he spent much wit and trouble on the refinement of the water-clock and fitted it out with a contrivance for announcing the hour. Ctesibius worked a great deal with compressed air, and even attempted to construct an airgun. The use of steam, of which we learn in Hero, is the most impressive proof of how close these scientists came to inventions of the greatest importance. Even though their inventions did not go beyond the stage of toys, these bore the seeds of the future when we see that motion was produced by means of escaping steam.

We have no work of Ctesibius. His follower Philo of Byzantium wrote a *Mechanics* (Μηχανικὴ σύνταξις, eight books), of which the fourth about engines of war has been preserved, and a few scraps in a Latin and Arabic translation.[2] We are well provided with works of Hero of Alexandria, who reviewed the whole field of mechanical engineering without blazing any new trails himself. His date presents a difficult problem; nowadays it is preferred to put him late in the first century A.D., if not even after Claudius Ptolemy, rather than in the Hellenistic era.[3] The portions of his work which have been preserved[4] clearly reveal the two directions of Hellenistic mechanical engineering indicated before. Ballistic engines (Βελοποιικά) and lifting machines (Βαρουλκός) are dealt with, while other works like the two books *Pneumatica* describe a large range of mechanical toys; his own treatise (Περὶ αὐτοματοποιητικῆς) introduces the construction of a small automatic theatre. The *Dioptra* describes a sophisticated sighting instrument and in an appendix an automatic road-measuring instrument which could have saved the surveyors in Alexander's retinue a great many foot-steps to be counted. Whenever Hero may have lived, it is Hellenistic technology that he reflects, limited, even at its zenith, both in achievement and duration.

Very little worth while was done in the Hellenistic age to follow up either Aristotle's zoological or Theophrastus' botanical studies. Activity in the sphere of medicine was all the brisker. During the peak of the Hellenistic era, especially

---

[1] Both by C. WESCHER, *Poliorcétique des Grecs*. Paris 1867. R. SCHNEIDER, *Gr. Poliorkęter. Abh. Gött. Ges. Phil.-hist. Kl.* 1908–12.

[2] Book 4 and fragments: R. SCHÖNE, Berl. 1893. H. DIELS and E. SCHRAMM, *Abh. Ak. Berl. Phil.-hist. Kl.* 1918/16 and 1919/12. The *Pneumatics* after the Arabic: CARRA DE VAUX. *Notices et extraits* 38. Paris 1902.

[3] Bibl. in REHM-VOGEL (*v. sup.*), 74. VAN DER WAERDEN (*v. p.* 786, n. 3), 276, 1.

[4] Edition: W. SCHMIDT–L. NIX–H. SCHÖNE–J. L. HEIBERG, Leipz. 1899–1914. E. M. BRUINS, *Heron. Metrica. Codex Constantinopolitanus, Palatii Veteris 1, containing Heron's Metrica in Facsimile, Transcription of Text and Scholia, with Transl. and Comm. Janus* Suppl. 2. 1960.

during the reign of Philadelphus, two great physicians were active, Herophilus of Chalcedon and Erasistratus of Iulis in Ceos. Both founded influential schools. Their common characteristic was a resolute application to anatomy, which could now base itself to a great extent on section, sometimes even on vivisection of criminals. Aristotle's notion of the heart as the central organ became obsolete, to be replaced by the correct appreciation of the function of the brain. Herophilus elaborated, for instance, the observations of the pulse of his teacher Praxagoras, and divided the nerves into sensory and motor.[1] Whereas he retained the doctrine of the humours as the basis, Erasistratus abandoned it and joined the side of the Pneumatics, probably under Diocles' influence (p. 577). His connections with the Peripatos through his teacher Metrodorus and the physicist Straton are also important. The most serious obstacle to the discovery of the circulation of the blood was that he separated the arteries as channels of the pneuma from the blood-carrying veins.

It should not be overlooked that these two important men of science did not eventually succeed in introducing anatomy into Greek medical science. H. E. Sigerist[2] compares the way in which it dwindled at the start with Aristarchus' inability to win general recognition for his heliocentric system, and points out that the two most successful medical schools in antiquity, the one of the Empiricists, which will be discussed presently, and the Methodic school, which flourished in Rome, denied the principle that anatomy was of medical use. It is still important to realize that the ancient civilized peoples studied anatomy as part of natural history, but did not make it the basis of a medical system. And so the important finds of Greek research in this field were not of real benefit to medicine. One wonders if a parallel can be drawn with the great mathematical achievements of Greek workers and the absence of any sizeable related technical development.

It was typical of the Hellenistic age that in the middle of the third century Philinus of Cos dissociated himself from his teacher Herophilus to found, under the influence of the scepticism of Pyrrhon of Elis and Timon of Phlius, the empirical school, which tended to be a trend (ἀγωγή) rather than a school. In open rebellion against the primacy of the Logos, every dogmatic basic concept was rejected, also the direction of medical research connected with aetiology. Only the results of experience were valid, and the method resulting from this was the collecting of experience. Side by side with Philinus, Serapion of Alexandria is mentioned as its founder. There were some distinguished advocates of this system, such as Heraclides of Tarentum in the first century B.C. and Apollonius of Cition, whose commentary in three books on Hippocrates' Περὶ ἄρθρων has been preserved.[3]

[1] The discovery of the nerves as an anatomically tangible reality has a prehistory going back to the philosophical speculations of the Presocratics. This is shown by F. SOLMSEN, 'Greek Philosophy and the Discovery of the Nerves.' Mus. Helv. 18, 1961, 150.

[2] 'Die historische Betrachtung der Medizin.' Arch. f. Gesch. d. Med. 18, 1926, 1 (esp. 13). Also important 'Die Geburt der abendländischen Medizin' in Essays on the History of Medicine. Pres. to Karl Sudhoff. Zürich 1924, 185.

[3] H. SCHÖNE, Leipz. 1896.

For the general bibl. we refer to p. 222, and give some additions here. There are useful references in H. BENGTSON's *Griech. Gesch.* 2nd ed. Munich 1960, 445. Special bibl. in J. MAU, *Der Hellenismus in der deutschen Forschung 1938-48.* Wiesbaden 1956, 149. Extensive summaries by J. L. HEIBERG, *Gesch. d. Math. u. Naturwiss. im Altertum.* Munich 1925 (*Handb. d.Altertumswiss.* 5/1/2), the excellent outline with copious bibl. of A. REHM and K. VOGEL, *Exakte Wissenschaften,* Leipz. 1933 (*Einl. in die Altertumswiss.* 2/5, 4th ed.) and B. FARRINGTON, *Greek Science,* Lond. 1953. Further: C. MARSHALL, *Greek Science in Antiquity.* New York 1955. *Histoire générale des sciences, publiée sous la direction de René Taton.* I, Paris 1957; in this work J. ITARD treats mathematics, J. BEAUJEU medicine in the Hellenistic and Roman eras. G. SARTON, *A History of Science II. Hellenistic Science and Culture in the last three Centuries B.C.* Cambr. Mass. 1959. On mechanical engineering: A. G. DRACHMANN, *Ktesibios, Philon und Heron. Acta Hist. Scientiarum Natur. et Medic.* 4. Copenhagen 1948. On mathematics: TH. L. HEATH, *A History of Greek Mathematics.* 2 vols. Oxf. 1921. K. REIDEMEISTER, *Das exakte Denken der Griechen.* Hamb. 1949. O. BECKER, *Das math. Denken der Antike.* Gött. 1957 (*Studienh. zur Altertumswiss.* 3). PER WALDAL, *Das Sieb des Eratosthenes. Eine Studie über die natürlichen Zahlen.* Dielsdorf 1960. A useful work for source material with Engl. transl. is IVOR THOMAS, *Selections illustrating the History of Greek Mathematics.* 2 vols. *Loeb Class. Libr.* 1951. – Technology: H. DIELS, *Antike Technik.* 3rd ed. Leipz. 1924. F. M. FELDHAUS, *Die Technik der Antike und des Mittelalters.* Potsdam 1931. Id., *Die Maschine im Leben der Völker.* Basel 1959. D. A. NEUBURGER, *Die Technik des Altertums.* Leipz. 1929; *Technical Arts and Sciences of the Ancients.* Lond. 1930. H. STRAUB, *Die Geschichte der Bauingenieurkunst.* Basel 1949. – Medicine: K. DEICHGRÄBER, *Die griech. Empirikerschule.* Berl. 1930. G. SPANOPOULOS, *Erasistratos. Der Arzt und Forscher. Abh. zur Gesch d. Med. u. Naturwiss.* H. 32. Berl. 1939. P. DIEPGEN, *Gesch. d. Medizin* I. Berl. 1949. – Editions and bibl. on the individual authors given in the notes.

10 PSEUDOPYTHAGOREAN LITERATURE

We follow up the discussion of the sciences with a survey of writings whose nature is utterly unlike the spirit of Alexandrian scholarship. They reveal, however, that broad substratum which, though it may have been present all the time, rises to the surface with increasing vigour in the latter period of the Hellenistic era. Holger Thesleff and Walter Burkert have done excellent research into these writings and clarified their context within the Hellenistic world.[1]

The tradition that the school of Pythagoras died out after a few generations goes back to Aristoxenus of Tarentum.[2] This has been accepted by modern

---

[1] H. THESLEFF, *An Introduction to the Pythagorean Writings of the Hellenistic Period. Acta Academiae Aboensis Humaniora* 24/3, 1961; with copious bibl. W. BURKERT, 'Hellenistische Pseudopythagorica'. *Phil.* 105, 1961, 16. 226. Id., *Weisheit und Wissenschaft. Studien zu Pythagoras, Philolaos und Platon. Erlanger Beitr. zur Sprach- u. Kunstwiss.* 10, Nuremberg 1962.

[2] Fr. 18 Wehrli. Diog. Laert. 8, 46. Iambl. *Vita Pyth.* 251; also Diod. 10. 10, 2; 15. 76, 4.

history of philosophy, which dates its end soon after the middle of the fourth century.[1] Consequently, when Neopythagoreanism was vigorously propagated from the first century onward, especially in Rome, by Nigidius Figulus and then by the Sextii, it could be aptly described as a *renovatio*, the term used by Cicero (*Tim.* 1). These are facts which are beyond doubt, but they raise the question whether there had been any link between the old and the new Pythagoreanism. Zeller and Carcopino have voiced opinions which are diametrically opposed. Zeller held that, although Pythagorean philosophy did not survive the middle of the fourth century for long, the religious movement persisted in cult-communities with an Orphic mystical background. Carcopino,[2] however, argued that there never was a break in the Pythagorean tradition, but he was unable to refer to corroborative material for the Hellenistic age.[3] The merit of both scholars is that they emphatically drew the Pseudopythagorean writings into the context of this complex of questions. Thesleff contributed an astonishingly voluminous catalogue which lists the few surviving fragments as well as the large number of attested writings of this kind.[4] It is certain that many of them were written in a literary Doric, so that within limits they provide material to study the development of a Doric prose style. Excluding the doubtful ἔχοντι of Alcmeon of Croton (VS 24 B 1), it began with Philolaus of Croton at the end of the fifth century and lasted until the middle and latter part of the third with Archimedes' mathematical writings. Thesleff wrote its history in a valuable chapter of his book; it led, for instance, to the 'Dorification' of the Ionian Pythagoras.

It was of supreme importance for this question that it was realized that a large number of Pseudopythagorean writings must be dated as early as the Hellenistic era, especially in the third and second centuries, in spite of the late chronology advocated so far. The main points only can be mentioned here, the rest can be found in Thesleff, who is also preparing a Corpus of these compositions.

Ancient tradition[5] reports that Pythagoras did not commit his doctrine to paper, but made it only accessible to initiates by instruction. This is the background to a letter under the name of Lysis, probably the Pythagorean who escaped the catastrophe of Croton and later was the teacher of Epimanondas. Copernicus and Matthias Claudius[6] translated the letter; it combined exhortation and instruction about the Pythagorean mode of living, which postulates a

---

[1] Thus E. ZELLER in his *Philosophie der Griechen* 3/2, 5th ed. Leipz. 1923, 103.

[2] J. CARCOPINO, *La Basilique pythagoricienne de la Porte Majeure*. Paris 1927. On the problem of the Pythagorean character of this subterranean place of worship bibl. in BURKERT (*v. sup.*), 227, 2.

[3] BURKERT notes correctly (*v. sup.*), 230, that the attempt of C. LÁSCARIS COMNENO and A. MANUEL DE GUADAN, 'Contribución a la historia de la difusión del pitagorismo'. *Rev. d. filos.* 15, Madrid 1956, 181 to infer the existence of Pythagorean congregations from the diffusion of the pentagram, has completely miscarried.

[4] Older surveys of the Pseudepigrapha in UEBERWEG-PRAECHTER, *Philosophie des Altertums*, 14th ed. Basel 1957, 45, and E. ZELLER, *Philosophie der Griechen* 1, 7th ed. Leipz. 1923, 366 and 3/2, 5th ed. Leipz. 1923, 92. 115.

[5] The passages in E. ZELLER (*v. sup.*) 1, 7th ed. Leipz. 1923, 409, 2.

[6] Reference in BURKERT (*v. sup.*), 18, 2.

purification of the soul, with an attack upon Hipparchus, who had broken Pythagoras' command of secrecy by philosophizing publicly. Of the two variants of the letter, one in Iamblichus' *Life of Pythagoras* (75–78) and another transmitted in epistolary collections (Hercher, *Epistologr.* 601), only the latter contains references to *Hypomnemata* which Pythagoras left to his daughter. Burkert has produced circumspect and shrewd arguments to prove that in all likelihood the second version is the original, contrary to the prevailing view, and that its purpose was to introduce the *Hypomnemata* which were published as Pythagoras' philosophy. According to the contents of Lysis' letter, which presupposes a rigid secrecy maintained so far, this forgery must be older than three very popular books which were also ascribed to Pythagoras, the so-called *Tripartitum: Paedeuticum, Politicum, Physicum.* Burkert has shown that it is likely, at least as likely as anything can ever be in these extraordinarily difficult questions, that the *Hypomnemata* are the ones which Alexander Polyhistor (*F Gr Hi.t* 273 F 93) excerpted. He dates them in the third century, but after Aristotle, for very good reasons; the *Tripartitum*, on the other hand, he allots to *circa* 200 B.C. Thesleff, who worked independently, came to an approximately identical date.

Pythagoras himself was supposed to have written a Ἱερὸς λόγος in hexameters and a Ἱερὸς λόγος περὶ θεῶν in Doric prose. Two treatises under other names have been transmitted complete, under the name of Ocellus[1] of Lucania the tractate *On the Nature of the Universe* (Περὶ τῆς τοῦ παντὸς φύσεως), dated by Harder in the second century B.C., but possibly much older. It shows a strongly Peripatetic trend. It has been transmitted in Koine, but was originally written in Doric, like Περὶ ψυχᾶς κόσμω καὶ φύσιος,[2] attributed to Timaeus of Locri, who was separated from him by a long time and mainly drew on Plato's *Timaeus.*

To fit this type of literature into the history of ideas, Burkert has made an important comparison with approximately contemporary work, such as the treatise of Nechepso-Petosiris (*v.* p. 698) or the Pseudodemocritean literature, to which Bolus of Mendes, whom Suidas calls a Pythagorean, contributed. It was not all pure Pythagorean that concealed itself under the name of Pythagoras and those of his adherents. Even the present concise review reveals the considerable influx of Platonic and Peripatetic elements. This apocryphal literature presented a pseudo-science sprung from philosophy, in which a trend towards the irrational sought a legitimate way to express itself with a semblance of profundity. It is the stirring of the same powers which at all times competed with the exact sciences and serious philosophy by adopting their rivals' arguments to ensure success. And so the Pseudopythagorica discussed here form part of a sort of pseudo-philosophical Koine. Obviously they have nothing in common with the cult and the community of the Pythagorean conventicles, and Burkert's

---

[1] The form of the name is uncertain, but Occelus and Ocelus have also been transmitted. On this and also on the relation with Eccelus, cf. R. BEUTLER, *RE* 17, 1937, 2361. The writing has been excellently dealt with by R. HARDER, *N. Phil. Unt.* 1, 1926. Also W. THEILER, *Gnom.* 2, 1926, 585.

[2] Cf. R. HARDER, *RE* 6 A, 1936, 1203.

phrase goes straight to the heart of the matter: 'In the Hellenistic age there is a deluge of Pythagorean literature, but there are no Pythagoreans.'

To illustrate the relation of this sort of literature with science here follows one example which was interpreted by Burkert. C. Sulpicius Gallus, who fought in the battle of Pydna in 168 as a military tribune, wrote a book on astronomy. Pliny (*Nat. Hist.* 2. 84) quotes from it that Sulpicius stated, in accordance with Pythagoras, that the distance from the earth to the moon amounted to 126,000 stades, that from the moon to the sun twice as much, from there to the Zodiac the triple distance. In an ingenious paper Burkert has shown that various sources lead to a treatise of the middle period of the Hellenistic age which had appropriated the name of Pythagoras. This was the source of Sulpicius' figures. Burkert also argued plausibly that in the same treatise the image of the music of the spheres as the gamut of the astral bodies was given concrete shape and linked with the determination of the distances which separate the constellations. This gamut of the spheres occurs first to our knowledge in Alexander of Ephesus, nicknamed Lychnus, of whose didactic poem with its geographical and astronomical orientation some fragments have survived.[1] The most astonishing point was already observed by P. Tannery:[2] the number of 126,000 stades which forms the basis of the celestial distances indicated is precisely half of the earth's circumference calculated by Eratosthenes. Thus one of the greatest achievements of Alexandrian science in this field was traduced into the foundation of a cosmic system which, with its amateurish mathematical dilettantism, was utterly ignorant of contemporary astronomical lore.

II JEWISH-HELLENISTIC LITERATURE

The Jews played an important part in the medley of races in the cosmopolis of Alexandria.[3] Even during the pre-Hellenistic centuries they had migrated to Egypt; now the rapid growth of the centre of Ptolemy's realm brought new groups of their people to the Nile. Of the five urban sectors of Alexandria two were considered to be Jewish, and Philo (*In Flacc.* 43) gives the number of one million for the Jewish population in Egypt. Alexandria represents an interlude in the antagonism between the tendencies to be assimilated and the forces of orthodox strictness which controlled the history of Jewry. Its special character is the reason for its insertion in the history of Greek literature. Some of the phenomena of the early empire will be included in this section.

To a large extent the Alexandrian Jews had lost the knowledge of Hebrew. It became necessary to translate the Scriptures, if knowledge of them was not to

[1] Ref. in BURKERT (*v. sup.*) 32, 1; cf. p. 752.

[2] *Recherches sur l'histoire de l'astronomie ancienne*. Paris 1893, 332.

[3] H. I. BELL, *Jews and Christians in Egypt*. Lond. 1924. Id., *Juden und Griechen im röm. Alexandreia*. Beih. z. Alt. Orient 9, Leipz. 1926 (with bibl.). V. A. TCHERIKOVER in collab. with A. FUKS, *Corpus papyrorum Iudaicarum* I. Harvard 1957 (in the introd. a history of the Jews in Egypt). Id., *Hellenistic Civilisation and the Jews*. Transl. by S. APPLEBAUM. Philadelphia 1959. TH. BOMAN, *Das hebräische Denken im Vergleich mit dem griechischen*. 3rd ed. Gött. 1959. M. HADAS, *Hellenistic Culture, Fusion and Diffusion*. New York 1959. The work by TH. REINACH, *Textes d'auteurs grecs et romains relatifs au Judaïsme*. Paris 1895, to be repr. by Olms/Hildesheim.

be restricted to a narrow circle. This need produced the *Septuagint*. We have the propagandist report about its origin in the *Letter of Aristeas to Philocrates*,[1] of the late second century B.C. Both the persons mentioned in the title and the contents are fictional. According to it Ptolemy sent for seventy-two learned men from Jerusalem at the instigation of the librarian Demetrius of Phalerum (who never had this function and who fell into disgrace at the accession of Ptolemy II); these scholars, who were highly esteemed by the king, completed the translation of the Torah in as many days.

According to the prevalent belief the *Pentateuch* was translated in the third century; various translations of parts may have been made earlier which were combined in the *Septuagint*. In the course of about the next hundred years the remaining writings of the Old Testament canon also found their way into the Greek bible.

Modern research[2] into the language of the *Septuagint* has strongly reduced the importance of the Semitic element in its stylistic and semantic character, but has, on the other hand, placed more stress on its Greek Koine nature.

The limits of the Old Testament canon as laid down by the synagogue were not felt to be equally obligatory throughout Hellenistic Jewry. Consequently, supplements to the canonical books and independent writings found their way into the Greek bible. Here we shall mention only a few examples from a richly developed and much varied literature. The *Prayer of Manasse* may serve as a model of original Greek writings, while the book of Jesus Sirach with its proverbial wisdom represents the far more extensive group of translated literature. The writer's grandson, who came to Egypt in 132 B.C., translated it soon afterwards.

The two first *Books of the Maccabees*, which could be dated at the turn of the second and the first centuries, claim a special place in this literature as notable historical sources. The first was translated from the Hebrew, the second appears to be an excerpt from the work of Jason of Cyrene in five books. It is probable that both original and epitome are of Greek origin. The two reports, which differ in many respects, contain one of the most important sections of the history of the Jewish sacerdotal state. In 200 it came under the rule of the Seleucids, who at first did not interfere with its special religious and cultural character. Antiochus IV Epiphanes was the first to break it up and to make Jerusalem into a Greek city. The substitution of the worship of Jahwe in the temple by that of Zeus Olympius in the year 167 meant the climax of a Hellenization for which to a certain extent the soil had been prepared in the higher classes. In Jesus Sirach and in the book of the prophet Daniel we hear voices raised in warning

---

[1] Edition of the work which is also important for Koine by P. WENDLAND, Leipz. 1900. Edition with Engl. transl.: M. HADAS, New York 1951. Engl. transl. by J. THACKERAY, 2nd ed. Lond. 1917. H. G. MEECHAM, *The Letter of Aristeas. A Linguistic Study with Special Reference to the Greek Bible*. Manchester Un. Pr. 1935. B. H. STRICKER, *De brief van Aristeas. Verh. Kon. Nederl. Acad. Afd. Lett.* N.R. 62/4. 1955/56. G. ZUNTZ, 'Zum Aristeas-Text'. *Phil.* 102, 1958, 240. Id., 'Aristeas-Studies' I. *Journ. of Semitic Stud.* 4, 1959, 21. II. Ibid. 109.

[2] E. SCHWYZER, *Griech. Gramm.* I. Munich 1939, 126; bibl. on p. 117; also R. MEISTER, 'Prolegomena zu einer Gramm. der Sept.'. *Wien. Stud.* 29, 1907, 228.

against this movement. The victory went to the adherents of the ancient faith and the old ways, who were led by the family of the Maccabees. As early as 164 Judas Maccabaeus could perform the new consecration of the temple and so start the development which within a few decades led to the complete liberation from Seleucid rule. This also determined the course of the Jews; one consequence was that Jewish Greek literature remained an episode. The translation of the Old Testament, the pride of the Alexandrian Jews in whose name the anonymous author behind Aristeas speaks, was disavowed and rejected. What we possess of Jewish Greek literature we owe to the stream of the Christian tradition.

The *Third Book of the Maccabees* has an entirely different content. In a fabulous manner it relates the story of the attempt made by Ptolemy IV Philopator on the temple in Jerusalem and the persecutions of the Egyptian Jews under this ruler. The *Fourth Book of the Maccabees* stands completely on its own. It was written a good deal later, perhaps not long before the destruction of Jerusalem, and contains a diatribe which develops the Stoic principle of the rule of reason over emotion, illustrated with examples from Jewish history. The work was at one time attributed to Josephus. The second part with the description of steadfast martyrs of the faith is a notable example of the Asianic style.[1]

A rare item of popular propaganda literature can be added here. Papyrus finds (no. 1732-1744; 1740 a- 1743 a P.) have revealed texts which extend from the time of Caligula to that of Commodus.[2] These fictional records present envoys from Alexandria, which feels that it is being elbowed aside in the world, who speak with astonishing freedom in front of Roman emperors. The point of the discussions is that the leaders of the Alexandrian Greeks have to defend themselves in Rome on account of their hostility to the Jews of the city, but this opportunity serves to air the hostile sentiments of the Greeks against the Romans.

Among the Jews there was also hate and contempt for the new mistress of the world. Impressive evidence for these feelings is found in the voluminous collection of *Sibylline Oracles*,[3] comprising fourteen books. This monstrous corpus has a long history. It begins in the Greek sphere with the words of Heraclitus (VS 22 B 92) of the Sibyl, whom the god impels to speak the untrimmed, unvarnished and plain truth. This figure probably came to the Greeks from the east; from Asia Minor, where it found a firm foundation, especially in Erythrae, it spread vigorously. It often had an important connection with the cult of Apollo. Varro (in Lactant. *Div. Inst.* 1. 6) drew up a sort of canon of the ten most famous Sibylls. Cumae and the role of the Sibylline books in Rome can only be recalled in passing. Finally Jewish and Christian propaganda took over the shape and style of this prophecy. The collection preserved combines the results of an

---

[1] E. NORDEN, *Die antike Kunstprosa.* I. 4th impr. Berl. 1923, 418.

[2] Bibl. in P(ack), further *Cambr. Anc. History* 10, 1934, 929. H. FUCHS, *Der geistige Widerstand gegen Rom in der antiken Welt.* Berl. 1938, 57. H. I. BELL, *Journ. Rom. Stud.* 31, 1941, 11. H. BENGTSON, *Griech. Gesch.* 2nd ed. Munich 1960, 509. H. A. MUSURILLO S.J., *The Acts of the Pagan Martyrs.* Oxf. 1954 (complete collection of texts and comm.).

[3] A. KURFESS, *Sibyllinische Weissagungen.* Munich 1951 (Tusculum-Bücherei), a selection with transl., comm. and a section about the subsequent influence. On p. 364 editions and bibl. For the anti-Roman passages cf. the book by Fuchs mentioned in previous note.

event which occurred mainly in the later Hellenistic era and the first century of the empire. Older oracular utterances were sometimes included or imitated. The analysis of the elements is a difficult task. The editor of the Corpus prefixed a prologue to it which proves to be largely an excerpt of the so-called Tübingen theosophy.[1] Since this belongs to the fifth century A.D., the compilation of the collection preserved took place in late antiquity.

In conformity with the pattern of Jewish Sibylline fiction, orthodox doctrine in verse was assigned to various Greek poets, among which the fictional poems of Orpheus were naturally not absent.

Matters are different where Jewish authors used the Greek forms to report or glorify the history of their people. The dramatist Ezechiel (*v.* p. 745) can serve as a good example of a group of authors. In Book 9 of the *Praeparatio Evangelica* of Eusebius several hexameters of a Jewish history in epic form by Philo the Elder and Theodotus have been preserved. As a prose-writer we add Demetrius, who wrote *On the Kings in Judaea* during the reign of Ptolemy IV. The Bible, which he used in the version of the *Septuagint*, was his basis. A work of the same title by Eupolemus is about half a century older, but the remnants reveal that for propaganda purposes he permitted himself considerable liberties with the biblical tradition. This brings us to the Jewish historians, of whom remnants of the excerpts made of them by Alexander Polyhistor (*F Gr Hist* 273) give us some idea. We discern (F 19) an Artapanus who combined Jewish tradition with Egyptian Hellenistic material in order to prove the precedence and greater age of the achievements of his own people. Alexander Polyhistor (F 102) bears witness to a similar mixture and trend in Cleodemus, also called Malchus. The writer of the *Letter to Aristeas* obviously also belongs in this group.

The most peculiar occurrence in this context was the controversy between the Jewish religion and Greek philosophy. Aristobulus remains a shadowy figure. In the second century B.C. he wanted to prove, if we may rely on the evidence, by means of an allegorical exegesis of the Old Testament, that it was the source of Greek philosophy. The authenticity of the fragments has often been doubted and many critics have been inclined to consider his work as a Christian forgery, but they have not succeeded in finding conclusive proof.

The most important representative of Alexandrian Jewry, Philo of Alexandria, is known to us through a relatively large number of surviving works. He came of a rich family connected in many ways with distinguished Romans of the time. His date is known through the embassy which went to Rome from Alexandria in the winter of the year 39 A.D. to obtain a decision of Caligula in the conflict between Jews and Greeks. At the time Philo was the leader of the Jewish section of the embassy and describes himself in his report on the mission as one advanced in years.

Our notion of Philo's intellectual world has become a great deal more profound lately, not least through the work of Hans Leisegang. No justice is done to Philo by ranking him with the Hellenistic Jewish authors who wanted, for the sake of propaganda, to derive everything foreign from their own doctrine.

[1] K. MRAS, *Wien. Stud.* 28, 1906, 43. H. ERBSE, *Fragmente griech. Theosophie.* Hamb. 1941.

Philo's Hellenism is not a subsidiary component of his intellectual structure, but the firm basis of his argument with the religious tradition of his own people. He does not adduce philosophical doctrines, because he needs them for certain purposes, but with nis erudition it is a necessity for him to think in their categories.

It is therefore likely that Philo's development led from the philosophy of the Greeks to the theology of his own people. In the same way his writing may be assumed to have begun with a series of philosophical essays which proclaim, in addition to his mainly Stoical attitude, his familiarity with the forms of Greek philosophy. Two of the earliest works, preserved in an Armenian translation, have the forms of dialogues. In both Philo converses with his nephew Alexander. In the first, called after this kinsman, they discuss the question whether animals have reason; in the second *On Providence* a cardinal notion of Stoic doctrine is the topic for debate. The writing *On the Indestructibility of the Universe* (Περὶ ἀφθαρσίας κόσμου) is a torso, the first part of which defends the indestructibility of the universe in opposition to the Stoa. As in the final sentence an exposition of the opposing argument is promised, the most likely solution is, in spite of all deletions and attempts to find an explanation, that Philo himself gave a synopsis of the arguments of the opposition which he refuted, or intended to refute, in a second part. The treatise *On the Freedom of the Morally Excellent* (Περὶ τοῦ πάντα σπουδαῖον εἶναι ἐλεύθερον) carried the Stoic principle in the title itself.

Philo's presentation of the Jewish religion is also guided by his philosophical education. What matters to him, imbued as he is with the spirit of Jewish monotheism and convinced of the importance of the law, is not prejudiced propaganda, but to approach the tradition of his people intellectually by means of philosophy. The chief work of this group is the book *On the Creation of the Universe* (Περὶ τῆς κατὰ Μωυσέα κοσμοποιίας), a collective picture of Philo's creed which is not without Platonic features. Of the biographies of the patriarchs who confirm the law by the example of their lives, only the ones of Abraham and Joseph have been preserved. These are joined by an essay *On the Decalogue*, while the special provisions of the Mosaic law are laid down in four books,[1] *On the Individual Laws* (Περὶ τῶν ἐν μέρει διαταγμάτων).

Side by side with these there are writings in which the aim to awaken an understanding for the Jewish religion in wider circles is more evident. Much of this is lost, such as the *Apology* ('Απολογία ὑπὲρ 'Ιουδαίων); the *Biography of Moses* (Περὶ βίου Μωυσέως), which is akin to the genre of Greek philosophers' lives, has been preserved.

Philo devoted a large part of his life's work to exegetical writings on the *Pentateuch*. He did not envisage a commentary following the Bible verse by verse. The *Allegorical Expositions of the Holy Law* (Νόμων ἱερῶν ἀλληγορίαι) are separate essays which deal with individual passages in the Bible. There is also a

---

[1] On the difficult transmission (in most manuscripts the four books have been taken to pieces and the separate parts have been given special titles) *v.* CHRIST–SCHMID–STÄHLIN, *Gesch. d. griech. Lit.* 2/1, 6th ed. Munich 1920, 641.

complete series of tractates. Independent of the rest there is a work in five books, *On Dreams*, which investigates the various kinds of dream images, verifying them with examples taken from the Bible. We have a large part of a second commentary on *Genesis* and *Exodus* in an Armenian translation with some Greek and Latin fragments; it was probably meant to encompass the whole Pentateuch.

Philo employed in his work the method of allegorical exposition in various degrees but on a uniform basis. It had been known to the Greeks for a long time, but he himself had learnt it especially from the Stoics.

Philo does not only reveal his familiarity with the doctrines of philosophy and his ability to operate with them, but his writings also permit insight into an event of the greatest significance in the history of ideas.[1] In Alexandria especially the philosophical tradition, in which Platonic elements were pressing vigorously and permanently to the foreground, came into contact with the world of the mystery religions. In the course of this clash and the resultant mutual influence, the philosophical search for God adopted numerous mystical notions (a trend which Plato had sponsored), while on the other hand these notions were given a new context. The enlightened vision of God becomes the proper aim of man's life, proclaimed by the various doctrines in externally differing, but fundamentally similar, ways. In Philo the Old Testament doctrine of revelation has been drawn within this intellectual sphere, but in many ideas and images the anticipation of the Gnosis cannot be denied.

Two writings dealing with the controversy with Rome are of importance for Philo's biography and the history of the Alexandrian Jews. The one *Against Flaccus* puts up the prefect of Egypt, A. Avilius Flaccus, as an example of the providence which watches over the Jews. The governor, originally a good man, persecutes the Jews after Caligula's accession, but soon afterwards he is banished and dies a shameful death. The report *On the Embassy to Gaius* (Φίλωνος περὶ ἀρετῶν πρῶτον ὅ ἐστι τῆς αὐτοῦ πρεσβείας πρὸς Γάιον),[2] describes in the surviving torso the grievous experiences of the embassy which took Philo to Rome to see Caligula in the year 39. The anti-Jewish group of Greeks was represented by Apion, the pupil and adoptive son of Didymus, a quill-driver who claimed to be following the line of Aristarchus' scholarship without having the ability. In addition to grammatical writings he produced an *Aegyptiaca* in five books.

Philo's language is as greatly influenced by Greek tradition as is his thought. His style is without Semitisms, and we do not even know if he was fluent in Hebrew. His vocabulary attests his wide reading. He made use of rhetorical

---

[1] This has been shown by ANTONIE WLOSOK in the penetrating chapter on Philo in her book *Laktanz und die philosophische Gnosis. Abh. Ak. Heidelb. Phil.-hist. Kl.* 1960/2, 48. She traces the course of these notions in the Hermetical Gnosis, Clement and Lactantius. In preparation: F. N. KLEIN, *Die Lichtterminologie bei Philo v. Al. und in den hermetischen Schriften. Untersuchungen zur Struktur der Sprache der hellenistischen Mystik.*

[2] A reconstruction of the lost second part which also justifies the title of the surviving section, is given by H. LEISEGANG, 'Philon's Schrift über die Gesandtschaft der alexandrinischen Juden und den Kaiser Gaius Caligula'. *Journ. of Bibl. Lit.* 57, 1938, 377.

ornamentation and Attic colouring, as shown, for instance, by his copious use of the optative, but generally his is the dry style of the scholar.

Since with Philo we have entered the era of the empire, we can also make room for the most important Jewish historian, Josephus. He was born in Jerusalem in A.D. 37/38 of a distinguished priestly family. In the year 64 he came to Rome for the first time. Here he gained access to Poppaea, Nero's consort; but the revolt in Galilaea (66) found him on the side of his compatriots in a position of leadership. In the year 67 he became a Roman prisoner, but was acquitted two years later by Vespasian, to whom he had prophesied the imperial crown. Since then he called himself Flavius. During the siege and capture of Jerusalem he was in Titus' camp, then lived in Rome for a long time engaged in literary activities; he probably died soon after the turn of the century.

In the seven books *On The Jewish War* he goes back in the introductory parts to the conflict of the Jews with Antiochus IV Epiphanes, but he mainly describes the events of which he had been an eye-witness. The work was originally written in Aramaic and then was translated, not without assistance, into Greek. In spite of all his attempts to write in a relaxed style with rhetorical ornamentation, Josephus was never able to hide the fact that Greek was not his mother-tongue.

We know that another Jewish historian and contemporary of Josephus, Justus of Tiberias, also wrote a *History of the Jewish War*, in which he criticized Josephus' presentation. The latter retorted with his *Autobiography* ('Ιωσήπου Βίος). But his main concern was to justify his loyalty to the Romans, and this gives to part of the treatise the displeasing effect which political justifications are generally wont to have.

Josephus' chief work is his *Jewish Archaeology* in twenty books, of which the first eleven relate ancient Jewish history, mainly according to the biblical tradition, but with much freer invention and ornamentation, while the rest of the work was carried on to the era of Nero, drawing on a variety of historical sources.

However much value Josephus may have attached to his good relations with the Romans, he never lost sight of the aim of Jewish apologetics. The treatise *Against Apion* entirely serves this purpose, but also in other works this aim is time and again discernible.

Bibl. on Philo in E. R. GOODENOUGH, *The Politics of Philo Iudaeus*. New Haven 1938. Bibl. also in A. WLOSOK, *Abh. Ak. Heidelb. Phil.-hist. Kl.* 1960/2, 50, 1. The authoritative edition is the one by L. COHN, P. WENDLAND and S. REITER, 6 vols., with an index-vol. by H. LEISEGANG. Berl. 1896–1930. In the introduction the copious transmission which varies from work to work has been presented; it is finally traced back to the library of Caesarea. Editio Minor in 6 vols. Berl. 1896–1915. R. BOX, *Phil. Alex. in Flaccum*. Oxf. 1939 (with comm.). R. CADIOU, *Phil. d'Alex. La migration d'Abraham. Sources chrétiennes* 47. Paris 1957 (bilingual with comm.). E. MARY SMALLWOOD, *Phil. Alex. Legatio ad Gaium.* Leiden 1961 (bilingual with comm.). Papyri: no. 1056-1059 P. With Engl. transl. F. H. COLSON and G. H. WHITAKER, *Loeb Class. Libr.* 10 vols. and 2 suppls. Lond. 1929–62. German transl.: L. COHN and J. HEINEMANN, 6 vols. Breslau 1909–38, repr. 1960. Fr. transl. R. ARNALDEZ, J. POUILLOUX, CL. MONDÉSERT, *Les œuvres de Phil. d'Alex. publiées sous le patronage de l'Univ. de Lyon.* 1 (Introd. *De opificio Mundi*); 9 *De agricultura,* Paris 1961. Latin translations of the works preserved in Armenian by J. B. AUCHER, Venice 1822 and 1826. The *Quaestiones et solutiones in Genesim et Exodum* now in English by R. MARCUS, 2 vols. *Loeb Class. Libr.* Lond. 1953. For the fragments the edition of TH. MANGEY, Lond. 1742 is still important; also J. R. HARRIS, *Fragments of Ph.J.* Cambr. 1886. Edition of the Armenian writings by F. C. CONYBEARE, Venice 1892. – A good monograph is represented by the *RE* article (20, 1941, 1) by H. LEISEGANG. Further: J. HEINEMANN, *Philons griechische und jüdische Bildung. Kulturvergleichende Untersuchung zu Philons Darstellung der jüdischen Gesetze.* Breslau 1932. Repr. with appendices in prep. by Olms/Hildesheim. M. POHLENZ, *Ph. von Alexandreia. Nachr. Ak. Gött. Phil.-hist. Kl.* 1942, 409. H. A. WOLFSON, *Philo. Foundation of Religious Philosophy in Judaism, Christianity and Islam.* 2 vols. Cambr. Mass. 1948. K. BORMANN, *Die Ideen- und Logoslehre Phil. von Alex. Eine Auseinandersetzung mit A. H. Wolfson.* Diss. Cologne (typescr.) 1955. A.-J. FESTUGIÈRE, *La Révélation d'Hermès Trismégiste,* 3rd ed. 2, Paris 1949, 519–72. E. BRÉHIER, *Les idées philosophiques et religieuses de Phil. d'Alex.* Paris 1950. H. THYEN, *Der Stil der jüdisch-hellenistischen Homilie. Ein Rekonstruktionsversuch. Forsch. zu Rel. u. Lit. des Alten u. Neuen Test.* 47. Göttingen 1955 (On Philo's allegorical commentary on Genesis). J. DANIÉLOU, *Phil. d'Alex.* Paris 1958.

Josephus: The basic critical edition is by B. NIESE, 7 vols. Berl. 1887–95; ed. minor in 6 vols. Berl. 1888–95; 2nd unalt. ed. Berl. 1955. On the basis of Niese's recensio: S. A. NABER, 6 vols. Leipz. 1888–96. With Engl. transl. H. ST. J. THACKERAY R. MARCUS, A. WIKGREN, L. H. FELDMAN, 8 vols. *Loeb Class. Libr.* Lond. 1926–64. *Against Apion:* TH. REINACH and L. BLUM, *Coll. des Univ. de Fr.* 1930 (bilingual). *Autobiography:* A. PELLETIER, ibid. 1959. O. BAUERNFEIND and O. MICHEL, *Flav. Jos. De bello Jud.* I (libri 1-3). Bad Homburg 1960 (biling. with comm.). – Transl. with introd. by H. CLEMENTZ, *Gesch. d. jüd. Kr.* Cologne 1959; *Die jüd. Altertümer.* 2 vols. Cologne 1959. W. WHISTON, *The Life and Works of Flav. Jos.* Philadelphia 1957. M. HENGEL, *Die Zeloten. Arbeiten zur Gesch. des Spätjudentums und Urchristentums* 1, 1961 (with critical appraisal of Josephus as a source). – Lexicon: H. ST. J. THACKERAY and R. MARCUS, 4 fasc. (A—Εμ). Paris 1930-55.

CHAPTER VII

The Empire

A Poetry

Before beginning a survey of Greek literature during the empire, we refer to the plan of this book as outlined in the introduction, in which it was explained why a different standard is set for this section and why a brief survey will have to do. There can be no question of making a detailed study of the many authors and of lost and largely insignificant works; we shall, however, trace the two opposing trends of development which characterize this epoch between the fall of Alexandria (30 B.C.) and the closing of the university of Athens by Justinian (529, the year of the founding of Monte Cassino). On the one hand there was a process of fossilization, brought about not only because the wells of vigour had dried up, but also as a result of the principles of a rhetoric controlled by classicism. On the other there arose a new world of ideas influenced by the Orient developing side by side with the irresistible advance of Christianity, which it approached internally even when repudiating it outwardly.

The period of more than five hundred years which this section comprises brought many changes of fortune to the Greeks inhabiting the great empire. Some brief remarks will have to suffice.[1] Ancient Greece became even less important than during the Hellenistic age. Though Athens had its Hadrianic renaissance, though Sparta could at least preserve the appearance of its ancient forms in peace into the third century and even if trade was a little brisker in a few places like Nicopolis, Corinth and Patrae, silence generally sank over the Greek districts which had belonged to the senatorial province of Achaea since 27 B.C. Large areas were suffering from depopulation, and the poverty of many a shrine bore witness to the prevailing economic distress.

In Egypt the Romans took over the bureaucracy of the Ptolemies in order to exploit the land on behalf of Rome. Although among the class of 'those of the gymnasium' Hellenistic culture lived on with relative vigour, the universal importance of Alexandria was a thing of the past; it was this very city which became the centre of anti-Roman sentiment; in the previous chapter we mentioned the 'Acts of Pagan Martyrs' as evidence of these sentiments. The Greek cities in Asia Minor developed more peacefully and so they formed the centres of Greek cultural life in the empire. In this area the tendency of the emperors to make the city a strongpoint of Roman rule worked out particularly successfully.

---

[1] Authoritative M. ROSTOVTZEFF, *The Social and Economic History of the Roman Empire.* Oxf. 1926. Bibl. in the *Cambr. Anc. Hist.* 10, 1934, 922 ff.; 11, 1936, 914 ff. U. KAHRSTEDT, *Das wirtschaftliche Gesicht Griechenlands in der Kaiserzeit. Kleinstadt, Villa and Domäne.* Diss. Bernenses Ser. 1/7. 1954.

There was no risk in granting municipal freedom to the cities, combined with a semblance of the ancient autonomy of the Greek city-states. The eyes of Rome were everywhere, and her hands were ready to intervene swiftly if things went against her will. To the cities larger territories with village settlements were joined where possible. Here a middle class developed which had made its fortune in commerce or agriculture; with much circumstance, but very often also with real devotion, these people took an interest in municipal duties such as building, worship, the gymnasia and games and, in times of emergency, the supply of wheat and oil. This is the class on which Roman rule rested and which at the same time remained the actual bearer of Hellenistic culture. Dedicatory poems and epitaphs, which occur so often in the inscriptions of this era, testify more or less aptly to the educational zeal of this class.

It is impossible to overlook the dark side of this system. A deep abyss separated the mass of the have-nots from the small number of the well-to-do; there were strong tensions in the social structure which easily exploded into disturbances in times of economic recessions. The circumstance that Rome depended on the propertied class meant a heavy burden, however, which at times threatened its very existence. In addition to the demands made upon the rich for their own community, those of the state became increasingly heavy. Egypt with its elaborate system of liturgies served as a model for compulsory tasks which were increased to an unbearable degree from the second century onward. The journeys of the emperors and their officials, liability for the gathering of taxes, enforced tenure of fallow land and other things consumed their substance and imperilled the economic and social structure. The attitude of individual emperors had, of course, a great influence on the social position and conditions of life of the Greek element. The variations were considerable. The first emperors were generally friendly to the Greeks (Alexandria is a special case); this tendency reached its climax in Nero's artistic activities and the theatrical declaration of freedom of the Greeks, copied from Flamininus. The Flavians looked more to the west; of the Greek opposition, which was vocal especially under Domitian, something will be said in connection with Dion of Prusa. Trajan and Hadrian brought the great change. The wars of the former against the Dacians and the Parthians created new opportunities for commerce with the east, and Hadrian's passionate philhellenism assured Greek culture of the first place in the empire. This provided the conditions for its flourishing in the time of the Antonines (138–180), a flourishing which represents the cultural climax of the epoch summarized here. But the picture changes already at the end of the second century; in the unhappy third century its features became particularly dismal. Epidemics and famines followed by social disturbances, afflictions from barbarian hordes, exploitation by the overlords, who needed money for their wars, destroyed a great deal of the prosperity of the preceding period and struck a grievous blow at cultural life. The reign of Gallienus (260–268), who approached the Greeks through their religion, especially through the Eleusinian mysteries, was a beneficial time for the Greeks. His reign coincides approximately with the last decades of the life of Plotinus. Diocletian (284–305) created entirely new conditions; in his bureaucratic state the last vestiges of the autonomous polis were finally wiped out. Constantine's edict of tolerance of 313 and the founding of the city named after him, the new Rome on the site of ancient Byzantium, represent new turning-points in a development which allowed ancient Greece to fade away and led up to the threshold of the Byzantine era.

With some simplification it could be said that the great genres of Greek poetry lost their inner life and meaning in the opposite order of their genesis. At the end of the Hellenistic age information about dramatic poetry in the ancient forms becomes scarce. There was apparently an attempt to revive drama in the time of Hadrian, but this did not last long. Any tragedies written in the first few centuries of the empire were probably meant to be read. Romans also tried their hand at it; we know that Asinius Pollio and the younger Pliny wrote Greek tragedies. But this form of literature was outdated, and this is clearly revealed by the information which attests its decline. According to Dion of Prusa (19. 5), part of the iambic passages were performed in the theatre, but the choral lyrics were neglected. An inscription[1] of the first half of the second century A.D. found at the Isthmus reveals how bits from ancient tragedy were served up for a show. It honours a certain C. Aelius Themison, who borrowed from Euripides, Sophocles and from Timotheus, the composer of nomes, for his own compositions. This highlights the problem of what is meant by the statement that Nero, according to Suetonius (*Nero* 21), 'sang tragedies'. It is difficult to answer the question to what extent these were passages from classical tragedies or products of the imperial dilettante himself.[2]

The theatricality of such solo-scenes could not command a very wide audience; the mime held practically undisputed sway on the stage. Its beginning goes back a long way (*v.* p. 240) and the Hellenistic age already saw it make vigorous progress. The few names and papyrus fragments at our disposal[3] have little bearing on the enormous output in this ephemeral genre. Much of it must have been mere improvisation. Philistion of Nicaea, who lived at the time of Augustus, remained famous until the end of antiquity. We have four versions of a *Comparison of Menander and Philistion* (Μενάνδρου καὶ Φιλιστίωνος σύγκρισις)[4] with aphorisms in his name; its authenticity is very doubtful. No less uncertain is the link which it has been attempted to establish between Philistion and the *Philogelos*, a collection of jokes of late antiquity,[5] with all kinds of itinerant narrative material and humorous stories of the Scholasticus, the absent-minded but sometimes pointedly witty scholar.

Among the remnants of mimes *Ox. Pap.* no. 413 (no. 1381 P.)[6] is the most important. The papyrus contains, partly even in two versions, a play with numerous characters which imitates the *Iphigenia in Tauris* in the most barbaric

---

[1] K. LATTE, 'Zur Geschichte der griech. Tragödie in der Kaiserzeit'. *Eranos* 52, 1954, 125.

[2] Cf. A. LESKY, *Ann. de l'Inst. de Philol. et d'Hist. Orientales et Slaves* 9, 1949, 396.

[3] Convenient summaries in O. CRUSIUS, *Herondas*. 5th ed. Leipz. 1914. D. L. PAGE, *Lit. Pap.* Lond. 1950, 328. P(ack) no. 1380 ff. and 1892 ff. For general bibl. *v.* p. 749.

[4] W. STUDEMUND, *Index Lect. Vratislav.* 1887. W. MEYER, *Bayer. Ak. Phil.-hist. Kl.* 19/1, 1891.

[5] Ed. by A. EBERHARD, Berl. 1869.　　　　　　[6] PAGE (*v.* p. 757, n. 1), 336.

fashion. Charition, a young Greek woman, has fallen into the hands of barbarians on the coast of the Indian Ocean. The king wishes to sacrifice her to Selene, but her brother, who has arrived by ship with other Greeks, saves her after making the barbarians drunk. A comic character and barbarian stammering (many try to recognize echoes of an Indian dialect) provide some coarse and primitive humour. The conclusion shows metrical forms in sotadean, iambic and trochaic verse. The second text in this manuscript is as little edifying and no less interesting. In eight scenes, linguistically expressed very concisely and composed with dramatic skill, a debauched woman condemns to death a slave because he denies her his services; she wants to poison her husband and though she seems to be successful in everything at first, in the end she fails. The conjecture that one actress, the archimima, played all the parts has much in its favour. The papyrus was written in the second century A.D.; the texts cannot have been much older. Another fragment of a mime in a London papyrus (no. 1383 P.)[1] is worth mentioning because of its motley metrical form; here a young girl seems to have got into the sort of trouble which we know from New Comedy.

The nature of the pantomime and its flourishing during the empire has already been discussed (p. 749). To the Pylades mentioned there we add the Alexandrian Bathyllus for the early empire; in contrast with the former he became famous through mimic dances of a comic nature. Admiration for stars is timeless; even in the fifth century a certain Caramallus was an idol both for the Greek east and the Latin west.

As far as we can judge, lyrical poetry occupied a minor place in the literature of the time, even if we include the epigram as a subjective utterance. Nevertheless, a fairly great activity is displayed in this sphere which reflects in its various aspects very faithfully the ups and downs during the centuries of the empire. At the end of the section in which we covered the history of the epigram up to Philodemus,[2] we already referred to Crinagoras as an innovator. This poet from Mytilene, who was sent by his city to Rome as an envoy in 45 and 25 B.C. and who was a client of Octavia, Augustus' sister, introduced a new trend in epigrams by stepping outside the ancient circle of themes into the whole sweep of daily life. The work of such poets as Antipater of Thessalonica, the friend of L. Calpurnius Piso, or of Philip of the same city, whom we met as the collector of a 'garland' (p. 741), echoed Augustan cultural policy in its bucolic idyllic features, in the praise of the heroic past or of the splendour of Rome. Under Nero a certain Lucillius developed elements of σκῶψις which also occurred earlier in this genre, into a concise epigram mocking social classes and types. We know almost nothing of his life (he is not the grammarian of Tarrhae), but we venture the conjecture that Italian delight in caricature played a part as well. This kind of epigram was perfected by Martial.[3]

This same epoch reveals serious marks of senility in epigrammatic poetry;

[1] PAGE (v. sup.), 366.

[2] P. 741 on the origin of collections of epigrams, also editions and bibl.

[3] Important for his connections with Greek: K. PRINZ, *Martial und die griech. Epigrammatik.* Vienna 1911.

Leonidas of Alexandria wrote epigrams whose lines produced equal numbers if the letters were assumed to be numerical symbols (ἰσόψηφα); Nicodemus of Heraclea wrote epigrams which could also be read backwards (ἀνακυκλικά). The Indian summer of Greek literature under Hadrian also produced the collection of epigrams of Straton of Sardes found in Book 12 of the *Anthologia Palatina*. Love of boys is the main theme of these poems which combine elegance and precision of form with a primitive sensuality. Balbilla, a lady-in-waiting of Hadrian's consort, wrote epigrams of which some were scratched on one side of the Memnon column in Upper Egypt.

In this sphere the third century also remained almost completely mute. In the fourth Christianity already begins to use this form (for instance Gregory of Nazianzus, to mention one), but the end of antiquity brings a very vigorous late flourishing of pagan epigrammatic literature. Palladas, a poor schoolmaster of Alexandria, who wrote in 400, rejected love themes entirely. He clothed his own displeasure with the world around him in verses of a personal nature;[1] he also wrote poems of a gnomic and popular philosophical type. Distichs are used more freely as well as the hexameter (the Homeric, not that of Nonnus) and the archaically constructed trimeter. In spite of their undoubted Christian confession Paulus Silentiarius, a court official under Justinian, and his friend, the lawyer Agathias, cultivated a playful prurience. Book 5 of the *Anthologia Palatina* (no. 216-302) offers plenty of scope to study the sensual enjoyment of these late-comers, but also their precise versification, which is influenced by Nonnus.

The subject matter of the Anacreontea (*v.* p. 177), which were specially cultivated in late antiquity, was closely akin to that of the erotic epigram.

Because of their metre we mention here the elegiac distichs of a certain Posidippus of Thebes (probably of Egypt)[2] which were found on some writing-tablets; they are a prayer to the Muses and Apollo, followed by a complaint of old age. The lines, probably written in the first century A.D., are very clumsy, but they have a personal ring.

In this epoch the hymn was relatively the most vigorous of all the ancient forms. This is borne out by numerous examples in E. Heitsch's collection of texts which comprises, as we think correctly, the hymns in the magic papyri. Originally three poems written by Mesomedes,[3] a Cretan and freedman of Hadrian's, were known. They were a prooemium to Calliopea and hymns to Helius and Nemesis, found in manuscripts which also contained musical notations. In the year 1906 eight poems in different lyrical metres were extracted from the Ottobonianus 59 (13th c.). Partly these are hymns like those to Physis

---

[1] C. M. BOWRA, 'Palladas on Tyche'. *Class. Quart*. N.S. 10, 1960, 118.

[2] PAGE (*v.* p. 757, n. 1), 470. E. HEITSCH, *Die griech. Dichterfragmente der röm. Kaiserzeit*. *Abh. Ak. Gött. Phil.-hist. Kl*. 3rd ser., no. 49, 1961, 21.

[3] Texts and comm.: WILAMOWITZ, *Griech. Versk*. Berl. 1921, 595. K. HORNA, *Die Hymnen des M. Sitzb. Ak. Wien. Phil.-hist. Kl*. 207/1. 1928. *Anth. Pal*. 14, 63 and *Anth. Plan*. 323 also belong to Mesomedes. On the hymn to Helius: E. HEITSCH, *Herm*. 88, 1960, 144. Id. *Die griech. Dichterfragmente der röm. Kaiserzeit* (*v.* prev. note), 23 gives the text of the hymns with app. crit. and the bibl. Cf. also his paper 'Die Mesomedes-Überlieferung'. *Nachr. Ak. Gött. Phil.-hist. Kl*. 1959/3.

and Isis, partly descriptions like the two poems on solar clocks. The most charming are those about a voyage in the Adriatic and a sponge which the poet gives to his sweetheart. The very simple language, which borrows freely except from ancient lyrical poetry, is 'coloured with Dorisms' (Wilamowitz).

Synesius of Cyrene, the Neoplatonist and later bishop, born between 370 and 375, was inspired by Mesomedes to write his hymns,[1] in which Neoplatonic and Christian elements were combined to express genuine religious feelings.

In addition we mention the surviving hymns of Proclus,[2] whom we shall meet among the Neoplatonists. They appropriate the hexameter tradition of the hymns and show that it was attempted to fit ancient polytheism into the system; they also reflect a genuine Neoplatonic uplifting of the soul. Nothing of this kind can be detected in the *Orphic Hymn Book*,[3] a collection of twenty-eight poems on various gods. Most of these are long-winded invocations with a great many epithets; we rarely find any true poetry; the nearest approach to poetic feeling occurs in the prayer to Sleep. The Orphic attitude shows itself in the central position of Dionysus, otherwise only in a few details. Goddesses like Hipta and Mise indicate that the hymn book is that of a community in Asia Minor. In spite of Kern it cannot be proved that it was Pergamum. The earliest date according to the language can be the end of the second century B.C., but the collection could be substantially later. The *Argonautica* also belongs to the literature of this time which borrowed the name of Orpheus for its own ends (*v*. p. 159) It is a sorry rehash of the old legend in which it is tried to place Orpheus strongly in the limelight and to effect variations from Apollonius' work.[4] Then there is the *Lithica*,[5] a didactic poem of sorts on the magic power of various stones. It has no connection with Orphic doctrine, but is rather a sample of the literature which passed on such superstition in prose and verse and was influential deep into the Middle Ages in a Latin version (Marbodus Redonensis). Mention was made earlier (p. 159 f.) of the *Rhapsodic Theogony* as a presumably late poem with a number of very early ancestors.

Epic poetry in various styles was still written with some frequency; it even produced, at the end of antiquity, an achievement of considerable quality. But first we must cast a glance at didactic poetry, which was cultivated with the same diligence during the empire as in the Hellenistic era. In this respect the second century was also particularly productive. Judging from the samples left[6] we can

---

[1] Edition: N. TERZAGHI, Rome 1939; repr. 1949. Interpr.: V. WILAMOWITZ. *Sitzb. Ak. Berl.* 1907, 272; now *Kl. Schriften* 2, 163.

[2] Edition by E. VOGT, *Klass.-phil. Studien herausg. von H. Herter und W. Schmid.* H. 18, Wiesbaden 1957. Id. *Rhein. Mus.* 100, 1957, 358. D. GIORDANO, Florence 1957 (text with transl.).

[3] Edition by G. QUANDT, 3rd ed. Berl. 1962. Cf. O. KERN, *RE* 16, 1936, 1283; V. WILAMOWITZ, *Glaube der Hellenen* 2, Berl. 1932, 513. R. KEYDELL, *RE* 18/1. 1942, 1321.

[4] Text: G. DOTTIN, Paris 1930. – H. VENZKE, *Die orph. Argonautika in ihrem Verhältnis zu Ap. Rhod. Neue Deutsche Forsch.* 292. Berl. 1941. Also H. HERTER, *Gnom.* 21, 1949, 68. On the Delphic metope, early evidence for Orpheus among the Argonauts: P. DE LA COSTE-MESSELIÈRE, *Au musée de Delphes.* Paris 1936, 177.   [5] Edition by E. ABEL. Berl. 1881.

[6] Edited by M. SCHNEIDER, *Commentationes philologae quibus O. Ribbeckio . . . congratulantur discipuli.* 1888, 124.

easily get over the loss of the forty-two books of the *Iatrica* of Marcellus of Side, who also wrote for his patron Herodes Atticus. We should prefer to have more than the few, though by no means contemptible, fragments[1] of the astrological poem of Dorotheus of Sidon, which exerted a strong influence. In the 1187 hexameters of his *Description of the Earth* (Περιήγησις τῆς οἰκουμένης)[2] Dionysius the Periegete charmingly concealed two acrostichs (109. 513) through which he revealed his origin from Alexandria and his function under Hadrian. This opuscule had a great success with its easily intelligible verses, cleanly constructed in the Callimachean manner. It became a textbook, often translated and commented on. We possess Latin versions by Avienus and Priscian, an extensive commentary by Eustathius, paraphrases and scholia. Of other works by this Dionysius a poem on birds (3 books) is known to us through a prose paraphrase.[3] The first of the two biographies preserved dates Oppianus of Cilician Anazarbus, the writer of the *Halieutica*[4] under Septimius Severus and Caracalla, but there is a great deal of confusion in this respect. In accordance with Suidas the dedication of the work should be linked with Marcus Aurelius. The five books of the poem describe fishing; the verse–construction, in which the frequent occurrence of spondees is striking, is smooth, but in spite of many interludes this versification of transmitted material cannot keep the interest alive. In form the *Cynegetica*[5] (4 books) stands on a lower level; its author was a certain Oppianus of Syrian Apamea, who dedicated his work to Caracalla. He versified this subject, which had long been a favourite in Greek prose (*v*. p. 621), with a great display of sound-figures, especially rhymes. The *Ixeutica* dealing with the catching of birds with the lime-twig is lost. Among late off-shoots of the didactic poem we mention Helladius of Antinupolis of the fourth century with his four books of *Chrestomathy*, of which we know through an excerpt by Photius. It is significant of a time which preferred an easier metre and one more suited to the new conditions of stressed syllables that the hexameter gave way to the iambic trimeter. Thus in 500 a certain Marianus transposed numerous Alexandrians like Theocritus, Apollonius and Aratus into trimeters.

Loosely connected with these is the surviving collection of verse fables by Babrius.[6] He probably was an Italian who lived in Asia in the end of the second

[1] W. KROLL, *Catal. cod. astrol. Graec. 6*, Brussels 1903, 91. V. STEGEMANN, *Dorotheos von Sidon. Die Fragmente*. Heidelberg 1939 and 1943.

[2] C. MÜLLER, *Geogr. Gr. min.* 2, Paris 1861, 102.

[3] Edition by A. GARZYA, *Byzantion*, 25-27, 1955–1957, 195. Part of the tradition gives the paraphrase as such of Oppian's *Ixeutica* (bird-catching with the lime-twig). GARZYA, 'Sull' autore e il titolo del perduto poema Sull' aucipio attribuito ad Oppiano'. *Giorn. ital. di filol*. 10, 1957, 156. Cf. also R. KEYDELL, *Gnom.* 33, 1961, 283.

[4] Edition: F. S. LEHRS in *Poetae bucolici et didactici*. Paris 1851. A. W. MAIR, *Oppian, Colluthus, Tryphiodorus*. (*Loeb Class. Libr.*) Lond. 1928; repr. 1958.

[5] Edition by P. BOUDREAUX, Paris 1908. A. W. MAIR (*v. sup.*). Scholia: U. C. BUSSEMAKER, Paris 1849.

[6] In 1843 Minoides Mynas discovered in an Athous 123 fables in alphabetical order according to the opening words up to about the middle of omicron; it is less gratifying that later he forged another 95. From the Vaticanus Gr. 777 came an additional 12, four more from wax-tablets of Palmyra and one each from Pseudo-Dositheus and Natalis Comes.

century. One of the papyri (no. 107 P.) preserving some of his verse is of this time. Modern scholarship has shown that it is doubtful whether the regular stress on the penultimate of the choliambs does in fact already reveal the influence of the changing conditions of quantity and accent.[1] Babrius proves to be a pleasing story-teller; he is dependent on Aesop's collection for his subject matter, but he also inserts novelistic material from other sources.

The epic form also flourished outside the didactic poem. Three fragments in Stobaeus produce seventy-three hexameters of a certain Naumachius,[2] gnomic poetry in the tradition of the hypothecae literature. The girl who relinquishes her maidenhood and chooses marriage as a career (the second best according to Naumachius) is given rules for her proper conduct as a woman. The verses flow smoothly, but the content is mainly plain home-spun. Following E. Rohde, R. Keydell[3] considers whether the author is identical with the Epirote who, according to Proclus (*In rempubl.* 2,329 Kr.), wrote on two problems connected with the myth of Er. Since he lived two generations before Proclus, this would date Naumachius in the middle of the fourth century.

A Strasbourg papyrus[4] contains an isolated group of seventy-eight hexameters, part of which are badly mutilated. They picture an impressive conception of the creation performed by Hermes at the behest of his divine father. He puts a stop to the war of the elements and forms the universe out of them. His son Logos is his collaborator. At the end of the lines preserved the foundation of a city is mentioned, which suggests a connection with Hermupolis. Egyptian elements have been forced into a poetical combination with Greek ones of various origins (demiurge, logos). There is a possibility that the author can be named. B. Wyss[5] referred to Suidas where an Antimachus ('Aντ. ἕτερος) is mentioned who came from Heliopolis and wrote a kosmopoiie in 3700 hexameters. The papyrus was written in the fourth century and could hardly be much older than the poem itself. As before, historical material was put into hexameter form. An epic poet Arrian, whose date is difficult, but probably late, and who is notable for a verse translation of Virgil's *Georgics*,[6] wrote an *Alexandrias* in twenty-four books. Alexandrian epic poetry on the foundation of cities was carried on in the poems of Claudianus about Tarsus, Anazarbus, Berytus and Nicaea; we are not certain whether he was the Claudius Claudianus who changed the language of his poems with his migration to Italy (394). At any rate the fragments of an epic *Gigantomachia* and seven epigrams in Greek are of the famous Claudianus. These epic poets were particularly fond of selecting themes of contemporary

There are also prose paraphrases in which the verse form can be detected. Editions: O. CRUSIUS, Leipz. 1897 with remnants of other hexameter and elegiac fables. Comm. and lex. in the ed. of W. G. RUTHERFORD, Lond. 1883.

[1] Cf. E. SCHWYZER, *Griech. Gramm.* I, Munich 1939, 394.

[2] HEITSCH (*v.* p. 811, n. 3), 92.   [3] *RE* 16, 1935, 1974.

[4] PAGE (*v.* p. 757, n. 1), 544. HEITSCH (*v.* p. 811, n. 3), 82. H. SCHWABL, 'Weltschöpfung'. *RE* S 9, 1962, 1557.   [5] *Mus. Helv.* 6, 1949, 194.

[6] The Greeks were customarily little interested in Latin literature, though there were exceptions; cf. F. DORNSEIFF, *L'Antiquité class.* 6, 1937, 232, 4; now *Antike und alter Orient*, Leipz. 1956, 36, 6. Cf. inf. on Quintus of Smyrna.

history, which necessarily changed into an encomium on the rulei. A papyrus of the second century (no. 1049 P.)¹ with Hadrian and Antinous on the lion hunt probably belongs to the epic written for the emperor by Pancrates, who is mentioned by Athenaeus (15. 677 d). The poem on the Parthian war of Diocletian and Galerius may be considered a sample of one type; of this work twenty-one lines have been preserved in a Strasbourg papyrus of the early fourth century (no. 1471 P.).² There is no support for its attribution to Soterichus, who described in epic poetry the destruction of Thebes (335) and the life of Apollonius of Tyana. Roman generals could also find delight in such hexameter homage, as shown by papyri of the fifth century (no. 1473, 1475, 1477 P.).³

Mythological epic poetry was also abundantly represented, and it was in this very sphere that a late splendour was to flourish. This does not refer to the epic poetry which rehashed the subject of the Trojan cycle. This trend produced such empty trifles as an *Iliad Omitting Letters* ('Ιλίας λειπογράμματος) by Nestor of Lycian Laranda, in which in each book one letter at a time was not permitted to appear. The same author also wrote a *Metamorphoses*. The fourteen books of the *Sequel to Homer* (Τὰ μεθ' "Ομηρον)⁴ of Quintus of Smyrna have been preserved; he meant with his epic to fill the gap between the *Iliad* and the *Odyssey*. His date is hard to fix, but the fourth century is the most likely. This sort of poetry shows that the richness of ancient epic is a thing of the past; this versifier works from mythological handbooks, even though he tells the story of his dedication as a poet in the manner of Hesiod. An interesting problem is posed by the correspondence of subjects with Virgil. R. Heinze's⁵ conjecture that they go back to common sources has been much applauded, but recently R. Keydell pointed out some similar traits which can hardly be accounted for unless it is assumed that Quintus knew and utilized Virgil.

Unlike Quintus, Triphiodorus⁶ and Colluthus seem already to be influenced

---

¹ PAGE (*v.* p. 757, n. 1), 516. HEITSCH (*v.* p. 811, n. 3), 51.
² PAGE (*v. sup.*), 542. HEITSCH (*v. sup.*), 79.
³ PAGE (*v. sup.*), 588 ff. HEITSCH (*v. sup.*), 99. 104. 120.
⁴ Edition A. ZIMMERMANN, Leipz. 1891. F. VIAN, *Histoire de la tradition manuscrite de Qu. de Sm.* Paris 1959. Id. *Recherches sur les Posthomerica de Quintus de Smyrne.* Paris 1959. To PHANIS I. KAKRIDIS, ΚΟΙΝΤΟΣ ΣΜΥΡΝΑΙΟΣ. Athens 1962, we owe a penetrating monograph which takes into account themes, style and metre.
⁵ *Vergils epische Technik*, 3rd ed. Leipz. 1915, 63. Also F. VIAN, *Recherches sur les 'Posthomerica' de Qu. de Sm.* Paris 1959 (Ét. et Comm. 30) denies that he used Virgil. He thinks of a Hellenistic Iliupersis as a source, apart from a mythological handbook. But there is no denying the partly very extensive parallels which were demonstrated by R. KEYDELL, *Gnom.* 33, 1961, 279. Especially impressive the passage with the testudo *Aen.* 9, 503-520, compared with *Posthom.* 11, 358-408 (also KEYDELL, *Herm.* 82, 1954, 254). K. BÜCHNER, *RE* A 8, 1958, 1475 also reckons with Quintus' using Virgil. KEYDELL goes a great deal further and assumes that he also knew Ovid and Seneca. The series of omens *Posthom.* 12, 503-520, can only be explained from Latin models. We must take into account the possibility that the general opinion according to which the late Greeks ignored Latin literature, needs considerable corrections. – MARIALUISA MONDINO, *Su alcune fonti di Qu. Sm. Saggio critico.* Turin 1958.
⁶ This spelling of the name is corroborated by the papyri and inscriptions; cf. R. KEYDELL, *RE* A 7, 1939, 178.

by Nonnus' strict rules of versification. Triphiodorus, who toyed with an *Odyssey Omitting Letters*, left a brief epic (691 lines) on the *Capture of Troy* ('Ιλίου ἅλωσις). Of Colluthus, who, like Triphiodorus, came from Egypt, an even shorter poem (394 lines), *The Rape of Helen* ('Αρπαγὴ 'Ελένης),[1] is extant. We are not grateful for it. Once more the chronology is difficult, but since Triphiodorus reveals the influence of Nonnus, and Colluthus on the other hand is dependent on him, he must be dated between these two in the second half of the fifth century.

From among the fragments of epic poetry which imitated the cycle, we refer to the remnants of twenty-one hexameters which occur in *Pap. Ox.* 2, 1899, no. 214.[2] The speaker alludes to the story of Telephus whom Dionysus in his wrath caused to trip over a vine during the battle with the Achaeans who had landed, and he prays to the gods for peace between Trojans and Greeks. It has been conjectured that this was the speech of Astyoche, who was afraid of Eurypylus. If the sparse remnants of twenty-two hexameters on the reverse side belong to the same poem, all these conjectures are useless, since they mention a ship's voyage.

While we have the impression that the cultivation of cyclical themes did not get beyond a scholastic traditionalism, another range of subjects proved to be considerably fertile. The Dionysian myths with their tendency to ecstatic transports, the breaking through of all bonds and their numerous possibilities of absorbing mysticism, magic and astrology, agreed with the mood of the time, quite unlike the ancient epic with its fixed norms. The same holds good for a subject like the gigantomachy which was used by the sophist Scopelianus under Trajan. A certain Dionysius also wrote a *Gigantias*; of him we have in a papyrus an important piece of Dionysiac epic poetry before Nonnus in the *Bassarica* (no. 244 P.).[3] Here the Indian expedition of the god already forms the theme; Deriades also appears as the hostile king. The verses, which undeniably have some poetic vigour, relate the remarkable episode of how Dionysius' companions forced an opponent into a deerskin and how the god tempted the enemy to tear to pieces and devour the supposed animal, a rare variety of the ancient Dionysian theme of omophagy. Unfortunately we cannot date this Dionysius accurately. The papyrus is of the late third or early fourth century, but the poem could be considerably earlier than Nonnus. Soterichus, whom we mentioned before, also wrote a *Bassarica* under Diocletian (Βασσαρικὰ ἤτοι Διονυσιακά, 4 books); fifty-seven lines of a hexameter poem about the punishment of Lycurgus (no. 1455 P.),[4] perhaps a hymn, belongs to the same period. The poetically insignificant lines, partly written in an awkward style, produced the unknown story that the blasphemer Lycurgus had eternally to scoop up water in a broken pithos in the underworld.

[1] Editions of Triphiodorus and Colluthus by w. WEINBERGER, Leipz. 1896; cf. p. 813, n. 4.

[2] PAGE (*v.* p. 757 n. 1). 534. HEITSCH (*v.* p. 811, n. 3), 58.

[3] PAGE (*v. sup.*), 536. HEITSCH (*v. sup.*), 60 with all the fragments of both poems. P(ack)'s identification with the Periegete is not justified.

[4] PAGE (*v. sup.*), 520. HEITSCH (*v. sup.*), 172.

So there was no lack of preludes to the last great poem preserved from antiquity, the forty-eight books of *Dionysiaca* of Nonnus[1] of Egyptian Panopolis. It is difficult to date him precisely, but he can confidently be put in the fifth century, preferably in the second half.[2]

In the broad sweep of this gigantic epic the story is told of Dionysus' Indian expedition and his battles against king Deriades, a legend which was the mythical reflection of Alexander's vast expedition long before Nonnus' time. Apart from this the epic contains a complete history of the god. In extensive introductory sections the events prior to his birth are told; the birth itself does not occur until Book 8, followed by his youth; Book 13 starts with the preparations against India. Deriades' fall (Book 40) is followed by numerous adventures on the march home, new proofs of the god's power such as Pentheus' punishment and finally his admission to Olympus.

In this bewilderingly colourful fabric the warp of Homeric origin is still noticeable, both in motif and form. The Muse is invoked at the beginning, there is a catalogue of the god's forces, the manufacture of beautiful weapons; Homer can be recognized in the battle scenes, funeral games, and even a deception of Zeus is perpetrated by Hera. This late epic also uses stock epithets, which actually run riot in it, and frequently repeated formulae. But how different is the woof under which the Homeric warp often disappears almost completely! The solemnity of tragedy exerts as powerful an influence as Alexandrian poetry with its penchant for the idyllic or for riddling paraphrase. But it would be doing Nonnus an injustice to characterize his work by an analysis of these elements. However many precedents there may be of motif and form, the *Dionysiaca* is a work with a personal stamp through the Dionysiac ecstasy which pervades the whole work. Classicist criticism could only find bombast and exuberance, and there are indeed passages which deserve such condemnation; but apart from these there are many through which there runs a deep emotion which throws off all restraint. With what exploding force the work begins! The cosmos is in commotion; Typhoeus has possessed himself of the fire of lightning and is threatening Zeus' world with destruction. Cadmus will be the saviour, his daughter will give birth to Dionysus. The wide spatial background is another of the baroque features of this poetry; the world is too small to serve as its stage.

So great was this poet's frenzy that the poem's composition fell a victim to it. He made neither careful preparations nor kept anything in reserve. In rich profusion stories of gods are interwoven with astral legends after the Alexandrian manner into a plot whose unity at times threatens to be overwhelmed by all the accessories.

The strictness of the hexameter structure is in a peculiar contrast with this lack of restraint. At the time of Nonnus the differences in quantity of Greek vowels were already disappearing, and it is significant that he not only constructed hexameters with correct quantities himself, but even found a following. He

---

[1] The name is not Egyptian but Celtic. Proof in FR. ZUCKER, *DLZ* 81, 1960, 120, 3.

[2] The arguments of P. FRIEDLÄNDER, *Herm.* 47, 1912, 43, are still noteworthy.

carried on the development from Homer to Callimachus, decreasing the permissible forms of the hexameter with a number of restrictions. The numerous dactyls and the predominance of the feminine caesura imparts movement and at the same time softness. On the other hand, the change of accent and quantity is revealed in the obligatory stress on the ultimate or penultimate syllable of the hexameter (suppression of the proparoxytone).

An epigram (*Anth. Pal.* 9. 198) mentions giants in connection with the poet, but since the adversaries of Dionysus were called so, this must be considered as a description of the *Dionysiaca* rather than an allusion to a *Gigantomachia*. A *Paraphrase of St John's Gospel* has been preserved which exhibits all the characteristics of the style of the poem on Dionysus. Did Nonnus write the *Dionysiaca* when he was already a Christian or are the two poems separated by his conversion to the new faith? Various opinions have been put forward, but elements of magic and astrology are so deeply rooted in the *Dionysiaca* that it is preferable to place its composition in a time when Nonnus was still a pagan.[1]

Among the number of Nonnus' followers we have already mentioned Triphiodorus and Colluthus. We add Musaeus, whose epyllion of Hero and Leander has been preserved. This love story with a tragic ending had been put into poetic form in the Hellenistic age, as we know from a papyrus (no. 1411 P., *v.* p. 758). In his use of metre and in many linguistic features Musaeus is Nonnus' pupil, but this does not apply to his much simpler form of narrative. Two poems in a Viennese manuscript (no. 1048 P.)[2] follow Nonnus' example. The first gives, after a brief iambic prologue, a very successful ecphrasis of the times of the day and man's activities during them. The battle of light with dark, of the warmth of the sun with damp cold, imparts movement to the whole poem. The second item offered by the papyrus is a fragment of an encomium on Patricius Theagenes, an Athenian archon and patron of the arts in the second half of the fifth century. In his edition H. Gerstinger has shown that it is possible that the author of this poem is identical with Pamprepius, who was born in Egyptian Panopolis in 445, rose from a primary school-teacher to be a professor at Athens and later an imperial diplomat, and died a violent death in 488.

At the turn of the fifth and sixth centuries we meet Christodorus of Coptus, a historical epic poet in this group. Apart from *Isaurica* and *Lydiaca* he wrote various histories of cities (Πάτρια). 416 hexameters of his have been preserved as Book 2 of the *Anthologia Palatina* with a completely unimportant description of some statues in the gymnasium of Zeuxippus. Considerably greater ability is displayed by Paulus Silentiarius, whom we already met as an epigrammatist and who must be mentioned here as a follower of Nonnus, in his description of the Hagia Sophia and the singer's pulpit (ambon) in this church.[3] He also wrote a description of the hot springs in Bithynia (Εἰς τὰ ἐν Πυθίοις θερμά). Ioannes of

---

[1] Thus H. BOGNER, 'Die Religion des N. von Panopolis'. *Phil.* 89, 1934, 320.

[2] H. GERSTINGER, *Pamprepios von Panopolis. Sitzb. Ak. Wien. Phil.-hist. Kl.* 208/3. 1928. PAGE (*v.* p. 757, n. 1), 560. HEITSCH (*v.* p. 811, n. 3), 108.

[3] P. FRIEDLÄNDER, *Ioh. von Gaza und Paul. Sil.* Leipz. 1912 (with the history of the poetical ecphrasis). The description of the Hagia Sophia was declaimed on the 6th of January 563, that of the Ambon soon afterwards.

Gaza, who described a picture of the cosmos in the conservatory at Gaza in two books of hexameters with an iambic introduction, is less important as a poet.

We wish to glance at one example of the degeneration of Greek poetry beyond the temporal limit which we have imposed. Some papyri[1] have preserved (it would be an exaggeration to say 'saved') a number of occasional poems by an official of Aphrodito in Upper Egypt called Dioscorus. They are encomia in hexameters and iambs, wedding poems and some mythological items in the form of the ethopoiie. He lived approximately between the years 520 and 585, was a Copt by birth and Coptic was his native tongue. His ambition to write Greek was not without an ulterior motive in his homage to high-ranking personalities. His style and verse structure are clear proof of the degeneration.

Nonnus: Editions: A. LUDWICH, 2 vols. Leipz. 1909/11. W. H. D. ROUSE, 3 vols. (*Loeb Class. Libr.*) Lond. 1939–41 (with Engl. transl.). The authoritative edition by that scholar who has performed such outstanding services in the whole field of literature R. KEYDELL, *Nonni Panopolitani Dionysiaca*. 2 vols. Berlin 1959. The Prolegomena contain important sections on language and metre, as well as a thorough description of the Laur. 32, 16, which Ludwich acknowledged as the basis for the text; the Berlin papyrus 10567 is valued for its importance for criticism; the extensive bibliography is also valuable; also KEYDELL, 'Mythendeutung in den Dionysiaka des N.'. *Gedenkschrift Georg Rohde. Aparchai* 4. Tübingen 1961, 105. – V. STEGEMANN, *Astrologie und Universalgeschichte; Studien u. Interpretationen zu den Dion. des N.* Leipz. 1930. – Metre and language; A. WIFSTRAND, *Von Kallimachos zu N.* Lund. 1933. J. OPELT, 'Alliteration im Griechischen? Untersuchungen zur Dichtersprache des N. von Pan.' *Glotta* 37, 1958, 205. – Musaeus: Editions: A. LUDWICH, Bonn 1912 (Kl. Texte 98). ENRICA MALCOVATI, Milan 1947. H. FÄRBER, Munich 1961 (Heimeran, biling.) with Pap. Rylands Libr. 486 and further evidence for the later influence of the poem up to the German folk song of the two king's children – Verbal index in the edition of A. M. BANDINI, Florence 1765. – G. SCHOTT, *Hero und Leander bei Musaios und Ovid.* Diss. Cologne 1957.

B Prose

I PLUTARCH

Plutarch demands a place of his own, because he occupies a fringe position compared with the prevailing currents of his age. Although he never tried to break new ground with original ideas or to shake the barriers of his time, he put the stamp of his personality so strongly on the vast mass of the tradition which he used so skilfully that it became often independent and exerted an influence beyond the times.

[1] HEITSCH (*v.* p. 811, n. 3), 127.

He was born a few years before 50 and died a little after 120, which means that he lived during the rule of the Flavians, their degeneration under Domitian and the renewed flourishing of the empire under Trajan. He was born in Boeotian Chaeronea where his family enjoyed great distinction.[1] Study at Athens was almost a matter of course. There he joined the Academy, especially through his teacher Ammonius; throughout his life he was faithfully devoted to the founder of this institution. He himself records his diligent mathematical studies (no. 24. 7; 387 f);[2] several of his works reveal that he occupied himself no less industriously with rhetoric. He discovered the extent of the empire on voyages which took him to Asia and Alexandria, and especially to Italy. We are badly provided with the dates and length of his stays in Rome, but they probably occurred shortly before 80 and soon after 90. They definitely did not last very long, for Plutarch states in his biography of Demosthenes (2) that politics and philosophy made such demands on him in Rome that he could not even learn Latin properly and only came to Latin literature in later years. His attitude to Rome was loyal and gave him no problems. Friends played a great part in his life, and he made some among distinguished Romans. Among these were L. Mestrius Florus, who procured him Roman citizenship and with it the gentile name of Mestrius, and Q. Sosius Senecio, the confidant of Trajan. According to Suidas, Trajan conferred the consular dignity on him and bound the governor of Illyria to obey his pleasure. According to Eusebius (on the year 119) Hadrian even made him governor of Hellas. Neither statement can be defended here.[3] It can hardly be decided whether these tales conceal some distinction in his old age.

Plutarch, who came to know considerable parts of the empire in the course of his journeys and to whom the houses of the great were opened, spent by far the greater part of his life in the small country town where he was born. His life is like his work; his glance had taken in wide spaces, but he always remained conscious of the restrictions which hemmed in his nature. Within these he achieved his best without striving for what his genius had denied him. What makes Plutarch so charming for us is the rich humanity which he unfolded within these limitations. Its main source was an exceedingly intimate family life, of which the consolation for his wife Timoxena at the death of their little daughter of the same name (no. 45) gives a particularly fine proof. In the tradition of the ancient polis, Plutarch did not shun the duties of his city. He directed the building activities and was eponymous archon. All these events occurred on a humble level; no doubt he benefited a great deal more from his connections with the ancient centre of Greek religious life, Delphi, which was conveniently close to Chaeronea. These connections pervaded his whole life and his writings; they were crowned by a position in the twin priesthood of Delphi, its highest religious authority, which function he performed for many years. Apart from his family, his civic activity and his Delphic service, the richness of

---

[1] K. ZIEGLER, 'Plutarchs Ahnen'. *Herm.* 82, 1954, 499.

[2] We refer to the individual writings of the *Moralia* with the numbers of the catalogue appended.

[3] *v.* the objections of K. LATTE in ZIEGLER *RE* (*v. inf.*), 658, 1.

his life was formed by an extensive circle of friends. Plutarch's house must rarely have been without guests; in his home he was something like a leader of a many-sided circle with a special interest in philosophy.

The diversity of Plutarch's interests is expressed in the mass of writings comprised under the rather unfortunate description of *Moralia*. However, only about one-third of Plutarch's works have been preserved, including the *Lives*. This information is supplied by the so-called catalogue of Lamprias, a very careless and quite incomplete list which cannot be the work of Plutarch's son Lamprias, for the simple reason that there was no such person.[1] It is not possible to go here into details of the numerous themes dealt with in the *Moralia*; we shall try to give a collective survey at the hand of the record of titles referred to, singling out a few items with constant reference to it.

A fairly large group is marked off by its strongly rhetorical character. These works were probably written in the early years, when Plutarch had not yet adopted his moderate, reserved attitude to rhetoric. He declaims in these on Tyche, her role in the life of Alexander and in the history of Rome, on the foundations of Athens' fame and numerous other themes (no. 8. 20-22. 27; also 32-34. 62). Much of this contrasts so greatly with the harmony of the other writings that scholars like Pohlenz and Ziegler have considered the possibility that immature early work was published from the legacy. Much room is occupied by popular philosophical tractates; the one on peace of mind (no. 30) characterizes their structure. Here, as well as in many other passages, the great admirer of Plato exhibits a strong influence of the Stoa. The object of serene peace of mind, to which all Hellenistic systems aspired, is praised here by one who contributed what was best for it in his own soul. For similar reasons Plutarch has also much to say that is useful about marriage (no. 12), and it should be noted that, though in the *Eroticus* (no. 47) he follows Plato's footsteps in praising Eros as the guide to the highest good, he makes homosexual love recede very much into the background.[2] Everywhere in Plutarch's writings we notice a strong didactic temperament. It is not surprising, therefore, that he also made some direct statements about matters of education (no. 2 f.).

Apart from many works composed as diatribes there are writings in which Plutarch attempts serious philosophical discussion. Without penetrating to the final depths of the problems, he has passed on to us a notable quantity of philosophical-historical material. The treatise on the doctrine of the soul of the Platonic *Timaeus* (no. 68 f.) gives an arbitrary and harmonizing interpretation, but it is interesting because it deals with the question of the evil universal soul. The *Platonic Problems* (no. 67) deals with individual passages, and the *Timaeus* is once more in the foreground. It is remarkable that of Plutarch's polemics against Stoics and Epicureans three each have been preserved (no. 70-72, 73-75). Ziegler's conjecture that this is the result of a selection is attractive.

Plutarch did not only write about the human soul – we have fragments of an

---

[1] The dedicatory letter, prefixed in some manuscripts, is a medieval forgery; K. ZIEGLER, *Rhein. Mus.* 63, 1908, 239 and 76, 1927, 20.

[2] Other popular philosophical works 4-7, 9, 11, 28 f., 31, 35-40.

extensive work on this subject – he was also interested in questions of the psychology of animals (no. 63). A curious item, and one whose authenticity has been a matter of argument, is the dialogue on the reason of animals with its mythological form (no. 64) which is reminiscent of the satirical attitude of Cynicism. The two books against the use of meat (no. 65 f.) are akin to the early rhetorical works; they reveal some Pythagorean influence.

The Pythian dialogues on the enigmatic E at the entrance to the Delphic temple (no. 24), the form of the oracles (no. 25) and their decline (no. 26) originated in the sphere of religion which meant so much to Plutarch. One of the most interesting works is the *On Isis and Osiris* (no. 23),[1] in which Plutarch, himself an initiate of the Dionysiac mysteries (no. 45, *c.* 10; 611 d) gives an interpretation, or rather a tangle of syncretistical and allegorical interpretations, of the mystery religion of Osiris. Osiris emerges as the main god who signifies the Logos and the Being above the world of Becoming, Isis as the goddess of wisdom gives man access to knowledge of the Highest, whereas Typho is the hostile principle of deception and blindness, the destroyer of the path of insight. This makes the treatise an important document for a mystery religion which absorbed Platonizing elements and envisaged the knowledge of a highest intelligible principle (352 A: ἡ τοῦ πρώτου καὶ κυρίου καὶ νοητοῦ γνῶσις).[2] There is much less implied in the dialogue *On God's late Judgment* (no. 41), which is staged in Delphi and takes up the ancient problem of divine justice. He does not penetrate to a profound depth, but Plutarch's pious faith in the righteousness of a god free from human reproaches is presented with the warmth of a personal confession. The concluding myth with its metaphysical vision has a very obvious affinity with the end of Plato's *Republic*.

The pedagogic trend[3] which is peculiar to Plutarch's work, is also evident in his writings on politics, such as the instructions for the statesman (no. 52, cf. no. 49-51). The fragment on constitutions (no. 53) is of doubtful authenticity.

Plutarch also occupied himself in his own way with scientific questions. The treatise *On the Face of the Moon* (no. 60, cf. no. 59. 61) combines various theories about this celestial body into a motley collection. In the final passage, a myth, he strongly stresses his belief in an intermediate realm of demons.[4] Here Plutarch writes in an Academic tradition which mainly follows Xenocrates.

The antiquarian medley of the *Roman and Greek Aetia* (no. 18) carries on a Hellenistic fashion. Cult naturally occupies a great deal of room in questions of the meaning and origin of various customs. His delight in anecdotes, which put its stamp on the *Lives*, is also evident in the treatise on womanly virtue (no. 17) and the collection of Laconic dicta (no. 16). Another collection of apothegms

---

[1] TH. HOPFNER, *P. über Isis und Osiris. I. Die Sage. Monog. des Archivs Orientalni* 9. Prague 1940 (text, transl., comm.); II *Die Deutungen der Sage.* 1941.

[2] Treated by ANTONIE WLOSOK, *Abh. Ak. Heidelb. Phil.-hist. Kl.* 1960/2, 56.

[3] Plutarch did not write the treatise on the education of children, but it has some importance as the only extant Greek writing which deals specifically with the subject. On the source analysis E. G. BERRY, 'The De liberis educandis of Pseudo-Plutarch.' *Harv. Stud.* 63, 1958 (Festschr. Jaeger), 387.

[4] G. SOURY, *La démonologie de P.* Paris 1942.

(no. 15) is spurious, but gives a notion of the sort of collections used by Plutarch. The *Table-talk of the Seven Sages* (no. 13, cf. p. 157) and the nine books of the *Symposiaca* (no. 46) may be added here for the sake of the diversity of their content which touches nearly the whole scope of his themes.

Plutarch, who read industriously, also devoted himself diligently to the great authors of his people. We know of expositions on Homer and Hesiod,[1] but he was dissatisfied with Herodotus (no. 57) because of the part which Boeotia played in his work. In a critical study (no. 56)[2] he significantly gave preference to Menander over Aristophanes, whose genius was beyond his grasp. As elsewhere, apocryphal material also has significance in this group, such as the *Lives of the Ten Orators* (Bernardakis VII 329) with a wealth of material from ancient Homeric philology. All these apocrypha are overshadowed by the treatise *On Music* (no. 76), one of our most important sources on this subject. Aristoxenus and Heraclides Ponticus have not only been extensively used, but large sections are verbatim copies.

The form of the *Moralia* is as motley as the contents. Many parts are cast as dialogues. His attempt to emulate Plato is shown in the details of the scenic framework, the artifice of having the dialogue narrated by one of the participants and the occasional insertion of myths, but the execution of the dialogue-form reveals marked differences, and the conversation is not rarely replaced by a complete didactic lecture. We singled out the rhetorical declamations, probably products of his early years, as a group with a special character. Other writings are purely factual essays, while in the popular philosophical tractates features of the diatribe can be observed.

It was not the *Moralia*, but rather his biographical writings, which established Plutarch's fame. He states himself (Prooem. *Aemil.*) that he started upon these through others, but that he then took a delight in them. In the same passage he gives an account of the meaning of this activity; the association with the great men of the past is meant to influence our own nature with their high qualities. But when he sometimes introduces us to a pair of doubtful morality, like Demetrius and Antony (on other respects one of the most brilliant of syzygies), he zealously assures us in the introduction that even a negative example can be of great use for the right mode of life. Albrecht Dihle has enlarged on the extent to which the biographical tradition of which Plutarch forms part, is influenced by Peripatetic doctrine, which assigns to man's actions the decisive importance in its ethical system. Fr. Leo has also referred to the importance of the Peripatos for biography. This does not mean that it is a matter of course that ethical qualities become evident in actions, but it refers to the Aristotelian doctrine[3] that the

---

[1] Printed in Bernardakis, VII.

[2] The surviving treatise is an excerpt of an essay which is probably by Plutarch and at any rate reflects his opinion.

[3] The first chapters of the second book of the *NE* are of special importance for this. K. V. FRITZ, *Gnom.* 28, 1956, 330 correctly stresses that it is strange that Aristotle especially should separate the formation of the ethos by action so sharply from the physis. Here a tradition, handed down from Pindar and Sophocles, has been abandoned. Euripides reveals how it became a problem.

'ethical virtues' are not naturally present before their manifestation, but come into being as customary modes of behaviour (given a disposition for them) with the action and through it. This connection between ἤθη and πράξεις stipulates for Plutarch's biography a description of character which takes its heroes' actions as its constant premiss. A great deal of historical material is, of course, also involved. Plutarch has often been censured for his way of dealing with history, and it would indeed be difficult to make a first-class historian of him. But he did not claim to be one at all. He stated this most clearly in his introduction to the *Alexander*, where he describes biography, and not history, as his business. He was never concerned with historical relations, or political aetiology in the meaning of Thucydides; he is only interested in the images of great men. Their traits, he states in the passage referred to, do not appear only in their great deeds, but much more in many a small gesture or utterance. This is the Plutarch of the anecdote, always ready to reach into his great stock and to impart, with numerous little tales, to his biographies the variety which is their charm. This is not the least reason for the influence which they exerted throughout the ages, so that their subsequent influence forms part of the history of European literature. In addition we mention Plutarch's considerable skill in dramatized narrative and duly stress that a warm understanding of humanity and a likeable moral optimism also give their character to the *Lives*, these being some important characteristics of these biographies. In the question to what extent Plutarch used independent sources or utilized available compilations, scholars are at present more inclined to acknowledge his personal achievement.[1] Of course he also had collections at his disposal which provided him with apophthegmata, anecdotes and literary quotations. He may even have prepared such aids himself.

Preserved are also twenty-two *Parallel Lives*, of which our catalogue gives a survey.[2] The pair *Epaminondas-Scipio* is lost; it referred to Scipio the Elder rather than to Aemilianus. Of the individual *Lives* we have those of Aratus and Artaxerxes, as well as those of Galba and Otho. Lamprias' catalogue mentions a whole series of others, among which those of poets (Hesiod, Pindar, Aratus) and one of the philosopher Crates, who was a Boeotian like Hesiod and Pindar.

The idea of combining a great Greek and a Roman into a pair is both in accordance with the time in which Greek tradition sought to maintain itself beside the power of Rome, and with Plutarch's own conciliatory nature, which attempted to unite historical realities within the framework of his view of life. Plutarch, to whom the sceptical conviction of modern historians, that there are no true parallels at all, was completely foreign, was sometimes quite fortunate in his combinations, as, for instance, with Demetrius and Antony, while in

[1] An instructive bibl. on this question in connection with the *Life of Pericles* by E. BUCHNER, *Gnom.* 32, 1960, 306.

[2] Agis and Cleomenes have been combined into a tetrade with the two Gracchi. We shall not go into the question of the relative chronology of the *Lives*. It is particularly difficult through the alternating quotations, among which there may well be later additions; cf. ZIEGLER, *RE* (*v. inf.*), 899. C. THEANDER, 'Zur Zeitfolge der Biographien Pl.'s' *Eranos* 56, 1958, 12.

other cases the possibilities of comparison may be very slight, but hardly ever miscarry completely. Even for Pericles and Fabius Maximus the stress on defensive warfare may be considered a modest link. Plutarch reveals the rhetorical tradition in the syncrisis,[1] the synoptical comparison with which he usually concludes a parallel life. This is often a *tour de force* or it is devoid of meaning, but nowadays no one would think of denying Plutarch's responsibility for these parts, as Rudolf Hirzel did.

Atticism was flourishing when Plutarch wrote, but here he also proved to be a man of moderation. The freeman of the city of Athens appreciated Attic culture and language, but he joined neither in the pursuit of rare Attic words, nor did he bar elements of Koine from his diction, so that his style belongs to the Hellenistic tradition. He adopted this same moderate attitude towards rhetoric, after shaking off the ties which were noticeable in the early declamations. He generally is so precise in his avoidance of hiatus, that this trait could be used as a criterion for authenticity. An attempt to introduce rhythm can be detected in the appearance of usual types of clausulae.[2] Plutarch's style owes its personal note especially to the broad sweep of his periods; he tends to be broadly informative, while at the same time his wide literary experience induces him to fit as many ideas as possible into the framework of one sentence structure.

The considerable difference between Lamprias' catalogue and the preserved writings proves that a great deal of Plutarch's work was lost during the dark ages. For the *Lives* an edition in two volumes in chronological order (according to the Greeks) can be identified, which was probably produced at the end of antiquity. Evidence for this is a manuscript in Seitenstetten (11th/12th c.) and one in Madrid (Matrit. 55; 14th c.). Early in the Byzantine era this edition was joined by another in three volumes which arranged the material in the first place according to the place of origin of the Greeks and only in the second place according to the chronological order. Manuscripts of this edition occur as early as the 10th c.: Vat. Gr. 138, Laur. conv. soppr. 206, Laur. pl. 69, 9, each for one book. The particular importance of Par. gr. 1674 (13th c.) for the edition in three volumes is stressed in the *Coll. des Un. d. Fr.* (*v. infra*) for which M. JUNEAUX did the collating. The transmission of the *Moralia* was decided by the work of Maximus Planudes from the end of the 13th c. to the early 14th c., combining the pieces transmitted in individual groups into one corpus. The unsuitable title of *Moralia* is due to the fact that he opened the corpus with the 'Hθικά. For the various stages of the collection, in the course of which Planudes also included the *Lives*, we have excellent evidence in the Ambros. 859 (C 126 inf.; shortly before 1296); Paris. 1671 (completed 1296); Paris. 1672 (soon after 1302). The tradition of the *Moralia* is abundant and varies greatly.

---

[1] On this notion: F. FOCKE, 'Synkrisis'. *Herm.* 58, 1923, 327. On Plutarch: H. ERBSE, 'Die Bedeutung der Synkrisis in den Parallelbiographien Plutarchs'. *Herm.* 84, 1956, 398.

[2] Ditrochee, cretic and trochee, double cretic, hypodochmius.

The old Teubner-edition of the *Moralia* by G. N. BERNARDAKIS in 7 vols. (Leipz. 1888–96) has already been almost completely replaced by the new one on which C. HUBERT, W. NACHSTÄDT, W. R. PATON, M. POHLENZ, W. SIEVEKING, I. WEGEHAUPT and K. ZIEGLER collaborated (6 vols., of which Vol. 5 is still incomplete, Leipz. from 1908; fasc. V/1.3; VI/1-3, were published in 1957–60 in reprint, often with appendices by H. DREXLER. For the *Lives* the Teubneriana of C. SINTENIS (5 vols. Leipz. 1852–55, often reprinted) has been replaced by the one of C. LINDSKOG and K. ZIEGLER (4 vols. in 8 parts, Leipz. 1914–39, I in 3rd ed. 1960; 2 in 2nd ed. 1959). In the *Coll. des Un. de Fr.* (biling.): R. FLACELIÈRE, M. JUNEAUX, E. CHAMBRY, *Plut. Les vies parallèles.* I (Thésée-Romulus. Lycurgus-Numa) 1957; 2 (Solon-Publicola. Thémistocle-Camille) 1961, based on new collations by M. JUNEAUX. We give next a complete survey of Plutarch's surviving works. The numbers between brackets refer to the new editions mentioned; for only a small part of the *Moralia* reference has been made to Bernardakis. Athetesis is indicated by bracketing the serial numbers, doubt by an additional ?, but in this connection it must be admitted that there is still uncertainty with regard to the criticism of individual writings.

Moralia:

(1.) *De liberis educandis.* Περὶ παίδων ἀγωγῆς (I 1). – 2. *De audiendis poetis.* Πῶς δεῖ τὸν νέον ποιημάτων ἀκούειν (I 28). – 3. *De audiendo.* Περὶ τοῦ ἀκούειν (I 75). – 4. *De adulatore et amico.* Πῶς ἄν τις διακρίνειε τὸν κόλακα τοῦ φίλου (I 97). – 5. *De profectibus in virtute.* Πῶς ἄν τις αἴσθοιτο ἑαυτοῦ προκόπτοντος ἐπ᾽ ἀρετῇ (I 149). – 6. *De capienda ex inimicis utilitate.* Πῶς ἄν τις ἀπ᾽ ἐχθρῶν ὠφελοῖτο (I 172). – 7. *De amicorum multitudine.* Περὶ πολυφιλίας (I 186). – 8. *De fortuna.* Περὶ τύχης (I 197). – 9. *De virtute et vitio.* Περὶ ἀρετῆς καὶ κακίας (I 204). – (10.) *Consolatio ad Apollonium.* Παραμυθητικὸς πρὸς ᾿Απολλώνιον (I 208). – 11. *De tuenda sanitate praecepta.* ῾Υγιεινὰ παραγγέλματα (I 253). – 12. *Coniugalia praecepta.* Γαμικὰ παραγγέλματα (I 283). – 13. *Septem sapientium convivium.* Τῶν ἑπτὰ σοφῶν συμπόσιον (I 300). – 14. *De superstitione.* Περὶ δεισιδαιμονίας (I 338). – (15). *Regum et imperatorum apophthegmata.* Βασιλέων ἀποφθέγματα καὶ στρατηγῶν (II/1, 1). – 16. *Apophthegmata Laconica. Instituta Laconica. Apophth. Lacaenarum.* ᾿Αποφθέγματα Λακωνικά (II/1, 110. 204, 216). – 17. *Mulierum virtutes.* Γυναικῶν ἀρεταί (II/1, 225). – 18. *Aetia Romana. Aetia Graeca.* Αἴτια ῾Ρωμαϊκὰ καὶ ῾Ελληνικά (II/1, 273. 337). – (19.) *Parallela minora.* Συναγωγὴ ἱστοριῶν παραλλήλων ῾Ελληνικῶν καὶ ῾Ρωμαϊκῶν (II/2, 1). – 20. *De fortuna Romanorum.* Περὶ τῆς ῾Ρωμαίων τύχης (II/2, 43). – 21. *De Alexandri Magni fortuna aut virtute or. I et II.* Περὶ τῆς ᾿Αλεξάνδρου τύχης ἢ ἀρετῆς λόγος α΄, β΄ (II/2, 75. 93). – 22. *De gloria Atheniensium.* Πότερον ᾿Αθηναῖοι κατὰ πόλεμον ἢ κατὰ σοφίαν ἐνδοξότεροι (II/2, 121). – 23. *De Iside et Osiride.* Περὶ ῎Ισιδος καὶ ᾿Οσίριδος (II/3, 1). – 24. *De E apud Delphos.* Περὶ τοῦ ΕΙ τοῦ ἐν Δελφοῖς (III 1). – 25. *De Pythiae oraculis.* Περὶ τοῦ μὴ χρᾶν ἔμμετρα νῦν τὴν Πυθίαν (III 25). – 26. *De defectu oraculorum.* Περὶ τῶν ἐκλελοιπότων χρηστηρίων (III 59). – 27. *An virtus doceri possit.* Εἰ διδακτὸν ἡ ἀρετή (III 123). – 28. *De virtute morali.* Περὶ ἠθικῆς ἀρετῆς (III 127). – 29. *De cohibenda ira.* Περὶ ἀοργησίας (III 157). – 30. *De tranquillitate animi.* Περὶ εὐθυμίας (III 187). – 31. *De fraterno amore.* Περὶ φιλαδελφίας (III 221). – *De amore prolis.* Περὶ τῆς εἰς τὰ ἔγγονα φιλοστοργίας (III 255). – 33. *An vitiositas ad infelicitatem sufficiat.* Εἰ αὐτάρκης ἡ κακία πρὸς κακοδαιμονίαν (III 268). – 34. *Animine an corporis affectiones sint peiores.* Περὶ τοῦ πότερον τὰ ψυχῆς ἢ τὰ σώματος πάθη χείρονα (III 273). – 35. *De garrulitate.* Περὶ ἀδολεσχίας (III 279). – 36. *De curiositate.* Περὶ πολυπραγμοσύνης (III 311). – 37. *De cupiditate divitiarum.* Περὶ φιλοπλουτίας (III 332). – 38. *De vitioso pudore.* Περὶ δυσωπίας (III 346). – 39. *De invidia et otio.* Περὶ φθόνου καὶ μίσους (III 365). – 40. *De laude ipsius.* Περὶ τοῦ ἑαυτὸν ἐπαινεῖν ἀνεπιφθόνως (III 371). – 41. *De sera numinis vindicta.* Περὶ τῶν ὑπὸ τοῦ θείου βραδέως τιμωρουμένων (III 394). – (42.) *De fato.* Περὶ εἱμαρμένης (III 445). – 43. *De genio Socratis.* Περὶ τοῦ Σωκράτους δαιμονίου (III 460). – 44. *De exilio.* Περὶ φυγῆς (III 512). – 45. *Consolatio ad uxorem.* Παραμυθητικὸς πρὸς τὴν γυναῖκα (III 533). – 46. *Quaestionum convivalium libri IX.* Συμποσιακῶν βιβλία θ' (IV 1). – 47. *Amatorius.* Ἐρωτικός (IV 336). – (48). *Amatoriae narrationes.* Ἐρωτικαὶ διηγήσεις (IV 396). – 49. *Maxime cum principibus philosopho esse disserendum.* Περὶ τοῦ ὅτι μάλιστα τοῖς ἡγεμόσι δεῖ τὸν φιλόσοφον διαλέγεσθαι (V/1, 1). – 50. *Ad principem ineruditum.* Πρὸς ἡγεμόνα ἀπαίδευτον (V/1, 11). – 51. *An seni sit gerenda res publica.* Εἰ πρεσβυτέρῳ πολιτευτέον (V/1, 20). – 52. *Praecepta gerendae rei publicae.* Πολιτικὰ παραγγέλματα (V/1, 58). – 53. (?) *De tribus rei publicae generibus.* Περὶ μοναρχίας καὶ δημοκρατίας καὶ ὀλιγαρχίας (V/1, 127). – 54. *De vitando aere alieno.* Περὶ τοῦ μὴ δεῖν δανείζεσθαι (V/1, 131). – (55). X *oratorum vitae.* Βίοι τῶν δέκα ῥητόρων (Bern. V 146). – 56. (?) *Aristophanis et Menandri comparatio.* Συγκρίσεως Ἀριστοφάνους καὶ Μενάνδρου ἐπιτομή (Bern. V 203). – 57. *De Herodoti malignitate.* Περὶ τῆς Ἡροδότου κακοηθείας (Bern. V 208). – (58.) *De placitis philosophorum.* Περὶ τῶν ἀρεσκόντων φιλοσόφοις φυσικῶν δογμάτων βιβλία ε' (Bern. V 264). – 59. *Aetia physica.* Αἴτια φυσικά (V/3, 1). – 60. *De facie in orbe lunae.* Περὶ τοῦ ἐμφαινομένου προσώπου τῷ κύκλῳ τῆς σελήνης (V/3, 31). – 61. *De primo frigido.* Περὶ τοῦ πρώτως ψυχροῦ (V/3, 90). – 62. *Aqua an ignis utilior.* Πότερον ὕδωρ ἢ πῦρ χρησιμώτερον (VI/1, 1). – 63. *De sollertia animalium.* Πότερα τῶν ζῴων φρονιμώτερα (VI/1, 11). – 64. (?) *Bruta ratione uti.* Περὶ τοῦ τὰ ἄλογα λόγῳ χρῆσθαι (VI/1, 76). – 65. *De esu carnium I.* Περὶ σαρκοφαγίας α' (VI/1, 94). – 66. *Id. β'* (VI/1, 105). – 67. *Platonicae quaestiones.* Πλατωνικὰ ζητήματα (VI/1, 113). – 68. *De animae procreatione in Timaeo.* Περὶ τῆς ἐν Τιμαίῳ ψυχογονίας (VI/1, 143). – (69). *Epitome libri de animae procreatione in Timaeo.* Ἐπιτομὴ τοῦ περὶ τῆς ἐν τῷ Τιμαίῳ ψυχογονίας (VI/1, 189). – 70. *De Stoicorum repugnantiis.* Περὶ Στωικῶν ἐναντιωμάτων (VI/2, 1). – 71. *Stoicos absurdiora poetis dicere.* Ὅτι παραδοξότερα οἱ Στωικοὶ τῶν ποιητῶν λέγουσιν (VI/2, 59). – 72. *De communibus notitiis contra Stoicos.* Περὶ τῶν κοινῶν ἐννοιῶν πρὸς τοὺς Στωικούς (VI/2, 62). – 73. *Non posse suaviter vivi secundum Epicurum.* Ὅτι οὐδ' ἡδέως ζῆν ἔστιν κατ' Ἐπίκουρον (VI/2, 124). – 74. *Adversus Colotem.* Πρὸς Κωλώτην (VI/2, 173). – 75. *De latenter vivendo.* Εἰ καλῶς εἴρηται τὸ λάθε βιώσας (VI/2, 216). – (76.) *De musica.* Περὶ μουσικῆς (VI/3, 1). – 77. (?) *De libidine et aegritudine.* Πότερον ψυχῆς ἢ σώματος ἐπιθυμία καὶ λύπη (VI/3, 37). – (78.) *Parsne an facultas animi sit vita passiva.* Εἰ μέρος τὸ παθητικὸν τῆς ἀνθρώπου ψυχῆς ἢ δύναμις (VI/3, 46). – Various excerpts and fragments in Bern. VII.

Vitae:

I/1: Theseus-Romulus. Solon-Publicola. Themistocles-Camillus. Aristides-Cato-maior. Cimon-Lucullus.

I/2: Pericles-Fabius Maximus. Nicias-Crassus. Coriolanus-Alcibiades. Demosthenes-Cicero.

II/1: Phocion-Cato minor. Dion-Brutus. Aemilius Paulus-Timoleon. Sertorius-Eumenes.

II/2: Philopoemen-T. Flamininus. Pelopidas-Marcellus. Alexander-Caesar.

III/1: Demetrius-Antony. Pyrrhus-Marius. Aratus. Artaxerxes. Agis and Cleomenes-T. and C. Gracchus.

III/2: Lycurgus-Numa. Lysander-Sulla. Agesilaus-Pompey.

IV/1: Galba. Otho.

In his *RE* article ZIEGLER quotes special annotated editions for the separate writings of the *Moralia*, while he gives a summary for the *Lives* (960). In add.: R. FLACELIÈRE, *P. Dialogue sur l'Amour*. Paris 1953. J. DEFRADAS, *P. Le Banquet des Sept Sages*. Paris 1954. F. LASSERRE. *P. de la Musique*. Olten-Lausanne 1954. W. H. PORTER, *Life of Dion*. Dublin 1952. S. GEVERINI, *Vita di Flaminino*. Milan 1952 (with transl.). EUG. MANNI, *Vita Dem. Pol.* Florence 1953. A. GARZETTI, *Vita Caesaris*. Florence 1954. R. DEL RE, *Vita di Bruto*, 3rd ed. Florence 1953. E. VALGIGLIO, *Vita di Mario*. Florence 1956; *Vita dei Gracchi*. Rome 1957. – Lexicon: D. Wyttenbach. Leipz. 1843; for the Index Graecitatis of the *Moralia* (vol. 8 of the edition of D. WYTTENBACH, Oxf. 1830) a reprint is in preparation by Olms/Hildesheim. – Plutarch was often translated; here only a selection of recent work is given: French: B. LATZARUS, *Vies parallèles*. 5 vols. Paris 1951–55. English: the bilingual ed. of the *Loeb Class. Libr.*: F. C. BABBITT, H. CHERNISS, W. C. HELMBOLD, *Moralia*, 15 vols. planned, partly still in preparation. Lond. 1927–59. B. PERRIN, *The Parallel Lives*. 11 vols. Lond. 1914–26; repr. up to 1959. – We have a comprehensive and weighty monograph in K. ZIEGLER's long *RE* article 21, 1951, 636–962. A fine characterization in M. POHLENZ, *Gestalten aus Hellas*. Munich 1950, 671. Important for P.'s religious sentiments: M. P. NILSSON, *Gesch. d. gr. Rel.* 2, 2nd ed. Munich 1961, 402. – On biography as a genre: W. STEIDLE, *Sueton und die antike Biographie*. Zet. 1, Munich 1951. A. DIHLE, *Stud. z. griech. Biogr. Abh. Ak. Gött. Phil.-hist. Kl.* 3. F. 37, 1956, with important sections on Plutarch and an analysis of the *Life of Cleomenes*. – Papers: H. SCHLAEPFER, *Pl. und die klass. Dichter*. Zürich 1950. M. A. LEVI, *Pl. e il V. secolo*. Milan 1955. R. WESTMAN, *Pl. gegen Kolotes. Seine Schrift 'Adversus Colotem' als philosophiegeschichtliche Quelle. Acta Philos. Fennica* 7. Helsinki 1955. E. MEINHARDT, *Perikles bei Pl.* Diss. Frankf. Fulda 1957. R. FLACELIÈRE, 'Pl. et l'épicurisme', in the collective work *Epicurea in mem. H. Bignone*. Genoa 1959, 197. W. C. HELMBOLD and E. N. O'NEIL, *Pl.'s Quotations*. Baltimore 1959. H. WEBER, *Die Staats- und Rechtslehre Pl.s von Chaironeia*. Bonn. 1959. A. M. TAGLIASACCHI, 'Le teorie estetiche e la critica letteraria in Plutarco'. *Acme* 14, 1961, 71.

LISETTE GOESSLER, *Pl.s Gedanken über die Ehe*. Diss. Basel. Zürich 1962. – Subsequent influence: R. HIRZEL, Plutarch. *Erbe der Alten* 4. Leipz. 1912.

2 THE SECOND SOPHISTIC

We saw that Isocrates and Plato sparked off an educational controversy which influenced intellectual life with a varying intensity until the decline of antiquity. In this battle for the prerogative of education both sides sometimes crossed the boundaries and attempted a reconciliation, since both philosophy and rhetoric claimed the whole of education for themselves. In the Hellenistic era, as defined by us, the new and the old schools of philosophy were vigorous enough to maintain their claim. This is very clearly expressed in Cicero's attempt to bring about a settlement of the demands of both sides. It was different during the first two centuries of the empire, before Neoplatonism once more stirred up intellectual life. Now philosophy had left large parts of the disputed field to rhetoric, which chiefly controlled advanced education and determined the characteristics of the literature of this time.[1] The edge had gone out of the struggle with philosophy; at times there was even a neighbourly relationship. The state extended its blessing to this development when, in the edict of the year 74, Vespasian conferred special privileges on grammarians and orators, and on physicians as well.[2] The same emperor initiated the establishment of chairs of rhetoric at a public stipend in Rome. Later philosophy received a similar endowment from Marcus Aurelius of four chairs in Athens, so that each of the great systems was given its due.[3] But any one who compares the intensity of rhetorical teaching in the empire with the importance of philosophy at this time soon observes which side predominated. A course of rhetoric was prescribed for all who aspired to a higher education. When primary schooling was finished, a course of wide reading and grammatical instruction introduced the theory of rhetoric. The student was trained by means of various preliminary exercises (pro-gymnasmata),[4] such as repeating a story, writing an essay which painstakingly enlarged upon some moral theme, a description (ecphrasis), proof or refutation of the facts of some assumed case, to mention only a few. It will be noticed how great the influence of this system still used to be in the schools of our days before it was considered better to let a child give free rein to his imagination with pen and pencil. Grammatical instruction was followed by that in rhetoric proper, which was supposed to produce the finished orator and was concluded with a declamation on some fictional subject.[5] The *Suasoriae* and the

---

[1] H. J. MARROU, *Histoire de l'éducation dans l'antiquité*. 5th ed. Paris 1960 (Engl. London 1956). D. L. CLARK, *Rhetoric in Greco-Roman Education*. New York, with copious bibl. Good material in W. KROLL, *RE* S 7, 1940, 1039 (esp. 1105 ff.); cf. also A. D. NOCK, *Sallustius*. Cambr. 1926, XVII.

[2] Inscription from Pergamum: R. HERZOG, *Sitzb. Ak. Berl. Phil.-hist. Kl.* 1935, 967. S. RICCOBONO, *Fontes Iuris Anteiustiniani*. I, 2nd ed. 1941, 420.   [3] LUCIAN, *Eunuchus* 3.

[4] On how the grammarians took over part of rhetorical instruction, KROLL (*v. supra*, n. 1), 1119, 33.

[5] W. HOFRICHTER, *Stud. z. Entwicklungsgesch. d. Deklamation*. Diss. Breslau 1935. Enumeration of the exercises in CHRIST-SCHMID, *Gesch. d. gr. Lit.* 2nd part/I, 6th ed. Munich 1920,

Controversiae of the older Seneca give a very upsetting picture of the bizarre imagination with which the most absurd stories were concocted as themes for these exercises.

Rhetoric had a twofold influence on the poetry of the time. Firstly it could not help having some influence, because most contemporary poets themselves passed through schools of rhetoric. But in the second place rhetoric – and this is the most important factor – cut the ground from under the poets' feet with its claims. The development which we saw begin with Gorgias is now completed. Whole genres like the encomium or the epithalamium, which once belonged to poetry, have now become the permanent property of rhetoric.

Even before the beginning of the empire, in about the middle of the first century B.C., the long anticipated reaction against Asianism set in, presenting itself as a return to the ancient Attic models of style.[1] This Atticism is met in Cicero's polemic as well as in Caecilius of Sicilian Caleacte and in Dionysius of Halicarnassus. We only possess some fragments of Caecilius' many works[2] which comprised technical treatises on rhetoric, exegetical and lexicographical writings, apart from a study of the slave war. His book *On the Ten Orators* ((Περὶ τοῦ χαρακτῆρος τῶν δέκα ῥητόρων) was probably responsible for the creation of the canon, but it was in any case largely influential for the development during the empire. This determined enemy of Asianism (κατὰ Φρυγῶν. Τίνι διαφέρει ὁ 'Αττικὸς ζῆλος τοῦ 'Ασιανοῦ) was a special admirer of Lysias, but he did not understand the greatness of Plato's style. The schoolmaster's mind of the stern Apollodorus of Pergamum still had some influence here; he was probably his teacher, as well as of Augustus. During the following generation he was opposed by Theodorus of Gadara, the teacher of Tiberius, who had a more liberal conception. The conflict of these two men, in which the contrast between analogy and anomaly rears its head again, was carried on by their disciples in a very remarkable manner. Caecilius wrote *On the Sublime* (Περὶ ὕψους), which he saw as a stylistic idea and with which he dealt in a purely technically descriptive manner. He was answered in A.D. 40 by an anonymous author who was the pupil of Theodorus in a treatise under the same title, which has survived in a fragmentary condition.[3] For him the sublime cannot be

---

461 and 2nd part/2, Munich 1924, 931. Three subjects for rhetorical μελέται with a pseudo-historical content now *Ox. Pap.* 24, 1957, no. 2400.

[1] For an understanding of this controversy the observations of v. WILAMOWITZ, *Herm.* 35, 1900, 1 are still important. Bibl. E. RICHTSTEIG, *Bursians Jahresb.* 234, 1932, 1. A. BOULANGER, *Aelius Aristide.* Paris 1923, 66.

[2] E. OFFENLOCH, Leipz. 1907.

[3] According to an incorrect ascription caused by the caption Διονυσίου ἢ Λογγίνου often called Pseudo-Longinus. O. JAHN-VAHLEN. Bonn 1910. A. O. PRICKARD, 2nd ed. Oxf. 1947. H. LEBÈGUE, 2nd ed. *Coll. des Un. d. Fr.* 1952 (biling.). Verbal index: H. ROBINSON, *Indices tres etc.* Oxf. 1772. Influence of Democritus' notion of enthusiasm conjectured by F. WEHRLI, *Phyllobolia für P. von der Mühll.* Basel 1946, 11. 23. On the work: J. W. ATKINS, *Literary Criticism in Antiquity.* 2 vols. Lond. 1952 (orig. Cambr. Un. Pr. 1934), 2, 210. G. M. A. GRUBE, 'Notes on the Περὶ ὕψους'. *Am. Journ. Phil.* 78, 1957, 355. HANS SELB, *Probleme der Schrift Περὶ ὕψους. Untersuchungen zur Datierung und Lokalisierung der Schrift sowie textkr.* Erl. Diss. Heidelb. 1957 (typewr.).

reached through rules, but it is present wherever a lofty conviction, remote from the commonplace, is expressed in such a way as to move our souls. This may happen through the passion of a Demosthenes, the force of tragedy or the Platonic vision. Our author does not attempt preciser differentiations. Not small streams, even if clear and useful, but mighty rivers seem to him worthy of admiration. He praises genius in its gigantic proportions. It is also a rejoinder to the Callimachean principle which used the same image to express the opposite idea (*v. p.* 710).

This anonymous, a talented lone wolf who was far ahead of his age and whose name we should be only too glad to know, has an understanding of the values of great poetry which appeals directly to the modern mind. In retrospect he could seem to represent the break between ancient and modern intellect, but in fact his treatise could not yet bring about such a change. However strong his influence may have been in modern times, as for instance in the *Querelle des anciens et des modernes* which had such momentous consequences for Homer, in antiquity he had to give precedence to those who were guided by canon and mimesis. Dionysius of Halicarnassus, who came to Rome in 30 B.C. and worked there for twenty-two years in close contact with politically and intellectually leading circles, was more prepared than Caecilius to adopt a conciliatory attitude. Though he spurned Asianism, his admired model is Demosthenes, not Lysias (Περὶ τῆς Δημοσθένους λέξεως. *1st Letter to Ammaeus. Letter to Pompeius Geminus*).[1] In this and in much else his kinship with Cicero is close. He also had a feeling for the immediate effect of great works of art,[2] but on the whole he became the harbinger of a classicism tied to Attic models. When he discusses authors of the past (Περὶ μιμήσεως. Περὶ τῶν ἀρχαίων ῥητόρων), they are mainly notable for him as samples of style. He delights with many intelligent judgments of his own or of other origin, but we notice that when he is faced with a figure like Thucydides (Περὶ τοῦ Θ. χαρακτῆρος *2nd Letter to Ammaeus*), he appears to be narrow-minded. His most important work (Περὶ συνθέσεως ὀνομάτων)[3] also means to give stylistic instruction. It deals with the two elements of style vocabulary (ἐκλογή) and the arrangement of words (σύνθεσις), the latter with a great many examples. Many of these observations, especially those on the combinations of sounds, may make us realize to what extent the effects of ancient literary language are no longer accessible to us. A *Handbook of Rhetoric* was attributed to Dionysius; its content is very varied, but it is not unimportant, probably belonging to the third century A.D. Dionysius the 'historian' will be discussed later.

Atticism must in the first place be understood as a reaction against Asianic bombast; it was, however, a sign of weakness and torpidity that it could only oppose with a linguistic and stylistic form which centuries ago had been the

---

[1] The texts by H. USENER – L. RADERMACHER, 2 vols. Leipz. 1889, 1904 with index by L. BIELER, 1929. Analysis by ATKINS (*v.* p. 830, n. 3), 2, 104. G. PAVANO, *Dion. d' Alic. Saggio su Tucidide*. Palermo 1958 (text, transl., comm.).

[2] Cf. WEHRLI (*v. sup.*), 16.

[3] Ed. with comm. and transl. W. RHYS ROBERTS, Lond. 1910; id., *Three Literary Letters*. Cambr. 1901.

exponent of great quality, but could be so no longer. This was not the start of a development which made the ancient forms useful for a new life; it seemed rather that all that mattered was the cultivation of a mummified style.

The most extreme expression of Atticism was the lexicographical collection of authorized linguistic material. The work of the Hellenistic age and its pursuit of glosses, which had had entirely different causes, was now carried on in a singular manner. In this confusion two centres of radiation were the Atticist collections of Aelius Dionysius of Halicarnassus and Pausanias of Syria during the Hadrianic period.[1] Later Atticists made extensive use of them; their source had been Diogenianus of Alexandria,[2] who can be traced back via Julius Vestinus to the Aristarchean Pamphilus of Alexandria. In the middle of the first century A.D. the latter recorded the lexicographical tradition in a lexicon of glosses in ninety-five books, in this way pointing back via Didymus to the great age of Alexandrian scholarship. Diogenianus is one of the main sources of the very valuable lexicon of Hesychius of Alexandria (5th c.).[3] We add here a reference to the Byzantine Suidas (10th c.),[4] who represents the last, often doubtful yet indispensable, reservoir of the ancient literature of collectanea.

To return to Atticist lexicography, a great deal of what was produced in the second century A.D. has survived. The boundaries of what was linguistically permissible wavered. Moeris is the strictest in his Λέξεις 'Αττικαί.[5] Another Atticist of strict observance was Phrynichus; we have excerpts of his two works ('Αττικιστής, 2 books, and Σοφιστικὴ προπαρασκευή, 37 books, dedicated to Commodus).[6] His successful rival in the competition for the Athenian chair in rhetoric, Julius Polydeuces (Pollux) of Naucratis, was less orthodox in linguistic matters and considerably more interested in technical questions. His Onomasticum,[7] preserved in excerpt, is an important source for many such matters as the stage and masks. The Orator's Lexicon of Harpocration (Λέξεις τῶν δέκα ῥητόρων)[8] of the same time uses good sources and being preoccupied with technical matters, it provides important material on the Athenian judicial organization.

Atticism was not unopposed. An anonymous lexicon, the Antiatticista,[9]

[1] For both v. the collection of fragments of H. E. ERBSE, Untersuchungen zu den attiz. Lexica. Abh. d. deutsch. Akad. Phil.-hist. Kl. 1949/2. Berl. 1950. The work offers a great many important observations on the origin and tradition of Atticist glosses. W. SCHMID, Attizismus 1-4. Stuttg. 1887-96 is still a mine of information, although the necessarily incomplete manuscriptural basis calls for caution.

[2] ERBSE (v. sup.), 36.

[3] The ed. of M. SCHMIDT, 4 vols. Jena 1858-68 (ed. min. 1867) is now being replaced by K. LATTE: I (A-Δ) Copenhagen 1953.

[4] Suda, not Suidas – a title, not a personal name – according to F. DÖLGER, Der Titel des sog. Suidaslexikons. Sitzb. Bayer. Akad. Phil.-hist. Kl. 1936/6. Edition: A. ADLER, 5 vols. Leipz. 1928-38.

[5] I. BEKKER, Berl. 1883 with Harpocration.

[6] 'Εκλογή from 'Αττικιστής: W. G. RUTHERFORD, Lond. 1881. Excerpt from Σοφ. προπαρασκευή: J. V. BORRIES, Leipz. 1911.

[7] E. BETHE, 3 vols. Leipz. 1900-37.

[8] W. DINDORF, 2 vols. Oxf. 1853, cf. supra, n. 5. The Lexicon rhetoricum Cantabrigiense, E. O. HOUTSMA, Lugd. Bat. 1870 is dependent on Harpocration.

[9] In I. BEKKER'S Anecdota, Berl. 1814/21, 78.

purposely enlarges the circle of admissible authors and linguistic usages. Lucian poured his ridicule over the hyperpuristic fanatics who profitably adopted a handful of ancient Attic slogans in order to be able to join in (*Rhet. Praec.* 16 f.). The last fling of this tendency is the κειτούκειτος (Athen. 1, 2 e) whose intellectual scope was exhausted with the search for verification in Attic (κεῖται ἢ οὐ κεῖται).

There was a great deal of opposition against this Atticism which broke off all contact with the living language (συνήθεια), but nevertheless its influence was decisive for the solidification of linguistic and intellectual life through its classicism, in whose soil no new growth could thrive. It was something exceptional that a writer like the astrologer Vettius Valens wrote his guide to the interpretation of the stars ('Ανθολογίαι, 9 books)[1] without Attic colouring.

It was indispensable to discuss Atticism for the review of rhetoric under the empire. But it would be wrong to call it despotic and to characterize the second sophistic through it alone. It is no less one-sided to describe this period simply as Asianic. The fact that many threads crossed one another in this epoch has long caused great confusion. It is Norden's merit to have demonstrated in his *Antike Kunstprosa*[2] that it is not a matter of either one thing or another, but of an antagonism continuing through late antiquity between Atticist classicism and the legacy of Asianism, which was never quite extinguished. In the theory and practice of the rhetorical style this applied especially to the *compositio verborum* (σύνθεσις), while in vocabulary (ἐκλογή) Atticism could gain more ground. Norden demonstrated that in each case the individual author demands special analysis of the influence that operated in his style.

The expression [second sophistic] is used by Philostratus in his *Lives of the Sophists*. Actually it is misleading, for on the one hand this period is essentially different from that of the old sophists, while on the other there is no question of a new beginning, but of a development which led from Gorgias via Isocrates, the Peripatos and the Hellenistic age in action and reaction, on to the empire. Philostratus (1. 19) considers that Nicetes in the epoch of Nero was the revivalist of the sophistic movement, followed by his pupil Scopelianus. Nicetes came from Smyrna, his pupil, a Clazomenian, taught in his teacher's native town; both orators followed the Asianic tradition. This also applies partly to Polemon, with whom we reach the era of the Hadrianic attempts at renewal. At the order of the emperor he was permitted to deliver the festive oration in front of the Olympieum in Athens on the occasion of its dedication in 131. We have two *Declamations*[3] by him in which two fathers of Marathon fighters killed in battle contend for the honour of giving the funeral oration. He gives more pleasure with his *Physiognomy*,[4] which is only known to us through an Arabic translation and the paraphrase of the physician Adamantius. Of the older group of these

---

[1] W. KROLL, Berl. 1908.

[2] 1st vol., 4th impr. Berl. 1923. Ibid. 353, 1 bibl. on the old controversy.

[3] H. HINCK, Leipz. 1873.

[4] G. HOFFMANN in R. FÖRSTER, *Physiognomici Graeci et Latini* I, Leipz. 1893, 98; FÖRSTER, ibid. 295.

sophists mention must be made also of Lollianus of Ephesus,[1] who carried on a rhetorical practice and wrote a *Techne*, in which he elaborated the status doctrine.

The early second sophistic brought forth a man who, though a product of his intellectual milieu, showed flashes of aspiration towards a higher form of expression. Dion of Prusa in Bithynia (*circa* 40–120) surnamed Cocceianus upon being granted citizenship under Nerva, and Chrysostomus since the third century, began his chequered career as an orator, occasionally writing polemics against the philosophers. In his *Praise of Baldness* Synesius has preserved a trifle (Παίγνιον) by Dion, the *Praise of Hair*. Eulogies on a parrot and a gnat are lost. Internal and external influences were to give his life another direction. Musonius Rufus, who was also Epictetus' teacher and against whom Dion had written in his early years (Πρὸς Μουσώνιον), won him over to the Stoa, whose elements of kinship with Cynicism had a special influence on Dion. In the year 82 he was condemned to exile by Domitian, probably in connection with the fall of his patron Flavius Sabinus, so that Italy and his Bithynian homeland were closed to him. Until the death of this emperor he led a wandering existence in needy circumstances, travelling far, especially in the north-east of the empire. The sentiments of his orations of this period are typical of the life of a Cynic beggar-philosopher. Under Nerva and Trajan he once more rose to distinction, but he remained faithful to his ethical mission. He combined his praise of morality with a Hellenism whose features originated in a romantically glorified past. Thus he also followed Attic models, but with moderation, just as generally what he had to say mattered more to him than linguistic artistry. The change of his style to serious dignity, which was connected with his approach to philosophy, is characterized by Synesius in an important passage in his *Dion*.[2] Under his name we read eighty speeches, of which, however, the *Corinthiaca* and the second declamation *On Tyche* belong to his pupil Favorinus.[3] This sophist, who also wrote compilations (Παντοδαπὴ ἱστορία, 24 books) wrote in a style which paraded sound figures and rhythmical combinations, and which is in striking contrast with the simpler diction of Dion. A Vatican papyrus, discovered in 1931, with a fragment of the treatise *On Exile* (Περὶ φυγῆς; no 330 P.) gives an idea of Favorinus' artificial style, in this case surfeited with quotations. Dion's genuine speeches are important documents in the history of culture, especially those addressed to cities like Rhodes, Alexandria, Tarsus and Celaenae (31–35). The *Euboicus* (7) with its picture of economic misery in Greece may be added here; it is read especially for the idyll of the huntsman's family whose simple withdrawn life is depicted to present a contrast with urban restlessness and

---

[1] About this city in the cultural life of the time J. KEIL, 'Vertreter der zweiten Sophistik in Ephesos'. *Öst. Jahrb.* 40, 1953, 5. There Dionysius of Miletus taught, Favorinus of Arelate settled part of his conflict with Polemon, Aelius Aristides won victory wreaths and Hadrianus of Tyre conducted a school for a long time. The sophist T. Flavius Damianus was a special benefactor of the city.   [2] In NORDEN, (*v.* p. 833, n. 2), 355.

[3] This is certain in the *Corinthiaca*, of which NORDEN (*v.* p. 833, n. 2), 422, gives an important analysis. There is much in favour of ascribing the *Tyche* oration to Favorinus. The 30th speech, the *Charidemus*, is also of suspect authenticity; cf. M. P. NILSSON, *Gesch. d, gr. Rel.* 2nd vol. 2nd ed. Munich 1961, 401, 2.

corruption.[1] The *Troïcus* (11) is one of the versions of Homer, the unconstrained kind of sport with the myths in which this era delighted. A presentation of the Trojan War which denied the fall of the city will have been welcome to the Roman public. The four *Royal Speeches* (1-4) belong to the philosophical debates on the ideal ruler. Dion's religious sentiment is beautifully manifest in the *Olympic Speech* (12) which contains some noteworthy remarks on the importance of art for the notion of the divine. When he uses the refined form of the diatribe to call with real conviction for moderation and self-control, he is at his most charming. The last thing we hear about Dion's life has to do with a lawsuit which he had to conduct against some malicious accusers in 111/12 before the younger Pliny as governor of Bithynia. The letter which Pliny wrote to Trajan on this occasion has been preserved (*Ep.* 81), and so has the emperor's answer, a fine monument to a noble disposition.

During the peak of the second sophistic, which coincided with the favourable economic conditions of the second century, we first meet the splendid figure of the Marathonian Tiberius Claudius Atticus Herodes (101-177). He was taught by Favorinus and Polemon, and numbered among his pupils successful orators like Aelius Aristides, as well as the imperial princes Marcus and Lucius. He stood in the centre of a rhetorical tradition which endeavoured to retain relations with philosophy. His rhetorical fame is matched by his renown as a patron of the arts. This rich and distinguished man, who held the office of consul in Rome in 143, erected through his generosity splendid monuments in numerous places in Greece, above all, of course, in Athens, where his Odeon is still the scene of concerts and performances in our days. This Attic writer, who called the style of the Asianic Scopelianus 'inebriated', knew the significance of moderation and adhered to it also as an Atticist, although he was instrumental in bringing about the dictatorship of an archaïzing purism. He wrote a great deal, letters, diatribes and other work; one speech, Περὶ πολιτείας,[2] has been preserved; its model was Thrasymachus' speech *For the Larisaeans* (v. p. 357). He managed the ancient style so well that time and again attempts have been made to date it in the fifth century.[3]

The second century is the most flourishing period of the orators whom Ludwig Radermacher aptly described as concert-orators. Their ancestry goes back to Gorgias, in that they excelled in the two forms cultivated by him, the improvisation and the carefully prepared declamation. The veneration in which these men were held can only be compared with the excess of the modern worship of film stars and the like. Aelius Aristides won the greatest fame among these people, not as an extempore orator but as the master of the artistic oration. He was born in Adrianutherae in Mysia in 129.[4] In his youth he travelled through Egypt. His lecture tours carried him far through the Greek world, but also to

---

[1] The interesting and successful experiment of translating the prose of the *Euboïcus* into German hexameters was done by H. HOMMEL, *Dion Chrys., Euboïsche Idylle*. Zürich 1959 (*Lebendige Antike*). [2] Edition: E. DRERUP, Paderborn 1908.

[3] So also H. T. WADE-GERY, *Class. Quart.* 39, 1945, 19, with survey of the controversy.

[4] His indication of the birth-constellation (50, 58 K.) would also agree with 117, but the late date is more probable.

Rome. He spent a great deal of time in Smyrna, whose pride he was. He died about 189. Aristides was a follower of Isocrates, for he, too, claimed the whole of education for himself and even wanted to take issue with Plato on this basis. His speech *On Rhetoric* (45 D.) turns especially against the latter's *Gorgias* and claims to prove the primacy of rhetoric as well as its character as a techne. These attacks were taken seriously in neo-Platonic circles; we know from Suidas that Porphyry retorted. In the speech *On the Four* (46 D.) he opposes Plato's devaluation of Miltiades, Cimon, Themistocles and Pericles. The same romantic glorification of the Athenian past also occurs in the *Panathenaicus* (13 D.). It is obvious that he was a convinced Atticist, as shown by his *Monody* (18 K.) on Smyrna after its destruction by an earthquake in 178.[1] He exerted all his influence for the reconstruction of the city, to which purpose he devoted his *Smyrnaïcus* (17 K.), as proved by the open letter to the Roman emperors (19 K.).

The highly artistic form cannot conceal the fact that the intellectual material of these speeches is mostly traditional stuff. It could be called an Atticism of themes. Nevertheless references to the historical situation are not completely absent. This applies especially to the *Roman Oration* (26 K.), which Michael Rostovtseff[2] has taught us to understand as the best description of the empire in the second century. It represents Rome as the great bringer of peace in a gigantic combination of city-states, which itself represents a polis.

The fifty-five speeches offer a variegated picture. Panegyrics on cities occur side by side with declamations on themes of classical history, occasional speeches and open letters. How the orators wanted to replace the poets everywhere is demonstrated by the *Addresses to the Gods* (37–46 K.), which were to precede the great speeches as once the 'Homeric' hymns the performances of the rhapsodes. The six speeches *On the Holy* ('Ιεροὶ λόγοι; 47–52 K.)[3] form a chapter of their own, interesting rather than attractive. For seventeen years Aristides suffered from a disease which the physicians could not cure, but of which Aesclepius cured him after a lengthy treatment. He feels that he has been singled out for the special protection of the god who made him healthy in Pergamum and ensured his road to fame. These records have much significance for us as evidence for the personal relations which a highly educated man of the second century entertained with a god, but Aristides' vanity, hypochondria and primitiveness which bordered on an Epidaurian belief in miracles is anything but attractive.

A rhetorical textbook, consisting of two separate parts, dealing with the political and the simple speech, was attributed to Aristides, probably not until a late date.

Philostratus is more colourful and interesting than the formally precise Aristides. But the question arises at once: Which Philostratus? And with this question an extremely difficult problem emerges. In some confused articles

---

[1] Important NORDEN (*v.* p. 833, n. 2), 420.

[2] *Gesellschaft und Wirtschaft im röm. Kaiserreich* I, Leipz. 1929, 112. Monograph with text, transl. and bibl.: JAMES H. OLIVER, *Trans. of Am. Philos. Soc.* N. Ser. 43/4, 1953, 871–1003.

[3] An excellent study in A.-J. FESTUGIÈRE, *Personal Religion among the Greeks.* Univ. of Cal. Pr. Berkeley 1954, 85.

Suidas presents three related Philostrati, to whom a fourth must be added, as we shall show. When we hear that the first of these, a writer of many speeches, lived in Rome during Nero's reign and was the father of the second Philostratus who worked in Rome under Septimius Severus, we already find ourselves seriously confused. Suidas mentions as the third a Philostratus who was a great-nephew and the son-in-law of the second. This may be doubted, but it must be admitted that such a double relationship is possible. Since the Philostratus who wrote the later *Icones* describes the writer of the earlier version (which in our opinion is the work of the second Philostratus) as his maternal grandfather, we have to take into account a fourth bearer of this name as well.

Various writings survive under the name of Philostratus, and the attribution to the various Philostrati poses a literary-historical problem. The solution which is the most likely (but no more than that) allots the surviving works to the second Philostratus with two exceptions, while the first remains in complete obscurity. This second Philostratus was born between 160 and 170, had as his teachers famous orators like Damianus of Ephesus[1] and Antipater of Hierapolis, the educator of Geta and Caracalla, and came to Rome under Septimius. It was probably his teacher Antipater who introduced him at court, where the Syrian Julia Domna, Septimius' ambitious consort, set the fashion. After the dramatic death of his patroness and her son Caracalla in the year 217 Philostratus probably returned to Athens to work there as a sophist. According to Suidas he died there under Philip the Arabian (244–249).

With complete confidence we assign to this Philostratus the *Lives of the Sophists* (Βίοι σοφιστῶν, 2 books), whose doctrinal importance we discussed earlier. The work begins with the founders of the ancient sophistical rhetoric, Gorgias being allotted the position due to him, and then passes on to the founders of the new direction up to the author's own era.

We are equally sure of attributing to him the *Life of Apollonius of Tyana* (Τὰ ἐς τὸν Τυανέα Ἀπολλώνιον, 8 books).[2] This absurd but interesting work, which chronologically preceded the *Lives of the Sophists*, is dominated by the interests of Julia Domna and the members of her circle. The historical Apollonius lived in the first century A.D. and wrote a variety of Neopythagorean works, among them a life of the Master. There may be some genuine letters among the seventy-seven preserved.[3] At an early stage tales of miracles were attached to this figure, which made him into a great magician. Philostratus, however, seeks to raise him from a γόης of a lower order to the level of a Neopythagorean ascete and prodigy, a true θεῖος ἀνήρ. By combining this sort of aretalogy with themes of the wonderful travel-romance, he has an opportunity to colour passages like the Indian sojourn of the sage with oriental touches and thus to cater for the taste of his high patroness.

---

[1] Cf. p. 834, n. 1.

[2] Apart from the analysis in F. SOLMSEN, *RE* 20, 1941, 139, also H. HELM, *Der ant. Roman·* 2nd ed. Gött. 1956, 62. On the type L. BIELER, Θεῖος ἀνήρ. 2 vols. Vienna 1935/36.

[3] On the letters v. WILAMOWITZ, *Herm.* 60, 1925, 307; now *Kl. Schr.* 4, 394. The text in R. HERCHER's *Epistolographi Gr.* 1873, 78.

The remaining works can be allotted only with some likelihood. There is the *Heroïcus*, this bizarre, but insufficiently utilized, dialogue about the local heroes between a vigneron in the Thracian Chersonese and a Phoenician traveller. The emendations of Homer which are inserted, are a literary game, but the defence of the belief in heroes should by no means be dismissed as such.[1] The *Gymnasticus*, which is valuable for the many details of contests, sports and training methods, also aims to give an appearance of importance to ancient traditional material by means of verbal artistry. Possibly the most charming work under the name of Philostratus is the *Icones* (2 books, but there is also a division into 4), the description of a collection of paintings in Naples, in which the ecphrasis, a standard exercise in the school of rhetoric, is turned into a masterly epideixis. Philostratus' main purpose is, of course, to allow his σοφία, his wit, full scope in learned references, interpretations and conclusions, but – whether the collection existed or not – there is no doubt of its relation to actual paintings.[2] This work affords the best opportunity for studying Philostratus' prose which, influenced by Atticist purism, still preserves a playful freedom and, in spite of all affectation, even achieves some charm in its best form.

The small dialogue *Nero*, in which the philosopher Musonius describes the tyrant's hybris, was transmitted with the tradition of Lucian. It is difficult to pass judgment on the *Collection of Letters*, transmitted in three versions, containing erotic trifles and letters to various addresses. The seventy-third letter, which defends the sophists before Julia Domna, is noteworthy. This much can be said, that no decisive grounds against their authenticity have been put forward.

To the third Philostratus, who was born in 190/91 and who achieved great fame as an orator, we can only attribute a treatise on epistolary style, the *Open Letter to Aspasius of Ravenna*, the imperial secretary and incumbent of the Roman chair of rhetoric. The *Dialexis*, added by Kayser, which seeks to settle the opposition between nomos and physis, is anonymous as far as we are concerned. The fourth Philostratus produced a later collection of *Icones*, in which he laboriously copies his grandfather.

The much-admired shows of celebrated oratorical performers, the endless conflict between the philosophical successors' realms, the steady advance of the irrational in the form of an escapist mysticism or banal superstition – all this is accompanied, during the Antonine era, by the laughter of a man whose outlook was scepticism and whose trade ridicule. Samosata, in which Lucian was born about 120, was situated on the upper Euphrates and was the capital of Commagene; he occasionally calls himself a Syrian and it is important to observe, apart from biographical interest, that he entered the Greek world from the outside and learnt its language at school (*Bis accus.* 27). His debut as a sculptor's apprentice with his uncle came to a swift and painful conclusion, as he tells in

---

[1] On the *Heroïcus* as an answer to Dictys, bibl. in w. KULLMANN, *Die Quellen der Ilias*. *Herm.* E 14, 1960, 104, 1.

[2] On the controversial question SOLMSEN (*v. sup.*), 168. Also A. LESKY, 'Bildwerk und Deutung bei Ph. und Homer'. 75, 1940, 38 in which the contradiction between Ph.'s interpretation and an apparently present object is evaluated.

the *Somnium*. His career then took him to the school of rhetoric, but his education gave him more than the skilful application of rhetorical rules. Wide reading gave him a knowledge of the range of forms of Attic prose as well as of Greek poetry from Homer to the Alexandrians. This does not mean that he penetrated to the problems of great poetry; he mastered the themes and the outlines. He has an abundant stock of quotations, or preferably, allusions. The richest treasure which the past opened up to him was the world of New Comedy. It has been aptly said that Lucian's linguistic Atticism is accompanied by a factual, though such an antiquarian attitude does not exclude the infiltration of contemporary elements.[1] Diligence and good taste achieved for the non-Greek an astonishing linguistic control of Attic Greek, which comes to a certain degree of life in the pleasant simplicity of his style. He was entitled to pillory the exaggerated purism of Atticism in his *Lexiphanes* and *Pseudologista*, for it was in the very moderation which he knew how to observe that the effect of his style was founded.

Initially Lucian was very successful as a bombastic sophistical orator. He travelled a great deal and visited many parts of the civilized world, Asia Minor, Greece, Italy and even Gaul, where he remained for quite a long time. Considerable evidence of his oratorical activity survives: practice speeches (*Abdicatus, Phalaris, Tyrannicida*), artistic descriptions (*De Domo* with the ecphrasis of a state hall, *Hippias* with one of a bath), the typically sophistical praise of the fly in the *Muscae encomium* and the prolaliae, little rhetorical appetizers which were offered before the longer epideixis.[2] Of these the *De electro, Harmonides, Herodotus* and *Scytha* probably belong to this period; this date is also possible for other prolaliae (*Bacchus, De dipsadibus, Zeuxis*), though the *Heracles*, which justified Lucian's renewed sophistical activity, shows that he wrote this sort of thing also in his old age.

His restless mind, which was always ready to take the opposite view, could not find lasting satisfaction in the sophist's occupation. In his *Bis Accusatus* (Δίς κατηγορούμενος) he had to defend himself, on the Acropolis of Athens against Rhetoric, which he gave up, according to his own indication (32) at the age of about forty. Later, in the *Rhetorum praeceptor* (Ῥητόρων διδάσκαλος) he poured all his ridicule over a trade which made impudent trickery a successful business. Stylistic pomposity is the butt of the *Pseudosophista*, which is akin to earlier mentioned writings against an exaggerated Atticism.

In the passage referred to above of his *Bis Accusatus*, which is important for its biographical details, he mentions his connections with the Academy or the Lyceum. It has been assumed that this denotes the beginning of a philosophical period and attempts have been made to utilize especially the *Nigrinus* to prove such a development. This difficult dialogue depicts Lucian visiting the Platonic

---

[1] Shown by DELZ (*v. inf.*).

[2] K. MRAS, 'Die προλαλιά bei den griech. Schriftstellern'. *Wien. Stud.* 64, 1949, 71, who discusses this form in Lucian, Apuleius, Dion of Prusa, Himerius and Choricius, singling out the formal affinity of the first two authors mentioned; cf. id., 'Apuleius' Florida im Rahmen ähnlicher Lit.'. *Anz. Österr. Akad. Phil.-hist. Kl.* 1949, 205.

Nigrinus in Rome. The story is put in the framework of the dialogue, preceded by a dedicatory epistle to the philosopher. It has been conjectured that the latter's lecture has been abbreviated and the dialogue form added later, though there is little to support this. On the other hand, it may be possible for the following reasons. In the first place there is a tendency to contrast in Nigrinus' speech an ideal Athens with the vain emptiness of Rome;[1] and secondly there is the fact that Nigrinus – the name is probably not a pseudonym – made an impression on Lucian. But this was not sufficient to make a philosopher of him, and he never was one. Modern scholarship[2] has rejected the image of a Lucian who passed through profound changes. Of course this vivacious, if always superficial, man also had dealings with philosophy. Cynics and Epicureans offered much to his scepticism, others like the Stoics repelled him, but he never came to an understanding with any of them.

The effect of Cynical popular philosophy on Lucian was much greater. He had already written dialogues before Menippus became his model. He even felt that the invention of satirical talks, in which elements of the Socratic dialogue and of comedy were utilized, was his special achievement (*Prom. in verbis, Bis acc., Bacchus, Zeuxis*). The *Dialogues of the Gods* (Θεῶν διάλογοι) belong to this early group of dialogue writing; the *Prometheus* is added to these, and they were carried on in the *Dialogues of the Gods of the Sea* (Ἐνάλιοι διάλογοι). In all of these he played an ironically naïve game with themes which classical poetry provided in abundance, without allowing the destructive trend to become evident. To Lucian the myths were no more real than they had been to the Hellenistic poets. But it is possible to observe a characteristic difference in subject matter. While the Hellenistic writers prefer to ferret out little-known local legends in order to indulge in their erudite sport, Lucian remains on the wide road of what every one knows. The *Dialogues of the Hetaerae* (Ἑταιρικοὶ διάλογοι) drew largely on comedy themes; the *Timon* with its story of riches regained and the warding off of parasites owes a great deal to comedy, but anticipates the dialogues which Lucian wrote under the influence of the popular philosophical diatribe of Menippus of Gadara[3] (*v.* p. 670). In this the sceptic and scoffer, the enemy of uncritical acceptance of tradition, has found the tool which suits him. In *Bis accus.* the personified dialogue itself states how the changes to which Lucian subjected it found their perfection in the form of Menippus. The dialogues of the years 161 to 165 show how much more cutting and nimble Lucian had become.

His rationalism aims its sharpest darts at religion. In the *Icaromenippus* the Cynic flies to Heaven to rise above the confusion of opinions; the *Iuppiter confutatus* (Ζεὺς ἐλεγχόμενος) shows the highest god in his doubtful position with regard to fate; the *Iuppiter tragoedus* (Ζεὺς τραγῳδός) shows an assembly of agitated gods, because their non-existence is to be proved in an Epicurean-Stoic

---

[1] Strongly stressed by AUR. PERETTI, *Luciano, un intellettuale greco contra Roma*. Florence 1946. Bibl. on p. 147; also CASTER, *Luc.* (*v. inf.*), 374. A. QUACQUARELLI, *La retorica antica al bivio*. Rome 1956.

[2] Esp. CASTER, *Luc.* (*v. inf.*).　　　[3] Details given in HELM's book mentioned inf.

debate; and in the *Deorum concilium* (Θεῶν ἐκκλησία) Momus complains of the influx of new gods. A good while later Lucian continued mockery of this kind in the *Saturnalia*. To what extent he depended in all this on literary influences is demonstrated by the observation that his attacks did not concern so much phenomena of his time, like astrology, belief in demons or the new mysticism, but rather the traditional picture of religion presented by poetry.

Such literature takes a specifically Cynic turn, when the impudent sport with the myths contrasts an insight into the happiness of those without desires with the folly and absurdity of the rich. This is the final wisdom which in the *Menippus* (M. ἢ Νεκυομαντεία) the significantly chosen title-figure learns upon going down into the underworld. *Cataplus, Charon, Dialogues of the Dead* (Νεκρικοὶ διάλογοι) and the *Gallus* (Ὄνειρος ἢ ἀλεκτρυών) move in the same sphere; in the *Navigium* (Πλοῖον ἢ εὐχαί), whose date is somewhat later, Lucian laughs at the folly of human wishes. The bitter scorn with which the figures in the underworld describe the fates of the rich and the powerful lets us hear the voices of the famished and suppressed who created the prosperity of the time without sharing in it.

Philosophy also gets its turn, as in the frequently mentioned *Bis accusatus*, in the *Convivium* ((Συμπόσιον ἢ Λαπίθαι) with its caning of philosophers, in the *Vitarum auctio* (Βίων πρᾶσις) with its auction of philosophical ways of life. A small piece of palinode is contained in the *Piscator* (Ἁλιεὺς ἢ ἀναβιοῦντες), in which Lucian defends himself against the degenerated progeny of the great philosophers. The *Fugitivi* (Δραπέται) also pursues this line of thought. In the *Philopseudes*[1] Lucian very maliciously made the philosophers themselves narrate the most fabulous ghost stories, among them the Sorcerer's Apprentice.

We add the *Toxaris* from among the dialogues without Menippean characteristics, because it offers, like the *Philopseudes*, a cycle of stories. Several of these dialogues introduce the writer under the Hellenized name of Lycinus. The most important among them is the *Hermotimus*, which rejects all dogmatic philosophy, the Stoa first of all, under the banner of scepticism, not with any scholarly profundity, but with great earnestness. The *Eunuchus* moves along the same lines: Lycinus depicts the struggle over the chair of philosophy of Athens (176) in all its deplorable details. In two dialogues (Εἰκόνες. Ὑπὲρ τῶν εἰκόνων) full of flattery for Pantheia, the mistress of the emperor Verus, Lucian confesses that he did not act much better himself. Of the Lycinus dialogues the *De Saltatione* (Περὶ ὀρχήσεως), at one time wrongly declared spurious, is the most interesting from a cultural-historical point of view.

Although Lucian had warned a certain Timocles earnestly against the life of a dependent court tutor in a letter *De mercede conductis* (Περὶ τῶν ἐπὶ μισθῶν συνόντων), he had to submit to such an existence himself in his old age, when he accepted a bread-and-butter post in Egypt.[2] His *Apology* justifies this step. Some more work of importance is produced in the later period of his literary activity, the dialogue making way for the form of the letter. The treatise *De*

---

[1] J. SCHWARTZ, *Phil. et de Morte Peregrini*. Paris 1951 (with comm.).
[2] Probably the one of secretary *a cognitionibus*; cf. CASTER, *Luc.* (*v. inf.*), 369, 11.

historia conscribenda (Πῶς δεῖ ἱστορίαν συγγράφειν),[1] written as a letter, turns against historiography as it was cultivated at the time of the second Parthian war. In the manner of Hellenistic argumentation it defined the aim and boundaries of the genre. The two books of the *Verae Historiae* ('Αληθῆ διηγήματα) form the incidental music to it, amusingly parodying the fantasy of the romances of adventure. Also in the form of letters are two writings in which Lucian continues his battle against the irrational, but now with reference to his own time. *De morte Peregrini* (Περὶ τῆς τοῦ Περεγρίνου τελευτῆς)[2] describes the theatrical suicide by burning of the fanatic Peregrinus Proteus in Olympia (165 or 167), the *Alexander* ('A. ἢ ψευδόμαντις)[3] the life and work of the fake prophet and founder of a cult Alexander of Abunotichus, the complete counterpart of Philostratus' miracle-believing *Life of Apollonius*. The work implies the death of Marcus Aurelius (180); it is unknown how long after Lucian died.

Lucian read widely and learnt a great deal in the school of rhetoric, but he did not have the gift of making the fruits of his learning his own property. On the other hand the opinion of modern scholars who would deprive him almost completely of imagination, goes a great deal too far. The *mise en scène* and composition of his works plead for the author. To what extent he did indeed depend on literature was already emphasized in connection with his attitude to the myths and religion.

An observation about the circumstances and background in which Lucian cast most of his works must be added here.[4] In this respect he is as much an Atticist as in his language, but it is obvious that his knowledge of the Attic world does not go beyond some particulars derived from literature, and does not penetrate any deeper. At times he mixes in some contemporary details and then it is hardly possible to decide whether he does so unconsciously or is playing an ironic game. In the repetition of words and phrases, too, he betrays himself as a hack who battens on tradition and is skilful at utilizing it.

Here we insert Artemidorus of Daldis in Lydia as an Atticist of a special kind, of whom we have a *Book of Dreams* ('Ονειροκριτικόν, 5 books).[5] He was probably a Stoic, and so he was permitted to make the belief in dreams into a system and to illustrate it with examples.

The industrious cultivation of sophistical show-speeches, together with training in rhetoric, which was compulsory for a higher career, are unthinkable without an abundant theoretical literature, of whose volume the surviving information and books give evidence.[6] In the beginning of this section mention

---

[1] G. AVENARIUS, *Lukians Schrift zur Geschichtsschreibung*. Diss. Frankfurt 1954, published Meisenheim a. Glan 1956, with ext. bibl.

[2] *v.* p. 841, n. 1.

[3] M. CASTER, *Etudes sur Al. ou le faux prophète de L.* Paris 1938 (with text and transl.).

[4] *v.* DELZ in the Diss. mentioned below.

[5] R. HERCHER, Leipz. 1864. Repr. in prep. by Olms/Hildesheim.

[6] R. VOLKMANN, *Die Rhetorik der Griechen und Römer*. 2nd ed. Leipz. 1885 (3rd ed. 1901) has not yet been superseded. Cf. also p. 829, n. 1. G. A. KENNEDY, 'The Earliest Rhetorical Handbooks'. *Am. Journ. Phil.* 80, 1959, 169. In KROLL, *RE* S 7, 1940, 1132, 42 an instructive list of occasions for oratorical epideixis.

was made of the controversy between Apollodorus of Pergamum and Theodorus of Gadara and its continued effect on their pupils. A brief sketch was also given of school exercises in rhetoric. The oldest, and at the same time most important, collection of such *Progymnasmata* which we possess is the one of Aelius Theon of Alexandria,[1] who probably lived in the later first century A.D. Its influence lasted well into the Byzantine era.

During the empire the most important author in the field of rhetorical theory was Hermogenes of Tarsus.[2] Born in 160 he shone originally as an oratorical prodigy, but when grown into manhood he turned his back upon this fashionable business to prove himself to be a theoretician of intelligence and good taste· He also wrote *Progymnasmata*. His main achievements, however, are the renewed formulation of Hermagoras' status doctrine (*v. p.* 789 f.) in the treatise Περὶ στάσεων, and the systematic treatment of the forms and medium of speech in the two volumes of his *Doctrine of Style* (Περὶ ἰδεῶν). It is entirely based on an analysis of classical models, especially Demosthenes, so that it would be permissible to speak of a rhetorical Atticism. Some similarity with the *Rhetorical Techne*[3] (*v. p.* 836), wrongly attributed to Aristides, proves that Hermogenes climbed up over his predecessors' shoulders, since this work appeared before his, although it was not simply his source. Other works by this author are *On the Finding of Subject Matter* (Περὶ εὑρέσεως, 4 τόμοι) and *On Aids for a Vigorous Style* (Περὶ μεθόδου δεινότητος). A section of the tradition ascribes to him *Progymnasmata*, but they have now been correctly athetized. Hermogenes' influence grew gradually, and became canonical in late antiquity. In the fourth century Libanius' pupil Aphthonius of Antiochea[4] successfully recast Hermogenes' system in his *Progymnasmata*, which partly supplanted its model and had a strong influence on the Byzantines. The *Commentaries on Hermogenes*[5] form a literature apart reaching from late antiquity into Byzantine rhetoric.

The unhappy third century was still quite fertile in the field of rhetoric, if fertile is the right word for it. The Anonymus Seguerianus (Τέχνη τοῦ πολιτικοῦ λόγου)[6] is important for the discussion of analogy and anomaly in rhetoric. The

---

[1] L. SPENGEL, *Rhet. gr.* 2. Leipz. 1854, 59. In the early Middle Ages THEON's *Progymnasmata* were read in Armenia. Edition of an Armenian translation with the Greek original by JA. A. MANANDJAN, *Eriwan* 1938. Information about the manuscripts in *Wyestnik Matenadarana* 3. Eriwan, Ac. of Sc. of the Arm. SSR 1956, 451. ITALO LANA, *I 'Progimnasmi' di Elio Teone 1. La storia del testo.* Turin 1959. A second volume will be devoted to the Armenian translation, which contains all the progymnasmata not occurring in the Greek tradition, except the last.

[2] H. RABE, *Rhet. gr.* 6. Leipz. 1913; cf. KROLL (*v. p.* 842, n. 6), 1127. 1135. W. MADYDA, 'Über die Voraussetzungen der hermogenischen Stillehre'. *Aus d. altertumswiss. Arbeit Volkspolens. D. Ak. Wiss. Berl. Sekt. f. Altertumswiss.* 13, 1959, 44.

[3] W. SCHMID, *Rhet. gr.* 5. Leipz. 1926.

[4] H. RABE, *Rhet. gr.* 10. Leipz. 1926. Id., *Jo. Sardianus, Commentarius in Aphth. progymn. Rhet. gr.* 15. Leipz. 1928.

[5] CHR. WALTZ, *Rhet. gr.,* 9 vols. Stuttg. 1832–36 is still the main source for the texts; Syrianus edited by H. RABE, Leipz. 1892/93. Surveys in CHRIST-SCHMID, *Gesch. d. gr. Lit.* 2nd part/2, 6th ed. Munich 1924, 935 and KROLL (*v. p.* 842, n. 6) 1137.

[6] Text in L. SPENGEL–C. HAMMER, *Rhet. gr.* 1. Leipz. 1894, 352.

tractates of Menander of Laodicea (Περὶ ἐπιδεικτικῶν)[1] and the earlier-mentioned pseudo-Dionysian *Techne* (p. 831) give rules for the various genres of oratory. Cassius Longinus, philologist, orator and philosophically interested anti-Roman counsellor of Zenobia of Palmyra and victim of her fall, is fairly clearly outlined as a person; apart from a letter in Porphyry's *Life of Plotinus* only some fragments survive of his commentary on the metrical treatise of Hephaestion and of his *Rhetoric*.[2] Another figure of the third century is Apsines of Gadara with his *Techne*[3] which has been preserved in a revised form.

Aelius Aristides

The tradition seems to point to old editions in groups. As regards the best manuscript, the Laurentianus 60, 3 (written in 917) B. KEIL found the first half in the Parisinus 2951 in 1887. Editions: W. DINDORF, 3 vols. Leipz. 1829 (scholia in the 3rd vol.); only partly superseded by B. KEIL, 2 vols. Berl. 1898; repr. 1958 (17-53 with new enumeration). The spurious *Rhetorica*: W. SCHMID, Leipz. 1926. F. W. LENZ, *The Aristeides Prolegomena*. Leiden 1959. A number of tractates about the author's life and work which so far had received little attention. – Papers: A. BOULANGER, *Ael. Ar. et la sophistique dans la province d'Asie au IIe siècle de notre ère*. Paris 1923. U. V. WILAMOWITZ, 'Der Rhetor Ar.'. *Sitzb. Berl. Ak. Phil.-hist. Kl.* 30, 1925, 333. C. A. DE LEEUW, *Ael. Ar. als bron voor de kennis van zijn tijd*. Amsterdam 1939.

The Philostrati

The tradition, which varies from work to work, in the editions of K. L. KAYSER, 2 vols. Zürich 1844-53, then Leipz. 1870-71. Special editions; *Gymn.*: J. JÜTHNER, Leipz. 1909 (with comm. and verbal index). V. NOCELLI, *La ginnastica*. Trad. e comm. Naples 1955. *Icones*: Seminariorum Vindob. sodales, Leipz. 1893 (with important indices). The later *Icones*: C. SCHENKEL and E. REISCH, Leipz. 1902 (with add. of the 14 descriptions of statues by Callistratus of the 4th century A.D.). In the *Loeb Class. Lib.* (with Engl. transl.): *Vit. Ap.*: F. C. CONYBEARE, 2 vols. 1912-17. *Vit. Soph.* (with Eunapius): W. C. WRIGHT, 1922; repr. 1952. The older and later *Icones* (with Callistratus): A. FAIRBANKS, 1931. The *Letters* (with Alciphron and Aelian): A. R. BENNER and F. H. FOBES, 1949. – The best monograph is the article by F. SOLMSEN, *RE* 20, 1941, 124. On the language W. SCHMID, *v.* p. 832 n. 1.

Lucian

The following writings, not mentioned before, complete the list of works: *Adversus indoctum; Anacharsis; De calumnia; Demonax; Dissertatio cum*

---

[1] L. SPENGEL, *Rhet. gr.* 3. Leipz. 1856, 331. It is not certain, however, which of the two tractates is Menander's. C. BURSIAN, *Der Rhetor Menander und seine Schriften. Abh. Bayer. Ak. I. Cl.* 16/3, 1882 (with text) ascribes the Διαιρέσεις τῶν ἐπιδεικτικῶν to Menander, the tractate Περὶ ἐπιδεικτικῶν to an anonymous.

[2] L. SPENGEL–C. HAMMER, *Rhet. gr.* 1. Leipz. 1894, 179.

[3] L. SPENGEL–C. HAMMER (*v. sup.*), 217; cf. KROLL (*v.* p. 842, n. 6), 1123.

Hesiodo; Ludicium vocalium; Pro lapsu inter salutandum; De luctu; De sacrificiis.
Much spurious material has found its way into the tradition, among it two
works which claim special interest. *De Syria dea* deals with the worship of
Atargatis in Syrian Hierapolis, in the Ionian dialect and in the manner of
Herodotus. Those who do not try to read parody and irony between the lines at
all costs, as partly done again by Bompaire (*v. infra*) must deny that this work of
religious-historical importance is Lucian's, as argued recently by J. DELZ, *Gnom.*
32, 1960, 761. The same holds good for linguistical reasons with regard to the
Lucius (Λούκιος ἢ ὄνος), in spite of several attempts to rescue it. The amusing
tale of the metamorphosis into an ass of a precocious young man is an excerpt of
the lost *Metamorphoses* of Lucius of Patrae, from which Apuleius adapted his
Golden Ass. On the relationship of the versions A. LESKY, 'Apuleius von Madaura
und Lukios von Patrai'. *Herm.* 76, 1941, 43, with a survey of the investigations;
Q. CATAUDELLA, *La novella greca.* Naples n.d.152. Further spurious works, for
which we follow Helm: *Amores; De astrologia; Charidemus; Cynicus; Demosthenis
encomium; Halcyon; Longaevi; Nero* (*v.* on Philostratus); *Ocypus; De parasito;
Patriae encomium* (athetesis uncertain); *Philopatris; Tragoedopodagra.* The epigrams
are also doubtful. – K. MRAS has done fundamental work for the tradition: *Die
Überlieferung Lukians. Sitzb. Akad. Wien. Phil.-hist. Kl.* 167/7, 1911. He traces
back the transmission to an ancient collective edition and a selection of the most
popular works. – Editions: Complete only C. JACOBITZ, 4 vols. (with verbal
index), Leipz. 1836–41, ed. min. 1871–74. The editions of F. FRITSCHE, 3 vols.
Rostock 1860–82, and J. SOMMERBRODT, 3 vols. Berl. 1886–99 remained
unfinished. F. N. NILEN only made a start: Fasc. 1/2, Leipz. 1906–23. Special
editions in the notes, in add. K. MRAS, *Dial. Mer.* Berl. 1930. Id., *Die Hauptwerke
des L. griechisch und deutsch.* Munich 1954 (with crit. notes; *v.* p. 539 for brief
history of the text and survey of the manuscripts). In the *Loeb Class. Libr.*:
A. M. HARMON, 8 vols. 1913 ff.; repr. until 1959 (with Engl. transl.). – *Lukian.
Parodien und Burlesken. Auf Grund der Wielandschen Übertragung* by E. ERMATINGER
and K. HÖNN. Zürich 1948 (*Bibl. d. Alten Welt*). – Scholia: H. RABE, Leipz. 1906.
– Still important R. HELM, *L. und Menipp.* Leipz. 1906. Also by him the *RE*
article 13, 1927, 1725. M. CASTER, *L. et la pensée religieuse de son temps.* Paris 1936.
AUR. PERETTI, *Luciano, Un intellettuale greco contra Roma.* Florence 1946. J. DELZ,
L.s Kenntnis der athenischen Antiquitätcn. Diss. Basel 1950. J. BOMPAIRE. *Lucien
écrivain. Imitation et création.* Bibl. Éc. Franc. d'Ath. et de Rome. 190. 1958. –
Later influence: A. V. COLL, *Luciano de Samosata en España* (1500–1700). La
Laguna 1959.

3 HISTORIOGRAPHERS AND PERIEGETES

Even though Dionysius of Halicarnassus and Diodorus were approximately
contemporary and their historical writings, if they can be given this title, consisted of compilations, we draw a firm distinction between them. While Diodorus
was mainly concerned with the collection of material, which he used without
much pretence of literary style, the literary critic and pace-maker of Atticism
wanted to put his principles into practice in his historical work. When he wrote

his *Ancient Roman History* ('Ρωμαϊκὴ ἀρχαιολογία)[1] and published it in 7 B.C., he had hardly any misgivings about the difficulty of completing Polybius with a historical study of Rome's early period from 264 B.C. upward. Where today we often still grope in the dark, he trusted the Roman annalists without second thought.[2] Historical criticism was foreign to him; his boundless admiration for Roman *virtus* made him erect a monument for the Romans which even his compatriots, so often otherwise inclined, were supposed to admire. Its rhetorical configuration is evident, especially in the many long speeches. Occasional attempts at dramatization betray Hellenistic tradition. The style, which borrows freely from the old historians and orators, attempts to achieve a classicist finish with Attic colouring.[3] Of the twenty books, the first ten are completely preserved, the eleventh in fragments. For the remainder we depend on Constantine Porphyrogennetus' collection of excerpts and a Milan epitome.[4]

More than a century and a half later another Greek undertook a history of Rome, this time the whole of it. Appian of Alexandria worked in Rome as a lawyer in Hadrian's era; Fronto, the champion of Latin archaism, was his friend; he was appointed procurator, probably in Egypt. He wrote a Roman *History* ('Ρωμαϊκά)[5] in his old age, probably finishing it in 160.[6] He differs from Dionysius in many respects. The style of his compact work is considerably less pretentious, while for the contents he could lay claim to an original, not badly contrived, arrangement, although it lacked a personal conception and critical penetration. Of the twenty-four books, which were still known to Photius, the first three dealt with the early history: 1. era of kings, 2. 'Ιταλική, 3. Σαυνιτική. Next follows the separate discussion of the individual peoples and countries as they had come to terms with Rome in the course of history: 4. Κελτική, 5. Σικελικὴ καὶ νησιωτική, 6. 'Ιβηρική, 7. 'Αννιβαϊκή, 8. Λιβυκή, 9. Μακεδονικὴ καὶ 'Ιλλυρική, 10. 'Ελληνικὴ καὶ 'Ιωνική, 11. Συριακή,[7] 12. Μιθριδάτειος. Then the five books on the civil war were inserted (13-17 'Εμφυλίων), which had a prooemium of their own, followed by Egypt (18-21 Αἰγυπτιακῶν), and leading up to the author's own time, 22. 'Εκατονταετία, 23. Δακική, 24. 'Αράβιος.

[1] C. JACOBY, 5 vols. Leipz. 1885–1925. With Engl. transl. E. CARY, 7 vols. *Loeb Class. Libr.* 1937–50. The fragments of a preliminary work Περὶ χρόνων F Gr Hist 251.

[2] Still important: E. SCHWARTZ *RE* 5, 1903, 934; now *Griech. Geschichtsschreiber.* Leipz. 1957, 319. E. GAIDA, *Die Schlachtschilderungen in den Ant. Rom. des D. v. H.* Breslau 1934. A. KLOTZ, 'Zu den Quellen der Arch. des D.v.H.'. *Rhein. Mus.* 87, 1938; id., *Livius und seine Vorgänger* III. Leipz. 1941.

[3] S. EK, *Herodotismen in der Arch. des D.v.H.* Lund 1942; id. 'Eine Stiltendenz in der röm. Arch. des D.v.H.'. *Eranos* 43, 1945, 198.

[4] Ambros. Q 13 sup. ANGELO MAI, *Romanorum antiquitatum pars hactenus desiderata.* Milan 1816.

[5] Teubner-edition: I. P. VIERECK–A. G. ROOS, 1939. II. L. MENDELSOHN–P. VIERECK, 1905. A papyrus no. 66 P. with Engl. transl. H. WHITE, 4 vols. *Loeb Class. Libr.* 1912/13; repr. up to 1955. E. GABBA, *App. bellorum civilium l. 1. Bibl. di studi sup.* 37. Florence 1958.

[6] In the prooemium Appian calls himself procurator of the emperors Marcus Aurelius and Verus, i.e. the years 161-169.

[7] The Παρθική appended here in the manuscripts is a Byzantine addition, due to Appian's promise (11, 51. 14, 18. 17, 65) of a Parthian history.

Books 6-8 survive complete, also the second part of 9 and 11-17, among them consequently all the five books on the civil war. In addition there is the introduction to Book 4, a piece about Macedon from 9 and various fragments. The question of sources[1] is particularly difficult. The desire to quote specific names has tempted many to make uncertain hypotheses. This much has been demonstrated, at any rate, that Appian did not pledge himself to only one source in the various parts of his work. He may not be counted among the important historians, but his *modus operandi* seems to have been less primitive than has sometimes been believed.

Even in this time with its retrospection and narrow linguistic purism, notable work could be done whenever a capable mind and clear thinking did not allow the fashions of style to interfere. Flavius Arrianus of Nicomedea in Bithynia[2] (*c.* 95-175) sought, like others, a model in a past which was 500 years away. He wished to be a new Xenophon, as he himself stresses several times.[3] Like his model he flirted with philosophy as a young man when he heard Epictetus in Nicopolis and to this circumstance we owe all that we know of this philosopher's doctrine. When after Epictetus' death unqualified writers published the notes which Arrian had made during his Stoic studies, he decided to publish them himself. Of the eight books of *Diatribes* four survive, as well as the *Enchiridion*, the summary of Epictetus' ethics dedicated to a certain Messalinus. Photius mentions twelve books of *Homilies*, which should perhaps be understood to mean that in addition to the eight books of *Diatribes* there were four books of *Apomnemoneumata* and that together they formed a corpus of twelve books. In the surviving books Epictetus' colloquial style has been preserved. They represent a valuable tradition, but not a literary achievement of Arrian's.

This Bithynian of a distinguished family, on whom his native city had conferred the life priesthood of Demeter and Core, entered upon a splendid career when the great friend of the Greeks was on the imperial throne. He rose to the dignity of consul suffectus, and administered the province of Cappadocia as legatus Augusti pro praetore. He probably assumed office in 130, and there is inscriptional evidence for his tenure in 137. He travelled extensively on imperial business, came to know Noricum and Pannonia and saw himself faced with such heavy tasks as defending his province against the Alani. His earliest known work,

---

[1] Still important, E. SCHWARTZ, *RE* 2, 1895, 216 = *Griech. Geschichtsschreiber*, Leipz. 1957, 361, who assumed Latin sources for the whole work, but warned against rashly assigning authors. More recent works in *Fifty Years of Classical Scholarship*, Oxf. 1954, 190, n. 119 f. P. MELONI, *Il valore storico e le fonti di libro maced. di A. Ann. fac. lett. Cagliari* 23, Rome 1955. E. GABBA, *A. e la storia delle guerre civ.* Florence 1956. Against an overestimation of Asinius Pollio as a source for this section M. GELZER, *Gnom.* 30, 1958, 216.

[2] A. G. ROOS, *Flavii Arriani quae exstant omnia.* 2 vols. Leipz. 1907/28 (without Epictetus, for whose editions v. bibl. on philosophy). Bilingual: P. CHANTRAINE, *L'Inde.* 2nd ed. Coll. des Un. d. Fr. 1952. E. ILIFF ROBSON, *Anab. and Ind.* 2 vols. *Loeb Class. Lib.* 1929/33. *F Gr Hist* 156. – Pap. Soc. It. 12, no. 1284 proved by K. LATTE, *Nachr. Akad. Gött. Phil.-hist. Kl.* 1950, 23, to be a fragment of Τὰ μετ' ᾿Αλέξανδρον. Best discussion in the *RE* article by E. SCHWARTZ 2, 1895, 1230 = *Griech. Geschichtsschreiber*, Leipz. 1957, 130.

[3] *Peripl.* 1, 1. 12, 5. 25, 1. *Tact.* 29, 8. *Cyneg.* 1, 4.

the *Periplus Ponti Euxini*,[1] which he dedicated to the emperor Hadrian in 130/31 is connected with his office. It is a combination of a report about an official voyage from Trebizond to Dioscuras in the eastern corner of the Pontus, which he had previously written in Latin, with two other passages, the whole forming the story of a circumnavigation of the Black Sea coast. His source was Menippus of Pergamum. During his governorship he also published his *Tactical Manual* (Τέχνη τακτική) in the year 136. Here, too, analysts have detected material from an official report on infantry tactics combined with a literary tradition which had a precedent in Aelian's *Tactics* and goes back to Asclepiodotus (*v.* p. 773 n. 3). The *Alanice* probably belongs to this group of writings, since Arrian had to protect his province from an attack by the Alani in his capacity as governor. The Florentine codex of tacticians (Laur. 55, 4) has preserved a section of it (῎Εκταξις κατ᾽ ᾽Αλανῶν).

Even before Hadrian's death (138) Arrian had left Cappadocia. We next find him in Athens in completely different circumstances. He was granted citizenship in the deme Paeana, was eponymous archon in 147–48 and later prytanis of the Pandionis.[2] We do not know to what extent these changes were due to his own wish or to political conditions. But this much is clear that Athens, the ancient cultural centre turned into a museum, meant in a sense a fulfilment for Arrian. Here he could devote himself to his literary labours with all his powers. The surviving *Cynegeticus* reveals by its title that he followed Xenophon. But his ambition went further; he now schooled his style with Herodotus and Thucydides, setting himself the object of becoming the historian of important epochs as well as of his own native country. Presumably the lost biographies of Timoleon and Dion, to which curiously one of the highwayman Tilloborus[3] is added, were preliminary exercises to his more ambitious undertakings. To this group of historical works of the first Athenian years belongs the work which has passed on Arrian's name through the ages, the *Anabasis of Alexander*. The title implies his reverence for Xenophon. The division into seven books no doubt had the same purpose, but the contents show that he is at least the equal of his model in historical ability. He was happy in his choice of sources (above all Ptolemy, also Aristobulus). He managed to separate the vulgate from the serious tradition and his was the great merit of having preserved the image of Alexander from being distorted in the fog of fiction. Arrian wrote the *Indice* to complete the *Anabasis*. Here he also succeeded in going to the right sources by consulting Nearchus (p. 578), Megasthenes (p. 771) and Eratosthenes. In this work the imitation of Herodotus was augmented by an imitation of the Ionic dialect. It is the same with the *Bithynica* which related in eight books the history of his native country from the mythical beginnings to the death of Nicomedes Philopator (74 B.C.). The Byzantines still knew this work. The *Parthica* (17

---

[1] Cf. R. GÜNGERICH, *Die Küstenbeschr. i. d. griech. Lit.* Münster 1950, 19. Another *Periplus Ponti Euxini* (*Geogr. Gr. Min.* 1, 402) is a late compilation. The inscription with his governorship DESSAU, *Inscr. Lat. sel.* 2, Berl. 1906, no. 8801.

[2] The inscriptional evidence in SCHWARTZ (*v.* p. 847, n. 1).

[3] On the form of the name L. RADERMACHER, *Anz. Akad. Wien. Phil.-hist. Kl.* 1935, 19; 1936, 8.

books) and the *History of the Successors* (Τὰ μετ᾽ ᾽Αλέξανδρον) are also lost. If we may trust Photius, the work had ten books ending in the middle of the events of 321; it probably remained unfinished.

Arrian also was an Atticist, but with Xenophon's simplicity for a model he avoided any exaggeration; he rejected the ornamentation of rhetorical figures and spoke a language which seems to fit all that we know of him.

A little more than half a century later another Bithynian, who also rose to the highest positions in the empire, became a historian. Cassius Dio Cocceianus[1] (*c.* 155–235) of Nicaea, a relative of Dion of Prusa, had the expectancy of a distinguished career through his father's senatorial rank and function as a governor. Soon after Commodus' accession (180) he came to Rome, entering the Senate during this emperor's reign. Under Pertinax he was made a praetor, under Septimius Severus he served as consul suffectus. In 216 he accompanied Caracalla on his journey to the Orient. Macrinus entrusted him as curator ad corrigendum statum civitatum with the settling of conditions in Pergamum and Smyrna. But he enjoyed the special favour of Severus Alexander, during whose reign (222–35) he administered the proconsulate of Africa as well as the imperial provinces of Dalmatia and Upper Pannonia; in 229 he became consul ordinarius with the emperor as his colleague. But at this point his career ended. The strict discipline which he maintained had made him unpopular with the soldiers and the guard, so that the emperor himself advised him not to spend the period of his second consulate in Rome. He left the city and the public service and withdrew to his native Bithynia, where he passed his last years.

He began his writing in the service of Septimius Severus, on whom, like others, he at first placed great hopes. He wrote of the dreams and signs which resulted in the calling of Septimius to the throne. In doing so he hardly committed a *sacrificium mentis*, since he combined a belief, unburdened with philosophy, in the control of providence with that in omens. He soon followed this up with a treatise on the death of Commodus and the subsequent events, also for the gratification of the emperor. He inserted excerpts from both in his great work.

When we hear of dreams which Cassius Dio believed to confirm him in his calling as a historian (72, 23), we may interpret this as referring to restraints which he had to overcome. To write a history of Rome from its beginnings was a gigantic undertaking, and it is easy to believe Dio's claim that he collected for ten years and wrote for another twelve until he had reached Severus' death (211). He carried his work beyond this date, concluding with his consulate in 229. Finally his *Roman History* grew into eighty books. The structural principle was the annalistical, as presented by a considerable part of his sources. Yet within this he attempts to combine relationships in time and space to the best of his ability. Inevitably there are considerable differences in the presentation of

---

[1] The justly praised edition of PH. U. BOISSEVAIN (5 vols. Berl. 1895–1931, new impr. of the first 4 vols. without alteration in 1954) contains in vol. 4 the *Index Historicus* of H. SMILDA, in vol. 5 the *Index Graecitatis* of M. NAWIJN. In BOISSEVAIN also the history of the transmission. Teubner-edition by J. MELBER, 3 vols. 1890–1928. With Engl. transl. E. CARY, 9 vols. *Loeb Class. Lib.*, 1914–26.

individual parts. A first long section (51 books) extends from Aeneas to Augustus as the founder of the monarchy. In this part especially Dio's conviction operates that the description of detail is incompatible with the dignity of history (ὄγκος τῆς ἱστορίας 72, 18) and its task of stressing the main features. Vividness of narrative was not his strong point generally, but on the other hand he did not reject dramatization altogether, as shown, for instance, in the Vercingetorix-scenes. Harsh Schwartz' judgment may be, but on the whole it must be said that in this part particularly the limits of Dio's powers of presentation are demonstrated. In the description of the empire up to Marcus Aurelius' death the intellectual control over his material was impaired by the fact that the loyal supporter of the monarchy saw it from the outset as a permanent reality and was consequently unable to do justice to the development of the principate. The speech in defence of monarchy which Maecenas delivers in Book 52 is written so much in the spirit of Dio's age that it was thought to be an intentional interpolation of a doctrine.[1] The description becomes, of course, more colourful and direct when Dio deals with contemporary history. He was aware of this and thought it necessary to offer a reason and an apology for it (72, 18).

The problem of sources is particularly difficult in this gigantic work. Even after the exhaustive discussion in the article by E. Schwartz there are many unsolved problems. For the first six centuries of Rome annalistical sources seem to be much in the foreground, from Book 36 onward Livy becomes important; it is difficult to evaluate the importance of Tacitus. Schwartz probably went too far when he wanted to deny the originality of the latter's picture of Tiberius in order to separate Dio from him altogether, although the same features turn up in his description. There is much uncertainty here, and this emphasis on single points must not conceal the multiplicity of the problems of sources.[2]

Of this work, which the Byzantines still possessed for the greater part, Books 36-60, extending from 68 B.C. to A.D. 47 survive, with some gaps in the beginning and end. There are also some fragments of Books 79 and 80 on twelve sheets of parchment of Vat. Gr. 1288. Some compensation for the lost material is provided by the Byzantines who utilized Dio. In the eleventh century Ioannes Xiphilinus recast Books 36-80 into a history arranged according to emperors. For Antoninus Pius and the early period of Marcus Aurelius he already found a gap present, according to his own indication (70, 2). Later, in the twelfth century, Ioannes Zonaras excerpted Dio 1-21 and 44-80 for Books 7-12 of his Ἐπιτομὴ ἱστοριῶν. Of other aids for the reconstruction special mention must be made again of the collection of excerpts by Constantine Porphyrogennetus.

Dio Cassius' style[3] should be re-examined, especially to ascertain how far varieties are due to the influence of his sources. His aim was an Atticist archaism, his models were Thucydides and Demosthenes, mutually very different authors.

[1] M. HAMMOND, 'The Significance of the Speech of Maecenas in Dio Cassius Book LII'. *Trans. Am. Phil. Ass.* 63, 1923, 88.
[2] Some bibl. in *Fifty Years* (*v.* p. 847, n. 1), 191, n. 122 f.
[3] Bibl. in *Fifty Years* (*v.* p. 847, n. 1), 191, n. 121.

He deviates from Arrian in using rhetorical artifices, also sound-figures, and especially in the frequent and long speeches.

Herodian,[1] a Hellenized Syrian, is a good deal below the level of Dio Cassius as a historian; he was about twenty years younger than his predecessor. He was also a public servant, though not in the high offices of Dio Cassius. His *History of the Emperors after Marcus* (Τῆς μετὰ Μάρκον βασιλείας ἱστορίαι, 8 books) goes up to the accession of Gordian III (238). The narrative of this gloomy period, riddled with flat gnomae, opens up no useful aspects and is only valuable as a source. The language is meant to be Attic Greek, but is only partly successful; it betrays the influence of the sophistical rhetoric of the time.

Finding an Attic author among the historiographers of the empire is nothing short of a miracle. P. Herennius Dexippus (*F Gr Hist* 100), who was born *circa* 210 and lived until the time of Aurelian, is surrounded by the splendour of the ancient Attic tradition. A member of the family of the Ceryces, he was the incumbent of a high priesthood (ἱερεὺς παναγής), basileus, eponymous archon and played a meritorious part in the great festivals (T4=IG II/III² 3669). But he also proved himself in the face of danger when he repulsed the Heruli from Athens with a quickly collected force in 267.

His main work was the great *Chronicle* (Χρονικὴ ἱστορία, in at least 12 books), which extended from prehistory to 269/270. Here a thread becomes visible which runs from the universal history of Ephorus via works like the *Bibliotheca* of Diodorus finally to the Byzantine universal chronicles in the style of Ioannes Malalas (6th c.) or Ioannes Antiochenus (7th c.).

Dexippus also wrote a *Scythica*, in which he dealt with the invasions of the Germans from 238 up to at least 270. The four books of *History of the Diadochi* (Τὰ μετ' 'Αλέξανδρον) we may fairly certainly consider to be an excerpt of the work of Arrian with the same title.

Dexippus' style was praised by Photius (*F Gr Hist* 100 T 5), sharply condemned by Niebuhr, warmly commended by Norden,[2] censured by Schwartz[3] as obscure and far-fetched, while Jacoby is non-committal. It is obvious that a standard is lacking which will keep our criticism at least free from the grossest subjectivity. It is clear that Dexippus was no mean stylist, that he observed Thucydides as his model,[4] and also that any modern criticism rests on a narrow foundation, as substantially only speeches have been preserved.

Eunapius of Sardes (*circa* 345-420)[5] joined on to Dexippus' chronicle the

---

[1] Edition: K. STAVENHAGEN, Leipz. 1922. A somewhat higher appreciation of the author in F. ALTHEIM, *Lit. u. Gesellsch. im ausgehenden Altert.* 1, 1948, 165. Opposing him, with analysis of the first book E. HOHL, *Kaiser Commodus und Her. Sitzb. Akad. Berl. Kl. f. Gesellschaftswiss.* 1954/1; cf. A. BETZ, *AfdA* 10, 1957, 255.

[2] *Ant. Kunstprosa* 1, 4th impr. Leipz. 1923, 398.

[3] *RE S* 5, 1930, 293 = *Griech. Geschichtsschreiber*, Leipz. 1957, 290. On Dexippus also ALTHEIM (*v. supra*, n. 1), 175.

[4] Cf. J. STEIN, *Dexippus et Herodianus rerum scriptores quatenus Thucydidem secuti sint.* Diss. Bonn 1957.

[5] The historical fragments of Eunapius and those of the subsequent historians in vol. 4 of Müller's old *Fragm. Hist. Gr.* The sophists' biographies: In the Loeb Class. Libr. W. C. WRIGHT (with Philostratus' *Vit. Soph.*) 1922; repr. 1952 (with Engl. transl.). J. GIANGRANDE,

fourteen books of his history ('Υπομνήματα ἱστορικά), which dealt with the period of 270 up to 404. This enemy of Christianity dedicated his work to his friend Oribasius, a medical author and court-physician of Julian. Only some excerpts survive in Photius, in Constantine's collection of excerpts and in Suidas. We have all of the *Lives of the Sophists* (Βίοι Σοφιστῶν), which deals mainly with the Neoplatonists. It is written in an artificial style, but it gives a glimpse of the life and work of orators and philosophers in fourth-century Constantinople and the Greek cities of Asia Minor.

Eunapius' historical work was followed in approximately chronological connection by that of Olympiodorus of Egyptian Thebes, which describes the period of 407 to 425 in twenty-two books and was dedicated to Theodosius II (408–450).[1] The sophist Priscus of Thracian Panion lived under this ruler and a good while after him. Apart from rhetorical exercises he wrote a *Byzantine History* (8 books), which probably extended up to 472. Only fragments survive. The most important of these with the description of the embassy to Attila, in which he participated in 448, occurs in the excerpts of Constantine. The latter and Photius have also preserved fragments of the *Byzantiaca* (7 books) by Malchus, who carried the history on to 480.

The six books of the *New History* (Νέα ἱστορία) of Zosimus,[2] who wrote in the end of the fifth century, have been preserved. They provide a concise survey of the emperors up to Diocletian, and a more extensive presentation of the years 270–410. The work is poor in style and in its utilization of sources, but it is noteworthy because of its trend; its writer explains the decline of Roman power through the renunciation of the faith of their fathers.

In accordance with the pattern of universal history, Hesychius Illustrius of Miletus (*F Gr Hist* 390) went far back, beginning his *Chronicle* with Bel of Babylon and carrying it on to Justinian's reign. Since the latter's capable historian Procopius of Caesarea with his eight surviving books on the wars of his imperial master belongs already in the Byzantine era, we conclude with Hesychius a series which began for us with Hecataeus, another Milesian.

We add here, though with the reservation of quasi-historical, the *Strategemata* (8 books) of the Macedonian Polyaenus.[3] He dedicated his collection of various stratagems in 162 to the emperors Lucius Verus and Marcus Aurelius as a sort of tactical aid; but it is not a soldier who speaks, but an orator who has literally gleaned his material and offered it with a poor attempt at Atticizing. The

Rome 1956, on the basis of a new collation including the important Codex Laur. 86/7 (12th/13th c.) refutes v. LUNDSTRÖM's thesis that Eunapius' *Life of Libanius*, transmitted separately, represents a personal recensio. Id., 'Vermutungen und Bemerkungen zum Text der Vit. Soph. des Eun.' *Rhein. Mus.* 99, 1956, 133; 'Herodianismen bei Eun.'. *Herm.* 84, 1956, 320; 'Caratteri stilistici delle Vit. Soph. di Eun.' *Boll. del Com. per la prepar. di Ed. Naz. dei Class. Gr. e Lat.* N.S. 4, 1956, 59. For all these authors Constantine's excerpts are important; edition by PH. U. BOISSEVAIN, C. DE BOOR, TH. BÜTTNER-WOBST, 4 vols. Berl. 1903–1906.

[1] The fragments, including an excerpt of Photius and a quotation in Zosimus 5, 27, 1, in MÜLLER, *Fragm. Hist. Gr.* 4, 1885, 58.

[2] L. MENDELSSOHN, Leipz. 1887; repr. by Olms/Hildesheim in prep.

[3] J. MELBER, Leipz. 1887.

Strategicus of Onasander,[1] who wrote under Claudian, and the *Tactica* of a certain Aelian,[2] who probably worked under Trajan and largely depends on Asclepiodotus, are not actually technical manuals either. In both cases the author makes a display of knowledge acquired through reading and deals with the subject matter from a scholar's point of view.

Basically the *Strategemata* is a collection of military curiosities, typical of a literature which had become sterile in its traditionalism and was prepared to seize upon the bizarre for stimulation. It is due to the malice of the transmission that we must here insert Phlegon of Tralles, a freedman of Hadrian's (*F Gr Hist* 257). His voluminous chronicle of the *Olympiads* ('Ολυμπιονικῶν καὶ χρόνων συναγωγή, 16 books; there was also an edition in 8 and an epitome in 2 books), extending from the start of the numbering of the Olympiads up to Hadrian's death, is lost. Also lost are his works on Roman topography and festivals as well as a description of Sicily. On the other hand, we have a treatise *On Marvels and Long-Lived People* (Περὶ θαυμασίων καὶ μακροβίων),[3] about ghosts, changes of sex, gigantic men, monsters and other matters of this kind.

A popular literary genre of this epoch was the medley, as whose representative we have already mentioned Favorinus of Arelate (p. 834). Claudius Aelianus (*circa* 172–235)[4] offers an opportunity to become familiar with this form of amusement, obviously a necessity in times without a firm intellectual structure. In Rome this Praenestinian was a pupil of the sophist Pausanias and acquired some ability in writing Attic Greek, of which he was extremely proud.[5] We have the seventeen books of *Animal Stories* (Περὶ ζῴων ἰδιότητος), the result of industrious excerpting and compiling, in which he hardly had recourse to the ancient authors but limited himself mainly to collections. The stoïcizing trend towards demonstrating the wisdom of nature is something like a guiding principle in this accumulation of zoological curiosities. Points of contact with the *Physiologus*[6] show that Aelian draws on some kind of widespread paradoxography. In its most ancient form this collection of marvels from natural history could have been produced in Alexandria in the second century A.D. Later, cast

---

[1] The edition of H. KÖCHLY, Leipz. 1860 has been superseded by W. A. OLDFATHER, *Aeneas Tacticus, Asclepiodotus and Onasander*. London 1923. A. DAIN, *Les Manuscrits d'Onésandros*. Paris 1930. On bibl. of military lit. cf. on Biton, p. 794, n. 1, and M. FUHRMANN, *Das systematische Lehrbuch*. Göttingen 1960, 182, 3.

[2] H. KÖCHLY–W. RÜSTOW, *Griech. Kriegsschriftst.* 2/1. Leipz. 1855. A. DAIN, *Histoire du texte d'Élien le tacticien des origines à la fin du moyen âge*. Paris 1946.

[3] With JACOBY, who gives the text in *F Gr Hist* 257, we assume a work with a double title, but this cannot be considered completely certain.

[4] R. HERCHER, 2 vols. Leipz. 1864/66. With Engl. transl. (with Alciphron's and Philostratus' letters): A. R. BENNER and F. H. FOBES, *Loeb Class. Libr.* 1949. The *Animal Stories* with Engl. transl.: A. F. SCHOLFIELD 3 vols. *Loeb Class. Libr.* 1958/59 (3 in prep.). A catalogue of the animals in Aelian by H. GOSSEN, *Quellen und Stud. z. Gesch. d. Naturwiss. u. d. Medizin.* 4, 1935, 18.

[5] Cf. the conclusion of the animal stories. Philostratus, *Vita Soph.* 2, 31, 1 commends him. His ideal of style was ἀφέλεια, artful simplicity.

[6] Edition: F. SBORDONE, Milan 1936; cf. M. WELLMANN, *Der Physiol. Phil.* Suppl. 22, 1930. O. SEEL, *Der Physiologus.* Transl. and comm. Zürich 1960 (Lebendige Antike).

into a Latin version and provided with Christian symbolism, it largely influenced the world of ideas in the Middle Ages.

The counterpart in the human sphere, as it were, of the *Animal Stories*, are the *Miscellaneous Stories* (Ποικίλη ἱστορία, 14 books), whose first part, however, also deals with matters of nature. The complete version of individual passages in Stobaeus and Suidas shows that what we possess are often excerpts. Twenty *Peasants' Letters*, Atticist in form and content, have also been handed down. Stoicizing treatises (Περὶ προνοίας. Περὶ θείων ἐναργειῶν) are lost.

We follow Aelian up with Athenaeus of Naucratis with his *Sophists' Banquet* (Δειπνοσοφισταί, 15 books),[1] but this juxtaposition should not conceal profound differences. Athenaeus revealed whose intellectual heir he was by the fact that he built up his monstrous collection as a banquet of numerous (29!) learned men with varying backgrounds at the house of the distinguished Roman Larensis, and carried his imitation of Plato so far as to use a conversational framework in the manner of the *Symposium*. The large quantities of antiquarian, grammatical and literary details reveal no views of any profundity, but the material which he pours out unstintingly is of the greatest value. Athenaeus made proper use of the library of Alexandria and has preserved a vast mass of worthwhile knowledge. He deserves praise for his mania for quoting and also for the care which he took in his references. What fragments of comedy he has preserved for us, to mention one aspect only! We would not be prepared to call him a scholar who went to the sources themselves. He mainly dipped into the broad streams of the tradition as represented by such names as Didymus and Tryphon. Nothing is known about his life. The ridiculing of Commodus (XII. 537 f) indicates that the work was published after this emperor's death.

In spite of the difference in subject matter Diogenes Laertius[2] can be added here. In the ten books of his *History of the Philosophers* (Φιλοσόφων βίων καὶ

---

[1] Book 1 to the beginning of 3 only in excerpts. Remarks in the main manuscript (Marcianus A, 10th c., brought from Constantinople by G. AURISPA in 1423) seem to indicate that there was also an edition in 30 books. The opinion that the present Athenaeus with his 15 books is an excerpt from a work of double the size in 30 books, which is also adopted by the Fr. editors, is opposed by G. WISSOWA (GGN 1913, 325), now also by H. ERBSE, Gnom. 29, 1957, 290. ERBSE also defends against the Fr. editors the thesis of Paul Maas that the Athenaeus-epitome should originate from the Marcianus A and from Eustathius. Editions: G. KAIBEL, 3 vols. Leipz. 1887–90 (with important indices). S. P. PEPPINK, 2 vols. Leiden 1936/39. With Engl. transl. C. B. GULICK, 7 vols. *Loeb Class. Libr.* 1933–41. With Fr. transl. A. M. DESROUSSAUX–CH. ASTRUC (books 1–3), *Coll. des Un. d. Fr.* 1956. – LAJOS NYIKOS, *Ath. quo consilio quibusque usus subsidiis dipnosophistarum libros composuerit.* Diss. Basel 1941.

[2] The city of Laerte in Asia Minor mentioned by Steph. Byz.; WILAMOWITZ, *Herm.* 34, 1899, 629 (=Kl. Schr. 4, 1962, 100) temptingly considered a nickname from Διογενὴς Λαερτιάδης. Text still C. G. COBET, Paris 1862. With Engl. transl. R. D. HICKS, 2 vols. *Loeb Class. Libr.* 1950. A. BIEDL, *Zur Textgeschichte des Laertios Diogenes. Das grosse Exzerpt.* Città del Vaticano 1955. P. MORAUX, 'La composition de la "Vie d'Aristote" chez Diog. Laerce'. *Rev. Ét. Gr.* 68, 1955, 124. O. GIGON, 'Das Prooemium des Diog. Laert. Struktur und Probleme.' *Horizonte der Humanitas (Freundesgabe Wili).* 1960, 37–64. G. DONZELLI, 'Per una edizione critica di Diog. Laerzio. I Codici VUDGS'. *Boll. per la Prepar. di Ed. Naz. dei Class. Gr. e Lat.* N.S. 8, 1960, 93. Id., 'I codici PQWCoHIEYJb nella tradizione di Diog. Laerzio'. *Stud. It.* 32, 1960, 156.

δογμάτων συναγωγή)[1] he also passed on a tremendous quantity of excerpts without any intellectual profundity, but he stored up invaluable material. He brought together writings on the succession in the individual schools of philosophy, doxographical works, collections of apophthegms and lists of books. He did not study any sources either, but his work is a visible sample of a voluminous mass of tradition, the remainder of which is lost. He seems to have had a personal affinity to the Sceptics. He also reveals something of his mental attitude by dedicating a whole book (10) to Epicurus, which he otherwise does only on the case of Plato(3). The work probably remained unfinished, for not a few parts convey the impression of formlessly combined excerpts. The nearest date that can be allotted to it is the first decades of the third century before the predominance of Neoplatonism. Diogenes also published a collection of *Epigrams*, the first book of which (Πάμμετρος) related in varying metres the deaths of famous men, except those of the philosophers, which he inserted in his history of the philosophers.

It is easy to understand that an era which produced such literature cultivated particularly the genre of anthology, which was already so popular in the Hellenistic age. Here, too, a great deal of lost material is concealed behind surviving work. In the fifth century Ioannes Stobaeus,[2] called after Stoboe in Macedon, collected several passages from numerous poets and prose authors in his *Anthology*. Here, too, it must be assumed that the compiler used collections which were already available. The arrangement of the four books of the *Anthology* is uniform. In each case the indication of the theme is followed by the passages from the poets and then by those from the prose-writers. A secondary division is responsible for the fact that in the Middle Ages the work was transmitted in two separate parts of two books each (*Eclogae* and *Florilegium*).

The only completely surviving work of periegetic literature, the Περιήγησις τῆς Ἑλλάδος by Pausanias (10 books)[3] was written in the second century. As far as we know it was the last of its kind. The writer remains obscure for us. Neither his identification with the historian Pausanias of Damascus nor with the sophist of Cappadocia, whom we know from Philostratus' *Lives of the Sophists*

---

[1] Other versions of the title in E. SCHWARTZ, *RE* 5, 1903, 738 (= *Griech. Geschichtsschreiber.* Leipz. 1957, 453), which can also be consulted on the problem of the sources.

[2] Edition: C. WACHSMUTH–O. HENSE, 5 vols. with appendix Leipz. 1884–1923; 2nd unalt. ed. Berl. 1958.

[3] Text: F. SPIRO, 3 vols. Leipz. 1903, repr. 1959. For the recension the edition of J. H. CHR. SCHUBART and CHR. WALTZ, Leipz. 1838/39 is still useful. Fundamental for criticism and exegesis, though obsolete in many details: H. HITZIG and H. BLÜMNER, 3 vols. in 6 parts, Leipz. 1896–1910. Bilingual: W. H. S. JONES and H. A. ORMEROD, 5 vols. *Loeb Class. Libr.* 1931–35. Abundant material (much of an ethnographical nature) in the commentary on J. G. FRAZER's transl., 6 vols. Lond. 1898; the 2nd ed. has only the addenda to the 1st ed. in the text. G. ROUX, *Paus. en Corinthe* (2, 1–15). Paris 1958 (with transl. and comm.). An excellent abbreviated Germ. transl. with important notes by ERNST MEYER, Zürich 1954 (*Bibl. der Alten Welt*); id., *Paus. Führer durch Athen und Umgebung.* Zürich 1959 (*Lebendige Antike*). The best monograph by O. REGENBOGEN, *RE* S 8, 1956, 1008. There and in MEYER (*v. sup.*), 726, bibl. Also A. DILLER, 'The Manuscripts of Paus.'. *Trans. Am. Phil. Ass.* 88, 1957, 169.

(2, 13) are more than vague possibilities. But the sound knowledge which this periegete has of Asia Minor shows that he came from there, perhaps from Lydia. A valuable indication for his date is his statement in 5. 1, 2 that Corinth had been a Roman colony for 217 years, which produces 173 for the date of composition of this book. Since furthermore the latest event mentioned is the invasion of the Costoboci (175), the work, on which Pausanias worked of course for a long time, may be considered to have been completed in the years shortly before 180. In the first book, whose original independence cannot be proved, Pausanias begins with Attica, extending in the next his periegesis over Central Greece and the Peloponnesus. Besides descriptions of localities and monuments such as are to be expected in a work like this, there are many excursuses of varying length on geography, history and mythology. Since information of this kind and the periegesis itself are approximately balanced in volume, it is not very easy to determine the nature and purpose of this work. Characterizing it as 'The Baedeker of Antiquity' is inadequate, although to a certain extent Pausanias could be a guide for travellers. But the thought of his reading public was uppermost in his mind, and for their sakes he took a great deal of care with his style. He firstly brings about some variety in the composition of the individual books. This is continued in the presentation of the material, especially in the necessary enumerations, and lastly in his personal idiom. Connected with this is the tendency to paraphrase names and things and the use of many artifices in the word order, while in his syntax he affects simplicity and avoids the long period. His predilection for archaisms is part of his imitation of Herodotus, although his style has little in common with the many possibilities exploited by the latter.

The sceptical attitude of the late nineteenth century turned Pausanias into a wretched copyist who had as little expert knowledge as Polyaenus of strategy or Aelian of zoology. Today the so-called Pausanias-problem has proved to be illusory. He was widely travelled; he spoke of numerous things from his own observation. He was also widely read, but in a better sense than the writers of miscellany. He certainly did not copy his work, or large parts of it, from elsewhere; the construction and arrangement of the details are his own creation. What he had observed and investigated during his travels, he combines with the fruits of his reading which was not restricted to compendia. It may be considered whether the frequent mention of Pergamum is connected with the importance which its library had for Pausanias. Occasionally we are granted a glimpse of his personality, as in 8. 2, 5 when he rejects the deification of men (read emperors!), and in 8. 8, 3 on the change which took place during his work of rational criticism of the myths to their symbolical conception. His interest in religion, especially the more primitive and obsolete forms, is characteristic of himself and the time in which he wrote.

Of the mythographical literature, which we have to assume as abundant from the Hellenistic times onward, the *Bibliotheca*[1] survives, which goes under the

---

[1] Text: R. WAGNER, *Mythogr. Gr.* I, 2nd ed. Leipz. 1926. Bilingual with comm. and copious ethnographical notes: J. G. FRAZER, 2 vols. *Loeb Class. Libr.* 1921. Analysis: v. WILAMOWITZ, 'Die griech. Heldensage' 1: *Sitzb. Akad. Berl. Phil.-hist. Kl.* 1925, 41; 2:

name of the great grammarian Apollodorus of Athens (*v.* p. 787). This has been shown up as a fraud by C. Robert in his dissertation.[1] Since the language of the *Bibliotheca* is not Atticist, the first century has been considered, but the second should be reckoned with as well, because in books of this nature stylistic trends work out least uniformly. The surviving book starts with the theogony and breaks off after dealing with various cycles of legends in the mythical genealogy of Attica. The epitome in the Codex Vatic. 950 (discovered by R. Wagner in 1885) and the Sabbaitical fragments (found by A. Papadopulos in Jerusalem in 1887) give us an idea of the rest which followed after Homer and the Cycle. This opuscule sports the name of ancient authors, but draws on a late-Hellenistic manual.

4 PROSE ROMANCE AND EPISTOLOGRAPHY

The traditional picture of no other genre in Greek literature was altered so completely by the papyri as that of the romance. For a long time Erwin Rohde's book dominated criticism in this field. At that time only Iamblichus' date was substantiated by solid proof. He was born before 115, and went on writing after 165, as proved by his mention of Soaemus, the Armenian king who was restored by the Romans. Rohde placed this Iamblichus at the beginning of a development which he believed to have ended in the sixth century with Chariton. This made the romance a product of the empire, and as such its value was extremely doubtful. Furthermore, his chronology suggested that it was a product of the second sophistic, and Rohde, following others,[2] emphatically defended this point of view.

These critics were completely confounded by papyrus finds with fragments of Chariton of the second/third century A.D. (no. 156 P.); lately a papyrus of the second century has been added.[3] The language and connection with historical events (*v. infra*) warrant the assumption that the romance emerged even earlier, perhaps as early as the first century A.D. We are at any rate forced to trace the beginnings of the genre back to Hellenistic times, for even the remnants of the *Ninus romance* point to such a dating. Further support has been provided by papyri of Achilles Tatius' romance (*v. infra*) which corrected its late dating (5th c.), at the same time upsetting the long-established point of view[4] that this author was dependent on Heliodorus.

The later Hellenistic era proved to be the time of the development of the Greek romance; we can follow it into the third century. Caution has to be observed with regard to the opinion that this century meant the end of this genre. The whims of transmission have deprived us of a great deal and the chronological distance between the literature of the Greek romance and its vigorous revival in the Byzantine era may be less than we think.

Ibid. 214 (= *Kl. Schriften* 5/2, 54). M. VAN DER VALK, 'On Apoll. Bibliotheca'. *Rev. Ét. Gr.* 71, 1958, 100.   [1] Berl. 1873.

[2] Of predecessors now forgotten, special mention must be made cf A. NICOLAI, *Übe Entstehung und Wesen des griech. Romans.* Berl. 1867.

[3] *Papyri Michaelidae.* Aberdeen 1955, no. 1.   [4] HELM (*v. inf.*) still clings to it.

At any rate a new insight into the chronology of the romance has done away with the hypothesis that it was born from the rhetorical activity of the second sophistic. In the splendid sketch with which Otto Weinreich followed up Reymer's translation of Heliodorus, he whimsically called the Greek erotic romance a mongrel which was the product of a liaison of the elderly epic with a capricious Hellenistic historiography. But, as indicated by Weinreich himself, other elements have to be taken into account, for the range of themes of the later genre is extraordinarily wide.

Travelling adventures and the passion of love are the stock subjects of the Greek romance. The stress on these aspects differs, but it is hardly advisable to separate the romance of travel from that of love as special genres, for in most cases the two themes are combined. The story of fabulous travels has a long ancestry. Among these the *Odyssey* occupies a place of honour, but we have to go back even further. Egyptian stories, like the one of the Middle Kingdom which deals with the shipwrecked sailor on the island of the mighty snake,[1] reveal ancient Mediterranean narrative stock. What was stated earlier (p. 218 f.) of the vivid interest of the Greeks, especially the Ionians, in faraway countries, explains the reason why genuine information and fabulous report found an equally ready hearing. Both of these had flowed into the Greek world in unparalleled abundance after Alexander's expedition, the fairy-tale dominating by far. What openings this offered for the later romance can be observed from the fact that Alexander's expedition itself became a romance with an unequalled breadth of influence.

The explanation of the unlimited power with which Eros rules in the romance must be looked for in the vigorous advance of erotic themes in Hellenistic writing. It is still one of the merits of Rohde's book that it singled out this fact clearly, while it also correctly evaluated this development as being anticipated in Euripides. The erotic element in the Greek romance is of a special nature. Love is nearly always a great passion, which is entirely in the line which connects it with Euripides. But in the romance only the secondary characters succumb to a guilty passion.[2] Their actions bring about the complications of the plot. The central couple are bound by a great and pure love, which is kindled at the first glance which they exchange. The goal which is reached after all the misunderstandings and confusion is not a fleeting pleasure, but the lasting union of two hearts which need one another.

This brief outline sketches the difference between the Greek romance and such stories as the *Milesian Tales* (v. p. 762) with their witty frivolity. Inclusion of the novella in the preliminary form of the romance must be completely rejected. The profound basic difference between the two genres permits only an occasional exchange of themes. What must be seriously considered is the question where

---

[1] Cf. L. RADERMACHER, *Die Erzählungen der Odyssee*. *Sitzb. Akad. Wien. Phil.-hist. Kl.* 178/1. 1915, 38. J. W. B. BARNS, 'Egypt and the Greek Romance'. *Mitt. aus der Papyrussamml. der Österr. Nationalbibl.* 5, Vienna 1956, 29.

[2] The Potiphar theme is traced by M. BRAUN, *Griech. Roman und hellenistische Geschichtsschreibung*. Frankf. a. M. 1934; *History and Romance in Graeco-Oriental Lit.* Oxf. 1938.

the romance acquired its erotic element which combines the greatest intensity with the greatest decency. How circumspect is, for instance, Heliodorus (5. 18, 8) in observing the separation of the lovers in their sleep! Now even Homer's epic, in spite of its freedom in sexual matters, already has a lofty conception of the honour of women, as borne out by figures like Penelope and Nausicaa. In the Hellenistic poetry of the preceding era, however, men are portrayed as unnaturally spurning all the charms of Aphrodite in the manner of Hippolytus rather than experiencing the love of young people, tender in spite of all vehemence, pure and reserved. It is not easy to give reasons for the origin of these features in the picture of Hellenistic love. It is possible that it is due to a large extent to a new conception of the nature of Eros which was founded by the philosophers, especially the Platonists. But we should not underestimate the influence of Oriental stories either, of which Xenophon's *Cyropaedia* with the story of the undemanding love of a highborn woman gives an impressive example. They must also have provided standards for the passion of men which excluded frivolity and voluptuousness.

In addition to Euripides' contribution drama was important for the romance in two other ways. In the first place it offered subject matter; those stories of children exposed and found again, of people who recognize each other after a long and grievous separation – the legacy of tragedy, utilized by New Comedy – play a part in the romance which is hardly less important. And if we knew a little more about the mime with its elopings, piracy and assassinations, it would be clearer how close the affinity is of theme and subject matter. On the other hand, dramatisation is an essential feature of the narrative technique of these products. Tension is raised with all kinds of artifices; the beginning of Heliodorus will give us a special example of this, Peripeteia takes place frequently and in quick succession, brisk dialogue occurs side by side with lofty mono-logues.[1] It should be borne in mind, however, that drama did not only have a direct influence, but also had an effect through dramatized Hellenistic historio-graphy, of which we spoke earlier (p. 764). We should also like to include bio-graphy with historiography in a wider sense, as in certain Hellenistic forms it gave plenty of scope for romantic features.

Earlier we rejected a theory according to which the romance was a product of the school of rhetoric of the second sophistic. Even chronologically this is impossible. This should not be taken to imply that rhetorical education, which demanded from the students a rhetorical elaboration of the most varied situa-tions from history, the myths or free invention, and from the teachers' models for this sort of thing, did not have some importance for the romance. Such an occupation must have led, at least for the more gifted, to a greater profundity of the intellectual processes and to a more refined elaboration of psychological details. Thus preliminary work was done for the romance also in this sphere.[2] The supposition, however, that certain specifications of the narrative form in

---

[1] Examples in H. RIEFSTAHL, *Der Roman des Apuleius.* Frankf. a. M. 1938, 86, 22. For Heliodorus reference is made, for instance, to the long tragic monologue of Chariclea (6, 8, 3)   [2] A synopsis of these features in RIEFSTAHL (*v. sup.*), 88, 25.

Cicero and Greek rhetorical writings referred to the romance has proved to be a fallacy.[1] It should also be stated at once that the ancient world never coined a definite label for this genre. Photius, for instance, speaks occasionally of drama, τὸ δραματικόν, or of comedy, when he means the romance, and avoids this difficulty by using the name of a well-defined genre.

Attempts have been made to derive the Greek romance entirely from Oriental myths, especially those about Isis and Osiris, and to seek its origin in the presentation of the deity's suffering and death.[2] In this extreme form the theory is untenable, although the influence of Oriental elements on the romance must not be underestimated. Nor can it be denied that the erotic conceptions of the romance often accord with themes of the mystery religions and it also contains linguistic borrowings from the same source; but this is not sufficient to derive the romance simply from the mysteries.

It is different with the aspects which are the result of the secularization of the Greek myths, and their development into fiction. We already saw in the case of Dionysius Scytobrachion (p. 782) that free composition continued side by side with the commonplace mythographical handbook. This went on during the empire. In A.D. 100 Ptolemy with the nickname Chennus of Alexandria wrote inter alia his epic Anthomerus, which advertises its purpose, the correction of Homer, in its title, and his Καινὴ ἱστορία (6 books; Παράδοξος ἱστορία in Suidas).[3] It is typical of such literature that the authorities for all these fictions were invented at the same time. A form of writing, typified in the Hellenistic age by the Troïca of Hegesianax from the Troad, is continued in the Troy-romances of Dictys and Dares. Until 50 years ago both were only known in Latin versions of late antiquity,[4] and were very influential in the Middle Ages and later. Particularly interesting is the part which the Troy-romance played in Goethe's planning of the ending of the Achilleis. In 1907 a papyrus of the early third century A.D. (no. 240 P.) gave certainty in the case of Dictys. Both authors may be given a date in the early empire. It is characteristic of this genre that they pretend to be contemporaries of the event, the Phrygian Dares on the side of the Trojans, and declare that the Dictys-romance was substantiated by wooden tablets which came to light from Dictys' tomb at Cnossos through an earthquake during Nero's reign.[5]

---

[1] K. BARWICK, Herm. 63, 1928, 261 ff.

[2] K. KERENYI, v. inf. Recently R. MERKELBACH has also proclaimed and energetically taken up the thesis of the origin of the romance from the mysteries in his book also mentioned below. He aims to prove that 'the romances are actually mystery texts'.

[3] W. KULLMANN, Die Quellen des Ilias. Herm. E 14, 1960, 141, 1 singles out Ptolemy Chennus, because he utilizes the sources of the spurious literature of his time more carefully,

[4] Editions by F. MEISTER, Leipz. 1872 and 1873. W. EISENHUT, Dictyis Cretensis Ephemeridos belli Troiani libri a Lucio Septimio ex Graeco in Latinum sermonem translati. Accedit papyrus Dictyis Graeci ad Tebtunim inventa. Leipz. 1958. Characterisation of the 'Dictys': JOHN FORSDYKE, Greece before Homer. Lond. 1956, 153. On Goethe's Achilleis: K. REINHARDT, Von Werken und Formen. Godesberg 1948, 311; now in Tradition und Geist. Göttingen 1960, 283.

[5] On the fiction of proof in hagiography: A. J. FESTUGIÈRE, Révélation d'Hermès Trismégisters, 2nd ed. Paris 1950, 309. On proof by means of finds in a tomb: W. BURKERT, Phil. 105, 1961, 240.

In theme and form the romance is the offspring of distinguished stock. Analysis is able to point out manifold threads which lead to other literary fields. But more important is the realization that it is the expression of a changed conception of life.[1] The myths have ceased to be a living force; the story of the Greeks who repulsed the Persians and waged a fratricidal war for the hegemony, had already become 'ancient history' in the Hellenistic era; contemporary politics was in the hands of a few leading men and did not reveal much coherence beyond threatening or securing personal civic existence. The realm of imagination dissociated itself radically and conclusively from private everyday life. The marvellous only occurred beyond its narrow confines. It was diligently sought and found in foreign lands and in the fates of lovers who proved themselves to be images of faith and constancy. Women must have had a stronger influence than ever before on the wishes of the reading public. It is difficult to imagine Gorgo and Praxinoa of Theocritus' *Adoniazusae* watching a play of Sophocles, but we would not mind handing them a Greek romance.

Two Berlin papyri (no. 2041 f. P.) give us a fragmentary idea of the *Ninus romance*, the oldest representative of the genre available. Ninus, whom Ctesias puts at the head of the series of Assyrian kings (*v.* p. 623 f.) and Semiramis, whose name does not actually occur in the fragments, are the lovers whose chequered fortunes, which end happily, already control the course of the plot. One fragment relates how the lovers, who are cousins, turn to each other's mother at different times in their ardent desire to be united. The discreet rhetoric of the young man, who stresses his chastity, and the modest bashfulness of the maiden, are contrasted with good effect. The other fragment shows Ninus before the battle against the Armenians. He has elephants and a Greek contingent with him, but that is one of the anachronisms often found in the romances. The fragments are of the first century A.D., but the romance was written a good deal earlier. The affinity with historiography, and linguistical details, such as the pronounced dread of hiatus, recommend an early date, probably the second century B.C.

In the Ninus romance the love theme is already firmly established, but it seems to be absent in Iambulus' travel story. We know its outlines from the excerpts in Diodorus' book 2 (55–60), which gives the *terminus ante*. In this case a date in the second century must also be considered. Iambulus' (the name is Syrian) adventures take him via Ethiopia to an island situated in the remote south, in which unusual inhabitants lead a happy life in fairy-land surroundings. Features like sharing wives in common are elements of the Utopian ideal state which already had a tradition at the time. Iambulus was allowed to share in the happiness of this south-sea island for seven years; then, cast out by the islanders, he returns home via India. Lucian, who wrote his *Verae Historiae* (*v.* p. 842) as a lampoon on stories of adventurous travels, nevertheless admitted the attractive execution of Iambulus' fantasies (1. 3).

Diodorus' excerpt provides no grounds for the supposition that Iambulus' romance contained erotic themes, although the possibility cannot be excluded.

---

[1] F. ALTHEIM thinks that the romance is particularly suitable to become the expression of times of revolution and crisis.

Such themes are, however, connected with the fantastic travelling adventures in the *Marvels beyond Thule* (Τὰ ὑπὲρ Θούλην ἄπιστα, 24 books) by Antonius Diogenes. We have an excerpt of it in Photius' *Bibliotheca* (cod. 166), to which excerpts in the *Life of Pythagoras* of Porphyry and a papyrus (no. 50 P.; 2nd/3rd c. A.D.) are added. As Photius realized, Lucian parodied the work in his *Verae Historiae*. As, on the other hand, the removal of the plot to Pythagoras' time, and all sorts of things which were reported about him, aptly fit in with the neo-Pythagorean wave of the early empire, the romance can be dated with some confidence in the first century. The elaborate attestation through tablets in a chest of cypress wood, found by Alexander at the capture of Tyre, is reminiscent of Dictys. They contained Dinias' report of his wonderful travels, which took him far beyond the borders of the inhabited world and even as far as the moon. The story of Dinias' adventures is interwoven with that of a brother and a sister who flee from an evil Egyptian sorcerer; it adopts fairy-tale themes, magic plays a large part, many motives typical of the romance are used such as separation and reunion, apparent death, poisonings. The love element is included, but it is not yet the centre as in the romances which will be discussed presently. Photius still reveals the skill with which the separate strands of the plot had been blended. Dinias' story was told in the third person; those of the others had been inserted in the same form.

Mention has already been made of the papyrus finds which necessitated a thorough change in the chronology of the romance of Chariton of Aphrodisias in Caria, and even made it possible to consider a date in the late Hellenistic era. The story of *Chaereas and Callirhoe* (8 books) contains free invention, but it still seeks a connection with history. At the beginning of the romance the name of Hermocrates occurs, the Syracusan general who led the victorious battle against Athens' expeditionary force (cf. p. 467). His daughter is the beautiful Callirhoe, whom Chaereas, the son of a political opponent of Hermocrates', wins as his wife with the aid of the people; next he loses her through the intrigues of his rivals and his own delusions, but he finds her again after endless perils to gain lasting bliss. Artaxerxes II and his satraps Pharnaces and Mithridates also appear as characters of the plot; a rebellion of the Egyptians against Persian dominion leads to the solution, but all these historical persons are unreal elements in this motley play of the imagination. The themes, which are shuffled in romances like playing cards, are nearly all present in Chariton: the couple's love at first sight, the suspicion of infidelity aroused by envious rivals, through which Chaereas is driven to maltreat his wife, apparent death and funeral, robbers who plunder the tomb and carry off the revived victim. The east attracts the plot with a mysterious strength. It moves by way of Miletus to the court of the Persian king; the Egyptian revolt brings the solution. In these romances it is always the unusual beauty of the heroine which causes her the greatest peril. Men of lofty station, even the Great King, desire her and contrive the most skilful intrigues, until the great ruler Tyche grants the much-enduring couple the certain bliss of mutual possession.

The dramatization of the narrative has been taken particularly far. In the powerful description of the trial before the Great King in Book 5 Chariton himself indicates that here the stage is going to be surpassed. Otherwise the story proceeds from episode to episode in a fairly straight line. Heliodorus' technique is entirely different. The cautious avoidance of hiatus supports early dating. Linguistical borrowing from the classical historians match a dependence on historical themes. A peculiar feature is the occasional sprinkling of verse, which has a remote resemblance in Xenophon of Ephesus. Our material, however, is not sufficient to enable us to characterize this as a peculiarity of the older romance.

The special frequency of related papyri reveals that the second century A.D., a period of relative prosperity, was also one of active reading of romances. Those of which we have such fragments may, of course, have been written substantially earlier. One fragment (no. 2046 P.) shows the separation of the lovers. Herpyllis' vessel is prevented from sailing by a gale, while her lover is in another ship at the mercy of the weather. Fragments of the romance *Metiochus and Parthenope* (no. 2047 P.) show the hero as a scorner of Eros who, of course, experiences its effects all the more violently. Another fragment tells of the ransoming of Parthenope in Corcyra. Suicide is often prevented and this theme occurs in a fragment (no. 1054 P.) which depicts the despair of a certain Calligone. Battles between Sauromati and Scythians, which separate the lovers, bring in the quasi-historical sphere of the older romance. Of two small scraps (no. 2053, 2057 P.) written during the transition from the second to the third century, the first shows a certain Anthea who handles poison; time and again suicide is planned in these stories. A parchment palimpsest (no. 158 P.) of the seventh century with a piece from Chariton, contains another of the romance of Chione, who is loyal to her lover in spite of all impetuous suitors. Similarities with Chariton can be discerned, which does not necessarily mean that he is the author; it is possible, however, that it also belongs to the older group. The fragments of the Sesonchosis romance (no. 2044 P.) should also be mentioned. They appear to contain the story of a conflict between the legendary king of Egypt and his son, who refuses the marriage planned by his father, probably because he loves someone else. The papyrus was written in the third or fourth century, but its quasi-historical character seems to point to an earlier date of composition.

The arrangement of the five books of the *Ephesiaca* (Τῶν κατ᾽ ῎Ανθειαν καὶ ῾Αβροκόμην ᾽Εφεσιακῶν λόγων βιβλία έ) of Xenophon of Ephesus is still open to many questions. Habrocomes, who wishes to rise above Eros (a theme pursued without any success) and Anthea see one another at the occasion of the procession for Artemis, they fall in love and are joined in marriage. The oracle of Apollo of Colophon, which forecasts the perils in store, plays a part in it. In order to avoid these perils, the relatives of the young couple send them on a journey. This, of course, releases the usual series of adventures: gales, shipwreck and pirates pursue the separated lovers, and time and again their beauty arouses dangerous passions. In Habrocomes' adversities the Potiphar theme plays a part. Among the many adventures of Anthea it falls to her lot to become the wife of a poor shepherd. But although he is of the lowest rank, his nobility of character allows her to preserve her purity. The return of a feature which Euripides had inserted as a bold novelty in his *Electra* is noteworthy.

For the dating the first important thing is that the romance contains reference to the institution of the office of irenarch by Trajan. It seems possible to deduce the *terminus ante* from the fact that the Ephesian temple of Artemis, which was destroyed in 263, plays an important part in the story. Admittedly the possibility that the writer moved the plot back in time and ignored the catastrophe should not be excluded, but the form of the *Ephesiaca* is so close to that of Chariton's romance that its date will not be very much after the end of the first century A.D.[1]

Suidas, who also knows of a history by Xenophon *On Ephesus* (Περὶ τῆς 'Εφεσίων πόλεως), assigns the number of ten books to the *Ephesiaca*. The composition of the romance, which strings numerous adventures together without much skill, exhibits in many passages a striking conciseness. There is therefore much in favour of Rohde's conjecture[2] that it is an excerpt. But in the case of this deplorable scribbler it may well be that these features are simply due to his lack of talent.

It was already mentioned that, owing to his autobiographical indications, the *Babylonica* of the Syrian Iamblichus can be placed in the last three decades of the second century A.D. The excerpt of the δραματικόν, which that voracious reader Photius offers in his *Bibliotheca* (codex 94),[3] gives a fair impression of the structure and contents of the work. The setting of the romance is pre-Persian Mesopotamia. The sea with its gales, shipwrecks and pirates is absent, but otherwise there is a good supply of all the well-known themes, to which are added a man-eating robber and a particularly generous share of ghosts and sorcery. This veritable witches' Sabbath of persecutions, bloody deeds and mistaken identities is caused by the fact that Garmus, the inhuman king of Babylon, desires Sinonis, Rhodanes' wife, for himself. The composition is very loose; Photius reveals insertions in the nature of short stories and excursuses on various customs. The vicissitudes of individual secondary figures have been quite skilfully connected with the main plot. The language of the fragments shows a strong influence of rhetoric. Suidas mentions thirty-nine books, whereas Photius ends with Book 16; it is hard to see what else could be told after the happy reunion of the couple. Two editions of different size could be considered, but we should remember how untrustworthy numbers are in manuscripts.

The romances of the sophist Nicostratus of Macedon, of which we do not even know any titles, and the *Metamorphoses* of Lucius of Patrae (cf. p. 845) also belong in the second century. Perhaps the Greek original of the *Historia Apollonii regis Tyrii* may be allotted a similar date, which is recommended by points of contact with Xenophon's *Ephesiaca*. There were several translations of the story

---

[1] HELM (*v. inf.*) 45 adheres to indebtedness to Heliodorus and dates Xenophon in the late 4th century. Neither is convincing.

[2] *Griech. Roman* (*v. inf.*), 429; cf. R. M. RATTENBURY, *Gnom.* 22, 1950, 75.

[3] A few fragments surviving in manuscripts are enumerated in URSULA SCHNEIDER-MENZEL (*v. inf.* under Iamblichus).

of king Apollonius, who passes through many perils to win the princess of Cyrene for his wife, only to lose her and his child as a result of the most singular misfortunes, and to find them again only many years later; it was especially in a Latin version of the fifth or sixth century that it became a popular romance.

The surviving material is sufficient to give us a picture of a prose literature whose scope is as wide as its level is low. Two works stand out to some degree, even though their stock of themes is quite typical of the genre. The papyri, as mentioned before,[1] have brought about a radical change in the dating of Achilles Tatius' (the Egyptian god 'Tat' is probably concealed in the name) *Leucippe and Cleitophon* (8 books). The finds correspond with the dating of F. Altheim,[2] who wished to place the romance between 172 and 194 on the basis of historical indications, even though these are not decisive in view of the *modus operandi* of the writers of romances.

This Alexandrian orator, to whom Suidas allots several more works of miscellaneous content, shows particularly in the opening that he wishes to rise above the hackneyed manner. After a stormy passage the author comes to Ephesus, where he admires a painting of the rape of Europa which he describes in the style of Philostratus, taking an obvious delight in rhetorical ecphrasis. Descriptions of this nature occur more often in his work. The Eros which impels the bull provides an opportunity for a conversation with a young man. He is Cleitophon and in the manner of the *Phaedrus* he tells in a grove of plane trees of the power of love as he has experienced it in wild adventures. As far as we can judge, the romance also had individual characteristics in that the development of the love between the youngsters up to the moment of their flight together is told with a broad sweep and subtle nuances. But next to elements of truly psychological description there are effusions about Eros in the old smart scholastic manner. A storm at sea, which carried the fugitives into the hands of Egyptian pirates, introduces a series of adventures told in a highly dramatic form with the aid of conventional themes. Time and again Cleitophon can scarcely doubt that his beloved is dead. Once he has to watch her being killed, though he does not realize that the whole thing is simulated by means of intestines tied on to her and with a stage–dagger; this is an example of the excesses to which the craze for inspiring overworked themes with new life was leading. In this romance constancy is also rewarded, as is proper to the genre. Unlike in Heliodorus there is an occasional dash of prurience in the story. It is, for instance, unusual that Cleitophon once has to oblige a woman whose passion largely

---

[1] *v.* p. 857. The first jolt was given by *Ox. Pap.* no. 1250 of the late 3rd or early 4th century. A problem is posed by substantial deviations from the manuscripts. c. f. RUSSO, who also gives a bibl., has shown in *Accad. dei Lincei, Rendic. d. classe di scienze mor. stor. e filol.* Ser. VIII, vol. X, 1955, 397, that it is likely that the papyrus has been altered in order to effect abbreviations. VILBORG expresses a cautious opinion in his edition (*v. inf.*), LXI. An even earlier dating was made imperative by a Milan papyrus of the 2nd century A.D., published by A. VOGLIANO, *Stud. ital. fil. class.* 15, 1938, 121. Bibl. on both papyri in QU. CATAUDELLA, *Parola del passato.* Fasc. 34, 1954, 37, 1. In add. a papyrus now lost: W. SCHUBART, *Griech. Lit. Pap.* (*Ber. Sächs. Akad. Phil.-hist. Kl.* 97/5) Berl. 1950, no. 30. which the editor places conjecturally in the third century.   [2] *Lit. u. Gesellsch.* (*v. inf.*), 121.

controls the plot of the second part. Its course runs along a fairly straight line in spite of various insertions; the actions of the secondary characters are closely connected with the main theme. The artfully simple form of language (ἀφέλεια) and the extensive use of figures show that the stylistic trends of the second sophistic have now taken hold of the romance.

The new chronology, effected by the papyri, proved that Heliodorus of Emesa was later with his *Aethiopiaca* (Σύνταγμα τῶν περὶ Θεαγένην καὶ Χαρίκλειαν Αἰθιοπικῶν, 10 books) than the romance of Achilles Tatius. Its more precise dating is still a matter of controversy. F. Altheim[1] has drawn attention to the description of a battle of Aethiopians against Persians, in which the cata-fractarii, the armoured Persian cavalry, play a part; this, by the way, is an extreme anachronism, for the plot was supposed to occur in the epoch of the Persian dominion over Egypt, and these catafractarii had first crossed swords with the Romans in the Persian war of Alexander Severus (232/33), but for our problems this gives only a *terminus post*. Neither the descriptions of the Blemmyans as submissive subjects of Meroe nor the story of the worship of the sun and its (sometimes exaggerated) importance in the romance provide a definite earliest date; most probably it is the second quarter of the third century, but the fourth century cannot be positively excluded.[2]

It is preferable to pay no attention to the information which first turns up in Socrates' ecclesiastical history (5th c.; 5. 22) that Heliodorus, who wrote the *Aethiopiaca* in his youth, later became bishop of Tricca and introduced clerical celibacy in Thessaly. In Nicephorus Callistus' ecclesiastical history (1320: 12. 34) this is turned into the fiction that a synod gave Heliodorus the choice of burning the work or resigning from his episcopal office. Achilles Tatius is also converted to Christianity by Suidas, and it is important in this connection[3] that in the legend of the holy Galaction and the holy Episteme (Migne 116. 93), the couple Cleitophon and Leucippe of the romance appear as their parents. This is part of the many attempts to make the two most widely read romances somewhat legitimate by connecting them with Christianity. Christian narrative literature drew very heavily on themes from the romances.[4]

Two qualities put Heliodorus' romance in a special position. There is in the first place the unusual virtuosity of the narrative technique. The opening is quite extraordinary. At break of day some robbers are looking out from an elevation at the Heracleotian estuary of the Nile and observe a rare sight; a fully loaded freighter without a crew or boats; on board some seriously wounded men, the remnants of a feast and a girl who is tending a wounded young man.

---

[1] *v.* prev. n., 108.

[2] For the later dating: M. VAN DER VALK, 'Remarques sur la date des Éthiopiens d'Héliodore'. *Mnem.* 9, 1941, 97, with the assumption that in several places Heliodorus is indebted to Julian; A. WIFSTRAND, *Bull. Société des lettres Lund*, 1944/45, 2, 36 ff. on linguistical considerations. M. P. NILSSON, *Gesch. d. gr. Rel.* 2, 2nd ed. Munich 1961, 565. That none of these arguments is effective is demonstrated by O. WEINREICH in REYMER's translation (*v. inf.*), 348.

[3] H. DÖRRIE, 'Die griech. Romane und das Christentum'. *Phil.* 93, 1938, 273.

[4] A great deal in HELM (*v. inf.*), 53.

Without any exposition the couple Theagenes and Chariclea are shown in exceedingly dramatic circumstances and so a tension is aroused which is only resolved through several skilfully contrived steps, by our understanding of the complex previous history, Chariclea is the child of the royal Ethiopian couple, exposed by her mother. She grows up in Delphi, where she arouses the love of Theagenes which she answers. Together with the young man and old Calasiris, whom the Ethiopian queen has sent out to search for her child, she sets out for the distant lands of which the oracle speaks in obscure words which promise happiness. Once more a chain of perils and adventures ensues, until Chariclea, about to be sacrificed together with Theagenes, finds her parents in Ethiopia, where she and her beloved are given a priesthood. The variegated nature of the plot is strengthened with great skill by the secondary characters, each of whom has his own exciting story. There is Cnemon who, being involved in a Potiphar story, took up a roaming life; Thyamis, the noble headman of the robbers, who turns out to be Calasiris' son. A hostile fate, which overtook him at the same time as the young couple, had thrown him off his course, but he returns to an honourable existence when he finds his father again.

Another aspect of the *Aethiopiaca* is that it provides evidence of new religious forces which pervade the period. Chastity is not a pose here, but a genuine inner commandment; the Ethiopian gymnosophists advance to the rejection of blood-sacrifice; divine justice is recognized in the issue of human affairs. It depends on the dating of the romance whether Neopythagorean or Neoplatonic features can be found in it.[1] There are Oriental influences in the lofty conception of the sun-god who is felt to be universal and is identified with Apollo. Astrology, belief in dreams and sorcery are present as well, but their lower form is separated from the wisdom of the priests.

It is clear in Heliodorus especially that the language of the romance is an artificial product. Particularly the mannerism of overloading sentences with an accumulation of participles leads to monstrous structures.

The pastoral romance of *Daphnis and Chloe* (4 books) by Longus of Lesbos is somewhat different from the other romances of love and adventure described so far. The author's literary skill has combined a great variety of elements, through which the work exerted great influence, and even aroused Goethe's admiration.[2] Remote countries remain distant in this romance, which is entirely enacted in the writer's native island. The adventures, an assault on Chloe, attempts to abduct Daphnis and then the girl again, are secondary episodes, just as the various obstructions which oppose their union. The bucolic world in which the events take their course is depicted with a broad sweep, but, in spite of the ornateness, also with charm. It is reminiscent of Theocritus' *Idylls*, but the distance which separates this trifle from the art of the Alexandrian should not be overlooked. In Longus everything is idyllic in the manner of the shepherd's poetry which continued this romantic world. The author places in this idyllic setting two foundlings who are serving as shepherds. His actual theme is the

---

[1] Following GEFFCKEN, the latter now favoured by NILSSON (*v.* p. 866, n. 2), 565, 5.
[2] Conv. with ECKERMANN of 20.3.1831.

awakening of their affection and the naïveté of their passion, which fails for a long time to find its way to fulfilment. This romance wavers between frivolity and naturalness, because the innocence of the two young people and the natural instinct of their desire is observed by the author in a lascivious mood and depicted accordingly. The dénouement follows the manner of New Comedy. Daphnis and Chloe find their parents, well-to-do citizens of Mytilene, and can get married. But they prefer the happiness of the shepherds' world, in which they grew up, to life in the city.

The turning point at the end with its profession of the innocent life in nature is reminiscent of Dion's *Euboïcus* (*v.* p. 834). The present tendency is to separate Longus not too far from him, and to date him in the second century. The previous later dating is not credited now, although the first half of the third century should be considered as well. The style, which aims at symmetry and makes a pretence of simplicity, agrees with this date.[1]

Epistolography, the favourite child of rhetoric which cultivated letters as a stylistic feature, is separate from the romance as a genre.[2] In its erotic varieties, however, there is some similarity of subject matter, and so a word about it in this place is justified. Mention (p. 838) has already been made of Philostratus' love letters and Aelian's *Peasants' Letters* (p. 854). The collection of love letters of the orator Lesbonax of the second century is lost. This is probably the same man of whom we have three deplorable declamations.[3] It is characteristic of the time that two of these imply historical situations of the fifth century B.C. The most gratifying products in this field are the letters of Alciphron, who also belongs in the second century. In the four books (*Letters of Fishermen, Letters o Peasants, Letters of Parasites, Letters of Hetaerae*) it is not merely an author who does his Atticist best (though he cannot avoid running off the rails occasionally), nor his assiduous antiquarianism which is revealed, but we also sense his warm love for his romantically radiant Athens. He also often succeeds in capturing something of the incomparable charis of this time in his letters. This applies especially to the fictional correspondence of Menander and his Glycera, of whom we already had occasion to speak (p. 645) There are also many delightful descriptions of nature, as in the first fisherman's letter and in the account of a trip into the country (4. 13). His treatment of love is conventional and reveals also the otherwise frequent borrowing from comedy. There are also such charming things as the letter of Lamia to Demetrius (4. 16).[4]

A much later offspring of this genre is Aristaenetus who, according to the mention of the pantomime Caramallus (1, 26 with Apollinaris Sidonius 23, 268) belongs in the fifth century. The use of accentuating clauses agrees with this. In his *Love Letters* (2 books) he copies whole sentences from Plato, the writers of romances, Lucian, Philostratus and Alciphron, to mention only these, in his

---

[1] In a preface to his book (*v. inf.*) R. MERKELBACH wanted to prove the kinship of the romance with the mysteries, especially those of Dionysius: 'Daphnis und Chloe'. *Antaios. Zeitschr. für eine freie Welt.* 1, 1959, 47; id., *Roman und Mysterium* (*v. inf.*), 192.

[2] On the letter and its theory: H. KOSKENNIEMI, *Studien zur Idee und Phraseologie des griech. Briefes bis 400 n. Chr.* Helsinki 1956.   [3] Edition: F. KIEHR, Leipz. 1907.

[4] Text and transl.: V. WILAMOWITZ, *Herm.* 44, 1909, 467 = *Kl. Schr.* 4, 244.

zeal to write Atticist Greek. But his subject matter is interesting, since he collects the erotic themes of antiquity from everywhere; 1, 10 and 15 draw on Callimachus' *Aetia*.

A non-erotic form of the epistolary romance is represented only by a collection of seventeen letters attributed to Chion of Heraclea. Like his fellow-conspirator Leonides, Chion had been a student at the Academy, and so was Clearchus, the tyrant of Heraclea on the Pontus, who was the object of their attack at the Dionysia of 352. There may be a faint reminiscence of Dion, Plato's friend, who fell a victim to a conspiracy in Syracuse which was the work of the Academic Callippus. It is no longer assumed that the letters which describe the events of the deed, were written by Chion himself. Apart from some isolated bits of historical knowledge, which are based on a good tradition, the author of these letters is a man of mediocre ability. Precise dating is difficult; the late Hellenistic age or the first century B.C. are considered.[1]

General studies of the romance: E. ROHDE, *Der griech. Roman*. Leipz. 1876; 3rd ed. 1914. E. SCHWARTZ, *Fünf Vorträge über den griech. Roman*. Berl. 1896. K. KERENYI, *Die griech.-orient. Romanlit. in religionsgeschichtlicher Beleuchtung*. Tübingen 1927. F. ZIMMERMANN, 'Aus der Welt des griech. Romans.' *Die Antike* 11, 1935, 292 (with samples of translation). E. H. HAIGTH, *Essays on the Greek Romances*. New York 1943. F. ALTHEIM, *Lit. u. Gesellschaft im ausgehenden Altertum*. Halle 1948; *Roman und Dekadenz*. Tübingen 1951. R. HELM, *Der antike Roman*. Berl. 1948, 2nd ed. Gött. 1956. BR. LAVAGNINI, *Studi sul romanzo greco*. Messina-Florence 1950. O. WEINREICH, *Nachwort zur Heliodor-Übers*. von R. REYMER. Zürich (*Bibl. d. Alten Welt*) 1950. R. MERKELBACH, *Roman und Mysterium in der Antike*. Munich 1962. – Collective editions: G. A. HIRSCHIG, *Erotici scriptores Graeci*. Paris 1856. R. HERCHER, *Erotici scriptores Graeci*. 2 vols. Leipz. 1858-59. P. GRIMAL, *Romans grecs et latins. Textes présentés, trad. et annotés*. Paris 1958. Q. CATAUDELLA, *Il romanzo classico*. Rome 1958. F. ZIMMERMANN, *Griech. Roman-papyri*. Heidelb. 1936; cf. P(ack) no. 2041-2067 and on the individual authors. Transmission: H. DÖRRIE, *De Longi Achillis Tatii Heliodori memoria*. Diss. Gött. 1935 (cf. R. M. RATTENBURY, *Gnomon*, 13, 1937, 358).

Chariton: W. E. BLAKE, Oxf. 1938. F. ZIMMERMANN, *Der Roman des Chariton*. 1 *Text u. Übers*. Berl. 1960. (*Abh. Ak. Leipz. Phil.-hist. Kl. 51/2*). It. transl.: A. CALDERINI, Milan 1913. B. E. PERRY, 'Ch. and his Romance from a Literary-historical Point of View'. *Am. Journ. Phil.* 51, 1930, 93. A. D. PAPANIKOLAOU, *Zur Sprache Charitons*. Diss. Col. 1963. – Xen. Eph.: G. DALMEYDA, *Coll. des Un. d. Fr.* 1936 (bilingual). – Iamblichus: E. HABRICH, *Iamblichi Babyloniacorum reliquiae*. Leipz. 1960. Analysis by URSULA SCHNEIDER-MENZEL in Altheim, *Lit*.

---

[1] Excellent edition with translation and commentary (also important for the language) by I. DÜRING, Göteborg 1951 (*Acta Univ. Gotoburg.* 57). He dates the genesis of the collection between the early Augustan period and Plutarch. O. GIGON, *Gymn.* 69, 1962, 209, relegates it to the late 2nd century B.C.

u. Gesellschaft (v. supra), 48. – *Historia Apollonii*: A. RIESE, Leipz. 1893. – Ach. Tatius: S. GASELEE, *Loeb Class. Libr.* (with Engl. transl.). Lond. 1917. E. VILBORG, Stockholm 1955 (with history of the transmission and bibl.); also C. F. RUSSO, *Gnom.* 30, 1958, 585. D. SEDELMEIER, 'Studien zu Ach. T.'. *Wien. Stud.* 72, 1959, 113. – Heliodorus: A. COLONNA, Rome 1938. R. M. RATTENBURY and T. W. LUMB, *Coll. des Un. d. Fr.* (with transl. by J. Maillon), 3 vols. 1935, 1938, 1943. 2nd ed. 1960. F. ALTHEIM, *Lit. u. Gesellschaft (v. supra)*, 93. V. HEFTI, *Zur Erzählungstechnik in H.s Aeth.* Diss. Basel, Vienna 1950 (with bibl.). O. MAZAL, 'Die Satzstruktur in den Aith. des Hel. v. Emesa'. *Wien. Stud.* 71, 1958, 116. Transl.: R. REYMER, Zürich 1950 (*Bibl. d. Alten Welt*). English: M. HADAS, Ann Arbor Univ. of Michigan Press 1957. – Longus: W. D. LOWE, Cambr. 1908. G. DALMEYDA, *Coll. des Un. d. Fr.* 1934, repr. 1960 (bilingual). Together with Parthenius: J. M. EDMONDS, *Loeb Class. Libr.* Lond. 1955 (bilingual). O. SCHÖN-BERGER, *Longus*, Greek and German with comm. Berlin 1960. German transl. L. WOLDE, Leipz. 1939. E. R. LEHMANN, Wiesbaden 1959. G. VALLEY, *Über den Sprachgebrauch des L.* Diss. Uppsala 1926. – Alciphron: M. A. SCHEPERS, Leipz. 1905. The Letters of Hetaerae: W. PLANKL, Munich 1942 (bilingual). With Aelian's and Philostratus' letters: A. R. BENNER and F. H. FOBES, *Loeb Class. Libr.* Lond. 1949 (bilingual). L. FIORE, Florence 1957 (bilingual). English transl. by F. and B. WRIGHT, London 1958. – Aristaenetus: For the text we are still dependent on R. HERCHER, *Epistolographi Graeci*, Paris 1873 (with Latin transl.), which often deals with the transmission in an arbitrary manner. Fr. transl.: J. BRENOUS, Paris 1938. Germ. transl. with introd. and notes: A. LESKY, Zürich 1951 (*Bibl. d. Alten Welt*). Id., 'Zur Überlieferung des A.' *Wien. Stud.* 70, 1957, 219.

5 THE SECOND SOPHISTIC IN THE LATER ERA

The fourth century is full of symptoms which indicate the changing of the times and anticipate the closure of the Athenian university, which represents our boundary. Most of the old families perished in the confusion of the third century. The losses of landed property had dealt an extremely heavy blow to the cities. The ephebia, this nucleus of Greek education, had vanished completely; the year 393 saw the end of the Olympic games, in which in 385 the Armenian prince Varzdates had been the last Olympic victor known.

But the great force in education, and for a long time the only, was still rhetoric. Its teachers, the sophists, controlled intellectual life. It had become torpid and desolate, but it should be borne in mind that this activity had contributed a great deal towards maintaining the Hellenic tradition. The great authors of the past were still the foundation of instruction and the models after which men aspired.[1]

In the more peaceful times of the fourth century this rhetoric was given a new lease of life. It cannot be denied that it had a close affinity with the traditionalist opposition against Christianity, whence the applause from this circle for

[1] On the forms of this later education the 6th chapt. 'Paidéia grecque et éducation chrétienne' in FESTUGIÈRE's book on Antioch (*v. inf.*) is important.

Julian. But on the whole they managed to live peacefully with the Christian rulers.

The most successful teacher of rhetoric, a typical sophist, was Libanius of Antioch (314 until about 393). After studying in Athens and travelling for some time, he opened his school in Constantinople in 340/41, withdrew to Nicomedea before the intrigues of his rivals in 346, and finally returned to his native city in 354 after a brief interlude in Constantinople. Among his students, who came from all the countries in the Orient, were leading Christians such as Ioannes Chrysostomus, Basil the Great and Gregory of Nazianzus. Libanius, the traditionalist, remained, however, aloof from the new trends; to him Julian's attempt at restitution meant the fulfilment of his wishes. Although the emperor could by no means have heard him in Nicomedea as a boy, Libanius still felt that he was his pupil. He dedicated to him, when he fell in battle against the enemy of the realm in the east, his *Monody to Julian* (17 F.) and his longest speech, the *Epitaph on Julian* (18 F.), in which we perceive the personal note much stronger than elsewhere. He expressed the close ties which bound him to his native city in the *Antiochus* (11 F.).[1] Libanius declaimed this oration, which is also historically important, at the Olympic games in Antioch.

The literary legacy of this teacher and orator, among which there is also an autobiography (1 F.), is extremely bulky, but not all of it has been preserved. In addition to occasional speeches there are numerous *School-declamations* and *Progymnasmata* for the various accomplishments demanded by the school of rhetoric. The *Hypotheses* to Demosthenes' speeches were written for the proconsul Montius, an admirer of Demosthenes, but the bulk of the surviving work is formed by the gigantic collection of *Letters*, which in late antiquity can only be compared, with some reservation, with the one of Julian and that of the Platonist and later bishop, Synesius of Cyrene.

Not everything that Libanius wrote was mere rhetoric. He is sincerely convinced of the primacy of Hellenic culture. But, however much his intellectual world may be made up of elements of the past, we learn from him a great deal about contemporary life. The *Letters* are outstanding for their value as source material. Nor should it be forgotten that occasionally he expressed himself freely about abuses in state and society. In style he is an opponent of Asianism, and adheres to the great ancient models. The example which he admired most was Aelius Aristides, who was already something of a classic for the latecomer.

In 353 Libanius declined an offer of the chair at Athens; he preferred to leave this field to others. At this time Himerius of Bithynia, who was born in 310 and died at an advanced age, enjoyed oratorical fame there. He started out upon his career as a sophist in Athens, where he had studied; he left the city for a few years, which may be connected with the defeat which he suffered in an oratorical contest with Prohaeresius. In 362 Julian called him to Antioch; he returned to Athens in 368. His eighty *Speeches* keep aloof from all politics; twenty-four of them survive, several others are known from excerpts by Photius. Through

[1] Bibl. *v. inf.*

871

Photius we also know of progymnasmata with the playful fictions of the rhetorical school. Demosthenes intercedes to have Aeschines recalled, Epicurus is denounced on the ground of atheism and such like. The *Polemarchus* survives, a festive oration attributed to the archon polemarchus at the Attic Epitaph festival. Generally, however, they are occasional speeches, addresses to high officials, while many of them are concerned with the life of the school. In contrast with Libanius' purism, Himerius, the 'friend of the divine poets' chorus' (*Or.* 4. 3) reveals a predilection for the diction of poetry which is unexampled in this time.[1] This rhetoric, which rivalled poetry, goes indeed to the very extreme. These speeches pretend to be hymns and lyrics; their writer feels that he is closer to the poets, especially the Lesbians, than the ancient orators, his natural models. An extenuating circumstance is that, in spite of his irritating pretentiousness, he has at least preserved in this way many fragments of ancient poetry.

None of these sophists was hostile towards philosophy; Libanius even mentions it with particular respect.[2] Some rivalry did exist, but they did not deny the philosophers' claims, they pretended to be philosophers themselves. The Bithynian Themistius, who probably lived from 317 to 388, is more closely allied with philosophy. Within his limits he remained true to it, having become familiar with it through his father. He shut himself off from the new spiritual movement of his time; the sharp intellect of Aristotle was his ideal, from which he seeks a bridge across to Plato, whom he often quotes. He wrote paraphrases of the two philosophers, of which the one on Aristotle survives. But the same Themistius passed through the rhetorical school, first at home and then in Constantinople; in 345 he began to teach in the new capital. Since he tried to serve two masters, he inevitably attracted attacks from both sides. In a series of speeches, of which the Βασανιστὴς ἢ φιλόσοφος (*Or.* 21) was the first, he defended his position in this war on two fronts. In the course of time, however, his position rose above such squabbles. This pagan, for whom, as for Libanius, Julian meant the fulfilment of his dreams, managed to be on excellent terms with the Christian emperors from Constantius II to Theodosius I. Under the first he entered the Senate of Constantinople in 355.[3] Theodosius made him prefect of the city and entrusted him with the education of Arcadius, the crown-prince. A large part of the surviving thirty-three speeches is formed of addresses to his imperial masters. They are a mixture of purposeful flattery and the proclamation of an ideal monarchy guided by philosophy. The speeches are also important for the political conditions of the time, especially two addressed to Constantius (*Or.* 1. 4). In style Themistius was a pure Atticist, which agrees with his outlook generally.

This is not the place to outline a picture of the emperor Julian and to trace the development which made this prince, oppressed and persecuted by Constantius, an enemy of Christianity, a victorious general in the west and finally the rival

---

[1] An instructive collection of passages in E. NORDEN, *Ant. Kunstprosa.* 4th impr. Leipz. 1923, 429.   [2] E.g. *Or.* 1, 131. 13, 13; ep. 1051. 1496.

[3] The imperial letter and the speech expressing gratitude (*Or.* 2) have been preserved.

emperor. His attempts at reform, conceived as a renewal of ancient paganism guided by Neoplatonic ideas, are a fascinating chapter in religious history, and that is where the story belongs. But Julian the littérateur demands some remarks. The years under Constantius had constrained his stylus; he had even been forced to write two eulogies (*Or.* 1 f.) on the object of his hatred, apart from the one on the empress Eusebia (*Or.* 3). When in 360 his elevation to the dignity of Augustus also gave him freedom of speech, he made extensive use of it in his struggle for his ideas. The ruler who wanted to put the clock back and who, moreover, had his hands full with urgent matters of state, produced a great deal of hastily written work, only part of which survives. A satire in the manner of Menippus, the *Symposium*, is of slight importance. It portrays great emperors at the Saturnalia during an Olympian banquet and evaluates them against contemporary ideals of monarchy. The *Oration to Helius* (25. XII. 362) and the one *To Divine Mothers* reveal how extremely confused were the emperor's syncretism and his philosophical ideas influenced by Neoplatonism. His literary zeal remained unaltered when, at first very slowly, he marched out against the Parthians. We get an impression of the polemic *Against the Christians* (Κατὰ Γαλιλαίων, 3 books) from the retort by Cyrillus of Alexandria. The *Antiochicus*, or *Misopogon* (hater of beards) has come down to us; this satire, which the emperor, roused to anger in Antioch, wrote shortly before his death on the field of battle, is an important piece of autobiography. The imperial wearer of the philosopher's beard took Cynicism very much to his heart and attacks the more violently those who seem to be untrue to its ideals. Thus in 362 he turned *Against Uneducated Dogs* (Εἰς τοὺς ἀπαιδεύτους κύνας), while the speech *Against the Cynic Heracleus* has a personal background. Problems of authenticity are involved in Julian's *Letters* and some *Epigrams* handed down under his name. Yet among the letters there are genuine contemporary documents, especially the letter to Themistius, which anticipates the problems of his reign, and the letter to the Athenians with an autobiographical statement of account.

Julian's legacy means a great deal for the image of the time and for the characterization of this tragic figure. The style of these products, rapidly written and dependent on fashionable models, has little of importance for us.

By way of appendix brief mention is made of the rhetorical school of Gaza, which began to prosper in the beginning of the sixth century and whose important representatives were all Christians: Procopius, who wrote strictly Atticist declamations, progymnasmata and letters, apart from theological works, and paid homage to the emperor Anastasius in a *Panegyricus*; his pupil Choricius, who is of special interest for his defence of actors and for his description of the churches in Gaza in his speeches to bishop Marcianus; Aeneas, of whom we have some letters and a dialogue *Theophrastus*, in which the philosopher is converted to Christianity.

Works on rhetoric, such as we traced into the third century (p. 843 f.), went on being produced until the end of antiquity. We know that Lachares of Athens, who belongs in the fifth century, wrote about prose rhythm. His most successful pupil was Nicolaus of Lycian Myra, of whom we have *Progymnasmata*. They have a certain value for the knowledge of a tradition which made do with the traditional material without creating anything new.

J. GEFFCKEN, *Der Ausgang des griech-röm. Heidentums*. 2nd ed., Heidelb. 1929. – Libanius: R. FÖRSTER, 12 vols. Leipz. 1903–27. J. BIDEZ, *Themistius in L.' Brieven*. Paris 1936 (critical ed. of 52 letters with comm.). L. HARMAND, *L. discours sur le patronage*. Paris 1955 (with transl. and comm.). P. WOLF, *Vom Schulwesen der Spätantike*. *Studien zu L.* Baden-Baden 1952 (with bibl.); 'L. und sein Kampf um die hellenische Bildung'. *Mus. Helv.* 11, 1954, 231. P. PETIT, *L. et la vie municipale à Antioche au IVe siècle après J.-C.* Paris 1956; 'Recherches sur la publication et la diffusion des discours de L.' *Historia* 5, 1956, 479; *Les étudiants de L.* Paris 1957. A.-J. FESTUGIÈRE, *Antioche païenne et chrétienne. L., Chrysostome et les moines de Syrie*. Paris 1959. This valuable book gives a translation of the *Antiochicus* with archaeological comm. by J. MARTIN, with the history of the activity of L. in Antioch and a selection of the letters in translation, all in chronological order. – Himerius: A. COLONNA, Rome 1951; id., 'Himeriana' *Boll. del com. per la prepar. della ed. naz. dei class. Gr. e Lat.* 9, 1961, 33. S. EITREM, L. AMUNDSEN, 'Fragments from the Speeches of Him' *Class. et Med.* 17, 1956, 23. – Themistius: The paraphrases of Aristotle in vol. 5 of the *Commentaria in Aristotelem Graeca* (*v.* p. 580). The speeches: W. DINDORF, Leipz. 1832; repr. by Olms/Hildesheim 1961. H. KESTERS, *Antisthène de la dialectique*. Louvain 1935. Id., *Plaidoyer d'un socratique contre le Phèdre de Platon. XXVIe discours de Th.* Introd., texte et trad. Louvain 1959. The edition is useful, the thesis that in this case Themistius has appropriated a writing of one of the Socratics, is untenable; cf. O. GIGON, *Mus. Helv.* 18, 1961, 239; O. REGENBOGEN, *Gnom.* 34, 1962, 28. G. DOWNEY, 'Education and Public Problems as seen by Th.'. *Trans. Am. Phil. Ass.* 86, 1955, 291. – Julian: J. BIDEZ and F. CUMONT, *J. imperatoris epistulae leges poemata fragmenta varia*. Paris 1922. J. BIDEZ, I/1: *Discours*; I/2: *Lettres*. Coll. des Un. d. Fr. 1932 and 1924 (bilingual). W. C. WRIGHT, 3 vols. Loeb Class. Libr. 1913–23. B. A. VAN GRONINGEN, *I. imp. epistulae selectae*. Textus min. 27, Leiden 1960. F. BOULANGER, *Essai critique sur la syntaxe de l'empereur Julien*. Lille-Paris 1922. J. BIDEZ, *La vie de l'empereur J.* Paris 1930. On his religious principles M. P. NILSSON, *Gesch. d. gr. Rel.* 2, 2nd ed. Munich 1961, 455. J. KABIERSCH, *Untersuchungen zum Begriff der Philanthropia bei dem Kaiser J.* Klass. Phil. Stud. 21, Wiesbaden 1960. – The old editions, quoted in Christ-Schmid's *Lit.-Gesch.* are still the only ones for the Gazaeans. Also the editions of Aeneas, *Theophrastus sive de immortalitate animae* by MARIA E. COLONNA, Naples 1958. Nicolaus: J. FELTEN, Leipz. 1913.

6 PHILOSOPHY

During the first two centuries of the empire philosophy was dominated by traditionalism, which however, allowed varieties of considerable breadth. While on the one hand the tradition continued in its external form, the ancient doctrines were also filled with a genuine inspiration. Compilation, initiated by the Peripatetics, was carried on. Large parts have been traced of a *Compendium of Tenets* (Συναγωγὴ τῶν ἀρεσκόντων) written by Aetius in the first or second century.[1] They are invaluable for the history of ancient philosophy, especially because Aetius proceeded only by quotation and did not introduce any personal exegesis.

The Peripatos maintained its ancient close connection with scientific work. The discovery of Aristotle's didactic writings and their republication (*v.* p. 578) laid the basis for an extensive activity in commenting. Mention was made of this with regard to Themistius. From among a fairly large number Alexander of Aphrodisias (early 3rd c.)[2] is singled out as a scholarly expounder who devotedly served his master. His teacher was Aristocles of Messana in Sicily, who belonged to the truly Peripatetic tradition with his voluminous history of philosophy (Περὶ φιλοσοφίας βιβλία ι').[3] The fragments, most of which are preserved in Eusebius' *Praeparatio Evangelica*, give the impression that the work was written with erudition and scholarly thoroughness; in its endeavours to trace the development of the various doctrines it was considerably above Diogenes Laertius' level. He also wrote on rhetoric (Τέχναι ῥητορικαί).

The Academy had temporarily come to a certain understanding with Scepticism as formulated by Pyrrhon (*v.* p. 685 f.), but its eclectical attitude again brought about an alienation; as early as the end of the first century this philosophy had undergone a process of renovation through Aenesidemus, who was once close to the Academy, but opposed it because of its defection from scepsis. Sextus Empiricus, a notable representative of the empirical medical school, with which Aenesidemus also had close connections, is our main witness of the struggle of this school against all dogmatism. He wrote at the end of the second century, leaving an *Outline of Pyrrhon's Doctrine* (Πυρρώνειοι ὑποτυπώσεις, 3 books) and *Sceptica*, composed of six books *Against Mathematicians* and five *Against Dogmatists*.[4] It must have been far from the minds of these advocates of sceptical opposition to the conquests of reason that it should have contributed towards preparing the way for mysticism.

Epicureanism still had its adherents, as shown by the information about the Epicurean interests of Plotina, Trajan's consort, or testimony like the inscription

---

[1] H. DIELS has recognized Aetius' work as the common source of Ps.-Plut.'s *Epitome* (on which K. ZIEGLER, *RE* 21, 1951, 879), excerpts in Stobaeus in Ἐκλογαὶ φυσικαὶ καὶ ἠθικαί and Ps.-Galen, Περὶ φιλοσ. ἱστορίας and has proved this in *Doxographi Graeci*, Berl. 1879, 273-444.

[2] P. MORAUX, *Alexandre d'Aphrodise. Exégète de la Noétique d'Aristote*. Paris 1942. F. E. CRANZ, 'The Prefaces to the Greek Editions and the Latin Translations of Al. of Aphr. 1450 to 1575.' *Proc. of the Am. Philos. Soc.* 102, 1958, 510. The fragment of a comm. on the *Topica*, which is at least 100 years older than the one by Alexander, *Pap. Fayum* 2 (ca. 100 A.D.), is important for the tradition of which Alexander forms part.

[3] The fragments both in MULLACH, *Fr. Phil. Gr.* 3, 206, and H. HEILAND, *Aristoclis Messanii Reliquiae*. Diss. Giessen 1925. F. TRABUCCO, 'Il problema del De Philosophia di Aristocle di Messene e la sua dottrina'. *Acme* 11, 1958 (1960), 97.

[4] His quotations from his own work produce the following chronology: Πυρρ. ὑπ., then *Against the Dogm.* 7-11 (against the dogmatic logicians, physicists, ethicists), then more work on the Πυρρ. ὑπ. 2. 3, finally *Against the Math.* 1-6 (on grammar, rhetoric, geometry, arithmetic, astrology and music).

of Oenoanda (*v.* p. 683). There is, however, no trace of a further development of the doctrine, which diminished greatly in importance in later antiquity.

In this time the greatest vigour is developed by the Stoa. It was decisive for its influence that it had conquered the Roman world. Who could, for instance, depreciate the influence which the Platonizing Stoic Areus Didymus of Alexandria exerted as Augustus' court philosopher and as a friend of Maecenas'?[1] L. Annaeus Cornutus of Leptis in Africa was the teacher of Lucan and Persius. Of him we have a *Concise Hellenic Theology* (Ἐπιδρομὴ τῶν κατὰ τὴν Ἑλληνικὴν θεολογίαν παραδεδομένων), which is wholly in the tradition of Stoic allegorizing as we came to know it earlier (p. 675) in an approximately contemporary writing of a certain Heraclitus. Another figure who well illustrates the linking of remote realms of culture is the Stoicizing philosopher Chaeremon,[2] who probably was head of the Museum at Alexandria after Apion (p. 804). After 49 he came to the imperial court as Nero's teacher and wrote historical and grammatical studies. A comparison of the fragments of an Egyptian history and the *Hieroglyphica* about the symbolical writing of the ancient Egyptians with the information that he performed the function of hierogrammateus in an Egyptian priesthood, suggests that he was a representative of the Egyptian-Alexandrian syncretism which had a romantic predilection for the past and was subject to Platonic and Pythagorean influences. The *Pinax* of Cebes, a surviving allegorical description of various ways of life, probably also belongs in the first century A.D. Roman Stoics wrote Greek so frequently that Seneca must almost seem to be an exception. C. Musonius Rufus, of an equestrian family of Volsinii, also used the Greek language. Stobaeus has preserved some notes of a pupil of his called Lucius.[3] What we learn from these shows that he followed the tradition faithfully. He must have been more influential through his personality. During Nero's last years he was banished to the island of Gyaros as a member of the philosophical opposition, but he was allowed to return under Galba. During the reigns of Vespasian and Titus the game of exile and return was repeated. The number of his scholars was considerable. Among them we find, besides Dion of Prusa, a man who gave an unforgettable personal stamp to the Stoical command of life.

Epictetus was born in Phrygian Hierapolis in the middle of the first century A.D. He was a slave and physically handicapped through lameness. To his master, the court-official Epaphroditus, he owed his freedom, as well as an opportunity to hear Musonius. He himself first taught in Rome, but had to leave in the course of the expulsion of philosophers under the imperial decree of exile. In Nicopolis in Epirus he gathered a large circle of students round him. He probably did not die until Hadrian's reign.

In his teaching he stressed questions of ethics even more than the ancient Stoa.

---

[1] Excerpts from his doxographical works on Plato and Pythagoras in Stobaeus, cf. H. DIELS, *Doxographi*, 477.

[2] A collection of the fragments with comm. by H. R. SCHWYZER, Diss. Bonn (*Klass.-Phil. Stud.* 4.) 1932. The fragments also in *F Gr Hist* 618.

[3] Editions by O. HENSE, Leipz. 1905.

This is splendidly expressed by W. Theiler,[1] 'with a minimum of metaphysics he gives a maximum of ethical power'. Although he came very close to the Cynics, he increasingly picked up the threads which had been of importance to the Stoa from the very outset. We do not hear the zealot who campaigns against the good things of this world, but the sage who with quiet superiority counsels abstention. For him, too, 'fata sequi' is the guiding principle, but he does not proclaim it with the heroic fervour of a Seneca, but with humble resignation to the will of providence. He expounds the ancient stoical cosmopolitanism in the accents of a true love of mankind. It is understandable that attempts have been made to detect Christian elements in him. He never wrote anything; what we know of him we owe to Arrian (v. p. 847), who, in the dedicatory letter to the *Diatribes* has given us a picture of the strong and direct impact of Epictetus' delivery.

According to Willy Theiler the last Stoic who had anything of importance to write was the emperor Marcus Aurelius. Through his correspondence as a future ruler with his teacher Fronto,[2] the significant turning point in his life can still be detected. Fronto and Herodes Atticus made sincere attempts to win the prince over to rhetoric, but the severity of his view of life led him in a different direction, towards philosophy, which remained his companion when he had to bear the heavy burden of cares of state after the long periods of peace under his predecessors. The Parthians, the plague, Marcomanni and Quadi, a revolt under Avidius Cassius, all these things kept him constantly occupied during his reign (161–180). His philosophy gave him the internal peace which he needed to perform his duties. Much of the twelve books of his contemplations (Τὰ εἰς ἑαυτόν) was written in the field, as, for instance, the second in the land of the Quadi, the third in Carnuntum. The aphoristical character, which is peculiar to all the books except the first, probably the last to be written, is accounted for by the nature of the author, but also by the conditions under which it was produced.

The Stoic doctrine had a different ring in Marcus Aurelius from that in Epictetus. To a slight extent this is due to other sources which he consulted, such as Posidonius. Nor is the difference in attitude a conclusive explanation, but rather a difference of temperament. In Epictetus we observe a warmth of feeling and a fine faith, while in Marcus Aurelius all is coloured by a profound resignation. The *Historia Augusta* (4. 27, 7) puts the word of the Platonic king-philosopher in Marcus Aurelius' mouth, but the emperor himself states it differently (9. 29): 'Do not hope for Plato's state, but be satisfied with the slightest step forward.' Thus speaks the man who without the illusions, unassaulted by temptation to take refuge in mysticism, followed along the path of duty the divine in his inner self which the doctrine of the Stoa taught him to acknowledge.

A Berlin papyrus[3] has preserved large parts of the *Ethical Elements* ('Ηθικὴ στοιχείωσις) of Hierocles of Alexandria, who was approximately contemporary

---

[1] *Gnom.* 32, 1960, 500.
[2] Particularly 1, 214 in C. R. HAINES, *The Correspondence of Marcus Cornelius Fronto.* *Loeb Class. Libr.* 1919, of the year 146; a fine transl. in THEILER's introduction (v. inf.), 9.
[3] No. 400 P.: the authoritative edition of H. V. ARNIM, *Berl. Klass. Texte* 4, 1906.

with Epictetus. This popularization of ancient Stoical ethics has little meaning for us.

The last great and influential achievement of Greek philosophy is connected with the name of Plotinus. His work occupies no more an isolated position in time than that of the other Greek thinkers; we can also still discern many of the lines which were focussed, as it were, in his philosophy, from which they exerted their influence along various paths far into the centuries. Once and for all the notion should be put aside that Neoplatonism is simply the subjugation of the Hellenic intellect by the Orient, a sort of revenge of the myth over its tyrant, the logos. On the other hand, Oriental elements, which were especially influential in the later epoch, should not be underestimated. In this sphere the investigations are mostly in a state of flux. In the case of Plotinus, however, it is valid to say that his building was founded in Hellenic ground and was mainly constructed of material of the same origin.

His philosophy was above all a truly renewed Platonism, although he did not adopt the full scope of it. The dialectic of the early dialogues had hardly any meaning for the new movement, and the same applied to Plato as a political thinker; in the imperial era his words found no echo. But the radical separation of the world of the senses from another which is only accessible to the intellect and which relegates the only thing which has value in man to the sphere of that intellect, these remained the determining and fixed prerequisites of the renewed Platonism. In Plato we recognize the beginnings of important elements of Plotinus' system. The being beyond being (ἐπέκεινα τῆς οὐσίας), which in *Republic* 509 b is adjudged to the idea of the good, anticipates the surpassing of all being by the One, and the curious passage in *Letter* 7 (341 c; cf. p. 514) about the light which suddenly flashes after long endeavour is comparable, in spite of many differences, with the way in which Plotinus conceives the attainment of the highest goal.

The connecting lines traced here should not, however, conceal the awareness that the new Platonism was not the immediate product of the tradition of the Academy; it entered the ancient world as something new which had been prepared in other quarters. The place of dialectical struggling, endless in accordance with its nature, is taken over by the proclamation and spreading of knowledge which has been acquired through the evidence of an inner vision. Within the circle of the Neoplatonists there may have been disputes about the manner in which the most varying problems of this knowledge are to be arranged and subordinated – the knowledge itself is beyond doubt. Such a new conviction may grow into intolerance. But the final goal is not mere knowledge of the divine being, but union with it, experienced in the mystical act. Philosophy has become religion.

This direction has been anticipated by various trends, but only to a slight degree inside the Athenian Academy itself. Of course, significant starting-points for the later doctrine can be detected in Speusippus and Xenocrates,[1] but during

[1] PH. MERLAN, *From Platonism to Neoplatonism*. The Hague 1953. Also H. DÖRRIE, *Philos. Rundschau* 3, 1955, 14; 'Zum Ursprung der neuplat. Hypostasenlehre'. *Herm.* 82, 1954, 331.

its development in the Hellenistic era the school received only few fruitful impulses. Nevertheless, eclecticism meant that other schools of thought were approached with an open mind. Platonism did this also outside the Academy. Thus Pythagorean influence can be pointed out in Eudorus of Alexandria, who is of importance for the renewed vigour of the Platonic tradition in the first century A.D.[1] Elements of the Peripatos and the Stoa also played an important part in the school of the expounder of Plato Gaius (first half of the second century A.D.), to whom we have access through the introductory Platonic treatises *Prologue* and *Didascalicus* of his pupil Albinus.[2] Gaius coined the phrase which dominated all future exegesis of Plato, that the Master's utterances should be interpreted sometimes ἐπιστημονικῶς, sometimes εἰκοτολογικῶς,[3] sometimes purely scientifically, sometimes as a reference or allegory. The writings of Albinus reveal that a form of Platonism was gaining ground which stressed the demiurge as the superior principle over the ideas as merely subsidiary causes of being; it introduced the twin notion of δύναμις-ἐνέργεια and the graduation of the divine in the Neoplatonic system. Celsus, who in the late 'seventies of the second century attacked the Christians in his *True Word* (Ἀληθὴς λόγος), was close to this circle. The extensive apology of Origin (Κατὰ Κέλσου, 8 books) makes it possible to restore it to a large extent.

Posidonius should be remembered regarding the Stoic influences to which reference was made just now.[4] It may be mentioned that Theon of Smyrna, who wrote under Hadrian, probably utilized a *Timaeus* commentary of the Peripatetic Adrastus for his *Mathematical Introduction to Plato* (Περὶ τῶν κατὰ τὸ μαθηματικὸν χρησίμων εἰς τὴν Πλάτωνος ἀνάγνωσιν),[5] while Adrastus drew on Posidonius.

In addition to Plutarch's conciliatory attitude, Maximus of Tyre is also a characteristic example of the way in which the boundaries between the systems were being obliterated. This wandering orator and philosopher opened up his Platonism to practically all systems except Epicurus, and combined a notion of the divine raised to transcendency with a broadly developed demonism. Of the lectures which he delivered in the era of Commodus, forty-one *Dialexeis* survive, tractates written for the sake of effect, in a style replete with mannerisms; they are mainly concerned with the traditional popular-philosophical themes.

The most important phenomenon in the prehistory of Neoplatonism is the revival of Pythagoreanism. In an earlier chapter we discussed its apocryphal existence during the Hellenistic age and the movement in Rome at the end of

---

[1] H. DÖRRIE, 'Der Platoniker Eud. von Alexandreia'. *Herm.* 79, 1944, 25. On the movement which began in Alexandria A. WLOSOK, *Laktanz und die philos. Gnosis. Abh. Ak. Heidelb. Phil.-hist. Kl.* 1960/2, 52.

[2] On his relation with Gaius: K. PRAECHTER, 'Zum Platoniker G.'. *Herm.* 51. 1916, 510. On his characteristics cf. H. DÖRRIE, 'Die Frage nach dem Transzendenten im Mittelplatonismus', in *Sources de Plotin. Entretiens sur l'ant. class.* 5. Fondation Hardt. Vandœuvres-Geneva 1960.   [3] Proclus *in Tim.* 1, 340, 25 Diehl.

[4] W. THEILER, *Die Vorbereitung des Neuplatonismus. Problemata* 1. Berl. 1930, attempted to prove his importance for Neoplatonism. H. R. SCHWYZER, *RE* 21, 1951, 577, is sceptical.

[5] E. HILLER, Leipz. 1878. J. DUPUIS, Paris 1892 (with transl.).

the Republic, which was connected with the name of Nigidius Figulus and Q. Sextus. It is difficult to assess how old collections of aphorisms like Pythagoras' *Golden Words* (Χρυσᾶ ἔπη)[1] are, but they were probably augmented in the course of time. In spite of the pretentious title, the wisdom which they pass on as Pythagorean is rather pedestrian.

The most impressive figure of the new Pythagoreanism in the first century A.D. was Apollonius of Tyana, of whom we have heard already (p. 837). Moderatus of Gades wrote at about the same time as Apollonius; he had a close kinship with Platonism and conceived the Pythagorean theory of numbers as a system of symbolic metaphysics. The doctrine which he passed on that the One is above Being (τὸ πρῶτον ἐν ὑπὲρ τὸ εἶναι),[2] is of importance in that it prepares for the central thought of Neoplatonism. It also looks backward to the notion of Plato's esoteric doctrine which recently became a point of controversy. In the second century Nicomachus of Gerasa in Arabia, also an author of a biography of Pythagoras, wrote an *Introduction to the Theory of Numbers* ('Αριθμητικὴ εἰσαγωγή),[3] much esteemed by the Neoplatonists and much commented on. For the close connection of Pythagoreanism with Platonism, for the stress on God's transcendence, for the evaluation of matter based on a dualistic view of the universe, no other thinker of the second century A.D. is so significant as the Syrian Numenius of Apamea.[4] The reproach levelled at Plotinus that he was indebted to Numenius[5] was superficial, but not entirely inexplicable. Numenius interpreted Platonism as opposition against the invasion of Peripatetic elements, to which the eclecticism of Antiochus of Ascalon (p. 686) had opened the door. The Platonist Atticus,[6] who lived in the second half of the second century, adopted the same hostile attitude to Aristotle. But in spite of his disavowal of eclecticism regarding Aristotle, he admitted many a Stoic element.

The attitude of the Pythagoreans, which is so important for Neoplatonism, their inclination towards a new mode of life and to a knowledge of the divine as its goal, must be seen in the wider framework of a movement which had its roots in the Hellenistic age and began to gain ground during the first few centuries of the empire. This dualism turned away from the world and aspired to save man in the knowledge of God and in union with Him. It is presented in a collection which, under the name of Hermes Trismegistus, combined a number of tractates which are of importance to the history of religion. The most important of these *Hermetica*, among which there are many differences, is the

---

[1] D. Fasc. 2, 82; now D. YOUNG, *Theognis etc.* Leipz. 1961, 86. There were other collections of sayings by Sextus (A. Elter, Bonn 1891/92), Secundus, Demophilus, Eusebius; judging from the remnants they were very colourless.

[2] In Simplicius, *In Phys.* 1, 7; cf. E. R. DODDS, *Class. Quart.* 22, 1928, 140.

[3] Edition by R. HOCHE, Leipz. 1866; An 'Αρμονικὸν ἐγχειρίδιον by him has also been preserved: C. JAN, *Musici scriptores Graeci.* Leipz. 1895, 237.

[4] G. MARTANO, *Numenio d' Apamea.* Naples 1960.

[5] Porphyry, *Vita Plotini*, 17, 1. The grounds which make this reproach intelligible are developed by E. R. DODDS in 'Numenius and Ammonius', his contribution to the *Sources de Plotin* mentioned in the bibl. on Plotinus.

[6] The most important fragments in Eusebius' *Praeparatio Evangelica* 11, 1 f. 15, 4–9. 12 f. J. BAUDRY. *Atticos. Fragm. de son œuvre avec introd. et notes.* Paris 1931.

Poemandres. This is not the place to go into the details of this Hermetic belief, this pagan sister of the Christian gnosis, but it must be allotted a place in the intellectual milieu of the evolution of Neoplatonism. The same applies to the *Chaldean Oracles*, which were very highly esteemed among Neoplatonists. They originated in Marcus Aurelius' time; the author is probably the theurgist Julianus. The remnants of these hexameter sayings (λόγια) show Pythagorean, Platonic and Stoic elements combined with an unmistakable Oriental influence.[1]

Plotinus, who evolved his system from all this confusing abundance into the last great creation of ancient philosophy, was born in 205. The place of his birth is unknown; an indication of Eunapius pointing to Lycopolis in Upper Egypt is unreliable.[2] He turned to philosophy at a late date, when he was 28. He was first disappointed by the scholastic philosophers in Alexandria, but soon found in Ammonius, later surnamed Saccas, the teacher who was decisive for his career.[3] Ammonius did not write himself. What we know about him, largely through Porphyry, points to a combination of Pythagorean and Platonic elements. There is no doubt but that he was responsible for the intellectual awakening of Plotinus, who studied with him for eleven years in a Platonic community of life and spirit. He then joined Gordian III's expedition against the Persians (243) in order to become acquainted with the wisdom of Indian thinkers.[4] But the emperor was murdered early in 244, Plotinus had to flee to Antioch and went to Rome in the same year. There he began to teach and continued doing so for twenty-six years, completing his instruction, after ten years of oral teaching, with the written word. In the year 269 he had to retire to Campania with a serious illness, and died there in 270.

We have already tried to understand the historical preliminaries to Plotinus' doctrine, of which we can only indicate some of the essential features. The controlling thought is the supremacy over all forms and degrees of reality of the One, which, however, must not be understood to be a numerical notion. It rather eludes any positive description, being the highest deity and the origin of all that is. Below this is the realm of the intellect which, as pure thought–force, is one, but is nevertheless already split into multiplicity. This is the location of the ideas which for Plotinus no longer occupy the central position in his doctrine to the same degree as in Plato's. In this graduated structure, which we traverse downward, the realm of the soul follows next; it is neither corporeal (Stoa), nor harmony (Pythagorean), nor entelechy (Peripatos). It is the organizational principle of all living organisms, of the cosmos as a whole as well as of each

---

[1] Bibl. in M. P. NILSSON, *Gesch. d. gr. Rel.* 2, 2nd ed. Munich 1961, 479, 1.

[2] FR. ZUCKER, 'Plotin und Lykopolis'. *Sitzb. D. Ak. Berlin* 1950/1 thinks that this indication is correct and points to the vigorous Greek educational elements in this Graeco-Egyptian world. He also discusses the surviving writing of Alexander of Lycopolis, a Neoplatonic who wrote *Against the Doctrines of the Manichaeans* (πρὸς τὰς Μανιχαίων δόξας).

[3] H. DÖRRIE, 'Ammonios, der Lehrer Plotins'. *Herm.* 83, 1955, 439.

[4] Porphyry, *Vita Plotini*, 3, 17. There is no support for the conjecture of E. BRÉHIER, *La Philos. de Pl.* Paris 1928, 107, that Plotinus should have borrowed essential thoughts from India.

individual living creature. Even matter, the non-existent in the sense of Plotinus' reality, acquires its form (the Aristotelian εἶδος) from the realm of the soul. The individual degrees of being have not evolved one from the other in time; emanation and origin are mere metaphors in this system; all these spheres or hypostases are mutually connected (an important passage 6, 5, 4, 23), forming one great, ultimately homogeneous structure, which determines the possibilities and tasks of the philosophizing human. The labour of his intellect can lead the soul back to the One out of the entanglement in the multiplicity of earthly things. Cleanliness of body and soul are self-evident conditions, as they are for the Pythagoreans, but with Plotinus the ultimate goal is no longer mere knowledge, but union with the highest principle, the unio mystica. It is attained after long preparation, in the rare moments when man is freed from himself in ecstasy. According to Porphyry (Vita 23. 16), this fulfilment fell to Plotinus' lot four times.

Plotinus made his writings accessible to his students, but in his lifetime he did not produce an edition for the book trade. In Porphyry's Life (4-6) we have a trustworthy enumeration of Plotinus' works in chronological order. This clearly demonstrates that Plotinus did not proceed systematically, but selected urgent questions as they occurred in the course of his teaching. From a scholium in some manuscripts after 4. 4, 29 we learn of an edition produced by Eustochius, a physician and one of the Master's most intimate scholars. There is much in favour of the theory that the quotations from Plotinus in Eusebius, which are so valuable for the tradition, go back to this edition. The edition of Porphyry, however, published somewhat later, between 301 and 305, has survived. It combined the writings in subject groups, which yielded three corpora (σωμάτια) of 27. 18 and 9 writings, i.e. six groups of nine as a whole; this was the reason for the title Enneads which has become customary. The so-called Theology, transmitted in Arabic, is a presentation of the doctrine bloated with paraphrases. An attempt to establish a correspondence between this and the σχόλια ἐκ τῶν συνουσιῶν, which Amelius, another pupil and companion of Plotinus', wrote in about a hundred books, lacks dependable support.[1]

Plotinus' most important pupil, the Syrian Porphyry of Tyre, originally called Malcus, was a scholar of extensive learning rather than a creative philosopher. He was pledged to Plotinus' doctrine by his ultimate concern, which was theological, the purification and salvation of the soul. He was born in Tyre in 234, studied in Athens and in 263 came to Rome to join Plotinus, whom he left in 268 after a great inner crisis, without giving up his faith in the doctrine. After a long stay in Sicily he returned to Rome. It may be assumed that he directed the school after Plotinus.

For his development the remnants of a treatise On the Philosophical Benefit of Oracles (Περὶ τῆς ἐκ λογίων φιλοσοφίας) are important, which he wrote while he was still in his native land. It is dominated by a belief in demons and a magic control over the gods. Later writings like On the Images of the Gods or the Letter

---

[1] Cf. H. R. SCHWYZER, RE 21, 1951, 505. A. N. SUBOS, Amelius von Etrurien. Diss. Munich 1954. Id., Amelii Neoplatonici fragmenta. Athens 1956.

to *Anebo*,[1] an Egyptian priest, both only surviving in fragments, do not point to a renunciation of these notions, but indicate that he tried to fit them into Plotinus' system. We already met Porphyry as his master's biographer and editor of his writings; characteristic of the Neoplatonist are the surviving *Life of Pythagoras* and the treatise *De Abstinentia* (Περὶ ἀποχῆς ἐμψύχων). What meaning in this conception of the universe the ancient instrument of allegory could assume is shown by the treatise *On the Nymphs' Cave* (Περὶ τοῦ ἐν 'Οδυσσείᾳ τῶν Νυμφῶν ἄντρου), which turns *Od.* 13. 102-112 into an allegory of the cosmos and the fate of the soul. Porphyry has the greatest personal appeal for us in the late letter *To Marcella*, his wife, in which he develops the basic features of his doctrine. This religious-minded author, in whose spiritual world demonism played a significant part, did serious scholarly work in a variety of fields. In his voluminous and versatile work there were a large number of commentaries on Plato and Aristotle. His preoccupation with Aristotelian logic, of which we have the Εἰσαγωγή, became an important chapter of the intellectual tradition. Among the loss of much else we particularly regret that of his work *Against the Christians*, which developed an extensive criticism in fifteen books.

The influence of Neoplatonism soon assumed tremendous proportions. Schools began to separate off which developed numerous variations without upsetting the foundations. The Syrian Iamblichus of Chalcis (*c.* 275 to *c.* 330) was of the greatest importance for this event. In Rome he heard Porphyry, but his path deviated considerably from his teacher's. Contradictions, which Neoplatonism carried within itself, are more sharply evident in him. All the gates were open now; superstition and magical practices entered unhindered, Oriental elements flowed in in an increasing degree. On the other hand, all this was carefully fitted into the system, and the result was an ingeniously contrived abstruse extension of the doctrine, mostly with the aid of divisions into trinities. With one exception, the surviving works are remnants of *Pythagorean Dogmatics* (Συναγωγὴ τῶν Πυθαγορείων δογμάτων, 10 books). There is also a *Life of Pythagoras*, a *Protrepticus* and three writings on the doctrine of numbers in the Pythagorean-Neoplatonic sense. The treatise *De Mysteriis*, whose authenticity is no longer doubted, stands on its own; excerpts of it were translated into Latin by Marsilius Ficinus (1497). It purports to be the answer of the Egyptian priest Abammon to Porphyry's letter to Anebo and is one of the most important religious documents in late antiquity. Among the representatives of the Syrian movement in Neoplatonism which originated with Iamblichus we mention his pupil Theodorus of Asine, who further elaborated his master's system of trinities.

The polytheistical-superstitious line of Neoplatonism is particularly evident in the Pergamenian school, founded by Iamblichus' pupil Aedesius of Cappadocia. Through Maximus, Aedesius' pupil, it strongly influenced Julian's

---

[1] A. R. SODANO, Naples 1958. F. ALTHEIM and R. STIEHL, *Porphyrios und Empedokles.* Tübingen 1954 have published excerpts from Porphyry's writings in an Arabic writing of Sakrastani, among which a fragment of the *Letter to Anebo* which is important for the pre-history of Iamblichus' *De Mysteriis*; cf. ALTHEIM-STIEHL, *Philologia Sacra* 1958, 100.

syncretical polytheism. This movement was advocated with an elementary introduction to Neoplatonism which Salustius passed on in his surviving work *On Gods and the Universe*. It is very likely that the author is the friend of the emperor to whom he addressed the fourth speech and for whose removal he consoles himself in the eighth.[1]

The Alexandrian school is in marked opposition to the directions mentioned. The religious and metaphysical components are superseded in favour of scientific elements. The spirit of the Museum is still active. On this basis contacts with Christianity were possible. Synesius of Cyrene, the later bishop, found his intellectual starting-point in these surroundings. We already met him as a writer of hymns (p. 812), and a glance at his prose works[2] will serve to complete the image of this attractive personality who brought about a personal synthesis of the various influences which converged in him. He was a pupil of the daughter of the philosopher and mathematician Theon of Alexandria, the philosopher Hypatia, who was murdered by fanatical Christians in 415. Synesius, born between 370 and 375, studied Neoplatonic philosophy, astronomy and mathematics under her and this instruction decided his career, while the Athenian schools at that time had nothing to offer. Personal observation had made him acquainted with Byzantium and its court and also in other ways he had been active in his own particular combination of the *vita activa* and *contemplativa*, when in 410 he was elected metropolitan of Pentapolis in his native country. If we are to believe the ecclesiastical writers[3] he was baptized after his election. But the hymns, of which part was written earlier, clearly reveal his conversion. In spite of this he never renounced his close connection with philosophy. Nothing shows this so clearly as the passage in one of his letters (*Ep.* 11 p. 648 H.), where he states that he felt his ghostly office not as an alienation from philosophy, but as its confirmation. He probably died about 415, but the precise date is uncertain.

The oldest of the surviving prose works is the speech Περὶ βασιλείας,[4] in which as an ambassador he developed his conception of the ideal ruler before the emperor Arcadius. In spite of its literary leanings it reveals a great deal of his personality, while in his *Dion* (Δίων ἢ περὶ τῆς κατ' αὐτὸν διαγωγῆς),[5] in which he defends his philosophical and 'musical' activities against all sorts of fanaticism by taking Dion as his model, his literary tendency contributes to an understanding of the author. In the Αἰγύπτιοι λόγοι ἢ περὶ προνοίας[6] he describes the vicissitudes of his patron Aurelian under the guise of the myth of Osiris-Typhon; the treatise Περὶ τοῦ δώρου accompanied a celestial globe which he had ordered. In Περὶ ἐνυπνίων he discussed dreams, especially their mantic meaning. The playful *Praise of Baldness* (Φαλακρίας ἐγκώμιον) was

[1] Cf. NOCK (*v. inf.*), CI.

[2] N. TERZAGHI, *Synesii Cyrenensis opuscula*. Rome 1944.

[3] Evagr. *Hist. eccl.* 1, 15. Nicephorus Call. *Hist. eccl.* 14, 55. Photius *Bibl. can.* 26.

[4] CH. LACOMBRADE, *Le Discours sur la royauté de Synésios de Cyrène. Trad. nouv. avec introd., notes et comm.* Paris 1951.

[5] K. TREU, *Synesios von Kyrene. Ein Kommentar zu seinem 'Dion'*, Berl. 1958. Id., *Syn. v. Kyr. Dion Chrysostomos oder vom Leben nach seinem Vorbild.* Berlin 1959 (Text and transl.).

[6] S NICOLOSI, *Il 'De providentia' di Sinesio di Cirene.* Padua 1959.

mentioned earlier (p. 834). He was fond of writing letters[1] at every stage of his career. The collection, which comprises 156 of them, represents a chapter of biography and cultural history dominated by the venerable personality of its erudite author. He gave his hymns, linked as they were with the form of a literary genre, a Doric colouring, but in his prose he attempted to write pure Attic.

Of Hierocles of Alexandria (5th c.) we have a commentary on the *Golden Words of Pythagoras* and considerable remnants of his work *On Providence and Fate*. This erudite school is most impressively represented in the numerous commentaries on Plato and Aristotle, for which the names of Ammonius, Olympiodorus and of Ioannes Philoponus, later converted to Christianity, will serve as testimony.[2]

The Athenian school, which had been greatly stimulated by Iamblichus regarding the principles of the interpretation of Plato and the scholastic expansion of the system, begins with Plutarch of Athens. One of his assistants, Syrian, is noteworthy, because he introduced rhetoric into the didactic activity.[3] The most successful representative of this direction, Proclus (*c.* 410–484), was a student of the two men mentioned. He was born in Byzantium, passed his youth in Lycia and at an early stage he found in the school in Athens the place for his activity. His biography was written by his zealous pupil and adherent Marinus. In a series of writings, of which we single out the surviving *Outline of Theology* (Στοιχείωσις θεολογική) and the *Physics* (Στοιχείωσις φυσική), as well as the numerous *Commentaries on Plato*, whose theology is summed up in the important Εἰς τὴν Πλάτωνος θεολογίαν, Proclus elaborated the Neoplatonic system by making increasingly minute subdivisions and interpolations, of which the insertion of units between the Original One and the intelligible was particularly characteristic of the Athenian school. In his versatility Proclus is reminiscent of many Alexandrians, though he is not up to their scientific level. He wrote on mathematics (e.g. a commentary on Euclid) and astronomy; he also commented on Homer and Hesiod. We have remnants of his interpretations of the latter. It is doubtful, to say the least, if the *Chrestomathy* is his (*v.* p. 81 n. 1). His hymns were discussed earlier (p. 812).

The last representatives of the Athenian school, Damascius,[4] in whom dialectic

---

[1] A. GARZYA, 'Per l'edizione delle epistole di Sinesio'. *Accad. dei Lincei. Bolletino del Comitato per la preparazione della Ediz. Naz.* Nuova serie 6, 1958, 29, and 'Nuovi scoli alle epistole di Sinesio', Ibid. 8, 1960, 47. Cf. also *Rendic. Accad. Linc.* 8/13, 1958, 1, and *Rend. Accad. di Napoli* 33, 1958, 41.

[2] KL. KREMER, *Der Metaphysikbegriff in den Aristoteles-Kommentaren der Ammonios-Schule. Beitr. z. Gesch. u. Theol. des Mittelalters* 39/1. Münster 1961. Of editions of the Plato commentaries of Olympiodorus of particular value L. G. WESTERINK, O. *Commentaries on the First Alcib. of Pl.* Amsterdam 1956. The comm. on *Phaed.* and *Gorg.* edited by W. NORVIN, Leipz. 1913, 1936; cf. also on Damascius.

[3] H. RABE, *Syr. in Hermog. commentaria.* Leipz. 1892/93.

[4] L. G. WESTERINK has proved in his enquiry *Damascius, Lectures on the Philebus*, wrongly attributed to Olympiodorus. Amsterdam 1959, that the comm. on the *Phaedo* and *Philebus* of Cod. Marc. gr. 196 fol. 242-337 actually belong to Damascius; he has also re-edited the texts on the speech with transl. and comm.

and mysticism blended once more in a singular manner, and the excellent Aristotle-commentator Simplicius, were among the seven philosophers who went east, to the court of the king of Persia, after the closure of the school by Justinian (529). The conclusion of peace in the year 533 made it possible for them to return to an Athens which was no longer to be the city of the Platonic Academy.

Sextus Empiricus: H. MUTSCHMANN; I: *Pyrrh. Hypoth.* Leipz. 1912, repr. 1958; II: *Adv. dogmaticos* (7-11) 1914; III: *Adv. mathematicos* (1-6) 2nd ed. J. MAU. 1962. IV: K. JANÁCEK 1962. With Engl. transl.: R. G. BURY, 4 vols. *Loeb Class. Libr.* 1933-49. Important for the text: W. HEINTZ, *Studien zu Sext. Emp. Schr. d. Königsb. Gel. Ges. Sonderreihe* 2, 1932. – Cornutus: C. LANG, Leipz. 1881. – Heraclitus: Edition of the Bonner philol. Gesellschaft. Leipz. 1910. – Cebes: K. PRAECHTER, Leipz. 1893. A. PH. FLOROS, '᾽Ο Κ. Πίναξ'. *Platon* 7, 1955, 287. C. E. FINCH, 'The Place of Codex Vat. gr. 1823 in the Cebes Manuscript Tradition'. *Am. Journ. Phil.* 81, 1960, 176. – Epictetus: W. A. OLDFATHER, *Contributions towards a Bibliography of Epictetus.* Univ. of Illinois 1927. A suppl. ed. by M. HARMAN, with a preliminary list of Epictetus manuscripts by W. H. FRIEDERICH and C. U. FAYE, *ibid.* 1952. Important for the text: REVILO PENDLETON OLIVER, *Nicolò Perotti's Version of Enchiridion of Ep.* Urbana 1954; also K. MRAS, *AfdA* 12, 1959, 107. Text: H. SCHENKL, 2nd ed. Leipz. 1916. Bilingual: W. A. OLDFATHER, *Discourses,* 2 vols. *Loeb Class. Libr.* 1926 (repr. 1952/59). J. SOUILHÉ, *Entretiens, Coll. des Univ. d. Fr.* 2 vols. 1948/49. PABLO-JORDAN DE URRIES Y AZARA. I. Barcelona 1957. H. F. W. STELLWAG, *Het I.B. der Diatriben.* Amsterd. 1933 (transl. with good comm.). Transl. W. CAPELLE, Jena 1925. J. BONFORTE, New York 1955. R. LAURENTI, *Epitteto. Le diatribe e i frammenti.* Bari 1960. Interpretation: B. L. HIJMANS JR., "Ἄσκησις—Notes on Epictetus' Educational System.' Assen 1959. An elaborate article on Epictetus by M. SPANNEUT in the *Reallex. f. Ant. u. Chr.* 5, 1961, 599. – Marcus Aurelius: H. SCHENKL, Leipz. 1913. The following four editions are bilingual: C. R. HAINES, *Loeb Class. Libr.* 1916. A. J. TRANNOY, *Coll. des Un. d. Fr.* 1925. A. S. L. FARQUHARSON, 2 vols. (with comm.) Oxf. 1944. W. THEILER, Zürich 1951 (outstanding, with excellent notes, bibl. p. 300). A translation by A. MAUERSBERGER, 4th ed. Leipz. 1957 (Samml. Dieterich 50). Various studies and papers: H. R. NEUENSCHWANDER, *Mark Aurels Beziehungen zu Seneca und Poseidonios. Noctes Romanae* 3. Bern 1951. A. S. L. FARQUHARSON, *Marcus Aurelius. His Life and his World.* 2nd ed. Oxf. 1952. F. C. THOMES, *Per la critica di Marco Aurelio.* Turin 1955 (Pubbl. d. Fac. di Lett. e Filos. 7, 5). CH. PARAIN, *Marc-Aurèle. Portraits d'histoire.* Paris 1957. Epictetus and Marcus Aurelius: M. POHLENZ, *Die Stoa.* 2nd ed. Gött. 1959. – Albinus: P. LOUIS, Paris 1945. New ed. in prep. by H. DÖRRIE. Bibl.: R. E. WITT, *Albinus and the History of Middle Platonism.* Cambr. 1937. J. H. LOENEN, 'Albinus' Metaphysics'. *Mnem.* S.4, 9, 1956, 296. 10, 1957, 35. – Celsus: O. GLÖCKNER, *Kl. Texte.* Bonn 1924. R. BADER, *Der 'Αληθὴς λόγος des Kelsos.* Tüb. Beitr. 33, 1940. A. WIFSTRAND,

'*Die wahre Lehre des Kelsos*'. *Bull. de la Soc. Royale des Lettres de Lund.* 1941/42,
391. H. CHADWICK, *Orig. contra Celsum.* Transl. with introd. and notes. Cambr.
1953. C. ANDRESEN, *Logos und Nomos. Die Polemik des K. wider das Christentum.*
Abh. z. Kirchengesch. 30, Berl. 1955 (A study of the philosophical personality
of Celsus utilizing the unprinted collection of fragments of H. O. SCHRÖDER,
which was present in Giessen as a Habil. writing in 1939.) – Maximus of Tyre:
H. HOBEIN, Leipz. 1910. – Numenius: E. A. LEEMANS, *Studie over de wijsgeer
Numenius van Apamea met uitgave der fragmenten.* Brussels 1937. R. BEUTLER, *RE*,
S 7, 1940, 664. – The relevant sections in M. P. NILSSON, *Gesch. d. gr. Rel.* 2, 2nd
ed. Munich 1961, 415. 426. 435, are important for the intellectual background
of Neoplatonism and the system itself. – Hermetica: The texts: W. SCOTT–A. S.
FERGUSON, 4 vols., Oxf. 1924–36. A. D. NOCK–A.-J. FESTUGIÈRE, 4 vols. *Coll. des
Un. d. Fr.* 1945–54; 1 and 2 repr. 1960. A tractate, not in the Corpus of Hermetical
writings, has become known in an Armenian transl. through *Der Bote aus dem
Matenadaran* 3. Eriwan. Ac. of Sc. of the Armenian SSR. 1956; Armenian text
by JA. MANANDYAN, Russian by S. AREFSHATYAN. Cf. H. DÖRRIE, *Gnom.* 29,
1957, 446. Of fundamental importance for the whole section the great work of
A.-J. FESTUGIÈRE, *La révélation d'Hermès Trismégiste. I: L'astrologie et les sciences
occultes*; II: *Le dieu cosmique*; III: *Les doctrines de l'âme*; IV: *Le dieu inconnu et la
gnose*. Paris 1944–54. A. WLOSOK, *Laktanz und die philos. Gnosis. Abh. Akad.
Heidelb. Phil.-hist. Kl.* 1960/2. 115. – Plotinus: Bibl. by B. MARIEN in the transl.
of Cilento (*v. infra*). For the history of the text P. HENRY, *Les états du texte de
P.* Brussels 1938; *Les Manuscrits des Ennéades. Ibid.* 1941; 2nd ed. 1948. H. R.
SCHWYZER, *Gnom.* 32, 1960, 32 on the passages of Plotinus quoted in the *Praeparatio Evangelica* of Eusebius. Editions: E. BRÉHIER, 6 vols. *Coll. des Un. d. Fr.*
1924–38; 2nd ed. from 1954 (bilingual). New critical edition, the only authoritative one: P. HENRY–H. R. SCHWYZER, I (Enn. 1-3). Brussels 1951; II (Enn. 4-5)
1959. Translations: R. HARDER, Leipz. 1930–37; new with Greek text based on
HENRY-SCHWYZER, and notes 1 a/b (1-21) Hamburg 1956. II a/b (22-29) edd.
BEUTLER-THEILER. 1962. V a/b (46-54) edd. BEUTLER-THEILER. 1960. V c
appendix. Porphyry on Plotinus' life and the order of his works. Ed. Marg.
1958. An Engl. selection in transl., H. A. ARMSTRONG, *Plotinus*, London 1953.
Italian V. CILENTO, *Antologia Plotiniana*, Bari 1955, by the same also the
valuable It. transl. of Plotinus, Bari 1947–49. The Engl. transl. by ST MACKENNA,
2nd ed. revised by B. S. PAGE, London 1957. An outstanding monograph is the
RE article (21, 1951, 471-592) by H. R. SCHWYZER with bibl. and a valuable
section on the subsequent history. PH. V. PISTORIUS, *Pl. and Neoplatonism. An
introductory Study.* Cambr. 1952. J. TROUILLARD, *La Procession plotinienne.* Paris
1955. *La Purification plotinienne.* Paris 1955. H. FISCHER, *Die Aktualität Pl.s.*
Munich 1956. K. H. VOLKMANN-SCHLUCK, *Pl. als Interpret der Ontologie Platons.*
2nd unalt. ed. Frankf. a.M. 1957. W. HIMMERICH, *Eudaimonia. Die Lehre des Pl.
von der Selbstverwirklichung des Menschen. Forsch. z. neueren Philos. und ihrer
Gesch.* N.F.13, Würzburg 1959. *Sources de Plotin. Dix exposés et discussions par*
A. H. ARMSTRONG, P. V. CILENTO, E. R. DODDS, H. DÖRRIE, P. HADOT, R. HARDER,
P. P. HENRY, H. CH. PUECH, H. R. SCHWYZER, W. THEILER. *Entretiens sur l'ant.*

class. 5 Fondation Hardt. Vandœuvres-Geneva 1960. E. BRÉHIER, *La philosophie de Pl.* 2nd ed., Paris 1961; in Engl. transl. by J. THOMAS, Chicago 1958. C. RUTTEN, *Les Catégories du monde sensible dans les Ennéades de Pl.* Bibl. de la Fac. de Phil. et Lettr. de Liège 160. 1961. – Porphyry: The editions of the individual writings in R. BEUTLER, *RE* 22, 1953, 278 ff. W. THEILER, *P. und Augustin.* Halle 1933. (Schr. d. Königsb. Gel. Ges. 10/1.) On this question also P. COURCELLE, *Recherches sur les Confessions de S. Aug.* Paris 1950. J. J. O'MEARA, *Porphyry's Philosophy from oracles in Aug.* Paris 1959 attempts to prove through Augustine that Porphyry's Περὶ τῆς ἐκλογίων φιλοσοφίας and *De regressu animae* in *Civ. Dei* 10, 29 and 32 are the same work which had great influence on Augustin; doubted by H. DÖRRIE, *Gnom.* 32, 1960, 320. Further on Porphyry: J. TRICOT, *Porphyre, Isagoge.* Transl. and notes. Paris 1947. H. DÖRRIE, *Porphyrios' 'Symmikta Zetemata'. Zet.* 20. Munich 1959 (with a reconstruction of the *Symm. Zet.* mainly from Nemesius and Priscian). – Iamblichus: L. DEUBNER, *De Vita Pythagorica.* Leipz. 1937. The older editions of the remaining writings in Christ-Schmidt, *Gesch. d. gr. Lit.* II/2, 6th ed. Munich 1924, 1054. On the *Protrepticus* W. JAEGER, *Aristoteles.* 2nd ed. Berl. 1955, 60. Important for the tradition the works of M. SICHERL, *Die Handschriften, Ausgaben und Übersetzungen von J. de mysteriis.* Berlin 1957 (Texte u. Untersuchungen zur Gesch. d. altchristl. Lit. 62); 'Bericht über den stand der krit. Ausgabe von J. de mysteriis'. *Arch. f. Gesch. d. Philos.* 42, 1960, H. 3; 'Ein übersehener Jambl.-Codex (Matrit. O 46)'. *Emérita* 28, 1960, 87. – Salustius: A. D. NOCK, Cambr. 1926 (with important introd. and comm.). G. ROCHEFORT, *S. des Dieux et du monde.* *Coll. des Un. de Fr.* 1960 (bilingual). Transl. also in G. MURRAY, *Five Stages of Gr. Rel.* 3rd ed. Boston n.d., 200. – Proclus: The editions of the individual writings in R. BEUTLER's comprehensive *RE* article, 23, 1957, 185. L. G. WESTERINK, *Proclus Diadochus. Comm. on the First Alcibiades of Plato. Crit. Text and indices.* Amsterdam 1954. E. TUROLLA, *Pr. La teologia Platonica.* Bari 1958. H. BOESE, *Die mittelalterliche Übersetzung der στοιχείωσις φυσική des Proclus.* Berlin 1958. Id. *Procli Diadochi tria opuscula (De providentia, libertate, malo). Latine Guil. de Moerbeca vertente et Graece ex Isacii Sebastocratoris aliorumque scriptis collecta.* Quellen u. Studien z. Gesch. d. Philos. 1. Berlin 1960. P. LÉVÊQUE, *Aurea catena Homeri. Une étude sur l'allégorie grecque.* Paris 1959 (important for Proclus). TH. WHITTAKER, *The Neo-Platonists. A Study in the History of Hellenism. With a Suppl. on the Comm. of Proclus.* 1928. Repr. 1961 Olms/Hildesheim. V. COUSIN, *Procli Diad. comm. in Platonis Parmenidem* reprinted after the 2nd ed. Paris 1864 in Hildesheim 1961. Minerva G.m.b.H. Frankf. a.M. is preparing a repr. of the ed. of *In Platonis Theologiam* of AE. PORTUS, Hamburg 1618. Ibid. since 1962 reprints of V. COUSIN, *Procli philosophi Platonici opera inedita* (after the 2nd ed. of 1864) and A.-E. CHAIGNET, *Pr. Comm. sur le Parménide.* 3 vols. (1st impr. Paris 1900–03).

7 THE SCIENCES

The élan of scientific research, which was especially distinctive of the early Hellenistic period, was succeeded, during the empire, by a broadening of scope which necessarily involved a decrease in depth. It also becomes quite clear in this sphere to what extent Greek culture in this epoch should be viewed in its relationship with Rome. Pure theory did not find a fertile soil there. For the rulers of the world, astronomy was meaningful if it helped to establish a serviceable calendar, natural science, if it improved agriculture, geometry, if it helped in surveying the provinces and the making of maps. Greek science had other aims and a few men had not lost sight of them even in this time, but they were exceptional.

Many were absorbed with grammar. As a curiosity, mention should be made of the erudite collector Pamphila; during Nero's reign this lady wrote thirty-three books of *Miscellaneous Historical Notes*. We reviewed the literary importance of the lexicographers' activity n connection with Atticism (p. 832).

Herennius Philon of Byblos, whom we met in another context (p. 95) as the rehabilitated author of the *Phoenician History*, should be mentioned here. He also wrote on history and grammar. There is little doubt that he produced the matrix of the lexicon of synonyms[1] which was attributed to Ammonius. He was the Alexandrian grammarian (and also a priest of the monkey-god) who went to Constantinople with Helladius after the destruction of the pagan temple.

The second century brought also a late flourishing of the study of grammar. Apollonius Dyscolus, who worked mainly in his native city of Alexandria, dealt with the parts of speech in a large number of writings, which are quoted by Suidas and by himself. Of these smaller works we only have three, but we also have the four books of his *Syntax* (Περὶ συντάξεως), in which he is the first to give a systematic summary of this material. He did not blaze new trails; he always takes his starting-point from the parts of speech and proves to be, as befits a true dyscolus, a pedantic analogist. In another field of grammar his son and pupil Herodian also carried out synoptical work. His *General Prosody* (Καθολικὴ προσῳδία) was written in Rome under Marcus Aurelius, to whom it was dedicated. The numerous individual writings are lost but for one on formal anomalies (Περὶ μονήρους λέξεως) and one small, probably spurious, Atticist lexicon *Philhetaerus*.[2] A third systematist did comparable work in the field of metre. Hephaestion wrote his large work Περὶ μέτρων (48 books) in the Alexandrian tradition, and he himself undertook the work of excerpting it, a labour normally left to posterity. The final result, the product of various stages of work, is the *Little Manual* ('Εγχειρίδιον), which has been preserved.

In the theory of music the standard activity is also one of summarizing and excerpting. An *Introduction to Harmonics* (Εἰσαγωγὴ ἁρμονική)[3] is preserved; as its authors, the mathematicians Euclid and Pappus, and also a certain Cleonides, are mentioned. The unimportant name is probably the correct one. The treatise

---

[1] KL. NICKAU, *Das sogenannte Ammonioslexikon. Vorarbeiten zu einer kritischen Textausgabe.* Diss. Hamburg 1959 (typesc.).

[2] A. DAIN, *Le 'Philétaeros' attribué à Hérodien.* Paris 1954.

[3] The text, with a Latin translation, was published in the 8th vol. of the Euclid edition by J. L. HEIBERG and H. MENGE, Leipz. 1916, 185 after C. JAN's edition in the *Musici Scriptores Graeci* 1895, 179. An analysis in M. FUHRMANN, *Das systematische Lehrbuch*, Göttingen 1960, 34.

gives rigid and conventional outlines of doctrines which are basically derived from Aristoxenus of Tarentum. A Leiden Aristoxenus codex reveals a manual of a larger size probably written between Aristoxenus and the *Introduction*. Its date is difficult to fix; the early second century is mere conjecture.

In the sphere of geography the descriptive historical and the mathematical branches proceeded along ways which led to their final degeneration. We already met Strabo of Amasea in the district of Pontus (*c.* 64 B.C.-19 A.D.) as a historian (p. 777). His large historical work is lost, but the seventeen books of his *Geographica* survive, although parts are missing. The first two books, in which he takes issue with predecessors like Eratosthenes, Polybius and Posidonius over the mathematical elements, reveal that this field was not his forte. The very fact that, under the influence of the Stoa, he considered Homer as a source, made it impossible for him to acquire a deeper understanding. The far lengthier parts about Europe (3-10), Asia (11-16) and Africa (17) are supported only to a limited degree by personal experience, although he travelled far. He is mostly dependent on his sources among whom, apart from the authors mentioned, Artemidorus of Ephesus (11 books of *Geographumena* in 100 B.C.) is especially singled out. Strabo writes simply, without an emphatically Atticist tendency. He is not important in any way, but we must be grateful for the survival of this geography with its wealth of historical data and variety of excursuses.

In the realm of descriptive geography we have already discussed Dionysius the Periegete (p. 813) and Arrian (p. 847); we add here the *Anaplus Bospori* of Dionysius of Byzantium, who probably still wrote in the second century. The treatise pretends to be literary art; its author tries to deploy all the artifices of Atticist rhetoric.

In this province antiquity also ekes out its final epoch with compilations, of which Marcianus of Heraclea on the Pontus (400)[1] has left some samples. The great lexicon of Stephanus of Byzantium, the *Ethnica*, of which we possess a few articles in the original and a great deal in excerpts, was probably written in the sixth century, or perhaps earlier.

The work produced by Ptolemy of Ptolemaïs in Upper Egypt (*c.* 100 to 170) in the field of applied mathematics can also be characterized as a synopsis resulting in considerable losses. But it should in all fairness be admitted that in this case intellectual penetration of the difficult material was demanded to a greater extent than elsewhere. Ptolemy, who lived in Alexandria, administered the great legacy of the Museum with propriety and reflected on the philosophical foundations of what he did. The small epistemological treatise Περὶ κριτηρίου καὶ ἡγεμονικοῦ shows that he followed the Peripatetic tradition, which he mixed with Platonic and Stoical elements. Relatively early – the astronomical observations quoted occurred in 127–147 – he wrote the work which comprises our knowledge of ancient astronomy, the Μαθηματικὴ σύνταξις. The current name of *Almagest* originated from the Arabic translation (9th c.), which in turn

---

[1] On the remnants of his epitome of Artemidorus of Ephesus and his descriptions of coasts: R. GÜNGERICH, *Die Küstenbeschreibung in der ant. Lit.* Münster 1950, 22. The texts *Geogr. Gr. min.* I, 515.

has its origin in a version of the title μεγίστη σύνταξις (or something like it). It presents the geocentric conception of the universe after Hipparchus and others. Aristarchus of Samos was destined not to gain acceptance again until Copernicus formulated his conception. The *Tetrabiblus* (Μαθηματική or 'Αποτελεσματική σύνταξις τετράβιβλος) may be considered as an astrological appendix to the great work. Of his astronomical charts a *Canon of Kings* (Κανὼν Βασιλειῶν) is preserved because it had been inserted in the chronicle of the Byzantine Georgius Syncellus. The *Geographical Primer* (Γεωγραφικὴ ὑφήγησις, 8 books), which tried to meet a demand which had existed since Hipparchus, is no less important than the astronomical work. Ptolemy gives references for about 8000 places according to longitude and latitude as a basis for the production of maps, but only a small part of the data is based on exact observation. Ptolemy borrowed a great deal from his predecessor Marinus of Tyre and much of his work rests on doubtful data and conjectures. Ptolemy did valuable intermediary work in his *Harmonics* (3 books) and *Optics*. Of the latter we have only books 2–5 in a Latin translation, which in turn has its origin in one in Arabic. We have only some fragments, Latin or Arabic translations of minor astronomical works, a weather almanac, a work on the movements of the planets, one on a sundial and about a planisphere.

Cleomedes, whose date is difficult, may have been a somewhat younger contemporary of Ptolemy. His *Encyclopaedia of the Celestial Bodies* (Κυκλικὴ θεωρία μετεώρων)[1] was a textbook and as such had an influence deep into the Middle Ages. It is important to us because the author, who has Stoic tendencies and is hostile to the Epicureans, is often dependent on Posidonius and is therefore one of the most important sources for him.

Astronomy's illegitimate sister, so exuberant in her degeneration, continued her career under the empire with an élan which the sources hint at rather than reveal. Paulus Alexandrinus, an Egyptian who resided in Alexandria and had acquired a broad Greek education, wrote in the second half of the fourth century an introduction to astrology which was probably entitled Εἰσαγωγικά.[2] Large parts survive. This pseudo-scientific mixture reveals both ancient tradition and new doctrines, Ptolemy's among them.

Among the mathematicians Menelaus still belongs largely to the Hellenistic tradition. We can estimate his achievements in spherical trigonometry through an Arabic translation,[3] which in turn formed the basis for Latin and Hebrew ones. For a long time Greek mathematics was dominated by geometry. For this reason Nicomachus of Arabian Gerasa, who wrote c. A.D. 100, occupies a special position in the history of this discipline, even though he was not a scholar of independent status. But he is the first to our knowledge to have given a coherent account of arithmetic. Himself a Neopythagorean, he summarized in

---

[1] Edition by H. ZIEGLER, Leipz. 1891. On the connection with Posidonius A. REHM, *RE* 11, 1921, 683.

[2] Edition by E. BOER, *Elementa apotelesmatica. Interpretationes astronomicas add.* O. NEUGEBAUER. Leipz. 1958.

[3] M. KRAUSE, *Die Sphärik von Menelaos aus Alexandrien in der Verbesserung von Abū Naṣr Manṣūr b. 'Alī b. 'Irāq*, Berlin 1936.

his *Introduction to Arithmetic* (Εἰσαγωγὴ ἀριθμητική)[1] the knowledge which Pythagoreanism had acquired in this field. Apuleius of Madaura and later Boethius translated the textbook into Latin. His numerical mysticism (Θεολογούμενα τῆς ἀριθμητικῆς)[2] is preserved in fragments only, interspersed with other tractates.

Owing to the original transmission we are familiar with Diophantus of Alexandria (third century), of whose main work, the *Arithmetica* (thirteen books), we possess the first six books; there is also a minor treatise *On the Number of Polygons*. The *Arithmetica*, a systematically arranged collection of problems, is important because hardly anything is known of any predecessors in the Greek world of the algebraical problems dealt with here. The two Alexandrians Pappus (probably under Diocletian) and Theon (*v. p.* 884) both wrote commentaries on the *Almagest*.[3] Eutocius, born about 480,[4] who commented on Archimedes and Apollonius, also belongs in this series. Of Serenus (fourth century) we have two treatises on conic and cylinder sections, of Domninus (fifth century) an introduction to arithmetic which reverts back to Euclid.

It was stated earlier (p. 793) that the dating of Hero, the mechanical engineer, is a problem, but that he may have to be considered as having lived under the empire. The achievements of technology were also important for warfare at that time. The Hellenistic literature on the techniques of siege warfare was carried on during the empire. Apollodorus of Damascus, Trajan's successful architect, dedicated his *Poliorcetica*[5] to the emperor Hadrian. Anthemius of Tralles, the mechanical engineer and architect, lived near the end of our period. From 532 until his death in the year 534 he collaborated with Isidorus of Miletus on the reconstruction of Hagia Sophia. We possess a fragment of his work on concave mirrors.[6]

Under the empire the science of medicine developed more independently than the other branches of learning, although in this realm, too, the achievements of the past were still decisive. There is much uncertainty about the details, but the following line can be traced regarding the Methodists, whose school advanced vigorously against the empiricists and dogmatists in the early first century A.D.[7] Asclepiades of Prusa in Bithynia, who came to Rome in 91 B.C. at the latest, built up his theory on a solid atomism, in the sharpest possible contrast with the doctrine of humours of the Hippocratic school. His pupil Themison of Laodicea deviated from his teacher (probably even before 23 B.C.)[8] to the extent

---

[1] Edition: R. HOCHE, Leipz. 1866. Transl. of the 6 introd. chapters: M. SIMON, *Festschr. M. Cantor* 1909. Engl. transl.: M. L. D'OOGE. New York 1926.

[2] In the old editions of the two writings by Ast 1817.

[3] Pappus' Συναγωγή: F. HULTSCH, Leipz. 1876–78 (with a Latin transl.). French transl. with introd. and notes by P. VER EECKE, Bruges 1933, repr. Paris 1959. Theon: N. THALMA, Paris 1821 (with transl.).

[4] Bibl. on Eutocius, Serenus and Domninus in REHM-VOGEL (*v. inf.* on Galen), 71.

[5] R. SCHNEIDER, *Abh. Gött. Ges. Phil.-hist. Kl.* N.F. 10/1. 1908 (with transl.).

[6] In A. WESTERMANN, *Paradoxographi.* Brunsv. 1839, 149. G. L. HUXLEY, *Anthemius of Tralles. A Study in Later Greek Geometry.* Cambridge 1959.

[7] Against Edelstein's attempt (*RE*, S 6, 1935, 358, 'Methodiker') to exclude Themison from their number: K. DEICHGRÄBER, *RE*, 5 A, 1934, 1632, 'Themison', and H. DILLER, *RE*, 6 A, 1936, 168 ('Thessalos').   [8] Cf. DEICHGRÄBER (*v. sup.*), 1634, 8.

that he made the condition of the walls of the foramina (tension, slackness, a mixture of the two conditions[1]) the centre of his theory. Thessalus of Tralles in Lydia, a physician with an alert eye for public success, who worked in Rome during the reign of Nero, elaborated the therapeutics of the school of the Methodists and may be considered to have completed the system. In spite of a certain primitiveness in aetiology and therapy, this school, whose aversion to anatomy was mentioned before (p. 795), produced one of the greatest physicians of the empire, Soranus of Ephesus. He was trained in Alexandria and worked both there and in Rome under Trajan and Hadrian; he entered medical history as the author of the best ancient study of gynaecology. He presented his material in the *Gynaecea* (four books), which survives in Greek, although the tradition presents great difficulties, and in two books of Γυναικεῖα κατ' ἐπερώτησιν as an instruction for midwives in the form of questions which has reached us in a Latin translation. Caelius Aurelianus has passed on Soranus' great work[2] *On Acute and Chronic Diseases* (Περὶ ὀξέων καὶ χρονίων παθῶν) in the same language. A *Life of Hippocrates* from a work on important physicians and a treatise *On Bandages* (Περὶ ἐπιδέσμων), with illustrations, have survived in Greek.

The background of the school of Methodists is formed by scepticism, which had been given new life by Aenesidemus (*v.* p. 875). The school of the Pneumatics, which Athenaeus of Attalea founded in Rome in the first century B.C.,[3] was strongly stimulated by the Stoa. The role of the pneuma was not an innovation in medical theories as is demonstrated by names like Philistion, Diocles (*v.* p. 577) and Erasistratus (*v.* p. 795). But Athenaeus no longer equated pneuma with air, but meant by it the warm breath which, in the meaning of the Stoics, differs from respiration and has its seat in the heart. It is the actual carrier of life; any change in it is responsible for both physiological and pathological phenomena. The next two generations of students are characterized by the names of Agathinus and of Archigenes,[4] who was also important as a surgeon. During this time there is an increasing trend, over and beyond the conflict of the sects, to come to a settlement through eclecticism, which largely controls the last stage of ancient medicine. This becomes evident in the case of one of the most important physicians of the empire, Rufus of Ephesus, who probably still belongs in the first century A.D. Of his innumerable works many fragments and some minor writings *On the Designation of Parts of the Body*, *On Diseases of the Kidneys and the Bladder* and *Medical Questions* have come down to us. In Aretaeus, a Pneumatic of the second century, the movement towards eclecticism can also

---

[1] Γένος στεγνόν, ῥοῶδες, ἐπιπεπλεγμένον. The share in the elaboration of the details of this doctrine is a point of controversy between Themison and Thessalus.

[2] E. DRABKIN, *Cael. Aur.* Univ. of Chicago Press n.d. (1950) with Engl. translation.

[3] F. KUDLIEN, 'Poseidonios und die Ärzteschule der Pneumatiker'. *Herm.* 90, 1962, 419 (421), has shown that contrary to the latest dating of WELLMANN (under Claudius), Athenaeus should be considered as 100 years earlier.

[4] C. BRESCIA, *Frammenti medicinali di Archigene.* Naples 1955. G. LARIZZA CALABRÒ, 'Frammenti inediti di Archigene'. *Boll. del Comit. per la prepar. della Ed. Naz. dei class. Gr e Lat.* 9, 1961, 67.

be recognized. Of him we have two works, of four books each, on the diagnosis and therapy of acute and chronic diseases. He writes in an Ionic manner and inserts many Homerisms.[1]

In this section we have spoken of summaries which involved losses in some spheres; this formula is not applicable to the most successful physician of antiquity. Galen, the eclectic, has indeed produced compilations in great volume, but he has really revised, tested critically and elaborated in many points what he took over. He was born in Pergamum, the city of the worship of Aclepius, in 129 (130?). While he was still in his native country he heard philosophers of various schools, but turned to medicine before setting out on extensive educational travels through Asia Minor, Greece and even Alexandria. These gave him a knowledge of different trends and teachers. In 157 he became the gladiators' physician in his native city, but after four years went to the capital, which alone could promise a great career. Once more after some years (166) he returned to Pergamum from Rome despite his successes, probably fleeing from the plague which at the time afflicted Italy. But Marcus Aurelius was not prepared to give up the physician who was then already famous; Galen was to accompany the emperor on the expedition against the Marcomanni. He managed, however, to achieve something which attracted him more than life in the field, he was appointed medical attendant of the crown-prince Commodus. Later Marcus Aurelius made him his physician-in-ordinary. Information about the last period of his life is defective. He died a little before 200.

It is hardly possible to review Galen's literary production. He included his own bibliography (Περὶ τῶν ἰδίων βίβλων) among the writings of his old age, enumerating 153 works in 504 books. But he is not complete, for much that survives is not included. Of his work we possess complete or in large parts 150 writings; some are also extant in Latin and Arabic translations. In the work just mentioned Galen himself proposes an arrangement of his works. One group comprises philosophy, in which he also reveals himself as an eclectic who only rejects Epicurus and Scepticism. His firm principle is proclaimed by the title of one writing: Ὅτι ὁ ἄριστος ἰατρὸς καὶ φιλόσοφος. His Protrepticus to the Art of Medicine and the great dogmatic work (Περὶ τῶν Ἱπποκράτους καὶ Πλάτωνος δογμάτων, nine books) reveal the physician who also aims to be a philosopher and so he wrote about logic and epistemology as well. Of the grammatical and rhetorical writings we know little more than the titles, excepting the first books of the work On Medical Names, which we possess in an Arabic translation from an intermediate version in Syriac.[2] The catalogue of works reveals his extensive occupation with the vocabulary of the Attic prose authors and of comedy. There was also a work Noteworthy Attic Words. In the treatise on the order in

---

[1] It is very doubtful if we may agree with c. j. RUIJGH, L'Élément achéen dans la langue épique. Assen 1957, 85, whether this can be explained from a tradition which goes back to the old didactic poems. F. KUDLIEN is preparing a monograph on Aretaeus; to him we also owe the chronology (by mail): 'A. belongs precisely in the middle of the 1st century A.D.' (Contemporary of Dioscorides and Nero's physician-in-ordinary Andromachus.)

[2] M. MEYERHOF and J. SCHACHT in Abh. Preuss. Akad. Phil.-hist. Kl. 1931/3. Also K. DEICHGRÄBER, Sitzb. D. Akad. Klasse f. Sprachen, Lit. u. Kunst 1956/2, 4.

which his works are to be read (Περὶ τῆς τάξεως τῶν ἰδίων βίβλων πρὸς Εὐγενιανόν), however, Galen himself states what can be inferred from his style; he has no wish to be a scrupulous Atticist, his overriding principle is clarity of expression (σαφήνεια).[1] The fact that he tries to effect this by means of immoderate expansiveness does not make it a pleasure to read his work.

Galen's medical writings cover in their gigantic proportions practically all the specialist fields existing at the time. For him the basis is faith in Hippocrates, which implies the importance of the theory of humours. But with this he combined ideas of other systems, excluding not even the Methodists, whom he opposes most vehemently. His writings are copiously interlaced with polemic, for throughout his life he remained aggressive, complacent and vainglorious *ad nauseam*. And yet it would appear that a picture of Galen, supported by a thorough interpretation (for which not much more than the beginning is available) will also reveal other features, features of a man who was genuinely concerned with imparting knowledge and giving an account of his life. Recently the autobiographical information of Galen in his work *On the Diagnosis of Different Pulses* (Περὶ διαγνώσεως σφυγμῶν) has been utilized by K. Deichgräber[2] in a way which enriches and widens the image of the man in the direction indicated.

Next follow the compilers of medical literature, of whom one must be singled out because of the purity of his work and his importance as an intermediary, Oribasius, Julian's physician-in-ordinary, of whose tremendous compilations, the Ἰατρικαὶ συναγωγαί in seventy books, twenty-three have been preserved, in addition to excerpts from others. We have also an abbreviated edition of the great work in nine books (Σύνοψις πρὸς Εὐστάθιον τὸν υἱόν) and four books *Euporista*, a sort of domestic pharmacopoeia.

We have yet to mention the most important pharmacological book which we possess from antiquity, Pedanius Dioscurides' *Pharmacology* (Περὶ ὕλης ἰατρικῆς, five books; 6 and 7 are later appendices). It was written in the second half of the first century A.D., its author being approximately contemporary with Pliny the Elder. His lengthy travels enriched his botanical knowledge, which he displays in the description of the curative properties of some six hundred plants. His medical interest, however, always overshadows the botanical. With Dioscurides a special treasure of the tradition appears at the end of our history. Manuscripts, foremost of which Vindobonensis Med. Gr. 1,[3] have preserved diagrams which eventually can be traced back to Cratevas, the pharmacological counsellor of Mithridates VI Eupator.

[1] The opening of book 2 of Περὶ διαφορᾶς σφυγμῶν (8,567 K.) is important for Galen's tolerant notion combined with a high esteem for the Greek language. Cf. DEICHGRÄBER (*v. sup.*), 26.

[2] *Sitzb. D. Akad. Klasse f. Sprachen, Lit. u. Kunst* 1956/3.

[3] The invaluable codex, written for the Byzantine imperial princess Anicia Juliana, is at present being preserved against impending ruin by specialized methods of preservation.

For general bibl. we refer to pp. 222 and 796. – Apollonius Dyscolus: R. SCHNEIDER and G. UHLIG, 3 vols. Leipz. 1878–1910. P. MAAS, *A. D. de pronominibus. Pars generalis.* Bonn 1911 (*Kl. Texte*). A. THIERFELDER, *Beitr. z. Kritik u. Erkl. des A. D. Abh. Sächs. Akad. Phil.-hist. Kl.* 43/2, 1935. – Herodian: A. LENTZ, 2 vols. Leipz. 1867–70. In opposition to his reconstructions R. REITZENSTEIN, *Gnom.* 5, 1929, 243. The *Philhetaerus* only in J. PIERSON in the appendix of his edition of Moeris 1750. – Hephaestion: M. CONSBRUCH, Leipz. 1906. – Strabo: The edition of the Vatican palimpsest is important for the tradition: W. ALY, *De Strabonis codice rescripto.* Vatican 1956, with an appendix on the more important manuscripts by F. SBORDONE. W. ALY, 'Zum neuen Strabon-Text'. *Parola del passato* 5, 1950, 228. Editions: A. MEINEKE, 3 vols. Leipz. 1851/52. G. KRAMER, 3 vols. Berl. 1844–52 (with app. crit.). C. MÜLLER, Paris 1858. With Engl. translation: H. L. JONES–J. R. S. STERRET, 8 vols. *Loeb Class. Libr.* 1917–32 (repeatedly repr.). A. SCHULTEN, *Estrabón. Geografía de Iberia.* Ed. transl. and comm. Barcelona 1952 (*Fontes Hispaniae antiquae*—6). W. ALY, *Strabon von Amaseia. Geographika.* Text, transl. and comm. Vol. 4, *Unters. über Text, Aufbau und Quellen der Geographika.* Bonn 1957. (*Antiquitas R.* 1/5). Critical of this A. DILLER, *Gnom.* 30, 1958, 530; W. HERING, *DLZ,* 80, 1959. – Dionysius of Byzantium: R. GÜNGERICH, Berl. 1927 (2nd unalt. ed. 1958; excellent critical ed.). – Stephanus of Byzantium: A. MEINEKE, Berl. 1849, repr. Graz 1956. – Ptolemy: Teubner edition: I: J. L. HEIBERG, *Almagest* 1898; II: Id., *Kleinere astron Schriften* 1907; III/1: F. BOLL–A. E. BOER, *Tetrabiblos* 1940; III/2: F. LAMMERT, Περὶ κριτ. 1952, 2nd ed. with indices 1960. *Almagest* in Germ. with notes: K. MANITIUS, 2 vols. Leipz. 1912/13. *Tetrabiblos* with Manetho: W. G. WADDELL and F. E. ROBBINS, *Loeb Class. Libr.* 1940 (with Engl. transl.). *Harmonics:* I. DÜRING, Göteborg 1930 (with comm.). *Optics:* G. GOVI, Turin 1885. A. LEJEUNE, *L'Optique de Claude Ptolémée dans la version latine d'après l'arabe d'émir Eugène de Sicile.* Louvain 1956. *Geographica:* F. A. NOBBE, 3 vols. Leipz. 1843–45. C. MÜLLER-K. FISCHER, Paris 1883/1901 only goes up to book 5. A serviceable collective edition is lacking, but the partial editing of several western countries by O. CUNTZ, *Die Geographie des Pt.* Berl. 1923, is all the more important. E. POLASCHEK, 'Ptolemy's Geography in a New Light'. *Imago Mundi* 14, 1959, 17. – Diophantus: P. TANNERY, 2 vols. Leipz. 1893/95. French transl. with introd. and notes by P. VER EECKE, Bruges 1926, repr. Paris 1959. T. L. HEATH, *D. of Alexandria.* 1885; 2nd ed. 1910.

For medicine in this time we refer particularly to P. DIEPGEN, *Gesch. d. Medizin* 1, Berl. 1949. Very useful for the separate editions, in so far as they have appeared in the Corpus Medicorum Graec., is the convenient survey given by K. DEICHGRABER, *D. Akad. d. Wissens., Schriften der Sektion f Altertumswiss.* Heft 8, Berl. 1957, 116. Only a limited selection of other editions and papers will be mentioned here. – Soranus: definitive *CMG* 4. – Rufus: C. DAREMBERG–C. E. RUELLE, Paris 1879 (with fragments) H. GÄRTNER, *Rufus von Eph. Die Fragen des Arztes an den Kranken* ('Ιατρικὰ ἐρωτήματα). Diss. Göttingen 1960; now *CMG* 1962. G. KOWALSKI, *Rufi Ephesii De corporis humani appellationibus* ('Ονομασίαι τῶν τοῦ ἀνθρώπου μερίων) Diss. Göttingen 1960 (Edition with verbal index). – For the Pneumatic school M. WELLMANN, *Die pneum. Schule. Philol. Unters.* 14, Berl. 1895, is still indispensable. – Aretaeus: *CMG,* 2 (now 2nd ed. 1958). – Galen: A serviceable collective edition is lacking; C. G. KÜHN, 20 vols. Leipz. 1821–33 is inadequate. Several works in *CMG,* 5 (*v. supra,* Deichgräber), also: F. PFAFF, *Gal. Kommentare zu den Epidemien des Hippokrates. Indices der aus dem arabischen übersetzten Namen u. Wörter. CMG* 5/10, 2, 4, Berl. 1960 with an edition of Galen's Περὶ προσπ. by K. DEICHGRÄBER and F. KUDLIEN. Other special editions in A.REHM-K.VOGEL, *Exakte Wissenschaften.* GERCKE-NORDEN, *Einl.* 2/5. 4th ed. Leipz. 1933, 77. Cf. A. J. BROCK, Περὶ φυσικῶν δυνάμεων. *Loeb Class. Libr.* 1952 (with Engl. transl.). Important for the Arabic tradition: R. WALZER's edition of the writing *On Seven-months' Babies. Rivista di Studi Orientali* 15, Rome 1935, 323. Id., *Galen, On Medical Experience. First Edition of the Arabic Version with English Translation and Notes.* London 1944; *Galen on Jews and Christians.* Oxf. 1949. CH. SINGER, *Galen. De anatomicis administrationibus.* Transl. with introd. and notes. *Wellcome Hist. Med. Mus. Publ.* 7, Lond. 1956. E. COTURRI, *Galenus de theriaca ad Pisonem,* Latin text, transl., introd. Florence 1959. J. EHLERT, *Galeni de purgantium medicamentorum facultate.* Tradition and edition. Diss. Göttingen 1960 (typescr.). F. KUDLIEN, *Die handschr. Überlieferung des Galenkommentars zu Hippokrates De articulis.* Berlin 1960 (*D. Akad. d. Wiss. Berl. Schriften der Sektion f. Altertumswiss.* 27). J. WILLE, *Die Schrift Galens* Περὶ τῶν ἐν ταῖς νόσοις καιρῶν *und ihre Überlieferung.* Diss. Kiel 1960. J. KOLLESCH, *Galen über das Riechorgan.* Text, transl., comm. Diss. Halle 1961. Two more enquiries deserve to be singled out: A. WIFSTRAND, *Eikota* VII: *Weiteres zu den Hippokrateskommentaren des Galenos.* Lund. 1958. O. TEMKIN, 'A Galenic Model for Quantitative Physiological Reasoning?' *Bull. Hist. Med.* 35, 1961, 470. Introductory: J. MEWALDT, *RE,* 7, 1910, 578. G. SARTON, *G. of Pergamon.* Univ. of Kansas Press 1954. – Oribasius: CH. DAREMBERG–U. C. BUSSEMAKER, Paris 1851–76, repr. Amsterdam 1962 (with transl. and notes). J. RAEDER, *CMG,* 6. H. MORLAND, *Die lat. Oribasiusübersetzungen. Symb. Osl. Suppl.* 5, 1932. – Dioscurides: M. WELLMANN, 3 vols. Berl. 1906–14; repr. 1958.

INDEX